The Valley

A Trilogy

by

C Louis Leipoldt

The Valley

A Trilogy

by

C Louis Leipoldt

GALLOWS GECKO ◆ STORMWRACK ◆ THE MASK

EDITED BY T S EMSLIE SC, P L MURRAY & J A J RUSSELL

STORMBERG
PUBLISHERS

2001

Distributed in southern Africa by Book Promotions,
P O Box 5 • Plumstead • 7800 • South Africa
Tel: (021) 706-0949 Fax: (021) 706-0940
email: orders@bookpro.co.za
and in the United Kingdom by Central Books,
99 Wallis Road • London • E9 5LN • England
Tel: 020-8986-4854 Fax: 020-8533-5821
email: orders@centralbooks.com

The Valley was first published by Stormberg Publishers in 2001

ISBN 0-620-27816-1

COVER DESIGN BY ANNE EMSLIE
SET BY EILEEN EAGAR
PRINTED AND BOUND IN THE REPUBLIC OF SOUTH AFRICA
BY CREDA COMMUNICATIONS

To the memory and spirit of C Louis Leipoldt

C Louis Leipoldt 1880 – 1947

Biographical Note

[from *The C Louis Leipoldt Papers* by Etaine Eberhard, University of Cape Town]

Christian Friederick Louis Leipoldt, poet, playwright, journalist, chef, botanist and doctor was born on 28 December 1880 at the Rhenish Mission House in Worcester, Cape Province, the home of his grandparents, Rev Louis Francois Esselen and his wife Catherine Wilhelmine, née Knobel.

His paternal grandfather, Johann Gottlieb Leipoldt, was trained as a Rhenish Missionary in Germany before being sent to the Cape in 1829. He founded the Mission Station at Wupperthal in 1830 and worked there until his death in 1872. In 1835 he married Carolina Jacoba Maria Lind in Cape Town. Three sons and two daughters were born of this marriage. Their son, Christian Frederick, was sent to Barmen in Germany to be trained as a Rhenish missionary. In 1870 he went to Sumatra to work among the Bata people. Anna Meta Christiana Esselen, second eldest daughter of Rev L F Esselen of Worcester, travelled to Sumatra in 1874 to marry him. A daughter and two sons were born there, the youngest of whom died when only a few days old. Mrs Leipoldt's health broke down seriously and her husband decided in 1879 to bring his family to the Cape. They settled in Worcester at the Rhenish Mission House where Rev Leipoldt assisted his father-in-law in running the Mission school. It was there that their fourth child, Christian Frederick Louis Leipoldt, was born.

In 1884, having left the Rhenish Mission field and joined the Dutch Reformed Church, Rev C F Leipoldt went to serve the congregation in Clanwilliam. He worked in this community until his retirement in 1910. Leipoldtville in the Clanwilliam district is named after him.

By all accounts he was a scholarly man of gentle habits and was a talented violinist. His wife, on the other hand, appears to have had a very uncertain temper and her relationship with her family does not seem to have been a very happy one. She would not allow her sons to attend school, nor would she let them mix freely with the children of the district. Their father took charge of their education and CLL was encouraged at a very early age to read widely on all subjects and was given a grounding in several languages and in the natural sciences, particularly botany and geology. Whenever the family visited Cape Town, where Rev Leipoldt attended the Dutch Reformed Church synod, CLL was sent to his father's friends, such as Professor P D Hahn, for special instruction.

CLL first made contact with Professor P MacOwan when he sent some dried plant specimens to the latter for identification. MacOwan exerted an important influence on the youth and encouraged him to send more specimens. In his Report for 1895, he stated, 'More recently good contributions have come in from Mr C L Leipoldt, of Clanwilliam, a district possessing a rich and somewhat peculiar flora, which I hope by his instrumentality to illustrate largely in the centuriae ...' In 1895 CLL was a boy of fourteen.

In 1893 CLL met the botanist Rudolph Schlechter who was travelling with a party in the Clanwilliam district on a botanical and zoological collecting trip. At Schlechter's request CLL was permitted to accompany the expedition into Namaqualand as a guide.

At about this time CLL also met Harry Bolus and, despite a difference of nearly 47 years in their ages, a lasting friendship developed.

CLL was without question a gifted child who showed early promise as a writer and undoubtedly benefited from the liberal, if somewhat eccentric, education he received. He is said to have written a play when he was eight years old and when he was eleven he won a prize of half a guinea and a merit award for a story he entered in a competition run by the *Boys Own Paper*. He was encouraged to write, and from the age of 14 was contributing news items to Cape Town newspapers on a fairly regular basis and a number of stories and sketches he wrote while still a teenager appeared under various pseudonyms.

After passing the matriculation and Civil Service examinations in 1897 and 1898 respectively, he worked as a journalist in Cape Town, at first on *De Kolonist* and *Het Dagblad* and later on the *South African News*. He was also a correspondent for various overseas newspapers, amongst which were the *Manchester Guardian*, *Chicago Herald*, *Het Nieuws van den Dag* (Amsterdam) and *Petit Bleu* (Brussels). When Albert Cartwright, editor of the *South African News*, was imprisoned for political reasons in 1901, CLL took over the editorship until the paper was closed down by the authorities later the same year. When this occurred he decided to go to England to broaden his experience as a journalist. He had always wished to study medicine but could not afford to do so. Before he left South Africa in January 1902 Harry Bolus suggested lending him money to enable him to study, and shortly after arriving in London he wrote accepting Bolus's offer. He studied medicine at Guy's Hospital and throughout his period as a student he augmented his financial resources by writing. During this period he also for a time edited *The Hospital*, a medical journal owned by Sir Henry Burdett.

In 1907 he obtained the MRCS and the LRCP and was awarded gold medals for both medicine and surgery. Later the same year he was appointed Assistant House Surgeon at Guy's Hospital, an honorary post but one which carried great prestige. This appointment came to an end in January 1908 and his work on *The Hospital* in March, after which he was free to travel on the Continent and to work in Milan. At Sir Henry Burdett's suggestion, he wrote articles assessing these institutions for *The Hospital*. He also went to Prague, Cracow, Warsaw and Moscow, during these seven months.

In October he was back in London and failed in his first attempt at the FRCS examination. After this disappointment he accepted the post of medical adviser to the American millionaire newspaper owner, Joseph Pulitzer, and spent four months cruising on his steam yacht, the *Liberty*. On his return to London he once more wrote the FRCS examination, this time with success.

Except for the first four months of 1912, when he travelled to the East, visiting Java and Sumatra, as ship's doctor on the *Ulysses*, he worked in hospitals in London and also as a medical inspector of schools for the London County Council.

He returned to South Africa in 1914 to take up an appointment as Medical Inspector of Schools in the Transvaal, the first such post in South Africa. Shortly after his return World War I broke out and CLL was drafted into the Army as General Louis Botha's personal doctor. He is reported to have saved General Botha's life when the latter was taken seriously ill during the South West African campaign.

CLL's interest in the School Journeys Association and school camps was kindled in England and he was actively involved in the movement for many years in South Africa. He also educated a number of boys over the years and often had several staying in his home at the same time.

In a letter to Mrs Eve Allen he makes the following comment which may throw some light on his reasons for helping children all his adult life: '... My position is simply this: when I was a youngster an old Englishman did far more than that for me, and all he asked was that in my turn I should do something to help an English boy or girl in this country. If they won't let me—well, I can only burn one more joss stick to the old man's memory ...'

In 1928 while visiting England with a group of school children, he adopted a seven year old orphan, Jeffrey Leipoldt, and brought him back to South Africa with him. In 1932 another English boy, Peter Shields, came from Stellenbosch, where his mother had settled after being widowed, to live at Arbury, CLL's home in Kenilworth. Later CLL regarded him also as an 'adopted' son and left the residue of his estate in equal shares to Jeff and Peter.

CLL was Medical Inspector of Schools in the Transvaal from 1914 until the end of 1922. During this time he travelled throughout the Transvaal and set up permanent clinics in some of the larger centres. He also advised the Provincial Councils of Natal and the Cape on the organisation of school Medical Inspectorates in those provinces.

He resigned from the Education Department at the end of 1922 in order to return to journalism and was appointed assistant editor of *De Volkstem* and worked under Dr F V Engelenburg who was at that time editor. In 1924 CLL accepted nomination as the South African Party candidate for Wonderboom in the general election held that year but was defeated. During the same year Dr Engelenburg relinquished the editorship of *De Volkstem* and was succeeded by Gustav Preller with whom CLL was unable to work. In 1925 he left the editorial staff and settled in Cape Town, setting up in practice as a children's specialist. Shortly afterwards in 1926 he became the first organising secretary of the Medical Association of South Africa and the first editor of the *South African Medical Journal*, posts he held until the end of 1944. In December 1926 he was appointed to the staff of the University of Cape Town Medical School as the first lecturer in children's diseases. By mid-1927 he wrote to a friend in Johannesburg that he had been given 18 children's beds in the hospital and had about 20 students. The hospital referred to was the New Somerset Hospital which was then used as the teaching hospital by the University of Cape Town Medical School. He gave up lecturing in 1939.

Throughout his life he wrote prolifically. He was almost constantly engaged in journalism, submitting articles to overseas newspapers on a regular basis, wrote poetry, plays and novels. He also wrote books on health matters, dietetics, food, cookery and wine as well as on historical subjects. Very often his books and poems were written in English and translated, by him, into Afrikaans before being published in the latter language. In 1915 he was elected to the *Maatschappij der Nederlandsche Letterkunde* and an honorary D Litt degree was conferred upon him by the

Witwatersrand University in 1934. That same year he was awarded the Hertzog Prize for poetry and in 1944 he won the Prize for drama.

Although the greatest volume of CLL's writing was in English, his importance as an Afrikaans writer was immense. The publication of *Oom Gert Vertel en Ander Gedigte* in 1911 was a major event in the development of the Afrikaans language. There is no complete bibliography of his writing available although a good deal of information can be obtained from the two existing bibliographies, *viz—*

1. Christiaan Frederick Louis Leipoldt (28 Des 1880 – 12 April 1947). Bibliografie, saamgestel deur SWR de Toit. Universiteit van Kaapstad, Skool vir Biblioteekwese, 1947.
2. C Louis Leipoldt, 'n Bibliografie van dr Christian Frederick Louis Leipoldt, 28 Des 1880 - 12 April 1947. Saamgestel deur NALN, 1979.

According to his passport he was 5 feet 11 inches tall and had neutral grey eyes and brown hair. From photographs it is evident that his hair was always a little unruly. In his home he spoke English and German, and, despite his missionary heritage, asserted that he was a Buddhist. From his diaries and letters it is evident that he suffered from heart damage following rheumatic fever which he had had as a child, and from asthma which he appears to have developed during a visit to New York during his late twenties.

After his death in Cape Town on 12 April 1947, his ashes were taken for burial to the Pakhuis Pass where a simple ceremony was held by a few of his friends.

Note on the Text

The text of C Louis Leipoldt's trilogy has been left as intact as possible, not only to preserve the flavour of the era depicted by him in each of the books, but also in deference to Leipoldt himself.

Those who read *The Valley* with sympathy and discernment will, we think, recognise in the 'omniscient author' a truly far-sighted thinker and commentator, and we suggest that, if anything, he was ahead of his time in the attitudes portrayed in these novels.

Readers unacquainted with Afrikaans culture should appreciate that the terms 'Uncle,' 'Nephew' and 'Brother' etc are not used literally, but to convey respect and affection, and are widely used in this manner in Afrikaans to this day. Thus a younger person will call his elder *Oom*, or Uncle, to denote respect, although there is no blood relationship between them or even if the elder is a stranger. Leipoldt's use of these terms is therefore intended to convey in English the everyday idiom of Afrikaans (or South African Dutch) usage at the times of which he wrote.

Leipoldt himself has been inconsistent in his use of capitals etc, so we have standardised according to what we considered appropriate in the circumstances. We have italicised foreign words, including Afrikaans words such as *meneer* (mister) used regularly throughout the text. — Eds

The old Village of Clanwilliam

Contents

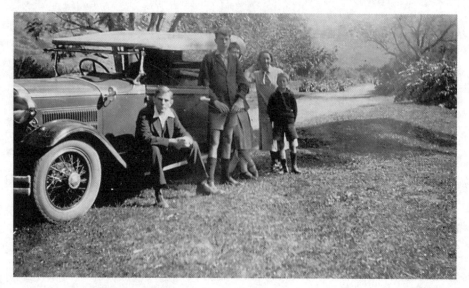

The author, seated, and companions, with his motor car

Introduction

This is the first publication of C Louis Leipoldt's trilogy of historical novels entitled *The Valley*. All attempts to have these works published during Leipoldt's lifetime—he died in 1947—were unsuccessful. An abridged version of *Stormwrack* was published in hardback in 1980 and in paperback in 2000, an abridged version of *Gallows Gecko* was published under the title *Chameleon on the Gallows* in 2000, but *The Mask* has never been published.

We have set out to make *The Valley* available in a form of which the author would have approved, and our guiding principle has been to be faithful to Leipoldt's own last edition of each of the novels. With respect to those who may differ, we prefer Leipoldt undiluted to any attempt to contain his *ipsissima verba* by wielding the editorial axe. We know that he is at times master of the long sentence, invariably—in our view— marvellously crafted in the best classical tradition, and reminiscent of the famously long first sentence of Alessandro Manzoni's *The Betrothed*. As with a Mahler symphony, if one 'relaxes' into it, the effort—or lack thereof—is richly rewarded. We maintain that only by reading the trilogy as a whole can one apprehend the true scale of Leipoldt's achievement, and that this is the appropriate context in which his efforts must be appreciated and evaluated.

Leipoldt said the following of his trilogy, which he entitled *The Valley*:

> 'These three are separate and independent but closely related books, that are designed to describe the history of a small semi-rural community in the Cape Colony from 1820 until 1930. Each book is complete in itself, but the three together are necessary to outline the environment and to explain the changes that have taken place in the course of a century in the relations between the English and Dutch speaking elements in the community.'

Our task of editing has been confined to matters of detail and consistency, and we have eschewed any notion of 'improving' upon Leipoldt as an impertinence, and set our course by faithfulness to his accomplishment in all its fullness.

The task of producing this trilogy from the typed manuscripts held in the Manuscripts and Archives Library at the University of Cape Town has been accompanied by a voyage of discovery of a wonderfully complex, versatile and endearing personality—a journey we commend to all who find themselves inspired by what is contained in these pages.

Leipoldt was a many-sided man of genius, whose '*traak-my-nie-agtigheid*' (devil-may-care tendency), bluntness and unpredictability no doubt contributed to the following remark after his death: 'He preferred to contradict. He was the apostle of the opposite view.' He was also much more than the seminal Afrikaans poet and writer that many English-speaking South Africans have encountered as the author of *Oom Gert Vertel* and other well-known poems. He wrote, in English and Afrikaans, books on *inter alia* cookery, and wine-making at the Cape; and he grew up speaking English, Dutch and German—to the extent, he said, that he would be hard-pressed to say which was his home language—reading Latin and Greek under the tutelege of his father, and adding French and Italian in due course. Leipoldt was in many senses a 'universal man,' and as 'omniscient author' of *The Valley* his versatility and subtlety are more and more manifest as the trilogy progresses.

Some knowledge of the life of the man is, we feel, helpful to an appreciation of the trilogy, for when one reads of botanical or medical or culinary matters, to mention but a few, it is worth knowing that the author was an expert in these fields and wrote from a wealth of knowledge and experience. Leipoldt's Valley, the Village and the District, are Clanwilliam and its surrounding mountains and valleys, extending to Wupperthal, though he does not mention these by name. This is where he grew up, with deep family roots, and where he returned in later life, botanising and camping out with his great friend Dr Nortier. The strongly autobiographical aspect of these historical novels prompts curiosity about Leipoldt's life, and for this purpose we have, with permission, included a separate biblographical note by Etaine Eberhard from her publication *The C Louis Leipoldt Papers*.

The books comprising *The Valley* were written in the early 1930s, and represent— we consider—the mature views of the 50 year old poet who had lived in the Cape Colony through most of the Anglo-Boer War (he left for England in January 1902, two months before the war ended) and expressed himself more stridently when he was a younger man. Could it be that *The Valley* was in a sense a culmination, a pulling together by Leipoldt of the various threads of his personal, political, geographical and cultural history, as well as those of the beloved country of which he writes with such sympathy and affection? His insights are remarkable, as for instance the broad-mindedness shown by the Dutch Reformed Minister to the artist Mabuis in *Gallows Gecko* compared with the narrow-minded and brutal silencing in *Stormwrack* of the violinist in Pastor Uhlmann—a regression from tolerance to intolerance. The latter incident happened to Leipoldt's father, the model for Pastor Uhlmann; he it was who on his deathbed called for his violin and actually died holding it. See pages 337 of *Stormwrack* and 532 of *The Mask*. Leipoldt even gives himself a cameo appearance as Louis, one of Pastor Uhlmann's sons—see page 293 of *Stormwrack*.

We wish to express our sincere thanks to the University of Cape Town, owner of the copyright in these works, for permission to publish the trilogy. To Mr Hugh Amoore, Registrar of the University, and Mrs Lesley Hart of the Manuscripts and Archives Library at UCT, thank you for the permission, assistance, courtesy and encouragement extended to us. Your support is greatly appreciated. To Anne Emslie, who took the cover photograph, thank you for your enthusiasm and for truly entering into the spirit of *The Valley*.

Trevor Emslie
St James

Paul Murray
Birkenhead

Alexander Russell
Oxford

October 2001

GALLOWS GECKO

by

C Louis Leipoldt

The Prologue

Ill at ease, self-conscious, though he hated himself for being both, the magistrate rose from his hardwood chair to greet his visitor. He did not offer to shake hands, and for one moment he pondered what he should do if the young man, true to the country's custom, held out his hand. But the visitor did not presume. He merely bowed respectfully, murmured the conventional, 'Good day, Sir,' and took the chair that the magistrate indicated.

'After all,' said the magistrate to himself, 'I am a fool. A damned fool. As if it matters one little bit what the fellow had to do ...'

Aloud he said, pleasantly, with the kindly intonation that he affected when not on the bench, 'I suppose I must congratulate you. We have heard all about your good fortune. It is several thousands, is it not?'

The young man—he really was not so young, the magistrate reflected as he looked at the care-lined face of his visitor—smiled, both with his lips and his eyes. Damn it, the fellow had quite a pleasant face when he smiled.

'Rumour always exaggerates, Magistrate'—the voice, the magistrate noted, was almost musical. 'We do not know the exact amount. The attorneys at Cape Town could only give me a rough estimate. It is largely in immovable property, which, as you know, Magistrate ...'

'Takes time to realise,' the magistrate nodded, to show that he quite understood that immovable property cannot be disposed of as quickly as other assets. 'Still, I hope they were able to give you something to go on with?'

'O yes, Magistrate. I brought back with me enough for my purpose. That is really what I came to see you about, Magistrate.'

'Whatever I can do—in my official capacity or otherwise—I shall of course be only too glad to offer. Let me see, now that your aunt's fortune ...'

'My wife's aunt, Magistrate. She was my wife's mother's sister, Magistrate. The de Lerchs were well-off, formerly, Magistrate, although with trade failing and the change of government—you must excuse me, Magistrate, if I refer to that ...'

'Certainly, certainly. But surely you were much too young to remember the change. Why, you must have been a mere boy at the time of the first occupation.'

'That I was, Magistrate. I am just telling you, Magistrate, how things impoverished the de Lerchs. That was one of the reasons I had to set up for myself as a harness maker, Magistrate. I might have had my own land, Magistrate ...'

'So you might ... so you might. But you surely do not complain. After all ... after all ...'

The magistrate paused, and to cover his embarrassment jerked open the drawer in front of him and took out some cheroots. His sister in India supplied him regularly with cheroots, and the magistrate found them excellent. He took one, hesitated, took another and proffered the second to his visitor.

'Grateful, Magistrate, but, with permission, Magistrate, I prefer my pipe. I am more used to it,' said the young man who looked so much older than he really was.

'Certainly, certainly, please yourself.' The magistrate struck a villainous looking sulphur match, and carefully lit his cheroot. The visitor produced an enormous pearwood pipe, which he proceeded to fill with coarsely cut tobacco from a woollen pouch, and lit from a brass tinder box after a few deft manipulations with flint and steel. What long, strong slender fingers the man had. The magistrate watched these fingers with a feeling of fascination that almost made him shudder. On one occasion those fingers ...

He jerked himself back into the present, and drew carefully at his cheroot, for unless they burned evenly his sister's offerings were apt to refuse to draw altogether.

'I am quite at your service,' he said, kindly. 'I can give you exactly half an hour. Then I must step over to the court.'

'I shall not keep Magistrate that long,' said his visitor. 'The matter on which I should like to have your advice, Magistrate, is a simple one.'

'Then, possibly, I may be able to help you,' replied the magistrate, encouragingly. 'So long, of course,' he added as an afterthought, 'it is something which does not conflict with my official duties.'

'Not in the least, Magistrate.' His visitor settled himself more squarely upon his chair, and blew clouds of blue white smoke from his pipe. 'Now that I have a certain amount of ready money, Magistrate, my wife and I have decided that we will leave this district.'

'In some ways a wise resolution,' said the magistrate, reflectively.

'We feel sure it is, Magistrate. Everyone here knows us. They will always talk ... about what has happened in the past, Magistrate. It is about this, Magistrate, that I have come to consult you, if you will be so kind.'

'Certainly, certainly. Have you made any plans? You do not, I hope, propose to follow those ill-advised persons who have left the boundaries of the Colony—one hears of them trekking every day. Stupid fellows ... stupid fellows ... they are just laying rods in pickle for themselves.'

'No, Magistrate. My intention is to buy land somewhere else. I want to farm—I feel sure I can make good at it, Magistrate.'

'Quite so ... quite so. I don't doubt you will, too. By all means. And what's more, let me know where you want to settle. There's plenty of government land, good agricultural land, and, you know, if we can do anything for you ... after all, we owe you something for helping us out of the lurch.'

'Grateful, Magistrate, very grateful. I do not know yet. My plan is to go and prospect. It will not do to buy a pig in a poke. I shall have to be careful. But I shall be grateful if you will expedite matters for me, Magistrate, in case it is vacant land I select.'

'There need be no difficulty about that. I will see that the Secretary gives you title as soon as you can fix matters up.'

'Thank you, Magistrate. Now there is another matter. I want to change my name, if that is possible. It can be done?'

'Certainly. It is done quite frequently, although to tell you the honest truth, I can't at the moment say what are the precise steps you must take to make the change legal. I can quite see why you wish to do so, and, if I may say so, I think you are acting wisely, especially if you go somewhere where you are not known. Personally, I do not know if what ... what has happened in the past is going to handicap you to any great extent.'

'I want to cut myself off from the old life, Magistrate. I have two children, and I should not like them to learn too soon about that.'

'Still, they must know about it, I suppose,' remarked the magistrate, drawing reflectively at his cheroot. The man was very sensible, after all. Sweep the past clean away ... yes, that was it. It was not easy in many cases, but a legacy of several thousands smoothes many difficulties. And he was a level-headed sort of fellow. As a harness maker he was quite a master. Everyone said so. And evidently a good businessman too.

'That would be quite all right,' said the magistrate. 'What you wish your children to know, or not to know, is your own concern. I should advise you to put the matter entirely in the hands of your attorneys at Cape Town. They will know what to do, and they will take all the necessary steps. All the arrangements can be made through them. Your share will be merely to pay the bill, and I presume there will be no difficulty about that.'

'Not the slightest, Magistrate. Thank you. I will follow your advice, Magistrate. Next week I go to Cape Town. I have to see them anyway, to fix up certain things. They have to sell my business here. It won't fetch much, but I have some stock-in-trade, and I do not much care what it brings in at the auction. Then I take the wife and children to Cape Town, and I go to look for my farm.'

'You have my best wishes,' said the magistrate, rising to show his visitor out. 'I am sure you have decided for the best. Let me know how you get on. Anything I can do for you I will do with much pleasure.'

'Deeply grateful, Magistrate. I shall not forget your kindness, Magistrate. Pardon me for having taken up so much of your time, but I wanted to be sure ...'

'Not at all, not at all. It is getting very hot again; I think it is high time we had some rain. Good day to you ... good day. Let me know if there is anything else ...'

The magistrate's voice trailed away as his visitor went through the door that opened on to the *stoep*. This time the magistrate had decided to shake hands, but somehow the visitor had merely bowed, and departed with the conventional farewell.

'I am really a cad,' reflected the magistrate. 'Amadeus Tereg did his duty, under very painful and embarrassing circumstances, and I have the effrontery to look upon him as someone quite outside the pale of humanity. It's damnable for a man in my position to be so cursedly sentimental. I might have been a little more friendly to the poor wretch.'

And the thought that he had been uncharitable tortured the official, who when not on the bench was a most kind hearted individual although he deemed it his magisterial duty to be as dignified and gruff as he could possibly be, and he went down to the court house in a state of irritability that boded little good for his underlings. He made the Native constable shiver with apprehension by finding fault with the set of his ill fitting tunic, and his one and only clerk blaspheme by insisting upon trivialities that could quite easily have been dispensed with.

'The *Landdrost*,' said Toons, the Hottentot interpreter, 'has had goat's chops for breakfast this morning. They always give the *Landdrost* acidity.'

'Don't you dare talk about the *Landdrost*,' snarled the clerk. 'You get on with cleaning that ink-pot and see that there's some decent sand. The last lot you brought in was all dust, and it dirties my records, fool.'

Chapter 1

The Valley, bounded by high hills that run length-wise from east to west, is a long, narrow tract of rich alluvial soil, through the middle of which courses the River. On the south the bounding hills are high, rising four thousand feet above the flat lands that stretch to the sea. On the north, the nearer hills are pygmies, compared with their southern opponents, but behind them soar a range of boldly buttressed peaks, weathered into strange shapes and coloured, by oxidation, with rich carmines and gaudy russets, wooded on the lower slopes by shrubs and aromatic bush, and higher up, where the cliffs are stark and sheer, by splendid, gnarled cedar giants which have for many hundreds of years looked over and beyond the Valley, and seen, from their points of vantage, the blue parallel mountains that were landmarks for the old Portuguese navigators.

Many years before Everardus Nolte journeyed hither to choose for himself a portion of land to be for him a farm and an abiding place, exploring parties, sent out under the auspices of the old Dutch East India Company, whose headquarters was the geometrically designed fortification on the sandy shore of Table Bay, had entered the Valley and reported upon its suitability for agricultural settlement. They had found the passage through the southern hills, high up to the east, a stone strewn pass, raked by the wind, with a gradient not too steep for their big wagon wheels. Crossing this, they had entered the Valley at its upper portion, and traversed it to that western point where it broadens out into open country, bare but for stunted shrubs and grey veld bush, and dreary with its wastes of river sand swept far inland by the fierce, gusty bursts of the east wind. The crossing and the traversing had been difficult, owing to the matted bush in the Valley itself, for in those early days the River boasted big fig trees, tangled with lianas, wild creepers, and prickly thorns, while its very bed nursed miles of thick grey-green sedge that fringed the sides of its deep, slumbering pools, the haunt of colossally big barbles and lithe, graceful silverfish. The early explorers encountered lions in the Valley, but as they were used to such beasts, which in those days were not infrequently met with even in the vicinity of the lands occupied by the employees of the Lords Major, they did not stop to chronicle their adventures with these animals. When, lower down in the Valley, they came across a troop of elephants, and, close by, were endangered by the forceful curiosity of a rhinoceros that seemed to be the twin brother of what Albrecht Durer had so faithfully depicted, they thought the event worth recording. Similarly they described the hot springs, the pride of the Valley, and the wealth of flowers, opening at midday, which made a gorgeous carpet of colour on the brown, hard baked clay of the lower hills' slopes.

The flowers are still there, and the hot springs, but the elephants have vanished with the rhinoceroses and the lions. Now the most savage animal that roams the hillsides and makes his lair in the *kloofs* is the leopard, to which the inhabitants of the Valley refer as the 'tiger,' and next to it comes the wild cat, untameable, savagely fierce, but graceful and sleek in its coat of red fur. Troops of baboons, raucously sounding their sentinel cries, patrol the mountains and adventure down to the river bank to drink. Otters swim ashore through the matted sedges at night when the moon silvers the yellow river sands, and leave their spoor in the mud. Weasels and martins and river rats lurk in the undergrowth, rarely seen though often heard, and on the dry, arid veld between river and hill there are many puff-adders, black spitting-snakes, and hooded yellow cobras.

Everardus Nolte, mounted on a sturdy horse trained to go for hours at that smooth, ambling pace that the inhabitants of the Valley call a 'tripple,' journeyed far beyond the Valley, carefully prospecting for land on which he could settle. He found many good sites for his farm, but the quest for the ideal led him to the country behind the big range where the magnificent cedars grew, and beyond that again to the wild, barren wastes of the Hantam Karroo. On his way he passed through the Valley, and its wonderful beauty, its serenity, and its boundless possibilities captured his imagination. He returned to it, and pursued his quest with patience and perseverance. It was not easy, but the hardship of travel was lightened by the kindness and hospitality that he received from all with whom he came into contact. Every night he slept at some homestead, where his hosts plied him with questions about himself, the condition of affairs in the district whence he had come, and the objects of his mission. He replied to their inquisitiveness, which he realised sprang not from mere curiosity but from an active interest, with answers which while they did not reveal what he wished to conceal, gave them sufficient reason to be further interested and helpful. The assistance he received was valuable, for on more than one occasion a talk with his hosts made a personal inspection superfluous, and enabled him to go farther afield to hunt for his ideal farm. The result was that when he returned from the north, he had already made up his mind where he wanted to settle. Somewhere in the Valley lay his farm.

There was much unoccupied, vacant land, government land, they told him, that could be bought for a pittance. There were wide tracts of such land, stretching from the river up into the mountains, unsurveyed, wild and for the greater part barren. They did not attract him. He wanted something that had already been reclaimed, at least in part, something that he could labour at and improve, with a chance of seeing the results of his labour before he was too old and spent to care much for what life could still give.

At last he found what he sought. Half-way down the Valley, just at the point where the River broadened and made a curve towards the south, the bounding hills on the north shelved down, revealing the massive, imposing escarpments of the higher range behind. A broad tributary valley, what the inhabitants of the Valley called a '*kloof*,' ran up towards the mountains and down towards the river. Through it sparkled a clear, brown tinted stream from some hidden rock fountain high up, and on both sides of the stream were acres of excellent black and red soil, rich loam whose value he could calculate at a glance. The road that ran through the Valley, following the river bank on its northern side, cut at right angles across the little stream, and close to the road stood a little mud walled house, surrounded by a few scattered oak trees planted some twenty years before. As soon as Everardus, ambling past on his trippling horse, saw this homestead, and noted its environment, he felt that he had reached his goal. Here was his ideal site. This was the place where he would settle.

Cautious and careful enquiry confirmed him in that opinion. The little farm was really no-man's-land. A freed slave, an old Mozambique Native, already bent with years and labour, had squatted there. He had built the wattle daub house, planted a few orange and loquat trees, and cultivated a small kitchen garden. Behind the house were a stretch of wheat land, a patch of maize and a field of pumpkins. Everything was as yet primitive, mean, makeshift. But Everardus glimpsed the potentialities of the place, and determined to become its owner. He found that this was by no means so difficult as he had at first thought it would be. The owner possessing no true title to the ground, was fully aware of the fact that his holding was precarious, and a generous offer found him perfectly willing to cede his claim in favour of Everardus, and to retire to squat elsewhere in the district. A hurried visit to the attorneys at Cape Town, an interview with the authorities, who he found to his regret refused to be hurried on any account whatever, and a generous expenditure of ready money to expedite the government surveyor's languid movements, resulted in a notice in the *Gazette* to the effect that Her Majesty's Government at the Cape of Good Hope, no man having submitted a prior claim or entered legal protest, had seen fit to grant unto Everardus Nolte, for the sum stated on the title deed, the unoccupied piece of crown land, in area three thousand two hundred morgen and so many square roods known as *Knolkloof* in the Valley district, subject to such annual quitrent as by law imposed.

His negotiations for the purchase of the farm kept him at Cape Town for many weeks, and he used his spare time to good purpose. His attorneys had done their share of his business. They had succeeded in publishing to the world, or such part of it that read the *Government Gazette*—though they hoped few people would notice the unobtrusive declaration printed in small type on one of the end pages of that uninteresting official publication—that Amadeus Tereg had, with the Governor's consent and approval, changed his name to Everardus Nolte. They had succeeded in realising part of the immovable assets of his wife's mother's sister, although they had pointed out, with the commendable disinterestedness that had given their firm such a fine local reputation, that further realisation, in view of the fact that the legatee would derive a reasonable income from certain city properties, would be inadvisable—advice which Everardus had gratefully accepted. Moreover, they had been helpful in many other ways, and had given him introductions to various firms with whom he could bargain for whatever he needed for his new venture.

As to the ultimate success of that venture, Everardus had no fears. He had always longed for a farm. He felt in him the urge to wrest from the land a living. His ancestors had been tillers of the soil. He too would be one.

With his decision his wife had cordially agreed. She, too, had yearned for the peaceful quietude of a rural life, although her own girlhood had been spent in the mild excitement of the garrison town where the Castle was the centre of all social activity and culture. When she married him they had removed to the little inland town where Amadeus had worked hard, and in a manner successfully, at his trade as a saddler. Here their two children, the daughter Catherine, and the boy Gottlieb, had been born, and here, too, she had lived under a cloud since that time when her husband had been persuaded to ...

When Everardus thought of these things, his rather weary looking face showed a contraction of the fine muscles around the mouth, and to efface that, which he knew made him look stern and morose, he quickly switched his mind on to other subjects of thought. He had shaved his chin and his cheeks when he worked as a saddler; now he let his beard grow, and cultivated his moustache, which changed his appearance, although Margaret, whom he called Magriet, said it improved him. Personally he thought it did. It hid, at least, his tell-tale mouth, with those very sensitive muscles that registered, almost as quickly as his eyes did, his annoyance or his distaste.

When he returned from his prospecting tour, he told Magriet about the Valley, speaking enthusiastically, as do all those who fall under the spell of its enchantment. He pictured to her, with the natural facility of description possessed by men who have learned to observe Nature closely and who know the varying conditions of soil and climate and have a vocabulary fitted to express these constant changes, the beauty of those stately sky-splitting peaks, garbed in crimson at the sunset and majestically blue at midday. He had made her vision, as he himself had done, the immense potentialities of its virgin soil for the growing of wheat, the breeding of cattle and horses, and the cultivation of fruits. He had given her a heartening account of the inhabitants of the Valley, judging, as was perhaps natural, the whole community from the few with whom he had in some measure become intimate, describing, with grateful recollections of their innate hospitality and old world courtesy, their way of living as in no way inferior to that of the communities which she knew. He had drawn for her, on the back of a discarded quittance for leather received many years ago, the curves of the River, showing her where, in olden days, the Company's exploring party had met the elephants, and where, at a later date, the travelling coach of a *Heemraad* had been overturned by an angry rhinoceros. Magriet had listened and nodded her head sagely while he explained, and when she had left him that evening, to put Catherine and Gottlieb to bed, he had won her over to his manner of thinking, made her eager to share with him in the new adventure, and stirred her to an enthusiasm akin to his own.

But neither was blind to the difficulties and the hardships that loomed ahead. Both knew that the earth disputes mastery with the settler, and that sheer hard work, unremitting toil, and endless sacrifice are necessary to curb and tame that virgin soil into the semblance of a home and a friend. Fortunately there was no lack of capital. The attorneys at Cape Town had provided ready money, and even after Everardus had paid the very moderate sum demanded by the authorities before the official announcement of ownership could be published in the *Gazette*, there remained enough to provide them with ample security for expansion and to tide over the lean years until their investment should become remunerative. It was Magriet who touched upon other subjects, of which her husband had not thought at all. It was she who took upon herself to wipe out, so far as she was able to do so, all links with the past, which both of them wanted to forget; she who intimated to their acquaintances that they were going away, far away, into undiscovered territory, following, as she suggested but never explicitly stated, those complaining *burghers* who had trekked beyond the great river to find in the no-man's-land beyond a refuge where they could be safe from the exactions of a government that they disliked. It was not to be wondered at, therefore, that those who knew the saddler and realised that he had come into some money and had sold out, bade him goodbye under the impression that he was going far beyond their ken. They pitied him for that, and some even despised him, for there were those who did not see eye to eye with the dissatisfied *burghers*, holding it more manly and courageous to remain and fight the evils they complained of than to throw down the reins in despair and seek salvation in flight.

Everardus did not much care what they thought. His life among them had been lived largely solitary, for that one event which had made an unaccountable shadow over it had driven him and Magriet apart from them. He had no real friends among them, even as he had no open enemy. But he had never been a part of them; he had never taken his share in their interests, and his poverty had restrained him from mixing with them as freely as he might have done had his wife's mother's sister's legacy come to him a few years before. Now, he decided, he would alter all that. In his new environment, there in that beautiful Valley, on his own land, his own master, he would play his part, win new friends, and take his due share in the affairs of the community.

Chapter 2

One of the oldest farms in the Valley district belonged to Martin Rekker. It lay, not in the Valley itself, but in a larger, more open valley behind the bounding hills, more than a day's journey from the spot that Everardus had selected for his holding. A straggling road, the continuation of the main road that ran over Everardus's farm towards the Village, climbed by a gradient ever increasing in steepness, over the first high ridge, reached its peak three thousand feet above sea level on the top of a picturesquely dangerous pass, and descended with almost precipitous directness, varied here and there by sharp zigzags that had to be negotiated with skill and some courage, into an immense amphitheatre of sheltered veld, in a nook of which, overshadowed by those imposing cliffs round which the pass had been made, nestled the *Hoek* farm. One of the earliest settlers in this part of the country, old Marthinus Rekker, now, as the Valley expressed it, long ago with God, had bought twenty thousand acres of land from the old Company for next to nothing, and had turned it into a flourishing, profitable farm. Because it lay angled between the mountain spurs, he had called it the *Hoek*, or Angle, and because he had possessed a soul that sometimes soared above sweet potatoes and yellow corn, and had had plenty of time and many slaves, he had amused himself by planting trees, oaks, white and Lombardy poplars, willows and wild figs, which with the years had grown into giants that shaded the old homestead and made a tangle of interlacing branches behind it where a large poplar bush had spread outwards and upwards to meet the hill slopes. He had planted an orchard and a vineyard, ploughed many acres of ground into well evened wheat land, and made, close to the house, a garden whose rich black soil gave abundance of vegetables and flowers.

A more satisfying farm than that of the Rekkers it would have been impossible to find even in the Valley itself. Its neatly whitewashed gables gleamed cool under the greenery of the overarching oaks; its attendant barns, sheep *kraals*, low walled threshing floor, and quaint sedge thatched huts for the slaves, impressed one with their cleanliness, their neatness, and their manifest utility combined with charm. Some of the more prosaic inhabitants of the Valley had shrugged their shoulders when they saw these adjuncts, so artistically disposed in a setting of artificially arranged greenery, with a background of imposing cliff and hill slope. But old Marthinus Rekker, now long ago with God, had had an eye for these things, and the means to indulge his fancy, and in time, realising that there was method behind his fancies, the Valley had ceased to jibe and learned to appreciate one who could even make his fancies pay in solid *riksdalers* when he sold his produce at the Village.

Long ago old Marthinus had died, and now one who to the Valley was known as old Martin, his son, reigned in his stead. He, too, had his fancies, and the Valley indulged him, bore with him, and respected him not only for his wealth but equally much for his solid good sense, his neighbourliness, and his character. His wife had died many years ago, and he lived on his farm in company with his eldest son, who was married and had a family. The second son farmed somewhere in the Valley, as successfully as his grandfather and his father had done at the *Hoek*, but Gys was a pure utilitarian, who looked to the immediate future and saw no reason why he should waste his time in beautifying his farm before he could make it pay.

Behind the homestead, tumbling wildly over a precipice, fell a magnificent waterfall, whose water, reduced to tameness in a neatly channelled canal fringed with royal fern and arum lilies, fed a large dam, which in turn gave its water to the mill-race and after that to the garden and the orchards. The mill-house, built under two large oak trees whose trunks still retained the iron staples to which old Marthinus had bound his recalcitrant slaves as a preliminary to the paternal correction which he was in the habit of administering when he thought it necessary to do so—and in justice to his memory it must be added that he rarely resorted to force, and that, when emancipation came, his slaves, one and all, refused to leave the *Hoek* but remained to serve him loyally as free men and women—had strong, home-made machinery inside, and a ponderous water-wheel outside, whose movement, when the sluice gates were opened and the water permitted to stream over the wooden partitions, made a monotonous but pleasant splashy sound in the cool air. Tradition clustered around that mill-house, for old Martin remembered how as a boy he had sought shelter in it from a troop of wild Bushmen who had shot poisoned arrows into the thatch, and how, on one occasion, the fierce Lord Governor had got his green velvet coat all floury with bran dust in trying to satisfy himself that the mill stones worked properly. That was a good while ago, while his father was still alive, for there had been talk of the Governor's stallion, and of entering one of the *Hoek* horses for the cup to be raced for on Greenpoint Common.

In the large dining room of the homestead, old Martin sat at a little side table before the window on the evening of a cool March day. The room was sombre, for the house had been built for coolness, because the Valley district is notorious for its oppressive heat in summer time, and famous for its mild, frostless winters. Above the rafters showed solid cedarwood beams, that held up the neatly worked thatch, revealing the cordage with which the straw sheaves had been bound together, and the underside of the straw itself, now darkened by age and smoke. From the horizontal beams hung mealies, double cobs fastened by their leaves and slung over the beam, balancing themselves by their own weight. The walls were whitewashed from top to within three feet of the ground, where the whitewash gave place to a dado of bright blue, glorified by arabesques and geometrical designs in red and yellow and green. The floor was of hard stamped clay, daily smeared with dung, so that a slightly aromatic scent lingered in the room, mingling with the odour of food from the adjacent kitchen. In the middle of the room stood a large cedarwood table, now bare of any covering for the maids had removed the cloth, and the light of the oil lamp merely served to show the fine polish of the wood and the equally fine graining. Here and there on the floor were spread skin rugs, the heavy pelt of the grey-maned jackal, the ocelli-spotted skin of a leopard, and the fantastically designed kaross made of goat's skin cut into triangles and circles and neatly sewn together with thin sinews. On the walls hung a few coloured lithographs, and over the massive stinkwood sideboard, laden with old Dutch earthenware mingled with cheap modern glass and still cheaper crockery, a large framed portrait of the Queen in very early Victorian court dress. On a tallboy at the other end of the room stood a fine Flemish glass carafe, flanked by several equally choice specimens of glassware, heirlooms in the Rekker family, jealously treasured since the time when Serafina Rekker, who had been born a Coursel and therefore allied by blood to one of the Lords Major, had brought them out from Arnhem in the *Ster der Hoop* as part of her dowry. Leather seated chairs, a home-made arm-chair and a comfortable stinkwood sofa, made more comfortable by the addition of fur covered cushions stuffed with goat's hair, and a number of small wooden footstools, shaped like little boxes and meant to carry in winter time the braziers of glowing coals with which the household warmed itself, completed the furniture of the room, except for that portion of it where old Martin sat at the window.

There he had before him a small cedarwood table, highly polished so that its surface reflected almost faithfully the two home made candles that burned in a tall, double-branched silver candlestick. On the table were set a couple of small silver dishes containing peeled almonds and raisins, a silver salver with a bottle of wine and a couple of wine glasses, a chess board, finely inlaid with ebony and bone, and a little velvet bag. On the other side of the table, facing him, was a large cushion-covered chair, now occupied by his old friend and crony, Doremus van Aard, a Valley farmer who had come to pay his usual bi-annual visit.

Martin Rekker was a tall, almost ungainly angular man, already on the wrong side of sixty, with a smooth, clean-shaven face, elongated into a sharp jutting chin. His complexion was tanned and brown, and his skin was wrinkled into innumerable little creases that, radiating from the outer corners of his eyes, spread downwards across his cheeks and upwards towards his temples. His wide, high forehead, his large grey-blue eyes, overhung by massive eyebrows whose pearly grey matched the colour of the remaining hairs on his almost bald head, and his regular features, with the sharp, finely shaped nose and the large, thin lipped-mouth, proclaimed him a handsome man, an aristocratic type that in youth must have attracted anyone with a sense of beauty, and with the discrimination necessary to discount such externals as a patched jacket, a snuff-stained velvet waistcoat, and monstrously ill-fitting corduroy trousers. His really beautiful hands, slender in the palm, with long, delicate fingers, and evenly rounded nails, were, like his face, browned by the sun-glare and hardened by manual work, but a glance at them and at the delicate wrists above them, strengthened the first impression that Martin Rekker came from a race finely framed and belonging to the best Nordic stock.

His companion, Doremus van Aard, was totally different in appearance, being a short, comfortably fleshy man whose round, chubby face, almost equally round short-cropped head, and podgy hands could not for a moment be compared with those of his friend. But what Doremus lacked in personal beauty he made up by his geniality, his good temper, and his solidity. His good humoured face radiated friendliness, cheerfulness, and good sense. His little hazel-brown eyes twinkled with merriment, and his chubby face, with the upper lip clean shaven and a fringe of greyish brown beard jutting out from under his chin, was perpetually wreathed in a smile that seemed to start from both corners of his full lipped little mouth and to spread upwards until it touched both his little ears. He looked like a grown up schoolboy enjoying a joke, and his short arms and legs seemed to share in the merriment that convulsed him, for his whole body shook with laughter, and his little twinkling eyes dimmed with the tears that his enjoyment forced from them.

'It is all very well for you to laugh, Brother Doremus,' said old Martin, in a voice that one would have expected from him, a carefully modulated, precisely enunciating voice, speaking the vernacular Dutch with a proper appreciation of gender. 'It is all very fine to laugh, but I can tell you, as I do now, that it is no laughing matter when one is expecting to find good wine to discover that it has all turned to vinegar.'

'I ... I ... really, Brother Martin ... I cannot refrain ... from laughing ... when I think that you, who are a ... a ... a, what d'ye call it?'

'I think the word you want is *connoisseur*, Brother. It is a French word, and means one who knows. From the Latin *cognoscere*, Brother.'

'Excellent ... you who know ... and you to be spoofed like that. It is choice, Brother Martin, choice ... You must permit me to laugh. As the good Book says, laughter is good for the soul. I have, of course, no desire to pain you, Brother ... but really ...'

'If you have had your fill of the enjoyment that the narration of my trifling mishap has given you, Brother Doremus,' remarked his friend, stiffly, but at the same time with a disarming smile that robbed the reproof of any sting it might have possessed, 'we might now, if you feel inclined for it, concentrate our attention upon something both useful and pleasant.'

'Quite, Brother Martin. You are, I believe, one up.' Doremus picked up the little velvet bag, and drew the purse string. 'But tonight I think you will find your match ...'

Gently he took from the bag the carved ivory chessmen, Indian work, dating back to the time when Aquaviva had attempted to convert the great Akbar and had failed in the attempt. He took a pawn in each hand and held them behind his back, and Martin, following the customary ritual, repeated the childish formula for choice of colour.

'You have red,' said Doremus, taking out his pear wood pipe, and filling it from his pouch. 'I therefore begin.' He placed his men carefully in position while his opponent did the same. 'Let me see, last time you beat me with the knight. This time I shall venture the Lopez.'

'Venture what you please,' replied Martin, cheerfully. 'I shall do my best, Brother, to defeat you.'

The first half-dozen moves were made with the celerity of accustomed chess players, for both knew them by heart. At the seventh move Martin paused. Deliberately he took out his snuff box from his waistcoat pocket—a large oval shaped silver plated box, and handed it to Doremus, who took a pinch between thumb and forefinger. Martin himself used thumb and ring-finger, delicately apportioning the snuff to each nostril, lingering over the aroma, and repressing the effects long after Doremus had ended his sneezing and resumed his pipe.

'It is a trifle too heavily scented for me,' he said, gravely. 'But it is good ratafia, all the same. I get it from the chemist in the Loop Street at Cape Town. It is the same make that old Somerset used. He sent my father a box of it, years ago.'

'It is indeed. I rather like it heavily scented, Brother. But it is your move if you please.'

'Then I move this pawn, so. Tell me, Brother, what impression have you formed of your new neighbour? I had a talk with the magistrate last week. He seems to think that the fellow is likely to be an acquisition to our District. But I have not met him yet.'

'I have met him several times, Brother Martin. You know when he first came to spy out the land, he overnighted with us. We found him a good fellow ... I move bishop, which threatens your knight, Brother ... but one cannot tell. Since then he has bought *Knolkloof* ... you know that, of course. I must say I think he has bought wisely. I always said that it is one of the best bits of land in the Valley, and it was wasted on that Black creature who had it. I am glad one of our people has it now.'

'But that is the question, Brother Doremus. Is he one of us? I am not so sure. I move my horse so ... now you can tell your bishop to attend to his parochial duties ... I am not so sure. I cannot recall his name. Nolte ... it is not known to me.'

'I really don't know where he comes from, Brother. But does it matter? I mean, cannot we take the man as we find him? And from what I have seen of him ... he stayed with us quite recently, and I saw a good deal of him ... in fact I shall see a great deal more of him, for I have promised to help him. As the Book says, one must deal neighbourly with one's neighbours.'

'Quite so ... quite so. I should not like to treat him in any other than a Christian fashion ... I move my pawn, so ... but, pardon me if I remind you, Brother, there are neighbours and neighbours. I do not speak of social standing, for that is sometimes of temporary quality, and may indeed be a passing phase. But there are such things as family and blood, Brother. You and I, after all, can look back upon honourable forebears, and you yourself, even though you do not look after these things as you should ... I have often told you that you should have your coat of arms properly displayed ... you yourself will admit, I am sure, that these things count for something. You cannot make wine out of wild grapes, and you cannot make a man out of indifferent stock. It is for that reason ... I give check to your queen, Brother ... that I am doubtful in my mind about our new fellow *burgher*. I fancy I remember my father speaking of Noltes, but they were in the eastern districts. Does he speak like one from there?'

'His speech, Brother, is more like that of the Cape folk. You know they clip their words, and they are not always correct with their genders. He is careless about these.'

'You have enquired, have you not, Brother? Asked him, cautiously and in a gentlemanly way?'

'Indeed I have, Brother. But he has told me next to nothing. I think he keeps his own counsel, and I cannot very well take it amiss. At least not until we know him better.'

'Perhaps not. I move my rook so, which gives check to your king. The position is precarious for you, Brother, but the Lopez is always like that. It is fierce at the beginning, like a flood that comes tumbling down the mountain, but if you manage to stop it, then it is as harmless as quiet water. As I was saying, my doubt is as to his standing. I do not wish to be hard on any man, particularly not on one who comes as a stranger and a beginner among us, but we have certain obligations, Brother, to ourselves, if I might so express it. You will, I am sure, admit that.'

'That I do, Brother. How on earth am I to get out of this? You must give me a little time.'

'Gladly.' Martin produced his snuff box, titivated his nostrils delicately, and helped himself to almonds and raisins. Doremus pored, with wrinkled brows and a pathetic look of annoyance on his face, over the chess board.

'I presume the fellow has some money. Else he could not buy the place. Or at least not start farming on the scale that I am told he is trying. They tell me that it is his intention to go in for horse breeding. Now that demands capital, ready money, and it is after all chancy.'

'He has money enough,' said Doremus, who had allowed his pipe to go out in his earnest concentration over the board. 'And I must say that from what he has told me, the fellow has some knowledge of farming. He is looking out for a young man as helper. I have thought of letting him have Matryk ...'

'The boy has the makings of a good farmer in him,' said Martin, pleasantly. 'I allow it would be a good chance for him, provided the new neighbour is the sort of man we hope he is. You know, Brother Doremus, we ought to be a little more careful. It is not so very long ago that we had all these newcomers ...'

'Some of them have turned out very good *burghers*, Brother Martin. Look at Seldon and Andrew.'

'I have nothing to say against either. But not all have turned out so well as Nephew Seldon and Nephew Andrew. And some of them were not of our class, Brother. They were strangers, and are likely to remain strangers.'

'But Nephew E'vrard is not a stranger, Brother. He is one of us. He speaks our language, though to be sure he can sling English almost as well as the magistrate or Nephew Seldon can. But he is manifestly one of us. He is of our faith ...'

'Has he delivered up his attestation certificate? It is a point I had in mind. You, as Elder, should know.'

'Now I come to think of it, Brother, he hasn't. I must look into that. But how the devil am I to get out of this? If I move my king then you jump my rook ... and if I move my knight then I lose my queen.'

'You can always hoist the white flag, Brother. So he has not handed in his attestation yet. That is curious. Do you by any chance happen to know what His Reverence thinks of him?'

'No. He has not been to see the parson, Brother. Doubtless he will, as soon as he visits the Village. I shall move my rook. I can only lose it, after all ... there.'

'Then I take that pawn, and give check again. You overlook that, Brother. If I may remark, little things make perfection but perfection, Brother, is by no means a little thing. To come back to that fellow Nolte ... you did not find out if he has any dependants?'

'I believe so. He has a wife and two children. But, Brother, as the Scripture by the word of the Preacher says, "yielding pacifieth great offences" ... though I know not in what I have greatly offended, I strike my flag. It is sheer bad luck, but you are now two up. I take red this time, and I shall play the Sjokko. It leads to a close game, but it is not so fierce as this damned Lopez.'

'Very well. But let us pour ourselves a glass of wine first. I have heard various things, Brother, some of which I cannot credit. There be those that say he has had to fly from justice. Do not think that I imply that there is anything in it ...'

'Did not Solomon remark, as the good Book tells us, that where there is no tale-bearer, strife ceases, Brother? And Timothy, whom Paul loved, did he not exclaim that there are tattlers and busybodies, speaking things they ought not? People will hazard all sorts of surmises when they don't rightly know where the truth lies. Your prosperity, Brother Martin.'

'Yours, Brother Doremus. It is just on the sweet side.'

'A good wine, all the same. Better than mine, this year.'

'You must let me taste yours, to compare. But you have not ripened yours yet, surely? I only started pressing my grapes last month. This is, of course, last year's.'

'I meant that. Seriously, Brother ... yes, here we are, all crowded together, and now the least little false move lands me in a mess ... seriously, I think Nephew E'vrard is all right. He is a good man, Brother. Mark my words, he will be an acquisition to the District.'

'I am glad to hear that, Brother Doremus. As a matter of fact, I take no pleasure hearing people tell tales about their neighbour. I value your opinion, for you have met and talked with the fellow. But I say again, we ought to be careful. Blood, Brother Doremus, will tell in the long run ... blood and family. We have kept ours pure, thank God, and I should regret it sadly if we failed to keep it pure in the future. Will you take another glass?'

'Gladly, Brother Martin. I quite agree with you. But, between ourselves, you need have no fear. Nolte is a White man just like you or me.'

'I did not mean it in that sense, Brother. But I should like to meet him, to judge for myself. I move the pawn ... so.'

'That can easily be managed. He has now gone to Cape Town, to buy things. But he returns next week, and will then live in a tent on the farm. He intends to start building before the rains come. He has already asked me to look out for some sheep. I thought about Nephew Barend's ewes ... he can easily spare fifty or even a hundred.'

'Very well. We must make a plan to arrange a meeting.'

Thereafter both the old gentlemen busied themselves in intricate schemes with the chessmen, and when they separated for the night Doremus had reduced his host's lead to nil. Which gave him such hearty satisfaction that he forgot to quote the apposite scriptural text which he had decided to recite in case he won two out of three games.

Chapter 3

What it could the Valley gave to Everardus Nolte. It gave freely, generously, ungrudgingly, with the courtesy and hospitality innate in a community so primitive in its conception of communal obligations. For the first month it looked upon the newcomer as an interesting and curious novelty. In the second month, it regarded him as a stranger within the gates, needing advice, help, and encouragement, and it proffered all three, with smiling insistence and interested eagerness. It told him, with much circumlocution and many deprecatory gestures, that life in the Valley was bound to be hard, and that the farmer's existence was embittered by many vicissitudes, acts of God that tore the remnants of patience out of a man's soul, misfortunes of Nature that made him despair of worldly salvation from tilling the soil. It adduced numerous examples, derived from a long experience and a vast memory of ill-chances encountered through several generations, but it spoke of all these things with a certain dignified cheerfulness that robbed the warnings of much of their effectiveness had they been addressed to anyone not so fully aware of their gravity as Everardus Nolte.

He, knowing the country and its kind, fully realised that what the Valley told him had not been tweaked solely out of the imagination of the tellers. There were too many proofs to the contrary around him. Years ago the Valley had received a sudden influx of immigrants, when a party of the 1820 settlers had arrived to occupy holdings in the District. Some of them had made good, but many of them had found the hardships of farming under conditions to which they were totally strange far too severe for them, and had departed, so that the Valley no longer knew them, and, if the truth must be told, scarcely cared to remember them. A few had prospered exceedingly, more through following a trade or profession than through attempting to compete with the older settlers on their own lines. There was Thomas Seldon, for example, who had arrived with the immigrants, a fresh-faced, active-limbed young Leicester youth, and was now regarded as one of the best men in the Valley, although it was admitted that he was an exception and that one swallow never yet made a summer. Young Thomas had not at first attempted to work his holding. He had gone to Cape Town and returned with a varied and variegated stock of negotiable wares, bought on credit from a wholesale firm. With these as his stock-in-trade he had tramped from farm to farm, selling his goods at a fair profit, making friends as well as customers wherever he went, and winning for himself a reputation for honesty, fairness, and comradeship that no one grudged him. In time he had exchanged his pack for a donkey cart and, his profits increasing as his clientele became larger and his ventures more successful, he had built himself a wayside store on his holding, handed over the cultivation of his land to a paid manager, and busied himself increasingly with his shop and his trading. Now Thomas Seldon could look back upon twenty and more years of hard work crowned with indubitable success. His wanderings on foot throughout the district had brought him into intimate relations with all the farmers; he knew each man's worth and standing; he knew their children, their pedigrees and their capacities; he had learned to speak their language, not faultlessly, for his tongue still refused to elide where elision was required and he had never fully mastered the glottic catch that he deemed to be a gutteral, but sufficiently well to be able to converse on equal terms with any of them. He had married, not indeed one of them—for he had chosen his wife from among the English settlers, but she had adapted herself so well to her new environment that nobody looked upon her as a stranger and an alien, for she too could 'sling' the language, and no one could say a word against the manner in which she ran her household.

Then there was Quakerley, another English settler, who had made good on a four thousand acre holding not very far from the spot that Everardus had selected, and was now breeding sheep and planting orange trees with a success that some of his neighbours envied. He too had acclimatised, and few, seeing him in his rough corduroy trousers and grey worsted shirt, would have taken him for what he really was—a member of an English country family.

These were two outstanding examples of newcomers who by their grit, their patient hard work, and their adaptation to their new environment, had made good. But on the debit side, as the Valley took care to explain to Everardus Nolte, there were others who had failed, who had sold or abandoned their holdings and had either left the District, to seek fortune in other parts of the Colony where the conditions were less onerous, or had settled in the Village to earn a living by trade or by manual labour. The very spot he had selected, Everardus was told, had been in possession of one of these settlers, but had been abandoned by him, and taken over by the manumitted slave. In the district were many graves of the men who had come out in 1820 and who had died before they had earned from the soil a competence and a home. The Valley spoke respectfully of them, and had pitied them when they died, but life was strenuous and exacting, and there was no time to waste on failure. So much Everardus gathered very quickly from his communion with the inhabitants of the Valley, and he saw clearly from the first that his success as a farmer, as one of them competing with them in friendly and neighbourly rivalry, could only be assured through hard work, a plodding patience, and an imitation of that all-concealing cheerfulness that masked whatever petulance resulted from these unfortunate acts of God or those disturbing mischances of Nature that on occasion prevented their best efforts from reaching fruition.

With that object in view he proceeded cautiously, soliciting advice from the seniors of the Valley community, deprecating his own lack of practical experience, and following such counsel as seemed to him to be based on mature reflection. Old Doremus van Aard, Uncle Dorie as he was known familiarly to all and sundry in the Valley who could not claim to be his immediate contemporaries, an Elder of the church and a man of considerable standing in the District, with the official status of a field-cornet or under-sheriff, was his immediate neighbour, although their homesteads lay several miles apart. Uncle Dorie owned the fertile *Sandvlei* farm, renowned for its fine vineyard and the excellence of its wheat and rye. There he lived, a chubby genial patriarch with a small squadron of children and grandchildren, and the much respected *Baas* or Master of a community of half-caste natives, the greater number of whom had originally been his slaves. He was a cheerful, downright old man, much given to quoting, and on occasion misquoting, Scripture, who esteemed good living, was friendliness personified, and withal a shrewd, level-headed farmer who managed to surmount whatever obstacles the acts of God or the mischances of Nature put in his way. To Nolte he had been a good friend from the first. It was on *Sandvlei* that Everardus had found a hospitable home when he had come to spy out the land; it was *Oom* Dorie who had cordially approved of his intention to purchase *Knolkloof*, and it was the Elder who, now that the title deeds had been secured, helped him in every way possible to settle down on his newly acquired land. At first Everardus had been doubtful about his welcome in the Valley. After all he was a stranger, an intruder, and he naturally imagined that as such the Valley would look askance at him, especially as there was that ... Of course, the Valley was not supposed to know what had taken place many years ago in a district far beyond its confines, but Everardus was diffident, self-conscious, and to some extent suspicious. The geniality of his reception at *Sandvlei* and the kindly interest of his new acquaintances showed him that his doubts were uncharitable. As he wrote to Margaret, giving her his fortnightly budget of news, no one could be more friendly or helpful than *Oom* Dorie had been. If it had not been for *Oom* Dorie's constant assistance, ungrudgingly given, his progress on the new farm would not have been so speedy nor so satisfactory.

In truth there was much to be done. His new holding was to all intents and purposes virgin soil, for the former occupier had cultivated but a strip of land, sufficient to bring in corn and mealies and pumpkins for his own subsistence. The little two-roomed shanty was of no use as a homestead, and Everardus found that as it occupied the best site for a dwelling house, it would be necessary to raze it and build new premises. With Uncle Dorie's help he planned his new home on cardboard, a roomy house, thatch covered with the thatching laid down on good solid popular rafters with oaken cross beams, and with a pergola-covered *stoep* over which he could grow vines. Seldon, the acknowledged contractor of the district, agreed to build it for him, together with the barns and out-houses and the cellarage that he needed. Uncle Dorie, accustomed to see beginners start with the minimum of dwelling space, had stared at this ambitious programme, but Everardus has smilingly assured him that the money for building would be forthcoming, and it was only later on that Everardus discovered that the Elder had stood surety for him with Seldon, a mark of trust and confidence that the newcomer cordially appreciated, even though he thought that it had been a superfluity. It was Uncle Dorie, too, who had helped him to get Natives for his farm. Many were needed, and Native labour was by no means abundant, for the wages, paid mostly in kind, were not sufficiently high to tempt those who lazied in the locations or squatted on the farms as hangers-on, doing odd jobs, but chary of engaging themselves for any definite period. It was Uncle Dorie who procured old Sylvester, a half-caste Hottentot with a strong strain of Mozambique blood in him, who had been a slave and had wandered into the Valley district in search of work. Sylvester brought with him his wife, whether by law or by custom no one had ever thought it desirable to find out, Regina, a wrinkled but podgy woman skilled at kitchen work and a mistress in the art of baking bread and griddle cakes. She too had been a slave, and both she and her husband had that respect for authority and that conception of loyalty which were innate in those who had been brought up under a system of paternal slavery. Everardus knew from personal experience that the lot of the average slave in the Colony had not been a hard or a bitter one, and that senior slaves of the type of his newly found cook and her husband were dependable servants who more than repaid whatever kindness or courtesy their masters showed them. Nor was

Sylvester amiss in gauging the value of his new situation. He had been perfectly willing to remain with old master Dorie, but he realised that at *Sandvlei*, where there were older servants who had been with the *Oubaas* (Old Master) for generations, he would have had to fill a strictly subordinate position, whereas with his new '*Baas*' he had a chance of becoming the headman or man-doer of the Native employees. He exerted himself to the full to prove himself worthy of such a position. Garrulous, good-natured, and easy-going, he was popular among the half-caste Natives, and it was not very long before he had established a small community of these on the new farm from which Everardus obtained such labour as he wanted. They selected a patch of land on the eastern side of the stream, where they built, very rapidly and with commendable neatness, a semi-circle of reed huts, a common outdoor fireplace, and a small enclosed garden which in time became the Native 'camp' of the farm *Knolkloof*.

Everardus laid out his new holding with an eye to the future. He had heard from *Oom* Dorie about the show farm in the district, the beautifully cultivated and artistically designed *Hoek* where old Marthinus Rekker had lived and died, and he could understand and appreciate the policy and the methods of that exemplary pioneer. So he planted oaks, poplars and wild figs, and centred these round about the homestead, building his cattle and sheep kraals outside their range, on the hill slope where the ground was too stony for immediate cultivation. But while he gave so much attention to the aesthetic side of his farm, he did not neglect, as Uncle Dorie had at first feared that he might, the strictly utilitarian. He cleared acres of land from bush and scrub, levelled them with the broad raking harrows, and made them ready for sowing wheat, rye and barley. He deep-delved a patch of black soil for a vegetable garden, and prepared another, and much larger, tract for an orchard, where he planted some hundreds of the little seedling orange trees that he had bought from Quakerley. Nearer to the homestead he made another and smaller orchard of fruit trees, peaches, mainly of the large yellow clingstone variety, apples, the big red-cheeked sort that Uncle Dorie procured for him from the mission station deep in the mountain ranges behind the valley, walnuts brought from Wellington through the good agency of his Cape Town attorneys, plums, figs, loquats, and mulberries. On the advice of his neighbours, though somewhat against his own inclination, for he was doubtful of his ability to make wine, he planted a vineyard, putting in thousands of muscadel, pontac and crystal cuttings, together with an additional thousand of white hanepoot.

These improvements took time, and while his house was being built, he lived in a reed hut, fashioned after the style of those inhabited by his Natives, but strengthened and cooled by an outer layer of clay. Seldon's workmen, half-castes who did their masoning, plastering and joinery with admirable skill and expedition, made good progress with the buildings, and by the time the first rains had deluged the District, the thatching was finished, and he could occupy one of the rooms.

He now set himself to furnish his house, and here again he found that his new friends gave him helpful advice. He had intended to have all his furniture made of stinkwood. The magnificent specimens of carpentry in such wood that he had seen in Cape Town and in other districts had fired him with the ambition to possess similar furniture in his own home, and on one of his visits to his attorneys he had asked them to have various pieces made to his specifications. But now he counter-manded that order, not before part of the goods had been made. He had seen and admired the lovely polish acquired by cedarwood furniture. Every homestead in the Valley possessed some article of furniture in cedarwood, locally made by artisans who had been trained at the mission station behind the mountains, and he determined to go there and see for himself what they could do for him. He wanted a large dining table, several wardrobes and chests of drawers, tall-boys, and a sideboard, *stoep* sofas and chairs, and all these, Uncle Dorie assured him, could be easily and cheaply procured in the District.

The rest of his household goods he obtained from Cape Town, at a cost, mainly for transport, that almost frightened Uncle Dorie. It took many weeks for the mule wagons to traverse the several hundred miles that lay between his farm and the capital, and the cost per hundred weight for transport was consequently high. But with the exception of such things as he could procure locally, at Seldon's shop, and in the larger store at the little Village, all his goods and chattels had to be imported, and as he had determined to have a complete installation before his wife came to share with him their new home, he did not grudge the money necessary to obtain what he wanted. It was a more difficult thing to stock the farm. Discussing the matter with Uncle Dorie, he had found that the Elder's imagination stretched no further than wheat growing, wine making, and gardening. Sheep farming, Uncle Dorie told him, was unsatisfactory, although of course everyone must keep a small flock for domestic purposes, while cattle were required for food and for draught purposes. There was, Uncle Dorie explained, far too small an area of grazing land for sheep on his farm; one estimated, according to the Elder, two acres of grazing land per sheep, and even then, with scab and the wasting disease, sheep farming was precarious. He advised a flock of goats, and a few sheep for table use, nothing more. But Everardus had set his heart on horse breeding, and when he told his friend of his intention to start with a few selected mares and a couple of Hantam stallions, Uncle Dorie nodded his head. There was something in the notion, the Elder acquiesced. The farm was good enough for horse breeding, although the extent of level land was not so considerable as it might have been. Very likely, however, Everardus could in time acquire the annexe, which was eight thousand acres in extent and unoccupied Crown land. And horse breeding could be made profitable, if it was properly undertaken. Several settlers in the country adjacent to the Valley had made a success of it, and the horses from the Hantam farms were justifiably renowned. There was the widow Louw, whose horses had been purchased, at magnificent prices, by the Governor himself. Yea, it was a matter to be considered, and Nephew Ev'rard might do worse than consider it.

Nephew Ev'rard did consider it. He considered it to such an extent that he bought his horses even before he had selected his furniture, and he bought wisely, though by no means cheaply. He knew the points of a horse, and he picked out likely breeding animals, adding to his outbuildings a suitable stable and wagon house. He bought, too, a span of oxen, heavy, long-horned Afrikaner oxen, uniformly red of coat, a perfect span that cost him more money than he had intended to spend, but of which Uncle Dorie most heartily approved when he saw them. He acquired some cows, four mules, and a couple of donkeys, and at a timely auction at the Village he invested, again on Uncle Dorie's advice, in a hundred sheep and half that number of goats.

Meanwhile his Natives had been capably organised by Sylvester, and had reduced what a few months before had been an uncultivated waste into some semblance of order. Progress was slow enough, and Everardus was impatient to see results. But he realised that he had to hasten slowly, and he felt, too, the need for further assistance. Again Uncle Dorie came forward with a suggestion. What Nephew Ev'rard required was a sub-manager; a white man, who could be trusted to look after things in Nephew Ev'rard's absence, not a partner—he would not dream of suggesting such a thing to Nephew Ev'rard—but a youngish fellow, not above learning from his elders and betters, a fellow who would not presume, who would know his place without having to be constantly reminded of it. As Nephew Ev'rard probably knew, the younger generation thought it had acquired knowledge by the spoonful—just as if the Almighty ladled it into one's skull, which Nephew Ev'rard knew was by no means the case, knowledge coming from experience. Did not the good Book say that 'in the sweat of one's countenance one had to acquire experience,' and did not the Apostle Paul counsel the Thessalonians to 'work with their own hands, that they might walk honestly toward them that are without, and that they might lack of nothing?' That being so, if he might so express himself, it would undoubtedly be to Nephew Ev'rard's benefit to obtain the services of a youth suitable for that purpose. If he happened to know of one? Why yes, otherwise—Nephew Ev'rard must forgive him for reminding him of a fact so patent—he would not have hazarded the suggestion. There was a youth, one Matryk Thalussen, on a neighbouring farm. A good youth, though folk did say that he had a line through his head, which meant merely that in understanding of things written and read his capacity was not ideal. A strong sturdy youth, with nothing so far as he, Doremus, knew against his moral character, neither given to sauntering nor to any vice, and, yes, indubitably, a member of the church, although to be sure the council of Elders and Deacons had showed some obstinacy in accepting him because he did not remember the proper answers to the short catechism. And talking of membership, might he remind Nephew Ev'rard that Nephew Ev'rard had not yet formally handed in his own attestation of membership? It was of course merely a formality. He would be the last person—yes, the very last, if he might so express himself—to question the fact that Nephew Ev'rard was a proper legitimised member of the church, but formalities were after all formalities, and without the production of his attestation Nephew Ev'rard could not be admitted to the Lord's communion table. Nephew Ev'rard must forgive him for broaching the subject, but as an Elder, and as such in some ways responsible for administrative matters in the church, he had certain obligations.

Everardus, who had entirely forgotten about his certificate, felt a qualm of conscience at the reminder. He wondered if it was possible to obtain a proper certificate that did not disclose his old name. He would have to refer the matter to his attorneys at Cape Town, and trust them not to make a mistake. Very likely it could be done. If it could not, he would have to invent some excuse, although he felt that any subterfuge would be dangerous and might land him in unpleasant complications. But apparently the Elder had no misgivings, and the conversation veered back to Matryk Thalussen. Everardus agreed to give the good youth a trial. He proved to be a gaunt, over-grown stripling, tremendously long in the leg and arm, with a vacant, stolid look on his face when in repose, but with an expansive smile when interested. There could be no doubt about his mental incapacity, for he could barely write his name, and his reading was elementary. But he seemed to be strong and willing and good natured, and Everardus decided to employ him. When he saw how well the boy worked, and how cheerfully he got on with the Natives, who treated him with great deference although they sometimes laughed at him, Everardus came to the conclusion that his choice had not been so bad after all. Almost daily the now rapidly improving farm was visited by members of the Valley community who came, partly out of sheer curiosity and partly out of a real desire to show their friendliness, and drank coffee, many cups of it, with Everardus on the newly built *stoep*. From the Village they came and from the neighbouring farms, men, women and children, all eager to make the acquaintance of the newcomer, and all perfectly friendly, though sometimes officious and, from Everardus's point of view, altogether too free with suggestion and question. In time he learned by experience to evade answering without offence, and to turn the conversation when it touched upon his past life and his career before he came to live in the Valley. There were some of his new acquaintances whom he instinctively liked at first sight. Among these were the Village magistrate, a plump, very upright little gentleman, who talked in a harsh voice, knew no Dutch and obviously a good deal about Everardus, but who inspired him with the feeling that he was utterly friendly, and the Village pastor, Reverend Sybrand de Smee, a courtly, wizened old cleric who wore horn-rimmed spectacles, talked a very correct and accented Dutch, and seemed wholly unlike most of the clergymen that Everardus had hitherto met. But above all it was old Martin Rekker who impressed him most. The old man's grave, stately courtesy, his imposing figure, his long delicately slender fingers, and his old fashioned manner were in striking contrast to the bluff geniality and the sometimes boisterous friendliness of the other visitors. Uncle Dorie had brought him one morning, and they had walked round the farm, inspected the improvements and the building operations, and taken coffee under the oak trees planted by the former owner. Old Martin, whom Everardus, following the custom of the Valley, had called Uncle as he called Doremus, had expressed himself satisfied with what he had seen, and had talked with the newcomer in a friendly but rather restrained manner. It was only after his visitors had gone that Everardus realised how subtly the old man had talked, how finely he had probed, without giving the impression of searching, and how much, possibly, he had learned. Yet Uncle Martin had so impressed him that the realisation did not bring him any discomfort but rather a sense of relief, for he was confident that the old man had not disliked him. Somehow he found that confidence very pleasant. He liked Uncle Dorie very much, but he was prepared to like Uncle Dorie's old friend even better. To Everardus it was as surprising as it was gratifying to find that among his new neighbours there were so many to whom he found himself attracted. He had imagined, when he came to spy out the land, that in these parts of the Colony, so remote from that chief centre of culture, the capital, he would be among men who were uncouth, good material indeed but roughly hewn with facets unpolished and with manners deteriorated through long absence from all cultural and softening influences. The hospitality and the innate kindliness he had anticipated; they were characteristics of his race and were to be found all over the Colony, even among those who had shaken its dust from their feet and had adventured into the unknown lands beyond the great river. But he had not expected to find old world stateliness and dignified courtesy such as Uncle Martin had exhibited, pleasant camaraderie such as Uncle Dorie had shown him, nor the culture and refinement that he had found in the home of the Seldons, and the sweet reasonableness of the old pastor. As he thought over these things, he felt that he had not yet learned all that there was to know about his new environment. He appreciated the homeliness of the Valley community, just as he appreciated its sturdy cheerfulness, its obvious good health, and, what had come to him as another surprise, the physical perfection of most of its male members. They all seemed to be taller, sturdier, better proportioned than the men he had lived with in his old district; their complexions, though tanned by the sun-glare, were healthy and fresh, in the younger ones fair almost to transparency; their musculature excellently well developed; their carriage and poise admirable. Comparing himself with the average, he could honestly say that he had no need to feel inferior. In education he was manifestly above their average, for he could speak both English and Dutch fluently, whereas even Uncle Dorie knew little or no English, and the magistrate no Dutch. There was little, so far as he could see, that leavened them culturally, and beyond their farming and their home interests they seemed to have nothing that could serve as immediate points of contact between them and the gay social world at the capital. But he realised that his knowledge was as yet imperfect, and that there were many angles which he had not studied. Already he had learned to love the Valley. It was to be his home, he hoped, until he needed no other than the little plot which he had already selected under the young poplar trees where he and Margaret, when their time came, would be laid to rest. Hitherto, he reflected, he had had no real home. Here, then, he would work for himself and for the Valley, and if it was his good fortune to win the friendship of such men as old Martin and the pastor, he felt that he had it in him to work successfully for both.

Chapter 4

Leading one of his new riding horses by the rein, and accompanied by a young Native who acted as his guide, Everardus slowly ascended the steep mountain pass that crossed the high range behind the Valley. He had undertaken the journey on the advice of Uncle Dorie, who had told him that a personal visit to the mission station, established many years before in one of the picturesque *kloofs* among the outliers of these high escarped peaks, would not only enable him to secure cedarwood for his furniture but would also bring him into contact with his new friends. Uncle Dorie had a high opinion of the mission station, and a still higher opinion of the missionary, who from his account was a most praiseworthy person, thoroughly different from those faddists and agitators whose only object in life, it appeared, was to create unnecessary friction between the White community and the Natives. The Neckarthal Mission was not a doctrinaire institution. It was, so Uncle Dorie asseverated with a great deal of insistence, a sensible group community, fully aware of the value of the Biblical admonition that man should live by the sweat of his brow. Its adherents were excellently trained and disciplined, and the tight control exercised by the superintendent was paternally despotic but wielded in such a manner that it carried away the full approval not only of the neighbouring farmers, who at first had been doubtful about the desirability of the mission, but also of the Natives themselves.

Uncle Dorie had given him a detailed account of how the mission had been started. Early in the century the missionary, a properly ordained priest though perhaps not belonging to the church of which the Elder was a member and therefore perhaps not quite on a par with the Reverend Sybrand de Smee, had entered the District, alone and unaccompanied except by a lay helper. Both had come out from Germany, knowing English, but ignorant, as yet, of Dutch, and both were quaintly strange in their habits and ludicrously unacquainted with local conditions. They had behind them, so the Elder had been assured, the resources of a rich and enthusiastic mission society at home, which had enabled them to buy from a Native chief whose title was not admitted by government, a vast tract of land, estimated at a hundred thousand acres, at the mouth of the River. Sandy, uncultivatable land, Uncle Dorie said, on which no sane man could settle in the hope of making a living out of it. Here they had started a mission, gathering round them a group of Native fishermen, and painstakingly improving their immediate environment. Then the government had stepped in and questioned their title, with the result that endless negotiations had ensued, a weary, vexatious period of anxiety diversified by bouts of bargaining and threats of legal proceedings. Finally the matter had been settled by the Governor himself, who had offered the missionary the choice of any two pieces of Crown land in the District and a sum of money in exchange for the fifty morgen of unprofitable land he occupied. Like a sensible man the missionary had come to the Valley to take counsel with those who knew more about such things than he did, and the Valley had unanimously advised acceptance of the government's offer, and had indicated to him the magnificent possibilities of those *kloofs* lying far away beyond the higher ranges on which the cedar trees grow. Uncle Dorie had himself accompanied the missionary, together with Uncle Martin, whose father was then too old to join the survey party, and after due exploration and careful consideration of the potentialities of various suitable spots, they had fixed upon a site for the mission station and on another for the mission farm. The government had been friendly and helpful, and in due course an area of land, in extent twelve thousand acres, had been transferred to the mission society. With commendable energy and expedition the missionary and his lay helper had exploited their new territory, and now, after nearly a quarter of a century, they had improved it to such an extent that the Neckarthal Mission had a reputation as well deserved as that of the far older Moravian station at Genadenthal.

Uncle Dorie had waxed almost dithyrambic in his account of the missionary. He represented the Reverend Johann Uhlmann as his ideal of what a missionary should be, and listening to him Everardus obtained the impression that the reverend gentleman was a cross between a saint and a very shrewd and businesslike administrator, well able to bargain in four languages, and endowed with a knowledge of all the arts and crafts. He discounted that impression, for Uncle Dorie's enthusiasm, as he had learned, admitted of exaggeration, but nevertheless the picture that his friend drew of that hard-working community in the mountains stirred his curiosity and made him eager to meet the workers there.

The way towards the mission was by a long and dreary road that led through the Village and onwards over Martin Rekker's farm, and then, by steep inclines and through heavy, wind-piled sand dunes, a circuitous road which took three days to traverse. But there was a shortcut across the mountains, a footpath trodden only by the Natives coming from and returning to Neckarthal, a path that could be travelled on horseback, provided the traveller was willing to climb stages of it on foot. It led through the minor glades of the mountains which bounded the River on the north side, debouched to the east in the next valley where it crossed the tributary that poured its meagre summer water into the River just below the Village, and zig-zagged towards a lonely farm that lay in the shade of a high pointed peak. From there it turned sharply north, rising by sudden ascents until it entered the gate of the pass, the summit of which was three thousand feet above sea level.

Everardus had started long before dawn, on a fine August morning, when the air had a nip in it and the rising sun could still gleam on innumerable dew-fringed gossamers on the stunted veld bush. At sunrise he had reached the pass, and started the climb, and as the sun rose higher and the morning air lay heavy between the walls of rock on either side of him, he had to concentrate all his attention on his footing and the management of his horse. It was only when he had gained the middle ridge, where the path broadened out, that he had time and opportunity to rest and assimilate the beauty of the scenery. Then, when he turned to face the way he had come, he looked upon an imposing panorama of valley and hills, the like of which he had not seen before, the magnificence of which made him gasp in sheer astonishment and admiration.

To the right and left of him towered high walls of rock, weathered and wind-scarred, and tinged with all gradations of colour, from the grey-white of newly split sandstone, to the ferruginous ochre of water-worn shale, interspersed with vivid masses of steel-blue, lilac, pink, and variegated beryl that owed their constantly changing tints partly to alterations of sunshine and shadow and partly to the effects of oxidation and lichen growth. Between and below these cliffs, in crannies and on numerous rock ledges, grew masses of vegetation, whose surface tints rivalled those of the rocks above them. Here and there he saw a gigantic wild fig, nestling in some cleft where its roots obtained a precarious hold; higher up were big gnarled evergreens, with spreading branches and twisted trunks, which his guide told him were specimens of the cedar that grew in these mountains. Bordering the path were bushes of magenta coloured midday flowers, and on the sides of the mountain stream that the path constantly crossed and recrossed were magnificent ferns with patches of lush green grass starred with diminutive sorrels, yellow and rose-red and white. Wherever his eye roamed it saw colour, colour in all gradations of tint, colour in shapes new to him, and over all hung the heavy aromatic scent of wild jasmine and blossoming buchu. Immediately below where he sat, with his horse idly cropping the fresh grass, was a field of waving mauve, made by the gorse-like blooms of some leguminous plant that grew gregariously all over the sides of the pass. Farther away was a gorgeous splash of red where the big protea bushes showed their coloured floral leaves, among which long-tailed sugar birds darted in search of prey. On the left a creeping mesembryanthemun sunned its saucer-big flowers, blush red and chrome yellow, in the glare, while on the right, peeping out through the tall grass, he could see the delicate bells of the blue gladiolus, and the starry, wax-like flowers of the adenandra.

Higher above him the footpath straggled, now less steep in its ascent, towards the skyline, a curved ridge of green which showed that behind it lay land more or less level. Below him it descended steeply, in places almost precipitously until it was lost to sight in the distance. He could see the pass broadening out below, the space between the high walls widening and the walls themselves decreasing in height, until they fell away on each side and the Valley and River lay below him, their northern hills dwarfed in comparison with these giant mountains on either side, so that he could look over them and glimpse, far away to the south, the range upon range that ended with the sea. The River lay ribbon-like under the midday sun, its banks darkened by the bush that grew upon them, its curves outlined with precision. From it stretched the green wheat lands, their colours perpetually changing as the breeze waved their crops backwards and forwards. He could see many farms, plots of greenery set in a frame of dull gold, for the midday sun, striking the level sand, cast reflections around them. Far away to the right he could glimpse the Village, a collection of tiny whitewashed houses embowered in green trees and bounded by the white sands where the River received its tributary. Beyond the Village lay ridge upon ridge of slate coloured mountains, following the course of the River westwards. To the left the Valley narrowed upward to be lost in a maze of peaks and *kloofs*. Here too there was colour wherever his eye could range—the pale blue of the sky overhead, the darker aquamarine of the hills, the heavy azure of the high peaks, and the watered sapphire of the lower slopes, hazed by the morning sun so that they still seemed misty, with their sharp edges blurred and their outlines obscured. He could trace almost the whole length of the Valley, and see his own farm, though part of it was hidden behind a mountain spur, and already he could note that its greenery made a splash against the dull yellow of the surrounding veld. He could see beyond the Valley, and glimpse the wide level country that lay behind, a seemingly endless space of variegated russet and black fading away into the distance.

Late that evening he arrived at the mission station. As it was already nightfall when he rode down the steep decline that led into the station, he could not form any idea of what its setting was. He halted his horse before the missionary's *stoep*, and as he descended he caught sight of the door opening, a flood of lamplight illuminating the budding vine shoots of the *stoep* trellis, and a tall figure advancing to welcome him. He shook hands, uttering the customary formula, 'Good evening, Your Reverence. I am Everardus Nolte, from *Knolkloof*, in the Valley.' He noticed that the hand that clasped his own was strong and bony, and that his host was a tall, thin man, but in the dark further details were impossible to determine. Already his guide had led his horse away and disappeared, and the missionary was inviting him to enter the house.

He found himself in a large, low ceilinged room, simply furnished but with a simplicity that showed taste rather than poverty. Plaited matting and skin rugs covered the floor, and from the open rafter beams an oil lamp hung over a dining room table of polished cedarwood which had obviously just been cleared, for the maids were still fumbling with a table cloth. The farther wall of the room was entirely covered by a home-made bookshelf liberally stocked with books and papers. On the other walls hung pictures and framed texts in German. Some Native curios, a shotgun and a powder horn, and a wreath of everlastings tied with a faded green ribbon. On the sideboard were several carafes of wine, a number of wine glasses and a vase of mountain flowers tastefully arranged. Close to the window was the usual side-table with a brass candlestick and a pair of candle snuffers. The chairs and sofa in the room were covered with skin cushions, and all the woodwork gleamed with a high polish in the lamplight, while in the air hung a mingled scent of tobacco smoke and raw linseed oil, a combination which was by no means unpleasant, for the smoke was that of cigars and the linseed smell emanating from the woodwork, daily rubbed with oil, was not pungent.

His host, whom he now could observe at leisure as the missionary bustled about and the maids relaid the table cloth and arranged for the guest a welcoming evening meal, was dressed in a rough fustian coat, black trousers cut rather narrowly, and home made leather 'veldshoes,' the leather of which had not been blacked nor polished. He was a man of middle age, with a pronouncedly dolichocephalic head, a long, angular face, accentuated by the straggly pointed beard on his chin, and large steel-grey eyes that had in them something wistful and childlike. His frame, though slender to the verge of delicacy, seemed tough, and his features gave no indication of hesitancy of character. It was rather the face of a scholar, Everardus thought, than of a shrewd businessman, and although the missionary was not dressed in clerical garb, he conformed to what Everardus had imagined he would be. When he spoke, in a quaint Dutch that had a strong German accent, his voice was a trifle harsh, but his demeanour and actions were friendly, and when Everardus sat opposite him at the table, munching sweet potatoes and cold meat, he discoursed amiably without apparently the slightest desire to find out what his guest wanted.

'My wife,' he remarked, pleasantly, pouring out a glass of wine for Everardus, 'is for the moment out. We have a guest staying with us, *Meneer* Nolte; a brother missionary, and a dear friend. He has come across the mountains by the eastern route from Cape Town, and his station is much nearer civilisation than ours. He arrived this afternoon, and my wife has gone with him to the church. They will be back in a minute.'

'Then perhaps, Your Reverence, I come at an inconvenient time ...' Everardus began, but his host interrupted him quickly.

'You are very welcome, *Meneer* Nolte. There is room enough and to spare, and believe me, we are only too grateful to have one from the outer world to commune with occasionally. You are very welcome indeed. We like to show our neighbours what we are doing here, and if you will honour us by accepting such hospitality as we can offer you and bide with us for a few days, you will be very welcome.'

'That is what I should like to do, Your Reverence, if it is not putting Your Reverence to too much inconvenience ...'

'It will be a pleasure, *Meneer* Nolte. If you have finished ... but yes, Elfrida, you may now clear away, and bring the coffee when the mistress comes. If you will be pleased to take a seat over here, *Meneer* Nolte. At the side table—so. Place the carafe there, and we will get an extra glass. Brother von Bergmann likes a glass of sweet wine before retiring for the night. Elfrida, you will please see that the master's room is ready. Ask the mistress for the clean sheets, and see that there is an abundance of water in the can. You will smoke, *Meneer* Nolte? I have cigars here ...'

'Thank you, Your Reverence, but if it is all the same to you, I prefer my pipe.'

'Certainly. Would you like to try some of our Neckarthal tobacco? It is villainously strong, but some people like it ... I will get you some ... here, you might perhaps like it. For myself, I find an occasional cigar is very soothing. Not that I get much chance of smoking them. We have made them here—we still do, but ...' the missionary shrugged his shoulders. 'However, these are what Brother von Bergmann brought with him as a present for me.'

He lit one, and smoked gravely, enjoying the fragrance. Everardus filled his pipe from the cut plug that his host had handed him, and found the local tobacco very much to his taste. It was well cured and, although decidedly strong, of a pleasant flavour with no bite in it.

'I must apologise, Your Reverence,' he began, 'for so unexpectedly planting myself upon Your Reverence ...'

'Do not, *Meneer* Nolte, do not. I assure you it is a pleasure. Just as it must have been a pleasure for you—was it not?—to have seen the beauties of our pass. It is stupendous ... colossal, *Meneer* Nolte. I have seen much that is beautiful ... *ach*, is not everything that is something that has a beauty in it, *Meneer* Nolte?—but rarely have I seen anything to surpass that scene when one stands atop of the pass and gazes down into the Valley. It is to me an inspiration, *Meneer* Nolte. If I had the poet's gift—which alas, *Meneer* Nolte, has been denied me—I would rhapsodise over it. I would make a sonnet ... an ode ... a paean ... And now, well now, *Meneer* Nolte, when things go awry here, and I feel, as one sometimes feels even with the best faith and the Lord's upholding of the spirit in trouble, that my strength is too little for the task before me, I go to the pass and look down upon that scene.'

'It is very wonderful,' said Everardus, who had been honestly impressed by the pass, 'I felt something like that myself, Your Reverence, although I am a plain farmer. And I am told that Neckarthal is quite as beautiful ...'

'I warrant you, *Oom* Dorie has been telling you that, *Meneer* Nolte. *Ach*, I have tried to beautify ... in time, when you and I are dead, *Meneer* Nolte, people will say that there is something beautiful here. In arrangement—disposition ... in our work that we have tried to do. But not yet. You must give us time ... but wait, here come my wife and Brother von Bergmann.'

He rose up to open the door, and Everardus stood up. The missionary's wife paused on the threshold and threw her husband an enquiring glance. She was a fair-haired, matronly looking woman, obviously much younger than her husband, with a pale complexioned face that was still beautiful to look upon. Behind her, much taller, loomed Brother von Bergmann, a broad shouldered, brown haired, clean-shaven man, with a determined chin, cleft in a dimple, and a finely modelled head, broad in the forehead, high above the ears ... a man carpentered by Nature on ample lines, forceful, virile, impressive. A glance at that strong, determined face, which could on occasion lighten up with a smile of captivating charm but habitually showed a grave, reposeful dignity, would have told anyone with a knowledge of human character that here was no weakling but one who steered his course with knowledgeable certainty towards a goal carefully marked. From underneath his bushy eyebrows he shot a long, steady glance at Everardus, and under that look Everardus involuntarily dropped his eyes.

'It is *Meneer* Nolte, from the Valley,' the missionary hastened to explain. 'He has but just arrived. We were conversing ... you will join us, Brother von Bergmann, in a glass of wine? Mother, if you will see to *Meneer* Nolte's comfort, we can have evensong in a few minutes.'

'*Meneer* Nolte ... from the Valley,' said Brother von Bergmann, slowly. He spoke in a high pitched voice, phrasing his Dutch carefully, but without the German accent of his brother missionary, a cultured voice that had something peremptory in it. Once more he glanced fixedly at Everardus, who did not return his look. Then, with a little shrug of his broad shoulders, he turned to the side-table, took up a cigar, carefully cut the end off with his pocket knife, lit up and puffed serenely.

'Yes, Brother von Bergmann,' said his colleague. 'A newcomer. He has but lately taken over the farm *Knolkloof*. That much I have heard ...'

'If the gentlemen will permit me,' interrupted the missionary's wife, 'I will leave them to look to *Meneer* Nolte's comfort. In ten minutes time, Johann ... if that suits you for the evensong.'

'Certainly, Mother.' The missionary courteously opened the door for her. 'We might as well sit down again. Yes, Brother von Bergmann, he came over the pass. He was impressed by it. You really must see it, Brother von Bergmann ... but there, you are so unfeeling—a philistine, Brother, a philistine.'

'Neither the one nor the other, Brother Johann. But *Meneer* Nolte ... interests me. Might I enquire ...'

'The matter, Your Reverence,' said Nolte, feeling ill at ease although he could not imagine what there was to make him so, 'is very simple. I have come to see whether it is possible for me to get someone to make me cedarwood furniture ...'

'Of course it is possible, *Meneer* Nolte' replied the missionary quickly. 'We can make anything from any design for you. And we have now quite a nice stock of well seasoned wood, some planks very choicely grained. Tomorrow you may see the carpenter's shop and the joinery, and choose for yourself, and if you will give us some idea of what your wishes are, we will design the things for you.'

'I should like that,' said Everardus. 'I had thought of stinkwood ...'

'Then think no more of it, *Meneer* ... Nolte,' said von Bergmann, decisively, and Everardus noticed that there was a tiny, almost undetectable pause before he spoke the name. 'I used to have a similar notion, before I saw what cedarwood is like. After rosewood ... which one does not get here—it is the finest wood I know. Even though I am a philistine, as Brother Johann expresses it, I know a beautiful thing when I see it.'

'You may regard that as settled then, *Meneer* Nolte' said Brother Johann. 'I will take you round myself tomorrow. And now it is time for evensong.'

The missionary's wife came in followed by a string of servants, men and women and small children. From a neighbouring room three little toddlers, two boys and a girl, came shyly forward, rubbing eyes that were already heavy with sleep, and were introduced to the strange Uncle. The eldest was little Johann, barely seven; the girl was Catherine, rising six, and the smallest was Christian, just turning five. They nestled alongside their mother on the big sofa, while the servants squatted on the floor in a double rank along the wall. Brother von Bergmann took the head of the table, and Brother Johann sat next to him. Everardus drew his chair up and sat facing them. Elfrida brought the large Bible, and Brother Johann read from it a few verses, pausing now and then, to explain, in very simple language, when explanation seemed desirable. Then the company sang, very melodiously and in perfect tune, with much more animation than Everardus had experienced at services in his own church, a verse of the Moravian evening hymn, after which they all knelt down and Brother von

Bergmann offered up prayer. He prayed frankly and simply, remembering daily wants and human hopes, and Everardus noted with surprise that he especially commended to the Almighty's care 'the two children of our beloved Brother Johann, Johann and Christian, about to be taken from him and from their dear mother, for Thy sake and for Thy glory and the justification of Thy faith,' and that while the father's 'Amen' was firm and precise, the mother's was barely audible and more like a sob than anything else. And after the company had dispersed, and the children been sent to bed, he noted, too, that Mrs Uhlmann furtively wiped her eyes with her handkerchief, and sought her husband's hand when he handed her the glass of wine. When she had left them, with the hospitable, 'Sleep well, *Meneer* Nolte. Your coffee will be brought you at six o'clock,' and the three sat round the little side table, smoking a last pipe and cigar before retiring to bed, his curiosity got the better of his manners and he asked a question.

'Your Reverence will pardon me, but I was struck with one sentence in the Reverend von Bergmann's prayer. It seemed so strange to me ... I mean where he asked our Lord to look after the two boys. If Your Reverence will not take it amiss ... of course, if I inadvertently ...'

'By no means, *Meneer* Nolte' said Brother Johann, with a smile that made his large grey eyes look even more wistful. 'It is merely because you are a stranger. My two sons are leaving us next week. They go to Germany, to the Mission House at Barmen. That is why we have specially commended them in our prayers to the good Father's care.'

'But, Your Reverence, these two ... blood-young chaps like that ... I can hardly believe it ...'

'They are not too young, *Meneer* Nolte. Johan is nearly seven, and Christian is five. They must be educated. How can they be here? I have no money to send them to Cape Town to a boarding school. Besides what are they likely to learn there, more than what I can give them here? They must earn their own living, and our Society, fortunately, has a special fund for educating our children. At the Mission House they have free board and tuition—very good tuition too, *Meneer* Nolte.'

'But so young, Your Reverence. How can their mother part with them?'

'It is through sacrifice that one is ennobled, *Meneer* Nolte,' said Brother Johann, calmly. 'Their mother ... my wife and I, we both feel it. Doubtless we will feel it the more when they have left. But when we came to work in the Lord's vineyard we realised that we would have to give up many things—our home, our friends, our children. Did not our dear Lord give up far more for us, *Meneer* Nolte? And after all, it is in the children's interests. That is one comfort.'

'You must not think that it is cruelty, *Meneer* Nolte,' remarked Brother von Bergmann. 'Often what looks like cruelty is kindness. It may seem to you that we are talking platitudes, but I assure you it is not so. My own children are going too ... it is true they are a bit older, but the parting is none the less a wrench for their mother and for me.'

'I really did not know ... I did not imagine,' began Nolte. But von Bergmann interrupted him.

'How could you? To most of you ... farmers, our lives and our doings are as unknown as those of the Israelites were to the Pharaoh who hardened his heart. You think we come merely to divide, to blunder, to bring the sword instead of peace. Know us, *Meneer* Nolte. Learn to know us, and bear with us when we make mistakes, as we often do, for we make them unwillingly, not with intention. You can do much, *Meneer* Nolte, here in your District ...'

'Now, now, Brother,' interrupted Uhlmann, 'you are on your hobby horse. I am sure *Meneer* Nolte has no *animus* against us. He has only heard about us, and if what he has heard is to our detriment, well, let us try to show him tomorrow that we are not quite as black as we are painted. And now, I think we should go to bed. I will show *Meneer* Nolte to his room—he is doubtless tired after that long climb. You know where yours is, Brother von Bergmann, and so I may say good night ...'

'With your permission, Brother Johann,' said von Bergmann quickly, 'I will take *Meneer* Nolte to his room, it is next door to mine, so you need not trouble yourself.'

'Very well. Then I shall say good night and sleep well, *Meneer* Nolte. And the same to you, dear Brother. Do not forget that we have prayer meeting at seven o'clock tomorrow in the church.'

Brother von Bergmann led the way with a candle in his hand. At the door of the bedroom he stopped, and turned round to look Everardus full in the face.

'With your permission,' he said suavely, 'I should like a few words in confidence. I do not like my old friend to be deluded, *Meneer* ... Tereg.'

'My name is Nolte, Your Reverence,' said Everardus, stubbornly, but Brother von Bergmann shrugged his shoulders, entered the bedroom, placed the candlestick on the dresser, and sat himself down on the bed. Everardus followed him into the room, angry, defeated, uncertain of his next move.

'I never forget a face, my friend,' said Brother von Bergmann, 'and though yours has changed, that beard does not disguise you to me. I know you are Tereg who ...'

'I pray Your Reverence, do not say it. I have put it behind me. I have changed my name by legal process ... Your Reverence will see it in the *Gazette* now almost three years back. I have come here, Your Reverence, to lead a new life, and nobody knows of it ...'

'Is it then that you are ashamed, *Meneer* ... Nolte?' asked von Bergmann, in surprise. 'What is there to be ashamed of? Forgive me, but I had thought that you had some intention, some bad intention—you must forgive me, but in the circumstances my inference was justifiable. Now that I think of it, I can imagine that you would ... Really, I beg your pardon.'

'It is nothing, Your Reverence. And now that you know, it is a load off my mind. If I may tell Your Reverence ...'

'Do. Sit down here, and let me hear all about it. I recognised you, for you may remember, I was in the room when you ...'

'For heaven's sake, Your Reverence, I implore you. I have put all that behind me. If you will permit me ...'

Brother von Bergmann shook his head when Everardus had finished. 'I do not quite like it, *Meneer* Nolte' he said, gravely. 'Nothing comes of hiding things, nothing good, I mean. Sooner or later the truth will out. I can understand why you and your wife wish to cover it, especially now that you are among new people who do not know you. But why not tell them frankly when you are asked? I see nothing very portentous in the disclosure. After all there must be some who know of it. The magistrate, for instance, he must be acquainted with the details. And from what I know of the people in the Valley, I do not for a moment believe that they will think any the less of you. Indeed, they will probably regard you as a hero, and give you some silly nickname. But sooner or later there will be complications, and then you will regret that you did not openly, manfully come among them without any secrecy. Think it over. Consult with your wife. And I must of course acquaint Brother Johann. You will see that for yourself. I may say that Brother Johann will not abuse that confidence. He will keep your secret. You have no objection?'

'No, Your Reverence. I should indeed like *Meneer* Uhlmann to know, now that you know.'

'That is settled then. But I think you are a fool. Pardon me. In my country no one would have dreamed of throwing mud at you. Not in the circumstances. As a regular profession that is a different matter. But that is not your case. Very well. I ask your pardon again for misjudging you. Sleep well, *Meneer* Nolte.'

Brother von Bergmann's peremptory, commanding voice and his imposing presence took themselves away, and Everardus undressed slowly, put out the candle and crept into bed. But it was long before he fell into slumber, and in the night his sleep was disturbed by dreams wherein he saw that strong, gravely dignified face menacing him from the top of a high, weather-scarred precipice that looked down into the Valley.

Chapter 5

The following day Everardus had ample opportunity to test the value of the superlatives Uncle Dorie had used in describing the mission and its work. At an early hour, when the daylight was scarce strong enough to filter into his room through the cedarwood venetians outside, Elfrida, the Hottentot maid, a cheerful but unattractive young female, brought him the morning coffee, together with a piece of must-biscuit, and announced that breakfast was at half past seven but if the *Baas* wished to attend prayers, prayer meeting was being held that morning in the church. Everardus, more keenly sensible of certain conventional obligations here in an environment to which he was in some degree antagonistic, decided to attend. When he came outside, and stooped to rinse his mouth in the water of the furrow in front of the mission house *stoep*, he saw the Natives walking quietly towards the little church, and followed them. On the way he could see something of the station, and he noted, and at once appreciated, the neatness, orderliness, and quaint precision with which it had been laid out and in which it was kept. There were several houses, ranging from the large, low, wide *stoep*-fronted mission house itself, to the tiny cottages, all covered with the thick foliage of the cerulean blue morning glory which grew luxuriantly wherever it found a space for its roots. The roofs were all of thatch, beautifully finished, the thatching of the mission house being a work of art over which the wind had already spread enough soil to make it a garden for various kinds of composites. In front of the small cottages were plots of cultivated ground, well-tended gardens, orchards, and patches of young maize; here and there he noted the creeping green of pumpkins and gourds, the quick growing Calabash that makes a screen against wall or tree trunk and produces huge fantastically shaped fruits which, when dried and cleaned, serve as water bottles, pans, and basins.

The station lay in a curious dell or hollow between high hills, the outliers of the ranges over which he had come the preceding day, and the spurs of the mountains lying to the north and west. For the most part these surrounding hills, which nowhere here reached a high altitude, as Neckarthal was itself already several thousand feet above sea level, were sandstone formations, with their slopes scarred and strewn by talus and scree, overgrown now, when it was early spring, with a wealth of greenery and variegated flowers. Between them stood out rounded slopes of a more ash-coloured, rubble-covered surface, deeply scarred by erosion and weathered, near the tops, to a uniform smoothness that appeared to be almost artificial. Although Everardus was no geologist, and could not have told the difference between diorite and shale, he knew that these strange, barren looking slopes were outliers of the Karroo composed mainly of alluvial shales and strewn with ferruginous nodules that gave them their ashy-brown colour. It was too early yet for their surface to be covered with flowers; later on in the spring, when the rains had penetrated more deeply into the loose soil, these slopes would show a wealth of green and colour, surpassing in richness the vegetation on the sandstone soil derived from the higher mountains. Their presence here told Everardus that Neckarthal could not boast of a uniform high rainfall on at least one of its sides, but the strong stream of limpid water that ran through the mission station, that fed the garden furrows and turned several mill wheels, came from the sandstone formation, which probably held hidden many perennial springs.

Of this abundance of water the Natives made excellent use. The trees, mainly poplars and oaks, were already in full leaf, and had grown so rapidly that they afforded a welcome shade to the road and over the cottages. There were many orange trees, still bearing some of their fruit, but already putting out buds for the next crop, and in the mission garden, he noticed shaddock, guava, and lime trees with a clump of tall date palms, graceful in the early morning sun. Beyond the cottages were the working sheds, the tanneries, the shoemaker's shop, the common store of the settlement, and the tiny church. The little wooden bridges that spanned the stream were well made and well cared for; the road was excellent both as regards planning and surfacing, and there was an absence of litter, a cleanliness and an orderliness that impressed him.

He walked towards the church, and stopped to talk to one of the Natives, who pointed out the several buildings, showing him where the school house stood and where the *kraals* for the cattle were. As he stood chatting many other Natives came along, on their way to the church, and he noted that they were all clean, healthy, cheerful looking. The variety of colour and physique among them was striking, many of the women obviously had Bushman blood in them; their short, heavy bodies proclaimed their blood even to those who did not know how to distinguish between the sharp features that betokened Mozambique, and therefore probably Arab descent, and the flat, broad-nosed faces that told of original Hottentot ancestry. They all greeted him respectfully and cheerfully singing out 'Day, Master' with monotonous insistency when they walked past him. Finally he followed them into the church, and made his way towards the front benches which he knew were reserved for the Whites. The little church was bare of ornament, with white-washed walls, a wood floor, and the usual open rafter work and thatch for ceiling; it had attached to it a tiny vestry, and on the floor were cedarwood benches, regularly spaced so as to leave the area in front of the pulpit vacant for the platform on which stood the altar covered with black cloth fringed with gold braid. On the altar stood a crucifix and a couple of vases filled with mountain flowers, which Everardus thought strange, for his own church had no altar and no one would have dreamed of bringing flowers, for decorative or any other purpose into it. He reflected upon this point and came to the conclusion that the community was probably Romish, but decided, for all that, to stay.

He had not long to wait for scarcely had he seated himself when the vestry door opened, and his host and Brother von Bergmann, now both dressed in clerical black, entered, followed by half a dozen Natives who defiled to left and right and took their seats on the benches arranged at right angles to those occupied by the congregation. The two missionaries stepped on to the dais, and stood in front of the altar. Brother von Bergmann gave out a hymn, which the congregation sung standing, and Everardus was struck, once more, by the surprising excellence of the singing, and by the fine quality of the voices. The short and simple service that followed, lasting a bare ten minutes, impressed him by its sincerity, and the *extempore* prayers, delivered by several of the Natives who sat on the side benches impressed him even more. Then Brother von Bergmann intoned the benediction, and the congregation filed out of the church to their daily work.

Outside Brother Johann and Brother von Bergmann greeted him cheerily. Brother Johann, when he shook him by the hand and asked how he had slept, looked at him a trifle searchingly with his wistful eyes, and Everardus knew at once that Brother von Bergmann had told him. But Brother Johann's demeanour was so friendly that he felt no annoyance at any disclosure that might have been made, and rather a relief that his host was no longer in the dark.

'I am glad that you have sufficient energy to join us, *Meneer* Nolte,' remarked Brother Johann, pleasantly. 'Doubtless the service is strange to you. Is it not that of your own church, which is strictly Calvinistic? We are, of course, in community with it; on general principles there is no great difference between us, but we are Lutherans and in some ways nearer to the old faith, especially as far as ritual is concerned.'

'I liked it,' replied Everardus. 'Especially the singing. That was fine, Your Reverence.'

'I am glad you think so,' said Brother Johann. 'We have tried to train them to use their voices. But they are far from perfect yet. You should hear Brother von Bergmann's choir.'

'Ah, you flatter me, Brother,' said von Bergmann, the austerity of his face relaxing, however, into a smile. 'If only you knew what difficulties I have had to encounter ... But I see Augustus over there. I must talk to him about the horses. I will follow you, Brother Johann. Don't, please, wait for me.'

'Shall we proceed to the house, *Meneer* Nolte? Breakfast is waiting for us. Afterwards I will take you to the shops. You will see much to interest you, I hope. We like people to see us as we are. But you must remember that we are young yet. Now Brother von Bergmann's station is something to see. There is a man for you, *Meneer* Nolte. Imagine, in a few years time he has built a church, a steepled church with a peal of bells, and a big school with more than two hundred pupils. Without asking a penny from the society at home, mind you, and even contributing to the fund that pays for all our stipends. He is a fine man, Brother von Bergmann. But it is like chopping wood with razors. He ought to be at the Mission House in Barmen, superintendent, not out here, doing the work he does. *Ach*, what am I saying, *Meneer* Nolte? It is after all the Lord's work, and I should not criticise.'

'Perhaps *Meneer* von Bergmann will go back,' hazarded Everardus, anxious to know something more about the grave, handsome man who had impressed him so much. 'You sometimes do, don't you?'

'If the call comes, *Meneer* Nolte. But we are free to decline, if we feel that we have good reasons for doing so. Nor do I think Brother von Bergmann will ever go back. He has rooted here. He has married—he wedded a baroness's daughter, a von Staffelberg von Hohenlaub—and he has a large family. Two of his boys go with Johann and Christian next month to Barmen. To be sure they are a little older, but even that is a wrench for him. No, I do not think he will go, even if he is called. I fancy he has been called, but he declined then and he will do so again.'

'It seems a great pity to send the children away so early,' remarked Nolte. 'They must miss much ... their mother's care, for instance. Your guidance, Your Reverence.'

'We know that, *Meneer* Nolte. But what would you have? They cannot remain here: I feel that; their mother feels it. I will not say there is no culture here, but there is much that we lack and that they should get which we cannot give them here. In their own interests, in ours too, we must give them up, for a time, *Meneer* Nolte. Brother von Bergmann ... you must talk to him about the matter. I cannot speak about it, for Heaven knows I am still weak, and there are times when I feel that I cannot let them go. But come,' Brother Johann made an effort to shift the conversation, 'here we are. Ah Mother, I hope you have some nice liver sausage for us, to show *Meneer* Nolte what kind of pigs we breed here. After breakfast, *Meneer* Nolte, we will go and look at the sties. I should like your opinion about a young Chinaman we are fattening up for Christmas.'

Breakfast was a pleasant meal, and as he listened to the cheerful conversation of the two Brothers, a conversation in which the children and the missionary's wife took part freely and easily, he wondered at the difference between that household and others with which he was acquainted. In the Valley children were not encouraged to talk at table; they certainly did not with their elders as little Johann did, nor did they directly question them as these children did. Not that there was anything amiss with the manners or deportment of the missionary's children. They behaved in an exemplary fashion, and it was really Brother von Bergmann who was to blame, for he gave them a finger and they promptly took the whole arm, right up to the elbow, and beyond.

'And so,' Brother von Bergmann was saying, 'part of all this was sea, an inland sea. What did you find at the cutting, Christian?'

'A stone shell, Uncle von Bergmann,' piped the child, excitedly, 'and Anta got another. Only Johann, because he won't look for them, didn't find anything at all.'

'Because Johann was studying his Latin, my son,' said von Bergmann. 'But you must show me the shell, later on, and we will wrap it up for you so that you can take it with you to Barmen and tell the Uncles there about our big inland sea that is now dried up. Bye and bye, I fancy, we will all be dried up, for it rains less and less every year. And then Anta will have nowhere to swim, and you'll all have to come to me and paddle in the duck pond.'

The children shrieked with delight at this possibility, and even their mother smiled while Brother Johann laughed with unrestrained glee. Really, it was remarkable that a grave man like von Bergmann should put such fancies in a boy's head. An inland sea ... and shells! In these mountains! Preposterous!

But a few hours later, when the Brothers took him down to the cutting, and showed him, encrusted in the shale, numerous specimens of spirifers, trilobites, ammonites, and pecten shells, Everardus changed his opinion. The evidence was too strong for doubt. It changed his outlook upon things, and he decided that he too should ask questions when he had an opportunity to do so.

That opportunity, however, did not present itself before the evening. There was far too much to see on the station, and he was interested in everything he saw. He visited the carpenter's shop, where an old, almost white headed European whose name, he learned, was Anton Fischer, was instructing some Natives in woodwork. Brother Johann told him that Anton had fought at Waterloo, attached to Blucher's Pomeranian Horse, and had come out with him as a lay Brother, and was now doing excellent work as a master craftsman in wood and iron. The specimens of his handiwork, and that of his pupils which Everardus saw in the shops and in the houses, fully bore out the encomiums of Brother Uhlmann. Most of the work was in cedarwood, which took a brilliant polish, but which Anton declared was too soft for his taste. He liked a better and harder wood, and he showed some samples of Native woods that he had seasoned. But Everardus had set his heart on cedarwood, and when he saw the broad, closely grained planks that were stored in the seasoning shed, he was loud in his admiration. Half the morning was spent in intimating to the craftsman what furniture he wanted and what designs he preferred. Anton was a good draughtsman, and by luncheon time he had produced plans for a table, a hanging wardrobe, and a set of chairs for the dining room which Everardus at once approved of.

After that he had to see the tannery, visit the shoemaker's shop, and inspect the common store. He learned that no money was in circulation within the boundaries of the mission station. The Natives were paid with counters, round discs of brass imported from the Mission House at Barmen; only these were accepted in exchange for goods, and each had its own monetary value. Brother Uhlmann explained that this had been decided upon to limit the possibility of introducing drink into the community. When the Natives went to outside farms to work, they were of course paid in ordinary money, and with that they could buy what they pleased at the Village, but in the community shop they could only trade with counters, and if they wanted to possess these they had to exchange them for money. He learned, too, that the discipline of the community was strict. There was a church council, consisting of the senior Natives who had entered the church in the wake of the missionaries that morning. Its members were elected by the Natives themselves, subject to the approval of the missionary, and it dealt with all ordinary transgressions against community law. Its highest and gravest punishment was expulsion, which was regarded as a dreadful disgrace, and was very rarely inflicted. For minor peccadilloes, laziness, inattendance at worship, and breach of the communal regulations, which were in the main simple and designed for the benefit of all, light fines or punishment work was given. For graver offences, among which were counted drunkenness and introduction of drink into the community, corporal punishment was meted out, and for recidivism the culprit was censured, which meant that he was placed in Coventry for a time, and if that did not help, he was expelled. Natives who wished to enter the community had to give proof of their ability to earn a living, and permission to settle on the station was only granted after due enquiry. Every settler received a plot of ground, to which, however, he got no title as the land was held in community. He had to cultivate his plot, build his cottage, and do his share of work in the tannery, shoemaker's shop, or mills, and he was expected to pay his share of the church dues. The missionary was also the field-cornet for that particular ward, and possessed a certain official authority, besides being the marriage officer, the postmaster, and an unlicensed medical practitioner. So far as Everardus could judge, the community was perfectly happy and contented, and regarded its pastor and field cornet with respect and admiration, as one whose wishes had to be obeyed not because he could exact obedience by virtue of his official position but because disobedience 'made *Meneer* heartsore.'

So interesting did Everardus find his new environment that he readily accepted Brother Johann's invitation to prolong his stay for a few days longer than he had intended to remain. The time passed all too quickly, for it was a time of infinite enjoyment to him. He found himself charmed with the homely simplicity and innate gentleness of his host, more and more impressed by the virile strength and exuberant vitality of Brother von Bergmann, and soothed and attracted by the quiet serenity of Mrs Uhlmann, whose pathetic resignation at the thought of giving up her children he marvelled at daily. In the evenings, the four of them would sit on the *stoep* or in the dining room of the mission house, and Brother von Bergmann would tell them of various and always interesting things. He had been to Europe the year before, and Brother Uhlmann was indefatigable in asking questions of the homeland which he himself had not visited since his emigration. Everardus found much in their talk that gave him food for profound thought, just as he found much to criticise in their manner of living and their outlook upon life, so profoundly different from what he had experienced elsewhere.

'You have asked me,' said Brother von Bergmann one evening when Everardus, taking his courage into his hands when Mrs Uhlmann had left them, had boldly broached the subject of the necessity for the children to be sent overseas, 'why we think it imperative for them to go. I will tell you, *Meneer* Nolte. You have in this fine country of yours—it is mine now; God willing, I shall end my life here, lay my bones among the people I have cared for, and wish for no other grave-stone legend than that which, with God's help, I shall engrave in their hearts—in this fine country of ours, then, we have nothing as yet of that which spurs a man on to self-sacrifice, to duty ... tradition. We are young, and we are, or imagine ourselves to be, superior to those other fellow citizens of ours whose skins are not the colour of ours. We, who are old, who are able to judge, to discriminate, and to know that a man's nobility resides not in his skin but in his soul, we can on occasion discount much. But the young child, brought up in such an environment as ours, does not learn to do so. He grows up—he must grow up—with a pride of caste that is as detrimental to his spiritual and intellectual outlook as it will be ultimately inimical to his social and economic interests. Believe me, *Meneer* Nolte, slavery is bad both for the slave and the master. It stifles human progress. The only tradition it leaves behind is a tradition of subserviency on the one side and of aggression on the other. No, do not interrupt me, please, I know what you would say. That we here have never mishandled our slaves, any more than we now ill-treat our servants. I grant that, I admit that I came here after our slaves were manumitted, but Brother Uhlmann has had experience of how they were treated, and he can bear witness to the truth of what you would say. So I grant all that. But the fact remains that slavery—the system, the premiss—has given us all here a false impression of human values ... no, Brother Johann, I withdraw that word. You are quite right. I see you still remember something of your Fichte. I substitute the word 'spiritual.' Does that satisfy you? Spiritual values, then. We have lost sight of the one all-embracing fact that all men are equal before God, and that inequality in spiritual relations is the result of environment, social conditions, food perhaps, economic factors. We start from the assumption—let me include myself, *Meneer* Nolte, in this general indictment. You have no idea how, at first, I resented the notion that a Hottentot could be my equal ... I who have generations of culture and civilisation behind me. But with God's help I have crumpled my pride, and applied that stern logic which excludes sentimentality. But I ask you, how can our children apply it if they have not learned to reason ... if they have had no opportunity to see for themselves that in that homeland of ours beyond the seas there are factors as inimical to civilisation as there are here? If they have not had the means of comparison ... if they have not had a chance of learning that each one of us must work out his own salvation, and that no man can depend, solely, upon what his father and his grandfather gained for him ...'

'But, Your Reverence ... Your Reverence will pardon me, but surely Your Reverence does not for a moment imply that we are no better than the Hottentots? Why, we White men are infinitely superior. They haven't got the brains, Your Reverence. They can never attain to our ... our civilisation, Your Reverence.'

'What makes you say that, *Meneer* Nolte? Do you really believe that one race, one civilisation, is superior to another? That another race cannot attain to what one race has reached? I doubt if there is any evidence, any proof, of that. So far as I read history, none. So far as I can judge, there is no reason why these aboriginals in this country of ours should not reach—aye, perhaps surpass—our level, if they had the opportunities that we have, if we gave them something of what we possess, share with them ...'

'That is because Your Reverence is a missionary. It is the missionaries who have always made trouble in this country ...'

'Again I will grant you something—not all, mind, of your premiss. We have made mistakes ... tremendous mistakes. We are still making them. It is human nature. But that does not alter the fundamental position, *Meneer* Nolte. There was a great man, *Meneer* Nolte, who wrote—

> *Was muss, geschehe.*
> *Fallen seh' ich Zweig und Sweige*
> *Und in Staube liegt die Eiche.*

You will remember *Die Ahnfrau*, Brother Johann? We have often read it together.'

'*Meneer* Nolte will not follow it, Brother,' remarked the missionary, mildly and translated for Everardus's benefit.

'No, I don't believe that for a moment,' Everardus burst out. 'We can never fall and perish. It would be impossible for God to will such a dreadful thing as that.'

'What God wills, my friend, we might leave out of the discussion. Neither you nor I know what is ordained by His will and foreknowledge. But look around you and ask yourself whether things are as they should be. What of our own people? You know them better than I, who am after all a newcomer. But have we reason to be content with what they are or with what they are likely to be in the future?'

'I really cannot follow Your Reverence now. What is wrong with us, then?'

'What is wrong with you? Why, man, open your eyes. Yes, Brother Johann, but I get warm when I see such wilful blindness. *Dass kann ich nich ertragen* ... I cannot bear that ... pardon me, *Meneer* Nolte, when I am warm I sometimes speak in my mother tongue, forgetting that you do not understand. But look around you. What schools have you got in the Valley? How many of you there can read and write? How many of you have even the shadow of some culture? When I came into this country, I was privileged to dine with one of our judges, a man who, I believe, knows our people far better than either of us do. He told me that there were two classes of folk here. One, in the towns and near to the capital, who were used to discipline, who recognised authority, and who had learned to control themselves. The second, a class of men who had for years flouted authority, with no law but their own, who brooked no interference. Is it true?'

'There is some truth in it, Your Reverence. I take it Your Reverence has in mind the folk who emigrated. I don't hold with them myself. I would have remained and struggled through. But I don't judge them, Your Reverence.'

'I do. And in your heart you do too. You know that your forefathers did not do that kind of thing. They did not trek. They stayed and fought for their just rights. They did not—how do you phrase it?—throw up the guide rope. And that is what I fear! I fear that if our children stayed here, they will learn to do as these men did, forgetting their traditions. How can it be otherwise? We shall inevitably degenerate unless we guard what we have. And are we guarding it? No ... no! You jibe at me, and Brother Uhlmann here—yes, you do, for you have not the faintest notion what we do, nor what our aims are. Let me tell you, in my own District I have started schools, not for the Natives, though they have theirs, right enough, but for the White children. Why don't you do that in the Valley? You are not poor. You all make a fair living out of your farms. Compare any of your Valley children with *Meneer* Seldon's boy—I have seen him; I have stayed with the Seldons. But what will Seldon's grandchildren be like if you do not guard what you have got? That is why we send our children overseas, *Meneer* Nolte.'

'But how can it go on, Your Reverence? Must we then send all the children away?'

'Ah, that is the question. Look, *Meneer* Nolte, there are other sides to the question. I have seen perhaps more of this country than you have. I have been in the northern Districts, across the Karroo. There folk are even more behind than they are in the Valley. I doubt, indeed, if it is a suitable country, the inland Districts, for us to settle on. But if we do settle there, let us at all events guard what we have. At present we are letting the children degenerate, and at the same time allowing them to imagine that, just because they are White, they will be all right in the future. That is a sin, and a shame, *Meneer* Nolte. Nature revenges herself for our neglect. She exacts punishment from us for our stupidity, and alas, often that punishment does not fall upon us who are stupid but on our descendants who have really not merited it, to the fourth and fifth generation as the Bible says. Let us get away from this stupid idea that we are inherently superior as a race. It will inevitably bring its own punishment in our children's shame when, in the future, they compare themselves with other white children from the homeland. Forgive my warmth, *Meneer* Nolte, but I rage when I see how much we neglect ourselves, and think only of our prestige as white men, of our boasted civilisation. What are they, after all? You deny it, but I do not see why the Natives, whom we now despise as sadly inferior, should not in time gain the same prestige and make the same civilisation, or a better one even, their own. I do not believe that one race is superior to another. It is a question of environment, opportunity, economics. But here I am, laying down the law, as my nature is, and you are angry with me, and good Brother Johann shakes his head.'

'Indeed I do, Brother von Bergmann. You are altogether too impetuous. You have given our good friend the impression that you are much more negrophilistic than those reverend brothers whom he so much dislikes.'

'I don't dislike them,' said Everardus, puffing at his pipe, and anxious to put his view of the case, 'as a matter of fact I have never met any missionaries before I met Your Reverences. And what I have seen here has opened my eyes. I do not think you come to sow dissent and promote strife. But you do not understand our people, Your Reverence, and that's flat.'

'Why do you say that, *Meneer* Nolte?' asked Brother Johann, mildly, while von Bergmann blew clouds of cigar smoke into the air.

'Because you have no sympathy with those of us who trekked, Your Reverence. After all, they had their grievances. They did not go into the wilderness for nothing. They braved hardship and danger with courage and self-sacrifice. Your Reverence surely sees that.'

'Yes, but you admit that they would have done a braver thing if they had stayed behind and worked out their own salvation. That is what Brother von Bergmann means. He implies, *Meneer* Nolte, that it would be difficult for our children, especially here in association only with a few Whites of their own class, and in constant association with Natives, to obtain a correct perspective ...'

'Exactly, Brother Johann. And then you belittle your own powers of exposition. That is the whole argument, if they so remain, if they get no chance to obtain what you call a true perspective of life, of its obligations ... of their special obligations as White men and White women, they must inevitably deteriorate, degenerate. That is the danger I foresee, even for those who are not missionary children. For them, perhaps, the danger is greater. You and I after all, Brother Johann, we are not quite normal ...'

'I think I may say, with *Meneer* Nolte here, Brother, that now I can't follow you. Why do you say we are not normal?'

'Because we are missionaries! A missionary must be abnormal! I recognise that myself. I don't say abnormal in a pathological sense. You and I and our brother missionaries are physically and mentally normal. At least I hope so! But we are abnormal inasmuch as we have an obsession to interfere with other people's business, even with God's. I see *Meneer* Nolte nods in agreement. But it is so. You, Brother, should have been a professor of exegesis, and I ... why I should have stayed at the cadet school and by now I would have worn epaulettes and rattled a sword. Instead of that I preach the Gospel to an inferior race that God has meant forever to be hired labourers for the superior race that lives in the Valley and out yonder on what was once an inland sea.'

'You would certainly not have made a good officer, even with epaulettes,' remarked Brother Johann drily. 'And from Anton's account they are particularly strict in most regiments. Whereas I could not possibly be a professor of exegesis. I would entangle myself in all sorts of difficulties. You know at college I was said to be difficult ...'

'Don't I remember. You once queried the genealogical tables, and your essay on the *logos* ... don't I just remember,' and Brother von Bergmann threw his well shaped head back and laughed uproariously.

'But I never stated that missionaries were abnormal, Brother.'

'If you did the inspector would have died of shock, Brother Johann. But, dear me, it is past eleven. And tomorrow I must be away by daybreak. Brother, Brother we are keeping late hours.'

'I entirely forgot. Of course you must go to bed. But I trust that our conversation tonight has not been entirely without profit to all of us. *Meneer* Nolte, you have your candle? Good. Then I will say well-to-rest.'

Everardus woke early before dawn to bid farewell to von Bergmann, who was leaving by cart on his return journey across the eastern mountains. The handsome, imposing missionary gave him a cordial invitation to visit his station when he was in that neighbourhood, and Everardus promised, willingly enough, to do so if he got the opportunity. He had been much impressed by the man's character and presence, and he looked forward to meeting him again. Little Johann and Christian were to go with von Bergmann, and the parting with their parents and with their little sister, whom they called Anta, affected Everardus so much that he walked away although he need not have done so, for the whole community had turned out to bid goodbye to the little masters and the big *Baas*. That afternoon Everardus himself started on his return journey, for although pressed to stay for another day, he felt that the missionary and his wife would prefer to be left alone with their grief. He had determined to go by road this time, and on his way to visit Rekker's farm which he could reach before nightfall. His visit to the mission station had been both interesting and profitable, for before he left he had seen part of his new furniture in the shaping, and he was quite satisfied that the work would be done admirably, while the estimate that Fischer had placed before him was eminently reasonable.

Chapter 6

An indifferent chess player, Everardus found himself overmatched by Uncle Martin, and when that facile exponent of the game had beaten him soundly in three games, he clamoured for quarter.

'I am really nothing like Uncle's equal,' he remarked deprecatingly. 'And I should much prefer, if Uncle has no objections to the proposal, to talk instead of play. It seems more sociable too.'

'That I do not admit,' replied the old man, regretfully replacing the chess men in their little green velvet bag, and laying them aside while he folded the inlaid chess board. 'There are some people who must for ever be chattering. They call that conversation, but it is nothing of the kind. I can converse with a man quite as well when I am playing chess and holding my tongue as when I am talking to him. Conversation, Nephew Ev'rard, comes from the Latin *conversari*, which means to consort, to turn in unison, to live with. It does not mean to chatter. Starlings do that.'

'Still it is pleasant, Uncle, to exchange views. To listen, for instance, as I am going to listen, while a friend tells me what I must know ...'

'And who tells you that it will not be I who will do the listening, Nephew? But there is method in what you say. One cannot always commune in silence. The heart strings must be infinitely in tune for that, and we have not known one another well enough for that to be, as yet. Now I come to think about it, I know very little about you ...'

'And I about Uncle.'

'Softly, Nephew Ev'rard. The cases are not parallel. Everyone knows about me. Ask whomsoever you will, and you will get the story of the Rekkers from the time my foremother landed out of the *Ster der Hoop* on the strand of False Bay and my forefather went road-making northwards. The Rekkers have no cause to hide their past. Look, there our coat hangs,' and he pointed to a framed bit of blazoning on the wall, 'if you knew anything about heraldry—which I doubt—it tells its own story. The halved tree trunk and the crescent moon, and the three annulets, which as you see are all gold—or, from the Latin *aureum*, they call it in the art of blazonry—set on a field of green—*vert*, that is, also from the Latin, through the French. I do not know French—regretfully—for there was no one to teach me in my young days, but, Nephew, my father taught me something about heraldry, and about the meaning of things one sees on coats of arms. They all tell their own tale; one has no need to enquire. But yours I do not know. I have never seen it. It may be that you are not armbearing—*armiger*, that is the Latin for it, and everyone is not that. Some lose it through being born on the mother's side—it is an involved business and I never found anyone who could quite explain it to me. But with us it has come down through the male line.'

'My wife has her family's coat on her grandfather's old snuff-box, Uncle. A hunting horn, and three birds that look like quails ...'

'Larks, Nephew, larks. That sounds like the de Lerchs, but I did not know there were any remaining in the country. Let me see. I mind my father telling me of one who was a merchant in Cape Town, long before the Company left us ...'

'I believe they all died out,' said Everardus, hurriedly. He had no wish to discuss the de Lerchs or his wife's coat of arms. It was trenching, he thought, on dangerous ground, especially when his inquisitor was so subtle and penetrating a connoisseur of coats of arms as Uncle Martin.

The two were seated at the little side-table in Uncle Martin's dining room at *The Hoek*. Everardus had arrived in the afternoon and had been received with hospitable kindness. The younger Martin, known to his servants as the *Kleinbaas* or little master, in contradistinction to Uncle Martin who was the *Oubaas* or old master, had shown him over the farm, and given him valuable hints about farming in general and the peculiarities of farming in the Valley in particular. Everadus liked the younger Martin, who was more or less his contemporary in age, and who was an agreeable, gentlemanly person, although he lacked the aristocratic, dignified appearance of his father. *The Hoek* was a flourishing farm, and Everardus liked everything he saw of it, and admired the manner in which it had been laid out and improved. It was beautifully run, though in a manner entirely different from the mission station. Here everyone worked for the *Oubaas*, who, although he had long ago given up active participation in the business, which was nominally entirely in his son's hands, maintained a general supervision like that of a superannuated general manager who could not tear himself away from the management. To Everardus it seemed that this duality of control must on occasion lead to difficulties, but the younger Martin told him that it never interfered with the smooth working of the farm. They all deferred to 'father's' opinion, as father obviously had more experience, and where it was plain that father's opinion ran contrary to sound common sense, as it sometimes, though admittedly very rarely did, they tacitly ignored it, and gave him credit for whatever profit accrued from such disregard. They made a good thing out of the farm, and had sent some of their produce to the Cape Town market where, despite the charges for transport, which were high, they had sold them at a reasonable profit. Their oranges and *naartjies* were famous in the Valley, and their wine fetched a good price, while among their other exports were protea bark, used for tanning purposes and for staining wood, as it possessed a fine log-wood colour, and buchu and bush tea, which were readily saleable in the Valley and beyond. After dinner, or rather supper—for like all the inhabitants of the Valley the Rekker household took its principal meal in the middle of the day—old Martin had invited his guest to have a game of chess with him. Everardus had readily agreed, for he would have ample time the next morning to visit the *kraals* with the younger Martin, and he wished very much to study the older man's acquaintance. During the play both had been quiet, Uncle Martin concentrating upon the game, and Everardus occupied as much in watching his host as in attending to the moves. He was not a good chess player and he knew it, so that his defeat did not disappoint him, and when for the third consecutive time he had admitted checkmate, he thought that he had done all that courtesy demanded of him, and eagerly looked forward to a talk with his host.

'I believe they have all died out,' he repeated, helping himself to the snuff that Uncle Martin tendered gracefully. 'If Uncle would care to give me a few particulars ... I am immensely interested in *Meneer* Uhlmann. And more in his friend, that upstanding *Meneer* von Bergmann ...'

'Oh, was he there?' exclaimed Uncle Martin, surprised. 'I should have liked to meet him again. Usually he returns by way of the Village, and spends a night with us. He is a fine man, *Meneer* von Bergmann. One would scarcely say he was a *predikant*. But hear him in the pulpit—I do not think there is one of our pastors who can hold a candle to him for eloquence. He is a veritable *Chrysostome*—which means a gold-mouth, Nephew, though it is not Latin; Greek, I fancy, but I am not sure. A fine, powerful figure of a man, and as fine inside as outside.'

'He has some queer ideas,' said Everardus, and he recounted some of these queer ideas, dwelling in particular upon the opinion von Bergmann had expressed about the condition of the country and its population. Uncle Martin listened with attention and nodded his head.

'I can almost hear him say it,' he remarked. 'We have before now discussed the same thing, and I fancy you give a true account of his opinions. I do not say that I see eye to eye with him in this, Nephew Ev'rard, but I fear there is a deal of truth in what he says. I can see for myself that we are not progressing as we ought to progress. In some ways we are falling behind. Sometimes I think it is only an old man's imaginings. You know, as children we always thought things were finer, larger, grander than they really were, and when we come back, grown men, and view these things again, we are surprised that they are so small and mean. Perhaps it is that. But ...,' he shrugged his shoulders deprecatingly, and took another pinch of snuff, delicately.

'It seems to me he overstates the case against us,' said Everardus argumentatively. 'It may be true that we neglect to give the children a right education and allow them to grow up without much more than what they learn in the catechism class, but after all we make them into good farmers, and they turn out good citizens.'

'Aye, there lies the pith of the matter,' said Uncle Martin. 'Do we? When you have lived long enough among us, Nephew Ev'rard, to know us all as doubtless you knew people in the District whence you came, you will find that there are many of us who are not as they should be, and you will ask yourself if it is not our fault that they are worse than they should be.'

'Surely Uncle does not hold with him that those people who left to find a home for themselves beyond the great River are blameworthy?' asked Everardus eager to have his own doubt on this point finally quashed.

'I gravely question the propriety of their doing,' answered the old man, speaking very seriously. 'Look you, Nephew Ev'rard, I recollect the time when we all grumbled against the Company. My father and my grandfather had their grievances. They were many and galling, some of them. Did you know, before any of them could enter into holy matrimony he had to travel to Cape Town and show himself and his intended wife to the Governor for approval? He could only marry there. You can picture for yourself what that meant. And later on when the English came, people grumbled at them and longed for the old Company! What happened? *Meneer* de Mist came out, and we had a new administration, and nobody was satisfied, and there were murmurings throughout the land. I am old enough to remember how angry my father was when he heard that they were going to levy a high road tax to make roads that were of no use to him or to anyone here. And then came the second occupation, and people remembered all the old grievances, and put them down to the English. It was no longer the Company; it was the English. Honestly, Nephew Ev'rard, I can't say that I think there was just cause for trekking. We had as much as they had, in grievance and complaint, I mean, although it is true they were more exposed to the wild Kaffirs and we had by that time tamed our Bushmen. Not that the Korannas did not worry us quite a lot. But I think, with *Meneer* von Bergmann, that it would have been better and more courageous for them to have remained and fought with us to get salvation. It is easy enough to fly from temptation, but a true man fights against it.'

'But the government has been unjust to us all. Uncle will surely admit that. Look at the way they dealt with us over the slaves.'

'Ah, that was mismanaged, badly. I know a little more about it than you do, Nephew. Father was too old to have anything to do with that business; he died just before the proclamation was issued. So I had everything to do with it. We lost a deal of money over that transaction, but I do not think the government was altogether to blame. And any other government would have done much the same, but naturally we throw the blame upon the English. We shall never get a good government until we have one of our own. That time is coming. Already we have some say, and if the hotheads will only work and have patience, we will get along much better than we will by trekking and complaining.'

'When you are with us a little longer,' went on the old man, warming to his subject, 'you will find that here too, in this District, we have hotheads. They talk without text or book, and they harp merely on one thing, that all our troubles are due to the English. Why, I believe they would ascribe the drought to the English, and the scab and the failure of fore-last year's wheat crop. They have lost all sense of proportion. They have not come into close contact with the English; some of them have never been to Cape Town even, and they believe all the other hotheads tell them. We had one such here. He came to collect funds for the Trekkers, though how much of what he collected ever reached them, I can't tell you. I did not like the chap. There was a strain of Black blood in him. But he could talk, and he upset some of us very much. We Elders had our work cut out to prevent some of our younger men from going with him, but we pointed out to them that they could do quite as much here as they could do out there in the wilds.'

He paused and took another pinch of snuff, tendering the box to his guest who helped himself and waited, for he felt sure that Uncle Martin had some further observations to make.

'If I may tell you so, Nephew' said the old man, reflectively, 'a man's liberty is something to be fought for, something even, on occasion, to die for. But it is one's *personal* liberty, and that, so far as I know, is not more circumscribed under our present government than it was under the old Company. In many ways we are much freer. You, of course, cannot compare, and that is a pity, Nephew, for without comparison there can be no adequate reasoning. That is what the hotheads do not understand. I may tell you that there are some among us who are so wanting in respect for authority and for those set above us that I have heard talk of their abstaining next year from celebrating the birthday of our beloved Queen. So far has the poison entered into their minds, that they no longer can compare things justly. Every year, since I can remember, we have celebrated our beloved Queen's birthday with the customary rejoicing, and it would be a grievous pity, I may almost say an act of disloyalty, that I for one would bitterly regret, if we failed to show our respects on a day like that.'

'I, too, have heard something about it, Uncle.' said Everardus. 'This year I was away at Cape Town, and could not join you, but I am looking forward to next May. I hear that you have a big gathering at the Village.'

'Yes. That is the best place, although I have often thought that we should have it alternately on the farms and at the Village. It would bring the matter nearer home that way. Look you, Nephew Ev'rard, I do not say that the government does not make mistakes. I indeed believe that if our good Queen knew of things that went on here, she would be profoundly shocked. In the old days the Governor came down among us; he mingled with us. I have had him sitting in that very chair where you are sitting, eating almonds and raisins, and enjoying them too, for after all they are men like you and me. Old Somerset came down in my father's time, and got his green velvet coat all dusty with flour in the mill house. He bought three of father's horses before he went on to the widow Louw's farm to look at his imported stallion. And he was by no means the best of the English, for he was haughty, and conceited, and talked through his nose, so that even the interpreter could not rightly follow him.'

'What *Meneer* von Bergmann—and he is a man for whom I have the most profound respect, for he does not talk without reflection and he has done great good although he is only with us for barely ten years—what *Meneer* von Bergmann said about the children, I am afraid, is gospel truth. Look you, Nephew Ev'rard, I do not hold with what he said about race. Blood, after all, will tell, but it must be good blood. Here in the Valley—I can say it in all honesty—we have kept ourselves moderately pure. There are some of us who have transgressed. You can tell them when you meet them, I mean their children, for a sin of that sort strikes at the young generations, Nephew, and passes us over. Perhaps not that, for a sinner never comes off quite scatheless.'

'I do not quite follow, Uncle' remarked Everardus, although he fancied that he could grasp the drift of the older man's argument. 'Do you mean to imply that they have married non-Whites?'

'No, no. Some of us did, to be sure. You have only to look into their pedigrees and when you find that there is some hitch, you may take it that there was a slave girl. Some of us married them openly. Everyone knows about it. There is no mystery made of the matter. But some did not marry those they took, and you will find bastard children who know their White fathers though none of them dare presume on the relationship. That I call a sin, Nephew Ev'rard. But it is there, patent. We do not talk about it, at least not in public, but if you keep your eyes open ... well, you will see. I do not say we have been the only sinners nor that it is something that has come upon us latterly. It was so in the old days, in the Company's days. Then, perhaps, there was some excuse for it, though I would be the last to excuse so flagrant a sin. Now there is none, and yet ... well, look about you, Nephew, and then ask yourself if everything is as it should be with us. I fear ... I fear, *Meneer* von Bergmann has got hold of the right end of the stick.'

'That sort of thing is everywhere, Uncle' said Everardus, again argumentatively. 'You cannot say that we alone are guilty of it. In Cape Town, why most of the black creatures are half-castes, and they must have had some white forebears. Not that it is always easy to tell ...'

'There you are mistaken, Nephew Ev'rard' said the old man, decisively. 'It is quite easy. If there is any doubt, the nose always tells.'

'The nose, Uncle? I thought the finger nails, the hands ...'

'Oh no. But feel the nose. You and I, Nephew' old Martin touched with his slender delicate fingers the tip of his own nose as he spoke, 'have a little cleft in our noses. I do not know rightly what it is, but it is there. When you have Hottentot blood in you, it disappears, and the nose is round, smooth, so that you cannot feel it. Yes, that is it,' for Everardus was now feeling his own nose and much relieved in mind to find that he could plainly detect the sharp edge of the nasal cartilage underneath the skin. 'And not that alone. There's the man's character, Nephew. You cannot always feel the nose—it would not be proper to do so. But from the character you can nearly always tell. If you meet one of us who is boastful, having little to boast of, and inordinately vain, disinclined to work, idle, and boisterous one moment and like a sodden dish-cloth the moment after, be on your guard, for the chances are there is bad blood in him. I know, Nephew, for I have had experience, to my sorrow and calamity.'

'But if what *Meneer* von Bergmann says is true,' ventured Everardus, 'is there then nothing we can do? He spoke of education. I have not had experience, but surely there is a school here.'

'There is one at the Village,' answered the old man. 'But few of the Valley people can send their children there. I have often talked to our parson on the matter, and at the next meeting of our church council it will come up for discussion. We should have a school at every central farm. But where is the money to come from? I could afford to give something, and so could others, but we have all been lax. Take my own children; Martiens has had no schooling, except what he got at the catechism class. I had none, but then I was for more than a year a boarder with our old pastor, who is dead now. He taught us Latin, and reading and writing and a trifle of arithmetic, besides, of course, Bible and church history. In many ways I had a much better education than I have been able to give my own children. That is where *Meneer* von Bergmann is so dreadfully right. We are degenerating, and unless we do something we shall go on degenerating. It is for the younger men among us—you, for example, Nephew Ev'rard, to help us. You are a newcomer, you are, I am told, rich, and from what I have seen of your farm and of you, I think that there is truth in what I have been told. You should bestir yourself, and help us. I will do what I can to assist, but I am an old man, Nephew, and the old look back, not forwards. It is you who must look over the mountains and spy out the new Canaan.'

'What Uncle has just told me,' said Everardus, much impressed by this admonition, 'will give me plenty of food for thought. I must admit that what I saw at Neckarthal impressed me profoundly. If so much is being done for these Native children—why, Mrs Uhlmann herself teaches in the school, and her own children sit on the same benches with these Black urchins—we should do something for our own children. I am not rich, and I have no right to be prodigal with my wife's money, but we have two of our own, and I should not like them to grow up without some schooling. When I get back I will have a talk with Uncle Dorie, and we will see what can be done.'

'That is right. That is what I expected of you. And Doremus will give you good advice; his head is set squarely on his shoulders, believe me. You will have a great deal of difficulty. Our people are not very wise in some matters, although they have a high opinion of their own wisdom in others. Consult with His Reverence as you go through the Village ... You have met him, eh? Very well. You will find him a true counsellor and a good friend, if you are yourself true and loyal. If he finds you insincere, Nephew, goodbye to any help that you may expect from him, for *Meneer* de Smee hates hypocrisy and deceit.'

Everardus was not quite sure if there was not some hidden meaning in Uncle Martin's last sentence, but he was not anxious to unravel it, and presently, after his host had poured out the sweet wine and he had drunk his share with the usual 'May it benefit you,' he parted from him for the night, and went to the outside room which had been assigned to him as a bed-chamber.

Under the myriad stars that spangled with iridescent glittering, the dark green night above him, the open *werf* of the farm lay sombre and serene in its quietude. Through the poplar trees came the far off sound of the waterfall, its roar dimmed to an interrupted monotone like the sough of wind through leafy branches. The innumerable sorrels that in daytime made a flower garden of the grass patches on the farmyard were curled up and closed, but from the garden came the scent of yellow jasmine and cactus flowers. In the background loomed the dark masses of the mountains, sharply outlined against the black green of the skyline. A fine light mist was gathering over the spurs and coursing down into the deeper dells of the amphitheatre, and in the air lay the fresh coolness of early spring. Everardus opened his door, and dragged his mattress on to the *stoep*, and lay down under the stars, and for a long time his reflections on what he had heard from Uncle Martin and from Brother von Bergmann kept him awake.

Chapter 7

The lengthening days of September found the building and furnishing of Everardus's homestead so far advanced that he could summon his family to share with him the wonders he daily discovered on his farm. As the spring advanced and gave place to summer, the country surrounding *Knolkloof* blossomed into a flower garden so diversified in hue and odour that it was almost impossible to enumerate the species of which it was compounded. Had Everardus been a botanist he would have classified these wonderful flowers according to their floral characters, the number of their stamens, and the shape and outline of their perianth leaves. Those scintillating, almost iridescently coloured blossoms that opened only in the sun-glare, and where everything else seemed to wilt and droop, expanded gorgeously into many-rayed stars of the fieriest primary colours, belonged to the aizoaceae, and there were so many kinds of them that the botanists had despaired of cataloguing them properly. They were mostly shrubs or small bushes, sometimes trailing or decumbent, perennials with succulent, fleshy leaves and fibrous stems, or with no stems at all when they simply protruded their two leaves from a rock crevice and starred the hard cliff with flowers, but some of them were annuals, tiny plants whose blossoms were almost bigger than the rest of the plant, which grew in myriads on the flat sandy banks of the River and everywhere in the Valley from early spring until mid-summer. So prolific were these midday flowers that Everardus, had he possessed the patience and the interest necessary for such a task, might have counted thousands of blossoms on one bush, and similarly thousands of flowered plants on favourable sites where the sand and the clay mixed to a combination most suitable for their growth. The most showy of the early spring flowers were of the iris family, which has three stamens and an inferior ovary, and an underground stem which is sometimes marble shaped and edible. To this family belonged the delicate silky-petalled moraeas, the dwarfed but splendidly coloured galaxias, the tall and wind-draggled holias, the fringed, velvety ferrarias, the star-like ixias, the sturdy blue and crimson babianas, the charmingly curved tritonias, the upright synnotias, the abundant lapeyrouseas that carpeted the ground in grey and silver, the odorous freesias, the many varieties of gladiolus, some slender and delicate both in stem and bloom, others tall, sweet-scented and fiery-hued, and the even taller and much more free-blooming watsonias. Their colours were startlingly bright, representative of every tint that Nature has at her disposal, but among them all there was none so amazingly pure in its vivid colouring as the wonderful aristea, whose beautiful blue is like nothing else on the earth or in heaven or in the seas. And the aristeas covered acres of veld, making splashes of brightness between the green and the grey that took one's breath away when one came upon them for the first time. There were all varieties of them, short ones and tall ones, pale blue ones and dazzling lapis-lazuli ones, all growing prodigally luxuriant in soil that seemed far too poor to nourish such splendour. Nor were these representatives of the irises without gaudy rivals. There were species of the lily family, which has six stamens and a superior ovary, whose colouring, and beautiful shapes vied with those of their neighbours. Bright crimson and variegated golden lachenalias, the flowers drooping gracefully on their short stems, large-leaved massonias full of strongly scented honey, plant aloes in the rock clefts, white and orange coloured ornithogalums, blue ornithoglossums, and sad-coloured drimias, grew everywhere, wherever there seemed space for them to congregate in clusters or room for even a single seed to germinate. With them grew representatives of the amaryllis family, which, like the lilies, has six stamens but an inferior ovary—the chaste waxy white or yellow hypoxis, the boldly outlined golden curculigo, the quaint, leafless haemanthus which is the colour of new blood, and the tender-petalled gethyllis whose fruit pods perfume the air for miles.

This floral harvest told Everardus that his land was good, although it also made him realise that most of it was virgin soil. His predecessor on the farm had burned large tracts of mountain and veld, and on these burned spaces the grass and the bush grew heavily, while the flowers were less abundant than on other sites. Early in the spring, just after the rains had ceased, the grass had sprung up, greening the Valley right down to the River's edge, and before October came the hills around were vividly green, and the bush on the river bank luxuriantly leafy. With the early summer warmth everything on the farm seemed to spurt into life, to burgeon and to quicken with almost amazing rapidity. The newly planted fruit trees started budding, the young oaks put out foliage, and the orange and *naartjie* trees blossomed so that their heavy, sweet scent hung over the orchard and was wafted towards the house.

Seldon had been quick with the building, and at the beginning of October the masons had left, and the new house was ready for occupation. Everardus went to Cape Town and came back with his family, and installed Magriet in a home that was very much to her liking. Anton Fischer came in person, with a party of Native workmen from Neckarthal, and superintended the fitting of the cedarwood furniture. He, too, had done his work well. When Everardus saw the finely polished dining-room table, large enough to seat twenty guests in comfort, the broad seated sofa, and the set of sixteen chairs whose seats were of intricately plaited leather thongs, he was amply satisfied, and his satisfaction increased considerably when he found that the price he had to pay for these useful ornaments was far less than he had anticipated.

During his first week in his new home, he and Magriet and the children found that the time passed all too quickly. From practically all the neighbouring farms came the curious, anxiously friendly and disposed to help, but also furtively inquisitive to gather whatever information they could glean regarding the qualities and antecedents of the new mistress of *Knolkloof*. Uncle Dorie and his wife came from *Sandvlei*, bringing with them a wagonload of provisions, delicacies like homemade brawn, spiced dried beef or biltong, sausages and bacon, new potatoes, wholemeal loaves made from home-grown wheat, and translucent slabs of watermelon preserve. They were so kindly in their fussiness, so utterly disinterested in their cheery officiousness, that Magriet found herself exchanging confidences with *Tant* (aunt) Sophrosina, a buxom, double-chinned dame with absurdly small eyes and a complexion which, owing to the fact that its owner almost always wore a large cotton headdress or *kappie* completely protecting her face from the sun and wind, had retained much of its youthful fairness and smoothness. *Tant* Sophrosina was a walking echo of her husband, whom she deferred to in all things, although those who knew the pair shrewdly suspected that hers was the really directing voice in the van Aard household. Her assistance was invaluable to Magriet, just as Uncle Dorie's help was of real value to Everardus, and on their side both Uncle Dorie and his wife were attracted by the newcomers. In these circumstances, the friendship between the two households rapidly ripened into a real intimacy that did much to strengthen the prestige of the owner of *Knolkloof* in the Valley.

The Valley, indeed, was quite prepared to accept Everardus as part of itself. After his return from his trip to Neckarthal, he had taken some pains to regularise his position among them. His attorneys at Cape Town had once more shown themselves capable of handling a delicate situation with tact and discretion, and in due course he had received his attestation of membership of the Dutch Reformed Church in which his name and that of his wife were given in complete accordance with the now forgotten notice in the *Government Gazette*. With that proof in his hand, he could afford to forget that such an individual as Amadeus Tereg had ever existed. It was true that Magriet still called him Ami, but that would be taken as a term of endearment, and need not necessarily give rise to any suspicion. On his visit to the Village he had called on the pastor and submitted his certificate, and he and Magriet had been received as full members of the local congregation. Uncle Dorie had even hinted that at the next election of office bearers it might be a good thing to propose him for the office of Deacon, which in time would lead to the more responsible senior position of Elder. At the Village, too, he had called upon the magistrate, who had been courtesy personified, and had talked in English on many subjects. The magistrate, although he had not committed himself to any definite expression of opinion, had yet given

Everardus the impression that officially he knew many secrets and that his official duty made it sternly necessary for him to guard such confidences as he held. Moreover, his manner and his speech had been such as to justify Everardus in concluding that officially there was nothing to prevent him from associating with one who in the past had done the government some small service under conditions that were not such that they could be published abroad.

All this was very satisfactory. Indeed, Everardus found a strange gratification in the thought that three men whom he much respected and would very much have liked to look upon as friends, shared a secret with him. He had instinctively liked the magistrate, whose blunt friendliness and official tactfulness he could appreciate, and he had liked Brother Johann even more. Brother von Bergmann, an altogether stronger personality, had given him, at first, some misgivings, but later on he had conquered those, satisfied that the action which Brother von Bergmann had taken in his case was justified in the circumstances, and rather glad, if the truth must be told, that such action had been taken. He told his wife all about it, and found her sympathetic but at the same time inclined to be critical. Magriet evidently shared Brother von Bergmann's views to some extent, and she pointed out that it was possible that the secret would leak out, now that three people already knew of it, and that it might be infinitely better if Everardus came into the open and disclosed it. But Everardus could not bring himself to do that. He had so carefully in the past guarded it, he had so masked it that even in his old environment no one could possibly have suspected that he, the village saddler and harness-maker, had ever ... No, the mere contemplation of confessing gave him gooseflesh. Later on, perhaps, when they were settled here ... when Uncle Dorie, for instance, and Uncle Martin were proved friends ... then perhaps. But not now.

Magriet made no further attempt to persuade him. She had made many in the past, when dissimulation and subterfuge had been more repugnant than they were now, and she realised that on this matter, as it touched him so intimately, he was not to be moved. She did not approve of his decision, for she felt that it was wrong, just as Brother von Bergmann had thought it wrong. But she hoped that circumstances would enable him to keep his secret, until such time as it would be necessary to proclaim it to the world. That that time would ultimately come, she had no doubt whatever, but meanwhile she was content to wait, and to help him in his task. It would not be easy, she told herself. One had to be on one's guard constantly. One had to evade questions; one had to steer round, tack and slant, which was always a wearisome business at the best. But possibly things might be better here at *Knolkloof*.

And *Knolkloof* came up to her expectations. It still looked bare, disorderly, uncared for. But she visioned its possibilities clearly. She saw that her husband had planned for the future on a scale which could almost be called grand. And already there were encouraging signs of success. The vineyard was sprouting; the orchard trees were blossoming, and although they could not expect either grapes or fruit this season, it was at least an indication that what had been put in was living and growing. The house pleased her. Its roominess, its excellent furniture, whose qualities she could fully appreciate, and its situation, delighted her. Old Sylvester and Regina she had been prepared to take on trust, her husband having written a glowing account of their capabilities, but the first day showed her that Everardus had not exaggerated their merits, and that she had secured in them two very valuable servants on whose loyalty and devotion she could depend. Under Regina served two indoor maids, and with this household staff Magriet was quite satisfied, for she took her household seriously and had no wish to shirk her home duties. She saw herself mistress of a house such as she had often dreamed of yet had never expected to own, and she realised, especially after a talk with *Tant* Sophrosina, how much she could do to help her husband to win the respect and popularity of the Valley.

With the Valley itself she was as much charmed as her husband had been, and as she became better acquainted with her environment, that charm increased. Most of those who live in the Valley learn to love it. It grips the imagination; it conjures with its beauty, with the subtle impression that it makes upon that aesthetic sense that lies dormant in each of us. No one can explain that influence of concentrated natural beauty upon those that are daily exposed to it, but it is chastening while it is uplifting, strengthening to the soul as well as to the mind, a very potent factor in the life of those who feel that mountain and river, with their age old serenity, bear the impress of forces that have moulded man's destiny in the past and will mould it in the future.

So the Valley had left its imprint upon its inhabitants for generations. It had influenced them, unconsciously. They could not, had they been asked to do so, express in words just in what manner it had shaped their lives. Most of them, indeed, would have been surprised if anybody hinted that these rugged ranges and that slow moving River that in winter overflowed its shallow bed and in summer dwindled down to mild trickles divided by lines of drift sand had had anything to do with their lives. None the less the Valley had stamped them, indefinably indenting upon them something of its own character, inevitably teaching them to look with liking upon its contours and ultimately to love every coign of it, every buttress that caught the wind in its seaward or inland sweep, every hill slope that lay brown under a blistering sun in late summer or blazed in purple and crimson and gold when the spring gave it a harvest of sorrel and saffron irises.

There was much to do before the sweltering mid-summer heat made outdoor work an economically unproductive task. Indoors, Magriet set herself to improve the house, and train her raw material derived from the huts, while on the farm itself Everardus, ably assisted by Matryk and Sylvester, worked hard to consolidate what had already been acquired and to accumulate new assets. By Christmas the evidence of this hard work was apparent. The buildings had been neatly whitewashed; the harvest had been gathered, and the horses were running circlewise round the threshing floor. It had not been a big harvest, but what it lacked in quantity it had made up in quality, and Everadus was well satisfied with the results of his sowing. He was equally satisfied with his horses and cattle, and knew that if he had no disasters, none of those acts of God which sometimes wrecked the best laid plans in the Valley, he might look forward to a far better success the following year. In this opinion he was strengthened by the criticism of his friends, who opined that he had done very well indeed for a newcomer. Uncle Dorie was enthusiastic in his praise, but suggested that much more might be done. Seeing that Nephew Ev'rard had ample capital at his disposal, he would suggest that a watermill be built, and that cement furrows—or, as cement was expensive and had to be brought from afar, merely paved channels such as our forefathers had found good enough for their purpose—should be made to carry the water from the stream to the mill. A dam above the farm where the little valley narrowed would also be an improvement. Nephew Ev'rard might not believe it, and indeed the weather this season had been singularly mild and propitious, but there were years when the rainfall in the Valley was lamentably low. Drought years came on an average in rotation every five years, and a prudent agriculturist made arrangements to meet them. Lean times had to be expected—after all, the world had not changed very much since Pharaoh's time—and it was folly to put all one's eggs in one basket or to expect that a pet dog could be allowed to run loose in the streets without sometimes being knocked down by a passing vehicle. He was merely suggesting, for Nephew Ev'rard had shown himself so thoroughly capable of managing his farm that any criticism, no matter how kindly it was intended, must necessarily sound like impertinence, which was by no means what he had in mind. But Nephew Ev'rard would have the common sense to see that the suggestion was a good one, and while they were talking about water furrows, he would have Nephew Ev'rard bear in mind that unchannelled water carried away a good deal of ground. Almost as much as the east wind did, though to be sure, *Knolkloof* was not so much exposed to the east wind as some other farms were. Nephew Ev'rard had no doubt seen *Brakvlei*, which in its time had been a good farm, carrying, easily, a hundred muids of wheat, but now had barely room for ten muids, all the soil having been swept away by the wind. A great pity, but farming in such exposed situations was a tempting of Providence, and no one could approve of it.

Everardus readily acquiesced in the suggestion, and the watermill was built. Anton Fischer came back from Neckarthal to fit the machinery and make the huge wheel, and he did it single-handed, with a skill that Everardus envied him and a taciturnity that was proof even against Magriet's courtesy. The artisan, who had fought at Waterloo, was a morose, silent man, much older-looking than he really was, who only expanded when he had Everardus's children around him. With Katryn and the little Gottlieb he would be friendly and even, on occasions, sportive. He made curious toys out of bits of wood and the fat triangular leaves of the creeping mesembryanthemum, whose fruits the children ate with relish, and he told interesting fairy tales in a Dutch that was barely understandable but which he eked out with wonderfully expressive pantomime. His son, too, Everardus learned, was in Germany, studying at the Mission House, and Anton had vague hopes that ultimately young Frederick might be found fit to carry the gospel into cannibal lands in the east.

For all his moroseness Anton was a good and quick worker, and his mill house was a marvel of neatness, much admired by all who came to look at it. He refused to stay over for Christmas, saying curtly that they knew how to spend that festival at Neckarthal, and accordingly, a week before it came, he trudged back over the mountains, disdaining the horse that Everardus had offered him. Everardus himself spent his Christmas and New Year—the latter regarded as a much greater event—at *Sandvlei*, where he made the acquaintance of still others of *Oom* Dorie's numerous family. On former visits to the farm he had already met a couple of dozen people who in some way or other claimed intimate relationship with the Elder, and it was rather bewildering to find that there were many others—sisters' children, brothers' children, grandchildren, and even second and third cousins—whom Uncle Dorie regarded as part of his legitimate family. The lavish hospitality, the unaffected cordiality with which every visitor was greeted and made welcome, and the cheerful ingenuity of *Tant*

Sophrosina and her daughters and handmaidens in disposing and boarding so numerous a visiting party, were things to be remembered, for neither Everardus nor Magriet had ever seen anything like them. Relays of guests sat down to supper in the evening, and beds were shared indoors while most of the men slept out of doors in tents or under improvised shelters made by hanging the heavy bucksails over the branches of the big oak trees. Every day a couple of sheep and many chickens were slaughtered, while from early morning until well after sundown the big soup pots boiled on the open fireplace. It was a time of holiday, and custom had decreed that while it should be suitably interlarded with occasions of solemnity, at which the Elder or some of the senior visitors officiated, it should also be celebrated with feasting and an abundance of good cheer. From it Everardus came away with yet other impressions of the Valley which were as pleasant and as encouraging as were some of those he had received in the past. He had seen another side of life, another aspect of their outlook upon it, and both had been to his liking.

In time he settled down to the routine of farm life, a routine that to many people might sound monotonous but which to him held infinite pleasure and was capable of endless variation. His old occupation as a saddler he found very much to his advantage; he could deal promptly and efficiently with repairs, and his skill with his awl, first witnessed by Uncle Dorie, soon became known to many of his neighbours, who often brought him leather work for opinion or adjustment. When his time allowed him to do so, he executed these small commissions, earning thereby much goodwill from the Valley, though he refused to receive payment for his work, exercising at the same time his privilege of refusing to undertake anything when he could not do so without infringing upon his routine work. He used his skill in other ways, and made an exhibition saddle with bridle complete for Uncle Dorie, a gift that is still treasured in the Elder's family although it is now no longer fitted for anything but exhibition purposes. His knowledge of English gained him a reputation as a *slim* or clever man, and if the truth must be told Everardus had much more book learning than the majority of his neighbours. He could read and write passably well in two languages; he spoke the vernacular Dutch with the fluency that comes from practice in childhood, and the more sonorous 'high' Dutch with a facility bred from long familiarity with the idiom. He could speak English, with a noticeable intonation it is true, but understandably, and he knew a smattering of Native tongues, although he could not have conversed with ease with any of his farm hands who was proficient in Koranna or Bushman. He had a knowledge of arithmetic up to the four rules, wrote a very neat script, could sign his name with a real flourish, and had been taught to sing from the notes at sight. Moreover, he had seen something more of the outside world than most of his fellow citizens in the Valley, and had possibly a slightly larger acquaintance with officialdom than they had. All of which went far to impress his neighbours with his learning and his ability. Some of them, like Uncle Martin, respected him less for these gifts than for what they found in his nature and temperament, but they recognised that he was an acquisition to the District and placed him in the same category wherein they had already listed Quakerley and the Seldons, remarking, when they did so, that Nephew Everard was at any rate superior to these latter inasmuch as he was indubitably one of their own people, even if they did not know where he came from or who his father and grandfather had been.

Chapter 8

Summer came with its scorchingly hot, wearisomely long days, relieved by the cool nights thick-scented with the smells of many flowers. Never before had Everardus encountered such midday heat. The Valley knew nothing of thermometers, but had one hung in the shade, under the eaves of the *stoep*, it would have registered over one hundred and eighteen degrees Fahrenheit, while outside in the sun-glare it would have jumped twenty degrees higher. It was a dry, motionless heat, that sucked the energy and the life out of one, and the Valley respected it as such and did not flout it. After the midday meal the Valley went to rest, sleeping in cool lofts, under shady trees, or in bedchambers with the inside blinds lowered and the outside jalousies closed. Only at four o'clock in the afternoon it woke to life, came into the dining rooms, and took coffee with biscuits and preserves, exchanged gossip, and resumed such work as there was to do, although it took care that in the late afternoons there was little that demanded toil or exertion. It was probably a habit that the Valley had inherited from Indian tradition, for many of the Valley's ancestors had known Java, had shuddered at Peter Elberveld's treachery, and looked upon the Boroe-Bhodoer as a monument of monstrous idolatry.

Everardus found the heat intolerable. As a newcomer, they assured him, he would find it so. Later on he would get accustomed to it, and take it as a matter of course. But they advised him to go to the seaside for the hottest part of the year, which was the latter end of January and February until the moon was full. Most of them went to the seaside for the sea was some sixty miles, as the crow flies, from the Valley, and there was a finely sheltered little bay, perfectly safe for the children, where they could camp, and where a few of them had their 'seaside houses.' Uncle Dorie, who went regularly after New Year, with his wife and family, to spend some weeks there, taking the opportunity to bargain with the fisherfolk who lived round the salt pans and inland lagoons, and returning home with his wagon laden with dried, curried and kippered fish, invited Everardus to accompany him, but agreed when Everardus declined the invitation, that it would perhaps be better if Nephew Ev'rard remained this year at home and looked after his embryonic farm. From Neckarthal came another invitation, written in a quaint, sloping script which Everardus found some difficulty in reading, but phrased with old world formality toned down by touches of homely idiomatic frankness. Would Everardus spend a week with *Meneer* Uhlmann, and bring his wife and children as well. *Meneer* Uhlmann would send a wagon, if *Meneer* Nolte found difficulty in securing transport. With their own children away, *Meneer* and Mrs Uhlmann would welcome having young folk in the house, and Mrs Nolte would probably find the upland coolness a pleasant change from the sultriness of the Valley. And the writer begged to remain, with an expression of cordial esteem, *Meneer* Nolte's brother in Christ our Lord, Johann Uhlmann.

Everardus was glad to accept this invitation. He had already bought a wagon, and increased his stock of transport animals, so that there was no difficulty on that score. He took with him a Native boy to help with the mules, and a Native to attend on Magriet and the children, and went by way of the north road across the steep pass that led to *The Hoek* and reached Neckarthal after three days' travel. One night he slept under the hospitable roof of Uncle Martin, the second night under the stars, and the third night in Neckarthal itself.

The Uhlmanns made them welcome, and were genuinely delighted to see them. Magriet and the children had plenty to occupy them, the former in long and intimate conversations with her hostess on household affairs, the latter in tumultuous play with the small playfellows they found on the station. Everardus's stay with the missionary was a pleasant holiday, for he learned much by intercourse with his host and by studying the methods employed at the station. Here the climate was not so swelteringly hot as in the Valley. In the afternoon and evening there was generally a soft breeze from the mountains that tempered the air, and during the day the abundance of shade afforded by the heavily leaved trees and the suggestive coolness of the purling station stream combined to alleviate the heat. The gardens were at their best, and yielded luscious sweet and giant watermelons, deliciously delicate young mealies, to be eaten from the stalk cob, and various kinds of gourds and squashes, while there was a surplus of fruit—large, fleshy black-mulberries, that made a vividly crimson stain when squashed, meltingly tender *Bon Chretien* pears, big sun-kissed free-stone peaches, blue plums, and even golden bananas. From the Karroo veld the Natives brought in bundles of morea corms, which grow deep down in the hard clay and have to be tediously dug out with a pointed stick, and gathered only by those who know the difference between the edible and the poisonous varieties. These corms were boiled in milk, and tasted like fresh chestnuts, and from them Mrs Uhlmann prepared thick soups and puddings which the Nolte family found much to their taste.

In the evenings Brother Johann and Everardus would sit on the mission house *stoep* and talk about all manner of things. The missionary amazed Everardus by his breadth of outlook and his wide general knowledge, even of matters upon which his guest could test him by his own experiences. His long, thin, wrinkled un-handsome face, with its wistful eyes, would light up with animation when he talked of his work on the station, and Everardus best loved to listen to him when he discoursed on his work. Brother Johann, now that the case of cigars had been exhausted, had fallen back on his large, long-stemmed china pipe, the bowl of which rested on his knees while he smoked. It was too large a pipe to be used at table or while he was walking about the station, but on the *stoep*, in the cool of the evening, it was a constant companion from which he seemed to draw inspiration and comfort.

'Yes, *Meneer* Nolte' he would remark, 'it is undoubtedly more pleasant here than with you yonder in the Valley. We are much higher, and there is always a breeze. You get only the hot east wind—you have not experienced it yet, but it will come, and you will not like it. That was one reason—the main reason, in fact—why I selected this place for a station. At the mouth of the river, where I settled first, it was almost as hot as in the Valley, hotter at times, for we had more level sand there, and although the breeze from the sea cooled the air, the reflection from the dunes made the heat sometimes almost unbearable. For here we are sheltered. We have, as you see, plenty of shade. My first care when I came here was to plant shade trees. Everyone of these oaks you see there I planted with my own hand. They have grown marvellously rapidly, and we plant more every year. You have seen the nursery, where we also have pines and cedars, but these grow very slowly. Perhaps the soil is not good for them;

their taproots strike stone too soon, I fancy.'

'You have indeed improved the place mightily, *Meneer* Uhlmann,' said Everardus. 'I will ... I promise you, take yours as an example to follow, and put in more oaks. They grow just as rapidly on my place.'

'You will be well advised to do so, *Meneer* Nolte. The more shade you have the better. I sometimes think that this hot sun—I am grateful for it, and I do not complain for the sun is a great purifier, *Meneer* Nolte, and we have much less disease here than we have at home, where we see the sun much more rarely than we do here. But I think one can have too much of a good thing ... no, I think I am putting it wrongly. What I mean is, I think one can abuse a good thing. The sun takes energy out of one; its light is so glaring, its strength, here, is so tremendous. That is one reason, *Meneer* Nolte, why it is not good for our children to be constantly exposed to it. I have a feeling that it is sapping to the strength of the body, that it enervates. It does so in the tropical parts of the world, and here we are almost tropical. You must yourself have remarked that in the Valley there is something which makes the people there lethargic. Now it is not so very apparent, but we must look to the future, *Meneer* Nolte.'

'Is it that *Meneer* Uhlmann thinks the same as *Meneer* von Bergmann does,' asked Everardus, 'that environment, rather than race, counts? I cannot quite believe that. It would mean that there is little hope for us here.'

'I would not go as far as that,' replied Brother Johann reflectively. 'Brother von Bergmann is a much cleverer man than I am, *Meneer* Nolte. He is a great man—a great thinker and a great administrator. You should see what he has achieved at his own station. But he is perhaps a dreamer, and he is apt to express himself too dogmatically. I think what he intended to convey to us when we spoke about the matter some months ago, was that if all races had the same chances, the same opportunities, there would not be marked differences between them. That I can very well believe. No man, after all, lives to himself, *Meneer* Nolte, and no man dies to himself. All our doings react upon our fellow men.'

'I think, myself, that he was a trifle too ... too insistent,' said Everardus. 'But his talk made me think, Your Reverence, about things. It would be a pity if we did not do something to improve matters in the Valley. I have thought about it and asked myself if it would be possible to have down there, something similar to what you have here. I fancied a school—I would build one, I mean a schoolhouse, on my farm. It would not cost very much. But the difficulty is to get a teacher.'

'That might be managed,' said the missionary, drawing reflectively at his long pipe. 'But you must bear in mind, *Meneer* Nolte, that book learning is not everything—not the best thing for some youngsters. We have found that out here, and indeed at all our stations in this country. The Natives are very avid of book-learning, but our results are not so very encouraging. They go up to a certain point, and then they seem to lack the capacity to improve further. Not all, of course, but the majority. That is why we teach them handicrafts. I fancy—I speak under correction, of course—that you will find it is much the same with our White children in the Valley. How far are you going to teach them? And what will you teach them? To read and write—yes, that everyone ought to know. But after that, what? I feel sure that if you were to teach them some simple craft—to use tools, to work with their hands, *Meneer* Nolte, you see what I mean? But, if I may advise, I would ask you to discuss the matter very carefully with your neighbours and with the *landdrost* and the Reverend Mr de Smee. These two latter, *Meneer* Nolte, are men who can give you invaluable help, and they know much more of the people than I do. I live very much isolated, as you see, *Meneer* Nolte. My interests are here—I daresay you think that I am doing superfluous work, wasting my time ...'

'No, really, I had no such thought, Your Reverence. Of course, now that Your Reverence speaks of it, I have thought that it is strange that men like Your Reverence, and women like Mrs Uhlmann, should come out here, to a strange country, and give up your own home and people to teach the Natives. I can't digest that yet.'

'It is not so very strange, after all, *Meneer* Nolte. You see—I am speaking for myself now, *Meneer* Nolte, though perhaps I may say also for Brother von Bergman and some of our other Brothers—you see, we felt the urge to work in the Lord's vineyard. We could have worked in it at home; I am sure there is much there that requires weeding and cultivation. But it was not for us to choose. The Society does that. Brother von Bergmann, now, he should have been at home. He should have been one of our administrators, one of our inspectors. But he wanted to come out and be a missionary, an apostle to the heathen. He and I had selected our field. It was to have been the East. From my youth, *Meneer* Nolte, I have looked towards the East— whence the light comes, you know. I read all about it. It has a glorious history, *Meneer* Nolte, for there were great kings and great empires in the East, and today there is much darkness, and a fertile field for the Lord's labourers. But it was not to be. Both I and Brother von Bergmann were at first destined for China. But difficulties arose, and we could not go. Then there was talk of sending us to Java, but that too could not be done. Finally we were selected to go to South Africa. So we came here. Brother von Bergmann went east and I went west, and we settled on barren ground and founded our stations. I sometimes regret that I did not go to China or Java, and I know Brother von Bergmann does too, but we abide by the Society's choice. I hope that my children will, if it is the Lord's wish that they should become apostles to the heathen, go out to the East and do the work that I have not been privileged to do, and then again I hope that they may come here and complete what I have begun. These are an old man's fancies, *Meneer* Nolte, and I ask your pardon for obtruding them upon you.'

'But surely Your Reverence has some choice—had some choice, in the matter. Or is it that the Society simply orders and you all obey?'

'We would be very bad missionaries if we did not obey, *Meneer* Nolte. We have a choice, of course, for the Society would not send out anyone who did not care to go. Unwilling workers, *Meneer* Nolte, spoil any work, as you have doubtless experienced. But it is a matter of conscience, of prayerful consideration. I do not mean to imply that there is any special direction vouchsafed to us—it would be an impertinence on my part to imply this. But both Brother von Bergmann and I thought—we still think—that we had a call to come here, and if we have regrets ... well, my friend, we are human after all. There is a field here, not among the heathen, perhaps, for all these men and women among whom we work have heard the gospel, but among people whom we may help. I consider that is our primary duty, to help. You—I do not mean you personally, *Meneer* Nolte, but the people, the White people, in the Valley—often think that we are doing more harm than good. There are different views about duty, and each one of us must make up his own mind about them. You have seen for yourself what we are trying to do and how we do it, and I hardly think that you will join in the voices that blame us ...'

'Indeed I don't, Your Reverence. Nor would anyone who spent a week here at Neckarthal and saw the work. It is sheer ignorance, Your Reverence. I am sure that those of us who know you and your work wish you every success. Why Uncle Martin and Uncle Dorie both speak in high praise of what you have done ...'

'*Meneer* Rekker and *Meneer* van Aard are very good friends,' said the missionary with a smile. 'I have tested their friendship on more than one occasion, and it has been solid. I owe a great deal to them for which I am very thankful. But they are not all like that in the Valley. There is still much prejudice against us. No doubt it is ignorance, as you say, but ignorance can do much mischief, *Meneer* Nolte. That is one of the reasons why Brother von Bergmann spoke as he did. It is not only ignorance of spiritual matters but ignorance of material things that we have to fight against. In the Valley—I speak in all sincerity and with no intention to pass judgement—there are few folk who have seen anything even of this country, and much less of the world outside. You know some of their prejudice ...'

'I have found out some of it, *Meneer* Uhlmann. It is all ignorance, ignorance and cheek. They think they know everything. To hear them talk about some things, of which they know nothing ...'

'But do we not do the same, *Meneer* Nolte? We affect to despise those whom we think lower than we are. We lack the virtue of humility, and without that there can be no greatness. Perhaps that is why we who are missionaries see more of the other side of the shield than most people do. I do not say we are as humble as we should be— Brother von Bergmann, now, he is not cut out for humility, and, as I have often told him, his pride is his great sin.'

'One can see that *Meneer* von Bergmann is not of the common people, Your Reverence,' said Everardus, who prided himself on the fact that he had once upon a time mingled with those who were not of the common people.

'It all depends,' said Brother Johann, cautiously, 'what you mean by common, *Meneer* Nolte. If you mean vulgar—what we call in German—*gemein*—which is just the same in your Dutch, then you are right. Possibly you may be right, too, if you mean that he comes from noble stock. I do not know. He does not know himself ...'

'How is that, Your Reverence? Surely he must know ...'

'Why surely, *Meneer* Nolte? Is anything quite sure in this world? The matter is very simple. Brother von Bergmann's father was a foundling; he was picked up in the streets of Paris during that horrible time when they cut off people's heads, a young child who did not know who his parents were, a poor creature who had had all his wits scared out of him. But the people who rescued him from heaven knows what fate saw that he was not a stupid child, and they gave him a good education, and in time he was taken into their business. Brother von Bergmann and his brother were sent to the cadet school, but our Lord disposes of us according to His wish, and Brother von Bergmann was called by Him and found grace to answer the call. He came to the mission house, and there I met him and we became friends. He has told me what little he knows of his family, but it is not family, any more than race, *Meneer* Nolte, that counts in a man's life, although I would not go quite so far as to say that tradition and upbringing and a long line of virtuous and upright ancestors have no influence upon a man's character.

Maybe Brother von Bergmann is of noble ancestry. I do not know and I do not very much care, for to me he is a nobleman because he is honest, God-fearing and upright. He has married into a noble family, but that is not a matter that need concern us, for his wife is, like him, one who is virtuous and upright.'

Brother Uhlmann gave Everardus detailed accounts of life at the Society's mission house. He seemed to like to talk about it, possibly because his reminiscences of his boyhood there deflected his thoughts from his own boys' miseries and made him vision the little exiles as enjoying all the excitements and pleasures he had himself enjoyed. He showed Everardus pictures of the Society's offices, and Mrs Uhlmann brought out the autograph album in which the great treasure was the signature of Goethe, which had been the hobby of one of the Brothers at the mission house and had come to the missionary's wife as a wedding present. Every Brother, from the *Herr* Inspector downwards, had written some text or apposite remark in it, and the diversity of handwriting fascinated Everardus, who could not understand the German. There was a sentence in Arabic, which Brother Johann said had been written by a young Brother who had long ago been eaten up by the Batta cannibals, and one in Hebrew, the contribution of a learned professor at Jena. Apparently Brother Uhlmann could read and, what was more surprising still, understand everything that was written in that book, and in his little study, where he received complaints, heard cases, and carried on his administrative work, there were many other books, some in vellum covers, and all totally incomprehensible to Everardus.

On Sunday he and Magriet and the children attended the mission church morning service and again in the evening; in the afternoon there was a Sunday school service for the children who did not attend the evening ceremony. The services were short, with much more ritual than Everardus was accustomed to when in his own church, and with fine choral singing, when slow, dignified melodies were intoned by the congregation. The missionary preached a short sermon lasting barely twenty minutes, with homely illustrations and commonsense reasoning, and although his Dutch was by no means perfect and marred by a terrible accent that some people might have found ridiculous, Everardus was edified and listened with rapt attention. The evening service was equally short and simple, and both were attended by practically the whole adult community. The Native women wore white sunbonnets and black dresses, the men, with the exception of the members of the church council who sat on the benches at right angles to those reserved for the congregation and wore black coats whose surface had been reduced to a shiny green by years of vigorous brushing, were dressed in everyday costume, clean and with coats. Among the congregation Everardus noted all sorts of faces, and some of the older members were obviously pure Mozambique Natives whom he judged must have been slaves.

He saw the school, and Mrs Uhlmann explained to him and his wife how she managed it. She was the teacher, and had under her a young Native girl whom she had trained to read and write and who looked after the infant class. Later on Anta would take her place, but at present Anta was herself a pupil in the school and not—her mother smiled sadly as she said it—one of the best behaved since her brothers had left. But one made allowances. Johann and Christian had been model pupils, for Christian, although only five, had been permitted to attend the infant class—'where, indeed, they simply play, *Meneer* Nolte, and try to pick out the letter blocks'—and had made excellent progress. Johann could read and write quite well, and had been taught a little Latin and the Hebrew alphabet. When Everardus expressed surprise at this, the missionary informed him gravely that Hebrew and Latin were considered essentials— for anyone who wished to understand the Scriptures. 'And Syriac,' he added, 'one must not be amiss in learning Syriac. It is the key to many things. Alas, I have had so little of it that I must depend on translations.' Brother Johann deprecated his own classical knowledge. 'Brother von Bergmann now, *Meneer* Nolte, he can talk Latin and write it as well as any Romish *pater*. He has a memory for these things, and here one rusts, *Meneer* Nolte, one rusts. Besides, there is so much to do that I have but little time to occupy myself with the classics. When little Johann was here it was different. Then I would look up something simple for the boy to tackle, and in so doing I would improve my own acquaintance with the books. But since they left ...'

When Everardus left Neckarthal on his way back to *Knolkloof*, he and Magriet had grown to love their simple hosts and thanked the kindly Providence which had brought them into touch with the Uhlmanns. Their week they would have lengthened out into a fortnight if it had been possible to do so, but their home imperatively called them, and reluctantly they had bidden farewell to the missionary family.

On the farm *Knolkloof*, life proceeded along the lines laid down by routine and convention. The sultry days of February gave place to the milder, more equable fair weather of March, but in April came the east wind, hot and dusty. It swept the farm, and tore the young trees, destroying most of the young oranges and ruining the beginnings of the flower garden that Magriet had made. When Everardus saw his lands, one morning after the wind had raged uninterruptedly for an afternoon and a night, he could well believe what Uncle Dorie had told him of farms which had been almost denuded of their soil by the east wind. But he knew that with care and cultivation he could guard his more stable soil against such waste, and he determined to plant wind screens, hedges of quince and pomegranate which could shelter the garden at least from the fury of that annual enemy of the Valley. The wheat lands could hardly be protected in that manner, but by selecting suitable sites that were more or less shielded by the mountain spurs, he could prevent wind erosion. The more he saw of his own holding, the more he realised that to make it, ultimately, a rival to the well established farms of the Rekkers and Uncle Doremus would need hard work, constant attention and unlimited patience. These he was determined to give, for the rewards that he stood to reap would be great. He could live in comfort here, and expect a fair return for the capital expended on the farm, and above all he could live in a manner which was particularly congenial to him, in the manner in which it had been his and Magriet's expectation to live if once they had the means to secure a holding of their own and an opportunity to return to the land. No man could ask for more, and if there were difficulties and dangers before him ere he could realise his ideal, it would only spur him on to greater efforts. The example of the missionary at Neckarthal, who had created a paradise out of a waste, and created it, apparently, with the expenditure of far less capital than he had available, though to be sure Neckarthal had had the advantage of almost unlimited labour, stimulated and encouraged him.

He built a small house, double-roomed, on the farm yard, within easy distance of the main dwelling, to serve as a schoolroom, and began to discuss the matter of starting a school with his neighbours. He found they were all heartily favourable to the project, and by mid-winter half a dozen children had been collected, the pastor had come down to open the *Knolkloof* school with due solemnity—an occasion that gave Everardus and Magriet their first chance to return some of the hospitality which they had enjoyed since their entry into the Valley—and the magistrate had promised to write to Cape Town and interest the authorities in the matter, with a view to obtaining a subsidy. Magriet undertook to teach the children, and the curriculum, as drawn up by the committee in consultation with the pastor, who was *ex officio* chairman of that body, was made as simple as possible. For the present the children would concentrate their attention on the three r's, with bible history and simple religious instruction. Later on the committee would try and secure the services of a teacher. There were difficulties in the way, not merely financial but practical, for teachers were few and scarce. But Everardus was glad that he had made a beginning, and when he saw the first class being held in the new schoolroom, he felt satisfied. *'Meneer* von Bergmann would approve,' he told himself. 'I know he would, and I shall write and tell him all about it.' But he did not know Brother von Bergmann's address, so he contented himself with a letter to Brother Johann, in which he gave his friend a detailed account of what he had done, in the hope that these particulars would be transmitted to the man who had inspired the undertakings.

Chapter 9

With the advent of May, Everardus found himself involved in a controversy which, while it caused him some mental perturbation and strained his good humour, sometimes to breaking point, taught him a good deal about the temper and disposition of his neighbours. The question at issue was whether the Valley should participate in the yearly Queen's Birthday festivities or whether it should stand severely aside, leaving all these celebrations to the Village folk. The Valley itself was sharply divided on the question. Year after year it had joined with the Village in honouring the young Queen by expressing, in the boisterous fashion which had been introduced during the preceding reign, its sense of loyalty by demonstrations on horseback and on foot. It had no direct reason to abstain from again taking part in these celebrations. As a matter of fact it yearned to do so, and had it been left to its own devices, had no agitating busybodies interested themselves in the matter and thrown out vague hints about the impropriety of following what had become an established custom, the Valley would probably have demonstrated as fervently and as sincerely as it had done in the years before. But busybodies had been about. One, a little man with a stutter which made his dogmatic statements all the more emphatic because th   were so frequently reiterated, had visited every farm in the Valley to collect funds f   the exiled Trekkers who, it seemed, were finding life in the uncivilised regions   to which they had travelled much more strenuous than they had anticipated. He t   harrowing tales of the difficulties and the dangers that had been surpassed—dange   rom Native hordes, from wild beasts, and from dissensions among the Trekkers themselves. He waxed passionately indignant when he recounted how Port Natal had been wrested from its lawful owners by the greed and rapacity of the English, and he told of the solemn obligation one Charl Celliers had taken upon himself, on behalf of the entire white community of the southern half of Africa, to set aside one day of the year as a feast in celebration of the glorious victory that the Trekkers had against the Kaffirs. The Valley took his enthusiasm for less than it was perhaps worth, for it had known pioneering hardships, and there were many of its older inhabitants who remembered dangers and difficulties at least equal to those which the delegate from the congregations beyond the Vaal so vividly described. But the little man was not content with the courtesy that went so far as to provide him with free board and lodging, an attentive audience to hear his stories, and the gift of various pieces of money and a good deal that could be turned into money provided one found a market for it. He wanted something more. He wanted to raise something of that discontented enthusiasm, which, in his opinion, had already achieved so much, and to achieve this he fell back on argument and exhortation by no means convincing or stimulating. He enjoined the Valley not to be pusillanimous; to remember that it sprang from forebears who had repeatedly thrown aside the yoke of slavery and grasped—these were the little man's words—the flowing garments of Liberty. Were they, he asked pointedly, to forget that England had bought them from a king who had no right to sell what was not his by inheritance or the grace of God? Could they, he demanded with passion, acquiesce in seeing their own kin being harried out of existence by these very English who were now fattening on the wealth of the land, after having burdened them with a heavier quitrent than any company had ever exacted, and after cheating them out of the money due to them for the slaves they had been forced to liberate? If so, he had nothing more to say, but he could not forbear to declare, with his hand upon his heart, that the Almighty, who would not let a sparrow fall to the ground unnecessarily, would see to it that they did not escape from the due punishment of their sin.

The seniors in the Valley, with few exceptions, found the little man's talk by no means to their taste. The pastor, indeed, had called him a 'pestilential fellow,' and publicly exhorted his congregation to turn a deaf ear to all who tempted them to forget that they were subjects of a sovereign to whom they owed allegiance and loyalty. Uncle Martin, who had been visited by the little man to whom he had been courteous and hospitable as he would have been to anyone who sought the shelter of his house, had shrugged his shoulders and hinted that the emigrating farmers would have done better to have sent another envoy. Uncle Doremus had been irritable and short-tempered, and had 'sent the chap about his business,' as he termed it. 'It is scandalous,' had been Uncle Dorie's complaint, 'it is scandalous to come and spread such tales abroad. What have we got to do with these men who have trekked? They have made their bed; let them lie upon it. If they find it hard, well, it is their choice. They took it with open eyes. We too have our grievances, but, man, we do not jabber about them all day long. We endure patiently, as the good Book teaches us to do, and we do not mis-say our rulers nor those set in authority over us.'

But the younger men, and it must be added the younger women, found the little man attractive and stimulating, and before long the Valley could point to a definite section which could be looked upon as adhering to the new doctrine that Uncle Martin, contemptuously, called the gospel of dissent. Everardus, who had no great feeling either way, found himself attempting to analyse the mind of this minority group, and failing miserably to come to any logical conclusion. He had himself lived under two authorities, the old Batavian *interregnum* between the first and second British occupations of the Colony, and the home government rule established before and confirmed after the cession in perpetuity to England in 1814. Of the first he could remember little from personal experience, but, judging from what had been told him of the events under that administration and under that of the old Company that had preceded it, he felt sure that matters had not been entirely different in those early days. Indeed, he was reasonable enough to realise that in many respects the new administration was an improvement upon the old. There had been mistakes, and there were still undoubted grievances, but his commonsense told him that the faults about which the little man spoke so earnestly had not been on one side only. He could not feel himself in complete sympathy with those who had trekked, for he agreed with Brother von Bergmann that it would have been more manly to stay and work out salvation in co-partnership with one's fellow citizens, rather than to adventure into the unknown and leave those who preferred to remain behind to achieve salvation unaided. The accusation of cowardice and want of patriotism, an accusation that the little envoy was fond of flinging at those who differed from him, left him cold, for he had no reason to think that the Trekkers were braver or more courageous than those who refused to trek. Nor could he agree that it was his duty to support those who had left by contributing to their keep or helping them to establish congregations in their new territory where they hoped to find an abiding place free of all intermeddling from the English. He had no grievance against the English, and so far as he could see no one in the Valley had any special *animus* against them. Some of the Valley farmers were English settlers, and two of them, Seldon and Charles Quakerley, had made good, and had so thoroughly identified themselves with the local community that they formed part of it and were accepted as part of it. Moreover, in his dealings with English officials, he had found much which he could honestly admire—a solid sincerity, a strict sense of duty, a conception of responsibility and a capacity for official business that had impressed him.

On the other hand, the majority of his neighbours had not had his opportunities. As Brother Johan had said, few of them had been to the capital; none, so far as he knew, read any paper, although the Seldons received regularly one of the two newspapers published at Cape Town. Few had any conception of what the change of government had really meant. Self-centred as a community, the events in other parts of the Colony had hardly affected them. These events had certainly not stirred them into anything like the feeling that the little man would have had them show, and the absence of such feeling could not, reasonably, be ascribed to any want of national solidarity or to a failure to conceive themselves as part of the large family to which the Trekkers belonged. The fact was that none of them lived outside themselves; none regarded it as his duty to harass himself with doubts as to what would happen to the White race if the Dutch speaking element did not, by finding a new country free from the usurpation of the English, act as a buffer between the degenerates who had stayed behind, content to linger under foreign bondage, and the vast hordes of Natives in the interior. Not one of the inhabitants of the Valley had the slightest fear of being swamped by the

Natives. It was perhaps not altogether a positive realisation of their own prestige, but rather an absence of those frontier experiences that had frightened the Trekkers, that gave the Valley the complacency which the little man found so maddening. But for all that, as he enunciated in his stutter, they could at least remember that they were of the same race, and that the English were foreign intruders, to whom they could owe no respect or loyalty. That, at least, should make them sensible of their duty towards their kin across the Vaal.

Unfortunately the majority of the Valley thought differently. National feeling is a complex of slow growth, the product of various emotions that react differently upon different individuals. It is developed by factors and conditions that antagonise as much as they may tend to encourage the cultural progress of a people, and it is directed into channels that may or may not benefit communal solidarity. Few of these factors and conditions were as yet operative in the Valley, where the inhabitants lived quietly, with no unsatisfied desires simply because their range of requirements did not extend beyond the Valley. Their forefathers had been, for the most part, solid, hard-working artisans in the Company's employ; a few, like the Rekkers, had been men of substance and some pretensions to family; none, so far as they knew, had been adventurers in the real and derogatory sense of the word. It is true there was in the Valley a legend that in its vastnesses in its upper reaches, there where the original passage into its level lands had been, a dissatisfied sergeant in the Company's employ had hidden from authority, recklessly raiding such primitive settlements as offered a chance of loot, until a posse of the Company's soldiers had routed him out and taken him to the Cape Town castle for summary execution. The older inhabitants of the Valley could still point out the spot, high up in the mountains, where his left arm had been exposed on a pointed stake, as an example to all evil-doers of the Company's justice and stern methods of reprisal, and to a similar spot alongside the wagon road where another stake had borne the right arm, until the jackals had cleared both exhibition poles. The sergeant's head, so legend related, had rested on a spike above the castle gate, until it had dried and become so much weathered by the east wind that it fell to pieces and was decently interred in unsanctified earth. But nowadays the Valley had no grievances; nothing that could spur it into animated, clamorous insistence upon its rights and privileges, for these had never been disturbed to an extent that warranted indignant complaint. The change from Company or Batavian to English rule had come so smoothly that the Valley had hardly noticed it, although it knew that at the capital important and stirring events had taken place, culminating in a constitutional modification of which the outward and visible sign, so far as the Valley was concerned, had been the substitution of large and ugly Georgian pennies for the smaller coinage current before, and the establishment of a magistracy where formerly there had been a *landdrost*, together with the introduction of a language altogether new. The Valley had taken these things philosophically. The Georgian pennies it had found excellent for other purposes than those for which they were meant; they could be used to weigh the ends of candlesticks and ash trays, and they were just the proper shape, size, and heaviness to put on the eyes of the dying to prevent the lids from gaping. Gradually it had become custom in the Valley for the newly married to give to each other, in addition to the dead shroud and, where possible, the coffin, a couple of these new coins, to be treasured carefully until the time came for them to be used in that last ritual in the death chamber. The magistrate the Valley had found to be a just man, new and strange, it is true, to local custom and conditions, but reasonable, and in many respects more helpful than the old *landdrost* had been. The new language had at first threatened a grievance, but the influx of the party of English immigrants in 1820 had rapidly altered the Valley's opinion about the absurdity of attempting to learn a tongue that only officialdom spoke. It is possible that the new settlers, coming at a time when the Valley was pros-perous, when the crops had been unusually good, and the Valley's mood consequently ultra-kindly, had done much to prevent the birth of that antagonism to all things English which Everardus was aware was at work in other portions of the Colony. The settled farmers had felt towards the newcomers, who were obviously quite unused to local conditions, and who as a result floundered and made mistakes and came for help and advice, that sense of protective superiority that excludes any feeling of enmity. One cannot be indignant with a kitten which does not know how to mouse and miauws in plaintive despair when it should sharpen its claws and vigorously attack all mice. The parallel was not exact, neither zoologically nor ethnologically, but the Valley had not troubled itself about possible dialectical fallacies in its reasoning. It had simply welcomed the English settlers as fellow citizens speaking a strange language and incapable of expressing themselves in the much more suitable vernacular. As communication by gesture and pantomime was obviously absurd among grown men, the Valley had set itself to acquire just so much of the strange tongue as would conduce to amicable intercourse between it and the newcomers, and it had found the acquisition of English by no means so difficult as it had at first imagined it would be. On their side the English settlers had been, with few exceptions, good fellows, who, although they knew little about local agricultural methods, prejudices, and superstitions, were unacquainted with weather lore, and even had a different religion, did not erect a barrier between themselves and the older settlers but communed freely and gave proof of their intention as neighbourly as circumstances permitted. Some of them, noticeably the Seldons and the Quakerleys, were popular and respected in the District, and they had introduced nothing to which the Valley could take exception. Nor did the Valley, as a whole, feel itself profoundly interested in political questions. There were such questions, fundamentally unsettling to those who dwelt nearer the capital, where politics had always been a disturbing factor in life, but the Valley did not feel disposed to grow warm in discussing them. There was talk about the new legislative assembly, and the new legislation that was meant to give the vote to a certain number of citizens. The Valley approved, in principle, of these innovations, but it did not discuss them with any great heartiness, and was content to abide by the opinions enunciated by its Elders and representatives.

In such circumstances the attempt of the envoy from beyond the Vaal to stir the Valley into enthusiasm for the cause of the Trekkers was a dismal failure. But the little man's oratory bore fruit in another way. It engendered a spirit of dissatisfaction among the younger and to some extent also the poorer inhabitants of the Valley, the landless and the herdless Valleyites who listened greedily to the account of how easily farms could be obtained in the new territory merely by staking them out on the old fashioned plan of riding around one's selected site on horseback for eight hours. Farms, too, unburdened by quitrent, on which they could live unharassed by laws other than those they could make themselves in assembly and could—a point which more strongly appealed to them—repeal or modify as they subsequently pleased when they found that their self-imposed restrictions were irksome. These men and women formed a minority in the Valley, but they repeated the little man's arguments and urged that something should be done to assert their independence, although, if the truth must be told, they had no definite idea of what they meant by that term.

Where such a spirit is abroad, it is inevitable that those moved by it should attempt to practise, where possible, part of what they preached, if only to show that they were serious in their imaginings. The Valley, unfortunately, offered no chance for any definite action that could be taken to imply a demonstration of its freedom from governmental supervision. That much even the theoretical malcontents had to admit. The roads were execrable, but then everyone railed against the Road Board, on which the Valley as well as the authorities were represented. The post came and went irregularly, but few in the Valley made use of it, and its vagaries scarcely constituted a legitimate grievance. The language, which had at first seemed an admirable peg on which to hang an indictment, caused them no worry. It was true that it was the official language which had displaced the high Dutch, but in practice they did very well with the vernacular, and the magistrate was accommodating and reasonable. There seemed nothing to warrant the accusation, so recklessly cast by the little man, that they were pusillanimously cowering under oppression with the English astride on their necks and exploiting them. Even the malcontents felt that there was something extravagant in the little man's dithyrambics, and in secret jeered at his attitudinising and his invective.

Openly, they fixed upon the Queen's Birthday celebrations as something which might and could be regarded as reprehensible. Many years ago, when the Queen had come to the throne, the Valley had been wildly scandalised. It was not, the Valley had said, quite the proper thing that a woman should be a ruler, and in open assembly it had resolved upon a protest, which the magistrate, being accommodating and reasonable, had accepted, pigeon-holed, then forgotten. The Valley had been sincerely glad that he had done so, and much preferred that that absurd resolution should remain hidden in the magisterial archives than that it should be remembered today. For the Valley's opinion of Alexandrina Victoria, by God's grace Queen of Great Britain and Ireland, and Defender of the Protestant Faith, had undergone extensive modification in time. She was generally referred to as 'our respected Queen' or 'our beloved sovereign' and the Valley pictured her, now that she was married and had a family whom it remembered in its household worship, as a wise and dignified matron, elevated above the rest of humanity, and intimately acquainted with her subjects. The picture would doubtless have pleased the Queen, had she known of the existence of the Valley, and she would have been doubly gratified to hear that her own slightly ash-coloured outlook upon life was shared by the majority of her subjects who lived there. Every year, on the twenty-fourth of May, they united to celebrate her birthday. It was a festival that came and was honoured as a matter of course. No one had ever dreamed of looking askance at it, but now there were voices raised in protest, on the ground that Alexandrina Victoria was after all a foreigner, who, although she was Queen *de facto*, had really no right to their loyalty *de jure*. A quiet abstention from the celebrations, these protesting voices argued, would in the circumstances be more dignified and more worthy of the descendents of those valiant men who had braved the frown of Alva and flooded their farms rather than submit to the tyranny of the wicked Philip of Spain.

These historical references were not generally appreciated by those who heard them enumerated, but that made no great difference. In time there arose in the Valley a small but active section hostile to the old custom and eager to prevent its repetition. Uncle Dorie came to sound Everardus on the subject. Uncle Dorie had ranged himself definitely on the side of the majority, and made no secret of his exasperation at and his contempt for the attitude of the malcontent faction. As he walked with Everardus in the garden, where Magriet's chrysanthemums and wild daisies were blossoming, he expressed his indignation with more than his customary vehemence.

'It is not as if we do not know about things, Nephew Ev'rard' he said. 'We do. We have lived under the Company, and we have lived under a Republic, and we have lived and are living under the English. But does it make any difference at all? I have never been able to see it. The good Book tells us in Exodus chapter 22 verse 28 that we must not revile the ruler of our people, and what are these people doing but reviling our beloved Queen? Does not the Preacher say "Fear thou Jehovah and the king," and "I counsel thee to keep the king's commandment, and that in regard of the oath of God," and does not the good apostle write to Timothy that all supplications be made for kings and for all that are set in authority? And are we not told "Thou shalt not speak evil of the ruler of thy people?" No, fie, it is plain to me that they are bent on stirring up strife among us, out of sympathy with those who have left this land because they are dissatisfied. I do not judge them, no, Nephew Ev'rard, the Book tells us not to judge others ... but I do not hold with them. What is there to complain about? And what is there to prevent us from honouring our beloved sovereign? After all, she is a woman, and she cannot be held responsible for every thing that is done even in her name.'

'I am of a mind with Uncle,' said Everardus, pausing to admire a magnificent chameleon which, struggling down from a chrysanthemum branch, was evidently preparing to seek winter quarters. The splendid green and gold of its colouring attracted Everardus and he put his hand out to stroke the little reptile, which turned a gaping, angry mouth at him. But Uncle Dorie snatched his hand violently away.

'How can you do such a thing?' the Elder demanded, almost in an angry voice. 'They are poisonous, these gallows-geckos. See how the thing breathes at you, almost like a goose. Fie, Nephew Ev'rard, they are horrible creatures, these gallows-geckos.'

'I think they are quite harmless,' said Everardus, slightly astonished at his visitor's annoyance. 'They are certainly not poisonous; I have often taken them in my hand, and Uncle knows they have no teeth. They can't bite as a gecko—a real gecko—does.'

'Aye, that may be. But I can't abide them. When I was a child I remember seeing them crawling on the gibbet which stood at Three Anchor Bay. It is gone now, Nephew Ev'rard, but in my time it still stood there, just where the lake comes close to the sea, you know. Horrible things, these gallows-geckos, I can't abide them.'

'It is only a *koggelmander*, Uncle, quite harmless. See.' Everardus took up the chameleon, which protested vigorously, and placed it on a lower twig. Uncle Dorie shuddered violently and closed his eyes.

'I don't like to see you do that, Nephew Ev'rard,' he remarked plaintively. 'As a favour to me, come away from the horrible creature. I hate everything and anything connected with a gallows.'

'But why, Uncle? I suppose there must be gallows, if we have to hang people. And I have never heard them called gallows-geckos before ...'

'Yes, it is my own name for them,' said Uncle Dorie, taking his companion by the arm and turning away from the hateful chameleon. 'They used to crawl upon the uprights of the gibbet, and I fancied I could see then swarming up the rope. Ugh ... the nasty things. I daresay there must be gallows, but our good Lord preserve me from having anything to do with such things.'

'You surprise me, Uncle' said Everardus, who had his own reasons for harping on the subject. 'I should have said that you would be one of the first to uphold the right of the state to kill a murderer.'

'I am not so sure about that, I am not at all so sure,' replied the Elder, vigorously shaking his head. 'I admit Scripture has it "An eye for an eye, and a tooth for a tooth," but there were sanctuary cities in those days, Nephew Ev'rard, and now we have them no more. But if it has to be done—and I suppose it has to be done sometimes—I don't wish to have anything to do with it. It is horrible taking a man's life even when the law commands. I know there are such people, of course. One came to this District years ago when they hanged a Hottentot for a murder. He put up at *Sandvlei*, and I had to show him some hospitality, for the creature was of our race, Nephew Ev'rard, and I did not at first know what his purpose was. I actually shook hands with the fellow—fancy that ...'

'But Uncle, after all he was an official. He had to do his duty. Does that make him unworthy of being shaken by the hand?'

'That may be,' answered the Elder, stubbornly. 'But a man is not altogether accountable for his whims. It may not be Christian conduct, but had I known who and what he was I would never have had him under my roof. He could have remained outside. I could have had a tent put up for him, if necessary, or he could have slept in the wagon. For he had a wagon with him, Nephew, a government wagon, and on it he carried the gibbet. I saw it—painted a dull green, it was, Nephew ... ugh. No, say what you like, but I don't like and I shall never abide anything that reeks of the gallows. And that is why I cannot bear these gallows-geckos. To you them may seem beautiful, but there is lots of muck in the world that appears fine in the sunshine and is after all nothing but muck.'

'I still can't see why Uncle is so down upon a man who, as an official, does his duty. Would Uncle refuse to shoot a man if war came and it was necessary to defend the country?'

'In my young days I would have thought nothing of it,' said Uncle Dorie. 'I have been on commando, and I have had a shot at the Bushmen in my time, and I doubt not that I hit a few, although I can't swear that I killed any. But that is different, although, mark you, I would not defend even that, except when one's own life was threatened. I think it is silly to make war, and shoot people who have no grievance against you and whom you have never harmed nor they you.'

'But the soldier has to do it, Uncle. Would you refuse to shake hands with him if he came back from the war, and you knew he had shot people?'

'Now you are talking sheer nonsense,' replied Uncle Dorie, irritably. 'Almost as inane as these youngsters who don't want to go to the village on the Queen's Birthday. An executioner is a different creature. He gets paid ...'

'But so does the soldier ...'

'Heavens, can't you see the difference, Nephew? Why, would you have me grasp a hand that had put a rope round a fellow creature's neck and dumped him into eternity—that I—yes, even if he did it by the Governor's order, I say.'

'It is Uncle who is unreasonable,' said Everardus, earnestly. 'A man must sometimes do nasty things as a duty. It is no worse then flogging a fellow ...'

'And you say I am unreasonable while you talk nonsense like that? If I give a Black servant a drubbing with my sjambok, is he any the worse for it? Am I accountable to God for his life? I would be if I tortured him to such an extent that he died, but then I would be a murderer ...'

'And who would have to hang Uncle? Somebody would have to do it.'

'Yes, I say there must be an executioner. It's sad enough, but while we have murderers and hang them, I suppose someone must do it. But it nauseates me to think of it, and I really can't see, Nephew, why you should go on talking of such horrible things. I came to discuss the Queen's Birthday with you, not to have my words twisted so that, as the Psalmist says, "I have not wherewith to answer him that reproacheth me." If you like the gallows-geckos, go on liking them; I can't stop you from liking them, for every little animal has its little pleasure, as the poet says. But please don't bring them to me, Nephew Ev'rard. I hate the creatures.'

'I was only interested in what Uncle said about the hangman,' said Everardus, whose face was very serious, and showed a sadness that the Elder put down to a feeling of regret at having, inadvertently, annoyed a guest. Uncle Dorie made haste to turn the conversation round to the subject which had brought him to *Knolkloof* that day.

'Very well,' he said. 'And having heard my opinion about hangmen, you can now pay some attention to what I want to say on another matter. As you know, all this talk has upset folk. It is not good for them, and they are thinking God knows what. At first it was our intention to have the celebration on one of the farms, and I placed my own at the disposal of the committee. As you know it is central, and I am man enough to entertain whoever comes that day. But now we have decided to have it, as usual, on the Village square. The magistrate thought—and we all agree with him—that it will not do to make any change just at present. People might think we have been influenced by what that little villain said. So we are following our usual custom. But the difficulty is that some of the youngsters have said that they won't come with the commando. Now you are a newcomer. We all respect you, and already you have a little influence with them. What we want you to do is to go and reason with them, and get them to come. I can give you the names—I have made a list; here it is. Will you do it for us? We have put you on the committee—the magistrate proposed your name and Brother Martin seconded it at the meeting last month.'

'I very much appreciate this, Uncle' said Everardus, who really felt touched by the confidence in him. 'I will do it with pleasure, but I doubt if I shall be able to effect much. Surely you and the other seniors could do more.'

'I am ashamed to say that we have not been able to do much,' said Uncle Dorie, with considerable annoyance in his voice. 'Some of the young men are very foolish— it is of course that little stutterer who has put all that nonsense in their heads, but the mischief is done, Nephew Ev'rard, and it is for us to counteract it.'

'I don't think you need take a very serious view of it,' Everardus consoled him. 'Probably they will all come round to your view before the Queen's Birthday. And if their don't, we can spare them. There will be enough to make the celebration a success.'

'Of that I have not the shadow of a doubt,' declared Uncle Dorie. 'But it is saddening to find some of our people are so misguided as to make trouble. It is not as if we really had something to trouble about. As I tell you, we have nothing. Do we not live free? Are we oppressed by the English? No, not more than we were oppressed in the Company's days. It is all this spirit of insubordination that is abroad, Nephew, when folk think that it is something derogatory to their dignity to obey those in authority over them. If it goes on, what is to become of us? We would be like a family divided, and division, Nephew Ev'rard, would be fatal to us. We should live in peace and amity, like good brothers, and not quarrel among ourselves about things that really do not matter a scrap. But this new spirit, of mis-saying everything because it is foreign and English, well, I don't hold with it. It is not going to do us any good. I don't see why we should be bad friends with a man simply because he is English, or why we should show disloyalty to our beloved sovereign simply because she happens to have been born abroad and not in the Valley. It makes me angry to think that we have among us some who differ from me in that opinion.'

And with that final expression of his sentiments Uncle Dorie followed his host to the *stoep* and drank innumerable cups of coffee while he discussed at length the arrangements that the committee proposed for the great day.

Chapter 10

The twenty-fourth of May dawned with the long, grey, mother of pearl pallor in the eastern sky that heralds the coming of a cold winter's day. Long before the streamers of gold and rose shot across the high tops of the mountains, long before the mother of pearl had broadened out until it paved the whole sky, dimming the stars, the Village was astir. For it was to be the day of the celebration of the beloved Queen's nativity, and it behoved everyone to be abroad early.

Everardus and his family had arrived the night before, and had taken their wagon to the wide and hospitable *agterplaas* or courtyard of Uncle Martin's town or 'church' house. The Village was composed of a number of houses, set in a straggling line with their backs towards the main road that led across the hills to the north, and with their fronts turned towards their gardens, with the River at the extreme northern end. To the east, or to the right, as one entered, lay the Native location, a collection of thatched huts and small mud-plastered shanties set in an expanse of barren veld, unrelieved by a single tree, whatever greenery there was being the result of self-planted, wild tobacco shrubs whose straggling branches were almost constantly in flower. To the left, at the other extreme end of the Village, the tributary river on which the Village was built ran into the great River of the Valley, itself the confluence of the streams marked by numerous yellow sand dunes and one large expanse of white, wind-tortured shingle. The sides of this desert of white sand sloped very gradually upwards until they merged into the slant of the Karroo hill that was in winter the delight and in summer the bane of the Village. For in summer it was unrelieved and bare, its parched clay reflecting sharply the sun's rays and helping, with the equally reflecting river sand, to concentrate the heat exactly in that part of the little valley where the Village had been built, making the place almost unbearable for those who were not inured to the distressful warmth of the Valley. In winter, and more especially in the latter end of it when spring had already entered into its short but beautiful reign, these Karroo slopes were charged with a wealth of green, that gave place later on to a fairyland of flowers, chief among which were the large, golden and orange, and white- and blue-centred daisies that covered acres and acres of veld. Some thirty miles away in the north and north-east were the mountains, marvellously blue with scintillations of orange and brown in the early morning sunlight, and as wonderfully dark azure with patches of jasper and turquoise during the late afternoon when the sun disappeared behind the lower ranges in the west where the River ran down to the sea. It was the same mountain range that Everardus had behind him on his farm, the same range amidst which lay the Neckarthal mission farms, and it was a beautiful range, renowned throughout the Colony for its bold outlines, its magnificent colouring, and its valuable forests.

The Village had been founded a little less than half a century before the time of the first British occupation of the Colony, when the District had been divided off from the neighbouring and, up to that time, much larger district, and had been given its own *landdrost*. Where the Village now stood had been a flourishing wayside farm, whose owner had been reputed to have made a fortune by stock buying and, if tradition could be believed, by trading in human cattle and by devious methods even more blameworthy. The Governor had found the place to his liking, christened it in honour of one or other of his overseas acquaintances, and decided to build on it a hunting lodge or *Drostdy* which would serve as official mansion for the magistrate. Nothing, however, had come of that project, and the official buildings in the Village could not boast of any architectural pretensions. Nor were the private dwellings in any better way. They were commodious, roomy houses, simply built on the compound system, with broad *stoeps* in front that looked towards the river and the gardens and with an enclosed yard at the back where the hens and livestock were housed. The gardens, indeed, could be looked upon as the glory of the Village, for they had been carefully laid out, were well-cultivated and planted with a variety of trees and shrubs, all of which had grown so rapidly that they had transformed the place into a shady oasis in an environment that was, at least in summer and early winter, singularly bare, although set in a framework of magnificent mountain scenery. There were some twenty houses, but the White population of the Village numbered scarcely fifty all told, old and young, and several of the houses stood empty and tenantless for the greater part of the year. They were 'church houses' belonging to the wealthier farmers of the Valley, who had built them for their accommodation during the few days that twice a year saw them congregated in the Village for the periodical *Nagmaal*, or communion services of the church. There was a fairly large and well built Dutch Reformed church, whose fittings inside were all of polished cedarwood; it stood on one side of the square or 'plain' having almost opposite to it the massively constructed

Village gaol. The much smaller English church, built by the settlers at a later date, stood lower down in the Village, at the back of the houses, facing the main road. Both churches were surrounded by a high wall, and in the church-yards straggling bush had grown between the graves, and the veld flowers had sown themselves in profusion.

Uncle Martin's church house was one of the largest and most pretentious in the Village. It stood in line with the others, having on one side the magistrate's official dwelling, government owned, and on the other a smaller house owned by Quakerley, whose neighbour again was the parsonage, flanked by another church house. It had, like all the other houses, a wide and commodious *stoep* or raised terrace in front, paved with slate slabs between which the winter grass grew several inches high. Descending the *stoep* the visitor could cross the little second street, a few paces broad, parallel with the main road behind, on the other side of which was a strong stream of limpid mountain water, bridged by rustic bridges constructed from sods and bamboo poles. Beyond the stream lay the garden, with its numerous fruit and shade trees, embowered among which was the washed bath-house fed by a bamboo pipe from the water furrow.

On the morning of the twenty-fourth of May, the Village was active long before cockcrow. Ordinarily it would have stirred much about the same hour, for in winter-time the sun rose late, and the Villagers were early risers, accustomed, in summer, to be up with the dawn and well abed before the southern cross had sunk towards the horizon. But the twenty-fourth was an exceptional day, and a little extra zeal was permissible and praiseworthy. That, then, was the reason why, when Everardus entered the large dining room of the church house when he had dressed himself and seen to the horse, he found the whole company awaiting him, and eager to start breakfast.

During the past few weeks Everardus had acquitted himself of the task imposed upon him with creditable success. He had personally visited several farms and talked, persuasively and convincingly, with the recalcitrants, and had been successful in swaying several to give up their intention of not participating in the Birthday festivities. With a few he had been less successful, but these were the hotheads, and he agreed with Uncle Dorie that their services could very well be dispensed with for the occasion. Thanks to his advocacy, the commando had been whipped up, and the number of farmers who had come to the Village was not below that which had graced the festivities on previous occasions. It had been arranged that the younger Martin should lead the commando, and that Everardus himself should form part of the more select group which clustered round the official representatives. The ceremony was timed to commence exactly at midday, but as everyone knew that midday differed from time in the various dependencies of the beloved Queen, it had been agreed upon that that the magistrate's watch should decide when the proceedings were to start.

At the breakfast table Everardus found several neighbours whom he only knew by name. All were welcome at Uncle Martin's hospitable board, which was served by the posse of retainers recruited from the Natives attached to the various masters who had come into the Village for the day. Accustomed as he was to the ways of the Valley, Everardus could not but feel some astonishment when he found that no fewer than twenty guests were present, and that these did not even include the women and children, who would breakfast in a second breakfast shift later on. The senior guest present, another Elder of the church, pronounced a long and rather rambling prayer, to which the audience listened on their knees. He prayed especially for the beloved Queen, her family and her dependents, and expressed on behalf of the assembled company the most profoundly loyal sentiments, to which most of those present, Everardus included, responded with loud and vehement 'amens' indicative of their unanimous approval. Thereupon Uncle Martin started the doxology which they all sang with gusto, and a junior guest, only, however, slightly junior to most of those present, read a chapter out of Samuel after which they all drew up their chairs to the table and attacked the breakfast before them. There was a winter's nip in the air, and the cold gave them a hearty appetite, but that did not impair their conversational powers and Everardus, preferring to listen rather than talk, was edified, instructed, and also amused by the senior Elder's reminiscences, dating back to the days when the custom had been initiated, of earlier Birthday celebrations. The company was cheerful, even hilariously so, although the only drink was coffee, doled out assiduously by the Native servants who went round constantly replenishing empty cups from the great black coffee kettles brought in from the kitchen.

When breakfast was over, the younger generation trooped into the room and settled down round the table, supervised by the women. The men went about their business and those, like Everardus, who had already seen to the comfort and care of their transport animals, grouped themselves on the *stoep* where they smoked and talked until it was time to go and dress for the ceremony. The Village, so much Everardus could see, was already bustling with suppressed excitement. Its population had been augmented by the influx of some two hundred extra White persons from the District, and the main street presented an animated appearance, not unlike that to be observed on a communion Sunday. On the farther side of it, away from the houses, where the road merged into the open veld, carts and wagons were drawn up, many of which had bucksails spread as canopies under which their owners had passed the night. More wagons and carts were arriving, and there was much cheerful bustle, the Native community participating in the excitement in a manner which showed that they, too, regarded the day as holiday. Nearly all the wagons and houses were decorated. From the parsonage gable flew a flag, the magistrate's flagpole flaunted the official bunting, and even in the location some of the huts bore coloured scraps which waved proudly in the slight morning breeze, while if one walked along the second street, past the *stoeps*, one could see in many windows the portrait of the beloved Sovereign, framed in cedarwood and flanked by masses of everlastings in old-fashioned china vases.

In honour of the day, the Villagers were dressed in their Sunday 'chest clothes.'

The senior Elder, Uncle Martin, and Uncle Doremus wore old fashioned frock coats, stiff, starched turned-down collars, and white ties that gave them a funereal look by no means in keeping with their cheerful, jovial expressions. The women turned out in a variety of dress and colouring that gave a touch of gaiety to the scene, and the children had new suits, or old ones renovated, and looked surprisingly neat and clean and healthily happy. Even the Natives had managed to furbish themselves up for the occasion, and some were resplendent in the cast-off uniforms of old regiments, whose vivid crimson facings made strong splashes of colour among the generally sombre apparel of the men. Outstanding among them was Augustus, whose surname nobody knew or cared to know. Augustus was the Native constable, usher of the court, and on

Sundays the sexton of the Dutch Reformed church, the acknowledged head of the Native location, and reputed to be the best lithotomist in the District. His father and grandfather had been slaves, but had won a similar reputation as 'cutters for the stone,' and Augustus had inherited their skill, liking for this gruesome trade, and capacity for making other people believe in his experience, with the result that when some unfortunate patient found himself in need of surgical assistance, the constable was called in consultation. Augustus was a middle-aged, middle-sized Native half-caste, whose features revealed his Mozambique descent, and he had all the half-caste's affection for finery, and much of that unfortunate's personal vanity. He was now dressed in his official uniform, but his dignity was somewhat marred by the fact that while his almost brand-new helmet, adorned with the official coat of arms which he had burnished until it shone like a little sun, and his neatly brushed coat proclaimed to every stranger that he was an official, his bare feet were presumptive evidence that he really belonged to the location and not to the Dutchmen. Nevertheless, Augustus busied himself in importantly striding up and down the main street, flourishing his baton at the little Native boys who giggled openly at him, and sang ditties disparaging his official duties. He officiously showed the newcomers where to outspan their carts and wagons, gave orders to his staff of underling Natives in a tone of voice that overawed all those who heard him for the first time, and gesticulated wildly when addressed by any of the White 'masters' to show his willingness to fall in with anything that was suggested, though the suggestion was directly contrary to the orders he had just given.

Gradually the Village moved towards the central square, which was not really central as it lay behind the main street, and between the houses and the huts. There, in the cleared space fronting the church on the one side and the gaol on the other, a party of Native prisoners in charge of the gaoler had brought out the little muzzle-loading gun, mounted on its wooden carriage, and placed it in a central position where Augustus could keep guard over it. Others had brought out the ram and cleaning rods, the bucket of cooling water in which the mops could be dipped after every discharge to clean the bore, and the tins of gunpowder whose startling red showed in strong and bright contrast to the dull grey ground on which they lay. Here the company grouped itself in respectful lines, and by and by the members of the commando, mounted on their finely groomed horses, some with plated bridles and gaudily coloured saddle-cloths, ranged themselves in line behind the crowd, on the veld side of the square, and sat stolidly, nursing their guns in the crooks of their arms. As the sun rose higher and higher, the cool of the morning gave way to a subdued heat, for although it was winter time the Village was always hot when there was no breeze and when there had been no rain. Today, however, it was cooler than usual, and several of the senior onlookers declared that it was even cooler than they had ever known it to be before on the twenty fourth of May. All agreed that it was a remarkably fine day, and one particularly suitable for the celebration of their beloved Queen's Birthday festival.

Everardus, who had also dressed himself in his best clothes, went with his host's house party to the square, and while most of his fellows mingled with the crowd, he and the seniors attached themselves to the magistrate's party which had now appeared on the scene. With the magistrate walked the Reverend Sybrand de Smee, in his Geneva gown with silk tassels and his starched, white linen bands, bareheaded. They took up a position some paces behind the gun, and the magistrate and the chief constable, who had official charge of the proceedings, consulted, with watches in hand. The crowd waited patiently but expectantly, the conversation and the cheery hum of noise hushed for the time being, although from the outskirts came the yells of the little Native boys until these too were cuffed into silence. When the watches corresponded, the magistrate motioned to the parson who came forward and joined him. The magistrate bared his head, all the male members of the crowd who possessed head-gear doing likewise, and lifted his hand for official silence.

'I now ask the Reverend de Smee,' he said loudly, 'to lead us in prayer as is usual on these occasions. Augustus, see that these little wretches keep quiet.'

Clearly, so that he could be heard by those farthest off, the pastor prayed for the safety, health, and long and prosperous reign of their beloved Sovereign, Alexandrina Victoria, through God's grace Queen of Great Britain and Ireland and the dependencies beyond the seas and Defender of the Protestant Faith. His prayer was a simple, manly one, short and to the point, and he did not use the opportunity of invocation to the Almighty to point a moral or explain a platitude. He contented himself with drawing the Almighty's attention to the fact that their beloved Queen was a fallible human being, just as much as every one else in want of Divine guidance, quite as likely as everyone else to be led astray by human error and the sin of pride, covetousness, and uncharitableness, earnestly beseeching for her that help in the undertaking of her immense responsibilities and the load of obligation that rested upon her weak and womanly shoulders, which could only be given by a heavenly Father, to Whom, he had no doubt whatever in saying it, she had been constantly loyal and in all things subservient. He prayed that she might be touched by the Divine grace to continue in the path of righteousness and godliness, and that through it she might act as a Christian woman, elevated to that high position she occupied, would act for the welfare of her realm, of her subjects, and of her own immortal soul. It was a prayer and an invocation that Alexandrina, had she been there to listen and had she been capable of understanding the high Dutch in which it was uttered, would undoubtedly have approved, although she might have flinched at hearing herself described with such painful anatomical preciseness. It carried away the full approbation of the assembled Villagers and the loud and sonorous 'amen' that greeted its conclusion testified to the fact that in what he had said the reverend gentleman had correctly interpreted the sentiments of his audience.

It was now the magistrate's duty to address the meeting, which he did in short, staccato sentences, halting at the end of every one to allow his reverend companion to translate them into the vernacular. His speech was short and to the point. He told his hearers that their beloved Sovereign, like himself, was a servant of the people, but that she, again like himself, represented the authority of the people, of law and of established order. 'You who are here today,' he said, emphatically, 'have had no opportunity of seeing our Queen. To all of you she is a name. I wish it were otherwise. I wish you could have an opportunity of seeing her yourselves. Her portrait does not give you a true impression of the Queen's dignity, her womanliness, or her real presence, I know, for I have seen her. It is true she was younger then, but I carried away with me an impression of a lady who is loveably human, and who above everything else is filled with a sense of her duty. That is the point I want to make today. Let us, too, be sensible of our duty; our duty towards her, as our Queen, as towards one who is set in authority over us, our duty towards ourselves and our neighbours, and our duty towards this country of ours over which she rules. I am now trenching on matters which some of you may think are out of place here on an occasion like this when we are met together to show our loyalty towards our Queen. But I should be failing in that very duty about which I am speaking if I did not deal with them. There has been among you lately much talk of abstaining from this celebration. If we had any real reason for so doing, if there were grievances against our Queen—and you know as well as I do that not one of us has the slightest grievance against her, not a vestige of a quarrel with her—there are times and opportunities for expressing our opinion. We are free men in this country, although you all know that we have not yet got our own government elected by the people. That will come, and matters are already in train towards that end, as you doubtless all know. But I would ask you all, and I do ask it very earnestly, gentlemen, that you will not allow yourselves to be carried away by the idle talk of outsiders who know next to nothing about us and our conditions here, and that you will not give ear to agitators who want to stir up discontent among you. I represent the government here, and I am always at your disposal—that is what I am here for, that is part of my work, to listen to what you have to say, and to act as a medium of communication between you and the government at Cape Town. Come to me when there is anything about which you are in doubt, and be assured that I will do my best to help you. Unfortunately I am not able to go among you and talk to you in your own language. I have tried to learn Dutch, and I have not succeeded in learning it well enough to speak it. That, of course, is my own fault, but it need not place a bar between us, for I can understand you and you can understand me, much better perhaps than you think you can. Let us pull together and work together. We have the same aims and objects—the welfare of this country that we all love, and even though we believe different creeds and speak different languages, there is no reason why we should not work in unity and co-operation for that common object. I thank you on behalf of Her Majesty, whose representative I am, and, if I may add, on my own behalf. I thank you for your presence here today, which is, if I may say so, a proof of your personal goodwill towards our sovereign lady the Queen. I have rarely seen a larger gathering here on the square or one more truly representative of the District, and I am fully aware of the difficulties some of you have experienced in coming here at all. I notice among you gentlemen who come from more than three days' travel from here. I notice many old friends and some new faces, and I am deeply grateful for their presence here with us today. Once more my thanks, gentlemen. Chief constable, you will now proceed with the business.'

The magistrate's address had been listened to in attentive silence, broken now and then by expressive 'Hear, hears' from the gathering. It had ended a few minutes before midday, and the crowd now waited for the church bells to ring out the signal for the salute to be given by the gaol gun and the muskets of the horse commando. Punctually on the strike of twelve, Augustus handed over the lighted spigot to the chief constable, who applied it to the touch hole. The report rang out sharply, and the little gun carriage skidded six feet backwards, for Augustus had been liberal in his charge of powder and paper wadding. Immediately the horse commando wheeled round, raised their guns in the air and fired a salvo. Again and again the little gun boomed and when the final discharge had been made, to the accompaniment of loud and prolonged hurrahs, the commando wheeled back into line, and joined the crowd in the singing of 'God save the Queen.' Everyone sang, with great fervour and animation, the Natives yelling at the top of their voices and the Whites keeping closely in tune. Three further hurrahs for the Sovereign lady, three more for the magistrate, and a final three for the commando, concluded the official proceedings, and Everardus found that he now had to accompany the magistrate's party to the *Drostdy* where an informal reception was to be held.

The events of the morning had favourably impressed him. There had been no formality; everything had gone off smoothly and the occasion had not been marred by anything to which anybody could have taken the slightest exception. The *landdrost's* speech had been tactful and edifying, and the demeanour of the crowd exemplary. Altogether he felt very much satisfied with himself and with everyone else. After all, there was a good deal in what the magistrate had said, and it was interesting to know that His Honour had himself seen the Queen. It was a pity she was so far away. Perhaps if she had been nearer, these recalcitrants would not have talked as they had done. But after all everything had gone off well, and next year, possibly, there would be no repetition of these unfortunate, disturbing elements. At the magistrate's house there was wine set out on the *stoep* tables, coffee and cakes, dried fruit and almonds, and the magistrate's wife was graciousness itself and dispensed hospitality to all who came, chatting in the most friendly fashion although he was sure that she did not understand half of what she heard. The magistrate took wine with them all, exchanged snuff with Uncle Martin, talked freely about the crops and the seasons, asked pertinent questions about horse farming, and showed himself rather an approachable, good fellow, quite different from what one had expected him to be. The Seldons were there and the Quakerleys, and Everardus, saw with some surprise how well these two Native-born Englishmen chatted in Dutch and were hail-fellows to most of those who crowded the magistrate's *stoep*. His own knowledge of English was passably fair; he could converse in it with moderate fluency, not idiomatically perhaps, but with some regard to grammar and construction, and he found no difficulty whatever in talking with the magistrate's wife. She was much interested in the school, and asked him many questions about it.

'It is too much to expect from Mrs Nolte,' she said, 'that she should take the whole burden of it on her own shoulders. You must try to get a teacher, *Meneer* Nolte. It is sometimes possible to get one. My husband will help you. Why not have a talk with Mr Seldon, and see if you cannot arrange something for mutual benefit? His own son must go to school very soon, and if you can get a good governess, it will be of a great help to you both.'

'I will try,' said Everardus, who had already considered the possibility of enlisting Seldon's aid.

'Do. By the way, this is the first time we have seen you here, Mr Nolte. I hope you will come again, and bring your wife and family. You must not stand on ceremony with us.'

'Thank you, Madam. I will gladly bring Magriet—that is my wife. The children are too young yet. And we should like to see you and His Honour at the farm. It is new yet, but we mean to make it a show farm.'

'I am sure it will be one, Mr Nolte. I have always admired that little valley where you are, and I have wondered why they let the Native boy have it all these years. He did nothing to improve it. Now my husband tells me you have already made the place look homely.'

'I am trying to, Madam, but it is uphill work. I was glad to learn something from the missionary.'

'Have you been at Neckarthal?' asked the magistrate's wife, with interest. 'I am so glad to hear it. Mr Uhlmann has made a wonderful station there. I have been twice and I am looking forward to going again before we leave here.'

'I hope His Honour is not going from us,' said Everardus, anxiously. 'I should not like to lose him.'

'My husband is a public servant, Mr Nolte, and must do as he is told. I don't think they will move him yet, but they may at any time. I should hate it just as much, for my garden—you must come some other time and look at it—is just beginning to look lovely.'

'I did not see Mr Uhlmann, or any of the Neckarthal people on the square,' said Everardus. 'Is it that they do not hold with the celebration?'

'Oh no,' answered the magistrate's wife quickly. 'But you see they have their own little celebration at Neckarthal. Quite as imposing as ours, I think. Of course they have no commando, and no salvoes, but they have an impressive little service and fire a salute, and in the evening they have illuminations and fireworks. You must see ours tonight. I have quite a lot of crackers and my husband has a few rockets to shoot off in the garden. Now I must go and speak to Mr de Smee. The poor man has had nothing to eat.'

In the evening Everardus saw the illuminations. They were not on a grand scale, and possibly Alexandrina Victoria, had she been there to see, might have considered them wholly unworthy of the occasion. But they were the best the Village could muster. There were rockets, sputtering candles, and detonations from Chinese crackers. The windows were dressed and the portraits of the beloved Sovereign lit up with homemade candles that had to be watched because the heat made them bend and there was a risk of the curtains catching fire. The little manual fire engine, the only one that the Village possessed, was placed in readiness, with its tank properly filled, for emergencies, but fortunately no occasion arose to call in the amateur fire-brigade, and Augustus reported no casualties from the location. As Everardus, after walking down the second street to inspect the decorations, wandered back to Uncle Martin's church house, he saw a small party of Natives emerging stealthily from the shadows and slinking furtively past him, hiding, as he thought, something beneath their jackets. Imagining them to be thieves, he stopped them to have a look at what they carried, but the first glance at their maimed hands, and their repulsive features told him the truth. They were lepers, searching for cast-off remnants of the festival fare that the feasters had dropped from the wagons. Shudderingly, he turned away and walked on towards the church house.

Chapter 11

Came winter with its rains, the steady drizzle starting in the morning and lasting through the day, soaking the hard, clay shale, impregnating the dry, fissured Karroo soil and the superficial layer of the loose earth derived from the weathered sandstone, and bringing with it new life to the seeds that lay dormant below, waiting for the warmth of spring to quicken into full and blossoming life. Came the boisterous east winds, soughing through the leafless trees at night, like lost souls clamouring for release, shaking from the orange and lemon orchards many of the young fruit whose smooth green carpeted the red soil below the trees, a pathetic and saddening sight for the farmer. And at last, almost miraculously sudden, the space of a night and a day, the spring, splendidly fresh, and verdant, daintily perfumed with the soft odours of infant leaf and bud of aromatic mountain and veld plants, making garden of what it touched and revealing untold glories in what had seemed a waste but a week before.

For that was one of the characteristics of the Valley, its sudden spasms of natural activity, its amazing leaps into life and sterility. A cold wind, sweeping through the gateways of the mountains, would warp and wither the tender shoots of the adenandra bushes, and dull them to a dingy grey; a snatch of warmth after the winter's rain would bring forth innumerable sorrels and make the veld cheerfully variegated for a short while. A hot blast in summer would sear it, so that the foliage showed its under-surfaces and the whole hillside looked bleak and bare, and in midsummer the veld would appear more barren than a desert, while in spring it would be hard to find on it a square inch not scented by some adjacent flower or not shadowed by some neighbouring leaf.

In winter the mountains filmed themselves, especially in the early mornings, in hazes of grey and pearl. Only towards midday, when the sun had gathered strength and the mists drew slowly, reluctantly, away, in wisps of cloud that lingered around the dells and in the wooded *kloofs*, their bold outlines were sharply silhouetted against the sky. Generally only the higher peaks were snow-crowned, but the snow had been known to come down into the lower slopes and tradition asserted that it had in one season even fallen on the banks of the River, doing incalculable damage to the young sheep. That, however, was far in the past, and only the oldest inhabitants remembered it, and preferred to forget that they had seen it there. On the mountain tops snow was another thing. It was something wonderful to look upon, something quite foreign to the Valley, yet not altogether unfamiliar, though few had taken the trouble to climb up to it and handle it, so as to be able to say, authoritatively, what it felt and looked like. Some, like the magistrate and the parson, who had travelled in foreign parts where snow actually fell on the ground and men careered over it with sledges and children threw balls made of it at one another, knew all about it, but the Valley accepted that knowledge as it did so many other things, with a philosophical calm that was almost indifference, with a tolerant smile that was more courteous than curious.

Everardus, as the months passed and life at *Knolkloof* became largely routine, had ample opportunity to study the psychology of the Valley. He was not by nature cast for the role of a scientific observer, but he had in him a detached strain such as, when developed, breeds cosmopolitanism and free thinking. Incidentally, his peculiar relation to his fellow men at a very early stage of his manhood had made him more inclined to look at things from another angle than that usually selected by his race. Having personally experienced the stings of intolerance, he had become more tolerant himself, owing to his wife's heartening support and her innate charitableness that served as an antidote to his own bitterness, and also to his own sense of fairness. The more extensive experience of the world beyond the Valley that he had had, in his relations with people at the capital and in other districts of the Colony, had broadened his outlook and smoothed down his inherent prejudices. He could view with detached amusement many of the conventional distastes of his new environment, and because he did so he rapidly attained to a position of some eminence among his neighbours, who considered his judgment to be impartial as it was less likely to be bent by local bias than their own, and listened to his comments, if not always with approval, at least with respect and attention. He had much strengthened that position when, at Uncle Dorie's insistence, he had gone among them to argue them out of their silly reluctance to observe what was after all merely a pleasant custom. Everardus had never bothered his head about political questions; there had been no occasion to do so, for no great event had occurred that could stir men's minds throughout the length and breadth of the Colony. Here and there things had taken place that had caused discussion and a ripple of temporary interest. The emigration of the Trekkers had been one such event, but here in the western part of the Colony it had had far slighter repercussion than in the Districts where the Trek had originated. The Valley got its information about the Trekkers from hearsay; it knew none of these complaining farmers personally, and although it had bonds of blood or family with some of them, these were too loosely attached to make them feel personally interested in the matter. Even the widespread agitation when the slaves had been emancipated had left the Valley cold. Its slave owners did not regard slavery as a sacrosanct institution, and, if the truth had to be told, were rather grateful than otherwise for an Ordinance which released them from responsibilities which they took very seriously and from which they had no reason to anticipate any difficulties in the future. They realised, indeed, that they were in a slightly different position from that in which slave owners in other parts of the Colony found themselves, and they were fully aware of the fact that these others had lost much through the curious methods which the government of the day had employed to indemnify them for the loss of their human cattle. The taxation, for emancipation purposes, of the Valley slaves under the Ordinance had been done by the local committee under the chairmanship of the magistrate, and payment had been made, in the usual fashion, by warrant, but the Valley had no real difficulty in discounting the warrants because Thomas Seldon and Andrew Quakerley managed the matter for them through their agents in England with altogether satisfactory results. While the Valley could therefore in part sympathise with those parts of the Colony where the affair had not proceed with equal smoothness, it had seen no reason to regard the failure of government methods elsewhere as proof of the allegation that the government was inimical to them and bent on their economic destruction. It thought that it had manifest proofs to the contrary, and up to the time when the stuttering envoy had entered the District on his collecting mission, it had found no good grounds to complain or to depart from its philosophic attitude towards the authorities in the capital with whom it rarely came into direct or indirect contact.

The little man's eloquence and his dogmatically expressed doctrine of independence, had, however, stirred in some of them those feelings which lie dormant in all men, awaiting only the stimulus of emotional appeal to be quickened into something like a sporadic activity. On the organ of class or race, the veriest amateur can play and evoke responsive sounds, and where class and race are so sharply demarcated as they are in South Africa, the response must of necessity be more spontaneous and more general, in due proportion to the large mass of the community that has not learned to look beyond superficial things into the core of matters that are usually viewed from a purely subjective and emotional point of view. Everardus could understand this, and he had the logical sense to differentiate between the sentiment of men like Uncle Dorie with whom he felt himself in cordial sympathy, and the exuberance of the recalcitrants whom he had endeavoured to persuade out of their sullenness. That had made him feel a useful intermediary, for in differentiating he could also sympathise, to some extent, with both views, and his advocacy of the one side was not clouded by a preconceived notion of its utter infallibility, nor his opposition to the other view based on an utter want of understanding that negated all sympathy. The result was that he made friends even where he found the differences of opinion so marked that no argument that he could use was of any avail. That was rarely the case for the recalcitrants were mostly young, landless, inexperienced men, who listened to him with respect, and admitted that their opposition to the Birthday celebrations was based purely on theoretical grounds and class sentiment.

These negotiations, which had taken some time, had brought him into intimate contact with nearly all the inhabitants of the Valley, and his part in them had undoubtedly given him a standing which he found useful and advantageous. Uncle Dorie had come forward, almost as the direct result of his success in persuading the young men to join the Birthday commando, with the proposal that Everardus should agree to have himself nominated for the church council. As Magriet approved of this, and as the position of Deacon would not entail duties which were beyond his capacity to execute, he accepted the offer and in due course attended the church *Nagmaal* or communion service and was consecrated Deacon. As such he had to wear, on state occasions, the long, black frockcoat and the white tie which custom had decreed as the official dress of members of the church council, to attend services in rotation with the other Deacons, to take the collection bag round during the singing of the closing hymn, and to be present at the final examination of those about to be confirmed, when he was allowed to put such questions to the candidates as he thought fit. Usually he contented himself, not being very sure of his own knowledge of biblical subjects, with a question on his favourite hero, Samson. His position as Deacon gained him a trifle of added respect, but he flattered himself, perhaps rightly, that his standing in the community was not so much due to the fact that he was a member of the church council as his membership was due to the fact that he was a man of some standing. That was probably the case, for all the members of the church council were men of standing and means, and although no one could say anything against them on moral or social grounds, there were in the Valley many others of equally blameless conduct who had never been nominated for membership simply because they could not, for all their purity of life, be looked upon as leading men in the community.

With Thomas Seldon his relations had improved so that the two families were now on terms of intimacy. Seldon was a man of outstanding character, simple in his way of living, unostentatious, although he was reputed to be very well off with a flair for business, a thrifty but by no means ungenerous disposition, known to all the Valley as one whose word was his bond. In appearance he was a lean, middle-sized, brown-bearded man with shrewd hazel-brown eyes and a pleasant, rather soft-toned voice. His wife, Agnes, was a plump, smiling little lady, who managed her household and served in the shop with equal ability and charm. Their eldest born, Tommy, was a bright, mischievous lad of ten, and following him came a string of four daughters, Maggie, Sarah, Dorothy and Alice, respectively eight, seven, five and three years of age. While English was the home language of the Seldons, as it was that of the Quakerleys, the magistrate and the other English inhabitants of the District, both parents and children had learned to speak Dutch with a fair amount of ease, Tommy and Maggie, indeed, speaking both languages with such freedom that they had manufactured between them a *lingua franca* composed of both in which they were accustomed to chatter when by themselves, for their mother frowned upon it, and insisted that they should talk correct English. That, however, was a matter of some difficulty, for already both had broadened their vowel sounds, clipped disyllables into monosyllabic sounds, and freely translated from the Dutch idiom with the result that they referred to the cart-hood as a 'tent,' and 'uncled' and 'auntied' male and female visitors instead of saying, as their mother had taught them, 'Sir' and 'Ma'am.' The Seldons felt that this was the price that had to be paid for exile and estrangement. Their children's education was a matter of great difficulty. They were not prepared, as the Uhlmanns and the von Bergmanns and indeed most of the missionaries were, to send their children away at an early age, away to that 'Home' which could only be regarded as home in the sentimental sense of the word, separated from the real home by more than six thousand miles of sea. In the Colony itself the facilities for education were still primitive at the capital, and non-existent in the rural districts. At the Village there was a small school, but its teaching was not such as to find favour with the Seldons, who preferred to keep their children on their farm and, at the risk of danger from alien influences which affected not only their speech, pronunciation and accent, but might possibly affect their ultimate character, give them such education as would enable them at a later stage to go to the capital as borders at some private scholastic establishment. Mrs Seldon taught Tommy and Maggie, and the younger girls attended the classes, which were held at irregular intervals, and frequently interrupted by the exigencies of the shop.

The shop was the great feature of the Seldons' farm. It stood close to the road, a long, low, reed-thatched building, with a roomy loft, to which an outside staircase gave access, and a *stoep* shaded by tall syringa trees. Inside, it was cool and dark, its atmosphere pervaded by the mingled smells of leather, buchu, hides, and haberdashery. Its broad deal-counter, roughly printed, was littered with odds and ends, which had to be cleared away to make space whenever a customer wanted to display his own wares or to inspect those which he came to buy. It was the recognised place of gossip, and as the farm was also a post-station, it served as post-office, the letters being stuck in a rack behind the counter whence they were handed out on demand by Mrs Seldon who functioned, gratuitously, as the government postmistress. It was she who had charge of the mailbag, who cut out the sheets of unperforated triangular stamps when postage was required and who stamped the letters with a roughly made, wooden impression-stamp. Seldon dealt in everything. He bought buchu and hides, bark and firewood, farm produce and thatching material, and he sold, or ordered and imported whatever he was asked for. His White customers came to him for groceries and provisions, for tea, coffee and sugar, the last in crystals, very expensive, and the first in lead wrapping and even more dear. As a result most of the Valley folk contented themselves with tea made from a local composite plant which was pleasant to the taste, contained much less tannin than the imported article, was healthier to drink, and had the added advantage of being procurable by all those who took the trouble to gather it from the hillside. His Native clients demanded beads and coloured yarns, and he did a good deal of his business, very profitably, by barter and exchange. From Neckarthal he obtained leather shoes and boots, made locally and much in demand in the Valley, and also planks for building purposes, wood for carpentry, dressed and tanned hides for saddlery, and quantities of buchu, protea bark, and the fruit of the wild almond, another species of protea, which could be used to make a kind of coffee known to the Valley as 'ghoo.' He drank of it himself and found it quite palatable, for it tasted not unlike a mild cocoa, and the cooked nuts were regarded as a highly nutritive food, but had to be specially prepared for they contained prussic acid in their fresh state and were exceedingly poisonous.

While the shop was Seldon's main business, he did not neglect his farm, which he had so much improved that it now yielded him a comfortable living and produced an entirely satisfactory interest on the on the capital which he had expended upon it. Moreover he had other activities. He owned the transport wagons that brought goods from the capital, and he shared in their profits with the White drivers whom he employed. Originally single-handed, he was now perhaps the largest employer of labour in the Valley, and he was known as a good master, who paid his employees well and who looked after their comfort. Altogether his reputation stood high in the Valley, and while he was nobody's enemy, he maintained a sturdy independence of thought and action that in an individual of lesser weight could have earned him some criticism. None, however, dreamed of criticising Thomas Seldon, who, while he gave generously to the funds of the local Dutch Reformed church, had given much more to build and furnish the little English church in the Village, and paid handsomely when called upon to contribute to the travelling expenses of the English ministers who visited the Village from time to time to conduct services for those not of the Dutch Reformed faith. The Valley respected him for his independence, but it also liked him for the manner in which he had acclimatised himself to local conditions. It regarded him as a good *burgher*, who, although he spoke English by preference, had so far identified himself with his adopted country that he had had learned the language and was able to take his share in such deliberations as the Valley might from time to time indulge in. He and his family were well liked, and his innate honesty, his known generosity and his cheerful urbanity were virtues that the Valley could, and did, fully appreciate.

Thomas Seldon would have laughed uproariously, with that mellow, baritone laugh of his, if anybody had told him that he was a missionary. Yet such, in effect, he was, and he played a part in the Valley which was in many resects similar to that acted by

Johann Uhlmann. He was a civilising force, operating unconsciously but none the less effectively upon the minds to whom practice appealed far more than precept. When the 1820 settlers had entered the Valley, the Valley had received them kindly, but had judged them for all that, according to local standards, and many of them had fallen below these, and had been condemned accordingly. But the Seldons and the Quakerleys had stood the tests successfully and had shown the Village that they could compete with it in fair competition, without favour asked or received, and the Valley had been impressed, and from a tolerant, protective attitude towards them veered round to accepting them as part of it, as co-equal, needing no more protecting beyond what Christian neighbourliness prescribed in a community so closely knit as that into which they had introduced themselves. Whatever sentiment of opposition had been aroused by the cession of the Colony in perpetuity to England, had been effaced, so far as the Valley was concerned, by the Seldons and the Quakerleys. That could be accounted a great achievement, but Thomas Seldon did not bother his head about it. He had left the homeland in order to better himself, and he frankly acknowledged that his new country was very much to his liking and that it had given him more than he could have reasonably expected at home. Nevertheless he did not forget the homeland, any more than Johann Uhlmann forgot the Mission House at Barmen, and Mrs Seldon took care that her children should know as much as she herself knew about the history of the land they had never seen. To her and to her husband, England was 'home.' To their children, that word carried no such definite connotation as it did to their Elders, for they knew it merely as the land where grandfather Seldon was still living and grandmother Allen had a sweet-stuff shop at a place called Chester, which had high, red-coloured walls and far more people than the whole Valley contained. Little Tommy knew that William the Conqueror had landed in 1066, and that King Charles had been beheaded by Uncle Oliver Cromwell, but it must be admitted that he did not know that the captains of King James had taken possession of the Cape, that Van Riebeek had planted the first decent garden under the shadow of Table Mountain, or that a battle had been fought on Blaauberg Strand between the English and the Dutch not so very long before his birth.

The relations between the nationalities in South Africa are today not yet what they might or should be, and there can be little question about the utter absence of such true standards of comparison as may be obtained by a conscientious study of their several histories, in other words, to the lack of real education and cultural development. Mutual respect in a community is the result, in such circumstances, of personal factors operating within limits. It does not transcend these limits, and it never probes down to root factors, trying to find a mutual basis of understanding outside and above national and sectional prejudices, conventions, and characteristics. This was the case in the Valley, as it is still today in many parts of the country. The Valley took the Seldons as fair representatives of the English, but it hugged, unconsciously or subconsciously, the idea that they did not represent England, and equally subconsciously, it ranked them very much in the same category in which it had placed the Trekkers. The Valley, being, in comparison, older and long-settled, had forgotten that its forefathers had also been immigrants. It had now so thoroughly identified itself with its environment that it was inclined to look askance at newcomers, especially if these came from foreign parts, and were strangers to its ways, its thoughts, its faith, and its customs and language. Its innate courtesy, its customary hospitality, and its subconscious sense of superiority made it tolerant and protective towards these strangers, but only when the newcomers had shown themselves proved fellow-citizens was it prepared to accept them as co-equals.

Thomas Seldon had discussed the question of the school with Everardus, and had readily agreed to contribute towards such expenses as it might entail, although he had refused to accept a seat on the committee. While his own son had already, thanks to his wife's tuition, progressed beyond the stage that the school could be expected to cater for, he thought that it would do Tommy some good if he could attend regularly, doing such homework in class as his mother could give him. Maggie, too, would be a pupil, and later on Sarah and Dorothy could attend. The farms lay several miles apart, but the children were good riders, and could be trusted to ride to and from school, and their transport therefore offered no insurmountable difficulties. But it was imperatively necessary that some more experienced teacher than Mrs Nolte should be found, one who could teach geography and history, and perhaps the rudiments of Latin and higher arithmetic. He would look out for a suitable candidate, and write to the authorities at Cape Town. There need be no difficulty about the money side, for he was quite prepared to pay the teacher's salary himself.

That was the stage of the undertaking when Everardus discovered Tins. The school had been at work for several months, the class numbering some ten girls and five boys, the eldest of the latter being the Widow Priem's overgrown and loutish lad Frikkie, who as yet could neither read nor write although he had passed his fourteenth year and was accounted a good shot and an able farm-hand. The children came from the farm immediately adjoining *Knolkloof*, some trudging on foot, some brought in by carts, and the two Seldons arriving daily on horseback. At midday Magriet gave them luncheon, for the school hours were from nine to three, with a midday interval of an hour. A couple of youngsters, whose parents lived beyond the mountains, were weekly borders, an arrangement which Magriet had made because she had room enough and to spare for them, and felt that both could be desirable companions for Katryn and young Gottlieb. The two, a boy and a girl, were bright, intelligent little persons, and gave no trouble whatever.

Everardus was sitting on the *stoep*, in the cool of the forenoon, listening abstractedly to the singing of the children, a clear, thin treble that blended with the hum of the cicadas in the trees, when Sylvester came to tell him of the stranger. The morning air was crisp with the tempered warmth of early spring, and the veld beyond the main road was lovely to look upon, starred as it was with sorrel blooms. The mountains melted away in a shimmering haze of blue; the River lay like a broad line of gleaming silver framed by yellow sand and patches of willows.

'There is a master lying under the sage bush alongside the road, *Baas*' said Sylvester, importantly. 'The master is, with permission, *Baas*, dead drunk. I could smell the smell of the wine, *Baas*, yards away.'

Everardus sprang up. 'Perhaps the *baas* is hurt, Sylvester,' he said, extenuatingly. 'You should have taken him up.'

'*Ag*, no. The *baas* is merely tight,' remarked Sylvester, rolling his quid in his mouth and expectorating upon the *kweek*-grass. 'Do I not know one who is drunk when I see him? *Baas* should come and look.'

'Let us go at once. Do you know the *baas*? Is it one from the Valley?' asked Everardus on his way towards the road.

'No, *Baas*. It is a strange face. I do not mind having seen it hereabouts, but one never knows. There, *Baas*, under that bush ... you can see his feet from here, and Almighty, *Baas*, I should be shamed to wear such boots.'

Everardus approached the sage-bush. In its shade was lying a thin, attenuated figure, clothed in torn and very dirty trousers and shirt, with boots whose soles and uppers stood sadly in need of repair. The man was lying on his face, his head covered by a large, brown felt hat. As Everardus and Sylvester came near, he raised himself on his elbow, and stared at them. Everardus saw a very white face, burdened by heavy black eyebrows and a beard of many days' growth, but before he could speak the stranger had risen, with some difficulty, to his feet, taken off his hat with a flourish, and, bringing his heels sharply together with a click, had made a graceful bow.

'I am delighted to meet you,' said the stranger, in a voice that was obviously not quite under control, so that Everardus could not fairly judge of its timbre. 'If you will permit me ... Pierre Mabuis, generally known by the nickname of *Blikkies* (Tins). To whom have I the honour of addressing myself?'

'I am Nolte,' said Everardus, nonplussed by this frontal attack. 'This is my place. I think you had better come with me to the house.'

He spoke in Dutch, the same language that the stranger had used, but he knew that his visitor was not one of his nationality, although he could not place him. The stranger was obliging enough to volunteer immediate information.

'Extremely kind, *Meneer* Nolte' he said, approaching Everardus and taking him by the arm while he carefully replaced his hat on his head. 'In consonance with what, if I might be permitted so to express myself, I have been told of the—ah—hospitality of these parts. Ravished to make *Meneer's* acquaintance. Though under unfortunate conditions, consequent upon the too liberal consumption of—ah, thanks, Boy, my bottle. It is unfortunately empty—*vide*. No importance! You may as well have it, Boy. For carrying milk in, or water. As I remarked, *Monsieur* Nolte, I am charmed to meet you. A long and, if I may say so a hazardous walk—precipitous pass there on the other side. My footgear, as you see, not good. One might say *epouvantable*. But one moment—somewhere hereabouts ... ah, there it lies. My flute, *Monsieur*, my flute. And now I am entirely at your disposal.'

The stranger had turned round, looking for some object, and Sylvester had handed him the two pieces of a flute which the boy had picked up from the grass. The man had put these in his trouser pocket, hitched that garment a little higher, so that Everardus could see that it was held up by pieces of string, and then resumed his grasp of the farmer's arm, and hobbled rather painfully along.

'By trade, occupation or profession, *Monsieur*, a player. Came out years ago, but originally of this country. Made here, *Monsieur*, made here and born here. *Papa* now—ah, with God, as the saying is, though I rather fancy the other gentleman has charge of him. Also a player. Not successful. Hereditary, *Monsieur*. *Certes*, it is the only thing on which I can consistently—ah, rely. A great boon, short grass, *Monsieur*. Especially after you have tramped on a hard road for miles in these damnable shoes.'

'You must come in and rest awhile,' said Everardus, thinking he had to do with someone who was not quite right in his head. The stranger was certainly one of the most extraordinary men he had ever seen. He was tall and gaunt, very much the worse for wear and tear and fatigue, and, Everardus suspected, for food as well, but his small, piercingly black eyes flashed vivaciously and he spoke in a rapid, high-pitched voice, which he gradually got under control. Evidently, so Everardus presumed, a man who could carry his liquor and sleep off the effects of it very well. His shirt was wet with dew, and his appearance was bedraggled, but he bore himself with a certain natural dignity that was impressive to those who could overlook the ludicrousness of his apparel and the strangeness of his gesticulations. He used words that were new to Everardus, who had some difficulty in following him, but he talked so quickly and manifestly so much to his own satisfaction that he evidently did not need a reply to anything he said.

'*Magnifique*, this view of yonder range,' he said, stopping Everardus and directing his gaze at the mountains. 'Beautiful. Quite unlike the mountain at the Bay. That is imposing, I grant, but not beautiful. Now here—ah, the blend is exquisite. Yes, Pierre Mabuis, *Monsieur* Nolte, formerly sergeant in the Hottentot's regiment. Known familiarly as 'Tins.' Now on tour to *le bon Dieu* knows where. Original intention to reach the copper mines—now departed from, the said destination being, as I am credibly informed by those who were good enough to give me the bottle of wine which I have just handed to *Monsieur's* blackamoor, several hundred leagues farther on. Impossible to reach without proper shoe-gear. Therefore all the more grateful to *Monsieur* for his invitation. By all means, let us go to the house.'

'*Meneer* Mabuis thinks of reaching Namaqualand?' asked Everardus. 'But that is dangerous and far. I do not think *Meneer* Mabuis would be well advised to go on.'

'Exceedingly ill-advised, *Monsieur*, if I may say so. *Diable*, can one walk several hundred leagues without boots? *Monsieur* Nolte comprehends that the question is pertinent. Unfortunately, the exchequer is deficient. Entirely exhausted, if I may so express myself.'

'In that case *Monsieur* Mabuis must stay here for a few days. Probably we may be able to hit upon some plan.'

'Grateful, *Monsieur*, grateful. There is so much goodness in the world, *Monsieur*, that if I had a farm so *charmante* as this of yours, I should christen it *la Gratitude*. The men of the Drakenstein did that. I have stayed on it, and drunk some of the best Jeropigo that has ever passed my—ah, lips. And talking of Jeropigo, *Monsieur*, I note that you have a vineyard. I noticed it when I was picking out the thorns under that damned bush. Figure you, *Monsieur*, I was like a—ah— *horisson*, all over prickles.'

'That's the little black man,' said Everardus, with a smile, knowing his visitor alluded to the spiky grass that pins its barbed seeds to whatever it can penetrate.

'They were terrible little black men,' said the stranger. 'They made me feel red all over. That,' his voice sunk almost to a whisper, 'that, *Monsieur*, is why the bottle is empty. I saw the light in the window, but I could not go and knock at the door with all these little black men over us. It would not have been *convenable*.'

'We should have thought nothing of it, *Meneer* Mabuis' replied Everardus. 'You should just have come as you are, and not spent the night under a sage-bush. It ... it is bad for the Natives to see a White man like that.'

'I ask your pardon. I ask ten thousand pardons, *Monsieur*. That point of view is to me new. But I can see its quaint reasonableness. Permit me, *Monsieur*, once more to ask your pardon. And to suggest, if I may be permitted to do so, that having spent the night under that darned sage-bush, you allow me to accept of your hospitality under this budding oak.'

'But you must come indoors, *Meneer,*' said Everardus, puzzled by the sudden sharpness in the gaunt man's voice and the manner in which his visitor had jerked his arm away.

'It would not be fitting, *Monsieur* Nolte,' said Mabuis, shaking his head. 'The Natives might not be benefited by it. If I may be permitted, with all due respect, to suggest—ah, a cup of coffee and a piece of bread partaken outside *Monsieur's* house—or yonder in one of the huts over there ...'

It says much for Everardus's sense of humour that he did not lose his temper; he merely took the stranger by the shoulder and pushed him on to the *stoep* and from there into the house.

'Sylvester,' he called out, 'tell Regina to fry some sausage and get us some coffee and biscuits quickly. And now, Mr Jackanapes, you sit down there and keep a still tongue in your head until you have had something to eat.'

Chapter 12

Cleaned, dressed in spare clothes that Everardus had lent him—flap corduroy trousers, a grey shirt, and a moleskin jacket—and with his stockingless feet shod in a pair of Neckarthal veld shoes, 'Tins' Mabuis looked a different man from the ragged individual who had been found sleeping off the effects of a bottle of Jeropico under the sage-bushes. After his much needed breakfast, to which he had done more than justice, eating, as Everardus observed, with gusto but at the same time with a certain fastidiousness that showed him to be above the common herd of tramps, he had borrowed a razor and removed his beard, preserving only his moustache, which he had twisted into fine points at the end and waxed with the application of a portion of his breakfast butter. Now, as he sat in the armchair on the *stoep*, puffing at a borrowed pipe, he presented an appearance that intrigued Everardus. His pallid face bore the marks of privation and poverty, but his features were undeniably good, and he bore himself with an air of dignity that seemed to be natural rather than adopted for the occasion. Indeed, what Everardus was especially struck with was his naturalness. The fellow made no pretence whatsoever; he seemed to take it for granted that he was on an equality with his host and hostess, and his company manners were undoubtedly good. When Magriet had entered the dining-room where he was eating his breakfast, he had jumped up, bowed two or three times profoundly, and when Everardus had presented him with his customary form, 'Mother, this is *Meneer* Mabuis. *Meneer* Mabuis, this is my wife,' he had not shaken hands as most sensible folk did but, when Magriet had extended her hand, he had lifted it with his fingertips and kissed it. He did so very gracefully, but Magriet had not liked it, and Everardus thought her first impression of the stranger distinctly unfavourable. It was only that evening, when he and Magriet were discussing the fellow in their bedroom, that he had learned that she had been favourably impressed. She had admired the fellow's pallor, his waxed moustache, his mannerisms. There was no doubt that the fellow had a manner. Everardus could not make up his mind whether that manner was something to be deprecated or something to be approved of, but he was certain that it was a strange manner, a foreign manner, not Valley-like, and therefore to be considered carefully.

Mabuis proved to be an entertaining fellow. He told Everardus that he had been a master, practically, of no trade and a jack at them all. He could paint a little, carpenter a little, knew something about wine farming, and had served as a wine blender for some weeks with a Cape Town wine merchant. Before that, so it transpired from his confidences, he had been a soldier. He had served as a sergeant in the Hottentot Regiment, but had left the service because—so he freely admitted—his sobriety had not commended itself to his superiors. Thereafter he had been a salesman in the capital, an assistant to a gardener, and a buyer on commission for a produce merchant. Formerly he had also been a teacher, but originally he had been an actor. He said little about his father, who, Everardus understood from such remarks as his visitor dropped, had not been an altogether satisfactory parent, but Everardus gathered that the Elder Mabuis had been one of the French players who had come to the Colony just prior to the first English occupation, when the French garrison was quartered in the Castle, and who had married a Colonial. Apparently both his father and mother were dead, for Mabuis declared that he had nor kith nor kin in the Colony, and that, although he had once been to Europe, he had no great wish to go back there.

His conversation was a strange mixture of Dutch and what Everardus took to be French, for it was inter-larded with quaint expressions, which had a nasal twang, and which he usually translated for his hearer's benefit. When Everardus spoke to him in English, he answered readily enough in that language, and he intimated that he had a smattering of German, as well as a working knowledge of Malay.

'*Monsieur* sees,' he said, waving his pipe in the air to emphasise his words, 'that these things come of themselves when one is forced to wander about the world. Not that I have wandered far, *Monsieur* Nolte. It has been from town to town, for the shoes wear through and the exchequer is not always easily replenishable. And then, *Monsieur*, my cursed inherited facility of picking up trouble. It is the only thing I can consistently rely upon, *Monsieur*. Whoever doled out man's fate, *Monsieur*, saw to it that Pierre Mabuis should have his share of misfortune.'

'My experience,' said Everardus sententiously, for he was not quite sure whether the man was worth commiseration or reproof, 'my experience is that a man makes his own lot, more or less.'

'There, if you will allow me to remark, *Monsieur* Nolte, you err. Fate administers the *frottée*—what you call the thrashing, *Monsieur*—more often to those who are already beaten than to those who have never felt the stick. The one leads to the other, *Monsieur*. I have been treated *froidement*—that is coldly, *Monsieur*—by the world, but I do not say it is the world's fault. Do not take it amiss, Sir. I do not complain. Indeed, I am myself largely responsible, as *Monsieur* has justly and very pertinently observed. It is, of course, *Monsieur's* privilege to draw attention to my failing ...'

'Heavens, man,' interrupted Everardus, who was getting exasperated with his guest's touchiness, 'no one has said anything of your failing.'

'It is so lamentably obvious, *Monsieur*,' said Mabuis contritely. *'Monsieur* has had occasion to observe me *ivre-mort*, and *Monsieur* has naturally an aversion to *ivrognerie*. It is natural; it is perfectly understandable in a man who has his own farm and who has no occasion to drown his miseries in Jeripico—which, by the way, is a much overrated wine, fit for the Natives, really, *Monsieur*. But if I may remark ...'

'I do not understand half of what you say,' interrupted Everardus bluntly. 'But it seems to me, *Meneer* Mabuis ...'

'If I may be allowed the remark, *Monsieur* Nolte, my friends, intimates and mere chance acquaintances call me "Tins." It is a familiarity to which I do not in the least object. Has it ever struck you, *Monsieur*, that a nickname makes intercourse between individuals more easy? It smoothes down the rough edges of malice, if I may say so, and it gives piquancy, geniality, to the talk which might otherwise assume a complexion more favourable to the court house or the barracks. I should esteem it a favour if *Monsieur* would bear that in mind.'

'I have known you for a few hours, *Meneer* Mabuis,' said Everardus, 'and it would ill become me were I to call you familiarly by a nickname. We are utter strangers ...'

'By no means, *Monsieur*. I can recall an occasion when I had the honour of meeting *Monsieur*.'

'Meeting me? You must be mistaken, *Meneer* Mabuis. I have never seen you.'

'More people have seen the ... let us call it the *landdrost*, the *magistrat*, than the *magistrat* has seen. Perhaps I am indiscreet, for *Monsieur* has told me his name is Nolte. And the gentleman I had in mind was named Tereg ...'

'How? When?' exclaimed Everardus, in displeased astonishment. 'Are you taking me for someone else?'

'Monsieur will pardon me, but I can see that the matter is one that is no concern of mine. I grieve that I have inadvertently touched upon it. *Monsieur* may take it that I have forgotten all I ever knew of the gentleman of whom *Monsieur*, for one moment, so marvellously reminded me.'

'I am sure you must be mistaken,' said Everardus, nervously. 'At any rate, it is of no importance.'

'It shall be as *Monsieur* wishes. I am not one *follement* to introduce my own fancies where they are not wanted. *Certes*, I have other things wherewith to occupy myself, and the present question is how am I to get to the copper mines. It is more than three weeks' journey hence afoot, *Monsieur*, and I am desolated to say that I have not the means.'

'For the present you must bide here,' said Everardus. 'We must make a plan and see what can be done for you. I have a notion we might be able to find a use for you ...'

'That would be a mercy for which I should be eternally grateful to the *bon Dieu*,' said Tins, with what Everardus fancied was real feeling in his voice. 'I have been footing it for weeks and months, *Monsieur*, having nowhere to lay my head, and doubtless there is some use in me. I do not know, but perhaps others can find it out. There is unfortunately my failing—*Monsieur* will permit me, this time, to raise the matter myself. It is, I believe, a hereditary failing. *Papa* was much addicted to it. Most players are. You see, *Monsieur*, it is the life, the errant manner in which the profession is of necessity conducted ...'

'If you were to remain here and be of use,' said Everardus, decisively, 'you will have to give up the drink. I tell you that frankly. I will not have a drunkard on the farm, and it is better that we should understand each other from the beginning.'

'Monsieur is perfectly right. But may I remind *Monsieur* that it is all a matter of opportunity. Pierre Mabuis is the soberest individual—*sec, Monsieur* dry, dry, dry— when there is no opportunity to get liquor, but when the opportunity is there—well, did not the good Lord tell us to pray not to be led into temptation?'

'I shall take care that there is no opportunity,' remarked Everardus, drily. 'That is, if we can arrive at some understanding. I do not yet know what I shall be able to do for *Meneer* Mabuis ...'

'Tins, if you please, *Meneer* Nolte.'

'I do not yet know,' went on Everardus, disregarding the interruption, 'but I daresay we will manage in some way. Meanwhile you must just remain as our guest. I shall have to talk to other folk about the matter, and we must find out what you are capable of.'

'An examination, does *Monsieur* mean? By all means. I do not of course know what *monsieur* has in mind, not being aware of the circumstances. But Pierre Mabuis is willing to do anything and everything, not inconsistent with what a gentleman may do, for a living. I could herd *Monsieur's* cattle, for instance, or water *Madame's* flower garden ...'

'That is Natives' work, *Meneer* Mabuis. We do not employ White men for these purposes here in the Valley. But come, it is time for midday dinner, and I think we can both do with a bite.'

Discussing the matter with his wife that night, in the seclusion of their bedroom, Everardus discovered that Magriet had already found a use for the stranger.

'Did he not say that he had been a teacher, Ami?' she asked. 'Why then, it is a God-send, if he be suitable for the job.'

'Do you mean as teacher for our school?' said Everardus, surprised, for he had not thought of employing Tins in that capacity. He had had in mind some less responsible position, a sort of under-overseer, co-adjunct to Matryk Thalussen, if Mabuis proved himself adaptable and could be kept from indulging too freely in his family failing.

'Why not? You must, of course, find out if he is capable of teaching, but that the pastor will be able to do. By the way, Ami, have you noticed that he is not of our faith?'

'No. What do you mean? He is a strange fellow, but that I did not notice. What makes you say that, Mother?'

'He crossed himself when you said grace at table. That is the custom of the Papists, Ami. And if he is a Papist it will create difficulties.'

'I rather think he will create difficulties all along,' Everardus grumbled. 'He said something that makes me almost certain he recognised me. He said he had known a Tereg. I was so dumbfounded that I did not know what to do, but fortunately he saw that there was something amiss, and he apologised for having referred to the matter.'

'There you have it, Ami. Why not let the thing go? Sooner or later it will come out, when we least suspect it and are least prepared to face it. Why not disclose it now, Husband? It is nothing to be ashamed of. You and I and our friends will know ...'

'We discussed all that years ago, Mother,' said Everardus, irritably. 'I cannot do it now. We are not settled, and ... and I should hate if Uncle Martin or the others ...'

'They must know, sooner or later, Ami. Why not now? Especially if there are others who already know of us. The Uhlmanns do, and you remember how kind they were to us.'

'With them it is safe, our secret, Mother,' answered Everardus. *'Meneer* von Bergmann said it would be, and I trust him. I trust *Meneer* Uhlmann as well. He is a saintly man, and he understands. He never once referred to it all the week we were at Neckarthal, and he treated me like a friend.'

'No one who knows us will do otherwise, Ami. But have it your own way. I only referred to it when you said that this new man knows something, and it may be that he is not to be depended upon. Not that I think he is that kind of man. He has frank eyes, Husband, and there is honesty in his face. That is why I am so sorry for him. I am sure if you help him you can get him away from the drink. We might give him a chance.'

'That is what I have in mind, Mother. But I must consult His Reverence about it, and the committee. And we must of course see if he is fit for the work. We have no proof that he knows anything at all about teaching.'

But the proofs were soon forthcoming. The Reverend de Smee, on his periodical tour of house visitations through the Valley, touched at *Knolkloof* and stayed there for the night. Everardus took the opportunity of introducing Mabuis to him, and ventured to suggest that the pastor should test him to find out if it was possible for the stranger to act as teacher, if only for a time until the school could procure a more suitable person. The interview took place in the dining room, and Everardus found himself soon entirely out of the conversation that ensued. The reverend gentleman became more and more animated, and Tins gesticulated freely and spoke with increasing volubility, and it was only the pastor's genial smile that prevented Everardus from interfering, for he thought that they were on the verge of quarrelling. But at the end, the Reverend Sybrand dismissed Mabuis, gravely stating that he had to speak to *Meneer* Nolte in private, and opened his mind.

'The man,' he said, 'is a strange mixture of worldliness and good sense, of culture and gipsyness. Look at his writing—it is the most beautiful script I have seen, and I have seen some excellent writing in my time. He could set copy for any class, and on that I alone would say, take him. But he has knowledge also of many other things. He speaks and reads well; his knowledge of figures is beyond nine—I have, as you might not perhaps know, Brother Nolte, a poor head for figures. I could never quite see the sense of all these involved calculations that I had to do in my university days. And he knows something of French and German, while his English is again better than mine. Look at that translation. It would do credit to *Meneer* Seldon or *Meneer* Quakerley. And I like the man. Yes, I like him, Brother Nolte. There is something fine about him, although there is also much that makes one pity him.'

'Then Your Reverence approves of my wife's plan?' asked Everardus, glad to find that the pastor's verdict was not unfavourable.

'I do. I do. But it is not for us to decide. It is a matter for the whole committee. We must ask Brother Martin and Brother Doremus to see him and talk to him, and their views may perhaps be in harmony with ours. On one point you are quite right. The man is a Roman Catholic. He is not of our faith, and in that I foresee difficulties.'

'Your Reverence thinks that makes it impossible for us to employ him as our teacher?'

'No, I would not go as far as that. But it certainly raises difficulties, although I think they might be overcome with a little tact and common sense. You know what our people are. They would not readily consort with a Papist, and to have him as teacher to our little ones ... There, Brother Nolte, lies the hitch. Personally, I do not think there would be any great risk in employing him. Sister Magriet might continue to take scripture and catechism, and *Meneer* Mabuis made it plain to me that in any case he could not undertake religious instruction. It was he who touched upon the matter, and I liked him the more for that. What you tell me about his failing, well, that is a matter which might lead to trouble in the future. My advice is that we go slowly. Let us follow the Latin admonition and hasten unhurriedly.[1] There is no haste. We can try him for a day or two, and see if he is really capable of teaching a class, and what his work as a teacher is like. But from what I have seen of him, I fancy that he will do well.'

'Then, if Your Reverence approves, I propose to invite Uncle Martin and Uncle Doremus to come and see him. They can put him through his paces, and if their verdict agrees with yours, Your Reverence, we can submit him to the committee as a candidate for the post.'

'That is exactly what I was going to suggest. The man has impressed me, Brother Nolte. He is in many ways a rough diamond, and we have not found all his facets yet, if you will pardon a metaphor so confused, for roughness excludes faceting, but you will grasp my meaning.'

'Very well, Your Reverence. I shall give him odd jobs about the farm, and see what he is capable of, and then, later on after Uncle Martin and Uncle Dorie have seen him, we can arrange something for him in the school. That is to say if the committee approves. Your Reverence will have to help there, for it will go against their grain if they know the man is a Papist.'

'I may be able to do something if the subject is raised,' said the pastor, not however very convincingly, for he knew the difficulties better than Everardus did. 'We need not anticipate trouble.'

Chapter 13

Tins shared a room with Matryk, who lived in one of the outbuildings. His personal belongings consisted of one flute, which an auctioneer would have catalogued 'ebony, in two pieces, with silver-plated mountings and ivory mouthpiece.' On the first evening he had put it together, and finding himself alone in the room, which was bare, mud-floored with the floor plastered with that sweet-smelling dung mixture with which the Valley invariably plastered its mud floors, he had played on it, softly, melodiously, with the feeling and tenderness of one who loved his instrument and

---

[1] *Festina lente*—Eds.

knew how to evoke the best from it. He had not noticed Matryk creep in behind him and squat on the window sill, nor the Natives who, attracted by the sounds of music, had gathered round the door outside and stood listening. He had gone on playing because it was a comfort to him to play.

But his playing had won him more friends than he had thought possible to find in one day, and when he had ceased and, looking round, had observed Matryk, he had noticed that the lad's eyes were wet. Matryk was a simple soul, whose emotions were not altogether under his control, and plaintive music affected him almost as powerfully as it did the Natives who revelled in the lugubrious. To cheer them, Tins played a gavotte, a mazurka, a waltz and, as they wanted more, he continued playing until it was far past bed-time.

The next morning he found that he had won a reputation. The Natives, from Sylvester downwards, who had been inclined at first to regard him as one who—not having upheld the dignity of the White man—could be looked upon as belonging to that crowd of unfortunates who fitted into neither camp, now touched their forelocks to him, and addressed him deferentially as *'baas'*. Sylvester, too, was no longer patronising, but almost servile, for Sylvester thought very highly of a *baas* who could produce music like that, and who did it, apparently, without any trouble, just as if he knew the notes by heart and could make the black tube do whatever he chose. Sylvester was altogether much impressed, and the episode of finding the artist dead-drunk under the sage bush was promptly relegated to the category of things about which no well-mannered Native obtruded his opinions in company. There were many things that Dutchmen did which a Native had no right to criticise. Sylvester had learned that lesson when young, and it had frequently been impressed upon his back with a quince stick before he had reached adolescence. In his mature age he was not likely to forget it, and in any case a *baas* who could play like that deserved more latitude than was usually granted to others not so marvellously gifted by divine and obliging Providence.

For the first few days, Tins was left much to his own devices. Magriet allowed him to attend at the school, to watch the proceedings, and there he sat on one of the back benches, engaged with a pencil and a piece of paper on which he drew heads, outlines of the mountains, and strange, weird-looking animals that interested the children. There was no doubt about his ability to draw, and there was no doubt about the fact that he could handle a class, keep them interested, and teach them something. On the fourth day, Magriet left him in charge and absented herself. When she came back she found Tins with the children round him, listening open-mouthed to a descriptive account of the Battle of Waterloo, in which, so he informed *madame*, his *papa* had taken a prominent part.

Thereafter he regularly assisted her, and she grew to have so much confidence in him that she gradually shelved the greater part of the school work upon him and attended personally to the singing and the scripture lesson only.

When Uncle Martin and Uncle Dorie, summoned by Everardus to discuss the matter and interview the new teacher, arrived, their verdict tallied with that of the pastor. Uncle Martin told Everardus in confidence that there was a Mabuis family that had come out in the days of Governor Swellengrebel, and as it was not French but Frisian, he suggested that it was the mother's name that Tins had taken, and that there was possibly no definite record of marriage. 'But that,' he asserted, 'made no great difference. The man, whether legitimately born or in the bush, as the saying is, is a man of parts, and so far as appearances go, honest. I should, Nephew Ev'rard, vote that we give him a trial. Let him take the school for a month. We need not regard it as a fixed appointment, which, after all, we have no right to do, seeing that the committee and not its individual members appoints the teacher. If the experiment—and it must be that only, Nephew Ev'rard, for the present, at least—is not a success, you can think of something else, though to be sure it would be a great pity to let the man return to his life of vagrancy and intemperance. That is my opinion. And yours, Brother Doremus?'

'I am inclined to agree with you, Brother Martin. As you say, the man is a man of parts. True, he has forgotten what the apostle wrote to the Thessalonians in, if I remember rightly, the first epistle and somewhere in the fifth chapter, where it says, "Let us who are of the day, be sober," and the result has been that he has not profited. That is according to the Word, for in Proverbs we are told—it is also in the fifth chapter if my memory serves me—"Who hath woe? Who hath sorrows? Who hath babbling, and wounds without cause and redness of eyes, but they that tarry long at the wine." Also, he is a Papist. These are faults, and grievous ones, Nephew Ev'rard, but who are we to judge them? Should we not rather, as Brother Martin here says, give the poor devil another chance? I, too, would vote for that, and would commend the counsel of Brother Martin.'

'Aye, I think that would be best,' said Brother Martin, reflectively. 'So it be that His Reverence has no objections to the man being a Papist, we may leave it to you, Nephew Ev'rard, to see that the fellow is not led into temptation. A little wine is good for everyone of us. I say nothing against it, and I do not hold with those who wish to destroy it for fear of the temptation. Rather, would I have our friend strengthened, through divine grace, so as to be able to overcome temptation.'

'Which, being a Papist,' remarked Uncle Dorie, doubtfully, 'is hardly likely to be vouchsafed him. But belike His Reverence can prove to him the error of his heretical ways and bring him into the true fold. That,' continued the Elder hopefully, 'would be an added reason for keeping him with us. A brand destined for the burning may yet be snatched away from it, and as Christian men we are admonished to bring him to repentance and confession.'

'From which I gathered in conversation with the fellow,' remarked Uncle Martin, drily, 'he seems to have mastered all the arguments in his favour. I should not like to contend with him on points of dogma, but happily that is the pastor's business and need not concern us.'

'There I am with you,' said Uncle Doremus, helping himself to a pinch of snuff from his friend's box. 'The fellow has parts, he is an educated fellow. Not, perhaps, with that modesty of demeanour that the apostle enjoins upon us, and with a devilish short temper, I should think. But these are human failings and, taking all in all, Nephew Ev'rard, I agree to the proposal and both Brother Martin and I will strengthen your hand when you lay the matter before the committee.'

That evening, when Everardus had gone off, after supper, with Matryk to look at a calving cow, Tins watched the two old gentlemen absorbed at their chess over the little side-table. Uncle Martin never travelled without his green bag and inlaid chessboard, and whenever he got time or opportunity to use them he did so. Now, as he made a devastating move that hopelessly endangered his opponent's queen, and saw that Doremus would take time to get out of the difficulty, he handed Tins his snuff-box—a great favour, and a proof that he considered the newcomer on terms of social equality. The delicacy with which Mabuis inserted his thumb and ring-finger, and the appreciative manner in which he allowed the snuff to enter each nostril separately, delighted the gentleman.

'Ah,' he said, commandingly. 'I see *Meneer* Mabuis values good snuff. That is pure ratafia, a little over-scented, unfortunately, but I am told that is now the mode.'

'It is, *Monsieur* Rekker, of the best snuff I have ever had the pleasure of using,' reported Tins, bowing gracefully. '*Monsieur's* very good health,' he sneezed gracefully—'and as for the scent, that is, as *Monsieur* rightly says, the modern fashion. For myself, I prefer it a trifle less aromatic, but everyone has his taste.'

'Aye that is so. No, Brother Doremus, it needs a genius to get out of that position. I do not like to boast, but you might as well strike the flag. The position is impossible for you.'

'I verily believe you are right, Brother Martin,' said Uncle Doremus, very dolefully. 'If I don't get out of it I may as well lose my lady, and then you take my rook. And after that I might as well resign.'

'Yes, that is the case, Brother. The position is much too strong. I do not think there is any chance of getting out of it.'

Uncle Doremus surveyed the board, pulled at his beard meditatively, and sighed with annoyance and chagrin. He looked so doleful and woebegone that Tins thought that he might interfere, although he knew very well that his interference might be resented.

'If the gentlemen will permit me to make a remark,' he hazarded, humbly. 'A remark applicable to the position in which *Monsieur* van Aard now finds himself owing to the excellent play of *Monsieur* Rekker.'

'By all means,' said Uncle Martin, graciously. 'You, Brother Doremus, would not object to *Meneer* Mabuis making a remark?'

'He can say whatever he pleases,' answered the Elder, with some heat. 'It is your game, Brother. I resign. I don't think anyone can get out of it.'

'I flatter myself it is a good position for me, and I think you are right, Brother,' said Uncle Martin. 'And now, *Meneer* Mabuis, we are all attention.'

'*Monsieur* van Aard having resigned, and being therefore no longer in a position to continue the game,' began Tins, speaking with quiet decision, 'I may perhaps presume to point out that the position is by no means so precarious for *Monsieur* van Aard as *Monsieur* Rekker is good enough to imagine. In fact, if the gentleman will permit me, I might say that for *Monsieur* van Aard the position is indubitably the more favourable, for he has *Monsieur* Rekker mate in six moves ...'

'What?' exclaimed Doremus, incredulously. 'Impossible.'

'I really should like, *Meneer* Mabuis,' said Uncle Martin in his most dignified tone of voice, 'to see how you deduce that. I had no idea that you were a player.'

'I know a trifle of the game, gentlemen. The position is easy, and the demonstration of its favourableness for *Monsieur* van Aard of the most facile. Permit me—he leaves his queen where it is, and moves the pawn forward—so. You, of course, take his queen. *Monsieur* must do so, or *Monsieur* is checkmated in four instead of in six moves. And if *Monsieur* does take it, *Monsieur* van Aard moves his pawn a step forward, so ...'

'Then of course, I move mine—so,' said Uncle Martin.

'*Pardon*, *Monsieur* is taken in passing, and the next step *Monsieur* van Aard makes a new queen, which, as *Monsieur* sees, mates in three. It is a pretty mate, but *Monsieur* was rash in leaving *Monsieur* Van Aard's pawn where it was. Of course the queen was a temptation ...'

'My good life,' said Uncle Dorie, who rarely permitted himself a stronger expletive, 'the man is right, Brother. It is amazing. And to think that I did not see it! My wits must be wool-gathering.'

'Yes, you are right, *Meneer* Mabuis,' confessed Uncle Martin, after he had studied the moves attentively. 'It is not only a way out, but it is a defeat and very excellently thought out, I must say. Brother Doremus, we may perhaps ask the gentleman to favour us with a game?'

'Certainly, Brother Martin. You play, of course, *Meneer* Mabuis? Very well, we will toss for choice, you and I, Brother. I say red. And now, *Meneer* Mabuis, we must toss for piece. Will you name, please?'

'The white,' said Tins, nonchalantly.

'It is red again,' said Uncle Dorie, who had a sneaking belief in omens, and was highly delighted that he had won the toss three times running. 'I take white. Sit you down there, *Meneer* Mabuis. Brother Martin will sit by me, but merely as an onlooker. I play ... yes, Brother Martin, it will serve to see what our friend is made of—I play the red Lopez.'

'A hazardous attack, *Monsieur* van Aard,' remarked Tins, genially, responding for the first three moves with exemplary speed and precision, 'but not, to my mind, the best. The bishop, gentlemen, should not attack. His eminence should defend, for law forbids him to shed blood. And to expose himself, as yours does, *Monsieur*, is good neither for his flock nor for himself. Away from his diocese, the reverend gentleman loses half of his merit, and even a miserable pawn may drive him back ... like this.'

'That I had foreseen,' said Uncle Dorie, 'so the bishop goes here.'

'And the pawn moves another stop, so,' remarked Tins, suiting the action to the word.

'Where I attack him with my other horse,' began Uncle Dorie, but felt his friend's hand convulsively on his own arm, and heard Uncle Martin's hoarse whisper, 'Brother, take care; it looks like a trap.'

'Oh no,' said Uncle Dorie, with supreme confidence. 'Traps do not develop so soon with the red Lopez. Now I shall be able to castle in comfort.'

'Whether *Monsieur* castles or not,' said Tins, smilingly, 'I am afraid *Monsieur* is mate. It is a matter of eight moves—so, so.'

The demonstration was conclusive, and although Uncle Doremus gasped, both with vexation and with astonishment, he had to admit that there was no possibility of escape. Uncle Martin took snuff vigorously, sneezed repeatedly, and so far forgot his habitual dignity as to ejaculate, 'Astonishing, perfectly amazing!' Nevertheless he was too experienced a player not to be able to admire the beauty of the newcomer's play, and although his expressed sympathy with Uncle Dorie, who persisted in calling it a piece of bad luck, lacked nothing in its sincerity, at the back of his mind glimmered the thought that his friend had been much too precipitate. He, Martin, would be more cautious. It was true he was a more expert player than Doremus, but so palpable a trap ... really there was no excuse for the defeat.

He glanced sharply at Tins as these reflections coursed through his mind, for he knew that men's characters reveal themselves in moments of triumph and defeat. A smirk on the part of Mabuis, an exaggerated expression of satisfaction such as a conqueror might have been expected to show—had he observed these on the pale face of the man who sat opposite his friend, Uncle Martin would have got up, bidden the newcomer a courteous good night, and listed him with those with whom one does not get on terms of lasting friendship. But the expression on Tin's face was such as Uncle Martin himself would have assumed under similar conditions. It showed no more satisfaction than was allowable, and a tinge of deprecatory negation that the old man found entirely praiseworthy. The man, he reflected, was a gentleman, who knew how to win like one. Very well, he would find out if the man could also lose like a gentleman.

'I shall have to guard our reputations, Brother Doremus,' he said, getting up to take the chair that his friend had vacated. 'I see *Meneer* Mabuis is a clever player, but we too have our tricks. If *Meneer* will be so good ...'

Tins held the pieces behind his back, and the old man chose according to the custom, 'Little one, big one, little one come; little one, big one, little one go,' and winning the toss, elected to play with the white. He started the *Giucco Piano*, and was gratified to find that his opponent seemed equally earnest and determined. The first few moves were made rapidly, for both knew them by heart, but the game developed, as Uncle Martin had meant that it should, into that close, cramped position which is characteristic of the *Giucco Piano*. Uncle Dorie followed each separate move with eager attention, and the play was conducted in tense silence, for when Tins had ventured a remark, Uncle Martin had silenced him with a peremptory gesture. Little by little, the old man developed his attack, and found to his satisfaction that his objective appeared to be hidden from his opponent. Cautious and careful, he studied his own position, but it appeared to be sound, and his play became bolder. When Tins checked his king, he moved it into safety, but apparently he had overlooked something for he saw checkmate to white in four moves ahead. Long and anxiously he pondered over the situation, but he could see no way out of it, and handing his snuff box to his opponent, he leaned back in his chair.

'*Meneer* has the better,' he said, trying to hide the disappointment he felt. 'It is a fair win.'

'If *Monsieur* had not been so bold as to move the queen,' observed Tins, deprecatingly, 'it would have been, possibly, *Monsieur's* game. The position was then even, but that move gave me the advantage. *Monsieur* is, if I may be permitted to say so, a strong player, and it has been a pleasure to engage with him. Now, if the gentlemen will allow me, I should like to watch them play.'

'Oh no,' said Uncle Dorie, sharply. 'You must give us our revenge. We cannot allow a newcomer to vanquish us like this, can we Brother? With your permission, Brother Martin, I shall try my skill.'

'Do so, Brother Doremus. And beware of traps. Our friend is a strong player— much the strongest among us, I daresay. But it is good play. I will get ...' He was going to say, 'I will get the wine glasses,' but he suddenly remembered the man's failing. It would not do to put temptation in his way. But a cup of coffee could do no harm. So while Doremus and Tins settled down to their game, the old man went into the back regions to find Magriet. When he came back, followed by Regina bearing the coffee cups on a tray, Uncle Dorie was desperately struggling to disentangle himself from a situation that to the expert eye was as hopeless as the one in the former game.

They played until a late hour. Everardus came in and sat down to watch them, but hardly dared speak, for their concentration was too intense. One game Uncle Martin, by brilliant boldness, snatched from his opponent, but against that Tins had five to his credit. When it was time to retire, the two old gentlemen shook him vigorously by the hand, and declared him to be one of the best players they had ever met.

'It is something one learns as one learns other things, *Monsieur* Nolte,' said Mabuis, as he prepared to go out of doors, for his bedroom was on the farther side of the house. 'Not altogether a pastime and not altogether a study, but something between. The gentlemen are good players, but *Monsieur* van Aard is reckless, and gives his opponent altogether too much credit for simplicity. Which is not good, *Monsieur* Nolte, for humanity is not simple. It is cunning, *Monsieur*. I wish you to sleep well, *Monsieur*, and I thank you again for your kindness to me. Pierre Mabuis has rarely had so pleasant an evening as this, and that with people who are not ashamed to play with him.'

Chapter 14

One of the peculiarities of the Valley was its frank acceptance of whatever was laid down by the ecclesiastical authority it recognised. Its deference to such authority amounted, indeed, almost to subservience, for it never questioned even though it might have misgivings about the practical or theoretical value of the opinion it was called upon to subscribe to. It had unswerving faith in the capacity of its pastor to lead it aright in everything that might be considered as belonging to the cultural or the spiritual side of life. In things more material, the church took care not to obtrude its opinion. Had it done so the Valley would, very probably, have acquiesced, as it did in everything else, but the strain might have been too great and a readjustment at some future date might have been difficult. But in matters of faith, social custom, education and ethical relations, the church decreed and the Valley followed. It is true, the Valley did not know, and would have been scandalised if someone had hinted, that it gave its conscience into the hands of its spiritual leaders. It would have been still more shocked had anyone declared that the difference between the congregation here and priest-ridden communities elsewhere was infinitesimal. Nevertheless it abnegated much of its own independence of thought in deference to what the church, or what had become ecclesiastical custom, laid down for its guidance.

Such willingness to accept matters that were not quite beyond criticism, on the mere opinion of the pastor, was useful now, when the question of Tins's appointment as teacher to the *Knolkloof* school came on the carpet for discussion. The magistrate, consulted by the pastor himself, had seen no harm in trying the newcomer, although he confessed that he had not been able to glean much about Mabuis's antecedents, and could only assert that officially there was nothing against the man. So Tins was instituted, on trial, as teacher. The pastor came down for the occasion, delivered a fatherly address to the assembled children and such parents as had turned up to be present, and exhorted all to give the new *'Meester'* (master) a patient and co-operative chance. He stayed to listen when Tins took the class in hand, and although he did not quite approve of the new teacher's methods in everything, he nodded his head as he listened, and went back to tell the magistrate that the man would do.

The Valley took Tins with philosophical calm, amounting almost to indifference at first. The fact that he was a Roman Catholic and therefore, in its opinion, little better than a heathen, had been discounted by the knowledge that the pastor had approved of him, and was further weakened by the pious hope, publicly expressed in many quarters, that it would not be long before Mabuis would see the error of his ways and enter the true fold, where to be sure he would be received with open arms. His quaint manner of speech, his absurd gesticulations, and his prickly touchiness—the Valley put that down to his foreign nature, for it firmly refused to accept him as 'one of our people,' although Tins spoke Dutch quite as well as most of those with whom he conversed, and the variation of it which in the Valley was used for conversational purposes and sometimes written for epistolary use, with fluency and idiomatic facility. In those days this variation of the parent language, which is now called 'Afrikaans' and which differs from high Dutch in its disregard of inflexions, its peculiar construction of sentences, and its predilection for the use of the double negative and of diminutives, had not attained to the dignity of official and semi-official recognition. The Valley talked it to its Native servants, whose only language it was, to its children who had not yet mastered the grammatical high Dutch, and familiarly when it conversed *inter pares* about commonplace things. It never dreamed of using it, when it addressed the Deity, officialdom, or superiors, for then the high Dutch was imperative, and the Valley had kept its high Dutch singularly pure and free from alien admixture. Seniors like Uncle Martin and Uncle Dorie spoke it with almost as good an accent, and certainly as grammatically correctly, as did the Reverend Mr de Smee who had received his education in Holland and could converse in several languages, including Arabic. For the Reverend Sybrand had passed his superior examination and had obtained his *Acte Classicale*, which permitted him to write the letters 'VDM' behind his name, and qualified him for an appointment in the East Indies. To obtain these distinctions, as everyone knew, he had had to prove his knowledge not only of the classics, but also of Oriental languages, and although he protested that these acquirements rusted very soon through disuse, it was generally understood that when he went to Cape Town he practised his Arabic on a Malay Imam and talked Latin with the learned pastor at the Paarl. In the Valley the Reverend Sybrand represented the acme of culture, and it was perhaps well for the Valley that such was the case, for the pastor was a mild-mannered, gentle-souled man, whose influence made itself felt far beyond his immediate environment.

Although more than a century had gone by since the settlement in the Valley had been established, the community, during that time, had made little cultural progress, for obvious reasons. It was far removed from the cultural influence that radiated from the capital, and it was absorbed in its daily task of earning from the soil that was sometimes so stubborn and always so wayward and undependable a living. It followed its humdrum, routine life with equanimity and philosophical calm, rarely troubling itself about things that lay outside its immediate sphere of influence, and it was, by nature and through such education as it had received, intensely conservative. In some respects it was even pig-headedly obstinate. It admitted of no other interpretation of its faith than that laid down in the short catechism, and it sternly ignored all innovation that presumed to criticise what it believed to be utterly beyond human criticism. It had been horridly shocked when the pastor had explained that the conjuration to the sun to stand still must be accepted symbolically, as there could be no doubt about the fact that it was the earth and not the sun which turned and completed a circuit in one day. That explanation had led to questions and interpellations at the church council, and the Reverend Sybrand had been hard put to it to defend his position. Only his pastoral authority had won the day for him, and since then the matter had never again been referred to.

Because of its isolation and its absorption in its own communal interest, to the exclusion of other interests beyond its immediate ken, the Valley remained in that blissful state of complacency which is characteristic of those who through ignorance and inexperience of the world are without proper standards of comparison. It felt no need for such standards, believing that it already possessed sufficient data to enable it to judge of a case or of an individual by the application of such measures as it was accustomed to employ within itself. It took a man for what he was, not for what he might be, and when it found that he was unfortunately a Roman Catholic, a species of which it had no certain knowledge, but about which it imagined various things that were not virtuous, it marked him with a black mark which, however, it was prepared to efface when it found that there was really no vice in the fellow. That was how it had received Tins, and it was quite ready to continue to look upon him with tolerant indifference until such time as he could do something against the canons of the Valley that showed him to be otherwise than what they had believed him to be capable of being.

It was three months after the arrival of Tins at the farm when the *Knolkloof* school committee met for its quarterly meeting in Everardus's dining room on a Saturday morning. Winter was still awake in the air, and the members of the committee were clad in their warmest clothing, fustian and corduroy predominating, and necks being wrapped round with several pieces of knitted scarf. As it was morning, there were no braziers of glowing coals such as would have circulated round the room had the gathering been held in the evening. On the side-table stood a coffee can, with a jug of hot milk and many cups and pannikins, ready for those who wished to refresh and warm themselves by partaking of this homely beverage, and on the sideboard were set out a carafe of sweet wine, a plate of almonds and raisins, and half a dozen old fashioned wine glasses.

Round the already polished cedarwood dining table that everyone admired, the members grouped themselves. At the head sat the Reverend Mr de Smee, *ex officio* chairman of the committee, wearing a little velvet skullcap to warm his bald crown. Next to him sat Uncle Martin, with the senior Elder whose surname was Dietleefs but who was familiarly and generally addressed as Uncle Roelf by those who were his juniors and as Brother Roelf by those who were his contemporaries, on his right hand. On the other side of the pastor sat a tall, gaunt-looking man, with a goatee beard, and an expression of discontent on his face. Jeremias or Mias Bartman, whose dignity in the community was similar to that of Everardus as both were Deacons, was a hypochondriacal individual who would have been classified today as belonging to the category of leptosomes whose fate, had he been a well-to-do man living in a community that boasted of modern medicinal refinements, would have been to wander from sanatorium to sanatorium and from quack to quack in the fond expectation of getting someone to cure him of diseases from which he certainly did not suffer. Here, in the Valley community, Nephew Mias was looked upon as a sterlingly honest, crabbed and rather pernickety fellow who had a 'stomach.' The Valley carefully refrained from particularising in what way Bartman's gastric organ was different from that of any other inhabitant of the Valley, but it put his ill-temper, his crabbedness and his total want of any sense of humour down to the fact that there was a difference, and it thought it a sin and a shame that so honest and sensible a man should go through life burdened by an ill-functioning part of his anatomy that the doctor could not put right. It forgave him, accordingly, his mannerisms, and indulged him to an extent that was calculated to spoil him and to strengthen him in his belief that he was suffering from incurable diseases. As a result his conversation generally tended towards medical therapy, and his devotional exercises were made contributory to an exposition, for the benefit of those who listened to them and immensely to his own satisfaction, of the state of disrepair of his bodily organs. As a matter of fact, Nephew Mias was a healthy, strong man who, when forced by circumstances to do so, could do a strong man's daily work on his farm and eat a hearty meal.

Next to him sat Uncle Dorie and, at the end of the table, facing the chairman, sat Pierre Mabuis, who as teacher was also *ex officio* secretary to the committee, and kept the minutes. He was provided with quill pens, which he sharpened finely with the end of a small pen-knife that he had himself manufactured from a portion of the blade of a pocket-knife, with a quire of blue ruled foolscap paper, and a pot of loose sand and an old-fashioned ink-horn. Between him and the senior sat Elder Everardus.

The proceedings were opened by the pastor with a short prayer, responded to all by the members with a subdued 'Amen,' succeeded by a general clearing of throats preparatory to discussion. The short account of the previous meeting, written down by Magriet at her husband's dictation, having been read and unanimously passed as correct, and there being nothing for discussion arising out of it, the Reverend Sybrand, fixing his horn-rimmed spectacles firmly on his nose, intimated that the committee had first of all to consider a complaint.

'Our new teacher has now been with us for a couple of months,' he stated, 'and so far as I am aware he has done his work well. There is, however, a verbal complaint which the Brothers committee members ought to take cognisance of. I had occasion, on my visit to the place of the widowed Sister Priem last week, to discuss the matter, of which Brother Mias already knows the gist, with the complainant, and I understood from the widowed Sister Priem that she had commissioned Brother Mias to lay the details of her grievance before this committee. Brother Mias, the word is with you.'

'Your Reverence and Brothers committee members,' said the gaunt man, speaking with a lugubrious solemnity that appeared to be in complete harmony with the expression of complete misery on his face, 'the widowed Sister Priem has, as you are all aware, a son of hers, her only son, attending our school. On several occasions, she asserts, and the assertion is a truthful one as I can personally vouch for, she asserts that her son has returned home much too late to attend to his duties on the farm, which consist in separating the calves from the mothers, preliminary to the evening milking. Questioned as to the cause of this dilatoriness, the youth asserted—and neither I nor the widowed Sister Priem can imagine any reason for the boy bluntly telling an untruth, as he is by nature inclined to honesty and open speech—asserted that *Meester* had kept him in because he had not done his share of copy-writing. That, Brothers, is the widowed Sister's complaint. She has no grievance against the *Meester*, but she is of opinion that discipline in the school should be maintained by other methods, less calculated to upset the working arrangements of her farm. The boy, after all, is her son, and she has a right to that part of his time not included in the period which we have agreed should be allotted to classwork. I have spoken.'

'Brother Mias has stated the complaint fairly, Brothers,' said the pastor. 'I may add that the widowed Sister Priem, when she discussed the matter with me, implicitly disassociated herself from any criticism of the methods of our teacher, and that I, for one, would not have condoned anything in the nature of adverse criticism, feeling that such would be a reflection upon this committee. The matter, therefore, seems to me a simple one. Perhaps the teacher, now present, would like to favour this committee with his remarks on the complaint as set forth by Brother Mias. In justice to him, Brothers, we should have his side of the question. *Meneer* Mabuis, you have the word.'

'Your Reverence,' said Tins, rising respectfully and bowing first towards the helm of the table and then to the right and left, 'that *garçon* of the *douairiere* Priem—its name, gentlemen, is Frikkie, and it is a *bête*—an animal, gentlemen, that is like an *âne*, what you call a donkey. Of a stupidity and a laziness *incroyable*, not to be believed, gentlemen. I set him a fair copy. I wrote for him an exhortatory sentence, "Regard the ant that is not sluggish and be like unto him," and I say, I order, gentlemen, the young man to copy it four-five times. I attend to the other children, who are not *cigales*—grasshoppers, gentlemen—and when I turn to Frikkie I find he has not done a line, not a letter, not a comma. Do I lose my temper, gentlemen? No! You would not like a teacher who loses his temper. You would say—quite rightly, gentlemen—this person is unfitted to teach our children how to control their tempers. I say briefly, "Boy, you will write those lines four-five times if you sit here until we see the cross shining in the sky." I do that one day; I do that two days; I do that the third day, and each day Frikkie goes home a little earlier. And each day I have four-five copies of Frikkie's writing, the second better than the first, and the third better than the second.'

'You have heard the *Meester's* explanation—sit down, *Meester*,' said the parson, 'and the matter is now open for discussion. Brother Martin, will you favour us with your views, please?'

'I am of opinion,' said Brother Martin, precisely, tendering his snuffbox to the senior Elder, 'that the complaint may be dismissed. We should, as a committee, uphold the authority of our teacher.'

'Yes, but ...' interrupted the senior Elder, waiting to express his views before titillating his nostrils with Uncle Martin's ratafia, 'there is another side to the question. We all know the lad Frikkie. He is a lazy young fellow, and inclined to be obstreperous ...'

'Having no father, Brother,' interrupted Brother Mias, with a little animation in his lugubrious voice.

'Having no father, as you say,' went on the senior Elder. 'Therefore all the more reason why he should be trained into habits of industry and obedience. And is it not for our teacher so to train him? Is it, I ask you, Brothers, a fit punishment for disobedience that a boy should be kept in? I speak under correction, but my own view is that the application of a quince stick to the lad's seat would be much more efficacious, and would at the same time serve as a wholesome example to the class.'

'Therein I wholly support you, Brother,' said Uncle Dorie. 'We have repeated scriptural authority, as His Reverence will bear me out in saying, for what you have just said. In the thirteenth chapter of Proverbs it is written, "He that spareth his rod hateth his son, but he that loveth him chasteneth him betimes," and in the fifth chapter—I do not remember the verse—we are told, "Folly is bound in the heart of a child, but the rod of correction shall drive it far from him." Nowhere in the good Book, as far as my memory serves me, are we bidden to keep a child in for his disobedience. I, too, do not wish to criticise our teacher, but I cannot refrain from expressing my conviction that scriptural methods such as those you have alluded to, Brother, are more likely to conduce to good upbringing and the eradication of sloth and disobedience than these new-fangled ways. If,' concluded Uncle Dorie, vigorously, 'my son refuses to do what he is told I lamn him, and I have found that he does not repeat his refusal.'

'The widowed Sister Priem,' remarked Brother Mias, in a voice as if he were intoning the litany, 'has nothing whatever against corporal punishment. In fact she confessed to me that she would thank the *Meester* if he administered a proper thrashing to the lad, he being now grown beyond her capacity to hit him forcibly enough to inspire contrition.'

'If the *Meester* is incapable of using the rod,' said Uncle Dorie, 'I daresay Brother Everardus, who is generally at hand, could be looked upon to undertake the task of correction ...'

'That would, I am afraid,' said the pastor, smilingly, 'hardly redound to the credit of our teacher, Brothers, if he were to call in outside help to enable him to maintain authority. I opine that *Meester* has been diffident in exerting his authority in the direction suggested by Brothers Doremus and Mias, because we have not, so far as I know, regularised his position. That being the case, Brothers, I suggest that it would be as well, before we go any further, to discuss his position. Are the Brothers agreed? Very well, then, I shall ask *Meneer* Mabuis to leave us while this point is under discussion. Brother Nolte, will you please act as amanuensis to the committee for the time *Meester* is absent from this meeting?'

Tins resigned his papers, ink-horn and quills to Everardus, and, bowing gravely to the committee, retired gracefully, and in his absence the members proceeded to deliberate. They drew up a formal contract, phrased in correct and impressive high Dutch, of which the following is a literal translation.

> Contract entered this 20th day of August in the year of our Lord one thousand eight hundred and forty-two between the Committee of the *Knolkloof* Farm School in the Valley District, on the one hand, as representatives of the parents, and Pierre Mabuis,

hereinafter designated as the Teacher, on the other hand.

1. The said Committee hereby contracts and undertakes to employ the aforementioned Teacher as Teacher in sole charge, subject to the qualifying conditions stated in clause 3 of this contract, of the *Knolkloof* Farm School, at an annual stipend of £50 (Fifty) pounds English sterling to be paid quarterly or at such periods as may be most convenient to the Committee.

2. The said teacher to be honest, sober, industrious, and conscientious, to give five hours teaching service daily, with the exception of Sundays and holidays and such periods as the Committee exempts as being periods of vacation for the school, in harvest or lambing time, such honesty, sobriety, diligence, and conscientiousness to be judged by the Committee which may, by majority vote, ask the said Teacher to resign if it considers that the said Teacher has been wanting in any or all of these requisite qualifications.

3. The said Teacher to give instruction in smooth writing, the tables of multiplication and simple arithmetic according to the four rules, reading and the use of the globe, but to abstain from giving any other instruction or in any way to interfere when such instruction is given by other persons properly appointed for that purpose, in scripture, hymn-singing, or the exposition of the short catechism, instruction in these subjects for the present, subject to such other arrangements as the Committee may make, being in the hands of Sister Magaretha Nolte.

4. The said Committee, realising that it conduces to the material and moral welfare of the said Teacher to feel that he is not wholly dependent upon his teaching efforts, and realising further that it is of importance to the community that the Teacher should feel himself settled and at home among us, undertakes, and hereby commissions on its behalf one of its members, to whit Everardus Nolte, Deacon and owner in freehold of the farm at *Knolkloof*, to present to the said Teacher at the expiration of each calendar year, four ewes sheep and six ewes goats to be kept with the herds of the said Everardus Nolte and to have free grazing together with their progeny. The accumulation from such sheep and goats to be, together with the mothers, the sole property of the said Teacher, by him to be disposed of as he may deem fit, provided they be not sold or bartered to Natives.

Considerable discussion arose at this point, it being considered that, in view of the teacher's well known 'failing,' a substantive clause should be inserted in the agreement prohibiting the pledging of the sheep as credit for the supply of liquor, but this was finally voted against, chiefly on the reasonable argument advanced by Uncle Martin to the effect that if the Committee started by distrusting its teacher, it might as well look out for a substitute.

5. The Committee delegates to the said Teacher as such full parental authority over the pupils attending the *Knolkloof* Farm School, subject to the aforementioned qualifying conditions stated in clause 3, and subject also to such regulations as may be made by government as a condition to the granting of a government subsidy to the said school. The Committee undertakes, on its part, to uphold the authority of the teacher in all reasonable matters, and to see that no outside interference militates against the welfare of the school or the authority of the teacher.

Signed on behalf of the Committee
Sybrand de Smee VDM, Chairman
Martin Rekker, Vice Chairman
Signed on his own behalf
Pierre Mabuis, Teacher

These preliminary proceedings for regularising the teacher's position having been satisfactorily concluded, Tins was recalled to fix his signature to the document, which he did, after hearing it, in his neat Italian script. Thereupon the pastor, in a few well chosen words, congratulated him on his new post and wished him God's blessing on his work, to which Pierre Mabuis responded with much emotion, which the Committee fully appreciated and understood, and resumed his place as scribe.

'Now, Brothers,' said the Reverend Sybrand, 'we must now return to the matter of the widowed Sister Priem's complaint. It seems to me that no good purpose will be served by further discussing it. Teacher has heard the views expressed by the Committee, and knows now that we have delegated full parental responsibility to him over the those who are *in statu pupillari* under him. He will doubtless know what to do in cases of insubordination, wilful neglect of duty or work, and such other delinquencies as we need not further particularise. Regarding the complaint itself, it seems to me that the best thing this Committee can do is to instruct its secretary to communicate its findings verbally to the widowed Sister Priem, which will at the same time enable Teacher to make the widowed Sister's personal acquaintance. It is surely right and proper that Teacher should be on a footing of personal acquaintance with the parents of all children attending our school and I am sure that Brother Nolte will arrange for him to visit the widowed Sister Priem at a time convenient for both parties. Is that agreed upon? Yes? Very well. The secretary will please minute accordingly. And now, Brothers, we proceed to the third item on the agenda, which is the matter of vacation time. Brother Mias, you have the word.'

The committee discussed the question of vacation time with due seriousness. Conflicting opinions were expressed, but the consensus of the meeting was that there should be four terms a year, with intervals at Easter, during the ploughing season, at harvest time, and at the end of the year. A preliminary timetable was drawn up, and the Committee then delved into the different subject of finance. It was agreed that funds should be raised through the church council, that Everardus should act as treasurer, and that the magistrate should be consulted on the point as to whether the school could hope for a government grant. Finally the pastor exhorted the committee to advertise the establishment of the school throughout the District, and to get pupils from the farther-lying farms, Everardus having undertaken to house these if their parents were willing to pay towards their keep.

'Brother Nolte's offer,' remarked Uncle Martin, 'is most generous and timely. I myself, unfortunately, cannot make a similar offer, for my homestead is too far removed from *Knolkloof* to permit me to take boarders for the school. But I am willing to bear my share, and I propose that we start a boarding fund to which I am willing to contribute fifty pounds a year.'

'Aye,' said the senior Elder, 'that is well offered and I, although in comparison with Brother Rekker a poor man, would willingly contribute a similar amount, but the question arises—do we do well to offer so much? Does anyone value what he obtains for nothing? I imagine not, Your Reverence. And for so valuable a thing as one's education one should be prepared to pay something oneself. I do not hold with having everything free, and running to the church council or the government to provide for us what we should, if we were man enough to do it, get for ourselves.'

'Precisely my own opinion,' chimed in Uncle Doremus. 'Have we not done enough, Brothers, in starting this school, guaranteeing the stipend of our teacher, and giving our friends the opportunity of educating their children? Should we do more? I think not. After all, as the apostle admonishes us in the second epistle to the Corinthians, in I believe the eighth chapter, "If there be first a willing mind, it is accepted according to what a man hath, and not according to what he hath not".'

'Education,' said the pastor reflectively, 'is such a valuable thing, Brothers, that I doubt if we should apply to it the ordinary qualifications we are accustomed to apply to daily things of more material value. I should like to see it free, and general, but the time for that is not yet. Still, there is much in what Brother Doremus has said, and I do not believe that there are many in the District who cannot make some sacrifice on behalf of their children. For those who are really destitute, however, we should make provision, and I think the Brothers may safely leave it to the church council to decide in what cases to extend the helping hand of charity.'

There being no further items on the agenda, the Committee adjourned, and Everardus found himself button-holed by Brother Mias and forced to listen to a long disquisition on the merits of lavender-water as a remedy against flatulence.

Chapter 15

In his fourth year of occupation of the farm *Knolkloof*, Everardus took advantage of the yearly repeated invitation of Uncle Dorie to accompany the Elder and his family after the New Year to the seaside. The preparations for this holiday were on a grand scale. The wagon was prepared, and the team of selected horses, ten in number, seemed to Everardus to be more than would be required for the journey, but Uncle Dorie assured him that he himself took twelve and only just managed to get through the sand, though his wagon was lighter and he knew all the deviations. Ample provisions—dried sausages, biltong, cured flanks of home-fed pigs, sacks of biscuits made from the must buns that Regina had baked assiduously, immediately after the New Year festivities, and a half a half-aum of wine—were loaded on the wagon, together with blankets, mattresses, utensils, and shooting-gear. *Knolkloof* was left in the charge of Matryk and Sylvester, who declared themselves quite competent to look after it in the master's absence, but Regina went with the mistress and the children, and Tins was invited to accompany them. A couple of Native boys to look after the horses, and a small Native girl to help with the housework, were included in the party, which set out one morning before daybreak on the road that lay along the River bank until it reached the Village and then turned sharply to the left, to cross the River and enter the barren, sandy tract that separated the Valley from the sea.

So late in summer the veld looked sere and dry, although the river still displayed clumps of greenery, and the mesembryanthemums still put forth late blossoms of vivid mauve and magenta on the hillside. The ford was deep and treacherous, banks of shifting sand making the passage dangerous to those who did not know it. But thanks to the guidance of his Native boys, Everardus, who sat on the front seat handling the ribbons of his long but perfectly trained team, reached the farther bank safely, and outspanned there to rest his horses and give his party the opportunity of having their midday meal. Under the shade of a large wild-fig tree, rooted in a rock cleft on the River bank, the blankets were spread out, and the Natives busied themselves with the preparation of a meal. The green rhinoceros bush, that is impregnated with a mastic-like gum, made excellent firewood, and over the perfumed ash that it left, the chops, cut the night before from the loin of a freshly slaughtered sheep, were broiled, gathering into their tender succulence the aromatic odour of the brushwood smoke, and emerging from their fiery ordeal as titbits fit for an epicure. Coffee was brewed in the large iron kettles that had made the journey suspended to the back axle of the wagon where they had tinkled in company with a gridiron and a frying pan. Rich, aromatic coffee, strong and black, which, when the grounds had been induced to settle by the simple method of stirring the decoction with a piece of glowing wood, was poured into the earthenware pannikins, diluted with fresh milk and sweetened with honey for the children, and with sugar crystals, which were expensive and had to be doled out carefully, for their Elders. Tins, to whom these camping arrangements, notwithstanding his vagrant experience, were new, cut the heavy homemade loaves, and buttered them liberally in the intervals that he could spare from his admiration of the scenery. To Everardus there was nothing very striking or admirable in the view, which he thought by no means so perfect as that which could be seen from his own *stoep*. But Tins had brought his sketch book, and made drawings of the mountains far in the north, sketching rapidly with great skill—to the admiration of the Natives who looked upon him as something of a wizard. After a couple of hours' rest, the journey was resumed, and soon Everardus began to realise that Uncle Dorie's account of the road had not been exaggerated. It was a mere sandy track, with the sand so heavy that the wheels of the wagon sunk deeply into it, and the team had to strain and tug to advance. More than once Tins and the Natives had to get down and push to help the vehicle out of some particularly clinging stretch of sand where the wind had blown the yellow dune on to the road itself. Here and there were welcome deviations, where other travellers had trodden a new path through stunted bush that yielded a better hold for the wagon wheels, and these were used wherever possible. But it was a long and wearisome road, through flat, unbroken country, bush-covered for the most part, but with areas that were open and windswept, sandy stretches encrusted with sparkling salt crystals, and sparsely grown with such grass as lives in this saline soil, with creeping mesembryanthemums, dwarf euphorbias, and the fleshy-stemmed stapelias whose beautiful, velvety flowers smell of carrion.

Everardus had planned to reach the Bay that night but out of consideration for his horses he determined to camp some ten miles away from his destination. A suitable site was selected, the canvas manger was stretched along the *disselboom*, or shaft of the wagon, and filled with a mixture of chopped chaff, handfuls of barley and crushed maize. The horses were knee-haltered and allowed to stray where they liked, one of the Native boys being told off to look after them until it was time to tie them up to the manger. The mattresses and blankets were spread out on the sand, and the mistress and Regina prepared the evening meal, while Everardus and Tins sat on the front seat of the wagon and placidly smoked their pipes. Round the camp fire that night Tins showed himself an admirable camp mate. He entertained the company, the Natives squatting respectfully round their own little fire a few paces away, segregated but yet part of the audience, to a selection of airs on his flute. He played sad airs, melancholy in the extreme, which delighted the Natives, and jovial tunes which pleased them still more, the *rigadoon* which heralded the approach of the prisoner about to run the gauntlet in his own regiment, the *mazurka* which in the Company's time grand folk danced to in the Castle, the *fandango* which the Creoles loved, and the weird syncopated chant of the stabbers at a *Khalifa*. He told them stories in his queer, outlandish Dutch, interspersed with words whose meaning none of them understood, of witches and demons and of wild cruelty in eastern lands. Regina and the Natives listened open-mouthed and wide-eyed, and Magriet forgot that it was long past bedtime for the children.

Under the stars that twinkled so grandly above, Everardus and Tins sat and chatted and drank coffee when the others had retired. It was the first time that Everardus had found an opportunity of really coming to grips with the man, and he availed himself of it and found it so intensely interesting that it was far in the night before he sought his blankets. It was a conversation that cleaned up much that had been mysterious to him. Tins, he found, had been in charge of a squad of the Hottentot Regiment on the particular occasion that Everardus remembered so well. It was there, as he frankly admitted, that he had seen *Meneer* Tereg, and now that *Meneer* Tereg, if he might so express himself, was really *Meneer* Tereg, although his name was Nolte, he might perhaps be permitted to enquire why these things were kept secret. It was of course none of his business, and he had given his word to *Meneer* Tereg, who was his bene-factor to whom he would be eternally and unequivocally grateful, but he would merely express his opinion that such things could not be kept secret for long. And *Meneer* Nolte would please bear in mind that there was nothing to be ashamed of in the business. Name of a pipe, no one had the slightest right to think that there could be anything to be ashamed of in the business.

'It is perhaps as you say, Teacher,' replied Everardus, wearily. 'But the fact is, I haven't the courage to declare myself. I cannot look my friends in the face, yet, if I spoke up to them and told them what I have done ...'

'But *Meneer* Nolte need not say a word,' exclaimed Tins, convincingly. 'If *Meneer* Nolte would be good enough to leave the matter to me ...'

'No—no—no,' said Everardus vehemently. 'That is not to be dreamed of. If it has to be known, I shall do it myself. But not yet. And I would ask Teacher to refrain from any allusion ...'

'That I will do,' promised Tins. '*Meneer* Nolte need apprehend no indiscretion from me. It is, as I have said, none of my business, and it is easy for Pierre Mabuis to forget that he was ever present at ... at something that *Meneer* Nolte wishes to forget. But all the same, it seems to me, if I may be permitted to voice my opinion, that *Meneer* is making a mountain out of a molehill. If *Meneer's* friends knew of it, why they would think of it as I do, and make a laugh of it, a thing for a smile, and the worst would be, belike, that *Meneer* gets a nickname.'

'I could not bear it, yet,' asserted Everardus, fiercely. 'And in any case I must ask Magriet—my wife has a say in the matter. So no more about it, Teacher. But I am glad that we have had this talk. It is ill going through life uncertainly.'

The following day, after several hours of slow progression through sand that seemed to become deeper every mile, they reached the Bay. A lovely Bay, rock-ringed on the left, with a half-circuit of smooth white sand, and a rocky island half a mile away from the shore, an island tenanted by millions of birds, penguins, snake-birds, cormorants, terns and gulls that flew in serried regiments to and from their fishing grounds. This was the seaside resort of the Valley. Here, on the sandy ridge some three hundred yards from high-water mark, some of the farmers had built themselves seaside houses, roughly made habitations of deal planks or bamboo thatched with sedge, with wooden steps, standing bare and forlorn in the sun, without a single tree to afford shade. Fresh water could be got from a spring some miles inland, or by digging between high- and low-water, but the little stream that entered the Bay was brackish and its water was scarcely suitable for domestic purposes. Uncle Dorie's seaside house was slightly larger and a trifle more pretentious than those of his neighbours, and in it Everardus and his family found hospitable shelter, and a noon-day meal ready for them. They could appreciate, after the weary journey in that scorching sun, the luscious sweet melon, whose slices were eighteen inches long and whose flesh was deliciously cool and fragrant; the firm, large-berried hanepoort grapes, whose golden translucency made them appear so inviting; the tender, full-flavoured Bon Chretien pears; and the monstrous mulberries which appeared at dessert.

The Bay was a picturesque little bit of the South Atlantic, whose shore stretched rockless and low for miles on either side, a line of dried seaweed, principally composed of the heavy sea-bamboo that grew so prolifically in the shallower water, marking the high level of the summer tides. Beyond that lay ridges of yellowish-white sand, sparsely grown with bush and creeping mesembryanthemums, and beyond that again the flat veld, bush-covered and grass-grown, stretched endlessly into the distance landwards, without a single high peak or tor to relieve the monotony of its levelness. But in that plain of bush-grown sand, as Everardus discovered afterwards, were the lagoons, the great salt pans where the Valley folk went to collect salt; brackish lagoons so shallow that one could walk through them without getting wet more than waist high, weed and sedge-ringed, with open water in the middle where innumerable waterfowl disported themselves. There long twin-lines of pink flamingoes stood, sunning themselves from early morning until sunset, when they flew away to the west, in serried ranks that wheeled overhead with matchless precision and orderly discipline, like a flock of starlings. There, too, the big coursers ran between the bushes, stopping to stare at the newcomers whom they had not yet learned to fear, while many species of duck, coot, and tern sported in the shallows and nested in the clumps of reed-grass that grew near the edges of the pan. In the country surrounding the pans there was plenty of game; partridges, whose clear, fluting calls were to be heard at daybreak and in the cool of the afternoon; bustards, whose rattling cry when they were flushed rang raucous through the quiet air; tall grey and blue herons; the ponderous pelicans that came sedately in from the sea and as regularly flew back to some islet where they nested; *duiker*-buck and grey-buck that lay lazily at rest between the stunted bushes; and big land tortoises that crawled through the long grass and made little pathways of their own towards the pan water. The veld was full of life, teeming with smaller animals and in springtime it was a garden of colour; but now, in late summer, it appeared dun-coloured and sere, and to anyone not knowing its wealth, almost lifeless and barren. Yet at sunset it flushed into beauty, for the long stretches of brown and grey took on coloured reflections from the sky, and wonderful waves of ruby and blush-rose seemed to pulsate over the landscape, harmonising with the grey of the bush and the brown of the uncovered clays, while overhead the setting sun died in splendours as vivid as those any mythical dolphin ever scattered over its polished skin before it expired.

At the Bay the community was nomadic, coming and going with the season which lasted only for a few months at the end of the summer, when the heat of the Valley induced many farmers to come to the seaside with their families, just as Everardus had come, and Uncle Dorie came regularly every year. There were some half a dozen houses, and on Sundays, when service was held on the beach, there were about fifty people present, or, when the Reverend Sybrand came out, as he did once every season, and the congregation was augmented by the attendance of the farmers who lived in the low-lying District immediately adjacent to the Bay, perhaps eighty or a hundred all told, with their Natives. On such occasions most of the visitors camped out on the sand above the beach, bringing their own provisions with them, but sharing in the good things which the temporary residents provided. Everardus found that Uncle Dorie had provided for nearly everything. Fresh vegetables were brought in daily from one of the nearest farms, and with them came fruit of all kinds, ranging from the huge, four feet long watermelons whose ripeness was tested by percussion, or, in the case of smaller specimens, by bending them on one's head to hear the crack of the flesh splitting inside, to the wild dune berries, and the thorny but deliciously cool fruit of the spiny cactus. Most of the temporary residents baked their own bread in ovens built in the sand, and fresh butter and milk were easily obtainable from the same source as that which yielded the fruit. Fresh water and firewood were difficult to get, and the visitors had to be content with bush for fuel and with the half-brackish water of the little river, though Uncle Dorie brought in weekly several casks of clear spring water which he obtained from a farm three hours' distance from the Bay. As in the Valley, though on a much larger scale, there existed a partnership and a camaraderie between the residents which were rarely broken by misunderstandings or quarrels. The families shared many things, and from experience of such partnership had evolved a number of communal conventions and usages which it took Everardus and Magriet some time to master, but which—when mastered—made their intercourse with their neighbours much more pleasant and friendly than it might otherwise have been. Here, too, as in the Valley, hospitality and an open-handed charity were communal virtues, honoured by the poorest as well as by those better able to afford such things as conduced to comfort and good living in a community where everything was of necessity primitive and simple.

There were two safe bathing places, the one reserved for the women and the other used exclusively by the men. Mixed bathing was unknown, for all went into the sun in utter nakedness, the smallest children accompanying the women, and the boys over ten years disporting themselves in the men's pool. Both pools were admirably sheltered, rock-bound, and at low tide, fairy pools of colour and form where many-coloured anemones peopled the rock crevices and rainbow-striped rock fish swam lazily in the still water. There was deep water beyond the pools, which at high tide were flooded by the incoming waves that dashed fountains of spray over the rocks, but most of those who bathed were good swimmers, and those who could not swim never ventured beyond the safety of the shelving slope of the pool. Indeed, one of the first things that had impressed Everardus had been the skill which the Valley youth showed in swimming, a skill acquired probably by familiarity with the deep, rush-grown pools of the River. Nor were they less expert in managing their boats, in netting fish with the heavy seine nets, or in capturing, with very primitive homemade sea-tackle, vast quantities of fish, which formed the principle item on the daily menu. Never before had Everardus seen so many different varieties of fish, nor sampled so many different ways of preparing them for the table. The finest, Uncle Dorie told him, talking with expert knowledge and with the considered gravity of one to whom eating was some-thing more than a means to live, were the elf and the galleon, the former to be soused in wine and eaten with fresh butter, the latter to be broiled over the hot coals on a grid-iron and served with white, spiced sauce. After he had tasted them in this fashion, Everardus agreed with Uncle Dorie that they were excellent, but his own taste preferred the fat, juicy belly-steak cut from a young *snoek*.

Besides these, there were the fresh herrings, the lordly hake, the flakily tender but bony stumpnose, the giant *geelbek* or yellowmouth, the scarcely less magnificent *steenbras*, the brilliantly coloured red stumpnose and the sharply ridged gurnard, together with the daintily coloured rock-fish which, fried in sheep's fat so crisply that their numerous bones could be safely chewed, had the flavour of fresh sardines. There were other sea denizens too, of which the women made attractive and appetising dishes, such as the rock-limpet, the mussels, the pearl-oyster, and the cuttlefish; and round the stems of the sea bamboos grew a species of agar-agar which, steeped in water overnight, could be boiled up with wine and sugar and spices into a nourishing and much-relished jelly. There were lobsters, too, and crabs, but these the Valley folk despised, although both appealed to the educated palate, and Magriet, when she found that Uncle Dorie liked them but could not persuade his own wife to cook them, made lobster rissoles, lobster curry, and crab stew which delighted the Elder's heart.

The island in the Bay was a source of never ending wonder to the Noltes. On it bred millions of sea fowl, chief among which were the penguins, so awkward and seemingly helpless on land, yet so active and lively in the water. Their eggs, hard-boiled and eaten with vinegar, salt and butter, were excellent, and had the appearance of enormously enlarged plovers' eggs, the white coagulating into a transparent jelly in which the yolk appeared as a green ball which, when opened, was butter-coloured. These eggs were to be had for the gathering, but they palled on one after a time, and the inroads that the residents made on the breeding-places did not disturb the birds.

Amid these surroundings the Noltes spent a pleasant and recuperative month. The children learned to swim, and Magriet made many new friends by her intercourse with the women, while Everardus, introduced under the aegis of the Elder, consolidated his position in the community by his good sense, his neighbourliness, and his reputation as a 'solid man.' Pierre Mabuis, on the strength of his position with the Noltes and the van Aards and as a teacher, was admitted by the fellowship of the Bay, and received the genial welcome that the community was prepared to give to every newcomer. His talents as an entertainer, and especially his skill with the flute, soon won him such a reputation that his services were in daily, or more properly, nightly requisition. Nor

were they ever called upon in vain, for Tins was by nature companionable, liking the
communion of his fellow creatures, and solitude only when one of his touchy fits was
upon him. He was the hero and friend of the Bay's youth which, in return for the
pleasure and entertainment that his gifts of narrative, drawing, dancing, and flute-
playing gave them, instructed him in the art of swimming, an art which the *quondam*
sergeant of the Hottentot regiment had, much to his own regret, never mastered. It was
an amusing sight when Tins, shepherded by half of the older boys, stood shivering on
the edge of the pool, watching admiringly but also despairingly each of his would-be
instructors taking a standing dive into the water. His own imitative effort was usually
an ungainly plump into the pool, which hurt his body, made his skin tingle, and caused
him to swallow more bitter brash than he had intended. Nor were his attempts to swim
more successful or fortunate. He could not achieve what the youngsters achieved so
effortlessly, and his want of success preyed upon his mind and made him touchy and
irritable for the rest of the time spent in the water. Only when he had dried and clothed
himself again did his natural cheerfulness, that had carried the vagrant through his
forty odd years of Ishmaelitish gipsying, re-exert itself so that he was prepared to joke
about his failure and make vigorous good intentions for the afternoon dip. His ill
success lay in the inherent fear he felt for water. His artistic soul loved the sea, as it
loved and delighted in the mountains and the variegated colouring of the veld, but he
loved the sea perhaps more than he did anything else just because he feared it. He lay
awake at night, listening to the roar of the breakers, and speculating on the chances of
those who were out in the Bay or in the wide ocean of which the Bay water was only a
cupful. He imagined himself drowned by one of those crisp, curled waves that came
rollicking inwards to reach the strand, one of those huge Atlantic combers whose
rolling turmoil it was a delight to watch, and his body, all tangled in the streamers of
the sea-bamboo, cast up beyond low-water mark to rest on a bed of pearl-lined shell
and the sun-reddened carapaces of the crabs. Then he would shudder, and start up, and
think that he would never learn to swim, and to solace himself he would take out his
flute and pipe something melodiously sad from his recollections of Bach. The sounds
would reach the Natives who slept under the stars outside, and they would turn over
and lie listening, delightfully whispering that 'the strange *baas* was making the
wooden thing sing.'

The community took those things, as it did most things, philosophically, but one
thing it deemed its duty to criticise adversely and, for so mild-mannered a community,
strongly. It tolerated Tins's Roman Catholicism, for as a matter of fact that deviation
from established convention did not obtrude itself. Tins attended the communal
services, sang with the rest and in good tune, and made no parade of his different faith,
although he crossed himself on occasion and everyone knew that he had not been
admitted as a communicant. But the pastor and the church council, apparently, had
vouched for him, and that, the Bay community felt, as the Valley community had felt,
was quite sufficient.

But when it came to drawing naked youths in pencil on paper—why that was a
matter altogether different. 'Do you know,' Uncle Dorie had asked Everardus, with
more surprise than annoyance in his voice, 'what Teacher has done? He has drawn
young Matie Kromhout—you know Ebenezer's boy, the fourteen year old who is with
his father and the rest of the family—he has drawn the youngster standing on a rock.

Naked, Nephew Ev'rard, naked, just like your bare finger. Poodle-naked, so that you can see the lad's posteriors. It is wholly indecent, Nephew Ev'rard, and the people have spoken to me about it.'

'Then you had better talk to him,' said Everardus, with a smile, although, knowing the community, he realised what a gross impropriety Tins had been guilty of.

'*Ach*—talk to him. It is easily said. But the fellow twists everything one says, and, really Nephew Ev'rard, I don't quite know what to say. You see, it is a good picture. I would not say it was a bad one. You can tell it is Matie—it is a wonderful likeness of the boy. But naked, Nephew, naked! Ah, here you are, Teacher. I was just saying to Nephew Ev'rard here, that you really must be more discreet. You must not bring newfangled fashions into our little world, and we expect, Teacher, we expect that our—a Teacher, should have some regard to decency and what is befitting.'

'It is to me astounding, *Messieurs*,' said Tins, shrugging his shoulders and twirling the ends of his little black moustache, 'that *Monsieur le doyen* should accuse me of a thing so *degradant*. I cannot see that I have merited a charge of a nature so monstrous ...'

'Here, Teacher,' said Everardus, quickly. 'It is only that you have drawn young Matie without any clothes on. Which you mustn't do, Teacher ...'

'*Certainement* I have drawn the little fellow,' expostulated Tins, energetically, drawing from his side pocket a mass of crumpled papers and sorting one from the rest, 'I have it here—*Meneer* Nolte can see it for himself.' He handed the sketch over to Everardus, who saw it represented a boy, in that interesting stage between boyhood and adolescence when every line and curve hint at a maturity yet hidden by a youthful softness, poised on the ledge of the bathing-pool, with arms outstretched above his head, preparatory to a dive. It was a part-profile view, and the excellence of the line drawing, and the boldness of the pose appealed to Everardus, who found Uncle Dorie peering over his shoulder as he studied the sketch.

'*Meneer* Nolte can see for himself,' resumed Tins, 'the *garçon* is of a shape most beautiful—alas that his face is not that of a *Narcissus*, but *le bon Dieu* does not give all at once. But his proportions ... Look, if you please, *Meneer* Nolte, at that buttock curve ... at that body; they are for the sculptor to chisel in marble, gentlemen. And my poor sketch ... it wants the colouring; it is altogether a poor thing ...'

'It is altogether an indecent thing, Teacher,' said Uncle Dorie, severely. 'If you wish to draw the lad—and none of us has any objection to your doing that, aye, even his parents would, I daresay, like to have a sketch of him, and Nephew Ebenezer is well enough off to pay you a riksdollar for it—then draw him, in heaven's name, decently clothed.'

'But it is his body that I wish to draw,' exclaimed Tins. 'What is there indecent in the young man's body? He is clean—he swims daily in that pool, even as I do and the rest, though *diable*, I cannot yet swim nor am ever likely to. But I do not want his clothes. They make him ugly, *laid*. But *déshabillé* he is of a beauty to make one want to draw him. I have watched all the others but there is no one to compare with him. I have here—see, the men, and the *garçons* too, but look *Meneer* Nolte, look *Meneer le doyen*, there is not one to be compared with him ...'

'I don't want to see them,' said Uncle Dorie, nevertheless taking the sketches that Tins handed him, 'and I must say that I do not think you should watch a fellow creature's nakedness. It is not good. It is forbidden in the Book, and it is anyway indecent ...'

'Will *Meneer le doyen*,' riposted Tins sharply, 'give me the citation in the Book where it is forbidden?'

'Hey? The text?' said Uncle Dorie, taken at a disadvantage. 'I do not at the moment remember the exact reference. It is somewhere in Isaiah where the prophet tells us to cover the naked ...'

'But that is to inculcate our duty towards the poor,' remonstrated Tins. 'The prophetic gentleman tells us to take the poor into our house—as *Meneer* Nolte has done unto me, for which I am eternally his debtor—but he in no way enjoins us not to draw a youth so gloriously proportioned as the *fils* of *Meneer* Kromhout.'

'I do not know if your and my Book agree,' said Uncle Dorie, taking refuge in the difference of faiths which showed that he was by no means sure of his ground, 'but there are other texts apposite to the occasion, although to be sure they have escaped my memory just now. But texts or no texts, Teacher, we cannot have you drawing the boys with nothing on. Why, the women may come to see it, and I ask you, what then?'

'And I answer, *Meneer* van Aard, that if the women cannot see how beautiful it is, that young man's body, then they are indeed devoid of any soul ...'

'But man, seriously, it is indecent. You surely do not mean to tell me that it is anything but grossly indecent to show that sketch to any woman?'

'They have all seen us naked, and they know what we look like *déshabillé*, *Meneer le doyen*. And when we are sick, does anyone care if they are naked when the women minister to them ...?'

'That is altogether something different, Teacher. You twist my words. I cannot pin you down. I say it is indecent, and there is an end to it. Why, if the thing becomes known—and many of us have already seen it, for you drew it openly, publicly, at the pool, and the other lads saw it ...'

'I did so, *Meneer le doyen*. Why should I not? Look you, *Meneer le doyen*, I have a proposal to make. Let us take my poor sketch to His Reverence, and abide by what he says. It was my intention to show it to him in any case.'

'Certainly,' said Uncle Dorie with alacrity. 'His Reverence is just across the way. I know how he will take it, and I am quite content to leave the matter in his hands.'

But to Uncle Dorie's huge astonishment, the Reverend Sybrand, after a cursory glance at the sketch, looked sharply at Tins, and then concentrated his attention on the drawing. He held it at arm's length, he peered at it through his horn-rimmed glasses, he took the glasses off and looked at the sketch at close range, and he nodded his head vigorously. At last he spoke.

'Teacher,' he said, with real feeling in his voice, 'let me congratulate you. It is a little masterpiece. The curve of that shin—now that might, I think, be a little less hard. But it is altogether a beautiful piece of work, worthy of so beautiful an object. What a pity it is that the boy Matie has not a mind to correspond with so well-formed a body.'

'But Your Reverence,' exclaimed Uncle Dorie, appalled that his arbitrator had so suddenly and unconditionally surrendered to the enemy, 'it is monstrously indecent. Impure, if I might say so, and indecent.'

'I do not see why you should say that, Brother Doremus,' said the pastor, mildly. 'There is nothing indecent about it. You would not call God's handicraft indecent, would you, now? There are sketches like this, statues of naked youths and paintings of them, and only those who are not pure themselves would call them impure ...'

'*Bis, bis,* Your Reverence,' exclaimed Tins, marvellously delighted. 'I said it, *Meneer le doyen,* that His Reverence would know which of us was in the right.'

'To the pure,' went on the pastor, disregarding the teacher's enthusiastic approval, 'all things are pure, as the good Book tells us through the lips of the apostle. And nowhere in holy writ, Brother, will you find that man's body is regarded as otherwise than something to be looked at with reverence and to be pondered at. Is it not made in His image? I know what is in your mind, Brother, and I will not say that it is fitting, at present, that these things should be publicly exhibited, as they are in other countries, where such a sketch would be extolled as the work of an artist. Indeed, it were perhaps better that our friend should keep them for such as can understand and appreciate them.'

'Will Your Reverence favour me by accepting the lad's presentment as a gift from the humble artist?' asked Tins, quickly. 'That would, meseems, be a fitting disposition thereof.'

'Gladly and with gratitude,' said the pastor, pocketing the sketch. 'I will have it framed and hung up—not in my study chamber, Teacher, for there are many among us who think not as we do. And you, my good friend, must favour me by following Brother Doremus's suggestion, and refrain from publishing your sketches, even though they are of youths so marvellously well-formed as this lad appears to be.'

With the pastor's tact and commonsense way of looking at the incident, the affair was settled, but Uncle Dorie was not altogether satisfied. Tins's skill with the pencil was now common knowledge, and he utilised it to sketch whoever sat to him, earning in this way many gifts in kind and from some of the seniors an occasional piece of money. In deference to public opinion, however, he refrained from using his pencil at the bathing pool, but no one could prevent him from continuing to admire the beautiful proportions of some of the youth who frequented it.

Chapter 16

To Everardus the most interesting part of his sojourn at the Bay was the time he spent at the salt pans, whither he had gone with Uncle Dorie and a party of young men for a few days' shooting. He found there a community of men, women and children who lived a life of their own, apart, in squalid misery—mitigated by their philosophical resignation, their patient acceptance of hardship and poverty, and their sturdy, hard-working independence. They inhabited reed huts covered on the outside with mud, dwellings a trifle more spacious than bell-tents, but devoid of any of the simple comforts that even the humblest *bywoner* or squatter on a Valley farm would have deemed indispensable. They cooked their fish and griddle-cakes made of unleavened rye flour on an open fire on the hard clay in front of their huts, and they hung their catches of fishes on tarred lines suspended between high poles out of the reach of marauding strand-wolves and the baboons which occasionally adventured within stone's throw of the pans.

There were some six white families living on the shores of the principal pan, and these received the hunting party with courteous hospitality, sharing with them their scanty stock of eatables, although Uncle Dorie had provided an abundance of good things. They were silent, almost morose folk, these pan-dwellers, but hardy and sun-tanned, although when they stripped for a swim in the pan, their skins showed milk white against the brown of the water. Tins, had he been there, would have exulted in their proportions, for a vigorous open-air life had moulded their limbs far better than any course of exercises, designed for that purpose, could have done. The men were strapping, upstanding fellows, bearded six-footers, with long, sinewy, hairy arms. The youngsters were oval-faced, under-fed, slender-limbed striplings, agile in the water and out of it, well versed in veld-craft, but ignorant of any schooling, quiet to the very verge of solemnity in the presence of their Elders or of strangers, and hardly loquacious when they were among themselves. Everardus gained the impression that they were all wearied, disappointed men, and that their women folk shared in this general depression, for like the boys they hardly ever spoke unless directly addressed, and their faces wore an expression of resigned gloom unrelieved by a flicker of interest in the conversation. Among the men there were faces that attracted, by reason of the regularity of feature and the comeliness of their open, honest expression, but the women appeared prematurely aged, bowed under by the care of a life that had in it so little that was pleasant and so much that was wearisome to flesh and spirit alike.

The pan-dwellers eked out an existence by cultivating small patches of *vlei* or marshland where they grew potatoes or beans. They had boats and nets, and harvested both the lagoon and the sea beyond it, going out in the early morning before the day had appeared to catch *snoek* in the waters beyond the Bay. Their fish they salted or dried, selling loads of these to the Bay visitors, and buying with the proceeds such necessities as they required from the itinerant hawkers. Rarely they travelled into the Valley, disposing of their produce on the way at different farms, and returned with tobacco, tea and coffee, which were carefully husbanded to serve them until the next fishing season.

Everardus marvelled at and admired their handling of a boat. They seemed to be born sailors, and Uncle Dorie told him that this was not a matter for surprise seeing that they were the direct descendents of some of the Company's seamen who had trekked into these wilds long before the English came to the Cape and had settled here, married, and lived in poverty and hardship simply because they had no mind to go further afield. Poor as they were they had their Native servants, and Everardus heard that their community was regarded as perfectly honest and that no one ever had any trouble from the pan-folk.

'They are,' said the Elder, 'quite content, Nephew Ev'rard. So why should we disturb them? When a man is content, let him be, say I. It is the one who always wants something that he hasn't got who gives us trouble in this life. And as you see, Nephew, they eat and they sleep, and they are content.'

'You might say that for us in the Valley,' expostulated Everardus, with a glance at the sombre children playing, scarcely with the happiness that one would have expected from such youngsters, engaged in a game with the leaves of the succulent mesembryanthemums that grow on the side of the pan. 'Look at those little chaps. Why, Uncle, with a little schooling one might make men of them.'

'I daresay, Nephew,' retorted the Elder. 'But men and men are different . If it is the good Lord's will to raise from those youngsters a leader in Israel, why, He has his own methods of going to work, and it is not for such as us to interfere with His fore-ordaining. You might as well say that we must interest ourselves in the Black folk's children ...'

'That is what *Meneer* Uhlmann is doing,' said Everardus, who had been much struck with what he had seen at Neckarthal. 'You would not say he was doing something of which we should not approve?'

'Nay, that I won't,' admitted Uncle Dorie. 'But that is a different matter altogether. Look you, Nephew Ev'rard, I do not hold with educating a man beyond his intellect. There are some of us who will have to be lower than the others. The good Book says there shall be masters and those under masters. Now our Black folk are good creatures. I say it and I should know. I have seen them bound to us, just like our cattle were bound to us, and I have seen them free men like you and me. But I ask you, do you consider them, for all that you have seen of *Meneer* Uhlmann's work in the Neckarthal, fit to be placed in the rank with us?'

'I don't know,' said Everardus, frankly. 'I have often thought about that. Once when I was at Cape Town, I heard *Meneer* Porter ...'

'So,' said Uncle Dorie, quickly and interestedly, 'you have spoken to *Meneer* Porter? Aye, he is a grand man, that. One of the best of the English there. I shall be interested to hear what *Meneer* Porter said, if you can recollect it, Nephew.'

'I heard him say,' said Everardus, 'that he would not say anything bad about our Black folk, but that the fact that they were so law-abiding and did not thieve and do crimes comes rather from their nature and from circumstances than from any fixed principles or morals. He said, give them teachers in mis-doing and they will be sure to learn. They don't know how to steal, he said, but once you teach them how to set about it they will become master thieves. That was why he did not want convicts to come out to us.'

'Aye, I know. He is a knowing man, that Mr Porter. And a straight man, too. I mind that it was he who gave us our magistrate. I have never seen him, Nephew, though I should like to meet him and grip him by the hand. But to come back to what we were talking about. You know there is talk of giving us our own government ...'

'I have heard something about it,' replied Everardus. 'It is a matter of voting, isn't it? I do not know the details.'

'No one knows them yet,' said Uncle Dorie, importantly. 'But the magistrate let slip a few words, and I sensed how the land lies. It is a matter of great difficulty, and we must have a talk about it as soon as we get back to the farm. But about these folk here. I do not see what we can do for them. It is not that I do not pity them, but they are content, and one cannot better them. Believe me, I have tried. There was the son of Gert Riks—he lives in that hut over there, and you must have seen the boy—a strapping fellow, as handy with a spade as with an oar. And strong—mighty, the lad can bend a horseshoe with his fingers. I offered to take him on the farm, to feed and clothe him and pay him a proper wage, giving him a heifer every half year and a couple of ewes. At first it was all right. He worked well, and I was satisfied with him. But soon he wanted to return home. He said he could not stand being away from the pan. It is so with all of them, Nephew. The salt has entered their blood. They must live and die on the pan.'

Many of them, Everardus heard, did so. There was a little graveyard on the veld, a few hundred yards away from the hut. Rude, slate grave-stones stood there on which, as rudely scratched with a nail, Everardus read of men and boys drowned in the sea or killed by accident on the pan. Every family had paid tribute to the sea; every family expected, with stolid resignation at Fate, which had decreed it, to pay still more. Out of the sea they got their livelihood, and if it called insistently to them to come forth and brave its dangers in open boats, they had no quarrel with it. Between them and it lay friendship and enmity, and none of them, had he been asked, would have been able to differentiate between them. Everardus felt in that respect he was akin to them, for what the sea was to them, the soil was to him. They were seamen, inured to the sea, always on their guard against it, familiarity with its varying temper breeding in them no contempt but respect for its savage strength and its wayward moods. He was a tiller of the soil and, like them, he had learned to respect the soil, not to fear it, but to know that it was something that had its moods, something to be treated gravely, with courage that on occasion did not shirk life and happiness to get what one could from it. And his heart warmed towards the pan fisher-folk, so that he spent most of his time in their company, going out with them in their boats, learning how to fish for *snoek*, and getting his hands horribly torn by the rushing lines when the fish snapped at the bait and rushed tearing away through the water. He made many friends, and even the silent youngsters came to him for advice, and by the time that his party broke up camp he felt that he stood on a footing of good fellowship with the entire community. He promised to return, and determined that he would not come empty-handed, for he saw how badly off they were for many of the bare necessities of life, and he knew that *Knolkloof* wasted much that to these men meant a great deal more than it did to him.

Riding back towards the Bay, he glanced behind him and saw the pan, a level line of silver, dotted with the countless moorhens and waterfowl, lying placidly under the declining sun. The serried ranks of flamingoes stood marshalled on the further side, half-way in the shallows, their backs reflecting the sunglow in pink and misty white. Beyond lay the sea, half hidden by the sand-dunes in the foreground, but its wide expanse, a shimmering haze of beryl, stretching out to meet the skyline. In the foreground stood the huts, with the pan-dwellers idly watching the retreating party and waving a last farewell. He was glad that he had visited them. They had given him something new to think about, and as he rode on, chatting to Uncle Dorie whose horse was heavily laden with the proceeds of the hunt, he made up his mind to do something for them in return. He did not know what he could do, but the Valley always had a plan. Probably he, too, could formulate one for the benefit of the pan-folk.

On their return to the Bay, the party found that Tins had distinguished himself and earned the reputation of a hero. A small boy had strayed from the women and idled on the rocks of the men's bathing pool at a time when no one was there to guard him. Tins had been sketching close by, and had idly watched the child playing on the rocks, and had only realised that the boy had slipped in and was struggling in the water when the women had rushed up and sounded the alarm. From the cottages the men and boys came running, but the child was already being carried out by the waves, and Tins had rushed forward, taken a sprawling header into the water, and managed to grasp the boy's pants before he himself went under. There had really been no danger, for the men and boys were promptly in the water and both the child and his would-be rescuer had been brought safely to shore where it appeared that the one most in need of assistance had been Tins. The women had made much of him, and in their attempts to restore him had dosed him so vigorously with brandy of all kinds, medicinal and otherwise, that when Everardus found him he was almost as helplessly intoxicated as he had been under the sage-bush on that memorable morning when Sylvester had discovered him.

Everardus and Uncle Dorie took him in charge and shepherded him to the latter's cottage, where he was rubbed down and induced to go to bed. But the Teacher had for months been a forced abstainer, and this excusable indulgence had its usual effects. The lamentable failing, hereditary in the Mabuis family, showed itself in a pronounced form, and for more than an hour Tins sat on the bed and behaved hilariously, to the no small indignation and alarm of Uncle Dorie, who complained that so sad an exhibition could not but be a most unedifying spectacle to the crowd outside. For the whole Bay community had followed the three to the cottage and now stood clamouring for the hero to come forth and make a speech. The little boy's mother was there, bearing a bowl of home-made brawn as a small tribute of gratitude; the boy's father, sisters and brothers pressed against the *stoep* door with urgent entreaties that *Meester* should give them a tune on his flute. And *Meester* sat on the bed, singing ribald songs in a high-pitched key, which Uncle Dorie fortunately could not understand else his indignation would have reached boiling-point.

Everardus got them away at last, promising that *Meneer* should appear when he was feeling a little better, and the company, knowing how sodden, pale, and nearly drowned Tins had looked when the youths had hauled him out of the water, expressed its sympathy in appropriate terms and dispersed to discuss the matter elsewhere. To the hilarious mood succeeded the state of somnolence, and Uncle Dorie had the satisfaction of seeing the Teacher fall back on the pillow and drop off into a drunken sleep.

The next morning Tins appeared in no way chagrined at his lapse. He took the stage with an appreciative bow, as it seemed, and swaggered in a manner that filled Uncle Dorie with disgust and Everardus with great amusement. To all who cared to listen, which everyone apparently did, he recounted his heroic effort to rescue the youngster, and every cottage made him welcome and pressed food and drink upon him. Uncle Dorie had taken care that the drink should be coffee only, but of that beverage Tins drank dozens of cups and a simple computation showed that he must have eaten as many slices of cake, as many preserved *naartjies* and green figs, and as many thick biltong and butter sandwiches. His triumphal march round the cottage ended up at the house of the rescued boy's father where he was regaled upon ginger beer and water-melon, a combination that would have sufficed to put any ordinary man completely out of action, but did not seem to have the slightest effect upon the teacher. He took out his flute and played handsomely in return for the hospitality received, and retired, panting and out of breath, but supremely satisfied with himself, to Uncle Dorie's cottage, declaring that he felt just hungry enough for his evening meal.

Supper was partaken of at the usual hour, and Tins did full justice to the good things that were put on the table. Uncle Dorie sat in unaccustomed silence, too shocked and disgusted to be his usual jovial self. He conducted evening service with more than ordinary solemnity, and in his evening prayer remembered 'our relapsing Brother, cursed, as Thou, oh Lord, knowest, with the sin of insobriety and unvirtuous boasting, whom we humbly pray Thee to awaken to a sense of his infirmities so that he might give hearty thanks to Thee for his preservation from a death for which, alas, he is not yet prepared,' allusions to which Tins responded with a fervent Amen, which the Elder hoped was the utterance of a truly contrite heart. So much was Uncle Dorie impressed by the spirit in which Tins had taken his outspoken criticism that he felt much more genially disposed towards the erring Brother, and when the rest of the family had retired and he and the Teacher were alone in the room, he thought it proper to improve the occasion by a friendly lecture.

'Before we part for the night, Teacher,' he said, clearing his throat, and affecting to adjust the wick of the oil-lamp, 'I should like to say a few words. I hope and trust, Teacher, that my words will not be taken amiss. They come from a friendly heart, which has been distressed—is still distressed—by Teacher's unfortunate lapse from the path of sobriety. I have never spoken to Teacher on the matter, being of the opinion, long with Nephew Ev'rard, that Teacher's unfortunate failing had been, through divine grace, conquered by fortitude and determination on the part of Teacher. It has been most distressing—most distressing, I reiterate, Teacher—to find that the Devil which lurks everywhere, has again caught Teacher, with the result that were it not for the tact and adroitness of Nephew Ev'rard, an unedifying scandal might have been revealed to our congregation. There are various passages in scripture to which I might allude, to show Teacher how wicked it is to give way to insobriety. There is for example the prophet Isaiah who said—I think it is in the fifth chapter—"Woe unto them that rise early in the morning to drink strong wine," and the apostle, who says in the first epistle to the Corinthians, in the sixth chapter and tenth verse, "Nor drunkards shall inherit the kingdom of God." I would not labour the point with Teacher, especially as I remarked earlier that a contrite feeling has now taken hold of Teacher, as I gathered when I remembered the occasion to our dear Lord in prayer this evening. But there is another matter, Teacher, and that I must touch upon, although I do so with pain. It appears to me that Teacher is boastfully glorying in what happened yesterday ...'

'But even so, *Meneer le doyen*,' interrupted Tins, grinning delightfully. 'Is it not something to be proud of, to have saved the mother's child?'

'You know as well as I do,' said the Elder, exasperated, 'that you did nothing of the kind. You did not save the boy. Indeed, if the others were not at hand you would probably have been drowned together with him.'

'Which perhaps would have been better for the twain of us,' said Tins, soberly. 'A lapsed Brother—a drunkard who cannot inherit the kingdom of the good God, and a *garçon* who—who knows? —may belike become worse when he grows to manhood— what better than death for the two of them?'

'There you go again,' said Uncle Dorie, plaintively. 'You do take a man up in a manner that is provoking. None of us would have liked to see you drown, and with God's grace, Teacher, you can conquer your failing and become a good man. Have we not welcomed you and given you a responsible position among us, entrusting to your care our children? Surely, Teacher, we can ask from you that you should be sober, not boastful and vainglorious, for does not the Book say, "Whoso boasteth is like clouds and wind without rain"?'

'*Monsieur le doyen,*' said Tins, gravely, 'may I ask *Monsieur* a question?'

'Ask me a question? Why, of course. But I do not say that I will answer it, Teacher. A fool can ask many questions which a wise man cannot reply to.'

'This is a simple one, *Monsieur*. Does *Monsieur* believe that if we die, we die *absolument*, or is it that *Monsieur* believes that we shall live again in the hereafter?'

'Why, what a heathenish question! It is just the sort of thing you Papists would ask. Of course we shall live again. Does not the Book say so, and are we not bidden to believe in the resurrection of the flesh ...'

'Aye. It is a comfortable faith, that, *Monsieur*. But if a man does not happen to hold it ... *Monsieur*, I am not frightened, even though I do not believe as you believe, of death. I have faced it before now, and now I do not boast. But of the water I am afraid, *Meneer* van Aard; at the sea I shiver. I cannot help it; it is my nature. I shall never learn to swim, *Meneer le doyen*, for the water, I distrust it too much, and it frightens me ...'

'The water, *Meester*, cannot really harm you. See how the lads swim in it, and you a grown man to be frightened at it.'

'That is so, *Meneer le doyen*. But as I say, *hélas*, I cannot help myself. It will come over me, this water-fright, which is not like that which the dogs get, but like the fear of children of the dark. Some time, perhaps, it will get me, this water, and I shall die in it, and of that, somehow, I am not frightened. But I was frightened, very much frightened, *Monsieur le doyen*, when I splashed in after the small *garçon*. And because I felt ashamed of my fright, I glorified in what the women-folk said. They made much of me, and I tried to think that I had earned what they said, and I drank, as *Meneer* van Aard knows, altogether too much for me. Does *Meneer* van Aard understand the position? It is not that I boast. It is that I am like a frightened lad who goes whistling and glances behind him on a dark night, imagining *hippogryphs* and *nyctalops* in the twilight, and keeps up his courage by whistling.'

'I don't know what these things are,' retorted Uncle Dorie. 'You sometimes, *Meester*, talk the most outlandish rubbish, so that no Christian man can comprehend you. But I take you, and if that is the case there is some excuse for you.'

'Indeed there is, *Meneer* van Aard,' said Tins, seriously. 'Look you, *Meneer*, it is that I am a stranger among you, a foreigner as you say, though that is not just to me, seeing that I am one of you, being born in this country and Native, just like *Meneer le doyen* himself. Is it my fault that my *papa*, now presumably with God ...'

'I wish you would not speak so irreverently when you allude to the Deity,' said Uncle Dorie, irritably. 'It is setting an example ...'

'Which no one but *Meneer le doyen* witnesses,' interrupted Tins, quickly. 'I do not speak disrespectfully of the good God, surely, when I say that *papa*, who was not altogether what a *papa* might have been, is now, *peut-être*, in bliss ...'

'Nor should you talk like that about your late, lamented parent,' remonstrated the Elder. 'The Book says plainly and clearly, "Children, show respect to your Elders." I have noticed, *Meester*, that in regard to these things your conduct leaves much to be desired.'

'I know, *Meneer* van Aard,' said Tins, contritely. 'It is my way of looking at things, which is not *Meneer's* way. But both our ways may be right, who knows? But to return to our sheep ...'

'We were not talking about sheep, *Meester*.'

'It is a mere way of expression, *Meneer*. To revert, then, to my unvirtuous behaviour. It is, *Meneer* will understand, the reaction against something that I did, almost without knowing that I did it, regretting it the minute that I did, and much comforted that in doing it I did myself no lasting injury. I cannot otherwise explain, *Meneer le doyen*. It is not as if I believed with *Meneer* that there is a hereafter ...'

'Why surely, *Meester*, even you Romans must believe in that? You could not be so utterly heathenish ...'

'It is one's way of looking at it, *Meneer*. I do not believe in *Meneer's* hereafter, which means—what does it mean exactly, *Meneer*?'

'What it means? Why everyone knows what it means, everyone who is not a Papist. It means that those whom our Good Lord has fore-ordained to taste everlasting bliss in heaven will inherit His kingdom.'

'And live happy, having no care, no pain, no sorrow or danger. Is it not so, *Meneer* Elder?'

'Even as you say, *Meester*,' replied Uncle Dorie, somewhat puzzled to know whither these interrogations led.

'And does *Meneer* really think that a life without action, without sorrow, without struggle, is life? Is happiness or bliss, *Meneer*? For me, I can picture to myself no such happiness where there is not something to be fought for, something to be conquered. *Meneer* would not like it if *Meneer's* farm yielded up its grain and its produce without any labour from *Meneer*, without any worry on *Meneer's* part. *Meneer* might think that he would, but ultimately, *finalement*, *Meneer* would get prodigiously tired of it and regard the scheme as altogether too bizarre for a real man to enjoy.'

'You misrepresent things, as usual,' said Uncle Dorie, querulously. 'I daresay there will be sufficient for us all to do in heaven, something for every idle hand and brain to occupy himself with, and something to be striven for. The good Lord knows human nature—after all He made it—and He will know how to deal with it. That,' concluded the Elder, sturdily, 'is what I believe, and if you, *Meester*, believe anything else, as very likely, being a Papist and therefore excluded from grace, you do, then it is your own look-out.'

'*Meneer* the Elder must not take it amiss if I differ from him,' said Tins, accommodatingly. 'My own beliefs – *voilá, Meneer*, they are not crystal clear. They will always have some of the lees of my unvirtuous life clinging to them and *Meneer* must take that into account. But *certainement* I could not believe that.'

'Then what, may I ask,' said Uncle Dorie, 'do you fancy happens to us in the hereafter? Just out of curiosity, I should like to know.'

'*Hélas, Meneer*, who can say?' answered Tins, taking up his candlestick preparatory to departure, 'Not the wise men who have attempted to enlighten us, nor the fools whose beliefs are all awry. *Omnia migrant* ...' [1]

---

[1] *Omnia migrant, / Omnia commutat natura et verlere cogit. De remum natura* Bk V line 830, Lucretius—Eds.

'You ought not to swear, *Meester*,' reproved Uncle Dorie, lighting his own candle and turning down the wick of the oil-lamp. 'Surely even a Papist knows that.'

'It is not swearing, *Meneer*. It is the word of the great poet—I forget his name but no matter; he was a great poet, and some of his words I remember. It means that we all change, and no one knows into what or how. There are the eastern folk, the men who twirl a ratched wheel and invoke the purity of the lotus-flower, who say that we come back, assuming new shapes ...'

'Now you are getting blasphemous, *Meester*,' remarked Uncle Dorie, severely. 'I do not wish to continue the discussion, and it is time to wish you a sleep-well. But I may just remind you that we are all Christian people, and that these heathenish notions will find no favour with us.'

Nevertheless Uncle Dorie pondered long and deeply over what Tins had said, and came to the conclusion that the *Meester* was a bit touched in his head, although not sufficiently so to unfit him for his pedagogical work. Still, as one never knew what might happen, he deemed it desirable to discuss the man with His Reverence. Again he found, to his surprise, that the Reverend Sybrand took the matter lightly, and only became serious when Doremus suggested that Tins should be induced to attend the confirmation class and be weaned from his heretical faith.

'Leave the man alone,' His Reverence counselled. 'God works in His own way, Brother, and if He wishes Teacher to become one of us, He will bring it about in His own good time. There is opportunity for Teacher; he is not debarred from the benefits we all of us enjoy, and it is for him to take such advantage of these as his own conscience and understanding may advise him. A man's faith is never forced, for in forcing it one destroys it, Brother. A word in season, that is another matter, but I notice that Teacher attends our services and that he joins with us in our devotions. Leave it there.'

And to Uncle Dorie's surprise, Brother Martin expressed the same views. He clearly did not think that Tins's lapse from the straight path of sobriety was a matter for congregational denunciation, and permitted himself a dignified smile when his friend recounted how hilariously Teacher had conducted himself on the evening of his adventure at the bathing-pool.

'His Reverence is perfectly right,' he remarked. 'Teacher is not a simple man, Brother Doremus. I suspicion that he has far more in that round head of his than most of us carry about with us, and when it comes to discussing the hereafter, why he must be worth hearing. Do you, Brother Doremus, see to it that he is free this evening so that we may have a few more games of chess. He really plays a most excellent game, even though he may, at times, be a *potator*—which, Brother, is the Latin for one who drinks.'

On the farm which he had named *Quakerskloof* lived Andrew Quakerley, the son of old Charles Quakerley whose career read like a miniature romance. *Quakerskloof*, whose name the Valley pronounced with a marked broadening of the first vowel sound, was reckoned the show farm in the western part of the Valley, for its owner had spared no expense, energy or labour in so assiduously cultivating it that it was now one of the most productive holdings in the District. It yielded corn, barley and rye; maize, forage, fruit, and garden produce; and its herds of sheep and cattle were good to look upon. Its homestead was a solidly built, attractive and comfortable dwelling, furnished inside with polished cedarwood and quaint, well made old things brought out from England.

The Quakerleys were not immigrant settlers, but owed their presence in the Valley to the initiative of old Charles Quakerley, who after wandering in various parts of the Colony, had wandered into the District, liked this corner of it, and patiently built himself a home in it. Somewhere overseas, in a county of England called Hertfordshire, one Andrew Quakerley, married to the honourable Alice Muscombe Downing, had won place and position for himself, becoming an MP and seeing sons of his rising to the rank of Admiral of the Red and holders of comfortable church livings. His youngest son, Charles, however, had occasioned his parent considerable annoyance and pain by his escapades as a small youth, and a sojourn at the Blue Coat School had not been sufficient to instil into the youngster those habits of discipline and correct deportment on which his brothers laid so much stress. Young Charles had accordingly been shipped to sea, in the ship commanded by his brother, whose severity and strictness proved a source of constant irritation to the young midshipman. The details of the young man's escape from the ship, while lying at anchor in False Bay off Simonstown, old Charles Quakerley never made public, but it was surmised that he and his fellow midshipman, having decided to abandon the ship, had been helped by some of the Cape Town residents. The fact remains that Charles Quakerley found himself, at the age of twenty-three, working as a clerk in one of the merchant shops of the capital, was placed on parole, along with other English residents, and sent for safety's sake to the District of Stellenbosch—thereby anticipating by almost a century the fate of other young Englishmen in disfavour with the authorities—where he continued until the Cape was taken in 1806 by Sir David Baird. The following year, under the governorship of Earl Clarendon, he made his peace with the authorities, family influence at home sufficing to condone his desertion from his ship, and on his father's death received his share of the family estate, amounting to some ten thousand pounds in English sterling. Some years later he married, his choice being the handsome daughter of one of the Stellenbosch farmers who had shown such hospitality and friendship during his exile at that place. And two years after his marriage he came into the Valley and bought the farm *Skurwekloof* or Rough Valley, changing its name to *Quakerskloof* and cultivating it in a manner that made the Valley folk stare.

Old Charles Quakerley, now living quietly on the farm, whose management he had turned over to his son Andrew, was a short, nervous-looking old gentleman with a white, closely-cropped beard, a much wizened, wrinkled but still healthily complexioned face, and hair which he wore long, and on state occasions still powdered. His fine clear blue eyes, and the fact that he never wore a hat—a habit probably dating from his Blue Coat days—had earned for him the nickname *'Oom Blou-oog Sonder-hoed'* (Uncle Blue-eyes Without-a-hat) which in time had been corrupted into *Oom Blonderhoed*, a variation which, as he freely translated it to mean 'Uncle Blunderhead,' afforded the old gentleman intense amusement. With Uncle Martin Rekker, who was his personal friend, with whom he had many habits in common, Uncle Charles was regarded by the Valley as one of its aristocrats, and such indeed, by right of lineage, he was, although in that community where descent counted for very little and a man's manner and personality much, the old man's genuine good breeding and gentlemanliness marked him out as the peer of those who, like Uncle Martin, could pride themselves on birth and breeding. Like Uncle Martin he was grave and dignified in his demeanour, impetuous by temperament—which had prompted his original desertion from his ship, and also accounted for the loss of some of his fortune in speculative ventures—and, while gentle and forebearing with his inferiors, apt to be curt and touchy in his intercourse with his equals. The result of this was that he had estranged himself from his family at home, with whom he corresponded only on very rare occasions when duty called for an expression of sympathy at the death of some near relative, while the grand folks at the capital, from whom he received marked attentions, being regularly invited to attend the Governor's receptions and as regularly declining in the most courteous terms to accept them, he stood on a footing of dignified aloofness. Although he had so thoroughly identified himself with his adopted country, he had never learned the second language, contenting himself wholly with English, with which, too, he had managed so well that he was perfectly friendly with the majority of the men of the Valley. With his wife, who in her youth had been tall and stately but in her old age was bedridden by arthritis, he talked in terms of old-fashioned courtesy, treating her with a deference and a consideration which the Valley found delightfully impressive. The Natives looked up to him with a great respect and admiration, and all those on his farm were freed slaves or the descendants of slaves, some of whom had followed him to *Quakerskloof* when he had settled there, and all of whom had elected to remain voluntarily in his service when they had been freed by law.

Uncle Charles's only son, Andrew, was a tall, broad-shouldered giant of a man, with a magnificent black beard that was the admiration of the Valley and the secret annoyance of his wife who liked him much better with the original moustache in which he had wooed and won her, when, as a young girl fresh from England, she had arrived in the Valley with her settler parents. Now she was a stout, attractive-looking little woman, an excellent contrast to her big, brawny husband, whose accent, manners, and deportment she unsuccessfully attempted to mould into the shape approved of by Miss Fitzjohn, whose four-volume novels she much preferred to the heavier *pabulum*[1] of Sir Walter. Andrew Quakerley, like his sister Joan, who lived with him on the farm, had acclimatised himself so well to the Valley ways that he

---

[1] Fodder—Eds.

slurred his words and broadened his vowel sounds almost as painfully as young Tommy Seldon, but his active language was still English, and his Dutch, idiomatic and grammatical as it was, was kept for use outside the home circle in his intercourse with his neighbours. His three little daughters were kept carefully away from the contaminating influences of Native and Valley children, and under the tutelage of their mother and aunt could have passed for typical English children from the ancestral country.

The relations of the Quakerleys with their neighbours in the Valley were excellent, and far more intimate than Mrs Andrew Quakerley sometimes approved of. She had never quite accepted the Valley as her permanent domicile. Her father and brothers had tried for a few years to get a livelihood from the soil, but, although heartily assisted by her husband and father-in-law, they had given up the attempt and migrated to the eastern Districts where the majority of the English immigrants had settled, and where they found their communal environment much more genial. The Valley had not regretted their departure, for it had instinctively felt that they were inassimilable and quite different from the Seldons or the Quakerleys and some of the other settlers who now resided in the Valley or the Village. Mrs Andrew would have liked to follow them, and had indeed urged her husband to do so, but she had found unexpected opposition both from him and her father-in-law. Old Charles had sarcastically hinted that if he could live pleasantly and in comfort in the Valley, there was surely no reason whatever why a yeoman farmer's daughter could not do the same. Her mother-in-law had simply refused to understand her feelings in the matter while her sister-in-law, a mild, timid creature, who scarcely had an opinion of her own, had impartially agreed with both sides when the subject had been under discussion. Mrs Andrew, who loved her husband very much, and who really had no royal grievance, had in course of time resigned herself to the inevitable, but, as was only natural, she had placed herself on a pedestal from which she affected to look down upon the Valley and all it contained. This had, equally naturally, made her less popular than her husband, and people said that Mrs Quakerley was stiff and 'English' in outlook and manner. As a matter of fact the heroes of Miss Fitzjohn's novels would have found her un-English in many particulars wherein she had insensibly absorbed something of the feeling and the spirit of the Valley. She did not know it, happily for her own peace of mind, and her ignorance made her blissfully unconscious of the fact that Mrs Seldon and Mrs Staples, the magistrate's wife, both regarded her as being petulant, affected and unsociable. She was in reality none of these things, being at heart a very generous, kindly woman, temperamentally disinclined to face realities and inclined too much to stress the value of theoretical things.

Her husband, on the other hand, was a matter-of-fact individual, a curious and very capable blend of his father's impetuousness and his mother's phlegmatic calmness, with the innate honesty and fundamental generosity of both his parents. His youth had been spent on the farm, with an interval devoted to study in the capital where his father had placed him at a small, private school kept by a retired English clergyman. He had learned sufficient to shine in the Valley as a man of education and culture, and he had carefully added to his store of knowledge by private study of his father's by no means insufficient library. The Quakerleys received the two papers published at the capital, together with such journals as from time to time came out from home by the mail, and their wealth had allowed them to purchase such books as could be procured by periodical visits to Cape Town. Nor were they dependent solely upon the resources of the Valley, for once a year Andrew took his wife and sister for a prolonged stay at the seaside, choosing for that purpose either the new and quite uninteresting town on the shores of Algoa Bay where his wife's father lived, or the more lively surroundings that could be obtained at Green Point, one of the seaside suburbs of the capital. On those occasions they wrote their names in the guest-book at the long, irregular government house, shaded by the old oak trees that the Company had planted, and received invitations to dances and receptions and an occasional dinner with His Excellency; visited Admiralty House at Simonstown where a Nephew of an Admiral of the Red was always sure of a warm welcome, even though his host knew that his father had deserted his ship, and attended the races on the Common where both Joan and Mrs Andrew invariably lost their money and Andrew invariably succeeded in spotting winners. These annual occasions were eagerly looked forward to by Mrs Andrew, who was in her element among her new surroundings, and who sighed when the time came to return to the farm, although both her husband and her sister-in-law declared that after so much gaiety the quiet of *Quakerskloof* was just the thing they desired. She hoped that in time Andrew might be induced to employ a manager on the farm and come to live at Cape Town, and she had visions of what that life would be. But she was a woman of some tact and forebore to trouble him with these expectations, experience having taught her that the expression of her hopes in this direction elicited from him merely a good-natured growl, like that of a big dog too harshly stroked.

At home old Charles toddled about the house, anxiously awaiting his son's return, for he hated to be dependent for his daily comforts upon the ministrations of the Native servants. In his old age he liked to have everything about him methodically arranged, for he had become a precisian in habits of life, if not altogether one in habits of thought. He saw really no reason why Andrew should waste his time at the capital, but he agreed that Andrew's wife, poor thing, should have some pleasure, and Joan, too, was all the better for an annual jaunt to the seaside. Though why they could not go to the Bay, whither he occasionally went, on Martin Rekker's invitation, spending an enjoyable fortnight among the temporary residents, he failed to understand. It was just because daughter-in-law imagined herself so mightily superior to the Valley folk, which after all she wasn't. He himself was quite aware of the respect due to one's family and all that sort of thing, but gentlemen never showed these things too openly, and daughter-in-law was at times rather trying, behaving distinctly so-so to men who were really excellent fellows in their way. Not that he would willingly say a word against daughter-in-law, who was, as far as daughters-in-law went—and he admitted that he was personally acquainted with one only of the species—not bad, but really of what earthly use was it to be so damnably affected? There was the occasion, he remembered it very well, when that really interesting fellow, the missionary chap von Bergmann, had overnighted on the farm. Daughter-in-law had really been trying on that occasion, and he, Charles, had had difficulty in restraining his sarcastic tongue and afterwards, when daughter-in-law had heard that the fellow was married to a baroness's daughter—really, you know, it was all very well, but that sort of thing was bad form, rank snobbery as a matter of fact. The sort of thing no gentleman did. However ...

And the old gentleman would gather his three little grand-daughters round him and shepherd them into the little summer-house in the garden, over which the wisteria scrambled in masses of purple, and tell them the ever wonderful story how as a boy he had stopped a gentleman on Hampstead Heath and asked the gentleman, who was fat and kindly-looking, to haul in an unmanageable kite.

'And, my dears,' the old gentleman would say, with a flourish of his arms just as he would make when he told them the story of the three bears, 'who do you think he was, the fat gentleman?' To which the three little girls, well trained in their responses to this recurring enquiry, would reply, 'Do please tell us, Gran'dad?' and Uncle Charles would say with impressiveness, 'The King, my dears, the King.'

Whereupon they would ask him to tell them about the Queen, and he would very patiently explain that it was all long ago, and that the Queen now was as old as their mother and had little children, as little as they were, and after that he would shepherd them back into the big, cool dining room, where Gran'ma Clara, who had such queer, bony fingers, all bunched up, and walked with the aid of a stick that was taller than she herself was, would give them transparently green, preserved figs out of a wonderfully cut-glass dish whose facets glinted with miniature rainbows.

Old Charles was a great favourite with his grand-children, and during their mother's absence from home it was he who supervised their simple lessons, and heard their recitations, and told them stories, and assisted at their being put to bed by the Native ayah. He was not quite easy in his mind about his conduct as maternal surrogate, for he never interfered with them when they babbled in Dutch to the ayah, and Mrs Andrew, when she came back from her jaunt to the capital, complained that they had picked up such vulgar expressions. They were not exactly vulgar expressions, these diminutives which the ayah used when she combed the long fair hair of the little girls, but they were endearments which have no real equivalent in English, and the children liked them and retained them. When she was present Mrs Andrew did her loyal best to counteract the Spirit of the Valley. In her absence old Charles, who had felt that Spirit and had found it not altogether bad, did not think it his business to follow her example. 'If they are to live here—and God knows there is no reason why they shouldn't,' he had remarked to his son—'the sooner they learn to talk the lingo the better. Why, darn it, boy, you knew it before you were ten, and it's a damn sight more good to you than the little French I tried to teach you. Not that I shouldn't like you to go across and see the old home. You will do that, Boy?'

'Some time, Dad, some day,' said Andrew, who really had no great desire to visit the old home. His mother's phlegmatic outlook upon life had become his, and as he grew older he was much less inclined to exert himself upon matters that brought no immediate and material profit. He had no curiosity, no restlessness, no wish to go outside his environment, and yet he felt that he owed a duty to the family, and had made up his mind that some time, some day, he would go and look up his uncle who was an Admiral of the Red. The old man was very sickly; the last letter, received five months back, had said that the great Dr Bright had been called into consultation, and that there was something badly wrong with the Admiral's kidneys. But this year there could certainly be no question of leaving the farm, and at any rate a long voyage of that sort could not be entered upon without due preparation. Dad would see that there was no sense in suggesting that one should go now.

Old Charles would agree, and betake himself to his journal. He kept a daily journal, in which he recorded such events as he deemed of sufficient importance to be chronicled for the benefit of those who could be permitted, after his death, to have access to his papers. Of late years he had been more prolix in his annotations, and there were times when he thought of sub-editing what he had written for fear that some incautious expression might cause annoyance to those he had no intention of wounding. Privately he would put down opinions of which he was afterwards ashamed, and one of his daily duties, which he never neglected, was to revise what he had written the previous day and scratch out such portions as were likely to be misunderstood by outsiders. So when he had written:

> 'Talked with A about his going home to look up brother Kenelm. Suggested that as K's kidneys are playing the very deuce with him, A had better get a move on. Felt queer myself, so took rhubarb grains twenty; bellyache next morning but felt brave for rest of the day. A seems averse from going. Have no wish to force the boy, for K can go to the devil so far as I am concerned. Still, a man's family is his family, and A takes things too lightly; is getting too much like his mother, who, poor thing, is horridly wrenched with gout. Daughter-in-law gave us a good dinner tonight; neck of lamb, stuffed roast goose and pancakes. Paid TS four shillings; more than the skin was worth but don't like to be niggardly in such things.'

He deleted the next morning all reference to his brother and to his wife, although the deletions were made so badly that the substance of what he had written was plain enough to those who subsequently would read the diary. Whether anyone would ever read it was a point on which he had by no means made up his mind, for there were days when he thought that he would destroy it as soon as he felt that his end was approaching, and there were other times when he did not care what became of it or who would read it. Had Uncle Charles been a little more egocentric and possessed a trifle less humour, he might have expanded his daily record into a volume of reminiscences which would undoubtedly have made interesting reading, for he had adventured much in his life, and he could narrate personal experiences of events that figure in history. But though he sometimes expanded when in congenial company, and embroidered on some of his experiences for the sake of his grand-children, whom he delighted to amaze, he usually preserved a quizzical silence and rarely gave his opinion, unasked, in conversation.

In the English community at the Village he held an acknowledged position as indubitably the premier resident in the District, a position to which his descent from a county family and his charming old-world manner entitled him. The English residents in the Village were of sound yeomen stock, none aspiring to social dignities to which they could lay no legitimate claim, and all quite willing to sink themselves, in the common democracy of the Valley, to the level of their neighbours, without imagining that by doing so they detracted from their personal prestige, won by sheer hard work and capacity. Staples, the magistrate, held an official position as the Queen's representative, and was, as such, the first in order of precedence, but who gracefully ceded pride of place to Charles Quakerley on such occasions when he could do so without compromising his official dignity. Below them ranked Farmer, who owned the Village store and was, after Thomas Seldon, the most prosperous tradesman in the District, Wicks, the chief constable, who was regarded more as a military man than as a civilian, and Trueman, the postmaster, who was really not of the Valley though in it, for he could be transferred at a moment's notice. These were all who could look upon England as 'home,' for all had been born there and had come out as settlers or in the government service, and none of them could truthfully say that he had so far identified himself with the Valley as to look upon it with the same feeling that Charles Quakerley had for it. All three had become proficient in Dutch, Farmer's knowledge of that language being almost as good as that of Thomas Seldon, and Wicks finding far less difficulty in making himself understood and understanding what was said to him than did his chief. All three had married English wives, and their home ways and home speech were English, though overlaid with that indefinable nuance of alien influence which the Valley cast over everything.

Between the English community and the Dutch-speaking people of the Valley there was not the slightest shadow of unfriendliness. The cultural differences between the two sections, with the resultant difference of outlook and opinion on ordinary matters of life, tended to keep the two from mingling as freely as they might otherwise have done, but both perhaps, or at least the more thoughtful and reasonable among them, agreed that these differences were being slowly effaced, and that in time there would come a complete understanding which might even proceed to assimilation, and produce a common basis of agreement on all subjects. Inherent prejudice had convinced each section that if such assimilation actually took place, his own culture and national characteristics, being so overwhelmingly superior to that of the other, would inevitably react so strongly upon the other side that the resulting amalgamation would show a preponderance of just those things that he cared for and valued more than did his neighbour. But that thought gave no enmity to his outlook upon the other side, although it naturally tinged his opinions and made him less inclined to allow for the slowly leavening influence of the very factors upon which he relied for the maintenance of his own ideals and prejudices. There was no sharp clash of views, no definite line of demarcation between the interests of the one section and the other, and with both the Valley was, for the time being at least, the chief and foremost influence which unconsciously reacted upon them, and ranged them in line, communally co-operant, to the exclusion of purely sectional interests that had more a sentimental than a practical value.

If anybody saw this clearly, it was old Charles Quakerley, who by experience and education was perhaps best fitted to institute standards of comparison between home conditions and his life in the Valley. A voluntary exile, he had chosen his life with his eyes open, and he had never regretted the choice. It was true that there were times when the longing came upon him to walk once more over the rain-swept Heath where the King had helped him with his kite—to see London lying in smoky haze, with the patches of sunlight glinting on church spires, to smell the hawthorn and lilac which he missed here, and to mingle with the crowd on Epsom Downs—but he suppressed it as something better dreamed about than done, and found solace and pleasure in reading such mail papers as his family sent him, and in the memories of the past which he could so easily conjure up. On his son he had impressed some of his ingrained and acquired convictions; the natural duty of every well-born man to be a gentleman, to be honest, to honour his obligations, not to whine in adversity but to take whatever came with a stiff upper lip, and to remember that race and descent, however intangible they might be, were nevertheless things that counted and that carried with them obligation well as privilege. He had found no reason to doubt that Andrew had profited by his teaching, and he did not regret that he had not more strongly stressed the importance of certain other things to which after all he attached less value than some of his own countrymen, exiled like him, did. He had found the Valley easy to live with, for its men reminded him of the rural communities which he had known and lived among in childhood and adolescence. They had many of the same traits, stubbornness, pigheadedness if you like, prejudices too deeply rooted to be shaken loose in a generation, a total lack of comprehension of what he called international values, and a pathetic ignorance, the result of the want of those standards of comparison which he himself possessed. But on the credit side there were many things of which he approved that appeared surprising when one took into consideration the fact that for generations they had lived far away from direct authority and cultural influence except such as radiated from the church. Although he himself set no great value on the church as an institution, and in matters of faith was inclined to think along the lines of Tom Paine, whose books he had read and admired, he realised that in the Valley the church had had something to do with the shaping of the community into the form he knew. The Valley had been fortunate in its pastors, and the Reverend Sybrand's two predecessors had been cultured and learned men, whose influence had been all to the good. The Reverend de Smee he liked, although the man's English was not quite so good as it might have been, while his French was really execrable. But there could be no doubt about the fact that the pastor was a man of considerable culture, a classicist who could cap any quotation from Terence—Uncle Charles remembered one exhilarating evening when they had discussed the *Phormio* and that very diverting *Hecyra*—and a sound, sober man who never got bosky but could take his wine like a gentleman, and could apprehend the way in which Joan had been taught to stuff the Muscovy ducks before they were roasted.

Uncle Charles had his fixed routine of life, and he rarely departed from it. If people wanted to talk to him, they could come to *Quakerskloof*, and so he infrequently visited the neighbouring farms, making an exception, however, in favour of his old friend, Martin Rekker, whose hospitality he enjoyed twice a year for a few days. There he learned whatever was to be gleaned from current gossip, giving in return the latest and most authentic news from the capital, gathered both from the papers he had received and from such letters as he himself or his son received from friends and business acquaintances at Cape Town. Once or twice a year, too, he went in to the Village, lodging for the night at the residency where he discussed gardening with Mrs Staples and high politics with her husband. The advent of Pierre Mabuis had intrigued him, and he had listened with great interest to Martin Rekker's account of the new school at *Knolkloof*, and had promised to contribute towards its funds. For Uncle Charles, although he had lost the greater part of his money in unfortunate speculations, still possessed what passed in the Valley for wealth, and was open-handed in his donations. He gave freely to the small committee which controlled the little English church in the Village, and he paid for the services of the English priests who came every quarter from Cape Town to officiate in it. He had even gone so far as to promise a fairly large annual contribution, with a guarantee that his son would keep it up after his death, in aid of the stipend for a resident English clergyman, and in his will, with Andrew's full consent, he had bequeathed his stock of books to the Village to form the nucleus of a library.

There could be no doubt that Charles Quakerley had identified himself with the Valley, and fallen under its spell; in his meditative moods he admitted it without any tinge of regret, and if there were times when he tried to look into the future and ask himself whither all this was tending and whether the new life and the new love necessarily meant a complete severance with the old ties, they had of late years become less frequent and of shorter duration that before. The future could take care of itself, and England, he felt, was strong enough and big enough to tolerate and to bless a younger generation which in lands across the seas had learned to love a home which they had helped to shape and whose interests would naturally come first with them. He could understand and appreciate that feeling, and understanding and appreciating it made him charitably tolerant towards the Valley, and inclined to be sarcastic when his daughter-in-law expressed contrary opinions and carped at the shortcomings of her environment.

That was one of the reasons why he had strongly dissented from his old friend Uncle Martin when the latter had expressed approval of the conduct of the Uhlmanns, who had sent their youngsters away to be educated abroad. He had called it stuff and nonsense. It was all very well sending a lad to a boarding school; he had been to one himself, and by Gad he remembered what he had had to stand, but, damn it, he had been all the better for the experience. But six thousand miles away and with no vacation visits home until the lads had reached manhood, that was a little bit too strong, by Gad, yes. And would Martin kindly have the sense to realise what that meant? Why, that the young men would come back absolute strangers to their own country, just as his own grand-daughters would be absolute strangers in England if they went there. Strangers to the manners, the customs and the thought of the country—why, it was the most preposterous nonsense he had ever heard of, and he was amazed, yes, by Gad, he was—that so sensible a fellow as Uhlmann, who for all his absurd whim-whams had his head screwed on the right way, could dream of doing such a thing. And when Uncle Martin had urged the benefits of free education, he had nearly gulped down his friend's ratafia in indignation. There were opportunities at Cape Town for any lad; had he not sent Andrew there, and was the boy anything worse for it? The expense—for Uncle Martin had mildly pointed out that the Uhlmanns were poor people and could not afford a high class private boarding-school at the capital— why that was rubbish. Uhlmann knew perfectly well that anybody would have accommodated him on his note-of-hand. He himself would have done so without the slightest hesitation, and damn the security, and he was sure that Martin would have done the same. It was all—but here the old man's sense of what one owed to oneself came to the rescue, and he gulped down his glass of sweet wine and muttered that perhaps that altered the case, and Uhlmann couldn't very well go begging for financial accommodation. That had to be thought out, by Gad, it had, and now that they were on the subject, what did Martin think of a reasonable sum in trust to found a school at the Village and prevent such preposterous nonsense in the future? A scholarship now— and he went on to explain the system of scholarships at Christ's Hospital, and adumbrated a scheme in which he and his friend, who was damnably more able to sump up for such a fund than he was, by Gad, figured as the largest donators.

Chapter 18

The Nolte family returned from the Bay to a *Knolkloof* already preparing for its mild winter sleep. As the days shortened, the oak leaves yellowed on the young trees, and the east wind shook them off in myriads, hurtling them rustling along the footpaths of the garden, and sweeping them into refuse heaps in the crevices just as the sea-foam gathers in rock clefts. When the early rains came down they soddened these leaf-heaps, and the rain water, storming down from the declines, left loads of sub-soil over them on which, later, grew mushrooms and toadstools and the quick sprouting composite which the Valley called the 'lean man.'

The transition from summer to autumn and from autumn to spring was almost as quick and as uneventful in the Valley as the daily change from day to night. The twilight was comparatively short, and the dark green of the night settled in idly and softly over everything, making, when the sky was unclouded, a strange luminescence in the air, so that the darkest night was never sombre, provided the stars were free to shine down and reflect from *kopje* and *kloof*, from clay and river surface, from the sheeny polish of the greenery and the grey facts and the synenite in the granite boulders, some of their splendour. Similarly summer gave place to autumn and autumn to winter and winter again to spring with almost startling suddenness, although its precursors made themselves felt before the final change came, just as the mosaic of colour in the eastern sky heralded the short twilight. With spring the change was perhaps startlingly sudden, for one would wake up one morning and find the veld, which the day before had showed no trace of colour except green, a sparkle with splashes of sorrel or dotted with great clumps of belladonna lilies whose leafless floral stems bore cream-pink flowers and whose pollen was reputed to inflame one's eyes. Summer changing into autumn was less peremptory in its abdication, for weeks of dry weather and scorching east wind had shaken all colour but dun and brown out of it. The veld bush had no time to clothe itself in that joyous, variegated mourning that in northern latitudes it would have spread over its foliage. Those that were deciduous shed their leaves under the hurtling gusts of the wind, and those that were evergreen hazed themselves with dust and became a dull grey, harmonising with their environment until it was time, under the warmth and moisture of the spring, to put forth new leaf-buds and appear in all their glory of freshly burnished green.

Under winter conditions *Knolkloof* did not show to advantage, for its trees were still too young to make much of a background to the sombre brown of its soil. Yet there lay a strange, alluring beauty in the scene on which Everardus looked when he sat on his *stoep* in the early morning, rubbing his hands to keep up his circulation and warming himself inside with copious cups of coffee. The grand mountain chain to the north loomed massive and bold against the skyline, its blue more vivid than in summer, its summits tinged here and there with snow dust which on the highest peaks, overlooking Neckarthal, formed dazzling white caps that glimmered in the sunlight. Over the River and the Valley spread morning mists, drawing slowly away from the hill slopes as the air warmed, while the River itself, swollen by the rains, lay, a wider and more turbulent River of ochre-yellow-brown, that lost itself among the trees where a mountain spur came down some miles to the east. From the hillsides coursed little rivulets, and when he looked towards the big range of mountains he could see white trails which marked down-rushing waterfalls that only appeared in the winter.

At night, the cold was by no means unbearable, for *Knolkloof* enjoyed a mild if somewhat damp climate in winter, and there was rarely any need to fill the little foot-stoves with glowing coals to keep up the temperature in the dining room. In the higher lying areas, where frost and extreme cold were common, these foot-stoves were indispensable articles of furniture. The maids filled them with glowing embers from the protea wood fire in the kitchen, and carried them into the dining room, one for each senior member of the family, who retained possession of it until he went to bed, when he either replaced it in the kitchen or carried it with him to his bedroom. They were cheerfully comfortable articles of luxury, and diffused a steady, genial warmth, but at *Knolkloof* they were rarely used, although Everardus had laid in a stock of them, fashioned, like most of his furniture, from the cedar wood planks which he had obtained at the mission station. In winter time, the family went to bed at an early hour and by nine o'clock the homestead was in darkness and its inhabitants were invariably asleep. They rose early, summer and winter, for even in the cold wet winter-time the farm had to be looked after, the cattle to be fed and counted, although it had to be done by lantern light, and the day's work arranged just as in summer. The maids came along with early morning coffee at five o'clock, and by half past five Everardus was at the *kraals*, superintending his Natives and working steadily until eight o'clock when breakfast was ready.

In winter, too, came the thunderstorms that reverberated round the hills and made alarming noise but rarely did any damage. Hail, that bug-bear of the farmer, was almost unknown in the Valley, though when it came it was a most deplorable thing, stamping down the young wheat and doing considerable damage in the gardens. It was altogether different from the soaking rains or from the heavy thunderstorms, both of which, to folk comfortably ensconced within their doors, were events that could be tolerated, admired and approved of. What, for instance, could be more beautiful than the sheets of lightning which lit up the Valley, and showed the cloud-covered outlines of the mountains and the turgid, turbulent River, its water foam-flecked in the eddies and its middle ridged into high waves where the stream was strong? What could be more comforting than to listen to the steady drip, drip of the rain on the thatch, and to feel that every drop fed the wide newly-sown lands which had been so laboriously cleared, ploughed, harrowed, and seeded during those strenuous weeks in anticipation of just these welcome showers?

Not that the rain did not have some drawbacks. It flooded the tributaries of the River which crossed and re-crossed the road, and made transport difficult and sometimes, though happily rarely, dangerous. The *Knolkloof* school was sometimes sadly depleted of its pupils because of these over-full rivulets, while on other days Magriet had to put up the pupils who could not go home because of the weather conditions. The school was progressing favourably, and Tins, who had adapted himself admirably to his new situation, had earned well deserved praise for the progress that his pupils showed when the pastor had come down for the first inspection. It had been a solemn occasion for the committee, and half the church council had attended to watch the proceedings, but Mabuis had been complimented upon the children's singing, and upon the way they had answered the simple examination questions which the Reverend Sybrand had put to them.

Tins had loyally carried out the instructions of the school committee, and on his return from the Bay had borrowed a horse and visited the Widow Priem to explain to her in person the methods of discipline he proposed to adopt at the school. The Widow Priem lived on the farm *Langvlei*, situated some miles from *Knolkloof*. Her husband had died many years ago, and she farmed on her own account, presumably with excellent success, for Tins saw that the lands and garden were in good condition, well kept, and that her house was scrupulously neat and clean although its furnishing was simple in the extreme and it lacked many of the comforts to which he had grown accustomed at *Knolkloof*. The widowed lady was a tall, angular woman, with a lean, long face, whose features were too strongly accentuated for beauty although they were indicative of considerable mental and moral vigour. She invariably wore a black crepe sun-bonnet, which concealed her hair, which she wore curled up at the back of her head in a little bun fastened with old fashioned brass pins, and she dressed herself in the plainest, and to Tins, the ugliest clothes that could be procured. When she came out of the house to receive him, she had on, besides the aforesaid sun-bonnet, whose side flounces effectually shielded her cheeks from the sun, a home made skirt of some coarse woollen material, grey-black originally, but now faded to a dingy fawn, and drawn up so high that the edges of her red flannel petticoat were plainly to be seen, and a close-fitting, long-sleeved jacket tacked on to the skirt, with a black shawl thrown over her shoulders. She had on neither stockings nor boots, and her long, well arched feet were still wet, for she had been leading water in the garden when she had espied Tins riding over the ridge beyond the house, and had come forward at once to meet him when he climbed down from the saddle.

The Widow Priem prided herself on her independence and her disregard of any but the most sacrosanct conventions of the Valley. She spoke in a high pitched, dominating voice, and she handled her horses, cattle and sheep as well as any of her male neighbours in the Valley, and this notwithstanding the fact that she had the reputation of being a highly skilled cook thoroughly acquainted with all the nomenclature and technique of the kitchen. She was not a Valley-ite by birth, having been born in the capital, from Swedish stock which, according to Uncle Martin, who was an authority on such matters, ranked with the best and richest in the Colony. Her husband had received with her a handsome dowry, which had helped to establish him in the Valley, but both had been hardworking, thrifty, and far-seeing, with the result that when he had died, he had left her with a good farm, a fair amount of ready money, and stock and equipment which were considered to be among the best in the District. Her eldest and only daughter had married, and was now living somewhere in the eastern districts where her husband was in government service; her second child had been killed by an accident, and her youngest, the boy Frikkie, whose misbehaviour at school was the cause of Tins's visit to her farm, was not yet of an age, and his mother doubted whether he would ever be of sufficient ability, to manage the farm and take his father's place as head of her establishment. The widow Cornelia Priem had therefore taken the management of things into her own hands, and under her able guidance the farm had prospered. Her Natives were contented and loyal; like those of many of her neighbours, they had been slaves, but they had elected to remain with her, and although the 'Old Mistress' had a reputation for severity and hard work, she was also known to be generous, just and as staunchly loyal to them as they were to her. Her Native overseer or man-doer, an old half-caste from Mozambique who answered to the name of Attico, enjoyed at *Langvlei* very much the same privileges which Sylvester had at *Knolkloof*, and like Sylvester he studied his employer's interests and got the most of his Native gangs that he possibly could. His wife, Cassandra, was a mixture of Hottentot and Koranna, who with advancing age displayed that curious lordotic shape which gave to her figure an ungainly and even an unprepossessing appearance, owing to the manner in which the lower end of her spine bent inwards and her hips came upwards and backwards. Notwithstanding this, she was an active, capable indoor servant, a good cook and washer-woman, and, second to the Old Mistress, the acknowledged leader on the farm, inclined, like her mythological namesake, to look upon the dull side of things, and, while preserving a smiling serenity of face, to harrow her husband's feelings by dire prognostications which were never borne out by facts. Attico and Cassandra were the Widow Priem's adjutants and they had for their old mistress a real regard, while she on her part, although her language might not have given an outsider that impression, respected and valued them for their honest loyalty and faithful, ungrudging service which they had given her for a quarter of a century.

To the Valley, the Widow Priem was an institution and a pride. It had followed her career with great interest and, finding that she had 'made good,' had admitted her, with the qualifications sanctioned by the good Book, which had after all declared that a woman could never be quite a man's equal, to common fellowship. Here and there, in the Valley and beyond it where the Widow's reputation had spread, this interest had become personal, for it had been felt that the admonition contained in the good Book, to the effect that it is not well for a man, and much less so for a woman, to live alone, was one that should be heeded. In consequence the Widow had been courted by several who aspired to the position once held by her late lamented husband. Indeed, it was a standing wonder to the Valley that the Widow Priem had not married again. It was known that she had had several good offers, and that she had dallied with more than one suitor. Gossip went so far as to declare that the government servant who was now her son-in-law had originally intended that the relationship between them should be far closer, and had finally contented himself in despair of winning the mother, with the daughter. Gossip, indeed, knew all about the love affairs of the Widow Priem, probably far more than she herself was willing to acknowledge. The latest aspirant to her hand had been a rich Hantam farmer, a widower with thirteen children and a cross-eye that gave him a rakish appearance. His visits to *Langvlei* had been frequent and long, and he had hinted that his intentions to the widow had not been entirely unreciprocated. But the cross-eyed widower had left very suddenly and, some months after his departure the Valley had heard, with mingled feelings of relief and amusement, that he had chosen, or been chosen by a 'blond young' girl from the Uplands—as the Districts around the capital were generally designated. The Valley, however, considered that sooner or later the widow would meet her fate, and was content to bide its time, secure in the conviction that it was 'God-impossible,' as it expressed itself, for a widowed woman to remain in that state for ever, especially when she possessed so much material and had no few encumbrances. To imagine that such a thing could be possible was to prove oneself incapable of logical reasoning or of profiting by the lessons of experience or the facts of history as revealed to the Valley.

Tins found the widow woman to be very much what his imagination, stimulated by frequent discussions on the subject with Matryk, had pictured her. His half-hearted attempt to kiss her soil-stained fingers was nipped in the bud by the vigorous way in which she grasped his palm and squeezed it in her hands. He found her tone of voice incredibly harsh, her manner of talking a shock to his ideas of female deportment; the way in which she unbridled his horse, disdaining his own frenzied efforts to do that work himself, an insult to his self-respect. He resented her tallness, which forced him to look upwards when he addressed her; he tacitly deprecated her mannishness which he contrasted, much to her detriment, with the womanliness of Magriet, Aunt Sophie-Rosina, Uncle Dorie's wife, and Mrs Uhlmann, and he shuddered at the coming interview when he heard her pre-emptory orders to the Native boy to take the *'Baas's'* horse and give it a rub down and feed. 'This female,' he muttered to himself, 'is of a temperament altogether savage. It is that one must step in a way the most wary not to irritate her.'

'And so,' said the Widow Priem, in her harsh, strident voice that unpleasantly reminded Tins of the noise made by a greaseless axle, 'Teacher has at last managed to find Teacher's way to *Langvlei*. I have it in mind, Teacher, that the visit is long overdue. But better late than never, as the saying is. Come in and drink a cup of coffee.'

As the Widow Priem gave him no chance of refusing, and as it would have been most undiplomatic even to have hinted at a refusal, Tins followed his hostess into the house. She led him into the dining room, which differed from the other dining rooms he had seen in the Valley merely in respect of the furniture, which was simpler, ruder, and more bare-looking than that which he had noted in other farm houses, and in the absence of any decorative mural embellishments. She made him sit at the table, jerked his hat out of his hand, threw it on to the sideboard, and whisked a salver in front of him, talking harshly and rapidly all the while, so that he got no opportunity of explaining his business. He wished to explain in a dignified fashion, doing most of the talking himself, and then to take a formal and courteous leave and get back to *Knolkloof*. But the Widow evidently had other intentions. She left him for a moment, and he thought of snatching up his hat and departing. But he did not know where the Native had taken his horse, and anyway it would not be the right thing to do. One had to be courteous to women, even if they were terrible widow ladies whose voices made him think of cart wheels. The Widow returned and set before him a cup of coffee whose aroma filled the room, a plate of home made biscuits, and a jar of exquisitely translucent green figs preserved in syrup. She produced a spicy cake, a cup for herself, and a coffee jug from which she filled her own cup, and sat down opposite him. He had no longer to look up to her; their eyes were now on a level, and that gave him a trifle more assurance.

'*Madame* is most kind,' he said courteously. 'A sip of coffee would taste admirably after so arduous a ride ...'

'Stuff!' said Widow Priem. 'I have done the distance on foot, and thought nothing of it, Teacher. And as to a sip, why the jug is full and there is plenty more in the kitchen. So drink, Teacher, and eat. Try the conserve. It is my own making and though I may say it myself, you will not find its like in all the Valley.'

She put two preserved figs in his saucer, and continued.

'It is not everyone who knows how to prepare them. You must get them early, but they must not be squashy. They must be firm, and you must scrape them well, but not too deeply, else you remove all the green. And that is not the way to eat them, Teacher. You should either bite them whole, which is the way the men do, or cut them in halves. Don't break them into little bits, Teacher. Only a finicky girl does that, and I have no patience with such.'

'*Madame la Douairiere* is embarrassingly kind,' said Tins endeavouring to follow instructions, 'and the conserve is of a taste the most delicious ...'

'Why does Teacher talk in that outlandish way?' asked the widow sharply. 'I don't hold with such affectations. We are not in Cape Town now, Teacher, and you may keep all that until the Governor comes to visit me.'

'I have no intention whatsoever of displeasing *Madame la Douairiere*,' said Tins, with a courtly bow that nearly knocked his cup off the table. 'It is my manner of speech.'

'Then it is a bad manner,' said the Widow Priem decisively, 'and Teacher should get out of the habit of it. People can talk quite well without those fall-lalls. Take another fig. There is plenty in the pantry, and I can see that you are not used to them. I would give you a glass of wine, Teacher, but I have heard that it goes to your head too quickly.'

Tins gasped and blushed, and to hide his embarrassment took a gulp at his coffee.

The widow immediately replenished his cup.

'I am glad you have called, Teacher,' she said in a less belligerent voice. 'I had a mind to come over myself and talk to you, but it is better so. Now we can have a talk in comfort ...'

'I must be back before the sun rests,' ventured Tins.

'It will not take you more than an hour's riding, as you well know, Teacher,' said the widow. 'Now, what I want to talk about is Frikkie. Why did I send the lad to school? Because he is a loafer here. He does nothing that is good and a lot that is bad, and he has got beyond me, Teacher. A year ago I could use a leather strap on his back, but now he is grown too much, and needs a man's arm. That is why I sent him to you. And what do you do, Teacher? You keep him in, instead of giving him a good, healthy drubbing so that he will dream of his grandma, and think twice before he disobeys again. That is not as it should be, Teacher. Is it now, I ask you?'

'I will take care in future,' said Tins, 'to carry out the instructions *Madame la Douairiere* is pleased so plainly to indicate.

'I don't know what all that means,' retorted the Widow Priem, 'but I take it that Teacher sees that one cannot train a big boy like that without making him feel that he has a master over him. I don't hold with all these new fangled notions, and as I said to the Elder, when we spoke about it, "Far better," said I, "to flog the lad until he has a contrite heart and a humble spirit than run the risk of having him burn in perdition hereafter." Take another fig. I said to the Elder that he must place my view before the committee, and I am glad to find that the members have been sensible enough to see my point of view. I am a lone widow, Teacher, with no one to help me ...'

'*Madame la Douairiere*,' said Tins gallantly, 'has innumerable friends, who would fly to her assistance at a moment's notice.'

'That you may believe,' answered the widow, a trifle scornfully. 'I have had some experience of these friends. Not that I blame them entirely. A person must look after his own interests first. But when my sheep had blue tongue and I had to fend for myself, I had precious little help from this legion of friends of which Teacher speaks.'

'They could not have been aware of the difficulty in which *Madame* found herself. I cannot figure to myself so distressing a contingency as ...'

'In heavens name, Teacher, speak so that a person can understand you. I meant that self is a better friend than next man, if you take me. Let me fill your cup, Teacher, and try this cake. It is a walnut filling which you will find tasty. If I have to pay for Frikkie, I must have value for my money. That you must admit. I cannot have the boy kept in when I need him here, especially now when the days are getting short. All I ask you is that you should prepare him for catechism, and teach him to read and write. That is enough for him to go on with. His father had no more, and he did very well with it. But Frikkie needs discipline, Teacher, and I look to you to see that he gets it. Else, not a stiver do I pay.'

'*Madame* may rely on me,' said Tins, who now felt much more at ease. 'Now that I know *Madame's* wishes in the matter, I will attend to it. Master Frikkie will give no further cause for complaint. On that point I offer *Madame* my profound assurances.'

'I am grateful, Teacher. Another fig? No more? Why, you hardly eat enough to satisfy a girl. Come, I will show you round the farm. There is plenty of time and the horse, too, must have its feed before you up-saddle.'

Tins saw the farm, and admired what he saw. The Widow Priem had improved it considerably, and she took some legitimate pride in showing him some of her most recent improvements. There was the dam in the little valley behind the *kraal* that was an improvement dating from last summer, and this winter's rains would test it. Not that the widow had any doubts about its stability. She had confidence in the strength of that neatly stone-paved retaining wall, built to her own design, and capable of withstanding whatever pressure might be applied to it by the water behind. Moreover, she had provided ample overflow space for storm water. The dam would give her sufficient water in summertime for her garden and for the nearer lands; the farther lying grain lands would still have to depend mainly on the rainfall which at *Langvlei* was not so great as at *Knolkloof* and other parts of the Valley. She showed him her citrus orchard, and he saw that the trees were all well cared for, with the soil raked beneath each tree, and the water furrows intelligently arranged. She took him to the *kraals*, and he admired the sleek, fat cattle, the full-fleeced sheep which would be sheared when the winter cold had gone, and the big, wallowing pigs roaming on the slopes of the hillside. He admired the mules and the horses, which, if not so good or well-bred as those at *Knolkloof*, were yet powerful, healthy animals. It was nearly sundown when they came back to the homestead, and by that time Tins had an altogether different opinion of the widow. He no longer regarded her as a terrible woman, but as one who was entitled to admiration and respect, for had she not evolved, out of as uncompromising material as that with which *Meneer* Nolte had had to work, a farm which in many respects surpassed *Knolkloof* though to be sure it was older, and a comparison was therefore not altogether fair.

He bade her farewell and found himself, to his astonishment, promising to come again soon and taste her Muscovies. He did not attempt to kiss her hand, but tried to return the pressure of her fingers, and when he looked up at her face, it seemed to him that her features were far more comely than he had imagined them to be at first sight. And when, half way up the rise, something made him turn and look back towards the farm, he saw her standing on the spot where they had parted, and he waved his hand and was gratified to find that she acknowledged the parting salute by waving back to him. He was very thoughtful on the way home, and when he reached *Knolkloof* and Matryk asked him how he had found the Widow Priem, he answered, quite shortly, that *Madame la Douairiere* was as well as could be expected. Matryk, who thought that *Meester* was in one of his touchy moods, did not pursue the subject, but started discussing the health of one of the cows which had lately been ailing, and Tins promised to drench it the next morning.

Chapter 19

The vicissitudes of farming, as Virgil pointed out long ago, tend to strengthen or weaken the character of the farmer, according to his temperament and his courage. Nowhere are these vicissitudes more frequent or more vexatious to the agriculturist than in South Africa, and at the time which is the period of this narrative there were fewer compensations for them than there are probably now. It was Everardus's good fortune that those which he met with during his first ten years of his Valley holding were not of a nature harsh enough to discourage him. The Valley admitted that Nolte had had good luck, and that he had been exempt to a large extent from those woefully annoying occurrences that had proved to many of them such deliberate obstacles to progress and advancement. Everardus himself admitted it freely. He had prospered beyond his best anticipations, and his prosperity was not due entirely to his own effort. He had started without that discouraging handicap, want of capital, and had therefore been able to obtain many comforts and conveniences which his neighbours lacked; he had worked hard and patiently, but so everyone in the Valley had done, yet few could look back on a decade of such progress and development as that which *Knolkloof* could show. His prosperity was due to causes which he could not clearly analyse, but he shrewdly suspected that among them were his ability to profit by the experience of others, the good seasons which the Valley had experienced during the time he had lived there, and the good fortune he had had in obtaining labour on which he could rely and an overseer of the type of Matryk. Matryk had grown into a dependable, capable worker. For all his natural simplicity, he was a good farm hand who understood how to manage the Natives, and although he did not possess much initiative, he could be relied upon to carry out an order, and on occasion act on his own responsibility on the lands or at the *kraal*. Between him and Tins a strange friendship had grown up, which apparently benefitted both. Mabuis had even tried to teach the young man to read and write, but Matryk's progress in this direction was infinitely slower than that of the junior pupils in the school. On the other hand he was expert with his hands, a good blacksmith, knowing how to shoe the horses and mules without harm to their hoofs, and able to do such repairs to the wagons and ploughs as could be done on the farm, so that Everardus rarely found it necessary to call in the help of the blacksmith at the Village. Anton Fisher, when he had installed the mill machinery, had taught Matryk how to look after it, and the latter had since done all that was necessary in the mill-house. He had grown into a tall weedy man, with a beard that could never be coaxed into regularity, and with a face that still retained its wooden expression of good-natured, smiling stupidity. In company he kept to himself, and he was far happier at work with the Natives than in conversation with his fellow *bywoners* on the farms, but his happiest moments were when he was with Tins, listening to the latter's flute playing or reminiscences of regimental life. The only time when he had been known to express a wish for something beyond what he could anticipate on the farm was when he had told Mabuis that he would like to be a soldier and had questioned him as to the best means of enlisting. Tins had promptly intimated that a soldier's life was a dog's life, especially in the Hottentot Regiment, and advised his friend to think of other things, and Matryk had never reverted to the subject.

Everardus, who at first had doubted the lad's ability, now had confidence in him, especially when he could also rely on Mabuis being at hand to help. The Teacher had a fund of common sense, obscured by his impetuosity and his careless, affected manner, and although he could not be relied upon to do any farm work himself, he could supervise such work. He was an admirable horseman, and trained Everardus's yearling foals, and had undertaken to make one of the three year olds fit for the race course. During his periods of teaching he was too much occupied to permit of his helping on the farm, but in the vacations he did his share, and occasionally made suggestions or deprecatingly offered advice which Everardus invariably accepted and found good. The period of his probationship had long since passed, and Everardus now had no scruples when passing the wine carafe across the table to Teacher, for Tins took his wine like a gentleman, and abstained from drinking anywhere but in the dining room at or after meals. He had developed into a staid, respectable personage, with a certain air about him that became him well, and his language had much improved. He no longer inter-larded it with foreign expressions and un-understandable ejaculations. Altogether, the Valley, which had watched him with interest and had indulged in many speculations about his probable future, admitted that he had improved, retaining many of his better qualities, shedding some of his worse, and acquiring others which the Valley thought even better than some which he had already possessed.

It was Tins who had first made the suggestion that Everardus should join forces with Thomas Seldon and engage in the transport trade. He had pointed out that the horse breeding was a success, but that there were now far more horses and mules on the farm than could easily be disposed of or economically employed in farm service. These, he suggested, could be made into teams and *Meneer* Nolte could invest in half a dozen wagons and carry on transport, not only in the Valley District, but in the adjacent Districts as well. He had broached the project to Seldon, on one of his visits to the store underneath the mountain pass, and the suggestion had been favourably received. Seldon had long thought of taking a partner for this side of his business. The government had declared its intention of altering and improving the main road, which meant considerable deviation work on the pass, and an accession of business with which Seldon was doubtful if he could cope single-handed. A discussion with Everardus settled the matter. Nolte would supply a certain amount of capital which would be invested in the business and Seldon would contribute a similar amount. The details of the small private company were quickly adjusted, and before the end of the year their transport wagons were travelling on the high road, carrying government stores for the road parties, and bringing in a reasonably fair interest on their capital after deduction of all working expenses. Everardus found that Mabuis had a working knowledge of bookkeeping, and his services were accordingly requisitioned, at an agreed upon wage, as bookkeeper and general secretary to the firm, on the understanding that such work should not be allowed to interfere with his teaching. This arrangement left Everardus free to devote most of his time to the personal supervision of his teams and his transport riders. He engaged some of the men at the pans and found that, notwithstanding Uncle Dorie's warning that he would only have 'sin and trouble' from the experiment, they served him well and faithfully, although, like Matryk, they possessed little initiative and had to be told everything in detail before they could be trusted to undertake a job. With his partner he soon became on terms of excellent friendship, and the relations between the Seldons and the Noltes increased in intimacy with the years. The children of both families played together, and when Tommy Seldon was reckoned too old and advanced to profit further from what Tins could teach him at the *Knolkloof* school, and was sent to Cape Town to the same private school which Andrew Quakerley had attended, Seldon urged that Gottlieb Nolte should accompany him.

'You would do well, Nolte,' he said, 'to give the lad proper schooling when he has a chance to get it. *Knolkloof* is all very well, but what, after all, do they learn? You want something more than mere preparation for membership of the church. For that a few weeks tuition with the pastor will suffice if the boy has a good grounding.'

Everardus, as usual, submitted the matter to his wife, and found that she heartily approved of the plan, while Gottlieb himself, a smooth faced, fair-haired boy whose English, owing to constant intercourse with the Seldons, was passably good, was eager to go. Accordingly, he took the boys in to Cape Town himself, travelling in his roomy spring-wagon drawn by a team of eight good mules, and arriving, four days after his departure from *Knolkloof*, within sight of the grand old mountain that he remembered so well. On his right hand lay the circular bay, faintly blue in the distance, with an East Indiaman at anchor in the roads; on the left curved the sweep of False Bay with Cape Hangklip far in the distance, and with the sharp point of the Little Paul's *Berg* on the nearer side, and in front towered the mountain, with its sheer cliff face reflecting ever-changing hues as he neared it, and a wisp of white cloud, the forerunner of a violent south-easter, stealing stealthily over the neck between it and Devils Peak. Under its shadow lay the capital, a straggling triple line of houses, variegated in colour and form, and stretching from the more thickly clustered part grouped in the vicinity of the old Castle to the fertile hill slopes on the left where the larger estates were.

Everardus spent an agreeable three days at Cape Town, finding much there to interest him. He visited his attorneys, whom he had not seen for several years, and was taken out by the senior partner to lunch at the latter's club, where he was introduced to several prominent residents, and had the honour of a few minutes talk with the Attorney-General, whom he found was a most charming and agreeable man, who reminded him of Brother von Bergmann, though the latter was indubitably handsomer and more imposing looking. He refrained from putting down his name in the Governor's visitors book, but he tramped into the Castle and had a look at the old Council Chamber where stood the cane seated chair on which, tradition held, Governor van Noot had died when he had been so suddenly called upon to give an account of his stewardship. He strolled on the pier and watched the fishermen landing their catches at Roggebay, and he walked up the Heerengracht, the principal street, to view the old prison.

All these recalled memories to him, some pleasant and others which he would gladly have forgotten, for they took his mind back to that distant date when his work had lain here and when for a bare livelihood he had been forced to do what he now regretted ever having done.

At Cape Town he heard of the new postal service, and his attorneys—whom he had told of his venture with Seldon, and had shown his contract, of which they had cordially approved—suggested that he should tender for the transport of mails from Cape Town to the Village. No one else was likely to tender, and he could make his own terms, within reason, they assured him. He could leave all the details in their hands, provided he gave them outside figures; the scheduled times would have to be fixed by the Postmaster-General. In view of his partnership with Seldon he would not definitely commit himself, but he liked the idea, and promised to inform them of his decision as soon as he had an opportunity of discussing it with Seldon.

The school to which he had taken Tommy and Gottlieb interested him vastly, for it was the first time he had seen anything like it. The master was an old, very mild looking clergyman, whose pronounced stoop and near-sightedness at first impressed him unfavourably, until he saw the old man in front of his class and witnessed his expert way of handling his pupils. They were taught Latin and French, besides the usual secondary subjects, but no Dutch figured on the programme, and he was told that its use was forbidden on the playground. The pupils were both day boys and boarders, and he left Gottlieb among the latter without any qualms, reflecting that the curriculum was one which he was not competent to judge, but that it must be good otherwise so many of the Dutch residents, whose boys he saw on the playground, would not patronise the establishment. The school fronted the large Greenpoint commonage, at the farther, seaward side of which lay the shallow lake on which the boys sailed their toy boats, and before he departed he took Tommy and Gottlieb for a walk along the beach, towards Three Anchor Bay, and tried to find the spot where the old gibbet had stood. He found only the iron staples which had fixed the standards into the masoned foundation, but on the bushes which grew on the common he saw several of the hissing chameleons which had so irritated Uncle Dorie on one occasion in his vineyard at *Knolkloof*. They looked harmless and beautiful, and he did not disturb them or direct the boy's attention to them, but the sight of them somehow made him feel uncomfortable and he was glad to turn back.

He travelled back the next day, starting before dawn to get over the rough road across the flats before it became too hot, and outspanned for the night on the bare veld. The following evening he was hospitably entertained at the wayside farmhouse, and the third night, to save his horses, he camped at the foot of the pass where the road gangs had pitched their tents, reaching *Knolkloof* in time for the midday meal on the fourth day. His visit to the capital had been a pleasant excursion, for although he regretted parting with his little son, he had felt that it was in the boy's interest that he should be placed at a good school, and he had been gratified in one way and secretly hurt in another to find that Gottlieb himself had shown much less feeling at parting from him than what he had anticipated would have been the case.

On his return he threw himself heart and soul into his work. His vineyard was now productive and the next season he had determined to make wine, and it was necessary to build cellars and provide cooperage. After discussing the matter with Tins, who declared that he was quite competent 'to make for *Meneer* Nolte such a wine as *Meneer* has never yet drunk'—an assurance whose dubiety did not at first strike Everardus—he decided to enlist once more the services of Anton Fisher. Although the Uhlmanns had visited *Knolkloof* several times, Everardus had found no opportunity of repeating his visit to Neckarthal, and as this seemed a good opportunity he inspanned his spring-wagon and took Magriet and Katryn with him, stopping on his way at the Village where he took advantage of the pastor's repeated invitation to accept his hospitality.

In the evening after his arrival at the parsonage, he found himself in company, in the pastor's roomy study, on the wall of which he noted the framed sketch which Tins had made of the naked youth at the Bay, with the Reverend Sybrand and old Charlie Quakerley, who had strolled over from the residency where he was a temporary guest, to drink a glass of wine and indulge in a bit of gossip. He had met and conversed with the old Englishman many times previously, but had never encountered him on terms of such equality, and he studied him with attention. He was impressed by the old man's stately courtesy, his old-mannered deportment—the way in which he took a chair was a revelation, the bow with which he opened the door to let the pastor's wife pass out was gracefulness personified—his well manicured hands, his meticulously clean and yet obviously coarse materialled clothing which he wore easily as if dress was a matter of supreme indifference to him. But above all he was impressed by the visitor's speech, so cleanly enunciated, so widely different from the English which the Seldons talked, a speech which slurred over some syllables so that Everardus had some difficulty in making out the words, and so carefully stressed others which he himself was in the habit of slurring. The talk was wholly in English, which the pastor spoke with a fierce Continental accent, and Everardus with the drawl and open vowel sounds to which he had been accustomed ever since he had mastered its rudiments, and on the whole it was vivacious, although the pastor and Quakerley did most of the talking.

'I hear, Mr Nolte,' said the old man, leaning slightly towards him as he spoke, 'that you have just returned from a visit to Cape Town. I have not been there for years, but they tell me it is no longer what it was.'

'It is very much changed, Mr Quakerley,' replied Everardus, choosing his words carefully. 'I hardly knew it, and it is not so very long I was last there. There is little water in the castle moat, and none at all in the street ditch.'

'But they are very excited, very, there,' said the pastor. 'Very excited, hey? I hear things. They talk of sending us the convicts. Good heavens, Mr Quakerley, what a disaster. I hope, I sincerely hope, it will come to naught, that plan.'

'If you were a betting man, Parson,' said old Charles tersely, 'you could put a pony on that. I don't know what has come over these idiots at home, though from Whiggery like John Russell's one may expect anything. And that ass Grey is not much better. Of course they don't know conditions out here—how could they? But Smith should enlighten them. I daresay he does his best, but I see that the *Neptune* is to sail with a load of riff-raff, and as soon as they come here, Parson, there'll be the devil to pay. Mark my words, the devil to pay.'

'Yes,' said Everardus, who while in Cape Town had heard much of the convicts but had not thought the matter of great importance. 'I heard talk about it. People are very much upset. So much I gathered, Mr Quakerley.'

'And wouldn't you be upset if they landed a gang of riff-raff in the Valley and plonked them down alongside of you, Mr Nolte? Of course you would. Not a doubt about it. But let me tell you this, Parson, it is one of the best things that could happen to us.'

'How so, Mr Quakerley?' asked the pastor in astonishment. 'It seems to me altogether a deplorable affair. How can it be good, except you take it that through God's grace all evil has in it something good.'

'I am not philosopher enough to argue that with you, Parson. But the thing is perfectly clear, to my mind at least. Listen, and I shall expound. I know something of this country; I have lived here almost forty years, and I may lay claim to knowing something about it, even though I haven't mastered the lingo yet and don't know a disselbum from a chucksky unless you show me the damn things—your pardon, Parson, but habit, habit. As I say, I know something about you. Just think for a moment. Here we all are, one side English and the other Dutch, though God knows few of us can honestly tell the difference. We the newcomers, you the old settlers, but neither with more claim than what is based on occupation or, if you like, conquest. Both, I am sure, though I admit there are exceptions—my daughter-in-law is one so I know—with the intention of living for this country and looking upon it as their home. Take me, Parson, as an example. I have no wish to go back. Here I stay until I die, and what I can give to this country I willingly give ...'

'That we know, Mr Quakerley,' interrupted the pastor. 'We look upon you as one of us ...'

'As one of us. Exactly. But, Parson, surely you can see that that is the very thing that tends to division and estrangement. Let us drop the possessive and start equal. Mr Nolte, I am sure, would not like to be called "one of us" if he decides to settle in England. Shiver me, Parson, but that is the very kernel of it and a ... a very unpleasant one it is too, far too bitter, sometimes, for the swallowing.'

'Ah,' said the pastor reflectively, 'I can take you. It has not struck me that way before, but I can see it. You object, naturally, to the ... how shall I say it ... toleration, hey?'

'Of course, any man would object to being tolerated when he thinks himself equal with the fellow who does the tolerating. You would yourself, Parson, and Mr Nolte here. But we shan't get away from it until we have a common grievance, and that is just what Johnny is about to give us. When the grievance is all on one side, as it is now, Parson, for we have none, and you have really none, except that you are still sore because instead of the little republics which you established when you were thirsting for the blood of the Orangemen, we came along and roped you all in. But that feeling is dying off; it was never strong in these parts; not as strong, certainly, as what I remember in other Districts. You are too sensible here, for you know that with our little population and with Cape Town as the key to India you would never be permitted to hold this country if England tomorrow withdrew from it and left you to your own devices. Up north, yes. There, perhaps, you might have found an independent state—they are busy doing that, I hear—but even that won't last very long. A country must have sea-ports, a trade. You cannot do without it. I know that feeling is not dead—I mean the feeling that you have been done out of something you regarded as your own—and at any rate the sentiment is still there, for when you talk of "us," Mr de Smee, you invariably think only of yourselves. We exist, you can't get a way from that, but we are not of you, and you don't regard us as being just as good citizens of this country simply because you still nurse that grievance. I don't say you, my friend—let us try and be impersonal—but I say that is the case with all in this country who do not belong to my section. Nay, Parson, I go further and I add, all those who do not belong to your section. Take Mr Uhlmann. The man is as good as any of us, better in many ways, certainly as good a citizen as you can find anywhere in this Colony. You will admit that he is quite worthy to be "one of us." But, honestly, if it happens that he does not agree with your section, will you feel the same regard for him that you felt—let me say—for one of your own parishioners, who speaks Dutch, goes to communion, and has, somewhere at the back of his mind, a vague feeling that England has cheated him of something that should by rights be his? Now, honestly, is not that the case?'

'Personally, of course,' said the pastor, 'I repudiate the charge, but I am afraid there is some truth in your indictment, Mr Quakerley. There is such a thing as national feeling, you know.'

'There is, Parson, and sometimes it is very so-so. But I have you in tierce, my friend, for national feeling presupposes a nation, and what you take for it is sectional feeling. That is just my point. If we had a common grievance, such as I say Johnny is about to give us, it may weld us together, and from that welding may in time spring a nation. But we are not that yet. Certainly you are not, although you are in the majority, and just as certainly we, English speaking Colonists, are not a nation. We are at the most clans, and clannishness is accountable for most of the misunderstanding between us.'

'That is so,' admitted the pastor. 'But you should take into consideration the difference in culture and outlook. In some respects they are radically different.'

'With leave, I deny that, Parson. What was your section, at first, but a heterogeneous combination of all sorts of people? Will you tell me that the French who came in 1688 or thereabouts were less different in culture than we English who came forty years ago? Indeed, I apprehend that if we properly discuss that point you will agree that there is far more national similarity between us and you Dutch, than between you and the Huguenots, and yet all these you regard as "of us" while you deny to us the right to claim common citizenship with you. Hardly fair, my friend, hardly fair. And now to wash the taste of the argument out of my mouth, a sip of your excellent wine.'

'I feel sure you overstate the case, Mr Quakerley,' said the pastor, pouring out three glasses of the golden brown Jeropico which he kept for special occasions. 'We have absolutely no *animus*, no *animus* whatever. But there is the difference of outlook, which you do not consider. You have not been born in this country, and you cannot understand ...'

'Can't I? My compliments on the wine, Parson; it is a trifle young, but sound and very pleasant to the palate. Does it really matter where a man is born? I do not go so far as to say with Tom Paine, whom you would scarcely approve of, Parson, that the whole world is my country and to do good is my religion, but I deny your inference, which is that a man cannot be a good citizen of a country unless he is born in it. In that case, your ancestors were but indifferent citizens, and those of us who came out as settlers can never be really one of you. What matters it where a man is born, so long as he loves the country, and is prepared to do his duty by it? And, speaking for myself, if I take this country to be mine, no matter under what rule it is, what right have you to deny me that privilege simply because I happen to have been born elsewhere? But I see, Mr Nolte is silent. I daresay he most cordially disapproves of all that I have been saying.'

'Indeed no, Mr Quakerley,' said Everardus, thus appealed to. 'I cannot follow it all—you both speak too quick, and my English, she is still young. But I think that you have right, in part. I was never in favour of all this talk against the English. When the younglings refused to attend the feast for our Queen, I went and talked to them, and made them see how they erred. I think such things create but ill-feeling, with which we are the better without.'

'I am glad Mr Nolte approves,' said Quakerley gravely. 'I wish I could speak your language as well as you do mine, Mr Nolte. And I am ashamed that I do not, for that is a fault which I much regret. Cato learned Greek when he was eighty—so they say— but I find it devilish hard to learn Dutch. I tried once, and I tried again, but it is hopeless. Very likely my own laziness, for Andrew learned it easily enough, and even my daughter-in-law can speak it although she affects not to be able to even understand it. So you must make allowances for me, although I grant you that my own case goes a little against my argument. A good citizen should speak the language of the country, and when there are two languages, as there are here, why, he should speak both. Therein, Mr Nolte, you are a worthier citizen than I.'

'That is what I had in mind,' said the pastor, nodding his head in agreement. 'The difference in language, in culture, and in outlook. It is always there, and you cannot get away from it. You talk of grievances and of feeling, Mr Quakerley, but have you considered how badly off we are against you English? So badly that we must be fighting constantly not to be overwhelmed by you, with your immense resources, your language, your culture ...'

'Stuff, Parson, and you know it! Behind you too lie ages of culture; your language too, has a literature as good as ours. Why, Milton borrowed from your Vondel, and just remember Grotius and Huyghens and the rest. You'll never be swamped unless you want to be swamped, and there is no earthly reason why we should not live side by side, bearing with one another, and working for the good of common cause and a common country. That is why I am glad that they are sending out those convicts in the *Neptune*. They will never land, believe me, and what is going to happen—you will see—will be that we'll get a common grievance, and Dutch and English, French and

Swede, and every man Jack of us will stand shoulder to shoulder in the fight for our common interest.'

'Pray God it may be so,' said the pastor fervently. 'If out of evil good comes, as you say, we will have much to be thankful for. But I fear that there will be much unpleasantness before we reap that good harvest.'

'You cannot have these things without a little unpleasantness,' said Quakerley. 'And before we understand each other, I apprehend there will be much more which you might call unpleasant. But we might at least pull together, and if what I hear is true, we shall have to do so. My latest information is that the home government is studying the report of the commission and that we may expect a constitution before very long. In that case, Parson, you should take time by the forelock and fix on somebody to represent you.'

'Is it as far as that?' asked the parson. 'Perhaps Mr Quakerley can tell us what has been proposed.'

'A variation of the scheme that Mr Advocate Porter suggested,' replied Quakerley. 'The details, of course, are not known, but I have private information to the effect that there will be two houses, with elected representatives.'

'To be elected by whom?' asked the parson, and Everardus listened eagerly.

'That I do not know with certainty,' answered old Charles. 'My information suggests that for the larger body all citizens will have a vote, provided they have certain qualifications, which I take to be similar to those at home.'

'All? But that is absurd,' exclaimed the parson. 'They would surely not suggest that the Natives also should vote. It is unthinkable!'

Uncle Charles shrugged his shoulders. 'You know what those Whigs are,' he said extenuatingly. 'It is sufficiently wonderful that they should insist on any qualification at all. It will of course depend entirely on what the qualification happens to be, and therein, my friend, I think we might with safety trust Smith.[1] I know what his views are, and in the main they agree with mine, and I fancy also with yours.'

'But is there to be no distinction of colour?' asked the parson, and Uncle Charles eyed him quizzically.

'There is none in the church, is there?' he suggested mildly. 'And I see no reason why a Native, if he is fit, should not have a say in the government of the country he lives in. Provided he is fit, and that, as I said before, depends on the qualification. I should like to see an educational qualification, which would exclude practically all our Natives'

'At present,' agreed the pastor. 'But what of the future? They can learn, and they are more numerous than we are ...'

'Again, my friend, that most disagreeable possessive spirit. You should really try and get rid of it. Why should you object to the Native voting if he is fit to vote? I object very much to the White man voting if he is unfit to have a share in governing the country, and the Native at present is not fit for the vote. That I readily grant you. But it would not be fair to exclude him forever, and thereby prevent him from becoming fit to bear his share of responsibility. But the subject is too wide to be

[1] Sir Harry Smith—Eds.

argued at this time of night, and Staples is sitting up for me. So I must away, my friend, after one more glass of your excellent wine. Thank you. Mr Nolte, your obedient; Parson, your very good health. And now to bed. I wish you a very good night, Mr Nolte. Sleep well, Parson. I thank you ... three steps, I am safely below. Goodnight.'

'A very fine old man, Mr Quakerley, Brother Ev'rard,' said the parson as he closed and locked the front door, 'but opinionated, opinionated. And worldly in his outlook. Given to reading godless books, Brother, like those of the revolutionary atheist Paine. But there is something in what he says and I shall remember that phrase, "The world is my country and to do good my religion." It is not so very different from what the apostle says for he defines true religion as being to visit the widow and fatherless and comfort them in their affliction. But it is disturbing what he said about the new constitution. I must have a talk with the magistrate on the subject, and we must see what can be done. Another glass of wine? No? Well then, let us follow our friend's example and go to bed.'

Chapter 20

At Neckarthal Everardus found that Brother Johann was in complete agreement with old Charles Quakerley on several of the points under discussion. The missionary, however, took a detached view of the position, and although he was not indifferent to its dangers claimed that it was a matter entirely for the country itself to settle.

'All the harm is done by those who interfere with us from abroad, *Meneer* Nolte,' he said judicially, puffing at his long china pipe. 'Now this constitution that we are about to get, and which we will get, is the product of theorists. Its framers are men who are completely unacquainted with the actual position here. Neither you nor I, *Meneer* Nolte, are fully cognisant of all the facts, and all the relations of these facts. We know the Valley, the District and possibly parts of the Colony, but we do not know their relations to the whole of Africa or to the rest of the world. A statesman would look beyond his own domains. He would ask himself "How is what I propose to do going to affect the rest of the world?" That is where we make our mistake. That, too, is where the English are apt to make mistakes. Their outlook is that of one safe at home, who has little concern with the rest of mankind. So, too, is ours, *Meneer* Nolte. It is perfectly natural, at present. But the time must come when what we do in the Colony, in South Africa, even in this Valley of ours, reacts upon humanity as a whole. We should bear that in mind, and go warily, and above all we should not do what we may later on have to regret having done.'

'Then Your Reverence is opposed to it?' asked Everardus. 'To me it seems silly not to make a difference between White and Black when it comes to voting.'

'I cannot say that the colour or race of the vote is an insurmountable difficulty with me,' remarked the missionary thoughtfully. 'My way of looking at that point is perhaps different from yours, although I can sympathise with your view. But I should be unfaithful to my convictions and to my upbringing—in fact, to my whole conception of Christianity and civilisation—if I admitted your premise that the difference between White and Black in this country is so great that the two can never be on an equal footing as regards civic rights. From what I have seen of the Native and the half-caste Coloured folk, who are, after all, descendants of White men or Asiatics who may lay claim to more civilisation than the aboriginals, I feel sure that they are capable of development which may in time bring their descendants into line with ours. You cannot conceive such a possibility; your whole nature revolts at the idea. But is not that very much on the same line as the prejudice which you tell me *Meneer* Quakerley complains about when he says that we who are not English-speaking at home mistrust and tolerate those who are English among us? Is it not merely ignorance and class prejudice? I confess I have felt something of it myself, and often I have discussed the matter with our brother missionaries. Some of them feel it as much as you do; others less strongly. It depends upon a man's temperament, his tolerance, and his outlook. Do you not agree?'

'When Your Reverence puts it like that,' admitted Everardus, 'there seems to be something in it. But after all the Natives and the Coloured folk are children. So long as they are happy and contented, why need we bother about giving them privileges which they do not want and which they might easily abuse?'

'Ah, you start from the assumption that children will remain children. That is never the case. I may be totally wrong, but my impression is that a considerable percentage of the Natives will progress, and I see no reason why they should not become as civilised as we are. As for the Coloured folk, why there can be no doubt about their ability, their adaptability, and their capacity for profiting by what they are taught. You can see it here at Neckarthal, and you will see it more clearly at Brother von Bergmann's station, at Genadenthal and at Amalienstein.'

'Then Your Reverence thinks that in time we shall have to admit them as full *burghers* ... and they in the majority. Where will it end?'

'Why, that our people in Europe might ask themselves, now that there is a movement to give votes to everyone, whether he possesses a qualification or not. It is democracy, *Meneer* Nolte, and if you admit the principle that all of us are equal, I do not see how you can object. In America they have laid it down in their constitution that all men are equal and free, yet they still keep their slaves. Which is illogical and absurd, and will very likely give rise to difficulties before very long. Now we have none of that here. We have admitted that it is not right that, as a great Englishman once expressed it, one man should be another man's property. And by admitting it we have tacitly implied that fundamentally one man is as good as another.'

'I don't dispute that,' said Everardus, 'so far as it applies to us Whites. But it can't possibly apply to the Natives.'

'You make a reservation in favour of the Coloured, *Meneer* Nolte. Then where would you draw the line?'

'If a man is not wholly white, he should rank with the Natives,' said Everardus stubbornly. 'His place is with them, not with us.'

'That, again, is not logical. What is not wholly white? You know yourself that in some families—I may say in many families—who pride themselves on being pure

White there is some colour. How many half-castes are there in this Valley of ours, for instance, who are of pure Hottentot and Malay blood without admixture of European blood? I know of White men who have married half-castes. Would you exclude their children, admitting them only to the full *burgher* rights and preventing the children from ever reaching the same privileges that you concede to the father?'

'I should exclude the fathers as well,' exclaimed Everardus vehemently, 'if they have so far forgotten their obligations.'

'Ah, then you would be more logical,' said the missionary with a smile. 'But I am afraid then you would stand very much alone, for none of us would like to go as far as that. Nor do I see how that is practicable. Where are we to draw the line? Believe me, *Meneer* Nolte, these things are not so easily settled as some people believe. There are natural laws—Gods laws, if you believe that God ordains everything according to His foreknowledge—which we cannot disregard or condemn for the sake of obtaining temporary peace or advantage. They rule the relations between races, and fix the position that men occupy in communities. We do not know what they are, though there is much speculation about them, but we do know that a race does not die out or succumb to another if it has the stamina to endure and to adapt itself to its environment. All I can say—I am too ignorant to judge of these things with the skill of an expert—all I can say is that in my dealings with the Natives here at Neckarthal, I have seen nothing to make me believe that they have no stamina and that they must inevitably give way to us White men, as they have done in some other parts of the world.'

Similar opinions Everardus heard when he returned to the Village on his way back to *Knolkloof*. The magistrate explained to him that his services were again required to calm another agitation that had arisen in the Valley, but this time his sympathies were wholly on the side of the agitators, and the utmost he could promise was that he would prevent, so far as was possible, the hot-heads from going to extremes. The anti-convict agitations were disturbing the Colony. At Simonstown lay the ship *Neptune*, freighted with a load of men condemned to penal servitude, among them John Mitchell whose *Jail Journal* contains a description of the excitement which prevailed at the time. In every town and District meetings were held to protest against the landing of the prisoners, and the Valley was no exception to the rule. At one of these meetings of indignation and protest, Everardus was asked to preside, and his capable chairmanship showed him in a new light to his fellow Valley-ites.

'Mighty, but Nephew Ev'rard can sling the words,' they said in open admiration. 'When the time comes we must get him as our representative.'

The time was not far off, for the Governor had already received the despatch authorising him to promulgate the new constitution for the Colony. The magistrate called a public meeting, which was largely and representatively attended—even Uncle Charles Quakerley riding into the Village with his son to be present at the deliberations. On the whole, the Valley approved. There would be, said the magistrate, an upper chamber, the members of which would have to possess immoveable property to the value of at least £2 000 sterling. The Valley cordially approved. And a Legislative Assembly, in which any elected representative would be entitled to sit provided he had the qualifications of a voter. The Valley was slightly dubious, but waited for an explanation of what these qualifications would be. The magistrate explained that to be a voter one had to be a male *burgher*, a major, and the owner or tenant of a house valued at £25 or in receipt of wages or salary to the amount of £50 sterling per annum. The Valley nodded its head and presumed that His Honour had left out the word 'White' before the word 'male,' but the magistrate patiently explained that the Ordinance would make no distinction between Whites and Natives. The Valley shook its head, and looked towards its spokesmen to voice its disapproval, but when Uncle Dorie rose to address the meeting, Uncle Charles was already on his feet, and the Valley heard, in surprised delight, his vigorous and emphatic declaration.

'It is just the sort of tomfoolery that they would timber together,' Uncle Charles said, speaking with cool deliberation tinged with a little bitterness and contempt. 'It's for us to take it or leave it, and speaking for myself alone, I should take it. Half a loaf is better than no bread, my friends, even though the loaf is, as you say, so expressively, speckled with mildew. You notice of course that the gentlemen at the head of the table will be responsible not to this newly elected Parliament but to the Governor. In other words, that your new government is to be representative so-so, but not responsible. That is the first blue bottle buzzing around the ointment, gentlemen. The second is this preposterously low qualification. You may think it isn't. I take you. You object, all of you, to being placed on an equality with the Native. I don't hold with you that that is altogether wrong. A man's skin and the colour of it have never troubled me much, provided the man himself was a man. But a man must have some stake in the country, and it is preposterous that those of us who have property should be placed on an equal footing, so far as the vote is concerned, with the vagrant who has none and merely tenants a house or earns a wage of £50 a year. And what about civilisation? While they were about it they might at least have suggested that the voters should be able to read and write and do a little figuring. Still, it's there, as you, Mr Magistrate, have pointed out, and my advice, so far as it goes—and you may take it or disregard it as you please, for I shall not be long with you to see what a mess you make of the business—my advice is that you take it, and see to it that in this Valley at least your registers are properly kept and that there is no fooling with them. I know what elections are; I have seen something of them in the old country, and all I can say is that you should bestir yourselves in the matter and make what you can out of what they have given you. It's not likely to remain there—not in that shape, Mr Magistrate—but it depends on yourselves how you use it and what advantage it is going to be for you in the end.'

Uncle Charles's speech was received with marked approval, and its sentiments were endorsed by the other speakers. A committee was formed, to which Everardus was elected a member, and it was decided that as soon as the Ordinance was promulgated, steps would be taken to elect a proper representative. Already there was speculation as to whom should be asked to allow himself to be nominated for that honour. Popular consensus demanded Martin Rekker, the acknowledged senior and premier of the Valley, but his English was imperfect and as the official language of the new Parliament was to be English, that was felt to be a drawback. Uncle Martin himself vetoed his nomination, declaring that he had no time to go to Cape Town, and much preferred to direct matters from his farm. He counselled patience and consideration, and to the hints thrown out that in the circumstances Thomas Seldon or Andrew Quakerley should be invited to represent the District, he replied that these matters would adjust themselves in time, and that meanwhile the Valley should wait and find out if it was to form an electoral District of its own or if it was to be merged in one of the neighbouring Districts. On this point the magistrate could give no clear indication of the government's intentions, and the meeting agreed that until this point had been settled it would be premature to do much more than to see that the new voters registers were properly drawn up.

After the meeting a private consultation was held at Uncle Martin's church house, which was attended by the principal residents in the Valley, all of whom had seats on the provisional committee. The discussion that ensued was long and involved, and reached no finality, but from it emerged the fact that the committee was unanimous in its decision that Everardus Nolte should be their choice when it came to nominating a representative for the new Parliament. None was more surprised at this decision that Everardus himself, who when the suggestion had been made, by Uncle Martin himself, had protested that he was totally unfitted for the task. The meeting, however, thought otherwise. They pointed out that he was not tied down to his farm or business as most of them were, and that he was wealthy enough to spare some of his time for public duties; that his knowledge of English was good enough to enable him to represent them in a gathering where English was the official and only language; and that his popularity in the District was such that, if the committee nominated him and Uncle Martin and Charles Quakerley supported him, no other candidate would have the slightest chance against him. In the circumstances he promised to think the matter over, and consult his wife about it. There was no hurry. It would take months before the Ordinance was promulgated, and probably there would be a new Governor before the elections came on. The committee felt that ample time could be allowed to Everardus for consideration and reflection, and after reiterating its perfect confidence in him, it adjourned until such time as the acting secretary, Andrew Quakerley, who was also to act as convener, should deem it desirable to call another meeting.

Chapter 21

Then enteric fever broke out in the Valley, in that memorable year when the Colony received its first constitution. It was inevitable that the infection should spread and reach farms which through no fault of their owners became *foci* of disease. Local conditions—the presence of *kraals* breeding innumerable flies, the primitive ways of disposing of night-soil, and the comparative ease with which food and water supplies could be contaminated—were favourable to the dispersal of the typhoid germs, and the Valley had little chance of adequately defending itself. Enteric fever was endemic; it had always been with them, and they had never found it so dangerous as it appeared to be this year. It attacked Natives, Coloureds and Whites alike, being in that respect as impartial as John Russell's government seemed to be, and it spared only the very old and the very young. On every farm there was an outbreak, and although there were few fatalities, those whom it attacked were dangerously sick for many weeks, and Dr

Anders, who was the only medical man available, was constantly in the saddle, riding from farm to farm and spending very few nights in comfort at his home in the Village. He was a silent, quiet man, parsimonious in his speech, but an old established Valley-ite and as such popular, although he hardly had the authority and the prestige to which his education and his profession entitled him. He lived in a straggling, low-walled compound house at the end of the Village street, and shared with old Charles Quakerley and the magistrate's wife a taste for gardening. Beyond this he had, apparently, no interests in life besides his practice. He had no children, and his wife was a shy, retiring personality, who rarely mingled with her fellow citizens, and as rarely went to church. At first the Valley had wondered at her isolation and speculated as to what her religious feelings might be, but it had soon tired of that amusement and now took no further interest in Mrs Anders, who, as a matter of fact, belonged to a small sect of Swedenborgians whose headquarters were in the capital.

At *Knolkloof* the first to succumb to the disease was Matryk, who was carefully and patiently nursed by Tins. It was Tins who had declared an entirely unauthorised vacation for the school, and had ridden into the Village, on his own responsibility, Everardus being engaged in political conversations on Uncle Dorie's farm, to fetch the doctor. It was Tins, too, who washed, nursed, and when allowed to, fed the patient, and who did most of the doctoring, for Dr Anders had contented himself with establishing the diagnosis, which in the circumstances was no great matter, as everyone knew that young *Baas* Matryk was down with the fever. But the doctor had told Tins quite frankly that no medicine was of any use. The disease, he had explained, was a self-limiting one, and the youth had strength and robustness on his side which ordinarily were so much in his favour that one need not be distressed. Unfortunately, in enteric fever one could never tell; the prognosis was distinctly worse where the patient was an adolescent. He had therefore ordered strict seclusion, rest, and a purely mild diet; and had warned Tins that the patient would rebel against all, but that on no account should Matryk be given anything solid to eat until convalescence had been well established.

Following Matryk some of the Natives contracted the disease, and Everardus came back in haste to give what aid he could. On the neighbouring farms the position was equally unfavourable, and everywhere the owners had their hands full, nursing members of their families or attending to the sick Natives. At the Village, too, there were several cases, and the magistrate resurrected—with the aid of Augustus, the Native constable—the squad of scavengers that had been organised some years before when the small pox scare had roused the residents to a realisation of the unsanitary condition of the Village location.

To *Knolkloof* came the Widow Priem, anxious, as she declared, to lend Niece Magriet a helping hand. She established herself in the spare room, rose at an unearthly hour in the morning when she kindled the fire in the kitchen and made the coffee long before Minerva, an early riser herself, had appeared on the scene, and gave help of such practical utility that Magriet warmed towards her. At first Magriet had not appreciated the Widow Priem. Her brusqueness of manner, her careless habit of dress—she seemed to have no flounced skirt and had brought no 'chest clothes' with her for her stay—and her directness of speech were apt to give her hosts a false impression of her virtues. Regina, on the other hand, had appreciated the 'Old

Mistress' from the start, and Magriet was glad to find that the presence of her guest in the kitchen had led to no unpleasantness.

The Widow Priem was assiduous in her attentions on Matryk. She shared the nursing of him with Tins, and for long hours the two of them would sit on opposite sides of the young man's bed, the widow engaged in knitting, and Tins occupied with his bookkeeping, neither speaking a word but each silently conscious of the other's presence. Only outside the sick room did they indulge in conversation, which was usually one-sided, the widow doing all the talking while Tins listened deferentially, agreeing as a matter of course to all suggestions which *Madame la Douairiere* might be pleased to make.

When Everardus himself fell sick, Magriet found the widow's help invaluable. Matryk was already convalescing when Everardus took to his bed and the Widow Priem, who had diagnosed his illness correctly, sent Tins to the Village for the second time to have her diagnosis confirmed by official authority. Dr Anders, dead beat after a round that had lasted the greater part of a week, had little to suggest when he saw the patient. Everything, he assured Magriet, was being done that it was possible to do. She could rely upon the Widow Priem who had had experience of typhoid and who could be trusted to nurse the patient with the requisite care and skill. Dr Anders made no secret of the fact that he regarded Everardus's condition as grave. The fever—which he measured by feeling the patient's forehead, declaring that his one and only thermometer, a huge instrument kept more for show than clinical use, had been broken—was high, and the patient's pulse was not what it should have been. Moreover, Everardus was delirious, and in the circumstances it would be well for Magriet to have assistance. He advised that Katryn should be sent to Uncle Dorie's farm, both to safeguard her from possible infection and to have her out of the way, and that Regina should take charge of the convalescing Matryk, leaving Tins free to devote himself to Everardus. This arrangement Magriet agreed to, but as in the days when she had first arrived at *Knolkloof*, she experienced once more the innate friendliness and charity of the Valley. Uncle Dorie, when he drove up to fetch Katryn, declared that he had come to stay. The little maid could go back with his wife; he would remain and help Magriet. And the following day Uncle Martin arrived, driven over by Andrew Quakerley, whose wife had sent jellies, reduced to a sticky liquid by the heat of the road, and chicken broth for the invalids. Uncle Martin and Uncle Dorie had no fear of infection; both had had enteric fever and regarded themselves as salted or immune to it, and both offered to remain at *Knolkloof* and take charge while its owner was ill.

Magriet gladly accepted their help, and during the first week of her husband's illness she fully appreciated the thoroughness of the assistance they gave her. Their encouraging cheerfulness helped her through a stage when she needed such help, for there had been times when Everardus had been violently delirious, and although the Widow Priem, used to such contingencies, would no doubt have managed the patient single-handed, Magriet felt that her two old friends were a tower of strength.

It was Tins who had drawn her attention to a possible source of danger which she had never suspected. At the end of the first week Everardus's condition was practically unchanged; he lay, with sores on his lips and open, staring eyes, muttering half-sentences whose import she could not catch, though she bent over the bed thinking that he wanted something. She was alone in the sick room, but at that moment

Tins came in with fresh water from the big canvas water bag that hung in the mill-house window where the circulating air cooled it to a pleasant coldness.

'*Madame*,' said Tins deferentially, 'it may be that *Madame* is *epuisé*—tired. Would it not be well that while *Meneer* is in this condition—*dans le deliré, Madame*—in which *peut-être*, something may be said which *Madame* would not like to be spoken about ...'

'Teacher ... what has he said? Have you heard?' asked Magriet, in a whisper. She had not thought of this contingency. It was quite possible. In delirium a man's secrets were not his own. They were spread abroad; they became public property. Teacher was quite right. She would have to be on her guard; she would not be able to leave Everardus. And she felt so exhausted, so terribly tired.

'*Madame* doubtless knows that *Meneer* Nolte has done me the honour of sharing his confidence with me,' said Tins, gravely. 'If *Madame* will retire, I will take it upon me to keep strangers away. It may be that *Meneer* Nolte says something in his delirium which ... which *Madame* would not have him say, for *Madame's* peace of mind and his, *Madame*.'

'Yes ... I know. Everardus told me you knew about it, Teacher. But it is nothing shameful, after all, though folk may think it is, not knowing.'

'*Madame* has reason. It is what I have myself had the honour of telling *Meneer* Nolte. But expressed as *Meneer* Nolte might now express it—listen, *Madame*, he is constantly referring to it. A man *malade* always does. It is what weighs upon his mind, and when expressed as he now expresses it, *Madame*, it is scarcely *niable*—what do you say—not capable of being gainsaid, *Madame*. Those who listen and hear—*helas*, *Madame*, even the things most innocent may by one's best friends be mistakenly construed to mean things they were not intended to mean. *Madame* takes me? I have no wish to distress *Madame*, but if I may make the suggestion, myself or the *douairiere*, we can be trusted.'

'But surely Aunt Cornelia does not know, Teacher?' asked Magriet. 'You, I know, for Everardus told me that you had seen him. But the widow does not know.'

'*Madame la Douairiere* is discretion in person, *Madame*,' replied Tins, with a touch of dignity in his voice. '*Madame* may rely upon her discretion and her perfect friendliness. I, Pierre Mabuis, vouch for her.'

'And a month ago you were so frightened of her,' said Magriet, smiling although she felt very miserable. 'She has soon twisted you round her finger ...'

'I entertain for *Madame la Douairiere* a feeling the most respectful and admirative,' said Tins with even more dignity, 'and there can be no question, *Madame*, of coercion or twisting around one's finger. I conceive that *Madame* uses the expression figuratively, but I would respectfully submit that it is derogatory to both of us.'

'I have no intention of hurting your feelings, Teacher,' exclaimed Magriet, contritely, realising that he had hurt him. 'I merely thought that as she did not know ...'

'It makes no difference whether she knows or does not know,' said Tins. 'The *douairiere* Priem is a woman of illimitable discretion and of a tact the most astonishing. It would not be convenable, in the circumstances, for *Madame* to leave *Meneer* alone with *Meneer* Rekker or *Meneer* van Aard, who might construe mistakenly what they heard *Meneer* Nolte utter *dans le deliré*. That is all that I had the temerity to suggest to *Madame*.'

'Thank you, Teacher. If you will be so good as to stay with him. I can ask the Widow Priem ... she is, as you say, excellent. And although she does not know ...'

'May I, most respectfully, *Madame*, venture a further suggestion. You permit? Very well, it is that you tell to *Madame la Douairiere* the tale, as you and I know it. I give *Madame* my assurance that *Madame la Douairiere* may be trusted to keep *Madame's* confidence as if it were uttered in the confessional, though she is not of the faith.'

Magriet shook her head.

'I cannot do that without my husband's consent,' she said. 'I have often asked him to reveal it himself. After all, why should he not? It is long past, and whatever shame clings to it ...'

'There is nothing dishonourable, *Madame*. I had the honour of telling *Meneer* that myself.'

'He would not do it,' said Magriet sadly. 'It should have been done when we came here. Then anybody and everybody would have known, and we would have lived it down by this time. But now ... now, when they have asked him to be their representative in Parliament ... Teacher, it is the most unfortunate time, and people will put their own construction upon it, and upon his silence all this long while.'

'Let them, *Madame*. The *canaille* will always yap and snap at their betters. It is of no importance what they say. But it would be better if *Madame* confided in her good friends.'

'I can't do that yet,' said Magriet dolefully. 'Perhaps when he is better. But not now. Look how ill he is, Teacher. Do you think he will recover?'

'I have seen much worse recover,' encouraged Tins with a decision that impressed Magriet, who wanted to be impressed. 'Were *Meneer* younger, the matter would be of an aspect altogether deplorable, but he is beyond the age when the malady is most dangerous. *Madame* may have good hopes. And now, seeing that *Madame* is fatigued, I permit myself the liberty of suggesting that *Madame* retires to her chamber for recuperative repose. I will look after *Meneer*, and I will keep *Meneer* Rekker and that excellent *Meneer* van Aard out of the room.'

In promising this, however, Tins had undertaken more than he could fulfil. Neither he nor the excellent widow could be at Everardus's bedside the whole time, and it chanced that when Uncle Dorie had been assigned, at his own urgent request, the task of watching by the sleeping patient, Everardus sat up in bed and, to the Elder's horror, talked in a mixture of English and Dutch of what he had done years ago.

Uncle Dorie was relieved in due course and came out of the sick room wiping the perspiration from his forehead. It was not the heat of the room that had caused him to sweat, although the climatic conditions may have had something to do with the prodigality of moisture on his brow. In the dining room he found Uncle Martin, seated at the side-table with the chess board before him, and the men invitingly set out.

'No, Martin,' he said, sinking into a chair and pouring himself out a glass of wine which he tossed off in a manner quite unlike his usual dignified way of sipping that liquid. 'No, I cannot play with you. I have had a most dreadful shock.'

'Shock, Brother Doremus?' asked Uncle Martin, who had noted that his friend had dropped the customary prefix when addressing him and felt that such omission could only be accounted for by great emotional stress. 'What shock? Is it that someone we know has crossed over. I should not be surprised, for there are several in a precarious condition, and we must be prepared for such tidings. Nor should you and I, who are old and on the brink, feel unduly distressed when we hear that our friends have gone before us. *"Quid mortem fles,"* as the Latin poet says, Brother, which means "why should you weep over your death?"'

'I am not weeping over my death, Brother Martin,' retorted Uncle Dorie indignantly, 'and you needn't fling these heathenish things at my head. If you want to quote something, quote from the good Book, in language which we both understand.'

'Why, Brother Doremus, you seem to be upset. Surely it is well with Nephew Ev'rard? Why, when I looked in he was sleeping peacefully, like a baby.'

'Aye, and that is how I found him when Niece Cornelia told me I could sit with him awhile. You know they have been keeping us away from him—why I could not think. But now I know. Brother, it is awful.'

He poured himself another drink and gulped it down. Uncle Martin placed the carafe of wine out of reach, and regarded him steadily.

'There is something gravely amiss, Brother Doremus,' he said reproachfully. 'I can see that someone has been walking across your newly sown wheat land. That is it?'

'I can hardly tell you, Brother,' said Uncle Dorie, energetically wiping his brow with the back of his sleeve, for his handkerchief was now saturated and no longer useful to absorb the moisture that trickled into his little eyes and from there on to his cheeks to find at last shelter in his wisps of beard. 'The man disclosed it in his delirium, and it is hardly fair ... But it gave me an awful shock, Brother, an awful shock! To think that such a thing is possible!'

Neither of the old gentlemen had remarked the entrance of Tins. He had come in through the kitchen door and had marked Uncle Dorie's agitation and Uncle Martin's perplexity, and he now came forward, drew up a chair and sat facing them.

'The gentlemen will forgive me,' he said suavely, 'if, by pure inadvertence, I have chanced to overhear part of what the gentlemen were discussing. It seems that *Meneer* van Aard has heard something which has given *Meneer* a turn ...'

'That you may well say, Teacher!' exclaimed Uncle Dorie vigorously. 'It would have given you a turn, Teacher, had you listened to what Nephew Ev'rard talked when he was rambling in the fever.'

'It may have, *Meneer*, did I not happen to know the circumstances,' said Tins, speaking with deliberation. 'Knowing them, I attach no importance to it ...'

'What! No importance?' cried Uncle Dorie, now roused to indignation. 'No importance, when the man said ...'

'Hush, Brother,' said Uncle Martin, raising his hand. 'As you have yourself said just now, it is hardly fair to disclose what a man said when he is rambling from the fever.'

'I pray *Meneer* to let *Meneer* van Aard expound,' said Tins. 'But as the matter concerns not us alone, not us materially even, but *Madame*, I would ask *Meneer* van Aard a moment's respite while I request *Madame* to honour us with her company. *Messieurs* have no objection? Very well, I go call *Madame*.'

During his brief absence, Uncle Martin took snuff delicately, and Uncle Dorie got up and fetched himself a glass of water. In the sick room Tins found Magriet bending over Everardus, who was again sleeping placidly, with the Widow Priem vigorously knitting at the foot of the bed where she sat primly upright on a wooden stool.

'It has come as we feared, *Madame*,' said Tins seriously. '*Meneer* van Aard has misapprehended what *Meneer* muttered in his delirium. He has conceived—the Devil alone knows what *Monsieur le Doyen* has conceived, but it is something unspeakably remote from reality, and it is for *Madame*, if she will have the goodness and the courage, to correct *Monsieur le Doyen*.'

'Yes,' said the Widow Priem, in her high pitched voice, 'Teacher talks sense, Niece Magriet. I have had my suspicions, but it is none of my business. But these sheep-heads, they may make a calculation and find that two and two come to five, and it is better that Niece Magriet should show them which road is the right one.'

'*Madame la Douairiere* has completely expressed my own feelings,' said Tins, with a bow towards the widow. 'Nothing, if *Madame* will permit me to remark, will be gained by further evasion—I ask *Madame's* pardon for a word which has perhaps an equivocal meaning. Will Madame be good enough ...'

'Now, Niece Magriet,' said the Widow Priem, getting up and gently propelling her hostess towards the door, 'be sensible and do what Teacher asks. I know nothing whatever about the business—it is none of mine—but I know that neither you nor Nephew Ev'rard here have any cause to be ashamed of whatever you have done and, why, if Nephew Ev'rard has ... but there, go, child, go and make these sheep's heads understand. Men are such fools. I will look after your man, Niece. Go.'

Ushered by Tins, who had always treated her like *une grande dame*, Magriet took the chair that Uncle Martin silently placed for her, and folded her hands on her lap. Uncle Dorie looked terribly distressed, and avoided her eye. Uncle Martin sat with a grave face, on which, however, she read unfeigned sympathy and great kindliness that gave her courage.

'What is it you wish to know, Uncle Martin?' she asked, addressing him in preference to Uncle Dorie who shifted uneasily on his chair. Tins stood behind her, respectfully silent.

'Why, Niece, nothing so far as I am concerned,' replied Uncle Martin. 'It seems that Brother Doremus here has discovered some mare's nest, and is anxious to tell us where the eggs are. It is he you must ask.'

'Look you,' said Uncle Dorie, 'it is a matter which is not for a woman to discuss with us ...'

'Your pardon, Uncle Dorie,' said Magriet, gathering courage as she spoke, 'but it *is* a matter for me to discuss. Will you tell us what you heard Ami ... Everardus say?'

'Niece, it is so horrible. I can scarcely believe my ears,' said Uncle Dorie, plaintively indignant, but obviously much distressed.

'But say it,' she reiterated. 'I cannot tell you unless I hear what he said or what you thought he said, Uncle Dorie.'

'It is so utterly unbelievable ... unthinkable!' exclaimed Uncle Dorie. 'I ... why Niece, one does not take what a ... man says in his rambling as gospel truth, but when it comes to murder ...'

'Murder!' exclaimed Uncle Martin. 'Brother Doremus, you forget yourself ...'

'Aye, you may think that, Brother Martin. I told you it was an awful shock. The man has killed a white man ... strangled him with his own hands. He said so. He dwelt on it, as a man does on past things in his frenzy when the fever is on him ...'

'Yes, as a man does in a nightmare, Brother Doremus,' said Uncle Martin scornfully. 'You speak and act like a child, Brother. And for that you plague Niece Magriet, and get her to leave her sick man and come and give you an explanation of such preposterous nonsense. Fie, Brother, and you a grown man and an Elder of the church! No wonder you want three glasses of wine to fuddle you still more.'

'Two only, Brother Martin, two only,' wailed Uncle Doremus. 'After that you snatched the carafe away. But,' he concluded stubbornly, 'I heard it with my own ears. Strangled him ... with his bare hands ...'

'Why not say cut his head off with his clasp knife,' said Uncle Martin sarcastically. 'The one is as believable as the other.'

'He said nothing about knives,' replied Uncle Dorie doggedly. 'But he mentioned the strangling ... repeatedly. It was awful ...'

'If you have nothing but his ravings,' said Uncle Martin, 'I do not know why we should trouble Niece here. She can go back to her man, and you, Brother Doremus, may have another glass of wine, since the other two have gone to your head ...'

'You know I can drink the whole carafe without it going to my head!' expostulated Uncle Dorie indignantly. 'It is only because of the dreadful shock, for fancy Nephew Ev'rard murdering a man! Besides, what are we to do about it, Brother Martin? It is out of his ramblings, indeed, but there is such a thing as our duty to the state and to our fellow men. What, I ask, are we to do about it ...'

'Forget it, of course,' said Uncle Martin, sharply. 'Forget it ...'

'No, Uncle Martin,' said Magriet, who had made up her mind. 'Uncle Dorie has misunderstood what he heard, but if you will listen, I can explain. It is not pleasant, and it is not quite right ... it is Ami ... I mean Everard's secret as much as it is mine, but Teacher here thinks that the time has come for you to know ...'

'If it is a secret, Niece,' said Uncle Martin deliberately, 'and not yours alone, Niece, it is not right for us to know or for you to tell. It were best, as I have just said, that we should forget it.'

'It can be secret no longer, Uncle Martin, seeing that Uncle Dorie has heard something of it. I have always prayed Ami to tell you, but he was stubborn. He thought you would despise him, look down upon him, and he hadn't the courage. I did not think so. I thought you would not think the less of him ...'

'Therein you were quite right,' said Uncle Martin. 'An ill friend would I be if I were to look down upon one whom I have called friend, and Brother Doremus says the same, although just now he only grunts. I do not care if he has a secret, for I know Nephew Ev'rard, and I know that he has nothing of which he need be ashamed.'

'Thank you, Uncle Martin,' said Magriet, genuinely moved by this declaration. 'But you should hear before you judge. Listen, and do not interrupt me, for I want your attention.'

'Go your gait, Niece. I am all attention. Brother Doremus, make no remark while Niece Magriet is having the word.'

'My husband,' began Magriet, choosing her words with care, 'was formerly called Amadeus. He was Amadeus Tereg ...'

Uncle Martin was the first to break his own prohibition.

'The Teregs came with Swellengrebel,' he said reminiscently. 'They had three amulets on a gold field, but no motto, so far as I remember. They were in trade.'

'Yes. Grandfather Tereg had a shop at Swellendam, but things went bad, and Ami's father was very poor. Ami did not know ... it is very difficult to tell, Uncle Martin. Ami was taught to work at the leather trade; he was apprenticed to a saddler. You know that ... there is no mystery about Ami's business. He was a young man when he married me, and like the Teregs, my family had become poor, although Uncle knows perhaps that they were of equal standing, for the de Lerchs were well born ...'

'Certainly, Niece,' interrupted Uncle Martin. 'Their arms were a couple of larks, sable, which is black, Brother Doremus, on a green field. With the motto *Blydschap* (happiness), which name they gave to their farm. Continue, Niece.'

'Yes, but the farm was sold long before my birth, Uncle Martin,' went on Magriet, finding it easier to tell her story, now that Uncle Martin's interruptions had given to it a tinge of heraldic commentary. 'And when we married we were very poor. Ami had only his saddlery to live on, and custom was poor; and there were times, at first, when we had very little, Uncle Martin.'

'But that is strange,' interrupted Uncle Dorie, notwithstanding a warning from his friend. 'How comes it then that Nephew Ev'rard can come here and buy a farm ...?'

'That comes later, Uncle Dorie,' said Magriet quickly. 'You must let me tell it in my own way. We had very little to live on. Ami went to Cape Town and worked there. He got to know people there, and in the old Governor's time—Lord Charles's time, you know, Uncle Dorie—he worked there and made some money with the horses. Then ... then they sent for him, and made him a proposal. He told me of it, Uncle Martin; he told no one else. Only the magistrate knew in our District, and some of the officials at the Castle at Cape Town. He would never have taken it ... he should not, perhaps, but we were poor ... dreadfully poor, Uncle Martin ...'

She hesitated, and Uncle Martin leaned over and patted her hand, for which Tins felt grateful. Tins himself thought she was telling her story well. Both her hearers were interested, and Uncle Dorie's face had lost its expression of horrified indignation for one of frank curiosity which he made no attempt to hide, while Uncle Martin listened with grave and courteous attention. *Madame* was doing the right thing, Tins reflected. She would make these gentlemen see how silly it was to accuse *Meneer* Nolte of anything dishonourable.

'So he went to Cape Town, Uncle Martin,' continued Magriet, 'and they paid him so much a year for it, and nobody knew. But I did not like it, nor did he, and it might be that he would be called upon, though he said it would not, ... could not happen ...'

'But Niece,' interrupted Uncle Dorie, 'what was it he had to do? What was the proposal they made to him?'

'Tell him, Niece,' said Uncle Martin gravely. 'I think I can guess. But tell him in your own words.'

'They said,' began Magriet, finding it difficult now to choose here words properly, 'they said that if anybody ... any White man was to be hanged, they had to have a White man as a ... as hangman. He would only be called upon if it was a White man; there was a Native executioner who could deal with all the others, but for a White man ... Uncle Martin, you will understand ...'

'Surely I do,' said the old man, patting her hand, while Uncle Dorie stared at her and muttered under his breath, 'So ... a public executioner ... a hangman. Now I understand. But who could have thought of it?'

'And one day they did call upon him,' went on Magriet, struggling to keep the emotion out of her voice, and he went. It was there that Teacher here saw him and *Meneer* von Bergmann, and it was the only time he went, Uncle Martin. He got paid for it, and nobody knew who he was, for it was far away from our District, and he was unknown to all, even to the magistrate who took him there. But our magistrate knew, and *Meneer* von Bergmann recognised him, and Teacher there ...'

'Yes, gentlemen,' said Tins breaking into the conversation for the first time. 'I was in charge of the guard, and I saw *Meneer* Tereg—I knew not his name then—but I recognised him, and the Reverend gentleman to whom *Madame* refers went with the condemned on to the scaffold. So he too must have recognised *Meneer* Nolte.'

'Unbelievably strange!' exclaimed Uncle Dorie, with more astonishment than indignation in his voice. 'That accounts for the rope that he talks about, and the strangling. To think that Nephew Ev'rard has been a hangman, a public executioner ...'

'Of a White man, remember that Brother Doremus,' said Uncle Martin sharply. 'That is a different matter, and in the circumstances, why, Niece, there is nothing to make a fuss about. Doubtless the tale strikes brother Doremus as strange—Brother Doremus has always had a horror of gibbets and such like—but he will get over it in time. Continue, Niece, continue.'

'There is little else to tell, Uncle Martin. My husband returned a fortnight later—it was far from us he had gone to do ... what he had to do. But he was determined not to do it again, and he gave up his post, and drew no more money from the government. Then my aunt died, and she left me her money, and that is how we became rich. Then we decided to leave our District, and to change our name—my husband's grandmother was a Nolte so he took that surname—and come here where we were not known. And that is all, Uncle Martin.'

Uncle Martin poured out a glass of wine and handed it to her. 'Drink, Niece,' he said kindly. 'There is nothing to be sad about. I only wish you had told me long ago, for then the telling might have been less hard to you. When a man does his duty, even as a common hangman, he is worthy of our respect. And what you have told us of Nephew Ev'rard does not lower him in my eyes. I am still his friend.'

'That is what I had the honour of telling *Madame*,' said Tins, highly pleased at the way in which the old man had taken the story. 'I said that *Meneer's* friends would not desert him because *Meneer* had done nothing of which a man need be ashamed. Why, it is no great matter to kill a man; I think I may have done it on occasion, though invariably my shots, I believe, went wide of their aim. The wonder to me,' he continued sagaciously, 'was how *Meneer* Nolte managed without practice. In the old times it would have been another matter; with a sword or a chopper it is no great skill to behead a condemned, but hanging is a matter of nice adjustment, gentlemen, and without practice ...'

'Will you hold your tongue, Teacher!' exclaimed Uncle Dorie, glad to have someone on whom to expend his emotion. 'It disgusts me the way you talk of the subject. And, Brother Martin, the matter is not so simple as you seem to imagine. If Nephew Ev'rard has been a common hangman, why, surely it makes some difference. Are we going to have a common hangman to represent us in Parliament ...?'

'Brother Doremus,' said Uncle Marin with gentle severity, 'I make allowances for you, for I know your characteristic horror of gibbets and such-like things. But you altogether misapprehend the situation. Nephew Ev'rard is not a common hangman. He is one of us ... a fellow citizen whom I am still proud to call my friend, and I withdraw nothing from what I have said when I suggested that he should represent us. If he will do so is another matter. This fact which we have learned from Niece Magriet can hardly remain hidden among us; that is too much to hope for ...'

'Just so, Brother Martin,' exclaimed Uncle Dorie. 'The people will come to hear of it, and then there will be all sorts of talk and magnifications ...'

'Such as we heard quite recently,' remarked Uncle Martin drily, 'when one of us suspected Nephew Ev'rard of being a common murderer. But,' he went on seriously, 'it is for us, Brother Doremus, who are leaders in Israel, to set the example. Nephew Ev'rard has hanged a man in the course of his duty; he was a paid official of the state, and in the interests of all of us, someone of us had to do that job. You would not have liked to see a Native hang a White man ...'

'No,' admitted Uncle Dorie, nodding his head. 'That would not have been seemly nor edifying.'

'Quite so. Therefore, when you come to consider it, we are really under an obligation to Nephew Ev'rard. Why, this Gallows-Gecko as you would call him, Brother Doremus, has done us a good turn. Why then should we be upset, as you were upset just now, when we heard about him, and what he did. Take my word for it, Brother, not one in the Valley will think the less of him for that. There may be some who will find it curious, but if you and I set the example no one will cast a stone at him. I should like to see anyone doing it, too.'

'Thank you, Uncle Martin,' said Magriet gratefully. 'It is a load off my mind. Ever since we came among you, it has burdened Ami and me, and often I have pleaded with him to tell you, but always he was shy, half-ashamed to admit what he had done ...'

'That was wholly unnecessary,' said the old gentleman. 'We know him for what he is, and as such we respect him. This will make no difference. Why, we will chaff him about it, belike, and nickname him Gallows-Gecko—it is a good name, that, Brother Doremus, don't you think?'

'Aye, that it is,' said the Elder, permitting himself for the first time since his exit from the sick room the liberty of a smile, 'and it may be that it is best to treat these things lightly, and make a joke of them. For all that, Brother, there are folk who might think differently, and who might have their own opinions. It may even be that Nephew Ev'rard may have to say with Job, "My brethren are far from me and mine acquaintance are verily estranged from me," and it may be that there will be those who, as the prophet Jeremiah tells us in his ninth chapter, will bend their tongues like their bows for lies, and will look askance at him ...'

'Nay, *Monsieur le Doyen*,' said Tins excitedly. 'Not one will do that. Is it not that everyone knows *Meneer* Nolte for an honourable man, *sans reproche*—what you say, without a stain? And if there be none else to do him honour, even though he has been a *bourreau*—what matter? So has many a soldier, for it is the sergeant who hangs, and the quartermaster aboard the ships, and who thinks any the less of them for it? But if there be none, why, Pierre Mabuis will remain with him and proclaim to the world that there is one friend—for *Meneer* Nolte has permitted me to call him that, having honoured me with his confidence—who is indebted to him; and to him he is as he has always been, a *gentil homme* to be respected. Why,' went on Tins, warming to his theme, *'Meneer* Nolte took me when I was *sauvagement* drunk; he clothed me with his own clothes; he gave me to eat and to drink, and befriended me. If *Monsieur le Doyen* quotes scripture so *savantissime*, he will perhaps permit me to quote to him St Peter who says that it is well to be fervently charitable among ourselves since charity covers many sins. And *Monsieur* Nolte has been of a charity the most amazing to us, for which I do him honour, gentlemen and *Madame*, and I will challenge whoever says the contrary. My *Papa* did kill in a duel one who slandered a friend, and it will surely not be accounted murder if I do likewise ...'

'Now, now, Teacher,' said Uncle Martin, who saw that Tins was working himself up to a pitch of enthusiasm that threatened to become hysterical. 'We may let it be at that. You will help us all more by taking it, as Brother Doremus says, easily, rather than by being furious about what nobody has yet said or imagined. And do you, Niece, go back to your man, and rest easy in mind. Brother Doremus and I and Teacher here, we will take a stroll in the garden, and make a plan.'

In the sick room Magriet told the Widow Priem what had occurred in the dining room. The Widow Priem listened with grim attention, and when the recital was over she delivered herself in a characteristically direct fashion.

'You are a fool, Niece Magriet,' she said, 'to attach so much importance to the matter. Murderers must hang, and somebody must hang them. I don't fancy any of us will think the worse of Nephew Ev'rard for having rid the world of one who is better out of it than in it. And now bathe your man's forehead, and I will make you a cup of tea for you need it. A grown woman like you should not cry about these things.'

Magriet found the Widow Priem curiously sympathetic and, while she bathed Everardus's forehead, wondered why she had not appreciated her guest's faculty of understanding before. When Everardus moved his head and muttered, she bent over him and spoke softly.

'They know about it now, Ami,' she said. 'You may sleep peaceably, for they are still our friends.'

And when the Widow Priem came back with a cup of tea, Magriet disgraced herself by unashamedly weeping on the widow's shoulder, an exhibition of weakness which the gaunt old woman reproved with an austere gentleness which the culprit found thoroughly satisfying.

Chapter 22

Convalescing three weeks later, from an illness that had sapped his strength beyond what he had thought an illness would have been able to do, Everardus awoke to the realisation that his well-kept secret was no longer his own, but was shared by his intimate friends and would possibly be common property before very long. Uncle Dorie had been perfectly right when he had hinted that such a thing could not be kept from the Valley, where everyone knew all about his neighbour's business, and it was accounted bad form to keep confidences apart from the general acquaintance of society. None knew how the first whispers arose; they certainly did not emanate from the four persons who had taken part in that conference in the dining room, but they gathered force as they percolated through the District, and by the time that Everardus was up and about and again able to count the sheep at the *kraals* and supervise the apportionment of the meat rations to the Natives, the Valley knew that he had been an executioner and had started life under another name than the one he now bore.

The Valley took the news, like a child who takes his first plunge into cold water, with a gasp expressive of astonishment, mild apprehension, and just a dash of indignation, and then settled down to enjoy it. Uncle Martin and Uncle Dorie set the example of treating the matter as something which could be discussed with a smile instead of a snarl, and both the pastor and the magistrate, with whom the two old gentlemen had consulted before they had taken up this eminently sensible attitude, were of their opinion. Against this quartet of authority, the Valley did not dare to embattle whatever contrary views it might have held. As a matter of fact, it held no contrary views and it took the story with evident relish, and agreed that what had happened long ago could most fittingly be commemorated by nicknaming Nephew Nolte 'Gallows-Gecko,' which appellation, provided one made it clear that it was not used in any derogatory sense, was euphonious, apposite, and had the added merit of sharply differentiating Everardus from such other Ev'rards as the Valley might at any time have to recognise. The Valley loved nicknames, which were freely bestowed, and which were sometimes very useful for purposes of differentiating between men of the same name. Usually its nicknames were, like the one now bestowed on Everardus, titles which bore some definite relation to the history, habits, or peculiarities of the individuals concerned, and in very few cases were they used sneeringly or with any deprecatory intention. In this case it was made perfectly clear to Everardus that no one had the slightest intention of grieving him by calling him Gallows-Gecko, but that he could rather look upon it as an honour, and as a proof that the Valley had sat in judgment over the episode which he had kept secret so long and had decided that it was something that need not be considered as detracting from the popularity which he had gained and the good will with which the Valley regarded him.

That was made perfectly evident when a deputation waited upon him to request him to allow himself to be nominated as candidate for the forthcoming election. The deputation was headed by Uncle Charles, who rode over specially from *Quakerskloof* for the purpose of leading it. Uncle Charles had received the tale of Everardus's activity as official hangman with interested incredulity, and had posted over to the residency to obtain confirmation or denial.

'Quite correct,' the magistrate had told him. 'I did not know about it, of course. None of my business, and besides they keep such things, naturally, secret at headquarters. Bless me, Quakerley, I couldn't tell you the name of the present functionary, and I doubt if anyone but the sheriff knows him. He may be someone who comes to dinner with us when we go to the capital. But Nolte—I knew his name had been Tereg, for we looked him up when he was put forward as a candidate for the Road Board, and there was nothing to his discredit—Nolte acted years ago. Best not rake the matter up. My own view is it will blow over very soon.'

'Shiver me!' said Uncle Charles. 'But what a how-de-do. It reminds me, Staples, of the Barry affair—you remember that good looking protégé of Lord Charles who turned out to be a woman, after pinking Captain Abernethy under the arm. A curious affair, Staples, and it rather complicates matters, for as you know we have our eye on Nolte for the Assembly. That is to say if it comes off, but I am not at all sure ...'

'You need have no fear about that,' the magistrate reassured him. 'I have it officially that the Ordinance will be promulgated this year.'

'I have no fear that it won't be tried,' said Uncle Charles drily. 'But I don't fancy, Staples, that it is going to do us much good. It's going to bring in all sorts of mischief; there's nothing like politics to play the devil with a mixed community such as ours. And these Dutchmen have some political sense—more, I fancy, than we from the old country, who have had our fill of politics and are sick and tired of the business. And the Natives too, Staples.

Mark my words, the thing will bring trouble to all of us in the long run, and trouble of a kind neither of us anticipates now. We can't, you know. Things change so damnably quickly here. There is no stability; there are no fixed interests. It's democracy in its best—or worst—form, and now that the qualification is so preposterously low ...' Uncle Charles did not complete the sentence but shrugged his shoulders suggestively.

'I don't quite agree,' said the magistrate, argumentatively. 'Politics will at least give them an outlet for their exuberance, a legitimate vent. They can formulate their grievances and discuss them, and they will have a hand, too, in shaping their own grievances. The Assembly will have to tax, you know.'

'None of them would object to that,' remarked Uncle Charles. 'They are used to it. The puzzle to me has always been why they disliked us so much when under the old regime they had worse to put up with.'

'Then it was a family affair, as they would say,' replied the magistrate. 'There was no foreign interference. I think we are apt to make too much of that dislike. To a certain extent it is natural. We hold by conquest, so far as they are concerned, and that, you will admit, is always rather galling. Now we are gradually changing our title and becoming holders by occupation, and in time the old feeling will vanish.'

'Yes, but it will be replaced by another feeling,' said Uncle Charles. 'I can foresee that, Staples. You can't keep a child at home forever, and when he goes abroad and slogs round for himself, why, shiver me, you can't treat him like a child and expect him to be at your beck and call when you want him to do something. That's where the trouble is likely to come from. It came in America and then we messed it up sadly. It may come here ... unless we keep our heads and act like sensible men.'

'I don't see why we shouldn't do that, Quakerley,' said the magistrate. 'This is but a beginning; sooner or later responsible government must come, but just now it would be awkward to grant it. Besides, the Colony is not fit for it yet.'

'There I am with you, Staples. So far as it goes, it's good, although I still protest against the terms. They should have put in an education qualification besides the property qualification ...'

'Which would mean that fully eighty percent of the Valley would not be able to vote!' objected the magistrate. 'It was discussed and turned down.'

'What matter? It would have given them a stimulus for education. By the way, I must have a talk with you on that subject some day. I want you and Anders to be trustees for a fund ... you *ex officio* and Anders as a sort of *amicus curiae*, but we can discuss that later. Now, as to Nolte. So you think that the man is still acceptable?'

'Why not?' asked the magistrate. 'If we had not heard about this past of his, would you have questioned his suitability? You accepted it on what you knew of his capability for the job, and that is still the same. I don't say that if there was a disputed election and if they managed things as they do in the old country, especially if feelings ran high, his past would not be dragged into the lantern light and made much of. But that is scarcely likely. You can put up whoever you like and the Valley will vote for him.'

'That is so,' admitted Uncle Charles. 'I myself should have liked to have seen Rekker nominated, but as he won't have it, and as Seldon refuses, I don't know of a man more fit than Nolte.'

'What about Andrew?' asked the magistrate. 'He talks both languages and he is popular throughout the District.'

'Andy has no political sense,' said Uncle Charles with a shrug. 'I sometimes wonder what sense he has got. Not that he isn't capable. He is, on the farm, and in business he has a rare way of picking the winners, just as he does on a race course. But we were none of us cut out for politics, Staples. My father sat for his borough, but I don't think he ever opened his mouth except to say Aye or No, and his value as a legislator was nil. I am disappointed in Andy, but one can't have everything one wishes for, and the boy is well enough as he is and I am a fool to grumble.'

Everardus received the deputation in the big dining room and treated it hospitably to wine and cake and coffee, and listened with becoming modesty to its eulogistic speeches. Magriet, the Widow Priem, and Tins were interested spectators, and the spokesmen of the deputation were Uncle Charles, who put the case in English, and Uncle Martin, who underscored the arguments in well-sounding high Dutch. The deputation withdrew with a conditional promise from Everardus to the effect that if he received a 'requisition' from the District, signed by fifty of the more prominent residents, he would consent to stand. There would be no difficulty about that, he was assured, and the assurance, and especially the manner in which it was made and the words in which it was expressed, told him that the Valley still regarded him as 'one of us,' with all the privileges appertaining to that appellation.

Magriet had told him how his secret had become common property. At first the shock of the revelation had almost stunned him. It had come at a time and in a manner which he himself, had he had any say in the matter, would not have chosen, and he regretted that the burden of explanation had fallen upon Magriet. That she had acquitted herself of her task ably and well he could not doubt; the evidence to that effect was too concrete to be doubted. But it had needed all his courage and manhood when in the early stage of his convalescence, he had had his first interview with his old friends, and had listened to their cheery congratulations, feeling all the time that they were itching to discuss the matter with him and only restrained therefrom by their habitual courtesy.

The discussion had been easier than he had imagined. He had told them all about himself, and had given chapter and verse to substantiate what his wife had said; he had even shown them the old *fiat* which he had kept, he knew not why, among his private papers. The name on it was apparently known to both of them, for Uncle Dorie had handed back the paper with the remark, 'he was an awful scoundrel, that fellow, but he was a White man, after all, and it was fitting that a White man should have hanged him.' And after that they had talked no more about the matter.

When he moved about in the District again, he experienced nowhere any of the mistrust and stand-offishness which he had told himself would be his portion when his secret had been divulged. Where reference was made to the subject it was made guardedly, usually in a half jocular manner, and in time he became reconciled to his nickname, which at first he had thought singularly distasteful.

'I don't see why you should object to it, Nephew Ev'rard,' Uncle Dorie had told him. 'It is given kind-like, and the good Book tells us that even the kings of Israel had nicknames. Besides, you told me yourself that you didn't mind handling the creatures.'

And Uncle Dorie told him of other men who had had even more distasteful nicknames and had been none the worse liked or respected because of them. There was a fellow in the Hantam, now, who was known as Koos Sore-Eye, and another for whom the Valley had coined the name of Koos Coffin-Lid, and a third Koos, somewhere in an adjacent District, who having been acquitted on a charge of shooting a Native, was known as Koos Murderer. No one thought any the worse of them for their nicknames, which had been given to them out of sympathy, and reminded the Valley of incidents in their career which could serve to distinguish them from the multitude of Jacobs with whom in conversation they might otherwise have been confounded. The explanation was not wholly satisfactory, but Everardus had to be content, for the Valley had decided upon Gallows-Gecko, and there was nothing more to be said. Nor did Everardus fare worse when he visited the Seldons and the Quakerleys. Both families received him with their usual courtesy and hospitality, and made no difference in their attitude towards him. Old Uncle Charles, who had manifested increasing interest in the political situation, talked to him on various aspects of it, and he gleaned much from his intercourse with the old man, whose varied experience and quick intelligence made him an excellent mentor for the aspiring Member of Parliament. Everardus found Mrs Andrew inclined to be distant and supercilious, but he remembered her kindness to him while he had been ill, and bore with her, so that ultimately she became one of his champions, and felt that she could safely entrust the destinies of the English-speaking community to one who had not been privileged to be born in Kent. He thought her a tactless, meddlesome woman, but never expressed that opinion openly, though her father-in-law made no secret of the fact that he, too, shared it. For Uncle Charles he came to feel a sincere regard, similar to that which he felt for his partner, Thomas Seldon, and for the big, bearded Andrew, who conversed in monosyllables and smoked bagfuls of coarsely cut home-grown tobacco, and developed more and more into a real Valley-ite, to the undisguised annoyance and vexation of his wife.

Now, when it became necessary for him to clarify his views on many subjects preparatory to representing the Valley in the Assembly, Everardus sometimes thought about the position of the two sections of the community and their mutual relations. He had never felt strongly on the subject of nationality or class. He had had no great sympathy with the grievance mongers, and at the time when the trouble had arisen about the celebration of Her Majesty's name-day, the arguments that had been advanced by them had left him cold. But his conversations with Uncle Charles had made him see that there were deep-rooted differences between his own outlook upon life and that held by his English speaking neighbours. Their conception of responsibility and obligation was not quite consonant with his own. He admitted that he had not yet crystallised his own views; he could not formulate a definition of what he regarded as national obligation, but he could confess to himself that it would not tally, if he did so, with either that of the stuttering little man who had represented the Trekkers or that of Uncle Charles. Outside the Valley—why, there he had no interests. Everything he loved, honoured and treasured lay in the Valley, and, the Valley being part of the country, it followed, logically, that his first duty was towards South Africa, and not to anything six thousand miles overseas. That was clear enough, but when it came to subtleties of convention, language, custom, and caste, he was still undecided. Mrs Andrew's pertinacious advocacy of things alien, her constant disparagement of local conditions, her continual reference to foreign standards as criteria of excellence, irritated and annoyed him, though he could not have explained why they did so. On the other hand, Uncle Charles's quiet criticism, though it tended in the same direction, did not displease him. It was true the old man had different canons of obligation and could not see eye to eye with him on many subjects. But so had Brother Johann, and, even more concretely and passionately, Brother von Bergmann, whose opinion he valued before everyone else's. Indeed, so highly did he value it that he determined, before he finally consented to stand as candidate for the District, to visit Brother von Bergmann and discuss the whole matter with him. In later years he looked back upon that visit as one of the tide-marks of his life. The Neckarthal mission had impressed him favourably; Brother von Bergmann's community, where the missionary was a definite power, respected alike by his Native and White neighbours, gave him a sense of entirely new values. The missionary's wife, the daughter of a baroness, and a woman of great beauty and dignified presence; the missionary's family, consisting of two grown up daughters and two little boys, whose Elder bothers had already gone overseas to that same mission hostel to which Brother Johann had consigned his sons; the missionary's well-stocked library; the cool, well ordered mission house, where he dined with a judge on circuit and listened to table talk ranging from the new comet to the Chartist disturbances and the coming election—all these things made a profound impression on him, which was enhanced by the feeling that he had that in that environment of culture and simple but dignified homeliness, Brother von Bergmann stood out as the predominant personality, a strong, virile character such as he had never before encountered. Even the judge deferred to him, and Everardus heard with no surprise that Brother von Bergmann had the entrée at Government House, and even chatted to royalty.

'I am glad, *Meneer* Nolte,' Brother von Bergmann had said when Everardus had confided his doubts and his difficulties to him and had asked his advice, 'I am sincerely glad that your secret is no longer your own. As I told you at Neckarthal, it was one that could not have been kept. Sooner or later it would have had to become public property, and you could not have accepted this responsibility, which you tell me you are thinking of accepting, unless those who are honouring you were aware of your past. Now that they know there is no reason why you should not accept. As for these other matters, your own good sense of what is right and wrong should guide you.'

'Nevertheless I should like Your Reverence to give me counsel on some points,' said Everardus. 'There is, first, this matter of the qualifications. Ought we to let it be? Should we not try and amend it? Is it right that the wives should be on an equal footing with us? Is it fair, Your Reverence, that those who have much property should be rated the same as those who have none, and those who are more ... civilised ... I mean ... who have had a better education, be treated just like those who are much inferior?'

'On those points, *Meneer* Nolte,' said von Bergmann gravely, 'we are likely to differ, but since you have asked my views, I give them freely. We are a very small White community, whereas the Natives are numerous. Most of us are civilised; the majority property owners. You cannot say that for the Natives. The vast majority of them are as yet uncivilised. It seems to me that the statesmanlike thing to do—which has not been done—is to put the qualification so high that while it excludes the uncivilised, it does not slam the door in their faces forever. The property qualification is far too low; besides, it is not a true criterion of a man's real value in this country— no, not even of a White man's real value. I make no distinction between race or colour, but I do make a distinction between moral, economic, and social qualities. And I think the franchise should draw such a distinction. You must remember that a child grows; that the Natives will progress towards civilisation, just as we have progressed. I am quite aware that there are people who deny that the Native can ever be on the same level with us, but I think they are wrong, quite wrong. And thinking that, I should be untrue to my convictions if I denied to them the right to have some say— however slight at first that share is bound to be—in the management of the political affairs of this country.'

'But in that case, Your Reverence, they would overpower us. They are far more numerous than we are.'

'We too can grow, as a community, *Meneer* Nolte. We have the whole of Europe to draw upon, and this country is wide enough to give shelter to millions of immigrants. I say wide enough; I am not so sure yet that it is a country that will bear White settlement on a large scale. On the coast, yes; but inland, that is another matter. But of that I am not competent to judge. At present the position is clear. We are a small community of Whites established as lords and guardians of a very large Native community, permanently settled here. Our Parliament, now to be elected, cannot in the nature of things be otherwise than a Parliament of the Whites; it cannot claim to be representative of the country. No Parliament can claim to be that unless it represents all the citizens; you must admit that. When we had slavery, it was another matter; the slave was not a citizen in the real sense of the term. But having abolished slavery, we have tacitly admitted that we are all citizens, and in principle this new constitution endorses that view. But it will take many years, centuries perhaps, *Meneer* Nolte, before the majority of citizens can take their part in ruling the country, and it should be our task to make them competent to do so, by setting them a high example. That the constitution does not do.'

'I can see that, Your Reverence. I, too, should like to see the qualification raised for even the White man. But this, after all, is our country, Your Reverence, not the Natives' ...'

'I don't see how you can say that. Rather say that it is ours as much as theirs and then I might agree. I think, if you will pardon me saying so, we are all a little frightened at the idea of sharing this country with others. Look at the feeling there is against the English. I do not say they do nothing to warrant it; sometimes their doings exasperate me, and I ask myself how sensible people can be so childish. But that is not quite the way our farmers here look at the matter. You know that as well as I do.'

'Yes, Your Reverence, that is another point. Are we never to call this country our own, then? Must we always be under England?'

'Until we are strong enough and able to stand alone, yes, *Meneer* Nolte. If England left us today, what do you think would happen? Some other country would step in and annex us. I can understand your feelings. I am not born here, *Meneer* Nolte, but I would live nowhere else, now that I know South Africa. I have made it my home; my wife was born here, and it is her fatherland, and my children's. I, too, may cherish the hope that some day South Africa will be a great country. But I am convinced that she can never be that unless she has the strength and the solidarity that comes from a united people, and gives to her Native subjects the same rights and privileges, and demands from them the same obligations, that she gives and exacts from her White citizens. That is my view, *Meneer* Nolte. It is unthinkable, unbelievable, that a country's destiny can be permanently shaped by a small section of her citizens. For a time, yes. It is inevitable that a small section must be leader and guide, but ultimately it must merge into the large commonwealth that is made up by all sections, Black and White and Coloured. You may dislike it as much as you please, but that is the position.'

Everardus felt that he did dislike the prospect very much indeed, but he had no arguments to oppose, and Brother von Bergmann went on.

'You will hear a great deal of nonsense talked about patriotism, *Meneer* Nolte. Patriotism is sometimes a virtue that a vicious man arrogates to himself. But it can never be a virtue unless it is based on righteousness. Nor can it be an effective virtue unless it takes cognisance of human rights and obligations. We have plain duties before us. We represent European civilisation here; we represent Christianity, education, economic development, social betterment—all the factors that combine to expedite a nation's progress. It is not right that we should say that these factors are for us alone and not for our Native fellow citizens. Why, even yonder, where some of our neighbours have established their own communities, they have had the good sense to see that and to say that they will not altogether her exclude the Native, provided he develops and shows that he is fit for his share in the government of a country which is as much his as it is ours.'

From his visit to Brother von Bergmann, Everardus came back to the Valley in as thoughtful a mood as he had returned from his first trip to Neckerthal. He had been given new apperceptive masses, and he had not had time or opportunity to develop them. That would come. Meanwhile, he decided to accept the committee's invitation and to allow himself to be nominated as a candidate. The decision was received with applause by the Valley, which formed itself into local election committees, and energetically scrutinised the new voters rolls in preparation for whatever might eventuate.

Chapter 23

A gloriously peaceful autumn twilight enveloped *Knolkloof* on that particular evening when Magriet and the Widow Priem sat on the *stoep*, awaiting Everardus's return from the Village, whither he had gone to attend his committee meeting. Over the high mountain ranges, still perfectly visible in their majestic ruggedness, stretched a green-blue sky, rapidly darkening to a deeper shade. In the *kloofs* and coigns of their rocky vastnesses lay massive splashes of denser shadow, coalescing slowly with their paler environment of slope and level veld. Over the River, winding westwards into the distance, the lights from the open Valley were reflected on the water and lost in the thick undergrowth of the banks. From across the road came the noise of lowing cattle, the bleat of the lambs shepherded into the *kraals*, and the innumerable sounds of farmyard activity preliminary to the quiet calmness of the evening's rest. From the garden the casual breeze wafted the faint perfume of the late-blossoming jasmine and the stronger scent of the dying amaryllis lilies.

The Widow Priem had shown a strange dislike to departing from the farm. She had protracted her visit long beyond the period for which she had stated she had come. Magriet was glad to have her company, for she had grown to like the old woman, whose directness, common sense, and experience she highly appreciated. But Aunt Cornelia had come to help her with her sick husband and Everardus was now perfectly well, and needed no further nursing. On two occasions the widow had mounted her horse and ridden out to her own farm 'to see how things were getting on there,' but both times she had returned and declared that she could trust the Black folk to go for a little longer and protract her holiday. Magriet had wondered at this decision, but as she frankly liked the old lady's company, and enjoyed her unconventional conversation, she had been glad of it, and in any case hospitality forbade her to comment upon it even had she wished to do so. It was an established custom in the Valley for friends to come on long visits, and no one would have dreamed of challenging so old and so honoured a practice. Now, as they sat on the *stoep* in the fading twilight, Magriet could observe that the older woman was not quite at her ease. She affected to be busily employed with her knitting, an occupation to which she invariably resorted when there was nothing else to do. Cornelia Priem was one of those who implicitly believed that Satan finds occupation for idle hands, and to save the Devil from any worry on her account, she was never idle. Mere conversation did not suffice for her activities; she desired something more, and found it in this incessant click-clack of her knitting needles, which had the added advantage of enabling her to emphasise her words when she wanted to do so by appropriately softening or increasing the sounds they made.

'Would you believe it, Niece Magriet,' she said tentatively, 'would you believe it, tomorrow I shall be forty-seven years old.'

'You hardly look that age, Aunt Cornelia,' answered Magriet, too well aware of the fact that the widow hated empty compliments, and expressing merely her sincere conviction. The widow did not look her age as she sat there busily knitting. The twilight softened her features, toned down her gaunt, angular figure, and gave to her face a mildness that it lacked in open sunshine.

'Yes, truly, Niece Magriet,' went on the widow. 'And my husband died fifteen years ago. Frikkie will be fifteen next May, and the boy was born after his father had gone to glory. I have had fifteen years of loneliness, Niece Magriet, though you may not think it.'

'Does Aunt regret that?' asked Magriet with a smile. 'I have heard it said that Aunt could have picked and chosen ...'

'So I might,' responded the widow quickly. 'For years they pestered me, the men. I might have had several, had I been so inclined. Not, of course, that one can marry several, as the Malays do, but you will grasp my meaning, Niece. I might have picked and chosen, as you say, but the fact is I did not do so.'

'And does Aunt regret not having done so?' queried Magriet. 'I have always thought that Aunt preferred being ... remaining single. Myself, I should not dream of marrying if I lost Ami.'

'It is not that, altogether,' said the widow reflectively. 'I have seen how it stands with you and Nephew Ev'rard. You are still in love with one another, as you should be. But with me it is different. Fifteen years do make a difference, Niece. My late husband would not have minded; he would have said, "Go your own gait, woman, and if you fancy the fellow ..." But somehow I fancied none of them, Niece, and for years I had no regrets. Not even for my Pieta, Niece, for he had a heart, a heart and asthma, Niece, and it was a God's-mercy he was taken, for he suffered much the last few years. Every night his chest contracted, and he wheezed something cruel, Niece. And when his legs swelled—he got the dropsy, Niece, as those with a heart do—and we knew that he was going, he told me not to worry. If I cared to take another, he said, he did not mind, Niece, so long as I had a fancy and the man was good. Naturally Pieta would not have liked to see me throw myself away upon some young, inexperienced fellow. It is ill-mating with those, Niece. But I was a grown woman when Pieta died, and I have my sense, so he knew that I would not judge rashly.'

'I am sure you wouldn't, Aunt Cornelia,' assented Magriet. 'It must have been difficult when the choice was so great ...'

'Not at all,' protested the widow vigorously, clicking her needles furiously. 'None of them had what I wanted, so I did not fancy any of them. But it is regrettable, none the less, that fifteen years have gone by, Niece. At my age one knows the value of time.'

'But Aunt Cornelia may still marry, if Aunt cares to do so,' suggested her hostess, 'I warrant there are others besides the gentleman from the Hantam who would like ...'

'If you refer to him who is cross-eyed,' remarked the widow with dignified primness, 'you need not scruple to say so. I am no longer a silly young thing, Niece. I know my own mind, and if Servaas—that is the fellow from the Hantam of whom you have heard; he was squint-eyed and he has since married a blood-young thing, though I say nothing against her—if Servaas were to be free tomorrow to ask me, I should say what I said then, namely that I would not marry him if he were the only man left alive after the deluge. No. I know my mind, Niece. And that makes the matter so regrettable.'

'What matter, Aunt Cornelia? I don't understand. Is there another suitor, and does Aunt fancy him?' asked Magriet, now thoroughly intrigued. She had not suspected anything like this, and wondered on whom the widow's favour had fallen. She rapidly reviewed in her mind the possible eligibles. There were several, but she could not imagine anyone in particular catching the widow's fancy.

'What we have been talking about,' said the Widow Priem tartly. 'Haven't I told you that sixteen years of loneliness does not stick in one's clothes? It is so much time wasted. The good Book says it is not well for a woman to be alone, and I only realised this when ... when it was too late. It is saddening, Niece, to a woman like myself, not too old to be a man's wife, to find that she has wasted all these years, and might have to go into her coffin without finding that solace of which the good Book speaks.'

'But if Aunt has a chance, and if Aunt wishes to marry again ...' began Magriet, bewildered, but the widow interrupted her briskly.

'It is not a matter of chance nor of wishing, Niece,' she said. 'It has ... has just arrived.' She ceased the clicking of her needles for an instant, and allowed the knitting to fall into her lap. 'It came over me sudden, Niece, just as if I was a silly young girl. These things are not of our own choosing. There is a providence in them, Niece, though you might not know it. How strong those Ceylon roses do smell ...'

It was not often that the Widow Priem referred to aesthetic factors. The fact that she did so now impressed Magriet.

'Perhaps I may be able to help, Aunt,' she said gently, and instinctively drew her chair closer to the old woman. 'If Aunt should confide in me ...'

'I have long wished to do so, my child,' breathed Aunt Cornelia, with a sigh of satisfaction or relief—Magriet could not be sure of the exact emotion vented in that sudden gasp—'I have long wished to do so, but there are things which the heart feels and the tongue dares not express. This is one of them. I don't know what has come over me—very likely it is the evening air and the smell of the Ceylon roses—that is very strong, Niece, and I always favoured Ceylon roses; my Pieta was buried with them on his breast and he looked lovely, although so swollen from the dropsy we could hardly get him into the coffin. Somehow I felt that I must tell you. Not that you can do anything in the matter—and of course you must keep it to yourself. Promise me,' exclaimed the widow wildly, as if suddenly realising that she had said more than she had intended, 'promise me, Niece, that you will not breathe a word of it ...'

'But of course not, Aunt Cornelia. I should not dream of doing so. Aunt can safely tell me all about it. And why should Aunt be distressed? Surely, it is a matter for Aunt to settle ...'

'Ah, now you talk without your catechism, Niece. There is nothing to settle, for an old woman's fancies are of no concern to anybody else but herself. That,'—the widow's voice had in it more indignation than Magriet thought the subject demanded—'is the misfortune of it. Could I foresee that in my old age I should hanker after another man, and take a fancy to him? Yet that is what has happened, Niece. I doubt, I much doubt, if he knows anything at all about it. That is what makes the matter so distressing, my child. I have heard it said that our gracious Queen, who also felt a fancy for a man, sat up with him of her own accord, but to my mind that is unseemly. Belike, it was different for her, and I have no wish to say anything, not the slightest, Niece, that in any way may detract from the respect we should bear toward our beloved sovereign, but I can't do that. It is not in me, my child.'

'Perhaps if Aunt would tell me,' suggested Magriet, now very much intrigued. 'It may be that we might make a plan, and find some way out.'

'I have thought over it and thought,' wailed the widow, 'but nothing has come into my mind. I did think of knitting him a pair of socks—now what do you think of that, Niece? Would it seem improper, immodest on my part, if I did that? I have noticed that his have holes in them, and time and again I have hinted that I should like to darn them. But men folk are so difficult, Niece. My Pieta was similar. He could never take a hint. I had to make everything plain to him, just like one does to a child, and even then he sometimes did exactly the opposite to what I wanted him to do. So difficult, my child. And he is even more so. He is all shyness and touchiness and pride. Why, I saw it the moment I clapped eyes upon him. He stood there as silly as if a wasp had stung him on his behind, and seemed like to bite my hand if I had given him any chance of doing so. Only when I made him eat ...'

'Teacher? Why, surely, does Aunt mean Teacher ... Tins?' exclaimed Magriet, too surprised to hide her astonishment.

'And of whom have we been talking all this time, if not of Teacher?' demanded the widow aggressively. 'And I do not like people to call him Tins. It is a silly nickname. He does not remind one of a tin at all. He is a proper man, although very touchy and full of pride. I like him for that, for a man should have respect for himself, and carry himself with dignity. Teacher does that. That is one reason why I fancied him from the moment I set eyes upon him. He is not like those others who sat up with me, and wasted my candles and my patience all for nothing. If I had only met him sooner ... but, my child, do say something sensible.'

'What can I say, Aunt Cornelia?' asked Magriet, very much in doubt as to how she should respond to this invitation. 'I had no idea that the wind came from that quarter. Why, *Meneer* Mabuis is ...'

'Don't say it, my child, don't say it. Of course he is, and so would anyone be who is like him, proud and dignified, with a head full of knowledge and sense, and a presence like ... like that of the Governor. What can a poor man do but drink when no one understands him and all the world is against him? Don't I know it? Why, sometimes I have myself felt the need for a sip of wine. Of course, if he has a wife to share the burden with him, there will be no need for him to get intoxicated, and at any rate he hasn't been that for ever so long. He has turned over a new leaf, and should make a good man ...'

'But, Aunt, he is not of our faith. He is a Roman Catholic ...'

'All the more reason he should have someone to look after him,' said the widow sturdily. 'Not that I care whether he is a heathen or not, Niece. When one has taken a fancy so strongly as it has come upon me, one does not ask oneself about these little things. They will adjust themselves. Do say something sensible, my child.'

'It is altogether too amazing,' said Magriet seriously. 'It must be thought about and considered; Aunt will see the sense of that. But I had no idea ... no idea at all ...'

'Nor had I,' admitted the widow, too agitated now to resume her knitting. 'It came upon me like a hailstorm in summer, and it beat down all my common sense; it sometimes does that, Niece, with a young woman when she gets her first fancy. But I had thought myself strong enough, with all my experience, my child, to resist. And I find I can't ... I simply can't, Niece Magriet. It is plain, sinful covetousness when I look at the man, and it is plain, sinful regret when I think of these fifteen-sixteen years I have wasted.'

'Aunt must be calm,' said Magriet nervously, for the Widow Priem displayed signs dangerously akin to breakdown. 'Perhaps we can make some plan. I must think about it. Does Aunt perchance know if Teacher ... if Teacher ... how shall I say it?'

'If the man reciprocates my feelings?' Aunt Cornelia said simply. 'Why, that is a question I have asked myself over and over again. Sometimes I think he does. The way he looks at me when he eats the preserve ... the manner in which he says good night to me ... the fashion in which he opens the door for me ... you might say they are foreign ways and popinjay tricks, but there are times when I fancy that they have deeper meaning, Niece. Probably the heart sees what it looks for to see, my child. Oh, I am so miserable, and you sit there and say nothing sensible.'

'But Aunt, what is there to say? If Aunt were the Queen, it would be simple enough, and now I come to think about it, why not? Aunt is almost the Queen of the Valley. Aunt is far richer than he is ... Teacher is a poor man, and I doubt if he has a hundred pounds of his own.'

'That does not make the slightest difference,' asserted the widow firmly. 'I have more than sufficient for both of us.'

'That may be, Aunt. But there is another matter. We none of us know much about Teacher, except what he has told us. Should Aunt not try and find out ...'

'At any rate I am certain that he wasn't a public executioner,' said the widow, and immediately added contritely, 'there, child, I did not intend to be vicious, but you do make it so hard for one to keep patience with you. What does it matter when a woman takes a fancy to a man ... I mean what does it matter if the man drinks or has no family or is poor? She thinks she can make up for all that, and make an angel out of the fellow. And that is what has happened to me, Niece. Belike, you cannot understand it, though if you felt for your own man ... there, I have hurt you again, for I know that you feel for Nephew Ev'rard, else you would not have borne with all him all these years. But, my child, have some consideration for an old woman who has wasted fifteen years in loneliness ... if I had only seen him before ... if I had only ...' The Widow Priem was now unashamedly weeping against Magriet. Her gaunt, bony frame was shaken by her sobs, and she yielded herself, with the pathetic confidence of a child, to her hostess's petting. It was some time before she was sufficiently calmed to discuss the practical side of the matter. Magriet had no suggestions to make; the situation was altogether beyond her. But she felt, and the widow agreed with her, that some certainty should be obtained before further developments were to be considered. Obviously the first thing was to find out if Teacher had any inkling of the widow's feelings. That was a matter which needed expert and wary handling, and Magriet was of an opinion that she could not proceed in it without consulting her husband. At first the Widow Priem was adamant in requiring that her secret should be kept, and it needed much diplomacy and tact on Magriet's part to move her from this position. Only when she saw that in such circumstances there would be the greatest difficulty in discovering what she so much wanted to find out, did she give her consent.

'You may inform Nephew Ev'rard of my inclination towards Teacher,' she said finally. 'He will bear with me, for he is a man of sense and experience, and he will know that in these matters one cannot control one's feelings. They come upon us unawares. I had thought that at my age ... but one is never too old to find out one's mistakes, and Nephew Ev'rard will not judge me too harshly. But it must remain between you two, Niece, and no third party must be added to the discussion. Promise me that. And now you must let Sylvester get my cart ready, for I must go to *Langvlei* tonight.'

'Surely not! Aunt can stay, and go over tomorrow,' urged Magriet.

'Surely yes, Niece. I should not like to encounter Nephew Ev'rard after you have told him. I am an old woman, and should be above such things, but I too have a touch of pride, and I could not bear that. Remember, Niece, I stuck up for you in your trouble ...'

'You did that, Aunt, and I am grateful to you for it,' replied Magriet fervently, for she had not forgotten the widow's staunch championship nor her faithful service when Everardus had lain sick with the typhoid. 'All that we can do for Aunt we will most willingly do. Aunt can rest assured of that.'

'I do, my child, I do. And now, please order Sylvester. One of the boys can go with me. I know the road and I shall be all right. Why, many a night I have travelled it and come to no harm. I shall be ready in a few minutes, just long enough for him to inspan the cart.'

The Widow Priem departed for her farm before Everardus returned from the Village. She left without saying goodbye to Teacher, who was engaged in totting up the proceeds of the month's transport riding. As she drove out of the farmyard into the road, she could see the candles burning on the little window table in the schoolroom where he sat at work, but she gave all her attention to the horses, and vigorously scolded the Native boy because the splash-board of the car had not been cleaned to her liking.

When Everardus came in, satisfied with his visit to the Village, where his committee had told him that his election would be unopposed, his wife told him the news. He was less surprised at it than she had imagined he would be.

'I had a suspicion that Teacher and Aunt Cornelia had something between them,' he said thoughtfully. 'It is a wonder to me, Mother, that you did not suspect it yourself. You women are keener on the scent of such things than we men.'

'I never for a moment suspected it of Teacher,' said Magriet frankly. 'About Aunt Cornelia, well, I did wonder what made her stay here so long. But even when she told me, I was hugely surprised. I had never thought that Teacher would find favour in her eyes.'

'One can never tell with you women,' said Everardus sagely. 'However did you come to have any inclination for me, Mother?'

'That is altogether a different thing,' said Magriet, blushing. 'And we were both young. Why, the moment I saw you—do you remember when you came to mend Uncle Roelf's harness—that day when the south-easter blew and all my washing flew off the clothes-line and you helped me to pick the things up ...'

'As if I should ever forget,' said Everardus, and hugged her. 'Or the night when I told you that the sheriff had asked me ...'

'Of that we will never speak again, Ami,' said Magriet gently. 'Now that it is past and done with, we will never refer to it.'

'But I shall never forget it, all the same,' said Everardus stubbornly. 'That is the sort of thing that a man does not forget, Mother. And if one feels like that, why, one can understand what the Widow Priem feels.'

'Yes, and we must help them, Ami. You must have a talk with Teacher ...'

'Steady, Mother, steady. That is more easily said than done. You know what he is like—as prickly as a porcupine. There's more harm done by interfering in these matters than by letting well alone.'

'But remember, Ami, she is alone, and has no one to help her. It would be different if she was a young girl with a father. Then he could do the talking. Now only we two know about the matter, and you have some responsibility in it.'

'Come, I fail to see that. What does it matter to us if the widow has an inclination towards Teacher?'

'Everything, Ami. You brought him here—or rather, you found him and took him up. I am glad you did. I like Teacher. I have always liked him. I think he is a good man—an honourable man—though I should never have said that he would be Aunt's husband. But if she has an inclination towards him, why then you should see if he is a proper man for her. And about that we are not sure yet, Ami.'

'I see,' said her husband thoughtfully. 'That is a point, certainly. There's the difference in religion. I fancy that would prove a bad obstacle for the widow to get over. Though I don't know. Haven't there been mixed marriages like that before? I can't recall any to mind, but there must have been. Why, they must have been common enough in the old days. However, that is a matter they can settle between themselves.'

'But what of his standing, Ami? Is he fit to marry her? After all, what do we know about Teacher? We don't even know ... why, Ami, he may be a married man for all we know.'

'So he might, Mother. Phew, the affair complicates itself. I shall have to do something, though I don't know what. Honestly, I don't like interfering in it, but as you say the widow must be protected. Where is Teacher?'

'At work on the accounts, in the school room. But not tonight, Ami. Sleep over it, and decide what to do in the morning.'

'Yes, certainly I had no intention of doing anything tonight. These things do not bear hurrying. And it's altogether too difficult a problem for me, Mother. I fancy I shall have to consult His Reverence about it.'

'You can't do that, Ami. I promised her.'

'Be easy, Mother. We need not give her away. I shall put a—how do they call it?—hypothetical case to His Reverence. About the religions, for instance. I don't know how far it would be legal if the two married. Where have the banns to be put up? There are complications, Mother. It is not quite so simple as you think.'

'No. I can see that. But do be cautious, Ami. I could not bear to hurt the old lady.'

'Be easy, Mother. She will not be hurt. I am learning every day to be more circumspect and subtle. Before very long they will call me Clever Gallows-Gecko in the Valley. You'd like that almost as well as Gallows—Gecko, wouldn't you mother?'

'I like you by any name, Ami,' said Magriet, nestling close to him as they went indoors. 'And I think Aunt Cornelia is perfectly right. One can't account for liking one's man.'

Chapter 24

Everardus felt diffident about broaching the subject with Tins, yet he could not but agree with his wife that he had some responsibility in the matter. It was he who had stabilised Teacher at *Knolkloof*. It was he who had arranged for him to remain there, rather than proceed on his gipsying towards the copper mines; he who had perhaps flouted public opinion by proposing a Papist for the job of teacher at his farm school; he who would now, in honour, have to prevent the Widow Priem from being imposed upon.

Fortunately for Everardus, Tins gave him more than one opportunity of discussing the matter. On the evening of the widow's departure, Teacher had been busily engaged with his accounts, for he had instituted a sort of half-yearly audit, and that had been the evening which he had taken for it. He had gone to bed very late, when presumably all the other units of the family had already retired. But the next morning he had been manifestly surprised when he had heard, at the breakfast table, that the Widow Priem had left the farm.

'That is indeed strange,' he said musingly, 'almost incredible. Did the *Douairiere*, *Madame*, by any chance leave a message for me?'

'No. Why should she have left one, Teacher?' asked Magriet brusquely, anxious to learn from his manner if there was any sentiment attached to the matter of the widow's departure. 'She had to go suddenly.'

'The *Douairiere* would have bidden her friends farewell,' he had replied stiffly. 'That is all, *Madame*. If *Madame* would have the infinite goodness to present me with another ration of sausage—a thousand thanks, Madame—you anticipate my wishes. Might I enquire, *Meneer* Nolte, if the political affair marches?'

'It goes well, Teacher,' said Everardus. 'It seems I shall not have to spend a penny. All is being arranged. Before May next year you will see yours truly a member of our gracious Queen's Parliament. And then I shall have to get a new frock coat and a new hat.'

'You want both very badly, Ami,' said his wife. 'I am ashamed of you when you take round the plate on a Sunday. The other members of the church council look spick and span, and my old man hurries down the aisle in a coat that dates from the year nought ...'

'*Meneer* Nolte can wear whatever he likes,' said Tins bellicosely. 'The clothes, *Madame*, do not make the individual. One may dress in miniver and yet be *canaille* ...'

'These matters you must argue with Uncle Martin,' retorted Magriet, noticing that Teacher was 'on his dignity' for some reason or other. She shrewdly suspected that it had something to do with the widow's departure, but forbore questioning him. That was Ami's duty, and Ami had never failed her.

So she left them on the *stoep*, smoking, and went to the kitchen to supervise Minerva's *sossaties*. Once a month the *Knolkloof* household feasted on these succulencies, and their preparation demanded a technique which was almost a ritual. Early in the morning Sylvester would kill the sheep, especially selected for the purpose because it was fat. From its tender muscle shielding the lumbar vertebrae, the meat would be cut in strips, and these strips would again be cut into small squares. A portion of the fat pork would be similarly cut up into large dice-shaped pieces, and the mutton and pork would be placed in layers in a big earthenware dish, and over them would be poured a pickle composed of vinegar, milk, curry powder, coriander seeds, tamarinds, almonds, and sliced dry peaches. Finally a layer of chopped onions would be added, and the basin would be placed in the coolest part of the pantry, where Minerva would stir it daily with a spoon, until the meat had extracted from its aromatic surroundings all that meat was capable of abstracting and absorbing. When the time had come for the *sossaties* to be prepared for the table, Sylvester would be sent out to fetch a piece of dried bamboo, which Minerva would split into several dozen ten inch long skewers, which had to be polished, pointed at both ends, and carefully dried before the fire. On these skewers the meat would be strung, each mutton square alternating with a piece of bacon fat in ordered sequence, and the skewered meat would be grilled over the wood fire, while the pickle boiled alongside in an iron pot. As accompaniment to these *sossaties*, rich, fried bananas, and poached eggs would be served, and on *sossatie* day the *Knolkloof* kitchen was kept busy all day.

On the *stoep* Everardus and Tins smoked for a while in silence, each occupied with his own thoughts. The Teacher appeared preoccupied and grave, and to the few perfunctory questions that Everardus asked him about the accounts, he replied shortly and without great enthusiasm.

'I shall have a request for *Meneer* Nolte,' he said at last, speaking abruptly. 'It may seem strange to *Monsieur*, but it is necessary that I make it.'

'Well, what is it, Teacher?' asked Everardus.

'It is that *Meneer* Nolte will permit me to leave him,' said Tins. 'The time has come for Pierre Mabuis to go on his travels again, like Telemachus—although that young gentleman went in search, if I remember rightly, of his *papa*, and I have no need to do that, being assured that my *papa* is now in such bliss as he probably deserves.'

'If Uncle Dorie were here,' observed Everardus with a smile, knocking out the dottel of his pipe against some of the *stoep* trellis poles, 'he would remark that Teacher should not refer to Teacher's parent in that disrespectful way. But as it is habit, like *Meneer* Quakerley's constant invitation to someone to shiver him, we may let it pass, and come to the business in hand. Why do you want to leave us? Are you not satisfied with what you have here? If it is a question of money, I daresay I could point out to the committee that it is time we increased our Teacher's honorarium.'

'It is not a question of *lucre*,' said Tins distantly. 'It is an affair purely personal, which, if *Monsieur* permits me to make the remark, I am not in a position more clearly to explain. But it is imperative that I should leave, and go on my travels again. *Meneer* Nolte will doubtless allow me to give him my sincere assurance that it is with unutterable regret that I make the request. *Monsieur* has been good to me; *Monsieur* has given me the inestimable privilege of permitting me to call myself his friend, and from *madame* I have had a charity the most Christian-like. It desolates me to have to forego these things, but the affair makes it inevitable that I should go.'

'What affair are you speaking of?' demanded Everardus. "I have found no fault to find with you, Teacher. The school progresses. If the work is too much ...'

'The work is as before, neither less *amusant, Monsieur*, than in times past nor more onerous. It has never been hard, for what these disciples demand from me is far less than what I should give in return for the kindness and the magnanimity with which *Monsieur* has treated me. The affair is one altogether separate from the school, or the farm, or *Monsieur*, or anything that *Monsieur* may have the honour to think of.'

'Then what in heaven's name is biting you?' asked Everardus. 'I suppose someone has offended you, and as you cannot run him through—as your *papa* might have done—and are too proud to tell me what your grievance is, you think the best way is to clear out, and start afresh elsewhere. But will you just bear in mind, Tins, that we are your friends here, and that we would grieve to see you go, no matter what the affair is. My friend, if it is anything in which I can help you ...'

'*Meneer* Nolte is most kind. *Meneer* is of a kindness that makes it all the more lamentable for me to have to decline to give *Meneer* further particulars, but *Meneer* will once more permit me to give him the sincere assurance that I should go and that the Valley should know me no more.'

'Well, if that is your fixed determination,' began Everardus, not without a touch of annoyance in his voice, 'you must go your own gait. But you cannot go today nor tomorrow. You are under contract with the committee ...'

'I had hoped that *Meneer* Nolte, in his goodness, would have the very great kindness to waive that condition,' said Tins hesitatingly. 'For the school, it is no great matter that I leave. *Madame* is quite capable of doing what I have done, until such time as *Meneer* gets another teacher ...'

'By no means,' interrupted Everardus quickly. 'I don't like to hold you to the contract, but there it is, in black and white, and you should give us due notice. What are contracts for? They are a mutual understanding between the two contracting parties, and I am sure that the committee will take it amiss if I dispensed with the notice you ought to give us.'

'In that case, *Monsieur*,' said Tins dejectedly, 'there is nothing more to be said. I stay. I stay until such time as *Monsieur* will give me leave to go. But *Monsieur* will have the goodness to inform *Messieurs* the committee members that Pierre Mabuis wishes to be relieved from his obligations under his contract as soon as may be convenable to the committee. I now have the honour to wish *Monsieur* a good day, being obliged to return to the business of adding up *Monsieur's* profits for the past six months.'

That may bide for a while, Teacher,' said Everardus. 'Sit you down, Tins. Sit you down. You and I must have a little talk.'

'It shall be as *Meneer* Nolte pleases,' said Tins, resuming his place on the cedar wood *stoep* bench.

Everardus remained silent for a few minutes. He was by no means certain of his procedure, for he knew the touchiness of his companion, and although he surmised that Tins's wish to leave the farm had something to do with his relations with the Widow Priem, he had little to go upon, and it behoved him to proceed warily. But Everardus was used to direct action; he loathed circumlocution and evasion, and he decided upon a frontal attack with all its attendant dangers.

'Tell me, Tins,' he said, trying to make his voice sound as nonchalant as possible, 'tell me, is there anything between you and the Widow Priem? I mean, have you any thoughts in that direction?'

Tins drew himself up on the bench and glared at his companion.

'I have not the slightest notion of what *Monsieur* refers to,' he said stiffly. 'Is it that *Monsieur* has in mind that I have by work or action shown myself to be other than what a gentleman should be ...'

'No, no, Tins. Will you come down from your high horse for a moment and listen to me. I am asking you in all friendliness. It is not a mere matter of curiosity—after all, it is none of my business ... directly that is. But indirectly, I am concerned ... we all are. And now that we are on the subject, we might as well have it out. Does your wish to leave us ... Has it any connection with the Widow Priem?'

'I have already assured *Monsieur*,' began Tins, but Everardus interrupted him sharply.

'Yes, you have assured me, but I have my own suspicions. When you heard that she had gone away without saying farewell to you, you showed—aye, I was looking at you when Magriet told you—you showed that you were annoyed ...'

'Not annoyed, *Monsieur*, not annoyed. I shall never be annoyed with *Madame la Douairiere*. I have far too much respect for *Madame la Douairiere*. But pained ... pained and grieved that I had, by mischance, given her any cause to shun me. I feel for *Madame la Douairiere*—why should I hide it from *Monsieur* now that *Monsieur* has detected what I would gladly have hidden—I feel for *Madame* the most sincere respect and veneration that it is possible for one so unworthy as myself to feel for a being so infinitely superior to himself. I admire *Madame la Douairiere*, *Monsieur* Nolte; I have done so ever since that afternoon I had the honour of partaking of Madame's hospitality on the farm *Langvlei*. When Pierre Mabuis is lying on his death bed, with the holy oil on his nostrils and forehead, he will still cherish the recollection of the happiness he has been privileged to have through knowing *Madame la Douairiere* even for the short time that he has been in her company. I have, *Monsieur*, had many happy days, through *Monsieur* and *Madame's* goodness to me, but I may say, honestly, *Monsieur*, that the supreme happiness has been the privilege of consorting with *Madame la Douairiere* ...'

'Very well,' said Everardus, interrupting this tirade briskly, 'then what in heavens name is there to drive you away from us? If the matter stands thus ... if you have an inclination towards Aunt Cornelia ...'

'*Meneer* Nolte will infinitely oblige me by abstaining from so vulgar an expression. It is sacrilege for anyone to have an inclination towards *Madame la Douairiere*. It is something far higher, far nobler that I cherish ...'

'No matter what you call the feeling,' said Everardus smilingly. 'I suppose in common, understandable language, you are in love with her?'

'If the snail may love the rose, the marmot the mountain,' began Tins, dithyrambically, 'or the commoner the Queen, *Monsieur*. Then, yes. I have done so since that day ... whereof the memory will never depart from me. I have loved *Madame la Douairiere* as a man worships from afar, for I have always felt that it is no dishonour to love the unattainable. It refines and ennobles the mind, *Monsieur*, and there is nothing dishonourable in so admiring what one can never possess ...'

'Now your are talking nonsense,' said Everardus practically. 'If you have an ... if you love the woman, why then you should tell her so. How do you suppose she is to know that you feel that way towards her? Be sensible, and look at the matter from a common sense point of view ...'

'That is impossible, *Monsieur*,' declared Tins. 'She is as far beyond my reach as these beautiful mountains which *Monsieur* sees before us. Would *Monsieur* have Pierre Mabuis, who is a vagrant, a drunkard—let me say through *Monsieur's* goodness and example, one who no longer gets inebriated to the extent customary in his family—a landless, penniless object, would *Monsieur* have him lay his heart on *Madame la Douairiere's* lap? Why, she would call in her excellent Black and say to him, "Remove this offal, Boy," and she would be perfectly right. It would be an insult, a degradation to *Madame la Douairiere* if Pierre Mabuis were to do such a thing. A scandal unutterable, *Monsieur*, a doing of the most despicable, a crime ...'

'I don't think so for a moment,' said Everardus, again interrupting the teacher's vehemence. 'It is all a question of whether she reciprocates your feelings towards her. That is the whole point, and to know that you would have to declare yourself. Come now, Tins, be sensible. Has Aunt Cornelia ever given you any indication that she shares these feelings? Have you ever ...'

'I should not dream of doing that, *Monsieur*. As for *Monsieur's* question whether *Madame la Douairiere* reciprocates, why, does *Monsieur* imagine that the Queen condescends towards the commoner? It is true there were times—*Madame la Douairiere* has been of a kindness the most tantalising towards me when we had the privilege of helping *Monsieur* to get over that damnable fever. She has permitted me, on occasion, to entertain her with edifying music upon the flute; she has been gracious enough to declare that I have some skill with that instrument; she has even vouchsafed me a posy of oleanders when I came upon her picking a bunch for *Monsieur's* table. She did me the honour of observing, on that occasion, that oleanders were her late lamented's favourite flower, and that she had buried him in a mass of them. She frequently referred to her late lamented, and she grieved that she had no protector, and that for fifteen years she had been a lonely widow. My heart bled for her, *Monsieur*, and there were times when I yearned to lay it—all bleeding, if *Monsieur* follows me, at her feet. But it would have been a sin ... a gaffe, *Monsieur*, what you call a stupidity, to have done so, seeing it was that of a vagrant and a drunkard, and she a woman of wealth and position, well born into the world ...'

'Come, come, Tins. Don't get so excited. I see that you are really in love with her ...'

'Of course I am, as *Monsieur* says, in love with her. Who would not be? But being in love and declaring oneself, as *Monsieur* puts it, are two different things, and *Monsieur* doubtless sees how wide is the chasm between them.'

'I don't see that. But we get no further, Teacher. Let me come down to hard facts. Supposing ... I say supposing, for one can never be certain in such matters ... supposing Aunt Cornelia fancies you? No, wait, let me speak ... supposing she said yes ... could you marry her? There is your faith, Teacher; she is of the Reformed faith and you are a Papist. That is one difficulty. Are there no others? Let us leave, for the moment, your position here. That can be adjusted. You need not go to her empty handed. Your friends will see to that. But there are other points. How do you stand?'

'*Monsieur* overwhelms me. I have never thought about it. Not in that light, for the idea of marrying *Madame* ... That was so far beyond me as the heavens are. But I take

Monsieur's intention.'

'Very well. I tried to be as plain as possible. Be likewise, Tins. Could you ... can you marry?'

'If *Meneer* Nolte means am I without bond or embarrassment? Why, yes. I am not—I have never been married, either in church or before the *landdrost*, or as they say behind the bush. I have had experiences—what young man has not had them, *Monsieur*? And a wandering life does not conduce to continency *Monsieur*, since we are now speaking plainly. But that lies behind, and there is nothing in it. Not even a nameless brat in Cape Town that does not know Pierre Mabuis for its father. On that score I come clean, *Monsieur*. Perhaps it is no credit to me—Monsieur knows what I mean. But it is so. There is neither bond nor encumbrance. And as for the difference of faiths, why that is no great matter. My own father was of the Faith, but my mother was a heretic. The good fathers took me at an early age, else I too had perchance become one. And those of the Faith marry heretics even now, and heretics marry into the Faith. There is nothing in that, *Monsieur*.'

'There may be more in it than you think, Tins. It strikes me that you will find some difficulty there, but that is your concern, not mine. I am glad to hear what you say. And now, let me give you some advice ...'

'I listen,' said Tins attentively, concentrating himself into attentive stiffness. '*Monsieur* is altogether too good.'

'That remains to be seen. Probably you will not like my advice, but it is sound, all the same, Tins. Go and have a talk with Uncle Martin. He knows everything about Aunt Cornelia, and it is quite likely that she, too, will consult him. Tell him what you have told me. It can do no harm, and he will keep your confidence as he has kept mine. But I warn you he will put questions to you. He will want to know all about your *papa*, for instance and your *mama*, ...'

'That I will explain to *Monsieur's* satisfaction,' declared Tins proudly. 'I will even draw for *Monsieur* Rekker my *papa's* armorial bearings, for at one time there was an ancestor who was *armiger* ...'

'I don't know what that means, Teacher, but probably Uncle Martin will. If you have a coat of arms, so much the better; he would like that, and it will give you some standing with him. But be frank with him, and if he approves, why, go to *Langvlei* and good luck to you.'

'*Monsieur* is unspeakably good. But Pierre Mabuis has no courage to do a thing like that. To converse with *Meneer* Rekker, yes. But to declare himself to *Madame la Douairiere*, no. That is impossible. Monsieur will realise the impossibility. I have nothing—I am bare, *Monsieur*, barer than your hand. With no worldly wealth, with no expectations—there is a little owing to me at Cape Town which I have never troubled to exact, but it is a drop, *Monsieur*—and *Madame* is a *Grande Dame* with wealth and well born. It is impossible.'

'Nothing is impossible when one is in love, Tins. Just get that into your head, and go and hear what Uncle Martin has to say on the subject. And don't think too much of your poverty. I tell you, you have friends among us, and we will not let you go bare when you go to sit up with Aunt Cornelia.'

'It is unthinkable,' said Tins slowly. 'Of *Monsieur's* goodness I have never felt a doubt, and of the charity of *Monsieur's* friends in the Valley I have had ample proof.

'Indeed, one can't. And I was feeling all-overish, Niece, if you take me, for I did not know—though being a grown woman with experience, Niece, I apprehended that he had not come merely to sell beans to me. Had I been free—I mean, had he not gripped my arm so tightly, Niece, of course I could have loosened myself had I wished to do so, for he did it kindly, if you understand, Niece, though masterfully, which I did not mind—but if he hadn't done it, I should have gone on in front and prepared coffee for him. *And* the preserve that he is so fond of—yes, he ate half a dozen green figs that afternoon, after we had settled the whole matter, and he ate them with delight, Niece, not just out of courtesy as some people, not having a sweet tooth, eat these things. So when we came in—into the dining room, Niece, you understand—he led me to a chair, and placed me in it, as grandly as if I were the Queen, and I doubt, Niece, if our beloved Queen has ever been handled more gently and respectfully by her men folk. And then he took off his hat and flung it into the corner—and you know he is always so careful of his hat, is *Meester*—and went down on his knees. Which was unseemly and indecorous, Niece; none of the others ever did that. My Pieta simply took me by my shoulders and kissed me and said, "Cornelia, you and I must be one" —but that was of course after we had sat up for several nights, you understand? He did not have his asthma then, my Pieta, nor his heart. These came upon him later on, and then he could not bear the night air. But I must say that I did not mind Teacher going down on his knees, even though I knew that it was unseemly for a grown man to do that. I had a sort of feeling that he did it for me, and that he would to it to no one else, which is as it should be, Niece, for one bows one's knees to God alone. On very special occasions now—well, I won't say there are exceptions, but it is generally speaking unseemly, and I told him so. But not scoldingly, you understand? Just by way of remark. And he said—yes, he did, though you might not believe me, "To God and the Queen, Mistress Priem, and to me you are my queen.' Which was very embarrassing to me, Niece, you understand, for it was quite unlike the talk I have been used to either from my Pieta or from those others who courted me. But then *meester* is not like those others, nor like my Pieta. It is not for me to draw comparisons, which are always bad, but I look upon *Meester* as in many ways far superior to all of us in the Valley ...'

'In many ways he is,' assented Magriet, feeling called upon to say something where the Widow evidently expected an interruption from the chorus.

'I am glad you comprehend,' went on Aunt Cornelia. 'I am telling you all this, Niece, not to glorify myself, but because you should know, knowing already what I felt, and because the knowledge might at some future date be of use to you. The more one knows about one's men folk, the better. They are very curious at times, and it is always best that we women should realise that in some things we are quicker than they, knowing their ways and what they are likely to do on occasion. That is where our strength lies, Niece, if you understand me. But I was telling you about what happened when he came for my yes-word. Where was I now?'

'When Aunt had reproved him for getting down on his knees ...'

'Not reproved him, Niece. That is not exact. Merely remarked that it was unseemly that a grown man should do that. But he didn't mind, although I pointed out to him that the floor had been newly dung-smeared and was not quite dry yet. There were stains on his knees afterwards, Niece, and I promised to wash his trousers for him and iron them, and gave him a pair that had belonged to my Pieta, which were of course too large for him, but they had to do all the same. I got him to see that it would be better for him to do the talking when we sat comfortably on the sofa, but he was like a live coal, jumping all over the place. Excitement, you understand. Myself, well, I have had more experience in these things, and after all it is not fitting that a woman should show her feelings too openly. So we sat on the sofa, and I ... why, Niece, you understand, I could not very well say anything, and he seemed to be tongue-tied as soon as he got off his knees. I waited and waited, and really, Niece, I thought that I should get seriously annoyed with him if he did not speak, not that it would have mattered very much, for these things were apparent in his eyes, Niece, you understand. So when he said that ordinarily he would have approached my *papa*, that being the correct thing, I quickly answered that I had no *papa*, father having been dead all these years, and mother having preceded him into bliss shortly after I had married Pieta. 'If you want anything, Teacher,' I said, 'you should speak to me. I am a lone woman, and have been one for fifteen-sixteen years.' And then he said, all a-quiver-like, Niece, if you understand, "If *Madame la*—there I can't say it the way he drawls it, but you know, Niece, you know—if I wanted I need no longer be lonely." He said he had the honour to ask for my hand, and he said that he hoped I would not take it as an impertinence—an impertinence, if you please, Niece, and him a grown man in whom my fancy saw everything that is proper in a man—an impertinence if he came to me for the yes- or the no-word. And he said it all with a stutter, almost like that of the rapscallion who came years back—you remember, Niece—to make trouble among us here, so I felt that he was anxious. And the best way, Niece, once you have made up your mind, is to let them know it, you understand. That has always been my way. When the cross-eye asked me to say the yes- or no-word, I did not hesitate. "Not if there were no other men left after the deluge," I told him, and he went away with a flea in his ear.'

'But you did not say that to Teacher,' remarked the chorus.

'Of course not. I did not say anything. I took his head between my hands, just as if he was a child, you understand, Niece, and I kissed him on the temple and on the forehead, for that speaks louder than any word, Niece. In a grown woman with experience, you might account it immodest, Niece, but I was so happy—and as I said, Niece, one can't control one's feelings on such occasions. And he did not seem to mind, for he—he kissed me also, Niece, and disarranged my sunbonnet doing so, which was unseemly, for one can do these things quietly. Indeed, I had some trouble to make him behave, but after a while we settled down to discuss things, and I found he had the most extraordinary ideas. Fancy, Niece, he proposed that I should let him go to Cape Town to make his fortune before we married! "And do you think I am going to wait until you have made it?" I asked him. "Haven't I got enough for both of us? Why, man, I am rich enough for us both, and what I have is yours." But would you believe it, Niece, the trouble I had to make him see sense? I almost got out of patience with him, but I have experience, you understand, and one must humour them when they are in that mood. So I told him that I proposed to see His Reverence about the banns in any case, and that he must look to it that his were put up properly.'

'It is all settled then?' enquired Magriet, who had not expected that the affair would run so smoothly and expeditiously.

'Of course. Do you think, Niece, that after fifteen-sixteen years of loneliness I am like to let slip a chance like this, and him the man of my inclination, too? What does the difference of faith matter? True, I don't like him being a Papist—did you see last week's paper? There was a piece in it about how the Papists burn folk who do not believe as they do, but that was in foreign parts and here there is no chance of that, thank God. Naturally, I should prefer him to be of the Reformed faith, but since he isn't, why then I must take him as he is. And I am grateful, Niece, for what you and Nephew Ev'rard have done, and for what you have been able to do for Teacher. He does not want to give up the school, but that we may talk over later on. If the government comes along with its inspectors and all that, they are sure to worry Teacher, and that I won't have. He is now my man, and his proper place is at *Langvlei*. And now let us talk about practical things, for time presses, and we must have the wedding before the winter is over.'

The news of Tins's betrothal to the Lady of *Langvlei* was received with mingled feelings by the Valley, and vied in importance with the political situation which daily became more interesting.

The Valley had learned that it was entitled to two representatives for the electoral division of which it formed part, under the new Ordinance, and stretched far back into the sparsely populated areas beyond the mountains. Between the committee and the capital there were many communications and consultations, and once more an attempt was made to induce either Thomas Seldon or Andrew Quakerley to accept nomination as co-member for the District. But neither was willing to stand, although it was known that either would be unanimously elected if he stood with Everardus for the suffrages of the Valley. In the circumstances other candidates offered themselves, and the cross-eyed gentleman from the Hantam came forward to solicit votes in the Valley. He received scant support, for popular opinion had decided that the Valley should be represented by a local resident and not by an outsider, however otherwise acceptable the latter might be.

Throughout the Colony the election fever raged. It was the first time that the *burghers* had been called upon to take an active, personal part in politics, and the novelty as well as the interest of the situation appealed to them. There were thoughtful residents like Uncle Martin and Uncle Dorie who did not quite like the popular excitement, and they were strengthened in their views by the outspoken opinions of Uncle Charles, who maintained that at all costs a contest should be avoided.

'Look here,' he said, on the morning when the Elder and Uncle Martin had visited him at *Quakerskloof* to have one more conversation with Andrew on the subject of his nomination, 'look what the paper says. It is clear that by working on the rabble, individuals will get into Parliament whom the people can never recognise as their representatives. There you have it. There lies the danger.'

'I have not seen this week's paper,' said Uncle Martin. 'I came away before I had time to open it. Is there any news?'

'They have caught Jack Hooper,' said Uncle Charles, 'and high time too. It is unpardonable letting that scoundrel rampage round the country. And they have really found gold in the new Free State—at Smithfield—a nugget. And the *Caroline Agnes* has brought a stock of new books for Marais's Bookshop, so I shall have to go to Cape Town and look them over some day. There is the Hessian state loan—a good investment that, Martin. You might do worse than look into it.'

'I fancied the new commercial bank,' said Uncle Martin thoughtfully. 'That should pay well.'

'Risky, risky,' said Uncle Charles, shaking his head. 'I should never trust a bank if I could get government securities instead. Besides, the situation is not at all nice. In Europe very much so-so. The Turks and the bears still at it, and we very likely to be drawn into the business. I should not mind that, for a good war would shake us all up, but conditions at home are not what they should be. All the more reason why we should try and be unanimous here.'

'We can be that if Andrew consents to stand,' said Uncle Dorie pugnaciously, 'otherwise we shall find one of these lawyers form Cape Town coming down with his bag, and pretending to be very fond of us for the moment, just as long as it needs to poll for him.'

'That is the danger,' admitted Uncle Charles. 'It is always the danger with representative institutions, and the paper is quite right. That is why I wanted a higher qualification for our voters. Now ... well, can you sum up things for yourselves. How many votes can we count on?'

'Out of a total of one thousand we are sure of seven hundred,' said Uncle Martin promptly. 'We can depend on all the Coloured voters from Neckarthal. They will just vote as *Meneer* Uhlmann tells them ...'

'Yes,' said Uncle Charles, with a shake of his white head, 'that is the very pith of the matter. A quarter of our voters are Coloured; most of them cannot write or read; they will simply have to make a cross, and they will make it not according to their views but according to the way their Masters look at it. Today we have Missionary Uhlmann with us—he is an honest, straight chap, and I have every confidence in him—but what about the others? What about the future? No, my friends, I believe in representative government, but then it must be really representative of the people who can rule, who have an interest in ruling, and who know what is to be ruled. And what is more, my friends, we are running far too quickly. Look what they are doing up north. I hear that the Governor's Proclamation is out, withdrawing the Queen's authority from the Free State ...'

'That is as it should be,' said Uncle Dorie, with a touch of truculence in his voice. 'Let them rule themselves. They are not beholden to England.'

'By all means,' assented Uncle Charles. 'An authority that is not effective means nothing, and authority without the approval of the citizens is merely despotism. I willingly concede that. But they too have framed a constitution which gives them a Parliament of sorts. There are anticipatory details in last week's paper—you will find it somewhere about, Martin, if your care to take it. The voters are to be White men only, with a property qualification of at least £200, but unfortunately no educational qualification. A pity. But it is at any rate different from ours.'

'You approve of it?' demanded Uncle Martin.

'I do and I don't,' answered Uncle Charles. 'It all depends on the way you look at us here. If we are to be the aristocrats, for ever remaining superior to the Natives, then it is all right, provided you make the qualification such as may be exacted from aristocrats. But it is not representative government, for a Parliament elected in that way represents only a class of the citizens not all the citizens. If you admit there is a ruling class, then it is all right, and fair according to your premise that the White man is the only fit voter. But even then you must surely draw a distinction between the White man who is—let us say civilised, although that does not mean much—and the man who is little better than a Native. It is easy to see that there may be Natives, just as we know there are Coloured people, who possess more than £200 worth of property. But don't call it representative government, and don't expect that it will last. That is the difficulty of the whole position, my friends. We here down south have a constitution which is really representative, although it is not what I had hoped it would be. Put that down to Whiggery, and to Johnny not knowing what our conditions are. Cathcart should have explained to him, and very likely he did, but I know these fellows; they are as stubborn as a pig and think they know everything. Up there in the north they have a wholly different system, which has all our drawbacks and is not representative. What is going to happen in the future? Which view is to prevail?'

'Theirs,' said Uncle Dorie. 'I don't hold with giving the franchise to the Natives or Coloured folk. I have always said so.'

'Very well. You hold the view that they are children, wards, and that you will always remain the guardians. You will always have a friendly despotism. I don't say you are wrong, at present. I have remarked that I think we are hastening too quickly. But sooner or later all civilised countries will have representative government, and where will you stand then? You don't imagine, surely, that you will be able to treat your Natives always like wards. Children grow up, van Aard, and when they are grown they demand their share. It is human nature.'

'All civilised countries ...?' said Uncle Martin reflectively. 'But is not America one, and there they still have slaves.'

'I apprehend that we will see an end to that before we die, old friend,' said Uncle Charles seriously. 'Already there are signs that America is coming into line with the rest of the world. And I know something of the Americans. They are logical, business-like folk. They will find some way out of the difficulty.'

'Yet you said—you advised—that we should accept,' said Uncle Martin. 'I did not like it much ...'

'I like it still less,' interrupted Uncle Charles passionately. 'I wanted a much higher qualification. That would have settled the matter once and for all. Put your qualifications high, but don't make them apply to one class of the community only. There you have a just and fair representation, and one which you can defend. Class representation, especially when your qualifications are so low, you can never defend while you plead that you have representative government. Shiver me, Martin, but I am one with you in thinking that we may make out of this country of ours a land worth living in and dying for, but we shall never do that until we have the courage to deal fairly with all its citizens and recognise that everyone of them has just as much right as we to a share in its government.'

'There is sense in what you say, Brother Charles,' said Uncle Martin, while Uncle Dorie sat in gloomy silence, digesting what he had heard. 'And it appears to me that we are merely on the eve of many things which neither you nor I would like to see. All this excitement, now—it is bad for us, it is bad for the Coloured folk, and bad for our children. But I doubt if we can mend it, and we must just put up with it. Neither you nor I, Brother Charles, will be here when the tangle has to be unravelled ...'

'For which let us thank whatever Gods there be!' exclaimed Uncle Charles fervently. 'Although it is a selfish spirit that prompts the gratitude, Martin. But we can at least do our best, and that is one reason why I should like to see the best of us come forward to represent us in Parliament.'

'Then make Andrew consent,' said Uncle Dorie, eagerly.

'I have done my best,' replied Uncle Charles, shrugging his shoulders. 'The boy won't. He has all sorts of excuses, but the long and the short of it is that he feels he is not cut out for the job. You should try Seldon again.'

'There is no hope in that quarter,' said Uncle Dorie sadly. 'There are others we have thought of—we have even thought of Teacher, now that he is to marry the Widow ...'

'I heard about that,' said Uncle Charles, with a broad smile. 'He has fallen very much on his feet, but I am glad of it, for Mabuis is a good fellow; eccentric of course, but every Frenchman is a bit of a mountebank, and he is no exception to the rule. But sound all the same. You might do worse.'

'We should be able to do better,' interjected Uncle Martin grimly. 'If there is no other way, why then, I should myself consent ...'

'That would indeed be the best way out of the difficulty,' said Uncle Charles with a nod of approval. 'There is really no difficulty. Your English is not of the best, but you will manage to make yourself understood, and before very long you would be able to address the Assembly in Dutch. Yes, that is only a matter of time. It is unthinkable that both languages should not be spoken in a representative gathering.'

'I feel that too. But at present I do not see my way clear. Like Andrew, it is not my business. But I have another in mind. You know Dr Snork, who used to be our District surgeon, until he got wild with the government for cutting down his salary ...?'

'An excellent man,' exclaimed Uncle Charles. 'He knows everyone here, and he is thoroughly familiar with the Valley. I should give him my vote at once, and I warrant *Meneer* Human would support him. That makes him sure of the Coloured vote. Can you get into touch with him?'

'I have already written,' said Uncle Martin. 'He is practising at Cape Town—or rather he is living there, for he has means of his own, and no need to practise. He knows both languages.'

'Exactly! And he is a man of culture and refinement, a strong man, though apt to fly off at a tangent. Get him, if you can. You have seen the *Gazette*?'

'Yes, the magistrate showed it to me. The election is to be April—on the 20th, I believe. There is plenty of time yet ...'

'Nothing to spare. Get a move on, and let him come. He must go round in the District ... see the people ... renew old acquaintances. Are you sure of him?'

'Yes, unless Andrew consents to stand ...'

'There is no hope of that. The boy simply won't. I can't make him. Very well, get Snork, and make it clear to the committee that he must be elected without a contest. For heaven's sake do your best to get that Hantam fellow to retire. We can't have a quarrel at the start. And anyway, he won't get a third of the votes.'

'I think I'll make him see reason,' answered Uncle Martin smilingly. 'Or Aunt Cornelia would. She still has some influence there.'

The committee, spurred on by Uncle Martin, reacted to the suggestion. Dr Snork reacted to the invitation. He came down on horseback from the capital, riding by relays provided by the committee, and arrived at the Village in record time. He was a tall, well-made, bearded old gentleman, irreproachably—even ultra-fashionably—dressed, and his first saunter through the Village street created a commotion, for most of the residents remembered him, and all came to pay their respects. In whirlwind fashion he rode from farm to farm, visited Neckarthal and the outlying mission stations at the mouth of the river, and his medical skill as well as his manners helped him to consolidate his interests. He spoke glibly, if not eloquently, and Everardus, who at first had been doubtful as to the advisability of the partnership, grew to like him for his common sense, his frankness, and his good humour. Dr Snork was an Irishman, and in medical circles he was esteemed as an able physician, but he undoubtedly had more interest in politics than in medicine, and he threw himself heart and soul into the campaign. The committee was thoroughly satisfied, and the Valley jubilant, for the aspirant candidate from the Hantam had gracefully retreated before the newcomer, and had promised his support to the committee's nominees. In these circumstances there could be only one result, and the Valley eagerly anticipated the day of the election, and looked forward to the time when it would have as its representatives Bartholomew Snork MD and Gallows-Gecko Nolte.

Everardus found that his fellow candidate shared in large measure the views which he had heard enunciated by Brother von Bergmann, with whom Dr Snork was well acquainted and for whom the doctor had a high regard. As they travelled in company from farm to farm in the Valley, canvassing for votes, in the unlikely event of a third candidate appearing in the field at the last moment, he told the doctor his own story, and found a sympathetic and appreciative listener. The doctor chuckled frankly over the episode, but suggested that it might be as well to allow it to sink into oblivion.

'It is improbable that anyone will resurrect it, Nolte,' he said seriously, 'but one never knows. Nor must you take this election as typical of what we may expect in five years' time. The whole thing is new to our folk, but they will learn politics and all its miserable wretchedness soon enough, and you will find that when it comes to a contest any stick will do to beat the candidate with. They will rake up whatever they can to discredit you, and they will put things in the very worst possible light. You have no idea how people lose their heads at election time, and how unutterably sordid the whole business is. I ... well, I suppose it's the Irish in me that makes me have a sneaking liking for an election.'

But the candidates found their way made easy by their universal popularity. No one troubled to ask their views on anything, which was just as well, for Everardus had as yet had no opportunity to crystallise his opinions on what might have been called current politics. He stood for the improvement of the District; new roads were wanted, a bridge over the river; schools were to be established; a better postal service was necessary. Local interests predominated and there were no great questions of policy at stake. Parliament was not responsible, for the government could rule without it, but it was to be a vent, and all that the Valley required from him was to voice its sentiments and further its interests.

Dr Snork saw further. He told Everardus much that was interesting and new. He hinted that before the election there would be war; not a frontier affair such as Everardus had lived through on several occasions, but a world-disturbing upheaval, which might or might not affect the Colony.

'I have no certainty,' he said, 'but I was told when I left Cape Town that every moment they expected the declaration of war between England and Russia. It is bound to come, and it is bound to affect us in some ways. Money will be tighter; credit will be shaken. We think we are isolated and nothing that goes on abroad matters, but that is a grave mistake, Nolte. Nowadays no country can live to itself, any more than a man can live to himself. Our interests are too complicated for that. We are part of a great nation, and we may have to do our share in the business, though God knows what that share is likely to be.'

He took a great interest in Everardus's horses, and advised him to get the prize-stud stallion Loadstone—by Touchstone out of Ildegarde, sister to Napoleon by Bob Booby. 'He will improve your breed,' he remarked, 'and you should get up races here. You have every facility for that. Form a racing club ... I will subscribe, but I can't take part, for I shan't live here. But Quakerley will come in willingly, and you might stir Andrew out of his lethargy ... heavens, that boy needs someone to prick him; he is getting monstrously fat and self-satisfied.'

Chapter 26

The east winds of April ruffled the river and blew the dune sand into the road, and winter came with its drenching showers, quickening the sorrel into premature blossom so that the veld looked like an expanse of burnished green flecked with spots of vivid colouring. In the air lingered the smell of the wet earth mingled with the scent of aromatic shrubs crushed on the hillsides by the tramping cattle.

On the nineteenth of the month, pursuant to the government notice of the thirteenth of March, the Valley held a court in the Village for the purpose of electing its Members of Parliament. The bald official return transmitted by the magistrate, who presided, to the Cape Town authorities gives but a meagre and uninteresting account of the proceedings on that eventful forenoon. It states that the Proclamation having been read, Doremus van Aard, field-cornet of Ward No IV proposed Everardus Nolte for nomination as representative of the Valley District, and Hendrik van der Westhuizen seconded; and that Martinus Rekker senior proposed Bartholomew Snork MD, and Andrew Quakerley seconded; and that there being no further nominations, the said Everardus Nolte and the said Bartholomew Snork MD were declared duly elected by the presiding officer.

As related by Uncle Dorie to his wife, Aunt Sophrosina, the affair was altogether more exciting.

'His Honour,' said the Elder, 'read the Proclamation, which was a waste of time, Wife, for we knew it all, almost by heart. But that is the official way, and once they get into it they cannot depart from it, though it does annoy one. Thereupon he called for nominations, and up I jump wishful to give Nephew Ev'rard the honour of being our senior representative, it being customary that the one who is first proposed, should there be no contest, is looked upon as the senior ...'

'But the doctor is that, Husband,' said Aunt Sophrosina placidly. 'You should have though of that.'

'He would not mind,' explained the Elder. 'It was the intention that Brother Martin should have seconded me, but that officious Nephew Hendrik, who never can keep his mouth shut, spoiled it by bawling out "I second," although no one had asked him to do so. Then Brother Martin proposed the Doctor, and Nephew Andrew seconded, and there was of course no further nomination. So *Meneer* Staples declared them duly elected, and our hearts being filled with gladness, as the good Book has it, we hurrahed to honour them. Whereupon the magistrate called upon them to speak, and Nephew Everard, being now the senior—though not in years—had to make the first speech, but remembering what David says in the psalm "... my heart is not haughty, nor mine eyes lofty, neither do I exercise myself in great matters or in things too high for me," he made way for the Doctor, who thanked us all and spoke for half an hour just as well as anyone can speak. It warmed my heart to hear him, Wife, for he spoke just as well in Dutch as he did in English, and I said to Brother Martin that we have no cause to regret having chosen so well-spoken a man. Then it was Nephew Ev'rard's turn, and for a moment I felt doubts, for coming after the Doctor it was no light thing to have to attempt. But Nephew Ev'rard spoke well, and no one can say that our Gallows-Gecko is not the equal of anyone they are sending to Parliament. Then the magistrate spoke a few words, and we sang *God Save The Queen*, and I went with them to sign the documents, and that was all. But it was very cheering, Wife, to listen to one's own representatives, and to think that at last we have come into our own.'

'So long as you don't think too much about it, Husband,' said Aunt Sophrosina mildly, 'it can do no harm. But all this excitement is bad for you, at your age. Why, it is not worth bothering about.'

'That is a woman's view,' said Uncle Dorie grandly. 'Women cannot be expected to understand politics. When they meddle in it, as Andrew's wife does, they only make fools of themselves.'

'I daresay the men will do that soon enough,' remarked his wife cheerfully. 'It is a sad business, and why they can't make laws without talking so much and getting so excited about it passes my comprehension. And now?'

'Now they will have to go to Cape Town,' said Uncle Dorie. 'Parliament is to meet on the 30th of June next, which gives us nearly two months to talk things over with them. The doctor has to go away this week, but he will come back and meet the committee, and tell us more or less what their intentions are.'

'Then there is plenty of time for the wedding,' said Aunt Sophrosina, complacently. 'Which reminds me that you have not yet told me what we are to give them. It is a sorely difficult matter, Husband, for she is rich enough, and he poor enough in all conscience, and one does not know what to do.'

'We have decided to give Teacher two years' salary,' said Uncle Dorie, 'and he will of course take with him his cattle and his sheep. They can now run on *Langvlei*. Have you women decided when and where it is to be?'

'Niece Cornelia decided that long ago,' answered his wife. 'On the second Monday in May and at the Village. From Brother Martin's church house and in the church, of course. You would not have them marry anywhere else, would you?'

'No, that would not be seemly. Is it to be a regular wedding, with maids and groomsmen and all that, or quiet-like?'

'Quiet-like, Husband. He must have someone to support him, and he wants Nephew Ev'rard, though Matryk would be better. But one cannot depend on Matryk. Now, will you have your coffee here, or will you come and sit on the *stoep*? It is a bit cold, but very refreshing out there.'

Uncle Dorie elected to remain where he was, in the comfortable warmth of his dining room. His wife filled the foot-stove with glowing coals, and he carried it to his arm chair and placed it between his legs while he read the latest papers which he had borrowed from the Quakerleys. The English ones he could read with difficulty only, but the bilingual Zuid-Afrikaan interested him deeply and he read eagerly until it was time for him to go to bed. He read out to his wife bits here and there, as she sat placidly knitting, and she made appropriate comments.

'Listen to this, Wife,' he said. 'A great diamond has been discovered in Brazil—that is somewhere in America, I fancy—weighing 254 and a half carats—I wonder, now, what a carat is—and its value is over £100,000. Prodigious. Fancy picking up a diamond like that. And there might be diamonds in this country, Wife. We might pick them up on the farm.'

'That would not do us much good, Husband. People would come traipsing all over the garden, and ruin the orchard,' said Aunt Sophrosina. 'Is there anything about the war?'

'Oh, plenty. Here is a bit that will interest you. On the Russian front it is stated that the troops have been encouraged by the appearance of the Virgin Mary in the skies. The incident is well authenticated. Well, well. I suppose they are all Papists, but it is curious that such a thing should have happened after all. Dr Oudenhoff of Utrecht—that as you know, Wife, is a town in Holland—has successfully operated on a boy with diphtheria—that is a hard word, but they explain it here in brackets; it means the white sore throat, Wife, the same that our own little Stephen died of—by cutting a hole in the windpipe and putting in a silver tube; it is the first time the operation has been performed successfully in Holland. Fancy that now. If that doctor had been here he might have saved our little Stephen. They have discovered more gold, this time across the Vaal at the Witte Watersrand—a man named Marais, it appears, found it, but the people censured him for doing so, and he has got little for his pains. And here is an account of a murder in Natal—but that won't interest you. Listen to what the paper says about our election ...'

At *Quakerskloof*, Mrs Andrew announced her intentions of visiting Cape Town for the Opening of Parliament, which she anticipated would be a great social function, even though the Governor would not be present, but a mere acting Lieutenant-General whom she did not know would officiate in his stead. Her husband was not at all anxious to go. He pointed out that his citrus trees demanded his attention, and that their usual time was at the end of the year when a sojourn at the seaside was a welcome relief from the sultriness of the Valley. But for once, Father-in-law came to her rescue.

'If Daughter-in-law will put up with an old man,' he said courteously, 'I will drive her up, Andy. I should like to look in at the bookshop and see what the *Caroline Agnes* has brought, and I might look in and hear what they talk about in their new Parliament.

It is years since I listened to that sort of twaddle, and it might be amusing.'

Mrs Andrew eagerly accepted the old man's escort. He had never been with them on one of their visits, and she knew that he had many acquaintances at the capital and would be treated with great respect. A brother of an Admiral of the Red commanded more attention than the Nephew of that great personage, and an invitation to the Governor's levee would come as a matter of course. They might even be invited to lodge at Government House, an honour which she had always looked forward to, but which her stupid husband had never thought of soliciting by those efforts which one might have expected from one who was in a position to command it. Andrew was really shockingly absent-minded, to put the most charitable construction upon his action or want of action. He could so easily have been a Member of Parliament, like his grandfather had been. Of course, it was not quite the same thing, being a Member of the House of Commons, and being a member of a paltry Colonial House of Assembly, but still it was unpardonable that he should have waived his claim as a representative of the District to a fellow of such questionable antecedents as Mr Nolte, who had been a public executioner. It was shocking that so gentlemanly a man like the doctor could associate on terms of equality with a fellow like that.

But really, public opinion in the Valley was something which Alice Quakerley had never fathomed. One could not, of course, expect much from these boors; they were all very well as simple agriculturists, and, not knowing the language, they could not improve their minds, poor things, but they should, at least, have proper respect for their betters, and not impose themselves upon the gentry. Now this election ... And Alice shook her head in painful but tacit expostulation, for she had long since given up the thankless task of making her husband see through her spectacles, and she had no idea that the glasses she herself looked through distorted more than they revealed. Her father-in-law and her husband were cosily settled in front of a cheerful fire, for the Quakerley homestead was one of the few which boasted of open fireplaces. A trunk of the resinous protea crackled in the dining room, and sent out a comfortable warmth, for the early winter air was chilly. She told the servant to bring in the warm toddy for the masters—Mrs Alice rarely did these menial duties herself—and went off to the nursery.

'Daughter-in-law a bit off colour tonight, Andy,' said the old man. 'She resents your incapacity to adjust yourself to her point of view. Well, well, ... You had your choice, my boy, and it is not for me to quarrel with it.'

'She's a good wife, Dad,' said the bearded Andrew. 'She steps rather high at times, but that is nothing to worry about. I make up for her shortcomings in that respect. I suppose I am dreadfully what I should not be.'

'Don't say that, my boy, don't say that. I should not like to see you pretend to be other than what you are. And you are good enough for me as you are. I sometimes wish, of course, that you had more spunk in you, but your mother liked an easy way, and still likes it. She is very poorly tonight, your mother, my boy, and I can see that she is breaking. I shan't survive her long. You know my wishes. That is one reason I should like to go to Cape Town. Probably it is for the last time.'

'Don't talk like that, Dad. You have a long life before you. All the Quakerleys are long-lived.'

'Yes, hard as nails and as sinful as old Nick. But it depends on the way one has lived, my boy. Mine has been a full life, and I am not complaining if it is not so long as ours usually is. I am not weary of it, but if your mother goes, I shall not regret following her. You have seen the Proclamation?'

'Staples got it just as I came away. So it is to be war.'

'Yes. I wish I could be there. These Russians were asking for it and after all, as the Declaration says, the Sublime Porte is our ally. The only thing that annoys me is that we shall have to fight along with the Frenchies. They are good soldiers—I heard the old Duke say they were the best, if properly led—but somehow it doesn't seem right. Maybe my prejudice, boy, but shiver me if I like it. It will be an anxious time in England ...'

'I don't suppose it'll make much difference, Dad. All the fighting will be in the Crimea.'

'And all the crying at home, boy. You have no conception of what war is like. How could you have? It is nothing like these frontier affairs here, though they are bad enough. But out there one never knows how far it will spread. England is not loved, Andy. You notice it here, although I really see no cause for the feeling that exists here. You don't yourself, do you?'

'There is no feeling here ... against England, I mean,' said his son. 'Some of us rub them up the wrong way—look at Alice; she can't see any good in any of them—and some of them don't get on with us. But that is all personal, Dad.'

'I wonder. I wonder now if you are right, my boy. You might have said the same in Canada, but when I was there I noticed things. It made me think, though I was young then. And take Snork, now. The fellow is Irish, and you can't expect him to love us, quite. But there is something more than just plain dislike to us in what he feels. Or Martin. He's not a fool, not by any means, boy. He's as level-headed as any of us, and an aristocrat—one of the gentry as Daughter-in-law would say.'

'But Uncle Martin does not hate us. He has never shown it at all events, Dad.'

'No. Not us, my boy. But what we stand for. Outside interferences—Johnny's Whiggery, perhaps, or Tory interference—call it what you like. Downing Street officiousness. Take this new constitution. Why couldn't they, while they were about it, make it responsible government? Why give half a slice when the whole would have settled the business?'

'We are hardly fit for that yet, Dad.'

'Ah, that is another matter. If we all think that. But how many do? Is there anybody here in the Valley who has the faintest notion of what England's rule here means for the Colony? Is there one—I except, of course—of those who have been abroad and know something, like His Reverence, and most of the missionaries, who realises what the connection with England brings with it in material benefit and prosperity? You know as well as I do that most of them think that if they cut the painter tomorrow they could stand on their own legs and be damned to the rest of the world. Why, boy, I sometimes fancy that you yourself incline that way.'

'I suppose if we have to stand alone, we'll manage somehow,' said Andrew, without much enthusiasm. 'I am not exactly longing to try the experiment.'

'I should hope not!' exclaimed his father. 'Where would you be? With your coasts undefended, open to the first one who wants to attack you. But there is not much chance of that. The Cape is the key to India, my boy, and England dare not give it up so long as she holds India.'

'Then why worry about it, Dad? I expect what you mean is only the sort of thing that puts one's back up when a small boy gives himself airs. They will outgrow it.'

'Perhaps you are right, boy. But some of these things go deeper than you think. They touch the root of things that matter—sentiment, honour, one's respect for oneself. Maybe I am too old to see things in a correct perspective, but sometimes I get angry when I think that what we call democracy is going to play the deuce with us all. There must be leaders and leadership, and there must be a sense of responsibility. That is what I miss here. We are playing with the present and remembering the past while we should be concentrating on the future. Well, it is, happily, no business of mine. I shall not live to see the outcome of it, but—there, my boy, you must forgive my crotchetiness tonight. Your mother's attack has upset me. I should go to her now. So good night to you.'

Chapter 27

On the day of the Widow Priem's wedding, the Village presented a scene of activity such as it had never shown, even on the name-day of the beloved Queen, and had rarely offered to the interested spectator—even at *Nagmaal* time, when the quarterly communion service was held and church members flocked in from all parts of the District. A wedding or a funeral was always an excitement for the Village, and this wedding was more than usually interesting, for it concerned two of the most popular members of the Valley community. Aunt Cornelia was known throughout the District; her fame, indeed, had spread beyond its boundaries, and had she wished she could have aspired to far more prominence that she chose to enjoy. She came from a well-known stock, and her former husband had been respected and liked. Moreover, for fifteen years the Valley had been waiting for her to re-marry, and had been deliciously disappointed in its expectations; deliciously, for so long as the widow remained single, so long did the Valley have a subject for speculation and that smooth gliding gossip that is based on presumption and never surmounts but always tries to circumvallate any plausible objection. The Teacher, too, had furnished material for prolonged and vivacious debate since the time when Sylvester had found him under the sage-bush and Everardus had given shelter, occupation, and the protection of his favour. His fame as a draughtsman and, more, as a maker of music, had percolated through the District, and even in the back blocks, far beyond the mountains—beyond even that forbidden-looking range behind which lay the copper mines and, according to rumour, anarchy and lawlessness—he was known for his eccentricity and his Roman Catholicism. Public prejudice inclined to the belief that the latter would prove an obstacle to his marriage with the Widow Priem, and this belief was cherished by those who were of the opinion that Aunt Cornelia was about to make an alliance derogatory to her dignity and to the prestige of the Valley. No great difficulty, however, had been experienced by the parties chiefly concerned in adjusting this matter. The Reverend de Smee, who had been consulted as soon as the affair had passed beyond the stage of expectation, had declared that it was fully competent for the widow to marry a Papist; all that was required was that the banns should be properly put up and that both contracting parties should prove that there were no legal impediments to their union. This had necessitated a trip to Cape Town on the part of the Teacher, who on his return had furnished such indisputable evidence of his eligibility that no further objection could reasonably be entertained by those who had constituted themselves the widow's temporary guardians. Aunt Cornelia had insisted that the union should be 'in community of property,' though Uncle Martin had strongly favoured an ante-nuptial settlement.

'If I started by distrusting Teacher,' the widow had observed bluntly, 'I could just as well have given him the no-word and ended the matter then and there. I don't believe in trusting a man in parts. I believe in trusting him entirely or not at all. And I trust the Teacher from the sole of his feet to the crown of his head; so, Brother Martin, do me the favour of not referring to this silly suggestion again.'

Needless to say the Widow's entourage took a great interest in the event. Nightly Atties and Cassandra held informal receptions in or around their hut on the *Langvlei* farm to which all residents, and every itinerant or squatting Native or Coloured was welcomed, for Cassandra dearly loved an audience. The two would sit, side by side, warming themselves over the small fire made in the centre of the hut, and in the doorway or grouped outside in the chill night air, the audience would dispose itself on its haunches and listen with attention and respect to whatever remarks either of them felt inclined to make. Spans of roll tobacco would be handed round, from which the men would cut inches of plug to serve as quids, and later on the girls would serve ghoo-coffee, liberally sweetened with the syrup of the protea bush.

'Ah, me,' Atties would observe in a sing-song voice, 'it is indeed gratifying to us all that the old mistress has finally selected a helpmate for herself. These fifteen years I have expected her to do so, but the mind of a woman, and especially of a White mistress, is hard to read.'

'For a stupid man like yourself, *Tati* (little father),' said his wife, in her cheerful matter-of-fact tone of voice, 'it would be, but not for a woman. We are all alike, no matter what the colour of our skins may be, and I saw from the first that the old mistress had an inclination towards the old teacher master. You remember I told you so. I prognosticated that they would make a match of it. And was I not right? Answer me that?'

'Little Aunt is always right,' chorused the audience, as it was expected to do. 'But then Little Aunt has tremendous experience.'

'Of course,' said Cassandra complacently. 'I have that. Ever since I was a little slip of a wretch, so high,' she indicated a distance of a few inches above the ground, 'and when Old Mistress Maria bought me at the sale of Old Master Sybreg's effects—he went bankrupt, else the old mistress would never have bought me so cheap, children, but they were bad times those, when a woman could be bought and sold, just like cattle, children. You should have lived in those times, children; it would have made you more experienced than you are now, and would have taught you a proper respect for your elders ...'

'Yes, Auntie,' said the audience, which had heard about the old times often before and was much more interested in the present, 'but go on about the old mistress.'

'What is there to say, children? What the heart wants it strives to get, and that is just the case with the old mistress and the teacher master. Mighty, but the teacher master blows beautifully on his flute. He will be able to make music when the old mistress is in a temper—and she gets like that sometimes, children—don't I know it.'

'It is a pity I don't know how to play on the flute, Cassandra,' remarked her husband in an audible aside, but Cassandra affected not to hear the observation.

'Of course,' she went on, 'the fact that the teacher master is a heathen is a great pity. We do not even know if he has had water thrown on his head, and unless you have had that done to you, you remain a heathen, children. But I daresay the Old Mistress will see that it's done. He can go to Neckarthal where they do that to grown people, though usually the White masters have it done when they are quite small. It is told, too,' she added gravely, 'that the teacher master has a string of magic beads, with a little idol at the end. I don't know how much truth there is in that, but I have seen him draw his finger across his chest—so—to tell the evil spirits to go away. I sometimes think that the teacher master knows something about magic, like the Malays do, but that is perhaps merely my imagination.'

'It must be,' said her husband brutally, 'or your stomach, Cassandra. Why do you come barging in with your talk of magic? What has magic to do with the matter?'

'Magic may have far more to do with it than you think, Atties,' she corrected him, mildly. 'It is wonderful what these Malay magicians can do. They can make you love a stump and dislike your heart's desire. They put something in your coffee, and before you know where you are you have an inclination towards someone upon whom you would very likely spit if you hadn't been bewitched.'

'That must have happened to me when I saw you, Cassandra,' said Atties, mischievously, 'though I don't remember seeing a Malay in the neighbourhood at the time.'

'They work from a distance, Atties,' said Cassandra quite seriously, and without the least trace of resentment in her voice. 'Very likely you had done something they did not approve of and so they put the *paljas*, the magic, upon you. Not that it hasn't turned out for your good, for I have made you a good wife, and I don't think the old mistress will make the teacher master a better.'

'That she can't,' chorused the audience approvingly.

'I don't go so far as to say that,' remarked the old woman generously. 'The old mistress has her faults—I should know, having lived all these years with her—but she also has her good points, and they are as many as there are quills upon a porcupine. It all depends on the man, children. A woman can do much with a man if she wants to, but if there is something wrong with the man, then God Almighty can't do much. Not that I would for a moment assert that the teacher master is the Devil's handiwork. I don't think he is, although being a heathen he probably knows more about the Devil than we do, children. The wedding is to be at the Village. Ah me, at first I thought I would not see my old mistress, but she is good, children, she is good. She said "Cassandra," she said, when she gave me that portion of flannel over there—it is a fine piece, isn't it, children?—"you may go to the Village with Atties, and attend the wedding. It is my wish." That was very delicately suggested, children. Ah me, but it made my heart warm towards the old mistress, to think that I should see her with the orange blossoms on her head and the veil over her face, just like a young thing going to her lord.'

'The old mistress has too much common sense,' interjected Atties, 'to make such a fool of herself. She won't have orange blossoms; there won't be any, either, as you ought to know, it being winter now. She'll be married in a proper, Christian-like black dress, with a hat, of course.'

'You know nothing whatever about it, Atties,' said his wife, displaying for the first time some irritation. 'It would not be a proper marriage unless she wore a veil. And we are already getting things ready for the baking. There will be many cakes, and hundreds of buns, not to mention the preserves. Early this year the old mistress told me to make much preserve, and I guessed then that she had something in mind. You children don't remember the old mistress's first wedding. Mighty, that was an affair. She was young then, a slip of a thing, and almost what you might call good looking, and Master Piet, he was a proper man—upstanding and with a man's vigour. I envied the old mistress then ...'

'Here,' said Atties sullenly. 'You had me, hadn't you?'

'I said the old master was a proper upstanding man,' explained Cassandra, so pointedly that the audience grinned and Atties wilted. 'You did not enter into comparison, Little Father. Not that I haven't found you useful, but that is neither here nor there. As I was telling the children when you interrupted me, it was a proper wedding, and we feasted—ah me, how we did feast. Turkeys, and guinea fowl and hares, and an ox roasted whole in a ditch they had dug in the garden, and mountains of cakes. Only one better feast do I remember, and that was when we gave the arval for the old master when he died of the dropsy. That was a feast if you like. Such a one had never been heard of in the Valley. You remember, Little Father? There were about a hundred guests, and His Reverence—not the present one, children, but his predecessor, him who died that same year of the galloping consumption—he was always a thin, scraggy man and he caught a chill at that same arval, standing bareheaded over the grave, which was a risky thing to do seeing it was in July with wetness in the air. Oh yes, that was a feast to remember, children.'

'Belike we shall have the same now,' suggested the audience, with a lively anticipation of good things to come. 'The old mistress is richer now.'

'That she is,' assented Cassandra, 'thanks to Little Father and me, who have worked so hard for her these fifteen years. But it is a pity, a great pity, it did not come sooner. I am not what I was. Eating is no longer the pleasure that it was fifteen years ago, children. The stomach revolts at greasiness and at sweetness. I get the sour, even when I just look at the good things, and I fear I shall not be able to do justice to them this time.'

'Never mind, Auntie. Auntie will be able to do something,' comforted the chorus, troubled with no such harassing thoughts of incipient dyspepsia. 'A little bite will do no harm.'

'No, I daresay not,' said Cassandra thoughtfully. 'Though I shall fortify myself with a draught of buchu tea beforehand. That settles the food, children, and prevents the wind from disturbing one. But have you thought about what you will give to the old mistress? We must show her our respect, and I have a fancy she might like to have a bunch of flowers. Plenty of flowers, indeed. If you children were to go out and pick them on the mountain the day before the wedding—there will be sugar bush in flower, lilies in the creeks and plenty of fern leaves. It will be a good thought, and the Old Mistress will appreciate it.'

So it came about that on her second wedding day, Aunt Cornelia found the dining room in Uncle Martin's church house in the Village, from where the wedding procession had to start for the church, encumbered with masses of flowers. There were beautiful protea heads from the mountains, bunches of freshly picked gladioli from the *kloofs*, bouquets of white adenandras and crimson lachenalias that grow in the sandy stretches on the river banks, and banks of fern. Her Native retainers had gathered these for her, and when she looked at them the Widow relaxed something of her stern gravity and the corners of her mouth drew up in a smile that brightened and softened her gaunt features. It was a wedding to be remembered, and even now, after all these years, the Valley speaks of it, for it was an event that possessed memorable features. There was something romantic about it that touched the Valley's imagination; something impressive that the Valley could feel and share in. Not only were the contracting parties older than the majority of those who entered into the contract of marriage, but both were characters in the Valley and as such had a claim to distinction which nobody thought of denying them.

Everardus acted as groomsman, very much to the satisfaction of all concerned and greatly to the Teacher's content. His office was no sinecure, for Tins was in a state of suppressed excitement, more absent-minded than Everardus had ever known him to be, and pregnant with suggestions that could not be carried out. Nevertheless, Everardus shepherded him to the church, where the ceremony was to take place, and saw to it that he was properly dressed in accordance with the customs of the Valley, which decreed that he should wear a frock coat and a black hat. The frock coat fitted him indifferently well, and accentuated the angles of his sparse figure, but what he lacked in appearance he made up for in dignity when the time came for him to draw up before the pulpit at the widow's side. Aunt Cornelia had not donned her first wedding dress as she had much wanted to do, nor had she put on a veil and orange blossoms. It was Magriet who had persuaded her that it would be better to dress as simply and as unostentatiously as possible, and against her inclinations the Widow Priem had followed her suggestion. She was clad in a neat black dress, with innumerable lace flounces, cut full so that its lower end ballooned out, and wore a big black straw hat trimmed with artificial roses and forget-me-nots, which made her look younger than she was.

The Village had turned out to a man, woman and child to witness the ceremony, and the large church was crowded when the procession marched up the aisle and stood at attention in front of the pulpit. Immediately in front stood the widow and Tins, both comporting themselves with a decorum which won approving nods from the congregation. Immediately behind were ranged Magriet, Aunt Sophrosina, Martin Rekker Junior's wife , Uncle Martin, Uncle Dorie, Martin Rekker Junior, and Andrew Quakerley, who much to his wife's annoyance had laughingly offered himself as a member of the wedding party. Everardus stood by the bridegroom's side, ready to coach him when the time came for him to make the proper responses. In the front pews sat the magistrate and his wife, the pastor's wife and family, old Charles

Quakerley, and Alice—mother-in-law had not been able to attend owing to her arthritis—and the Chief Constable and his wife, while behind them sat the Seldons, the postmaster and his family, and behind those again the chief residents of the Valley with their wives and families. The hindmost pews were given over to the Natives who also clustered round the door, where Augustus, now in his capacity of sexton, ordered them about with the same insistent authority he had displayed on the occasion of the beloved Queen's Birthday. It was a full audience, and exemplified both the interest which the Village and the Valley took in the wedding, and the good feeling existing between the different sections of the community. Even Alice, who had been persuaded to allow her daughters to attend, and who was still feeling sore about her husband's freakishness in so prominently allying himself with the wedding party, grew conscious of a pleasant satisfaction stealing over her as she glanced over the cheerful, expectant faces. They were common enough, and it was nonsense making so much fuss about the marriage of a two-penny-half-penny teacher, even though he was marrying one of the richest women in the District—who, unfortunately, did not fulfil Alice's conception of what a lady should be like—but after all, there was no harm in allowing herself to be pleasantly interested in the proceedings.

She could not follow them, for they were all in high Dutch, but the words that the Reverend Sybrand—clothed in his Geneva gown with tassels and with bands—read out reverberated sonorously round the church, and the singing was good, although she had heard better. Everardus, listening to the marriage formulary, wondered how anyone could like it; it sounded so harsh and forbidding, and at times positively indecent. What, he reflected, did Tins think of it? Perhaps the man did not comprehend the words, for they were archaic, but that could scarcely be, for the Teacher knew high Dutch very well. But Tins kept a grave, impassive face, and did not even grimace when the formulary touched upon matters which are usually left to the indiscretion of sex-muddled novelists. Everardus wondered what the Papist wedding service was like, and got comfort from the thought that very likely it was much the same, for had not all these liturgical formulas a common origin, so that even this Calvinistic service might be a translation from the Latin. He had never seriously though about it, and he jerked himself back from his thoughts when it became time for the pastor to approach the climax of the ceremony. He nudged Tins when His Reverence began the sentence, and the Teacher responded in the appropriate words. The Widow needed no reminder; she had been through the ceremony before, and she knew exactly what to do. The congregation would have applauded, had the circumstances allowed of such vociferous approbation, when it heard her firmly intoned, 'I will, Your Reverence, till death us do part.' As it was, it contented itself with that silent consensus of approval which anyone who is accustomed to a crowd can feel although none can describe how it comes to be felt.

Thereupon the wedding party retired to the vestry. Uncle Charles and the magistrate and Thomas Seldon followed, to sign the register, and other acquaintances, whose status in the Valley warranted such a liberty, came after them for the same purpose. The widow received the sisterly kiss from His Reverence, and Uncle Dorie and Uncle Martin claimed the same privilege which was graciously accorded. Uncle Charles, having seen Andy follow suit, did as in Rome the Romans are accustomed to do, and was heard afterwards to declare that he had enjoyed the experience, although he hoped that no one would tell Daughter-in-law about it. Congratulations were showered upon the newly wedded pair, and much light-hearted and good-natured chaff was indulged in, which Tins took with impassive dignity. Outside the church the children of the *Knolkloof* school were drawn up, and when the couple left the church, the children welcomed them with the customary hymn.

The wedding luncheon was held at Uncle Martin Rekker's church house, where all who came were cordially welcomed, but late in the afternoon a move was made towards *Langvlei* where the real celebration, carefully prepared by the Widow and her friends, was to be held. There the hospitality was on a tremendous scale, and the farmyard resembled a small camp, for many of the visitors, knowing that the homestead could not accommodate them all, had brought their tents with them. Dancing was kept up till a late hour, and Tins condescended to play on his flute, although he was indefatigable in his attentions to the married and unmarried female guests. His wife looked on indulgently, for she felt that it was a special occasion, and she too took the floor with her partner, in order of seniority. His Reverence came first, protesting that his dancing days were over, but nevertheless acquitting himself well in the polka, while Uncle Martin and Uncle Dorie both excelled in the *quadrille*. Even Mrs Andrew Quakerley displayed some animation, and was graciousness itself when Everardus asked her for the honour of a round, and was please to compliment him on the accuracy of his steps.

'You dance very well, *Meneer* Nolte,' she said mincingly. 'I did not expect it. Nor did I expect to find that a clergyman would take part in such ... such gaiety.'

'Oh, there's no harm in it, Mrs Quakerley,' said Everardus smoothly. 'It would not be proper for His Reverence to attend every dance, but this is a special occasion, and His Reverence is far to broad-minded to object.'

'Where are they going to spend the honeymoon?' asked Mrs Quakerley with interest. 'I should have thought that they would go away at once after the wedding.'

'The honeymoon?' asked Everardus frowning, for the word was new to him. 'Oh, you mean the white-bread days, Mrs Quakerley. We don't have them ... that is to say, it is not the custom ... our custom. They won't go away at all. Very likely you will find them both at work tomorrow, clearing up the place. It'll need some clearing up too.'

'I should fancy they might leave that to the servants,' said Mrs Quakerley scornfully. 'Mrs Mabuis is surely able to afford a visit to Cape Town. But perhaps she does know anyone there. I might be able to give her an introduction to some friends ...'

'Oh, Aunt Cornelia, Mrs Quakerley, is an old Capetonian. She belongs to one of the old families there, and she knows many folk alt the capital. But she does not care to go ...'

'How surprising!' exclaimed Alice. 'I should have thought that after being so long cooped up on the farm she would have jumped at the chance of visiting Cape Town. Especially now when you are going to have such grand doings. I am coming to hear you speak in the Assembly, Mr Nolte. You must be a credit to the Valley, you know.'

She said it condescendingly, for she had no doubt that he would not be a credit to the Valley. A common executioner ... really ... and with a quick movement she disengaged herself from his arm.

'I really must get back to Andy,' she said. 'No more, Mr Nolte. I have enjoyed it immensely, but I have promised Andrew a dance, you know. There he is waiting for me.'

Everardus strode back with her to where Andrew was waiting. He felt that Mrs Alice had repented of her first generous impulse, but he was not annoyed with her. He only wondered why the woman could not take a sensible view of things, and behave like a sensible person instead of giving herself airs.

'Well, Mr Gallows-Gecko,' said Uncle Charles smilingly, tapping him on the shoulder. 'We are amusing ourselves grandly, hey? Shiver me, but I never yet saw a parson foot it more glibly in the polka than His Reverence did. And I like it, begad, Mr Nolte, I like it. Do you know, it is the first time I have been at a hop like this. It's given me an altogether new impression of you all.'

'If *Meneer* Quakerley would come more frequently,' said Everardus 'he would get to know us better.'

'Shiver me if you aren't right, Nolte,' said the old man. 'There's far too much aloofness between us, you know. We should rub shoulders more, and then we'll rub the angles off. You're right, Nolte, you're right. And I'm glad Andy sees it that way. Now I am too old for that sort of thing. I can't mingle ... it's my fault, my fault entirely, but I belong to the old generation, and it's the new one that counts.'

'The old one too,' said Everardus firmly. 'Mr Quakerley can do much ... Mr Quakerley is doing much already, if I may say so. I have never yet thanked Mr Quakerley properly for Mr Quakerley's support to me ...'

'Don't mention it, my dear fellow, don't mention it. A pleasure. Begad,' the old gentleman smiled slyly. 'Begad, it was something of a joke, if you take me, Nolte, getting an ex-high sheriff into Parliament. But don't make too much of it ... don't make too much of it. Remember, there are other ways of looking at it, and when it comes to a contested election they might let you hear far more of it than you like.'

'Not now,' said Everardus with conviction. 'After this, Gallows-Gecko is a name to conjure with. It'll win me the next election, no matter who stands against me. Don't you think so, Mr Quakerley?'

'I do believe your are right, Nolte. There's nothing like a popular nickname to give you strength in a District like this. But tell me, where are the Uhlmanns? I had hoped I would meet him here.'

'*Meneer* Uhlmann sent his regrets,' said Nolte. 'They are still worrying with the fever at Neckarthal, and one of his children is ill. He could not come. Has Mr Quakerley seen his present to Tins? A lovely dinner table of cedar wood—polished so that it shines. It is in the dining room.'

'Then let us go and see it,' declared the old gentleman. 'I feel confoundedly thirsty, and I know the widow has some excellent wine.'

In the dining room the refreshments were set out, and Uncle Charles sampled the golden-coloured Jeropico and found it so much to his taste that he took three glasses of it. Tins, who had scrupulously avoided the dining room, was prevailed upon to join in the toast to his health, but on this occasion his firmness did not need the vigilance of his wife to support it; he took his wine like a gentleman, diluting his second glass with water, and excusing himself from drinking a third on the plea that it was his duty to see to the disposal of his guests. Uncle Charles nodded his head approvingly, and told Andrew that it was time to inspan the spring-wagon, for the Quakerley party was determined to return to *Quakerskoof* in the early hours of the morning.

It was indeed morning when *Langvlei* farm settled down to its normal state of quietude, but its period of rest was short, for the *kraals* had to be attended to, the sheep counted before they were sent out to graze in charge of the little Native herds, and the cows to be milked. The Widow appeared as fresh, when she superintended these duties, as when she had received her guests the evening before, but even then her work was not done, for there were many to cater for at breakfast, and from time to time newcomers arrived to offer their congratulations and partake of such hospitality as they knew would be awaiting them. Only on the second day after the wedding was it possible to clear away the litter and settle down to ordinary routine. The Native girls came from the *kraals*, carrying buckets of dung mixed with water, and with big brooms of river-sedge they swept the rooms and smeared the floors with the aromatic concoction, tinged with bullocks blood to darken it, drying quickly to a smooth evenness which exhaled a faint, ethereal smell. The Natives cleaned up the farmyard, and Cassandra sent baskets of pickings to the huts where until late that night the chorus revelled in sedate feasting, drinking the health of the Old Master and Mistress in numerous pannikins of ghoo-coffee, while in the large dining room of the homestead Tins sat on the sofa and played on his flute for the entertainment of his wife. He selected soft, dreamy airs which he thought would please her, and she was too happy to tell him that she preferred quicker music. But he felt her mood instinctively, and gradually changed into a more spirited tempo until at last Atties, who stood outside on the *stoep*, with other Natives who had been attracted by the sounds, heard the strains of the rigadoon, and declared that all was well with the Old Master and Mistress for they were now dancing as man and wife should do.

Chapter 28

'I really enjoyed it,' declared Uncle Charles. He sat by the side of his wife's bed in the large front bedroom at *Quakerskloof*. The warm winter sunlight streamed into the room, making golden splashes on the floor. The twitter of yellow finches, building their nests on the poplar trees, and the call of the yellow bush shrike, the bakbakiri courting his mate, came through the open window together with the faint breeze that brought the scent of sorrel and wild pelargoniums blossoming on the hillside.

In her stiff starched night dress and her laced cap, old Mrs Quakerley looked less pale than she did in her black household clothes, but her frailty and her old age were apparent enough, and her husband noticed how much weaker she had become of late. The gnarled hands, with the joints of the fingers enlarged to ugliness, lay outside the coverlet, the left idly turning the leaves of the book she had been reading. It was, her husband noticed, a devotional book in high Dutch. Of late she had lost her interest in novels, and had taken to her old favourites, which were mostly Dutch and all religious. The Quakerley library was well stocked, and Uncle Charles was a great reader. What was more, although he rarely corresponded with his own family at home, he occasionally wrote to someone whose books he had read, and in that way he had drifted into a correspondence with several well known authors. There were autographed presentation volumes from Sir Walter, from Thomas Burchell, and from Byron in his library, but his most valued literary possession was a well-annotated copy of Wordsworth with the poet's letter to him pasted in at the back. His wife did not share his love of reading, but she read dutifully the novels which he thought might interest her, and discussed them with him when he talked about them. So far she had entered his world, but he knew that although she had identified herself with him, she had retained her love for her own people, and he felt that as she was getting older the habits and conventions which had been ingrained in her in her youth were reasserting themselves. Between Andrew and her there appeared to be a closer bond. Andrew understood his mother; he shared much with her, divined her wishes before they were uttered, and paid her a devotion which his father appreciated but which Alice thought sentimental and overdone.

'Yes, I liked it, my dear,' said Charles Quakerley. 'I only regretted that you were not there to share the fun with us. You should have liked it too. It brought back to my mind the old days when I was an exile at Stellenbosch, and your father—all of you, indeed—and your mother were so good to me. The same sort of boisterous joviality; the same dances, my dear; almost the same kind of higgledy-piggledy—you know what I mean, my dear; everyone on an equal footing for the time being, and nobody asking who was country and who was common. I fancy Daughter-in-law did not quite like that, my dear.'

'You wrong Daughter Alice, Father,' said the old lady. 'It is her nature; we cannot help our natures. God gave them to us.'

'As He did everything else, my dear. But we can at least shape them, and daughter-in-law does not try to shape hers the right way. She rubs them up against the grain, which is tactless, my dear, tactless.'

'Perhaps it is,' said the old lady slowly. 'But Charles, they do want rubbing sometimes. I know my people, better than you do. But let us not speak about that. It does not interest me now. It used to, formerly, when I wondered how you and I found courage to mate. Now I know that these outward things do not matter in life. Did you do what I asked you, Father?'

'About the will? Why, yes. I have made a memorandum, but the lawyers will have to lick it into shape. If I can leave you—you look very frail today, my dear, and I don't like leaving you ...'

'No, no, Charles. You must go. You must put things in order. What did you decide about it?'

'What we agreed upon, my dear. It shall be as you wish. Your money will all go to Andrew and the children; he will of course make his own will and leave what he has to Daughter-in-law with reversion to the girls. The farm goes to him, naturally. A thousand to the Village when I die, for the library; they must have funds for upkeep. A couple of thousand—that is all we can spare, my dear, but Andrew will be able to add to it later on—for the nucleus of an educational fund. We discussed all that, you know, and the details will have to be settled by the lawyers. I want to tie it up so that they can't play fast and loose with it; and I want to be fair to both sections, but it is difficult. I should like the boys to go to that new school of the Bishops. There is much to be said for it, but the magistrate tells me that would be a mistake. He advises that we should attach no conditions to the grant, but leave it to the trustees to decide what the scholars will have to do. Perhaps that is best.'

'Yes, I like that way better. You will never make real Englishmen out of them, Charles, if they have Dutch fathers or mothers. Look at Andy. But you do not regret that, do you, husband?'

'No. Andy is all right. So long as they turn out like him I have no quarrel with them. If it comes to that, my dear, you won't be able to make real Dutchmen out of them, either, if they have an English mother or father, so it cuts both ways. We must assimilate; that is the only way. I don't see why we should not. We come from the same race—we are the same race. If we only knew more about each other, things would right themselves. Last night was a revelation to me. It reminded me of your people's ways at Stellenbosch, but it reminded me also of our own folk at home. The tenants' ball, you know, my dear. I have often told you. It is a pity we never went home, my dear. Then you would have seen how similar we are in many respects.'

'It was not necessary, Charles,' said the old lady, wearily. 'You were enough for me and, knowing you, I accept the rest on trust. I am sure things will come right. But this political business—I have a feeling sometimes, dear, that it will cause trouble. But don't let us speak about that. There is something else I want to talk to you about. It is about the children. They have never been to see my people. They go to see Alice's folk, which is right and proper, but they should know something about their grandmother's people, shouldn't they? I know Alice won't like it ... that's why you must say nothing about it until I am gone. It will be easier for her then to consent; she will remember me more kindly, dear. Now we must make allowances for her.'

'Daughter-in-law will have to do as she is told,' said Uncle Charles sternly. 'I beg your pardon, my dear, but I have never thought about the matter at all. I will see to it at once ...'

'No. Not until I am gone, dear,' said his wife decisively. 'I have already spoken to Andy. He will do what he can, but Alice must take them of her own accord, else the visit will do more harm than good. They can go and see the grand-aunt at Paarl. Alice will be mightily surprised, I daresay, for the girl hasn't seen the best class of our folk that you have, dear. And my nieces in Swellendam—you know them, and you can assure her that they are gentry. Do this for me, Charlie, when I am gone, but do it gently, dear, so that she does not set them against their kin by her talk. I should dislike that. I should not like my grandchildren to be ashamed of their grandmother's folk ...'

'Trust me, they'll never be that,' said Uncle Charles. 'Andrew will see to it, my dear, Andrew will see to it.'

'Andy goes his own gait, dear. He does not trouble himself with what people think or say. He lives to himself, and will do so until something brings out what there is in him. It may never show, dear, but when it does, you may be sure that it will show strongly. Do you go to Cape Town and let Alice see some of our people. Don't be so selfish, dear. Don't refuse the invitations. I will write and tell them you are coming, and then you can take Alice with you and show her what we are like. She does not know, and that is why she does what she does. And people in the Valley are not the same as some of our folk. The old families, you know, dear. She should meet them, get in touch with them, and then she won't ... she won't dislike us so much.'

Uncle Charles said nothing. He bent over her with caressing fondness, and stroked the grey curl that had crept from under her cap.

She went on, 'It is the same with the rest of you, dear. The Seldons ... they understand better, for Thomas is an understanding man. But they don't see as you do. They are still apart from us, from my people, I mean.'

'The children will better all that,' he said at last. 'We old folk are rooted in our prejudices, my dear. You must leave it to the younger generation. They will assimilate. They must. There is nothing between them.'

'I hope so,' she replied, but he fancied she spoke without much conviction. 'It will depend upon their upbringing, and that is why I asked you to see to it that the children get to know my people. There will be something coming to them from my side, too, dear, and that is another reason they should remember them. Do this for me. Promise.'

'I promise,' he said gravely. 'It shall be as you wish, dear, and now that I know it, it is my wish too. They shall see both sides. I will make Andy take them to England, and they shall visit your own folk, whatever Daughter-in-law may say.'

'Do not let her say it. She won't if you put it properly. Alice is a good girl, but she does not know, and she thinks they are all what they ought not to be. So many of your people think that, dear. I know you don't, but you are an exception. That is why you married me and remained here instead of taking me with you to your home, as so many others would have done. That was much to do for me, Charles. I have been grateful to you for it all these years.'

'It was nothing,' he declared. 'I, too, have come to love this country. I don't know what it is, but shiver me if I would leave it now. We are both concerned, my dear, and it shall be as you wish. Entirely as you wish. You have my promise.'

'I knew you would see it, dear,' she said. 'And about Andy ... let him be. He will go his own way; don't try and force him to think as you do. Remember he has some of my folk's blood in him as well as yours. Remember he is of this country; this is his home, not overseas, dear.'

'I do,' said Uncle Charles. 'I have always remembered that, and I have always let him go his own way. He is a sensible fellow, Andrew, although he needs riding on the snaffle. We need have no fear about him. He will do the right thing when he has to choose.'

Uncle Charles went to Cape Town, escorting Daughter-in-law but not Joan, who had elected to remain behind, and on the way he stopped, as Everardus had done on his journey to the capital, at farmhouses where Alice was introduced to folk who rather upset her ideas about the inherent want of culture and breeding with which she had associated those who were not in the Quakerley class. She dined with an old fellow who had been a crony of Lord Charles Somerset, and who behaved with the courtliness of one of the heroes in one of her favourite romances; she took tea with a hook-nosed old lady who had been received at court—a distinction which daughter-in-law had often dreamed of but had lately come to regard as one of the eventualities which would never occur in a waking state—and she was asked to dance with a young fellow who, the new Governor informed her, traced his descent back to a French *marquise*. In a Strand Street salon, in a drawing room furnished with just the kind of furniture which she had seen in the Valley, she found a salon attended by a party from

Government House, and the conversation was such that she could do no more than listen to it. Her father-in-law took her to various houses, and wherever she went she found gentle-folk, though they had Dutch names and their English was not unlike that of the Valley people, just as their hospitality was as generous and as homely as that of the Valley. She attended the opening of the Assembly, a ceremony that was as gorgeous as Cape Town could make it, and one Sunday she went with the old gentleman to *Groote Kerk* in the renamed Heerengracht which, in honour of Mr Adderley—a Member of the House of Commons who had vigorously protested against sending convicts to the Cape—had recently been re-christened Adderley Street. It was the occasion of the solemn day of prayer for the success of Her Majesty's forces in the Crimea, and the service was attended by the Acting-Governor and his suite, by the Admiral and the officers on the ships at Simonstown, and by the elite of the capital. She could not follow the service, except the short part of it which was in English, but she was impressed by the gathering and by the solemnity of the proceedings. Later on—for Uncle Charles protracted his stay for several months and Alice had such a round of entertainments and gaieties that she began to long for the quiet of *Quakerskloof*—she saw the reception of the new Governor, and was again impressed by the deference he showed to the old Dutch residents and their ladies, and by the cordiality with which he greeted her father-in-law.

Uncle Charles took her everywhere; he was indefatigable in attending receptions, dinners, levees, and parties, and he received more invitations than he could possibly accept. Formerly, when she had come to Cape Town with Andrew, she had on occasion found the time hang heavy on her hands, for Andrew did not care for these things, and never did any more than what social obligations exacted from him. But Father-in-law entered into the spirit of things, and seemed to like it. Alice never knew how wearisome that round of visits and entertainments had been to old Quakerley, but she did realise that the old man had some purpose in it, and to her surprise she found that she did not resent that purpose.

Once, when he had taken her to one of the old farmhouses where the rococo gables gleamed radiantly in the spring sunshine, and the clustered old oaks made a mosaic of gold and shadow over the time-worn thatch, she had questioned him about their hostess, whose deportment and quiet dignity had impressed her, just as much as the rich and varied appearance of the stately old house had impressed her—the gleaming silver and scintillating cut-glass on the sideboard, the solid beauty of the old furniture, the simple yet rich luxury of the bedroom, and the quality of the rugs and upholstering.

'Her grandfather was a Councillor of State in Holland, my dear,' he had answered, 'and her grandmother a *ferule*, which means a lady in her own right. Perhaps I have not got the right sow by the ear, but they were quality, Daughter-in-law, quality. Get that into your head. Many of these plain looking folk—aye, even in our Valley—are the descendants of families who in Europe were country folk, though titles are rarer there than with us at home. I doubt if I can show as long a pedigree as old Martin Rekker, and I doubt if any here can equal him in lineage. There's class and class, Daughter-in-law, and descent is not everything, but it is a hall-mark, even though the silver is rubbed down so thin that it bends and breaks when you use it. Your mother-in-law, my dear, comes from the same line as our hostess. Did you think I did wrong, my child?'

'No, Father. Not now. I used to think ...'

'Doubtless all sorts of things, my dear. But have a care that you don't wander too far from your text. Look at that heath. Have you seen more glorious colouring anywhere in our Valley?'

She was grateful to him for changing the subject, for she reflected that she might have pointed a moral from her own ancestry. Yeoman farmers were not country, and her father and brothers could not rival these people with whom she had dined and danced on terms of equality. It was a thoughtful and subdued Alice who returned to *Quakerskloof*, and her mother-in-law was gratified and surprised at the questions she asked and the eagerness she showed to hear about Andrew's maternal ancestors.

Chapter 29

To Everardus the six weeks that he spent in the capital, attending the meetings of the first House of Assembly in his capacity as Member for the Valley District, were monotonous during the first third, interesting during the second, and absorbing during the third. Every fortnight found his eagerness and his alertness doubled, for as he became more confident in himself, more acquainted with the procedure of a gathering which was not quite sure of itself, and more firmly convinced that practically everyone of his colleagues felt the same diffidence and the same shyness which he did, his interest waxed and he became strangely, as he himself felt, absorbed in the business of political intrigue, bargaining, and wrangling. It was surprising to discover that points over which he and another member had been hotly debating were, when he came to consider them in calm earnest, very minor ones indeed. It was more surprising to find that opposition, argument, and debate jarred upon him, made him aggressively active to vindicate his own point of view, less tolerant towards the other man's phase of thought, more sure that his own opinion was right.

This attitude disquieted him, for Everardus had always been logically inclined and apt to take a detached view of affairs. On his return from Cape Town, he visited Brother von Bergmann, with whom he had now become so far acquainted as not to need a formal invitation, although the missionary's hospitality did not exclude those who came without such a guarantee of amicable interest.

'I expected that, *Meneer* Nolte,' said Brother von Bergmann, offering him a fine Havana cigar, 'a gift from the Governor,' he explained. 'It is not often that one gets such good ones and this you really must smoke. I expected you would find that out for yourself, in time. Politics—political wrangling—gives one an utterly false sense of psychological values. Indeed, one is forced to take an untrue perspective as being real, simply because there is no chance for one man to stand alone in an assembly where each vote counts equally and where every member has made up his mind beforehand how he is going to vote.'

Everardus was inclined to agree with this opinion. He had made two speeches—or rather, he had bluntly, less haltingly than he had at first expected that he would, given the House his impression of certain proposed legislation, and although the House had listened to him with attention, it had not showed itself in the least impressed. One man there was who seemed able by his words to stir the members to something like vehement dissent or as audible approval—a little fellow of a man, bent dwarf-like, with a large head, black hair, fine dark eyes, and a calm, dispassionate demeanour. He told Brother von Bergmann about him, and was not surprised that the missionary knew all about the little man.

'That is *Meneer* Solomon,' he said. 'A strong man, because he is a just man, and honest. He will not pacify his conscience with words, nor try to placate it with a peroration—as he well might do for he has eloquence and speaks with the fire of conviction. But I am afraid he will not be able to do much; circumstances—the whole system and all it stands for—are against him. In time you will find that it is so. That is why I consider it unwise, as yet, to have representative government in the Colony. We are not ripe for it. In theory it is admirable; in practice ...' Brother von Bergmann shrugged his shoulders, leaving Everardus to guess what his opinion was of representative government in practice.

Everardus had a shrewd suspicion that it was not a favourable opinion, and he felt that he might even be inclined to endorse it. For his six weeks in Parliament had not given him a high idea of the value of that institution, and it had shown him that it presented possibilities that might not be advantageous in the long run to a community not yet shaped into a homogeneous whole. He felt the attraction of the political fight; the satisfaction of advantage obtained by judicious intrigue or carefully planned arrangement. It agreed with what lay in his blood. Years ago Brother von Bergmann had remarked—and Everardus had mildly resented the remark, although now he felt that there was germ of truth in it—'You and the Natives are the only folk in this country with any political sense. We others have none, because we think there are other things that matter more.'

Were there? Everardus wondered as he rode home to *Knolkloof* after his term of activity at the capital. What, after all, had he done during those many weeks he had spent in the House of Assembly? Increased his experience of affairs and his knowledge of men—certainly. But was it necessary to go to Cape Town for that, and had it been worth the time, the energy, and the trouble which he was conscious of having expended? It was his duty, naturally, to do what the Valley required of its representative, and he had done his duty conscientiously as far as in him lay. But were there really other, more important things than the legislation about which they had talked so much, which, now that it was passed and proclaimed, seemed to be of so little value in comparison with what had been spent on achieving it?

He thought of the Valley, and wondered. It lay before him in all its glory of early summer efflorescence, its general hue a subdued green merging into the deep blues of the mountains and the umbre of the harvested wheat lands, with farms dotted over it, and the River winding though it. It was his Valley now, as much as it was Rekker's and van Aardt's and the newly wedded Mrs Mabuis's. He had identified himself with it, and the Valley had taken him and made him one with it. And he could feel its influence upon him, the subtle urge of its very passivity that had made its inhabitants what they were. Generations might come and go, but the Valley would always remain; its influence would always be there. Its fierce daylight, its splendour of sun-glare, its enervating warmth, its very soil, at once an incentive and a disappointment to those who tilled it, would exert their influence, subtly, unconsciously, upon those who lived in it. What would be the outcome of it all? Wither were they all tending? Everardus was acute enough to realise that conditions were changing, and that the old ways were no longer the wisest ways. And above all he was sensible of the fact that the Valley did not take kindly to the new ways, and that progress outside might make little impression upon it unless those who were in a position to do so helped to bring it within.

'I wonder if the missionaries are right after all, Wife,' he said to Magriet as they sat on the *stoep*, on their first evening after his return home. 'I wonder if it is possible for us White folk to do everything and to leave them outside. It seems to me rather as if it is our own case over again, Wife. You and I—we came here, hiding our heads as it were—and what would have happened to us if people stood aside from us and left us alone? I expect I should have been bitter by now, having the taste of sour figs constantly in my mouth.'

'We have to thank our good friends for what we have, Ami,' said Magriet, 'and ourselves for what might have happened if they had not proved themselves our friends.'

'Aye. But that is not what I have in mind, Wife. I have thought over these things. Times are changing, and the opportunities you and I have had are not likely to come to Gottlieb and Katryn. It is of the youngsters I am thinking, Maggie. What is to become of them, unless we create new opportunities?'

'That must be our work, Ami,' said Magriet, firmly. 'It must be your work. You must see to it that they get educated—not only Gottlieb and Katryn, but all these children in the Valley that now have no chance of it. After all, you and the doctor are our representatives. In the other Districts they have schools. Why not here?'

'I will do my best—I have tried already, but there is no money, Wife,' said Everardus despondently. 'But it is not education alone. Even that perhaps may do more harm than good. That, at least, is what *Meneer* Uhlmann thinks. Do you know what he wrote me while I was at Cape Town?'

'No. I hope it was nothing disturbing, Ami.'

'In a sense it was. You know Anton Fisher's boy is over there in Europe, at the Mission House, getting free education. It is the old man's wish that he should qualify for the mission service, but the boy wants to be a doctor, and Anton is much perturbed about it. What is more, Christian, Uhlmann's younger lad, wants to be a musician. The old gentleman is very sad about it all; he wrote to me that he did not know what to do, but that a musician was quite out of the question, though he did not see why Anton's boy should not be a doctor and a missionary at the same time.'

'I expect they will settle it for themselves,' said Magriet, with her sound common sense. 'Everything settles itself, Ami, if one does not entangle it in all sorts of irrelevancies.'

'That is very comforting, Wife!' exclaimed Everardus impatiently. 'But in practice things don't turn out so well as all that.'

'It has in our case, Ami. Look what we gained by making difficulties for ourselves, and yet at the last it settled itself. If anyone had called you Gallows-Gecko when you came here first—why, Ami, you would have cuffed him over the head, and there would have been a court case about it. And now, why, they use it as a compliment to you, and you take it as such.'

'And they made their Gallows-Gecko their Member of Parliament, Wife,' said Everardus, with a touch of pride which Magriet found entirely justifiable. 'Very well, I will show them what he can do. The Valley has chosen Gallows-Gecko, and Gallows-Gecko will serve the Valley. I don't know what I can do, yet, but a man can try, Wife, and find out the work that God created him for. And it seems to me I have not found it yet.'

'It lies here in the Valley, Ami,' said his wife. 'Here among our people.'

'That I, too, believe, Wife. Let us take it as God gives it to us, and work, as Mr Uhlmann says, for the future.'

STORMWRACK

by

C Louis Leipoldt

Chapter 1

Not to all men is given the power to remain faithful, in their later life, to the loves and attachments of their youth. With the changing years the passions and emotions alter their flow into directions other than those into which they were forced originally. The defensive love of the child gives place to the proprietary, protective instinct of the adolescent, which in turn merges into the complacent masterfulness of the middle-aged, to dwindle, finally, into dispassionate, objective contemplation when the fire has burned out, leaving only the comfortable warmth of grey ash behind.

In Andrew Quakerley the passions that stir men in early youth had long since given place to that detachment which comes from the realisation that the results of most of them are evanescent. His temperament, derived from those subtle, inherited qualities of which we know so little, although science attempts to postulate so much about them—the inherited dominants and recessives dormant in ancestors, the fine adjustments of glandular tissue, the nuances of endocrine ferments, and the fleeting impressions the mind stores up for stray use in emergencies—all that had gone to the making of him—had paved the way for him to achieve that realisation which in most men is the result of poignant disappointments and hateful failure. Because he had not fixed his hopes beyond the reach of his grasp, he had been spared much of the smart with which love sometimes stings. He had married early in life, driven thereto as much by convention as by the desire to have companionship and an outlet for the purely animal urging which Nature provokes in every male adolescent. His married life had been happy within the lines and limits he had himself laid down. It had never been passionate. Andrew's inherited calmness and equanimity of mind had prevented any exuberance of feeling. He had taken his marital relations as he had taken his everyday life, as things which should be considered soberly, as a gentleman considers them, and not extravagantly as a young man might. His wife found him, on occasions when her own emotional necessities demanded a warmer response, too cold and matter-of-fact. She had complained that Andrew had wooed her as if she had been a piece of furniture, and later in life, when her handsome, sensually attractive features had degenerated into the sharpness old age brings, and the smoothness of her complexion had become marred by wrinkles, she had secretly harassed herself by the thought that she was losing his love. That was because she had allowed herself to dally with the thought that he required, for the persistence of his attachment to her, the same allurements which she imagined had attracted him in his youth. She judged him by herself. In her own case it was his handsome bearing, his regular features, his fine bodily proportions, that had aroused in her the desire to possess him. Her love had been a purely sensuous, sex emotion which she had never outlived and had never attempted to sublimate into a less selfish and more disinterested passion. She had never understood him, and her want of understanding had made her ascribe to him feelings and prejudices such as she herself experienced.

Yet it was easy to understand Andrew Quakerley. The descendant of an impetuous, passionately self-centred father, and of a phlegmatic mother, under whose veneer of calm impassivity had smouldered fires of feeling as hot as those that sometimes flared up in her husband, he had inherited more from his mother than from his father. In temperament he was singularly like the old lady who in her adolescence had trusted herself to the handsome young English naval officer who had deserted his ship in False Bay, at the time of the first English Occupation of the Cape, and had fled to Stellenbosch, to be hospitably received and hidden from pursuit on the farmstead of a wealthy Dutch resident. The Quakerley romance was known to all who were acquainted with the history of the Valley, but its details were no longer common property, and about some of them Andrew himself was not particularly well informed. He knew that on his father's side he was descended from a prosperous English county family; his father's father had sat in the House of Commons as representative of a rotten borough; one of his uncles had been an Admiral of the Red. His father had told him these things when he was but a lad, and had impressed upon him, in a mildly sarcastic manner, the fact that if he ever wished to go to England, he could go there as an Englishman, with the privileges and the rights, the loyalties and the prestige, that belong to such. He had never taken advantage of this satisfactory dispensation of Providence, for his ways were the ways of his neighbours and from the time when he had been capable of thinking, he had identified himself with the country of his birth, caring little, in the concrete, for that of his descent. Men who knew him said that he was indifferent, a 'deep fellow,' whose taciturnity verged on sullenness, but in reality that was only his diffidence and his entirely logical mind, both of which he had inherited from his mother.

For Andrew Quakerley was, without knowing it, an artist. He delighted in what seemed to him beautiful, and he saw beauty in many things in which other folk saw merely the commonplace. As a youngster he had made, in the rain-sodden soil of his father's farmyard, little gardens of delight, pansied with sorrel petals and the ultramarine blossoms of wild tulips. He had built furrows of Karroo nodules and terraces of weathered sandstone, all in miniature such as a child produces, and his father, capable beyond the rest to understand what lay behind these childish amusements, had encouraged and had presented him with a glorious paint-box on his seventh birthday. But Andrew was no painter; he was not even a colourist, and within a few weeks, when the novelty of the new possession had worn off, the paint-box and the sable brushes had been consigned to the big cupboard in his room, and he had resumed his occupation of building miniature gardens. The artist is a creator, and Andrew's creative faculty seemed to concentrate itself upon this game of laying out flower plots in the sand and studding them with blooms picked from that great natural garden that in springtime blossomed in such profusion around him, the veld.

Then had come school, at Cape Town, where, in the little suburb of Green Point, within a hundred yards of the flat rocky coast against which the same Atlantic Ocean lapping the shores of his country of descent washed its emerald waters, a retired clergyman presided over a select school for sons of gentlemen. Here for eight years he had worked in moderation, played with a little more zeal, and thought with all the intensity of introspective youth. In an environment whose quiet beauty could make an appeal even to the normal boy, Andrew had grown up to strengthen his fervent love of form and colour and composition. The tremendous mass of the mountain behind the school, its steep, imposing escarpment butting up into the sky beyond the rolling contour of Signal Hill, the flat expanse of Green Point Common, diversified by its lake fringed with mild muntia bushes that in early summer were laden with a profusion of sour-sweet berries, and the far horizon of the sea, broken by the outline of Robben Island, round which the merchantmen passed on their way to England, were important factors in shaping his aesthetic education, and of these his preceptor had made full and intelligent use. His headmaster was a cultured and refined personality whose humanity had not been etiolated by too violent a classicism nor misdirected by too fanatical a piety. The Reverend Mr O'Callaghan was housemaster as well as principal, and he regarded his boarders as part of his family. They took their meals at his table, and he had frequent guests, who came indiscriminately, from Government House as well as from the East Indiamen that entered the harbour, and were always interesting, informative, and good company. Andrew was privileged to listen to the discussions on art, literature, and science that took place at the hospitable old gentleman's board, and the fact that the headmaster was himself a clever draughtsman and an intelligent, knowledgeable critic, was a guarantee that his artistic guidance was along sound lines. It served, at least, to inculcate in him a more disciplined appreciation of form and colour than he would have been able to cultivate had he been left to his own devices and his miniature gardens on the farm.

It was fortunate for Andrew that his preliminary training, at the hands of *Monsieur Ommes*, a Belgian 'newsletter writer' of uncertain age and unprepossessing appearance, who acted as instructor in freehand drawing at Mr O'Callaghan's Academy, was sufficiently thorough to make him realise that he could never aspire to be even so mediocre a painter as his tutor. It was more fortunate for him, perhaps, that the Reverend Mr O'Callaghan, while thoroughly sharing that conviction, had seen no reason why his pupil should not continue the course.

'It will, at least, enable you,' the reverend gentleman had told him when Andrew had lamented his inability to compete with some of the more facile students in the drawing class, 'to understand what is correct drawing and composition, and appreciate beauty when you see it. My dear boy, everyone does not learn that, more's the pity, and I think—ahem—that it should form part of every—ahem—gentleman's training.'

Indeed, but for his headmaster's understanding of the boy's character and temperament, Andrew might have passed his eight years at Green Point without benefiting more from that cultured establishment than most of the reverend gentleman's pupils did. He was slow in the uptake, he learned painfully and ploddingly, rather than with the minimum of effort and application. He had his Dutch mother's patience, a certain indomitability that ensured him a fair standing in class, and a certain language sense that made him take kindly to the Latin and even tolerate the Greek. In the playground, although the rule of the school was that only English should be spoken, Dutch, and the vernacular variant of it now known as Afrikaans, and at that time regarded as less a language than an inelegant *patois*, were freely used, and he learned both easily, picking up at the same time a little Hottentot from the

Natives and a smattering of French from *Monsieur* Ommes. Most of his playmates and fellow pupils had in view a post in the Government service or the entry into one of the learned professions, for which they would have had to go to Europe since the Cape Colony in the first half of the nineteenth century offered no opportunities for the study of the law, medicine or theology. He was more fortunate, for his father had sent him to a boarding-school in order to fit him, so far as such education could be adequate preparation, to take charge of the home farm. The Quakerleys were rich folk, and there would be no need for him to become a civil servant or a professional man, although paternal authority would put no obstacles in his way if, later on, he elected to qualify for either. In the circumstances Andrew might have lazed, and the temptation in the way of a big, strong, good-looking boy to do so was strong at an establishment run on such unconventional lines as that of the Reverend Mr O'Callaghan. The pupils were permitted an amount of liberty which would have scandalised most housemasters, and boys being what they are, it was not to be wondered at that some of them abused their privileges. Andrew himself had a standing invitation to dine at Government House once every term, where the Governor, Sir Benjamin D'Urban, patted him familiarly on the shoulder, enquired after the welfare of his father, and suggested that Andrew should in his next letter home 'present my compliments and ask why the devil he does not give us the pleasure of his company occasionally,' thereafter turning him over to the youngest of his aides and paying no further attention to him. Andrew dutifully delivered the Governor's message but his father never came to town, contenting himself with his solitude on the mountain-ridged farm in the Valley where he was a man of position and influence. Similarly Andrew was made free of the Admiral's House at Simonstown, which he much preferred to Government House, for the Admiral was a bluff, genial sailor who understood boys, although he had a poor opinion of Andrew's uncle, his colleague of the Red. At Simonstown there was much more fun to be had, for the midshipmen were wholesome, sport-loving lads who were not above companioning a civvy of their own age whose father was undoubtedly a Nabob and whose uncle was equally undoubtedly high in the service.

But what Andrew in his pupillage loved best of all was to ramble on the common, climb the slopes, and occasionally to the top, of the imposing mountain whose grandeur of outline and massive majesty came in time to impress him less profoundly than the wealth and beauty of its vegetation. When the term started, in late January, when the Common lake was almost dry, the mountain rivulets still coursed down their dark amber-coloured water, impregnated with the peaty acids derived from the flat table-top of the range. One could follow these rivulets until they dashed sheer over a declivity that was unclimbable, and admire the gorgeous red disas studding their banks, with the vividly coloured butterflies, named in honour of Governor Ryk van Tulbagh by the encyclopaedically clever Linnaeus, hovering over their broad, wax-like lips. In autumn, the giant proteas blossomed on the slopes; in spring thousands of composites sprang up and made a garden of Signal Hill—a garden such as young Andrew saw in his dreams and determined to create for himself once he became his own master and had plenty of money to indulge his whimsies.

It was O'Callaghan who divined the direction in which his pupil's tastes lay. The headmaster knew all about Andrew's parentage, and he had sufficient knowledge of human nature, and more especially of the nature of the adolescent humanity entrusted to his charge, to be able to mould it along the lines which, rightly or wrongly, he considered desirable. He exerted himself to rouse Andrew's interest in botany, a science in which he himself had dabbled. In later life Andrew Quakerley, when he could be induced to speak about himself, referred with some amount of excusable pride to the fact that he had strolled, on one memorable Sunday afternoon, with Johann Franz Drege up the slopes of the Devil's Peak, where the great botanist, who ranks next to Thunberg and Burchell in the history of Cape Botany, had initiated him, frankly and unaffectedly, into the mysteries of sex with the help of a silver tree and a fir cone. He could cap this reminiscence by adding that later on Dr William Harvey, Treasurer-General of the Colony, had been a frequent visitor at the Academy, and that he had often accompanied that indefatigable botanist on his rambles in search of new species.

The headmaster's experiment proved an undoubted success. There was no attempt to teach formal botany, but the natural treasures of the mountain and Common proved apperceptive masses upon which the mind of the country lad seized with avidity. The old, infantile love of gardening gained a new stimulus, intensified by frequent visits to the garden that lay on the other side of the old Company's oak avenue, fronting Government House, and to the still more interesting horticultural masterpiece owned by a certain Baron Ludwig on the lower slopes of the Kloof Nek. Here young Andrew revelled in the contemplation of exotic species of flowers and shrubs, admired the wonderful arrangement of borders and beds, appreciated even the technical niceties of pruning, oculating, grafting, and layering, and learned, by insatiable cross-questioning of the good-humoured Native gardeners, a great deal about the habits and cultivation of plants. Already at that early age he felt stirring in him that feeling for a garden which a great philosopher has likened to a man's love for a beautiful woman. In a boy barely beyond puberty such a feeling is sexless, less an emotion than an expression of a determination, but its ethical influence is no less tangible than if it were the result of an innate urge to satisfy emotional requirements. Good teachers understand and appreciate it, for they know that settled concentration upon what some parents dismiss as a passing hobby is of incalculable value in a child's education. It stimulates, refreshes, even exalts, and acts as a spur and incentive to disciplined work. In Andrew's case, as his headmaster had hoped, it produced excellent results, for it gave to his study of Latin a real, practical fillip, quickened his already well-developed powers of observation, and intensified his desire to become acquainted with the geography of the countries from which so many of the plants which he saw in the gardens had come.

When he was eighteen years of age, Andrew left the hospitable Academy where for eight years he had worked with passable diligence and thought with boyhood's intensity. He was a tall, well-grown, absurdly good-looking lad with a serious, adult expression of countenance. Fluent in three languages, with a moderate knowledge of Latin, less of Greek, and still less of philosophy, he left school a member, by confirmation, of the Church of England and with the expectation of being a farmer all his life. There waited for him in the Valley the fine estate of *Quakerskloof*, bought by his father twenty-one years ago when it was a barren, unimproved ravine between two spurs of the surrounding ranges, but now, after much capital and labour had been expended upon it, a flourishing wheat, citrus, and sheep farm. His father expected him to take over its management, for old Charles Quakerley had never taken kindly to farming, and had left matters very much in the hands of a paid manager. His son, he presumed, would take kindly to it, for the boy's predilections were always in favour of gardening and such-like things, and between gardening and managing a farm there was, after all, no great difference. A farm was only a garden on a large scale, and aptitude and inclination for the one would surely justify the presumption that they were also adapted for the other.

Young Andrew did not see things entirely in that light nor from that perspective, but he was obedient, as a good son of a Dutch mother should be, and he attended to his father's behests. Farming gave him no great pleasure, but he did his duty to the farm which, aided by good seasons and that luck which in agricultural pursuits is so irritatingly vacillating, flourished and brought in sufficient interest on the capital invested in it to satisfy its owner.

In due course young Andrew married. It would have been strange for so eminently desirable a young man to have escaped that consummation, especially in an environment which looked upon marriage as the natural, God-ordained crown and sequel of every male human being's endeavours. He went about the business with the calmness and dispassionate seriousness which characterised his action in all things, taking no one, not even his mother, to whom he was devoted, into his confidence. His choice fell upon the daughter of one of the English settlers who in 1820 had entered the Valley and established themselves on farms within it. Some of them had made good, but the majority had rid themselves of their farms and settled in the Village as traders or had migrated into other districts. Among these latter were the luckless father and brothers of the young woman whom Andrew had chosen for his wife. She was English-born, the daughter of a working farmer who had left his small rented holding in the homeland to come out to South Africa to make his fortune, but had found that occupation so hazardously difficult when it consisted in tilling a soil utterly different from that to which he had been accustomed that he had sold out at a loss and rejoined his fellow immigrants at Algoa Bay, where he found a more congenial occupation in running a store with the help of his sons.

Neither Andrew's mother nor his father approved of his choice, but both were much too wise to oppose it. His father shrugged his shoulders, and expressed the hope that 'daughter-in-law' would at least have the sense to keep her relations at a distance, but he looked quizzically at his son and wondered what that excellent fellow could really have seen in a young woman so patently inferior in race and breeding to the Quakerleys. His mother shook her head and remarked, more as an aside than as an expression of settled conviction, that a man must 'make his own bed.' The engagement was short, and the wedding, celebrated with unusual display of the Quakerleys' hospitality, was a year's wonder for the District. In the absence of an English clergyman it was solemnised by the Dutch Reformed parson according to the ritual of that Church, and clinched by a civil ceremony before the magistrate. Old inhabitants, who clustered to congratulate the couple, told the bridegroom, who was generally popular and respected in the Valley, that he was lucky that he had married so late in the century.

'Had you lived under the old Company,' Uncle Doremus van Aard assured him, 'you would have had endless trouble! Most worrying trouble! As the Psalmist says in the good Book, "vexation and weariness of spirit!" I know. I had it all when I married my wife. We had, both of us, to journey up to Cape Town for the Governor so see my intended before we could get permission to put up the banns. Yes, no; we live in a better time now that we are under the rule of our good sovereign lady Alexandrina Victoria—God bless the woman! And you too, Mrs Quakerley.'

The marriage made no difference in Andrew's life. His wife, who was sincerely attached to him, largely by power of the immense physical attraction of his handsome face and his fine proportions, found herself elevated to a position for which she was unfitted by nature and education, though by no means by inclination. She committed solecisms in speech which set her father-in-law's teeth on edge, and made false steps in society which her mother-in-law gravely rebuked, though her husband saw neither of them, and would not have greatly cared had he done so. With her sister-in-law, Joan, old Charles's only daughter, who lived with them on the farm and was a mild, sweet-tempered woman, slightly older than Alice, she got on remarkably well, and it was mainly owing to Joan's encouragement and help that she learned in time to adapt herself to her changed environment and to bear herself with the dignity and restraint befitting a Quakerley's wife. She bore Andrew two daughters, Kathleen and Anne, and insisted that the children be brought up on strictly English lines to prevent any contamination from the Dutch or Native environment. Towards her mother-in-law, whom she knew to be the representative of one of the oldest and best Dutch families in the Colony, she displayed the best side of herself, in an attempt to ingratiate herself with the old lady, an attempt that seemed at first to be doomed to failure. When Mrs Quakerley Senior realised that her daughter-in-law, notwithstanding her want of birth and upbringing, was at heart sound, although superficially flighty and uninteresting, and that she loved her husband with an eagerness that, while it was passionately animal in its emotional expression, was at the same time capable of self-sacrifice and a real desire to make herself worthy of him, she received these advances with more cordiality. In time the relations between the two became filial, and although on both sides there were strains that threatened to rend the bonds of affection between them, such a catastrophe was always averted by the innate good sense of the elder and the anxiety of the younger to do nothing that could in any way displease her husband, of whom she was so passionately fond.

Chapter 2

In the early years of the last century, when England was warring with France and the greatest person in White civilisation was, by general acknowledgement, a little Corsican of tremendous energy and unbounded ambition, the Valley was part of a huge District comprising almost the entire north-western half of the Cape Colony. So large and unwieldy a fiscal entity could not be administered with ease, and the powers at the Castle, with the entire consent and approval of the Lords Major, who formed the

Directorate of the old Dutch East India Company, decided to deliminate the District into two *landdrosties* or magistracies. For the one a centre was already in existence. For the other a town had to be created in the Valley, and the preliminaries for it had already been sanctioned when the disastrous Battle of Blaauwberg Strand, where Sir David Baird defeated General Janssens, put an end forever to the Company's rule at the Cape. At that time the Valley was peopled by industrious, careful and competent settlers, who derived their title to their farms from direct purchase from the Company, or effective occupation of waste lands. They were the descendants, mostly, of employees of the Company, small men who had struggled to win a personal independence, who valued what they had won and were eager to better themselves by farming in a district far enough from the capital to permit them to be exempt from the disturbing interference of officialdom that persisted in regarding the population as merely an appurtenance of the Company. There were among them men of finer breeding with more pretensions to culture than their neighbours, who could look back to ancestors who in Europe had owned estates proportionately as large as these they now held, who had had the right to armorial bearings, and who had played some part in their home country's history. Such were the Rekkers, whose immediate ancestor had been a Count, and the Gersters, who derived from a Councillor of the Empire. Although the language of these settlers was Dutch, spoken with all the grammatical complexity which in those days characterised that language, they were not by any means all Dutchmen in the true sense of the term, although all had been Dutch subjects under the Company's rule. Germans, French, Walloons, and Hanoverians were to be found among them, an occasional Swede and Dane, and as occasionally a true Friesian or Amsterdammer. With the Second English occupation, there was added to their community a small nucleus of English and Scotch folk, officials of the new regime who came to administer the District. Yet diversified as the community was, in point of nationality and type of settler, it was homogeneous in one respect, namely, that it was composed wholly of adherents to the Reformed religion. There was no Roman Catholic, Jew, or Heathen to be found in it, for the Coloured half-castes and the Natives, not to mention the imported slaves on the farms, were all supposed to be members of the Dutch Reformed Church, which was attended by the few Europeans who were not officially members of it. Where an area became settled, the Church established an ecclesiastical centre. The congregation helped nobly by donating land for a township, and the government assisted by adding whatever the community thought a reasonable extension at the expense of crown lands.

In that manner the Village had come into existence, and as the congregation wished to show the new English Governor, Lord Caledon, that it had no *animus* towards him but was on the contrary imbued with feelings of loyalty and respect, it petitioned him to grant to the Village a name, and to dignify it with the presentation of a coat of arms. To the first request His Excellency readily agreed, fixing on a name which, while it was typically English, was at the same time euphonious and unlikely to be mangled by those to whom its pronunciation was a matter of considerable difficulty. To the second he responded by transmitting to the College of Heralds a request that, if possible, the Village should be indulged in its whim. As the Village had never possessed a coat of arms, it may be assumed that the College, for reasons which will readily be understood by those who are familiar with the way in which such things are managed, found itself unable to comply with the Governor's request. The refusal made no difference either to the Valley or to the Village. The former went on farming in the old-fashioned style, and the latter started to prove itself worthy of its name. It laid out its plots in what it understood to be the correct manner, built houses and stores on them, made a hard road which at the same time served as a street, and invited whoever cared to live in it to take advantage of these improvements. The Valley responded by building a neat residence for the pastor, and a number of 'church residences' to house the more wealthy farmers when they came in to attend the quarterly communion service or *Nagmaal*. In time the Village became the centre of activity of the Valley, the seat of a magistracy, the headquarters of the police and the post office, and last, but in the opinion of the Valley by no means least, the site of an imposing gaol built of hewn stone and adorned, over its gateway, by real fetters gracefully festooned between two iron hooks.

It gave to the Valley farmers a centre where all the things to which they attached importance were presumably concentrated. It introduced, too, a cleavage which from the very beginning exercised some influence, intangible but none the less effective, upon the two sections of the community, the urban and the rural. In the early stages, the interests of these two sections were so closely linked that there could be no question of antagonism, still less of enmity, but as time went on, and the Village became more and more the home of those who had no direct interest in tilling the soil while the Valley had no great concern with trade, the distinctions between the two sets grew more pronounced, socially and culturally as well as industrially and, at least, politically. That the process of differentiation was a slow and almost imperceptible one was caused by the fact that while the population of the Valley was large and to a great extent independent of the Village, that of the town was small and in the beginning utterly dependent for its existence upon the goodwill and co-operation of the farming community.

The agricultural community was composed almost entirely of the Dutch-speaking element. Only after the Village had been established for some years did an Englishman enter the Valley as a settler. This was old Charles Quakerley, who had married a Dutch lady and had received from England a large sum of money on the death of his mother. To the Valley he was an utter stranger, and his arrival, with the avowed intention of purchasing a farm and settling down in the District, was looked upon as an innovation on which adverse opinions were expressed. But old Charles, then by no means entitled to the prefix, had rapidly and with amazing success won a popularity which made him one of the most respected and important citizens of the Valley. He never attempted to learn Dutch, which he spoke, when driven to it, with singular incompetence. He never scrupled to declare his views with facility in the language he understood, and his views were not always those which the Valley, as a community, could wholeheartedly endorse. But the leaders of public opinion in the community— the scrupulous Rekkers, the sternly correct Gersters, and the good-humouredly pious van Aards—whose opinion carried immense weight, had marked him down as an aristocrat, as one who, although by no possibility superior to them in lineage or breeding, was yet their equal in descent and perhaps a little more than their peer in culture and education. They had taken him up, not patronisingly, for that was not their way, but with the old-world courtesy and dignified seriousness to which his own conception of what constituted gentlemanly behaviour could so easily and frankly respond. He had come among them with the vague notion that he would have to fight a lone battle, the Valley was uncivilised and lay far from the capital, so that the leaven of culture from the Castle could have little influence upon it. That much he had assumed, and his wife, who knew much better than he what sort of individuals he would meet, had merely smiled when he had talked of the possibilities of hardships engendered by animosity from ignorant neighbours and actual opposition from jealous competitors. To his surprise he had found hospitable reception, friendly fellow-feeling, and a society which, although wedded by usage and convention to old-world fashions, contained men and women with whom he could associate on terms of intellectual and social equality. He had been astonished that old Martinus Rekker could quote Horace, and that Uncle Doremus van Aard could talk knowledgeably about chess gambits, though to be sure he mispronounced the Spanish and Italian names and insisted that the *Ruy Lopez* was the best attack. He had been agreeably flattered when Pastor de Smee had deferred to his interpretation of a line in the *Hecyra*, and still more surprised when he had found that the Reverend gentleman had no objection to a square dance. But what had astonished him most of all had been the perfect friendliness with which they had received him, the deferential manner in which they had given him neighbourly counsel about what parts of his new farm were suited for this or that, and the grave and polished courtesy which they invariably showed to him and his wife. With them he discussed political matters—it was inevitable at a time when change was in the air, and when Europe was recovering from a shock that had threatened to shiver the foundations of monarchy—and found, again to his surprise, that they had no great bias, and that they were prepared to give the new government a fair trial and thought, on the whole, that from what they had seen of it so far it was a trifle better than the old Company's autocratic rule. There was difference of political opinion among them, for some favoured the Orange Party and some were inclined towards republicanism, but they debated these things as if they were of academic, not of practical, interest, and they seemed to him to be frankly of Johnson's opinion that the best Government is that under which a man is contented and free in such measure as freedom is compatible with the interests of all concerned. As he was inclined towards that view himself, he found them eminently reasonable.

With the advent of the 1820 settlers, a party of whom came into the Valley and settled on government farms, the small English element, of which old Charles was the head and acknowledged leader, was augmented. Quakerley found his fellow countrymen less to his liking than the neighbours whom he had already learned to respect and regard as personal friends. That was not to be wondered at for the newcomers were not of his class. They were not folk to whom he could look for congenial companionship, and while he appreciated the motives that had led them to emigrate and cast their lot with the dwellers in the Valley, he considered that they had made a mistake, because they lacked the necessary capital, experience and aptitude to become successful citizens in a farming community. His expectations proved correct, for the majority of them soon abandoned their farms and settled down to industrial or trading occupations in which their prospects of securing a livelihood were much better. His own farming operations, thanks to the assistance and advice which he received and was not too proud to accept and act upon, were amazingly profitable. His neighbours, who were experienced agriculturists, had helped him, and he readily admitted that without their co-operation he would probably have made a mess of things.

One of these neighbourly neighbours had been old Martin Rekker, an aristocrat whose farm had at one time been one of the show places in the Valley. Rekker had provided Quakerley with a *kneg* or overseer, to whom could be entrusted most of the expert work of the farm. In time old Charles had come to depend more and more upon his manager, and when his son had come back from school to take charge of the estate, the old man had practically retired, content to look on, a mild critic, occupying himself largely with his reading and relegating the management of the farm to young Andrew.

For all that, old Charles had influenced the Village in many ways. When he came to live in the District he had found himself practically the only Englishman who had a vested interest in it. His fellow English residents had been government officials, some of whom had served under the first English administration of the Colony. Nearly all were, like him, newcomers and profoundly ignorant of the conditions and men they encountered. The transition stage between the government by the old Company, so autocratic in many ways and so exploitative in its policy, and the first English occupation had been too abrupt to permit those who had lived under the old regime to draw effective comparisons. The period of government by the Dutch, after the coming of de Mist, had been too short to leave a permanent mark upon them. When the second English occupation came, the change was scarcely noted in the Valley. Its inhabitants accepted that change with resignation. No one resented it, and no one looked for a revolutionary upheaval. The Valley had its own ideas; it lay beyond the sphere of intrigue and agitation prevalent in other districts, where the new yeast of revolution and advanced liberalism had produced some results in the shape of dissatisfaction with existing states of things. For that reason the Valley had not been affected by the rebellion in the eastern districts, nor by the northward trek which was to produce such far-reaching consequences in the future. One or two incidents had, indeed, stirred it and created a temporary excitement. While on the eastern frontier the settlers were endangered by Kaffir marauders, those in the western districts were harassed by aboriginals no less active and in some ways more irritating. The roving Bushmen, armed with their poisonous arrows, were a danger constantly to be guarded against, and the Colonists of the Valley could, if they wished to dilate upon their heroism, which as a matter of fact they did not feel inclined to do, have told of pioneering work no less arduous and no less indomitable than any which could be ascribed to their fellow Colonists in the eastern districts.

Another happening that had produced less agitation and excitement in the Valley than in other districts was the emancipation of the slaves. Thanks to the presence of English settlers in their midst, thanks also to the efforts of old Charles Quakerley himself, the slave owners of the Valley had not materially lost by the Ordinance. Their valuations had been accepted and had been paid with less discount and more promptly than in other districts. They had all been humane and kindly owners; slavery with them had been less a vice than a traditional institution, and many of their slaves could be looked upon as old retainers, friends almost, of the families to which they were attached. There were, of course, exceptions, but these were so few that their names have become legendary in the Valley which today recounts, as one would tell a fairy story, of masters who immolated their human property and mistresses who won an unenviable reputation through their inhumanity to man. The fact that such exceptions were enshrined into legend serves, better perhaps than a mere denial, to emphasise the absence of any gross cruelty on the part of the Valley slave owners. The added fact that on every farm the slaves remained as willing workers after they had received their freedom strengthens that assumption.

The Village, of which the Valley was proud as one is proud of a family relation who has prospered, a pride tinged with a trifle of envy, was a happy combination of mild activity and placid quiet. With the years it had prospered and added to its buildings. The English settlers had made a small community, which had brought about considerable changes in some directions. Landed from the *Fanny* and the *East India* they had marched across the veld and settled in the Valley. Some of them had definitely remained; others, the greater number, had left. Those who had remained had found an interest in the Village, and there the nucleus of a separate community had been formed which at first had been definitely demarcated from the older inhabitants, but in time became assimilated with the latter. Such assimilation had progressed by inter-marriage but more patently by the recognition of a mutuality of interest which even the difference of language and convention could not permanently prevent.

In such assimilation the influence of men like Quakerley had played a part. Old Charles had felt it an obligation upon him to do what he could for his compatriots. He was wealthy, and although he did not look upon himself as a settler, he was not altogether indifferent to the interests of men who spoke his language, belonged to his church, and represented, although perhaps indifferently well, his culture. Of his money he gave freely. He bought a plot of ground for the new church, helped to build it, and gave a considerable amount towards a fund for the erection of a vicarage and the payment of a stipend. At first the little community was ministered to by chance visiting priests, to whom the Dutch Reformed parson offered the hospitality of his manse and pulpit. Later a resident vicar was appointed with a parish so large that it needed a journey of several days' duration for him to traverse it.

Of these early days Andrew Quakerley knew little from personal experience for he had been too young to remember them. As he grew older and his father, on the occasions when he came home for his holidays from the Green Point Academy for the Sons of Gentlemen, talked to him with that restraint which on such occasions is almost natural between father and son, he found that he had almost as many ties with England as with the country of his birth. His mother, from whom he had learned Dutch simultaneously with English, was a calm, silent woman, so sure of herself and so convinced of her perfect equality with her husband that she never discussed these relations with her son, who in time had come to accept her own straightforward standard—a standard which other aristocrats of the Valley approved of. Old Charles Quakerley's wife came from a high-bred, reasonably proud lineage, socially and culturally as far removed from the ruck of Dutch colonists as he himself had been superior to the majority of the 1820 settlers. She had married her English lover with the intention of sharing his, not making him share her, life. As a result of this decision, which old Charles had neither asked for nor quite approved of, the intimacy between her own relations and her husband and children had gradually slackened. Young Andrew learned to like and respect his maternal grandfather, whose English was rudimentary just as old Charles's Dutch was meagre, and to feel at ease in the company of his numerous maternal aunts and uncles, but his mother had never encouraged him to grow more intimate with them so that he could really feel that he was of them and they were of him. Her attitude had always been rather a defensive, negative one, which her husband found perfectly reasonable but which her son had never troubled himself to analyse. It was long after he had married that his father had discussed the point with him one day, and the discussion had been a revelation to him.

'Your mother's point of view, my boy,' the old man had said in his precisely intoned voice, 'now would you believe it, I found it demn'd quaint, once. Now I can allow for it. You see, Andy, there's such a thing as breeding and quality, and when that's on a level, why, shiver me, my boy, there's not much else that matters. You're lucky—I can say it without boastfulness for my share in it has been little enough—you're lucky in having clean blood on both sides of you, and good at that. Why, demn it, your mother's grandfather came from the same house as Lamoral van Egmont, and ... well, well, it's not for me to boast of the Quakerleys. So there's no difference between good English and good Dutch and good anything else, but your mother holds—God bless her for it—that a woman should stand by her man and cleave unto him, as the Scripture puts it, "Thy country shall be my country" and that sort of thing as in *Ruth*, you know. And because you cannot see anything of my people here, and cannot become intimate with your Quakerley cousins six thousand miles away, she thinks that it is not fair that you should see too much of her folk. A quaint notion, my boy, but women take these patsies and no harm's done with this. Mark you, Andy, when it comes to demn'd pride there's not much—a sliver this way or that way makes no odds—to choose between us.'

So young Andrew had grown up in a home where English and Colonial Dutch tradition had seemed to mingle, although, as a matter of fact, the English element supplied by his father, by the literature that was chiefly read, by the language and to some extent by the daily formularies, could hardly weigh against the preponderating Dutch influence, especially in an environment where, outside the immediate home circle, the colonial tradition ruled. But Andrew felt, very early in his adolescence when in his quiet, introspective way he had tried to grapple with such things, that his father's philosophy, which affirmed the oneness of all traditions founded on equivalent principles, was essentially sound.

His early manhood had been spent on the farm, but in such close touch with the Village that he had virtually come to associate himself more with the urban than with the rural section. No other farmer in the District had possibly such intimate interests with the Village as he, and in time these interests were enlarged and added to as he found it necessary to invest his profits. In the middle of the last century the difficulties in the way of investing them safely were perhaps greater than they are at present, and for obvious reasons the Quakerley money remained in the District. Only much later when old Charles had been buried in the little English churchyard, where his Dutch wife already lay, had his son found investments outside that promised a larger and more lucrative yield. The discovery of diamonds along the Vaal River had brought about a great development of trade, and had led to a rapid expansion of which the Valley had felt the repercussions. Andrew had journeyed to the capital and looked into things, using his shrewd common sense and his inherited caution, and had expended a thousand pounds in the purchase of shares. He had followed this up with equally judicious investments, buying not for speculative purposes, for his temperament was not that of the gambler, but for investment. So fortunate, or so shrewd, had he been that in his old age he could look back with complacency upon his manner of employing that talent which had been granted him. He was a rich man—far richer than the Village, who looked upon him as a well-to-do resident, supposed—a man able to indulge in what he pleased without constantly referring to the counterfoils of his cheque-book to find out how much he had spent.

That fortunate position was attained when he was already an old man, a confirmed inhabitant of the Village, though still the owner of the family farm and still entitled to call himself a farmer. During the years that preceded it his energies had at first been concentrated on his agricultural interests, which he dutifully supervised without, however, feeling enthusiastic about them. Later on, when it was possible to delegate these to paid helpers, very much after the manner in which his father had acted, he had cut himself loose from his country interests, without altogether separating himself from them, and retired to the Village, where he had built himself a moderately fine house and had set himself to plan and establish a really fine garden, his one ambition, his single enthusiasm, from boyhood upwards. The artist in him, struggling for expression, had tried various means of becoming a creator without finding the satisfaction of succeeding with any. There remained his love of gardening, something more specialised than what he could achieve on the farm where conditions of climate and soil made it impossible to concentrate on the very points to which he attached so much importance. As soon as he knew that he was independent, that he had the means to be care-free and to indulge his hobby, he had decided to give himself up to it and to attempt the realisation of the dreams of his boyhood.

Circumstances were favourable. His father and mother were dead; his two daughters, finished at an expensive private school at the capital, much preferred town life, and his wife had always found the farm too quiet and uneventful for the life that she was determined to live. His sister, Joan, who had never married but who had devoted herself wholly to her parents, to the father with whom she had much more in common than had her brother, and to her invalid, arthritic mother, would doubtless have been perfectly content to remain at the farm, where she had spent a quiet, calm life from girlhood to middle age. But she had not demurred to the change, and in the new house in the Village she had found congenial occupation. It was Joan who ran his establishment, efficiently, smoothly, without fuss or worry, very much along the lines in which his mother, during her lifetime, had managed his father's house. Alice, his wife, who had never taken kindly to the dull routine of housekeeping, acquiesced contentedly in this devolution which left her free to play the part of hostess and *grande dame* to which she aspired, but for which she was scarcely fitted by nature or education. Old Charles Quakerley would never have admitted, even to his best friend, that his son had married beneath him; a Quakerley simply could not do a thing like that, for naturally a scion of the house ennobled the fortunate female whom he married. But old Charles in his own mind had never had any doubts about the innate vulgarity of 'daughter-in-law,' while his wife, an equally shrewd judge of character, had secretly regretted the marriage. Both, however, had made the best of the situation, and had been helped immensely by the tact and self-sacrificing action of their daughter who had taken her sister-in-law in hand and unconsciously moulded her into something which would ultimately be a credit to the Quakerleys. Joan had succeeded in her efforts, and before her father's death she had harvested the gratitude which he felt for her help.

'She'll do,' the old man had said reflectively, two days before his death when he sat on the padded arm-chair under the homestead oaks, idly fumbling with a pipe which he could no longer use. 'There was a time when I had my doubts, Joanie. That time I took her to Cape Town, you know, and gave her her fling at Admiralty House. I thought then that she would never do for our Andy, my dear. So did your mother. So did old Martin, demn him. But it's owing to you, my dear, and ... well, it makes me a trifle happier. There, child, get me the Terence and let's have some more of *Phormio*.'

Mrs Andrew Quakerley—no one discriminated nowadays for there was no need to do so, there being only one Mrs Quakerley on the scene—had profited by her sister-in-law's example and precept. She made a passably good great lady in the environment where comparisons were difficult because the younger generation no longer had before it the means of comparison. With the exception of a rather florid taste in dress, a penchant for gaudy colours and for showy jewelry, and some minor solecisms of speech, the stray lapses into the habits of long ago when she had assisted in serving drinks behind a counter, her manners and demeanour could be accounted correct. She still spoke her mind freely, still displayed a degree of intolerance in her opinions that was by no means a true index to her real charitable, good-natured disposition, and still, on occasion, gave way to passion that threw her into early Victorian hysterics. But she had aged agreeably, for the years had toned her beauty into something richer, patinated with the geniality that is the result of placid self-satisfaction and the consciousness of having nobly done one's duty.

That she could truthfully declare she had done. She had been to Andrew a good wife. She had brought up his two daughters with credit to him and to herself, and she had loved him passionately and lost, through the years, nothing of the devotion she had lavished on him from the first. If she had a grievance against him, a possibility which she scrupled to admit to herself, it was that he had done so little for himself. According to Mrs Quakerley's opinion, Andrew should have interested himself not in the childish delights of gardening, which were all very well as a hobby but led nowhere, but in material matters which might bring fame, reputation, an official position in the capital, a seat in the cabinet, the prefix 'Honourable' and the possibility of a decorative title in which she too might share. It had galled her when he had refused to stand for Parliament; it had enraged her when he had declined honours thrust upon him. Andrew had no ambition; he was too meek and brotherly, she had almost said too mild and motherly, for a man cut out by nature and by circumstances to be a leader of men, a force in the community, a power in the land. More than once she had tried to spur him on, to stir in him something of the spirit of daring and doing which she had recognised in her late father-in-law. She had even enlisted the half-hearted co-operation of Joan in the attempt to make him accept a nomination for the Legislative Council, but he had treated the matter as a joke, and the honour had gone to old Gerster whose English was fragmentary and whose manners were terrible.

Andrew had never aspired to leadership. He had taken no interest whatever in local politics, and the only honour, if honour it could be called, which he had accepted was the appointment of Justice of the Peace, which he felt would widen his sphere of usefulness to his fellow men. When the first candidate for Parliament had to be nominated, in the early fifties of the nineteenth century, he had been approached, and his father had favoured the notion that he should stand. But he had resolutely refused, and the District had elected a well-to-do farmer who bore the nickname of 'Gallows-Gecko' because once upon a time he had helped the authorities to execute a European murderer.

To one acquainted with the political movements of the time and the place, such want of interest might have appeared inexplicable except on the assumption that he was callous to possibilities lying dormant in the situation. That assumption would not have been correct, for Andrew, with all his devotion to his hobby, was a shrewd, practical fellow, very well acquainted with the tendencies operative in the District and with the opinions of his fellow citizens. The period from the early fifties to the late eighties was one of emergence from tutelage into the responsibilities of constitutional representative government. It saw the creation, on the borders of the old Colony, of two sister states, the nearer one still favouring, to a certain extent, the tradition of the south, the farther one, on the contrary, developing rapidly a tradition of its own, and one altogether strange to the conception of constitutionalism cherished in the Colony. It was inevitable that the purely local or regional political issues should become tinged with a graver aspect as the differences between these traditional outlooks developed. The process of development was very gradual, almost imperceptible to those who did not know the history of the District nor the change in the nature of its population. To Andrew, who had lived all his life in the Valley, the change was marked and disturbing. The older, more solid element, characterised by a sturdy independence of opinion, a strong sense of communal solidarity, and an innate respect for constituted authority, was gradually dying out. It was being replaced by a looser element, less responsive to the call of tradition. That was after all the case everywhere, for economic and industrial changes had effected similar developments the world over.

The District, the Valley, was solidly Dutch. In the Village there lived half a dozen families whose home language was English, although none of their members, with one solitary exception, had been born in England. They were the descendants of the early settlers, and nearly all had contracted ties of kinship with Dutch and German families in the Colony. Their position was by no means anomalous, for from the first the Village had been predominantly English in its conventions, its outlook and its temperament. The District frankly accepted it as such, and no one had ever remarked upon it or objected to it, just as no one in the Village had ever jeered at the District for being predominantly Dutch. On festive occasions, notably on the anniversary of the Queen's birthday, Village and District joined hands in loyal celebration. All the English of the Village, with the exception of the one English-born inhabitant, spoke both languages, and the landowners and most of the younger generation of the District understood both. There were no differences wide enough and grave enough to occasion antagonism between the two sections, between which there existed a co-operation which was based on mutuality of interest and aim.

In other parts of the Colony there was marked friction between the two sections, friction that could be put down to the political agitation of parties, to the introduction of canting slogans for electioneering purposes, and to the inevitable competition and rivalry between urban and rural areas. But these influences, Andrew told himself, should not be operative in the District, where there had never been, and possibly never would be, a clash of interests with the Village. Yet the permeation of the subtle poison of sectional disagreement seemed to affect the District and insensibly, unconsciously, to spread into the Village, disturbing its calm quietude, and raising at times issues which threatened to interfere with the friendly relations between English and Dutch.

The last election had been a hotly contested one, and although Andrew had taken a part in it, he had never been able to see what all the bother had been about. For years Gallows-Gecko had been returned, together with his colleague member, a carpet-bagging doctor who paid flying visits to his constituency and had been greatly popular, unopposed, since there was no one who doubted his ability or questioned his right to be the representative of the District and the Village. But the old man had died suddenly of apoplexy, and things, within a few years, had changed with amazing rapidity. In the District a Farmers' Association had been formed, which was in reality a branch of a great political movement organised by the rural electors to safeguard their interests. It was not a sectional party so much as a regional one, but it rapidly assumed the complexion of a sectional association because, while the rural population was essentially Dutch, the urban electorate was essentially English.

It affected the District, as it affected all other districts in the Colony. It presented the electors with new issues, to be discussed with amazing vehemence, issues in themselves slight but in their ultimate effects graver than those who had so lightly raised them could by any stretch of the imagination have foreseen.

Andrew Quakerley had shaken his head when he heard of these things. He had almost decided to give heed to his wife's constant urgings that he should take a hand in the game of politics. In the Valley men knew him, respected him; some were old and close friends, with whom he had never had a disagreement, for he knew their ways of thinking and he was convinced of their innate honesty.

He discussed the matter with his intimate friends, who urged him to stand. But they could not deny that it would have to be a contest, and one in which feeling would probably run high. After considering the matter carefully, he declined to allow himself to be nominated, and threw the weight of his personal influence, which counted for much, in favour of the more moderate candidate.

The election was fought with energy, but hardly with any ill-feeling, and reflecting on the proceedings after everything was over and the more moderate candidate had secured the seat, Andrew asked himself if his forebodings had been exaggerated. A little excitement was inevitable in any contested election, and here after all the pent-up feelings needed some safety valve for their escape. He was glad that he had declined to mix himself up in the business. He would certainly have been elected, but his election would have created some ill-feeling, and would have bored him very much. He had no wish to go to Cape Town and attend committees and listen to the interminable speeches in the House of Assembly. At his age it was stupid to think of such things.

Nevertheless he absented himself from his beloved garden and took the post-cart to the nearest railway station, a hundred odd miles away, on a fleeting visit to the capital. He wanted some roses, a new araucaria that had been advertised in a seedsman's catalogue. Not that he would see it rival the giants already glorifying his garden. Araucarias grow slowly, and he had not got very much time before him. But it might be worth while getting it, all the same.

At Cape Town he discussed things with his friends, of whom he had many. They took a gloomy view of the situation, but were hardly explicit in their statements. He gathered that it was as he had thought, a clash between northern and southern tradition.

At a cheerful hostelry, which had an interesting menagerie at the back, he lunched with the Prime Minister and several of the Dutch Party. He came away tired and feeling that he had done well in declining to mix himself up with politics so long as there were better things, like gardens, in which he could interest himself.

For there still remained his garden, the wonderful garden he had created, the solace and comfort of his ageing years. No one could take that from him; nothing could destroy that!

Chapter 3

Andrew Quakerley's house stood at the western end of the Village flanked, with a respectable interval between, on either side by a church house, the one belonging to the van Aard family and the other to a widow farm-woman who had leased it to the postmaster. All the Village houses were thatched, with pointed gables, solid walls, and a *stoep* on the northern aspect, facing the front street which was little more than a broad footpath, and overlooking the gardens. At the sides and in front and at the back of the houses grew trees, old oaks with gnarled trunks shedding in winter-time their myriads of dead leaves on to the front street; evergreen eucalypti, whose leaves twisted to meet the sun's rays, so that the mass of foliage presented a problem to any painter who tried to capture it on canvas; giant magnolias with broad burnished leaves; tall, straight Lombardy poplars, skimpy Grevilleas blossoming yellow in spring; and shapely white wattles graceful in outline of feathery branch and well-shaped crown. On the *stoeps* grew orange and tangarine trees, in holes made in the flat sandstone paving. Immediately beyond the *stoep* ran the front street, and beyond that coursed the sparkling Village watercourse bridged by rustic traverses of bamboo laths overlaid with sods. Beyond that lay the gardens.

Every house in that long, straggling street possessed its garden, and every garden in the Village was well cultivated, with a dignity of its own that seemed to resent meanness and to challenge comparison with the greenery of the veld in winter. Most of them had orchards and all, at their farther end, miniature barley fields meant for the production of green forage.

Of all the gardens, that of Andrew Quakerley was indubitably the finest as it was also the largest and best cared for. It comprised several acres, a far larger space than that allotted to its fellows on either side, and extended right down to the banks of the sluggishly flowing river whose waters joined those of the larger Valley stream three miles beyond the Village. It gained, like all the other gardens, its water supply from the furrow, from which subsidiary longitudinal channels had been constructed towards the broad drainage furrow at the lower end, from which again ran smaller channels that ended in the river.

Andrew Quakerley had selected the site of his residence with great care, mainly concerned not so much with the situation of the house which had to be in line with the other houses, as with the soil on which he proposed to grow his exotics and where he intended to found his garden. He had built his house in accordance with the generally accepted traditional convention of the Village, which implied comfort, quiet, shade and protection from the fierce summer sun, and ample security from the harassing east wind that in autumn and early spring whirled the leaves off the tress and danced palsies on the *stoeps*. Tradition made it imperative that the walls should be high, substantial, thick; that the windows should be shuttered from outside with jalousies; that the roofs should be smoothly thatched, so cunningly and so firmly that even the boisterousness of the wind could not disturb the fine bevelling of the eaves; that the rooms should be large, spatial, suggestive of wide, well-shaded anchoring places lying under the pleasant shelter of over-arching boughs; that the ceiling should be of cedar, planed and polished, and the floors of deal stained with the logwood of protea bark; that the kitchen should have a large, old-fashioned fireplace, even if it was no longer necessary to use chains in it nor to make a wood fire upon it, and that there should be ample pantry and cellar space. Tradition could be indulged, for he had the means and the leisure to build his house according to his desire.

It must be confessed that Andrew had not troubled himself much about the details of his new residence. He had been content to leave these in the hands of the contractor, who had also been the architect, and who had found that Mrs Quakerley was much harder to satisfy on some points in connection with the building than her husband. Alice had wanted everything of the best, for in the new house she had decided she would outshine all her neighbours and prove to the world at large and to the Village in particular that the Quakerleys were something more than mere Valley folk. Andrew had allowed her practically a free hand, and her interference had resulted in making the house a warren of rooms, connected by narrow corridors that meant much more work and worry for the housekeeper than the conventional model would have given. The rococo gables had been her suggestion, and Andrew admitted that they gave to the house, when it was finished, a touch of distinction which the houses of his neighbours lacked. But he had grumbled at the multiplicity of rooms and would much have preferred a smaller dwelling.

His own interest lay chiefly in the surroundings of his house. These were his care, and he had supervised the laying out of the little estate, to which he had meant to retire when the time came, with keen attention to detail and with meticulous consideration of the conditions which would be required to secure perfection. He had selected the erven at the western end of the Village deliberately, although at the time when he had bought them that part of the settlement was not considered to be the most fashionable. The centre of the street, where the government had built a house for the magistrate and where the Rekkers had erected their distinguished looking church house, was reputed the finest site, but an outcrop of sandstone ran diagonally across the gardens there, and it would have needed blasting and excavating to suit his purpose. The western property was rich alluvial, the age-old silt of the two rivers rankly overgrown with sedge and matted grass, giving promise, under proper cultivation, of a rich yield; sheltered, too, by old oaks planted long ago when the first settlers had developed it, and owning, near the river, some of the original shrub, waterwood, wild willow, and coppices of dark green rhus bushes clustered over with trailing smilax and bordered with huge brunsvigias which in winter sprouted forth their large leathery leaves, and in summer showed the splendours of their pink lily-like blossoms. It held grassland and sand, loam, clay soil, and gravel; it possessed everything that he wanted for his garden, and in time he could make from it a glorious estate, such as he had dreamed of in those boyhood days when he had admired the marvels of the Baron's demesne on the Kloof Nek.

With an enthusiasm that was akin to love, that was love itself because it was the sublimated worship of beauty, he had taken his task in hand from the moment he had signed the deed of purchase. Gradually he had arranged for his farm to be independent of his own management. While his father was still alive there could be no thought of leaving it, for old Charles had no desire to reside in the Village, and his son had no wish to displease him by suggesting such a change. But old Charles knew perfectly well that the new house being built at the Village was destined to be the headquarters of the Quakerleys in the future and in a sense he approved of it, and tacitly allowed it to be understood that he had no great objection to the plan provided its execution was delayed until he himself was out of the way.

'You will bury me in the churchyard, of course,' he had told his son, nonchalantly, as a gentleman talks about such things. 'I do not like this custom of lying in farm ground, boy. Not that the consecration matters much to me, but your mother lies in the churchyard and you must bury me next to her. That's why I bought the plot there. By the way, the gardenias want pruning, and you might see to it when you go in.'

Andrew had said 'Yes, father,' dutifully, and had journeyed out specially the next day to prune the gardenia bush over his mother's grave in the little English churchyard that surrounded the little English church, so quaintly reminiscent of those parish churches of his father's country which he had never visited. The Quakerleys had an interest in church and churchyard, for old Charles's money had acquired the land and contributed towards the building. It was right and proper that the Quakerleys should lie there, even though Andrew's mother, who had always remained a member of the Dutch Reformed Church and had been buried with the ceremonies of that denomination, might have considered it alien ground. There was no proof that she had ever done so. She had taken her marriage vows solemnly and had felt herself in life one with her husband, and desired in death to lie where he himself, when his time came, would choose to lie.

Under Andrew's fostering care his estate had improved so much that before the thatch of the new house had accumulated enough sand to give harbourage to the wild plants that yearned to grow upon it, the Village unanimously agreed that Quakerley's place was the finest in the District. When his father died the house was finished and the garden already in course of development. Andrew moved rapidly after that. He had brought his family to the Village and had installed them in the new house, which he had furnished partly with old furniture from the homestead and partly, out of deference to his wife's wishes, with new furniture manufactured in Cape Town. He still had duties at the farm, but it had not taken him long to find an efficient and dependable manager to whom these duties could be entrusted, leaving him finally free to devote himself entirely to his new interests and pleasure. He could not bring himself to sell the farm although he had had tempting offers for it, for it was his ancestral home, and he had something of his mother's attachment to the past.

His new hobby, which in reality was the avatar of his youthful yearning to plant a garden, engrossed him almost to the exclusion of other interests. He threw himself with avidity into the work of planning, perfecting, and ennobling the magnificent creation which he had in mind. Long ago he had laid, in imagination, the foundations of it, sketched in outline the salient features, filled in the details, and studied the combinations upon which he had decided. The comparatively small space in which he had to work prevented the conception of anything on a grandiose scale, but that did not disturb him, for he did not wish to emulate, in quantity or extent, the horticultural achievements of Buitenzorg or the Company's garden at Cape Town. He wanted quality, a choice, delightfully patterned series of plots, in which practical utility should neighbour aesthetically satisfying arrangement, a collector's garden more than a nurseryman's, a dilettante's more than a professional's. He spent anxious hours in considering how the best effects could be obtained, whether by massing or by single, ungrouped sorts, and eagerly read and assimilated everything that could be of help in arriving at a wholly satisfactory decision. All this preliminary work took time, time that was not wholly wasted for it allowed for the growth and development of his trees and sheltering hedges.

With these he had been fortunate. An old quince hedge ran round the property, and it needed only pruning, restoration with new cuttings here and there, and careful nursing to get this into proper order. Close to the water furrow, overshadowing the old bath house which was a relic of the original homestead that had stood on the one erf but which had been demolished to make room for the new house, grew a fine magnolia, one of those magnificent efforts of nature to combine a flowering shrub with the dignity and impressiveness of a stately tree. Its large waxed flowers glistened imperiously between its burnished foliage and its smooth, virescent trunk sheered upwards in sharp contrast to the whitewashed wall of the bath house. Lower down a row of oak trees spread their strong branches to meet a younger neighbouring row which in time would make of the passage between them a delightfully shaded avenue. Behind the bath house grew, wild and tangled, a small forest of bamboo, fed by the overflow water which ran through a little gutter into the affluent channel, but so often overran into the surrounding soil that it had made a small pond filmed over with sweet-smelling waterweed and fringed with masses of tall arum lilies. A clump of date palms, graceful and dignified, rose against the sky still further down the erf, and the remains of what had been a fair-sized orchard of apple, pear and citrus trees grew close to it.

Such was the virgin material with which he had to work, and once he had thought out his plan, and sketched the broad outline of his scheme, it was comparatively easy for him to adjust his designs to what he found growing and dovetail these valuable assets into them. He started by planting trees, selecting their positions carefully so as to give room for what he wanted later on. The orchard was re-fashioned, the best of the old trees being left and the unnecessary specimens ruthlessly uprooted; the vacant spaces were restocked. The sheltering hedges, of Native plumbago whose pale delicate blue blooms practically all the year round, or of wild tecoma flowering profusely in orange in early spring, were planted to shield selected plots from the wind. Australian myrtle and the sweet-smelling low-growing variety ridged the smaller plots. He corresponded with foreign growers, soliciting cuttings and seed from Java and Japan, from England and India, and even from America, in the attempt to collect a selection that would be distinctive, however little it could claim to be catholic. It was not his intention to make a botanical garden in the ordinary sense of the term. That would have meant more space, more time, and more unprofitable work than he cared to give. But he did want to make his garden as closely akin to that ideal garden of which he had dreamed when he had fashioned it in miniature on the sodden sand of the veld in the days when he had been in knickerbockers and had known nothing about the Latin names of plants.

Now, when he was an old man, nearing the fourscore years allotted to the average denizen of this world, he could look with pride, with that cheerful satisfaction of an idealist who sees the realisation of at least a part of his ideal, upon his garden. Many years had gone to the making of it. Hard work, unremitting care, watchful attention, and a jealous, unabating vigilance had shaped it into the beautiful, satisfying thing it was.

The Village took pride in it, but familiarity with its many excellencies had blunted local appreciation of its merits, which were perhaps better recognised by visitors than by residents. Abroad, the Quakerley garden was well enough known to those who took an interest in such things. At Cape Town its virtues were lauded by the government botanist, and endorsed by the comparatively few rivals who in the Peninsula had attempted to achieve similar success on a smaller or larger scale. They drew comparisons between Andrew's garden and others and these were not altogether unfavourable to the former. Everyone who knew about such matters, and was competent to judge, declared that Mr Quakerley's garden was the one thing that raised the Village into a position above that of other communities in the Colony. That, perhaps, was not quite fair, for the Village was itself a beautiful spot. It lay in an amphitheatre of blue mountains whose weathered outlines stood out strikingly against the blue background of sky; mountains whose sheer escarpments were glorified, in the early morning or late afternoon, by colour combinations so startlingly magnificent that admiration was for the moment overwhelmed by astonishment; mountains that in winter were white-topped, and in spring were redolent of aromatic scents and gorgeous with a profusion of wild flowers; mountains that from time immemorial had borne on their high cliff ledges, four thousand feet above sea-level, the ponderous cedars whose trunk girth exceeds the combined clasp of three men's encircling arms. From these mountains came the river that ran at the foot of the gardens, coursing slowly along a bed that had altered its position from time to time, so that at varying distances from the stream there remained huge water-holes, reputed in former times to have been the haunt of hippopotami. Between the river and the mountains lay broken ground, rising immediately in front of the Village into a rounded Karroo hill, whose uniform brown in summer was suddenly changed, in spring, to vivid green when the lush grass, refreshed by the early rains, sprang up on the fertile soil. Miles to the west the river joined the greater River that ran through the Valley. Both streams, in flood time, formed impassable barriers to traffic, but the smaller one was spanned by a wooden wagon bridge at the extreme end of the Village.

Set in an environment of green, the little Village, with its neatly thatched, cleanly whitewashed houses, gleamed like a jewel. One came upon it suddenly, as one ascended the sharp spur over which the main road wound its way, and saw below the variegated gardens, with waving palms, dark oaks, lighter green orange groves, the greys of the underside of the leaves of the silver poplar lightly stirred by the wind, the tall spire of the Dutch Reformed Church, the flat glistening roof of the gaol, the green expanse of the treeless park laid out, but never finished, in honour of Queen Victoria's Jubilee, the blue mountains to the north, and the white ribbon of the River. Its beauty stirred, held; the peace and calm of it touched and thrilled, as a placid expanse of water, in which are reflected the shapes of far-off things, touches and thrills.

Nor did a nearer acquaintance with its details remove that first impression of attractiveness. The squalidity of the Native location, the barrenness of the dune lands immediately behind the second row of houses, which had no gardens and fronted the main road, and the ugliness of some of these later creations with their iron roofs, seemed but to bring into prominence the intrinsic allure of the older part of the Village where every house was thatched, tree-shaded, and garden-environed. The primitive simplicity of these older buildings, their solidity and their dignity accentuated their charm. Especially on a hot summer's day, when the heat was stifling and the leaves of the eucalyptus trees slanted downwards, with their edges turned towards the glare, in a protective attempt to withstand the sun, the Village attracted by its oasis-like beauty, its impression of decorous coolness, its charm of dappled shade and sunlight filtered through green leaves.

That is why it was perhaps unfair to call Andrew Quakerley's garden, fine as it undoubtedly was, the one item that gave to the Village its distinction. It enhanced the prestige of the Village, but that prestige was already conferred by the environment, by its own whitewashed, black-thatched houses, and by the simple dignity of its rusticity and old-fashioned unpretentiousness. Few great agitations had stirred it. Its inhabitants had lived placidly and peacefully for half a hundred years, and although it had had, in its early days, sufficient of strife and movement, of peril even and adventure, the latter years of the century had given it little disturbance beyond the passing emotions evoked by political elections and local disagreements. It represented much of what was best and most worthy in the Colony, a quiet out-of-the-way village, mildly famous, within a limited circle, for the excellence of its wine, for the flavour of its peaches and seedling oranges, and for the garden which Andrew Quakerley had created.

Chapter 4

In its eighty years of existence the Village had developed characteristics which, cumulatively, expressed its soul. It was somnolent, not with the sleepiness of repletion, but with the sense of complacency that is the result of victoriously overcoming small difficulties. The Village had matured like a fine Burgundy wine, in which time, climate, and repose mellow the acids into esters and the alcohols into aldehydes. Nothing revolutionary had ever happened in it. Tranquil through the years, it had devoted its energies to the tame villatic interests which had absorbed all its attention. It had concentrated upon them an enthusiasm and a forceful energy that elsewhere, directed into other channels, might have achieved great things.

Here, in an environment essentially peaceful, these factors had produced a stereotyped routine which had stamped the Village almost as indelibly as if someone had impressed upon it a gigantic official stencil. No one ever hurried in the Village. With the outside world it was in touch by its bi-weekly post. The post-cart, a two-wheeled hooded vehicle drawn by six mules and driven by a half-caste boy approaching middle age, arrived at the Village on Wednesdays and Saturdays, according to schedule precisely at four in the afternoon, but, in deference to the vagaries of the road, the weather, and the moods of the driver, usually much later, although the contract stipulated that a monetary fine could be exacted for every hour's delay. Its arrival was a matter of profound local interest, and from four o'clock the greater part of the male population crowded in the street opposite the post office, ostensibly for the purpose of being more expeditiously served with the mail but in reality to exchange gossip and to take preliminary stock of such strangers as might arrive in the post-cart. The nearest railway station to the Village was a hundred miles away, and the road lay across a steep and, in winter-time, owing to the clayey nature of the surfacing which facilitated skidding, a dangerous pass. Those who kept their own carts, wagons, and transport animals could traverse this stretch without relying upon the post-cart, but that meant a two days' journey and a considerable outlay. The busy Villager, who had to go to the capital, invariably made use of the post-cart, the fare for which was reasonably cheap while the time occupied in travelling by it was estimated to be the minimum necessary for the journey. The main road through the Village was the great northern artery running to the western part of the Colony, and on that account alone, if on no other, the Village could plume itself on being a centre of traffic, a half-way house between the capital and the lone outposts in the sandy, desolate areas beyond where the rainfall was sometimes calamitously frugal and the European population lamentably small.

All things that mature slowly carry in themselves a capacity for permanency. The Village was no exception to this rule, though few of its inhabitants would have been able to define just which of its prevailing characteristics were the more likely to endure. The old-fashioned air that nestled about it—the rococo gables of the brown-thatched houses, the trellised vines that made arbours in the gardens in summer time, the quaint dignity of wooden gates and *stoep* seats plaited with leathern stripes—all these would vanish before the onrushing tide of novelty which year by year broke down the old barriers and transformed the nooks and corners into open spaces, more sanitary perhaps but far less picturesque than what they had been before. Few of the Village inhabitants minded these inevitable changes, which came so slowly that their effects were hardly recognised before they had achieved such permanency that they could be reckoned as part and parcel of the environment.

Perhaps that was the tragedy of the Village—that it acquiesced in changes which it could not forbid, and while acquiescing, was incapable of realising what it lost.

For more than a hundred years—a great age in a Colony whose Nordic population could look back on merely little more than two centuries of effective occupation—the

Village had slept on, tranquilly, without upheaval. Its maturity had not lined it, nor scarred it with remembrances which it would much rather have forgotten. What it held in memory was wholly pleasant, satisfying the dull requirements of a community that regarded peace and content as the greatest possessions to be aspired to. Twice a year it held festival. On the outgoing of the old and the incoming of the new year, and on the twenty-fourth of May, the anniversary of the birth of the Sovereign Lady whose portrait hung in every withdrawing room, the Village put on its best clothes, furnished itself and its visitors with its best viands and liquors, and orated, publicly and in private, with much zest and real sincerity. Intermittently, three times a year, it became animated, when the surrounding population poured into it on the occasions of the periodical communion service or *Nagmaal*. It was true that this important event concerned more especially the Dutch-speaking section, for it was a festival of their church. As a matter of plain fact, however, it interested everyone. On Friday the carts and wagons began to outspan in the yards of the 'church houses' or in the open veld behind. Tents and improvised shelters were erected for those whom the church houses could not conveniently accommodate. The Village store worked overtime, and the few professional men did likewise, for the incoming flood of country visitors took this opportunity of profiting by the leisure and attention they could give to such duties as needed, for their due elaboration, the counsel or advice of attorney or doctor or agent. On the Saturday more carts and wagons came in, and the church bazaar took place— an important function most necessary for the proper increase of the funds from which the annual stipend of the pastor had to be paid. The visitors brought with them produce to be sold by public auction for the benefit of the church funds, and the Village auctioneer gave his services free, and made an entertainment of the business which was hugely enjoyed by all. Nor was it such a simple business as outsiders might have supposed it to be. On the contrary it was sometimes exceedingly complicated. Brother Marius, for example, might have brought a pumpkin of monstrous size in aid of the church funds, but as pumpkins are common enough, and grown by everyone who has any land, the demand for it could hardly be said to be eager, with the result that the real value of the vegetable would be assessed at a few pennies. For that it was knocked down by the auctioneer, to be immediately donated by the purchaser, re-auctioned, re-sold, re-donated, and re-bought, until the gathering had tired of that particular item, but not before the total income from it had far exceeded its intrinsic value.

On Saturday afternoon, the bustle and excitement died down, for at two o'clock the 'preparation service' started, and it was seemly and fitting that a pall of solemnity and seriousness should descend over the scene. At this service the new members of the church were formally presented to the congregation, having already been examined by the church council and privately admonished by the pastor. On the Saturday evening there would be a further service, while on the following day there would be no fewer than five services, a prayer meeting in the early morning before breakfast, the long and important communion service, lasting from nine o'clock until half past twelve, the thanksgiving service on Sunday afternoon, a special children's service following it, and the final evening service. The Village and the Valley took religion seriously but by no means sadly, and these *Nagmaal* gatherings were as much occasions for reunion and good fellowship as for the observance of ritual.

In practically unbroken sequence the Village had carried on since its establishment.

Its oldest inhabitant could not remember that the anniversary festival of Her Most Gracious Majesty Alexandrina Victoria—for it was customary to give to the Queen her full name—had ever been omitted, or that the *Nagmaal* gatherings had ever been postponed. Legend stated that one or both had at times been celebrated with less unequivocal enjoyment, if that term may justifiably be applied to the observation of events so dignified in themselves, than usual. When the Valley had been ravaged by the outbreak of smallpox, eighty years back, the attendances had been small at the *Nagmaal* service. When men's minds had been disturbed by the events in the eastern part of the Colony, fifty years back, and when agitators had toured the District and inveighed against the authority and prestige of the good Queen, there had been difficulties about arranging the birthday festival, but these had been overcome, by tact and common sense and pertinent, timeous references to the authority of Scripture, and since then nothing had marred the good feeling and camaraderie displayed on such occasions.

That was due in part to the complacency of the Village itself, and in part to the good-humoured logicality of its inhabitants. From the first it had assumed the inherent equality of the two sections that comprised its little commonwealth. Its isolation from the great world outside had helped it to be tolerant, quickened its understanding of common difficulties, and enhanced its sincere desire to live peaceably. Solitariness may at times be a wholesome check on assertiveness and communal impudence. There is in communities, as there is in the individual, a consciousness of effort, a desire to achieve. Such consciousness is not always furiously active. In the case of the Village it was largely dormant, but it was there, nevertheless, and it influenced the life and the ideals of its community.

That, very possibly, was the main reason why the Village had remained practically untouched by the friction, erroneously styled 'racialism,' evident in other colonial centres where Dutch and English lived in community of interests. There is no racial difference between these two sections. Both are branches of the same stem, closer akin in blood, language and temperament than is usually taken for granted. What is mistakenly called racial conflict between them is merely the clash of cultural divergencies which owe their origin to differences in training and in the interpretation of a tradition common to both. Naturally, where the exigencies of environment have forced into dominance one or other of these different interpretations, with the result that there is an unconscious insistence upon its presumed truth to the exclusion of the equally presumable warranty of its opposite, there results, inevitably, an antagonism which, even if it is not expressed, is usually felt, and sometimes resented. On the other hand, where communal interests are so intertwined, and intercourse between the two sections is so frank and free as to obviate undue stress upon the differences in conception and interpretation, the tendency is for both sections to develop side by side without creating a sense of inferiority in one and an overbearing pride in the other.

That, fortunately, was the case in the Village, and to a lesser extent in the District of which it was the official centre. Although the community was preponderantly Dutch, in the sense that most of the inhabitants spoke Afrikaans, it had originally had a large accretion of English settlers, who had freely intermarried with their colonial-born neighbours, and had, on the whole, earned the respect, and not merely the toleration, of their fellow *burghers*. Indeed so complex were the relationships in the

District, and therefore also in the Village, that it would have been difficult for many of the inhabitants to regard themselves as wholly Dutch or wholly English. Nearly every family in the District was allied to some other family by ties of marriage and blood relationship, and those that were not so allied could yet claim kinship with families in other parts of the colony. The Quakerleys were a case in point. Although there was no one in the District with whom Andrew could establish blood affinity directly, there were some who were distantly related to him, on his mother's side, through alliance with third cousins of his maternal grandfather, the prosperous Stellenbosch farmer who had given shelter and security, and afterwards his youngest daughter, to the wilful young English midshipman who had deserted his ship in False Bay.

The Village, had it possessed the ability, the desire, and the knowledge necessary for self-analysis, would have recognised that the absence of sectional friction, of cultural clash, within its community was much less the effect of the wide, Christian tolerance which it sometimes vaunted than of the realisation that there was really nothing at all to quarrel about and that the interests of both sections were identical.

There remained the political situation. In the late nineties of the nineteenth century, the Colony had had almost fifty years of responsible and representative government and the District had found it good, eminently suitable for its needs, and undoubtedly to its advantage. There was, by general consent, no outstanding matter on which issue could be joined. There were numberless minor points on which there might exist differences of opinion, but so far as the Colony itself, and the District as a part of the Colony, were concerned, there was nothing upon which the Village could concentrate with the fanatical enthusiasm with which men concentrate upon a bone of contention. Outside the limits of the Colony, however, the case was different. In the north lay the two Republics of the Orange Free State and the Transvaal. While their internal affairs were of comparatively little interest to the District and the Village, the rumbles of what took place in one of them reverberated through the land, and faint echoes of them reached even into the Valley. The discovery of gold and the influx of many settlers into the Republic beyond the Vaal had created a new situation which all men recognised as disturbing to the state of mind that desired nothing better than to be left alone in untrammelled possession of its own conventions and tradition. It was not that the Village and District wholly and unreservedly approved of those conventions or wholeheartedly subscribed to that tradition. In fact both mildly deprecated such innate conservatism as that which was presumed to exist in the Transvaal, and as mildly thought that new settlers, so long as they paid taxes, were law abiding, and of European descent, should not be prohibited from having some say in the management of affairs. But they refused to take the situation seriously, or to contemplate that disturbance so far away from their borders could, by any stretch of the imagination, be considered to involve themselves.

The Village had never been enthusiastic on the question of republicanism. It, as well as the District as a whole, looked upon that question as altogether outside practical politics, and regarded the discussion of it as just as much a waste of time and energy as had been expended upon other political issues of equal impracticability. Its daily life was, therefore, not visibly perturbed by political or party strife, and the vicarious interest which it felt in quarrels that stirred other communities with which it had far-off bonds of contact, manifested itself in amicable debates which never transgressed the limits imposed by a tolerance as sincere as it was natural to folk who appreciated the cultural differences between the two sections.

The District, perhaps, felt a certain complacent pride in the fact that the party to which its sympathies, as a whole, went out was now the party in power, under the chieftainship of a man whose reputation transcended that of the republican leaders in the north. Mr Rhodes, the Prime Minister, had visited and had been charmed by the Valley. His geniality, his bluff, direct manner, and his evident goodwill towards them, had impressed the farmers and towns-people alike. The fact that he, an Englishman of the English, had allied himself with the party of their choice, the Farmers' Party, generally known as the South African Bond, and that he was shaping his policy in conformity with the wishes expressed at a recent conference, had done much to satisfy them, and they were quite content to entrust the direction of affairs to him.

Chapter 5

On an early December morning in the year of grace 1895 Andrew Quakerley stood on the *stoep* of his house, looking down over the blossoming gardenia hedge on the glory of his garden below.

It was a brilliant, sunshiny morning, with the promise of a load of heat later on, but now fragrant with the varied scents of summer flowers and vocal with the music of the finches aswing on their nests in the poplar trees. A haze of blue shimmered over the outlines of the high mountains beyond the river, softening the patches of colour on the cliffs where oxidation had painted them luridly and darkening the shadows in the deep, overgrown ravines. A cloudless sky spread overhead, translucent in its shimmering intensity of pale beryl.

As he stood idly looking at his garden, Andrew Quakerley presented the appearance of a man who had grown old with singularly little disturbance of his serene virility. Neither his face nor his figure gave evidence of senility. His neatly trimmed beard, with some reddish strands still apparent among the grey, his sparkling eyes, his clear, wholesome skin, and his loose, well-made tweed suit which set off his tall, spare, but finely proportioned figure, combined to give the impression of an alert, healthy, vigorous old man, whose oldness had in it no attribute of decline but suggested a rich maturity, mellowed by time and dignified by age. A handsome, well-shaped man, would have been the verdict of whoever saw him standing there, and no stranger would have guessed that he had recently celebrated the seventy-fifth anniversary of his birthday. There lay upon him a calmness, a serenity of bearing, and a dignity that stamped him as a gentleman by birth and upbringing, and in his face the forceful placidity of one who knows his own strength.

Beside him, modestly hanging back a bit, as convention and good manners demanded, stood his grandson, Charlie Crest, a slender, supple boy whose open shirt revealed the smooth white of a skin not yet bronzed by the semi-tropical sun, and the marked contrast between bone and flesh that is the hallmark of a lad just emerging from childhood. Six months ago Andrew had welcomed back his widowed youngest daughter who had returned from Australia to spend that period of indecision when the executors are struggling to settle the estate and when there is no certainty that what has been left will be sufficient to warrant the setting up of an independent establishment, in her father's house. Andrew had welcomed the family without realising what its intrusion into the routine of his ordinary household life would mean. He had lived so long in the companionship of his wife and his unmarried sister that he had grown accustomed to a quiet regularity which brooked no interruption and resented change. The arrival of three young people totally strange to the customs and prejudices of the Village had at first jarred upon him, with the result that he had devoted himself more to his garden than to familiarising himself with the peculiarities and temperaments of his grandchildren. His house had for many years been childless, and children's influence, as a factor in daily life, had counted for little in it. Now, as he allowed his eye to stray from the belt of greenery below to rest upon the little figure at his side he felt, suddenly, a strange and wholly incomprehensible sense of satisfaction at the thought that he could claim some share of ownership in this straight, manly little fellow. For a moment it irritated him, for it seemed as if that sense of satisfaction carried with it some implication of disparagement of the things in which he had hitherto been interested—a suggestion of disloyalty to his beloved garden—a suspicion of an alien pride which the plants that he had carefully tended and that he loved so dearly, might justifiably resent.

His irritation was gone in a moment, overmastered by his real appreciation of the charm that he sensed in the boy. He had never realised the beauty of contour, the round sweep of limb and cheek, the straight line of shoulder, the shapeliness of head, the attractiveness of the tousled fair hair and above all the amazing vitality of the boy beside him. It struck him that the child's skin had a shine on it, a bloom such as he loved to see on the petals of a flower, a velvety richness too delicate for a finger's touch. With the slender straightness that implied power and strength in the slight figure, the boy stood silently, shyly, shifting from one foot to the other, waiting with a child's wistfulness for an advance which he did not dare to make himself. His grandfather reflected, with a tinge of shame at the thought, that he had never tried to induce confidence or invited advance. Something in the eager, longing face of the boy appealed with an appeal that was irresistible to the old man, and he bent down. 'Would you like to walk round the garden with me, Charlie?' he asked. The little boy slid a hand into his and nodded. It was the first time since his arrival that granddad had displayed any interest in him beyond intimating, in a rather dignified tone of voice, that it was time for little boys to go to bed, or enquiring if he wanted a second helping of pudding. Andrew liked the feel of the little paw that clasped his fingers. He felt absurdly pleased with the sense of comradeship that it seemed to impart to their relations, and at the same time rather annoyed that he should feel delighted.

They wandered into the garden, and as they strolled down the carefully tended path, bordered by big veld daisies blooming late in the season, he felt tongue-tied and even more foolishly delighted than on the *stoep*. He stooped to flick off a crawling beetle, gorgeous in tufted metallic green and gold, from a border carnation, and found himself chatting easily before he realised that he was doing so.

'That,' he pointed to a giant araucaria, 'comes from Norfolk Island. And this,' he touched the leaf of a tree under which they were passing, 'is the sacred ginkgo. Look at the leaves, Charlie—just like a fern, aren't they? And there—what do you think that is? You'd never guess. It's the oldest plant in existence—a stangeria. It comes from the forests, and represents all that remains of the old trees from which we get our coal nowadays. Look, there's another sort—*encephalartos altensteinii*—and three more down there. They are cycads and closely related to the pines. Look at that cone—I'm proud of it, though I shouldn't be, for these things are very easy to grow. They just take root wherever you plant them, and nothing seems to kill them. Now this,' he touched a lilac bush whose flowers had already faded, 'is ever so much more difficult to grow, though it grows quite easily in England. And those big poppies over there— they come from America, and I can't tell you how troublesome they were at first. But now they're all right, and they do make a fine show, don't they? Look at the white and the yellow of them. Yes, that's ginger over there, but it's the root that you get in the syrup, the root and the stem, sometimes. We don't preserve it here; we get all we want from China. That? Oh, that's another difficult Johnny. I had no end of trouble to get it to grow, and it simply won't flower. It's a peony, and in England it flowers amazingly well, but here it won't bud. I've given it guano, and bone meal and stable manure, but it simply won't. And it's far finer than a dahlia, my boy. Look at my dahlia bed over there. Did you ever see such colour. And the cannas over there. I got that dark red chap—that big one there—from Java. Seeds. Now it grows wild. But they're greedy things, cannas. They want all the water they can get. That's why we planted them close to the water furrow. And here's something you ought to know, but it hasn't flowered yet. It's a waratah, and lovely in flower. Perhaps next year—well. There's one of your old friends—a bottle-brush from Australia. Now come along, and see what we can get you to pick. There should be plenty of guavas, and I daresay we'll find a plum or two. The rose apples are too green yet, and you know where the *naartjes* hang.'

He found the boy surprisingly quick at understanding, with a vigorous curiosity, and an eager attention that stimulated him to explain the beauties of his garden in which he himself took such an absorbing interest. 'The kid is certainly bright,' he told himself. 'I wonder why I never noticed it before. And a handsome little chap, by gad. More like a Quakerley than his sister. I really must ...'

He broke off his reflections to answer an eager question, and explained, in a way that his own love of the things he cared for made interesting, the difference between succulents and water plants. He lingered over the epiphytic orchids, growing on the trunk of the big oak trees, and stopped on their way to the orchard to explain the fertilisation of the orange trees, over whose late blossoms the honey bees were buzzing in excited activity. The garden was too large, its contents were too varied, its treasures too many, to be dealt with in one ramble. So when the guavas, ranging from the large, green-rinded fruits the size of an apple, to the smooth red berries smaller than a cherry, had been sampled, and the loquat trees plundered of what remained of their belated harvest, he reluctantly intimated that grandma was waiting for tea on the *stoep*, and that courtesy demanded that she should not be kept waiting.

As he drank his tea and listened, abstractedly, to the talk around him at the tea table, his eyes followed the boy playing with the terrier on the lawn. They made a pretty picture, these two, and his aesthetic sense responded to the appeal of their lithe, clean beauty. Looking at them, he felt the satisfaction he had frequently experienced when admiring some lovely flower.

'You aren't listening, Andrew,' said his wife querulously. She sat at the tea table, in the large Madeira chair, with her hands encased in silk mittens, reading the papers which had arrived by the previous evening's post, and eating citron preserve in the mincing, delicate manner in which she had been taught to do these things in her youth. She was an old woman looking her age, which was eight years younger than his, for she had not 'worn well.' Her lower eyelids showed their red, and the skin of her face, dead white in colour, was wrinkled and creased, lacking altogether the smooth colourful healthiness of his. She still sat upright, dignified in her poise, and still retained something of the beauty that had originally attracted him, but her outline was gaunt, and her voice had grown sharper, and in her old age retained the querulous ring which it had possessed in youth. His sister, Joan, too, had aged, but then she was seventy-three and she had never given the same care and attention to her appearance that Alice had done.

As she sat facing him, pouring out the tea for her niece and grand-niece and grand-nephews, acting, as usual, as hostess since Alice took no interest in and had no liking for such things, Joan appeared a placid, good-natured, uninteresting old woman, unaware, apparently, of her sex and thoroughly domesticated. No one would have taken her for a Latinist who could read Terence with understanding, or for a girl who had danced at Admiralty House and had been reckoned a 'toast' by that Don Juan of Governors, Sir Henry Pottinger. She had given the best part of her life, that youthful part of it that should rightly belong, almost exclusively, to love and desire, to her father, and she had never regretted doing so, or at least had never proclaimed her regret to her brother. Between her and him there existed the intimate relationship established by years of community of interest, a relationship that, however intimate, had never challenged rivalry or presumed to be exclusive.

Between her and Alice sat Anna Crest, Quakerley's youngest daughter, dressed becomingly in what may be described as the mufti of widow's weeds. She did not possess sufficient character to fix attention, nor sufficient personality to assert herself, but she had inherited her mother's tall lithesomeness and something of her mother's early beauty. Her daughter, Agatha, a winsome girl of twelve, with no trace of the Quakerley regularity of feature, sat at her feet on a skin mat feeding a kitten with sops of bread dipped in milk, and her youngest son, Aloquin, a boy of six, lolled on the *stoep* sofa at play with another kitten.

'I beg your pardon, my dear,' said Andrew, setting his cup aside to give his attention to what his wife was saying. 'I really did not know that you were talking to me.'

'You never do,' complained his wife. 'Here I have been telling you about the Christmas decorations, and you pay no attention whatsoever. Whatever is the use of my getting all those catalogues and working night and day when you don't pay the slightest attention to what I say?'

'Joan's there to help you,' said her husband. 'You know I am no hand at these things. Have whatever you fancy. I'll pay the bills. I can't say fairer than that.'

'If you would only pay a little attention, Andy,' remonstrated his wife, a little less querulously. 'I have a whole list of people to whom we must give something, and I can't make up my mind. Now there's the children. I'm sure I don't know what to give them.'

'Why not ask them?' suggested Andrew, taking up his cup, which his sister had refilled.

'Do have some sense, Andy,' exclaimed his wife. 'What's the use of a present if you know what it is to be? Besides, how do they know what is good for them? I'm sure I never let Anna choose for herself ...'

'I often wished you had, Ma,' said her daughter. 'I remember your giving me a string of china beads which I didn't want at all. I had four necklaces at that time, and couldn't wear any of them.'

'I certainly never gave you chiny beads, Anna,' said Mrs Quakerley, in dignified protest. 'Coral, very likely, but chiny, never. I should never have allowed my gells to wear chiny bead necklaces. It would have been too common. But I suppose a bead necklace would do for Agatha?'

She dropped her voice as she asked the question and looked askance at the little girl who went on calmly feeding her kitten.

'Anything, Ma, anything you like,' said Mrs Crest. 'I haven't spoiled my children, that's one blessing. I know what I'm going to give them, anyway.'

'Then perhaps we may join forces,' said Andrew, beginning to take an interest in the conversation. 'I should like to do my share. Now that little chap ... what would you suggest for him?'

'Charlie? O, his dearest desire has always been to have a gun,' said the widow, 'but I'm so dreadfully nervous about giving him one.'

'You needn't be,' said her father. 'I learned to shoot when I was younger than Charles, and I daresay we can teach him to look after himself when he has a gun. Do you know, Anna, I like that youngster of yours. There's something about him ... Joan, have you looked at him? Doesn't he remind you ... ?'

'Of you when you were his age,' said his sister, glancing at the struggling pair on the lawn. 'I don't know how you know, but that's just what he does remind me of.'

'You were much handsomer as a young man, Andy,' said his wife, querulously again. 'Charlie is not likely to look so distinguished as you did. I remember when your father took me to the Governor's ball ...'

'Never mind that, Alice,' he interrupted hastily. When his wife became reminiscent about the time when her father-in-law had taken her on a never-to-be-forgotten visit to the capital, where she had had an impressive reminder every day of the worth and high standing of the Quakerleys, it was difficult to deflect her current of conversation, even in a family circle which was thoroughly conversant with all the details of that memorable adventure of forty years ago. 'You and Anna and Agatha can go to town. Only we shall want you to be here at Christmas. Why, Joan, do you know this will be the first Christmas we've had with children in the house since Anna and Winnie grew up?'

'I suppose it will have to do,' said Mrs Quakerley. 'We can have the spring-wagon and stop the night at the Seldons, as usual. It will suite you, won't it Anna?'

'So long as Pa foots the bill, Ma,' said her daughter, 'I should love to go.'

'Very well, then. We'll call it settled,' said Andrew, rising. 'I'm going down to the magistrate's house for a minute, Alice. By the way, Anna, your youngsters ought to go to school, you know. What about letting Charlie come with me to be introduced to Mr Mance-Bisley? I'll be passing his house on my way.'

'Oh, Pa, I haven't thought about it yet,' his daughter replied. Her father's suggestion was in the nature of a distinct hint. It meant, if it meant anything at all, that he would be responsible for her children's education, and Mrs Crest had enough of her mother's business sense to realise that such an arrangement would be materially to her benefit. The post had brought her a statement of account from the executors from which it was painfully clear that the estate of her late husband would not permit her to refuse any help that she could get from her relatives. 'But if you think he ought to go to school here, perhaps it would be better to get Mr Mance-Bisley to see what he's fit for.'

'For the present, at least, here,' said the old man, decidedly. He had already made up his mind. The boy should remain with him. Later on, perhaps, the question of a boarding-school might have to be considered. But now ... he glanced towards the lawn, and nodded his head. 'I'll see about it,' he said, gruffly. 'Don't you worry your head over it, Anna.'

He went indoors, and took his hat and stick from the hat-rack in the hall and his old pair of gloves from the pocket of his greatcoat, and came back.

'Tell the boys to mix some manure water, please,' he said to Joan. 'And let them have some soot ready. We'll have to plant out the schizoglossums for the new bed. They'll just flower in January if we deal with them now. I'll be back in time for lunch, Alice. Charlie ...'

'But, Pa, he must go and get dressed first,' exclaimed his daughter, as the boy came running up the steps in answer to his grandfather's call. 'You can't go like that, Charlie. Go and get into your blue shirt.'

'If you don't mind, Anna,' said her father, 'I'd like to take him as he is. Get your hat, though, young man. The sun's rather too hot for an Australian. Now, then, don't worry, Anna. Mance-Bisley won't think any the less of him because he hasn't a tie. If he only plays cricket ... he does, doesn't he?'

'I suppose so. I never asked about it,' said the boy's mother, nonchalantly. 'They all do, in Australia. But he really is too piggy, Father ...'

'Not a bit of it,' said Andrew, as he took the boy's hand in his. 'He's just as he should be. Come along, young man. We're going to interview the beak ...'

Chapter 6

The Reverend Claude Mance-Binsley could pride himself, if he were pleased to do so, on the fact that he was the only male inhabitant of the Village who had been born overseas in England. He was a Master of Arts of the University of Oxford, and had in early life won some distinction by his edition of a Latin classic which he had prepared for school use. He had been ordained shortly after the publication of this first-born of his literary children, and had come out to South Africa where, after filling various posts in various parts, he had finally been inducted as rector of the Village. He now acted also as schoolmaster, and under his very able tutorship the Village school had already won almost the same degree of distinction which his edition of the Latin classic had gained for him. In person he was a short, rotund, chubby looking man, with large nearsighted eyes and an expression of perpetual anxiety on his smooth, almost juvenile features, an expression that was by no means a true index to his temperament which was impetuous and daring to a degree that often exasperated his wife. Mrs Mance-Bisley overtopped her husband by almost a foot and, both in appearance and in temper served as a complete contrast to him. She was gaunt, angular and bony, determined, cautious and dogmatic, as befitted one who came from a family that had served the church for many years, almost for generations, and who was fully aware of the dignity that appertained to a rector's wife.

The Reverend Claude's predecessor at the rectory had been a staid, homely man, who had built up the Village school from an insignificant private class to an institution that could rank with the best of the smaller urban schools in the Colony. The Village had mourned his departure for he had endeared himself to all who had come into contact with him. He had given his successor some good advice, and had patiently explained the peculiar circumstances of the Valley, and hinted at the desirability of consolidating the foundations which he had already laid so well.

'My dear fellow,' he had told Mance-Bisley as they had sat on the bench on the rectory *stoep* in the cool of the evening, 'You will find that people will take you just as you wish them to take you. If you are high and mighty, they will treat you in the same way. If you show them that you despise them—their want of culture, their language, and their local conventions may not seem, at first, all they should be to you—they will despise you. But if you take them for what they are—really honest, fair-minded, and in their own way tolerant fellows, you'll have no difficulty at all. You must remember that our congregation here is a very small one. We have about a hundred Coloured half-castes and about thirty Whites, all told. There's half a dozen Romans somewhere about, and the rest of the community is solid—very solid—Dutch Reformed. But you'll find that they will be very friendly, very friendly indeed. They'll let you go your own way, if you'll let them go theirs. That does not mean that you should be indifferent to them, or that they will be indifferent to you. Not at all. Take Uhlmann for example. He's the *predikant* here—to all intents and purposes the Pope of the Valley. You'll meet him tomorrow, for I'm going to take you with me when I pay my farewell call, and you'll find him—well, I'll leave you to form your own opinion. But let me just say that Uhlmann is probably one of the best Oriental scholars in this or any other country. He's translated the New Testament into some strange eastern tongue—I don't quite know what it is, but the British & Foreign Bible Society has published it—and he was a missionary out there for donkeys' years before he became a *predikant*. He's a man of culture and refinement, and I can only say that I esteem his friendship and am grateful—profoundly grateful—for the help he has often given me. Now Uhlmann may ask you to join with him in a funeral service ...'

'Surely not,' ejaculated Mr Mance-Bisley. 'Am I expected to do so?'

'I think,' said the out-going rector gently, 'that that is a matter you must decide for yourself. But I may remind you that we used to hold our services in the Dutch Reformed Church over there formerly, by courtesy of their *predikants*, and that Bishop

Gray more than once preached from a Dutch Reformed pulpit.'

'That,' said the Reverend Mr Mance-Bisley, with a stubborn expression creeping over his youthful features, 'seems to me decidedly derogatory.'

'Bishop Gray did not think so,' his host retorted. 'Nor do I. There is nothing derogatory in being—ahem—courteous. When it is a question of principle, of course, it is a different matter. The question of communion, for example—that is quite a different thing, although even there one fancies that there might be means of arranging a what d'you call it, *concordat*. But you will find that people will regard you—us, I may say—as very much akin to themselves, and that they are disposed to look upon us as not very different from them in creed and as being Protestants sundered only by difference in ritual and administration.'

'I should not like to subscribe to that,' said the Reverend Mr Mance-Bisley, with intense determination in the tone of his voice. 'I do not admit that for one moment ...'

'My dear fellow, surely you do not think that anyone here, with the exception of Uhlmann, perhaps, knows or cares a button about our church tradition? Uhlmann, yes, he takes an interest in the matter and I often discuss things with him. He admired the Latinity of the Bishops' encyclical, but he jibbed at their arguments, and you'll find, if you discuss the matter with him ...'

'I shall certainly do no such thing,' said the Reverend Mr Mance-Bisley, even more determinedly than before.

'You might do worse, my dear fellow, you might do worse. Just bear in mind that he was brought up as a Lutheran, and so far as I can see they stand very much closer to Rome than we do. But here we are discussing church politics, and there's so much else I ought to be talking of. Let me give you a word of advice—I am sure you'll take it in good part. We—I include myself, for I am a South African born and bred—we are just a bit sensitive, touchy about ourselves. We take ourselves mighty seriously. Don't try to be—you won't take it amiss if I say it—too English. Or too ... anything. There's a convenient *via media*. Stick to it. Take the school. Many of your pupils come from homes where no English is spoken; their parents know no English, but they are all keen to learn it, and you can pump it into them as hard as you like. You'll find them docile and the parents will back you up. And wonderfully keen on their work, though of course there will be exceptions. Don't hesitate to use the stick if necessary. People hereabouts believe in the old aphorism which they still take to be a Bible text— wonderful, isn't it? How few of us can place a quotation correctly. But go warily, until you feel your feet and know the people. You won't make a mistake then. You might easily if you barge into things straight off. Try and learn the language here; you ought to find it quite easy, for it is not difficult. And bear in mind that our own people, your parishioners, know as little about England as the others. There are exceptions, of course. Old Quakerley is one, and so is his sister, though neither of them has ever been outside this country. You'll find him a great standby, but you'll rarely see him at church. He'll put his hand into his pocket whenever you ask him, and you can depend upon him. Don't scruple to ask, either; he's got far more than he can spend.'

The next morning the Reverend Mr Mance-Bisley met the Reverend Christian Uhlmann, and revised his notions about the Dutch Reformed clergy. But he retained much of his prejudice and tried to translate some of them into practice. The Village English church got the reputation of being 'high.' Mrs Quakerley began to speak of attending compline, and the old Cornish carpenter, whose father had been born at Marazion but who had never been farther than Kimberley, declared that the service was getting too 'papistical' for him. But the Village took these things with commendable calmness, and the Reverend Mr Mance-Bisley found that there was no active opposition to his innovations. Perhaps that damped his zeal, for he proceeded no further on the road to Rome and forgot his desire to have candles burning in his church in daylight.

His reforming activity was as evanescent where his school was concerned. He started by instituting the system of prefects, only to find that loyalty to his fellows interfered with the prefect's loyalty to his headmaster. He found his pupils interesting enough, with enough juvenile depravity among them to give scope for his disciplinary genius. But they failed to respond to his initiative. They did not resist his reforms. No one objected to the changed curriculum, the alteration of the time table, and the new-fangled regulations which he had, after consultation with the government inspector, who had smiled but acquiesced, attempted to enforce. There was no insubordination. But there was a complacent, stolid negativism that baffled him, and made him feel that he was hitting at a soft jellyfish that yielded but could not be quite squashed. It was all very annoying and irritating at first, but when he found that there was no one besides himself, with the possible exception of his wife, who sympathised with him, even though she did not altogether approve of his school reforms, who could see in it a defiance of his authority, he gave up the struggle and returned to the old path, with excellent results to the school and the scholars.

There was one matter, however, upon which he was determined that his will should prevail, and that was cricket. To the Reverend Mr Mance-Bisley it was unbelievable that there should exist in the British empire a school, with a secondary top containing sturdy, well set-up lads preparing for their matriculation, which did not play cricket. He was horrified when he found out that not one boy in the Village possessed a cricket bat, and that a set of wickets and a few broken bails were all that could be procured after a careful canvass. He promptly sat down and wrote to a firm at Cape Town, and in due course several sets of cricket implements arrived with the post-cart and were taken to the school. At morning assembly he spoke enthusiastically on the subject. He took 'cricket' as his text, and although he was too conscientious a man, and too experienced a teacher, to refer to the possibility that some future South African battle might be won on the cricket field, he made it clear that he expected every boy to consider it his duty to learn to play cricket. That afternoon he took his senior lads to a grassy patch suitable for such excitement, and explained, with meticulous care, the layout of a cricket field. The next morning he reverted to the subject, and daily he impressed on the boys the importance of practice at the nets. He was gratified to see quite a large gathering on the field when the first practice took place. The Coloured youths from the location had turned up in force to watch the proceedings, and they were interested and critical spectators, who quickly made their own stumps and manufactured bats from cedarwood planks and proved enthusiastic proselytes. But his own school was singularly lukewarm. When his boys were supposed to be bowling or slogging, they would be punting a ball about the field. Football had been their one and favourite team game, and they had seen no reason why it should be made to give place to cricket. Nevertheless the Reverend Mr Mance-Bisley persevered, and in time, after a struggle that would have done credit to a more important enterprise, he succeeded in getting up a passably good eleven that played matches with scratch teams made up from adolescents who good-naturedly agreed to humour them. It remained a regret to the Headmaster that his boys were so singularly unappreciative of the noblest game that in his opinion the boyhood of any country could indulge in. They were in other respects, apart from this singular apathy about cricket and their equally strange desire to play football at all seasons of the year, quite normal boys, presenting the usual problems that pedagogues have to deal with and that Mr Mance-Bisley was peculiarly qualified to handle.

Mr Mance-Bisley was dozing in the garden, with a handkerchief over his chubby face to keep the flies off him, and Max Nordau's latest sensation, which he very much disliked but which had immensely interested him, lying on the grass beside his chair, where a patient chameleon was trying to crawl over it, colouring itself in the attempt to a shade closely akin to the scarlet binding. *Conventional Lies* had not been intriguing enough to prevent the rector from succumbing to the soporific influence of the warm, syringa-scented morning. His snores came gently through the handkerchief, a regular, rhythmic drone that kept pace with the buzzing of the bees hovering over the honeysuckle.

Andrew Quakerley, leading his grandson by the hand, stopped and swished his walking stick in the air, and Mr Mance-Bisley roused himself with a start, shook the covering handkerchief off his face, and sat up and blinked.

'Good morning, Rector,' said the old man. 'I must apologise for disturbing you, but I had no idea that you were taking your afternoon nap so early. Mrs Mance-Bisley said that you were gardening, so we came out to find you.'

The rector rose and shook hands.

'I fell asleep over a silly book,' he said picking Max up from the ground, thereby disturbing the chameleon which hissed with rage and blew out its pouch with annoyance. 'Dear me, here's one of our curiosities,' said the rector, pointing with his finger to the little reptile. 'Yes, you may pick him up, my boy. He's quite harmless, and there are plenty of others in the garden. Shall we go in, Mr Quakerley?'

'No need, Rector, no need. I merely came to introduce this young shaver to you. He's my grandson. I daresay you know ... Mrs Crest's boy, the elder. There's a girl, too, Agatha—this chap's name is Charles, though why they didn't call him Andrew I can't make out. From Australia, you know. I thought you might like to have him in your class. It's demoralising for these youngsters to laze about for so long.'

'Term's almost at an end,' said the rector, studying the boy who stood stroking the chameleon. 'He'd better enter in January. What standard is he in?'

'I really don't know. I suppose the Australian schools have different standards from ours. You might put him through his paces, Rector, if you please. Come, Charlie, tell Mr Mance-Bisley what you can do.'

'Sums and reading and writing,' said the boy, shyly. 'And map drawing and history, Grand-dad. And we started algebra just before we left.'

'How old are you?' asked the rector, noting with satisfaction that the boy had good manners, bore himself with a certain childlike dignity, and spoke without a trace of the 'colonial' intonation so annoyingly prevalent among the Village youth.

'Ten, Sir,' came the reply, and the rector was still more satisfied with the answer.

Obviously the lad had been well taught. The Village schoolboys tacked on 'Sir' to their replies as an afterthought and usually omitted it altogether. There was something strangely likeable in the little fellow, something that reminded one of small boys in an English preparatory school, something altogether different from the brown, sturdy boyhood in this semi-tropical part of the world where the co-existence of two languages played havoc with accent and correct speech. Old Andrew had moved away, his interest caught by something that grew in the garden, but although the boy's eyes followed his grandfather he made no movement to accompany him, but stood respectfully at attention, his long, slender little fingers idly stroking the still protesting chameleon.

'We shall have to see what you can do, Crest,' said the rector. 'I think you'd better come to me this afternoon and bring your books with you. Have you started Latin yet?'

'No, Sir.'

'Hm, you'll have to make a start with it sometime, and you might as well begin now. You should have started long ago. I suppose Mr Quakerley wishes you to matriculate. Well, we'll see about that. Perhaps you may be fit for standard five, or four at least.' He turned to the old man, who was interestedly examining a clump of yellow flowers that grew on a sandy patch close by. 'Perhaps you'll let him come and see me this afternoon, Mr Quakerley ...'

'Yes, yes, any time you like. But where did you get these from, Rector? Do you know what they are? Coryciums ... I think *corycium crispum*, but I am not sure. They grow in this District, I know, but I've never seen them in a garden. You must let me have a bulb or two.'

'I have never looked at them before,' said the rector frankly. 'I really do not know what grows in the garden, Mr Quakerley. Perhaps they are self-sown. By all means take them if you want to.'

'No, no. Not now. Wait until they are withered. These orchids are finicky things. I have some disas—have had them for years, and I can't get them to flower. I should like some of these, if I may have them, Rector. So you will take Charlie? Run away and amuse yourself, Son. I want to talk to Mr Mance-Bisley. You see, Rector, I did not uite know what Anna was going to do. That's my daughter, Mrs Crest, the boy's mother, you know. But this morning I made up my mind. He's too good a boy to be lost sight of and if you will take him in hand ... or later on, if you think he'll do for College—but not yet. I should like him to stay a while with us, Rector. My wife and I have been ... how shall I put it? We'd like to have some of the youngsters around, and from what I can see, he's a good goy, and uncommonly smart.'

The rector looked at the boy and agreed. Charlie, told to run away and play, had obeyed his grandfather to the extent of wandering towards the water furrow and the little bath house, shaded by leafy oak trees, and had found, leaning against the bath house door, a cricket bat with which he was now blocking imaginary balls whizzing past the bath house steps. Mr Mance-Bisley felt an emotion that surged up in him like a wave. There was grace, action; there was evidence of that instinctive liking whose absence among his boys he had so often deplored. He startled the old man by bounding forward, and crying—for Mr Mance-Bisley was impetuous and excitable—at the top of his voice, 'Wait, wait! I'll get the ball and bowl to you.'

Mr Quakerley found the ensuing quarter of an hour mildly interesting. The rector revelled in its revelations. He divested himself of his coat, turned up his shirt sleeves, shortened his braces by two holes, and bounded, with an agility which one would scarcely have expected from a person so sleek and so chubbily rotund, over the garden path while he bowled. How his spectacles remained on during those vigorous exhibitions of arm- and leg-play was a miracle, but they did, and they evidently served him well, for he bowled with skill, maintaining a good length and varying his pace. The little batsman took the bowling with some trepidation at first, but steadied in a manner that both grown-ups liked to see, and snicked and blocked with commendable judgment. Old Andrew admired the easy grace of the boy who, flushed with excitement and eagerness, handled a bat obviously too large for him with a dexterity that showed that he had had some practice. The rector noted the faults, the imperfections that revealed bad training, the wasted effort in strokes that should have been made differently, but he also observed the quickness of eye and hand, the alertness of the player, and the courage with which the boy faced the bowling. The youngster was untrained but he had style, and there were the makings of a fine cricketer, or at least a fine batsman, in him.

The rector, heated by his exertions, handed the ball to Charlie. 'Let's see what you can do with the bowling,' he remarked. 'Just a minute, Mr Quakerley, but I really must try him with the ball.'

'There,' he said, after he had dealt with the bowling and noted once more that although there were plenty of faults to be corrected in the boy's action, there were certainly also points which any cricket coach would have appreciated. Mr Mance-Bisley, who adored cricket as he adored few mundane things except his wife, and who had for years been looking out for a promising youth who could be inspired with something of his own enthusiasm for the game, felt that he had at last found what he had been seeking.

The realisation of this, like so many other realisations coming upon us rather suddenly and unexpectedly, sobered as much as it pleased him, for he was a conscientious man, responsive to his obligations. The immediate thought leaped into his mind how selfish it would be to keep this promising cricketer in the Village, where no-one except himself seemed to care for cricket, and how much more honest it would be to say to Andrew Quakerley, 'Take him and send him to College, where they will look after his Latin, but much more conscientiously after his cricket, where he will have the benefits of a coach and the rivalry of real cricketers, not the limited enthusiasm of those who prefer, even in the summer, the robust attractions of rugby football.' Being human as well as conscientious, he found no dishonesty in dallying with his obvious duty, and as he walked towards the house with the old gentleman, Charlie following sedately behind still hugging bat and ball, he discreetly probed into a selfishness akin to his own and found he had a fellow-conspirator to deal with.

Eleven o'clock morning tea was one of the Colonial customs the Reverend Mr Mance-Bisley had taken kindly to, much as he had at first resented it as un-English and redundant to anyone fortified by a good wholesome breakfast of staple porridge and bacon and eggs. His visitors had already had their share, but they stayed to bear him company, and the boy found entertainment in a Doré-illustrated Milton, the sunlight filtering through the leaves of the orange trees on the *stoep* making eyots of brightness on his fair hair.

Mr Mance-Bisley and Andrew Quakerley discussed standards, and exchanged views on country schools. Andrew, dipping far back into his own recollections, recalled some of his experiences at the private school where, more than sixty years ago, he had been indulged in his love of botany. From such practical issues they wandered into matters more theoretical, and discussed the intricacies of the situation in the north where, from all accounts, mischief was brewing. They discussed it as if it was something that did not affect them, something to be dealt with, so far as they were concerned, from an academical point of view, by no stretch of the imagination destined to influence their own lives or conditions in any serious sense.

'The news in Monday's paper, Mr Quakerley,' said the rector, 'is distinctly disturbing. It seems that the reformers are bent on forcing the issue. I can't say that I blame them, do you?'

'I find some difficulty in deciding, Rector,' said the old man, reflectively. 'The position is too intricate for me to judge. I have never given much thought to it, you know. These are matters that hardly affect us.'

'But they do concern us,' said the rector, vehemently. 'It seems an almost intolerable situation up there. I was reading Mr Leonard's speech yesterday, and he puts the case so clearly that I cannot see how there can be any effective rebuttal.'

'Leonard is a lawyer,' replied old Andrew lightly. 'A lawyer can make a good case out of anything. That's what he is there for. But I am afraid the main points of the indictment are perfectly true. It is the old, old trouble over again ... the clash between advance and conservative stubbornness. The two are incompatible, but it has always seemed to me that time and tact settle these difficulties without asking us to interfere in any drastic way.'

'Do you really think so? I confess I feel disheartened when I read about the way in which these Outlanders are denied the common rights of citizenship. I should have expected more sympathy from people here. Don't they taken an interest in the matter?'

'They do and they don't, Rector. Bear in mind most of those on the farms hardly ever read a newspaper. If you were to ask them what the trouble is all about, I hardly think you'd find one who could give you a correct explanation. To the majority it is purely a matter of settlement without outside interference, and honestly that, too, is my opinion. I don't think matters will come to a head. We talk much more than we act, Rector. I can remember in 1880, there was just as much excitement as there is now, but in the end it did not affect us at all. I expect that is what will happen now.'

'You know more about these people than I do,' said the rector. 'Tell me, do they really imagine that they can keep the clock back for a century? When one reads these reports, one fancies that there must be gross ignorance at the back of that idea ...'

'So there is,' interrupted Andrew. 'If our people here are still conservative and ignorant, those in the Transvaal are doubly so. Education is only now being attended to there, and if you went through districts like Waterberg and Zoutpansberg, which are off the railway line, you would find a primitive community still firmly attached to old prejudices and old customs, the same that their forefathers had when they trekked north in '36. At Johannesburg you have a mushroom city, preposterously well-to-do because of the gold and the employment that the mines give, and hardly in tune with the old population. Numerically strong and threatening to swamp the old *burghers* by sheer weight of numbers. That is the old President's difficulty, and I assure you that I can sympathise with him in his trouble. He is a shrewd old man, Rector, and it would not be easy to jolt him. That is my main hope—that old Kruger will not give ear to the extremists on his own side.'

'He must be a singularly obstinate old chap,' said Mr Mance-Bisley. 'I suppose the stories one hears about him are largely fables, Mr Quakerley?'

'I hardly think so, Rector. I met him once—when I went up north to have a look round. I found him a very likeable old fellow, but that may be because I could talk with him in his own language and smoke his tobacco. We spent quite an interesting morning on the *stoep* in Church Street, consuming many cups of coffee. He kept the State carriage waiting all the time, and I daresay somebody told somebody else that we were discussing politics. As a matter of fact, he was telling me how difficult he had found it to build his first church. He built it without help—made the bricks himself and felled the trees for the rafters, and found that his plaster would not stick on.'

'How odd,' said the Reverend Mr Mance-Bisley. 'But he wasn't President then?'

'Oh, no. He was merely a field-cornet. He was made one when he was sixteen, you know, which gives you some idea of what the community must have been like. But I have no doubt that they chose the best man for all that. He is a remarkable old fellow, Rector. Immensely strong, bodily, and with a shrewd commonsense such as one finds in these old Dutchmen who have had to fend for themselves all their lives and have a fund of experience to draw on. But I really must go. I am so glad you will be able to take Charlie. Where is the boy? Oh, there you are, Charlie. Say goodbye to the rector; you can come up this afternoon and bring your books.'

Chapter 7

Christmas brought with it that year a sense of anxiety to those who read their newspapers and took an interest in affairs outside their local circle. Such were not many, for the majority of the inhabitants troubled themselves little about what went on in the great world. The summer had been one of unprecedented drought. In the adjoining districts the sheep were dying and the wheat crop had been a dismal failure, but in the sheltered Valley the harvests had been good, and the fruit season this year was no worse than in the preceding year. Those who studied their papers read with mild interest the cable news, chronicling the death of the Duke of Leeds; the birth to the Duchess of York of a son; the advent of Captain Baden Powell in command of the Native scouts at Prahau in Ashantee; the return of Khama and his two colleague chiefs from a visit to England; the resignation of the Spanish Ministry, and other equally exciting events, which did not even furnish material for conversation. A few, more deeply interested in what went on in their own country, found matter for discussion in the controversy then raging in the public press on the education system of the Colony. The Reverend Mr Mance-Bisley read with keen interest and profound dismay about the first match between the Colonial team and Lord Hawke's visiting team—a match which had resulted in the collapse of the visitors, who had made 79 runs against their opponents' 115.

The few who found cause for anxiety in what they saw in the papers fixed their attention almost entirely upon the news from the north. In the Orange Free State a Presidential election was in process. A short despatch from Pretoria stated that the guns ordered from Europe had arrived, and even briefer notices hinted at trouble at Johannesburg, where the Outlanders were agitating. Over everything, to those who took a far view, seemed to loom the more distressing trouble of complications between England and America on the Venezuelan difficulty.

One of these anxious ones was the Village magistrate. A conscientious, hard-working civil servant, a direct descendant of the families that had entered the Colony as English settlers in 1820, Albert Storam had grown attached to his environment and had thoroughly assimilated its many pleasant features. He was well liked as an official and as a man. He knew everyone and everyone knew him. On the Bench he preserved a staid, judicial calm; at home he was a jovial, hospitable neighbour, addicted to whist, game shooting and croquet, which last he would probably have given up for golf had that game been known to the Village.

Albert Storam understood his community even better perhaps than any other official that had ever ministered to it. He knew that there were undercurrents in it of which he could take no official cognisance, but of whose existence he was well aware. He was acquainted with the agitation that had gone on in other districts and with the interest that was being taken elsewhere, and mainly for political reasons, in the north, and he felt some anxiety about what in these later days would be called its repercussions upon the District. Already there was talk on the farms about the subject, but fortunately there was a chance that the trouble would remain localised and that the Colony would not be dragged into it. In other districts, where the relations between English and Dutch were not so cordial as they were in his District, the political situation might become acute, but he hoped that would not be the case here.

That was why he grew anxious as he studied the papers, and more anxious still when he read the semi-official telegrams that came from the Department of Justice to keep him informed, as much as the Government deemed it necessary, of the general situation. They told him little enough. The news from the north filtered in slowly. On Boxing Day there had come but hints, so cryptically phrased that the magistrate kept them to himself instead of pinning the announcements on the Court House notice board, as was his custom with official despatches not marked 'Strictly Confidential.'

Christmas week had been a week of unparalleled excitement. On the day following the public holiday, the telegraph had told of the Outlander manifesto, publishing to the world at large, with an eloquence and sincerity masking much of its special pleading, the grievances under which the non-*burgher* population of the northern Republic groaned. Saturday's papers had brought a more complete summary of this document, along with controversial reports from correspondents, the gist of which was that matters were shaping towards a clash. On the Sunday, the pastor had referred to the situation in his general exhortation to his congregation, and Mr Storam, who made a point of attending service in the Dutch Reformed Church in the morning and of patronising the Reverend Mr Mance-Bisley's evening performance in the English Church, had listened with approval to Mr Uhlmann's grave pleading for tolerance and charity.

The last day of the year, Tuesday, found the magistrate a trifle more confident, for his official telegrams had led him to believe that a way had been found out of the difficulty, and that a settlement could reasonably be expected. He told his wife of his hopes as they sat at the breakfast table, in the front room of the Residency. Through the big, low-silled windows, the sunlight, filtering through the screen of orange trees on the *stoep*, slanted into the room and made golden splendour on the carpet. Already the air was stiflingly hot, without the slightest breeze to shake the heavy haze of heat shimmering between river and mountain.

'I expect it will blow over,' said Mr Storam, referring to the political and not the atmospheric sultriness. 'After all, my dear, we should trust Mr Rhodes. He knows people thoroughly, and he's not likely to be stampeded into doing anything to upset things.'

His wife faced him across the breakfast table, the only other occupant of which was his son, Martin, a healthily tanned, lean, sinewy lad of fifteen who, despite the heat, ate a meal the caloric co-efficient of which would have amply satisfied the requirements of a body twice his size.

'I don't know where you stuff all that marmalade, Martin,' said his father, eyeing him with a twinge of envy. 'It's as much as I can do to eat a scrap of toast in this hot weather.'

'I need all that, Pa,' said his son, grinning. 'Old Mance kept us at the nets all yesterday afternoon. That new kid is shaping very well, Pa. You should see him snick a ball ... My, he does know how to handle a bat. Not that he's much good at football. But I say, Pa, if it comes to a fight, which side are we going to be on?'

The magistrate was startled by the vehemence with which the question was put. A peremptory rebuke trembled on his lips, but he refrained from voicing it and asked, with some curiosity, 'What makes you think there's going to be any fighting, Martin? What do you know about it?'

'Oh, everyone is talking about it,' replied his son, frankly. 'There's bound to be a rumpus, isn't there, Pa? Old Kruger won't allow the Outlanders to do just as they please, will he? After all, it's his country, not theirs ...'

'My dear boy,' expostulated his mother, 'do eat your breakfast and don't talk about things you don't understand. Isn't it too bad, Albert, that the children are encouraged to talk about such things in the playground. I do wish you would speak to the rector about it.'

'Old Mance can't make us keep quiet, Mother, even if he wants to,' said her son, stoutly. 'And he had better not try, either. We're about fed up with his everlasting cricket. Football's good enough for me.'

'That will do, Martin,' said his father. 'There's no harm in cricket, and you should help the rector—you're head boy of the school, and it's up to you to support him.'

'So I do, Pa,' grumbled his son apologetically. 'But some of the kids are perfect duffers at it, and it's a sheer waste of time. They'll never take to it, and they do take to football. It's just Mr Bisley's rotten prejudice against things which are not English.'

'Just remember, my boy, that there's a good bit of English in you,' said his father gently, 'and don't make the mistake of thinking what's English must be bad, just because your schoolmates take that view. I should regret it, Martin, if you hadn't enough moral character to form your own opinion and just followed other people in their opinions.'

'It isn't that, Pa,' the boy's voice was subdued in his eagerness, 'but one does get fed up at times. You should hark to that new kid bragging about what they do in Australia, and just because they're all English there, old Mance makes a pet of him, and we're not good enough to lick his boots. It does make you wild, Pa. After all, we're just as good as they, even though we happen to be South Africans, aren't we, Dad?'

'Not if we can't see where they beat us, my boy. At cricket, now. If I were you I'd show the new kid—I suppose that's young Crest, isn't it? A nice, likeable lad, and you might at least copy his way of speaking, Martin. He does not clip his words, and he certainly does not say "wull" for "will."'

'There you go again, Dad,' exclaimed Martin. 'I never say "wull"—only the farm boys do, and you can't blame them. They don't speak English at home.'

'But you forget sometimes that you do, my boy; and remember, please, that we're not English and Dutch but South Africans. You ought to be more sensible than to think that all this clap-trap about English and Dutch is going to make us any better. I had no idea that you were so stupid as to pay any attention to such foolish talk. Seriously, my boy ... what is it, Magriet?'

The magistrate interrupted his conversation as the Coloured maid came into the room. It was rarely that he was disturbed at the breakfast table, but official duties took precedence over private affairs and he was always ready. This time it was the chief constable, asking for an immediate interview. With the natural impatience of even a conscientious official, interrupted in the midst of a serious conversation, the magistrate took a final sip from his tea-cup and stalked from the room.

'You see how shocked your father is, Martin,' said his wife when he had gone. 'I have told you often enough that you ought to be a little more careful. Father is in a difficult position, and as the magistrate's son, and head boy besides, you should set an example ...'

'So I do, *Mater,*' replied Martin, again attacking the marmalade. 'You should see me coach the little fellows ... my, some of them are stupid. But *Mater*, don't you think there's going to be a bust-up? And would you mind it if I cut in ...'

'Martin,' exclaimed his mother, 'don't say such things. Whatever makes you think anything is likely to happen? Wherever did you get the idea from?'

'Oh, they all say that there's going to be a rumpus, *Mater*. It's bound to come. I was listening to old Ras—he was in the last scrap at Majuba, *Mater*, you know—and he said ...'

'I don't want to know what Mr Ras said,' declared the magistrate's wife, sharply. 'It's bound to be wrong, whatever he said. He's not one of our people, my dear; he comes from the north, and he's one of those who are always trying to make trouble. And there's trouble enough in this world, Martin, without dragging in politics to make things more difficult.'

The magistrate came in. He carried in his hand a sheaf of telegrams, and his face was stern and tense. The boy, aquiver with curiosity, felt himself suddenly sobered by his father's grave seriousness.

'What is it, my dear?' asked the magistrate's wife. 'Is it bad news?'

'The worst possible' the magistrate sat down in his chair and drank his lukewarm tea, fingering the telegrams in his hand. 'I may as well tell you—it'll be common knowledge within the next hour, and what will happen then goodness alone knows. I can't take it in yet. It seems so utterly fantastic ... so damnably silly. Yes, excuse my language, my dear, but that's just what it is ... the silliest, most damnable nonsense that I ever heard of ...'

'But what is it, Albert? What do you mean?' exclaimed his wife.

'A force of Chartered Company's police, under the command of Dr Jameson, has crossed the Transvaal border,' said the magistrate. 'The Colonial Secretary wires me that a proclamation will be issued repudiating this step on behalf of the Crown. They cannot do anything else, either. It is the only sensible ... the only honourable thing to do. But now the fat's in the fire, my dear. Jameson is Administrator of the Chartered Company's territory, and he has been lying on the border with those men for weeks, evidently preparing for this. A pretty kettle of fish. Give me another cup of tea, my dear, and then I must go to the office. Don't expect me back for luncheon. I shall have to be at everyone's beck and call this morning; and Martin, for heaven's sake remember what I've just been telling you. Keep out of the talk when it comes round to this. Don't let your feelings carry you away, my boy, and remember that I am the magistrate and that you have some responsibility, just as I have.'

'Yes, Dad, I'll try,' said young Martin, soberly. 'Is it going to be war now, Dad?'

'God knows,' said the magistrate, rising. 'It looks very much like it, but there's just a chance or two ... It all depends on what is going on up north, and evidently the wires are cut, so we can't hear any news for a day or two.'

He took his leave and walked to the office along the little front street that was merely a footpath, regarded as the private right of way of those whose houses abutted on to it. It was a shady walk, shadowed by the old oaks and tall Lombardy poplars growing alongside the water-furrow, from which the little bath houses in the gardens were fed. The refreshing coolness of the old oaks, the faint sound made by the water splashing into the cement baths, and the strong green of the grass bordering the furrow, tempered the sultriness of the morning, but the magistrate scarcely felt the heat as he strode quickly along the little street. Through the lanes between the houses he could see into the main street behind, and already it seemed to him that there was a grater activity there than was normal. Of course it was Old Year's Day and New Year's Eve, and that possibly accounted for the unwonted bustle, but he fancied that the news had already got abroad and had evoked this excitement.

At the office he found most of the principal inhabitants of the Village gathered to interview him. Many prominent farmers from the District had come to the Village for the New Year's celebrations, and some of these too had taken the opportunity to call upon him. Normally there would have been very little work for him at the office on Old Year's Day, which was a day of leisure on which as little official business as possible was transacted. But today it was different.

He read out the telegrams he had received, and noted that the reading was listened to in tense silence. No one made any remark, but all looked intensely serious. To relieve the situation, he adopted a tone of genial exuberance, not entirely in keeping with his own feelings.

'There it is, gentlemen,' he said. 'But you must not take it that it means war. Not by any means. All that it means, all that we really know, is that a filibustering expedition has made an attack upon the Transvaal, and that our Government, quite rightly, has tried ... is trying ... to stop it. Whether the Government will succeed in doing that I don't know. I can't tell. None of us can. But you may take it from me, speaking officially as the representative of the Government here, that this is a totally unprovoked, unauthorised inroad, which the British Government will promptly repudiate.'

'But, Magistrate,' said one of his hearers, a field-cornet and a man who carried much weight in the District, 'that means war ... bloodshed, and you cannot easily put out a fire once you have lighted it.'

'I know, I know, Field-cornet. But that is a matter not for us. It is in other hands. If the Transvaal wants help, you may be sure that the Government will give it such support as will suffice to maintain its authority. I will only ask you all, gentlemen, to do your best to keep feeling quiet. I can understand ... in a measure I can sympathise with your feelings. They are largely my own. We all know that these difficulties can be settled without war or bloodshed if people will only be reasonable and tactful. We should work to that end.'

'I think a public meeting should be called, Magistrate,' declared another farmer, whom the magistrate knew as one of the strongest supporters of the political party in power, and of whose talents he had no great opinion. 'I imagine that the people here would like to have this matter explained to them, and that a united protest against this crime should go forth from us.'

'That,' said the magistrate hastily, 'is a matter for consideration. Certainly not one to be hurriedly decided. I cannot, of course, prevent you from calling a meeting of protest, but I should most strongly advise you to wait a bit. Let us celebrate the New Year in quiet, no matter had badly it seems to have been ushered in. Afterwards, when we know where we stand, we can consider the advisability of calling a meeting. Unfortunately it appears that the wires are cut, and it may be some time before we have any authentic news. In the meantime I need not warn you against believing rumours that may be without the slightest foundation. One thing you may be certain of, and that is that our Government will do nothing—has done nothing—that need cause any of us alarm. It will act, as it has acted throughout, with perfect honesty and fairness.'

'Aye,' said the field-cornet, 'I reckon we can trust our Government. But I do not like the look of things, Magistrate.'

'Nor do I, Field-cornet,' said the magistrate, frankly. 'The thing has come upon me like a bolt out of the blue. That is all the more reason for us to be cautious, and to refrain from doing anything to make the position worse. You will of course discuss it, and I hope that you will do so quietly and temperately.'

'You are an optimist, Magistrate,' said the old field-cornet, with a wry smile. 'I was one once. I am not any more. When people's feelings are stirred—and this will stir them, Magistrate—they are apt to be bitter and warm. But for my part I will do what I can. It is the young blood, Magistrate, that will have a vent.'

    *   *   *   *   *

The Old Year went out with a sunset gorgeous in fiery crimsons and beryl greens, flooding the west with colour so that the sky seemed a sea of variegated tints under which the deep brown of the landscape, still panting under the oppressive heat of the afternoon, lay like a heavy pall. Custom demanded that the New Year should be welcomed with gaiety, with gunfire and cracker detonations, with frolic and festivity in which old as well as young took part. But the Village hardly responded to the appeal of custom on this thirty-first day of December 1895, and the New Year's Eve exuberance was confined to the children of the Village who saw no reason why they should be debarred from their customary privilege of shouting and enjoyment simply because Dr Jameson had been foolish enough to cross the Transvaal border. Not that this folly on the part of a gentleman of whom they had never heard did not affect them. Hot discussions took place in yard and garden, leading sometimes to flights in which the combatants had no clear notion why they had quarrelled. At midnight, when custom decreed that the New Year's glass of wine should be solemnly drunk, the elders pledged each other with unaccustomed gravity, and set down their glasses with a sigh, wondering what the New Year had in store for them.

Chapter 8

It brought, in its first week, the excitement of uncertainty balanced by the anxiety that from the conflagration in the north redundant sparks might settle on the inflammable stubble in the south.

An outlet for such excitement was provided by the arrival of the post-cart which brought more detailed news than what could be gleaned from the curt official communications pinned by the magistrate on the notice board of the court house. These communications had been curiously brief, indecisive and tantalising because of the things they omitted to mention. The Village knew that the Government had repudiated the Raiders; that the Raid itself had proved a fiasco, and that the gentlemen adventurers who had planned it had surrendered and were now prisoners at Pretoria. But it was far more interested in the influence of these unhappy events upon their own affairs, and there was as yet no certainty about what was taking place in the capital where the trusty and well-beloved Mr Rhodes gave no sign of that active effectiveness which had bred confidence in the past and helped to inspire trust in his capability and sane levelheadedness. Action, it seemed, had passed into the hands of the Governor, whom the Village had hitherto regarded as merely an ornamental figurehead, symbolising, it is true, the prestige and power of Alexandrina Victoria, but admittedly a far less stately figure than the Prime Minister. Probably there were few in the Village who really grasped the significance of Mr Rhodes's abdication. But there were many who felt that so strange a silence and so complete a surrender of responsibilities as that which it seemed to presage was an ill omen, and they shook their heads and awaited with anxious eagerness the arrival of the weekly mail that might bring more detailed news of a crisis whose gravity none presumed to deny.

The main road through the Village formed the back street. The majority of the houses turned their backs towards it, but the two churches, the gaol, and half-a-dozen other buildings erected on the bare veld behind the Village, fronted it. Between their frontages and the yard walls of the regular line of houses was a comparatively wide space, so that the back street was a broad thoroughfare, bare except for a few bluegum trees and the straggling shrubs of the yard hedges. The court house, in which were the Government offices, the library, the post and telegraph office, possessed two fronts, one overlooking the back street and the other abutting on the shadowed, tree-screened walk between the gardens and the *stoeps* of the houses. Its own *stoep*, wide and grass-grown, was rarely used, for most people approached by way of the road, and its front door, which could also be called its back door, opened on the back street. That door gave admittance to a passage with the post office on the right and the magistrate's room on the left, which led into the big court room overlooking the *stoep*. Against the outer wall, immediately below the window of the magistrate's room, stood two iron and wood benches, government property but used indiscriminately by whoever waited to transact business at the court house. On the left hand side the brass slit of the letter box gleamed in solitary grandeur. No bench was allowed beneath it, for such would have blocked up the approach to it. An ancient thorn tree, relict of a couple that had been there before the court house was built, overshadowed the door and letter box, its meagre foliage a mass of golden blossom in mid-summer, and its scarred trunk worn smooth in patches from the reins of countless horses which had been tied to it.

Here, in front of the court house, the Village, or at least the adult, adolescent and older juvenile male portion of it, congregated on mail days. Some of them came to get their letters and parcels, but the majority had no expectation of any postal harvest but loitered for the simple reason that attracts any crowd—the chance of a gossip, of novelty in some form or other, of interest, or of mild excitement, a chance ever present when the only link between isolation and the larger civilisation three hundred miles away lies in the arrival of the weekly mail. Such occasions were made the opportunity for the interchange of opinion, for discussion between the older and more sedate members of the community, and for mild bickering and horse-play between the juveniles, who on these weekly gathering days were allowed more liberty of action than was usually considered advisable in so conservative a community.

The post-cart was scheduled to arrive promptly at four o'clock in the afternoon, but the experienced knew well enough that the schedule was never strictly adhered to and that considerable latitude was granted to the driver. In winter, when the air was cold and rainy, few grouped themselves around the thorn tree much before sunset, and the gatherings were always smaller. In summer, when the heat of the day had died down and the air was pleasantly cool, it was another matter. Then there was no discomfort in loitering underneath the thorn tree, chatting with one's acquaintances, observing with mild interest what went on, and smoking, in leisurely satisfaction, the fragrant home-grown tobacco whose smoke curled lazily into the air. There was no loss of dignity attached to that democratic intercourse, and in consequence the Village had no scruples in attending. On such occasions one could see not only the magistrate, the chief constable, and the local attorney among the little throng that clustered in the vicinity of the thorn tree, but practically everyone who counted for anything at all in the Village, including the Reverend Mr Mance-Bisley, who took advantage of these opportunities to discuss the various questions with the parents of his scholars, and the Reverend Christian Uhlmann, who, with a gravity befitting his position and with a childlike shyness which was temperamental, stood modestly aside and engaged in conversation only when he was directly approached. It took some time to sort the mail, and when the doors of the post office were opened there was a rush towards the counter and a quick dispersal of the waiting crowd homewards.

On this first Saturday in the New Year, the attendant Villagers found a common subject for discussion and debate. That subject was the Situation, as yet so nebulous and unclarified that it permitted of a variety of conjecture and conclusion to be anxiously canvassed and furtively submitted or eagerly defended according to the bias of the debater.

The post-cart was late. Somewhere in that hundred mile stretch of road which it had to traverse from the railway station to the Village it had been delayed. A broken trace, a strained hoof—such things were beyond the foresight of even the best contractors, and could be indulgently overlooked on ordinary occasions. But today was not an ordinary occasion. The little waiting crowd was pent up with eagerness. During the week there had been a summation of stimuli sufficient to pitch men's minds to that impatience which can neither condone nor extenuate delay.

The Reverend Mr Mance-Bisley gave voice to it when he spoke to his companion, the chief constable. The latter was a burly, sunburnt police officer, whose spruce semi-military uniform and pointed moustache ensured him more respect and administration than did his undoubted efficiency as an experienced patrol leader and detective. Sam Chumley was colonial born, a descendant of an 1820 Settler family, but well liked and respected in the Village and District not only because he was a good police official but also because he was a good fellow, sympathetic with an understanding insight that had made him thoroughly cognisant of the different peculiarities of the various units in the community which he served. His wife was the daughter of one of the local farmers, and at home he spoke English and Dutch with an impartiality that in time had done much to ruin his command of both languages. In that respect he could be called the most perfectly bilingual person in the District, and his services as interpreter were often called into requisition in court.

'I think it is high time,' observed the rector, plaintively, 'that the government enforced the fine for these vexatious delays, Mr Chumley. Every mail day, for the last three months, the post-cart has been late. It is simply disgraceful. And today of all days ...'

''Taint Seldon's fault, Sir,' rejoined the chief constable, screwing his moustache point into a more tenuous end. 'You must blame the driver. Not that Ampie isn't a good driver. One must make allowances, sir. If you've driven in this heat, Sir, as I have done, you would make 'lowances, Sir. You want to stop, 'casionally, to give the mules a breather, Sir, and to take a *sopie* yourself, Sir.'

'That is all very well,' said the rector, impatiently, 'but the man should know that we are all waiting. We have had no reliable news at all today ...'

'Bar this morning's telegram, Sir. You've seen that? They are making a rare mess of things, Sir. That comes of trusting to *ametjoors*, sir. If you want to get things done properly you have to do it yourself, Sir.' An equally burly farmer approached, and greeted the rector and the chief constable civilly.

'Good day, Your Reverence, good day, Chief Constable,' he said, speaking English with a pronounced intonation but intelligibly. 'It is so that we are going to have war, now?'

The chief constable shook hands. 'Who's been putting that flea in your ear, Uncle Berend?' he asked genially, for the rector's benefit, and then lapsing into Dutch, 'For the Lord's sake, Uncle Berend, don't go about putting the wind up on people. You ain't a youngster, and you should know better at your time of life. What's there to fight about ...'

'That you may well ask,' replied Uncle Berend van As, stroking his beard reflectively. 'That is what I ask myself. But it's always this blasted interference. Why can't they leave us alone? Now these Outlanders ...'

The rector turned aside. He could not follow the conversation, though from the vehemence with which the words were spoken he could guess something of its import. Nor could he altogether blame the point of view which he felt more than heard the newcomer express. These people had their sympathies. They naturally took a one-sided, biased view of affairs in the north. Perhaps, too, they had resented the implication that their own trusted leader had failed them at a critical moment. He preferred not to be drawn into the conversation, and walked briskly to meet the magistrate who came up at that moment to join the crowd.

'Is there anything further, Mr Storam?' he asked anxiously.

'Nothing of importance, Rector,' the magistrate replied. 'You know of course that His Excellency has arrived at Pretoria and that, incidentally, Mr Rhodes has handed in his resignation. It is now a matter of settlement between the insurgents in Johannesburg and the Boer Government, and I have every confidence in the Governor.'

'I am not so sure about that,' said the rector, gloomily. 'I am told that he has been singularly weak. The papers tell us that Mr Hofmeyr practically forced him to draw up that Proclamation. I still feel rather sore about that, Mr Storam. I don't like the idea that we left Jameson in the lurch ...'

'My dear Rector,' exclaimed the magistrate, 'whatever else was there to do? You surely do not imagine that any government, any civilised government, could have done anything else but repudiate so flagrant an act of brigandage? Do get things in their right perspective ...'

'I try to do that,' said the Reverend Mr Mance-Bisley with dignity. 'It is all very confusing, I admit, but I do not like the idea that an outsider can dictate to Her Majesty's representative what to do in an emergency. And that is practically what has been done.'

'You've got it all wrong,' said the magistrate, patiently. 'Mr Hofmeyr is not an outsider. He is a member of the Executive Council, and virtually the leader of the party in power. Moreover—and get that clearly in your mind, please—the acknowledged mouthpiece of that party. I do not see how he could have acted differently, and it seems to me that he has acted throughout with the greatest correctness. There has been no dictation—none whatever, Rector; and I should not like that idea to get abroad. May I appeal to you,' he sank his voice confidentially, 'not to add to the difficulties that we have got to face, Rector. I am quite aware that you think

Jameson's action is one—let us say—dictated by humane motives, and all that sort of thing. I beg to differ, but let us agree to differ, Rector. Only bear in mind that people do differ, and will differ, on the exact interpretation to be put upon this unfortunate affair, and don't please make it more difficult for us all to adjust our differences. Here is Mr Uhlmann. You will see in a minute what his point of view is.'

The Dutch Reformed *predikant* who approached them lifted his rather shabby flat clerical hat in courteous salute as he came forward. He was a man of middle age, tall, angular, but upright of carriage, with a certain poise that betokened muscular strength. His clean-shaven face was tanned and wrinkled, regular of features, and settled in an expression of grave kindliness to which his fine brown eyes lent vivacity as well as charm. He was dressed in clerical garb, with black cloth trousers and an old frock-coat that fitted him badly.

'I thought I should find you here, Mr Storam,' he said, speaking English with a rather slow, careful intonation. 'But not you, Mr Bisley. You do not often waste your time at the Post Office, I think so? But no doubt the anxiety ... yes, Mr Storam, we are all anxious. These are tragic times. I have had callers all day. Do you know, I have been asked ...'

'I know, Mr Uhlmann,' interrupted the magistrate hurriedly. 'They came to me too, but I shooed them off. A public meeting just now is the very last thing we want. It would do far more harm than good ...'

'So I expressed myself,' said Mr Uhlmann, gesticulating with his hands, a habit which his brother clergyman thought undignified and foreign and as such disapproved of. Mr Mance-Bisley had not made up his mind whether he quite liked his colleague— whom he would never have alluded to by that designation—or disliked him. There was something in the *predikant's* mild, almost defensive, attitude which he resented because it implied a want of courage, and Mr Mance-Bisley put courage among the major virtues. He could respect the man's sincerity—his acknowledged learning, and his quiet, unostentatious activity. But he found Mr Uhlmann's mildness an incentive to himself to become more aggressive and militant when they discussed controversial matters, and although he tried his best not to give way to his feelings he realised that there was an antagonism, subtle indeed but real, between him and his fellow clergyman. He felt it now. It was not quite the same feeling of disagreement which he had experienced when the magistrate had discussed the Raid with him, but it was something akin to it.

'What should there be a meeting for?' he asked, belligerently. 'And what business is it of yours ...'

'No, my dear Rector,' said Mr Uhlmann quietly, 'that is what I said. That is indeed what I tried to express. These matters are in higher hands than ours. This is not the time to interfere. You agree, Mr Storam?' The magistrate nodded emphatically and lit his pipe. 'I said to them—they came in a deputation last night to see me—I said that I would not be a party to any agitation. Not, at least, until we knew more. More facts, I mean. You agree with me, don't you, Mr Bisley?'

'I hardly see that you are called upon to make any decision, Mr Uhlmann,' replied the rector, stiffly. 'It seems to me that,'—he was going to say 'we should keep out of it,' but felt that that did not quite express what he had in mind, and changed it to 'there is enough excitement already.'

'Mr Uhlmann, unfortunately,' interrupted the magistrate, 'has something to do with it. They come to him, as they do to me, for advice and guidance, and it is his duty to give both. I think you did perfectly right, Mr Uhlmann. If you could make some reference tomorrow, in your address ...'

'I will do so, Mr Storam, I will do so. I will do my best to calm feeling and allay fear. But it is little one can do, is it not? The people have received a profound shock. You, Mr Bisley, hardly realise how profound. You have not been long enough among us to understand what this means.'

The Reverend Mr Mance-Bisley did not like that tone. It implied that he was unable to form his own judgment, and such an implication savoured of impertinence.

'I am quite capable of realising that there are many here, Mr Uhlmann,' he remarked stiffly, 'who are in sympathy with the—ah—retrogressive administration in the Transvaal. Quite a number, too, who would like to see the—ah—English swept into the sea. I have only to read the papers to realise that ...'

'Ah, the papers,' Mr Uhlmann gesticulated with his hands in the way that his colleague found so foreign, 'you should not believe all they write. Nor, do I think, should you accuse us of—Mr Storam, you must help me out with the word—is it disloyalty? But no. Disloyalty to what? Sympathy, yes. They are blood relations, Mr Bisley, and blood ... you know the saying. But there is no more in it than that. Mr Storam will bear me out. There is no active support of what you call the retrogressive administration of the Transvaal. On the contrary, there is considerable fellow-feeling with the *Uitlanders*. We, too, have suffered. My brother-in-law—he is up there, and he has taken some prominent part in the movement. You should not judge us harshly, Mr Bisley.'

He spoke so mildly, with such obvious sincerity, that the rector felt a twinge of conscience. Uhlmann, he knew, was related by marriage to one of the leaders of the Progressive Party in the Transvaal, a man who had a reputation for integrity. He hastened to apologise, for the Reverend Mr Mance-Bisley, for all his belligerency, was a gentleman with a gentleman's instincts.

'Forgive me, Mr Uhlmann,' he said cordially. 'I had no right to say that. But really, in these circumstances one does say more than one ought to.'

'That is the pity of it,' said Uhlmann, gravely. 'And if we—we are more or less responsible citizens—allow ourselves to be carried away by our feelings, Mr Bisley, what allowances must we make for others who are ignorant and irresponsible? But is there no further news, Mr Storam? Is anything settled at Cape Town?'

'Nothing yet,' replied the magistrate. 'If the resignation of the Prime Minister is accepted ...'

'Then of course the ministry goes,' interjected Uhlmann quickly. 'That means— well, what do you think it will mean, Mr Storam?'

'I really don't quite know,' replied the magistrate. 'Sprigg, I suppose, if Hofmeyr cannot or will not carry on. An election pretty soon, at all events, and that is not desirable just now. There comes the post-cart. Now we can get the papers, and I can assure you that I am longing to read them.'

'I too,' said the rector. 'I should really like to know why they lost. There must have been some reason for it. Of course, the weather may have had something to do with it, but I can hardly accept that as a sufficient excuse. It seems to me sheer bad management ...'

'Oh no,' said the chief constable, who had come up to them, having finished his talk with uncle Berend. 'It's just bad soldiering, Sir. Against Cronje's commando they had no earthly ... Besides, what can you expect after fifteen hours in the saddle ...'

'I was referring to the cricket,' said the rector crossly. 'Not to the fighting.'

'Oh that,' the chief constable's voice was slightly contemptuous. 'We none of us take much account of cricket when there's something more serious on the carpet, Sir. But Western Province is not to be despised, Sir. I remember when they played ...'

The chief constable was left soliloquising, for the arrival of the post-cart had broken up the groups, already keenly on the alert, for the driver had sounded his bugle a mile away to give warning of his coming. The Post Office clerk rushed out of the seclusion of his office and, helped by willing volunteers, off-loaded the bags and bundled them into the office, locking the door to give himself and his chief the necessary privacy for the sorting of the mail. The bystanders clustered around the cart and plied the driver with questions, which the stolid old Coloured man answered to the best of his ability. The sunset splashed the horizon with gorgeous colouring, but the afterglow lingered, and before twilight set in the mail had been sorted, and those who were fortunate in receiving letters or papers had been handed their post and trudged homewards.

The Reverend Mr Mance-Bisley walked along the street with his clerical *confrere*. Each bore a parcel of letters and papers, and both were eager to find out what these contained. The rectory was a few yards away from the post office; the parsonage at the extreme end of the street. At the back entrance of his house, the rector took leave of his companion.

'Tell me, Mr Uhlmann,' he said, as he shook hands, a courtesy which Village convention imperatively demanded even after such a casual meeting, 'do you really think that this ... this trouble in the Transvaal will have any repercussions here? What you said just now, and what Mr Storam has told me ... I am really anxious to know.'

'I cannot tell you, Mr Bisley,' said Mr Uhlmann, gravely. 'One can only reason from experience, and there is no experience here to guide me.'

'But you have the experience of twenty years ago,' the rector retorted. 'I imagine feelings must have been much more disturbed then.'

'Then I was not here,' replied the *predikant*. 'From what I was told, there was no trouble here then. But things have changed since then. When I came here, Mr Bisley, the people were not so much interested in politics as they are now. They are different today. I do not know what has made them different, but I think that what has happened, what is today happening up in the north, has had some influence in causing that difference.'

'I should like to talk it over with you, if I may,' said the rector. 'Not now, of course. I can see that you are itching to read you mail, and I am just as eager to read my *Times*. But some time on Monday, if you care to discuss things with me. At your own convenience.'

'With pleasure. I shall be at your disposal whenever you like. Perhaps by Monday we may have clearer light. Just now it is very much like this twilight, and one is afraid it may be dark too soon. Goodnight.'

The Reverend Mr Mance-Bisley settled himself in his study, for once glad to find that his wife had not yet returned from her round of visits, and opened his bundle of newspapers. He found to his astonishment that his *Cape Times* had a leading article in Dutch alongside the usual leader in English, and he read with strained interest the latest detailed communications from the north. They were unpleasant reading, and from time to time he took off his strong reading glasses and rubbed his eyes. He found, when he had finished reading all that the papers contained about the situation in the north, that he had no great desire to read particulars of Lord Hawke's first match. Even cricket seemed to have sunk into insignificance before this disaster at Doornkop. And a filibustering raid such as that about which he had read did not seem like cricket. He recognised the fact that it implied something very much unlike cricket.

'I really cannot understand how men can be such fools, my dear,' he said to his wife when she came back. 'It is unbelievable. And the worst of it is, my dear, that it has given British prestige a shock—yes, my dear, a shock. Mr Uhlmann tells me that I don't understand—that I have not been long enough in this country to realise what it means. But I fancy that I can realise it well enough.'

'I should think so,' said Mrs Mance-Bisley in her decisive way. 'It is incredible stupidity, that's what it is. But that's no reason why we should not have dinner, Claude. And remember you have your sermon to prepare. So come along.'

Chapter 9

The mind of a small boy is not a clean-wiped slate upon which every passing impression leaves an indelible mark. It is the product of forces yet imperfectly understood, forces stretching back to that period before birth, even to the time before conception, when emotion and passion are material factors in moulding and modifying those subtle temperamental traits which we are pleased to call innate tendencies. The academical battle between those who hold that heredity has a larger share in our lives and those who maintain that we are all insensibly shaped into what we ultimately become by the influence of our environment, has not yet been decided. The man of common sense will abide by the results of his own experience, the sum of which seems to be that both environment and parental characteristics, familial peculiarities, and racial attributes combine to fashion the child into what he becomes, all sharing, though perhaps in diverse proportion, in the reactions that he ultimately shows to the stimuli that touch him in daily life.

To the making of Charles Crest had contributed on the maternal side, from which the boy is popularly supposed to derive the major share of his temperament, the cultured, physically perfect and mentally wholly sound Quakerley strain, blended with the equally satisfactory blood of the Stellenbosch Dutch farmer whose forefathers had been Frisian noblemen. In appearance the boy, as his grandfather had discovered, was a perfect Quakerley type, with the lithesome grace, gracile but with no indication of weakliness nor of effeminacy, that had characterised the manhood of the family. In temperament, as Andrew gradually found out, young Charlie approximated to his great grandmother. He possessed something of Andrew's mother's assured reserve, a shyness that was less a lack of initiative and self assertion than a disinclination to demonstrate what was palpably self-evident. Andrew himself possessed something of that calm, phlegmatic assurance upon which his father had often sarcastically complimented him, but he knew that withal he had much more of his father's impetuosity and capacity for passion latent in him than his mother had ever evidenced. In his grandson he now observed, or fancied he observed, some of the traits he had admired and respected in his mother. Youth is at no pains to curtain its feelings, not having learned, by experience, to hide what it holds, whether the holding grieves or pleases it. Its reactions to emotion are unschooled and naïve, registered in expression and behaviour with a certainty more convincing than any that maturity can supply. Old Andrew found himself analysing these reactions in his grandson, an occupation so interesting and so instructive to one whose mind, while not painfully introspective like Lamb's, had yet been trained by circumstances and by his own predilection for communion with himself, that he devoted more time to it than he could conscientiously spare from his garden.

The intellectual ability of the boy was what had attracted him in the first place, though, when he pondered over the matter, he admitted to himself that the appeal of the lad's physical beauty had been an equally powerful attraction. The combination of intelligence and bodily grace had influenced him in much the same way as a beautiful plant, where delicacy of structure and perfection of colour were enhanced by odour or utility, would have done. He found Charlie avid for information, quick, as an intelligent child is, to collect facts, impressions, views, and opinions, and he observed, too, that the boy had an unusual, almost precocious, instinct to adapt himself to new standards, as if he were capable of assessing values and discriminating between them. Every day as they rambled in the garden, the boy gave evidence of these qualities. He had been given a patch to till for himself, and with the help of the Native garden boy he had already made a passable collection of veld-plants. The old man refrained from trying to teach him formal botany. He had himself found, in his own boyhood, that a knowledge of nomenclature was no indication of the man's knowledge of the science, and his teaching was therefore in the nature of what he himself had experienced in his rambles with the old botanist on the slopes of the Devil's Peak. He took the boy for walks into the River valley and the neighbouring hills, where the weather-worn sandstone boulders gave shelter to succulents so small that an expert eye was needed to detect them. Such excursions yielded a host of apperceptive masses, of which good use could be made, and old Andrew, himself a naturalist by choice as well as by inclination, exerted himself to draw from them whatever could be extracted. He showed Charlie the tiny window-leaved mesembryanthemums, half-buried in the sand; the modest flat-topped sort that mimics the surrounding stones but is magnificently revealed, despite its care to conceal itself, by the gorgeous magenta bloom which it proudly expands at midday; the queerly fringed Ferrarias, that blossom in the dry sand, and whose flowers look like brown irises; the spider-like Bartholina orchids; the giant roridula fly-catchers, whose leaves are covered with a sticky gum on which roving ants and unwary beetles are trapped; the curious parasite growing on the roots of the milkbush, whose seeds are carried downwards by ants, and whose fruit is esteemed a delicacy, tasting of sweet custard flavoured with pine kernels; the prickly, fat-stemmed sarcocaulons, dwarf octogenarians so richly resinous that they burn readily; the rambling sour figs carpeting many square yards of veld with their rich gold and vivid violet, and their cousins, the low-growing, poisonous *Kougoed* from which the Bushmen extracted their arrow poison.

On these excursions the boy and the old man would talk familiarly, for when he was in his grandfather's company Charlie lost much of his reserve and shyness. Grandfather seemed an understanding sort of old chap, who took it for granted that a fellow had some sense. At first grandfather had appeared to be a rather terrifying personality, smelling pleasantly of soap, and hardly taking any notice of one. But from the time grandfather had taken him into the garden and shown him all its treasures, a change had been apparent. He could now talk freely to grandfather, who was really interested in all sorts of things. He could talk about Australia and about cricket; he could ask questions about kangaroos and opossums, of which, if the truth must be told, young Charlie knew very little, and he could be very patient and explain things in a manner that one could understand, even though he sometimes did make use of hard words that sounded like so much gibberish.

In the Village Charles had made friends with several of the boys, some of his own age, some older. Martin Storam, the head boy of the school and the magistrate's only son, was the acknowledged leader of the new society into which he had plunged even before he had been admitted to Mr Mance-Bisley's school. Charlie liked him, but stood a little in awe of his height, his long arms, and his quick temper. Not that young Martin ever bullied him. The relations between the boys at Mr Mance-Bisley's school were normal, and from the first Charlie had been subjected to the usual tribulations which beset every junior. Perhaps in his case they were slightly more pronounced, because the newcomer's acquaintance with local customs and prejudices was microscopic, and the class resented, at first, the implied superiority that came from experience derived from a school overseas, and from an accent that somehow did not seem to blend with the English spoken in the Village. But Charlie had soon acclimatised himself, although he still retained some of the juvenile expletives which were strange and novel to his mates, just as theirs had seemed bizarre to him when he came. The excitement about the situation in the north had found a distinct echo amongst the boys, who, hearing what their elders thought of things, reflected these opinions vicariously when they discussed the matter in the playground. There were three distinct sections among the boys, just as there were three distinct sections among the Village community. One, a distinct minority, affected to stand outside the debate, too apathetic or too aloof to argue either way, adopting a strictly Laodicean attitude which was distinctly unpopular. Of these the leader was the gaoler's boy, John Tomory, who had imbibed from his father far-fetched socialistic ideas, and who hinted that nothing mattered very much and that the whole thing was a put-up job in which the interests of the Boers on the one side, and those of the Transvaal Outlanders on the other, were merely pawns in a damnable comedy played by the capitalists. The second section, to which the Storam boy, notwithstanding his father's warning to remain outside the controversy, belonged, was fiercely pro-Boer, and wildly aggressive towards those who had anything to say in favour of the Raiders. The third section joined forces with old Mrs Quakerley, protesting their loyalty to British interests and equally vehemently championing the interests of the Outlanders.

Mr Mance-Bisley was too good a schoolmaster to be unaware of these undercurrents among his scholars, and far too sensible to try to turn them into other channels. What piqued him was to find that among what he called the 'Republic group' were boys of undoubted English descent, whose forefathers had belonged to the old settlers and whose sympathies, one would have thought, were entirely with the English-speaking section. Martin Storam was an example. The boy revelled in sport; he subscribed regularly to several English journals, among which the *Boys' Own Paper* and the *Leisure Hour* were his favourites; he was good at English history; his home language was English, and he behaved, as the rector was fair enough to admit, just as any normal, well brought up English schoolboy behaved. Yet, on the few occasions when the subject had cropped up incidentally, the rector had been surprised to discover that Martin's view of the case was not quite that which it might have been supposed he would hold. It suggested, if it did not implicitly state, that there had been something 'not fair' in the manner in which the Outlanders had handled their case; a possibility that the Raid, now so much discussed, was something not consonant with the spirit of sportsmanship which the headmaster was trying to inculcate. Mr Mance-Bisley was fair enough to admit that this point of view was reasonable. A boy like Martin could not be supposed to know that there were extenuating circumstances, points that could be pleaded for the defence, arguments cogent in mitigation of guilt. Indeed, the rector himself, when he had read everything that he could find in the newspapers and calmly reviewed the facts, confessed to himself that in strict justice that view was eminently rational. One could excuse the Raid; one could not, honestly, condone it. He himself had argued the matter at length with his wife, who had from the first declared, with her usual outspoken directness, that it was a 'sorry business, calculated to damage us no matter what happens, my dear,' and who had never shared his own initial burst of admiration when he had heard that a small handful of armed men had rushed in to the help of a sadly enslaved English community. Gradually he had come to realise that there was very little cause for admiration, and that there was, on the contrary, considerable justification for those who shared his wife's opinion that the small handful of impetuous men had done more harm to the cause he had at heart than anything else that had happened since the time he had arrived in the country.

He found that Mr Quakerley agreed with this latter view. And he had much respect for Mr Quakerley's opinion. The old man represented what to the rector appeared to be the best type of colonial Englishman, the type that had made good, that had succeeded, and in the process of acquiring success had refrained from losing those essential characteristics which were the hallmark of a gentleman. There could be no shadow of doubt about Mr Quakerley's loyalty. Loyalty to the principles which Mr Mance-Bisley regarded as primary principles, loyalty that could not be expressly defined in so many words, loyalty that recognised the predominant fact that this was an English Colony whose inhabitants owed, at least, the ordinary obligations of citizenship to the motherland. The rector knew, more from what he had read in the press than from what he had actually experienced in the Village, that there was a section among the inhabitants of the colony that held these obligations to be somewhat loose and optional, that coquetted with republican sentiments, and talked about ties of race and kin that could override their loyalty to the Crown. He vaguely opined that the political party which had installed Mr Rhodes as Prime Minister, the Bond Party, largely sympathised with this section, and that it was trying, insidiously, to undermine the loyalty of colonists of the stamp of Quakerley. It was all very disturbing and very conflicting, and the events that had taken place during the past few months had made the situation even more involved.

'You would do me a kindness, Mr Quakerley,' the rector said as he sat on Andrew's tree-shaded *stoep* drinking eleven o'clock tea, 'if you would explain just what the position is. It is most embarrassing, sometimes—I mean, one finds it so difficult to understand what these people really want. And, as you know, it is distressing to ... to ...'

'You shouldn't take any notice of what the boys say, Rector,' said the old man smilingly. 'They just repeat what they hear their elders remark. It's so much hot air, Rector; nothing else. Of course, I regret just as much as you do that these things are talked about. It must engender bad feeling in the long run ...'

'It does, it does,' exclaimed the rector, plaintively. 'There was a most unseemly squabble in the playground this morning. I had to cane three of them, and I do not yet know if I did the right thing, but one must have discipline. I have talked to young Storam, but to tell you the truth, Mr Quakerley, I am disappointed in the boy ...'

'You surprise me, Rector. I should have thought Martin the best head boy you have had so far.'

'So he is ... in a sense. But since ... since all this excitement, Mr Quakerley, I don't quite know what to make of him. This morning, for instance. It's his duty to keep order in the playground. You know I do not in the least object to a good stand-up fight if there is something to be fought for, and the lads know it. Officially, of course, I am not supposed to know when such affairs take place, and I take no cognisance of it officially when they do. But this morning's squabble one can hardly overlook ...'

'What actually did take place, Rector? Charlie told me his version ...'

'Ah yes, your grandson was implicated, but I let him off with a warning. It seems the whole matter started from one of these silly arguments about Jameson and the Outlanders, and a free fight developed before the debate had lasted many minutes. When I taxed Storam, his excuse was that he could not prevent the lads from discussing the matter, and that young Tomory and some of the others had "asked for it," to use his own expressive phrase. Crest, I must tell you frankly, contributed not a little to the disturbance. At the height of it, I found him perched on the fence singing *God save the Queen* at the top of his voice.'

'That's his granny,' said the old man, with an indulgent smile. 'Alice is fiercely militant, Rector, and Charlie is young. You must make some allowance.'

'So I do,' the rector's voice became plaintive again, 'but the whole thing is so thoroughly upsetting. There is no rhyme or reason for it, and I simply cannot have it in my school.'

'I quite agree, Rector. But it is difficult to stop it. Your school population is, after all, merely a reflection of what lies outside, and I can tell you, what you probably know quite as well as I do, that much the same things go on outside. This Raid has made a cleft between us here, Rector. You may not realise it, but I do. I have lived here all my life, and I know what its influence is, and I think I can foretell what it is going to be in the future. Eighteen years ago, when the war was on in the Transvaal, matters were different. We weren't in touch with folk up north then. Our associations were different; our outlook too, was not quite the same as it is today, Rector.'

'That is what I am told, Mr Quakerley,' said the rector, soberly. 'But that is just what I cannot understand. If you will kindly explain. Believe me, I am trying to understand. I should like to see matters from their standpoint—you know what I mean?'

Old Andrew nodded. 'I quite see, Rector. But it is difficult to explain. Let me try to make my own position clear to you ...'

'I have never for one moment imagined that you, Mr Quakerley, felt anything but what I feel,' interjected the rector quickly. 'Our English point of view is perfectly clear ...'

'Yes, but is it?' his host interjected in turn. 'Take Storam—take myself, Rector. We are English, in your sense of the term, although both Storam and I have Dutch or French blood in us. We are not pure English as you are, or as Mrs Mance-Bisley ...'

'I should say "Colonial" and let it go at that,' interjected the rector again. 'There is a considerable strain of French blood in my wife's family.'

'Quite so. And the non-English section, what you would call the "Dutch" section, Rector, are just as little Dutch—pure Dutch, that is—as we are pure English. Take the Reverend Mr Uhlmann; he's without a drop of Dutch blood; purely French and German, Hanoverian like our Royal family. It's a misnomer to call him Dutch ...'

'I should not take him to be at all typical of the Dutch section,' said the rector.

'And yet he typifies them,' remarked Quakerley. 'Take the Rekkers, pure Dutch, aristocratic Dutch if you like. You will find no more "loyal" man in our community than Rekker. I remember in my youth how his old father—a character, Rector, if ever there was one; a fine chess player, an aristocrat to his finger tips—used to lead the crowd on the square in singing *God save the Queen* on the Queen's Birthday. In those days we had a republican party—we have always had it, ever since the Company's rule went—but we had none of this ... this sectional feeling. Some people call it race feeling, but I don't, Rector. There is no difference, after all, racially between Dutch and English. But there is a difference of tradition. You, fresh from home, come with a different outlook. You have a different tradition from what we, who are Colonists, have. Yours may be better, just as that of the Dutchman, fresh out from Holland, may be better; but we have, at all events, a right to ours.'

'That I willingly grant, Mr Quakerley. But in what way does yours differ from mine? That is just the point I should like you to explain.'

'I can only speak for myself,' said old Andrew, reflectively. 'I suppose everyone has his own explanation, his own interpretation, and I can only give you mine. But I do believe, Rector, that you will find a certain agreement between mine and that of others who like myself are born here, no matter whether we are descended from Dutch or English or Hanoverian ancestors. And I also believe that each new generation gains new—how shall I put it?—new stimuli which tend to strengthen these differences in tradition. I have noticed that. You must have noticed it yourself. Take young Storam, for instance, as you mentioned just now. The boy ought to live wholly in what I may call the "home" tradition, but he doesn't. He is more strongly "Colonial" than I am ...'

'I should not class you as Colonial in that sense, Mr Quakerley,' protested the rector, sipping his tea and helping himself to another buttered scone.

'Yet I am, Rector. Thoroughly. If you would only divest your mind of the suspicion that "Colonial" means—implies—something antagonistic to England. I grant you it does imply—it necessarily must imply—something antagonistic to outside interference. Indeed, I should say that definition is a sound one—the only sound one we can find. We are a young community; like all young people we are a bit too big for our boots—a good sign, Rector, a good sign, for only old age brings us wisdom to realise our limitations. We resent interference, and there has been interference all along the line. What more outstanding proof of this can you want than this Raid? Well meant, of course; I do not say that whatever interference has taken place has ever been intentionally to our detriment. On the contrary. But ever since we have had responsible government we have felt ourselves fit to manage our own affairs, and any interference from outside, no matter how well intentioned, has put our backs up. I suppose in time all our crown colonies will become separate, independent units, bound to the motherland by ties of sentiment. I see no other logical development, Rector. It must come naturally. My only fear is that interference of the kind we have seen lately may lead to complications which will inevitably bring about not a fusion of the various sections but a widening of the gulf that already exists.'

'To that extent I am with you,' said the rector, ungrudgingly. 'I can imagine myself, in time, obtaining this tradition, if you call it that. I am anchored here, voluntarily, and I suppose I am like your father was, Mr Quakerley, still too strongly attached to the homeland entirely to share your tradition. I can understand it, and I can quite easily understand the growing sentiment, aspiration, or whatever you like to call it, in the colonies to become self-dependent. No one grudges them that, and it would be childish to cavil at it. But here things seem to be slightly different. I observe— pardon me for saying so—more than a feeling such as what one would expect in Australia. I have never been there, but I am told that colonial sentiment is quite as strong there as it is here. But it has nothing—let me qualify and say, little—in common with the sort of anti-English feeling that one notices here ...'

'Only lately, Rector,' interrupted old Andrew, quickly. 'You will do us the justice to admit that there is little of it here ...'

'But, to judge from what I read, much elsewhere in the Colony,' said the rector, shrewdly.

'Possibly. And so long as there remains in the north an administration which is definitely antagonistic to England, there will always be something of that feeling, Rector. I confess that the attitude which the Transvaal has lately adopted fills me with misgiving. It is calculated to cause much trouble in the future. When one bears in mind that these northern parts were settled by people who were dissatisfied here and who deliberately separated themselves from our traditions and adopted their own, which are in many respects not such that all of us can subscribe to them, one can easily understand that there is a clash. I agree that there is a section—a strong section—here that finds the northern tradition more congenial, and that propaganda is being made for it. Myself, I do not think that such propaganda will succeed. Our people here, whether Dutch or German or English, are much too sensible to give up substance for shadows. But interference such as we have lately seen is playing directly into the hands of these agitators, and I fear that we are in for considerable trouble. Nothing, you know, Rector, manures a grievance so well as opposition. And that is what is being done now.'

'You think there is a grievance, Mr Quakerley?'

'No community is ever without one, Rector. If you read our Cape history—let me recommend Theal; you will find him pretty impartial—you will discover quite a lot of grievances. I do not say they are such as to make me feel hot all over. Misunderstandings mostly; authority ignoring local interests; unfortunate lapses by officialdom. Just now we are—or some of us are—making a good deal about language rights. Myself I do not think that means much. But while there are two languages in a community, it is just as well to recognise them. Let the better one win in the end, but I fancy that it is bad statesmanship to try and anticipate the future. That, of course, is merely my own view.'

'Then you do not think that the Bond is out to make this colony a separate republic, or to attempt to bring about a union with the Transvaal, Mr Quakerley? One hears so much about a conspiracy ...'

'You will hear much more, Rector. But use your common sense. The Bond—I am not a member of it, for I have never troubled my head much about politics; I have always voted for the man rather than for the party—but the Bond is not, so far as I can see, separatist. It is not even distinctly pro-Transvaal. Some time ago, you may remember, it adopted a very sensible attitude on the closing of the Drifts by the President. It has kept Mr Rhodes in power, and I don't think you can question his loyalty. I don't like that word, Rector, but I use it in the sense that we now seem to imply. My father used it sometimes, but it seems to me in an altogether different sense. I think, to go back to the Bond, you may take it that it is an agrarian party and as such opposed to what one might call the urban interests. That seems the natural cleavage—the cleavage between conservatism and progress in the political sense of these terms. There are many points of similarity between the two parties, but at present the real issues are obscured by this racial business, and the situation has been terribly complicated by this Raid. I confess I do not like it. I look to men like Mr Uhlmann and Rekker to counteract such mischief, but you know how these things spread.'

'Indeed I do,' said the rector fervently. 'It has even reached my school.'

'There you can easily deal with it,' said Quakerley with a smile. 'By the way, I shall have to talk to Charlie and tell him not to imitate his granny so much. My wife, Rector, is one of the extremists on the other side, and it is the extreme section that creates all our difficulties.'

'I quite agree, Mr Quakerley,' said the rector feelingly. 'But what is one to do? I am in a difficulty myself. Mrs Mance-Bisley is keenly interested in the temperance movement. She wishes to start a Band of Hope in the Village, and she has been in correspondence with temperance interests at Cape Town. Now I understand that we are to be favoured by a visit from a prominent temperance man, and I am expected to make arrangements for a public meeting. That was one of the matters I wished to discuss with you.'

'I am sorry to hear it,' said Quakerley. 'The Village is not intemperate, Rector. Drunkenness is comparatively rare in the location. We are a wine-growing District, and such a visit will be unpopular, to say the least. But you might speak to Mr Uhlmann about it.'

'My wife has already done so,' said the rector, 'and I gather that he is much opposed to the plan ...'

'I am not surprised at that,' interrupted his host. 'In a way it is a sort of reflection upon him, don't you think so?'

'I should not like to say that. But the astonishing thing is that Mrs Uhlmann is heartily in favour of the gentleman's visit and offers to put him up, while she promises that her children will be the first recruits for the Band of Hope. I do not know much of them—they do not attend school, you know. Their father, I believe, teaches them. But Mrs Uhlmann's enthusiasm has greatly stimulated that of my wife, and I fear that we are going to get the temperance mission.'

'It will interest the Village,' said Quakerley, mildly, 'and it cannot do much harm, although I don't think it is likely to do much good. If I can be of any assistance—my house is at your disposal, and I presume whoever comes ... we must not fail in hospitality, Rector. And the Uhlmanns are perhaps not quite in a position ...'

'I don't see how we can get round Mrs Uhlmann's invitation,' began the rector nervously. 'My wife proposed that we should have the missioner at the rectory, but I do not like that ...'

'I am thinking of Mr Uhlmann,' said Quakerley, laughingly. 'I fancy he is much of your opinion, and that is all the more reason why he should not be placed in an invidious position. Mrs Uhlmann will not object if the missioner comes to me, and that solution will relieve both you and the pastor from any direct responsibility. And now, Rector, you really must come and have a look at my new salvias. I have a heavenly blue one in perfect blossom just now. And some luscious grapes. Come along.'

Chapter 10

The coming of the temperance missioner was an event which turned the mind of the Village, and of the District no less, for a time into other and fortunately more impersonal, though still highly controversial, channels. It occasioned considerable excitement, for a whirlwind campaign such as the allies of what was miscalled 'temperance' proposed could not but arouse feelings that had lain as dormant through the years as had that germ of national consciousness now striving towards the luxury of recognition.

It became noised throughout the District that the missioner was coming. The Reverend Mr Uhlmann had not seen his way clear to make a parochial publication from the church pulpit; that had seemed to him to be undignified, altogether too secular to be for a moment entertained. Mr Mance-Bisley had cordially agreed, and this consensus had robbed the enterprise of much of the advertisement on which its supporters had counted. But placards, printed in Cape Town and lavishly displayed on walls and telegraphs posts, had informed all who would read that on such-and-such a date Mr Caspar Silverbottom would address a public meeting in the Village court room on 'The Need for Prohibition.'

The announcement was received with mixed feelings by those who read and were prepared to discuss it. The District, although pre-eminently a wheat and wool growing area, contained many vineyards. Some farmers made a fair and reasonable profit out of wine and brandy, continuing with success an industry which had been started in the old Company's day by their grandparents. Here and there a farm had become noted for the good quality of the wine produced; one, indeed, had achieved a reputation that extended beyond the boundaries of the District. This was the old *Knolkloof* farm where, in the early part of the century, Everardus Nolte, formerly known as Amadeus Tereg, the public executioner, had settled down to become a shining light of the community. With the help of a vagrant teacher of French descent, one Pierre Mabuis, who had reformed from the role of what Pastor Uhlmann would have called *'potator strenuus'* and had subsequently married the rich Widow Priem, Everardus had planted a noble vineyard and made excellent wine.

Pierre, oenologist as well as oenophilist, had perfected a vintage wine which was in considerable demand and had earned the ungrudging praise of the Acting-Governor, Sir William Cameron, who on a visit to the Village had drunk of it at Quakerley's table and had assured his host that it reminded him of a good Sauterne. Indeed, so much had the Governor appreciated the *Knolkloof* wine that he had sent four bottles of what he called 'the world's best' to old Andrew with a request that one bottle should be presented to the owner of *Knolkloof* as a token of gubernatorial gratitude. As Pierre Mabuis was no longer there to drink it, and old Everardus Nolte lay dying of a stroke, the bottles had been put down in Andrew's capacious cellar, for their recipient knew much more about garden shrubs and exotic trees than he did about wine, and could hardly be expected to guess that the 'world's best' was the famous Chateau d'Yquem 1874. To the owner of *Knolkloof*, or rather to his son, who now had charge of the farm, it was much more to the purpose that the Controller of the Household had ordered four half-aums of the wine to be sent yearly to Government House, a commission which was repeated for a couple of years and gained for the *Knolkloof* wine the reputation which it still possessed. There were other wine farmers, whose vineyards yielded luscious, sun-kissed grapes in quantities far too large to be merely eaten or turned into raisins. They made passable wines, which they drank at home, gave to their farm servants, or sold to their neighbours. They regarded their industry as honest, useful, and by no means anti-social, and they would have been more amused than shocked to hear that there were folk who thought differently. In their way of life they were strictly temperate, and to the extent that lay in their power they enforced temperance upon their servants. Drunkenness, as Mr Quakerley told the rector, was not common in the District or in the Village. Altogether the District and the Village felt that a campaign in favour of temperance, however admirable that virtue might be in theory, was not called for in the circumstances. But they preferred to wait and see what the missioner had to say before they committed themselves to a definite opinion on the question. Their diffidence was so great that the special committee, self-appointed to make arrangements for the reception of the missioner, found a difficulty in providing a chairman for Mr Caspar Silverbottom's first meeting. The acknowledged head of the community was the Queen's representative, the magistrate, but Mr Storam excused himself on the plea that he was an official and could not take part in controversies. Andrew Quakerley, next appealed to as being the most respected and influential private member of the community, declared himself willing to extend his cordial hospitality to Mr Silverbottom, but quite unwilling to take the chair at any meeting. Pastor Uhlmann shook his head; the rector, notwithstanding the pressure exerted by his wife upon him, refused the invitation, and as a result the committee found itself at a loss. It was very provoking, but there was a possibility that, by the time Mr Silverbottom had introduced himself, a suitable chairman would be found, in default of which the committee would itself appoint one of its members to act in that capacity.

On the afternoon of Mr Silverbottom's arrival the clearing outside the post office presented almost as animated a scene as on that memorable day when the Village had gathered there to await tidings of the Raid. The onlookers saw descending from the dusty post-cart a short, squat, heavily-bearded man, who wore an alpaca dust coat and a white cork helmet that reminded one of the pictures in Stanley's book. He was followed by an equally short and bulky woman, whose face was concealed by a thick gauze veil, and whose ample figure was also shrouded in a dust coat. Mr Caspar Silverbottom, having descended from the cart, gave his arm to his wife, and drew himself erect in the attitude of one who is conscious of his dignity and awaits formal recognition. The deputation from the committee came forward, introductions were made, and Mr Silverbottom was graciousness itself, shaking hands with all and sundry and expressing himself in suitably appreciative terms in a voice that carried his words well into the throng of Coloured people from the location who had clustered on the outskirts of the group to share in the Village's reception to him.

That reception was kindly and hospitable. There was none among those present who harboured any feeling of enmity towards the newcomer. All were tolerant, curious but not critical, for the Village was by nature and tradition charitable, neighbourly, and generous. A critical audience might have cavilled at the missioner's air of assurance; a sensitive community might even have resented his complacent superiority, his aggressively loud voice. But those who had come to welcome him were prepared to take him on trust. They saw in him one of themselves, and that impression was strengthened by his cheerful, full-featured face, dripping with moisture, and his general appearance which strongly suggested that of a farmer, bucolic in gesture, gait and manners.

Andrew, with Charlie Crest in his wake, shepherded his guests to his house. Beside Mr Silverbottom, the tall, dignified figure of the old man seemed accentuated, just as his crisp, courtly speech seemed to contrast with the boisterous bass of the missioner and the high-pitched, jerky accents of the missioner's wife. The sun was setting, and the long range of high mountain in the east was tinted with gorgeous gradations of colour, with the Valley lying beneath in deepening shadow. The sight seemed to arouse Mr Silverbottom to dithyrambic enthusiasm. He gesticulated with violence, and called his wife's attention to the beauty spread before them. He enjoyed it vociferously, so clamantly that to Andrew, to whom it had been familiar for more than seventy years but who found in it, perennially, matter for silent, soulful admiration, there was something unnatural, artificial, and forced in his appreciation. Andrew Quakerley loved beauty, with that simple, child-like love that one finds in natures that are supremely artistic without being conscious of it. Such a love is not expressed in adjectival exuberance, in a verbosity as meaningless as it is repugnant to one who feels that silence is the best, the only, tribute to the beautiful. For a moment Andrew was conscious of a vague dislike towards his guest. Mr Silverbottom's enthusiasm was too loud-voiced to be wholly sincere. Gradually that feeling of antagonism became stronger. It was no doubt a mistake on Alice's part to put a carafe of wine and wine-glasses on the hall-table; had Joan been there it would not have happened, but Alice had no tact. Nevertheless it had been no less tactless on the part of Mr Silverbottom to lift up his eyes in holy horror and to declaim against the sin of wine-bibbing before he had known his host for half-an-hour. Andrew ordered the servant, more sharply than was his wont, to take away the silver salver and to serve tea. He attempted no excuse, none was needed. Custom had decreed that the guest should receive a glass of wine and a biscuit. There was no harm in it, and even for a teetotaller, a courteous refusal would have been sufficient in defence of a principle that denied the validity of such custom. A tirade was unmannerly, uncalled for, and therefore objectionable.

Mrs Quakerley, dressed in her finest black satin, greeted the guests hospitably, though with a certain reserve as befitted one who was not quite sure of their social standing. Her daughter seconded her efforts but the Silverbottom couple needed no encouragement to make themselves at home. They acted and spoke as if they had known the Quakerleys for generations; they exuded a familiarity that charmed Mrs Quakerley, who found that they had mutual acquaintanceships, mutual likes and dislikes, and few points upon which they could quarrel. Old Andrew found the conversation uninteresting. It veered from local topics and a discussion of fashions at Cape Town to politics and the political situation. On this last point Mr Silverbottom spoke with as much energy, vivacity and loudness as he had lavished on the sunset. He was loyalist through and through; he condemned, in very forcible language, the misrule and corruption of the administration beyond the Vaal.

'Mark my words, Mr Quakerley,' he boomed, energetically wiping his face with a not too clean handkerchief, 'there will be no peace in this land until we have had war. There are some things that can only be settled by a stand-up fight. Much as I deplore a conflict, which as a Christian and a man of peace is altogether abhorrent to me—and you agree with me, Eulalie, I know you do—I feel it is inevitable.'

'I differ altogether from you,' said old Andrew, quietly. 'There is nothing to fight about, Mr Silverbottom. If only the newspapers would keep quiet ...'

'The newspapers, my dear sir,' exclaimed his guest vehemently, 'the press is merely the mouthpiece of the people. It voices exactly the feeling that is strong among us at present—a feeling of resentment, Mr Quakerley, a feeling of disgust, if I may say so—and I feel you will agree with me, Eulalie—at the mischievous, misguided, I may even say malignant policy of President Kruger's government. Mark you, Mr Quakerley, mark you, there is an insidious propaganda afoot. It has its tentacles twisted around every village, every district, in this Colony—Republican propaganda, disloyal propaganda, rank treason, my dear sir. You will agree with me, Eulalie, I am sure you will.'

'Certainly Caspar,' said his wife in her high-pitched voice. 'Mr Quakerley too, I feel sure, would agree if he knew what we know. We travel a good deal, Mrs Quakerley. Caspar's work for the Cause makes it necessary for us to travel a good deal, you know. And wherever we come, in the country districts, we feel there is a leaven of disloyalty ...'

'Which will culminate in war,' boomed her husband, thumping the tea table to the violent danger of the crockery. 'In war, Mr Quakerley, in war. And it behoves every one of us, everyone, I say—and, Eulalie, I'm sure you will agree with me—who has English blood in him and who is jealous of England's prestige. We cannot—I say we cannot, Mr Quakerley—allow England's prestige to be impaired in this country.'

'I do not think that it is likely to be impaired, Mr Silverbottom,' said old Andrew. He did not want to be drawn into a discussion on the subject, but at the same time he did not like to hide his own view.

'I do—I do,' exclaimed his guest. 'We have been far too lenient—far too forbearing. Sir Hercules let us down sadly, and now this unfortunate Raid has damaged our prestige further. I am glad to hear that we are going to have a stronger man at the helm here, very glad indeed. I said to Eulalie as soon as I heard—you remember, Eulalie, when we were discussing the matter?—I said that it was high time we had a stronger pilot in charge of the ship. You have not heard? You surprise me, my dear sir. It is an open secret. We are getting Mr Goschen's right-hand man, an excellent man. I do not know Alfred Milner personally, but I am told that he is a very strong man, a very strong man indeed. With him in charge, I have no fear that these disloyal tendencies which I have everywhere, wherever Eulalie and I have gone on behalf of the Cause, observed are increasing in strength and proportion, I say I have no fear that these disruptive elements will succeed in their intention of driving us out of this country.'

'Surely,' ventured old Andrew mildly, 'you have seen no evidence of such a movement, Mr Silverbottom?' But his guest interrupted him loudly.

'I speak from experience, Mr Quakerley,' he declared, impressively. 'Ever since Mr Hofmeyr started the Bond, the intention has been evident. The ostensible purpose, the cloak for all this intrigue and underhand bargaining, has been the interests of the agricultural population. I ask you, what has the Bond done for the agricultural interests? In what way has it justified its name as the Farmers' Party? No, sir, no! Its prime, its only purpose, is to sow disloyalty, and to make the cleavage between English and Dutch greater than it already is. The intention of its leaders, Sir, is to disrupt the Empire, to tear this Colony from its adherence to the Crown.'

'I think you exaggerate, Sir,' said old Andrew, smiling at the vehemence of the accusation. 'I remember Mr Hofmeyr's advocacy of preferential tariffs and of a contribution to the fleet. That seems to me evidence which points rather the other way.'

'To deceive, to deceive, Mr Quakerley,' cried the missioner. 'Mr Hofmeyr is a clever, far-seeing intriguer, and he knows quite well how to play to the gallery. He works in secret. You have only to look at the way in which he bullied poor Sir Hercules in this last unfortunate affair. Actually bullied, sir, actually bullied him into issuing that Proclamation. I said to Eulalie at the time ...'

'But the Proclamation was necessary,' his host ventured. 'Surely you, Sir, do not condone Jameson's conduct?'

'I should not like to go as far as that,' interrupted Mr Silverbottom, quickly. 'Not that there are not extenuating circumstances. In fact, I go so far as to say that if we knew all the facts—all, mind you—we would find that there was ample justification for what the poor fellows did. Just now, of course, they must bear the blame, and they are doing that like men. But there was no need for such precipitate action, and the Governor should have used the occasion to better purpose. As it was he played into President Kruger's hands, and Mr Hofmeyr practically dictated his policy. Yes, Madam, I should like another cup of tea—three lumps, please; I like it sweet. And it is a great pity—Eulalie, I know, agrees with me—a great pity that we did not have a stronger man on the spot at the time. A splendid opportunity missed. Mr Quakerley, a splendid opportunity missed.'

Quakerley saw no reason to prolong the discussion. His guest's impassioned vehemence was distasteful to him; gentlemen could, and should, discuss such things calmly, dispassionately. His guests had drunk their tea, but they had not divested themselves of their dust cloaks and seemed more disposed to chat across the tea table than to seek their room. He diffidently suggested that they might like to retire, and Mrs Silverbottom accepted the hint, although her husband showed signs of wanting to continue the discussion.

'We must talk it over after dinner, Mr Quakerley,' the missioner said, rising. 'Although I daresay I shall have my hands full then. I believe the committee intends to discuss arrangements for the campaign with us tonight. All right, Eulalie, I am coming, my dear.'

At dinner the Silverbottoms monopolised the conversation. The missioner told, in his loud bass voice, of the repeated triumphs he had scored over opponents of the Cause. He gave statistics, he quoted from blue books, he laid down the law on temperance with an authority that brooked no contradiction. Not that anyone wished to contradict him. Old Andrew felt glad that Joan was not there to listen to him. Joan had gone on a visit to Cape Town, and it was not a mere coincidence that she was absent when her brother had to entertain his guests. When she had heard of the campaign she had spoken her mind with her accustomed gentleness which, for all its suavity, held a considerable amount of determination. 'Father would have shoo-ed them off, Andy,' she told her brother, 'and you must excuse me if I run away. Alice can manage very well in my absence. The maids know what to do. Send me a wire when they go, and I will return at once.'

At the time he had thought that Joan had shown some lack of family feeling, but now he could sympathise with her. Mr Caspar Silverbottom gave promise of being rather a trying guest.

He allowed nothing of his inward disquiet to show at the dinner table. There he was the courteous, old-fashioned host, who, out of deference to the principles of his guest, had countermanded the order to place wine-glasses on the table and had himself removed the wine carafe to the sideboard. He had noticed that Mr Silverbottom's eyes had strayed towards the old Queen Anne decanter, and that a disapproving look had rested on his guest's face. During a momentary lull in the flood of oratory which represented the missioner's table talk, he had himself referred to what, to a supporter of the same cause, must have seemed a direct challenge.

'You were looking at our wine decanter, Mr Silverbottom,' he remarked, pleasantly. 'It is well worth looking at.'

'Alas,' boomed the missioner in a melancholic voice, 'that it should be turned to such a use which I cannot do otherwise than condemn, Mr Quakerley. Because vice is attired in alluring raiment.'

'Nay, Mr Silverbottom,' old Quakerley's voice held the mild, sarcastic intonation that he had inherited from his father, 'I should hardly call table wine a vice. If it is, we are all very vicious here. But,' he got up from his chair and walked to the sideboard and brought the decanter to the table, placing it before his guest, 'it is well worth looking at. Notice, Mrs Silverbottom, the beauty of the pattern. It comes to me from my grandfather, and I cherish it not only for its old associations but equally much for its loveliness. I am sure you like good glass, Mrs Silverbottom.'

'It is beautiful, Mr Quakerley,' the lady admitted, 'but I agree with my husband that it deserves a better fate than to hold a mocker.'

'There we may agree to differ,' said her host, pleasantly. 'Myself, I like to see the sparkle of good red wine, such as this is, against the glass. See the reflections from the facets, Mrs Silverbottom. It is an almost perfect specimen. The height is exactly the same as the circumference of the brim.'

'Surely not,' the missioner was interested, and put on his glasses to observe the decanter more attentively. 'I should say twice, three times round the brim would be about the height.'

'Then you would be wrong. See!' His host measured the circumference of the brim with the edge of a table napkin, and demonstrated that it was exactly the height of the decanter from base to brim. 'That is one of the tests of a good Queen Anne decanter, I'm told. I have early Flemish decanters that are patterned similarly. You do care for good glass, Mrs Silverbottom?'

'I know so little about it, Mr Quakerley,' the missioner's wife answered, and Andrew liked her for her frankness. 'You have beautiful things in that wall cupboard—indeed, all your things are beautiful.'

'They are family heirlooms,' interjected Alice, with conscious pride. She did not share her husband's passionate love for these things, but she realised their value and the sense of superiority that their possession gave. 'My husband is frightfully keen on such things. He buys up all the old stuff he can lay his hands on. This service,' she swept her hand towards the Rockingham soup tureen, 'I should much prefer a new one from home—there are some delightfully quaint patterns at Cartwright's, you know, but he won't let me have a new thing in the house.'

'Yours are ever so much better than anything one can buy nowadays,' said Mrs Silverbottom, consolingly, and Andrew felt that she was sincere. He threw her a glance of appreciative thanks. Her husband was pompous, tactless and loud, but she at least was human, with some understanding. He made up his mind that he would show her his garden, early in the morning, when the dew was on the lawn and the yellow bush shrikes were calling in the shrubbery.

After dinner they retired to the large, stiffly furnished drawing-room, overlooking the *stoep*, where tea was served, and where they were joined by visitors who came to pay their respects to the newcomers. The Quakerleys kept open house, and custom had sanctioned the evening visit as being less formal than the afternoon call. Mrs Quakerley had rebelled early in her married life against the stilted etiquette that tradition had imposed on the Village. At the time of her marriage these social calls were strictly regulated by a code of unwritten but perfectly well understood rules which it was deemed the height of unmannerliness to infringe. Her mother-in-law, Andrew's mother, had been in the habit of sending a maid with a posy of flowers to acquaint whomsoever she wished to visit with her coming in the recognised formula: 'Missis Quakerley's compliments, and would it be convenient for Missis So-and-So to receive her this afternoon at five?' The maid would return home with the equally stereotyped reply: 'Missis So-and-So presents her compliments to Mrs Quakerley and has much pleasure in thanking her for the flowers and will make it convenient to be at home this afternoon.' Without such negotiations there could be no call, just as no visit would be adequately honoured with the fine Souchong flavoured with crystals of sugar candy. But Alice had set the example of 'running in' upon her friends and had allowed her acquaintances the same freedom which she herself took. From the time when she became sole mistress of the large house in the Village she had been lavish in her hospitality, for she delighted in gossip and had the means and the inclination to entertain. Once a week she held an evening at home, to which no one was specially invited but which was attended by everyone of her own circle and by some who were outside of it but who were made welcome and tolerated because she liked to see her drawing-room crowded. Old Andrew took little share in these entertainments, and his sister attended them as a matter of duty. There would be singing, much gossip, and some whist, a game which Alice was devoted to and played with considerable skill.

That night the newcomers had a chance of observing Mrs Quakerley in her role of gracious hostess. In her white lace cap, with her silver hair dressed in the old-fashioned way, she looked dignified and, in a dim light, even beautiful, although her wrinkled face and sallow complexion plainly showed her age. A commencing cataract in one eye necessitated the use of a tinted glass which, set in a frame of rolled gold, gave her a distinguished appearance. She wore old-fashioned silk mittens, extending to her elbows, and simpered and curtsied in the old-fashioned way. A stranger would no doubt have thought her affected, insincere, and sometimes vulgar, for although, out of love for her husband, she had schooled herself all these years to adapt herself to her new conditions of environment, on occasions her inborn temperament asserted itself in conduct and speech. Then she showed herself to be vain, pretentious, and shallow, but even then her natural friendliness peeped forth from beneath the cloak of dignified superiority with which she tried to cover her social shortcomings.

Mrs Quakerley's reception on the evening of the Silverbottoms' arrival could be taken as a proof of that regard and respect which people felt, if not for herself then at least for the family to which she was allied, and for its chief. Shortly after eight o'clock the guests began to arrive. The first were the Reverend Mr Mance-Bisley and his wife, with Mr and Mrs Storam hard upon their heels. Then came the young doctor and his newly wedded wife. Dr Gerhard Buren was Irish by descent, Colonial born, and acknowledged to be a first-rate professional man. His grandfather had been a deported Irishman, whose son had successfully settled in an eastern district and acquired wealth and prosperity by sound business methods.

The doctor had shown himself a tolerant, easy-going member of the Village community, who kept whatever political views he held strictly to himself and managed to remain the friend of everyone and the enemy of none. His wife adapted herself to the Village environment easily with the result that both became highly popular, a popularity enhanced by the fact that the doctor was known to be singularly lax in sending out his quarterly accounts and prone to overlook the indebtedness of poorer patients.

Following these came representatives from the District who had come into the Village in anticipation of the missioner's meeting. Jeremiah Gerster, a well-to-do, aristocratic farmer, a widower, who brought his daughter, Maria, fresh from finishing school at the capital, and his upstanding son, Jeremiah junior; the Rekkers, Martin the second, and his sister Gertrude, about to be married to Jeremiah junior; the Seldons, descendants from the 1820 Settlers and now flourishing farmers and storekeepers in the District. With them mingled the lesser lights of the Village, the van Derens, the Chumleys, the de Smidts, and the van Aards. Only the Uhlmanns were unrepresented, for the Reverend Christian and his family rarely attended Mrs Quakerley's receptions, limiting themselves to the more formal afternoon visit.

Mr Caspar Silverbottom and his wife were introduced to all these, and found themselves involved in conversation which, while it maintained an almost even tide of English, held at the same time an undercurrent of Dutch, with which everyone seemed familiar. The missioner noted with regret that whisky and brandy figured among the refreshments lavishly offered, and that some of the members of the special committee did not disdain to avail themselves of these aids to conviviality. He had around him a little group of guests, vivaciously discussing the matter to which he habitually referred as 'the Cause,' and heard with dismay that he might be forced to act as his own chairman.

'That,' he exclaimed, 'will never do. It is unheard of. Wherever my wife and I have laboured for the eradication of this vice of drunkenness we have at least had the support of the leading inhabitants of the towns we have visited. You, Mr Storam, as magistrate ...'

'Just because I am that, Mr Silverbottom,' interrupted the magistrate frankly, 'do I think that I should not act as your chairman. I have every sympathy with the cause of temperance but, if I may say so, I doubt very much if it is altogether tactful to imply, by inference, that our District is intemperate.'

'Every district is, where wine is made and sold,' declared the missioner sturdily. 'Your Village can be no exception to that well-established rule. The insidious way ...'

'Well, well,' interrupted Dr Buren, cutting short the missioner's rhetoric, 'if no one else will step into the breach, I shall have to do it myself. Although I differ entirely from you—bound to do, you know, being Irish—I'll take the chair for you and introduce you. But you must not expect me to support you.'

'I do not ask that,' said the missioner, more soberly. 'I even invite criticism, argument, opposition. My case is too strong to be damaged by these. All I ask is the opportunity to state it, clearly and unequivocally. My wife and I desire, before we leave you, to see established here a strong Lodge and an equally strong Band. We look to the youngsters, to the coming generation, gentlemen, to root out this evil from among us. Already we are promised strong support. Mrs Mance-Bisley has been good enough to assure me that we will find a dozen lads and lasses who are willing to come under our banner. With such a beginning, gentlemen, with such a beginning ...'

'Oh, you'll find all the boys willing enough,' replied the doctor humorously. 'You see, it's something new, and isn't there a sort of uniform attached? That'll appeal to them. But my experience, Mr Silverbottom, is that interest in a novelty soon wears off. I should like to hear you three months hence. But come and talk to Rekker. He makes a lot out of his wine, and you may be able to convert him to your way of thinking.'

When Mr Silverbottom retired to his bedroom that night he confided to his wife his belief that the doctor would not make an ideal chairman. 'He is far too frivolous, Eulalie,' he said, 'far too frivolous. And it is a slight upon us that Mr Storam does not take the chair. Do you know, Eulalie, I have half a mind to write to Mr Graham about it. After all, a magistrate has certain responsibilities. He is a public official, a public servant. The excuse he gives is absurd. You will remember, Eulalie, the magistrate has invariably presided over our first meeting.'

'I should not bother about that, my dear,' said his wife. 'Dr Buren strikes me as being a very sensible man, and his help might be useful.'

'One can never tell what will happen when one has a frivolous chairman,' grumbled the missioner. 'A word out of place, a single jibe, my dear, may do incalculable harm. However, let us hope that the man will not try to make a joke of it.' And with that comforting reflection Mr Silverbottom turned round to go to sleep.

Chapter 11

Mr Silverbottom's meeting was not an unqualified success. The court room was crowded, and the heat, engendered by the flaring oil lamps and the mass of perspiring humanity crammed into its limited space, was distressingly great. On the wall behind the dais, the missioner had pinned large, luridly coloured engravings, depicting, in a somewhat imagiNative manner, the appearance of the various internal organs of alcoholic persons. The doctor shook his head at these bizarre aids to propaganda but refrained from comment. The audience looked with spellbound interest at them and commented freely, with personal references which were taken in good part by those concerned.

While the front of the hall had been reserved, as custom dictated, to the white audience, the rear was crowded with men and women and children from the location who had been lured to listen by the notification that the lecture would be illustrated. They expected a magic lantern, and their disappointment at its absence was keen.

Dr Buren acquitted himself ably of his task as chairman, contenting himself with briefly introducing the missioner, and stating that the audience came with an open mind and was prepared to be convinced by argument. Thereupon Mr Silverbottom launched forth on a vigorous attack on wine, taking as his text: 'Wine is a mocker; strong drink is raging.' His address followed the usual lines favoured by teetotal advocates, statement succeeding statement, emphatically declaimed but devoid of such proof as could appeal to impartial judgment, impassioned rhetoric taking the place of reasoned argument, and reiteration amplifying the dogmatic assertions. He showed the drunkard's liver, hobnailed and scarred; the drunkard's kidneys, shrunken and inefficient; the drunkard's gizzard inflamed by the corrosive action of alcohol. The representatives from the location were suitably impressed; their excitement verged upon the hysterical. But the front benches displayed a languid interest; their attitude, indeed, reflected the bored expression upon the chairman's face. Mr Silverbottom, who honestly believed in his extravagant statements, became more extravagant. He permitted himself to enunciate dogmatic assertions which he could not have justified before a jury of experts, and the audience became restless. He reflected upon the enormity of the conduct of those who could manufacture poison to steal away men's brains, and old Martin Rekker shifted angrily in his seat and glared protestingly at the magistrate. But the Village knew its manners, and the protest went no further. Mr Silverbottom was allowed to finish his address in a perfervid peroration liberally besprinkled with tags from Shakespeare and Lowell, and sat down feeling that he had not done so badly.

The audience waited. No one seemed inclined to say a word. Dr Buren called for comment, but the invitation was not responded to. Usually, again as custom indicated, someone on the dais would rise and propose a cordial vote of thanks. That was the invariable rule, and the Village could not recollect, even in election time when feeling ran high, that this precedent had ever been overlooked. But no one appeared to be disposed to thank Mr Silverbottom who, hot and perspiring, sat in an attitude of satisfied martyrdom, awaiting his reward, whatever it might be.

It was the Reverend Christian who came to the rescue. He rose slowly, his ungainly, lanky figure accentuated by his long clerical frock-coat, and stepped forward. Speaking in Dutch, he remarked that while they had all listened with interest to Mr Silverbottom, there were some among them who did not quite agree with all that had been said. Nevertheless they respected the conviction with which it had been said, and the intention that lay behind the words, and the least they could do was, in accordance with time honoured custom, which the Village had never failed to observe, to thank the speaker for his address. He for his part could wish Mr Silverbottom success in his efforts to make the world temperate, but he could also assure their guest that he happened to be among people who did not drink to the extent pictured in those shocking placards on the wall.

They cheered Mr Uhlmann, and it was noticed that old Andrew Quakerley, usually too dignified to be demonstrative, joined cordially in the applause. Mr Silverbottom returned thanks in a chastened mood, and the meeting broke up after the usual vote of thanks to the chair.

Opinion was sharply divided upon the merits of the lecture. The location, to which Mr Silverbottom's flamboyancy appealed strongly, was ecstatic in its praise; the Village as a whole was critical, even cynical. It was understood that Dr Buren had been heard to say that the pictures were all wrong, and Dr Buren would know what a person's innards looked like. The farming community felt a little indignant at the aspersions cast upon it, but soon regained its tolerant attitude of bored amusement. No vineyards were rooted up. Martin Rekker declared his intention of ordering another copper still.

Meanwhile Mr Silverbottom, ably supported by his wife, held meetings in the location, in the schoolroom, and in private houses. He gained several influential supporters, among those being the pastor's wife, a lady of strong temperament and a power among the Native population. With their help and active assistance, two lodges were established, one, named the 'Realisation,' for the Coloured people, and the other, the 'Ebenezer,' for the European teetotallers. Mrs Mance-Bisley and Mrs Silverbottom succeeded in forming a Band of Hope which at its first meeting contained practically the whole of the Village European youth. The members wore gaily coloured scarves, promised to eschew alcoholic liquor, tobacco, and expletives, and took the keenest interest in electing officers, and performing the elaborate ritual with which the meetings opened and closed. Charlie Crest became an officer; his sister functioned as a vice something or other, and Martin Storam was elected to the Chair, an office which he filled with commendable energy and with the same impartiality with which he acted as head boy of the school.

The results of Mr Silverbottom's campaign, to judge from these happenings, could be regarded as successful. Indeed, Mrs Silverbottom made no secret of her delight at what had been obtained. Her own tactful manner of procedure certainly counteracted much of her husband's impetuous advocacy and gained adherents where his preaching would only have raised opposition. The Village knew him as a fiery, injudicious crusader, and looked upon his enthusiasm with amused toleration. But among the children Mr Silverbottom showed another side of his character. He managed to win their confidence and to keep their interest. He could talk to them as if they were his equals forgetting, in their midst, his exaggeration of speech, his sledgehammer rhetoric, and his unbending dogmatism. At the Band of Hope he told them stories, described, in simple language, what he had seen on his travels, and recited some of the stirring poetry of the Emancipationists. He dealt with them individually for he had been a teacher, and as a matter of fact he was a better teacher than missioner. He discovered the latent talents of the pastor's younger son, a dreamy, rheumaticky boy who was not allowed to mingle with the Village boys and was taught at home with the result that his knowledge was surprisingly unequal. Young Louis Uhlmann could write Latin, read Hebrew, and quote Goethe and Heine, but was hopelessly at fault when it came to calculating how long it would take for a cistern to be filled or a ditch to be dug according to the conditions so exhaustively detailed in Hamblin Smith's arithmetic. His mother had pressed him into the Band, together with his elder brother Johann and his sister Christine, but his shyness prevented him from taking a very active part in its doings, although he attended with praiseworthy regularity and joined heartily in singing: 'John went in to have a drink ... Oh, oh, the crafty drink.' The Band provided him with an opportunity of associating with boys of his own age, and he struck up a friendship with Charlie Crest. Mr Silverbottom found him an eager listener, and finding that he had never read Lowell, provided him with Stead's penny extracts of that author, and introduced him to Batcheller's stirring poem *The Baby Corps*, recently published in the American *Century*. Young Louis had no firm convictions on the subject of teetotalism. At home wine appeared on the pastor's table, and the children were allowed a glass after dinner, but from the time that the temperance campaign started Mrs Uhlmann, herself a member of both Lodges, had forbidden the use of wine at table, and consigned the carafe to a closed cupboard in her husband's study. For Mr Uhlmann, although he said nothing to prevent his children from attending the Band, showed no inclination to emulate his wife, and took his daily glass of wine, as he had always done, without ostentation but also without any qualms of conscience. When his children had asked his opinion on the matter he had told them frankly that they were old enough to judge for themselves. 'It will do you no harm to give up wine and tobacco,' he said. 'I have not heard you use bad words, so the third promise hardly affects you. But I do not like you to promise what you cannot perform, simply because you do not know what you promise. Nor should I like you to think that because you are members of the Band you are better than other children who do not belong to it. After all grandpa, who you know is a good and clever man, smokes his cigars and drinks his wine, and has never been the worse for either. Cannot you reason it out for yourselves, children?'

Young Louis had reasoned it out for himself, and decided that there was something wrong about it. But the attractions of the weekly meeting where he could sit next to Charlie Crest, and where the ritual appealed to his sense of the theatrical, together with the implicit instructions of his mother, prevented him from rebelling. He soon found out that his fellow members did not take the Band very seriously. John and Martin used expletives on occasions of great stress; they were harmless expletives but would undoubtedly have shocked Mrs Silverbottom had she heard them. Some of the other boys smoked, a few, from the farms, because they genuinely liked to smoke, the others simply because they imagined it manly to do so. Martin dealt with those in a highhanded manner, not because they had broken their Band promise, but on the assumption that it interfered with their wind and jeopardised their places in the team.

Mr Silverbottom, who understood boys and held more liberal views, strangely enough, where they were concerned than did his wife, dealt with these recalcitrants in a common sense way, which earned the applause of Mr Mance-Bisley and the grudging admiration of the recalcitrants themselves. He pointed out that wiser and better men had on occasion failed to keep their promises, and that one might fail in duty twice or more and yet prosper.

There could be no doubt that so far as the juveniles were concerned Mr Silverbottom was an influence for good.

Among the seniors, the results of his whirlwind campaign were less obvious. The larger Lodge was the 'Realisation.' The location folk, Coloured half-castes for whom all sections of the community could be held responsible but to whom no section dared to acknowledge its responsibility, were emotional, unstable, and temperamental. The uplift of Mr Silverbottom's eloquence had stampeded them. Old and experienced inhabitants of the District remembered that years before a similar stampede had resulted from the visit of a Salvationist, but the local branch of the corybantic Christians had endured for but a few years and died through inanition. They prophesied the same result for the 'Realisation' Lodge. Its contemporary creation, the 'Ebenezer,' functioned more steadily. Its chief protagonist was a young attorney's clerk, one Elias Vantloo, already regarded as a very astute and clever youngster who had risen from obscure beginnings to a position which qualified him to be looked upon as one of the inhabitants who counted. No one quite understood how he had managed to do so. He had matriculated at an early age from the Village school before the time of Mr Mance-Bisley's headmastership, gained a scholarship, and gone away. He had returned to take up a position as head clerk in van Deren's office, and it was whispered that he was really the junior partner in the business. He was a deferential, treble-voiced young man, good-looking and well-dressed, liberal and persuasive, and a favourite on the tennis court, where he played a good game. He now manifested a keen interest in Mr Silverbottom's mission, acted as secretary to the committee, and was elected one of the Lodge officers. Mrs Mance-Bisley and Mrs Uhlmann found his assistance invaluable, especially when it was accompanied by a generous donation towards the funds of the two lodges. The gold filigree for the regalia was expensive, and the first subscriptions did not entirely cover the expenses. Mr Vantloo came forward with an offer to bear the whole expense, which was thankfully accepted. Henceforward he was an important and influential member of the Lodge, and Mr Silverbottom felt that in him the Cause had secured a worthy defender and a staunch friend.

Mr Silverbottom's campaign, while it achieved these results, which were to him eminently satisfactory, accomplished something else which old Andrew for one was thankful for. It gave the Village and District some other subject of interest and discussion than that which some months before had threatened to be a means of discord and strife in the community. He said as much to his guest a few days before the latter's departure. Quakerley had not found the missioner an attractive personality, perhaps because he had only seen one side, and that the worst, of his guest. He had not seen Mr Silverbottom telling stories to the children; he had not heard Mr Silverbottom recite 'Lines on the Capture of the Fugitive Slaves.' Had he done so he would have credited the man with more sincerity than he did. To him Silverbottom was a teetotal fanatic, wholly without humour, inclined to be untruthful and unfair or at least partial to the edge of treason to the truth, and singularly lacking in the sense that appreciates beauty. Mrs Silverbottom was different. She could see a joke, even against herself; she had the feminine virtues which old Andrew was prepared to respect well-developed and, moreover, she could, with all her acquired—for he refused to believe that it could be inherent—prejudice in favour of her husband's strange fanaticism, see beauty in things beautiful and appreciate in silent content. He had shown her over his garden, and had been impressed with the manner in which she had listened to his explanations. 'You love it not only because it is beautiful, Mr Quakerley,' she had said, softly, 'and I have seen only one garden more lovely than yours, but because it is something of yourself. It is your child, and you have lavished upon it the love that a mother feels for her child. I can understand that.' He had been surprised, impressed, for she had said it with moving sincerity, and had told him of her own little boy ... An understanding woman, totally different from her silly husband.

Towards that misguided and tactless man he had preserved a demeanour of studied courtesy, persevering in it in the face of provocation that might well have annoyed a less courteous host. Mr Silverbottom had found no great pleasure in the garden. He had suggested alterations which he had implied would be improvements; he had contradicted Andrew about the name of one of the indigenous trees. Quakerley had not troubled to answer either provocation, the man was so obviously an ignoramus. Once only had Andrew's patience almost given way. That was when Mr Silverbottom had rudely told old Rekker, who had addressed him in Dutch, that he had no use for that language.

'One thing I am grateful for, Mr Silverbottom,' he said, as they sat on the *stoep* after dinner. 'Your lectures have shaken us up a bit, so much so indeed that we have had no time to discuss politics. I only hope that your quieting influence may endure.'

'In a sense I agree, Mr Quakerley,' said his guest, and Andrew was glad to hear that his voice was less aggressively dogmatic than usual. 'In another sense I should be sorry that anything I should have done should make you overlook the real seriousness of the situation. You will pardon me if I speak very frankly, Mr Quakerley. I am aware, Sir, that I am not—how shall I express it?—let us say quite sympathetic towards you. We do not see eye to eye. Let that go for the moment. But believe me when I say that I am sincere in this at least, Mr Quakerley, that I too love this country. I was born here; I shall die here; I shall be buried here. I look upon myself as a South African. Like you, Mr Quakerley, I am half-English and half-Dutch. My mother was a Dutch South African like yours. I have never learned Dutch because, as I have frankly said—and I saw that saying it annoyed you—I have no use for it. I look upon anything that divides us in this country as treason. I see the future of South Africa—the only future to which I, notwithstanding my mixed blood, can look forward to with pride— as similar to what the United States are today—a united country, part of the British Empire saturated with English tradition, English-speaking, knit to England by bonds of interest. I can see no future to be proud of in a divided country, bilingual, rent by conflict between two warring ideals. Therefore I stand wholly and frankly on the side of those who oppose all these attempts to placate the implacable.'

'Do you think that is quite a fair way of putting it, Mr Silverbottom?'

'Mr Quakerley, fairness must not be one-sided. It has been "give" on our side all through. That is what I honestly believe, and that is why I think that we should make an end of it.'

'I am not sure that I agree when you say "we," Mr Silverbottom. My own opinion is that these things settle themselves in time, without any quarrels or wars ...'

'No, no. We are already at war, Mr Quakerley, although it is not open war. That is why I should almost welcome open hostilities. If you go round the country, as I have done, you will see how deep-seated the trouble is and how fiercely the doctrine of hatred towards England is being inculcated. It is, of course, the influence from the north. Their tradition is altogether different from ours, and sooner or later there must be a clash between the two. Only one can be master in this country. That is why I urge that our own government should take up a strong attitude. That, too, is why I, at the risk of being thought intolerant, dissent from those who are constantly trying to placate those whom I call implacable.'

'And these are?' queried Andrew.

'All those who at heart are anti-English, Mr Quakerley,' answered his guest with conviction. 'There are many such in this Colony. They receive their inspiration from the north. They cannot get over the fact that sixteen years ago we ignominiously gave it to them ...'

'There again, Mr Silverbottom, I differ from you,' said Quakerley, earnestly. 'My own impression is that Mr Gladstone's action, in restoring self-government to the Transvaal after the disaster at Majuba, was an act of magnanimity which the Boers appreciated and which they still appreciate. So far as our local Dutch are concerned, I am sure that they do not think that England acted under compulsion ...'

'They do not think so now, Mr Quakerley,' interrupted his guest quickly, 'but they are being urged to believe that that was the case. There is an insidious propaganda going on. I am talking of what I know, and indeed it is an open secret. Surely you can see for yourself that the intention is to create a strong republican party in this Colony, to eliminate the imperial factor gradually, and to attach, ultimately, this Colony to the two Republics in the north.'

'That,' said old Andrew reflectively, 'need not be altogether a bad thing. A union of states with common interests ...'

'Ah, I am with you there. It must come in time. But it must not be a combination antagonistic to the Empire, one in which we, who are of English descent, have no say whatever and are tolerated only on sufferance. And that is the intention. The republican ideal in this country, Mr Quakerley, is not a true republican, democratic ideal. It is the ideal of government by a clique, by a bigoted, intolerant group, just as is actually the case in the Transvaal today.'

'Then you agree with those who regard the Transvaal Government as retrogressive, corrupt, and illiberal, Mr Silverbottom?'

'I do not go so far as to say the Government is. There is perhaps some corruption—much less than is alleged—but my own belief is that that is due largely to the Outlanders themselves. If there has been bribery to obtain concessions, the bribing must have been done by those who obtained the concessions. My quarrel with the Transvaal is that it represents a point of view altogether obsolete. The whole *burgher* system with its limitation of the franchise to a small group from which practically all the progressive elements are excluded, is an anachronism, and one that would be ludicrous if it were not so dangerous.'

'I can see that. Indeed, to me it is a puzzle why the President does not give way on the question of the franchise. But I imagine that the forces behind him are too strong, and that his *burghers* think that if they admit the newcomers they will soon be swamped.'

'Inevitably. But must the minority—and such a minority—continue to rule the majority? The present prosperity of the country is due to these newcomers. But I am not so much concerned with them as I am with our own people, here in the Colony. At this moment they are being urged to believe that they have decided grievances against England, and that the time has come for them to assert themselves. You and I, Mr Quakerley, know that there have been grievances—that there will be grievances in the future. We can both give instances of interference by Downing Street which have been tactless. But I can find none that would warrant a tithe of the resentment which is being fomented by those whose object is to drive English authority out of this country.'

'You take too serious a view of the situation,' said Andrew quietly. 'I have lived through a great deal of excitement, and my experience has always been that these things tend to settle themselves.'

'I do not think this will,' said Mr Silverbottom, lugubriously. 'I look upon the situation as serious, very serious indeed. We know that the Transvaal is arming. She is a state whose independence is guaranteed by Great Britain; no one can attack her without attacking Great Britain. Why then should she arm? No, Mr Quakerley, the whole of her policy during the past few years has been to pin-prick England, to rouse the sympathy and the fellow-feeling of the republican element in this Colony, and to prepare for the time when these forces will be strong enough to enable her to declare war upon us.'

'You must pardon me, Mr Silverbottom,' said his host with a smile, 'if I say that that seems to me too far-fetched to be credible. I cannot believe that the Transvaal will ever declare war on us. Why, it would be civil war, in a sense. And it would be a senseless war. Anyone who knows England's strength must see that it would be impossible for the Transvaal to win.'

'Yes, but how many here know what England's strength is? They do know that we have had some difficulty in squashing Cetewayo, and that at Majuba a small force of Boers beat an English general. It is this ignorance, abysmal in the country areas, where, as you know, there is no real education, that I fear.'

'Let us hope that your fears are groundless, Mr Silverbottom,' said old Andrew with a tinge of impatience. He had listened with interest to the missioner's remarks, but this continual harping on dangers which he though unreal, grated upon him. He thought his visitor knew as little about local conditions as the rural areas knew about English history. That alone could explain Mr Silverbottom's pessimism.

'I share your hope, Mr Quakerley,' said the stout man, shaking his head. 'But there are portents ... however, I shall say nothing more except this, Mr Quakerley, that I trust that when the time comes this beautiful Village of yours will be far removed from the conflict.'

The Silverbottoms returned to wherever their home was, and the Village settled down to think of other things. The whirlwind campaign left its two Lodges and one Band of Hope behind, and the wine farmers smiled and pruned their vines. In the location the Coloured folk, even those who were members of the 'Realisation' Lodge, agreed that the 'old master from Cape Town' had given them value for the money they had never expended in going to the lectures. The old master could 'throw the words' in an altogether amazing manner. And those who could afford it drank a tot of shilling Jeripico to his health—a culmination that would have sadly grieved Mr Silverbottom had he been there to observe it.

Chapter 12

Mr Storam rapped on the table with the end of his pencil. 'We must proceed in an orderly fashion,' he exclaimed. 'The first thing is to elect a committee. Will somebody please propose?'

The court room was full to overcrowding. The Village was there, and as much of the District as could find accommodation. On the front benches sat the seniors, Andrew, very neat in his grey tweed suit with a prize carnation in his buttonhole; Martin Rekker, dressed in his Sunday best, his 'chest clothes' reserved for communion wear; old Hendrik van Aard; Gottlieb Nolte, whose father had been a member of Parliament after having been the public executioner; old Seldon, Andrew's contemporary but his junior by seven years. All old men who could look back to childish memories sixty years back, dim, misty memories hardly now to be visualised into definite shape, but memorable none the less. Memories of the time when the District had met in almost similar conclave to discuss the accession of Alexandrina Victoria, whose coming to the throne had denaturalised so many of her subjects who had been Hanoverians.

Behind them sat the younger, the middle-aged, the very young, all male, for custom decreed that in these public gatherings the women should have no share. Augustus, the Coloured policeman, guarded the door in a semi-official capacity. His superior officer, Chief Constable Chumley, sat among the audience, part, for today only, of the public, with a vote and a voice, no longer merely its paid servant.

Among these younger members of the meeting there were many who could remember the previous meeting, exactly ten years back, when the Village had met to discuss the Sovereign's Jubilee. Now they were met to discuss the sixtieth year of Alexandrina Victoria's reign. How much water had flowed down the river those ten years! How much snow had melted on the high peaks of the glorious ranges overlooking the Valley! How times had changed! There was not one of those who remembered the Jubilee Year of 1887 who did not realise that conditions, opinions, viewpoints, even prejudices, hates and predelictions, had changed since then. There had been no hampering sense of division then; there had been no suppressed reservations in their expressions of loyalty.

Mr Storam's predecessor in office had told him how that meeting had been conducted. With enthusiastic unanimity, with sincere co-operation between all parties of the community, the Village and the District, collaborating after prolonged discussion, had selected for Her Majesty's jubilee gift a case of oranges and tangerines. Everyone who owned an orange orchard had contributed, and as the difficulty of selection was very great, it had been decided that only those oranges large enough comfortably to nestle in the magistrate's top hat, and those tangerines heavy enough to scale over what was considered a fair weight for such fruit, would go to Windsor. That had been the District's loyal gift to Alexandrina Victoria, but in memory of her glorious fifty years' reign the Village had fenced in a portion of the town-lands and planted an oak tree in the middle of the paddock.

Today Mr Storam felt that the sentiment of the meeting was not quite like that which his predecessor had sketched. There had been no warring political squabbles then. Mr Rhodes had been a mere name; now he was almost an execration to some, to others a hero to be defended at the cost of breaking a friendship and insulting a neighbour. The Bond Party had hardly existed then; now it was a nightmare to some, a harbinger of the millennium to others.

The meeting was opened by the magistrate who asked if the audience desired to elect a chairman. He was only there in an official capacity, as chief public servant, to initiate the proceedings at the request of several prominent citizens who had asked him to call them together to decide what should be done to honour Her Most Gracious Majesty, who for sixty years had reigned happily over the Colony. The meeting intimated that it desired no other chairman. From the back benches came a plaintive request to get on with it and not to keep them waiting. The seniors in the front row turned their heads protestingly at the interruption. Old Martin Rekker whispered to his neighbour that someone was trying to stir up trouble. Old Andrew leaned over and made a suggestion to Hendrik van Aard, a burly, big-boned farmer, an Elder of the church, and a man respected not only because he happened to be the son of his father, who had been their representative in Parliament, but also because he was an honest man and a highly successful agriculturist.

Slowly old Hendrik got on his feet; as slowly he walked forward, ascended the dais, and stood alongside the magistrate, resting his knotted, arthritic fingers on the magistrate's table.

'Friends,' said the old man, shifting his steel-rimmed spectacles higher up his nose so that he could glance under them, 'friends, I am one of those who signed the requisition to his Honour to call this public meeting. I look back for sixty years, and I mind me how as a small boy my father told me that we had a woman to reign over us. I mind me how he told me that there were folk who feared that a woman's rule would not be strong enough. They were for praying the government to have a king instead of a queen. But that could not be, such matters being ruled by the law of the land which gives to the children the rights that are theirs. So we abided by that law, friends, and I say we have had a good queen. We have none of us seen her, except perhaps our two clergymen who are with us today, but we know what she looks like, and we know that she is a Christian woman, God-fearing, a decent body who has ruled wisely and well. Ten years ago we met in this room to do her honour. Today we meet again for that purpose. I know'—his voice became stern—'I know there are folk that are dissatisfied today as they were when she came to rule over us. I say they have as little cause as had those then. I do not want to go into that now—to do so would be to talk politics and this is not a political meeting. We shall have enough of that by and by when we have to vote. Now we are come together to do her honour. I say to those who do not wish to join with us that this is a matter which we can discuss without them. Let them leave us if they want to have no part in honouring a lady to whom our respect and our loyalty are due, not only because she is our rightful, God-appointed sovereign, but also because she is a woman who through years of tribulation and sorrow has been a good woman. I have said.'

The old man's speech, made in correct, old-fashioned Dutch, was greeted with cheers and counter-cheers, and when he sat down on the chair which the magistrate had placed for him on the dais, it was apparent that there were occupants of the back benches who were not pleased with what he had said. Several began to speak at once, and the magistrate rapped for order.

'The gentleman at the back, there,' he called out.

'He has no business here,' said old Nolte, taking snuff and presenting his rappee to the magistrate with a courteous gesture. 'He is not one of us. He is one of the mischief makers, Magistrate. He should not speak.'

But the gentleman at the back had already shouldered his way forward and now stood before the dais, holding up his hand to command silence. He was Gideon Ras, a well-dressed, bearded, middle-aged man, who had recently come into the District and had visited many farms to buy horses. His name had just been placed on the voters' list, for he had bought a small farm and had announced his intention of settling down upon it.

'I rise, Magistrate,' he began, 'merely to say that there are many of us here who do not see eye to eye with Uncle Hennie in this business. We have no obligation towards the Queen. We have no wish to honour her any more than we need honour the President of the Transvaal. Indeed, I may go so far as to say, Magistrate and Friends, that we owe more to our old President, and that if we are true Afrikanders, true to our tradition, our race, our religion, and the customs of our great pioneers, who led us out of the wilderness of English oppression, injustice, and tyranny into the wide lands where we could live free and untrammelled, we should honour *Oom* Paul and not Queen Victoria. I confess I feel ashamed of my own people when I see them busying themselves in trying to curry favour by these pretences of loyalty to something to which we owe no loyalty ...'

'Magistrate,' exclaimed old Martin Rekker, rising from his seat in indignation, 'is this to be permitted? I have never heard ...'

'You will hear now,' shouted Ras, who had worked himself up and was gesticulating theatrically with his arms. 'It is high time that you were told the truth. Here where we are justly irritated because that very Queen whom you wish to honour sent her pirate soldiers to war treacherously upon our neighbours, our blood-kin across the river, you come with your soothing syrups and your affectations of loyalty. We want none of that loyalty. We want ...'

The meeting became voluble. The magistrate rapped on the table, and the back benches chorused indignation and approval. To old Quakerley, an interested observer of what was happening, it seemed that the two sections, the loyalists and the supporters of Ras, were about equally divided. The older men present looked worried but made no attempt to interrupt the speaker who went on, although frequently called to order by the chairman.

'I speak as the representative of most of those present,' declared Ras in a loud voice. 'I shall not allow myself to be brow-beaten by you, Mr Chairman, nor by anybody else. I say we want to have no part or share in this honouring of your Queen. She is not ...'

'That's right, Nephew,' yelled old Martin, but his approving shout was not directed at Ras. It was meant for young Jeremiah Gerster, who had jumped out of his seat, rushed forward, and forcibly removed the mouthpiece of the opposition, a task in which he was ably seconded by some of the older men. Mr Gideon Ras was lifted bodily and escorted to the door, where the Native constable stood grinning but aloof, perfectly well aware that this was a matter which the White folk could settle between themselves. The Ras faction attempted no retaliation, though vigorously exhorted to assert themselves like men by the struggling leader, but a number of them followed him out of the hall and, with the help of the crowd of location folk who had gathered in the street, held an opposition meeting in front of the court room.

'And now,' said old Nolte, closing his snuff-box with a snap, 'if there is anyone else who wishes to tell us what we have no wish to hear, let him stand forward and say his say. Is there no one? Come, there were some who applauded when our friend from goodness-knows-where spoke so heatedly. Have they no voice now?'

'We didn't know he was going to say such foolery,' cried a voice from the back benches. 'We don't hold with him, Uncle Hennie. Not so far as the Queen is concerned, anyhow.'

'That is to the good,' exclaimed the old man, scornfully. 'But if you hold with him in other things, then go with him.'

The back benches, now thoroughly tame, reassured him. 'He speaks for himself. After all, he doesn't belong here.'

'Nay, that he does not,' said the old man, resuming his seat. 'Magistrate, we can now proceed.'

The meeting elected a Jubilee committee on which every section of the community was represented. It drew up and circulated a subscription list, headed by Andrew Quakerley with twenty pounds, and by Martin Rekker with a like sum. Funds were needed for the celebrations. There would be a mounted commando; illuminations, fireworks, a feast for the location people. But the subject that came in for animated discussion was what form the official presentation to Her Majesty should take. There was a feeling that precedent should be followed and that once more a case of citrus fruit should be despatched to Osborne or Windsor, or wherever Alexandrina Victoria might happen to be. But the magistrate, who had been warned by his predecessor that such a gift engendered endless heartburnings, backbitings, jealousies and recriminations, pleaded for an address. After consideration, the meeting decided upon an address, in English and Dutch, to be delivered in a locally-made wooden casket enclosed in a leather cover elaborately tooled and gilded.

Mr Mance-Bisley walked home with Mr Uhlmann. He had understood little of what had transpired before the meeting settled down to business, for he could not follow the Dutch of old Nolte or of Gideon Ras. But he had felt the jarring note that the latter had introduced, and had marked the peremptory way in which young Jeremiah had ejected the disturber. Now as he trotted alongside Mr Uhlmann, whose legs were long and strides prodigious, he expressed his surprise that such disturbance had taken place.

'I fear it is only an indication of the trouble that is with us, Mr Mance-Bisley,' said the pastor, sadly. 'There are elements at work for disunion. What you have seen and heard today is a proof of it. But you have also seen that there is at bottom a sound common sense that I hope and trust will counteract the mischief.'

'I gather,' said the rector, 'that the impassioned gentleman was altogether against any celebration of Her Majesty's jubilee. That seems to me rather ungracious, to say the least.'

'It is a pity you did not follow Mr Nolte's speech,' remarked the pastor. 'He stressed what we all feel. Mr Ras is really not one of us. He comes from over yonder,'—he swept his arm towards the north—'and he tells those who will listen to him—alas, there are many such—that we are oppressed, tyrannised over ... Good gracious, Mr Bisley, I have lived under three governments, and never have I felt more free, less oppressed, than under English rule.'

'I should have said that needed no demonstration,' exclaimed the rector.

'Not to you, nor to me,' retorted the pastor. 'But some of us are living in total ignorance of what real freedom means. We have been a slave-owning community, Mr Bisley; you must not forget that. To some of us freedom postulates licence, the liberty to be lawless, or at least to have one law for the strong and another for the weak.'

'That seems to be the case in the Transvaal,' said Mr Mance-Bisley. 'I really cannot conceive how people who talk so much of freedom can tolerate a whole population standing outside, disfranchised and powerless, though taxed and with all the obligations of citizenship.'

'I do not know enough about that to discuss it with you,' said Mr Uhlmann, diffidently. 'My brother-in-law is in the Transvaal, and he has sometimes expressed himself in terms of strong disapproval of what takes place there. Whatever it is, it is a disturbing element in the country, and I pray that it may be settled. Not by war, Mr

Mance-Bisley, but by friendly agreement. As you have seen, our people are at heart sound. They have enough common sense not to be led astray by agitators of the stamp of Mr Ras. Believe me, the incident of this morning does not reflect the true feeling among us. We are not enemies of the Queen, and we do not, all of us, feel that because,'—he smiled as he said it and his smile robbed the words of any discourtesy they might have implied—'you do not speak Dutch you are treating us like inferior animals.'

'I haven't the remotest intention ...' began his companion, but Mr Uhlmann interrupted him.

'Language,' said the pastor, reflectively, 'is a great factor in building up national consciousness. But one can make too much of it, and I think some of us are doing that. There is first the feeling of inferiority in not being able fluently to speak that which is not one's own, and secondly the impression that because others do not speak one's language they are at heart unfriendly towards it and despise it. Here both come into play. English, with its fine literature, its tremendous commercial importance and its official prestige, has an unassailable position. Dutch, which is difficult—far more difficult than English, because it is partly an inflected language, Mr Bisley—is losing ground. Now there is a feeling that our dialect Dutch, which is not inflected, which is easy to speak and generally understood even by those who are illiterate, should be looked upon as our language. Well, I have no feeling against it. It may in time become a great language, like English, but at present it is a baby in swaddling clothes. Unfortunately there are many of us who cannot, or will not, see that. They want us to force the pace, Mr Bisley. And they are making it a matter of—what do you call it? You see, I cannot express myself well in a foreign tongue. I learned English as I learned Latin, and speak both about equally badly.'

'I only wish I could talk Latin as you speak English,' said the rector, fervently. 'Intonation, of course ... I daresay my Latin pronunciation would shock you, Mr Uhlmann. Yours is the continental, I presume. But you were saying ...'

'I tried to tell you that there are some of us who would seek in this matter of language an apple of discord. They go so far as to make language a test of patriotism.'

'And do you think that it will succeed?' asked the rector, interestedly.

'What? This attempt to put in place of Dutch our local dialect? I cannot say. Nor do I think that it much matters. So long as English remains it must be the predominant tongue; nothing can conquer it, and even if Afrikaans, our local dialect, supersedes Dutch, which it possibly will after a few generations, it can never have the same cultural significance that English has. Not to our generation, nor our children's, at least. Now, I must bid you good-day.'

And Mr Uhlmann, with old-fashioned, somewhat stilted courtesy, lifted his shabby, wide-brimmed clerical hat and turned in at his back gate.

Chapter 13

The Diamond Jubilee of Alexandrina Victoria was celebrated in the Village with the traditional ceremonies when the time came for it. The small section that had promised opposition, from political motives, yielded graciously to the expostulations of older citizens who pointed out that Alexandrina Victoria could scarcely be held responsible for whatever had been committed by Chamberlain.

The Village was illuminated on Jubilee night. The location held holiday on the smooth sward on the river bank where the winter rains had raised a luxuriant crop of grass between which sorrels gleamed like many-coloured stars. In the morning there was a meeting on the Village square attended by all who could find time and opportunity to come into the Village. The District sent a mounted commando under young Jeremiah Gerster; the two Lodges paraded in their regalia, and the Band of Hope, equally resplendent, its juvenile members the secret envy of the District youth who had accompanied their elders to the celebrations, brought up the rear. The Native constables fired the old muzzle loader that had been kept in the gaol yard since the time of Lord Charles Somerset. The magistrate made a speech; Mr Mance-Bisley said a prayer in English and Mr Uhlmann one in Dutch. Everyone joined lustily in singing *God save the Queen* and in the three hurrahs that were given on the suggestion of old Mr Rekker. At private dinners Alexandrina Victoria was toasted. Old inhabitants of the District compared the celebrations with those that had taken place ten years before, and found nothing to complain of. But when the cheers and the shouting had died away, there were some who considered that this ebullition of loyal feeling, however well-intentioned and expressed, was merely a shame-faced, sensitive reaction to a generous impulse stimulated by custom and tradition. Mr Storam, writing semi-officially to a friend in the Attorney-General's office, explained that he did not attach much importance to the Jubilee celebrations.

'They are the natural result of the event,' he wrote. 'For sixty years our people have considered the Queen as a personality standing outside politics. Of their personal loyalty, in so far as she is the personification of authority, there can be no question. But you must not take that to mean that it will prevent them from allowing full rein to their sympathies, which are now being played upon by agitators from the Transvaal, who are taking advantage of the rising spirit of what one may call nationalism, which has manifested itself since the Bond Party started. Mind you, I do not think that these sympathies are naturally anti-English. I may say—and you might tell Sir Gordon from me, if you discuss the matter with him—that we have had very little racial feeling in this District. Practically none. Our English settlers have pulled well with the others who, as you know, are all Dutch, although Dutch is the prevailing language spoken in the Village and District.'

Mr Storam's opinion was shared by the pastor who, like the magistrate, knew his people and was aware of what was astir. Mr Uhlmann had relations on both sides of the Vaal. His brother-in-law occupied a high office under President Kruger's government, but belonged to the anti-Presidential Party that favoured the candidature of General Joubert. Another brother-in-law, also in the Republican service, was a zealous partisan of the President. Between them they kept the Reverend gentleman informed of all the conflicting views prevalent in the north as well as in the south.

Jubilee year went out in a summer of unprecedented drought. The Karroo hillocks on the outskirts of the Village town-lands, burned bare of all but succulent vegetation, loomed against the sky in sombre brown desolation. None but a botanist would have found upon them matter for praise or interest. The botanist would have revelled, for the heat had matured the fleshy plants and brought them to unwonted flowering splendour. Between the hot iron-stone nodules bloomed the retiring dwarf midday flowers, the mesembryanthemums, whose delicately fringed petals shone in all the colours of the rainbow. Star-like gethyllis flowers, waxy in their whiteness, sprang without leaves from the dry clay; pale dropping anacampseros plants blossomed on the smooth slates where there was almost no soil for their roots to grasp, and prickly aloes threw aloft spikes of florid crimson and yellow. Between the leafless bushes grew the foetid-smelling stapelias and carellumas, their square, podgy stems laden with strange velvety blooms. Only the thorn trees had leaves and these were not green but grey and dust-covered, and fell to the ground when touched.

The District panted through the summer, for everyone felt the heat and the drought. Old Andrew Quakerley, who had more money than he could usefully employ for the development of his garden, obliged many by a loan, on first and second mortgage.

The drought brought penury to many farmers in the District. One or two sold their farms for what they would fetch and departed to other districts, some to the diamond diggings that lured every penniless vagrant and every gambling spirit to misery or riches, and others to the Transvaal where the chances for the adventurous were said to be equally great. The fine old homestead which had belonged to the Priem family and had by marriage passed into the hands of old Pierre Mabuis, was sold. Its owner, bankrupt, died a tired, broken man as a pensioner on one of Andrew's farms. His son, a roistering youngster, emigrated to the Transvaal, and was said to be doing great things there on the stock exchange.

Andrew had done his best for the Mabuis family, for he remembered old Pierre, a strange, eccentric, reformed drunkard with a cultivated taste in music and wine, who had for many years lived as a teacher on the bounty of Everardus Nolte, the ex-executioner, and had ultimately married the rich Widow Priem and settled down to a quiet country existence. His one son had married the daughter of a store-keeper in a neighbouring district, but had inherited much of his father's unbusinesslike temperament and, although respected as a good churchman—whereas his father had been a Roman Catholic—and citizen, had never been looked upon as a competent farmer. Drought, cattle disease and locusts had wrecked him, and with his death the Mabuis family, so far as the District was concerned, had died out.

Andrew, when he pottered around in his beloved garden, thought sometimes that the history of the Mabuises epitomised the history of the District. The good old families were dying out, degenerating, the third and fourth generations showing themselves much inferior, in initiative, in energy, and in ability, to their forebears. There had been a dearth of new blood to invigorate the old stock, but that alone could hardly be the cause of the deterioration that he could see all around him. After all, the original stocks were good—fine Hanoverian, Frisian and English yeomen. Three generations of them should have produced better, fitter men and women, but he looked in vain for these. It was like his perennials. His perennials were the bane of his life. He got them as seed from the best seedsmen in England and Germany, and the first season they were a delight to look upon, but the next they failed miserably, running to root and stem, and lacking foliage and flower.

With the advent of the new year came renewed political agitation. Some of the local excitement was reflected in the doings of the Parliament in Cape Town. Andrew read with interest, not unmixed with a trifle of indignation, that although the Assembly had risen to do honour to the dead Gladstone, it had passed Mr Schreiner's motion of no confidence in the Sprigg Government. Late in June, a June that promised to be as chary of rain as its predecessor had been liberal, the District and the Village heard that Parliament had been dissolved and that a new election, this time for the Assembly, would take place in September.

The District had the right to elect two representatives to the Assembly. In time a tradition had grown up that one of the District's representatives should be selected from those actually residing in the District and his colleague from someone living in the capital. The first two members of Parliament had been the ex-executioner representing the District, and an excitable Irish doctor, who had once practised in the District but had retired and lived at Cape Town. Following these, who had retired through extreme old age, had come a Rekker from the District and an attorney from Cape Town, and they now held the position. Both, however, were regarded as not quite staunch in the new faith, which demanded from them more clamorous support of the Bond Party to which neither, in fact, belonged.

That Party was now actively at work in the District. It had established a branch at the Village, of which the energetic secretary was the young attorney, Elias Vantloo, who had developed such exemplary teetotal views, and had organised an active opposition to the sitting members. Formerly no one had taken it amiss that Mr West, the attorney from Cape Town, resided three hundred miles away from his constituency; that want of propinquity rather added to than detracted from his qualifications, it added lustre to the District's choice that its chosen should live in the very shadow of the Houses of Parliament at the top of Adderley Street. But now it was alleged that local representatives were needed and, above all, men who could show by words and action that they could remain unimpressed by Mr Rhodes's cajoling, and stood firmly in the ranks of the Bond Party.

The election could be fought on one issue only, and that issue was Rhodes or the Bond. What did it matter if the principles enunciated by both sides were more or less the same, differing in so little that few of the electors could distinguish between the niceties of interpretation attached to them? In all controversies where the points of variance are overshadowed by the personalities of the debaters, the real importance of the issues is likely to be outweighed by the popularity of those who as leaders on either side formulate their doctrines in slogans that may serve as catchwords. Here even these slogans were somewhat dubious as to meaning and intention.

To the electors it did not matter that Mr Rhodes had in the past shown himself singularly sympathetic to those ideals which the party that now opposed him had placed at the head of their programme of principles, nor that Mr Hofmeyr, popularly referred to by those who followed him as 'Our John' and by those who opposed him as 'The Mole,' had supported many of the principles for which the Progressive Party stood and publicly declared himself in favour of Imperial preference, a contribution to the Navy, and a greater measure of tolerance towards the Outlanders of the Transvaal.

Sensible men, like Andrew Quakerley, deplored the agitation that had culminated in such bitter animosity and now threatened to create a chasm between the two sections of the community that had for some many generations lived in amity, co-operating heartily for the common welfare. They realised that much of it was artificial, stirred up by personal hate and prejudice, but that at bottom there lay differences which had their being in the difference of tradition and outlook of the two sections.

Much had been hoped from the new governor, but Sir Alfred had not shown himself equal to the task of understanding and sympathising with their difficulties. He had neglected to tour the districts. The Village had not had the honour of entertaining him, and knew him only by what it could read of his doings and utterances in the press. And these utterances failed to inspire them with confidence in his capability to deal with the involved situation. At one meeting he had addressed a deputation in what old Andrew irritably called 'a schoolmaster's fashion.' He had stressed, needlessly according to old Andrew, the advantages of the Imperial connection and had opined that it would be monstrous if the deputation were not loyal.

'Loyal to what?' old Andrew grumbled, as he read the report of the speech in the *Cape Times*. He sat in the big dining room where the reflection of the protea logs burning in the fireplace flickered over the polished silver on the sideboard. 'I wish he would not use such general terms. One almost despairs of any settlement when people talk like that.'

'But Andrew, dear,' interrupted his wife, lifting her eyes from the *Argus* which had fallen to her share from the week's mail, 'it's perfectly splendid of His Excellency to give it them straight from the shoulder. Just a little firmness—that is all that we want. And you know how timid dear old Sir Hercules always was. He couldn't have said "Boo" to them.'

'This isn't saying "Boo," Alice,' said Andrew, sharply. 'It's—damn me, it's very much like insulting them. And we won't get much forrader by doing that. If Sir Alfred would go about and get to know people, he would learn that at heart the Colony is perfectly sound.'

'You know it isn't,' retorted his wife. 'What with all this talk of fighting and driving us into the sea ...'

'Stuff, Alice, stuff,' exclaimed the old man, contemptuously. 'A few young hotheads ... why, Father used to tell us—you remember, Joan?—about what was said and done in his day in England. Nothing very much came of it. Nothing much will come of this, if we keep our heads and act like sensible folk.'

'That will just make them more impertinent,' complained Mrs Quakerley. 'We had a report at our meeting this afternoon ...'

'Really, Alice,' interrupted her husband in his turn, 'I do wish you would not go to these League meetings. They do no good.'

'I most certainly shall go to them, Andrew, dear,' said old Mrs Quakerley, bellicosely. 'Even if there are only one or two—and we have already three members, and Miss Marradee will join us, I am sure.'

'Miss Marradee is much too sensible,' said her husband, with a smile.

'She's too frightened, that's all,' said his wife, flourishing the *Argus* as if to emphasise Miss Marradee's timidity. 'But as I was saying, even if there are only three of us, it will show people that we at least are loyal.'

'There you go again,' grumbled her husband. 'Loyal ... you all talk of loyalty and disloyalty. What do you really mean by it? Surely you don't imagine that men like old Rekker or Mr Uhlmann or Mr Seldon are disloyal? That would be altogether too silly.'

'Then why don't they come forward and prove their loyalty?' asked his wife sharply. 'It's just these men who do all the mischief. They sit quiet and allow all the rest to insult and irritate us.'

'Now please don't get excited, Alice,' warned her husband. 'I've never yet heard of anybody insulting us.'

'Of course not, not us, personally. But England, the Empire. I heard one of the maids say that ...'

'If you listen to kitchen talk,' retorted old Andrew wearily, 'you will probably hear all sorts of things that you won't like. But honestly, Alice, I see no reason for your League. If you had a vote it might be different, but now it seems rather silly for three ladies to meet every week and to discuss politics, of which, if you will allow me to say so, I think you and I know very little, my dear.'

'I know quite enough, thank you,' said Mrs Quakerley with asperity. 'I know that if we do not make a stand we are going to be underdog here very soon. You should just hear the children talk. And of course they are merely repeating what they hear their elders say.'

'I had hoped that we had made an end of all that,' said old Andrew reflectively. 'Things went rather well at the Jubilee meeting, don't you think so, Joan?'

His sister, thus directly appealed to, nodded her heard. She sat by the side of her sister-in-law, stitching with meticulous, eye-trying fineness, the hem of a cambric cloth. In the reflection of the firelight her pale, sharp features and delicately slender figure, crowned by a mass of silvery-grey hair, were outlined against the shadowy background of her large arm chair. She rarely took part in the conversation, contenting herself with occasional interjections of approval or dissent, seldom followed up by more elucidative remarks.

'I fancied so,' she now said, 'to tell the truth, I thought that things were very much better since we had the meeting. And I agree with you, Brother Andrew, that most of it is talk. We used to have it in Father's time, and he always said "Let well alone".'

'He wouldn't say that now,' interjected Mrs Quakerley, quickly. 'Father would have been the first to assert his rights. After all, Andrew, you are a Quakerley, and the Quakerleys have always been loyal Englishmen.'

'And will remain so, I hope,' said her husband. 'My dear, there are loyalties and loyalties. I do not think it is disloyal—not in the sense you imply, my dear—to vote against Mr Rhodes or to say that the Transvaal is being treated badly.'

'Surely you wouldn't say that, Andrew. What could be more fair ...'

'No, I don't. I am not talking about myself. I am only trying to show you their point of view.'

'I don't care to hear about it,' said Mrs Quakerley, pursing up her lips in the prim manner which she had learned in the days of her youth when such had been the fashion among young ladies who wished to express disdain. 'I am quite aware of their views, thank you. But, if ingratitude and impertinence are not disloyalty, what, I ask, is? And what can be more disloyal than what they write in their stupid press.'

'Which you can't read, Alice,' said her husband, with a smile. 'Now I do read it, occasionally, and I must say that although they do use expressions which are not polite, I see nothing very bad in what they write. It is just the natural ebullition of feeling at a time like this, eh, Joan?'

'*Recte edepol spero*,' quoted Joan, who had read Terence to her father until she had most of the text in her head.

'My Latinity's too rusty for that,' said her brother, 'but I catch your meaning. After all, President Brand said much the same.'

'I don't care what Joan has to say,' commented Mrs Quakerley, angrily, 'and she might as well say it in sound English while she's about it. But I think it is high time that these people were taught a lesson. And that is why I am so glad that Sir Alfred has spoken as he has. I am sure it will do a world of good.'

'Let's hope so,' answered her husband. 'But I am afraid that we are going to have a disturbing time here with this election.'

'You should put your foot down, Andrew,' said his wife, less sharply. 'If you wished you could do so much. Why, half of these people owe you money. If you were to tell them that you want them to vote for ...'

'Alice, I wish you would not meddle with these matters. Let everyone vote as he wishes. I shall certainly not try to influence anybody in that way. You know very well that this District is preponderantly Bond and that the Bond nominees will romp in. I don't see much harm in that myself. As a matter of fact, I believe that with a Bond majority in Parliament there is every likelihood that things will go better. There is nothing like responsibility to sober a party.'

'I think I shall go to bed,' said his wife, plaintively. 'If you can be so mean as to stand aside and see these people make fools of us, there is nothing more to say.'

She kissed her sister-in-law with the customary peck, and submitted to the same salutation from her husband, who got up and opened the door for her, and departed, nursing her *Argus*.

Andrew threw himself into his chair. 'I suppose you can't manage to keep Alice from these meetings, Joan?' he asked, tentatively.

His sister shook her head. 'I shall not try to,' she replied. 'It is just natural ebullition of feeling at a time like this, eh, Andrew?'

'Confound you. I don't happen to know a single quotation from Terence to hurl at you, Sister.'

'I'll give you one,' said his sister, stitching industriously. '"*Quam forte saepe temere, eveniunt quae non audeas optare*. But I won't translate it for you. You must ask Mr Bisley to explain.'

'I imagine I can thrash out its meaning for myself, Joan. Let's hope you are right.'

The District was stirred to its depths. Excitement, such as it had not known since the days when an uprising of the faraway Native tribes had called for a volunteer commando, ebbed and flowed through it. The Government had dissolved the House of Assembly. An election was imminent.

For the majority of the voters in the District the issues were personal as much as political. It was to be a struggle between Mr Rhodes and the Bond Party, Mr Rhodes safely entrenched in the urban areas, his opponents invincible in the rural constituencies. And the District was wholeheartedly rural, its feelings sharply anti-Progressive, its sympathies unfeignedly Bond. The nomination meeting, held in the Village court room, resulted in the adoption of four candidates, two Progressives and two Bond nominees. The two former were well-known, eminently respected citizens, in many ways fitted to represent the constituency. But they knew from the start that their election was an impossibility, for their two opponents were men who had local interests, who were loud in their denunciations of Mr Rhodes, or what they imagined was Mr Rhodes's policy, and who could command the majority of votes. Never before had such a clash of sentiment shaken the District. There were many, Andrew among them, who regretted this clash.

Mr Uhlmann, walking alongside Andrew in the latter's garden, whither he had been taken to admire the on-coming daisies, said as much in no uncertain voice.

'We have never, Mr Quakerley,' he stated in his precise, rather curiously intonated English, 'had these personal issues raised here. It is lamentable. It introduces a new note that is utterly discordant. My people,'—he shrugged his shoulders expressively—'what would you have, Mr Quakerley? They are ignorant. They cannot see that these ... these clamorous sentimentalities are little to the purpose. What we want is good government, not merely disciplined voting as the party wishes.'

'You are sure then, Mr Uhlman, that the Bond will come in?' asked old Andrew, touching the silky petals of a newly-opened veld daisy whose gorgeous crimson and black flashed vividly in the morning sun. 'Myself, I confess I have a doubt.'

'I have none,' said the parson sharply. 'Every rural constituency will return an anti-Rhodes man. I feel sure that the balance of power in Parliament will be in the hands of the Bond.'

'And why should you object to that?' queried the old man, mildly.

'Because I do not think our country members are as yet capable of running—that is the word, is it not, Mr Quakerley?—the country. Government is a matter of training ...'

'Quite. But the country is governed by the departments, by the permanent heads, Mr Uhlmann. Administratively it does not matter what party is in power. I am more concerned about the impression that a Bond victory will have upon our friends on the other side of the Vaal.'

'You, too, think that it will strengthen the war spirit there?' asked Mr Uhlmann, anxiously. 'I hope, I pray, Mr Quakerley, that it may have the reverse result. You see, with a Progressive Party in power here, our friends over there may think—will think, I am sure—that we must necessarily be antagonistic to them—unfriendly, not eager to meet them half-way. With a Bond Party in power they may be willing to meet us, to concede what they should have conceded long ago. A man is less disinclined to admit he is in the wrong to a friend, Mr Quakerley, than to one who is not a friend.'

'That is quite true. I hope you are right. But the mere fact that we are in for a disturbing time here is enough to vex any of us. I don't like the feeling that there is among us. On both sides, Mr Uhlmann, on both sides.'

'I regret it as much as you do, Mr Quakerley. It is a feeling of antagonism where no enmity or unfriendship should be.'

'Then you feel it too, Mr Uhlmann?'

'Why, certainly. One meets with it everywhere, even where one does not go to seek it, Mr Quakerley.'

'And its explanation?'

The pastor shrugged his shoulders. 'One need not be a psychologist,' he said, enunciating the 'p' in the foreign manner, 'to explain it. It is the clash of tradition, or rather the emerging of a new tradition, that does not altogether respond to the older. You will find it everywhere, Mr Quakerley, where the ties that bind Colonists to the Motherland get loose, and where the younger generations no longer have cause to respect or cherish those things which we, who are of the older tradition, have been taught to keep in honour.'

'The Native born,' said Mr Quakerley with a smile. 'I can understand. I feel that way myself, sometimes, and you must too, Mr Uhlmann.'

'Yes, certainly. But there is more in it than that, Mr Quakerley. There is this personal appeal—this sense of injustice which my people—I merely use the possessive pronoun, Mr Quakerley ...'

'Quite, I understand ...'

'Very well, then. This feeling against Mr Rhodes. It dates from the Raid, of course, and it is being ridden to death by Mr Rhodes's personal political opponents. But all the same, it is having its effect. Most men here, as you know very well Mr Quakerley, have no deep feelings on political questions. There have been no matters that needed a sharp conflict of opinion to adjust. Or am I expressing myself badly?'

'No. Go on. I quite agree with what you say, so far.'

'I am glad of that. Look, Mr Quakerley. I have lived under four governments, and I can safely say that I have nowhere lived more happily, with less misgivings about ... about all manner of things that have to do with politics, than here. Under the administration of an English Colony in which we all who are Her Majesty's subjects have a say and a hand. There is, so far as I can see, no matter that need evoke such clamorous excitement as this election promises to evoke. Nothing—except that personal spite against Mr Rhodes, which is translated—is that the correct word? Yes?—into a common hatred of all that he stands for.'

'There I do not quite agree,' said old Andrew, reflectively. 'Do you not think, Mr Uhlmann, that at bottom there is another sort of feeling? The feeling that the manner— let me put it in the least objectionable way—the manner in which negotiations are carried out with the Transvaal tends to put their backs up?'

'There is that too, I admit,' said the pastor, thoughtfully. 'No doubt many of our folk feel sore at the thought that the Transvaal may have to eat humble pie. But I don't think that is really at the base of this ill-feeling. Every one of us has a certain amount of—again I do not know how to express it—I mean in each of us there is a capacity for what the Germans call *Schadenfreude*, the little delight we take mischievously in the small difficulties of our friends, as the French philosopher says. That discounts the sense of injustice felt at the humiliation of someone who has not, after all, behaved exactly as a friend should behave. Once before—you know when they closed the Drifts—we were prepared to be quite unfriendly, although I was glad to see that the matter went no further.'

'Then is there more behind it all, Mr Uhlmann? Is there really anything serious in it?'

'Not yet. But it may become serious, Mr Quakerley. Through agitation such as we are experiencing in this election. Most of all, through organisation, for party purposes, of feelings and sentiments that should not participate in politics that, like ours, are merely bread and butter politics. We have no great outstanding questions that need split us up into groups. Of course we have the clash, sometimes of agrarian against urban interests, economic matters, Mr Quakerley. But over these those who speak English and those who speak Dutch need not quarrel simply because they belong to different sections.'

'I am sure you are mistaken, Mr Uhlmann. Surely here, if anywhere, there is a clash of rural and urban interests ...'

'Ostensibly, Mr Quakerley, ostensibly. But in reality, no. Simply because the urban interests are identified, for the moment, with Mr Rhodes and with the Progressives, they are, for that reason alone, anathema to the rural areas. And simply because what is Dutch-speaking is identified with the Bond, it is equally anathema to the urban centres. That is an utterly false and artificial orientation, Mr Quakerley ...'

'Merely temporary, I should say.'

'Possibly. Let us, at least, hope so. If it were not for politics, as now organised, Mr Quakerley, we should have no sectional feeling in this District, nor, I think, anywhere in the country. We never had in the old days, when there were temporary matters which were of vastly greater moment than this matter which is now agitating us. We are grabbing old cows out of the furrow—I can give you instances of that; I had occasion quietly to reprove one of my Deacons the other day who took advantage of his position to refer to one such anachronism. It had its ludicrous side, Mr Quakerley, but it had also its serious side, and I regret to say no one saw anything funny in it.'

'What was it? You must tell me.'

'Then it must go no further. I do not tell tales out of school. This was at a prayer-meeting, and the fellow drew a parallel between Mr Chamberlain and Pharaoh's evil counsellors—an utterly uncalled for *mal à propos* analogy. I am sorely afraid that in this excitement we shall have more of these things. You will remember that at the time of the Raid there was all that talk about Slagter's Nek ...'

'I do. A mistake, that, of course, but it is rather hard that it should be brought up now.'

'History is full of mistakes, Mr Quakerley. But it is one thing to judge mistakes objectively, historically, and another to use them merely to inflame prejudice.'

'Politics,' said old Andrew, irrelevantly, 'is a dirty business, Mr Uhlmann.'

'I do not see why it should be that,' said the pastor, bending down to examine a budding mesembryanthemum. 'What a beauty this is. From the Rekkers' farm, is it not?'

'No. As a matter of fact, I do not know where I got it from. But it is a beauty. Now, why can't men interest themselves in such-like things, MrUhlmann, instead of ...'

'Men are not made that way, Mr Quakerley. Politics gives scope for passion that otherwise has no outlet. And all passion, uncontrolled, is likely to go to excess. That is one reason why I regret that politics is becoming a business, an organisation. Look, we have had our own methods in the past, and they gave us good men. We got up a requisition to the best man, and we did not allow party or sectional interests to knee-halter us in accepting him and assuring his election.'

'Would you allow me to ask you what you think of the two nominated candidates, Mr Uhlmann?'

'You know them as well as I do, Mr Quakerley. Better, perhaps.'

'Nevertheless I shall value your opinion, Mr Uhlmann. I have my own. Between ourselves, I shall not support the two others.'

'Is that so, Mr Quakerley? You surprise me. I thought ...'

'That I was anti-Bond? No, Mr Uhlmann. I am not anti-anything just because it has an unpopular label. I am not a member of the Bond, but there is nothing in its constitution at which I can cavil. Its methods ... well, I am a little old-fashioned, and I do not like to be forced, by a big party organisation, to sink my independence as a voter. There I am Native-born with a vengeance.'

'Then you do not think the Bond is disloyal?'

'You must define what you mean by loyalty, first, Mr Uhlmann, before I can answer that. I can only say that it seems to me that so far as loyalty to Her Majesty is concerned, there is nothing to choose between the two parties. I have no fear that the Bond Party will do anything that is treasonable, if that is what you mean. But I have not said that I am going to support it, have I? I should like your view of its two candidates first.'

'Well,' the pastor frowned thoughtfully and chose his words with care, 'I can say that both are honest men, according to their lights. Both are practical farmers who have made a success of their farming. Neither is cultured in the ordinary sense of the word. One is an Elder of the church; the other is now Deacon and will probably be chosen as Elder next year.'

'That does not help me very much,' said old Andrew. 'What I wish to know is ... where do these men stand? What will they do if they are elected? Will they help to bring into play these forces of disunion and distrust to which you have just now alluded, or will they try to prevent things from going worse?'

'I cannot answer that,' said the pastor, gravely. 'You must talk with them yourself.'

'But you have done so, Mr Uhlmann. You have seen both. Do not tell me that they allowed their names to go forward without consulting you?'

'That is so. Both came to see me and both asked my advice. The one I advised not to stand. I do not think he is the best man for a member. The other I cordially advised to allow himself to be nominated, as I think that he is a better man then either of the two members that we have had.'

'I think I know whom you mean,' said old Andrew. 'And your word is good enough for me, Mr Uhlmann. I shall have to think over matters.'

'Please do not let me influence you,' said the pastor, hastily. 'My own view has always been that the old members were quite good enough for us. This other matter is a Party matter, and I still think that we should keep Party feeling out of it ...'

'That is impossible,' said old Andrew curtly. 'You must see that for yourself, Mr Uhlmann. This is a Party election, if ever there was one, and the issues are Bond or Rhodes.'

'I am afraid it is,' admitted the Pastor, lugubriously. 'One has it dinned into one's ears ... the papers have nothing but politics in them nowadays, politics and the situation up north.'

'Yes, it is an interesting situation,' said his companion, leading the way towards the *stoep*. 'I am glad we have had this talk, Mr Uhlmann. We see too little of each other. You must come and visit me sometimes. I am an old man and you must not expect me to come up to modern notions, but we have something in common here and there.'

'I shall be delighted to come, Mr Quakerley. Your garden is a joy to the eye. I have enjoyed it ...'

'Yours is rather a waste land, Pastor,' retorted Quakerley, with a smile. 'I hate to see it like that. What about improving it a bit? I can send ...'

'I beg you not to give yourself the trouble, Mr Quakerley. A garden needs constant attention, care, regard, such as one gives a child ...'

'Aye, you may say that,' exclaimed Quakerley, fervently. 'More, Mr Uhlmann, more. Mine has been my hobby, my darling as you say.'

'I can see that, Mr Quakerley. But I have neither the time nor the energy to devote to mine, and it must linger on as it has all these years. You were always a gardener, I remember, at the farm you had a fine one. I came as a child with my father, and saw you gardening there. You were a young man then, and I was much impressed when you brought my mother a bunch of sweet-smelling waxy flowers such as I have never seen ...'

'That was stephanotis from the summer-house,' said the old man, quickly. 'I grew them better there than here. Do you really remember that? I have a dim recollection of it—that is to say, of your mother, and making up a posy for her. We always made posies in those days. We were much more formal. Nowadays all that has gone. People are off-hand and there is a want of courtesy that sometimes—I confess I am old-fashioned, Mr Uhlmann—distresses me. Ah, well, will you come in and have a cup of tea? I should like to show you my orchids.'

Chapter 15

The excitement of the general election simmered gently, almost fastidiously, in the District. Deep-rooted tradition, still too strong to allow old-established custom to be violently disregarded, denied to it the satisfaction of ebullient overflow of passion. Like a stew pot relegated to the tempered warmth of the cooler part of the range, it became pleasantly excited, no more; and although it recognised, as something disturbing and terrific, the radiating effervescence of heat from the centre of disturbance, it remembered what it owed to itself and the traditions of the past, and conducted its own election with a moderation and restraint in remarkable contrast to the ill-feeling and animosity displayed by neighbouring constituencies.

The assistant-magistrate, ordinarily rated as a first-grade clerk, came to enlist the services of Charlie Crest. There were half a dozen polling stations in the District, and over each one two officials had to preside whose first, and it appeared sole, duty was never to allow the ballot box out of their sight. Mr Chisholm thought that Charlie might like an outing to one of the far-away polling booths.

Early on the morning preceding the polling day a Cape cart, with its hood down, drawn by eight horses, driven by the Native constable Augustus, called for Charlie. The flush of dawn tinged the high mountain escarpments in the east with mother of pearl; a grey mist, slowly dispersing before the gathering warmth of the day, covered the river valley and shrouded the slope of the hills. The spring morning air retained something of its winter tang, soon to be replaced by the shimmering heat of the forenoon.

They reached the polling station as the sun was setting over the low, grass-grown dunes separating the wheat-lands from the sea. They drove past the sheep-kraals, square enclosures of ashlar provided with wire gates, now open to admit the sheep returning from the veld in charge of the Native herds; past the circular threshing floor, wherein after the harvest the horses circled at a jog-trot, treading out the corn in the old-fashioned style; past the little garden wherein the fruit trees were already in blossom, and up to the old avenue of dying date palms, towards the homestead with its neatly white-washed walls, its rounded gables, and green-painted windows. In front of the house was a low *stoep*, ornamented with a dozen tins containing flowering shrubs, and shaded by a rickety pergola festooned with budding bougainvillea. Out-buildings flanked the main house, the thatched chaff-house and stables that formerly had been the slaves' quarters. To the left, clustered in an irregular semi-circle, were the huts of the Native labourers, the free men who had replaced, since the time of the Emancipation Ordinance, the slave labour on Uncle Mias's farm, *Salt Pan*.

That evening they supped with Uncle Mias in the large dining room, with its long cedarwood table and its open, unceilinged rafters showing the neat thatching of the roof from underneath.

Uncle Mias was a stout, burly old gentleman, only saved from being double-chinned by a strong jaw that needed much more flesh to disguise the rigid line of the bone. He was clean-shaven, with a skin heavily tanned by exposure to sun and wind, and his eyes, though small and rather deeply set, were shrewd and kindly. He had the reputation of being one of the richest farmers in the District, hard-working and old-fashioned, with a liking for solid investments and a profound distrust of towns and townsmen. Rumour stated that long ago he had lost some thousands in the failure of a bank, and since that time he had hoarded his profits in the mill-house. The mill-house was one of the old out-buildings modified to house the machinery for grinding wheat, the power being supplied by a blindfolded mule that walked round and round a central pole and turned the cogwheels activating grinding machinery. In stacks between the rafters of the mill-house Uncle Mias was popularly supposed to store his banknotes.

Another peculiarity of the old farmer was that he went barefooted. Everyone knew of this habit which had earned him the nickname of 'Barefoot Mias.' Rumour, again, stated that he had worn boots on three occasions only, when he had gone to church to be confirmed, to be wedded, and to christen his first-born. Now as he sat in his great, massively-made arm-chair at the little side-table on which the oil lamp stood, he looked a mild, gentle-faced old patriarch, and Mr Chisholm found him a remarkably well-informed and shrewd conversationalist. After supper the servants had trooped in, and Uncle Mias had conducted evening service, reading, with homely dignity, a chapter out of the Bible, starting in a well-trained bass a simple hymn in which all present joined, though few with such attention to the notes as the host displayed, and finally kneeling down to deliver an *extempore* prayer in which the guests were considered, the coming election brought to the Almighty's attention, and the state of the crops, the weather, and the country described in a few well-chosen sentences. After that the servants trooped out sing-songing their 'Good night, Old Master ... good night, Old Missis, good night, Sirs,' and the grown-up sons took Charlie away to bed.

'Sit, Assistant-magistrate,' invited Uncle Mias, taking his chair at the side-table and motioning Chisholm to a seat opposite him. 'Here are almonds and raisins, and wine. Help yourself. No, not for me. I smoke my pipe and snuff my snuff. At my age that is enough for me. But you will find the wine good. It is old stuff, and tender.'

They talked in Dutch, Mias using the old fashioned grammatical form and his guest the more popular Afrikaans which has shorn itself of inflections and genders. Mias used the same dialect when talking to his servants, but for polite conversation he preferred the old form.

'So you have brought the boy to help you, Assistant-magistrate,' he said, stuffing his pipe and tendering the tobacco bag to his guest. 'He looks a good little chap. Comes of good stock, too. I mind his great grandfather—much before your time, Assistant-magistrate—but I mind him well. He was one of the elect in the land, was old Quakerley.'

'So's his son,' commented Chisholm. 'The one we call old Quakerley now.'

'Aye, Andrew, you mean,' retorted the old man. 'He is not so very old. He can give me five years at most, I think, and I shall be seventy come January. But his father was of different metal, Assistant-magistrate. Andrew is softer—more woman-like, if you take me. He was never a farmer. He's a town's man through and through. Why should a grown man bother about flowers and such-like things? Leave it to the woman, say I. And the waste ... he spends more on that flower garden of his than I do on my whole farm! And what does he get out of it? Nothing ... nothing but trouble and disappointment, Assistant-magistrate. But Andrew has something of his father's obstinacy in him, and he goes his own gait. He's got money to indulge his whims.'

'After all, he made it, Uncle Mias,' said his guest, 'and from what I know he's not been such a bad farmer after all.'

'Aye, let's be fair,' said the old man. 'I grant you that, but that was years ago, and he's made more out of speculation and business than out of the farm. I admit that Andrew would have made good had he gone on. I withdraw what I said ... that he's not a good farmer. On his place almost anyone could have made good. It's good soil. You just put things in ...'

'Are you quite fair in that, Uncle Mias?' asked Chisholm, with a smile. 'I fancy there were others who had just as fine farms, and they haven't made good.'

'Aye, but that is the truth. Do you know, Assistant-magistrate, that is a matter I have often thought over. We have had good farms, good stock, good men, and what have we left? Everything seems to degenerate, somehow. It's the same with my sowing.'

'And Mr Quakerley tells me it's the same with some of his plants, Uncle Mias. They flourish for a couple of years and then they die out.'

The old man nodded. 'Even so, they kill themselves in three years,' he said reflectively. 'I mind the men I've known. There were families as good as my own, and look at their descendants. Perhaps, Assistant-magistrate, an old man compares things unfavourably, always prejudiced in favour of his own contemporaries. My own sons, my own offspring—there's an example for you. Soft, though they look strong enough and there's nothing the matter with them, but soft compared to what I was at their age; and not wise, Assistant-magistrate, not wise. That is what troubles me more than anything. In my day—I speak of fifty years past, Assistant-magistrate—we paid less attention to externals, more to the inner worth of things; less to the tinsel gilding than to the core, if you take me. Now, well, it's wealth that you can see, that you must make folk see, that you rub under their noses and flaunt in the road, that gets you consideration and respect, and that's wrong, Assistant-magistrate, that's wholly wrong.'

'It's a passing phase,' said Mr Chisholm, soothingly. 'Every younger generation has it. You've got an old proverb, Sir, that everything rights itself ...'

'Aye, but you must quote it properly,' interrupted the old man quickly. 'If everyone does his duty ... that you must add if you would quote the proverb fairly, and nowadays who does? You will see tomorrow, Assistant-magistrate. There are two hundred and eleven voters in this ward. I know them all. And you'll see barely a quarter of them turn up to register their votes. They talk ... my heaven, how they do talk! But if it inconveniences them to vote they will not turn up, although so much depends on them. I suppose I must not ask you what you think; after all, you are a government official.

'Not tonight, Uncle Mias; I am merely your guest, eating almonds and raisins with you and helping myself to a pinch of your excellent snuff.'

'So, forgive me; the box is beside you. I did not think that you favoured a pinch. I am glad to see that you have the habit. Then I talk to you as one man to another.'

'I should feel honoured, Uncle Mias.'

'Well, then, you can tell me what you think of it all. Here at *Salt Pan* we are out of the world. I get the paper, but I hardly ever find time to read it, and the reading does not tell me much. Not the inwardness of things, if you take me, Nephew. There, you must forgive me, but one gets into the habit, and you are still young.'

'But certainly, Uncle Mias. I like it much better than the stilted 'Assistant-magistrate,' and I am that merely for a time. If you really want my official title it is First Clerk.'

'Then I shall say "Nephew," if you do not mind. It goes better, Nephew. Now tell me, is it really true that Rhodes wants war with the Transvaal?'

'I do not suppose that Mr Rhodes wants war at all, Uncle Mias. And the Transvaal must know that if it comes to a war, it will not have a dog's chance.'

'Of that I am not so sure, Nephew,' said the old man, blowing a cloud of smoke away from him. 'It is a big country, and a bad one in which one can go on warring for quite a long time. That does not matter. What matters is what will happen here.'

'I agree, Uncle Mias. That is why I think war is quite out of the question. And it seems to me you make altogether too great a bogey of Mr Rhodes. It is not for him to say if there is to be war, and I rather imagine that war will suit his purpose as little as it will suit ours.'

'I, too, think that. I saw Rhodes once—he is just an ordinary man, strong and I fancy kind, if you take me, Nephew. He talked to me—I have a little English and I can manage very well with one who does not speak my language—very sensibly. I liked what I saw of him, and I liked what he did for us that time he was our leader and chosen chief. If he did what they say he did, he made a great mistake. But everyone of us can make mistakes, and I doubt not that so sensible a man will regret that he made one and learn his lesson.'

'Then you would be prepared to trust him, Uncle Mias?'

'Not just yet,' said the old man sharply. 'He must bide his time. It will come, and if he is really wise he will wait for it. Look you, Nephew, just now men's passions are astir; they do not think quietly and wisely. There has been, as you know, great agitation. The Raid—now you mind what it did and what an impression it made upon us? Even here at *Salt Pan*, my boys were so excited they wanted to go up north. I said to them they had no cause to go, but youngsters are foolish, Nephew, and they talked of blood and kin and injustice ... I know, I know!'

'It will pass,' said Mr Chisholm cheerily, helping himself to another handful of almonds and raisins.

'Doubtless, but it may leave a *spoor*, Nephew. And some *spoors* stay for a long while and confuse the track for honest men. Now tomorrow ... I do not want to pry, but my own mind is in a doubt ... if you take me ...'

'You want to know how I am going to vote, Uncle?'

'Yes. If it is not indecent to ask. But do not tell me if you do not wish to. Still, you are a townsman. You know something more about things than we here at the *Pan* ...'

'I needn't make a mystery about it, Uncle Mias. I've thought over things and I shall vote for the two Bond candidates. I think most people will.'

'And why? Now, Nephew, you intrigue me. You, an Englishman ...'

'As little as you, Uncle Mias. My great-grandfather came from England, but my mother was a South African, like yours.'

'So! Glad to hear it. Yet, as I was saying, you who by kin and custom should be on the other side ...'

'But that is just it, Uncle Mias,' exclaimed Mr Chisholm, who found himself slightly irritated. 'Why will you make it a question between Dutch and English—between Mr Rhodes and Mr Hofmeyr? They don't count in the long run. What counts is our common welfare ... the country's. It's as much mine as yours, isn't it?'

'Aye, you speak wisely, Nephew. I have felt that ever so long, and it eases me to hear you speak it. But even then, why do you wish the Bond to come in?'

'Simply because I think it would make matters more even. It's our system of Party government, Uncle Mias. Give the opposition a chance, let it have the responsibility of government, and you will find that it suddenly becomes a champion of what it has formerly attacked. I do believe that a Bond majority in Parliament will be good for the country.'

'Do you indeed?' the old man sighed heavily. 'I am glad to hear that. I had a notion that it would only tangle things up more. But now that you reason it out, I have a mind to agree with you. I, too, must vote that way then ...'

'Surely you did not intend to vote Progressive, did you?'

'I had not made up my mind, Nephew,' answered the old man, cautiously. 'And I like their candidates better, though I have nothing against either of the Nephews that are standing as Bondsmen. But they are inexperienced, and the other two, although they are doubtless Rhodes men, have experience and can express themselves. These things weighed with me. But now I shall sleep on it. And you, Nephew, you have a trying day before you. Have you what you require in the guest room? Yes? Then let me say, rest well.'

Chapter 16

After an early breakfast, Mr Chisholm and his young assistant, accompanied by Uncle Mias and his three stalwart sons, took the black japanned box and the piles of voting papers to the booth. A little ceremony was conducted there, as the law demanded. The black japanned box was opened, to show that it was empty, and then solemnly sealed with red tape fastened by big blobs of sealing wax. Charles was allowed to drop the molten wax on the black japan where it burned dull patches on the tin. The sealed packets of voting papers were opened, counted, the official forms filled in and the signatures witnessed. Then, at eight o'clock sharp, the assistant-magistrate declared the booth open, and Uncle Mias and his three sons came forward as the first voters, were properly marked off the voters' list, given their voting papers, entered properly on the counterfoils, and dispatched to the side table where they pondered for some time as if undecided where to put their marks. When finally they came forward, holding out the slips of paper on which their choice was plainly to be seen, they were directed to fold them up and deposit them solemnly in the black japanned box.

'Well, that ends our business,' exclaimed Uncle Mias, cheerfully. 'I shall have to see to my work now, Assistant-magistrate, and my young men will have to go to theirs. So I can't stay to pass the time with you, but the others will be here pretty soon. The wife will see that you don't starve. If you will just look in at about ten o'clock ...'

Uncle Mias and his sons walked off, greeting on their way a couple of farmers who were dismounting from their horses in front of the house *stoep*. The newcomers hitched the reins over the gate post and came briskly forward.

'Good morning, Field-Cornet,' said the one. 'I am Booysen.'

'Good morning, Field-Cornet,' said the other. 'I am Franken.'

They shook hands solemnly with Chisholm and the boy, and took the voting papers gravely.

'Which must we put our marks against?' they asked, but Chisholm shook his head.

'The polling officer must not influence the voter,' he said sharply. 'You must choose for yourself. Go over to that table and mark the paper, fold it so that I cannot see what you have marked, and put it in this slit.'

'You might help a chap, you know,' grumbled the one as he went over to the little table. 'But I'll just do as Cousin Mike here does.'

Later on came a Coloured boy. He protested volubly that it was a shame to take folk away from the sheep at this time of the day, and when the voting paper was handed over to him, after he had been traced in the register, he eyed it askance.

'I can't read the Masters' names, *Baas*,' he said. 'And I don't care which it is either. It's no matter to me, *Baas*, Adoons will vote for all the four masters. Adoons has never had any harm done to him by any of them. They must be all good, *Baas*.'

'In the old days,' said the boy, returning with his paper which he had omitted to fold and which Chisholm could see had been spoiled by four big crosses, 'we didn't go to all this fuss. You just said whom you wanted, and the world went on just as well as now. *Ai*, my Little Master, but it's a bad world nowadays when one must do everything with the pencil or the pen. Good day to you, my Master, and good day, my Little Master. Adoons must go look after the sheep.'

A cart drove up to the house and outspanned. Men rode in on horses; one came in a donkey-cart, another rode in on an ox; more Natives came to vote, and by ten o'clock some fourteen had demanded voting papers. There were now several carts and a spring-wagon outspanned on the grass, but although these had conveyed quite a number of men and women, the visitors seemed to prefer the hospitality of the house to the ceremonial attendance at the polling booth. The sun streamed down upon the vacant chairs, and the maid brought coffee and biscuits. Both the polling officers found the interlude pleasant after the monotony of waiting for voters who did not appear.

Shortly before eleven o'clock there came an old man whose appearance and gait at once attracted attention. He was tall, standing several inches over six feet, lean almost to emaciation but erect with a posture that betokened health and strength. A long, narrow face, dark almost to swarthiness, large dark eyes almost violet in their shade, a thin, drooping, white moustache and white hair so inordinately long that it fell on to his shoulders, were sufficiently impressive to single him out in any crowd. He was dressed in shabby but well-fitting black cloth, and walked with a curious, high-stepping gait, as if he wanted to avoid something that lay in his way. As he came closer he waved his hand in friendly greeting, and even before he had reached the door of the polling booth he had introduced himself.

'I am Sablonniere, Amadeus Sablonniere, Mr Official,' he called out. 'You will find me on the register, though the number has escaped me. But I am there all right. Yes, Young One, look it up, but it is there.'

He put out a long, lean-fingered hand and shook hands cordially. Chisholm noted that his grip was vigorous, altogether unlike the perfunctory, flabby handshake of the other visitors who had preceded him. The business of voting took seconds with him, whereas it had taken minutes with the others. When he had placed his folded paper in the box, he bent down and genially took the polling officer's arm.

'Come and sit in the sunshine,' he invited. 'You can keep an eye on your box well enough from there. In here you get no sun, and it is the sun that I want. Come and sit outside.'

'I don't see why not,' said Chisholm. 'So long as I am on the spot. Very well.'

The old man proved to be an engaging personality, a character such as the assistant-magistrate had not expected to find at the *Salt Pan*, and one utterly unknown to him. When he intimated as much the lean man nodded his head vigorously.

'That is simply because I do not choose to come into town, Mr Official,' he said briskly. '*Surement*, there is no need to. Why should I go trapesing around when I can live quietly, sweetly, on my own farm, which lies yonder behind the hills. You must come and visit me there, Mr Official ...'

'Chisholm, my name is ...'

'Grateful! But it is customary to say so at once. Not that I did not know it, no. We all know our *landdrost's* right-hand man. Precisely. And I was exalted enough to imagine that my own was familiar to officialdom.'

'I have not had the pleasure of meeting you, Mr Sablonniere. Your name, of course, I knew. But I did not expect to find you ...'

'As you find me? Precisely. One often has that experience. There is a Frideaux—he calls himself Verdoos, but he is a pure Frideaux, all the same—that you would take to be one of our host's Anakian sons. Myself, now I am not what I seem. I have a little left in me of what I have inherited from my French ancestors, but that is little enough—a mannerism of speech, perhaps the appearance—old-fashioned and out of the way, Young Sir, you may find it, but it suits me and I have no reason to quarrel with it, and what other than my friends say of it leaves me frigid. You must not go by appearances.'

'I should take you to be French through and through, Mr Sablonniere, although you speak Dutch well enough ...'

'Dutch, Afrikaans, English, German ... I speak them all. *Ich lernte ja alle vier als Kind* ... and my little English'—he spoke it easily and fluently, and henceforth conducted the conversation in it—'was sufficiently tested when I was in Simonstown. You will not find a Frenchman hereabouts, Mr Chisholm. The last of that crew was old Pierre Mabuis, and he was half-and-half. A weird creature, somewhat like myself I have heard say, but he was before my time, for I am comparatively speaking a newcomer in this District. Here comes the coffee. Put it down on the bench, my girl, and tell the Old Missis in an hour's time we might need another cup. I shall take my meal with the Masters here. Tell her that, my girl, and if there is chicken, intimate to her that I like the brown flesh of the bird. Not the white meat. That is only succulent when it is made into a blancmange, with cream and spices. You should come to my place, Mr Chisholm, to eat a proper old-fashioned blancmange.'

'I always thought that was a sweet,' said the assistant-magistrate, drinking his coffee.

'Nowadays, I grieve to say, it is. But it should be the white meat of the chicken, Sir, pounded with cream and butter, and spiced with nutmeg and crushed coriander seed. Lightly steamed, like a pudding. I am fond of it. You have no doubt perceived my affliction. It is not, though you might think so, a nervous disease. My way of walking sometimes leads even experts to diagnose it as that, but they are mistaken. It is a matter of minor importance to you, Mr Chisholm, but to me it is of some gravity, and I have found that only a serious attention to diet prevents it from being a confounded nuisance.'

'Really, I did not think that there was anything the matter, Mr Sablonniere ...'

'Then you should have,' said the lean man, who talked almost as he walked, jerkily, but with considerable vigour, and no slurring of his words. 'Any one would have thought there was something the matter, seeing me walk as if there were serpents in my way. With a trifling amount of medical experience one would say at once, "Aha, *locomotor ataxia!*" Or one might even go further and guess disseminated sclerosis ... yes, Mr Chisholm, I know them all, for I have made a study of such things. But in my case there is nothing of the kind. If you are interested at all—it is not everyone that is, and it is not my intention to bore you. There are plenty of other, perhaps more amusing, subjects to talk about. But an old man likes to find someone to listen to his complaints—it is all one has to live for after one has left seventy years behind.'

'By all means,' said Chisholm hurriedly. The man was obviously mad, and it was best to humour him. And at any rate his talk was amusing.

'Oh, no, I am not in the least mad,' said Mr Sablonniere, who appeared to divine his companion's thoughts. 'That is the very last thing you must think of, although I am quite aware that it is the very first that you will think of. There are many who take me to be mad, but I assure you that I am not. Perhaps I shouldn't assure you. I am aware that a madman always does. Assures other people that he is not mad, I mean. But my affliction is not a matter of madness. It is merely a misfortune. In my youth I was magnetised. Magnetised by a Malay. You have heard of their magic, eh? And doubtless disbelieved all you heard. Well, in me you have a tangible proof of its effects.'

Mr Chisholm was more than ever convinced that his singular voter was mad.

'Hypnotised, I suppose,' suggested Mr Chisholm, gravely, but the old man shook his head.

'Mesmer and Sequah,' said Mr Sablonniere, "I know of. The one I have read about; the other I have allowed to draw one of my teeth, and bitterly I regretted the painlessness of it. I never experienced such agony in all my life, but of course the drums drowned my voice and afterwards I was too ashamed to protest. You mustn't think that I am unsophisticated. I am not quite a fool. The matter is, after all, very simple. When I was a child, my father—he was a harness-maker at Simonstown and did much business with the Malays down there—unwittingly offended one of them, and I was poisoned as the result. Deliberately hocused, Mr Chisholm. They put something in my food and I was ill for many weeks after. I have since wasted a lot of time and trouble to find out what it was. I am told it was 'magnet,' which I take to be powdered haematite—the magnetic stone you get in the Karroo. Probably that had some arsenic in it, and what I really had was arsenical *neuritis*—yes, I have studied the subject, and I am well up in these terms. So I am not at all mad. I am simply stating facts. My walk—I am told the children call me Uncle Ostrich because of it, but I do not mind; did not one of my forebears say that their age knows no pity?—my walk is merely the result of what the Malay did to me when I was a youngster.'

'I have never heard of such things,' said the assistant-magistrate, 'but,'—his official soul was shocked at the suggestion—'was nothing done to them? I assume it could be brought home ...'

'Perhaps. But my father was much too frightened to take steps. You know, Mr Chisholm, what superstitious folk we are. Take our host, now. You would say, to look at him, that no more level-headed, sober, solid man could be found anywhere in this

District. But do you know that he will not allow a Malay, not a strolling wagon painter, not a wandering Malay fisherman, to sleep on his farm? He is too much afraid of 'paljas,' which is magic. He firmly believes that I am 'magnetised,' that I can pick up needles by just putting my hand over them, and that I can cure people by making passes in front of them. I do sometimes. Merely suggestions, Mr Chisholm. They will tell you that I can stop bleeding, for I have done so. There was a reaper on my farm who cut himself a deep gash, right across the wrist artery, Mr Chisholm, with his sickle. How he managed it, I can't say, but he did it, and when they called me he was bleeding pretty badly. I stopped the bleeding—it is easy enough to control the main artery, at the elbow—and it impressed them very much. Since then ...' he shrugged his shoulders, took out an elaborately chased old snuff box from his waistcoat pocket, and presented it to his companion. 'I daresay you despise so old-fashioned a custom,' he said, invitingly, 'but it has its hygienic uses. There's another of the crowd. Attend to him, Mr Official, and come back. I like someone to talk to.'

The new voter did not take long over his business, and Chisholm came back and resumed his seat. 'Do you farm hereabouts, Mr Sablonniere?' he asked. Direct questions were allowed by custom, even more intimate enquiries being permitted than merely to investigate a man's occupation.

'Over there ... behind the hills,' said Mr Sablonniere, 'if you can call it farming. You may take it that I have retired myself, and that I amuse myself with agricultural experiments which bring me in very little money but give me some pleasure and my neighbours plenty of amusement. They look upon me, thanks to my affliction and the story of my magnetisation, as a sort of unregistered doctor. I am afraid my registered colleague at the Village does not altogether approve of me. Just now I am selling quite a lot of electricity. I suppose you have heard of it? No? You astonish me. There is a certain Italian Count—I daresay he is as much a Count as I am, but no matter, he is a smart fellow all the same—who has discovered that there are just as credulous folk in Europe as we have here. He has put up green, blue, and red and white electricity— nothing but coloured water, as a matter of fact—in little square bottles and advertised them as sure cures for cancer and all sorts of incurable diseases. What with postal and import charges—take another pinch, do—the cost per bottle is about a sovereign here, and you would be surprised to hear how many dozen bottles I have already disposed of. I tell them it is nonsense—I am a fairminded man, Mr Chisholm—but they do not believe me, and in some cases it seems to do good. Suggestion, again, but ...' he shrugged his shoulders once more and took snuff. 'If the public wishes to be deceived, Sir ... A credulous public, and nowhere will you find credulity more rampant than here, Mr Chisholm. The pother about this election is a proof of that. Not one of your voters, yourself excepted, knows what the pother is about. Not one but, if he met Mr Rhodes unknowingly, would esteem that diabolical gentleman as one of God's very good fellows, and Sir Gordon, why, if Sir Gordon came down here they would take him to be an Elder of the church, which I believe he really is. And between you and me, if they went to the Transvaal and were cold-shouldered there, as I am told most of us Cape Colony folk are, they would be very loud in venting their indignation and calling upon the government for reprisals.'

'You are, I suppose, a Bondsman, Mr Sablonniere?'

'We all are, hereabouts. But that says little, Mr Chisholm. Were there a branch of the Progressive Party, and were its propagandists to explain its principles in Afrikaans, we should probably belong to that. It is all a question of presentation. Granted certain fundamental principles, understandable by the mob, there will always be a sufficiency of members for any party. Party government—I speak from a ripe experience, Mr Chisholm, and perhaps I may say after fifty years' profound thought—Party government in this country is a mistake. Only the Native and the Dutch, as you would call them, possess a political sense. You English do not care for abstractions.'

'I suppose you tell them that, sometimes?'

'Why should I? There is no sense in opposing the stream. Swim with it, or drift, if you like. But when you have reached my age, young man, you will know that in religion, love and national prejudice there is no reasoning that will convert the man who holds an opposite opinion.'

'You take things very easily, Mr Sablonniere. Perhaps you are of my opinion in the matter ...'

'And that? What might that be?' asked the old man, curiously.

'I told our host last night. He asked me the same question. My opinion is that a Bond majority will ease matters. Give them a chance of assuming responsibility, and things will settle themselves. Do you agree?'

'No.' Mr Sablonniere shook his head decisively. 'As I see it—I may be prejudiced but that is my view—a Bond majority will make no difference whatever. Look around you, Mr Chisholm. Can you honestly imagine that what is going on is for the good of this country?'

'What do you mean? This agitation? Surely you do not subscribe to all that silly rubbish in the press—a conspiracy to drive us English-speaking folk into the sea on the one hand, and a grinding tyranny to suppress the Republics on the other? That is too silly to be discussed.'

'Baldly put, like that, it is,' the old man's voice was grave, although it still held its jerky intonation. 'But where there is smoke, ever so little, there must be something burning. Up there in the north, what have we? A small state, raised from poverty and insignificance by enormously wealthy gold mines into what, compared with ours, is wealth. A small state placed, by virtue of its geographical position, in a position where it is secure from any foreign foe ...'

'How do you make that out?' asked Chisholm, more and more surprised at his companion's talk. He no longer regarded Mr Sablonniere as mad, but he wondered at the old man's display of knowledge and his grasp of the situation. 'The Transvaal borders on Portuguese territory ...'

'Bah!' exclaimed Mr Sablonniere, contemptuously. 'Portugal is but England's little brother. I mean, no foreign power can do anything against the Transvaal without England's permission. That independence about which we hear so much—and believe me, it has been dinned into our ears for months now—what is it, after all, but the result of the protection of England? All this quarrel about whether there is or is not an English suzerainty—it is little to the purpose. The fact remains that if the Transvaal were vulnerable to foreign attack—which it isn't—those gold mines would not remain here for long. But while England is—what do you call it?—the party chiefly interested, no foreign power will dare attack the Republic. That is common sense and, being common sense, many of us cannot admit it. Has it not struck you, Mr Chisholm, that the most obvious facts are the ones we most commonly overlook?'

'I grant you all that. Still, that very fact does not seem to me to imply what you stated just now ...'

'Its implication is equally obvious, Mr Chisholm. The Transvaal has become a spoiled, quarrelsome, provocative child. All spoiled children are provocative. They are too stupid, too childish, to see where their provocation may lead to. In this instance, it leads to dangerous agitation. The root fact is that the men who left this Colony years ago to found new states beyond the government's marches, represent the majority in the north, and a growing minority here. Their tradition—call it freedom, license, grieved resentment, justifiable jibbing against authority—remains. It is a tradition which the majority here have always resisted. At bottom, Mr Chisholm, there is no difference between the English- and the Dutch-speaking Colonist here, but there is a profound difference between the Colonist here and the Voortrekker. The latter is an individualist, and an intolerant individualist at that. I do not complain of that. Here, perhaps, we give too little attention to the individual ...'

'As a lawyer I must dissent from you. I happen to know that the laws of the Transvaal—their *Grondwet*, for instance, and their Gold Law are quite as good as any of ours ...'

'I shall not dispute with you as a lawyer. I suppose all laws here are more or less based on that old absurdity which you call Roman-Dutch law. You might as well say their religion is the same as ours. Perhaps I go too far in using the word individualist. What I mean is rather an individualism in communities, if you will permit the contradiction. You have not been there? No? I thought so. Well, I have. I have even sold some of Count Mattei's cancer electricity there. It is a rich field for exploitation, for credulity there is even more rampant than here. Ant it is a credulity cradled and reared in tradition. You must not breathe a word against the forefathers: what they did is sacrosanct. They represent the best, the cream, of South Africa's White population ...'

'A very laudable ancestor worship, Mr Sablonniere. I expected you to admire it. I do. After all, they were plucky chaps, you know.'

'Pluck, my young man, is an animal virtue which I, too, admire within reason. But there are other civic virtues which I admire much more, and one of those happens to be tolerance. Perhaps because I find so little of it here. But it is refreshing to be able to talk like this once in a while. You will readily understand that I do not indulge myself to this extent when I chat with our worthy host, for example. He could not follow my highly philosophic argument ...'

'Nor do I, Mr Sablonniere. If you will come to your muttons ...'

'Excellent. A good old-fashioned phrase that. Well, I will herd them for you, Friend. My premise is this. Here are two opposing views, two opposing schools of thought. The one has reigned in this Colony of ours since its foundation, with variations into which we need not go; the other has reigned for some fifty years in the Transvaal, and now finds itself up against modernity. It is too proud, or too stupid, to adapt itself to new conditions; it merely opposes, propagandises, and sulks. Now that is dangerous. Do you imagine that there is none here who asks himself, in his ignorance, why South Africa as a whole should not be like the Transvaal, independent, rich, free from foreign domination, able to do what it pleases with its Black population—and that, Friend, is really the crux of the quarrel—without interference, tolerated in its intolerance? No; there are many who ask themselves that question, and there are many who think that, with the Transvaal as lever, with its tradition and its wealth behind us, we may achieve on a large scale what it has achieved on a small one.'

'Possibly. One has only to read the press to agree with you there.'

'Ah. Now to my second. Sooner or later these views must clash. This country is not wide enough for both to reign. And—it is my own opinion merely—England cannot, in her own interests, allow the northern view to triumph. To do so would be to play the traitor to history, to our White civilisation in this country. There stands its emblem— your polling booth and your ballot box. They are there for every citizen, White or Black, who is fortunate enough to have been born a man and not a soulless woman. But I daresay in time even the soulless woman will find a place on our registers ...'

'You'd better not hint as much to Uncle Mias.'

'Indeed, Friend, you will find Uncle Mias by no means so opposed to the notion as you think. His wife influences his politics quite a lot. But let us stick to our sheep. England, I say, cannot allow it. She must put her foot down, and a Bond majority will not help her to do it gently. A Bond majority at present—I, too, should like to see them in power, for at bottom I do not think there is anything much to choose between the two parties in their outlook upon internal politics—a Bond majority at present will simply strengthen the Transvaal in its obstinacy. I fear, I much fear, Mr Chisholm, that this is a case in which there will be some blood-letting. Perhaps not in my time—I am an old man. But sooner or later the clash will come.'

'Honestly, Mr Sablonniere, I cannot agree with you. I don't see that there is any reason to fear war. I don't see how such a war is even possible. It is unbelievable.'

'The unbelievable has happened before in this country, Friend. But go attend to your business. There is another contingent for you. I fancy so far you have not had a single Progressive voter. If you are a betting man, I could lay you odds against the Progressive candidates having a minority below sixty per cent of total votes cast.'

'No, thank you,' laughed the assistant-magistrate. 'I doubt if they will poll one per cent in this ward. Will you wait for me?'

'Certainly. I find it most exhilarating to chat to someone who is as tolerant as you are. Especially now that you no longer think me mad.'

Mr Sablonniere smiled ghoulishly, and pulling out a large, well-coloured meerschaum from his pocket, proceeded to stuff it with Boer tobacco, while Chisholm attended to the new voters. There were half a dozen White men whose Native servants, also voters, respectfully halted behind to give their Masters precedence, and then came forward shyly to make their marks, hurrying away immediately after. The White voters stayed to chat. More voters came from the big house, where it was understood that Uncle Mias had provided refreshments.

At midday the maid brought out a small table, and set it out in the shade of the wall. Chisholm and Charlie and Mr Sablonniere took their luncheon in the open air, and the farmyard fowls came cluck-clucking for scraps. Mr Sablonniere proved an entertaining and cheerful companion. He told stories of desperate fights with old 'man' baboons, gave hair-raising accounts of Malay magic, and narrated wonderful experiences of boys who had been born with the caul. Charlie listened in open-mouthed amazement, for the old man's English was excellent and one soon got accustomed to his jerky intonation. Like all lean men, he ate heartily, but he watered his wine and drank sparingly, and refused the preserved watermelon, delicately transparently green, on the plea that he had 'reason to believe that there was a predisposition to diabetes in his family.'

After luncheon there was a lull, and Mr Sablonniere went away for his *siesta*. 'I grieve, but I must leave you,' he said, apologetically. 'Man and boy, I have rarely missed my afternoon sleep, and much as I esteem the privilege of conversing with you, Friend, I go to get it now. At four o'clock I come back to take my coffee with you. You, too, I should advise to have a sleep. No one will come before four.'

Nor did any one come. The fowls cluck-clucked around on the grass, and the gaudily coloured bee-eaters, uttering their woebegone cries, flew low down, like swallows, before the polling booth and over the outspanned carts. A drowsy peace settled on the farm. Against the white gables of the homestead the sun-glare was dazzling. The assistant-magistrate settled himself on the garden bench and went to sleep.

The afternoon passed slowly. Mr Sablonniere came with the maid bringing the four o'clock coffee, with more biscuits and preserves and a plate of almonds and raisins for Charlie. His conversation enlivened their solitude, which was unbroken by other visitors. No voters turned up. But the booth had to be kept open until eight o'clock, a provision ordained by an enlightened Legislature, which had obviously had no experience of so uninterested a locality as the *Salt Pan* ward. In the cool of the early evening, the officials watched the flock of sheep being shepherded into the *kraals*, the cattle being milked by the Native maids, and the horses and mules being inspanned, for the visitors were departing. Mr Sablonniere, too, announced his intention of riding off.

'It is a pity,' he said, when the Native boy brought his horse for him, 'but I fear I must go. To me it has been a pleasure to make your acquaintance, Mr Assistant-Magistrate. I trust it will grow into a friendship, for I like tolerant men. I rarely come to the Village. There is nothing to attract me except a talk with His Reverence and a look at your grandfather's garden, youngster. These pleasures I afford myself once or twice a year, when I will do myself the honour of renewing our acquaintance. But my farm, yonder behind the hills, has some little stock of game, and I have a good dog. You are welcome there any time you like to come.'

He mounted his sad-looking horse and rode away, a queer Don Quixotic figure, and waved to them from the road before he disappeared in the distance. Uncle Mias and his stalwart sons came and kept them company, the boys bringing an old pack of cards with which they initiated Charlie into the mysteries of casino. The maid brought candles which were lit and placed on the table beside the ballot box, but the visitors stayed outside, for none but the voter was allowed inside. As the evening darkened the air became chilly and a cold wind crept round the angles of the little out-house.

With Uncle Mias as witness, the voting papers remaining were checked and counted, sealed, and enclosed in the large official envelopes. The slit in the ballot box was covered with gummed paper and sealed, and the official tapes were tied round it and also adorned with red blobs of sealing wax. Then the small party moved to the house. Polling day was over so far as the *Salt Pan* ward was concerned.

Chapter 17

The Bond candidates headed the poll with nearly a thousand votes to spare. The two Progressive candidates barely polled a quarter of the number of votes obtained at the previous election.

In this manner the District registered its emphatic protest against what it conceived to be the dangerous policy of Mr Rhodes.

The newly elected members, in short and exaggerated patriotic speeches, conformed to the custom of thanking the officials, and the defeated candidates honoured tradition by congratulating their successful rivals and seconding the vote of thanks. Much of the excitement seemed to have died down; enthusiasm, on polling day violently vociferous, had burned itself out.

And that feeling of fatigued satisfaction was an excellent index to the general state of emotion in the District. The election fight had been fought and won. There was no need to harbour resentment or indulge in ill-feeling. What the District expected from its newly elected representatives was to carry on the tradition instituted many years ago when it had sent the ex-executioner as its first representative to the new Parliament. They were expected to keep an eye on rural interests, to insist on economy, and to exert a restraining, carmiNative influence upon what it had now become the custom to style the 'jingoes,' who were bent on war with the northern states.

The magistrate reported in this sense when he wrote, unofficially to his friend in Cape Town. Officially he could not voice his opinion, but privately he wrote: 'The result is only what was to be expected. The defeated candidates are not to blame for their want of success; in normal circumstances they would have been elected without opposition, for they have done their duty by this constituency, and everyone respects them personally and for what they have done in the past. But this time they represent a party which the District suspects, and they have had to suffer for this suspicion. The newly elected members are capable men, but of course with no experience or knowledge of parliamentary procedure. Of one thing, however, you may be assured; they will vote exactly as they are told to vote in matters that do not directly affect agricultural interests of which they know enough to have an opinion of their own. It all depends on what is going to happen when Parliament meets. Sir Gordon would be ill-advised if he did not take this decision as final, for the present at least, and I see no reason why the Bond, which now has a majority, should not govern quite as well as its opponents.'

The magistrate's forecast was verified within a few months. The Sprigg government resigned, and the Bond majority formed its ministry, not, as most folk had expected, with the veteran who had always and consistently opposed the Bond, Mr Merriman, as Prime Minister, but with the comparatively untried and youthful lawyer, Mr Schreiner, the son of a missionary, as its leader.

The District, when it heard the news, shook its head, but acquiesced as it could not very well do anything else. After all, the two stalwarts, Merriman and Sauer, the former as vigorously anti-Progressive now as he had formerly been anti-Bond, and the latter a master of debate and well known throughout the Colony as a staunch upholder of what could be called the southern tradition, were both included in the Cabinet, and could be counted on to lead even their nominal chief in the path that the District felt convinced the new government would steer.

Meanwhile the District assimilated what news it received with stolid calmness. Everyone felt that the imminent danger had now been safely circumvented. The new government meant stability, peace, and an amicable settlement of the grievances that in the north had threatened to disrupt the friendly relations between the Colony and the Transvaal.

This feeling was strengthened by the emphatic declaration of the Acting Governor, General Butler, who in opening an agricultural show, had expressed the view that no surgical operation was necessary to relieve the situation. The District cordially applauded.

That was Mr Quakerley's view. Old Mr Quakerley had now got into the habit of strolling down towards the parsonage for an occasional talk with the parson. He found Mr Uhlmann's quiet temperament sympathetic, and he liked the cultured simplicity with which Mr Uhlmann had responded to his own overtures. Old Andrew was feeling his age, his isolation, and his helplessness. His long life had been passed in a blissful serenity, for the one great passion of it, his love for his garden upon which he had spent his energy, his time, and his interest, had ousted all other interests, and almost all other emotions. Now, however, in his old age, he felt that there were other influences at work upon him, influences to which in the past he had paid but little attention. His garden still maintained the first place in his thoughts, for a lifetime's devotion cannot be extinguished so easily, but there were other interests which he found he could not, and did not wish to, ignore. One of these was his grandson, to whom he had become more attached than the great difference in their ages and temperaments seemed to justify. He delighted in the boy's eager freshness, his abundant vitality, his splendid boyishness, the physical perfection of which pleased the old man as much as did the natural splendour of his horticultural achievements. He found himself making plans for the boy's future, speculating on what would be the outcome of generously cultivating the undoubted talents which still lay dormant, building castles in the air for Charlie's habitation just as formerly he had planned, in imagination, wonderful gardens in miniature. It was too early yet to assess the youngster's vocational bent. On this subject the Reverend Mr Mance-Bisley could not advise him. The rector looked upon Charlie as a promising young cricketer, one who, with careful coaching, would be able, in time, to take part in the play for the selection of a Colonial team, but did not report very favourably on his pupil's intellectual accomplishments. The boy held a good place in class, and was promoted with satisfactory regularity, but there were others in the Village school who showed better promise. Neither Mrs Quakerley nor Mrs Crest was satisfied with Charlie's progress at school and both were eager that he should be sent to Cape Town as a boarder. His grandfather did not like this suggestion, but he recognised that his dislike to it was rooted in selfishness because he could not bear the prolonged absence of his favourite that such separation would involve. After consideration he agreed to the plan, and early in the new year he took his grandson to Cape Town, travelling down to the railway-siding, a hundred miles from the Village, in his spring-wagon with a team of ten mules. He left Charlie in much the same way as sixty years before his own father had left him at the boarding establishment, and he came back wondering if his father had felt the same heartache and the same sense of isolation that he felt, and whether he, too, had shown the same stolid indifference that his grandson had manifested when the final goodbyes had been said.

He blamed himself, unjustifiably, for his emotional sentimentality, for Andrew was a fair-minded man, who ruled his life by common sense principles. Between his father and himself there had been a closer bond than that which he could expect to exist between himself and his grandson. The disparity in age and association had not been so great. Besides, Charlie was probably more sophisticated than he had been at that age, and it was not the first time the lad had changed his school. In Australia the boy had been a boarder ... But, for all that, the sense of loneliness that oppressed the old man on his return journey persisted, even when he came back to his beloved garden and found that the peonies, which for almost a decade had refused to blossom, were in full flower.

He found little consolation at home. His wife was absorbed in her whist parties and in the little social world in which she reigned supreme. His daughter and his grandchildren did not interest him in the same way in which Charlie had interested him, and he felt that he had little in common with them. Mrs Crest was in some ways a modern reflection of her mother. She shared old Mrs Quakerley's prejudices and likings, tempering but not refining both with an excessive gentility that did not allow her to display passion or exuberance of spirit or emotion. Old Mrs Quakerley was absorbed in her own limited interests, which her husband found increasingly irritating. She was now the Lady Chair of the small local League of Loyal Women, a post which satisfied her yearning to shine in whatever circle she found herself, as well as her prejudice against everything she considered antagonistic to the peculiar brand of imperialism she flaunted. Her husband had long ago ceased to expostulate with her. Expostulation with Alice served no useful purpose, even though it reduced her, at times, to tears; the elasticity of her likes and dislikes made her bound back to her original position as soon as the immediate effects of argument had subsided. She read her papers with bloating assiduity, and was loud in her aggressiveness that permitted of no excuse or extenuation of the disloyal 'Dutch.'

The Village, it must be confessed, did not take her seriously, nor the League of which she was the leader and inspirer. It smiled tolerantly when she talked disparagingly of the 'Dutch,' and broadly when she complained of slights and insults that existed in her imagination alone. Its respect for her husband, and for the family into which she had married, was too great for it to feel annoyance at her ignorance and stupidity, both of which irritated her husband. He suppressed his irritation, and at first tried to argue with her, but he soon gave that up and permitted her to go her own way.

In his sister, Joan, old Andrew found support and encouragement where he had scarcely expected to find it. Joan had always kept herself to herself; she had been her father's right hand, but from her brother in the past she had always been slightly aloof, a fact that he had recognised and justified by telling himself that she was much more cultured than he, and that she had interests in which he could not share—her books, her household cares, her welfare work in the location. Now he found, to his surprise, that she stood much closer to him than he had imagined. She was in agreement with him on the political question, and looked askance at her sister-in-law's prejudices. He could understand that, for Joan was an aristocrat like her father, much more an aristocrat than he himself was, and could make allowances where Alice could only see what strengthened her dislike and bolstered up her prejudice. Joan could be broadly tolerant without mitigating by a particle her own sense of the fitness of things. She got on excellently well with the Dutch-speaking members of the community, for she spoke the language as well as her brother did, and respected the old-fashioned homely courtesy to which it could give expression. She knew, too, exactly the social values of the families, their genealogical trees, the subtle differences that divided them on the social scale, and this knowledge prevented her from falling into the indiscretions to which her sister-in-law was subject.

Andrew Quakerley, who had for many years found complete satisfaction, spiritual and emotional, in his devotion to his garden, began to realise that he was passing into old age without having played his part on the stage for which his wealth and his position had fitted him. The discovery came like a shock, for hitherto he had deemed himself an entity that needed no strength or support from outside, and consequently demanded no fulfilment of obligation on his part. If he had any ambition, it had been the ambition to realise the vague, inchoate ideals which the dormant streak of artistry in his temperament had set as the limit to his practical aspirations—the desire to make a garden that would not only satisfy his sense of perfect beauty but would also remain as a monument to his taste and his horticultural skill. For years that ideal had contented him, just as his simple, uneventful, quiet home life had contented him.

His sister, who understood him better than he did himself, knew that he was no longer contented. She had marked and watched his growing interest in his grandson, and had hailed it as something to be encouraged, to be played upon, to be used as an instrument for stimulating him to attend to other interests. She had hoped that among these would be politics, which she envisaged as something larger and finer than mere Party squabbles. But as time went on she realised that not in this direction would her brother's latent activities find manifestation. His confidence in himself, which had always been great without being pointedly egotistic, was gradually fading. His mother had been like that, emotional to a degree, but with her emotions so rigidly controlled that they had become easily suppressed rather than sublimated. And although Miss Quakerley had no knowledge, expert or otherwise, of modern psychological jargon, she had practical and useful experience of the salutary effect of sublimating emotion so as to make it responsive to other stimuli than those that had originally evoked it.

The slow months dragged on, and the Village and District busied themselves in their ordinary routine of work, pleasure, and reflection, finding in all three sufficient to keep them from worrying unduly about the political situation. Mrs Quakerley held her evening receptions, her afternoon tennis parties, to which the invited guests came in stiff, starched collars that barely lasted one set, and smart straw hats that considerably interfered with the play, and her milder whist drives, which were now confined to members of the Loyal League and usually concluded the weekly sessions of that rather fatuous society. Mrs Mance-Bisley, who had formerly concentrated her energies upon the Band of Hope, now found an almost equally congenial sphere of work in the League. For the Band of Hope and the two Temperance lodges had languished; many of the members had lapsed, and the meetings were no longer regular and well attended, while the amount of outstanding subscriptions was a source of daily worry to the respective treasurers. No one really knew what was the object or aim of the League. Those who were antagonistic towards it said frankly that it was merely an association designed to cause ill-feeling between the two sections by sharply differentiating between the aggressive loyalties of the one section, and the tolerant, negative attitude of the other. The ladies who supported Mrs Quakerley and Mrs Mance-Bisley vigorously denied any such implication, and maintained that the League existed for the sole purpose of demonstrating their own affection for 'Home' and for all that this word denoted, and that nobody had any right whatever to prevent them from manifesting their feelings, even if such manifestation called out, from the other section, a response that could not be regarded as wholly friendly.

The Village and District were not alone in possessing such a League, for branches of it had been formed all over the Colony. The correspondence and controversy in the press covered columns. There were many who, like Mrs Quakerley and Mrs Mance-Bisley, honestly believed in the giant conspiracy of which the election had been only the opening act. There were many who were as firmly convinced as the Bond organisers that there was, on the part of the new Governor, a settled determination to complete the work that had been so miserably mismanaged in the Raid. Between these two factions stood a minority to which, it must be admitted, the most responsible inhabitants of the Village and District belonged, that was of opinion that no drastic interference was necessary, and that matters would right themselves if only Time, that great healer of dissension and misunderstandings, could be given a fair chance.

Andrew and his sister fell in this last category. Joan attended the meetings of the League, for she acted invariably as hostess, her sister-in-law having long ago abdicated control of the household in her favour, and even enjoyed them. For the meetings were usually merely of a social and literary nature, and the formal business transacted at them was limited to the passing of resolutions drawn up by the head office and sent down for ratification to the various branches. The tenor of these resolutions was an almost monotonous reiteration of the resolve of the League to support the 'Home' Government in its demand for justice and fair play to the Outlanders on the Rand, or to have complete confidence in Her Majesty's representative, Sir Alfred Milner. After having passed these resolutions, the meeting, in desultory fashion, discussed the position, airing with mutual satisfaction the views garnered from perusal of the latest leading articles in the press, and read, for general edification, some of Mr Kipling's poems. Mrs Quakerley 'simply adored' that gentleman's recently published new volume and knew most of it by heart, although there were portions of it that she deemed highly unsuitable for public reading, even in so intimate a circle as League gathering. Joan, who frankly admired the force and rugged beauty of *The Mary Gloster*, had been in a minority of one when she had proposed that this poem should be read. Mrs Mance-Bisley, who acted as chief censor on these occasions and held it her duty to suppress the skittish irresponsibility of Miss Marradee, the librarian and assistant teacher, had firmly and tactfully launched and piloted her amendment 'that we now read Mr Henley's beautiful verse *England, my England.*'

When the League gathered at his house, old Andrew felt that he had sufficiently acquitted himself of his obligations as host when he had brought bunches of cut flowers out of the garden for the decoration of the drawing room, and baskets of whatever fruit was in season. His presence was not required, and although it was not certain that he really did disapprove of the League, it was felt that his attitude towards it was not so cordial as it should have been. As a matter of fact, most of the ladies who were married recognised that their husbands did not heartily support them in their efforts to demonstrate their loyalty. They had a suspicion that even the rector, whom no one could possibly suspect of the remotest disloyalty, tolerated rather than encouraged them.

Needless to say this made them all the more eager servitors of the League, and all the more vigorous in its defence, even where no one dreamed of attacking them. It was primarily the League meetings that had driven old Andrew to wander further afield than his garden. He had begun by strolling down to the river, planning ways and means of extending his horticultural domain on that side. He had strolled farther, along the soft, grass-grown river banks on which abutted the gardens of his neighbours. Every garden ran down to the river, but no garden was a rival to his. He frowned when he looked at them, for with a little care and attention all of them could have been made, not, indeed, pleasaunces like his own, but respectable, well-tilled, beautiful gardens. And the worst of them were the gardens of the rectory and the parsonage. They were not gardens at all. They were wildernesses, without the charm and ingratiating mellowness that decay and disorder spread over forsaken gardens, but merely ill-kept, badly planned, higgledy-piggledy arrangements of vegetables and shrubs and fruit trees, uncared for, unpruned, and neglected.

The parsonage garden was undoubtedly the worse of the two. Originally it had been laid out with some care. So much he could see. That avenue of oak trees, now teeming with dead boughs and hollow trunks, had been planted with skill, but had been neglected, disgracefully neglected. It was all wrong to say that an oak tree would not last in the Village climate. It lasted quite well, if one only cared for it, tended it, looked after it, in the way it deserved. His own oaks were a glory to look on in summertime, ample of bough, leafy, compact, stately. Two of them, he knew for a fact, were eighty years old, probably more. The big magnolia was nearly two hundred years old, and a magnolia needed as much attention as an oak tree did. And that horrible swamp, overgrown with arum lilies and high flowered reeds, right in the middle of the garden where it acted as a pond to receive the overflow from the bath houses—that had originally been a perfectly respectable, even a beautiful lake. He could see the brick masonry below the verdant growth of the arums. If it had been in his garden, now, he would have cleaned it out, rebuilt the upper and lower walls, embanked the sides, and turned it into a wonderful water garden. His own was far too small; he lacked space, as it was, for his cannas, but cannas would grow gloriously here. They were gross feeders anyway, and the overflow from the bath houses would keep them watered all day and all night. Just the site for them. A mass of crimson cannas, backed by that magnificent, almost black, scarlet that did so poorly in his own garden—why, here it would be simply beautiful against the green of the oaks, and the darker shade of the compact pomegranate hedge behind. But he was trespassing on another man's property, and old Andrew drew himself away and returned to the river bank. There the parson found him and invited him to the house for a cup of afternoon coffee. It was not the first time that Andrew had been in the pastor's house, for he fastidiously adhered to the Village conventions which made formal calls upon neighbours compulsory. He had often entered it, and could easily remember the first time he had done so. That was when, as a boy, he had accompanied his father on a formal call upon the Reverend Mr de Smee, the sixth in line of Mr Uhlmann's predecessors. Mr de Smee had been a cleric of the old school, in knee-breeches and a long coat from the sleeves of which peeped out frilled cuffs, a cultured, genial old fellow, respected by all who knew him for his tolerance and his scholarship. Then had come the five successors, all of them men who had had personality, charm, culture, although few of them could talk to him in English. Of Mr Uhlmann he knew comparatively little. There had been the usual neighbourly association between the two houses, and he had perhaps seen more of the parson than of his predecessors, but yet he felt that he knew comparatively little about him. Their intercourse had been largely formal, on matters of business, parochial affairs, educational questions. Only quite recently had he come to like the parson, and he felt that it was due to himself alone that he had not profited by the acquaintanceship long ago.

Old Andrew found his host sympathetic, a good listener, a quiet talker. The study into which he was ushered was a large, plainly furnished room, one side of it taken up by roughly-made shelves, well-filled with books. When the parson went out to order coffee, Andrew got up and inspected the shelves. Most of the books were theological, but there were many scientific works, a few classics, some professional tomes, and many dictionaries. On the top shelf stood an array of chemical apparatus, and on the window sill a collection of minerals and rocks. Opposite the bookshelves was placed the parson's work table, littered with papers and books and oddments, as neglected, Andrew told himself, as the parson's garden.

On the following week, when the League met at his house, old Andrew strolled down to the river and again found himself in the parsonage garden. But this time he went up to the house, no longer feeling like a trespasser, although convention demanded that he should have come by way of the front street. And before the summer had waned and the first winter rains had come, the stroll had become a habit, and the parson knew that on Wednesday afternoons, somewhere about four of the clock, Mr Quakerley would be coming up the garden walk for afternoon coffee and a chat.

Chapter 18

The weekly visits of Andrew Quakerley to the Parsonage were productive of a close friendship between the two men so widely different in their temperaments and personalities. The parson was a quiet, studious, gentle-minded man, bred in an atmosphere of repressions that had robbed him of much of his initiative. His diffidence and want of self-assertion sprang as much from his culture and his intellectual discipline as from a natural disinclination towards aggressiveness. Similarly Quakerley's calm disinterestedness sprouted out of a confidence in his own capacity, the seigniorial assumption that the Quakerleys were supreme and that it did not greatly matter what other people thought and did, so long as the family remained true to its traditions. He could respect in others qualities that he valued in himself, and above all he valued self-control, self-discipline, consciousness of personal worth, instinct of race, all the high concomitants of what in his opinion were associated with the title of gentleman. There lay in him still too much of the prejudice which he had inherited from a long line of ancestors to enable him to give that rank to one who was obviously of the people, unless he was convinced that such a one represented that point of divergence from which his own ancestors must obviously have sprung, for his common sense and logicality forbade him to ascribe direct divine interposition in the manufacture of the better breed of mankind. In the District were many who by descent could claim inclusion in that superior category, but most of them, especially of the younger generation, lacked the polish and culture in his mind inseparably associated with the idea of gentleman. Yet Andrew Quakerley would have been unable, if asked to define what he meant by that idea, to put it in words, to draw demarcating limits, or to defend his innate prejudice in favour of the one and his distaste of the other. He took his stand on a general, to him a perfectly common sense, recognition of temperamental values that, of course, agreed largely with his own conceptions of what was right and proper. Those of the older generation, who in life had learned to use authority with discretion, and power with restraint, conformed to that standard. Their fathers, if not they themselves, had been territorially and domestically great men, holding property in man and in lands, goods and money; solid men, capable of voicing an opinion even if such were wrong, and as capable of granting to others who held different views the right to maintain their own. Perhaps it was this generous tolerance that Andrew esteemed most of all, for it suited his own large toleration that had made him, as some of his friends hinted, so lethargic and so much disinclined to live up to the position of chief personage in the District and Village. He had never given the matter much thought, content to do his duty as he saw it, and influenced, no doubt, by the repressive traits which he had inherited from his Dutch mother. His father, more suited by temperament and upbringing to aggressive action, had early developed a cynical indifference to position, dignity, and honours, and this attitude had insensibly reacted on his son. Andrew had never displayed the slightest wish to visit his well-born relations in England. He had never left the country of his birth, although he could easily have done so. He had sent his wife and his daughters, and had been mildly interested in their tale of experiences in his far-off ancestral halls; he had corresponded, more or less dutifully but without much interest, with his uncles and his aunts and his grandfather, the English baronet, but he had never even had the curiosity to examine *Debrett* to find out for himself where he stood should the nearer heirs to the title become extinct. He had always found sufficient in himself, content and satisfied with what his father and mother had left him. He was not given to self-analysis. Had he been, he would have found it an interesting study to elucidate his own feelings on this question of 'loyalty' of which there was so much talk. He felt no great, abounding love for England; certainly nothing like the attachment that he had towards the Village, his farm, the District, even the Colony as a whole. With these latter his whole life had been associated; they were to him real entities, while England was to some extent a shadow land, interesting indeed, and to be reckoned with, but not comparable, so far as realities were concerned, with them. On the other hand, he had never felt the slightest animosity towards England, and he loved and sincerely esteemed many things English, just as he did not care, honestly and sincerely, for many things Colonial. In his mind, however, there could never be a clash between the two; the possibility of such a clash he could only imagine if the great things that really mattered, individual liberty, freedom of conscience, material benefits, and the personal rights indistinguishably linked with political privileges freely conceded by England, were attacked or threatened. He admitted to himself, candidly, that such a possibility might arise. It had arisen within his own recollection, for he well remembered the agitation about the plan to settle convicts in the Colony, and dimly the fight for the freedom of the press in the unsettled days of Lord Charles Somerset. His common sense told him, however, that such possibilities, pregnant with disturbances of which the effects might be far-reaching, were as likely in England itself as in the Colony, and he could not, and would not, entertain the idea that public opinion in England could ever tolerate interference that verged upon injustice in the affairs of a self-governing Colony that for half a century had conducted itself, in fortune or adversity, with indisputable propriety. For all his Laodicean loyalty to the motherland—which he really did not regard as his mother land—he had innate in him the conviction that the England of his father and his ancestors on his father's side was an England of solid justice and equity, just as the Holland of his mother's ancestors was a Holland of sober, ample, stolid law and order, and unequivocal rectitude.

The pastor was in much the same position, though his convictions in this matter of loyalties was founded on conceptions that were different. Mr Uhlmann was the son of a Hanoverian missionary and a South African-born daughter of a Dutch merchant. His father had come to the Colony in the early part of the century, and had settled behind the mountains, devoting himself exclusively to the development of his mission station, which he had made one of the best in the Colony. At the accession of Queen Victoria he, who had deemed himself, being a Hanoverian, a subject of the King and as such the equal of his fellow colonists, found himself, by the considered opinion of the Attorney-General, to be an alien, as Hanover was no longer a part of the royal dominion. He had promptly taken out new letters of naturalisation. Mr Uhlmann still kept the imposing document, signed by Governor Pottinger and counter-signed by the Registrar of Deeds, the Surveyor-General, and the Superintendent of Police, by which his father had been reinstated in his rights as a British subject. The pastor had been sent 'home' to Germany as a boy of five and had lived there, first at the big mission hostel where the sons of the missionaries were educated, and later on at the University of Utrecht, where he had graduated and qualified for service in the mission field in the Dutch possessions in the East. On his way thither he had touched at the Cape to visit his parents, and had there become engaged to a missionary's daughter, the descendant on the one side of a Silesian baron, and on the other of a French indigo-manufacturer. Mr Uhlmann and his wife had lived for many years in the cannibal district on the shores of the Toba lake in Sumatra, and had finally returned home, where he had entered the ranks of the Dutch Reformed pastorate and accepted a call to the District where he now served. He had lived under four different Governments, had seen much of the world, and by training and discipline had learned to adapt himself. The tradition of his family had been the missionary tradition, zeal, and self-sacrifice for ideals, conformation rather than reformation, the enthusiasm of the student and the apostle rather than the fanaticism of the reformer. Both tradition and training, added to his natural disposition that made him averse from obtruding himself and inclined to the peaceful calm of a student's life, had made him far more cosmopolitan than he realised himself to be, and had dulled in him even that dim spark of nationalism that still flickered in Andrew Quakerley's soul. He felt no attachment to Germany, or Holland, or England, or even the Colony. If the truth had to be told, his heart sometimes yearned for the verdant luxuriance of that tropical beauty amidst which he had spent fifteen years of his best life among the Battas of Sumatra. There he had lived in contentment, though not in ease, arguing without loss of dignity or prestige on either side with the Imams on the principles of the Trinity, and with the monks from the *Singha Monga Radjahs lamaserai* across the lake on the attributes of the Ultimate Perfection, teaching, in his little *atap*-roofed house, the proselytes whose numbers had remained so lamentably small. He hardly liked to confess, even to himself when he thought quietly over these things, that his contentment there had been in some measure treason to his faith and to his principles, and that he had found as much intellectual satisfaction from his study of Buddhism and Mohammedanism as in his student days he had found from the perusal of Lange and Christlieb. Yet he knew, for he was more introspective than Andrew Quakerley, that he had not exerted himself as he might, as he should have done, for the faith, and that even now he was merely an exponent and not an apostle of the dogma that he preached. He knew, moreover, that that dogma, the narrow Calvinism of Dort, made more rigid by the intolerant interpretation of Scottish Presbyterianism, found him unsympathetic, and that he expounded it in a manner that, while perfectly satisfactory to himself and to the congregation to which he ministered, might have seemed too elastic for the orthodox. The District had always been tolerant in its religion as in its politics and its intercourse socially. It had tolerated even Roman Catholics in the days when Roman Catholicism seemed, to the Colonists, akin to atheism; and among the members of his congregation were many who had formerly been, like him, attached to the Lutheran confession. His predecessors had been cultured, gentlemanly clerics, who had preached what they practised, and Mr Uhlmann was content to follow in their footsteps, conforming, where he thought it expedient to do so, to the prejudices, which, with one exception, he had found mild, of his Church Council.

That one exception had saddened him, even though he had subscribed to it. From his earliest youth he had been passionately fond of music, and he had received a good musical training. In his Utrecht days he had devoted himself enthusiastically to the violin, and had pleaded with his father to be allowed to become a professional violinist. That could not be permitted in a missionary's son whose career had been mapped out from the day of his birth, and whose life had been consecrated to mission service. But while he had given up the idea of earning a living with his fiddle, that instrument had been a solace and comfort to him for many years. He played it in Sumatra, and his playing had won him a mild reputation which he had brought with him to the Colony. After his induction as parson at the Village he had played it often, in the quiet afternoons and the quieter evenings—Bach and Beethoven and Mozart, Hungarian, Russian, Polish and Italian compositions, improvisations of his own. The Village had listened and admired, and the location, that appreciated anything that could be fiddled with any semblance of tune, had been in ecstasies. But the Church Council had called on him as a deputation, and asked him, for the sake of his cloth and the edification of the congregation, to refrain from playing 'fiddle music.' No former parson had fiddled, and it was beneath the dignity of their parson to descend to such vulgarity. A less self-disciplined man would have laughed at them, and argued with them; one with more knowledge of men would have played to them, and mastered their prejudice by the wizardry of his art. Mr Uhlmann did none of these things. He gave them coffee and cake, and locked up his violin in his study cupboard which he never opened, although he had listened in silence and had given them no promise. But he never played the violin after the deputation had left. No one but he knew what the sacrifice had meant to him. There remained the piano in the drawing-room, and the small organ in the church, and these he could play on without wounding the prejudiced susceptibilities of his Church Council. He acted as he thought it was his duty to act; 'be ye conformed' was an injunction that had scriptural warrant.

Between two such men as Pastor Uhlmann and Andrew Quakerley there was thus bound to be a temperamental affinity that both realised as soon as they found opportunity for communion of thought. Both were cursed or blessed—the choice of the correct verb may be left to the reader's conception of real values—with the artistic temperament, though neither would have admitted as much, each accounting himself sternly practical. In Andrew that impulse towards creation, which is the hall-mark of the true artist, found expression in such arrangement of beauty as could be achieved by horticulture; in the parson it sought for an outlet in music. Both men felt and respected each other's bent, though neither knew or recognised that the sympathy which drew them so closely together was based on that mutual love of beauty, that innate appreciation of concord, order, and arrangement that each loved and lived for.

Their friendship had not fruited in a day. It had been a slow, careful approach, circumventing the natural shyness both had felt in breaking barriers that barred them from intimacy. As their friendship progressed, communion became easier, for they touched and held, without difficulty, matters that interested them both, though in different ways. While Andrew Quakerley lacked the almost erudite scholarship of the parson, who was a trained philologist and an amateur chemist, he possessed the excellent gift of understanding. The parson, again, knew nothing about botany or horticultural science, but he, too, had sufficient sympathy and knowledge to follow his friend's trend of thought when the conversation veered to these subjects. The difference in their ages was discounted by the large experience on the part of Uhlmann; neither was conscious of it, though the pastor instinctively deferred to his friend as the senior, for he had been educated in the old school that gave to age, whether it was worthy or not, its due honour.

They found much to discuss, but there were some points which by a tacit understanding between them were never made the basis of discussion. One of these was their personal relation to their families.

Not that there were not counter-attractions, verging upon family matters, that invited, nay demanded, animated discussion which would occupy the two friends for hours. On Andrew's side there was the course and progress of his grandson, in whom Mr Uhlmann took a lively interest, for possibly the same reason that had interested Quakerley—an appreciation of the boy's physical beauty and a liking for his mental liveliness. On the pastor's side there was his eldest son's adventure to be discussed. Educated at home, partly, when the whim to teach took her, by his mother, and, almost as intermittently, by his father, whose parochial affairs often took him away from home for a week or more, the pastor's elder son had that year obtained the parental permission to seek work in the Transvaal, where his uncle was said to have some influence in government circles. Apparently work had speedily been found for him, and he wrote glowing letters home, abounding in expressions of admiration for the way people lived on the Rand, and intimating his intention of joining the State Artillery and becoming a professional soldier.

'Though what the Transvaal wants with soldiery, I fail to grasp,' exclaimed the father as he sat with his friend beneath the orange trees on the *stoep*, whiling away the time until the League meeting should have finished its business in Quakerley's house.

'Ah,' said his friend, 'you must not take it too seriously. The boy was always bent on adventure. He has something of your missionary spirit, Uhlmann.'

'With permission, Mr Quakerley,' the pastor was almost formal in his phraseology when he was on the defensive, even to his friend, 'I must demur to that. It is not the missionary spirit to fight and be warlike. Not that I have not had my moments of— shall I call it martial exaltation? I saw something of the Franco-Prussian war, as a young student. My brother-in-law—we were all missionaries' sons at the old hostel over there, and intimate long before I met my wife—my brother-in-law was a first year recruit, and I was attached to the ambulance at Gravelotte. I saw war then, Mr Quakerley, and later I saw something of it at Sumatra. In Atjeh they were constantly fighting, and we were close to them. But that is altogether a different matter from playing at soldiers as they seem to be doing up north. Johnny is attracted by the uniform, no doubt, and the talk, and both are bad for him; as both are bad for them.'

'I should not take it seriously,' said Andrew, soothingly. 'There seems to me to be less likelihood of war now that there was a year ago. Nothing to quarrel about, you see, and besides there is every chance that things will settle themselves.'

'Pray God they may,' said the pastor fervently. 'But I like not the boy's letters, Mr Quakerley. They breathe a spirit that ... that is foreign to us here. A spirit of boastfulness, almost of enmity ...'

'Tut, tut, my dear friend. The boy is only echoing what he hears, I daresay. There is not much friendliness towards us in some quarters over there. I know that, for I have been there.'

'So you have, I forgot that, Mr Quakerley. You should know, first hand, how the land lies over there. And it gives me some comfort to hear that you are still optimistic.'

'Of course I am. And so are you, at heart, Uhlmann. You can no more imagine a war between England and the Transvaal than between us and England ...'

'In 1870 who would have imagined a war possible between Germany and France, Mr Quakerley? These things come like a thunderclap out of a clear sky, when one least expects them.'

'All the more reason to be confident here, Pastor. War is simply unimaginable. Yes, I know them. I found them very human; the old President above all. He is a simple soul, and I really believe that he will do his very best to keep the hot-heads in order.'

'But can he do it, Mr Quakerley?' asked the pastor, anxiously. 'It seems to me that what you call the hot-heads are much in a majority, and that they are urging him on. Things are being done that are not to my liking. And I must confess, Mr Quakerley, that I sometimes stand astonished at what the government in England tolerates. It does not seem quite fair to me, but then I am old fashioned and unversed in the ways of modern diplomacy.'

'I think you underrate yourself, Pastor. Seriously, have we any cause for anxiety?'

'I do not know. I wish I could be convinced that my fears are wholly wrong, Mr Quakerley. But these despatches—this constant harping on abstract propositions and this equally constant avoidance of getting to grips with the questions that matter—I like it not. There must come a time when Mr Chamberlain's patience gives way.'

'There are others who do not think with you that Joe is very patient. I believe myself that he has set the pace ...'

'You must not misunderstand me, Mr Quakerley,' said the pastor, eagerly. 'I do not hold entirely with those who blame President Kruger for all the trouble, for I can easily imagine myself in his position, and realise what his feelings are. I would share them were I in his position. But all the same, I cannot but feel that he is not improving matters by debating subjects which are really of no practical interest.'

'You mean the suzerainty question? Surely that is a matter of practical interest to him?'

'Is it not *res judicata*? Whatever it may be in theory—I am no lawyer, Mr Quakerley—the practical point is that the Transvaal owes her independence to England, and maintains it by England's goodwill ...'

'That of course I grant you. So do we.'

'Precisely. What then is the object of raising the matter in so—so debatable a form as he has done lately?'

'I see from Saturday's paper,' said Andrew, 'that attempts are being made for the President to meet Sir Alfred. That should smooth matters.'

'Possibly. No doubt if *Oom* Paul and our Governor could meet informally, here on my *stoep*, or in your garden—your garden for preference, for where could they get a more beautiful or peaceful spot?—they might forget provocation, suspicion, and resentment, and settle things in a friendly way. But I hear they are to meet at Bloemfontein, and the atmosphere there is not ... well, not decidedly friendly towards us.'

'That is what Storam says,' remarked Andrew meditatively. 'But I can't agree with either of you. The Free State has no part in this quarrel, and it will throw its weight on the side of peace.'

'It has such a part as an ally of the Transvaal has, Mr Quakerley. There is an alliance between the two Republics. It is common talk that the Free State is heart and soul with the Transvaal in this matter.'

'But the Free State President is a sensible fellow,' argued his friend. 'He is an educated man, a judge, and I cannot conceive that he will be so foolish as to force the issue. No, my friend. I think you are needlessly anxious. In a month's time you will laugh at your fears.'

'I sincerely hope so. None would be more glad to do so than I. But of late, Mr Quakerley, I have felt dispirited. If war should come ...'

'Even if war came,' interrupted his friend, quickly, 'it would be a matter of a few weeks, and it would not touch us, Pastor. We are far removed from its orbit ...'

'Do not say that, Mr Quakerley. You cannot mean it. You know enough of conditions here to realise that it must be, in a sense, a sort of civil war. We are kin to them and they to us. It must affect us, just as it affects them, and even if it is a short war, and ends as you and I know that it must inevitably end, it will leave an aftermath of misery and trouble behind it. At all costs let us try to prevent it, Mr Quakerley.'

'You and I can do very little, Pastor, to prevent it.'

'I know. Yet you have some influence—it has often struck me, if you will forgive me saying so, that you do not use your influence. If you will permit me—you have influence in England; yours is one of the big families there ...'

'My dear Uhlmann, I don't even know my relatives over there. I sometimes write, but that is all. And so far as I can tell, they are all behind Joe as solidly as Alice and the League here.'

'That unhappy League,' sighed the pastor, lugubriously. 'As if we had not enough trouble without a ... a ...' he stumbled over the word.

'I feel with you,' exclaimed Quakerley, with a laugh. 'It is distressingly foolish, especially here where there is really no necessity for it. But it just shows you how little real influence I have if I can't even prevent my wife and Mrs Mance-Bisley from behaving foolishly.'

'Yet in other ways, my friend, you may prove influential. The Governor would listen to you; the President would, as you are known to him. Oh yes, I assure you that he knows and respects you—who does not know Andrew Quakerley in South Africa?'

'As a gardener, perhaps,' exclaimed the old man with pardonable pride, 'but as a politician ... no.'

'It would not be as a politician that I should like you to exert yourself, Mr Quakerley. It would be as a South African, as one who loves his country, and his ancestors' country, as one who believes that England is great enough and strong enough to be magnanimous, and to act fairly.'

'And just now you wondered at England's patience, Pastor.'

'*Ach*, do not take me up so sharply. Seventy times seven, and even more—there lies the strong man's strength. A word in season now may be of untold importance, Mr Quakerley. I do my best, I. But what can I do but talk with those that come to me, and try to temper their passion ...'

'We know what you are doing, my friend. Go on doing it. Storam tells me that your influence throughout the election has been for good.'

'I am beholden to Mr Storam for his good opinion. But you can do ever so much more, Mr Quakerley. Why not write to the Governor? Or go and see him. I think you owe him that. You have always done so in the past, as a matter of courtesy, as your father did ...'

'But he has not visited us, Pastor. I cannot force myself upon him.'

'It would not be that, Mr Quakerley. It would be like a grand *seigneur* seeking audience of the king, and talking freely and openly. I believe you can do much good in that way. And besides, you might write to the President. A word from you, a word in the right sense—you know what I mean—might do much.'

'I don't know,' said Andrew hesitatingly. 'I have been out of things for so long now ... Tell me, you saw him when you were at Cape Town for the Synod. What was your impression of him?'

'Of Sir Alfred? A few moments' talk at a garden party does not give one much chance of forming true impressions, or estimating a man's spiritual values. What I saw of him I liked. I put him down as an honest man, a strong man, and an obstinate one. What he has decided upon he will do, never counting the cost, but his decision—that, at least, is my impression—will be an honest one. Hard, perhaps; his face is that, and I think he lacks humour, which is always bad in an official, Mr Quakerley. But a far stronger fellow than old Robinson, or Lord Loch.'

'Easily influenced, should you think?'

'I wonder ... I should not care to say. On the whole, I doubt if he could be diverted from a course he has decided upon taking, but I have had no opportunity of testing him. It is for you to do that, Mr Quakerley. Go to him and have a frank talk. It cannot do any harm, and it may do good. And you know the others as well. Go to them also. Mr Rhodes, now ...'

'He wants war as little as you and I do. Of that I am positively sure. But just at present he is under a cloud, and no good can come of an interview with him. I might do more with the others. I do not say I can or shall do anything, but I will think it over, Pastor, I will think it over.'

'Do not wait, I implore you, Mr Quakerley. Strike while the iron is hot ... don't leave the matter until it is too late.'

'Well, well, we'll see. I had thought of running over to have a look at Charlie. His last report is excellent, Pastor. But I should like to see more of the boy than merely in the holidays. You do not approve?' he asked anxiously, for the pastor had frowned.

'Not altogether, Mr Quakerley. But I can feel with you, and an occasional visit will do no harm to the young man.'

'I believe you are right,' sighed the old man, submissively. 'My dad did not visit me, and honestly ...' he sighed again "I have wasted much of my life, and now—when there's so little of it left—I feel that I must hurry up to make the most of it.'

Chapter 19

Spring had come again, after liberal winter rains. The veld on the outskirts of the Village was gloriously spangled with flowers; the hill slopes were vividly green. Wherever the eye looked it fell upon fields of white and golden daisies, carpeting the ground, miniated with marvellous colouring.

Mr Quakerley's garden was a wonder surpassing even its miraculous magnificence of five years previously, when its luxuriance had astonished all. There were beds of hyacinths so startlingly varied in colour and size that even their owner, who was a stern critic, was fully satisfied. There were rows upon rows of tall daffodils, laden with blooms which had been in the ground for three years, and had never blossomed with greater prodigality.

Mr Quakerley's satisfaction was shared by his neighbours and by the farmers in the District, for never before had the oranges been better, the tangerines more succulent, the wheat-lands more promising, and the grazing better. In the circumstances, the District would have been happy and care-free had it not been for the brooding shadow that lay over the north, a shadow that nothing seemed to lighten, a shadow that was growing more ominous as the months passed and spring merged into early summer.

The abortive Bloemfontein conference, from which so much had been hoped, had merely added to the darkness of that shadow. The interchange of despatches between the negotiating parties had done nothing to lift it. The Village read these despatches without admiration for the verbal agility displayed by both parties. Where anxiety and apprehension were so much in the foreground, it was impossible to admire dialectical subtleties or diplomatic ropes of sand. It read the report of speeches, in Parliament and out of it, with a sickening sense of dismay at the want of substance in them.

There were some who, being confirmed optimists, refused to allow themselves to be depressed. Mr Mance-Bisley was among them. The rector, probably as a defensive reaction to his wife's aggressively pessimistic attitude—for Mrs Mance-Bisley had more than once roundly declared at a League meeting that nothing else but drastic measures could improve the situation—had developed what amounted to almost an irritating cheerfulness. When he discussed the situation, daily, he dwelt on the bright highlights, persistently ignoring the shadows. He had, he declared, profound faith in Mr Chamberlain's good sense, and equally sound faith in Mr Kruger's sincerity; there was no reason at all for anxiety; the pourparlers were shaping quite nicely, and if people would only leave the two negotiating parties alone, matters would undoubtedly right themselves. He condemned both sides with impartial equanimity, mildly chaffed his wife on her League activities, and as mildly deprecated, when he could understand it, the provocative asides of those who were already gaining for themselves the appellation of pro-Boer. Yet he read his papers with increasing carefulness, and ruled his school with a severity that provided some outlet for feelings which had to be worked off in some way. Even so confirmed and cheerful an optimist had his moments of depression.

He had been at some pains to study his environment. He had found the speech of the non-English section of his community a difficulty which could be overcome by application; he could now follow a conversation in Dutch with ease, and could even venture to take part in it, though he did so with the utmost diffidence as he was sadly conscious that his pronunciation of the vowel sounds, especially of that curious 'u' so frequently used, left much to be desired. The District met him half-way, accepting with grave courtesy his quaint idioms at which his pupils, less courteous, frankly smiled. Intercourse with District farmers enabled him to sound their views. At first these were such that he felt disposed to dismiss them as of no importance, but as time went on and his own logical sense rose superior to ingrained presumptions, he found his own attitude influenced by some of the considerations submitted to him. Conversations with Quakerley and Uhlmann, both of whom he sincerely respected, gave him an insight into what he called the 'Colonial mind'—the Native-born's desire to exist not by sufferance but by right, the younger brother's privilege to live independently, without prejudice but also without animosity. He found this viewpoint intensely interesting, and studied it as a naturalist studies some specimen of woodland fauna in which he is interested. In a way he could sympathise with it, although he could not share it. He had no doubts about the situation; no qualms about the right of interference that England possessed, and the obligations that his own country owed to herself, as a great power in Africa, to insist on justice. His loyalty to England was instinctive, intuitive, and he was genuinely incapable of believing that her diplomacy in this matter was tinged by mercenary considerations, just as he was honestly unable to imagine that she would act provocatively, like a bully, to obtain her ends. At the same time, he was reasonable enough to realise that any action on her part, however forbearing it might really be, would seem to some of the native-born, jealous of their privileges and rights, an assumption of superiority that might be resented.

The rector had tried to make his wife look through his cheerful spectacles and cultivate something of his own complacent tolerance, but Mrs Mance-Bisley was frankly belligerent. So, too, was Mrs Quakerley and, strange to say, Mrs Uhlmann, whose opinions were greatly influenced by what her son wrote about the manner in which Coloured people were treated in the Transvaal. The pastor's wife was militantly negrophilistic, and had on occasion been tactless in publishing her feelings in a community where Coloured and Native were and had always been tolerated, kindly treated, with fairness and justice, but never elevated to the pedestal on which she wished to place them. The difference between Mrs Uhlmann and the rector in their attitude on this question was that of a virulent protestant and a nonchalant outsider. The rector had no colour prejudice in the sense that the District understood the term. The District, for all its kindliness to the Natives, a kindliness that dated back to the old slave-owning days when Coloured folk were chattels too valuable to be misused, believed that colour prejudice was a natural instinct, inborn, and as inevitable in a White man as the primitive emotions of sex or hunger or self-preservation. It could not stomach the view that such prejudice was the result of environment, training and circumstance. From the District's mild and tolerant colour prejudice to the full orthodoxy of the northern view, which was a prejudice rendered all the stronger by the fear of a small community living in the midst of a much larger Native population which in the past had been a source of danger and trouble, was but a question of degree. Mrs Uhlmann, like her husband, had been brought up in a missionary atmosphere, where the natural, humane reaction against the gross injustice of that orthodox prejudice had been intensified by both ethical and sentimental considerations. In her reaction against the orthodoxy of her community she allowed these considerations to have more weight with her than would have been the case were her sympathies deflected towards the poor of her own race who stood in want of her help. For her the political situation was not so much a question of preserving the integrity of the country as a part of the Empire as of forcing the northern Republic to recognise its obligations towards its Native subjects.

Mr Mance-Bisley often discussed these matters with his friends, among whom he counted Miss Marradee and also that strange anachronism whose acquaintance Mr Chisholm had made on the *Salt Pan* farm. Mr Sablonniere, who openly avowed himself a free-thinker, came infrequently to the Village, but when he appeared invariably made a point of attending service in the English church. He stayed at the Village Boarding House, a sedate and homely hostel whose permanencies were Miss

Marradee, the post-master, and a couple of clerks who worked in the Village store. He liked, he said, the evening collects, the music, and the ritual of the Anglican service, and Mr Mance-Bisley, who had added much to the ritual in the teeth of some opposition that had long ago died down, was gratified by his admission, and in time came to entertain for him a warm regard. The old French Colonial was a gentleman by education at least, and even if his past was somewhat obscured and his present not always unequivocal, he was a man of character, understanding and parts. In the little Village community there were other characters whose study the rector found equally interesting. There was, for instance, Ambrose Crawley. He lived in a little granadilla-embowered cottage, half-way down the Village street, which was both home and workshop to him, for he was the Village carpenter and had the reputation of being a coffin master. Crawley made all the coffins for the District and had done so since he had helped his father, a born Cornishman who, in the early part of the century, had settled in the Village. He was an old man now, a widower and childless, a wizened little man who went about with a velvet skull cap on his bald head, and talked English and Dutch with equal fluency. Then there was William Wain, who lived as a lodger in old Crawley's cottage, acted as linesman, and in his spare time gave lessons in boxing and single stick to the youth of the Village. Wain was a rolling stone who had finally covered himself with moss in his retreat. He had seen service under Sherman and could tell stories of the great struggle between the North and the South in the sixties; he had been a sailor before the mast and could make beautiful models of frigates, which he sailed on the placid waters of the River. He was a tall, lean, bony-faced man, with a coarse, white moustache and fierce blue eyes that belied the honest kindliness of his nature. Neither he nor Crawley belonged, strictly speaking, to the rector's fold, for Crawley was a 'Roman' and the ex-Federalist a Methodist, but both occasionally attended evening service in the church, and Mr Mance-Bisley regarded them as, provisionally at least, under his care. Once a year a Roman Catholic priest came down by post-cart from Cape Town and said mass in Crawley's workshop to a very small congregation of the faithful, some of whom travelled many miles to attend. The Village regarded this with the same good-humoured tolerance with which it looked upon the Loyal League. It had never been fiercely hostile to Roman Catholicism, for it had for many years had a highly respected member of the faith, the first indeed with whom it had become acquainted, in the person of the eccentric Pierre Mabuis who had married the rich Widow Priem. Indeed, the presence of so many different creeds and denominations as were to be found in the Village had tended to increase the traditional tolerance of which the community, not without reason, boasted. German, French, Hanoverian, English, Swede, Coloured, Hottentot and Griqua, ritualistic Anglican, almost equally ritualistic Lutheran, dour Calvinist, Roman Catholic, Salvationist and Wesleyan—they were all to be found in the District in microscopic minorities so far as the creeds were concerned, for the community was preponderantly Dutch Reformed and as such Calvinistic, but the mixture blended and nothing had hitherto happened to make its various components separate out into antagonistic sedimentary layers. That the oncoming shadow of war in the north might not have that disastrous effect was the fervent prayer of those who, like Mr Uhlmann and old Andrew Quakerley, knew how incongruous some of these ingredients were.

Nearer and nearer came that shadow. In August, when the oak trees were in bud and the blue gladioli were scenting the hillsides, the Village read of war stories pouring into Pretoria, of acrimonious debates in Parliament. September found Parliament still in session, and the cables purring with despatches.

Then came the news of the garden party at Highgate, splashed in the press under thick captions. The sands were running out. Even diplomatic patience has its limits. The metaphors were involved, but the sense, the meaning, was abundantly clear. So clear that the League meeting moved and unanimously carried a telegram of congratulation to the High Commissioner, applauding the determination of Her Majesty's government to formulate its own demands. 'That ought to have been done ages ago,' said the meeting, and drank tea and ecstatically smelled Mr Quakerley's lovely hyacinths.

Old Andrew thought it rather silly, and said so. Old Andrew, too, was losing his patience. He felt old and tired. He, who had scarcely had a day in bed by his doctor's orders, became aware of fatigue after a moderate afternoon's work in the garden. It did not alarm him, for he knew that he was ageing, trotting on for eighty, which is a goal that cannot be reached without travail. What worried him more was that he was losing his habitual calmness. Little matters that in the past would have given him no annoyance, now irritated him, and although he kept his temper under control he could not hide from himself the fact that these trivialities touched him and made him aware that he had a temper. His garden still soothed him, and the boy's return for the holidays had given him a great deal of pleasure. Young Charlie had come back much grown, and in some ways much improved. Yes, undoubtedly the school had done him good. He was friendly, confidential about his school experiences, and, as he had always been, popular with the other Village boys. His boyish grace, his good looks, and the fact that he was regarded by everyone as his grandfather's heir who, although a Crest, was destined to carry on the Quakerley tradition, enhanced his popularity. His prestige would have been greater had not Martin Storam, who had recently passed his civil service examination and was now a junior clerk in the Attorney-General's office, come down for leave at the same time, and detracted something from the glamour that clung to a boarding-school boy. Martin and he had their time fully occupied, but neither could be prevailed upon to attend the Band of Hope meetings, which were now rarities. The Band scarcely existed, though Miss Marradee still occasionally put on her regalia, and Mrs Mance-Bisley endeavoured to promote the annual picnic under the big boulders at the river.

In the circumstances old Andrew found Mr Uhlmann's companionship a solace that he appreciated almost as much as he did his garden. For both men the friendship had become a necessity. It had cemented between them a confidence founded on mutual respect, a confidence all the more intimate because both found in that companionship a surrogate for something denied to them at home. Both were lonely men, unconscious of their loneliness, trying, each in his simple way, to sublimate strongly repressed yearnings into emotions to which they could respond without fear of unmanly sentimentality. The psychologist would have explained their attitude in terms of a scientific formula; they were content to accept it as a fact without worrying themselves to account for it.

Probably the only individual in the Village who was capable of analysing that attitude was the Village doctor. Dr Gerhardt Buren had bought the practice of his predecessor and had won a deserved reputation in a comparatively short time. Colonial-born, he was the son of the descendant of an Irish father who had emigrated to South Africa to escape what he had called 'foreign tyranny.' Young Gerhardt had been brought up in an atmosphere of virulent anti-English sentiment, although his home language had been English and his baptism by a Church of England clergyman. Probably the very fierceness of his father's denunciations and his grandfather's tearful whinings had been the means of inducing in him an attitude towards these matters quite different from the parental orthodoxy of rebellion and protest against everything English, and his professional education at Dublin had not tended to change it. Here in the Village he was regarded as having neither Bond nor Progressive leanings, as one who kept himself strictly to his job and carried out the duties of his profession without the slightest regard to the political feelings of his patients. As he was a good doctor, though young, fully bilingual and without any of the failings of his predecessor, who had been a four-bottle man, he was popular and respected, a member of the school committee, a Justice of the Peace, and a man of standing in the community.

Dr Buren had had ample opportunity to study at his leisure the community in which he worked. He had watched with particular interest the gradual change in its oldest inhabitant, for from the first Mr Quakerley's position in the Village, his history, and his temperament had stimulated a curiosity that was as much scientific as it was personal. The old man had appeared so self-centred, so stately in his isolation, that the doctor had almost been chilled when he had first called upon him. But later acquaintance had entirely effaced these early impressions, and he now saw no reason to change the view that he had subsequently formed of Quakerley's character. The sudden development of the friendship with the pastor he could understand; it was a natural reaction from the awakening of emotions long dormant by the stimulus of the old man's love for his grandson, on the one side, and from the repressed emotions of a lonely middle-aged man who had hitherto found no congenial fellowship at home or in his immediate environment. As such it was to be encouraged, and the doctor knew enough of both to be convinced that the friendship would prove beneficial. In his quiet way he had helped them, although neither was aware that he had done so. But he had a profound liking for them, and he had understanding. That was part of his trade, not to be accounted a virtue. So he had set himself to win the grandson's confidence. He had taken Charlie for rides, and the boy had been easily impressed to the point of enshrining him in a blaze of hero worship, a state of mind suitable for careful suggestion that blossomed out in little graceful acts to gladden old Andrew's heart who thought them spontaneous when they were merely the results of Buren's judicious hints.

In his quiet way Dr Buren influenced all with whom he came into contact. From his point of view the District was lamentably behind the times. Its traditional tolerance was to a large extent a disinclination to exert itself sufficiently to condemn or criticise. It preferred acquiescence where such acquiescence did not involve the denial of first principles and exacted no great activity of mind or body. When it came to first principles, to prejudices long ingrained, the District could be vigorous enough and push its opposition to the verge of intolerance and even bigotry, but hitherto no such clash had occurred. There was a probability—he put it like that, for he had long ago decided that it was much more than a possibility—that now such a clash might come. Around him he saw emotions being stirred such as he had experienced, perhaps vicariously, in his youth at home, when his grandfather had whiningly told him of the sufferings of Irish refugees, of the Irish convict ship that had anchored in False Bay and that had carried a great patriot on board, when he had been taught that patriotism meant the innate preference for one's own kith and kin and a slavish subscription to the creed that one's country could do no wrong. Since then he himself had conceived it as something grander and nobler, but he was well aware of the fact that in the District that conception had not yet taken root. The District's idea of patriotism, indeed, had not yet crystallised, sharply faceted and clear, out of the liquid emotions stirred by the situation in the north. The agitation for a republic and for complete independence had made some headway among the younger men, but had left the older citizens cold. For its success demanded an appeal to sentiment founded on a realisation of injustice and wrong done to an unoffending part, and that was totally lacking. The Colony had possessed self-government for many years; it was prosperous, contented, and its grievances were local, the result of its own doing. Dr Buren, viewing the matter from the angle of one who could look at it with a bias in favour of what was called the pro-Boer side, had come to the conclusion that even if war came the District would remain quiet. It would never make the war in itself the cause for local disturbance, and it would offer no opposition beyond a formal protest. It would remain neutral, with an inclination to be amicably critical, and not averse to seeing both sides mildly chastened by the adversity of war. That was the opinion freely expressed by responsible old citizens like Mr Rekker, who, when Buren had discussed the situation with him, hinted that matters would very likely follow the lines in 1881. England, so the District thought, would never take away the freedom she had given to the Republic in the north, but would content herself with securing ample guarantees that her own subjects there would be placed on an equality with the Transvaal nationals, her own subjects including the citizens of her Colony at the Cape. The District had never thought that Majuba had the importance with which some of those who referred to it invested it, and had always given Mr Gladstone full credit for a magnanimity that it had appreciated and applauded. If war could be avoided, so much the better, for there was really no necessity at all for war; but if, by some mischance, it had to come, the District would be tolerant and acquiesce, fully convinced that such a war would be localised, short in duration, and unlikely to affect the Cape Colony.

With these views Dr Buren, like Mr Storam and Mr Uhlmann, only partly agreed. He realised that conditions were no longer what they had been in the early eighties, and that national consciousness was astir, although as yet its manifestations were slight and its emotional response barely perceptible. War, however, would stimulate it, especially if that war came nearer home than it had done in 1881. If the danger could blow over, sectional patriotism might, and very probably would, sublimate itself to serve other and more useful purposes than mere recrimination; it might even merge into a larger common patriotism to which both sections could own allegiance. But if war came, there was a possibility that it might run amok, overstep the bounds of common sense and reason, and be the cause of much misery and trouble.

Chapter 20

The Village still remembers with what consternation it received the news that war had actually been declared. It remembers quite clearly—which is all the more remarkable, for events crowded so fast and in such quick succession that its memories of the initial happenings might very well have been merged into that haze of unsubstantial recollection in which nothing is of outstanding importance, all being of the same memorial value—how fine that October month of 1899 had been. It is the pleasantest, best month in the District, the month wherein spring has not quite abdicated its quiet, subdued beauty for the more dazzling colour and glare of summer; a month still green enough to frame the gorgeous tints that make so lovely a flower-carpet on the hills, with still enough moisture in the air to form fleecy clouds, translucent in their whiteness, against the pure beryl of the sky and the darker blue of the mountains. That October was surely the finest that the District had known, the veld gloriously green with lush grass, slopes whitened and made golden with patches of daisies, ridges starred with boldly coloured midday flowers, damp riversides odorous with scented orchids, mountain valleys splashed with the bronze and brown of sugar bush clumps. The wheatlands were turning golden, and the ripening grain, as it caught the reflections of the setting sun, rippled in iridescent gleams when the late afternoon breeze played over it. A good harvest, good grazing, a more than average crop for the fruit orchards, a record yield for the vineyards—these were the promises that bountiful October held out.

In the Quakerley garden the double stocks, mauve and lilac and white, grew in masses whose almost rank perfume floated in waves, lazily, across the second street. The herbaceous borders, already in blossom, were a delight to the eye, for they held colour in all shades, prodigally splashed to secure the most effective contrast. The tall, showy anchusas formed a blue background for the lighter beds of cynoglossums; beds of fine crimson tritonias set off the pure white of ornithogalums and watsonias, and in the bulb beds the clumps of gladioli were putting forth their buds, eager for the warmer weather to unfold their petals and make them the proud peers of all, contributing to that galaxy of floral splendour. In the orchard the trees were laden with blossoms, and in the background the rich, polished green of the magnolias, the love apple trees, and the guavas stood up like a rampart of shadow, giving to the eye, sated by the colour of the flowers, an impression of delicious coolness.

The news came with sudden, sickening finality, in the shape of an official communication from the government on the Thursday. The Monday's newspapers which the Village had received on the Wednesday afternoon had emphatically declared that the rumours of an ultimatum were 'totally unfounded.' His Excellency, interviewed on the Sunday, had scoffed at the suggestion that the Transvaal would proceed to extremes; he had, he declared, every confidence the matter would be peaceably settled. The Village had read that communication with relief, for the second week in October had been a week of alarms and vague uneasiness. It had retired to rest on the Wednesday night, blissfully unaware of the fact that at five o'clock that afternoon war had actually begun.

On the Thursday morning there were few who witnessed Mr Storam's agitation when he pinned to the notice board in front of the court house the official communication which he had that morning received. But the news spread very quickly, and before noon there was a large gathering before the notice board. It held a couple of flimsies, the usual light lilac sheets on which official telegrams were transcribed, and the Village read, with silent amazement, their curt content.

'From *Lex* to Magistrate—For your information. Stop. Government South African Republic handed to Her Majesty's Representative, Pretoria, on Monday afternoon, long despatch concluding in the following terms: "Her Majesty's unlawful intervention in the internal affairs of this Republic in conflict with the Convention of London 1884, caused by the extraordinary strengthening of troops in the neighbourhood of the borders of this Republic, has thus caused an intolerable condition of things to arise whereto this Government feels itself obliged, in the interests not only of this Republic but also of all South Africa, to make an end as soon as possible, and feels itself called upon and obliged to press earnestly and with emphasis for an immediate termination of this state of things, and to request Her Majesty's Government to give the assurance:

(*a*) That all points of mutual difference shall be regulated by the friendly course of arbitration or by whatever amicable way may be agreed upon by this Government with Her Majesty's Government.

(*b*) That the troops on the borders of this Republic shall be instantly withdrawn.

(*c*) That all reinforcements of troops which have arrived in South Africa since the 1st June 1899 shall be removed from South Africa within a reasonable time to be agreed upon with this Government, and with a mutual assurance and guarantee on the part of this Government that no attack upon or hostilities against any portion of the possessions of the British Government shall be made by the Republic during further negotiations within a period of time to be subsequently agreed upon between the Governments, and this Government will, on compliance therewith, be prepared to withdraw the armed *Burghers* of this Republic from the borders.

(*d*) That her Majesty's troops which are now on the High Seas shall not be landed in any port of South Africa.

This Government must press for an immediate and affirmative answer to these four questions and earnestly requests Her Majesty's Government to return such an answer before or upon Wednesday the 11th October 1899 not later than 5 o'clock pm and it desires further to add that in the event of unexpectedly no satisfactory answer being received by it within that interval it will with great regret be compelled to regard the action of Her Majesty's Government as a formal declaration of war, and will not hold itself responsible for the consequences thereof, and that in the event of any further movement of troops taking place within the above-mentioned time in the nearer direction of our borders this Government will be compelled to regard that also as a formal declaration of war." Stop.

To this communication Her Majesty's Government has replied that it feels itself utterly unable to discuss the requests made, and has instructed Her Majesty's Representative at Pretoria to ask for his papers. Stop. A state of war consequently exists between Her Majesty's Colony of the Cape of Good Hope and the South African Republic as from 5 o'clock on Wednesday, and a proclamation to this effect is being issued forthwith. You will please give widest possible publicity to these facts. Ends.'

The majority of those who read the telegram hardly understood its full significance. It was in English, which had to be translated to many who could not readily follow the involved phraseology. It evoked widely different reactions among those who read it. Mr Storam, standing in the shade of the blue-gum tree, interested himself in trying to analyse some of these reactions. They were, he felt sure, a replica of his own turbulent but, at the same time, dazed emotions, which ran the gamut from fierce indignation at the effrontery which had penned so amazing a challenge, to profound regret that the consequences of such rashness would now be inevitable.

The rector joined him. Mr Mance-Bisley read the telegram with undisguised horror. He had been firmly and frankly convinced that there would be no war, and had gasped, literally and metaphorically, when, disturbed by the news that an official declaration of war had actually been posted on the notice board, he had hurried down the street and met the chief constable on the way, from whom he learned that the rumour was correct. He read the telegram twice, first with amazed incredulity, and secondly with amazed indignation, and it was clear to the magistrate that the latter emotion had completely mastered him.

'The impudence of it,' he exclaimed, loud enough for those around to hear him. 'Are they mad? Surely, surely, Mr Storam, there must be some mistake. No one in his right senses would have written such rubbish ...'

'It is official, Rector,' the magistrate replied, shrugging his shoulders.

'I know—I know,' the rector was almost breathless in his vehemence 'but such language ... unheard of ... scandalous ...'

'It is an ultimatum,' said the magistrate. 'It's meant to be provocative, but I think, I fancy, Rector, that its very provocativeness is a good thing for us. I do not know, of course, what the whole despatch reads like. We shall get that later on, I daresay. But if you read what the Attorney-General—the telegram is from him—has wired, you will see that even in the short passage of the preamble to the actual demands there is something which is decidedly undiplomatic ...'

'The whole wretched thing is undiplomatic,' Mr Mance-Bisley burst out. 'It is the most bare-faced impudence I've ever heard of. Its implications are lies ...'

'Would it not be fairer to say that they are one-sided, Rector? Come, let us be fair. From their point of view there is something to be said. But we need not go into that. Wait a bit, though. Here comes Mr Uhlmann. I should like to hear his opinion.'

The pastor approached them, detaching himself from a small group that had surrounded him where he had been reading the telegram pinned on the notice board.

'So, it has come at last, Mr Magistrate,' he said quietly. 'Good morning, Rector. It is an ill day for all of us. My poor people ... you must help me, Mr Storam. We face grievous possibilities, I fear.'

The magistrate felt instinctively that the stilted, precise English was some indication of the pastor's suppressed emotion. They shook hands—a grip of understanding and fellowship—without quite realising why they did so. The rector was far too much occupied with his own indignation to respond to that unspoken sympathy. His cherubic face glowed, partly from exposure to the sun and partly from his own feelings.

'You are right, Mr Uhlmann,' he said, nodding to the pastor, 'and I was egregiously wrong. But have you read that ... horrible thing there? It is unheard of ... I have never been so shocked in my life. Have you read it?'

'Over and over, Rector,' said the pastor, and made a gesture with his hand as if to brush something aside. 'With your permission, Magistrate, I will make a translation. You can pin that alongside. Some of them will grasp its import better then. Now, alas, they are not sure. Will you not speak to them, Mr Storam?'

'Not now,' said the magistrate, hastily. 'It will serve no purpose. I have asked Chumley to convene a meeting of all field-cornets tomorrow. Then we may have more information to give them. I am awaiting instructions. So far that,' he pointed to the notice board, 'is all I have.'

'But what do you think of it, Mr Uhlmann?' asked the rector. 'Surely you must realise how preposterous it all is ...'

'Is not all war preposterous, Rector? For myself, I ... how do you express it? I feel shocked that it has come, even though I anticipated it. Not in this form ... it is, as you say, shocking. But in a way it clears the air. It may even make our task here less difficult.'

'Ah,' interrupted the magistrate, 'you have noticed it too?'

'It is so obvious, so open, Magistrate. And it should be used. If I may say so, it gives us an advantage ...'

'I don't know what you are talking about,' interrupted the rector, peevishly. 'It seems to me that all we can do now is to stand shoulder to shoulder and show these people that they have made a bad mistake. I am a man of peace, but there are limits, Mr Uhlmann, as you will admit yourself.'

'Mr Uhlmann refers to a particular sentence in the preamble, Rector,' explained the magistrate. 'Perhaps you have noticed it yourself. In the sixth line you will notice the words "this Government feels itself obliged, in the interests not only of this Republic but also of all South Africa." That seems to me very important. Isn't that your view, Mr Uhlmann?'

'Yes,' replied the pastor. 'It is a proof, as I take it, of that arrogance—that overweening vanity that presumes to speak and act on behalf of all of us—that has made this colossal blunder possible.'

'But the whole ghastly rigmarole is a tissue of arrogance,' exclaimed the rector. 'Just imagine ... Her Majesty's government's unlawful intervention is the cause of all this trouble—unlawful, mark you, unlawful! And the strengthening of troops ... why, everyone knows that there aren't enough forces in this Colony to protect it.'

'It is an ultimatum,' said the pastor, repeating Mr Storam's words unconsciously. 'I am not sufficiently well versed in these things to know how they are usually drawn up. In fact, now I come to think of it, Rector, I have never before read an ultimatum. In the German war, of which I have some personal knowledge, there was no formal ultimatum. But I suppose it really means a letter of demand, written in such a style that it can only have one reply.'

'That certainly is the case here,' remarked the magistrate, drily. 'I should much like to read the actual answer that Chamberlain composed. From the AG's telegram I can see that it was dignified, which is more than one can say of the Transvaal's letter. But I suppose that's a translation, isn't it, Mr Uhlmann? It strikes me the grammar is weak, in spots, but the intention is perfectly plain.'

The crowd round the notice board increased, and from it small groups detached themselves to discuss the matter apart. Some of the readers joined the three men under the shade of the blue gum tree, greeting the magistrate and his two companions courteously, but obviously agog with expectation and excitement. The conversation drifted into Dutch, but the rector had enough of that language to be able to follow what was said. He heard expressions of regret, amazement, incredulity, but none of exultation, none that could be construed into covert disloyalty. He felt a trifle less indignant when he understood that the general opinion was that now that the die had been cast, the matter would be speedily settled.

That, however, was not the view held by those whose opinions counted for anything in the Village or the District. That evening Mr Storam worked hard in his office, assisted by the chief constable and his clerk. He drew up a report on the state of the District, in which he was at pains to point out that while the mass of the population could be depended upon to remain quiet, there had been considerable agitation, and there existed some danger that irresponsibles, mainly recruited from the landless class, might cause trouble. He recommended that the store of arms and ammunition in the Village gaol should be quietly removed, and that authority should be given to call a meeting of the ward field-cornets, to whom special powers should be given to deal with possible disturbances. These were reasonable precautionary measures. While Mr Storam had no faith in the assumption that there was in the Colony a well-organised and far-spread conspiracy to engineer a rebellion in order to support the Republic cause by force of arms, he was well aware of the fact that *burghers* from the Republics had visited friends and relatives in the District and had worked on their feelings, and succeeded in leaving behind the impression that the Republican cause was one worthy of the active support of all right-minded Colonials. He was equally well aware of the fact that this impression was not shared by the more solid inhabitants of the District. The District was Bond, whole-heartedly in support of the Schreiner ministry, but that support was based, not on the extravagant claims of extremists, but on the growing political consciousness of an agrarian group slowly awakening to a realisation of national ideals. Their reactions were perfectly natural and understandable, and although at first these reactions might assume a distinctly sectional—for Mr Storam was too acute to call it racial—complexion, with time they would settle down into the ordinary routine of party politics. No opposition to constituted authority, an authority of their own choosing, was thinkable without a grievance great and stimulating enough to warrant rebellion. There was no such grievance, although attempts had been made to make one out of the Transvaal troubles. But the magistrate knew that the war held possibilities which no one could quite calculate. While there was no reason to suppose that anything more than its shadow would touch the District, and that the reality would affect only those districts that bordered on the two Republics, it was undeniably true that it would be, in a way, a civil war in which many families in the District would be personally interested. So far as he had been able to ascertain, about sixteen inhabitants of the District were now *burghers* of the Republics, among them being Mr Uhlmann's son, who was a cadet in the State Artillery, and as such would be among the first called upon to fight. Many families were closely related by marriage to families in the Republics; almost none had no family connection with men who would be commandeered to the Republican ranks. In these circumstances it was natural that the District should view the coming onset with keen anxiety, an anxiety which was as personal as if the fighting took place in their immediate neighbourhood.

Mr Storam concluded his report by expressing the hope that the precautionary measures which he suggested might be superfluous and that the District might be kept entirely outside the periphery of operations.

He was justified in his opinion by the emphatic manner in which the Prime Minister, Mr Schreiner—the man whom the Bond Party had put into power as the supreme representative of constitutional authority in the Colony—had expressed the same sentiment, the same hope and the same suggestion in his public speech in Parliament. Mr Schreiner, too, had been gravely aware of the inter-lacing familial and sectional bonds that knitted the population of the Colony to that of the two Republics. He, better than any other, knew how wildly untrue was that accusation of a pan-Afrikander conspiracy to drive the English into the sea, but he knew also how fervently the Transvaal hoped that some portion of the awakening nationalism in the Colony might crystallise into an active support that would not shun sacrifice nor even the sin of witchcraft. Like everyone else, he supposed the war would result in only one way, the crushing of the two Republics, and an aftermath of sullen resentment to be vigorously exploited by agitators with lamentable consequences to the whole of South Africa. In Parliament he expressed the hope that in the welter of war the Colony at least would remain an oasis of peace. An impossible definition of a neutrality, as unconstitutional as it was fatuous, expressed in a speech so moving in its almost rhapsodical passion and earnestness that his hearers overlooked its want of logic in their sympathy with the lawyer whose human feelings refused to recognise the patent facts of the situation.

The Prime Minister's tragedy, a tragedy no less poignant because it did not involve death but only the destruction of long-cherished ideals, found its counterpart in many a household in the Colony, in many a family in the District. Now that war had broken out, made inevitable by that presumptuous, childish challenge, those who from the outset had struggled to secure peace, at the cost of being misunderstood, at the risk of having their loyalty impugned, found themselves faced with a new difficulty. Could they go on working for peace, protesting against a war none of them had wished or contemplated, when war was a fact, and when they, as subjects of Her Majesty Alexandrina Victoria, were now the established and lawful enemies of Stephanus Johannes Paulus Kruger as representing the government of the South African Republic? Their clear and obvious duty, as citizens of a country at war with another country, was to do their utmost, to strain every effort, to ensure the success of their own arms. Their duty was to their country, not to sentimental ideals of liberalism. Condonation of that gross effrontery of which the government of the Republic had been guilty could no longer be regarded as an expression of academic opinion; it became tinged, at once, with the savour of treason, for it implied condemnation of Her Majesty's government's immediate repudiation of the demands made in the ultimatum. Whatever had been their views about the negotiations that had preceded that declaration on the part of the Republic, now that war had actually been proclaimed it behoved them to do nothing that by word or deed could give assistance or comfort to the enemy. That under the term 'enemy' would be understood some of their own relatives who in the far north were equally against settling disputes by force of arms, made no difference. It was a hopeless, preposterous tragedy, and again no less poignant because no one dreamed that it might involve them in one still greater.

When Mr Storam met his field-cornets the following day, these considerations had already been canvassed in private, and were discussed with subdued animation in public. Further information, conveyed in telegrams from *Lex*, had been received, from which it was clear that the Orange Free State Republic was joined with the Transvaal in the presentation of the ultimatum. The local branch of the Bond Party received, from its head-committee in Cape Town, a condensed statement of the position which it had no hesitation in handing in to the magistrate before the meeting. The tenor of all these telegrams was monotonously the same. They urged that everyone should keep calm, implicitly obey constituted authority, and do nothing that could in any way be construed as impeding such authority in the execution of its constitutional duty.

The magistrate found that there were many among his audience who had no business to be there. The rector was there and the pastor; Mr Saxon Miller, the Village photographer, in his capacity as *Reuter's* local correspondent; Mr Amadeus Sablonniere who had come down in his neighbour's spring-wagon, and many others who were not field-cornets or assistant field-cornets. The solitary woman, seated next to Mr Saxon Miller, was Miss Marradee, the librarian and local correspondent for a Cape Town paper, who had insisted upon being present as a second representative of the press. In the background stood the Native constables; on the *stoep* outside, the Village and the District congregated, trying to hear through the open windows something of the discussion.

Mr Storam explained, simply and clearly, that a state of war now existed between the Republics and the British Government, in which the Colony, as a part of Her Majesty's dominions, was as much involved as was England herself. He read the proclamation, and the despatch of the Republican Government of which the concluding portion formed the ultimatum, first in English and then in the Dutch translation which Pastor Uhlmann had prepared, and he emphasised the last part of the despatch so as to bring out clearly the more blatant sentences. The reading was received in gloomy silence; his address was listened to with equal gravity, and it was only when he stepped aside and asked the pastor to address the meeting that the audience seemed to take an active part in the proceedings.

The Reverend Christian Uhlmann began by deprecating his ability to speak to them on so important and momentous an occasion. He had only consented to do so, he declared, because the magistrate had asked him to say a few words.

'To many of us,' he went on, 'today will seem to be the worst day that we have experienced, for it is a day that sees our hopes crashing about us, and the dark cloud from the north, under whose shadow we have lived these several years, sweeping down upon us, like our own thunder storms from the mountain bearing hail and lightning. God grant that it may sweep past us. But let us not, in our selfish hopes, forget that hail and lightning will strike other parts of our country, and destroy what is near and dear to us. Let us remember that we have duties, civic duties, *burgher* duties, our duty to be loyal to our allegiance. These duties do not exclude loyalty to the sympathies that our Lord has set in us as human beings who feel the bonds of blood relationship and kin. There can be no clash between these obligations if we hold fast to our faith and remember that we are not called upon to judge others but ourselves. To you who are officials of our Queen, who have sworn your oaths of office and for so many years lived in peace and prosperity under a government of our own choice, I can only repeat what the magistrate has already expressed. Acquit yourselves like men, as the Apostle bids you to do; prove to all of us who have put our trust in you, by electing you as leaders, that you are meant to be relied upon. To you, as well as to you others who are fathers and guardians of the young, we look to set an example to those more inexperienced, more passionate, more eager to let their passion sway them than their faith to guide them. Take to heart what our leaders have written to us. Let us strive to be calm, and let each one of us go about his daily work, doing his duty as he sees it, and avoid leading himself and others into temptation ...' He stopped for a moment and looked at the magistrate, who nodded sympathetically. 'I know that there are some here who are directly concerned in what may happen elsewhere. They do not stand alone. I, too, have a son over there. I pray that he may do his duty to his allegiance. My friends, I feel with you, as I know you feel with me. The Lord has put upon us a bitter trial, but He will assuredly give us strength to bear it. That is all.'

A murmur of sound rippled along the hall as the pastor sat down; it was not applause, but merely the quietly-voiced reaction to the emotion of the moment. Mr Sablonniere got up.

'Although I am not privileged to be a field-cornet,' he said, in his queer, staccato speech, 'I take it that this is not so much an official as a public meeting.' The magistrate nodded. 'I thank you, Sir. I am not unused to war. I know what it means. War has a way of wounding friends and enemies alike. You cannot keep it in a strong-ringed *kraal*; it leaps over the fence and runs into your backyard. Unless you take precautions. When there is a danger of fire, a prudent man makes things safe. I think I am voicing the opinion of all, Magistrate, when I say that we would like you to appoint a committee to work with you, to help you to make things easier for those who, belike, may have to do unpleasant things in the interests of safety. I have said.'

Mr Sablonniere's proposal found favour with the meeting. The magistrate pointed out that his intention in calling the meeting had been to form the field-cornets into just such a committee, but after discussion it was agreed that some of the older farmers of the District should be added to it. Various names were proposed, and the rector found that the meeting became quite animated in discussing the merits of the respective candidates. To him the meeting had seemed to serve no useful purpose, beyond giving the public such information as they could not have gained from the notices posted up on the board at the office. He had come to it with the intention of cordially supporting something in the nature of a vote of confidence in the Governor, some expression of satisfaction at the stand Her Majesty's government had taken up, a loyal resolution similar to what had so frequently, and so uselessly, been passed at the meetings of the Ladies' League. But nobody had moved such a resolution, and the discussion had been desultory rather than definite. Mr Mance-Bisley, who still felt very indignant, and was seething with honest resentment at what he took to be perfectly gratuitous insults expressed in perfectly preposterous language, felt uneasy and dissatisfied. He leaned across towards Mr Uhlmann, his nearest neighbour, and whispered in an audible aside:

'Would it not be ... ah ... desirable to move a resolution of confidence and of approval, Mr Uhlmann?'

'Do you think so, Rector?' asked the pastor, mildly. 'The magistrate and I discussed it. We sounded some of the men here. It would be carried, of course ... what do you say, Mr Storam?'

'Yes, of course, Rector,' said the magistrate, in an undertone. 'But what real significance could be attached to it? An expression of lip-loyalty, would it have any value, apart from that given to it by those'—he nodded to where Miss Marradee and

Mr Saxon Miller sat, busily writing on their sheets of foolscap which they held on their knees and scribbled over at a furious rate so as to give the bystanders the impression that they were taking the discussion down in shorthand, which neither of them had practised.

'I suppose it wouldn't,' admitted the rector, lugubriously. 'But then, Mr Magistrate, what is the purpose of this meeting?'

'Primarily to meet my field-cornets,' answered the magistrate, 'and to explain things to them. We shall have a private consultation afterwards. But I am not saying that this general meeting, although it is not what I had in mind, will not do any good. It will do a lot of good, Rector, and I look to you and Mr Uhlmann to help me further.'

'Your task will be easy, Mr Bisley,' said the pastor. 'Mine more difficult. I hope you understand. And I hope, too, that I may rely upon your help ...'

'Certainly, certainly,' interjected the rector, moved by the pastor's appeal. 'But I don't see that we need have any fears. If these people are representative of all in this District, we can rely upon them.'

'Unfortunately they are not,' said the magistrate, sinking his voice. 'You know that those who are here are leading men, farmers of substance, but there are many in the District who are landless and belong to the labouring class. There may be trouble with them. Not that I anticipate any difficulty, but it is just as well to look facts in the face, and there has been a lot of agitation. I am glad to see Sablonniere here, he has more influence, Mr Uhlmann, than we think he has. And if he will use it on the right side it will help us considerably.'

Their conversation was interrupted by the two press correspondents, who came forward to ask the magistrate to look over their reports of the meeting. Miss Marradee had written hers in an emotional vein, and had dwelt on the excitement and consternation in the Village. The magistrate felt that he could safely leave the sub-editorial blue pencil to deal with the superfluous adjectives with which her narrative was inter-laced, but suggested minor modifications, and the addition of a paragraph stating that the meeting had manifested unanimous approval of the steps so far taken in the interests of all. He asked the field-cornets and the chief of police to remain behind, and with a repeated request to all to take things calmly and await developments, he closed the meeting, which dispersed to discuss the situation outside the court house.

Chapter 21

Andrew Quakerley did not attend the meeting at the court house. Not because he was not interested in the matter to be discussed, but because he felt that his presence would not be necessary. His position in the community was assured. Everyone knew that he would be on the government's side. There could be no question of his loyalty. If it came to a division on a sectional basis, he stood, by virtue of tradition, upbringing, and habit, on the English side, at the head of the English-speaking community in the District, just as Pastor Uhlmann could be said to be the chief representative of the Dutch-speaking section. Neither of them would have admitted that it was a question of sectional interest.

Andrew had read the ultimatum with his customary dispassionate, almost indifferent, calmness. Those who came—and there were many—to enquire what Mr Quakerley thought about the business, found him ready to discuss it without betraying more emotion than he would have done in discussing local news, and with far less animation than he would have shown in refuting horticultural heresies. When they questioned him as to what was his opinion about the probable course of events, he replied frankly that he thought the Republics had harmed their own cause by precipitancy and by adopting an attitude of aggressive impulseness.

'You must know,' he told old Mr Rekker, who had sought counsel from him on the Thursday night, 'you must know that we have never been altogether in favour of their methods and their manners. We have been friendly critics, and when we thought that they were being pressed too hard, some of us said so. Apparently they have taken that to mean that we are willing to support them to the uttermost.'

'That is so, Mr Quakerley,' his visitor replied. 'I have had my doubts about it, and as you know, Mr Quakerley, I have said so, and gained some hostility from my own folk in saying it, Mr Quakerley. Not that I think that the war is right. That I will never agree to. For why should we—for, after all, we are the Queen's subjects—for why should we kill our own countrymen, Mr Quakerley, to put things right in the Transvaal for the Outlanders? Could it not have been managed without canon and Mausers, Mr Quakerley, with a friendly talk between all concerned? I ask myself that, Mr Quakerley, and I say it could, and I blame us as well for it as I blame them, Mr Quakerley, for being so hasty and overbearing.'

'I dare say you are right, Rekker. But the time to blame has passed. We are at war now, and I really do not see how England—how we could have done anything else but accept the challenge. You'll admit that?'

'Aye, Mr Quakerley, but the old Queen might have had some patience with them. It is like with a youngster, Mr Quakerley, who sometimes says things in heat, wound up, like, with his feelings, so that he forgets whom he is speaking to.'

'But I imagine, Rekker, if your own youngsters were foolish enough to be impertinent to you, you would teach them a lesson, and a pretty sharp one, too.'

'That is true, Mr Quakerley. *Ag*, it is a bad state of affairs, Mr Quakerley. Cannot we do something to mend it? Do you think if we petitioned the Queen to stay her hand ...'

'That is nonsense, Rekker. Things must take their course. Better let it be a short, sharp lesson, for then we'll have peace all the sooner, and an end to all our troubles.'

'If I could believe that, Mr Quakerley,' said the old man, shaking his head and passing his snuff box towards his host, 'I would willingly abide in it. But I have a feeling, Mr Quakerley, that we are in for difficult times. I have a pre-sentiment, Mr Quakerley, that it will be a long struggle.'

'You do not suppose, surely, that the Republics will be able to make a long fight of it, Rekker? Why, England can put an army in the field against them bigger than the total population of both the Transvaal and the Free State. Or are you one of those who believe that England was conquered at Majuba?'

'No, Mr Quakerley. I have my age, and it has brought sense to me. I am not so stupid as to think that the Transvaal conquered England in the last war, though many will have it that it is so. I am not so foolish, Mr Quakerley, for I know that the Queen has many soldiers and great resources, against which the Transvaal and the Free State are as wind. But there is all sorts of talk, Mr Quakerley, and there are those that say that it will not be a fight against the Republics alone, but that other lands will be involved.'

'You can give the lie to such talk right away, Rekker,' said Andrew, with a frown.

'Aye, Mr Quakerley, I do my best, but there it is. That is what they say. They assert, Mr Quakerley, that France and Germany and Russia will never allow the Transvaal to lose its independence. You see, Mr Quakerley, it is all this talk of independence, and being the equal of England, that has brought us to this pass. I never held with it. I always said, when folk nagged at me because I was not hot enough on the subject, Mr Quakerley, I always said that we were free, just as free as anybody in the Republics, and much less likely to be harmed because we have behind us the Queen's might. But there are those who think differently, and who say that we should have our own flag and our own men abroad, as the Transvaal has, to make new friends for us. Mr Quakerley, it always seemed senseless talk, that, to me, but there are many here who believe in it.'

'That I know, Rekker. You know that the Transvaal never was free in that sense, never the equal of England, or even, for that matter, of us. Why, we have representative government, which they never have had.'

'Aye, Mr Quakerley, there you speak a true word. As I was saying to Brother Mias but the night before yester-night, "Mias," I said, "if they have a President—and, Brother," I said, "let them have their President; I have nothing against it, not at all— we have our Prime Minister, chosen by ourselves, by all of us, and not only by a small number." You must not think, Mr Quakerley, that I hold by everything that the Transvaal has done or said. Between you and me, I think they have done very foolishly, like one who plays away all his cards at casino, Mr Quakerley.'

'I quite agree with you Rekker. But the question now is, we are at war and we must do our duty, hard as it is. You must go to the magistrate's meeting tomorrow, and help to calm the people.'

'I am no longer field-cornet, Mr Quakerley. I resigned years ago, as I thought it right the young men should have a chance.'

'But you are one of the fathers of the community, Rekker, so you must go. It is your duty, and Mr Storam will welcome you. If I may presume to advise ...'

'That is what I came for, Mr Quakerley. Counsel from you, old friend, is what I came to seek. You may speak freely.'

'Very well, then. You know how matters stand. There are two parties here, not so much in the District as in the Village. There are your people, in sympathy, to a certain extent, with our friends across the river. I don't blame you—I can't blame you, for they are, after all, countrymen, and some of them kin. There are others who have no such feelings, but who are swayed, just now, by other emotions, indignation for one, and the wish to teach the Transvaal a lesson. That, too, you must admit, is natural. We who are of English descent feel very strongly—I do myself, although I am as much a good South African as you are ...'

'One of us in marrow and bone, old friend. I will say that for you.'

'Very well, then. Do your best to prevent any clash between these two parties. Do not let your feelings run away with your discretion. You may be able to do much. What I specially want you to do is, if somebody proposes a resolution—I hear there is talk that that will be done—to express an opinion about things—you know what I mean—stifle it in the bud. Don't discuss what has led up to the war, or the war itself, whether it is right or wrong. The time for that has gone by. No one can expect you to say you cordially approve of the war, now it has come, but we do expect that all who are loyal subjects of the Queen will remember that they are loyal subjects.'

'I understand. There is talk of forming a committee, to help the magistrate. Our members, as you know, Mr Quakerley, are in Cape Town, but we expect they will come down ...'

'That too, Rekker, you must prevent it—I mean political meetings at this time. There must be nothing that will disturb the people. Meetings can do no good. Your committee might. There will be excitement enough, and some of our youngsters ... do you know, already there is talk of enlistment and recruiting ...'

'*Ag*, that is true, Mr Quakerley! It is the young blood. But we will see to that; you need not be afraid, old friend.'

'I am not afraid. I am one of you, Rekker, and I know what you feel, but I know, too, that you will not flinch from your duty. You have seen Mr Uhlmann, of course?'

'Yes, I saw Reverend this afternoon. He agrees with you, and for him it is a bad business. You see, Mr Quakerley, his son is over there, and if it comes to fighting, Johann will be one of the first to be called upon. So will young Berend Smit and the Mabuis boy—they are both *burghers*. And the widow Sandstrom's son-in-law that married Kato, Nephew Peter's daughter from *Doornvlei*. It is a bad business.'

'Indeed it is. I quite agree with you. But we have to face it, however bad it is. Have you any news about what they are likely to do?'

'Nothing definite, Mr Quakerley, nothing definite. But there are all sorts of rumours, which belike are nothing but hot air. Nephew Peter tells me that Kato wrote last month saying they were all prepared, and that she had been making biltong in case her husband was commandeered. She thought there would be a move towards the Natal border.'

'Yes, I suppose that is all they can do—strengthen their borders and entrench themselves, and then it will be a difficult job to come to grips with them. They are good fighters.'

'With the Martini, yes, Mr Quakerley, but with these new-fangled Mausers ... I don't know. And I don't fancy they will skulk behind the rocks, either, Mr Quakerley. My own thought is that they will split up into commandos and raid into Natal and into the Colony.'

'God forbid,' said old Andrew fervently. 'That would mean endless trouble and might involve us. They would be stupid if they did that.'

'I am not so sure about that,' said his visitor shrewdly. 'It is far better to attack than to wait until you are attacked, Mr Quakerley. I imagine that is what they had in mind when they sent their letter. You must not underrate them, Mr Quakerley.'

'I don't do that. Indeed, Rekker, I am well aware that it'll be a tough job, but I think it will be a short one, for all that. However, we'll see. Must you go? Very well, come and see me after tomorrow's meeting. I shan't go. It will be best for me to remain at home, and, as you know, you can always find me here.'

When Rekker had left, old Andrew sat for a long time brooding over the matter that had formed the subject of their conversation. His talk with his old friend had brought no new considerations for him, for Rekker's attitude towards the situation was one which he understood and could sympathise with. In giving his advice to the old farmer he had been more outspoken than was his wont, for latterly he had been anxious about the relations between the two sections of the Village community. He recognised that one of the factors of disturbance was the aggressive, pugnacious activity of the Loyal Ladies' League, which made up for their want of numbers by their vigorous propaganda, propaganda that was not always judicious or tactful. Now that war had been declared, the League would probably have the good sense to recognise that its usefulness could be exerted in a different fashion and directed into different channels. Hitherto it had been rather fatuous, more blatant than beneficial to all concerned, but there had been some justification for its propaganda. Andrew was fair enough to admit that, but he felt that whatever good the Ladies' meetings had done had been largely discounted by the tactless manner in which they had offended local susceptibilities and flaunted a virtue that, however praiseworthy it might have been by itself, suggested to those not wholly in sympathy with its objects something artificially fostered and cultivated by weekly doses of sentiment doled out by a press out of touch with a large mass of the people. Mrs Quakerley and her fellow-members took themselves very seriously. While the situation was still undeveloped, no great friction had been caused by the League's activities, for the Village looked upon them with a tolerant, if somewhat mocking eye, but circumstances were no longer the same, and it was possible that such propaganda might in future lead to difficulties. It was the League that had suggested that the magistrate should propose a motion of full approval of the action of Her Majesty's Government, of confidence in Sir Alfred, coupled with a pledge to do everything in its power to bring the war to a successful issue. Andrew had no personal objection to such a motion. It expressed merely his own opinion and that of every loyal subject of the Queen, but he thought that it was injudicious to propose it, in the form suggested by his wife—for Alice had written out sentences almost as fiery as those of the ultimatum—and had argued with her on the subject.

'Why not take it for granted?' he had asked. 'What purpose is likely to be served by such a resolution, my dear? Particularly when you know that it will not quite truthfully express what they feel.'

'That's just why,' his wife had retorted, glibly. 'Half of them are rebels at heart, Andrew, and now's the time to rub it in. They've had it all their own way so far, and now that we've taken up the right attitude we must make them feel sorry for themselves. You know they are dying to do us down, and yet you want to spare their feelings. They haven't spared ours, have they, dear?'

'You should know them well enough by this time, Alice,' he had answered, 'to know that you are grossly unfair. You have no evidence, no evidence whatever, that they are rebels. And I won't have you call them rebels, mind.'

'Of course you'd take their part,' said his wife, querulously. 'You are almost one of them yourself.'

'And so are you,' he parried. 'We've lived here seventy years and more, Alice, and had nothing but kindness from them. We are South Africans as they are ...'

'No, thank you,' exclaimed Mrs Quakerley, indignantly, tossing her head so that the lace edging of her cap shook ominously. 'I am English, and I do hope, Andrew, that you will remember that. I can make excuses for you; being, as you are, Colonial-born, you would naturally ...'

'Really Alice, do try and be a little more charitable. Try and look at things from their point of view—from Mrs Uhlmann's for instance. You know her boy is bound to be called up ...'

'That's not her doing,' said Mrs Quakerley, quickly. 'She was always against his going. And he had no right to go. It should have been stopped. Do you know, Andy,' she sunk her voice confidentially, 'it's my belief Mrs Uhlmann is altogether with us. She would attend our meetings and become a member, but of course, being the *predikant's* wife, she can't show her feelings openly ...'

'And you'd better not make yours so patent,' warned her husband. 'I know you won't listen to me, Alice, but let me beg of you not to force the pace ... you know what I mean. Especially not now. Anything that is likely to stir up feeling just now, my dear ...'

'That's what you said all along,' protested his wife. 'At first we had to hold our tongues for fear of hurting their susceptibilities, while they could just talk and do as they pleased. What did they care for our susceptibilities? And now we must remain quiet for fear of irritating them. That's a pretty sort of loyalty, Andy. It won't do for me. Now that it's war, I say let's proclaim that we are Britishers and that we fear no one, no one, I say.'

'All right, my dear. You need not raise your voice. I can hear you quite well. Nor do I want to muzzle you ...'

'You sometimes talk as if you did. You try to make me feel that what we are doing is silly and mischievous, Andy, and that is very unkind of you, for you are English, after all, even though you may kid yourself that you are Colonial.'

'I don't kid myself. I am Colonial, just as Anna is, and Joan. You knew that when I married you. You knew that I have Dutch blood in me, as good as what comes from my father's side ...'

'That,' said Mrs Quakerley, with finality, 'I shall never believe. Father-in-law came from a county family.'

'Yes, and Mother-in-law was a descendant of Count von Egmont, so there is little to choose between them,' said Andrew with a smile. His wife was really too stupid to argue with, and arguing always made her either lose her temper or dissolve into tears.

'I only want you to be a little more careful, my dear,' he said gently. 'No doubt your society can do a great deal of practical good work just now—working for the soldiers and so on ...'

'That's what we are going to do, too,' interrupted Mrs Quakerley, eagerly. 'We are appointing a comforts committee ...'

'*Bravo!*' interrupted Andrew in his turn. 'That's the very thing. Remind me to write you out a cheque—you may have a hundred guineas to go on with ...'

'Oh, Andy, that's too much. I think fifty ...'

'No, make it a hundred to start with. And I'm sure you'll want more. So long as you are practical and really help, I'll do my best for you, but don't please, Alice, don't stir up trouble.'

'But they do make me wild with their talk,' said his wife, plaintively. 'They take it for granted that they will drive us out of the country, and really it is enough to put one's back up, the way they go on ...'

'Never mind,' retorted her husband consolingly. 'Don't listen to them. You know that there is nothing in it.'

'But there is,' exclaimed his wife. 'Don't you remember that awful man—wasn't his name Ras?—who insulted the Queen? And Miss Marradee tells me even the young boys are sneering at us ...'

'I am sure Miss Marradee never said anything of the kind, Alice,' said old Andrew, sternly. 'You have been talking to the maids, and they have retailed location gossip. Don't listen to it. But my dear, just bear in mind that we've all got to do our bit just now, and get your committee started. It might be a good thing to get Mrs Uhlmann on it—if you like I'll speak to her husband. And some of the Dutch ladies—there's young Mrs Gerster and Miss Maria Gerster—they would do splendidly. Why don't you ask them?'

'But they are on the other side, Andy. Old Jeremiah is one of the worst influences in the District ...'

'There you go again! You know absolutely nothing about it when you say such things. What other side? There is no other side. We are all subjects of the Queen, and all willing to help.'

'I am not so sure about that,' said his wife, darkly. 'Anyway I won't have the Gerstners. They're sure to pull the wrong way. Mrs Uhlmann, that's a different matter, and perhaps if she is on the committee it might have a good influence. Will you see about it, Andy?'

'Very well. If you will promise not to make trouble—I mean, not to pass any more resolutions for young Miller to telegraph to the papers. It doesn't look nice, Alice, coming from one section. A resolution should be unanimous to have any value, you know. But let me hear more about what you propose doing. We might have a bazaar or something to get funds. Just let's put our heads together, my dear.'

On this amicable note his interview with Alice closed, much to his own mental relief. He hoped that he had induced her to be less aggressive, more practical, although he was fully aware that hers was not the dominant personality on the executive committee of the Ladies' League. But Mrs Quakerley, as the senior member and the wife of the most influential townsman, carried some weight after all, and if she only wished to do so she could divert the League's activities into more practical channels. Andrew was satisfied with what he had gained, and was too wise to press for more.

With his sister, he discussed the situation from an altogether different aspect. Joan was sensible, level-headed, with a better brain than his, and with more imagination than he possessed. He deferred to her opinion in nearly all matters that did not touch his hobby.

'We're in for a bad time, Joanie,' he said, when she brought him his night-cap of sweetened brandy and water flavoured with a chip of lemon rind. 'I've just had a talk with Martin Rekker.'

He got up and with his old fashioned courtesy drew his arm-chair forward for her while he seated himself in the swivel chair alongside. She had brought her own glass of warm milk, and he arranged the little Indian table, a gift from his uncle who had been an Admiral of the Red, between them for the glasses.

'I suppose he is very much agitated,' she said, sipping her milk slowly. 'You know, Andy, it must be a terrible trial to some of them. And, after all, it is going to affect us too.'

'I don't see that, quite,' he replied, puzzled.

'Mother's family, you know,' she explained. 'There is Uncle Sam in the Free State ...'

'Good heavens, so there is,' exclaimed her brother. 'I had quite forgotten, Joan. Of course, the Free State Egmonds will be in it. Honestly, my dear, I never thought of them.'

'You wouldn't,' said Joan drily. 'It must be twenty-five years since you saw any of mother's crowd, but I had a letter from Jessie only the other day. They are in exactly the same position as we are, Andy, only on the other side. If it wasn't so tragic, it would be funny. I suppose it wouldn't be tragic without some element of humour in it. Tantalus and Tityus may have appeared funny to some people ...'

'For heaven's sake, Joan, be serious. I see nothing humorous in civil war.'

'That doesn't necessarily mean that even civil war hasn't its humorous side,' retorted Joan, who had inherited her father's passion for hair-splitting. 'Tragedy is the inevitable, and the gods sometimes laughed at it. Can we do better than they, Brother?'

'I am not going to argue with you on abstract questions,' he said severely. 'The thing's too hideous, my dear. Why, here we are, all of us, involved in it, and all equally helpless to prevent or control it ...'

'That is the tragedy of it,' interrupted his sister.

'Don't go on repeating it. I know. Haven't I told myself that all the time I was talking to Rekker? And then I did not for a moment think that it came so near home as it does. What an awful thing! Here we are, English, I suppose, in sympathy and feeling—and there they are, our own relatives on the other side, forced to fight against us, though God knows the quarrel is none of our or their seeking. If I had remembered the Egmonds ...'

'You couldn't have said anything different to Mr Rekker,' interjected his sister. 'I am sure he remembered it well enough; everyone knows about mother's family, and understands our position. There is nothing we can do, Andy. And, frankly, I don't see what other solution there is. It may be a wrong solution—I daresay it will prove to be that in the long run—but it is the only practicable one I can see.'

'You mean war had to come? But why, Joan, why?'

'You know it as well as I do. The position was intolerable, impossible from our side ...'

'Yes, but wiser counsels could have prevailed. The Transvaal could have yielded gracefully. Everyone, their best friends, Sir Henry—Hofmeyr—Schreiner—Merriman—everyone pleaded with them.'

'Yes, to retreat so as to be able to jump better next time. But it is not a matter of incidents, Brother. It is a matter of ideals and principles, as Father would have said, of tradition. A clash was bound to come, and perhaps it is better that it comes now than later.'

'There is something in that. But Joan, you surely don't share Alice's views? You know our people too well—you can't believe in this conspiracy business, can you?'

"Not in the way Alice believes in it. Of course not. That is sheer nonsense. But haven't you sometimes felt that we could manage better if we were given an opportunity to deal with these things ourselves, without interference from Downing Street?'

'Certainly. I think that is generally admitted. But the desire for greater liberty of action does not exclude loyalty to the Empire, does it?'

'My dear Andy, "what do they know of England who only England know?" Forgive me for quoting it, but you asked for it. What do you yourself think is going to happen here?'

'That depends on the results of operations. My own opinion is that it will be a short, sharp war. Modern weapons and all that, you know. We're not in the eighties now, and to me it is unthinkable that there can be any other result than a speedy victory by force of arms. In that case it will be the task of the politicians who have got us into this unholy muddle to extricate us from it. I suppose that will be managed somehow.'

'And if the Boers come into the Colony, what then?'

'My dear, I sincerely hope they will not be so ... so damned stupid. Why it would simply mean that they would be annihilated ...'

'Come, come, Andy. Father used to say that a few bodies of armed men could maintain themselves for years in this country against anything that might be brought against them. You know how he harped on the chances that a desperate gang of bush-rangers would have, robbing the mails and stealing the diamonds. He used to say that only a little organisation was wanted. And if the raiders found sympathy here ...'

She paused and sipped her milk reflectively.

'You must admit, Brother, that they are likely to find many friends. I say nothing against our people, but there will be temptation, and you and I, Andy, are not the best folk to judge.'

'I see what you mean. I hope to God nothing of that kind happens. I confess I cannot contemplate the possibility of it. Of course, in the border districts there must be some disturbance. I admit that. But we are much too far away from the fighting-line for anything of the kind to happen here.'

'I hope you are right. But it's a tragedy, whichever way one looks at it, and it may become more tragic in time. I wish you would give Alice a hint ...'

'I have already done so. But you are one of them, Joan. You can do as much as she to help things along.'

'The meetings are a safety valve. I don't think they do much harm. And now there is a chance of doing some real good. We shall come to you for funds, Brother, for I don't suppose there is much chance of getting up a public subscription. You would not advise that?'

'No. I doubt if it would be wise. Not just now, at any rate. But I told Alice to draw upon me. Yes, Joan, there is scope for real hard work. Storam tells me that there is already some talk of recruiting.'

'That, too. I wonder how many recruits this District will furnish? Not many, I should say. But the location men will go, won't they? There must be a demand for drivers and Natives. You know what that means, Andy?'

'I am afraid so. Really, Joan, the more I look at the matter, the more it seems to me likely that we are going to be drawn into it, whether we like it or not. If I were not so old ... one does feel rather out of things when one gets old. But perhaps there is something you and I may still be able to do, Joan.'

'Lots, Brother. And, for an old fogey, you look surprisingly fit.'

'It's the gardening and the open air, Joan. I am beginning to feel the strain. Well, good-night, my dear. And if you can damp the ardour of your good fellow-members ...'

Old Andrew sipped his night-cap reflectively. He got out the atlas and refreshed his memory on geographical points. Yes, the District lay altogether outside the zone of possible military activity, more than a thousand miles away from the nearest point on the Republican border. Between were many other districts, rough, mountainous country, scored by high-banked, waterless rivers only filled after the winter rains. Operations in such country would be difficult, and have no tangible objective, for the main line of the railway was several hundred miles distant from the District's boundaries. There was no reasonable possibility that the war would ever come close to those boundaries. It was much more likely that the challenge would be fought out within the Republics themselves. And that, after all, was just, for they had invoked war.

Andrew Quakerley went to bed thinking about his kinsmen in the Free State, and wondering whether it would be right to let them know, by letter, that he had thought of them with sympathy.

Chapter 22

The east wind had blown almost continuously for a week, and it had brought as aftermath days of intolerable heat, heralding an even more unbearably hot New Year. The watercourse ran no longer glibly, with little eddies and swirls which its impetuous plenty made; it coursed moodily, sluggishly, and those who fed their gardens and their bath houses from it complained of the scarcity of water. The mountains were shrouded in a haze that made an intense, shimmering blue over their drab spurs. The main road was a dusty, baked thoroughfare upon which every passing vehicle or passenger raised a cloud of yellow dust.

December came with its customary, blistering heat—December that brought, as compensation, early apricots, grapes, and luscious water-melons, young sweet maize that was eaten in the cob, juicy dwarf squashes, delicately flavoured, and the large Kelsey plums with a bluish bloom over their dark maroon.

For more than two months the Village had lived in a palpitating gush of excitement. It had been, it was true, vicarious excitement, for matters had gone on in the old way, no item of daily routine being changed despite the war, but it had been excitement none the less. The past nine weeks had been thronged with incidents happening far away, whereof the news, chronicled in the papers or in special telegrams that came from *Lex* and were duly posted by Mr Storam on the notice board, evoked feelings that ran the gamut of emotions. The attack on the armoured train at Kraaipan had been the first intimation of actual, overt hostilities, and it had been followed rapidly by the isolation of Mafeking and Kimberley, where Mr Rhodes was shut up with every possibility that the Boers would catch him. The Village and the District speculated on what they would do with him if they caught him, and came to the conclusion that whatever it might be it would be something memorable. From the Far East had come the news of Elandslaagte, reported a great but a sterile victory for Alexandrina Victoria's troops, Dundee and Ladysmith, the death of General Penn Symonds, the investment of General White in Ladysmith, and the invasion by the Boer forces of Natal. From the north came the news that Boer commandos had appeared in some of the border districts, proclaimed them Republican territory, and commandeered the farmers to join the Boer forces. But the Village had taken all these reports with equanimity, for it thought them grossly exaggerated. The main line to the north was safe, for there lay General Lord Methuen with a strong force, flanked by the eastern force under General Gatacre, and at Cape Town the Commander-in-Chief, Sir Redvers Buller, was preparing for an advance in force.

In the District all who discussed the matter shook their heads and expressed their doubts about the Boer strategy. The investment of Ladysmith and the overrunning of the Natal border were perhaps to be defended from a purely military point of view, and there was something to be said for the siege of Kimberley and Mafeking. But the invasion of the Colony itself, and especially the annexation of the invaded districts, were generally regarded as on a par with the officiousness in the ultimatum that declared intervention in 'the interests of all South Africa.' The District was mildly disposed to resent such officiousness and to express its opinion in terms that, although still amicably polite, left no doubt about its disapproval.

In the Village that disapproval was voiced much more energetically. Andrew Quakerley, when he heard of the annexation of the parts of the Colony that had been entered by Schoeman's commandos, had spoken his opinion sharply in words that carried away his wife's complete and applausive agreement. Mr Storam had sworn at the breakfast table, and his wife had thought the expletive apt for the occasion and would have liked to echo it. To his son the magistrate's visible annoyance presented an opportunity which was too good to be let slip. Martin had come down, ostensibly for a holiday but really to obtain his father's consent to join a volunteer corps raised by Colonel Brabant. The war seemed to have effected a sudden change in Martin's sentiments. During the time of the Raid he had been enthusiastically on the Boer side, posing as the exponent of young South Africanism. During the negotiations, too, he had championed the Republican cause, much to Mrs Quakerley's annoyance, for she was very fond of the handsome young man, who flattered her as nobody else dared or desired to do, and whose only vice was that he laughed at her League and was not vociferously loyal enough to her constantly enunciated imperial sentiments. But the ultimatum had changed all that, and Martin had become intensely bellicose, so much so, indeed, that his father had expostulated with him. Mr Storam saw no reason why his son should enlist, and said so, but Martin, undaunted by refusals, persisted in the attack, though so far with little success. On the morning when Mr Storam opened his *Cape Times* and read the report of the annexation, Martin felt that the time was opportune for another sally.

'Well, now, Father,' he grinned across the table, 'I suppose you'll admit that there's some reason for me to go.'

'I'd go myself if I could,' exploded the magistrate, angrily. 'Excuse me, my dear, but this is a bit too much. Yes, Martin. Come with me to the office, and we'll see about it at once. That is, if your mother agrees.'

That had been the beginning of excitements such as the Village had not experienced at any time during its hundred years of existence. Its tolerant complacency was rudely shocked when the telegrams came to announce, successively, with short intervals between, Modder River, Enslin, Stormberg, Magersfontein, Chievely, Colenso, and the newspapers published casualty lists.

The Saturday before Christmas day, which that year fell on a Monday, had brought details of the fight at Colenso, in which, so rumour had already bruited, the Commander-in-Chief had been defeated by the Boers, and all chance of relieving Ladysmith had been destroyed. The weekend telegram from *Lex*, on which the magistrate now depended for confirmation of the reports that came from no one knew exactly where, contained an item of news that was at least consoling. Her Majesty's government was determined to prosecute the war with all its energies, and had decided that Lord Roberts of Kandahar was to take command of the forces in the field against the Boers, with Lord Kitchener of Khartoum as his Chief of Staff. The papers by the Saturday mail cart brought further confirmation, with a list of the Colenso casualties. The Villagers read these in the street, sweltering in the hot sun, and discussed them long after the dusk had fallen, sitting on the *stoeps*, where the air was slightly cooler than indoors, and speculating on what the New Year would bring.

This year both days were quietly spent. It was felt that joviality and exuberance of spirits were out of place with the shadow of war that hung over the Colony, and that a curtailment of pleasure, and of expense entailed by pleasure, was fitting. The Village and District celebrated their first war Christmas in a staid and eminently subdued fashion.

Old Andrew spent the morning of Boxing Day in his garden, pinching off the old spikes of the cannas, antirrhinums and lupins, watering the summer sweet peas with manure water, and tying up the giant dahlias whose weight of blossom threatened to snap their slender stems. He was adept at these horticultural expedients by means of which the expert gardener prolongs the flowering period of his plants indefinitely, getting new blossoms from old stems that seem almost too weakened for further floral progeny. And to Andrew his garden was still a solace, a comfort and an inspiration. The sheer, sensual pleasure that he got out of it was something intoxicating, for it gave him a satisfaction such as an artist feels when he creates. In fact, there was no difference between an artist and him. He was an artist, born with a sense of beauty, with a feeling for form and colour and line.

When he had completed his morning's work to his satisfaction, he went indoors to the coolness of the big dining room where Joan was knitting at the side table. There he had his morning tea, and read the papers. After the midday meal, of which he ate sparingly, he dozed quietly in his armchair, and in the cool of the afternoon, after four o'clock tea, he visited his garden once more. Finally he walked over to the parsonage, taking the footpath on the river bank where he could stroll under the shade of the old, arched oak trees.

He found Pastor Uhlmann in the parsonage garden, though that name could scarcely be applied to the muddled collection of vegetables and flowers for which the pastor's outdoor servant was responsible. It satisfied all the conditions needed to cause annoyance to the expert horticulturist, but Andrew had long ago ceased to discuss its demerits with Mr Uhlmann. Now he noticed that the pastor was unusually disturbed, and as he came forward, holding out his hand in greeting, he felt that something was amiss.

'A sad Christmas for us, Mr Quakerley,' said the pastor, shaking his hand, and speaking before he could voice his Christmas greetings, 'but to you, at least, I can wish a prosperous and happy one, so far as it is possible to be happy in these troublous times.'

'Is it Johnny?' asked Andrew. 'I hope nothing serious?'

'Yes, he is reported wounded,' said the pastor, nodding. 'We have only this morning received the news—I still do not know how we got it. Some friend at Cape Town must have seen his name in the lists of casualties on the Boer side, Mr Quakerley.'

'How? Where?' asked Andrew. 'Probably it is only a rumour. They get about so, you know.'

'Yes, but I feel that this time it is true. I have felt for some days that the boy was in danger. I cannot tell you why—I mean, why I felt it. But it is not the first time, Mr Quakerley. Out in Battaland, when I was a missionary, I once had this kind of feeling, when my colleague was in danger.'

'What makes you think it is true? Surely you have had something definite? He wrote to you, didn't he?'

'Our last letter was dated in November. Since then we have had nothing direct from him. He wrote that he was posted to the machine-gun section, and that has always been his fancy, Mr Quakerley. But we had a telegram this morning from Cape Town. A friend of my wife saw his name in their casualty list. Wounded, in several places. It is not stated how seriously, nor where, but it must have been at Colenso. He was on the Natal side, with the Pretoria commando.'

'You must not take it too seriously, Uhlmann. Besides, if he is only wounded, it will keep him out of the fighting, for a time at least. And there is going to be much more fighting.'

'That I believe, Mr Quakerley. From now on, the struggle will be to the death. Will you come to the house with me? My wife is lying down. She feels it uncommonly hard. Johnny was always her beloved, though he is not our first-born.'

They went up to the house and sat on the *stoep*. The maid brought out coffee and rusks, but Andrew left his cup untasted and the pastor did not touch his.

'I shall not try to condole with you, old friend,' said Andrew, noting how the pastor knit and unknit his fingers. 'The time for that has not come yet. I won't believe that anything serious has happened to Johnny. He's always struck me as a boy who can look after himself, and to be wounded, even in several places, is not such a serious thing after all.'

'You would try to console me,' retorted the pastor, with a wan smile lighting up his crinkled features. 'I have said that to myself over and over again. It is not that—I mean, I do not so much mind that he is wounded. It is the thought that someone of his own kin may have shot him. For this is civil war, Mr Quakerley, civil war.'

'I agree with you. But it is rather far-fetched, all the same. I don't think there were any Colonial troops at Colenso—certainly none from our part of the Colony. They're with the middle division, you know. Storam had a letter from Martin. He's with Gatacre's force.'

'It is not Johnny alone. There are others, Mr Quakerley. At Magersfontein young van Aard was killed; he's Erasmus van Aard's nephew, as you will perhaps know. Erasmus' brother's son, who settled in the Transvaal in the Ermelo district. At Labuschagne's Nek Piet van Tonder fell. He's a grandson of Jan van Tonder of *Suurvlei* here.'

'I know. I saw their names, and I saw Uncle Jan and condoled with him. It is awful. But it is war, Uhlmann. We can't help it.'

'No, that is why it is so bitter. So hard to bear. Not that I should complain. I have only the one on the other side. Others have more than one.'

'Your brothers-in-law, Uhlmann?'

'Ah, yes. But somehow I do not mind them so much. They have been *burghers* for many years. You, too, have kinsmen over there, Mr Quakerley.'

'Yes. My Mother's family. They are Free Staters. Joan keeps a good look out for their names, but so far we have seen no mention of an Egmond in their casualties.'

'We do not get all the names, Mr Quakerley. And one has a feeling that they hide some of their casualties.'

There seemed nothing more to say. They sat and watched the lights changing over the mountain tops as the sun began to sink. Blues and greens chased over the high cliff walls, miles away yet looming in the transparent, clear air, startlingly close, blues and greens, succeeded by warm lilac pink and red. From the disordered, neglected garden came the sound of the Native boy cutting grass for the cows.

Andrew glanced at his companion. He had never before seen the pastor so disturbed. There was something in Uhlmann's face that reminded him of the look he had seen upon young Charlie's when the boy had been on the point of tears, yet had kept tears down by conscious pride—by a boy's determination not to play the baby. He felt sure that it was not pride with the pastor, nor a sense of shame, that had drawn that expression.

'If he doesn't bend, he'll break,' said Andrew to himself. 'I must get him out of this.'

A sudden inspiration came. He laid his hand upon the pastor's arm.

'Uhlmann, I've never heard you play. They all say you're wonderful with the violin. Let me hear you. I'm not much of a judge—my father was, but I'm not—but—it may be good for you,' he ended lamely.

The pastor smiled again, wanly.

'And you would not condole with me,' he said, quietly but sadly. 'No, I cannot play the violin for you. I made a promise to my church council; I cannot break it. I cannot fiddle anymore. But on the piano ... yes, if it will not bore you. Come then.'

He led the way into the drawing room at the end of the *stoep*. It was Mrs Uhlmann's domain, and was furnished with some taste, though the chairs were Victorian and the carpet was much worn, and there was a monstrosity of artificial flowers, made from fish scales, under a glass shade on the window table. But the grand piano was bare of ornament or cover, standing well apart. Both the pastor and his wife loved music, and both had a sense of what a musical instrument deserved.

Andrew sat down in one of the hard-backed hair-upholstered chairs and the pastor took his place on the piano stool and opened the grand.

'What shall I play?' Uhlmann asked, running his fingers soundlessly over the keyboard.

'Anything you like. I am no judge of music.'

Although he was no judge, Andrew, when he heard the first bars, felt that he was listening to someone who loved music almost as much as he himself loved his garden. There was no tune in what the pastor played, but there were rhythm and melody, and grandeur and passion, warmth and colour and consolation in it. To listen to it was like listening to waves dashing on sea-shore rocks, to rain pattering on the leaves of his big magnolia tree, to bees humming in his cynoglossum patch on a summer's day. Joan played, and Alice, but not like that. No, not like that, though Joan could always make the melody sing. Joan at her best always reminded him of a rich wine, the sort that, as his father used to say, sparkled like a peacock's tail, though perhaps that wasn't quite the correct expression; anyway, a wine that brought an infinity of after-flavours to the palate. But the pastor's playing was quite different. It reminded him of flowers, of his garden, of the veld in late September when starred with daisies and iridescent with the sheen of velvety geissorhizas, of the mountains aglow with the reflected light of the sun's setting; of the big poplar bush at *Quakerskloof*, with the leaves turning silver as the breeze swept over them, of pontac vineyards turning a rich crimson in the autumn. It stirred him, and at the same time it soothed him, a paradoxical feeling that he could not, and did not, attempt to explain. He leant back and enjoyed it.

The pastor played on. Uhlmann seemed to be oblivious to his listener, to be entirely absorbed in his music. He improvised; he passed from Beethoven to Mozart, and from Mozart to Scarlatti, pausing between the various themes, and sometimes resting his head on his hands, almost touching the keyboard. Andrew could see that he was profoundly moved as he played, and that the playing soothed him too. At last Uhlmann withdrew his hands from the keys and let them fall limply by his side.

'Play some more,' said Andrew, eagerly.

His host smiled.

'I must have been playing for nearly an hour,' he said. 'Look, it is getting dark, and Mrs Quakerley and Miss Joan will be wondering what has become of you.'

'That does not matter, Uhlmann. I have enjoyed it thoroughly. Play something more.'

The pastor put his hands to the keyboard and played softly. Andrew found himself strangely stirred by the simple melody. It carried him back to his childhood days, more than seventy years ago, for there were cadences which he seemed to remember, although he could not place them. It was a very short piece, and came to an end all too soon. The pastor stood up and closed the piano.

'That,' said old Andrew, rising with some stiffness, for the hair-backed chair had been uncommonly uneasy, 'that was the best you've played, Uhlmann. Sometime you must play it again for me. Whatever is it?'

'A child's theme, Mr Quakerley,' said the pastor, who seemed to have recovered his spirits and spoke with his accustomed serenity. 'Johnny used to like it. He could strum it with one finger on the piano. But it is a delicate bit for all that.'

'It is a splendid bit,' said old Andrew, enthusiastically. 'You must play it again for me some time, Uhlmann. But what do you call it?'

'It is by Schumann,' said the pastor, smiling. *'The Canon of Alexis*. A child's theme, but pretty.'

Chapter 23

Andrew Quakerley, reared in a tradition and atmosphere of elect liberalism, had constantly believed that the fundamental principles of the British government were incontrovertibly sound. The etymological squabbles about the imperative meaning of the word 'suzerainty' had left him cold, for he believed, honestly, that Great Britain was the paramount power in the country, and that the Transvaal was a protected state, depending for its political existence upon the goodwill and the protection of England. He had never thought out clearly what he meant when he believed that, but generally speaking it had suggested to him the analogy of an elder brother's right to give counsel, assistance and candid criticism to a younger, not indeed still living in the family mansion but near enough to trouble, by injudicious action or extravagant pretension, the cordial relations existing between the various members of a family. Just because he thought like that, he had never contemplated the possibility of the elder brother forcibly interfering with the younger, and compelling the latter, by methods that savoured of bullying, to fall into line. England was great enough, liberal and fair enough, to be as magnanimous and as strong as she had been after Majuba. The little brother was no doubt spoiled, obstinate and unmannerly, but little brothers sometimes developed these childish peculiarities, and in time would outgrow them. That had been his opinion, to which he had held firmly until he read the ultimatum.

The arrogance of that document roused in him a mild indignation, just as it stirred the ire of many of his fellow citizens whose sympathies with the Republican cause were far warmer than his. Yet, after the first gust of anger at the insolence of the demands, the impertinence of the language in which they had been couched, and the presumption crystallised in the statement that 'this government' had taken up a challenge thrown out to the whole of South Africa, had cooled down, he had set himself, as a fair-minded man, to consider the rights and wrongs of the position. The result of his deliberations was that, while he felt that the business had been grossly mismanaged, he could not make up his mind on which side lay the greater blame. Now that war had been declared, there was only one possible course of action left open to those who were Her Majesty's subjects and that was to do nothing that might in any way injure Her Majesty's cause or prestige. That, he had made up his mind, was the right thing to do, the correct attitude to take up.

No one could foresee the results of this war. He himself hoped that it might be short and conclusive, but its progress, so far, had not strengthened that hope, and as the months went by it seemed that the waves of conflict encroached farther and farther upon the country, bringing with them complications that had at first seemed unbelievable but had to be accepted as tangible facts.

The first few months of war had not changed the life of the District or Village. Everything went on in its accustomed monotony. There was even some semblance of increased prosperity, for the Village and District shops did good business. From the location many Natives and Coloured men left, to be employed as drivers and sutlers with the imperial troops operating along the main line or as workers in the base camps. Oxen and mules were freely sold to imperial agents, and Elias Vantloo, the wide-awake young Village attorney, was understood to be making good money as a buyer on commission. He had come to Andrew for a loan, with which he proposed to buy up horses and cattle, and had calculated that he would be able to pay ten per cent easily. Andrew had not seen his way clear to let him have the money, but he must have obtained it somewhere, for he now had a good office, rode a fine government horse, and drove about the District with a team of excellent mules, and was said to be employing half a score of assistant-buyers. There was a demand for transport, and some of the farm hands had volunteered for this work, for the pay was good and the conditions of service appealed to them. In time the farming community came to complain of a lack of labour, and the committee appointed to assist Mr Storam reported that there was considerable dissatisfaction in the District because the Natives and Coloured boys demanded better pay and left for war service when they could not get higher wages.

From the Village there had been a few recruits for the volunteer force which under General Brabant had been raised to co-operate with the Imperial troops. Two of the store clerks had joined; Mr Chisholm had applied for leave to join but had been refused. The Prime Minister had thought it wiser that no civil servants should enlist. But when Martin Storam had departed, resplendent in his new khaki uniform that fitted him so amazingly well that he unconsciously swaggered in it, just as years before he had swaggered in the regalia of the Band of Hope, Mr Chisholm had renewed his application and he too had gone to the war. Mr Saxon Miller, with only one lung, Ambrose Crawley with a load of years upon him, and old William Wain, the veteran of Sherman's army, were bellicose without being convincing, for everyone knew that they could not join, and most people thought them very lucky at being able to stay out of trouble with a free conscience and the satisfaction of having tried to do their duty. Augustus, the Native policeman, allured by the higher pay offered in the camps, had resigned, but Mr Storam had refused to accept his resignation, and curtly told him to carry on as he was doing government service just as much in the Village as he would be doing government service in the camps. He had been loathe to accept the order, for his location mates had told him that life in the camps was attractive enough, and that no great danger attached to it provided you were not told off with a convoy, while the wages were magnificent. Even his wife's vigorous argument with the help of a saucepan had only made him rebellious instead of repentant. But he had finally acquiesced in his fate, and it was possible that his acquiescence was directly due to the report that two of the location drivers had been shot by the Boers. The location had, early in the struggle, heard about such happenings, and there was a general belief that the Boers gave no quarter to Coloured or Native boys attached to the columns. The location viewed the war as something that was meant for its especial benefit, and nowhere in the District was the communal feeling so wholeheartedly in favour of the British. There was considerable justification for this, for the Natives knew that in the Transvaal the liberal tradition of the Colony did not exist; beyond the Vaal there was no room for the Coloured, except as drawers of water and gatherers of firewood. If you were not the colour of old red sandstone, you were simply a 'creature' in sharp contradistinction to those whom the Almighty had gently and considerately fashioned with His hands.

Chumley, the chief constable, enlisted early in the summer, although he had been refused permission to do so. He departed without leave, and Mr Storam had been put to considerable trouble to get his dereliction condoned and to obtain a new police head in his place. The newcomer remained only a short period and then he too left for the war, so that Augustus found himself the solitary representative of law and order in the Village, a state of affairs that everybody considered perfectly scandalous. The committee called for volunteers, and for a few weeks these patrolled the Village, until a couple of disgruntled mounted police were sent down from headquarters. But Mr Storam worked hard to get his old assistant back, and when Chumley, wounded in a cavalry raid somewhere near Kimberley, had been sent back to the base, he was successful in getting the chief constable transferred back to his old duties, and the Village applauded.

The chief constable came back looking sunburned and fit, though he carried his left arm in a sling. His presence was needed, for Natives returning from the camps were proving a source of trouble in the District. Whatever good influence the Temperance Lodge might have had, it certainly had not been permanent so far as these derelicts were concerned, and drunkenness and sheep-stealing and petty theft became common. The community had always been law-abiding, but war and its attendant opportunities, the increased wages, and the demoralising effect of camp life, contributed to unsettle the Native element, and in consequence there was much work for Chumley and constable Augustus.

The District accepted the war as a sore trial, a dispensation from heaven, a calamity. At intervals came reports of direct local interest, such as the death of van Aardt's nephew, who had been killed fighting on the Boer side at Colenso, the wounding of the pastor's son—fortunately not fatally as a later communication made clear—on the Boer side, and the killing of one of the store clerks with Gatacre's column. In the Republican casualty lists were names of *burghers* who were linked by family ties to inhabitants in the Village or District. In those of the Imperial forces there were names of as near relatives. What else was to be expected in civil war?

The District shook its head, and remembered the dead and wounded in its evening and matutinal communication with God.

Meanwhile, by common consent, no political meetings had been held. When the representatives of the District, hurrying back from the session of Parliament in Cape

Town, had announced their intention of holding such meetings, the committee had intervened, with the result that the local members had contented themselves with private explanations of the situation. Their attitude was correct and irreproachable. They regretted the war, but deprecated any agitation as likely to do more harm than good, and the common sense of the District cordially agreed with them. They told how high feeling was running elsewhere; how in the annexed districts, far away, citizens had been commandeered to join the Republican forces, under the pretence that they were now *burghers* of the Free State; how the action of these rebels had complicated matters and justified the declaration of martial law in districts not yet invaded, and how under martial law, which is a negation of law, many things had happened which were intensely to be regretted. The District listened, shook its head, and congratulated itself that no such incidents could possibly take place there. It pitied profoundly the poor folk who had been swept into rebellion, but it was fair-minded enough to reflect that there were extenuating circumstances, and that it, too, when similarly circumstanced, might have found difficulty in squaring a theoretical loyalty with actual pressure of combined sympathy and alleged legal obligation.

'Damn it all,' Mr Storam had burst out, when he discussed the matter with one of the members. 'That is about the most dastardly thing I know of, Renselaar. It is simply pressing them by a legal fiction.'

'Of course, that is Mr Schreiner's opinion too. But they are fighting with their backs to the wall, Magistrate.'

'All the more reason why they should fight fair. Do you know, Renselaar, the Republics are alienating sympathy by their actions. They have played their game with almost childish stupidity. I take no stock of the alleged atrocities. These occur in every war, and probably three-quarters of them are lies. But this annexation ... you know as well as I do, it must be effective if it is to be legal. And it is about as effective as our proclamation would be if we annexed the Transvaal.'

'These people do not know that, Magistrate. They see the proclamation posted on the wall, signed by the President or the General—we don't yet know who signed—and they think that they are now subjects of the Free State, and as such liable to be commandeered.'

'That's just it. It's damnable. The Republicans must know that every man who joins them under these conditions is a rebel, and liable to be shot when captured. I can understand the Boers making full use of volunteer rebels ...'

'There have been very few, so far. We are told that the Republican forces have been much disappointed because more men did not join them when they crossed the border. That is probably why they annexed the districts. They wanted to make people think that they could join safely!'

'Of course, that is the idea. And that is why it is so terribly unfair. Just suppose it happened here ...'

'It can't, Magistrate. We shall never see them here. Why, it is more than a thousand miles away. And I feel sure that if such an extremely unlikely contingency were to occur, our people would be sensible enough to keep their heads.'

'I sincerely hope so. But I have my doubts, Renselaar.'

'I find our people very quiet, Magistrate.'

'They are that. We have had some trouble with the Natives returning from camps.

You know that. A few exemplary sentences have ended that business, I think. But I must say that there has been nothing in the least that has given me any anxiety—I mean about agitation and such things.'

'I never thought there would be, Magistrate. We are loyal, although God knows some of the things that are happening elsewhere make anybody's loyalty shake.'

'You must not harp too much on that. It is war, you know, and under martial law much must be permitted which would otherwise be illegal. I think it would be a good thing to put the whole Colony under martial law, and place the matter properly in the hands of the police and the civil authorities. It would accustom people to the changed condition, and it would help to keep things quiet.'

'You have practically everything that you are likely to gain by proclaiming martial law, Magistrate. Why, you've even prevented me from holding my usual meetings.'

'Don't say prevented. We've merely suggested to you that you and your colleague should see people privately rather than talk in public. A public meeting just now may give rise to undesirable incidents. You admit that.'

'Yes. That is why I fell in with the committee's wish. There is no sense in agitating, and a public meeting will look like it.'

'I am glad to see that you take it in the right spirit. You'll be pleased to hear that the ladies are not so clamorous as they used to be when you fought your election. The League is doing really useful work collecting comforts for the troops, and so on. You've got to thank Quakerley for that. They draw on him to an unlimited extent.'

'Yes, I know. We all owe thanks to Mr Quakerley, Magistrate.'

'You do indeed, Renselaar. Tell me, what is the talk down there about all this. Their real opinion ...'

'Can there be any question, Magistrate? At first there was some suggestion that we might try to intervene—offer to mediate between them. But that is out of the question now. We can only look on and abide by whatever happens.'

'And what do you expect will happen?'

'What must be, Magistrate. The troops will push on to Pretoria. The Transvaal will be conquered. England is too strong ... it is a tragedy.'

'Yes, it's that right enough,' said the magistrate, still probing. 'But would it not be the best thing after all? To make an end, and have the whole country from Pretoria down to the Cape under one authority? Or are you of those who detest being under British rule?'

'We are not under English rule, Magistrate,' retorted Renselaar, with some spirit. 'I have always deprecated this talk as if we were subservient to England. She has never molested us. In this matter, now, she has bullied, yes, that is my view, Magistrate, and I say so freely; we are not under martial law yet—but I do not think that she really wanted war. I think, and many agree with me, that if the Transvaal had been more—how shall I express it?—more diplomatic, things might have improved. The ultimatum was a mistake ... a great mistake. They should have given in ...'

'Now, yes, to jump better, as the French say, later on. Is that your meaning, Renselaar?'

'Say, Magistrate, you do not think that we are rebels? I know that. Then why suggest that we have any hidden motive? You know what underlies all that we have done.'

'I have a notion. But go on. Give me your view.'

'We do not like being treated like children. We are major. We have our own constitution, and we should be allowed to settle our own affairs. And this trouble in the Transvaal is our affair, not so much England's. We could have dealt with it just as effectively as Chamberlain can, and we should not have used cannon and shells to settle it. Sooner or later South Africa must be one—you cannot keep on competing against one another in railway rates and tariffs and such-like things. And now all that has been broken up. How long will it take to mend things when this war is finished, Magistrate?'

'I see what you mean. Your view is that if England had kept out of it we might have settled the Outlander question and brought about some kind of federation, but now all that has been indefinitely postponed?'

'Yes, the one thing the war has done, Magistrate, is to broaden the cleft that is between some of us. It was gradually getting narrower, and if we had been left alone it would have disappeared altogether, or we would have made a bridge across it. But it is wrong, when a country has self-government, for a section of the people to go constantly somewhere else when they can't get what they want and appeal, as it were, to some outside authority. That is what has caused the war, and it will be difficult to remove that impression afterwards.'

'It will be difficult to remove many impressions, Renselaar. The war is bound to leave scars ...'

'Infinitely more unsightly than anything that the past has left on us, Magistrate. To my mind the most hideous part of the whole business is that we are so helpless. We cannot move either way without being disloyal in some respect. We are pulled two ways—one way by our own ideals, and the other by our sense of duty. That is why I sympathise so much with those rebels, even though you don't.'

'But I do! Don't for a moment imagine that I don't. My sympathies are all with them, and that is why I blame the Boers for having acted in this perfectly damnable way. But sympathy, my dear Renselaar, won't help them when the troops get there. Have you considered that aspect?'

'We have indeed, Magistrate. It has caused us much thought and there is a wide difference of opinion on the matter. You know, of course, that there is a sharp division in the House ...'

'Yes, that is obvious from the reports. A pity. At such a time you might sink your party differences ...'

'There is no chance of that, Magistrate. Feelings are too deeply stirred, and the House is merely a reflection of what goes on outside. The opposition, even moderate men like Innes, are in favour of dealing with them in a way we think harsh. They suggest total disfranchisement.'

'I should imagine that is the least punishment possible, and after all it is not much of a punishment. What value do men place on their civic rights if they are willing to forego them at the call of the enemy the moment he enters their country? And probably half of them are voteless youngsters.'

'Oh no, Magistrate. Many of them are well-to-do farmers. There are even field-cornets and Elders among them. That is the greater pity of it. We think that total disfranchisement is wrong, a wrong punishment altogether for it has a political aspect and is not really a punishment. Most of them would never have had the courage to join if it were not for the Republican proclamation. And in some cases, from what I hear, Magistrate, there has been actual force used to press them to join.'

'I am not surprised to hear it,' exclaimed the Magistrate. 'You might do worse, Renselaar, than explain matters to people here—quietly, you know, in the sense of our conversation. Make a point of laying stress on the illegality of the Republican proclamation, and the fact that they know it to be illegal. To me that policy of bludgeoning and cajoling men into rebellion, well knowing that the poor fools must inevitably suffer while real Republican subjects are immune from reprisals, is perfectly damnable. But I fear that is what we may expect if the Boers are not driven out from the districts, or if they come further south.'

'I am told there is no probability of that, Magistrate. Frankly, I hold that they have shot their bolt. They have done marvellously well—better than their most sanguine supporters could have expected—but they lack the men and the means to keep it up. I suppose it is wrong to say so, Magistrate, but I confess I have admiration for the way in which they have fought. Magersfontien and Colenso were great battles, and well won.'

'There I am completely with you. They are brave fighters and good fighters, and that is just why I dislike to see them callous and cruel. I don't like the way they maltreat our Natives.'

'It is our fault, Magistrate, or at least the fault of the troops. They should not use Natives to fight. As you know, it is right against our tradition.'

'Rubbish, my dear Renselaar ... the Boers use as much Native labour as we do for military purposes, and as a matter of fact we use less, perhaps, for our Tommies have to fend for themselves, and most of the Boers have Native after-riders. And so far as I know we have never used Coloured or Native boys as soldiers in the field. But a Native policeman in uniform, doing the duties he is bound to do, gets short shrift from them if he is caught, and that again, I say, is damnable. For every Native shot by them in cold blood I should, if I had my way, exact exemplary punishment, and I say that without withdrawing my admiration of them as brave fighters.'

'These are only rumours, Magistrate. There are no authenticated cases of shooting Natives.'

'Perhaps you are right. But there is a lot of uneasiness among our Native boys here, and I don't like it. What I especially object to is the cool assumption that if the Republics declare war, their opponents must fight according to special rules which conform to their idea of what is fair. If they had France instead of England to deal with, they would have had the whole of the Native territories mobilised against them, and the Kaffirs would have been only too eager to take part.'

'But that would have been wholly wrong,' declared the member, shaking his head gravely. 'We must keep the Natives out of this. It is a White man's civil war, and must be fought out by White men.'

'I agree. But you can't altogether dispense with Native and Coloured labour, and it is only fair play and common humanity to treat such labour just as you would treat combatants. Thank God it has nothing to do with us here. I am only apprehensive of what may happen if it goes on.'

'I think you need have no fear, Magistrate. That was a point on which our government has definite assurance. And I fancy what you have heard about the shootings are mere rumours.'

'I am relieved. But tell me—I don't suppose I am asking too much—how do you pull in the House? Is there not frequently friction?'

'In caucus, often, Magistrate. I tell no tales out of school, but some of the party are displeased with the Prime Minister and with Solomon. They imagine more can be done to keep us out of the trouble. Some think that he is not doing his best.'

'In what way? I think Mr Schreiner has done his utmost.'

'Letting the police share, for example. And allowing the troops to use our rolling stock ...'

'But my dear Renselaar, Schreiner is a Minister of the Crown, and this is after all Her Majesty's Colony. Surely you do not imagine that he can refuse to put at the imperial government's disposal everything that is necessary? Why, the moment he suggested such a thing, Sir Alfred would dismiss him.'

'I—most of us, Magistrate—see that, of course. But the very fact that we see it, and understand it, makes us dissatisfied. If we are really self-governing, we should have a say in these matters, and not be forced to do just what we are ordered to do.'

'It's galling, no doubt, but where are you going to draw the line? Who is to say what the Colony really wishes?'

'What can I say, Magistrate? I know that it is wrong—we are subjects of the Queen, but it goes against the grain, especially since we were not asked whether we approved of the war or not. They might at least have asked us first ...'

'You would have swallowed the ultimatum, Renselaar ...?'

'I don't say that, Magistrate. It was surely an impudence. But a rebuke might have sufficed, and why should the whole country suffer for the foolishness of the Transvaal? What is the reason we are warring? Didn't Mr Chamberlain himself say that three-quarters of what was wanted had been obtained, and that the remainder was hardly worth fighting for?'

'Something of the kind. But that was before that preposterous ultimatum was launched. You know, Renselaar, I felt just as you do, until I read that nonsense.'

'It was most unpleasant reading, Magistrate. I blushed myself. But that has been their way all along. They have not been quite neighbourly and friendly to us.

'Ah, I am glad you see that. I was going to tell you to stress that point as well when you talk to our people, but I am afraid I am coaching you too much in war propaganda, and you may complain about me to the Attorney-General. Seriously, Renselaar, you must help us here. The people will listen to you and you could nip anything in the bud—you grasp my meaning?'

'Certainly, Magistrate. But you need not be alarmed. Nothing will happen here. We are thousands of miles away from the war.'

As he walked to his office Mr Storam reflected that there was something in that assurance after all. It was propinquity that had bred rebellion in the northern districts, propinquity and that damnable policy of the Boers to press ignorant *bywoners* into their ranks. That policy made his blood boil and alienated whatever sympathetic feelings he had for the Republicans. It was, of course, a civilian's trick; no honest soldier of the type of de la Rey or Joubert would have stooped to such infamy.

Thank God it cold not be paralleled here. The District was thousands of miles away from the scene where illiterate farm hands were being told that now that their farms had become Republican territory they were absolved from their allegiance to Alexandrina Victoria, and could with safety take up arms against the British troops. Such things could not happen here.

Chapter 24

The New Year, ushering in the new century—though on this point there was some justifiable doubt—brought no relief, but happily also no new trials. The District heard of the abortive attempts to relieve Ladysmith, the disaster at Spion Kop, the various skirmishes, wasteful in their toll of human lives and useless in their direct effect upon the campaign. Then, suddenly, the fortune of war seemed to change. Paardeberg could be looked upon as a decisive blow, and in rapid succession came the occupation of Bloemfontein, the relief of Ladysmith, the rolling back of the Republican forces into a crumpled remnant no longer capable of organised, effective military resistance.

The news of these victories, confirmation of which came from official sources almost as soon as the rumour of them had percolated to the Village, was received with mixed feelings by the District. No one dreamed that it did not portend a speedy end to the war, that end which had always been looked upon as a possibility, although there were many who hoped that the agony of surrender to men who had fought so valiantly against such odds would be made bearable by terms such as could honourably be accepted. The war was at an end; now it was for statesmen to see that its aftermath would not be more cruel than its actuality had been, that its results would not add to the scars already so apparent upon the body of South Africa.

Andrew Quakerley was feeling the strain of these strenuous, unhappy days. He was nearing his eightieth year of life, and although he had known no serious illness, and had always been a strong, healthy, robust old man, he had lately begun to take life more easily even than he had done before. To him advancing age had brought no alarm or regret. When he had passed his fiftieth year he had had periods of uneasiness, for he had always been physically strong, and looked forward with distaste to anything that savoured of valetudinarianism. But these transient twinges of moodiness had passed when he found that he could easily adapt himself to circumstances, and that his bodily machine continued to do its work with reasonable exactness, provided he did not overload it. Joan had given him, years ago, as a Christmas present, a copy of Cornaro's book, and he had made it his guide, within limitations. He did not cut his diet down to the ascetic proportion demanded by the Venetian, but he indulged in moderation in what he fancied, and led an ordered, sheltered, unemotional life. The war and its disturbance altered the routine of that life very little, but it supplied emotional excitement such as had been carefully excluded from it in the past, and inevitably the old man had reacted to such excitement. His psychological make-up had enabled him to withstand such reaction up to a certain point. He did not, for instance, get wildly excited, as Alice did, when he read the newspapers; he did not give vent to his feelings with the same naïve freedom in which Mr Mance-Bisley voiced his indignation or approval. Most people, in fact, thought him emphatic, even callous. But that was merely his nature, and under his placid, gentlemanly calm moved surges of passionate sentiment which he had schooled himself to restrain from his boyhood onward.

Sister Joan knew how tense her brother's heart-strings were stretched. She herself had inherited, if such things be hereditable, her father's cynical outlook upon life. She had no ideals beyond those that had formed part of her training and upbringing by a parent who had placed honour even above godliness, and had exalted family tradition into a creed. On this question of the rights and wrongs of the war she was cynically impartial, damning both sides for their sheer stupidity, but on the whole inclined to the view that such things settle themselves. But she knew that her brother's outlook was different. Andrew was as sentimental as Alice, though in a different sense. Her sister-in-law's sentiment Joan contemptuously regarded as sentimentality, the product of her age and her education, something that aped that aristocratic appeal to tradition which her brother had a right to make but which in Alice was unwarranted presumption bordering on impertinence. Andrew's sentiment was based on a real tradition of England's liberalism, that had made her the champion of freedom and had given her subjects constitutional rights, so that even the youngest brother shared in the privileges of the mother. The war—all that had preceded it more than its actual outbreak—had rudely and disturbingly shaken that traditional conception of the motherland. It had not, indeed, shattered it, but Joan felt that her brother had had a struggle, and was still struggling, to adjust his long-cherished conception of the ideal to the facts. She could not materially help him in that readjustment. Those papers that expressed something of the sentiment that Andrew harboured—there was only one of them in the Colony, a newly established English daily, to which Andrew subscribed and read with increasing distaste—were scarcely likely to assist him in the task. They were too blatantly pro-Boer and little-Englander to satisfy his longing for impartial criticism. Being essentially fair-minded, Joan admitted that it was a very difficult task to steer between the Scylla of pro-Boerism and the Charybdis of Chamberlainism. Here and there she found passages that seemed to her to have achieved this object, and she had marked those and discussed them with her brother. Mr Merriman, that trenchant champion of the tradition which Andrew so much loved, had spoken once or twice with an eloquence that had strongly impressed her, and she had admired, too, Mr John Morley's address to his constituents. Both had, as it appeared to her, justified her brother's assumption that loyalty to British interests, to everything that stood for that liberalism which, throughout all the mistakes that had been made in the past century, had marked England's dealing with her colonial subjects, could be compatible with an earnest and non-epideictic protest against a policy so calamitous as that which had led up to the war.

That the war was a calamity she did not, could not, doubt. She had no uncertainty in her mind as to the result of the campaign. There could be only one result—the subjugation of the Republics. When Andrew had moodily pointed out that the war was costing England nearly a million a week, and that there was a possibility of intervention, she had scorned the supposition that either argument carried the slightest weight. But in her heart she knew that the inevitable end of the campaign could not be considered the inevitable end of the struggle, and that the wounds of civil war tend to leave scars whose sensitiveness is not always dulled by time. From whatever angle one looked at the situation, it was calamitous.

As the months passed, matters in the Colony itself became more and more involved. The Bond ministry resigned on the question of the treatment of those Colonists who had gone into rebellion in the invaded districts.

Mr Quakerley thought that the fall of the Schreiner ministry was altogether to the good. Schreiner had been in an impossible position once war was declared; it would have been better and more dignified if he had resigned when the ultimatum came instead of waiting until circumstances forced his hand. Sir Gordon, after all, could be trusted to uphold the Colony's traditions, and to act fairly, for there were men in his cabinet as fair-minded and as South African in sentiment as Mr Schreiner himself. And from what could be gathered, the Sprigg cabinet was working well in these trying circumstances. A special court had been appointed to try the rebels, and the trials had been eminently fair, the sentences imposed reasonable, erring on the side of leniency rather than on that of vindictiveness, and the government of the country was being carried on with the minimum of dislocation.

With his innate common sense, Andrew realised that age brings with it an increased sense of irritation with trifles. He schooled himself against giving way to this, and found the discipline harder than he had expected it to be. Alice, with her outbursts of childish enthusiasm when something happened to give her an opportunity to show how excessively loyal she was, annoyed him; Mr Mance-Bisley's fits, complacency alternating with despondency, irritated him; Mr Storam's anxieties about the District made him petulant. When he found himself in this antagonistic mood, he talked with Joan, or voyaged in his garden, or visited Mr Uhlmann, who played him into peace, for *The Canon of Alexis* was indescribably soothing. Joan now played it for him almost every evening, but she thought it childish and much preferred something more classical.

Charlie came home from school for the Christmas holidays that year, bringing with him the frank freshness of youthful interests which even the calamity of war could not mar. Andrew found his grandson companionable and congenial, and enjoyed his company. Charlie had grown into a strapping lad, undeniably good-looking, though still angular and lacking the smooth roundness of matured adolescence. Joan thought him lankier than Andrew had been at his age, but Alice, whose eye for physical beauty was more expert, found him as pleasant to look upon as Martin had been. Martin was soldiering somewhere in the Free State, and occasionally wrote home, always tacking on to the end of his letter a message to her which Mrs Storam communicated laughingly. Old Mrs Quakerley valued these tributes to her personality, and smirked and preened herself when she listened to them in a way that the magistrate's wife thought thoroughly unbecoming to an old woman.

When it became known that the Republics had made advances for peace, excitement in the Village once more welled up in a wave of public interest. Mr Storam was asked to allow a meeting to be called to support the Republican plea, and consulted Andrew about the matter.

'If you think it will do the slightest good, Mr Quakerley,' he said, 'I am prepared to consent. Not that my consent is material. They can do it without asking my permission.'

'They won't do that,' replied Andrew. They were talking in his garden, under the spreading branches of the big magnolia tree, and the magistrate had opened the conversation by expressing his admiration of the herbaceous borders. 'You must admit that, so far, they have played the game. But this is another matter, Storam, and I hope you will think seriously about it before you agree.'

'Then you do not feel that it is likely to do any good?'

'How can it? Their premises are wrong. I almost said "as usual," for one expects them to do just the wrong thing. To make peace now would be to leave things entirely unsettled. You see that, don't you?'

'Of course. Nor do I think Her Majesty's Government will agree. But the general feeling is—even the rector shares it—that we have recovered our prestige now that we have fairly beaten them, and that it would be a good gesture to put our proposals forward.'

'Have you spoken to Uhlmann? No. Well, I have. He is as much against it as I am, Storam, and for exactly the same reasons. No matter what the facts are—they are as plain to me and to you as they can be—there will be the suggestion that if England makes peace now, even if she obtains much more than we asked for at the Bloemfontein Conference, it will be due to the pressure that has been exerted upon her by the Republican resistance during the past six months. Besides I don't see what other terms there can be than unconditional surrender and annexation. Do you?'

'I fancied that something in the nature of a protectorate might be offered, with self-government but with implicit guarantees against a recurrence of the old policy of armaments and agitation, with, of course, a liberal franchise, and the repeal of legislation restricting trade and industries.'

'All that would be very difficult to work in practice, Storam. Besides, is there the least likelihood that public opinion, in England, would be satisfied with a solution that seems a stalemate?'

'That is the point about which I am very doubtful, Mr Quakerley. Such information as I have—none of it is official, though—leads me to believe that you are right. But would it do any harm to express the opinion that we are in favour of terms being proposed?'

'Not if it were our unanimous opinion. But is it? You know perfectly well that there are many in this Colony—some even here among us—who will not be satisfied until there is an end to all this. And it may very well happen that your meeting is not unanimous, in which case more harm than good will result. Besides, some of us—you see, I include myself in the generalisation—some of us may express our feelings in a manner calculated to arouse ill-feeling.'

'That is what I feel, Mr Quakerley. That is really my difficulty.'

'It is a very real one. If I may advise, why not see Uhlmann. He has a great deal of influence.'

'What does he suggest?'

'He talked of the possibility of getting up some kind of petition. That seems to me much better. You could draw it up yourself, you and your committee, and I believe there would be no great difficulty in getting it representatively signed. I think you would get some of the members of our Ladies' League to sign it, provided it was worded tactfully.'

'That is Rekker's opinion, too, Mr Quakerley. He is even more against the meeting than you are ...'

'I can believe that. Rekker has had some experience. What about Renselaar and his colleague?'

'I have seen them both. They favour a public meeting. They tell me that such meetings are being organised in other districts ...'

'Very likely. On instructions from headquarters. All the more reason we should not do the same.'

'The position is very unsatisfactory,' said the magistrate. 'So far as we can ascertain, the Republican forces are still an entity. They are still capable of resistance, and there is still an authority to deal with. But what may happen if they disperse and we get guerrilla warfare, without some central administrative authority, that can speak and act for them?'

'Isn't that already the case? I suppose if England really proposed terms, they would say that these terms will have to be discussed by their respective *Volksraads*. There would have to be an Armistice, and there would be interminable discussions, with the press in the background distorting everything. Why, we should be back in the pre-war agitation with feeling much higher. An intolerable position.'

'I am inclined to agree with you there. But what is to be the outcome of it all, Mr Quakerley?'

'Annexation, I suppose. What else is there?'

'Crown Colony rule for them, and representative government for us and Natal. Isn't that just as intolerable, in the long run?'

'It needn't be for very long, Storam. Krugerism is a vanishing quantity. If it were not for this war—if we had played our cards well—it would have been dying by this time. We have given it a little longer lease of life, and we must wait patiently for its passing. I still have faith in England's liberality, and the good sense of Englishmen in general.'

'So have I, Mr Quakerley. Although one's faith is stretched to the breaking point, sometimes. You yourself must feel that.'

'I do, as you say, sometimes. But is England responsible for everything that happens? I cannot think it, Storam, I really cannot. Take these unfortunate happenings under martial law ...'

'I always said that if they gave the military an experienced civil servant, who knows the local community, martial law would give rise to no ill-feeling. We might have it here, and no one will be disturbed, any more than they are disturbed now by our local committee.'

'Yes, if you were in charge. But I daresay that you would be called away and some unknown Jack in office put in your place ...'

'Well, we need not discuss that,' said the magistrate, shortly. 'There is no probability of this District being under martial law. I take it that we shall see the end of the war before the year is out. There can hardly be more than thirty thousand Boers in the field now, and they haven't got any reserves. The thing will peter out by attrition.'

'Let us hope so. But see Uhlmann, Storam. And dissuade them, if you possibly can, from holding a public meeting. No good can come of it.'

No public meeting was held, but the District and the Village signed a petition to Her Majesty in which it expressed the hope that now that the superiority of the imperial arms had been vindicated, peace might be made on terms that would still leave the Republics their independence. Andrew Quakerley signed the petition, and induced his wife to do so. The rector signed it, Mr Miller signed it, and most of the English-speaking members of the community signed it. The only ones who refused to affix their signatures were Miss Marradee and the veteran from Sherman's armies, whom even his old friend, the carpenter, could not persuade to do so.

'I'd give the b——s hell,' said old William Wain, 'same as Grant did and my old chief, I would. That's what war is—hell, and don't you forget it, Ambrose, my lad. Let them as take up the sword perish by the sword. And don't you go signing no blooming petitions.'

Nevertheless, Ambrose signed, and the Seldons signed, and Mrs Corner, the boardinghouse-keeper, signed, and Mrs Chumley and her husband, although the latter had some doubts as to whether his official position didn't forbid him doing so. Augustus, the Native constable, wanted to sign too but was not allowed to. Mr Storam refrained from signing, not because he was not in sympathy with the petition, which he had drawn up himself, but because he was the magistrate and as such had to take charge of the document.

In due course he received a curt intimation that the petition had been considered but that Her Majesty's Government saw no reason to depart from the policy that had been clearly laid down.

'Somebody,' said old William Wain, pouring a dash of whisky into his friend's tea, 'has enough sense left to know what's what. And now the b——s will have to sing *God save the Queen.*'

Chapter 25

With the annexation of the two Republics there seemed to come a lull in the fighting, and communication with the northern parts, that had been so much interrupted, once more became possible. Letters from relatives in the Transvaal or Orange Free State, which had come in by stealth, smuggled in through the kind courtesy of officials or mutual friends of the correspondents, now passed through the mails, arriving with the coloured strip marked 'Opened by Censor' pasted over one end. The District and the Village learned much more from these letters than from the condensed accounts in the press.

Both Joan and her brother could now correspond with their mother's relatives in the Orange Free State, and the first letters that came through showed that the Egmonds were still on their farm where life went on, apparently, with the same routine monotony as in the Village. The Egmonds lived under martial law, in a land occupied by the enemy, but from what they wrote Andrew gathered that their lot was far easier than had been the fate of British subjects living in districts occupied by the Republican forces, or even in adjacent districts where the Boers had never penetrated, but which had been placed under martial law.

'Perhaps it is policy,' he said, discussing this interesting phase with his sister, 'but I really can't see why we should be harsher with our own people than with the enemy's subjects. Of course this letter is written so that it can pass the censor. Otherwise, I am sure Cousin Hester would have expressed her opinion of us much more cogently.'

'She'll do that,' smiled Joan, who had found the unimportant details in the letter interesting. 'Did you notice that she hints that one of them might come down? There it is, that passage. Curious, isn't it?'

Andrew read the sentence aloud. Mrs Egmond, whose father-in-law was Joan and Andrew's first cousin, had married a Free State official, and her grown-up sons were *burghers* of the Republic that had for so many years been a model neighbour to the Colony, but had thrown in its lot, to its own detriment, with the sister Republic in agreeing to the despatch of the ultimatum. Two of her sons had been killed; another was with his commando somewhere—the Censor had scratched out the name of the place, which irritated Andrew who thought that it really did not matter where young Arno Egmond's commando careered. But a fourth son had been seriously wounded and was now convalescent on parole, and his mother hinted that if Cousin Andrew would use his influence, Conroy might obtain a permit to complete his convalescence with his Colonial relatives. He could as easily report himself daily to the magistrate in the Village as at Bloemfontein, and such privileges were allowed to the favoured few who had friends influential enough to intercede for them. And Mrs Egmond had remembered that Cousin Andrew had in his time been *persona grata* at Government and Admiralty House, and that his paternal uncle had been an Admiral of the Red in the British Navy.

'Hm,' said Cousin Andrew, dubiously. 'I daresay it could be arranged. But, Joanie, does it not strike you as queer that the military should allow this sort of thing?'

'Why not?' retorted his sister. 'They must have their reasons. It is scarcely likely that they will allow an able prisoner of war such privileges, but Conroy, from what his mother writes, is disabled.'

'I shall have to see Storam about it,' said Andrew. 'I've no objection, if it can be managed quietly and without any fuss. But there may be complications ...'.

'I don't see why there should be,' interrupted his sister. 'If he is on parole he won't be able to talk politics, and of course he'll be on his good behaviour. Besides, he is only a lad.'

'He's nearly thirty,' said Andrew. 'Hester married young, and Conroy is her eldest. Will you speak to Alice, my dear? She might not like it.'

'You may leave Alice to me,' replied his sister firmly. 'If the lad is anything like what his father was at that age, Alice will take him for another *beau*. She'll flirt with the Devil himself provided he's good-looking.'

'I don't mind that in the least,' said Andrew, 'so long as she does not start arguing about the war. Alice can be very trying at times, Joanie.'

'You may be sure she won't offend a guest,' Joan consoled him. 'But we are talking about something that may not happen at all. You'd better see the magistrate about it before we make any arrangements.'

To Andrew's surprise Mr Storam raised no objection to the proposal. He explained that several prisoners of war on parole were in the Colony as guests of relatives or friends, and that others were living quietly abroad—some, like Mr Uhlmann's brother-in-law, who was, or had been, an official of the Republican government, even in England. Being on parole meant, in a military sense, being out of the war. The prisoner had to report daily or weekly, according to the letter of the parole he had signed, to the nearest military or civil authority, and to remain quiet. Nothing more was exacted from him, but if he transgressed the spirit of his parole, steps would be taken to transfer him to one of the prisoners' camps. Mr Storam promised to arrange the matter with the authorities.

In due course Conroy Egmond arrived. Although Andrew tried to keep the coming of his guest secret, the news leaked out, and on the afternoon of Conroy's arrival there was a larger crowd than usual under the eucalyptus tree in front of the post office. The Village was naturally curious to see the first Republican fighter, and frank curiosity was nothing to be ashamed of.

The stranger was a tall, strapping young fellow, with a clean-shaven, bony, but not unhandsome face, who smiled cheerfully when he was helped out of the post-cart, and immediately won the sympathies of the crowd when it was seen that he dragged his leg and had to use a crutch.

There were many who came forward to be introduced and to shake hands with him, a customary ceremonial to which Andrew could not take objection.

He was himself favourably impressed with the young man's bearing and good-humoured friendliness. Egmond obviously was surprised and pleased with his reception, but he quickly countered what might have become a demonstration by what Andrew thought was a sensible speech. 'I am glad to be among friends,' said the young man, holding old Martin Rekker's hand for a moment, and glancing at the crowd round him, 'although most of them are new. I have not even had a chance of knowing my old cousin—or is it third cousin, or grand-cousin? I really don't know— Mr Quakerley here. But I am a prisoner of war on parole, and I cannot say anything more than to thank you for your welcome.'

He linked his arm in Andrew's, and hobbled off on his stick. The welcoming group, their curiosity satisfied for the moment, discussed him at length while the mail was being sorted, and then went to the counter to get their letters.

Conroy Egmond quickly made himself at home in the Quakerley household. Grand-cousin Alice petted and spoiled him, as she had tried to pet and spoil Martin, and found him ever so much more interesting than Charlie, who was after all only a schoolboy, while Conroy was a grown man, obviously with much experience of life and quite equal to the task of acting as an old lady's cavalier. Joan thought him an agreeable, sensible young fellow, more staid than the types of his contemporaries she had known in the Village, and quite unlike what she had supposed a fighting *burgher* to be. Her brother shared her opinion, especially when he discovered that Conroy, who in civil life was a practical farmer, was an expert arboriculturist and loud in his admiration of the wonderful garden. The rest of the Village community, when they came to know the stranger, expressed unqualified approval of him, and before Conroy had been among them for a fortnight it was easily apparent that he was popular and respected for himself quite as much as for the cause which he represented.

He reported himself daily at the court house, spending half an hour at the office in a chat with the magistrate. His game leg made progression through the street a slow affair, but as he was not fit to mount a horse, and refused to go about in Andrew's cart, he swung himself along on his crutch and seemed none the worse for it. Everyone liked him, and stopped in the street to greet him when he crutched along. He had made friends early with both the rector and Mr Uhlmann, and was a frequent and welcome visitor at the rectory and the parsonage, while the Storams invited him to dinner once a week, and invitations from the farms were showered upon him. These latter, however, he invariably declined, excusing acceptance on the justified plea that his parole forbade him to leave the Village. One exception to this rule was made when the magistrate invited him to accompany him on a visit to Martin Rekker.

The Rekker farm lay on the farther side of the high range of mountains that formed the northern rim of the valley in which the Village nestled. The main road to it led over a steep pass, through most picturesque scenery of wind-worn sandstone rocks splashed with variegated colours, high cliffs overgrown with fern and brushwood, deep, narrow dells through which tiny mountain streams trickled, and bare, sunburned hillsides that in early summer were carpeted in colour. At the bottom of the pass, in a long, narrow valley, lay the farm, embowered in splendid old oak trees planted more than a century ago, with the imposing mass of the mountain towering behind, a sheer wall of rock indented at one place by a sharp cleft in which a waterfall fell down two hundred feet to race tumultuously in the high-banked channel until it reached level ground behind the homestead. The Rekkers' farm was one of the show places in the District, for old Martin's father had spent much money and care upon it, so that it now represented the high water mark of what could be achieved with such soil and in such surroundings. The house with its rococo gables and white-washed out-buildings, the vineyard with its rows upon rows of regularly planted vines, the citrus orchard, and the wheat-lands, made a picture as pleasing to the eye as it was satisfying to the practical farmer.

Here, in the large, cool dining-room, on the walls of which hung portraits of the Queen, of the Prince Imperial at Isandhlwana, and of General Smit on horseback, old Martin entertained his guests in the old-fashioned hospitable style which he affected. With old-fashioned courtesy he gave precedence to the magistrate, the *landdrost*, passing him the Bible when the evening meal was finished, for the customary chapter to be read while he himself led the singing of the evening hymn, and intoned the *extempore* evening prayer in which he remembered the war, Her Majesty, and 'all those who are in peril tonight, whether, O Lord, they be of our kin that are dear to us, or men unknown to us.' No possible exception could be taken to that petition, but then, the magistrate reflected, old Martin was a man of sense, loyal in the best sense of the word, reared in the honourable traditions of his house that had always served Alexandrina Victoria faithfully and well.

When the Native servants retired, Martin and his guests sat round the side-table, while young Martin, a married man with a family of five, and his wife, who kept house for her widowed father-in-law, sat on the leather-plait seated sofa. The men smoked, and Mrs Martin junior worked at a canvas square with multi-coloured wools to produce those curious effects known as crewel work. Sweet wine in an old Flemish carafe, and shelled almonds and sun-dried raisins were on the table as after-dinner refreshments for those who cared to partake of them.

'And now, Nephew Conroy,' said the old man, turning to his crippled guest, 'if Mr Storam will allow it, you must tell us something about the war. I do not mean about things that should not be spoken of. You have given your word not to do that, and an honest man must keep his word. But mayhap there are other things of which you can freely speak. Is it not so, magistrate?'

'There is no reason why he should not tell us some of his experiences,' replied the magistrate, thus appealed to. 'His parole does not prevent him from doing so. And we should like to hear about them, Egmond, if you care to tell us.'

'There is very little to tell,' said the prisoner of war. 'You know all about what happened on the eastern front; that's where I was. I saw something of the fighting round Dundee and Elandslaagte, but all that will be old news to you.'

'You might tell us how you were wounded,' said the old man. 'And generally about things.'

'I should like to know,' interjected his son, blowing out a cloud of smoke, 'if it is not trenching upon what must not be told, what in the world made you fellows come into the Colony. It has not done you any good, and it has done us a lot of harm. It needs some explanation.'

'I had nothing to do with that,' said Conroy. 'Although it was a Free State commando that went in first. But you know, Uncle Martin, there were many who thought that people here would rise when war came, and hurry to our help.'

'Aye, that I know. But were you fool enough to believe it, Nephew?'

'Better men than I believed it, Uncle. And they still believe it.'

'That is all very well,' said the younger Martin, truculently, 'but you fellows took a lot upon you, didn't you? First of all arrogating to yourselves the right to speak for all of us, which you hadn't really.'

'That again is politics, Uncle. You must excuse me, but I cannot go into that. The magistrate will tell you that.'

'Certainly, Egmond,' said Mr Storam. 'We'd better keep off that topic. But I suppose—it is rather difficult to suggest what you may tell us—but couldn't you tell us something about what was taking place on your side when you were still there? That is so long ago that there is no question about giving the show away.'

'Very well. In the Transvaal Botha is leader, with Beyers somewhere in the north. Botha took charge when Joubert died, you know, and he's our second best man ...'

'Why second best, Nephew?' asked old Martin, helping himself to snuff.

'Just in a manner of speaking, Uncle. We all think de la Rey is the better general, the better fighting general. Botha is too cautious. But he's a grand organiser, and it is due to him that there are still so many commandos in the field.'

'I suppose,' said the magistrate, diffidently, 'he has a fairly hard struggle to keep things going. We are among ourselves, Egmond, and can talk freely, without trenching upon politics.'

'You may say that,' exclaimed Conroy, answering the first part of the magistrate's remarks. 'Indeed, Mr Storam, you have no idea what a struggle it is. Sometimes it is almost amusing. I'll give you an instance. You know on the highveld there are lots of horses running wild, now that the owners are away on commando. Well, Beyers came along and took a couple of hundred to remount his men. He brought them into the lowveld, where there is horse sickness, you know, and plenty of them died. Then a deputation of *burghers* waited upon Botha to complain about it. He sent them about their business, of course, but they actually felt aggrieved that we had taken the horses down into the lowveld. You see, many of our people up there are still rather stupid, and they are not accustomed to obeying orders implicitly. They will argue a point before they obey. That is our real difficulty—has always been.'

'Aye,' said the old man, nodding his head. 'It is even so. Here, too, there is want of obedience to authority. There is no discipline. In the old days we had it, but there were many who did not like it, and tried to get away from it, trekking north to escape from it.'

'That's a dig at us,' smiled Conroy. 'I won't say you are wrong, Uncle. We have at any rate paid dearly for it. But even ordinary things, ordinary to you and me, are strange to them, and it is sometimes ludicrous to see what mistakes are made. I remember an instance which may amuse you. We had captured a small convoy, and the men looted the wagons. Every one took what he wanted, and there was plenty for all. I saw an old chap riding off with a Blickensdorfer portable typewriter, and wondered what he wanted to do with it, for the old fellow couldn't write. The next morning I met him and he called out to me, 'Say, son, I have been playing this auto-harp all day, and I can't get a note out of it. You might have a look at it and see what's wrong.'

The anecdote effectually dispelled the nuance of seriousness that young Rekker's reference to the invasion of the Colony had imparted to the conversation. They pressed for more, and Egmond told them tales of commando happenings, of the long rides through the park-like lowveld, where in mid-winter the air is mellow, and the hill slopes are symphonies of russet and gold, and in summer the tall monkey thorn trees are ribboned with the crimson-fruited creeper, of adventures on the highveld with its interminable stretches of wearisome, monotonously green grass. He talked well, without disparagement of the men he had fought against, and without undue emphasis upon the prowess of his own side, sliding rapidly over the personal and concentrating upon the general.

When they retired for the night, Storam and the prisoner of war shared the big guest room, with its quaint headpiece of carved wood. That, too, was customary and traditional. The room smelt pleasantly of raw linseed oil rubbed on the cedarwood furniture, and on the dressing-table Mrs Rekker junior had placed a porringer filled with early roses.

'I suppose,' said the magistrate, as he stooped down to unlace his boots, 'I mustn't ask you the one question I am burning to ask?'

'That I can't answer until I know what it is,' rejoined Conroy, with his pleasant, humorous smile. 'You should be the best judge of what I may talk about. I hope I have not been indiscreet tonight ...'

'You have been discretion itself. Let me congratulate you on your powers of description. You should have been a war correspondent, young fellow.'

'And I failed for my matric, Sir. I merely told them what I had seen.'

'That I can well understand. And you need not have matriculated to be able to use your eyes and your tongue. Can I help you?'

'Don't trouble, sir, I can manage very well, by holding on to the table. What is your question?'

'You ought to guess it, Egmond. But as you won't, I'll ask it. How long do you think this business is going to go on? And what do you people imagine you are going to get by prolonging it? There, don't reply if you'd rather not. I admit it is an unfair question.'

'I don't know, Sir. Honestly, I really don't know. Personally, I should say it is all over bar the shouting, when I think of some things. And then, again, I should say it is just about starting in earnest when my mind switches back to other things. Between them I am incapable of judging.'

'You think the Republics can continue in the field and make effective resistance?'

'As they are doing now, well yes, sir. You see, they have no lines of communication to keep up; they are mobile, much more so than the troops. And they know the country. Those are great advantages, Sir.'

'If that was all, Egmond, I should feel fairly easy. But I do not. You heard what young Rekker asked you. Very well, that is what makes me devilishly uneasy. I'll be frank with you. I admire what you people have done in the field, where you have proved yourselves as wise and capable—with a few exceptions, of course—as you showed yourselves clumsy and impotent in the negotiations. You need not agree with that, of course, but it's my opinion all the same. But what I do not admire, what I very much condemn indeed, is the way in which you led so many poor devils into rebellion, knowing full well that they and not you would have to bear the consequences. That I find hard to forgive, and what makes me uneasy, Egmond, is the thought that you might try it on again.'

'I have never thought about it from that point of view, Sir. Honestly I haven't. You see, we naturally looked to all Dutch-speaking South Africa to sympathise with us, and when we proclaimed these districts—we did that in Natal, I remember, but I know nothing about what happened in the Colony for I wasn't there—we naturally thought that we had safeguarded them by making them *burghers* ...'

'Surely you weren't so foolish as to think that, young man? A subject cannot throw off his allegiance so easily. Only duress can force him to overt treason, but in these cases, so far as I have heard, there has been no actual force or restraint used.'

'Now you point it out, I see what you mean, Sir. Of course, they need not have joined us. In Natal they didn't ...'

'That is a subterfuge, Egmond. You know that most of those who joined were of the lowest class of farm hand, *bywoners*, ignorant and illiterate. Everyone of them could have been shot. If they hadn't surrendered under Brabant's proclamation, they would have been, too. And you know what means were used to make them join.'

'I hardly think you need be afraid of anything like that happening again, Sir. People will be more cautious now.'

'I am not so sure about that. And I tell you again that that sort of thing will defeat you more quickly than anything else. There are many people here who sympathise with the Boers—up to a point. Between you and me, I do myself—up to a point. But don't stretch that point, my boy. You may play old Harry if you like within your own borders, but ... There, I won't say another word on that subject. It makes me too mad. But you haven't answered my question yet.'

'I did, so far as I'm able to, Sir. Of course, there are many of us who look to something happening abroad—some intervention by the other powers ...'

'You may put that out of your mind at once. There is no likelihood of such a thing happening.'

'That's what I think too, Sir. But there it is, some of us believe in it. Just as they believe that something may happen here in the Colony. Do you know, Sir, Uhlmann's brother-in-law suggested from the first that our forces should sweep down to Cape Town and occupy the ports and the lines of communication.'

'That would have been sound strategy,' remarked the magistrate. 'Much better from your point of view, and much worse from ours, than annexing a few districts on the border and forcing our citizens into rebellion. But the time for all that has passed. I don't see how you can possibly hold out against Kitchener's force.'

'Neither do I, Sir,' said Conroy, getting into bed, 'but few of us would entertain the idea of unconditional surrender just now. They might listen to proposals, but what sort of proposals are we likely to get? England can't very well withdraw the proclamation annexing the Republics, and to accept anything short of some shred of independence ... well, I don't see our people agreeing to that.'

'Still, it must come to that finally,' argued the magistrate, getting in on his side. 'Ugh—I do dislike feather beds. I suppose this sort of thing is customary up your way too.'

'With the old folk, yes, Sir. But we are not really behind the times up there. My own farm is quite up to date, I assure you, and if you favour me with a visit after the war, you shall have twin bedsteads and a spring mattress.'

'There mightn't be any farm left if this goes on,' grumbled the magistrate as he drew the coverlet over him. 'The Lord only knows what may happen if your people don't come to their senses.'

'Would you take it very much amiss if I retorted "if yours didn't come to theirs," Sir?'

'No, I shouldn't, young man. It's six of one and half-a-dozen of the other. But it's devilish trying, all the same. Good night to you.'

Chapter 26

Andrew Quakerley's Christmas, like most others in the Village, was not a joyous one, but it could not be said to have been a gloomy festival. Conroy's presence at the table brought the realities of war closer to all those who sat down to the turkey and plum pudding that convention had decreed should figure on the menu. The prisoner of war had improved vastly during the few months he had spent in the Village; he could now limp about without his crutch, and although his physique was of that lank, bony kind which only puts on superfluous fat with old age, the rest and the good living that he enjoyed had restored colour to his pale face, and smoothed out some of the premature folds around his mouth and eyes.

His conduct had been unexceptional and continued to be so. At first he had attended Mr Uhlmann's services in the Dutch Reformed Church, for after all there was nothing in his parole that prevented him from joining in the devotions of the church of which he was a member. But both the parson and the magistrate realised that such attendance, in the peculiar circumstances, had an effect which could not be looked upon as altogether satisfactory. The wounded prisoner of war was a constant object of commiserating sympathy for the congregation, and it was inevitable that his presence in church should stir men's feelings and lead them, however unwittingly, to read more in Mr Uhlmann's carefully impartial references to the calamity of war that overshadowed the Colony. It was difficult to put the matter into words, and Mr Storam felt that he had no right to speak to Conroy on the subject. But he broached it with old Andrew and found the old man quite in accord with him on his main argument.

'The difficulty,' said Andrew, meditatively, 'is to suggest a way out. Would it suit you, Storam, if Conroy alternated between Uhlmann and the rector's services? We used to attend both formerly. My dad, as you perhaps may not know, sometimes attended the Dutch Reformed Church and sometimes the English service, just as he pleased.'

'It is not a question of what suits me, Mr Quakerley,' answered the magistrate. 'I was merely thinking of the effect that he has upon the congregation as a whole, and I suppose it would be much the same even if he attended the rector's evening service. He would still go to the Dutch Reformed Church in the morning.'

'But you cannot prevent him from attending. That, surely, would be asking too much, Storam.'

The magistrate shifted uneasily on his chair. He saw the difficulties, and no way out of them.

'I thought,' he suggested, half-heartedly, 'that you might speak to him, Mr Quakerley. It would come better from you than from me.'

'Yes, but what do you suggest? I can quite see your point. You think his presence is emotionally disturbing.'

'The whole position is anomalous, Mr Quakerley. Egmond is an exceptionally acceptable parole prisoner, but that only makes the position more awkward for us all. My own view has always been that combatant prisoners of war—and I would even add, civilians on parole—are better away from an environment where their presence is likely to rouse active sympathy. All sorts of difficulties are likely to arise. I did not realise that when I tried to help him to come here, and now it is rather too late in the day to raise objections. I see that, but I still think that no great harm would be done if you were to put our point of view to him, and let him decide for himself.'

'Very well. I will do that. Have you any further news, Storam? Not bad, I sincerely hope.'

'Nothing good, anyway. I cannot tell you much, but that is simply because I do not know much. There are rumours, however, that things are not going well, and there is some evidence that two Republican commandos cannot be definitely located, and that the probability is that they are on their way towards the Colony.'

'I doubt that. I doubt it very much, Storam. They would be running right into the net if they did that.'

'Don't be too sure. The Colony is admirably suited for guerrilla tactics—it is, in parts at least, much less open than the Free State or the Transvaal. From all accounts, both the Transvaal and the Free State are untenable to them.'

'That is so. I hope all is not true that one hears. That confiscation proclamation ... I can't get over that, Storam. It is too low-down ...'

'You need not pay much attention to that, Mr Quakerley. It seems to me it was merely a threatening gesture, as abortive as it was silly. Technically, of course, it is perfectly legal. The Republics are now British possessions, and their subjects British subjects ...'

'Isn't that exactly on a par with what the Boers did when they invaded our territory, Storam?'

'No, not quite. Ours is effective occupation. Our civil administration functions in both states; the Queen's writ runs in both. Legally that makes all the difference. But in practice, of course, there is a similarity, and if the Boers re-conquered their territory they could, and probably would, regard the proclamation as null and void, and deal with those who acted upon it very much in the same way that we are dealing with our Colonial rebels.'

'In other words, law and right do not count for much. Only effective force counts.'

'I am afraid that is the case. But it has always been so. That is one of the reasons why guaranteed independence is, to my mind, practically valueless. One must have the power to defend one's independence. The very word implies that, doesn't it?'

'Quite. But what you have just told me is damnably disturbing, Storam—I mean the possibility of a new invasion of the Colony. Do you seriously think that there is anything in it?'

'Frankly, I do not know. I doubt very much if they have the enterprise and the—I suppose I must say pluck, although it would be effrontery more than pluck to do such a thing. If they came here ...'

'Good God, man. They are not likely to do that. Why, we are a good thousand miles away from them, and there are the mountains in between. Besides, what are they going to get when they come here? There's no column operating hereabouts, and we are far from the railway. There is no object in their coming here.'

'Their one object would be to give as much trouble as possible to the troops. Operating in a district like ours ...'

'Don't for goodness sake harp on that. It is out of the question.'

'In a district like ours,' went on the magistrate, calmly, ignoring old Andrew's irritable interruption, 'they would be operating in a field that is exceedingly difficult for anyone but a mounted rifleman to work effectively. Infantry columns would be of no use, no use whatever. The only way to cope with them would be to adopt the same principle that Kitchener has adopted up north, and that is to erect a line of block-houses along the main roads, and corral them bit by bit. It would take up time, and they would be working in an enemy's country where some, at least, of the enemy would be sympathisers. You see the difficulties, Mr Quakerley.'

'But you do not mean to tell me that our people here would help them, Storam? Sympathy is all very well, but they can't live on that.'

'Our people might be forced to help them. And then it would not stop at sympathy. They would get supplies, information, assistance, in many ways. It would be a terrible position, I grant you, and I sincerely share your hope that it will not come to that. Between you and me, Mr Quakerley, I am very uneasy about the matter.'

'Have you put it to your committee, Storam?'

'I mean to do so. You know we removed all the arms more than a year ago, and I have had them make out a list of what remains in private possession. I shall suggest that even private guns and rifles be given up—handed over to me for despatch to Cape Town with, of course, the promise that the owners will receive them back after peace has been declared.'

'Yes, that is a very good move. I think there are a couple of sporting rifles somewhere in my house. I haven't used them for years, and you are welcome to them. And there must be many on the farms.'

Old Andrew spoke to his guest, and Conroy fell in readily enough with the suggestion.

'Now I come to think of it,' he remarked, with a smile, 'there is something in it. I really did not know that I was making a public exhibition of myself, and I can well understand that it is not quite playing the game.'

'It's making a lot of fuss about a very little thing,' declared Mrs Quakerley, angrily, tossing her lace cap in the correct early Victorian way to express her indignation. 'As if it mattered one little bit what these people think. We know that in their hearts they are all rebels, and whether you are there or not, Conroy my dear, they will just go on praying for the success of the Boers and maligning His Excellency. If I were you I should go to church as often as I pleased. Not that I agree with what Mr Uhlmann preaches, and perhaps it would be better for you to go to Mr Mance-Bisley's services ...'

'I'll go with you whenever you want me, Aunt Alice,' said Conroy, gallantly, for he knew that Mrs Quakerley rarely went to evening service. She much preferred to doze in her chair at home, and had been known, in the early days of the rector's ritualistic activity, to express herself very strongly against 'Popish practice.' Since the outbreak of the war she had been more regular in her attendance, but that was due entirely to the fact that she identified the rector's church with what was loyal and superbly English and Mr Uhlmann's with everything that was its rebellious and unrighteous antithesis.

The year that had begun, from Mrs Quakerley's point of view, so well with the surrender of Cronje at Paardeberg and the effacement of the stain that Majuba had left, ended with what even Alice, with all her enthusiasm, could not regard as eminently satisfactory. There were set-backs and little disasters, not important in themselves but disturbing in their general effect, and annoyingly irritating, because their cumulative evidence showed that the Boer forces were still active. It was the activity of hornets chased away from their nests, of mosquitoes incessantly buzzing around, whose wearisome drone made rest and quiet impossible. The Government called for more volunteers, to release the regulars from guarding the lines of communication threatened by these marauding troops. Marshall's Horse, a Colonial force, was raised, and even the pro-Boer paper published in Cape Town contained large government advertisements offering five shillings a day for recruits to the Imperial Light Horse.

Sir Alfred Milner received a viscountcy, and meek Sir Walter Hely Hutchinson came down from Natal to assume the Governorship of the Colony, while his greater predecessor went north and remained Her Majesty's High Commissioner. At Cape Town the Sprigg ministry administered the government without the help of Parliament, and the opposition held meetings which were misreported in the press. The opposition, now solidly ranged against its former chief who, with one or two followers, philosophised in his cave of Adullam, had decided to send a deputation to England to appeal for more favourable terms for the Boers. In the District the news caused a brief flicker of excitement, and the Committee sought Mr Storam's advice on the question of supporting the deputation. Such support could only be financial and moral, and there was no objection to its being given. The District thought that Her Majesty's arms had been vindicated, and that a prolongation of the war was both unnecessary and un-Christian, and it saw no harm or disloyalty in expressing that thought and in sending its pennies to Cape Town towards the fund for the deputation.

Renselaar, the more active of the two local members, went about soliciting subscriptions, and had no difficulty in obtaining them. Old Andrew gave twenty-five pounds, merely stipulating that his name should not figure on the list to save him from acrimonious criticism from Alice. Old Martin Rekker gave ten pounds, and Mias Swart fetched a five pound note from his hoard in the mill-house, while the quack doctor contributed a couple of guineas with the cynical observation that they were the profits of a few bottles of Mattei's electricity which he had sold to Elias Vantloo, who had refused to subscribe. For Elias was now a wealthy fellow, having made much money out of his contracts with the military authorities. He swaggered about in a tailor-made suit, and drove a Cape cart with two splendid Hantam horses, and was understood to have matrimonial ambitions centreing round the daughter of old Jeremiah Gerster, who lived on the farm *Eisleben* and was reputed to be one of the richest men in the District.

'I do not see what good can come of the deputation,' Martin Rekker had said when he gave his donation, 'but it cannot do any harm. And there must be money, so you may have ten pounds, Renselaar.'

'Yes,' said the member, 'that, too, is our opinion, but you see, Uncle Martin, there is a possibility that they might influence public opinion in England. England is war-weary. She would like to end the war if she could. Every day it goes on costs her more money—hundreds of thousands, they say ...'

'Even if it cost millions,' said old Rekker, stubbornly, 'she can afford it. Don't tell me she can't. I am not a child, Nephew Renselaar. I know what this war means to her. As much, belike, as to us, although in a different sense.'

'You were always a bit English-minded, if you'll forgive me saying so, Uncle Martin,' said the member.

'No more English-minded than you are,' retorted the old farmer, quickly. 'No more so than the magistrate is, or Mr Quakerley. But I never held with those that thought all that Paul Kruger did was right, and all that Alexandrina Victoria's servants did was wrong. I have my intelligence, Nephew, and when I saw how things were going, I saw that we were sliding down a decline just as rapidly as the small boys slide down a shoot on the buttertrees. And it is not so easy to stop yourself when you are sliding on a buttertree, Nephew, as you perhaps know.'

'Still,' retorted the member, writing Rekker's name down on his list, 'it is well that we should put our view before the English public. They do not know that this is civil war, and that the longer it goes on, the less likely it is that we shall have peace ...'

'There I agree with you,' said the old man, reflectively. 'And that is why I give you ten pounds. You may have more if there is need for more, but if everyone gives his mite, there should be no difficulty in paying for the deputation. And perhaps they may effect something. I doubt if they will, but there is no harm in trying. What are they to ask for, by the way?'

'We want the war ended, Uncle Martin, but we do not want the Republics to be crushed. They must retain some degree of independence. It will be difficult to plan— we know that—but it should not be impossible ...'

'You should talk to Mr Quakerley,' said old Rekker. 'He knows about such things. He has influential family relations over the water, and you must remember, Nephew, that he is also allied to us by close ties of kin.'

'I have seen him, Uncle Martin. He is quite sympathetic. He has given us twenty-five pounds—more than anyone else has given. But he is breaking up, don't you think? Why, he must be close on eighty now.'

'He is good for many years yet,' replied Martin. 'I, too, am not a chicken, but he can give me points. As erect and as strong as his father was, though Old Quakerley didn't reach that age. But he comes from a long-lived family on his mother's side as well. So he agreed with you?'

'He did not quite agree. He sympathised. He said it could do no harm, though, like you, he doubted if it would do any good.'

'Aye, he is an understanding man, is Quakerley. But I daresay they can make speeches and show what things are like here. Hofmeyr—he has been over there for months now, and he has done nothing. But Sauer ... if anyone can do anything, it is he. What a pity it is that you have not got Schreiner as well ...'

'He is impossible,' said Renselaar, angrily. 'He let us down, Uncle, he let us terribly down. If he had remained firm ...'

'Then the fat would have been in the fire, Nephew. Nay, he should have resigned earlier. That would have been a good thing, a grand gesture. He would have shown them then that we did not like the war, and that we would not have anything to do with it ... But there, what is the good of talking about it? Now, I see nothing for it but to go on.'

'I don't think it will go on long,' said Mr Renselaar, confidently. 'From what we hear, there is only one strong commando in the field, and that is the one under Botha. The others will be rounded up in time, and will have to surrender. And it is better that there is an end now when there is something to be saved. Then we can go on afresh ...'

'No, Nephew, you must not talk that kind of talk here. It has struck me when reading our papers how some of us harp on that matter ... as if we are one with those who are fighting, and as if their cause is our cause. It is not so. Before this war came we had no cause to complain; we had no quarrel with England. I speak as one who knows. I have lived for seventy years and more and done my duty to Alexandrina Victoria, and I have no grievance against them. And I do not like this talk of grievances that do not exist, Nephew, and this pretence that if the Transvaal loses, we too lose.'

'If the Transvaal loses,' declared the member, roused by this rebuke, 'it means that our Afrikander nationhood is lost ...'

'Our Afrikander nationhood existed long before the Transvaal was heard of,' interrupted old Martin, drily. 'We fought for our rights here, and we have our rights. We have nothing to learn from the Transvaal, but it seems to me, Nephew, the Transvaal has still much to learn from us. And the matter, so far as the Transvaal is concerned, is settled. She has lost. She lost on the day when she flung down that presumptuous challenge, in which she dared to speak not for herself only, but for us all who did not ask her to be our champion.'

Chapter 27

He sat in a grass chair in the shade of the big magnolia. It was a gorgeous January morning. There had been a soft shower of rain during the previous night, which is rare in January but generously welcome. The parched veld had been lightly sprayed, and exhaled a soft, sweet, earthy smell, that mingled with with scents of the flowers in the herbaceous borders, where pink godetias, multi-coloured zinnias, and crimson and blue verbenas blossomed in profusion. The splendidly polished leaves of the magnolia threw a deep shadow on the ground, and from where he sat, Andrew, looking up through the branches, could see the large, waxy buds and blooms between the leaves, and beyond them the tall cliffs of the mountains, outlined against a sky of pellucid blue.

He sat huddled in his chair, his fingers still idly retaining their grasp on the newspaper which he had opened at the breakfast table. He had glanced at the news columns without much interest. He had not expected to find much to interest him. The usual inspired notes about the progress of the various columns, stray bits of sensation from Johannesburg, the short, incomplete casualty lists that mentioned the names of places which had never before figured in the news—these he had looked for and found. But his eye had lighted upon a splashed paragraph, the reading of which had evoked emotions long dormant with that painfulness that we experience when something touches our heart-strings.

Alexandrina Victoria lay dying at Osborne!

His mind went back to the day when as a boy he had first heard her name. He recalled the occasion quite easily, although it was sixty-four years ago. He remembered how his father had read the proclamation, reverently, as one honouring an authority greater even than that of the family, and how, for many years, the rudely printed paper had been given the post of the privileged among the framed documents hanging on the study wall in the old farmhouse at *Quakerskloof*. He could even recall some of its phrasing, for he had learned it by heart, conning its print over and over again because his father had attached so much importance to it. Now some of the paragraphs flashed before his eyes as they roamed over the herbaceous borders, seeing not the coloured blossoms but merely the heavy lines of black print.

'Whereas it has pleased Almighty God to call to His Mercy our Late Sovereign Lord King William the Fourth of blessed and glorious memory, by whose decease the Imperial Crown of the United Kingdom of Great Britain and Ireland is solely and rightfully come to the High and Mighty Princess Alexandrina Victoria saving the rights of any issue of his Late Majesty King William the Fourth which may be born of His Late Majesty's Consort.

We, therefore, the Governor of this Colony of the Cape of Good Hope, assisted by the Members of the Councils and Members of the Civil and Military Authorities and principal inhabitants of the Colony do now hereby with one voice and consent of tongue and heart publish and proclaim that the High and Mighty Princess Alexandrina Victoria is now by the death of our Late Sovereign of happy memory our one lawful and rightful Liege Lady Victoria by the Grace of God of the United Kingdom of Great Britain and Ireland and of this Colony of the Cape of Good Hope and the Dependencies thereof Queen ... Defender of the Faith, saving as aforesaid.

To Whom, saving as aforesaid, we do acknowledge all faith and constant obedience with all hearty and humble affection, beseeching Almighty God by Whom Kings and Queens do reign to bless the Royal Princess Victoria with long and happy years to reign over us.'

And now Alexandrina Victoria lay dying at Osborne!

He remembered how late in the day that proclamation had been issued—in September, although Her Majesty had been lawfully acknowledged in May—and how much the District had argued about the matter. Some had held that there was no precedent for a woman reigning over the Colony. Old Mr Uhlmann, the pastor's father, had consulted Mr Quakerley, Andrew's father, about what steps should be taken to regularise the position of Colonists who, like himself, were subjects of England by virtue of naturalisation in Hanover. He remembered that there had been quite a pother about that matter. Mr Attorney Porter—a good man but fearfully obstinate in some things—had flatly denied that a Hanoverian subject was an English subject, and that, too, in the face of the ruling of the counsel for the Crown in England who had held a contrary opinion. Mr Attorney Porter's opinion had prevailed—he was an excellent lawyer though an obstinate man, and Irish—and Mr Uhlmann and the other Hanoverian Colonists had had to be re-naturalised. Of course it had made no great difference, just as little as the mild expostulation of the District against the accession of a woman sovereign had made any difference. And for sixty years at least Alexandrina Victoria had reigned over them, and they had given her all faith and constant obedience with all hearty and humble affection. Of that there could be no shadow of doubt—for sixty years!

And now Alexandrina Victoria lay dying at Osborne!

And in her Colony of the Cape of Good Hope there were disunion and dissension, tradition opposed to tradition, kinsmen against kinsmen in the field, subjects imprisoned for treason, citizens suspected of rebellion, men's minds in a turmoil of doubt and perplexity, civil war ...

He cast his mind, without a conscious effort, back to those early days, contrasting and comparing the present with the past. Then there had been no question of the sincerity of their loving affection and humble obedience. There had been times—he called to mind the vehemence of the anti-convict agitation, and the passions engendered by the local differences between east and west that had at one time threatened a division of interest—when the national emotion of a Colony ripe for self-government had been profoundly stirred by the mistakes and trivial interferences of Downing Street, but these could not be compared with the deeper emotions that now surged, like an undertow on some dangerous coast, below the apparently calm surface of their lives. The war and, perhaps more than the war, the events that had preceded the outbreak of the war, had stirred these deeper passions, which had made some of her subjects forget the loyal obedience and faith they owed her. Not perhaps in the District, and certainly not in the Village, Andrew reflected. There her example, her personality, her prestige had always evoked loyal and sympathetic response. No one there had forgotten, when her crowning day came round, to beseech Almighty God by whom Kings and Queens do reign, to bless her with long and happy years to reign.

And now Alexandrina Victoria lay dying at Osborne!

The news had come with almost the same astounding suddenness as the declaration of war. There had been no preparatory communiqués, and at Christmas time she had been hale and hearty, although, being old and spent with years, her time could not be far off. Like him, she could not look for many more years, but like him, too, she had always been strong, never ailing in a manner to inspire anxiety. But these cables were very definite. Guardedly worded though they were, there could be no mistake about their import. The Queen was dying.

He wondered if the event of her death would affect the war. It was inexpressibly sad that she should end her reign while her vast empire was beating down the resistance of two small states, and her loyal subjects of her Colony of the Cape of Good Hope were being burdened by circumstances they could not deflect or change. It had been a long and glorious reign, in which the glory far outshone the slight shadows that had been cast by temporary disasters or passing humiliations. There had been that awful mutiny in India—there had been the fall of Khartoum and the death of Gordon—there had been Majuba and the Raid.

What did they matter, after all, in the sum of what had made her reign glorious in the history of Great Britain, prolific in goodness, in human progress, in real and lasting betterment of whatever counted in human values? A broad all-pervading, all-impregnating liberalism had been the keynote of that reign, an influence of far-reaching toleration, a potent fertiliser to that great tradition of fair play and fair dealing which had made England strong among the world's nations and ensured her the respect even of her opponents. A glorious reign, marred, at the ending, by what seemed a negation of much that had made it glorious, by a tragedy no less tragic because it was limited to one corner of the Empire and to a handful of Alexandrina Victoria's subjects.

Her death, he reflected sadly, would not, could not, affect that tragedy. It would merely add one more poignant reminder of the difference between that far-away September when she had been proclaimed Queen of her Colony of the Cape of Good Hope, and today when that Colony was directly involved in civil war. No one could blame her for that. One could only pity, sympathise, and pay to her passing the homage that one owed to a life and a personality so vivid, so exemplary, and so nobly a typification of sovereign womanhood.

He had never seen her, and now that she was passing away, he regretted that he had not seen her. He could so easily have seen her, even spoken to her, kissed her hand, perhaps not with the same grace as that with which his father would have rendered that homage, but certainly with dignity and with hearty and humble affection. Alice had had that privilege, but he had never been to England, and had felt no inclination to visit his father's home. Joan had been, and had told him much about the beauty of riverside and green meadow lands, but for him his garden had been all-sufficient. Perhaps too sufficient, for after all a man of family had obligations, duties. It was quaint to think that in this war he had obligations to both sides, if ties of family counted for anything. On his mother's side he had, he supposed, some fifty kinsmen who were *burghers* of the Republics; on his father's as many who were actively engaged in the war, although in neither case had he kept in touch with them. He had had a letter from a cousin, an officer in the Suffolks wounded in the action at Labuschagne's Nek, and Alice kept a roll of honour on which she wrote down the names of other relatives whose names had figured in the casualty lists. She had been to Cape Town and had been entertained at Mount Nelson Hotel by a spruce grand-cousin and had returned home highly indignant with Lord Kitchener for having ignored that promising scion of the house of Quakerley. What a mess-up it was.

From the old oaks came the chattering of the red winged starlings, and from the orchard the shrill cheep of the finches looting the ripe figs. On the air hung the cool reek of the rain-washed soil, gradually dispersing before the heat of the sun. From where he sat he could see his wife talking to Mrs Mance-Bisley on the *stoep*. He knew they were discussing the news. Everyone would be discussing it. Alexandrina Victoria's passing would overshadow even the war news, but the war would still go on ...

He knew how the District and the Village would take it. To both the Queen had been a great exemplar, almost an ideal. They had carefully refused to identify her with the war, preferring to believe that she had had no immediate part in bringing it about, and that she sorrowed with them because of it, and prayed for its ending. They recognised her helplessness. That was the tragedy of it all, that hopeless helplessness when she and they were eager to help, with no possibility of helping. In their prayers they had always remembered her. He could not, would not, believe that hypocrisy tinged those prayers, and that even the war had quenched that affectionate respect with which she was regarded by all. And lately there had been evidence that where she could make her influence felt she had not hesitated to use it. The District had, rightly or wrongly, presumed that it was by express royal command that the Maori contingent, offered by loyal New Zealand, had been tactfully declined. That meant, people said, that the Queen felt that Colonial tradition should be respected, and they honoured her for that solicitude.

Her birthday in the past year, the first time when its celebration fell in the war period, had been very quietly remembered. For the first time in its history the Village made no high holiday, shot no salvoes, and did not marshal its mounted commando. The magistrate and the committee discussed the matter at length and came to the unanimous conclusion that such outward display of loyalty was unnecessary, and that as meetings were not to be held for other public purposes it would be undesirable to have the customary celebrations on the square in front of the gaol. There had been considerable opposition to this decision, and the Loyal Ladies' League had entered a protest against it. But the committee had had its way, and though the flags had been hoisted and the committee had sent, in the name of the District and on its behalf, a loyal congratulatory telegram to the High Commissioner, there had been no fireworks and no illumination. Miss Marradee had reported to her paper that this was the work of the Bond party, but the Village had been tolerant as usual, and had let it go at that. Miss Marradee was an enthusiastic local correspondent, but no one took her communications seriously, and everyone felt that she had to do something to earn her commission, or whatever it was that she got for sending stray scraps of news to the press.

Andrew knew that the omission to celebrate the Queen's birthday in the past year had not been due to any disloyalty or want of that faith and constant obedience which the proclamation of 1837 had acknowledged, but merely to the committee's anxious desire to do nothing that might in any way stir feeling at a time of emotional stress. He had thoroughly grasped their point of view, and had been in cordial agreement with it, although it clashed with the pronounced opinions his wife had expressed on the subject. It had seemed to him that a lip loyalty needing emphatic demonstration was of no value either way, for it could not prove passive loyalty and could add nothing to active loyalty manifesting itself everywhere in deeds. Even in the Transvaal the Queen had been personally respected and her birthday celebrated before the war. Alexandrina Victoria's prestige was untouched. As a resplendent, royal figure she would keep her place in the memories and affections of all her subjects, no matter whether the machinations of Joseph Chamberlain or Cecil John Rhodes disturbed the Empire, or President Kruger dreamed of a South African Republic from Quoing Point to the Zambesi.

There would be hushed voices and reverent whisperings on the District farms when the news of her passing became known. The portrait in the dining-room, showing her as the jubilee Queen with a tiny crown on her head and a fan in her hand, would be ringed round with crepe. Some would place a gardenia flower, emblem of mourning, below the frame. All would be reverent, respectful, sad, speaking in softened voices to show that they felt her passing. For Alexandrina Victoria, who now lay dying at Osborne, had been for sixty-four years a queen, beloved, respected, and honoured by those who on that day in September 1837 had acknowledged all faith and humble obedience to her, and by their children and their children's children who had grown up in a tradition that had made her more than a mere name to them.

Of that there could be no doubt. Andrew, as he sat in the shade of the magnolia tree, felt curiously saddened, as if something personal had gone out of his life, and in his calm, dispassionate way he tried to analyse his feeling. He had never been a royalist more royal than the King. He had accepted her sovereignty as something unquestionable, natural and legal, just as he had accepted the Gregorian calendar and the validity of the laws that the Colonial Parliament passed. Some things were axiomatically simple, and belief in them strained no one's credulity; some things were the reverse, and there were, of course, other things that lay in a borderland between the two, where argument for or against was allowable. There was, for instance, the question of whether plants really benefited from the manure given them; he had often thought about that matter, and although empirically it was almost a foregone conclusion that they did, something could be said in favour of the opposite view. So, constitutionally, something could be said in favour of the Republican institutions, and in theory it could be argued that a sovereign six thousand miles away was a useless extravagance, whose hold on the affections of subjects, to whom her immediate entourage appeared to be composed of foreigners, would inevitably dwindle and finally become extinct. But he himself had never approached the subject from that point of view. In all his discussions with those who had championed the Native-born's interpretation of nationalism, Andrew had consistently maintained that the Crown stood above and outside constitutional quarrels. To him Alexandrina Victoria had symbolised that silken tie, elastic, slender, and far-stretched, which bound the isolated communities originally settled from the mother-lands of Europe to the only mother they had ever known. The time might come when both mother and offspring would no longer need even a coloured ribbon attachment to prove their oneness, but when it came the separation would be by agreement, a friendly devolution of duty, not a frigid repudiation of filial affection in favour of self-interest. The figure of the great Queen, emblematical of the life of the mother-land, of its routine, even of its prejudices and passions, its conventionality, formalism, conservatism, awkward liberalism, exploitive commercialism, insular standoffishness, dominated his mind-picture of the relations between the Colony and England. So long as that figure stood there, to be revered and loved because of its historical and traditional associations, there could be no question of cutting the painter, if such severance meant anything that could infringe on the respect that was felt for the Queen and all that she represented as Queen.

There had been times in the past when old Quakerley, his father, had expressed sentiments as distinctly adverse to Downing Street rule as those now being bruited about by men who knew far less about the real facts of the case than the old aristocrat had known. At the time of the anti-convict agitation such sentiments were almost general in the Colony, and Andrew had felt himself mildly stirred by them. They had not changed his creed, for he had always looked upon the Queen as distinct from her government, as one who stood outside Party controversies and diplomatic wranglings, serenely conscious of her obligations towards all her subjects in her wide-flung Empire. The war had demanded a readjustment of his conception of such obligations, but it had not materially interfered with his ideal. He still held that England was a great country, potent for good, still exemplifying that large-minded toleration which was the tradition of gentlemen. Passing events might smudge that picture, but the stains were not ineffaceable, and so long as the Queen lived, a great lady in the best sense of the word, that tradition would be respected and honoured.

He thought as he sat there of her own personal sorrows in which so many of them had vicariously shared—the death of her Consort, of her son-in-law, of her grandson. On those occasions of grief, men and women in the Colony had sorrowed with her, remembering her trial in their prayers, beseeching Almighty God by Whom Kings and Queens do reign and Who had been pleased to inflict on her unhappiness such as is the lot of all mankind, to endow her with strength and faith and fortitude. When some mad fellow had shot at her, they had joined in a demonstration to show their loyalty towards her person and what she symbolised, and their detestation of the miscreant's action. Then there had been no talk of conspiracy and rebellion and treason. Even when, twenty years ago, the shadow of war had fallen over South Africa, threatening as much as was now lamentable reality, their faith in her had not swerved, and when her government had shown its magnanimity they had applauded it as a signal proof of her own good sense of what was fair and just and honourable. No doubt she had been actuated by as noble and kindly motives during these long months of war; no doubt she felt, as they did, that it was a calamity that the closing years of her reign should be clouded by mistakes, disasters, and disturbance. But she had been helpless to prevent war, as she was helpless to mitigate its suffering or lessen the burden that it laid on her loyal subjects at the Cape. That was her tragedy as much as it was theirs, and in their introspective self-pity they could spare a thought for her.

And because he realised that the Queen could not interfere, Andrew felt his heart go out in sympathy to her now that she lay dying at Osborne. He could imagine how conflicting must have been her emotions when the arbitrament of war had been forced upon her, and he was fair-minded enough to agree that if she had had any say in the matter war would not have come in the way it did. She would have liked to end her reign in peace, to have all her subjects united in their sorrow at her passing rather than to crave from them part of the mourning for so many others, friends and relatives, killed in the war. It was pitifully tragic that that should now be the case, and that the great Queen should not get the undivided lamentation of her people.

And were they her people? He himself, born of an English father and a Dutch mother, Native-born with all home ties here in the country of his birth, with merely a fast-fading sentimental attachment to his father's homeland, could he be considered hers, as he considered her his, his Queen, the personification of a vague ideal formed by tradition and fostered by boyhood's memories? How often in the past fifteen months had he been harassed by doubts, perplexed by fears, and worried by despondencies, just because the appeal of tradition seemed to clash with the hard, saddening facts. And his position was easier, far, than that of many other of her subjects—men like Martin Rekker, being Native-born, had lost grip of their parents' ideals and acquired new birthright, and made for themselves new privileges. He could still point with pride to what England had achieved in the past; her honour was still something that mattered to him; injustice and wrong on her part could still by him be felt as a personal disgrace.

Those others could have no such sentiment, for to them all that mattered was South Africa. They had retained their affection for the Queen, but it was a personal, individual affection, which did not extend, he supposed, to the length his own was prepared to go. Like the faint, terrestrial smell that lingered in the shade of the magnolia tree, it would be dispersed before the burning heat of national sentiment evoked by this horrible war, just as the cool fragrance of the morning air, tempered by last night's rain, would be overwhelmed by the midday sun's heat. Some might say that that was inevitable, but he doubted the fact. There was no inerrancy in a creed such as his that made loyalty to his father's homeland compatible with an equal loyalty to his own. It was a question of degree, of adjustment, of common sense. Alexandrina Victoria, who now lay dying at Osborne, was an example of such divided but unmitigated loyalties.

But what a mess-up it was—what a mess-up!

He sat for long under the magnolia tree, and when the maid came to summon him to luncheon she found that he had dropped asleep with his hand still clasping the newspaper.

'The Old Master,' reported the maid in the kitchen, 'is sure getting older every day.'

Chapter 28

Two days later church bells tolled and flags were dragged down to half-mast. Alexandrina Victoria had died at Osborne.

The cables had prepared the Village for that event, but even with such preliminary warning the news came as a shock. The Village and District mourned, not ostentatiously, but sincerely, with a simple humility of reverence that proved more convincingly than any demonstrations how deeply they felt her passing.

Memorial services were held in the Dutch Reformed and in the English church, and to both came members of all sections of the community. As in peace time they had celebrated her birthday by sinking all sectional differences in praying for her welfare, they now joined in common sympathy to mourn her decease.

Carts and wagons flocked into the Village, and the square in front of the gaol resembled the bustling activity before a quarterly communion service. Only now the activity was more subdued, and limited to the essential necessities of the case. Round the little obelisk on the bare bit of veld, part of the town lands that at the time of the 1887 jubilee had been laid out as a Jubilee Park, but where the oak trees had obstinately refused to grow despite constant watering by the convicts in the charge of Constable Augustus, they deposited wreaths to her memory. Mr Quakerley sent the finest, made of white lilies and gardenias backed by shining, glossy magnolia leaves. Mr Renselaar, the member, and his colleague sent one of crimson everlastings, and the location contributed one of weeping willow intertwined with blue agapanthus. From a remote farm came one of faded lemon blossoms. The Ladies' League sent an anchor made of pale pink cannas, and the Bond branch a cross of carnations with ribbons suitably inscribed.

On every farm, in every house in the Village, which possessed a portrait, the mourning tribute of crepe and lowered blinds was paid to Alexandrina Victoria. Nowhere was that tribute more sincere or more loyal than where the farmers, who could not attend the memorial service in the Village, gathered together in dining room or wagon-house to remember the Queen in a simple service conducted by one of themselves who held office as Deacon or Elder of the church.

On the morning after these official and private solemnities, when the Village was still under the impression of them, Mr Storam walked into Andrew's garden in a state of suppressed excitement.

'I have come,' he said, hardly permitting himself the customary morning greeting in his impatience, 'to ask your advice, Mr Quakerley. I am ... really, I can hardly express myself ...'

'What is the excitement about, Storam?' queried Andrew in astonishment. The magistrate was usually a calm, matter-of-fact individual, who seldom permitted his feelings to get the better of him; his official training and his experience on the bench had schooled him to suppress them.

'You'll be excited enough when you read this,' answered the official tendering a telegram to the old man.

Andrew put on his glasses, and held the paper at arm's length.

'I see it is marked "Secret and Confidential",' he observed. 'Do you wish me to read it?'

'Certainly, Mr Quakerley, I can trust you wholly, and this is a matter that concerns us all. It is a "clear-the-line" despatch from *Lex*. But read it ... read it.'

The old man's brows drew together in a frown as his eyes travelled over the script, and as he read he mumbled the words audibly.

> 'Clear-the-line. From *Lex* to Magistrate. Information just received that two commandos of Boers have crossed river with presumed intention to invade Colony. Scouts report both moving your direction. Our forces in touch with most western body of invaders report strength of commando approximately five hundred men. Ample confirmation necessitates immediate steps being taken to put District in state of defence. Government considering advisability proclaiming martial law throughout Colony, and definitely your District and adjacent districts by proclamation to be issued tomorrow. You will receive communication from military through General Commanding Lines of Communication, at whose disposal you will place all necessary facilities; reporting in triplicate to this office. Suggest that you at once forward detailed report on state of District, together with lists of all disaffected, and information as to possibilities of defence in case of eventualities. Steps are being taken to deflect troops, but should like your views on possibility of raising local force for defence purposes. Acknowledge.'

'There,' said the magistrate, when his companion had read the telegram, 'there you have it. Just as I said—exactly what I feared.'

'But is it true?' asked Andrew, incredulously.

'True? It is at any rate official, and I suppose their information is reliable. As a matter of fact, Mr Quakerley, we knew that these two commandos had crossed over and entered the Colony, but the general impression was that they were moving towards the east. Now it seems they are converging upon some point much nearer at hand ...'

'You do not suppose, Storam, do you, that they are likely to enter our District?'

'How should I know? But it is by no means unlikely, Mr Quakerley. They have caught us napping—or rather they have caught the troops napping. We can do nothing in the matter. It is tomfoolery to suggest that we should put up any defence. Why, with the exception of Chumley and Augustus—whom we cannot use as a combatant—we have no force at all, and as for raising a local force ...' he shrugged his shoulders expressively.

'Where are they now? Have you any idea, Storam?'

'No more than you. I should say about half-way between our border and theirs—that will be about three hundred miles from us. But that they can easily cover in a week.'

'It is scarcely credible. There must be some mistake. What could be their object, Storam? It seems to me sheer cussedness ...'

'From their point of view it is the best—one might almost say, the only—way of attacking.'

'If it is true, then it is damnable,' said the old man, harshly. 'I cannot see anything that can possibly condone it.'

'From our point of view, yes. Nothing. But this is war, Mr Quakerley, and from their point of view everything is allowable. Bear in mind that they are worrying their enemy, and that the Colony offers them an unlimited field for guerrilla warfare. Besides, there are no block houses here, and no real defensive measures have been taken. They will find it an easy task to over-run our districts, and if they penetrate as far as this District we shall be at their mercy.'

'You think they can adventure to us? With all these columns in between?'

'Oh, the columns won't be able to stop them. It'll be like hunting for a needle in a bottle of hay. The commandos are much more mobile than our troops, and they act more quickly. With them it'll be a matter of cut and run, and come again. Make no mistake, Mr Quakerley, if they come here, we'll be in a devil of a mess, and God alone knows how we are to get out of it.'

'I quite agree with you, Storam. How awful it all seems. And only yesterday ...'

'Yes, yes,' interrupted the magistrate, impatiently. 'But the time has passed for sentiment, Mr Quakerley. I hardly think you quite realise what that telegram means.'

'I think I do,' said the old man, quietly. 'I noticed the suggestion about the disaffected.'

'Ah, did you? Somebody's damned impertinence, that. But when all our officials are jumpy one must make allowances for them, and I daresay Sir Gordon has been told that we are all rebels in embryo here. I shall clear up that point at once. So far as I am aware, there is no disaffection here; none, at any rate, that I cannot deal with. That, Mr Quakerley, is really what I came to see you about. We cannot keep this news secret— you know how things leak out, and sooner or later this will be public, probably with exaggerations and additions. I thought we might draw up some sort of statement, and post it up, and Mr Uhlmann and you could arrange to address a meeting. We shall have to call one, I fear, if only to arrange for eventualities, and to tell them plainly what may happen if the commandos come here. I am not going to let our people here suffer as people did in other districts when the war started. They must know, definitely, that under no circumstances can they join merely out of sympathy or dare-devilry. We have many quite ignorant and illiterate farm-hands, who are easily led into mischief simply because they haven't the backbone to resist. Poor devils, they will have a hard time of it when the Boers come.'

'Yes, that might be a good thing,' said Andrew, answering the earlier part of the magistrate's remarks. 'But it would have to be arranged quietly. The committee will help you there, and Uhlmann. Does he know?'

'I am going to the parsonage now,' replied the magistrate. 'Then there is the matter of raising a local force. We could, of course, get boys from the location, but that is out of the question. Indeed, Mr Quakerley, one of the most difficult matters will be to keep the Natives out of this. If the Boers do what I am told they did in other districts— that is, wantonly shoot Coloured men who are helping our troops as non-combatants, or Coloured or Native constables in uniform—I am afraid there will be—there must be—reprisals. To obviate that, I should suggest that we call upon our people to volunteer for service as non-combatants—drivers, you know, and camp followers. I don't quite see how we could ask them to give actual military service, although of course they would be in duty bound to serve if called upon. Still, that means that Gerster might have to shoot his cousin, or that you might be potted by one of the many Egmonds remaining in the field.'

'Have you any idea what commandos are coming? I mean, whether they are Transvaalers or Freestaters?'

'I should say Transvaalers. But it does not matter where they come from. What matters is that among them there are sure to be some who are directly related to people in this District.'

'After all, that was the position from the start, Storam. This is a kind of civil war, you know.'

'Don't I know it, Mr Quakerley. But it is no use exclaiming against it. There it is, and we must make the best of a bad job.'

'I suppose martial law will have to be proclaimed, eh?'

'Of course; by this time the proclamation will have been issued and I suppose I'll get it "clear-the-line" by tonight. It will be only a group of districts, possibly only those that are directly threatened by this invasion. I can't see why they should have it over the whole Colony. Of course, had they done it when the war started, as a matter of course, it would have been another thing, and a wise thing, too, I think. But the sea-port towns will resist martial law as long as they can, for all their loyalty, Mr Quakerley. It upsets things too much; it means dislocation of trade and restrictions all round.'

'What does it exactly imply, Storam? You would still be the chief representative of the government, I suppose?'

'That does not follow. When martial law is proclaimed the military take control, full control. They may delegate the non-military part to a civilian, and probably in our case I may be allowed to function as magistrate, subject to whoever is commandant. The commandant will be the responsible authority, and he will be simply a dictator, amenable to his military superiors alone. That has been the rule everywhere. In some cases it has worked very well indeed, where they had a man who was used to administration, and with some experience of human nature. But in others it has been a bad failure, and where difficulties have arisen they have almost always been due to the fact that the commandant in charge of the area has been an officer without the slightest experience of civil administration.'

'A bad look-out for us, Storam. You could not influence the authorities to delegate powers to you?'

'I could do a bit. As a matter of fact, as soon as I got this wire, I telegraphed to the A-G hinting at some such arrangement. But you see what the official view is. I am to await a communication from the military and place all facilities at their disposal. Everything will depend on the manner in which they interpret their orders. If we are not invaded—if the commandos are crushed before they get very far into the Colony, I am hopeful that matters may be much simplified. But if military operations are actually to take place in this District, I am afraid we'll have our difficulties. You see, Mr Quakerley, when it is a question of military safety, the commandant will naturally make everything subservient to ensuring this. You can't very well blame him, but the danger is that in such circumstances panic measures may be decided upon, and they may be horribly drastic.'

They strolled down the path towards the house, and the magistrate resumed.

'For one thing I am profoundly grateful, Mr Quakerley. And that is that there is, so far as I can see, no bitter feeling between our two sections anywhere in this District. We are likely to be spared the anonymous informer, and the ultra-loyalist who seeks to curry favour with the authorities by denouncing his fellows. There has been far too much of that in other districts, and I put it down to the inexperience of the commandants. I can't very well believe that they are all of them bullies and cads, can you?'

'No. I never believed half of what is alleged about the administration of martial law. It is hard, of course, and no doubt it is sometimes very annoying to those who are used to ordinary civil administration, but we must put up with it. I rather fancy that our people will bear it with stolid good nature. As you have doubtless seen for yourself, Storam, we are very tolerant as a community.'

'I have noticed that trait. It does you credit. I suppose it is due to the fact that you were originally such a cosmopolitan crowd that you had to give and take.'

'Partly that. Partly, too, I believe, because our original settlers were a better class than in some other districts. Our old people were gentlefolk, Storam, and calmness and restraint were accounted virtues in those days.'

'They are hardly that now. From what goes on in the other districts, if one is to believe the reports, there seems to be a good deal of tall talk. Fortunately we have had none of that here. I think we have our committee to thank for that, but also, as you say, our local tradition. Between you and me, Mr Quakerley, if there have been any offenders they are not among the disaffected but among the ladies who are so clamantly loyal.'

'Since the war started they have been too busy for propaganda,' said the old man with a smile. 'All they have done recently is to congratulate Milner on his promotion. And you cannot object to that.'

'No, certainly not. Besides, the man deserves everything he gets in the way of promotion. No one has worked harder than Sir Alfred.'

'So I am told. But the question is, has he always worked well, Storam?'

'I really think that is a matter we must leave to posterity to decide, Mr Quakerley. My own opinion is that he came to make peace at any price, and studiously tried to adjust himself to what I may call—I know it's rather a silly expression, but it will serve—the pro-Boer view, but that he has found out that it will be impossible in the long run to square Republican aspirations with England's prestige in this country ...'

'I should rather say, northern tradition with our southern, Storam.'

'That is a mere matter of words, Mr Quakerley. You are thinking of the tradition as something ideal. His Excellency thinks, no doubt, of the material, practical result of the agitation. But I don't think there can be the least doubt about his sincerity and honesty, whatever people may say, and I know that he has had a hard time, and is bound to have a harder. It cannot be easy to reconcile all these conflicting interests— indeed, you will see how difficult the task is, should we have martial law here.'

'I do hope we shan't have it. But tell me, in the event we do get it, who makes the regulations—I mean about curfew, and this, that and the other? Is there a model code, or does the commandant do it?'

'The commandant invariably draws up a local code of regulations. I presume he consults with the local civilian administration, but he is not bound to do that. It all boils down to a question of tact. Provided the officer in charge is tactful, I don't see why we should anticipate any trouble or unpleasantness. Apart, of course, from what these commandos are going to bring us if they succeed in getting as far as this.'

They parted in front of the *stoep*, the magistrate excusing himself from taking eleven o'clock tea because he had still much to do at his office.

Old Andrew took his tea in reflective silence, hardly reacting to the conversation at the tea-table, and, as soon as he conveniently could, withdrew into his study, nodding to Conroy an invitation to follow him.

'I hardly know if I am in order, Conroy,' he said, when they found themselves alone, 'in telling you something that the magistrate has just told me, but you are one of the family, you know, and I think I can trust you ...'

'If it is a secret of any military importance,' said his guest promptly, 'you'd better not tell me.'

'You'll hear about it soon enough,' interjected the old man, wearily. 'Your people have crossed over again, and are said to be converging upon this District ...'

Conroy emitted a low whistle.

'That about puts the lid on,' he exclaimed. 'I knew they had some such plan; it was always being talked about. But I hoped they would have sufficient sense not to try it. Of course, if there is the least chance that it will remove pressure from us up here, I ought to say nothing about it, but, speaking as a member of the family, Grand-Cousin, I should hate to see the war come to you here. I know what it means; you don't, yet.'

'We shall have to bear our share,' said Andrew, 'and I daresay things would be different from what they were in a conquered territory. But what about you, if they come?'

'I am on parole,' said his guest, curtly. 'I cannot take any further part—actively, that is.'

'But they might force you? No? I don't like it, Conroy. I think you should apply for leave to go to Cape Town. Not that I want to chase you away, but there are bound to be difficulties if you stay. You are the only prisoner of war here, and although no one has the slightest feeling against you—it is rather the other way about, as you know—there may be trouble when we have martial law here.'

'Martial law? Is that likely?'

'Almost a certainty, I understand from Storam. The proclamation has already been drawn up. Its promulgation will depend on circumstances.'

'In that case I think I should go, for all our sakes, Grand-Cousin. Will you arrange with the magistrate? The sooner the better, for if there are military operations here I may find some difficulty in getting leave. And you yourself, Uncle Andrew? Why not go too? Or send Aunt and the children away ...'

'We might do that, Conroy. Neither Joan nor Alice would go, I am sure. They would stay and see it out. Keep this to yourself, will you? Possibly it will be common property before tomorrow, but at present it is still a secret. And you'd better make a written application. You'll find paper and envelopes on the table there.'

The Village heard the news soon enough, and speculated on its meaning and possible consequences. Late that night a 'clear-the-line' telegram arrived from the military, reporting the detrainment of detachments at the nearest railway station, a hundred miles away, and instructing the magistrate to take certain precautionary measures. All horses and mules were to be brought into the Village from neighbouring farms, and all ammunition still remaining in private hands was to be collected. The military evidently imagined that Mr Storam had a posse of police to help him. The local committee met for the last time, and agreed to dissolve.

'If martial law is proclaimed,' the magistrate told them, 'there will be no need for you to meet, but remember you are still leaders to whom the people look for an example. Remain calm, and remember your obligations as subjects of His Majesty.'

The telegraph office was kept open all night, and shortly after midnight Mr Storam received another despatch, informing him that a special *Government Gazette* would be issued on that day proclaiming martial law over the District and the surrounding territories, and instructing him to act as commandant pending the arrival of a senior military officer who was already on his way.

Chapter 29

Charlie Crest, pedalling along the main road on his new bicycle, met the van of the column marching to occupy the Village.

Events moved rapidly during the two weeks following the memorial services to the late Queen. Carts and wagons had driven into the Village and been parked behind the church on the open veld. These had not been the peaceful vehicles of farmers or communicants, but transport wagons, heavily laden with supplies, commissariat wagons, ambulant wagons, ammunition wagons, wagons of all descriptions and sizes pressed into service to meet the emergency. The military acted with astonishing quickness, and the District, unused to organisation on so elaborate a scale, had been profoundly impressed.

The advance guard of mounted troops rode into the Village late at night, when the lights in the houses had all been extinguished, so that few people were aware of the occupation.

The proclamation of martial law had taken place in front of the court house in the presence of the usual village crowd. A copy of the Proclamation had been sent to all field-cornets and assistant-field-cornets, some of whom had been members of Mr Storam's voluntary committee. The magistrate appointed the chief constable as his deputy, and set himself to interpret the many, and sometimes conflicting, instructions that came to him, almost hourly, over the wires. He was to issue regulations according to the Code telegraphed, but it was left to his discretion to vary them to fit local conditions. As he read the Code it seemed to him that few of the regulations fitted in with local conditions, but that could not be helped. He was further required to close all canteens and bottle stores, to requisition supplies for the troops, and to draw up a list of all the inhabitants of the District 'known or suspected to be disaffected and likely to cause trouble.'

Fortunately for Mr Storam's peace of mind, he was spared the vexation of weighing the varying loyalties of all those in the District with whom he was personally acquainted, by the arrival of the military authority charged to supersede him.

Major Mallom, to whom this duty had been entrusted, was a red-faced fair-moustached, fierce-looking, middle-aged man, who hid under his bluff curtness a character essentially gentlemanly and frank. The magistrate, who had been disagreeably impressed by his curt, incisive manner of speech, and by his forbidding frown, found, after he had talked with the man, that there was something human and kindly about him. As Mr Storam noted the newcomer's efficiency, his manner of dealing with inferiors, and his quick grasp of facts presented to him, the magistrate revised his first opinion, and confessed to himself that the Village was singularly lucky in having obtained so capable a commandant.

'Now, Mr Magistrate,' the Major had begun, after he had formally taken charge of the court house and the office, which he proposed to use himself, 'it is beside the point to make an apology for dispossessing you. We are both officials, and it will be no fault of mine if we do not work harmoniously together. I take it that you would prefer to have no responsibility—better for you, my dear fellow; you can then blame me for whatever goes wrong. But I should like you to advise me. If you care to have it, I can appoint you Provost Marshal—that is, our legal adviser, prosecutor, and so forth. Think it over. And now, where's that list, please?'

'I presume you mean the list of disaffected that I had to draw up, Major,' said the magistrate. 'As a matter of fact, there is no need to make a list. So far as I know, there is no one who is disaffected in the sense implied ...'

'Come, come, my dear fellow! Our information is fairly precise. You have two Members of Parliament here who are known to be disaffected.'

'Pardon me, Major, but I do not see how you can infer that. I have no doubt that there are quite a number of names which might go on such a list for the same reason that you suggest Renselaar ...'

'Look here, Magistrate, I daresay a great deal of all this is nonsense, but we can't take any chances, you know. The Boer forces are within a couple of hundred miles from where we sit, and any leakage from this side must be prevented at all costs. I have seen your reports—both your official reports and your private, confidential reports to your departmental head, and I may say I had a talk with the A-G before I left. Let me tell you that in Cape Town they are not disposed to accept your views in their entirety. You are perhaps, if you will pardon me saying so, biased.'

'I am not in the least bit biased,' exclaimed Storam, vehemently. 'What I have reported is my conscientious opinion, based on facts, Major. And do let me pray you to acquaint yourself with the facts before you jump to any conclusions.'

'That is my intention, Mr Storam. But my first duty is a military one. If there is the slightest suspicion that military operations may be interfered with by ... er, let me say, injudicious sympathy on the part of the people here, it is my duty to forestall that by taking the proper steps, and to do that I must go on what appears to me to be precise information.'

'You can rely upon me to help you in that,' said the magistrate, eagerly. 'If you have read my reports carefully ...'

'I have done that. Indeed, if I may say so, I admired your meticulous attention to detail, and I am quite with you where you suggested that martial law should be proclaimed over the whole Colony. It seems to me there you rather gave your case away.'

'On the contrary, Major. The danger here is not from disaffection but from sheer stupidity. There are some hundreds of ignorant farm hands in this District, all more or less related to people in the Republics, who may be pressed to commit overt acts of treason ...'

'That is why we are here, Magistrate. You may take it from me that no one need be pressed, but for all that they should understand that even with such pressure they should not commit treason. I have some names here,' he drew a paper from his pocket and consulted it. 'Perhaps you can give me your private opinion, without prejudice, of course. The Reverend Christian Uhlmann has a son fighting on the Republican side; brother-in-law, official of the Transvaal, now prisoner of war; another brother-in-law, still in the field with Republican forces ...'

'Add,' interrupted the magistrate, quickly, 'a nephew killed in the defence of Kimberley; another nephew serving in Kitchener's Horse.'

'I will make a note of that,' said the Major, imperturbably. 'To go on, Dutch Reformed minister, has much influence in District, and is known to be actively and aggressively pro-Boer ...'

'Who has given you that rot?' exclaimed the magistrate, indignantly. 'Mr Uhlmann—but there, Major Mallom, I think the best thing you can do is to have a talk with him yourself ...'

'I propose to see him, Mr Storam. To proceed. Martin Rekker, farmer living at—I cannot make out the name, but it is a farm hereabouts—active Bondsman; has contributed large sums to propaganda; is said to have financed deputation to England ...'

Mr Storam burst out laughing.

'If that is a ground for suspicion,' he exclaimed, 'we are all suspect. I believe I was the only one who did not subscribe, and I couldn't very well do so because I was the magistrate, you see. But Mr Quakerley gave the biggest subscription in this District.'

'I have that down here,' interrupted the Major, glancing at his paper. 'Yes, here it is. Andrew Quakerley, resigned as sheriff two years before war broke out; has several uncles fighting on Boer side; was said to be a strong supporter of the Bond at last election, has great influence in the District and, although old, is still very active. There is a cross against his name, Mr Storam, which means that I shall have to keep my eye on him.'

The magistrate fought down his rising wrath.

'Who on earth,' he exclaimed, contemptuously, 'is responsible for your Intelligence Department, Major? Let me just tell you that Mr Quakerley has—or had— an uncle who had the honour of holding Her late Majesty's commission as an admiral of the Royal Navy, another uncle who was a member of the House of Commons, and that his grandfather is an English baronet. But,' he calmed down under the major's cool stare, 'it is no use talking. You must see these men, and talk to them. Good heavens, I had no notion that this sort of thing was being done. It explains a lot of things ...'

'Mr Storam,' said the Major, quietly, 'I have read you these few extracts from a report which is fairly comprehensive in order to show you what I am up against. Do me the favour of looking at the matter from my angle. I cannot ignore this report, but I have, as yet, a perfectly open mind, and I am quite aware that in the circumstances one must be careful to distinguish between reasonable presumption and innuendo. Let me tell you that our experience in other districts has been that reasonable presumption almost always proved correct, and that many against whom suspicion was not half as strong as against some of those whose names I have here, turned out to be rebels. No, just let me go on. It is my intention to assure myself that this is not the case here. I cannot take your word, much as I should like to do so, that these men are beyond suspicion. To your mind it may seem preposterous that they should be suspected, but it is my duty to make sure.'

'My dear fellow,' he went on, 'put yourself in my place. Do you imagine that I have any choice in the matter? Why, I'd far rather be anywhere in the field than cooped up here acting as commandant of your pretty little Village. But this is war, although so many people seem to forget that fact. And it may quite possibly happen that through the act of one or other of someone here, the Boers may obtain a momentary success at our expense, of which the effects may be incalculable.'

'I quite see, Major, that your position is difficult. But I do hope that you will not start by giving any belief to such absurd insinuations. Once it gets known that you attach any belief to these things, why, you will have all sorts of denunciations, and all manner of trouble will be stirred up.'

'We'll see to that, Mr Magistrate. You must come with me, and introduce your leading citizens to me. Now let me see ... we must arrange about quarters and supplies, and all that sort of thing. Perhaps you have already done so ...'

'I thought you might occupy the vacant house next door, Major. It is Rekker's church house, and there would be no difficulty. With regard to the other matters ...'

'Very well. Captain Thomas will see to that. Now about that Proclamation. I shall be glad if you will just cast your eye over my draft and sub-edit it, so to speak.'

The next morning the major's proclamation was posted on the notice board in front of the post office, and copies were circulated throughout the District. This very brief and concise document read as follows:

Martial Law
Notice to All Concerned

Whereas the District has been invaded by commandos of Republican forces, whose exact whereabouts cannot at present be ascertained, all subjects of His Majesty are called upon to give their loyal assistance in expelling the enemy, and to do nothing that can in any way aid or abet him.

Information about the movements of the enemy must be promptly reported to the nearest military post, and failure to do so will be punished under martial law. Stores or supplies that are in danger of falling into the enemy's hands must be destroyed.

Subjects of His Majesty the King who allow themselves to fall into the enemy's hands will be guilty of high treason if they do anything to aid and abet him, even if compelled to join him.

Signed Malcolm Mallom (Major)
Commandant

Mr Storam thought the Proclamation, especially its last paragraph, tragically ludicrous, but he had not sub-edited it. The responsibility was not his, but the Commandant's.

The long column of khaki-clad men marched stolidly along the main road, raising clouds of dust that hung about their flanks and settled down lazily upon the wild veld bush. There were mounted men and foot soldiers, and behind came the guns, dragged by the mule teams. Charlie drew to the one side of the road to watch them as they went slowly by, the rattle of the iron-shod wheels as they passed over the rutty road making a monotonous melody in the still afternoon air. Some of the men stopped and spoke to him, and he felt proud and important because they had done so. He pointed out the various places in the Village, lying far below in the valley in a shimmering haze of a summer afternoon. A young officer rode by on a charger and urged the men on; he remained chatting to the boy for a little while, and presented him with a cigarette, which Charlie forgot to light, but put in his pocket as a treasured relic of the encounter.

The column halted outside the Village, and camped on the bare veld. The boy, pedalling slowly behind, keeping in touch with the gunners, watched them as they pitched tents and prepared their bivouac. He had seen soldiers in Cape Town, but this was the first time he had seen them in the field. It was exciting to think that he was now in the midst of them, and that tomorrow those guns might be actually engaged in shelling the enemy. Already the location and the Village youth had turned out in full strength to welcome the soldiers. Charlie joined the little group of boys who stood shyly admiring the guns. An officer in a stained, dusty tunic galloped up to them.

'Hello, kids,' he called out, 'can you tell me which is Mr Quakerley's place?'

'That big house over there, Sir,' Charlie answered. 'I am going there, Sir, if you'd like me to show you the way.'

The officer climbed down from his horse, and handed the reins to one of the boys.

'My orderly will come for him,' he said, nonchalantly. 'Just hold him a mo. Lead on, youngster. I should like to meet Mr Quakerley.'

Charlie wheeled his bicycle and stepped by the officer's side, glancing shyly at his companion. He saw a tall, sun-burned, good-looking man, with rather large, humorously twinkling eyes, and with a captain's stars on his khaki shoulder straps.

'I suppose you know Mr Quakerley?' asked the captain, lighting a pipe, and accommodating his long stride to the boy's smaller pace.

'Yes, Sir. He's my grandfather ...'

'What? Then you must be Anna's boy. Here, let me have a look at you,' he grasped the lad's shoulder and swung him round. 'By the Lord, I believe I am right. You're a Crest, aren't you?'

'Yes, Sir. Charlie Crest.'

'The Australian kangaroo, eh? Well, my lad, I am your uncle Jim. I daresay you've heard about me.'

'Then you must be Aunt Kathleen's husband,' said Charlie, who knew enough of family history to know that Aunt Kathleen had married a civil servant somewhere in the eastern districts, and lived in a part where bananas and paw-paws grew naturally, and blue monkeys came into the garden to sport on the lawns.

'Right, first shot,' said the Captain, shaking his hand. 'So now you can introduce me. Do you know, my lad, I've never been here before, and Katie always told me her Village was beautiful. I see she's right. It's quite a lovely little bit down there. And the great garden is still magnificent, I presume.'

'It's looking very fine just now, Sir,' said Charlie, overwhelmed by the avuncular cheerfulness. He had known that Uncle Jim was a civil servant, but had never heard that Uncle Jim was an officer, and a fighting one at that.

'Might as well call me Uncle,' said the Captain, reloading his pipe. 'I find this Transvaal tobacco burns out ever so much quicker,' he proceeded irrelevantly. 'I suppose you're not full up, are you? I mean, I can barge in and get a bed and a decent bit of supper ...'

'Oh yes, Uncle. Now Cousin Conroy's gone ...'

'Didn't know about him. Who's Cousin Conroy?'

'He's Grand-dad's brother-in-law's grandson, Sir ... Uncle, I mean. He's a Boer on parole, and he stayed with us while he was wounded ...'

'You don't say. Do you mean to tell me they've actually had a scrap here, already?'

'Oh no, Uncle. He was wounded up north somewhere. Long ago.'

'I see. Came down to convalesce with his dear relatives, did he? No wonder ... hm, hm. Charles, my lad, is this the family mansion?'

'Yes, Uncle. That's Grandpa, in the garden there. The others are indoors ...'

'Well, I must surprise the old chap. It's years since I saw him. Hello, Father-in-law ...'

Old Andrew, however, was not surprised. His daughter had written to him some time before and told him that her husband had been detailed for service in the new area of military operations, and expressed the hope that he might turn up at the Village. He greeted his visitor warmly.

'My dear chap, I am glad to see you. Of course you must billet with us. I daresay that can all be arranged. You might have wired, though. Then we could have killed, well, not the fatted calf exactly, but a couple of Muscovy ducks for you.'

'That's all right, Sir. What a lovely place you've got there. It is a sight for sore eyes, and I can tell you mine have been smarting with the dust since we started. What horrible roads you have, too. Yes, Katie is bobbish, and the kids are growing up. Three of them, and one, as you know, is your god-child. Will I have a drink? You bet, I will.'

Dinner that night at the Quakerleys was merrier than it had been since Conroy's departure. For Conroy had been sent to the base, where nobody, apparently, bothered about him, for his letters reported that he was living quietly in a boarding-house in Cape Town.

Captain Overbury had something of Conroy's cheery amiability, but he was also a cultured, well-informed man, and had been a favourite with both Joan and Alice. When the table talk veered round from family affairs, he gave them inside information about the progress of the war, describing his own experience with a humorous objectiveness that appealed to Joan. His pronounced 'Colonial' views did not appeal to Alice, who thought that he took matters much too lightly and was inclined to overlook the dangers to which the empire was exposed by the great South African conspiracy.

'Just to show you how damn silly all that rot is,' remarked the Captain, cheerfully, as he peeled an apple, 'I may mention that there's some suspicion about you, Sir, not to mention your local magistrate. It's the greatest nonsense, of course. I know Storam— we passed our civil service in the same year; I remember he failed in tots and didn't get a first-class. But he's as straight as you make them, Mother, and to suspect him ...'

'You never know where you are,' said Mrs Quakerley, plaintively. 'I have even heard Mr Mance-Bisley—our rector, you know, James, and one of the most loyal men we have—express himself in a manner that I strongly disapprove of.'

'Quite likely. Everyone who does anything we strongly disapprove of must be disloyal. Hand the whole lot and be done with it. But really, you know, looking at the matter seriously, I expect you are in for considerable trouble.'

'I am afraid so, Jim,' said his father-in-law. 'But I expect we can rely upon you. And I must say, our commandant seems to me to be an excellent man.'

'So he is, too. Mallom is a gentleman, and that's saying much. But he is inflexible when it comes to what he considers his duty. He has the reputation of being a martinet with his men, and as a civil administrator, as a commandant under martial law, he will interpret regulations strictly according to the letter. You've got them, haven't you?'

'Oh, yes. Some of them appear to me to verge on foolishness. I can't see why we should have no lights after eight o'clock, nor walk across the street without a pass ...'

'That's a detail. It is of course to make patrolling easier, and to obviate any chance of signalling, and so forth. But there won't be much disturbance unless there is actual fighting. And you'll find that the regulations are in your favour now that the Village is our headquarters, you know. With a few thousand men and goodness knows how many camp-followers hanging around, it is not so easy to police the place.'

'I can't see that the soldiers being here alters the matter very much. They are under discipline, aren't they?'

'Supposed to be. But on active service ... well, it is sometimes difficult to prevent the civilians from being troubled. Now I must be getting back, Mother. I'll try and get leave to quarter myself here—it may be difficult or it may not. One never can tell. I don't know yet what the arrangements are.'

The arrangements, apparently, were very accommodating. Captain Overbury of Marshall's Horse, in civil life assistant-magistrate, was allowed to quarter himself in Mr Quakerley's house, and, being a popular officer, brought many friends to tea, tennis, and dinner. The Quakerley house became much more lively than it had been for many years; it formed a rallying point for those officers who could escape from duty for a few hours, and Mrs Quakerley's soirées, which had been interrupted by the war, were resumed, and once more supplied her with the chance of posing as a *grande dame*.

Major Mallom had his interview with old Andrew and Mr Uhlmann, and returned from it thoroughly in agreement with the magistrate. He had sufficient experience of men to know that neither the parson nor the squire could by any stretch of imagination be ranked among those who could be styled dangerous or suspect. Their names were scratched off his secret list, and he felt himself honoured by their acquaintance and hoped that in time it might fructify into friendship.

Chapter 30

Martial law, as administered by Commandant Mallom, proved to be no great hardship. Routine went on as before, with the exception that curfew was enforced and that anyone who wanted to go beyond the townlands had to be provided with a special pass, while every inhabitant was registered and given a permit to enable him or her to move outside the dwelling house. The Village tolerated this, for it soon saw that these apparently senseless regulations served some definite object, and that they were being enforced without unnecessary harshness. There was at first a natural reluctance to obey anything that savoured of an infringement of the individual privilege of perfect freedom such as the Village had always enjoyed, but this speedily gave way when it was understood that the restrictions applied to everyone, and that no exceptions were made. The military police were everywhere in evidence, and did their duty so well that there was no trouble with the mass of Native servants who had accompanied the column, and swelled the location community. Certainly Chumley and Augustus could not have dealt with that large influx of outsiders, whose language and demeanour left much to be desired from the point of view of the Village, and the military police dealt with them promptly and effectively.

Indeed, when the excitement caused by the proclamation of martial law and the arrival of the troops had died down, the Village recovered its equanimity and scoffed at the suggestion that it might be still further involved in the vortex of war. It carried on its business, finding a larger market for its products than ever before, and refused to take the situation more seriously than during the previous year.

Its complacency was rudely shattered during the first week in February, when, for no reason that was apparent, unwonted activity was manifest in the camp, while it was noted that orderlies hurried to and from the commandant's office, and that the teams were being harnessed to the gun carriages. Those who happened to be present in the early morning, when the column moved out, wondered at the precautions that were taken. Mounted scouts rode far in advance, spreading out fan-wise across the open veld on both sides of the road; the foot soldiers moved briskly, and in their wake followed the ammunition carts, while far in the rear the red-crossed ambulance wagons, with their fluttering red-crossed flags, rumbled along in a trail of dust.

Soon the Village heard the news. A Boer commando had actually penetrated into the District, and there had been fighting not fifty miles away. Particulars of what had actually occurred filtered slowly through the seepage of rumours that had driven the Village wild with excitement, but the first authentic details were communicated in a notice posted up in front of the court house:

Martial Law

A Boer commando, estimated to be of considerable strength, crossed the border of this District last night and occupied the farm *Ondervlei*, which has been looted and destroyed. A detachment of Marshall's Horse was attacked but succeeded in repulsing the attack, losing two killed and five wounded in the engagement. The enemy's casualties are believed to be one killed and several wounded. Two Natives living on the farm *Ondervlei* were shot by the enemy, although unarmed. In view of the fact that the enemy is now active in this District it is imperatively necessary that anyone who is in a position to give information about his whereabouts should at once report to the nearest military post, and failure to do so will be punished under martial law. The Commandant once more draws attention to the regulations prohibiting any communication with the enemy, and calls upon all subjects of His Majesty the King to co-operate with the authorities in the defence of the District.

Signed Malcolm Mallon, Major
Commandant

The Village had barely digested this communiqué when it was shocked to hear that another commando had entered its far western border and penetrated as far as Martin Rekker's farm, twenty-five miles distant from the Village itself. When the detachments, hurried across the mountain pass to intercept this commando, reached the farm, they found the old homestead burned, the orchard plundered, two of the farm Natives killed, and Martin Rekker junior missing. They arrested old Martin Rekker and brought him into the Village, where he was lodged in the gaol. As soon as Andrew heard of it, he walked down to the commandant's office, where he found Mr Uhlmann waiting on the *stoep*.

'You have come on the same errand as I,' said the pastor, greeting him.

'About *Mynheer* Rekker, of course. I heard of it just now, and I thought I must see the commandant ...'

'Yes, certainly. It is absurd to put the man in gaol. What has he done, after all? Can he help it if the Boers occupied his farm? Really, Uhlmann, I cannot conceive that this has been done with the commandant's sanction ... yes, yes, we are waiting to see the Major. Come along, Uhlmann ...'

They followed the orderly into the office where the Major sat busily writing at the magistrate's desk. He nodded curtly as they entered, but made no remark.

'We have come, Major,' said the old man, 'to ask you on what grounds Mr Rekker has been imprisoned. So far as we know ...'

The commandant raised his hand, and pointed to the door. 'You may go, Jones,' he told his orderly. 'I will see Captain Thomas when he comes in. Now, gentlemen ...' he motioned them to take chairs. 'I am afraid the matter is outside my province. Mr Rekker has been brought in as a prisoner, and I must refer you to Colonel Cautley who is in command, as you know. I do not even know what the charge against him is. But I understand that his son has joined the Boer forces ...'

'That I cannot believe,' interrupted the pastor. 'Young Martin would be the last man to do that. There must be some mistake, Commandant.'

'I can only tell you what has come to my knowledge. It seems that the old man's son was seen riding at the head of the commando when it cleared off the farm. There is no doubt about that, and the inference is that he is guiding them ...'

'After they have burned down his house, and shot two of his boys?' old Andrew interjected, stirred out of his habitual calm. 'It is too preposterous for words ...'

'I give no opinion on that,' said the Major, briskly. 'But, if it is any satisfaction to you, I may tell you that even if the son has joined the Boers, it does not necessarily mean that his father is implicated. However, the matter is out of my hands. It is one entirely for Colonel Cautley's discretion. If you care to see him, my orderly can take you across to him, but I doubt if you'll find him today. We have our hands full, Mr Quakerley, and as I really can do nothing more for you ...'

They took the hint, and left. Colonel Cautley was difficult to find, and when, after searching for him in all likely offices, they were at last informed that he had left with his staff and would only be back the following morning, they decided to visit the prison. A permit would be necessary to see their old friend, but Mr Uhlmann had always had free entry to the gaol in his capacity as chaplain, and Andrew had been sheriff. The gaoler, Monk, would surely not refuse to admit them.

He answered their ring at the gaol door in person, but shook his head when he heard what they wanted.

'I don't know as if I'd dare let you talk to him, Mr Quakerley,' he said, guardedly. 'Not as I've had special orders not to, but if it's likely to get me into trouble ...'

'I will take all responsibility, Monk,' said the old man, quickly. 'It may be a bit irregular, but it is necessary that we should see him, and in any case he cannot be prevented from seeing his friends so as to arrange for his defence. Where is he?'

'I've made him as comfortable as I could,' said the gaoler. 'Not that I can do much, Mr Quakerley. It's the first time I've had a White man in here since I've been in charge, and to fancy that it should be him of all persons. Not that he minds, Mr Quakerley. He's sort of dazed-like, and does not seem to take it in where he is, or what it is all about. As a matter of fact, I thought of asking the doc to call and have a look at him.'

He led them across the courtyard, and unlocked a cell. They saw that he had furnished the bare room with such simple necessities as the Government allowed to White prisoners, and had even gone out of his way to provide an iron bedstead and an improvised wash-stand with basin and ewer. 'Here's Mr Quakerley and the parson to see you, Mr Rekker,' he said, motioning them to go in, and closing the door behind them.

Old Martin Rekker sat on the bedstead, nervously pulling at his greying beard. He looked haggard and unkempt, and his eyes were bloodshot and moist as if he had been weeping. As they entered, he raised his head and smiled wanly at them.

'My dear friend,' Andrew shook his hand, and released it for the pastor to grasp in his turn. 'We'll have you out of this before the day is over.'

'Be assured of that, Brother Rekker,' said the pastor, trying to infuse cheery encouragement into his voice, although he doubted their ability to carry out the promise. 'But come, you must not despair. Tell us rather what has taken place ... we are in the dark; we know nothing, except that you are here, a prisoner for something that we know you have not done.'

'I thank you, Reverend, and you, Old Friend,' said Rekker with a catch in his voice. 'It is the first time,' he went on, whimsically, 'that I am unable to give my guests even a chair. You must sit on the bed ...'

'That doesn't matter,' exclaimed Andrew, seating himself alongside his old friend, while the pastor stood leaning over the low iron headpiece. 'Tell us what we can do for you ... tell us what happened.'

'I doubt if I can do that,' the prisoner responded, again fumbling with his beard. 'Yesterday afternoon they came. We had no notion that they were anywhere about, but Adoons, who was tending the sheep in the lower lands—where the *kloof* narrows, as you know, Reverend—came back about two, and said he had seen men on horseback against the sky-line. My son went to look, but could not see anything, and came back and sent Adoons to keep a look-out. About when we were having our afternoon coffee we heard the shots; quite close they were. That was when they shot Adoons. A head shot, Reverend, and him one of my best herds that never harmed a soul, although he did take a liking to sweet Jeropico when he came into the location. And they shot Stompie in the road where he was hiding behind a bush. They rode up to the house. I had gone out to see what it was, and Martin had gone to the out-house. They came up and shook hands ... they were friendly enough, and laughing and chatting. I did not know then that they had shot the boys, else ... They talked to me, and then Martin came round, and they began with him. They said that he was a coward, and English-minded, and they taunted him ... You know what he is, Mr Quakerley, he hasn't fallen on his mouth, and he gave them back what they gave him. They grew angry at that, and told him he would have to show them the foot-path across the mountain, guide them, Reverend, to the upland farm where there is a fountain and good shelter. It is not an easy way to find for those who do not know it.

Martin said he wouldn't, and then they seized him and tied him on a horse. I could do nothing. Then someone called out that the troops were coming, and they started firing. I could not see anything, but they were scared, and rode off.'

'Did they do any damage? We heard that the house is burned down.'

'Not burned down. They fired the thatch, but we managed to put it out. Two rooms, perhaps, and the out-house. I was working at that with the children and Gertrude when the soldiers came and arrested me.'

'Did you know any of them?' asked old Andrew.

'Aye, to my sorrow I did. Gideon Ras was among them, and Org Bons, the half-wit. They were the loudest in taunting Martin, and there were a few others of our folk whom I did not know by name. But only a few. The others were all strangers, but men like us, Reverend, talking our language ... I felt ashamed when I heard what they had done to Adoons and Stompie ... I do not hold with shooting boys in cold blood like that ...'

'But surely they gave some explanation ...'

'Oh, yes. They said the Natives had spied on them ... that they were employed by the military. They told me they shot every Coloured man whom they caught in khaki. Not that Adoons was in khaki. He was my herd boy, as harmless as you make them, and a good boy ... I don't hold with that. It is wanton wickedness. I don't say anything about setting fire to my house. Perhaps that is in return for what was done to their own homes up north, and we can repair it. But they should not have killed Adoons ... no, nor taken Martin. That was wicked, Mr Quakerley, and I say it, although they are our own people.'

'But what made the soldiers arrest you, old friend? Surely you explained ...'

'They gave me no chance. They seized me as I was getting down the ladder, and the officer—he is a colonel, I think, and he has no time for us—asked me why Martin had left with them. I said that they had forced him, and that he went against his will. They did, Your Reverence. They put him between two of their men, and tied his legs beneath the horse, and he rode with a Mauser on each side pointing at him. He could not help himself. But the Colonel would not believe me. Nor would he believe Gertrude ...'

'Is she still there?' asked the parson, anxiously.

'No. I told her to take the children to the lower farm where there are neighbours who will look after her. She has gone by now.'

'Then there is nobody left on the farm?'

'Only the Natives. But I can trust them, Mr Quakerley, and Martin will come back ...'

'But do you realise, Old Friend, what that means?'

'Aye, that they will take him and make him out to be a rebel against our Queen ... I know that. And she but dead a month ago ...'

'And what happened then? I mean, what did the Colonel say? What did he accuse you of?'

'He said that I was suspected of having brought the enemy to the farm and that I was a prisoner and must go with them to the Village. I could do nothing. They put me into a cart, and two of the soldiers climbed in after me and sat alongside me with their guns loaded. When we went over the pass we nearly had an accident, and would have had one if I did not manage the horses. They let me drive after that, and on the whole they treated me well. Mr Monk, too, he has been kind. I will repay him if I have the chance. But now, you see for yourselves, Old Friends, I can do nothing.'

The gaoler came in, looking worried. 'There's military police a-coming, Sir,' he said to Quakerley, and added, 'You'd best be going now. I can let you out at the back.'

On his way home, Quakerley stopped at Elias Vantloo's office. He did not like the young attorney, but he recognised his cleverness, and Elias was indebted to him for many small favours. Old Martin would need legal advice, and Vantloo was in touch with the larger law firms at Cape Town.

'You must get him out, Elias,' he insisted, as he put the case to the attorney. 'The commandant tells me that he has no jurisdiction in the matter, and that it is entirely one for the military. Do what you can. If necessary, apply to the Supreme Court for his release.'

'I will see what I can do, Mr Quakerley,' promised the attorney. 'But we are under martial law, you know, and it will be very difficult.'

'Even under martial law they cannot keep an old man in prison without a charge,' said Andrew, indignantly. 'There is not a shadow of a case against Rekker, and if there is, he should be properly charged, and told of what he is accused.'

'The court would not interfere in an area where martial law has been proclaimed, Mr Quakerley,' rejoined the attorney, shaking his head. 'It has been tried repeatedly, and the court has always decided that it would grant no order which it could not enforce. That is sober common sense, Mr Quakerley. Still, we can try it. Of course, you know it will cost money to brief counsel ...'

'I will write you out a cheque now, Vantloo. Don't spare expenses. But get a move on. I can't bear thinking of my old friend staying in gaol. It is too preposterous altogether. See Colonel Cautley, and give him any assurance he wants. Rekker can stay at my place on parole if he likes, but it would be best for him to return to his farm. Someone must be there to look after things.'

'That I am afraid I can hardly hope to obtain, Mr Quakerley. I have reason to fear that there are others who will soon be keeping Uncle Rekker company in gaol. The military police have just brought in Mias Swart and his two sons, and I am told that Amadeus Sablonniere is for it too ...'

'Good heavens, man, have they taken leave of their senses? What is there against these men? And they are not even within the area of military operations ...'

'Excuse me, Mr Quakerley, but they are. The Boers are all round us, and there was a skirmish on Mias's farm this morning. Six of our side were killed, and eleven wounded. It was a very warm engagement, and there is no doubt that the commando was guided to our positions.'

'This is shocking, Elias. Are you sure of your facts? But even then, neither Swart nor Sablonniere had anything to do with it. Of that I am sure, as sure as I can be of anything. If they are gaoled you must act for them as well.'

'I must have some authority, Mr Quakerley.'

'See them, man, see them. Meanwhile I authorise you, until you can get instructions from them. Here, give me a pen; I'll make out a cheque for you now. You can go up to a thousand—this is for five hundred as a start, but I shall expect you to act quickly.'

'I'll try and get a permit to see them at once,' said Vantloo, drying the cheque on the blotting pad. 'But I am afraid it can't be done so quickly, Mr Quakerley. These things take time.'

'Very well. While you are about it, get leave for us to send some comforts in to them. I suppose there won't be any difficulties about that?'

'Hardly, Mr Quakerley, but ...' the young attorney's voice was insinuating, 'have you thought about the possibilities of the case, Mr Quakerley? I mean,' he went on hastily, 'the possibilities that Mr Rekker might be tried? On some charge or other ... there have been numerous cases elsewhere, and it is so easy, Mr Quakerley, to arraign him on some specific charge of having infringed martial law regulations. It would be better, perhaps, to see the commandant ...'

'He tells me he has nothing to do with the matter,' interrupted the old man.

'That, Mr Quakerley, is really only an excuse. Of course, strictly speaking, a prisoner brought in by the police from outside would fall under the military, and not, properly speaking, under the commandant. I am not quite sure on that point. But in any case, Major Mallom is in charge here, and Colonel Cautley is the officer commanding the troops. I think I should see both, of course, but Major Mallom would ultimately have to deal with Rekker's case. He will have to make the affidavits if the matter goes to court.'

'Do what you think best, Vantloo. Only do it quickly. It is damnable that men of Rekker's standing should be in the common gaol.'

Old Andrew walked home. He was much upset; again his conceptions needed readjustment, and although he tried to view the matter from the angle of the military authorities, he could not rid himself of a growing resentment against high-handedness that on such slight pretext created these unheard of difficulties. It was all very well to safeguard military interests, and no doubt the activities of the Boer commandos were most annoying—he cursed them heartily and felt far less sympathy with them than he had ever done before—but this sort of thing, imprisoning staid and respectable citizens who had held Her late Majesty's commission as Justices of the Peace, was a bit too bad.

There were no telephones in the Village, and Andrew called the garden boy and bade him take a note to Mr Storam, asking the magistrate to call at his convenience. He felt very tired after his unusual morning's activity, and even the sight of his prematurely flowering daffodils in the garden did not rouse him out of his despondency. Normally he would have been excited by the sight of these star-like blossoms; they had no business to bloom at this time of the year, and unless something was done they would degenerate and be effete when the time came for their proper flowering, in spring. Now he merely glanced at them, and told the boys not to water them.

In the coolness of his study he rested for a while on his big armchair that had belonged to his father and had been brought from England almost a century ago. Then he roused himself and began to write letters to his own legal firm in Cape Town. It was a firm of high standing, and the partners were violently anti-Bond, but Andrew was a valuable client and he had no fear that they would not take up the case if there was anything in it. By the time he had finished the second letter, Mr Storam walked in.

'I have done my best, Mr Quakerley,' he said, shaking hands with the old man, and subsiding into a chair, 'but I am afraid it is of no use. If it were a matter for the Major, I feel sure that there would be no difficulty in getting Rekker out of gaol, on parole, but the Colonel does not see eye to eye with us. Yes, I have seen him; just now. He was most curt, almost offensive, but one must make allowances for his state of mind. The position is most unsatisfactory, Mr Quakerley, and there is every reason to be anxious.'

'Surely there is no danger, Storam. There's nearly a thousand men here, with guns, and surely they should prove sufficient for a bare two or three hundred of the enemy.'

'Oh no, as a matter of fact we have nearly five thousand men, and I believe an additional two thousand are on their way here. But double that number would be needed to round up the commandos. At present they are as elusive as a will-o-the-wisp, and no sooner have they been cleared out of one area than they bob up at some other place. There is constant sniping going on, and the District is thoroughly alight. I am afraid quite a number of our people have joined them, and of course there is always the active sympathy which they are sure of getting when they appear.'

'But that is no reason for imprisoning Rekker,' exclaimed the old man. 'If he and the others were free they would use their influence to prevent our people from making fools of themselves ...'

'I used that argument,' said the magistrate, shaking his head, 'but Colonel Cautley countered by saying that they might also use their influence against us. Come, Mr Quakerley, one must admit that there is some justification for the attitude he takes up. My own feeling is that if we could remove all the people from the farms into the Village there would be less chance of anything untoward taking place, and it would be best in their own interests. I suggested that to the Colonel, but although Mallom agrees with me, Cautley wasn't impressed. His opinion is that if the "suspects" are in gaol, the rest will behave themselves.'

'You need not be anxious about Rekker,' he went on, reassuringly. 'I have arranged with the Colonel that the prisoners may see their friends, and that comforts and anything they require may be sent in. Here, by the way, is a permit for you to visit the gaol whenever you like. Vantloo tells me that you have asked him to deal with the case. You know, of course, that Vantloo is the last person in the world to do anything that is likely to antagonise the authorities. He knows which side his bread is buttered on, does that young man. But perhaps, just on that account, he may be the best man to deal with the matter. Of course you know, too, that it is extremely unlikely that the courts will interfere ...'

'I don't see why they shouldn't, Storam. Do you mean to tell me that a man can be imprisoned without any charge being laid against him? Isn't there such a thing as *habeas corpus*? Couldn't the court order Monk—who is, after all, a civil servant and amenable to its authority—to show cause why Martin shouldn't be released?'

'In normal times, yes. But the Supreme Court has held, over and over again, that it cannot interfere in an area where martial law has been proclaimed. It has in one instance interfered where the military imprisoned a man of Rekker's standing, but before the order could be served, the authorities removed the prisoner to a gaol in a martial law area, and although it was manifestly contempt of court, the court refused to make a further order.'

'But this is unbearable, Storam. Are we to be deprived of our ordinary rights as citizens simply because the military get into a panic?'

'Martial law gives plenary and absolute power to the military authorities, Mr Quakerley. It is the negation of all law, in one sense, but it is a logical method of safeguarding interests which transcend those of the individual and the community. It is a measure of public safety, and as such we must submit to it. I like it as little as you do, and you may remember that I told you everything depended on the manner in which it is administered. Now in Major Mallom we have, if I may say so, an almost ideal administrator. The man is a gentleman, with the instincts of a gentleman, and he is the last person to act hastily, or in a panic. The trouble now is that there is apparently a higher authority, and that the Major is subservient to the officer in chief command in the field, who naturally enough has the immediate military interests in view. I am afraid we must just bear with it, and hope that it will not last long. But I confess I am very anxious, for if the commandos are not forced to surrender very soon, there may be terrible disorganisation and all sorts of difficulties.'

'Have you any idea of what is actually taking place, Storam?'

'Mallom lets me see the latest reports; they come in every hour, and there has been desultory skirmishing all over the District. You know how difficult the country is; in these rugged hills and in that sandy, bush-grown country round about Swart's farm, it is easy enough for a couple of hundred men, well-mounted and guided, to play old Harry for a while. Of course, there is no doubt that in the end their efforts will be utterly futile. That is what makes me so savage when I hear how they are going on, shooting harmless Coloured people and terrorising our own people. They know perfectly well that if they are caught they will be treated as prisoners of war, but that anyone who has joined them here will stand his trial as a rebel, and will probably be shot or hanged.'

'I thought it was agreed that the penalty should be disfranchisement?'

'No, that is only for those who joined when the war started, and who surrendered under what is known as Brabant's Proclamation. It does not affect our people, I am afraid. They will be treated like rebels, and if caught with arms in their hands, will either be shot straight off or condemned by court martial. Personally, Mr Quakerley, although it seems brutal to say so, I should much prefer to have them shot immediately, or killed in the fighting, to seeing them led into town as captured rebels. Indeed, I sincerely hope that none of them will be taken. It would be too awful to have a public execution here of someone we know.'

Old Andrew stared at the magistrate. His indignation had given place to a vague fear as he realised the boundless possibilities of the situation. Hitherto he had thought only of the irksomeness and the annoyance of martial law, of its petty officiousness and unwarranted interference with individual liberties, as exemplified in Rekker's case, but what Storam said postulated much graver danger. It brought vividly to mind what Rekker had told him about some of the District folk that had been seen with the commandos, and the serious position of young Martin Rekker who had been taken as a guide. He thrust the thought from him; it was incredible that such things could happen. Had the world gone mad?

'At all costs, Storam,' he said, struggling to keep his voice even, 'we must prevent that. I can scarcely conceive that they would go to that extreme ...'

'Mr Quakerley,' said the magistrate, seriously and gravely, 'we must not blind ourselves to facts. Take my word for it, the position is desperately serious. It could not be graver than it is. With the exception of one or two—I have in mind men like Gideon Ras and a few others who are fortunately not our people, although they are Colonials—not one of our people has joined voluntarily. All have been pressed. You know what sort of pressure has been used, and you know what these young, ignorant farm hands are like, and how such pressure, and the glamour of fighting on commando, reacts upon them. I think it is wicked and cowardly to entice these men, but it has been done, and we must face the consequences.'

'Can nothing be done, Storam? Anything I can do ... if I can go out and speak to them ... I may have some influence ... I will do my best ... or Uhlmann ... surely Uhlmann can be of use ...'

'I have done what I could, Mr Quakerley. I have already seen Mr Uhlmann. Major Mallom intends to issue a proclamation calling upon all those who have joined the commandos to surrender unconditionally, but Mr Uhlmann is to go out and try if he cannot move them to come in before it is issued. In that case they will be dealt with leniently—I have the Major's word for that. As to your going, I have not thought of that, but there would be some risk.'

'I am prepared to take that,' said the old man, staunchly. 'I daresay I can still manage to sit a horse, but at any rate with a cart ...'

'Let me put it to the commandant,' suggested the magistrate. 'I am to see him this afternoon. Could you walk over to the parsonage this evening—before seven, say? Then we can discuss the matter further.'

'I'll be there,' promised the old man, eagerly. 'If you can induce the commandant to come too, do so. Somehow I have an idea that Uhlmann and he get on very well.'

The magistrate took his leave, and Andrew busied himself with his correspondence, in an attempt to distract his mind from brooding over the situation. But he wrote badly; his thoughts kept wandering towards young Martin Rekker, and they were not pleasant thoughts. The maid came to announce afternoon tea. Alice was having a tennis party, and tea would be served under the big magnolia tree.

With a sigh he pushed his papers from him, and got up to join his guests round the tea table.

Chapter 31

The contrast between the atmosphere under the magnolia tree and that of the cool, darkened study he had just quitted was not merely climatic. True, the heat of the late summer shimmered in undulating gusts over the garden, and the slanting sun-light, reflected on the burnished canna leaves, dazzled one's eyes. Even in the shade of the magnolia tree it was hot. The heavy green of the foliage, and the light, immaculate dress of the guests seemed to accentuate the heat. But outside under the magnolia tree there was a spirit of light-hearted gaiety, as if everyone there was carefree, bent on seizing the happiness of the moment, counting today's gain whate'er befall. The tinkle of glass and china, suggesting fragrant tea and cool, iced drinks, the medley of voices, laughter, gesture, all indicated that Mrs Quakerley's tea party was a success.

Andrew went from group to group, exchanging a few banal conventionalities with his wife's guests. They were more Alice's friends than his, although he had nothing against them, and liked many. Most of the Village residents were represented, but he noticed that Dr Buren was absent and that Mrs Uhlmann, who sat quietly talking to Mrs Mance-Bisley, looked unhappy, although she tried to adjust to the gay company in which she found herself. His son-in-law, in shirt sleeves and khaki shorts, was acting as master of the ceremonies, and his cheerful cackle of laughter occasionally rose high above the hum of conversation. Seeing Andrew looking about for a chair, he brought forward a camp-stool and placed it a few yards away from the main group.

'Come and squat down here, Sir,' he called out. 'I'll bring your tea round to you, and Miss Marradee can tell you how she lammed us at tennis.'

'Oh, but I know the court, Captain Overbury,' chirruped the lady teacher, consuming her third éclair. 'And oh, Mr Quakerley, imagine for yourself what a victory it was when we only won six-five, and every game a deuce game ...'

'But it wouldn't have been if you had not played so magnificently, Miss Marradee,' said the Captain, gallantly. 'Your partner has no idea of placing. But I see Mrs Chumley is looking for you. I think they want to make up another set.'

'There,' he continued, seating himself on the grass, when Miss Marradee had gone off to the tennis court, 'now I may have a chance to chat, Sir. I tried to get you this morning, but nobody seemed to know where you could be found. Then I had to go on duty, and when I came back Mother wanted someone to shepherd this crowd. You wouldn't think, Sir, would you, that we're in the middle of a war, and within range of a Mauser, with all this jollification?'

'You seem to be enjoying it just as much as the others,' remarked his father-in-law, grimly.

'So I do. I can tell you it's a blessed change after being in the saddle and careering over the veld for sixteen hours at a stretch. But let me take your cup, Sir. Another? No? Well, if you don't want to play host—and mother's doing all the needful, so far as I can see—what about walking down to the orchard, Sir? I'd rather like a little chat with you.'

Andrew rose from his camp stool, and the two wormed their way, politely disengaging themselves from the little groups they met, towards the lower end of the garden. There they could still hear the sound of the animated conversation and the shrill cries of the tennis players, but could talk without being disturbed.

'Do you know, Sir,' began the Captain, taking Andrew's arm and steering him into the shade of the large-leaved shaddock trees, 'I have been thinking over things, and I have come to the conclusion that you and mother, Aunt Joan, and Anne and the children ought to go down to the coast while the going's good. What about having a holiday down at my place—you owe Katie and me a visit, and you will find ... well, things are not as bad there as they are likely to be here, Sir.'

'You think they will be bad here, James?'

'Think! I am sure of it,' exclaimed the Captain, in positive tones. 'I don't know if you are aware, Sir, of what is actually taking place now? Do you realise that we have fought five engagements, and that the District is as unsafe for any force that cannot cope with these commandos as the Transvaal would be? In fact, I believe that it would be safer for me to go on patrol on the highveld there than to go out here.'

'Storam hinted as much, James. But I can scarcely credit it. Here we have a strong force, with guns and all that, and yet it seems we cannot put a few hundred Boers in their place and prevent them from turning the District into a hell. I must confess that it makes me feel ashamed. After all we should protect our people ...'

'It is not so easy as you think, Father. As a civilian, I may at times share your view, but as a soldier of some little experience, I must say that we have a tremendous task before us. I doubt if we realise it. And if it comes to protection, I am not at all sure that if the Boers make an attack we'll be able to hold on to this place. It is far too exposed, you see. We shall have to fall back into the Valley. And that means that you and all the rest here will be at their mercy ...'

'I hardly think they can be more brutal ...'

'Now, now, Father, don't let your indignation carry you too far. I am quite with you as regards what is going on here. But you don't know what the position is. Storam can hardly put you wise, but I may drop a hint without impropriety.'

'What are you implying? Is there something worse than what I've heard, James? I am quite prepared for it, after what has happened so far.'

'I think you'd better be prepared for much worse,' replied the Captain gravely. 'Mallom is not quite *persona grata* just now. It is said quite openly that he is far too lenient, and he feels his position—anyone would in the circumstances, and this sort of work is distasteful enough to a civilian and must be a hundred times worse for a soldier, especially when there's fighting at the front door, so to speak. Now Mallom has played the game—you must admit that. And if he goes, well, if I were you I would just take the family and go down to the coast.'

'Is Major Mallom likely to be displaced, James?'

'I think, quite likely. There is little love lost between him and Cautley; their interests are in a way not identical, and naturally the Colonel is exceedingly worried, and thinks that if Mallom had been more strict and had acted on the hints given him when he came here, there would not have been half this trouble ...'

'If the commandant had been as foolhardy and as hasty as the Colonel seems to be, James, I can assure you that things would have been infinitely worse. I know our people. They are tolerant and long-suffering, but they are men with a certain amount of courage, and you can't deal with them as you are doing now.'

'Again, I agree. But the point that matters is what the Colonel thinks, and we cannot blame Cautley for taking every possible precaution. To you and me, Father, who are unaccustomed to war and attached to everything that stands for civil war, this sort of treatment may seem monstrous. No doubt it is, judged by our standards. But from a military point of view there is a good deal to be said for it.'

'That is what Storam impresses upon me,' growled the old man, disgustedly. 'James,' he broke out with a ring of passion in his voice, 'is this the sort of thing we Englishmen can stand for? We have always fought clean—my father harped on that in a way I sometimes found boring—England's prestige, her magnanimity, her sense of fairness. What becomes of it all when this sort of thing is going to be remembered long after the war is done? Do you think Rekker is going to forget this indignity that has been put upon him, or Swart, or Sablonniere? Is there a particle of evidence against them that justifies what has been done to them?'

'You really do not know if there is or not, Father. On the face of it, they would not have been dealt with in that way unless there was at least sufficient to make a *prima facie* case against them ...'

'That I will never believe, James. I know them, and I know that they are utterly incapable of treason ...'

'Yes, but Colonel Cautley does not know them, and Mallom is unable to interfere. You must look at the matter from a reasonable point of view and reserve judgment ...'

'Why is Mallom unable to interfere? After all, he is commandant. It is for him to say what should be done, not Cautley.'

'Ordinarily, yes. But I am not sure what exactly are the privileges of the commandant, and what those of the officer commanding the troops, and I fancy the former has only a limited jurisdiction. He can deal with offences against the regulations, but I doubt if he has any say in the treatment of prisoners of war. That is a matter solely for the officer commanding, whose decisions are, of course, subject to the approval of the commander-in-chief.'

'Do you mean to tell me that they may bring Rekker before a court martial and sentence him to what they please ...'

'I am afraid,' interrupted his son-in-law, seriously, 'that is exactly what they can do, and what they mean to do. Father, you must face the position, and it will be much the best way for you to get away from here until the affair is settled one way or the other.'

'That I shall never do,' said the old man, harshly. 'It would be the rankest cowardice, James. My father would not have done so, nor my mother, Boy. I shall stay, and while I have strength I shall do what I can for my old friends. But I think it would be as well if you spoke to Alice and Anne. You need not trouble to talk to Joan. She won't budge for all your Cautleys in the world.'

'It is you I want to get away,' urged his son-in-law. 'You and the children. This is no place for them, and you are ... well, Father, you're not quite the tactful old codger you imagine yourself to be. You are much too emotional. Do let me persuade you.'

'That you will never do,' said the old man, nervously fingering his chin as he spoke. 'I am not a bit emotional—ask Joan about that. But I get indignant when I see such ... such brutality. Any man would. Get Alice and Anne away by all means. You may tell them that the Village is unsafe, and that it is precautionary measure. I suppose we may go as far as that, James?'

'We may go much further, Father. Honestly, the position, from a military point of view, is dangerous. These commandos are all over the District. This morning we located one of them in a *kloof* in the mountains, and when our men came there they found only a few snipers who killed three of our fellows.'

In the cool of the evening Andrew strolled down to the parsonage. He drank coffee with the parson on the *stoep*, and they waited for the magistrate. Both men were too busy with their thoughts to talk. Uhlmann looked worn and anxious, and his lined, hatchet-like face had lost colour. When Storam came, bringing with him the young attorney, whose jaunty, detached manner seemed almost offensive to old Andrew, they adjourned to the study for consultation.

The magistrate had little encouragement to give. The prisoners were in charge of the military authorities, and amenable to a military court martial if it was decided to put them on their trial. The parson nodded his head as he listened.

'That is only what I expected,' he said slowly. 'It is war, and in war things take place which in peace time would shock us. I do not think we can complain ...'

'But, Uhlmann,' old Andrew interrupted, 'surely you do not justify their action? It seems to me to be the stupidest thing they could do.'

'Mr Quakerley,' said the clergyman, impressively, 'although it seems like that to us, it is what may be expected. War is harsh—cruel, unjust, but it is war. You,' he waved his arm so as to include his three listeners in its suggestive sweep, 'you have had no experience of its harshness. I have. I tell you, if you knew what happened in the Franco-German war, if you knew what took place in the war in Atjeh, you would not wonder at this, but you would be thankful that it is no worse. A civilian in arms is shot out of hand ... a farmer shielding the enemy is hanged on the nearest tree ... that is war, my friends; but our people do not know this, and they think that in war crime and suspicion of crime must be tried by the softer civil methods.'

'You are quite right, MrUhlmann,' assented the magistrate. 'I have been trying to make Mr Quakerley realise that all day.'

'I do realise it,' said Andrew. He felt very tired, physically and mentally. Only his strong sense of indignation bore him up and gave him strength to go on. 'But there is no reason to suspect these men of having committed a crime.'

'There is some evidence,' interjected the young attorney, glibly. 'I have had a talk with Colonel Cautley. He tells me that Rekker has been in correspondence with the enemy ...'

'I explained that,' Mr Storam broke in. 'They were duly censored letters from his relatives in the Free State. The latest is dated seven months back, and contains merely such information as relates to family matters ...'

'The Colonel spoke of a code,' interrupted Vantloo. 'But that, of course, is not the only evidence. The main point against him is the fact that his son undoubtedly guided the commando. That is a fact, and in the circumstances it seems to me that they are justified in detaining Mr Rekker.'

'Yes, I don't see that we can call their action entirely unjustifiable,' admitted the magistrate. 'You remember, Mr Quakerley, I suggested that young Martin's case might be much more serious than we think. I have no doubt in my own mind that he was coerced ...'

'Nor have I,' said the parson, stoutly. 'Young Martin is far too sensible to have done a thing like that.'

'But don't you see,' suggested the attorney, briskly, 'how much that tells against him? The prosecution will of course say that he made them coerce him—that the tying on to the horse and the loaded Mausers were carefully arranged beforehand, so that if he got captured he could claim that he had been forced ...'

'If that is the case, if they are going to allege that,' exclaimed Andrew, 'where is it going to stop?'

'Aye, that is the question,' remarked the parson. 'Mr Storam, did you convey to the commandant my proposals?'

'Yes, Mr Uhlmann. he referred me to the Colonel. By the way, the Major could not come tonight. He tells me that it is doubtful whether he will continue to act. He has asked to be relieved in order to go back to his command in the field.'

'That would be a great pity,' said the parson, shaking his head. 'We may not get so good a commandant if he goes. And the Colonel, what did he say, Mr Storam?'

'I am afraid, Mr Uhlmann, I would shock you if I repeated his words. The gist of them is that he fears you may do more harm than good by going out to talk with these men.'

'I was afraid he might think that.' The parson's sincerity was evident. 'It would have been utterly irregular, and the military mind dislikes irregularity of any sort. But there was a hope that he might consent, and I thought I might be able to persuade some of our people. Now I can do no more.'

'You must prepare yourself for something worse, Mr Uhlmann.' said the magistrate. 'The Colonel thinks that it would be desirable that there should not be any services. I understand that this is one of the reasons for the friction between him and the commandant.'

'What? Am I not to be allowed to minister to my people?'

The magistrate's distress made him reply in a hurried, shame-faced way. 'I understand that is the intention. I need not say, Mr Uhlmann, that such an interdict will have the worst possible results. I ventured to point that out, but his answer was that he was the best judge of the matter.'

'In that case I, too, must be the best judge of what I shall have to do,' said the parson, firmly. 'I have been brought up, Mr Storam, to obey authority in all temporal things, even when its orders are harsh and cruel, as they must of necessity be in war time. But I have a duty to my people and to God. An order like that I can only obey if I am forced to obey.'

'And you would be quite right to resist it,' said Andrew, indignantly. He had been so purged of emotion that he had deemed himself incapable of further resentment, but this new stupidity exploited a latent store of indignation of which he had not believed himself possessed. 'Vantloo, you must take this up—at once. Your wires will be censored, so you must go yourself. You must spare no expense. See the Governor, Sir Gordon, anyone, but do something to prevent this. It is scandalous ...'

'Better wait until we have it in black and white, Mr Quakerley,' said the attorney, soothingly. 'I daresay the Colonel was in a paddy when he spoke. He could hardly go that length, unless there is an actual military reason for closing the church. In that case, of course, Mr Uhlmann would have to consent.'

'Yes, that would be different,' said the parson. And I agree with you, Mr Vantloo, that it is probably only a threat. Let us, as you say, wait until we have to do with a fact. Am I to take it then, Mr Storam, that the Colonel objects even to my circulating a pastoral letter such as I submitted to you, and of which you and Major Mallom approved?'

'No, he will let you do that. The commandant is having copies typed, and they will be distributed. But I doubt very much if they will be effective. Have you any idea how many have joined?'

'I have tried to get information, but it is mostly hearsay and very unreliable,' answered the parson, glancing at old Andrew, who sat in moody silence, digesting his thoughts. 'Probably some twenty-five in all, and not one of them a man of substance or education. All poor Whites, and all like chaff driven before the wind.'

'That will not help them if they are caught,' muttered the magistrate. 'I know that. But so far no one has been captured. Two have been shot, in the fighting. That I know. If any are caught ...'

He did not finish his sentence. The magistrate got up.

'Come along, Vantloo,' he said. 'We must be home before eight o'clock, or we may have to spend the night in gaol. We'll see you home, Mr Quakerley. The military police are very active just now. Last night Miller got into trouble, and I had to go down to the office to release him.'

Chapter 32

During the week that followed, Captain Overbury persuaded his mother-in-law and the Crest family to retire to one of the coastal ports where martial law had not yet been proclaimed. Mrs Quakerley thought that Cape Town offered the best scope for her activities; she had many old friends there, and proposed to stay at one of the seaside hotels with her daughter, who would be near Charlie.

Andrew resolutely refused to shift, and his sister did not even condescend to argue the matter with her nephew-in-law.

'Get Alice and Anne away, by all means,' Joan had said, when the subject was first broached. 'They are worse than useless here, James. And if Andy chooses to join them, so much the better. I doubt if it will do him any good to remain here. But someone must stay, and I see no reason why it should not be I.'

Alice and Anne and the three Crest children had accordingly left in a spring-wagon, travelling by easy stages, and at their own responsibility. Captain Overbury had obtained leave to go with them as far as the railway station. The journey was accomplished without any misadventures. The travellers saw no signs of the marauding Boers, but wherever they outspanned at a wayside farm they found the country folk intensely nervous, jumpy and suspicious. Martial law had already created its special, pernicious atmosphere in the District, and the action of the invading commandos had done nothing to lessen the high-pitched emotional excitement that everywhere prevailed.

Captain Overbury, fluent in Afrikaans, talked with the country people whom he met, and the impression he got was that most of them were in a state of dire perplexity, torn between the innate respect for law and authority, and their resentment at the manner in which authority now enforced its orders. From the farms all horses and mules had been removed; ploughing and agricultural operations had to be carried on with donkey teams or by hand, and as practically all the supplies of grain had been seized, there was a want of seed, while owing to the scarcity of Native labour very little could be done on the lands. The wayside farms presented a neglected, in some cases almost a ruined, appearance. Some had been visited by the Boers, who had destroyed out-buildings, and done damage to the orchards and the vineyards. But even more wanton damage had been done by the troops which had passed along that road and had bivouacked upon the farms. They had broken down doors for firewood, requisitioned whatever they had required from the homesteads, and plundered the gardens and orchards. The farmers told him of wanton destruction and senseless looting, but admitted that all this had been put a stop to as soon as the officers had interfered. Their attitude was a mingling of apprehension and resentment, an apprehension as much of what they might have to suffer at the hands of the invaders as of what they might have to endure from the military, and a resentment directed equally against the enemy and the defenders.

This attitude was eloquently expressed by Thomas Seldon, who farmed at the foot of the pass over the mountain, and who had been a prey, successively, of the invading commandos, of the columns marching towards the Village, and again of the small parties of Boers sweeping down unexpectedly into the Valley. He had a large store, for his father, who had been one of the early English settlers in the Valley, had built up a flourishing business both as a trader and as a farmer. Thomas Seldon bought hides, bark, buchu, bush-tea, and wood in large quantities, and sold Birmingham wares, groceries and haberdashery in return. At his store you could get anything that you required, from a harmonium and a double-furrow plough to delicatessen imported in jars and tins. He was a typical first generation Colonial, burly of build, clean-living and honest, straightforward in his views, with a natural bent in favour of his father's homeland and all it stood for. Without having behind him the aristocratic tradition of the Quakerleys, he could look back on an early training which had inculcated in him an appreciation of English love of liberty, of civic freedom, and untrammelled tolerance. From the first he had been consistently anti-Bond, and had voted and thought Progressive, championing the cause of the Outlanders, even when such championship had seemed to endanger his business transactions. It had never really done so, for the District was tolerant, and allowed each man to have his own opinions on political matters, but before the war Seldon had often expressed himself warmly about the vacillating policy of the President, and when war broke out his support had been wholeheartedly on the right side. His son had volunteered for active service, and had been killed somewhere in the Transvaal. When the District became involved, Seldon had offered what he had in the way of transport and supplies. He had served on Mr Storam's committee, and was generally respected throughout the District as a man of substance and character, who, for all his 'English-mindedness,' was nevertheless a good Colonist on whose staunchness one could depend.

Like many another 'loyalist,' Seldon had found his position increasingly difficult when the war encroached upon the District. The Boer commando, galloping upon his farm in the middle of the night, had looted his shop, slaughtered his prize sheep, burned a rick, and devastated his garden. He had been forced to give them coffee and biscuits, which he did not much mind as it was the custom to extend such simple hospitality to those who touched at his place. But he had an uneasy feeling that even such simple hospitality as had been forced upon him might be construed as 'comforting the enemy,' and he had sent a boy secretly to the Commandant to inform him of what had occurred. The Boers had intercepted and shot the messenger. When the relieving patrols came to the farm, Sheldon had had some difficulty in proving that he had acted under duress. More than one column had passed over his farm since then, and every one had taken toll. The wire fencing had been snipped through; his cattle and sheep had been carried off, and all he had to show for them, as well as for the requisitioned stores, was a bundle of 'chits' illegibly signed, of which he doubted the commercial value.

'It was deucedly awkward, Captain,' he told Overbury. 'I am brow-beaten by some loutish commando commandant, and told that I am disloyal to South Africa because I do not fall on his neck when he trespasses on my property, and the very next day I am slanged by one of our own officers because I did not make enough resistance. What resistance can I make? I haven't even a shotgun on the place, and if I had one, what would be the use of the damned thing? I am supposed to give information about the movements of the Boers—how can I when the first thing I hear of them is when they are off-saddling in my farm yard? And how can I send information when there is no protection for my boys? And if that is my position, Captain, what must it be for my neighbours who have even less means than I have? All this won't beggar me, and I can put up with it, but they cannot. If this mess is cleared up, there will be a greater mess which we'll find much more difficult to clear up. And that's what frightens me.'

'We are fairly well organised now,' said the Captain. 'The main road is safe, I should say. There's no further risk of your being attacked here ...'

'Oh, isn't there?' interrupted Seldon. 'I can tell you, Captain, that the Boers are moving just where they please, and when they please. It is no use trying to round them up with these heavy columns. You should have a mobile force. Take a leaf out of their own book, and run them down with small, mounted bodies. Chase them right into the mountains. That is the only way.'

'Of course it is. I have always said so. But,' the Captain shrugged his shoulders, 'we Colonials must not express our views on these things. You were talking about your neighbours just now. What is your opinion of them? Are they helping the enemy? I mean, are they actively sympathising?'

'I know every one of them,' answered Seldon forcibly, 'and I can tell you this, Captain. If by sympathising you mean, are they doing what I did when they came here—talking civilly to them, giving them a cup of coffee, and listening to what they have to say—then there is sympathy enough. But that's natural. That's our way. When it comes to actually endangering our lives, I daresay most of us hereabouts will draw the line, martial law or no martial law. There's such a thing as natural feelings, Captain. But I can vouch for it that no one of any importance has helped them in the sense you mean—that is, giving them information, or helping them to fight. When you come to think of it, Captain, our way of acting is nothing to be astonished at. We don't want them here, and we think it is silly and stupid of them to come here. Of course, they say they do it for military reasons, but that is all Betty Martin. They did, and they do, expect that some of us would join them, and my own opinion is that now that they have found out their mistake, they will scurry back as soon as they can. Unless they can get a substantial number of recruits here—and that they won't—there is not much sense in dividing their forces as they are doing now.'

'How many recruits have they got? Have you any notion?'

'It would be difficult to say, Captain Overbury. So far as I could see, none of the faces in the commando that came here were familiar to me. I daresay, however, that they were not all *burghers*, and that about twenty-five per cent were Colonials. Not from our District, though. Hereabouts I know of only two who are absent and said to be with the commandos, and both are poor Whites.'

'That is also our information in the Village. But if this goes on, others might join, you think?'

'I am sure of it, Captain. Look you, people will say that if it is a choice between joining and being imprisoned and court-martialled for something you never thought of doing, the odds may be in favour of joining. Then you'd have a run for your money, and be something of a hero, too. There's many a youngster hereabouts, Captain, who might see it in that light.'

'I'm afraid you're right, Mr Seldon. But their position would be awful, all the same. There is no possible doubt about the result of the war—this incursion is a flash in the pan, and before the year is over it will have been quashed.'

'That's what I tell them, when I have a chance of speaking to them, Captain. But somehow it does not seem to impress them. If you were to get a move on and obtain some decisive result, the matter would be different. You have no idea how these men on commando cajole our boys.'

'Yes, that is one of the worst points in the case. I can imagine how dreadfully hard it must be for the poor beggars to resist all that tommy-rot about their duty as patriots, and so forth.'

'You may well say that. And it is tommy-rot. There's not a valid reason in the wide world why any one of us should lift his little finger to bolster up the sort of Republicanism they've had in the Transvaal. But I am getting doubtful about whether there is any good reason why I should risk my life and property for something that treats us in this step-motherly fashion. When it comes to loyalty, I'm as loyal as anyone, but I don't hold with what is being done hereabouts now, Captain. I don't indeed.'

'Have a little patience, Mr Seldon. It's a mess-up, as you say, and one must make allowances. I have seen much the same thing in the eastern districts, and things have come fairly right there. I expect that will be the case here unless we get complications.'

'There are sure to be complications,' said Seldon, gloomily.

In the Village the weeks passed without much to chronicle. There seemed to be a lull in the activities of the commandos. The general opinion, not shared by the military, was that the Boers had left the District and were operating farther afield.

The three prisoners in the gaol remained there. The young attorney's efforts on their behalf had been fruitless. The Supreme Court at Cape Town, sitting in the old building where in the days of Lord Charles Somerset the commissioner in charge of the slaves had his office, had had before it the case of *Rekker & Others v Military Authorities*. Counsel for the applicants had demanded an order calling upon the Keeper of the Village Gaol to show cause why the applicants should not be immediately released. Counsel had talked glibly about the liberties of the subject, and had declaimed apposite extracts from Burke. The Attorney-General, for the respondents, had put in an affidavit from the Officer Commanding in the District, in which it was stated that for military reasons it was imperative that the applicants should be incarcerated. Counsel for the applicants had protested that this was not enough. There had, he argued, been no fighting of late in the District; so far as was known, there was nothing to fight; the commandos had vanished. A specific charge should be intimated. The gaol-keeper was a civil official, amenable to the jurisdiction of the Court. He quoted cases in support, American cases, English cases, a Colonial case. The Court took two minutes to decide. It regretted that it could not interfere, as it was bound by its own decision in previous cases, where it had laid down that it would not grant an order operative in a district under martial law as it had no power to enforce such an order. The applicants would pay the costs of the application.

Andrew Quakerley, although warned by Mr Storam that such a decision was inevitable, was highly indignant. He wrote frantic letters to his firm of attorneys, urging them to spare no expense to take the case to a higher court. The firm wrote back soothingly, pointing out that it would be injudicious to take the matter to the Privy Council, as there was no doubt whatever that in a legal sense the Court was perfectly right. Andrew wrote to the Prime Minister, curbing his indignation so far as to confine himself strictly to what was relevant, although he much wished to pour out his heart to Sir Gordon. He received a short note of acknowledgment from the private secretary. He wrote to the Governor, almost a replica of his letter to the Prime Minister, although he enclosed a copy of the letter. The result was the same.

Mr Storam, more wary or more wise, had long ago given up his faith in Governors and Prime Ministers. He had set himself to woo Colonel Cautley, who, as the military situation cleared and the load of anxiety became lessened, had improved so far that he no longer broke off an important conversation in the middle, and much less frequently called upon the Creator to emphasize his opinions. Colonel Cautley had been worried, and had taken the line of least resistance. He would have liked to clap the whole suspect population in gaol, and his threat to stop the services in the Dutch Reformed Church had been an expression of his irritation which in calmer moments he had since regretted. He made no attempt to enforce it, and Mr Uhlmann continued his ministrations every Sunday, although his congregation was sadly depleted. The magistrate, who had correctly gauged Colonel Cautley's irritation, allowed some weeks to pass before he ventured to approach that irascible officer again. He did so with some cunning and diplomacy, between which there is indeed only a difference of degree. When the Supreme Court proceedings ended, he suggested that it would be a good thing if the Colonel cut the ground from under the feet of 'these worrying people' by allowing his prisoners on parole. It would make an impression, tend to pacify feelings, and be at the same time absolutely safe, for the prisoners would have to remain in the Village and report themselves daily. Rekker could lodge with the Quakerleys—the Colonel would remember that Mr Quakerley was Captain Overbury's father-in-law, and Mrs Quakerley was the lady chair of the Loyal Ladies' Guild. Swart could stay at the parsonage—a stone's throw from the gaol, where any prisoner could easily be held under surveillance, and Sablonniere could come to the residency. The Colonel, who was heartily sick and tired of his three prisoners, against whom he had been unable to find sufficient evidence to warrant the holding of a court martial, agreed, without any expletives, to Mr Storam's proposals, but intimated that this must be considered as a temporary arrangement, without prejudice, and that he held himself free to act on his own responsibility if ...

The magistrate was quite aware what that qualification portended. Rekker's son was still missing; none knew what had become of him. There was unfortunately no doubt about the fact that he had been seen at the head of the commando when the Boers had left the Rekker farm, and that the commando had safely negotiated that dangerous cliff footpath—a mere bridle track—that led to the safe seclusion of the upper farm. There was a *prima facie* case against young Rekker. Unless he could prove that he had acted in fear of his life, and had been demonstrably coerced, it was difficult to see how a court martial could fail to find him guilty of aiding and abetting the enemy. In that case young Rekker was 'for it.' The magistrate hoped that Martin junior had by this time either made good his escape, or had fallen in the fighting that had taken place in the mountains. It would be terribly distressing to have so prominent a member of the community arraigned on a charge of high treason, with so extremely likely a probability that he would be condemned to death for it.

The Village, happily, had been spared any tragedies of this nature so far. It had experienced the full tragedy of war in other ways that had brought home to the community the stern realities of the situation. There had been military funerals, in which the Village had shown its active sympathy. Funerals were rarities in the Village. In normal circumstances, it might have said, with Heine—

'Oh God, how monotonous are our days
Only when they bury somebody do we get any excitement'

and for that reason funerals had always been exciting, much more so than weddings, confirmations, baptisms, or the quarterly communion service. And these military funerals were conducted in an exciting manner, soberly but exciting notwithstanding. The street re-echoed to the salvoes that were fired over the grave, and to the plaintive strains of the *Last Post*. There was always an impressive procession. Mr Mance-Bisley leading the way in his scarlet hood, and the simple funeral ritual was inspiring in its solemnity. Two funerals had been those of members of the Dutch Reformed Church, where Mr Uhlmann had officiated; the funeral of a rebel who had been shot in fair fight, and of a Republican *burgher* whose body had been found on the veld. The Village had attended all these services, making no distinction between friend and foe, for Death levels or exalts all. 'In the midst of life we are in death ... I am the Resurrection and the Life to come ... I was born in corruption ... I was raised in corruption.' There was no difference between English and Boer. In death there was a sameness ... death levelled all differences, smoothed all excrescencies of creed, race or Party. When they stood around the open grave the Village could sink, in the sympathy it felt, all divergencies of opinion and sublimate its passion, its sentiment of the hour, to the common factor that allied it to humanity and that made friend and foe alike.

The solemn processions, passing down the second street to the graveyards of the Anglican and Dutch Reformed churches, gave further evidence of the close-knit inter-relationship between the two sections of the community. Men who belonged to the one denomination attended the funeral services of those who were of the opposite religious sect. Mr Mance-Bisley and Mr Uhlmann walked side by side on these occasions, the one in his plain Geneva gown, the other hooded in scarlet. The ritual for the dead was the same for all, a relic of the pagan past, adapted by time and convention to suit the circumstances of the moment, appealing to the common sympathy of English and

Dutch alike, ignoring differences of race or creed. The fact that among those who died in the camp were so many Colonials who were members of the Dutch Reformed Church was significant in another sense. It denied by implication the supposition that those who were fighting for England, those who were proving their loyalty to the empire by risking their lives against the Boers, were not all so thoroughly English that they belonged to the English Church. Mr Uhlmann would not, of course, have used that argument, had he argued at all about an organised rebellion or a conspiracy against the English in the Colony. He knew that in matters ecclesiastical there were among the ultra-loyalists almost as fierce differences of opinion as existed on matters political. The rector, curiously enough, had always shown sympathy with those who held the broader, Colonial view. Mr Uhlmann might have smiled at that, for it was, after all, merely a reflection of the larger nationalism that had made the Native-born's attitude towards local problems so aggressively assertive that even Sir Alfred Milner had resented it, and seen in it a faint proof of rebellion and disaffection. But Mr Uhlmann was far too busy with realities to occupy himself with speculations about the development of an idea that would have to wait two generations before it could crystallise into the blessed words 'Dominion status.'

So far, the Village had not been called upon to pay its last respects to a dead enemy. A few of the invaders had been killed, of that there could be little doubt, but their corpses had either been carried away by their fellows on commando, or had been secretly buried where they had fallen. A few *burghers* had been captured, and these had been sent to the prisoners' camp at Green Point, where they would await transport to India or the Bermudas. The Village had not even glimpsed them, for they had been marched by devious ways to the nearest rail-head, a precaution which the Colonel had considered necessary to obviate any demonstration of sympathy.

Major Mallom, working at high pressure, under conditions that were not conducive to light-heartedness or optimism, had long ago modified his views about the disaffection prevailing in his area. He had moved among the people, and although he could not talk their language and had to conduct much of his conversation through an interpreter, or be content with answers in English which he felt might not fully express what was in their minds, he had by this time formed a definite opinion about their attitude. He thought that the vast majority of citizens who had any responsibility and any real interest in the District resented the incursion of the Boer commandos as a gratuitous impertinence, calculated to throw doubt upon their allegiance to their own government, and to bring disorder and chaos in a community which had hitherto been, and had always wished to remain, neutral, but which had now been forced by circumstances to be actively hostile to men for whom it had always had a sneaking sympathy. The Major felt rather contemptuous towards that attitude. He would have preferred the resentment to have been stronger, and to express itself in vigorous, organised action and not in verbal protestations. But he could readily understand it as an attitude that did not necessarily imply opposition to the military, or anything in the shape of covert treason. Indeed, he was sure in his own mind that no responsible farmer would voluntarily aid and abet the enemy to an extent that would handicap the military, or impede the measures taken for the defence of the District. Because of that certainty he had been against the more drastic measures of administration advocated by the officer in command of the troops. That difference of opinion was now happily settled, and his administration was running smoothly. His resignation had not been accepted, and he had remained on, working smoothly with the magistrate, whose local knowledge and experience were valuable assets of which he made constant use.

Chapter 33

When the early sorrels had begun to blossom, making carpets of colour on the brown hillsides, there came disquieting news that robbed the District in one night of its almost carefree tolerance and complacency, and stirred it to emotional depths not plumbed before.

From the mountains had come down a strong Boer commando, reinforced by recruits from the north. Rumour stated it to be a thousand strong, which was probably a gross exaggeration. About its destructive activity there could be no doubt. It had fallen upon a military outpost and captured it. It had swept down to the main road and mopped up a convoy just beyond the border of Seldon's farm.

The Colonel acted with energetic promptness. A column under Captain Overbury was hurried to the spot where the commando had last been seen, and a strong force was despatched to close up the pass. During the night there was a fight on Seldon's farm, where the commando was firmly posted in a rocky outlyer of the main range that ran down to the river. By midday the Village received the news that there were many casualties on both sides, but that the invaders had been dislodged from their position and were retreating across the mountain.

The rector, hurrying down the front street towards the Commandant's office to read the daily bulletin posted up on the notice board, met Mr Storam hastening in the same direction.

'This is a bad business, Rector,' exclaimed the magistrate, falling into step with his companion.

'It is indeed, Mr Storam. After we had congratulated ourselves that the worst was over ... too bad, too bad! But I am told that the enemy has been driven off.'

'They have shifted their position, that's all,' said the magistrate, impatiently. 'We must be prepared for anything. Even for an attack on the Village. Didn't you notice that they are placing guns in position to shell the further river bank over there? That's where we may expect them to come from if they turn up.'

'Surely they wouldn't dare,' cried the rector. 'I am a man of peace myself, Mr Storam, but if it is necessary to use arms to defend ourselves, I would ...'

'No, no, Rector,' interjected his companion. 'We've got plenty of men, and there has never been any intention to ask for volunteers for a local town guard. But it is quite on the cards that they may attack.'

'But where are the troops then, Mr Storam?' asked the rector anxiously. 'If you expect an attack, surely our men would have taken up their positions by now?'

'I fancy everything has been carefully arranged, Rector,' replied the magistrate, soothingly. 'Give Colonel Cautley credit for knowing his work. You have evidently not heard the news.'

'No, what news?' asked the rector, halting in his stride, in his astonishment.

'Why, at last night's affair on Seldon's farm, our men caught a couple of them who turn out to be our own people. Rebels, Rector; two of our people who have joined them. They are now in gaol—they were brought in under armed escort early this morning, and the matter, I am glad to say, has been kept quiet. I even do not know who the men are. In fact, that's what I am going down now to find out.'

The rector took off his glasses, and pursed up his lips as his habit was when he was faced with a problem.

'I suppose they would have to be court-martialled,' he said, softly. 'But,' with an eager quickness that showed how anxious he was for substantiation of his hope, 'they might have been unarmed, you know.'

'I don't know the particulars,' responded the magistrate, gloomily, 'but I gather that they were not only armed, but took an active part in the fighting, and one is stated to have shot one of our wounded under particularly distressing conditions. Here we are. Will you come in with me and see the Major, Rector?'

'I ... I really do not think it would be advisable, Mr Storam. Do you? I think it would be better for me to wait outside while you see him. Perhaps I might more usefully call on Mr Uhlmann, and bring him down to see you. He would naturally be most keenly interested.'

'That will do excellently, Rector. I know that he has been asked to attend here, but he may not have received the message. Do you mind?'

'Oh, not at all, Mr Storam. I'll go at once. Dear me, it is, as you say, a bad business.'

The rector walked off, omitting in his hurry to study the notice board, which would not have given him any further information than he already possessed, for this morning there was no typewritten bulletin adorning it. The magistrate passed into the office.

Major Mallom, looking careworn and stern, got up as he came in and strode forward to meet him.

'Good morning, Storam,' he said. 'I am glad you came so promptly. This is a devilishly serious matter, as you no doubt understand.'

'Good morning, Major. If you refer to the rebels, I quite agree. But I know nothing as yet. If you will be good enough to tell me ...'

'Sit down,' said the Commandant, drawing a chair up to the table for his visitor, and resuming his place behind the desk. 'Here are the reports. You might glance over them and give me your opinion.'

The magistrate took the papers, and as he rapidly read them he whistled softly.

'Well,' said the Commandant, 'a pretty kettle of fish, isn't it?'

'It is indeed, Major,' replied Storam. 'I presume all this can be vouched for?'

'It will have to be,' said the Major, curtly. 'That will be for the court to decide; I mean the evidence. But as it reads, it seems pretty damning. Do you by any chance know either of them?'

'I know both,' Storam answered. 'And, between you and me, Major, I am relieved to find that neither is a man of the slightest standing or importance. I had an uneasy feeling that one of them might be young Rekker. By the way, have you any information about him?'

'No, nothing. The fellow has disappeared. From his point of view as well as ours, it is the best thing he could do, and it won't worry me if he never turns up again. What about these two? Who are they?'

'This one,' the magistrate tapped one of the papers, 'this Org Bons, is a lad of about twenty-two. His parents are *bywoners*—farm hands who own no land of their own. The boy is half-witted—I should almost say mentally incapable of realising what he has done. I know him as a harmless, hulking fellow, easily led and influenced ...'

'That might be argued in extenuation,' interrupted the commandant, grimily, 'but a court martial is unlikely to attach much importance to it. Even a half-wit can kill one of our men, and as you see this one shot one of our wounded. What about the other?'

'The other is quite a different brand, Major. I may be prejudiced, but I have always considered Gideon Ras as an agitator of the worst dye, and he has played the part of *agent provocateur* in this District to some purpose. Fortunately, he is not one of our people—I mean, he is not of this District, although he has lived here some time now.'

'As you see, he was armed and took part in the fighting, although, it seems, a very mild part. As a matter of fact, he was the first to surrender, and claims to be a Republican subject. There would have been no trouble for him—he had been placed with the other prisoners whom we were sending to Simonstown—if it hadn't been for Seldon, who spotted him. I should like your opinion on that point.'

'I cannot tell you off-hand,' said the magistrate, reflectively. 'Now I come to think of it, he certainly passed himself off as a *burgher*, but I fancy he is on our voter's register ...'

'If that is the case, then there cannot be any doubt about the matter, Storam. The one bit of satisfaction one can gather is that neither will be much loss to you if he goes. The boy's case, of course, is bad from every point of view.'

The Commandant played idly with his pen-holder. 'You see for yourself, Storam,' he said gravely, 'what the position is. I need not tell you that I am not very happy about it. Whatever we do, we are sure to be blamed, and the least we can do means ... you realise what it means, Storam?'

'Perfectly, Commandant. Unfortunately there is no option. These men must be court-martialled, and, if found guilty, I suppose there is only one sentence. I take it you will have to deal with them.'

'Under the Colonel's instructions, yes. Not ordinarily. Personally, I think they should have been dealt with on the field. That would have saved us a lot of bother. But the Officer Commanding thinks it would be well to make a public example of these men, and they will be tried here.'

'May I enquire,' said the magistrate, 'what happens if they are sentenced? There would be no possibility of appealing, I take it?'

'Not from a field court martial's decision. The commander-in-chief would of course have to ratify the sentence, whatever it is. In this case, if they are found guilty, there can be only one decision.'

'You mean they would be shot?'

'Not necessarily. They would be condemned to death, but they might be hanged. Or the commander-in-chief might commute the sentence to penal servitude. In any case, it's a devilishly bad business. I am sick and tired of all this, Storam. I should like to do something better than this kind of thing. It's necessary for someone to do it, of course, but it's not my line. But there, just forget that I have let myself go, will you, and let's go into this. Will you look up that chap's record—find out if he is a voter, and so on—and get together what you can about the lad as well.'

'Could either of them be represented by counsel, Major?'

'I suppose so. Yes, I am certain they could. If they are not, the court would assign someone to act for them. Have you anyone in mind?'

'I'd better consult with Mr Uhlmann about that, Major. He might be able to help.'

'Do so. You know, of course, Storam, that this will create no end of fuss. There have been a few executions in other districts, but there I gather things were quite different from what they are here. Very few of your people, as you call them, have gone over to the enemy.'

'That is quite true, Major. Do you suggest that making an example of these men might react in another way?'

'I suggest nothing, Storam, but I have my own views on that subject. Forget what I said. The responsibility, thank God, is not mine. I have merely to carry out my instructions.'

'Very well, Commandant. I will see Uhlmann, and give you a report on the men. That is the least I can do. Is there any further news?'

'No,' the commandant's voice was wearied; Storam noted the tired look in his eyes, and the droop of the wrist that spoke of physical fatigue. 'Nothing of any importance. That is what makes it so unsatisfactory, Storam. We've a tremendous task before us.'

'I always said we would have,' commented the magistrate, drily. 'And we're making it harder for us by being sentimental and unbusinesslike. I'm with you right through, Commandant, as to the futility of some of our methods, but if we want to bring this war to an end, we ought to put sentiment aside and conduct it as a business.'

'Of course that's the right way, Storam. But in that case you should train us all up to the business, as they do in Germany. We've never had experience of war, and an honest statement of the case would rouse a fierce shout of protest in England. They want us to end all this and at the same time forget that this sort of thing is going on ... it is impossible to do both, Storam.'

'I said that from the first, Major. Take this shooting of the Natives. We are practically being forced by the enemy to fight according to his own interpretation of the rules. Any other country would have brought up all its manpower—no matter whether that includes Indians or Esquimaux or Jews or Pagans—and crushed the opposition quickly and effectually. I'm sure Germany would have done so. But not only do we make no use of our full manpower, simply because there is colour prejudice against using the Native as a combatant, but we even allow the enemy to shoot our non-combatant Natives ...'

'It is deucedly difficult to prove that they are being shot in cold blood, Storam. If we can prove that, I think we shall exact reprisals, and that will soon put a stop to the business. But I must say your colour prejudice here has certainly complicated matters a good deal. It is not only the Dutchman who would object to our using Basutos or Kaffirs. Our loyal Colonials would shriek with indignation. Do you know, Storam, you loyal Colonials puzzle me a good deal at times. I can see the Dutchman's point of view—after all, he is a subject by conquest—but you are different, or should be.'

'I think our colour prejudice is the result of economic conditions, Major. As you say, both English and Dutch have it, but it is most evident among the lower classes, if I may use that expression. Mr Porter used to declare that we were nourishing a feeling of caste, leading to the creation of the foulest and most disgusting of all aristocracies, the wretched aristocracy of skin.'

'I should feel disposed to agree with Mr Porter, whoever he was,' commented the Major. 'But that does not resolve our difficulties, Storam. If we carried on this war as it should be carried on, I don't believe we could have greater difficulties than we have at present, and our system now creates danger and difficulty all along the line. Look at this unpleasant job before us. If public opinion realised what high treason means, no one would say a word if these men were summarily executed. But now ...' he shrugged his shoulders, and the magistrate nodded his agreement.

'I certainly don't believe that we have attained that conception of treason as yet,' Storam remarked. 'No doubt this trial, whatever its ending may be, will raise a storm. But your duty is perfectly clear, Major, and, as you say, the responsibility is not yours. The final decision rests with the commander-in-chief.'

'But we shall be blamed for it. Well, let it be so. I have decided that Major Thomas is to preside at the court, with Overbury and Fellowes as the additional members. What do you say to putting you on as legal adviser? Or would you rather not? Personally, I hope you'll agree.'

'If you put it like that, Commandant, of course. Perhaps it would be a good thing— make a better impression. Overbury is a Colonial and his experience as assistant-magistrate will be invaluable. When is it to take place?'

'As soon as possible. I should like to get the affair over. We are not out of the wood yet.'

'Is there any chance of clearing the District, Major?'

'I hope so. We are gradually rolling them back. There may be some more fighting. I am going out with a column this afternoon, but I daresay it will be a wild goose chase again. Our information is that the main commando is somewhere on Rekker's farm behind the mountain, and we are concentrating upon that.'

That afternoon the column moved out, a long line of horse and foot, with the guns trailing in the rear. The location cheered them as they swung through the second street, taking the main road that led northwards towards Rekker's farm. The Village, too much confounded by the news that two of the District community lay awaiting trial as rebels, looked on in silent interest, divided between its innate sense of loyalty and its futile pity.

The Village, although it had not yet fully realised what the war connoted, shuddered when it thought about the coming trial. It had read about similar processes elsewhere, and was under no misapprehension as to the probable outcome of this one. It had gathered that the evidence against the two rebels was grave, but it was not unanimous in apportioning guilt to both. For the half-witted lad, Org Bons, there was a general feeling of pity, and a fervent hope that his known irresponsibility would be taken into account at the trial. For his companion there was no great sympathy, for Gideon Ras was not a popular member of the District community, and had never been looked on with any favour. Nevertheless, to him too, their pitying sympathy could be extended in the same way as one could pity a person who has acted passionately, but without intent to do grievous harm. That was the tragedy of the Village, that it did not as yet grasp the full implication of an act of rebellion, or of the breaking of that solemn declaration of faith to Alexandrina Victoria when she had been declared Queen and Defender of the Faith so many years back.

Chapter 34

Andrew Quakerley sat in his great arm-chair in his study. Opposite him sat the pastor, the rector and the magistrate, and in the far corner of the room, in the shadow cast by the lamp shade, old Martin Rekker. Old Martin's health had not been good of late; he had complained of sharp pains in his left arm, and Dr Buren, diagnosing *angina pectoris*, had advised calm, and the avoidance of all emotion, and had prescribed liquor trini-trini in three minim doses.

The company looked depressed and anxious. Even the rector's cherubic cheeriness seemed to have evaporated; the corners of his mouth were drawn down, and he betrayed his nervousness by fidgeting with his glasses, and by restlessly crossing and uncrossing his legs. The pastor's deeply lined hatchet-face was overcast, and he too appeared nervous and ill at ease, while the magistrate, studying a file of papers which rested on his lap, drew furiously at his cigar and blew great clouds of smoke that lingered like a halo around his head. Old Andrew thought this was a senseless way to smoke a decent Havana. He, too, felt constrained and unhappy, but that was no reason why one should waste good tobacco.

'Well, Storam,' he said, gruffly. 'We are waiting to hear your opinion.'

'I don't see that I can add to anything that I have already said,' replied the magistrate, removing the cigar from his mouth, and clearing the smoke screen around him by waving the file of paper like a fan. 'You were there, Mr Uhlmann, and you, Rector.'

'But I wasn't,' said Quakerley. 'Nor Martin. You might just enlighten us as to what took place. I expected James to do so, but he has not been here, and I have had no chance of talking with him.'

'Captain Overbury left with Lieutenant Fellowes as soon as the court delivered its verdict,' said the magistrate. 'He has to report to the Colonel, who is in the field, as you know. But the facts are as Mr Uhlmann has stated. Against Bons there were five counts in the indictment. He has been seen under arms at two different places, and he was taken with arms on his person at Seldon's farm, where he had taken an active part in the fight. But the gravamen of his offence was shooting that wounded Tommy. There were three independent witnesses to that murder, and under cross-examination their evidence remained absolutely unshaken. I am afraid there is no getting over that point, and of course on the other counts the court had no option but to find him guilty. Against Ras there were five charges, all supported by evidence which the court had to accept, as there was absolutely no rebutting evidence.'

'In both cases,' said the pastor, interrupting, 'there might have been witnesses to prove that these men were forced ... coerced is the word, isn't it?'

'I am afraid, so far as the boy is concerned, his own admissions disproved that. Of course, one cannot take what he said very seriously. His whole demeanour showed that he did not realise his position, and that he has no conception of what he did. That, of course, I pointed out, but it could not influence the court, although I hope that it may have some influence with the commander-in-chief, when he reviews the case.'

'I thought,' said old Andrew, 'that Ras claimed to be a *burgher*. Did that affect his case?'

'Yes, naturally. But, unfortunately for him, his name appears on our register, and there is actual proof that he exercised his right as a voter. A lawyer might have spun out his case in a civil court, but with that proof in front of them the court had to find him guilty. He showed up badly when the decision of the court was made known.'

'He is not a brave fellow,' remarked old Martin, who had been following what was said with careful eagerness. 'He was always loud-voiced and boastful, but there is no backbone in him. Still, it is hard upon the man.'

'And the boy?' asked Andrew.

'The lad did not seem to understand what was said,' replied the pastor, sadly. 'I translated for him, and I made it clear that he had been found guilty of killing one who was no longer capable of defending himself. But he merely smiled—you know his way, Mr Quakerley.'

'Yes, yes. I have seen him sometimes, but I scarcely know him. Only by reputation, and as a poor specimen all round.'

'Not physically, Mr Quakerley,' objected the magistrate. 'And from what we gather he was highly useful to them, although he does not seem to have much recollection of what he did. I am afraid there are others like him whom these people have driven into rebellion.'

'It's cowardly,' declared the rector, nervously polishing his glasses. 'I must say I think we ought to have given these lads some protection ... I don't know what, but there is some excuse for them. Not, of course, for acting as he did ... I don't for a moment extenuate the murder ...'

'That was out of the question,' said the magistrate, sharply. 'And only actual force, actual duress, can justify a man in going with them. It may seem hard to you, Rector, but that is the fact.'

'That is what happened with my son,' said old Martin, nodding his head. 'They forced him to go. I can bear witness to that, and so can Gertrude and the children.'

'Then there can be no question of overt treason, Mr Rekker,' asserted the magistrate, 'and if Martin is captured, or comes in of his own accord, as I hope and pray that he may do ...'

'I sincerely hope he will do no such thing,' old Andrew interrupted, 'if he is to be hauled before a court martial with no chance of getting his witnesses to testify. Yes, Storam, I cannot get over this business. It revolts me. What is the reason for such haste? Why not keep these rebels locked up, and try them when things have settled down, and when there is a chance of their being able to get witnesses from the commando to prove what actually happened?'

'You mean try them by the Treason Court, as is being done in some districts, Mr

Quakerley? You must bear in mind that that is being done under a special Act of Parliament passed to deal with special cases of those who surrendered under a particular proclamation which guaranteed them their lives. Here there is no such proclamation, and you may remember that they have been warned that any act of treason would be summarily punished. As a matter of fact, both Bons and Ras could have been tried by a drumhead court martial and shot out of hand.'

'I suppose they might,' admitted the old man, ruefully. 'But as they weren't, what harm would there have been in postponing their trial for a few months?'

'My dear friend,' said the pastor, laying his hand on the old man's knee, 'you know that I feel as deeply, as sorely, as you do. These are my people—the sheep of whom I am the shepherd, for whom I shall be called to account. But I tell you this, that in time of war such things must happen, and will happen, and you cannot blame the soldiers for them ...'

'That is your damn German mind,' old Andrew broke out, angrily. 'You have been disciplined to submit to anything. Military necessity condones every violation of liberty, to you. But I'm not built that way, Uhlmann. I was brought up to believe that British fair-play and British justice are superior even to military necessity. What are we doing here but exactly the same sort of thing against which we protested in the Transvaal ...?'

'You are not quite fair, Mr Quakerley,' interrupted the magistrate. 'We are in a state of war, and that in itself means that ordinary law, and ordinary methods of dealing with crime, are abrogated. I hold no brief for the military, but in this matter they have acted within their rights.'

'Yes, I suppose so,' muttered the old man, grudgingly. 'And now? What is the next item on their programme? What does this decision mean exactly?'

'The verdict of the court was guilty, and the sentences imposed were the death sentences. The papers will now go to the Colonel, as officer commanding, for his ratification, and then the commander-in-chief will be notified. His decision is final. He may allow the sentence to stand or he may alter it, just as he pleases.'

'Is there any chance of an appeal? Can the civil courts be asked to interfere? There is such a thing as an injunction to restrain ...'

'Get that out of your mind, Mr Quakerley. No civil court has any jurisdiction in an area where martial law prevails, and ordinarily no civil court has the power to review the proceedings of a court martial. These things are controlled by the Army Act, so far as the soldier is concerned, and here, now, by the plenary powers given to the military authorities.'

'But if they do things that are wrong, Storam? If they do palpably wrong acts ...'

'Then a civil action would lie as soon as martial law no longer prevails. But usually there is an Act of Indemnity passed before that happens, which may or may not—it all depends on the manner in which it is drafted—make them absolutely safe against any prosecution. Come, Mr Quakerley, if you will bear in mind that such powers must be granted to the military in time of war, so as to enable them to deal with all emergencies, you will admit that, however bad it may be, it is necessary. In this case I am afraid there is nothing more that we can do.'

'There I do not quite agree with you,' said the parson, quietly. 'Mr Storam, it seems to me that a great deal will depend on what the final decision of the commander-in-chief is ...'

'There cannot be much doubt about what Lord Kitchener will do,' interrupted the magistrate. 'He will simply ratify the sentence. There is not the slightest hope that he will modify it.'

'Not even in the case of the lad Bons, Mr Storam?'

'No. I may be wrong—I hope I am—but there are aggravating circumstances in that case, as you must admit. From the military point of view—from any honest point of view, in fact—his was a cold-blooded murder.'

'But is his state of mind not to be taken into consideration, Mr Storam?'

'Mr Uhlmann, in a civil court that point might be of considerable weight, but here it hardly counts. From the military point of view, the lad is merely a physically capable, rather cunning rebel, who had committed a particularly atrocious crime. I know there is a tendency to extenuate murder when committed by a murderer who is not quite responsible for his action—it is the result of our humanitarian sentiment— but I am not quite in agreement with it. I think it has been overdone, and, when you come to consider it, which is worse—to be executed, or to be condemned to penal servitude or imprisonment for life?'

'Yes,' said the pastor, nodding his head. 'Mr Quakerley will probably say that it is my disciplined German mind, but I agree with you that it is unlikely that the lad's state of mind will be taken into consideration, though I suppose the court has made a note of that ...'

'Oh yes. I stressed it, and it received proper attention. They asked me if he was insane, and I had to admit that in a legal sense he is not. He is quite aware that he has done wrong, but of course he does not comprehend the extent of his wrongdoing. I daresay many of our poor Whites who have joined are in the same position.'

'Then we must accept the fact that the sentence will be carried out, Mr Storam. And there, it seems to me, we can still do some good. If we could prevail on the authorities that it be carried out elsewhere. I suppose that could be managed?'

'I doubt it very much, Mr Uhlmann. Remember, the intention of these military executions—of all military punishments in war time, as you have yourself admitted— is primarily deterrent. It is retaliatory only in the case of reprisals. You cannot call it reformative, and I don't think you can say it is vindictive. And if it is to be deterrent, it must be made to have an effect where there is a possibility that others might commit similar crimes ...'

'Surely you don't mean to imply, Storam, that these men will be publicly shot,' exclaimed Andrew, once more roused to indignation by the conversation.

'No, I don't think they will go as far as that. In the field, of course, a drumhead court martial sentence would be publicly carried out. But here, I fancy, the execution would take place in the gaol, but it would be known, and the fact that it had taken place would be published. You cannot complain about that, Mr Quakerley. From a military point of view—from the point of view of the state, which looks upon treason as one of the few crimes punishable by death—there would be every justification for such publicity, and for ordering the executions to take place here. In civil practice that is invariably the case.'

'I remember only one White man ever being executed in the Village,' remarked old Martin. 'Mr Quakerley might remember him, too. He murdered his wife. It upset us all terribly. It was long ago, before you were born, Magistrate, or you, Reverend.'

'This will upset us too, *Mynheer* Rekker,' said the parson, sadly. 'It may bring further trouble upon us ...'

'Indeed, that is a possibility,' chimed in the rector. 'I do hope the authorities have considered that, Mr Storam. Of course, I may be utterly wrong, but doesn't it strike you that deterrent punishments of this sort sometimes—I may almost say, commonly—have an opposite effect? In this case particularly, it may prevent those of our District who are with the commandos from voluntarily surrendering. Would it not be better to let them do so under the same conditions that, as you said just now, Mr Storam, were granted formerly?'

The magistrate shrugged his shoulders. 'I am afraid it is too late in the day for that,' he said. 'I did suggest it, and I may say that Major Mallom was at first inclined to adopt some such policy. He was overruled, I fancy.'

'Do you think it would be seemly for me to make any reference to the matter next Sunday when I preach?' asked the parson. 'I should do so circumspectly ...'

'That is a matter you must judge for yourself, Mr Uhlmann. I do not like to advise you one way or the other. You may be perfectly certain that whatever you do say is likely to be misconstrued.'

'That has not deterred me in the past,' said the clergyman, simply. 'I have made reference to our dangers, and I have laid stress on our obligations as loyal subjects. I am aware that some of the things I have said have been misunderstood and misrepresented. Mr Bisley here gave me a friendly warning on one occasion ...'

'That was merely because it was reported to me,' said the rector, hastily, 'that you had been incautious in criticising some things. I did not believe that you had ever said such a thing, but I knew that the Colonel imagined that you did. I represented to Colonel Cautley that he was entirely mistaken.'

'I know that,' said the pastor, with a smile. 'I saw the Colonel about the matter, and he was good enough to inform me that you had already interceded on my behalf. He told me that you had been rather strong in your views ...'

'I may have spoken rather heatedly,' interrupted the rector, vigorously polishing his glasses, 'but I thought the occasion justified my remarks. It was so patently an attempt to malign you, my dear Mr Uhlmann, and it emanated, I am sorry to say ...'

'We will say nothing more about it, if you please, Mr Bisley,' said the pastor. 'Doubtless there will be occasions in the future when I shall be grateful for a further good word from you. But if Mr Quakerley will now excuse me ...'

'I must be going, too,' said the magistrate, rising. 'And I'd better see you home, Mr Uhlmann. You have no special permit, I believe.'

'Indeed I have, Mr Storam. I would not go out otherwise. It is my duty to set an example, even in small things. My permit allows me to be out until ten o'clock. It is not that yet.'

'Well, if you must go,' said Andrew, shaking hands with them. 'But the Rector need not go yet. Stay for a few minutes, Rector. I should like you to, if you don't mind. Martin goes to bed punctually at half past nine, but I don't settle down before much later. And Joan would like to see you too.'

'Certainly, Mr Quakerley. I am not permitless either, and it's just a few steps to the rectory.'

The magistrate and the pastor said good night and left, and Martin Rekker followed their example. At the farm he kept early hours, and here, as a guest of his old friend, he forced himself to remain up longer than he was accustomed to do at home. There were several things in the Quakerley household that, notwithstanding his friendship and liking for both Andrew and his sister, the old man scrupled to countenance, although his natural courtesy prevented him from openly expressing his disapproval. The Quakerleys held no evening service, and the muttered grace before meals was more a convention than a real invocation, such as the old farmer was accustomed to. Moreover there was waste, an absence of frugality and thrift, such as old Martin disliked. Andrew was wealthy, of course; everyone knew that, but did not the preacher say: 'Set not thy heart upon thy goods, and say not, I have enough for my life?' But of such things one speaks not when one is a guest, especially such a guest as old Martin was, taken out of the common gaol by favour, and made a sport to the contumelious ... No, indeed one didn't.

So Martin retired early to his bedroom, where he read his Bible by the light of a tallow candle so heavily screened that it constantly smoked, and as he had no snuffers for it—though he might have obtained a pair from Joan had he asked for it—he probably damaged his eyesight by poring over the thin brevier type that he read.

'This,' said the rector, re-seating himself in his chair, from which he had got up in courtesy to the leaving visitors, 'this is a sad event for us all, Mr Quakerley. I daresay Mr Uhlmann feels it doubly as the men are of his church, but it touches us all, and although I am almost an outsider, and possibly take a different view from yours, I am only too ready to express my sympathy with you.'

'It's not so much sympathy, Rector,' said old Andrew, querulously, 'that we want, as encouragement. I have no sympathy with rebels and murderers. Ordinarily, I should not trouble myself about them, and should consider we are well rid of them by hanging them as speedily, and with as little expense, as possible. But here the case is slightly different. Technically every rebel who shoots one of our soldiers is a murderer, and everyone of our people who joins the enemy is a rebel.'

'But that is the law, Mr Quakerley. I remember quite recently reading that we had the death penalty for only four offences—murder, high treason, piracy on the high seas, and burning the King's arsenals. Rebellion, the sin of witchcraft, as the prophet calls it somewhere, is high treason, isn't it?'

'Isn't it a question of degree and shade, Rector? Don't think I am excusing these men, but you have always given me the impression, somehow, Rector, that you are reasonable and humane. Uhlmann is too hard ... I suppose it is his Calvanistic upbringing that makes him so ...'

'No, say rather that it is my innate selfishness that prevents me from having Mr Uhlmann's staunchness, Mr Quakerley,' said the rector, deprecatingly. 'I am so sorry for these poor people—I so much regret that this beautiful country should be the scene of war—that I allow my sentiments to overrule my judgment.'

'Is that wrong, Rector? No, do tell me. I have often asked myself that question. My father, who was as staunch as Uhlmann when it came to a matter of right or wrong, would have looked at this matter as I do. At least, that is what I think. Joan looks at it in the same way, and I cannot see that we are in the wrong ... I ask myself that question every day, and the longer this thing lasts, the less sure I am that my own answer is correct.'

'I think I see your difficulty,' said the rector, reflectively. 'It is one that every Englishman must feel when he reads about martial law, and the way things are carried on. One naturally regrets that there should be any necessity for such drastic action, and everything that interferes with liberty is distasteful. But what else can be expected? It is a military necessity; Mr Uhlmann, who has some experience of war such as we fortunately lack, assures me that what is being done here is not a patch on what was done in the Franco-German war ...'

'But that is different, Rector,' interrupted the old man, vigorously. 'That was against an enemy in occupied enemy's country. Here it is civil war, and can you give me an instance in any civil war that is on all fours with what we are having here?'

'Off-hand I cannot supply instances,' said the rector. 'But I am sure that civil war, if we only knew what happened, has nowhere been more humane than any other kind of war. Are you not confusing the issues, Mr Quakerley? I should say your quarrel is less with the military for acting so drastically than with the imperial authorities for giving them such very wide powers. Isn't that it?'

'Perhaps. Really, Rector, it is so difficult to express what I feel. My mind is nowadays a jumble of conflicting emotions, and I hardly know where I stand. Two years ago, if you had asked me, I should have said that England would never have waged war in this country in this way. I would simply have refused to believe it possible. Then, when the ultimatum came and I saw clearly that England had no option but to fight, I hoped that the struggle would be short and decisive. Now ... now I sometimes ask myself, is this ever to end? How are we going to live in peace, when peace comes, with the memory of these things upon us, Rector? I, who have plenty of English blood in me, how am I going to uphold English liberty ... our tradition of fair-play ... Rector, I don't see how it's to be done. When I think of it, it seems to me that England has lost us ... I mean, those here who have both English and Dutch blood in them ... I don't see how we can get out of it ... how we can reconcile the ideals we held with what we are experiencing now.'

'To a certain extent I agree with you, Mr Quakerley. I can quite understand the development of national aspirations, and I don't believe that there is the slightest objection to it. It is perhaps only natural for me to take it for granted that in this quarrel England is eminently in the right ...'

'I have always felt that, Rector. I have never had a doubt in my mind about the rights of the case against the Transvaal, and I will go so far as to say that it was imperative that England should prevent her prestige from being broken in South Africa, for that would have been a calamity.'

'Your grievance, Mr Quakerley, is against the manner in which the war is being carried on, then. But we are not responsible for that. If the commandos had not invaded our District, none of these difficulties would have arisen.'

'No, indeed not. When I think of that piece of folly, Rector, I get indignant the other way about, if you get me. But I do think that the authorities might take into account that there is such a thing as loyalty to family and race, and make allowances for some of our people who have joined.'

'But what else is there to do? In this case of the two rebels, would you advise leniency? Would it not conduce to further law-breaking? Be an incentive rather than a deterrent?'

'Rector, every way one looks at it, the matter seems impossible. This is just the end of a long string of little things that have shocked us, and a greater shock may pull us together again. Take Rekker's case. Why is the man on parole at all? What possible harm can there be in letting him return to his farm ...?'

'But supposing the commandos come there and force him to join them? Do you not think, Mr Quakerley, that it is in his own interests to keep him under surveillance here?'

'No, I don't. I should resent it very much if it were done to me, Rector, and so would you. We know perfectly well that it would not be done in our case. And why? Simply because we happen to be English, you wholly, I mostly, although as a matter of fact I suppose it's fifty-fifty in my case—simply because the military authorities seem to go on the principle that if a man has a Dutch name he must be a rebel at heart. That is what I can't stomach, Rector. I know that it is a fallacy ...'

'I quite agree with you. I believe the mass of our Dutch-speaking community is as sound as you or I.'

'Of course. They have never had a grievance that was worth fighting for—worth going into rebellion for. And now we are giving them one. I think it is wickedly silly, and I can imagine what the result will be. There you have a man like Seldon—English in his way of thinking, a member of our church, Rector, as loyal a man as you may wish to get anywhere in the Colony. And look how he is pestered and hampered by our own men—by those who should defend him and stick up for him. If there is a disaffected man in this District now, it is Thomas Seldon, and if there is an election tomorrow, he'll vote Bond. So will I, I can promise you that ... perhaps with a reservation.'

'Things might have been much worse, Mr Quakerley.'

'Of course they might. I take off my hat to Mallom; he has played the game, I must admit that. But isn't his attitude just another proof of what I mean? Here you have the man who should know best, who is on the spot, who has no local prejudice, and his suggestions are simply ignored. We know that Cautley and he are at loggerheads, and it is Cautley's interference that one objects to. If Mallom had a say in the matter, Martin would have been back on his farm the day after his arrest, and young Martin would have come in. Now, can you imagine young Martin putting his head in a noose just to show his loyalty to us English?'

'I never believed that the old man's son was a rebel, Mr Quakerley. I have said so repeatedly. Nor do I think he would run any risk if he surrendered voluntarily.'

'You may not, but would the District as a whole agree with you? I am afraid not, Rector. I was never so much disappointed in my life as when I heard that the Supreme Court had refused an order. I see now that it could not have granted one—one gets wiser every day, Rector, and I find that my education is damnably hard. I beg your pardon, but that just expresses it. An old man gets impatient, Rector, and I am no longer young. Perhaps that is why these things annoy me so much. But honestly, Rector, it is not so much annoyance as grief. I didn't think that I would have to live through such times, and see such things in my old age.'

'We none of us imagined it was going to be like this,' said the rector, soothingly. 'You must not allow yourself to be unduly worried by it, Mr Quakerley. I can't tell you to look at the brighter side—this case does not seem to have a bright side to it at all—but I do ask you not to lose faith. That would be a tragedy indeed.'

'I try not to,' said the old man, cheerlessly. 'But it is deucedly hard to keep one's faith. I suppose my trial is not any harder than that of the others ...'

'It is much harder than mine,' interrupted the rector, sympathetically. 'I can look at the matter almost objectively. You, Mr Quakerley, must look at it from quite a different point of view, and I can very well understand how you must feel. If it is any consolation to you, I may say that I sympathise very much with your attitude. You think that your ideals are being shattered, but is it not rather the ideal of an ideal that you have hugged? England—the traditional England, on which you and I pin our faith—that still exists; it is still sound at heart. That, Mr Quakerley, is my belief, and I feel that any injustice that has been done will be righted, so far as it is in the power of England to right it.'

'I try to believe that,' said the old man. 'I do, really, Rector. I read Henley's poem last night—Joan turned down the page for me—and it ... it strengthened me, Rector.'

'Yes,' said the rector, '"the faith that endures ... England, my England." I like the way he puts it. It is an encouragement for all of us in these times, and it breathes the spirit of our sacrifice. For there must be some sacrifice, Mr Quakerley, and there has been much ...'

'Even of our ideals?' asked the old man, mildly. 'Well, let us hope that it will not be all on our part. But come along, Mr Mance-Bisley, I think Joan has coffee waiting for us in the dining room, and she will be interested in the case. You might tell her what took place.'

'I should like to forget it,' asserted the rector. 'I went because I thought it my duty to go, but it was an unpleasant affair. Most unpleasant when they announced their decision, and the man lost control of himself. Most distressing indeed.'

'Well, come along. You need not mention that, although Joan has no sentiment about such things. She inclines to Uhlmann's view, you know. Thinks all this drastic action is necessary, and will speed up matters. I sometimes think Joan's a little hard, Rector, but perhaps that is an impression I got when she refused to let me eat too many preserved figs when I was a small boy. Come along to the dining room.'

Chapter 35

The Village was agog with excitement. The District was profoundly stirred by emotions, although different from those that in the dignified, gentlemanly disturbances experienced during an election, in a time that seemed so long ago, had mildly rippled over its surface. Since then it had thrilled with other convulsive spasms, but none had more severely shocked it, or proved so keen a plough-share of deeper passion ripping down to the primitive rock of human sentiment.

The immediate cause of it was a notice pinned to the board on the outside wall of the court house, a neatly typewritten bulletin which read—

Martial Law

It is notified for general information that the sentences passed by the Court Martial on the rebel prisoners, Gideon Ras and Org Bons, having been confirmed by the Commander-in-Chief, will be promulgated on the Village Square on Saturday morning next at 10 am. All loyal subjects of His Majesty the King are warned to attend the promulgation. All shops and places of business will be closed from half past nine to half past ten on Saturday morning. Failure to observe this order will be dealt with under Martial Law regulations.

Signed Malcolm Mallom, Major

Commandant

Copies of this notice had been despatched to all field-cornets, and posted in prominent positions on the District farms. Their reading gave rise to tumultuous emotion and excitement. Everyone was aware that the prisoners had been found guilty, and most people knew that the sentence of the court could only be a death sentence, but few had realised that there would be a further official ceremony. The ambiguity of the second sentence of the notice was commented upon, and caused much uneasiness. Under martial law locomotion was severely restricted. Farmers could not leave their farms and come into the Village without permits, and the time was too short to allow of these being applied for. Did the warning apply only to the inhabitants of the Village, or did it include all loyal subjects of the King throughout the District? And what was the meaning of the adjective? Were they not all loyal subjects? Or was it the intention of the authorities to make attendance at the promulgation a test of loyalty, and would those who failed to attend be arrested as rebels?

Moreover, did the command include women and minors, who were, after all, also loyal subjects?

The Village and the District pondered over these difficulties of interpretation, and the magistrate, more experienced in gauging the impression that ambiguity would make upon the rural as well as upon the urban mind, suggested a modification, that appeared late in the afternoon, and was published throughout the District.

Martial Law

Notice To All Concerned

The Commandant wishes it to be clearly understood that all registered voters in possession of permits allowing access to the Village on Saturday, and all registered voters who are resident in the Village, except those who are expressly exempted from attendance, are ordered to attend the promulgation of the sentence of the Court Martial on the date and at the time and place stated in the notice already published.

About this command there could be no ambiguity. Its terms were too clear to permit of any misunderstanding. So clear, indeed, that Mr Storam shook his head, and Mr Mance-Bisley took off his glasses and polished them so vigorously that the quartz lenses must have suffered in the process. 'This,' exclaimed the rector, 'is really ... really, Mr Storam, I can hardly find words to express my feelings.'

'Then you'd better not try, Rector,' answered the magistrate, drily. 'Especially not in that tone of voice. I daresay they will be vicariously expressed for you. You'd better come to the residency with me. This will need some thinking over.'

'I should say so, indeed,' said the rector, lowering his voice, however, as he saw the crowd round the notice board listening to their conversation.

They walked through the alley that led into the first street, fronting the *stoeps* of the houses, a quiet, tree-shaded lane, with the water-furrow as its farther boundary. On or before the *stoeps* of the houses, little groups were to be seen, privately discussing the notice. That, the rector reflected, was one of the worst things about martial law; it created an atmosphere of furtive secrecy, of suspicious stealth, an atmosphere that bred uneasiness and demoralisation.

'Let me say at once, Rector,' began the magistrate, as soon as they were alone, 'that I have had nothing to do with that order. Nor has Mallom. It emanates from higher authority, and it is no earthly use for us to contest it. Whatever unpleasant taste it may leave in your mouth, and I confess that to me it's a most unpleasant taste indeed—we've got to swallow it.'

'But really, Mr Storam, I have never heard of such a thing. Have they the right to order me to be present? I am a registered voter, but this is the first time that I am told that my obligations as such include being present at a ... at an unpleasant ceremony like this. It would be most distressing—it really would.'

'Make up your mind that you are going to witness much more unpleasantness, Rector,' said the magistrate, with some sternness. 'The military authorities intend this to be an example, and from their point of view they are quite justified in ordering the civil population to attend.'

'That I refuse to believe, Mr Storam. I cannot conceive that any officer has the right to order me to do this. It is not something in defence of the Village ... there is no shadow of justification for it. I shall most certainly protest, and emphatically ...'

'Better not, Rector, better not! Whatever protesting was possible has already been done. No one could have been more emphatic than I was. I told the Commandant that the second paragraph of the notice could easily have been left out altogether. All that was necessary, even from their point of view, was to close all business offices and stores for an hour or so. Most people would have attended, out of interest or curiosity. This order will only irritate people—set their backs up ...'

'I should say so,' exclaimed the rector, indignantly. 'I should say so. No one with any self-respect ...'

'One moment, Rector. If *you* adopt that attitude, what must the others feel about it? You can readily imagine what their feelings must be—men like Mr Uhlmann, Seldon, even Wain, and the man in the street—or let me rather say, the man on the farm. And disobedience, Rector, will certainly be punished—by fine or imprisonment, I should say. Don't make any mistake about that. I feel as strongly about this as you do—so does Quakerley, Uhlmann, Buren, all of us, in fact. But if we set an example, if we ignore this order and overtly disobey it ...'

'I don't care, Mr Storam,' said the rector, bellicosely. 'Let them fine or imprison me, if they dare ... I am quite willing to take that risk. But this is really too much ...'

'Now, do look at the matter in a sensible way,' argued the magistrate, smiling involuntarily at his companion's pugnacious attitude. 'Granted that it is altogether wrong—and on that point we agree—undignified, and in a sense unjustified, are we justified in setting an example which you may be sure will be followed by many others whose motives will at once be misunderstood? Look at it in this way. You stay away. Your absence may or may not be noticed: if it is, I doubt very much if the commandant will take any steps against you—you are altogether beyond and above suspicion, and after all you are the rector and proceedings against you under martial law will not look very nice. But supposing Rekker stays away, or Swart, or Sablonniere? You see what I mean?'

'I do indeed,' said the rector, more calmly, re-polishing his glasses. 'That aspect did not occur to me. You think that they might be suspected of being disloyal ...'

'Certainly. "All loyal subjects," mind you, all loyal subjects. The presumption is, of course, that those who stay away are not loyal. I imagine the military mind argues something like this: here's a nice edifying spectacle which should gladden and encourage every real loyalist.'

'Really, Mr Storam, this is not a matter for levity ...'

'Nor am I joking, Rector. But you will admit that some people who flaunt their loyalty might take that view of the case. And the inference, to the military, or let me rather say, the jingo-loyalist, mind, for I feel sure that the average soldier finds this sort of show quite as distasteful as it would be to you or me—the inference would be that those who are absent stay away as a protest, not against attendance, but against the sentence to be promulgated.'

'There's something in that,' admitted the rector, unwillingly. 'But that does not really touch the rights of the case. I maintain that no one has the right to order me to attend such a spectacle—why, no civil judge has the right to order a citizen to be present in court when he passes sentence of death ...'

'I am not so sure of that,' interrupted the magistrate, with a smile. 'There is, I believe, an old *plakaat* that gives the judge a right to have an audience on such occasions. But that does not affect the matter. Martial law gives the authorities all the powers they think needful to ensure military success. And in this instance they are of opinion that it is necessary that we should attend to hear what sentences are to be inflicted on the rebels. My point, Rector, is simply that we are bound to obey the order, however undignified it may seem to do so, otherwise we may indirectly prejudice the authorities against others who are already suspect.'

'I see that, of course. But it goes against the grain, Mr Storam, it does indeed. I shall certainly take steps to make it known that this sort of thing goes on ... I am sure the British public will not tolerate it for a moment.'

'That you may do. I, too, intend to take what steps I can to obviate such things in future, but at present there is nothing to be done. And so long as martial law remains in force, we are helpless.'

'If I were to see the commandant ...'

'Perfectly useless, Rector. I have already seen him. He told me quite frankly that he hated doing it, but those were his instructions. I even saw Cautley for a few minutes. He was as usual offensively curt, but I gathered from him that it was not his suggestion, although he said nothing to intimate that he did not approve of it. I should say that both he and Mallom would be better pleased if the affair was managed without any great publicity, but, apparently, that is not the view entertained by the superior authorities. The idea, of course, is to make the thing as deterrent as possible, but I rather fancy that they are overshooting the mark. However, that is beside the point. My vote, Rector, is in favour of obeying.'

'I shall have to think it over,' said the rector grudgingly. 'What you say certainly alters the case to some extent, but even supposing that your arguments are correct, I still hold that we ought to protest against high-handedness of this kind. I can see no necessity or justification for it.'

'Yes, yes,' said the magistrate, impatiently. 'You've said all that. We are in full agreement on that, but the fact remains if you stay away you set an example that may have an effect which you may regret, while if you attend, under protest if you like—I think it would be a good thing if you did protest publicly—you show that you are prepared to obey the authorities, even when they are manifestly in the wrong ...'

'But that is just what matters, Mr Storam,' expostulated the rector, agitatedly. 'Wouldn't it be sheer casuistry? Am I justified in obeying an order which is ... which ... really, I cannot find words to express how revolting the matter is ...'

'Here comes Mr Uhlmann,' said the magistrate, nodding to the parson, who was striding along towards them. 'Let us see what he thinks about it.'

'Yes,' exclaimed the rector, eagerly. 'Mr Uhlmann, did you see that awful notice? Ordering us all to attend on Saturday morning. Mr Storam and I are just discussing it. I hold that it is a most iniquitous order, and that we are certainly justified in refusing to obey it.'

'And I have pointed out to Mr Mance-Bisley,' remarked the magistrate, 'that to disobey it would lead to results which we may all have to regret, while obedience, under protest if we like, commits us to nothing.'

The parson nodded his head.

'It is a tactless and offensive order,' he said, slowly, 'but I should not call it iniquitous. That implies wanton wickedness, and I do not think that is intended here.'

'An etymological quibble,' the rector retorted, heatedly. 'Call it wanton injustice, then ...'

'No,' interrupted Uhlmann. 'There is nothing wanton about it. Does the word mean doing something thoughtlessly and playfully? There is nothing of that sort here, Mr Mance-Bisley. This is calculated, studied policy. It is, I believe, in accordance with the usual custom in such cases.'

'Your German mind, as Mr Quakerley would say, Mr Uhlmann,' said the rector, smiling in spite of his indignation. 'I do believe you would find some precedent for everything they do.'

'That would be easy,' said the parson, wearily. 'This order, Mr Storam, is nothing unheard of. We must obey it, of course. Disobedience would entail punishment which we might be able to bear, but which others would find hard. For the sake of everyone we must obey. And what is there in it, after all? You and I, Mr Mance-Bisley, may have to do much more distasteful things before long. I, at least, anticipate an hour which I would give much not to live through.'

His companions understood to what he referred, and the rector's mood swung round from indignation to a warm, broad-minded sympathy.

'My dear sir,' he said impulsively, 'if I can be of any assistance to you ... if my presence would be a comfort ... they are of course not of my church, but if I can be of any help ...'

'Thank you,' said the parson, gratefully. 'I cannot say yet. It may be—I am hoping against hope—it may be that some modification has been made. But if it is to be, why, I should be grateful if you could be with me when I have to go to them at the end.'

'You have been already, of course?' said the magistrate.

'Why yes, every day. There has been no difficulty about that. Every day I have seen them. The boy takes it very calmly—I do not think he realises even yet how dreadful his position is. The man Ras is moody; at times very contrite and dejected, and then again outrageously self-assertive and vain.'

'Have you been able to glean anything about young Rekker?' asked the magistrate.

'I have carefully avoided asking them anything, Mr Storam. That is not my business, and to do so would be to transgress the spirit of my permit to minister to them. But Gideon Ras had dropped driblets of information when he talked about what they had done. Sometimes he is vain-glorious and boastful—he has not yet found peace. I gathered that young Rekker is still with the commando, and that he is being detained against his will and kept as a sort of hostage. Indeed, Ras hinted that if anything was done to him, young Rekker would be made to suffer for it.'

'That is quite likely,' said the magistrate. 'They might even go to the length of implicating him. Really, Mr Uhlmann, the more I think of it, the less I like their methods. The one good thing about this sorry business is that our people will learn just what sort of people these would-be deliverers are.'

'My German mind might even find excuses for them,' remarked the pastor, a faint smile lighting up his tired and lined face. 'And I have no doubt that their disappointment is as great as is the disillusion of our people. They expected to find us all welcoming them with open arms and ready to join with them in throwing off the hated English yoke, and they find us resenting their coming and quite content to remain loyal. Naturally they would be annoyed, and would treat us all as hostile.'

'I shouldn't mind that in the least, Mr Uhlmann,' said the magistrate. 'What I do resent is the way in which they try to cajole our poor ignorant *bywoners*. They are morally responsible for that lad's death if he is to be executed, and they know perfectly well that they themselves are safe, while everyone who joins them goes about with a noose around his neck. I call that cowardly. Say what you please, I call that monstrous, and if I had my way, every commando that contains a rebel would be treated as if they were all rebels.'

'That would be altogether too drastic,' replied the pastor. 'But I agree with you that it is cowardly and wicked. How to avoid it, how to prevent it—ah, that is another matter. Only the conviction among our own people that it is wrong and wicked can prevent it, but I am afraid that they are not yet convinced.'

'No, and if we go on like this, it is highly probable that these marauding commandos will go down in history as heroic bands, and the rebels whom they forced to join them will be looked upon as great patriots. It is really absurd, when you come to think of it. Now, Rector, I do hope you've changed your mind?'

'I think I shall do as Mr Uhlmann does,' said the rector. 'We might go together,' he suggested. 'That is, if you have decided to go?'

'Yes, I shall go. And I shall be glad if you will go with me, Mr Mance-Bisley. I am glad you suggest it.'

'Very well. I will call for you a little before ten. Will that suit you?'

'Admirably. If you will think of those others, Mr Bisley, it will not seem so hard and undignified. Good day, Mr Storam. Good day, Mr Bisley.'

At the rectory, Mr Mance-Bisley found his wife occupied in nervously knitting socks for the hospital patients. Mrs Mance-Bisley had hitherto refrained from comment or criticism; she had, like so many others in the Village, acknowledged the fact that this was war time, and that it behoved everyone to set a good example. But now she was obviously agitated, and when her husband entered, she thrust her knitting aside, and beckoned him imperiously to her side.

'What is this I hear, Claude?' she asked, tersely. 'I am told that we are all expected to be present on the square when the sentences on these two rebels are read out ...'

'Not everyone, my dear,' explained the rector, hastily. 'All voters only who are resident ...'

'If that is an order,' remarked his wife, pursing her lips, 'I think it is a very silly one, and I hope you will tell Major Mallom so with my compliments. I should have said that in common decency they would have carried out these things with the least amount of publicity.'

'I am afraid, my dear,' said the rector, finding himself relegated to the role of defender of the military, 'that they have their reasons for acting in this manner. It is hardly fair to ...'

'Whether it is fair or not,' interrupted his wife, vigorously, 'it is bound to be resented. A gratuitous attempt at intimidation, that is what I should call it. And very hard on us, Claude. You may not look upon it like that, but just think what an effect it must have upon all these people who are already only too prone to think the worst of us ...'

'I know, my dear,' said the rector, miserably. 'Mr Quakerley said the same thing, and honestly I am inclined to agree with you. I think it is a mistake, and when I read the notice I was as indignant as you are ...'

'I am not indignant,' protested his wife, who was one of those people who seem to resent immediate agreement with their views. 'I am merely sorry that such stupidity should be allowed. But it is on a par with what we have been doing all along. Now we can expect to have the whole District going into rebellion, and they will at last have a grievance. Surely, Claude, Major Mallom cannot be such a fool as to think that he can intimidate all of them ...'

'I don't think he wishes to do so, my dear,' the rector responded. 'Major Mallom is carrying out his instructions, my dear, and we should carry out ours ...'

'You don't mean to tell me, Claude,' demanded Mrs Mance-Bisley, in the voice she reserved for important occasions, 'that you intend to obey this preposterous order? I should have said that you would have enough self-respect to see how undignified it will be, and I am certain that most people in the Village will take no notice of it.'

'But that is just the point, my dear,' her husband interjected. 'Mr Storam was most definite on that point, my dear. He explained that if they stayed away there would be a presumption—not an unnatural presumption, my dear, in the circumstances ...'

'That they are all disloyal? Of course. But do you think, Claude, that the majority of them are loyal to the extent that they will forget their own feelings? You can hardly ask that, can you? And it seems to me much better if Major Mallom will take the presumption as proved, and act on the supposition that some people's feelings are too strong for them. Take temptation away from them, and protect them against themselves, I mean. I can't say that I have seen much protection yet. Mrs Seldon tells me that they are practically helpless on their farm, and if the Boers come there they must just do as they are told. As you know, the Seldons are loyal to the core, Claude.'

The rector took a chair, and began to polish his glasses.

'Now, don't fidget with your spectacles,' his wife warned. 'You really agree with me in everything I say, but you are too obstinate to admit it.'

'But what is there I can do?' asked the rector, plaintively. 'Both Storam and Uhlmann say that it is our duty to attend, and I thought, my dear, that you would see it in that light. When I read the notice I really made up my mind not to go ... it is a bit too much ... and one naturally resents that sort of thing.'

'And now, because Mr Storam tells you that if you don't go, some of our Dutch-speaking friends may follow your example, and be accused of disloyalty ... That's all very well, Claude, but couldn't you help them much more if you showed that you felt that this disgraceful order is unfair and degrading? If you would see Major Mallom, and point out to him—as you can do very easily as the one English-born resident here, and in a sense the leader of our community—point out to him that he is doing his best to alienate the Dutch from us and drive them into the enemy's camp, you would do much more for them.'

'But, my dear, Mallom is carrying out his instructions. He knows perfectly well that all this may have a contrary effect to what the authorities imagine it will have.'

'Then the man's a fool,' declared Mrs Mance-Bisley, incisively. 'He ought to know better by this time. All I can say is that if we go on in this way, we may win the war— I'm sure enough about that—but we may lose South Africa. Still, if you've made up your mind, I suppose there's nothing more to be said. But you can at least write and tell people about what is taking place here. Judging from the papers, they don't seem to have any idea of how serious things really are.'

At the Quakerleys, old Andrew received the news from his son-in-law, who looked in for luncheon.

'The CC has confirmed the sentences, with modifications,' Captain Overbury told him. 'The wire came last night, with special instructions. One of these is that all residents have to attend the promulgation of the sentences on the square ...'

'All residents? Do you mean to say that Joan and I are ordered to be present, James?'

'No. Not the women, naturally. But all males, which I presume means all persons capable of bearing arms. The wire says "all loyal subjects," which is a bit ambiguous, as Storam pointed out to Mallom. So it's been changed to "all resident voters." That includes you, Father, I'm afraid, and your guest as well.'

'Let's have this clear, James. I don't quite follow. Am I—is Rekker—ordered to be present, whether we like it or not?'

'That's the instruction, Father. It's no use kicking against it and, if you take my advice, you'll go. If you don't, there'll be old Harry to pay. Look here,' the Captain laid his hand affectionately on the old man's shoulder, and spoke earnestly, 'this kind of thing sticks in my gullet just as much as it does in yours, Father, but there is no help for it. Just now martial law is supreme, and under it they can do jolly well whatever they please. Don't make it harder for us all by kicking, and just remember, Sir, that your kicking won't help the slightest bit. It will only get other folk into trouble.'

Andrew gestured with his hands, as if trying to shake something from him.

'Is there no end to these insults?' he asked, his voice trembling with emotion. 'First all this injustice to loyal men like Rekker, and Swart, and now this attempt to drag us all into a detestable business. Are they in their senses, James? Can't they see that this sort of folly is the surest way to create disaffection and difficulties?'

'I fear not, Sir. Remember, these things—the whole policy, in fact, all that is being done—are dictated from headquarters. We have no say in the matter, and headquarters does not know what the condition of things is here. Nor do I think headquarters sees anything extraordinary in issuing these instructions. They have been followed elsewhere, Sir, and it is quite a usual thing to order the community to attend promulgations. Let me advise you, Father, not to jib at it. Just go quietly, and stand at the outskirts of the crowd—there's sure to be a crowd—until the thing's over. I am afraid I can't be with you, as I shall have to play one of the leading parts. It'll be over in a few minutes.'

The old man shook his head.

'When is it?' he asked. 'Saturday—the day after tomorrow? Very well. Something may happen before then. James, I suppose I may not ask what the sentences are?'

'It's not supposed to be known, Father, but I may tell you in confidence. Our verdict was of course "Guilty"—we could not make it anything else—and on that we could only give one sentence. The CC has confirmed it in the lad's case—more's the pity, I think. He is to be hanged. Ras, who is a scoundrel if there ever was one, gets penal servitude for twenty years—a life sentence, but most likely it will be commuted when the war's over. I should have liked to see it the other way about, for the lad's not quite all there, but I daresay the charge of murder against him clinched the matter.'

'And nothing can be done? There's no appeal?'

'No, Sir. There is no appeal after the CC has confirmed the sentence. He has legal advice, of course, and there is always the question of expediency. Don't brood over it, Father. It is a damn unpleasant job, but we'll have to go through with it now, and I sincerely hope it may have some effect, although I doubt it.'

'I have no doubt,' declared the old man, energetically. 'A policy of repression never succeeds. Human nature makes it fail. We're playing with edged tools, James, and ... but there, we've had all this before. Go and get your luncheon now. You might tell Joan that I do not require anything. I'll try and lie down for a bit.'

Chapter 36

Mr Storam sat in the commandant's office, facing the Major behind his desk.

Both men were flushed and agitated. There was an atmosphere of restraint and uneasiness in the little office which would have been felt immediately by anyone who had chanced to be present at the interview.

The Saturday morning had been a damp, drizzly forenoon. The winter sun had vainly struggled to pierce the heavy mass of cloud that hung over the mountain and billowed far overhead into the sky, but it had succeeded only in momentary spasms, when the cold sunlight, glinting on the rapidly greening veld, had served to accentuate the frigidity of the north wind.

On the square there had been a good audience for the promulgation of the sentences on the two rebels, and the spectacle had not been without a certain dignity that had impressed many of the beholders. The commandant had read out the charges and the sentences in English, and Mr Storam had translated them into Afrikaans for the benefit of the majority of those who were there to listen. The crowd had gasped when it realised that Org Bons was to be executed, and it was fully prepared to extend a similar mark of fellow-feeling to Gideon Ras. When it heard that the latter was to escape the death penalty, its sympathy veered round to the half-witted lad, whom it thought much more worthy of mercy than the agitator, whose demeanour had always roused some resentment. It slowly broke up when the prisoners had been escorted back to gaol, and the cordon of bayoneted soldiers surrounding the square had been dismissed, and retired to discuss the matter in private.

Mr Storam had walked back with the commandant, at the latter's request.

Major Mallom had been unusually stern, his voice harsh and unsympathetic to a degree which had been commented upon by those who heard him reading the sentences. The magistrate, however, knew him well enough to realise that these comments were wrong. Mallom had done his job efficiently and conscientiously; his private feelings were his own, and the manner in which he tried to conceal them did not deceive his companion. As they walked across the deserted square towards the office, Storam refrained from addressing the commandant, and the Major made no attempt at conversation, but strode along steadily, acknowledging the military salutes he received on the way in an automatic manner. He preceded Storam into the little office, dismissed his orderly curtly, flung his military cap on the desk, and plumped down in his swivel chair, motioning the magistrate to take a seat.

'Have a look at this,' he said, unlocking a drawer and taking from it a typewritten paper, 'and give me your opinion, please.'

Mr Storam took the paper handed to him, and read it closely. He read it twice before he fully grasped its meaning, and as his eye travelled down towards the neatly typed list of names at the bottom, his face became suffused with red, and his legs involuntarily stiffened.

'Well,' said the Major, breaking the silence, and tapping with his finger on the blotting pad. 'What do you say to it?'

The magistrate rose from his chair. Very deliberately he put the paper on the commandant's desk, and drew himself up.

'I should prefer not to express my opinion, Commandant,' he said stiffly, controlling himself with a strong effort. 'If I gave you my frank opinion you would have no option but to arrest me.'

'Come, Storam,' said the Major, with some sternness in his voice. 'This is not the way to take it. You are my chief civil official and your opinion, whatever it is, I must have.'

'Just because I am a civil official,' said the magistrate, with rising indignation, 'I utterly refuse to have anything to do with what seems to me to be flagrantly opposed to the most elementary conceptions of civil justice and common fairness. If you want my frank opinion, you may have it. I think the instructions you have done me the honour to show me are calculated to do an infinity of harm and to shock the whole community if they are carried out, which I sincerely trust will not be the case.'

'Storam,' said the Major quietly, 'these instructions will be carried out to the letter. I have sent in my resignation again, and I have every reason to believe that I am about to be relieved, but while I am commandant any instructions I get will be carried out by me to the best of my ability, as you would carry out yours, whatever might be your opinion about them.'

'I beg your pardon, Major. But I told you that my opinion would be frank, and that you might resent it. I do not imply anything personal, but speaking for myself, there are some instructions that I would hesitate to carry out, even under protest.'

'I cannot allow myself that liberty of conscience, Storam. I am a soldier, and it would be subversive of all military discipline and efficiency if a soldier were to query an order, and to submit it to private judgment before executing it. These instructions are definite. I cannot alter them in any way. But you will notice that the list is in the way of a suggestion, and that I am allowed a free hand as to the number and kind of witnesses that I am ordered to summon. It is on that point I should like to have your views.'

'The whole thing is so intensely revolting,' said the magistrate, agitatedly walking up and down the little office, 'that I cannot yet grasp it. I cannot see any justification for it, and it is contrary to all precedent and to all our notions of decency.'

'Sit down, Storam. Don't let our emotions play the fool with us. I shall not argue with you on that point. You may remember I refused to discuss with you the ethical side of this morning's stage management. This is a much more serious matter ...'

'It is a much more damnably detestable matter,' broke out the magistrate, angrily. 'It is sheer downright brutality.'

'I am not concerned with that. I would merely remind you that my instructions have to be carried out, and that you may help me to carry them out in such a way as to do the least possible amount of harm ...'

'Ah, then you admit that the principle is wrong ...' began the magistrate eagerly, but the commandant cut him short.

'We need not discuss that. I think I have already said enough to show you—and you alone, mind—how I regard them. The point that concerns you is the list. Here, take it ... here's a pencil. Now let us take them name by name ...'

'I refuse to have anything to do with it,' said the magistrate, fiercely. 'I refuse to be a party to it in any way whatsoever ...'

'I may order you, Storam. No, wait,' as he noted the magistrate's whole body stiffen with passion. 'I am reminding you that you are still an official. But I will do more than that. I should like to remind you of the fact that your help here can be of incalculable value to these people. Just face the facts. I am ordered to summon "a number of loyal and disaffected residents of the Village and District to be present in person at the hanging of the aforementioned rebel." These are my instructions. A suggestive list of the 'loyal and disaffected persons' is attached for my information. I have told you these instructions must be carried out. Now I ask you to help me to draw up a list of those who should be summoned. Come, let us take the list there, name by name. The first, you will notice, is Quakerley ...'

'Mallom, the man is well over eighty. It would be sheer cruelty—cold-blooded vindictiveness—to force him to witness a hanging ...'

'Hasn't he been sheriff? I doubt whether his age ought to exempt him, and you'll agree that he can be put in the category of 'loyal'. But strike him out. Now, Thomas Seldon ...'

'If you want to turn the man into a rebel straight away, that's about the best method you can choose ...'

'Doesn't that argument apply to everyone, Storam? Seldon is a sensible man, and will take the matter in a sensible way. He is a good representative of the English-speaking Colonial in this District, and is not related to the prisoner in any way. We'll let his name stand. Now, there's Uhlmann—there'll be no difficulty about him; he'll attend in his professional capacity. What about Mance-Bisley?'

'If you order him to come, he'll certainly refuse, Commandant. But I heard him offer to stand by Uhlmann, and if you leave it at that, there should be no difficulty.'

'That's three, then. Now there are the three prisoners on parole—you will note they are mentioned. Cross out Rekker's name ... with his son still missing, it would be a real cruelty to subject him to this. Leave Swart and Sablonniere ... by the way, the old quack doctor seems to me to be very sound on general principles. He is much too wary to do anything that can bring him into trouble. Now we have five. A round dozen would satisfy these ... should be sufficient. What about the other names?'

'This one here is a Coloured man, Commandant. You surely would not have him present?'

'No, certainly not. You see, Storam, you are really of great assistance. Strike him out.'

'This one is a bedridden old fellow, who wouldn't be able to come unless you carried him. Buren can vouch for him. Cornelius Nolte is a boy of sixteen—why, Commandant, this list is as preposterous as that of your suspects which you showed me some months ago.'

'Very well, scratch out their names. But give me seven others. What about the MPs?'

'If your audience is to be representative, they should figure in the list, Commandant. But there is such a thing as privilege ...'

'Not under martial law, Storam. This affair will cause a commotion, you may bet on that, and one more or less does not matter. Put down their names. Any other five you can suggest?'

'There's Wain, the old Sherman veteran; and Crawley, the carpenter. The latter will be there, I presume, in any case, as undertaker.'

'Never mind, stick him down. Have you any objections to the elder Nolte?'

'Gottlieb? No. If you must have these men, he is as good as any of the others—thoroughly representative of our staunch loyal Dutch,' said the magistrate, bitterly. 'And you might include Hendrik van Aard—he's another; and Frikkie Gerster, or Jeremiah Gerster, or both.'

'That makes thirteen. Perhaps that's better. I am much obliged to you, Storam. You and I must of course be present, and Buren and Chumley. That will make sixteen from the Village and District. Thank you. I will have them notified in good time, and see that they are called for.'

'May I appeal to you, Major ... You can have no idea of what this will mean ... it will cause a revulsion of feeling ... it will add twenty per cent to the recruits that the commandos are going to obtain in this District. It will have an effect upon the whole Colony ... I am sure, I am positive, Major, that it is a damnable mistake ...'

'I cannot discuss that with you, Storam,' said the Major, curtly. 'If you like to draw up a memorandum explaining your views as to the probable effect it will have on the military situation—couched in official language—I will have it transmitted by wire to the commander-in-chief as a "clear-the-line" despatch. But you must hand it in before four o'clock. The execution takes place on Wednesday morning at eight. That is as far as I can go.'

The magistrate saw it was useless to continue the conversation. He picked up his hat and rose.

'I'll write it at once,' he said. 'Can I take it, Major, that these men will be notified privately, and that you will put it to them in such a way as to spare their feelings?'

'My instructions are definite, Storam. A notice is to be posted warning these men to attend, and the fact that they are ordered to attend is to be made known. The intention is that the execution is to be a warning and an example. I have no power to modify my instructions in any way.'

'And should any one of them refuse, Commandant?'

'Ah, then I shall have to take cognisance of such refusal, and compel him to attend. The notice will be served by a corporal's guard in each case, and that should be sufficient to compel attendance. There would further be a fine or imprisonment for those who resisted.'

'Would it be in order—would you object if I wrote a personal note to some of those on the list—I have in mind more particularly Seldon, van Aard, Gottlieb Nolte, and the two Gersters—advising them to attend?'

'You should not ask me that, Storam. Use your own discretion, but do not tell me officially what you propose to do. I asked you here to advise me in the selection ... that ought to convey to you what I cannot tell you outright.'

The magistrate held out his hand. 'Good day, Major,' he said, trying to make his farewell greeting sound perfunctory. 'I quite understand. If I can be of further use to you, pray command me.'

As he walked back to the residency, Storam's calm official mind considered, with growing uneasiness, the probable effects of the step that was contemplated. He could easily imagine the flood of indignation that would sweep over the community when it was made known that so many prominent citizens had been ordered to attend the execution. The order to attend the promulgation had been resented by the comparatively few to whom its harsh, overbearing crudity of expression, and the underlying suggestion of intimidation had appeared insulting and derogatory. The community had not taken it so seriously, although it implied that the authorities considered that they were in need of warning. But this new order would rouse very different emotions, shared by the educated as well as by the ignorant *bywoner*. Its implication was much more direct; its violation of the ordinary accepted canons of decency and propriety too flagrant to be misunderstood. Those men who had been selected to witness the hanging of the unfortunate half-wit would be considered scapegoats for the community, representatives of that disaffected section that had to be over-awed by methods and measures of intimidation altogether repugnant to every fair-minded man, and altogether opposed to the traditional conception of English fair-play. It was like picking out a few of a class to witness the flogging of a boy who had something which the class admitted deserved punishment, but who still deserved sufficient pity to deny him the added load of publicity and open exposure of his shame. The magistrate had sufficient experience of boys to realise that the selected few would resent their selection, and that the class would equally resent the attempt to intimidate it. And the District was very much like such a class of boys. It had its old tradition, its conventional regard for decency, its ingrained distaste of anything that looked like harshness and intolerance. For more than a hundred years there had been no public execution in the District. There had been a few hangings in the gaol, but these had been conducted in decent privacy, and the Village had always on such occasions preserved an attitude of dignified aloofness, studiously avoiding anything that smacked of excitement or interest in the proceedings behind those grim walls. Hanging was something disgraceful, not to be spoken of by decent men, except when there was need to talk of them, and then with proper modulation of voice, and a deprecating air such as one adopts when referring to an unpleasant and ugly subject. Indeed, the District was sensitive on the matter, unduly sensitive, for once upon a time it had numbered among its most respected citizens one who had been a public executioner, but had made himself a much respected and prosperous member of the community.

The magistrate felt that the order to be issued was a blunder of the first magnitude that would be interpreted promptly as a proof of calculated, brutal bullying, and as such would be fiercely resented by everyone, just as he had resented it when he had first become aware of it. That resentment could not find vent, under martial law, in open protest, or in a meeting of indignation which could pass a resolution, and get rid of the ebullient passions that had been aroused by ordinary constitutional means. Under martial law there was no safety valve left open for these turbulences. They would have to find outlets, or remain simmering in the dark until such time as they could conveniently be discharged. And unhappily there was one way in which some members of the community could actively express their indignation and their eagerness to avenge what could not but be considered an insult gratuitously and wantonly flung at them. Without the grievance of such an insult, there had been no particular inducement for many of the poorer and more ignorant to join the commandos, and for the better-class farmer there had been none at all. The magistrate was quite aware that the insidious propaganda on behalf of an academic patriotism that overlooked tradition and the facts of history had found few partisans. He knew of none who would willingly exchange the comfortable liberties that the Colonies had enjoyed for the peculiar republicanism that had denied to Outlander and Colonist their ordinary rights of citizenship. But now they would look at things in a different light, finding in the attempt to intimidate them a proof of the allegation that to Colonists of Dutch descent the traditional liberties of English subjects did not apply, and that loyalty for them meant slavish submission to insult and to indignities that were degrading to their self- respect. If the better class of farmer, the more educated and cultured class, could take that view of the situation, what would the poorer and more ignorant class do, subjected as they were to the constant baiting of the invading commandos, harping continually on the need for every South African to be patriotic to the extent of dying for his patriotism? The immediate result of what was contemplated by the military authorities would be, Mr Storam felt sure, that the commandos would gain more recruits than they would otherwise have succeeded in obtaining, and that the bitterness of feeling against the imperial authorities would be immensely accentuated.

That afternoon the Village read with amazement and anger that a number of its most respected citizens had been ordered to attend the execution of the rebel Bons in the Village gaol. It discussed the order with bated breath, generally in indignant disapproval which it had no means to vent in public protest. Its customary tolerance degenerated into a sullen submissiveness, ominous of more active opposition when the moment for such resistance was more favourable than it appeared to be at present. Even those who had openly expressed disapproval of what the condemned lad had done now shook their heads, and muttered that after all there might be extenuating circumstances if a man resisted an authority that had recourse to means like these, and had no consideration for common decency.

Martial law prohibited the gathering in the streets of more than four individuals; five, apparently, constituted a crowd, and the presence of a crowd was repugnant to the military mind. So one saw groups of three or four in the second street, or on the *stoeps*, anxiously debating what attitude should be adopted on the Wednesday fixed for the execution. On the Tuesday the rumour spread that the executioner had arrived. A transport wagon had been observed at the entrance to the gaol, on which the curious had seen the large mass, shrouded by a tarpaulin, that was undoubtedly the gallows. Coloured boys had removed the covering and dragged into the prison the scaffold of thick wooden beams painted a dull green-grey, under the supervision of a small, wiry man dressed in faded black, who had a gentle, careworn face, and who was attended at every step he took by an armed sergeant. This, the curious understood, was the hangman, who was taken in charge by the gaoler and had to be penned in a cell until such time as he could emerge to perform his duty. Rumour had it that he had been an assistant to Berry, the hangman in England, and that in private life he was a small grocer with the hobby of cultivating sweet peas.

Mr Uhlmann, who had been in constant attendance upon the condemned prisoner, saw the ugly green wooden erection being hammered into shape and position in the gaol yard. The high walls hid even its top from being seen by the curious outside, but the hammering could be plainly heard. If it were not for the martial law regulations that forbade the people from crowding in the streets, many would have congregated under the gaol walls to listen to what was going on within. As the pastor stepped out through the little gaol postern, and saw groups dotted about the streets, he reflected with sorrow that to many the tragedy of the following day held something that evoked a morbid curiosity transcending even the poignant emotions stirred by the event itself.

Chapter 37

The Village conducted itself, on that memorable Wednesday morning, with decorum, with a solemn propriety such as it had a few months before shown out of respect for the dead Queen, Alexandrina Victoria. Blinds were drawn down, no one ventured outside on the *stoeps*; even in the location, children were kept in the huts. The day dawned cold and rainy, but in the early morning the morbidly curious ventured outside to watch the procession of thirteen men who, shepherded by an armed guard, trudged up the second street, halted at the small postern, and were admitted to the gaol precincts. Everyone knew that these were the citizens ordered to attend Bons's execution, and the sight of the party trudging grimly and silently through the rain raised mixed emotions in the breasts of those who watched them.

Before seven o'clock the street and the square had been heavily picketed by troops. Mounted military police patrolled the second street; a corporal's guard sentinelled the first street, that private thoroughfare in front of the *stoeps*. Shops were ordered to be closed until ten o'clock. Over the camp, the public buildings, and the gaol, the Jack fluttered in the breeze; none hung at half-mast as on the day when there had been the memorial service for the late Queen. A sullen calm brooded over the Village, a quiet less of respect for the lad who was to be hanged than of burning irritation against the authorities who had decreed that his execution should be made doubly degrading to the whole community.

Andrew Quakerley, whose indignation had been loudly and vehemently expressed when he heard of the intention to summon these citizens to witness the rebel's end in the gaol yard, rose early in the morning, but found his guest already in the dining room. The two old men greeted each other with a nod; their feelings were too deep to allow them to indulge in the conventional morning greeting, and each knew that the other had passed a sleepless night. The maid brought in early morning coffee, and as they sipped it they stared moodily at the carpet. Shortly before seven Captain Overbury appeared; his spurs jangling in the passage had given notice of his approach.

'I am just off, Father,' he said, helping himself to a cup of coffee and a biscuit. 'I suppose you and Mr Rekker will stay indoors? Yes, that would be better, but don't take it too much to heart. Go into the garden— have breakfast—do something, Sir.'

'Shall we know when ... when it is over?' asked old Andrew, turning his head away as he spoke.

'Not officially,' answered the Captain. 'No such thing as a black flag, and so on, you know. But I daresay the usual notice will be posted.'

He shook hands with the two old men, and they submitted gravely, without enthusiasm, to his handclasp. When he had left the room, old Andrew took his guest by the arm and went into his study.

'Sit down, Martin,' he invited. 'There, take my arm-chair, and put this pillow behind your head. And it is no earthly good our looking like funeral mutes. Let's face this thing, Martin.'

'I can't yet, Mr Quakerley. Perhaps later on, but not yet. I am thinking what I should say to my son if he asked me, now, what he has to do ...'

'You would say to him, Martin, what I should say to mine, if I had one and he asked me that question. You would say, "Remember that you are a subject of the King, and that you have never had cause to complain of being ill-used." That is what I would say, and that is what you would say if young Martin came to you tomorrow!'

Old Rekker nodded his head.

'Aye, all night I have said to myself, in the words of the Psalmist, "Blessed is he whom Thou chasteneth, O Lord, teaching him in Thy law that Thou mayest give him patience in time of adversity." It is not for myself that I grieve, Mr Quakerley, but for those of our people who are not patient, and to whom this thing is an evil thing.'

'I know that, Old Friend. But you and I must try and help them to have patience. God knows we are sorely tried. I am tempted to lose patience myself, but I know that we are not alone in condemning this manner of doing things.'

'It will be hard to make them understand that, Mr Quakerley. There will be many that will say, "Tush, the Lord shall not see, neither shall the God of Jacob regard it." And they will say this is being done by the English, and their hearts will turn from their faith and doubts will oppress them. And when a man doubts, Mr Quakerley, he does things which he afterwards regrets, and that will be the case here.'

'Then you and I must prevent them from doing wrong things, Martin. We must try and make things right for young Martin. That must be our first thought.'

Old Rekker shook his head doubtfully.

'If I knew where the boy was,' he said, despondently, 'there might be some chance of getting a message through to him, but I have no notion where he can be. Sometimes, Mr Quakerley, I hope that he may be dead. It may be sinful to hope that, but I should not like to see him playing a part in such a spectacle as is now going on in the gaol.'

'I am afraid I am a poor comforter, Martin,' said his host, sadly. 'A month ago I would have told you that you are worrying yourself needlessly; now I can't say that. No one is safe under this horrible system which has no respect for decency or humanity. And yet, old friend, I tell you to hope. Don't despair. This may be the darkest hour for us, and after that there is the dawn.'

'No, Mr Quakerley. It may be only the twilight. I tell you, this thing, this execution, will make a stir hereabouts, and before the end of the week you will see more trouble among our people. They cannot understand that this is not an exception. They will say that it is going to be the rule, and if that is so, it were better for them to die in the field.'

'There is no hope that way,' retorted old Andrew, energetically. 'And two wrongs don't make a right. If they give way to their feelings they'll simply be playing into the hands of those who are responsible for what has happened here.'

'That I know, Mr Quakerley. But they will not reason that way. They will not reason at all. When people are hurt like that, Mr Quakerley, they get wild, like a horse that has been stung by a gadfly, and they simply kick out, not caring if they hurt friend or enemy.'

'Have you any reason for believing that many will take that line? If so—if you know any who are likely to ... to forget themselves, would it not be better to warn them? Even to prevent them by timely action, Martin?'

'Who shall say what people think, Mr Quakerley? I cannot tell you who is likely to go, but I suspect that some of the younger bloods will go, all the same. Many, I am told, threatened to do so on Saturday, when they were called upon to attend the reading out of the sentences. What is the time, Mr Quakerley? Is it eight yet?'

'No. don't let us think of it, Martin. It is just punishment, according to law. Harsh, perhaps, but just, according to law. It is not to the punishment that I object, but to the brutality that accompanies it.'

'Aye, but the lad is irresponsible. He has not got his intelligence. They might have taken that into consideration. If they do that to the green wood, Mr Quakerley, what will happen to the dry?'

'I fancy they will see that they have made a mistake. When this gets known, Martin, there will be revulsion of feeling. I cannot conceive the British public tolerating this sort of thing. It fights clean. It has never terrorised and adopted Russian or German methods. I hardly believed the stories that were told of the way in which martial law was enforced in some districts, but now I can credit them all.'

They sat for a few minutes in silence. The clock in the hall chimed eight.

Martin rose.

'You are not a believer, Old Friend,' he said simply, 'and I cannot ask you to join with me, but if you will excuse me now, I go to my room to pray.'

'I shall not say you wrong me,' said his host, accompanying him to the door, 'but perhaps we both believe the same thing in different ways. Go, by all means. There are many this morning who will join with you, and you know that my sympathies are wholly with you.'

Alone in his study, old Andrew walked restlessly up and down. He took up a catalogue of garden seeds and tried to immerse himself in its intricacies, but he found no help in it. Joan, coming to summon him to breakfast, found him in his arm-chair, idly turning over the leaves of his *Henley*.

'It is past nine, Andy,' she said, gently touching him on the arm. 'Mr Storam has been here, but we didn't like to disturb you. It is all over. Come in to breakfast. I have sent something in to Mr Rekker. He would prefer to have it in his room.'

She spoke in a matter of fact tone, and he felt grateful to her for adopting it. Sympathy or condolence at this moment would have jarred on him; they were not his due; he was part and parcel of those who were doing what called for sympathy from others as a mark of their disapproval of what was being done.

'Has James returned yet?' he asked, getting out of his chair.

'He looked in for a minute, but said he had to go to the commandant's office at once. It appears there is some trouble already ...'

'They might have expected it. But so soon?'

'It won't do any good, Andy. By the way, there is a boy in the kitchen who particularly wants to see you. I don't remember his face, but he says he wants to talk to you.'

'Then I'll see him now, Joanie. I don't feel like breakfast. Let me have a cup of soup later on, and a bit of crust. I'd better go into the kitchen ...'

'No, I'll send him out to you. Go in, Andy, and eat something. You can talk to him while you're eating.'

His sister turned towards the kitchen, and Andrew went into the dining room. He sat down in the chair at the top of the table, facing the heavy sideboard with its old glass and silver. Now that he was here, he might as well have his breakfast. It could do no good to get sentimental over the business.

The boy came in—an old boy, creased and wrinkled of skin, lean and sinewy of limb, old, but young compared with the 'old master,' who nodded curtly but not unkindly to him. Andrew thought the boy had more Bushman and Hottentot blood in him than White; he had the yellow-brown skin and flat cheekbones of the Hottentot type. These boys were all very much alike, and this one's features were strange to Andrew. Strange boys were not welcome in the Village. There were stringent regulations about them, and Andrew frowned when he saw the stranger, who shuffled into the dining room with almost a secretive air.

'Have you a pass, Outa?' he asked, sharply.

'Aye, Old Master. Old Kees has a pass, properly ink-signed and stamped,' said the Native boy, sidling closer. 'From the soldier master at the mission station, where we now have this Goddam war, Old Master.'

'So. You are from the mission station. I might have guessed it. And what do you want here?'

'I have something for the Old Master's ear,' said the Native, in a whisper, 'and for Old Master Martin's ear, if it be, as one is told, that he now lodges with the Old Master.'

'If it is something to be whispered,' said old Andrew, shortly, 'I do not wish to hear it, Outa. It is dangerous to speak things in a whisper these days. One never knows who might overhear.'

'Aye, that it is, Old Master. But the Old Master need not fear old Kees. Old Kees owes too much to Old Master Martin's father to do Master Martin a hurt. The Old Master need not be suspicious of old Kees ...'

'One should be suspicious of everyone, these days,' said Andrew, regarding the Native boy keenly. 'I know nothing about you. If you have anything that should be known, you should go to the commandant's office ...'

'Oh no, Old Master. Old Kees, he chooses the day when the commandant master is too much occupied, and all the soldiers too, Old Master, to pay any heed to old Kees. That is why I come now, Old Master. To tell Old Master and Old Master Martin the news ...'

'What news, Outa?' Andrew's heart seemed to miss a beat. Was it possible that this was a messenger from young Martin? Or was the Native boy merely a trap, to get old Martin into trouble? A month ago that suggestion would have been resented by old Andrew as implying an utterly unjust reflection upon the military authorities; now he could consider it calmly, just as objectively, indeed, as he had considered that morning's execution.

'Yes, Old Master,' whispered the Native boy, importantly. 'When the Boer masters galloped away across our lands, it was Master Martin, Old Master, who beckoned to me—they keep him with the horses, Old Master, and he does the sort of work that old Kees used to do when old Kees accompanied Old Master Jan to *Nagmaal*—and told me—very quickly, Old Master, for there was barely time for more than a wink and a hiccup—to try and get to see Old Master Martin and tell him the young master was well. But in a sad case, Old Master, in a sad case, with his breeches all torn, if old Kees may be permitted to say so, and his shirt in tatters, with the Old Master's permission to mention it ...'

Old Andrew got up from his chair, and went to the door which he closed and locked. He strode to the window and drew the curtain, although it was day and no light could filter out on to the *stoep*. The Native watched him in silence, and nodded his wrinkled old head on which the little stunted tufts that proclaimed his Hottentot ancestry could be plainly seen straggling from beneath the red bandana that he wore as a headcloth.

'Tell me, Outa,' said Andrew, coming back to the table. 'Was the young master ill? Was he wounded?'

'But no, Old Master. He was sound and well, but oh, so woebegone of face, like our little Lord in the garden of the olive trees, Old Master, where the cock crew when Master Peter, him that was the Apostle, denied him. And just skin and bone, Old Master, with his veins standing out like tree-roots, my Master, which is not good for a youngish man like Master Martin, my Master. And I almost not knowing him, him being so altered, so that I nearly made a fool of myself, Old Master. Which would have been bad, my Master, for the Boer masters, curse them, my Master, have no patience with us Black creatures. They'd as soon shoot as speak us fair, my Master, and so old Kees had to be circumspect.'

'When was this, Outa? Be careful, now.'

'Oh but, my *Baas*, I am careful. My wife—she's my third one, my Master, and the worst of the three, but she can count, my Master, which is something—my wife she told me this morning when I left—for I left early this morning, my Master, us knowing that all the people in the Village would be too much occupied, my Master, in grieving for your Master Org who is to die, my Master, to give heed to old Kees if he crept in through the hedge at the bottom of Old Master's garden. She told me, my wife, I mean, my *Baas*, to remember that it was three days since ...'

'That would make it Sunday,' muttered old Andrew. 'Did they come while you were having service, Outa?'

'Aye, my *Baas*. With no respect for the Lord's day, and for the harmonium that was singing ... no respect at all, my *Baas*. And they took all the bread there was, my Master, and threatened to burn down the shop, because there were no little fish in the red tins which they wanted.'

'They did no harm, did they? Shot no one ...'

'Aye, but they did, my *Baas*. Young Mok at the mill, my *Baas*, for being cheeky, they said. We found him dead, my Master. And they beat his brother, my Master, with a *sjambok*, but—praise the Lord—they did not shoot him. Not that it would have mattered much, my Master, such things happening on a Lord's day when the harmonium is singing, and the Reverend is telling us about the hereafter. Why could they not pick on another day, when one is not in one's chest clothes ...'

'And *Baas* Martin was with them?'

'But yes, my Old Master. Looking after the horses. Just behind the quince hedge where I was hiding. For my Master, Master must know we all ran out of the church and hid ourselves from the Boer masters, and with the women screaming and the brats yelling, my Master, there was a great to do, and old Kees does not hold with running into danger needlessly, my *Baas*. So I hid behind the quince hedge, and Master Martin he spotted me, just as soon as I did when he came round leading the horses. My, old

Kees got goose flesh then, my *Baas*, for old Kees saw he had no gun, my Master, old Kees he looked again, more manlike, my Master, and not like a Muscovy duck that tries to get away from the maids, my Master, and old Kees he saw that it was Master Martin, my Master, which was a miracle, my Master, for what should he do there with the Boer masters?'

'Yes, yes,' interrupted the old man, eagerly impatient. 'Did he talk to you?'

'Surely old Kees is telling the Old Master what he talked. He said, did Master Martin, in a whisper-like, "Outa, he said," not knowing old Kees, which is not surprising, my *Baas*, for why should Master Martin remember an old Hotnot like old Kees, who has never worked for him ...'

'Yes, yes! But what did he say, Outa?'

'Old Kees is surely telling the Old Master,' said the Native, not hastening in his speech, to his listener's great impatience. '"Outa," he said, in a whisper-like, for the Boer masters were not far away, and old Kees could see that it was a matter not to be discussed from the front *stoeps*, my Master. "Outa," he said, "if you go to the Village—carefully" he said, "so that the soldiers do not catch you, nor the Boer masters, you will tell the Old Master in the big house with the wonderful garden that you have seen *Baas* Martin, who cannot get away." And that is not all, my *Baas*, for he said to old Kees, "Tell the old master that if I can manage it, I will come, when it is safe." And then the Boer masters came along, my Master, and spoke roughly and most unkindly to *Baas* Martin, and old Kees drew back into the quince hedge until they were gone, my Master. But when the Boer masters had gone, old Kees went to the missionary, who was sorrowing in the church, my Master, because the Boer masters had come to us, and old Kees told him. And *Baas* Uhlmann said old Kees must go as soon as it is safe to go and tell Old Master, so old Kees he come, my *Baas*, when it is safe to come.'

'Very well, Kees. I'll see you don't suffer for it. But now you must go to the commandant's office—I will give you a slip of paper which will make it right with the soldier masters—and you must tell them what you have told me. Everything, mind. Just as you've told me. And you must tell the commandant master all you can remember of the Boer masters—how many there are, and how many horses, and which way they were making for. Can you do that?'

The Native touched his head cloth.

'*Baas* Uhlmann gave me a slip, my Master,' he said, simply. 'Old Kees carries him here, until the commandant master can read it. But first old Kees comes to the big house.'

'That is all right. Go back into the kitchen, and get the maids to give you something to eat and drink. You'd better stay there. At least, until the commandant sends for you. 'I'll go and see him myself.'

He escorted the Native boy to the kitchen, and saw him safely occupied with a bowl of mealie pap and a pannikin of coffee, and then went to old Martin's room, where he discussed the matter with serious attention to the various possibilities. There could be no doubt, both old men agreed, that the Native's story was substantially true. The mission station lay at the back of the mountains, in a lonely valley reached by a rough road. So far it had remained outside the turmoil of war, and the missionary, Mr Uhlmann's younger brother, had kept his small congregation in peace, for the discipline of the station was strict, and martial law was not needed to enforce the orders of the small local council that controlled it. But now, apparently, the Boer commandos had invaded it, and the fact that they were on that side of the mountain was disturbing. Old Martin agreed with Andrew that the commandant must be informed at once, and that no time must be lost in seeing him.

Outside it was still raining. A steady, winter's downpour made puddled mud in the street, where the feet of the soldiers and the hoofs of the horses had pounded the loose dust into miniature morasses. The mountains were invisible, shrouded in the haze of rain; the sky overhead was a leaden grey, and from the north blew a chill wind. In cheerless solitude stood the Village street, for everyone had retired indoors, and all the blinds were drawn, while the store attracted no customers. The Village was still deeply under the impression of the tragedy at the gaol.

Major Mallom received them with courtesy, but hardly with enthusiasm. He acknowledged their subdued greeting with an equally curt conventional rejoinder, and waved his hand towards the chairs, set at a properly respectful distance from his desk for the accommodation of those whom he had to interrogate officially.

'I can listen to no protest, Mr Quakerley,' he began, as soon as they were seated, 'and you must know that this is not the time, nor the place, to bring forward any protest. What has been done has been done after due consideration of all the facts. Nor can I allow the body to be buried outside the gaol. Please understand that at once.'

'We did not come to plead with you, Commandant,' said old Andrew, with dignity. 'We fully understand that you are merely executing your instructions. Our purpose is to make you acquainted with something that has come to our notice this morning. If you will allow me to tell you ...'

The commandant nodded, and listened gravely to the statement. He rang the bell, and told the orderly to march a guard down to Quakerley's house and bring the Native boy to his office.

'I am glad, very glad, Mr Quakerley,' he said, when the man had saluted and left, 'that you have been so prompt in notifying me. This is important information, if it can be substantiated. Curiously enough, we have had no report from the mission station, but your informant is probably the first to get through.'

'I believe he is,' said the old man. 'And he tells me that he has a written report for you. He should have come straight to you, Major, but you will perhaps forgive his lapse when you realise how eager he is to do something for Mr Rekker, whose father, it seems, placed him under some obligation.'

'Yes, I can understand that. Don't worry about that, Mr Quakerley. And if this about your son, Mr Rekker, can be supported by evidence—other evidence, mind you—the sooner he comes in, the better. I can hold out no hopes that his case will be more leniently judged if he cannot prove his statements ...'

'May I suggest, Major, that it is British custom to hold a person guiltless until his guilt has been proved? Under martial law,' said old Andrew, his indignation getting the upper hand over his determination not to allow his feelings to prejudice the issues, 'it seems to me you reverse that custom. You expect the accused to prove that he is not guilty.'

'It is not quite that, Mr Quakerley,' said the commandant, shortly. 'The mere fact that he is found with the enemy is presumptive proof of his guilt, which he must rebut by evidence. But we need not go into that. If there is the slightest evidence that justifies the inference that he has been forced, at the risk of his life, to join them, no court will find him guilty. You must accept that, but you must also accept the other conclusion. That is all.'

He ushered them out of his office, but at the door hesitated, made up his mind to get rid of an unpleasant duty, and addressed old Martin.

'I am sorry, Mr Rekker,' he said, not unkindly, 'but my instructions are to give you back your parole, and to transfer you back to gaol. You may have until this evening to take what steps you please, and I need scarcely say that anything your friends may do to make your detention more comfortable will be allowed. I am sorry, but my instructions are positive.'

Old Martin drew his friend away from the office. Andrew would have stayed and argued the case with the commandant, for the decision had come as a slap in the face. He was not to know that the Major had extended his friend's parole for much longer than his instructions had permitted. Quakerley saw in this new insult merely an added load to the heavy burden they were all called upon to bear, an unjust burden, an injury that shocked his sense of fairness and equity.

It was old Martin who comforted him.

'Perhaps it is better so, Mr Quakerley,' said the old farmer. 'In the gaol we'll be safe, at least. There we are out of temptation. Only it is sad to think that we old men should be spared while the others, who are younger and less able to resist, remain exposed to the dangers. And today I feel that I can bear anything. Come, old friend, do not take it so much to heart. For us who are old, it does not matter. It is for the younger ones that I grieve.'

Chapter 38

The three prisoners on parole were reincarcerated in the Village gaol, but this event, which ordinarily would have served as a topic of discussion for weeks, hardly stirred people's emotion. The summation of stimuli experienced by the Village during the past few months had exhausted its capacity for being surprised, astonished, or irritated. It had engendered a moral fatigue, the inevitable reaction after the emotional tetany caused by the sensational happenings in which the recrudescence of the commando activity had plunged the District.

This recrudescence was now very evident. Twice the outposts near the town had been attacked, and twice the commandos had been beaten back with some difficulty. The widespread area that had to be policed and defended made it difficult for Colonel Cautley to spare many men for the defence of the Village, and at first he had scorned the suggestion that the Boers would attack it. But on the day after the execution of Bons, the Village heard, for the first time in its existence, the sound of shots fired in actual warfare within its urban boundaries.

After the eight o'clock curfew, the Village was accustomed to peace and quiet. The only sounds heard were those emanating from the camp, the rumble of passing wagons, the tread of the patrols on the street, and the miscellaneous, damped noises that came from the horse lines. But that evening the guns had been hurried out, and men had taken up positions at the bottom of the gardens, facing the river where the ford was. On the other side, along the low ridge that in the daytime was starred with winter flowers, those who possessed binoculars could make out the figures of men afoot and on horseback, hurrying between the boulders and protea bush. Shortly after curfew, the first shots came from that direction and half an hour later the little force that defended the gardens was busily engaged. It spread out in a long line, positioned in the gardens themselves, and its fire was answered from the opposite ridge in a brisk fashion that showed that the attacking force was numerically strong enough to attempt to force a way across the river. Old Andrew, sitting in his study with Joan, could hear the sound of the firing quite plainly. It came in regular volleys; that was the defending force; it came in desultory cracks from beyond the river. Once a bullet struck the window, shattering the glass, and repeatedly could be heard the thump of a concussion on the woodwork, or the soft plump of a missile impinging on the thatched roof. The war was very close, unpleasantly intrusive, but the old man had no thought of danger. His one anxiety was now for his garden.

In the dark, drizzling rain that continued to fall throughout the evening, he watched the soldiers taking up their positions in the gardens. They hauled the guns through the hedges, over the flower plots; they chopped down trees to get a clear view. He felt too anxious to stay and watch what they were doing, and, besides, there were definite orders that all civilians should be indoors, all lights extinguished. There was nothing to do but sit in the study, listening to those nearby sounds, and to imagine all sorts of things, none of them pleasant to think of, all disturbing, all tending to bring out the sharp contrast between the quiet that had reigned here before Alexandrina Victoria's death, and the present wreck of his ideals, his hopes, and his peace.

He was sensible of his age, his tiredness, his irritability; sensible, above all, of a deep disappointment which he could not analyse to his own satisfaction because it was compounded of so many essentially different apperceptive quotients. For eighty odd years his life had been a moderately calm, pleasant, successful one. He had never known want; he had always been equal among his peers in the Colony, and, in the Village, easily first by virtue of his connections, his wealth, and the respect with which the name of Quakerley was regarded. Within reasonable limits he had obtained what he desired; there were of course things that he wished to have which were beyond the boundaries of reasonableness for him to get. His innate appreciation of beauty, inherited probably from some artistic Dutch ancestor of his mother, craved for far more than he had been able to develop and create in his garden.

His garden ... as he thought of it, a wave of strong emotion passed over him, and his fingers involuntarily grasped the arm-rest of his chair. Now there was fighting going on in his garden ... men were dragging the gun carriages across the paths; the wheels would make deep ruts in the gravel, but that was nothing—that could be repaired. But the guns would do much more damage, and so would the horses ... what a mess ... what a mess! It surprised him that he could not feel himself indignant, fiercely angry, when he thought of what his garden was suffering—that he could not transfer, as it were, part of that suffering to himself, glorying in it as martyrs for a faith glory in the contumely they suffer for it, yet passionately resenting it as something done to humiliate him. A month ago, he felt sure, he would have raged, however impotently, and used very strong language, such as his father would have used on similar occasions, to express his anger. But now, somehow, words, rage, anger, expletives, damnatory adjectives and rhetorical extravaganzas seemed banal, out of place, unworthy of the occasion and of the depth of his feeling. The irregular beat of the rifles outside and the steady drip of the rain falling on the *stoep* were too depressing to permit of the luxury of self pity.

He remembered, as in moments of anxiety one sometimes remembers trivialities, how, long ago, the rector had once asked him, 'Mr Quakerley, what do you really consider yourself?' At the time he had thought it a stupid question. What could one consider oneself but an Englishman, an English subject? Now, as his thoughts dwelt on the past few months, the question appeared to him to be less stupid than he originally considered it to be. He wondered what Joan would say—Joan, sitting there so calmly, reading the *Brothers* of her favourite Terence, finding, very probably, consolation in the philosophic talk of Geta, and the whimsicalities of Sostrata. English-Dutch colonial, Native-born first or second generation ... Transvaaler or Free Stater; did it matter very much what you called yourself? What counted was the tradition behind one, the ideal one had formed of one's nationality. And even that was a matter of vanity, unworthy of an honest man, perhaps. Accident of birth and place ... was that something to be inordinately proud of ... something to boast about ... something to throw in other people's teeth when it came to assessing national values? It was not his, Andrew's, doing that his father had been an Englishman with an unblemished English ancestry, and his mother a Dutchwoman who could look back upon an ancestor like Lamoral van Egmont, executed in Brussels for rebellion against his liege lord, King Philip of Spain. Yet the Egmonds, who now spelt their name differently, and made no claim to be *armiger*, referred, in spasms of pride, to their beheaded forebear; they would not look upon the execution of the great Lamoral in precisely the same light in which they would regard the hanging of that half-witted lad who had also rebelled against his liege lord, King Edward. History had dealt kindly with the men who had resisted Alva; was it absurd to think that it would deal kindly with the few ignorant farm hands who had transgressed the martial law regulations of Major Mallom? Were these narrow distinctions of nationalism material to the real issues about which men might quarrel, that a sane man could debate in conformity to the tradition in which he had been reared? What was he, Andrew, in this issue that was being fought out—the issue of English supremacy? In feeling, sentiment, association, he was Native-born, thinking, if he thought at all, about the effects some particular event or situation would have upon him as a Colonial, with no in-bred antagonism to England, and no resentment against English rule, tradition or association. Yet, in the present ebullience of academic patriotism, he supposed he and his would be classed as English, while those who had the least pretence to pure Dutch ancestry would be admitted to the ranks of the patriots, reckoned true South Africans, while he was regarded as English-minded, suspect because his father had been English, and because he doubted the justice of the Republican cause. He asked himself if there were any grounds for his doubts, and came to the conclusion that, no matter what happened, no matter how much martial law outraged his preconceived notions of English fair-play and equity, he could still cling to the hope that these notions were fundamentally sound, and that what had happened, what was daily happening, was no sound index of the real heart of England, beating in sympathy with his ideal, six thousand miles away.

If there, six thousand miles away, men and women could make sacrifices for their ideal, surely he could render them too, confident that in the end justice and right would prevail, and the ideal would emerge untarnished from the mire that now encrusted it.

Joan raised her eyes from her book, and the movement brought him back to the realities of the moment.

'Listen,' his sister said, 'they are firing from behind, Andy. Can you hear? I wonder what that can be?'

As she spoke there came sounds from the *stoep*. Andrew stepped towards the door and opened it cautiously. In the dark, hazy drizzle he could see the flashes in the garden, and make out the forms of men and horses massed under the trees. On the *stoep* were a few soldiers, in charge of a corporal, stooping over a wounded man. Andrew held the door wide open.

'Bring him in,' he said. 'Miss Quakerley and I will do what we can. Who is it?'

'It's the Colonel, Sir,' said one of the men. 'The stretcher is just a-coming ...'

'Never mind the stretcher,' said the old man, briskly. 'Lift him up, and carry him in. Tell the doctor, some of you, that he is here, and we'll take care of him ...'

'E'd better wait for the stretcher,' said the corporal, doubtfully. 'This ain't no such safe place, Sir. They're all about us, the b——y Boers. They shot 'im at fifty paces, an' they've broken through the line on the left. Best wait for the stretcher, Sir.'

'No. Take him in. We'll look after him. Tell Major Mallom, if he's there, or Captain Overbury ...'

An officer ran up through the garden, followed by two men.

'What are you doing here?' he asked breathlessly. 'Get back ... get back! The stretcher party will attend to all wounded ...'

Andrew recognised the Major. 'I suggested taking him in, Major Mallom,' he said quickly. 'I think that would be the best. And any wounded we can have here—there is plenty of accommodation.'

'Very well. Carry him in, then. And keep indoors, Mr Quakerley. He was shot quite close here. I'm afraid the doctor is too busy at the moment—we are having a hot time of it, but I think we've beaten them off.'

They carried the Colonel indoors, where Joan had already roused the maids, and prepared for his reception. The Major remained for a moment, rapping out curt orders to the men, and then disappeared into the darkness. The noise at the back increased, the sounds of the rifles following in quick succession, crackling bursts that seemed to be very near. From the *stoep* Andrew could see a dull glow of light on the left, the cause of which he could not understand. As he turned to go indoors, Dr Buren and an army medical officer dashed up and followed him into the house.

'As hot a little scrap as you'd care for,' exclaimed the Doctor, mopping his face. 'They've got past our right flank, and fired a house down the street.'

They left the old man in his study, where he sat in his chair, listening to the confused sounds outside. The firing was so brisk and so near that he could no longer tell the direction from which the sounds came, but he guessed that the centre of activity had shifted from the gardens to the back of the houses, and that hand-to-hand fighting was going on somewhere in the second street. There was nothing he could do. The two doctors came back. 'Pretty bad, Mr Quakerley,' said Buren, and his colleague nodded. 'We'll have to leave him here for the present. I don't think we can get him through to the hospital, and anyways he's all right here for the present.'

'And you?' asked the old man. 'Can I get you anything, Buren? It will only take a minute ...'

'No, no. We must get back. Do you realise that we have some thirty men to attend to out there, Mr Quakerley? We're holding our own, but unless we are reinforced I expect we shall have to fall back on the camp.'

'Surely not. You've got the guns ...'

'Their shooting is damn accurate. They picked off the gunners, and they've got the range to a yard or two. If you ask me, I should say they're being guided by local men who know every inch of the ground. We'll get some of our wounded here, if you don't mind, Mr Quakerley.'

They were gone before he had fully grasped the situation, and he went back to his chair and picked up his *Henley*. But he could not read. Even when the sounds outside died down and he could hear no noises, not even the drip, drip of the rain on the *stoep*, his thoughts refused to rest. They went wandering into the past, to the days of his boyhood, when he had listened to tales of the frontier, where pioneers were clearing a way into the wild interior, to the days when men still referred moodily to the misdeeds and tyranny of the old Company, and there were Orange and Republican sections almost as antagonistic as English and Dutch nowadays. They went back to that recurring question of nationality. What was his position in this imbroglio, in which ideals seemed all jumbled, and pre-conceptions all wrong? Culturally, traditionally, he was as much Dutch as English, for the two were one, after all, when everything was said and done. Both came from a common root-stock, each blossoming in its own way without sapping the other's strength, or clouding the other's glamour. Both had a past upon which a people could look back with pride and satisfaction; both had made mistakes from which had sprung much misery; both would probably make similar mistakes in the future. But there was no necessity for this sullen hatred, this clumsy antagonism of tradition which the war had called forth. Between enemies who stood apart in race and custom, such an attitude might be the result of economic forces; here it was merely evidence of distorted cultural values, rooted in contempt on the one side and a feeling of inferiority on the other. It was this feeling of inferiority, Andrew told himself, quite rightly, that was being strengthened and added to by martial law. Such events as the public promulgation of the death sentence upon local rebels, and the summoning of prominent Dutch-speaking citizens to be witnesses of the execution, were calculated to inspire the Dutch-speaking section with the feeling that their English fellow-citizens, as represented by the military authorities, were contemptuous towards them, and the recognition of such contempt was in itself an acknowledgment of inferiority, just as the constant reiteration on the part of the Transvaal that it was a sovereign independent state was an open acknowledgment of the fact that it had serious doubts about its ability to maintain its independence. One who was certain of himself did not hate, nor struggle to prevent his rights from being trodden underfoot.

He could stand aloof, indifferent to what others thought, supreme in himself, fighting fiercely enough when assailed, but not worrying himself about attacks when silence and contempt were the best defence. That was what England had done in this war, and could he really blame her for fighting, when attacked, when her prestige was threatened?

And yet ... he could not feel that victory, so evident, so inevitable in this war, would give him great pleasure, or, for him, increase that prestige and make him feel more proud of the English blood that ran in his veins, any more than the inevitable defeat of the Republics would make him ashamed of his Dutch blood. There would be those who might think it was necessary for them to rehabilitate themselves in their own eyes, possibly also in the eyes of their kinsmen who had invaded the King's Colony, by denying their allegiance and allying themselves with the King's enemies. That would be a natural reaction, similar to that which makes the small boy wilfully damage something belonging to a grown-up who has slighted or injured him, in the attempt to recover his own self-esteem, and make himself feel less a small boy. Normally, he would not have been conscious of his immaturity, but the sense of impotence would create the feeling of relative inferiority.

Normally, people like the Rekkers, the Gersters, and the van Aardts would not worry over their standing in a community where tradition had fixed certain essential values, reckoned not by standards of nationality, but in terms of human worthiness, which their families had possessed for generations. Their allodial excellence needed no demonstration; it was evident by contrast with the less generously endowed landless citizens, and by the greater contrast of the large Native and Coloured population that had originally been chattels to be bought and sold. But now they too would feel that something had happened to detract from these essential values, and they would naturally attempt to demonstrate their superiority, or at least equality, as a protest against the derogation to which they had been subjected ... what a mess it all was ... what a mess!

Andrew heard the clock strike twelve. He started out of his reverie, and was surprised to find that everything was so quiet. There were no sounds from the garden, and the shooting in the back street had long ago died down, although he had not been conscious of its cessation. The study was cold, and the oil in the lamp was exhausted so that the flame smoked. He turned it down, not minding the darkness, rested his feet on another chair and, thrusting his hands into the pockets of his heavy tweed jacket, decided to sleep. He had often done so, and formerly it had been easy for him to sleep. Sleep came as he willed it, a habit which he had cultivated and found very useful. But tonight he could not fall asleep. His mind refused to give up those disturbing thoughts that had disquieted him when awake, and each one seemed to bring associations that demanded further and equally disturbing consideration. The sound of the firing had been a distraction, it had kept him in a state of strained expectancy. Now that he no longer heard it, he wondered what was taking place in the Village. Had the commando been driven off? What were the troops doing? Why didn't they bring the wounded to the house as the doctors had suggested? What was the result of the fighting in the gardens?

As he turned restlessly in his chair, a faint sound from the window reached him. Someone was lightly tapping on the pane. At first he believed that he was hearing a sound such as comes in that state of semi-consciousness between waking and sleeping, but when it was repeated he sat up in his chair, and strained his ears. He heard the faint knocking quite distinctly.

He got up, pulled the heavy curtain aside, and opened the inside blind. Outlined against the window was a dark shape, bending forward and touching the pane. A man, obviously, who wanted to attract his attention, but the secretiveness of the method used irritated him. He swung round and strode towards the door opening on to the *stoep*, and unlocked it.

'Who is it?' he called out. 'Do you want me?'

'Hush, Mr Quakerley,' answered a voice which he thought he recognised, although he was not sure. A man came quickly out of the shadows into the slightly less dark part of the *stoep* where the faint reflection of the corridor light made a haze over the wet stone pavement. 'Let me in ... it is I ... Martin.' He made way, and the man walked into the house past him, and Andrew followed him, closing and locking the door behind them. Under the hanging corridor lamp the intruder was plainly visible, and Andrew saw before him old Rekker's son, Martin junior, dressed in a tattered shirt and trousers, wearing a slouch hat and worn-out veld shoes. A gaunt, weary-looking man, whose bearded face showed obvious traces of hardships endured and of emotional agonies which had left their impression upon it.

'Martin,' he exclaimed, involuntarily sinking his voice, 'what are you doing here? What,' he seized the man's hand and wrung it, 'what have they done to you? By heaven, my boy, you look done in ... sit down there ... sit down at once, man. I'll get you something ...'

'No, Mr Quakerley,' interrupted the young man, quickly. 'That would be too dangerous. There is no time to be lost. I have just managed to get here to tell you ...'

'Wait, Martin, wait,' the old man interrupted in his turn, 'I feel ashamed to ask you, but I must ... are you ...?'

'Have I joined them, Mr Quakerley?' Martin retorted quickly. 'No, not of my own will, Mr Quakerley. But they have kept me with them these months, and I am a rebel, I suppose, though I have never carried a gun and done nothing to make me a rebel. But that does not count now. If I am caught, Mr Quakerley, it'll be a court martial for me and a firing party. But that is not what I came for ...'

'Never mind what you came for,' said the old man, with decision. 'Now you are here, you will stay here, Martin. You have escaped and you will give yourself up. That is the only thing you can do, and for your father's sake, for your own sake, for the sake of us all, Boy, you must stay. We'll all help you ...'

'I am not going to risk it, Mr Quakerley. I have risked enough coming to tell you. Listen, Mr Quakerley. You must go to the commandant, now, at once, Mr Quakerley, and tell him that at dawn there is to be an attack on the camp at *Kromdraai*. This affair here is only to keep the troops here—the real attack is to be at *Kromdraai*. That is what I came to tell you, and we must not wait. You must go now ... I'll slip away— they'll never catch me—but I thought I must tell you. Now let me go, Mr Quakerley. You can't do anything for me, and I must get away.'

'Wait a moment, Martin.' The old man went to the sideboard and poured out some brandy into a glass and added water. 'Drink this first. Have you had anything to eat?'

'Nothing to speak of, Mr Quakerley. But never mind that. Let the commandant know. If they hurry troops out there, it will be all right. But if they delay ... thank you Mr Quakerley, this is good. I'll put these in my pocket.'

'No, sit down and eat them. Joan always puts a plate of sandwiches out for me. No, wait, wait, man ...'

There was a sound of footsteps on the *stoep*, and Martin sprang up.

'Get into that room—there,' whispered the old man. 'I expect that is the doctor— we've got a wounded man here. Stay there, Martin, promise me ... it'll be all right ...'

'I'm not going to be hanged—let me get to the kitchen ...'

'Be quiet. Just go in there.' He pushed the young man into the room, closed the door and stood with his back to it, just as Major Mallom, followed by Dr Buren and Captain Jobson, walked in.

'Commandant,' he said, before his visitors greeted him, 'is there a camp at *Kromdraai*?'

'Yes. Fifty of Marshall's horses are there. Why, Mr Quakerley?' replied the Major, regarding him curiously.

'I have information, Commandant, that they are to be attacked at dawn today by a strong force of Boers. The attack on the Village was to draw off your force ...'

'Quite likely. May I ask how you acquired this information, Mr Quakerley?'

'If you will sit down, Major, I will tell you in a moment. Doctor, you will find my sister with your patient. You know your way?'

Old Andrew felt quite calm. The room into which he had thrust Martin had been Charlie's bedroom, a small inner room with a window too small for a man to get out of. The only way out of it was through the door leading into the dining-room, facing which Major Mallom now sat awaiting his explanation.

'I have a confession to make, Commandant,' said the old man, simply. 'A few minutes ago, just before you came, a man knocked on my study window. I let him in, and he told me that he had come to warn you of an attack by the commandos on the camp at *Kromdraai* ...'

'Where is he? I must see him. This is important, Mr Quakerley. I confess I have had some anxiety about the camp. Was he one of our men?'

'Yes, Major, he is one of our men. As a matter of fact, he is Martin Rekker's son, who has been held prisoner by the commando, and he escaped, somehow, tonight with the intention to give you this warning.'

'That is very good of him,' said the Major, drily. 'But you will readily understand, Mr Quakerley, that information from such a source is scarcely likely to be reliable.'

'Major Mallom, may I beg you to believe me when I say that young Martin is thoroughly loyal, and that any information he gives you, you may depend on. He came to me simply because he knew I was here, and he knew that if he went to your office he would be arrested, and possibly get no opportunity of making a statement in time for you to act on it.'

'There is something in that, Mr Quakerley,' said the Major, rising. 'I take it' ... he looked fixedly at the old man ... 'that your informant is still here, and that you will hold yourself responsible for him?'

Quakerley nodded, but made no remark. 'Very well, I must go at once, Mr Quakerley ... this matter must be attended to immediately. But a guard will be detailed to secure the man ... you will see yourself that this is imperative.'

'I quite see that, Major,' said Andrew, mildly. 'But I am an old man, and you cannot hold me responsible if my ... my visitor leaves me before your guard arrives ...'

'Mr Quakerley, I do not think you need fear any personal violence if you tried to restrain your impetuous friend sufficiently to keep him safe until my guard arrives. If his information is reliable, and if we can profit by it, you may be sure that it will count very distinctly in his favour. I cannot promise any more.'

'I thank you, Commandant,' said the old man, courteously, escorting the Major to the *stoep*. 'I'll bear in mind what you say, but I, too, cannot promise any more.'

He came back, and went directly to the little room. Martin sat on the bed, with his head in his hands. As the light from the open door fell on him, he lifted his head and glanced mournfully at his host.

'Why didn't you let me go when there was time, Mr Quakerley?' he demanded, reproachfully. 'Would you, too, take a delight in seeing my father's son hanged like a Hottentot who has murdered somebody?'

'No, Martin, but I should not like your father's son to be a coward, when he has proved that he is made of better stuff. Come into the dining room. You heard? I spoke loud enough, for your benefit.'

'Oh, I heard all right. But what does it matter, Mr Quakerley? They will never believe me. But there—it is done now, and to tell you the truth, Mr Quakerley, it is a relief. Better to have it over and done with than to go about day after day knowing that sooner or later they will get you. Although I did think, once I had got free of them, that I would be able to make my way down to the coast, and escape out of the country.'

He sat down, and Andrew mixed a glass of brandy and water for him, and took one himself.

'You are wet through,' he said. 'Now, be a sensible boy and give me your promise that you will stay here, no matter what happens, and I will go and get you dry clothing. Or better come with me, and rig yourself out. There are clothes enough in the drawers. But promise first.'

'Very well, Mr Quakerley. I'll stay.'

'Good. Come along then. Do you hear that? They are moving, I think.'

The sound of wheels, of horses, and of marching men came from the back street. Reinforcements were being sent to the camp at *Kromdraai*. Old Andrew led his prisoner to his own bedroom. 'Make yourself at home,' he said, hospitably. 'When the guard comes, you'll have to be presentable, you know. You'll find Kropp razors in the top drawer, and I'll get you a jug of hot water from the kitchen.'

Chapter 39

The guard arrived sooner than Andrew expected. He had hardly returned to the dining room when there was a knock at the front door, followed by the tramp of the armed soldiers entering the corridor.

'He is just shaving, Corporal,' said old Andrew. 'You can go in there, if you like, and see for yourself.'

'That'll be all right, Sir,' said the corporal, apologetically. 'We'll wait for him here, Sir.'

'Very well. Perhaps one of you might make some coffee or cocoa if you care to take any. You'll find everything ready in the kitchen. If you stay here, Corporal, where you can watch the door ...'

'Oh, that's all right, Sir,' interjected the corporal. 'But we're on duty, Sir, and we can't do it, Sir. Thank you all the same, Sir. So long as he's not too long, Sir.'

'No. I'll tell him.' Andrew went to his bedroom and informed Martin that his guard had arrived. 'I know the corporal,' he said encouragingly. 'He's one of the best. And Monk ... but you know Monk. I told them you'd not be long ...'

'I'll be there in a minute, Mr Quakerley. There's no sense in spinning it out. If I have to go, I might as well go now.'

Andrew went back to the dining room, where the corporal and his two men were standing stiffly at attention, their gaze solemnly fixed on the open door.

'Your prisoner will be here in a moment, Corporal,' he said, briskly. 'By the way, he is a gentleman whom I know very well, who has been captured by the Boers and only succeeded in escaping last night. He came directly to me to ask me to notify the commandant that an attack was to be made on the camp at *Kromdraai* ...'

'We was told he's a ...,' the corporal hesitated over a suitable adjective and decided, out of deference to the 'squire,' to do without one ... 'rebel, Sir ...'

'So he is, technically, I suppose. That is to say, he's a British subject who has been with the Boers. But we needn't go into that. Here he is. Corporal, this is Martin Rekker, for whom I have been responsible until now. I hand him over to you. I suppose you will have to take him to the gaol?'

'No, sir. Orders is we've got to bring him to the commandant's office.'

'In that case, you might as well stay here. I don't suppose the commandant will be back much before noon today ...'

'Sorry, Sir, but that's orders, Sir,' said the corporal, firmly. 'Come along ... Sir.'

'I'll come round and see you as soon as possible, Martin,' promised the old man, shaking hands with his departing visitor. 'And I'll see that some breakfast is sent over at seven. Don't be down-hearted, Boy. We'll have you back on the farm before the week's past.'

Martin shook his head gloomily. He did not seem to respond to the encouragement. The corporal saluted, and let him out.

Andrew took his half drunk glass of brandy and sat down on the big sofa, whose seat was made of plaited leather straps. The incidents had excited him, and made him momentarily forget his fatigue and his infirmities. Now, when the inevitable reaction came, he felt tired, worn out, and dispirited. Under the emotion of the moment he had imagined himself courageous to the verge of martyrdom. His self-communion in the dark had produced in him a kind of exaltation which had immediately and instinctively responded to Martin's passionate appeal. That exaltation of spirit had remained during his short interview with the Major and with the corporal, but now, when he was again alone, doubts thronged upon him, pitilessly assailing his mind with their semblance of probability. Martin was technically, actually, a rebel. He had been with the commandos for several weeks, and the *onus* of proving that he had taken no part in their activities would be on him. Andrew had a harassing doubt whether that *onus* could be discharged to the satisfaction of a court martial. In his own mind he was convinced that Martin had been loyal; it was simply unthinkable that a member of a family reared in the tradition of the Rekkers, whose sense of honour and obligation was as strong as that of the Quakerleys, would have done anything even remotely disloyal in a furtive and underhand manner. If a Rekker wished to go into rebellion he would do so openly, not glorying in the publicity, but simply because his code of honour demanded that his repudiation of obligations he no longer considered binding should be indisputably declared to all men whom the matter concerned. Very many years ago a Rekker had actually defied the old Company, but before intimating that he had no desire to obey the commands of the Lords Major, and indeed would take every step in his power to nullify these commands. He had written a dignified letter to the Governor, wherein he had accurately stated the details of his plan of rebellion, giving the government full warning of his intentions. So much had the Governor been impressed by this courteous disobedience, that he had gone out of his way to save the writer from the inevitable consequences of his rebellion, and the matter had been adjusted with satisfaction to both sides. No, there could be no possible doubt about Martin's loyalty in the minds of those who knew the Rekkers. But the Major, the military, and the court would not know the Rekkers. Evidence of character would count for very little; it might even aggravate the seriousness of the charge, and if the court had not taken into consideration the fact that the lad Bons was half-witted, it would very likely pay no attention to the fact that the Rekkers were traditionally incapable of covert treason. The main difficulty would be for the court to realise that any Dutch-speaking inhabitant of the District was constitutionally incapable of covert treason.

'Give a dog a bad name,' said the old man to himself, bitterly, 'and hang him.' That was the trouble. Even so fair-minded a man as Major Mallom had sneered—yes, actually sneered—when he had heard that Martin had come in at the risk of his life to give information that might save a British force from capture or annihilation. If Martin had been a Quakerley, a Seldon, or a Miller, Major Mallom would certainly not have sneered. He might not have believed what he had been told, but he would have been angry, or pained, or simply incredulous; he would not have been sneeringly incredulous. If Major Mallom held that view, what would the average British officer, the members of the court martial, think? Would they not characterise Martin's version as 'poppycock,' a cunningly constructed web of fact and fable suitably intertwined, meant to extricate him from a position that was untenable in any case? As this view of the situation struck him, old Andrew winced, and his fingers beat a nervous rat-tat on the leather arm-rests of his chair. Had he done right in appealing to Martin's sense of honour? Would it not have been better to have let the man go? The information about the contemplated attack could have been given just as easily without dragging the informant into the matter, without putting Martin to a danger that was after all very real. The boy could have escaped—he knew every inch of the ground round about the Village; he knew the District almost as well as he knew his own farm—he could easily have managed to hide until his case had been forgotten. Now all that had been made impossible. Martin would have to stand his trial, and the more he thought about that trial, the more old Andrew doubted whether he had acted rightly in opposing the man's departure. His duty ... as a loyal subject ... but it was a duty laid upon him to deliver up to military justice, that was so cruelly unjust, a friend's son about whose innocence he had no manner of doubt. Even as a gesture of exaltation, it would have been more dignified for him to have connived at Martin's escape, and then to have come boldly forward and confessed his share in the business. It would have been aiding and abetting the King's enemies—comforting was, he believed, the legal expression invariably used—and he would have been court-martialled himself, and fined or imprisoned. Well, he could have borne either or both these punishments gladly, for Martin had acted honourably and his conscience would not upbraid him. But the Quakerley tradition would have suffered. What was that quotation that Joan had read of the *Brothers*?

'Minume miror qui insanire occipiunt ex iniuria ...'

But even men's madness did not justify an action that went against the Quakerley tradition ...

Joan entered, bringing a newly-filled lamp to replace the old one, whose flame had long ago expired. As usual she looked calm, detached, disinterested, although he knew that beneath her placidity stirred an undertow of passion as deep as his own. Briefly he told her.

'Poor Martin,' she said feelingly. 'Andy, we're paying dear for the privilege of being English ... No, no, you did quite right, Brother. Even if he has to die, let him die with clean hands.'

'Why should he die?' demanded the old man, fiercely. 'What harm has the boy done? If the Boers captured me and carried me about with them while they looted and shot Natives in cold blood, am I to be held responsible for them or for not having escaped from them? And what chance has the lad to prove his story?'

'None, I should say,' she replied, dispassionately, so dispassionately that if he was not convinced of her fellow-feeling in the matter, he would have burst out in protest. 'He would have to get witnesses to prove that he was actually forced. His own word would not be accepted ...'

'There you have it! His own word would not be accepted ... the word of a man who is a Rekker ...'

'Yours or mine wouldn't be accepted in such circumstances, Andy,' she interrupted, mildly. 'Isn't the *onus* on him?'

'Why should it be? They left his farm unprotected. We gave these men no assistance—even now, we do not protect them—and yet we say that if they allow themselves to fall into the enemy's hands they will be considered rebels. "Allow themselves to fall"—did you ever hear the like? Is this our British justice, Joan? Is this fair-play? It is enough to make anyone rebel when loyal subjects are treated like that, and when a man's word is doubted just because appearances are against him ...'

'No, dear. This is martial law, and Mr Storam says martial law is the negation of all law. But that does not mean that we are going to let Martin suffer for what he hasn't done. You'll have to see Mr Vantloo—don't let things go on as they did in that other case. Get Mr Vantloo to defend him. Don't give up hope, Andy. We'll do the best we can, and if it fails, well, it is just part of the tragedy. Come along now and have something. I've made you a cup of beef-tea and some sandwiches. Dr Buren and Captain Jobson are in the dining room.'

He allowed himself to be led into the dining room, where the two doctors were drinking a nasty tea. They had already been to the hospital and back, arranging for the accommodation of several wounded in the house. He listened with some show of interest to their account of the fighting that had taken place in the gardens, and learned that a flank attack had been made by the Boers, who had succeeded in penetrating into the second street, where they had fired the court house. Its thatched roof was now a ruin, for it had been impossible to put out the fire. The library at the back had suffered the most. Most of the books and the shelving had been destroyed.

'A very great pity, Jobson,' Buren told his colleague. 'We had a splendid collection of books. A good many autographed copies of standard works, presented by Mr Quakerley's father. Tennyson, Browning, even Scott and Jane Austen and George Eliot, you know. We didn't appreciate them, but all the same it is a great pity they've been destroyed. Casualties? Well, Mr Quakerley, the fighting was pretty hot, and at close range, too. We've five dead, and about fifty wounded—that's about it, Jobson, hey?'

'I don't think you need fear another attack, Quakerley,' said Captain Jobson, noticing Andrew's rather anxious expression. 'Besides, there's a strong column on its way, and before noon we'll be in a sound position.'

'I am not worrying about them attacking us,' interrupted the old man. 'I know our troops are quite able to defend the town.'

'Then you're worrying about something else, Mr Quakerley,' said Dr Buren, shrewdly. 'Better tell us—that is, if we can be of any help to you.'

He told them as succinctly as he had told his sister. Dr. Buren suspended his tea cup in mid-air.

'Wheugh!' he exclaimed. 'My dear sir, you should have looked the other way, and let him find the door himself. Jobson, my sympathies are very much with the prisoner, and you needn't look so outraged. There is no sense in running your head into a noose ...'

'I'm not so sure he's doing that,' interjected Captain Jobson, eagerly. 'You don't appear to realise what the man has done. Even if he's a rebel—and I must say, appearances are very much against him—this action of his goes far to condone it. They'll certainly not hang him now. Unless, of course, there are other accusations against him.'

'And these are easily trumped up,' said Dr Buren, aggressively. 'You must know yourself, Jobson, how simple it is to prove that one of our men was killed in an engagement in which the commando that captured Martin took part. That would justify a charge of murder against him ...'

'Technically it might,' argued his colleague, 'but it will have to be shown that he was armed, and took part in the action. If he is to be relied upon ...'

'The man's a Rekker,' said Dr Buren, anticipating old Andrew's indignant protest. 'And all Rekkers are reliable. You don't catch them telling taradiddles, even to save their skins. If he says he wasn't armed, he wasn't. Take that from me ...'

'The question is whether the court will take it from you,' retorted Captain Jobson, drily. 'I don't know the gentleman in question, but, if you'll excuse the remark, I can't say that I've found some of our friends hereabouts exactly George Washingtons. And in these times of stress, a little prevarication may go a long way ...'

'I am with you there,' said Dr Buren heartily. 'I've heard some tall things myself, even in normal times, but, my dear fellow, you must differentiate between men like Ras and the poor *bywoner* class, and men like the Rekkers. The Rekkers—Mr Quakerley will take no offence at the comparison—are as much aristocrats as the Quakerleys ...'

'Of course not, Doctor,' came Andrew's quick rejoinder. 'The Rekkers are every whit as good as my own family, and I needn't boast when I say that, Captain Jobson. But do you really think that his coming and telling me about the camp at *Kromdraai* will be taken into consideration?'

'About that you can make your mind easy, Mr Quakerley,' said Jobson, and his tone carried conviction. 'Unless there are aggravating circumstances about which we know nothing, it will tell very much in his favour. No, I don't suppose for a moment they will hang him.'

'I hope, for his sake,' said Dr Buren, gravely, 'that he'll be able to prove that he's been forced, so that this other matter does not come up.'

'Why?' asked his colleague in surprise. 'It will tell very much in his favour, Buren.'

'I know it would—from his and our point of view, Jobson. But bear in mind that we'll have to live in this country after you fellows have gone comfortably home ...'

'I don't see what that has to do with the case,' interrupted Jobson.

'Ah, but I do,' went on Dr Buren. 'My father used to ding into my ears his opinion of folk that played informer, and you may bet any money you like that my old man's feelings on the subject will find plenty of echoes here when the war is over.'

'Rubbish, Buren. They aren't wild Irishmen,' retorted Captain Jobson, while old Andrew looked disturbed. He had not thought of that side of the matter, and it suddenly struck him that Buren was right.

'No, but they have pretty long memories, Jobson. This war will leave behind it a feeling of resentment long after we have forgotten what there was to resent, and Martin's action, however praiseworthy it is from our point of view, is sure to be misrepresented. It always is, you know. I'm sure when we are all at peace again, and some busybody makes up these things, for political purposes, you know, there'll be many who say that Rekker was a traitor to his own people, while some folk we know about, who are making good money out of the war, will probably pose as patriots and national heroes. I know all about it, for I've had experience of it, and my old dad and my grandfather were constantly harping on the subject.'

'I suppose there is an analogy between South Africa and Ireland,' remarked Captain Jobson, meditatively, but Buren interrupted him with a laugh. 'Don't you believe any such thing,' he said, vehemently. 'Ireland has the religious difficulty, and the difference of tradition and outlook between the two sections. We have neither here. We are merely reacting to stimuli in a perfectly natural way, and if the authorities would only realise that fact, there'd be no great difficulty. Now they won't. They persist in imagining that our people are eager to see the last of the English, and that they are making common cause with the Boers.'

'Well, isn't that a fact?' asked Jobson. 'I know little about your politics—it's none of my business—but I am told that the whole Colony is practically seething with discontent and rebellion.'

'Then you're told something which isn't and never has been a fact,' said Dr Buren, hotly. 'When this war was started, you wouldn't have found six persons in our District who would have gone into rebellion. You would possibly have struck sixty who hoped that the Boers might teach England a lesson, and six hundred who thought that the war was unnecessary. Myself among them,' he added, sturdily. 'But you would have found quite as many who keenly resented being patronised by the Republics, you know, being told that this was a war of liberation, and so on. And when the commandos invaded our territory, you wouldn't have found three people of any standing who didn't condemn that more as a gratuitous piece of folly on a par with the ultimatum. Now I admit things are different. And between you and me, I can't say that we've done much good by martial law methods such as we've had here. But we must be getting along, Jobson. It's nearly dawn, and there's a lot to do, Mr Quakerley. Captain Jobson will send a couple of hospital orderlies along to help, Mr Quakerley, and we'll move the Colonel as soon as he's fit to be moved.'

'Is his condition serious, Doctor?' asked Quakerley, sympathetically.

'Yes, very. He's shot through the spine, poor chap. When he realises that, he'll probably wish that he hadn't come through. That's to say, if he does, which I doubt. Come along, Jobson. And you, Mr Quakerley, you'd better see Vantloo as Miss Quakerley suggested. He's one of those who is making good money out of our troubles, and probably one day he'll be a national hero. My Irish experience, you know. Come along, Jobson.'

Chapter 40

The rain had cleared the air, and the heavy mass of cloud lifted from the mountains, disclosing a faint sprinkling of snow on the higher peaks and terraces of steep sandstone cliffs, shining blue in the distance, on which the morning sun glowed. When old Andrew came out in the cold morning air, he saw from the *stoep* the havoc that had been wrought in his garden. He had not given much thought to it; he had been far too much occupied with other things. But his garden was a very serious matter, and as he looked down from the *stoep* and realised the wreck that last night's operations had made of it, something rose in his throat, and he had to swallow hard to save himself from gasping.

He hurried down the steps. The rustic bridge spanning the water-course was a ruin, but he easily stepped across the narrow furrow. The tall gardenia hedge on the farther side was almost razed to the ground; the fine old magnolia tree under which he had loved to sit was still there, but most of the ornamental trees had been hacked down. Where his beautiful herbaceous borders had been there was now a welter of mud, for the horses had trampled the flowers to pieces. His bulb garden existed no more; it, too, was a ruin, the tall-stemmed gladioli broken and bent, the freesias browsed down by the mules that had been parked there. As he wandered disconsolately down the path, no longer a path but merely a track through ground that seemed to have been mischievously ploughed over to destroy every vestige of its ordered arrangement of bed, border, rockery and slope, he realised how little remained of what the day before had been a thing of joy and pride, a beauty and a solace that had perpetually cheered him in his old age.

A child sobs over its broken toy. Andrew, walking among the ruins of his garden, was too grief-stricken to cry, for the consolation of tears is denied to age. A lifetime of repression had schooled the old man to remain calm in the midst of such misfortunes as had hitherto come upon him. There had not been many, for his had been a sheltered, easy, unburdened life, wherein the war, with its concomitant irritations and these later catastrophes, had been the first cloud of any magnitude to overcast the sunshine which had been his share. He had never felt the sharp, searing pain that he experienced now. The sheer cruelty, the hideous savagery of it all, not only appalled him, but tore at the very heart-strings of his innate devotion to beauty. These flowers that he had plucked reverently, not so much because he wanted them for indoor decoration, but mainly because judicious picking benefited them and made them bloom more profusely, had been trampled underfoot wilfully, wantonly. Bewildered by the pain that the sight of their remnants, sticking out of the wheel-rutted mud, gave him, his mind could not entertain even the reasonable extenuations with which he had soothed himself the night before, when he had heard the horses and the men taking up their stations in the gardens. Then he had comforted himself with the thought that this was war, and that everyone must be prepared to make sacrifices; that men lying snugly ensconced behind hedges and tree trunks would not, could not, do much damage to their environment, and that they would spare his garden as much as possible under conditions which he admitted were irregular and unusual. A pathway broken up, a flower bed trodden down, the neat leading furrows interfered with so that the water would overflow, the fountain with its lazy gold fish and large blue nymphae lilies perhaps dented here and there, and dirty—that was about the extent of the damage which he had anticipated. He was quite unprepared for the scene of devastation he now saw before him. Where the orchard began, at the bottom of the well-kept stretch of black soil that was the result of the silting up of the river in flood time, bringing down the fertile mud from the clay shales many miles away, the men had dug trenches, and thrown up a rough embankment of sandbags. They had improvised these sandbags by filling empty sacks with garden soil, and they had dug this soil anywhere, paying no attention to the arrangement of his beds. It tortured the old man's soul to glance at every spot where a spade or shovel had been inserted into the soft ground to remove enough of that rich, fertile soil, so carefully tended year after year, and season after season, so judiciously blended with fertilisers to suit the peculiar conditions of the various plants destined to grow in it. Every gaping hole—and there were many of them, some isolated, as if the destroyer had made a chance dab at the ground, others aggregated together to form miniature craters, and others, again, in array, so close together that they collectively resembled a long, badly-constructed circumvallation trench—cried to him in derision, just as it seemed to him that every tormented blossom and stem, not yet dead enough to have lost all semblance of life, called out for pity.

In the garden the air was sweet with the freshness of the morning, washed by last night's rain, cleansed by the cold wind that blew gently across the river, bringing with it a tang of those faraway snows crowning the high mountain peaks. Its very devastation had added to the garden's varied and cumulatively attractive scents. When the morning wind gently stirred the fallen leaves of the Lombardy poplars, it flushed, as it were, from the mass of wreckage that encumbered the garden, the smell of verbena, rose, violet, early hirsute gladiolus, jasmine, and freesia. Their blossoms or opening buds lay trampled in the mud, but perfumed the air, as if they wished to render a last, despairing tribute of affection to the artist who had planned and perfected their colour harmonies to blend with the green and white and pink of the tall oleanders on the left.

Old Andrew stood speechless, almost breathless, before the first savage onslaught of the reality of all this wreck. As his eyes travelled from one ruin to the other, his feet made little forward movements of which he was quite unaware, as if they wanted to push him towards the things for which he had cared so much and that were now beyond care. Without being conscious of his wanderings, he shuffled down the length of the garden path, halting to sorrow over some particular plant that he had cultivated with tender attention and loving solicitude. Here was the feeble, anaemic little quinine tree, a lineal off-shoot of the plants that had been cultivated from Ledger's seeds in the garden at *Buitenzorg*. He remembered how many, many years ago he had, with the exuberance and impertinence of youth, written a letter in Dutch to Tyesman, the world-renowned *hortulanus* of that wonderful garden, and how delighted he had been when the first seed arrived. The quinine tree was four inches high then, and it had always been feeble, for it wanted moisture and warmth combined, such as the Village summers, which were fiercely hot but deliriously dry, could not give. Nevertheless he had cherished it; after the fine ginko, with its memories of temple courtyards and barren women praying to Buddha for sons. It was his most treasured horticultural possession, and now both it and the ginko tree were irretrievably ruined. The little quinine tree had its stem snapped off an inch above the ground; its anaemic leaves still clung to the prostrate stem as if protesting against this outrage; the ginko, like many other trees in the garden, had been ruthlessly chopped down. There was the beautiful melatti hedge, grown from slips sent from Sumatra by Mrs Uhlmann when she was a missionary's wife on the shores of the Toba lake. He remembered the day those slips had arrived along with a letter telling them all about the wonderful high priest, the Singha Mongha Radja, whom Mr Uhlmann had visited in a *lamaserai* on the shores of the sacred lake. There had been a footnote, 'We are sending you some slips of melatti, the fine jasmine which we use for funeral wreaths; don't, however, look upon it as a *memento mori*.' That had been Mrs Uhlmann's joke, and Joan and he had smiled at it. Now the melatti hedge might well be looked upon as a *memento mori*, for it represented, in its draggled, devastated beauty, the whole garden, and exemplified, in its forlorn, hopeless vestiges of former fineness and symmetry, the ruin of everything on which his horticultural soul had leaned for pleasure and solace in his old age.

He wandered into the orchard, through the broken and bent fences, into the neighbouring gardens. These had never been comparable to his own, although none of them had ever been so neglected as those of the rectory and the parsonage, but now they, too, were ruined, for everywhere there were abundant traces of the struggle that had gone on in them during the night. There were soldiers still posted behind the heaped sandbags, tired-looking men in khaki who regarded him with curiosity as they saw him stumbling along. If he had been conscious of what was going on around him, he might have heard their muttered, 'What's the old buffer a-searching for, Jock?' and been cheered by the coarse, yet kingly, sympathy of the low, 'Cawn't yer see, fat-'ead, 'e's lost sumting that ain't 'alf worth seekin' for.' But he neither saw nor heard them.

He had gone out with the fixed intention of visiting Vantloo to ask the attorney to take charge of young Martin's case. After that he would have sought the parson, and together they would have waited upon the commandant. He had merely intended to make a cursory inspection of the garden, noting what replacements and repairs would be required, for he had never dreamed that it would be a ruin. And now he no longer thought about Martin, the commandant, or the parson. Not even about his garden. There was a blank in his mind from which all thought, all desire, and all passion were deleted. He felt very tired and ill, and with no conscious effort of his will allowed the little forward movements of his feet to propel him where they pleased, maintaining his balance intuitively by shuffling forward when he threatened to fall. In a wide semi-circle he stumbled along, emerging between the leafless oak trees where their long avenue opened on to the front street, half a dozen houses higher up than his own.

Miss Marradee, on her way towards the hospital with a basket of comforts, met him there, and dropped her treasures on the wet street in her eagerness to help him.

'Whatever is the matter, Mr Quakerley?' she exclaimed, taking his arm. 'Whatever has happened? You look frightfully ill ...'

'It's ... it's nothing, my dear ...,' he said, indistinctly, his life-long, ingrained, old-world courtesy making him attempt, feebly, to lift his hat. The effort was too much for him, and he collapsed in her arms as she shrilled for help. A couple of khaki-clad figures ran up. 'We'll take him, Miss,' they volunteered. 'Where's he wounded?'

'I don't know ... I don't think he's wounded at all,' Miss Marradee squealed. 'It's old Mr Quakerley from the big house down there. Can you carry him there? Oh, be careful. I'll run along ...'

They carried old Andrew home. He made feeble protests on the way, declaring himself perfectly fit to walk, but as they paid no attention, his rambling protests became fainter, and when they reached the *stoep* steps he lay perfectly still, his cheeks puffing out slightly with every expiration, and one side of his face very placid. When Joan saw him, her lips tightened, and she silently motioned the men to carry him in.

'My brother has had a stroke, I think, Miss Marradee,' she said, calmly. Joan did not lose her head in emergencies. 'He has had far too much excitement lately. Could you get Dr Buren for me?'

Miss Marradee fled down the front street towards the doctor's house, stopping on the way to inform Mrs Mance-Bisley. 'Mr Quakerley has had a stroke,' she panted. 'I believe he's dying, Mrs Mance-Bisley, and it might be a good thing if the rector went at once. Oh, no, thank you, I can't possibly stay. I must find Dr Buren, and then there's my basket, too. I left it lying in the mud when I saw Mr Quakerley. You've no idea how queer he looked.'

'They usually do,' commented the rector's wife. 'At his age I don't wonder at it. He must be well over eighty.'

'Eighty-five, I think, Mrs Bisley. But do tell the rector, please. And now I must really fly.'

When the rector, a few minutes later, called at the big house, he found that the news had already spread. Notwithstanding the regulations that prohibited a crowd from gathering in the street, a number of men and women clustered on the *stoep*, whispering sympathetically. Their eagerness to be helpful to one so universally respected as old Andrew had overcome their habitual caution, and when the military police came along and disturbed them, they broke up into little groups, obeying the letter of the regulations but still infringing the spirit. But the police were complacent. They, too, had learned to respect the old man, whom they looked upon as the squire of the Village, and they too knew that he was lying ill in the big house where Colonel Cautley was temporarily lodged.

'Certainly, Rector, you may see him,' said Joan, shaking hands with Mr Mance-Bisley. 'He is quite conscious, I believe, although rambling, and I hope it is nothing very serious, although the one side of his face looks queer to me.'

'Have you any idea what caused it?' questioned the rector. 'I know Mr Quakerley took things very much to heart, and at his age ...'

'I can guess what it was, Rector,' she answered. 'If you look over there,' she swept her hand towards the garden, 'he went to see it this morning. I would have kept him away had I known ...'

'Dear me, dear me,' exclaimed the rector, vaguely conscious that his exclamation was utterly inadequate to express his sympathy and commiseration. 'What an awful place ... Of course, it is like that all the way down, right down to the plantations, Miss Quakerley. And behind, it is not much better. The court house burned—the roof quite ruined, Miss Quakerley, and the library, I am afraid, utterly destroyed.'

'So I heard, Rector. Andrew takes these things to heart, as you say. But come in, Rector.'

Chapter 41

The parson and the magistrate sat in the commandant's office, waiting for Major Mallom.

'You know, Mr Uhlmann,' said Storam, beating out his pipe against the commandant's desk, and refilling it slowly from his woollen pouch. 'Cautley's being wounded makes the matter just a trifle better. Mallom's in command now.'

'Have you heard how things are going, Mr Storam?' asked the pastor, anxiously.

'Badly,' answered the magistrate, shortly, lighting his pipe, 'badly, in some respects, that is. We drove them off last night, and the column has gone in pursuit, though I daresay they'll find that their birds are flown. The worst point, Mr Uhlmann, is that our men have captured quite a few rebels—ten all told, I believe. And most of them men who attended here on the square when the sentences were promulgated. That's bad, very bad.'

'I am afraid that is not all,' said the pastor, sadly. 'There are others who rode away after the execution. Two of them let me know that they intended to go ... I could not stop them, Mr Storam, could I?'

'If you mean that you had no moral right to stop them,' said the magistrate, 'I do not agree with you ...'

'Oh no, Mr Storam; had I been able to communicate with them I should have remonstrated with them. I should have told them plainly that it was their duty to remain quiet, true to the faith they had sworn. But I had no chance to do that. They sent me a note by a Native. I have it. Would you care to see it?'

'Good heavens, no, man! Destroy it! Burn it! Forget it!' cried the magistrate, angrily. 'I wish you hadn't told me ...'

'It can make no difference ... now,' said the pastor, quietly. 'They will glory in what they have done, Mr Storam. They have a grievance now, and will listen all too readily to what the commando men say. I should not be surprised if others followed their example.'

'Nor I,' admitted the magistrate, grudgingly. 'Mr Uhlmann, it's the very devil of a mess, and I am not sure if we're not to blame for it. If Mallom had had his way, we wouldn't have been in it. Very few would have joined, I'm sure.'

'Now there are others. There's ...'

'Don't tell me, don't tell me! For heaven's sake, Mr Uhlmann, don't tell me their names. I'll know soon enough. The main issue now is to try and save young Rekker, and God knows how we're to do that, I don't.'

'But, Mr Storam, won't the fact that he gave himself up ...?'

'He didn't. He was captured here. That's a fact. Of course, there is another way of looking at the matter ...'

'That's what I mean. He came in to give warning ...'

'Quite so. But how can that be proved? And it may be argued that he did so to save his skin ...'

'Martin is brave, Mr Storam. He would not surrender just to save himself. He came to save others ...'

'That's what you and I believe, Mr Uhlmann. We know the Rekkers. But to the authorities, the Rekkers are suspect, like all the rest who are supposed to be sympathetic to the Boers, who are Boers themselves.'

'That is hard and unjust, Mr Storam.'

'Quite so. Much that is hard and unjust is taking place right now. But it is reasonable, especially after so many others have gone into rebellion.'

'They might say they were driven into it, Mr Storam.'

'They will say that, Mr Uhlmann. It will always be said. But would you accept such a plea?'

'In extenuation, yes.'

'Very well. But that does not apply to Martin.'

'He was forced, Mr Storam.'

'Can he prove that?'

'I don't know. But Martin would not tell a lie, Mr Storam. If he says he was forced, I believe him.'

'So do I. But bear in mind that belief is of no value as evidence. I believe myself that Martin was forced, but if I were a member of the court martial that had to try him, my duty would be to find the boy guilty, unless he can prove that he acted in fear of his life when he guided them.'

'And would his warning count for nothing, Mr Storam?'

'Ah, that I can't tell you. It all depends on what its value is from a military point of view. Off-hand, I should say that the CC would take it into consideration and commute his punishment if he is found guilty. Do you think Martin would like that? And have you considered the other aspect of the matter?'

'What other aspect, Mr Storam?'

'If Martin gets free on the plea that he gave the military authorities warning of the attack on *Kromdraai*, don't you see what our people will say? They will call him a traitor. Now it does not matter much. But afterwards ...'

'He must bear that, Mr Storam. One must sometimes bear burdens that seem insufferably hard.'

'Yes, I suppose so. And I rather think that when this rumpus is over we are all going to be burdened with loads that will tax our patience heavily enough. The real struggle will come when peace has been declared. But here's the Major, if I'm not mistaken.'

The commandant strode in, and the two visitors rose at his entrance. Major Mallom, who had been for many hours in the saddle, and had just come from a hot engagement, greeted his visitors curtly, turned to give a rapid order to someone outside, closed the door behind him, and sat down in his swivel chair, which he wheeled round so as to face them.

'Well, gentlemen,' he said, briskly. 'We've beaten them this time at their own game.'

'I am very glad indeed,' said the magistrate, sitting down and motioning the pastor to do the same. 'We've heard something about it, but I daresay the report has been exaggerated.'

'No, not if you mean our casualties,' rejoined the Major, affably, lighting a cigarette. 'Poor Overbury stopped one in the chest. Thomasson and Dalton are killed. But we managed to clear them out, and I have hopes that by tonight that part of the District will be free of them. Now, gentlemen, I take it that you are not here to enquire about what took place at *Kromdraai*?'

'No, Commandant,' said the pastor. 'We took the liberty of coming to see you about the young man Rekker, who as you know ...'

'Mr Uhlmann,' said the Major, tersely, 'I am fully aware of everything that you can say about the young man Rekker. By the way, I heard that Mr Quakerley is dying? I hope that is not true, Storam?'

'The old man has had a stroke, Major,' replied the magistrate. 'I went to enquire just before coming here, and was told that he was doing as well as can be expected.'

'That's good. I am sincerely sorry that this affair has had this unfortunate result ...'

'You need not worry on that account, Major. Mr Quakerley's illness has nothing to do with Rekker's case, I believe. It was the shock of finding his garden destroyed that proved too much for him. His garden was practically the only thing he valued, and after last night's fighting you can imagine what it looks like this morning.'

The commandant shrugged his shoulders. 'What can he expect?' he asked. 'All the gardens are pretty much in the same condition. He must thank our friends the enemy for it. But now about Rekker. The man must stand his trial.'

'We see that, Major. But I hope that time will be granted him to get his witnesses ...'

'The court martial will be convened for tomorrow afternoon,' said the Major. 'His is not the only case. There are five others who will have to be tried.'

'May I point out, Commandant,' said the magistrate, quickly, 'that in that case Rekker has no hope of an acquittal. Obviously, he would require witnesses to prove that he was forced. I had hopes, Major, that his action in warning us of the attack on *Kromdraai* might be taken into consideration ...'

'I can give you the assurance that it will,' interrupted the Major, extinguishing the stub of his cigarette against the ink-stand, 'and I may add, for your information alone, please, that we have captured several of the members of the commando. I took the precaution of questioning them about Rekker, and from their remarks, which I fear the interpreter toned down for my benefit as he did not understand what I was driving at, you need have no fear that they look upon him as one of their friends. Believe me,' he bent over towards them and spoke earnestly, 'the best thing for Rekker is to stand his trial immediately. It is a pity Mr Quakerley cannot testify, but my own evidence on that point ...'

'You are prepared to appear as a witness on his behalf?' asked the magistrate in surprise.

'If necessary, yes. But I don't suppose it will be necessary, Storam. I may use my discretion as it is and liberate Rekker, but in his own interests it is better that he should stand his trial. I have no doubt—no doubt whatever—that his statements are true, and that they can be substantially corroborated. If that is the case, the verdict must be one of acquittal, and the other matter to which we have just now referred need not be brought up at all in court. If there is the least likelihood that his statements cannot be substantiated—a great deal will depend on the witnesses, as you know, Storam—credibility, and so on—then you can always raise that point, though I feel sure that it is unnecessary.'

'I am much relieved, Major,' said the magistrate, rising. 'May I give the gist of what you have just told us to Rekker?'

'Leave that to me,' said the Major. 'I intend to see him, to thank him for informing us about *Kromdraai*. That I can do semi-officially. Does he talk English, or shall I have to take an interpreter with me?'

'Martin is a matriculated student,' said the magistrate, smiling, 'and talks English quite well. You'll find him a highly intelligent man, Major, a chip of the old block.'

'Will you allow me to ask, Commandant,' said the pastor, diffidently, 'if nothing can be done for those others? Is there no way of saving them from the consequences of their rashness?'

The commandant shrugged his shoulders. 'They were taken with arms in their hands,' he said shortly. 'I scarcely see what defence they have. I am sorry, gentlemen, but I am afraid I cannot hold out any hopes in that quarter.'

'Would it be possible,' hazarded the pastor, 'would it be possible, Commandant, to remove them after the trial ...'

'I see what you mean,' interrupted the Major, shaking his head. 'It would be quite possible, of course. Whether it would be advisable is another matter. In the circumstances, it is likely that the commander-in-chief will order the sentence to be carried out here. It is an unpleasant position, gentlemen, but ...' he shrugged his shoulders to disclaim all responsibility for the unpleasant position, and turned from them with a nod of dismissal.

'That will only make matters worse,' sighed Mr Uhlmann, as he walked down the *stoep* steps of the commandant's office. 'Mr Storam, cannot you use your influence ...?'

'My influence?' The magistrate barked out the words with passionate contemptuousness. 'My dear man, I have no influence left. And if I had, I doubt if I could use it in the way you suggest. The military authorities are perfectly justified in shooting these men out of hand when they catch them ...'

'That would be better,' interrupted the pastor, quickly. 'Far better than to make a public show of their execution.'

'Perhaps. But from their point of view it would lack just what they want it to possess. These punishments are meant to be a deterrent.'

'You cannot deter men who are blinded by passion,' said the pastor. 'You only create martyrs, and these are the seed of the faith ...'

'I know, I know! And it doesn't matter if the faith be true or wrong, more's the pity. However, neither you nor I, Mr Uhlmann, have any say in the matter. We must be thankful that Mallom takes such a reasonable view of Rekker's case. I confess I was much perturbed when I went, for I saw no possible way out of it. It is something to be devoutly thankful for that we've captured these Boers, who will be able to testify on his behalf.'

'Do you think they will do so?' asked the pastor, anxiously. 'If they hear that he gave information, they may get vindictive ...'

'Quite likely. We'll have to go warily. Between you and me, Mr Uhlmann, I don't think it is a wise move to ask Vantloo to undertake the defence. A better plan would be for him to have no counsel, but to conduct his defence himself. I can assist him, and probably there would be no objection to the court appointing me as his defender in case he is not represented by counsel.'

'If you think that best ...'

'I do indeed. Vantloo is currying favour with both sides, and he is not the man I would choose for this case. A slip might do much harm, and while I do not say that he would make a mistake intentionally—he wouldn't dare to do that, but he's clever enough to mask it—I prefer not to take the risk. You know that there has been no love lost between Martin and Elias ...'

'I regret it, Mr Storam, but I know that there has been bad blood between the two. The fault is entirely on Vantloo's part ...'

'Quite so. We need not go into that. I just don't quite trust Vantloo, and I think Martin will manage his case better himself. It will give the court a better impression, too. These military officials are always rather prejudiced against civilian counsel. Now, one more thing, Mr Uhlmann. When you get home, burn those letters. Don't keep them a moment longer than necessary. And forget who wrote them.'

Mr Uhlmann walked slowly home, drawing his coat tightly round his body, for the wind had risen, and although the sun shone brightly the cold breeze from the mountains chilled him. He passed the ruined court house, whose blackened roof-rafters stood out over the dirtied walls, a blot of ugliness in the neat orderliness of the Village. The road that here became the main street was no longer deserted. It was full of soldiers, vehicles coming and going, ammunition and store wagons, water carts, troops of horses and mules. Everywhere around him was bustle and activity, far exceeding what he had seen before. Evidently large numbers of reinforcements were arriving. He met Sam Chumley, the chief constable, hurrying with a despatch from the commandant, and stopped him to ask what was going on.

'There's a big drive on,' the chief constable replied. 'We've located them at two spots, Sir, and with a little luck we ought to get most of them before the week's over. Not that I'm particularly anxious to collar them, Sir. That'll only mean more unpleasantness for us all. But we'll drive them out of this District, anyway.'

'Don't you think, Mr Chumley,' asked Uhlmann, hesitatingly, 'that if I were to go out to them—on my own, you understand—and talk to them ...'

'Don't you believe it, Sir,' said the chief constable, decisively, 'they won't pay the slightest attention to you, Sir. You'd only get kicks for your pains, Sir. Them that's gone out, Sir, won't listen to what you or I can say. They're just fanatics, Sir, a-thinking they can help to make this Colony a Republic same as the Transvaal used to be. And anyone who thinks that, Sir, is balmy, and it's no use whatever trying to convince him that he is.'

In the middle of the street the pastor turned and retraced his steps towards the big house. There were still a few people lingering on the *stoep*, and as he came up they greeted him respectfully, and asked how Mr Quakerley was getting on. He spoke a few words with them, urging them to go home quietly, and went into the old man's study, where he found the magistrate seated in the big arm-chair, toying with Andrew's copy of *Henley*.

'Look here, Mr Uhlmann,' said Storam, holding out the book, 'he was reading this all last night and the better part of the morning. And from it he went out and found his garden ...'

'I know how fond he was of it,' said the pastor, placing the book on the table. 'One can understand it, Mr Storam. Mr Quakerley had a great deal of sentiment in him, much more, I should say, than in the average Englishman.'

'Yes, you're right. Got it from his Dutch mother, I suppose. I must say I never put him down as a sentimental man. He was always so calm and assured. Just like his sister.'

'That was merely his upbringing, Magistrate. Old Mister Quakerley—I allude to Mr Quakerley's father, who used to live at *Quakerskloof* when I was a boy, taught him never to show his feelings. It is in some ways a good thing, but it tends to repression, and there comes a time, Magistrate, when it is very difficult to repress one's feelings utterly. My own opinion has always been that the best plan is to switch one's emotion off to something different ... to change it, as it were, if you know what I mean.'

'I think I follow you. Perhaps that was what he was trying to do with *Henley*. There's a robust faith in *Henley* that survives most shocks. I expect he found it stimulating.'

'Yes, Mr Storam. But our people do not know *Henley*. Nor do they know the trust and confidence that Mr Quakerley felt in his traditions. That is our tragedy, Magistrate. We are slowly gathering tradition, and we have nothing to fall back upon ...'

'Don't say that! ... Don't say that! I should hate to think that I have no tradition, nor you, Mr Uhlmann. Our families have been here for generations, and we've behind us not only the massed tradition of the old country, but all the Colonial tradition as well ... pioneers and all that.'

'That is true. But that is not exactly what I mean, Mr Storam. We have had no great testing shocks from which a nation forges its credentials by hammering out principles that are vital to its existence. It's these principles that create tradition, Mr Storam. Mr Quakerley's ancestors made them for themselves. We must make them for ourselves. Perhaps this war ...'

'If there's any tradition growing out of this war,' said the magistrate, interrupting, 'you may be sure it won't be a tradition that is worth treasuring.'

'You can't say that, Magistrate. It was civil war in America in the sixties, and the German-Austrian war was almost civil war. Yet out of both grew something of which later generations can be proud. Perhaps out of this, our civil war, too, may grow something of which our children can be proud. Today there is nothing to link our two sections. But this war may give us the germ of a common tradition—of suffering and endurance if you like—which may really weld us into a nation in time to come.'

'It certainly is a satisfying faith, Mr Uhlmann. But isn't there another side? The side of hate and resentment, such as must be inevitable here.'

'Of course. But, Magistrate, that side need not be taken into account as a permanency. Hate is not constructive. It can never build up tradition that lasts. It must be kept alive by artificial means, by propaganda, as is being done in France today. Here our interests are one, not separate, and hate cannot keep us always apart. My father used to tell me, Mr Storam, how bitter was the hatred here between Orange and Republicans in the old days, but that didn't last. It couldn't, for the associations that kept it alive faded, just as I hope and believe the associations that make for hatred after this war will fade away.'

'I can hardly imagine Rekker having any great love for the English after this, Mr Uhlmann. Or the families of those who are to be tried by court martial the day after tomorrow.'

'When one individualises, Mr Storam, it is very difficult to be logical. Individual sentiment and feeling—Mr Quakerley's sorrow at the ruin of his garden, for example—are small factors compared with those larger ones that count in the destinies of nations. But here we are talking ...' he hesitated for a word, and the magistrate broke in.

'Political philosophy, I should say, Mr Uhlmann. And we ought to be seeing our poor old friend.'

'Yes. But don't call him poor, Mr Storam. I cannot grieve for the man who goes out now, while we are still in the pangs of labour. And Mr Quakerley will be spared the regrets and the disillusionment which so many of us must be prepared to meet. Can we see him, do you think?'

'Miss Quakerley said she would let me know as soon as he was fit to be seen. She tells me that he is quite conscious, and no longer rambles. He just lies quiet, and there is no sign that he is really paralysed.'

'That means that there has not been a bleeding,' said the pastor. 'But at his age the question is if he has strength enough to overcome the shock. But here comes Miss Joan ...'

He went forward to meet the old lady, and expressed his sympathy.

'You are all very good,' she said, gratefully. 'Mr Storam has been a real help. Especially in getting the news through to Alice. We telegraphed for her and Anne and the children. They should be here in a few days' time. And Dr Buren does not think there is any immediate danger. But you can't see him, so you must just give me your messages for him, and I'll take care that he gets them.'

'We really came to tell him about young Martin Rekker,' said the magistrate. 'You know about him? He came last night ...'

'Oh yes. As a matter of fact, I heard my brother speaking to him, and later on my brother told me all about it. I would have done the same, Mr Storam, and I am sure you, too, Mr Uhlmann.'

'I doubt if I should have had the courage to do it,' said the pastor, frankly. 'But Mr Quakerley was always brave.'

'Oh no,' said Joan, with a faint smile lighting up her severely calm face. 'Andrew was never very courageous. He hated fuss, and always took the easiest way out. In this case I think he acted on the impulse of the moment, and he afterwards regretted what he had done. I'm sure he does now. So your message about Mr Rekker had better not be delivered, Mr Storam, if it is going to upset him.'

'But it isn't going to upset him, Miss Quakerley. At least, I hope not, for it is good news.'

'What do you mean? Has young Rekker escaped? But, Mr Storam, they will get him in the end, unless he leaves the country ...'

'No, no! I mean his innocence is proved—will be proved. There are witnesses, and the commandant has practically assured us that he will be acquitted. Mr Quakerley will be glad to hear that.'

'Yes. My brother will be delighted, Mr Storam. But is it reliable? It would be too awful if the worst happens.'

'I think you may take it that this is reliable. It is confidential, of course, but Major Mallom has no objection to your knowing about it. He said as much, for he seems to think that something is due to Mr Quakerley for preventing the attack on *Kromdraai* ...'

'Yes. My brother is young Mr Rekker's godfather, Mr Storam. Didn't you know that? That's what made the position so hard for my brother. You see, it was practically sending the lad to gaol when he urged him to remain here, when he might so easily have escaped. And Martin would scarcely have come to anybody else but Andrew. He trusted Andrew.'

'We all do, Miss Quakerley. I am sure if Mr Quakerley could go out—he volunteered to go, as you may remember—and talk to the men who have joined, he would induce them to return. But it is too late to think of that now. Will you tell him about Martin? At your convenience, and when you think fit. And don't worry about anything else but about him, Miss Quakerley. I'll see to everything else. You must just tell me what you want, and if it is possible I'll see that it is done.'

'There is one thing you might do for me, Mr Storam,' said the old lady. 'He is constantly asking about the garden—whether the beds have been watered, and if the dahlias have been taken up. All little things, such as he would have attended to himself if ... if things had been just normal, you know. And as soon as he is able to move, he'll want to see his garden, if only from the *stoep*. But you know what a state it is in ... I can hardly bear to look at it myself, and I've not had the courage to walk down and see what damage has been done ...'

'I'll see about it at once,' promised the magistrate. 'I'll get a gang of convicts and clear up the litter, and improve matters a bit in the front. I'll see about it at once.'

Chapter 42

The court martial assembled in the school room, for the court room was now roofless and likely to remain so for some time to come. The proceedings were short, and the audience listened in strained tenseness to the curt interrogatories, and the equally terse answers. Martin Rekker, whose case was taken first, pleaded not guilty. The only evidence led against him was to the effect that he had been seen riding with the commando on the night when his father's farm was attacked. There was no cross-examination of the military witnesses, who, in answer to the court, declared that he had never been seen armed, and that when he was riding away they had an impression that he was guarded and tied on the horse. Formal evidence of his arrest was given.

For the defence, the prisoner's own statement was put in. He declared that he had been asked by the leader of the commando to join them, and that he had categorically refused; his father, wife, and two children had been present on the occasion, and of course the various members of the commando, who, with two exceptions, were personally unknown to him at the time, but whose names he had since learned. Two of them, he now understood, were prisoners of war, and could be called to substantiate his statement. He had been abused for his lack of patriotism, and been asked, further, to guide the commando up the mountain bridle path to the place where there was a fresh water spring, and ample grazing ground; on his repeated refusal, he had been seized, placed on a horse, his legs tied together so that he could not get off the saddle, and two men had been told off to ride at his side, and threaten him with their rifles. In this manner he had been carried off, and been kept with the commando, until he had a chance of escaping. He had seen no opportunity to do so until the night of the attack on the Village, when he had been left unguarded, and had slipped away in the darkness and walked several miles to Mr Quakerley's house to give himself up. In his statement he said nothing about what had induced him to go to Mr Quakerley's house, and the court asked no questions on that point. Cross-examination was directed to shaking his evidence on the amount of pressure that had been used to induce him to stay with the commandos, and here the prisoner's answers were perfectly clear. He had never, he asserted, been left alone and unguarded until the night of the attack on the Village, when there was considerable confusion, which had given him the opportunity to escape. Questioned about his actions when the commandos were raiding the farms, he declared that he had never given them the slightest information, and had never had a weapon in his hand, or taken any part in the fighting. The two prisoners of war, when called upon, corroborated his statements with, what seemed to the court, contemptuous indifference, which the official interpreter softened for the benefit of the court. Rekker had been of no value whatever to them; they had taken him with them merely as a warning to others, and would have sent him about his business were it not for the fact that it was in their interests to keep him with them, so long as they were operating in the District. The court forbore to question them in detail.

Considerable astonishment was caused when Major Mallom, the commandant, gave evidence in favour of the prisoner. The Major related, briefly, that he had been communicated with by Mr Quakerley, who had told him that the prisoner, who he understood was Mr Quakerley's godson, wished to surrender himself. A guard had been sent down, and the prisoner taken in charge. Through Mr Quakerley the prisoner had been of assistance to the military authorities, but the witness was not prepared to disclose in what way, as that point had no bearing on the question of his guilt or innocence. The witness had personally known the prisoner as a man of substance, and one whose loyalty, he was glad to say, he had never called into question. The witness had no personal knowledge of what had taken place on the Rekker's farm on the evening when the prisoner had been carried off by the commando, but the official reports he had received tallied with the prisoner's statement that he was under armed guard when he left the farm. Dr Buren testified that Mr Andrew Quakerley was too ill to attend on behalf of the prisoner, who was not represented by counsel.

After a whispered consultation, the court directed that the prisoner should be removed, and proceeded with the cases of the five rebels who had been captured during the *Kromdraai* fight. When the evidence had been heard, the court was cleared, and it was announced that its decision would be given later on.

Walking up and down under the leafless oak trees in the front street, Mr Uhlmann and the rector, who had both attended, and had only refrained from testifying on Martin's behalf because they knew that nothing they could say would have the slightest effect on the point at issue, passed the time of anxious waiting in moodily discussing probabilities. Mr Mance-Bisley, not impressed by the absence of ritual, to which he attached importance in a court of law, nor by the curtness of the questions that had been asked, was highly pessimistic.

'I fail to see how they can acquit him, Mr Uhlmann,' he said, lugubriously. 'We ought to have got Mr Vantloo to defend him. A lawyer would have shown how weak the case for the prosecution is, and would have got much more out of Major Mallom. Why, the fact that Rekker gave us valuable information was not even properly presented to the court. It was slurred over, and it is just that point that should have been emphasised.'

'I think that was done with an object, Mr Mance-Bisley,' said the pastor, who, unlike his companion, had been much impressed by the way in which the Provost Marshal had refrained from pressing points that told against the prisoner, and the curtness of the questions that the court itself had asked Martin. 'I fancy it would have done more harm than good to have laid stress on the fact that Martin gave that information. It can have no bearing on the point whether he joined or not. The court has to decide if he committed treason, and not if, after committing it, he did something to extenuate his treason.'

'That is all very well,' declared the rector, 'but wouldn't it have been better to bring out these extenuating circumstances? That is, I believe, always done in criminal trials. I have not had any experience, Mr Uhlmann. As a matter of fact, I have never been present at a criminal trial, but I understand that is always done.'

'I don't think that was necessary,' said the pastor. 'Nor would the court have been impressed, Mr Mance-Bisley. But see, they are walking in again. It must be about time now. Shall we go in?'

'I suppose we must,' grumbled the rector, polishing his glasses with his habitual nervousness. 'But really, Mr Uhlmann, I do not think I am equal to it. If you don't mind, I should prefer to wait outside. It would be altogether too painful ...'

'Very well. Let us walk down the street, Mr Mance-Bisley. They will tell us the verdict soon enough.'

They watched the audience struggling to gain admission to the little school room, which was far too small to hold the crowd. The other entrance to it was at the back, and there a guard of armed soldiers shepherded the prisoners waiting to be called upon to hear the court's decision. There was a stir in the crowd. Mr Storam shouldered his way through it, and came down the *stoep* steps towards them. His face was grave, but as he came near he smiled, and Mr Uhlmann heaved a sigh of relief.

'Acquitted on all charges,' said the magistrate. 'He has gone back to gaol to see his father. I'm going to tell Quakerley. He'll be glad to know ...'

'And the others?' asked Mr Uhlmann, quickly.

'What could you expect,' answered Storam, 'with not an atom of defence? Guilty, of course. I'm afraid there was no other verdict possible.'

The rector polished his glasses uneasily.

'What is their sentence?' he asked.

'That will be announced when it is confirmed,' said the magistrate. 'But I fear there can be only one sentence, although it is quite possible that the commander-in-chief will modify it. I'm not quite sure, but I believe in such cases the court can only inflict the death penalty, leaving it to the commander-in-chief to modify the sentence, as his legal advisers suggest. But don't build any hopes on that.'

'Alas, no,' said Mr Uhlmann. 'But one might make an attempt to induce the authorities to be lenient. It can do no harm. You yourself, Mr Storam, could write to the commander-in-chief ...'

'That would almost certainly defeat our object,' retorted the magistrate with finality. 'Lord Kitchener would not decide such matters on outside considerations. He would go entirely by what his legal adviser suggests, and that gentleman—I've no notion who he is—will take everything into consideration.'

Mr Storam's anticipations were realised. In due course the sentences were promulgated on the square in front of the gaol. This time the notice, signed by the commandant, merely intimated that the promulgation would take place on such and such a day, and ordered that the various shops should be closed; there was no formal command for all loyal subjects to attend, an omission received with a sigh of relief by the Village, the main part of which, nevertheless, attended to hear the sentences read out.

These, to everyone's satisfaction, were much less severe than had been expected. Two of the rebels, against whom charges of murder had been made, and who had been found guilty of actively participating, not only in the commando fights, but in the killing of Natives who had been sent out to report the presence of the invaders on various farms, received the death sentence. Their execution, by shooting, would take place outside the Village on the day after the promulgation of the sentence. The remaining three were sentenced to penal servitude for ten years.

The Village heard much, but saw nothing, of the execution of the two rebels. It was carried out at dawn, somewhere on the banks of the river, a few miles above the plantation, and with the exception of Pastor Uhlmann, who rode in the ambulance cart with the condemned men, no Village resident took part in it, and to this day the Village does not know where are the graves of those who were shot. This secrecy, so totally unlike the blatant publicity with which the half-witted Org Bons had been hanged, impressed the District. Org Bons had been buried in the gaol yard, and in due course his coffin could be removed to the local cemetery, but these men had been carted into the veld, shot in the grey dawn of a winter's morning, and buried where they fell. Mr Uhlmann probably knew the place, but he refused to disclose it, contenting himself, when people questioned him on the subject of his last ride with those two unfortunate members of his congregation, by declaring that both had died like men, facing death bravely. To Mr Storam and Mr Mance-Bisley, who had volunteered to accompany him when he had received from the commandant the intimation that the prisoners had expressed a wish that he should attend them on their last journey, he was less reticent.

'I am glad,' he said, 'that I have had the courage to go. It was much less painful than I imagined it would be—nothing like the hanging, Magistrate. And it was over in less time, or so it seemed to me. They took me back to the ambulance wagon, and I did not see where they buried the bodies. It does not matter. There will be many who will feel scandalised that there was no burial service, but that was said before they were shot. I do not think they minded that. And I am glad, too, that it was done in this way. If it had to be done ...'

'There can be no question about that,' said the magistrate.

'Very well. Then it was better done in that way. I understand that the chairs—did I tell you that they sat on chairs?—were broken up and buried with them.'

'That is the usual custom,' explained the magistrate. 'Such things are handed over as morbid relics. That's the reason.'

'Aye, I know. And it is perhaps better so. Now there only remains the memory of what was done. And that will remain for long, Magistrate.'

'We'll turn this country into a second Ireland,' said the rector, morosely.

'We can do nothing, Mr Mance-Bisley,' answered the pastor, wearily. 'In war these things happen, and I am grateful to Major Mallom—for I am sure we have to thank him for his intercession on behalf of those others—for what he has done. If Colonel Cautley ... but we must not talk of it, Mr Storam. It is better for us to be silent and bear our trial. One of your poets, Rector, has an appropriate maxim for us, where he bids us be silent when we feel crushed by what seems to us needless sorrow. It has always struck me as one of the most beautiful verses ... you know it, perhaps?'

'You have repeated it so often, Mr Uhlmann,' replied the rector, with a smile, 'that I know it by heart.'

'Hushed be every thought that springs
From out the bitterness of things'

he quoted. 'And you have always added a rider to it, you know!'

'How? A rider?' asked the pastor, puzzled. 'What is that?'

'I should say a reservation, my dear friend. One always falls back upon something of that sort even when one fancies oneself strong enough to bear things without complaint. Mr Quakerley goes to *Henley*; you to Schiller. Don't you remember, *"Denn alle Schuld recht sich auf Erden"*?'

'I try to remember it, Mr Bisley,' said the pastor. 'Though perhaps I do not apply it in quite that sense—as a sort of reservation when I think of the things that are now so bitter.'

'I am afraid our people won't be so philosophical,' said the magistrate, with a shrug of his shoulders. 'I fear they will even see in the commutation of the sentences of the other three something to complain about, some derogatory differentiation that will only increase their bitterness. That is the pity of it all. I said to Mallom at the time when that foolish notice, asking us all to attend, was issued, that the worst thing about it was that it would create just this feeling of resentment which you inspire when you try to impress your superiority upon others. If you ask me, the worst thing we shall have to face when all this is over is our own people—we Colonials, I mean—our own people's feeling of inferiority. It will make them jealous of all criticism, impulsive like children who wish to show off, and as an excuse they will always be able to plead that it's England's fault. And that's what makes me so mad, Rector, it isn't England's fault at all. It's the fault of these beastly commandos, running about where they have no business to be.'

'But that may seem to them good military tactics, or strategy, or whatever you call it,' said the rector. 'Anything to harass the enemy. Don't you agree, Mr Uhlmann?'

'With his German mind,' said the magistrate, hotly, 'he probably would.'

'No,' said the pastor, reflectively. 'Somehow even my German mind, as you call it, thinks it wrong. Just as wrong as it would have been had our Government called upon us all to take up arms against the Transvaal, which it never did. But that is not what most people would say ...'

'I know that,' interrupted the magistrate, vehemently. 'When all this is over, who do you think are going to be the popular heroes? Not men like Martin and Swart, and that old nincompoop who sells quack medicines but is man enough to tell the commandos to go to the devil when they ask him to join them to free South Africa from the hated English. Oh no! The fellows who came in here and started all this trouble, and turned this District into a little hell for us! They'll be the national heroes, and they'll look down in infinite scorn on the Dutchman who remained loyal to his oath, and refused to imagine grievances that did not exist.'

'Do you realise,' he went on, turning to the rector, 'do you realise what a man like old Quakerley must feel just now? Here he's been all these year nourishing his conception of a mother country with high liberal traditions, always leaning towards the right, championing small nations, and so on—you know what I mean. And then comes this war, which seems to upset that conception because the diplomatists handled the thing so infernally stupidly. Only that absurd ultimatum could put that right. It twisted his conception back into alignment, as you might say, although that stupid diplomacy still left a bitter taste in his mouth. And then he finds that his loyalty is suspected, that he has to make sacrifices such as he never dreamed of, and put up with things that leave a further bitter taste behind. With, mark you, the probability that when the mess has been cleared up to the satisfaction of the diplomatists, he is left with a situation that bristles with unpleasantness. You know we have never had any racial feeling here—though why people should call it racial when we are all of the same race, I have never been able to see. But there has always been good feeling and co-operation between those who, like you and me, Rector, are English-speaking, and those like yourself, Mr Uhlmann, who are Dutch-speaking. We respected each other's tradition and point of view and, although we differed here and there, as happened during the last election, we did so in a nice, gentlemanly, dignified sort of way. Now all that is changed ...'

'I sincerely hope not,' exclaimed the rector. 'I see no reason why the old feeling should not continue. Why, you and I, Mr Storam, we deprecate and regret these bitter things as much as Mr Uhlmann does ...'

'You won't be given the credit for that, Rector. You'll be lumped into one class— the English, who shot men in this District for rebellion—which will of course be patriotism, though no one will be able to define quite what made it patriotism—and buried them in unknown graves without Christian rites, and hanged half-witted *bywoners*, and forced decent men to come and look on at the hanging. Mr Quakerley, who is as much English as your wife, Rector, is French, and who is as good a South African as Rekker, or any of us, and I warrant ten times as good a South African as any man in the commandos—else they would not have come here, and tried to force men into rebellion—Mr Quakerley, I say, will be included among the English. They'll forget what he has done—what he has been. They'll tell their children how his son-in-law fought against them—for they'll identify themselves with the commandos, never fear—and transfer a little of the hate they feel against the English to him. Oh, I know what is going to happen, Rector. You don't. You're a newcomer, and you probably have much the same conception of England as that which Quakerley held up to a few months ago. But I can tell you what's going to happen. When this war is won—as it will be, of course; I have no doubt whatever on that point—England will say, "Now settle down and be good boys, and don't let's have any more trouble with you." And I daresay there won't be any trouble in the Transvaal and the Free State. There never is when you've thoroughly drubbed your opponent, and made it impossible for him to attack you again, and I don't think even our stupid diplomatists will be stupid enough to leave the Republics with a vestige of power for mischief. But here in our Colony there will be the deuce of a mess. Look at the political aspect. Look at the disfranchised voters in the eastern districts. Of course, they've been let off lightly. Mr Uhlmann's German mind will agree that they could all have been shot. But they weren't. They've been disfranchised, and that, to our Dutch-speaking friends, means social death—political death ...'

'Surely you exaggerate, Mr Storam,' ventured the rector, mildly. 'Personally, I should much prefer to lose my vote to being shot ...'

'You would! Only the Native and the Dutchman in this country have a real political sense, Rector. Just bear that in mind. Remember how the last election was fought. Think of what the vote means to a man in this Colony. If we had manhood suffrage, as some people want us to have, it wouldn't matter so much, but our qualification is a high one, and to be deprived of it means a lot. I rather think they will resent deprivation of the vote more than they would have resented some of them being shot. There's the personal factor, Rector. One doesn't much mind what happens to others, even if they are fighting in the same cause, but when one is placed in a derogatory position, one resents it. So will they. And at the back of their mind there will always be a sense of the unfairness of it, politically—the feeling that the whole thing has been gerrymandered so as to give a preponderance to the urban population at the expense of the rural, which, as you know, is largely Dutch-speaking. No, I don't want to be pessimistic, but I must say that the outlook is deucedly unpleasant.'

'I fear there is much truth in what you say, Mr Storam,' said the pastor, nodding his head, 'but I hope that you are unduly pessimistic. It is only a small percentage of our people who joined, and there are others, men of influence among us, who, despite all the bitterness, will remain sober-minded and just. And a little leaven ...'

'Our District is only a small part of the Colony, Mr Uhlmann. Think of what has been going on in other districts. Not all of them have had commandants like Mallom. I admit I did not at first believe everything I heard about martial law, but now I can believe all I hear. And what one hears is not at all pleasant, Mr Uhlmann. In some districts ill-feeling is running so high between the two sections that there exists practically civil war between neighbours in the same street. Overbury—you'll be glad to hear that he is doing very well indeed—Overbury told me a horrible story of how a good lady got hold of the nails in the chair in which a rebel was shot, and sent them to the rebel's wife with her compliments as a warning how all disloyalists would be treated. He assured me that the woman is really a kindly soul who ordinarily would not willingly upset anyone. But in these days, and under these conditions ...' he shrugged his shoulders and left his remark unfinished.

'As I was saying,' he went on, after a pause, 'our District is only a small part of the Colony. The rest will have its day, too. It is the collective feeling that counts, and people here will inevitably react to that feeling. Our military policy has been almost as stupid as our diplomacy. If we had adequately protected this District, for instance—we had ample warning and could easily have done so—the commandos would never had had a chance to enter it, and none of our people, not even the half-witted Org, would have been led into temptation. It is our want of protection that gave the commandos the opportunity to cajole our people into joining them, and we ought to have seen that, and altered our policy accordingly. If Mallom had had his way, I believe it would have been done. But there, it's no use crying over spilt milk. We'll have to make the best of a bad business, and combine to set our house in order when this affair's finished.'

'Is there any hope that it will be soon?' asked the rector.

'Every hope,' said the magistrate, confidently. 'I saw Mallom this morning, and he tells me the District is practically clear. By the way, Rekker and Swart and the quack doctor have been released. They can even go back to their farms, without parole. How I wish we had had Mallom in full command here when martial law was proclaimed. He would have handled things differently.'

Chapter 43

The Coloured boys in the location whistled *Goodbye, Dolly Gray* and cheered shrilly when the main troop moved out of the Village. The large camp on the veld behind the church was broken up. Where the tents had been, circles of dull yellow gleamed amid the greenery of the spring grass and the iridescence of the sorrels. Even where the horse lines had been, where the ground had been trampled so that it resembled the surface of a threshing floor, veld flowers had sprung up. The cold of winter was giving way to the cheerful warmth of spring, and from the mountain peaks the last traces of snow had long since vanished.

The war still dragged on, but the District was no longer a centre of it, and although martial law still reigned, its regulations had been considerably relaxed. Colonel Cautley had departed, rumour said, to England. Many people pitied him, for he had been so severely wounded that it was doubtful if he would ever be able to walk again, but no one regretted his going. Major Mallom had gone, and many deplored his departure, although the District as a whole considered that one commandant was as good, or as bad, as another. The District did not know what Major Mallom had done for it.

The new commandant was a different type of man, who fretted at the military inactivity to which he was doomed, for the District was now happily rid of the commandos. These were still operating in various adjacent parts, but there was little fear that they would once more be able to come down into the Valley and attack the Village. Formerly they had reached the coast, but that was at a time when they had been able to do pretty much as they pleased. Now there were lines of wire fencing stretching across the District, with blockhouse guards along the main road, and what happened in a remote corner could be reported almost immediately to the commandant's office. Occasional skirmishes with little rebel parties still occurred in those adjacent districts, and martial law there still exacted a heavy toll from the community.

That would continue until every commando had been rounded up, and every rebel caught. From a military point of view, that happy consummation was a foregone conclusion; it was only a matter of time.

The District shared this opinion, not with any feeling of satisfaction, but accepting it as an inevitable certainty. By no stretch of the imagination could it now envisage a triumphant Republicanism dictating terms to a beaten England on behalf of the whole of South Africa, as it had so arrogantly asserted its intention of doing. The war was dragging on, without benefit to anyone but the contractors. Elias Vantloo, for instance, had made much money out of it, though how much was known to the military authorities alone, and to his bankers. The location, too, had profited, although it felt it had a grievance because it was not allowed to spend the money it had earned at the canteens. But no one else had gained any benefit from it.

The Village rested, like a battered wreck that had drifted into a backwater where the eddies continually washed in stray bits of flotsam, from the excitement of the preceding three months and more, and took stock of its losses and scars.

It had been a beautiful Village when it had mourned the dead Alexandrina Victoria. Its environmental beauty remained. War could not rob it of that, nor could martial law interfere with the gorgeous wealth of blossom and leaf that the fecund veld was creating. But the Village itself was marred and blemished. The court house stood as a blackened ruin. Several of the church houses had been burned, none knew how, but there had been frequent fires, and at one time there had been talk of incendiarism, and the military police had been active in pursuing clues that had led nowhere.

Trade and industry, such trade and industry as the Village and District had had in the past, were stagnant; both would take time to recover, for the regulations had interfered with them, and it takes time to restore confidence. Trees had been ruthlessly chopped down, for firewood and to clear space for military purposes; most of the gardens were, like Quakerley's, a mockery of what they had once been. No new buildings had been erected. The only addition to the Village had been those graves in the two cemeteries.

At the big house Andrew Quakerley lay on the large four-poster bed which had been his mother's. He had been born on it, he had had measles on it when a boy; it had been the family bed of the Quakerleys, an heirloom made by skilful craftsmen who had delighted in working with their lathes and carving chisels, a quaint piece of old-fashioned furniture which would have gladdened the heart of a connoisseur. Its black stinkwood head- and foot-boards shone with polish as if they had been lacquered, reflecting on their surfaces the stray gleams of light that slanted towards them, and mirroring faintly the objects around.

The old man had changed very much. His face was seamed and thin, the malar bones prominent under the eyes, the frontal bone sharply defined through the thick, bushy eyebrows; his figure was massively bony, for he was a big man, and his leanness accentuated the sharp angles of his frame. The slight paralysis on the one side of his face was scarcely noticeable as he lay there on the bed; it betrayed itself when he talked or smiled. It could not detract from the wan beauty of his features, the strongly modelled lower jaw, the firm, well-chiselled nose, and the sensitive curve of the lips partly hidden by the neatly trimmed grey beard.

He was dressed in a tweed suit that hung loosely about his frame, showing how much more lean his illness had made him. From the time the two soldiers had carried him into his house he had been ill, seriously at first, and then, in the opinion of his friends who came to se him, much less so. It was common talk in the Village that Mr Quakerley was on the mend. Although he had never left his room, it was understood that he got up every day, was dressed, sat in his arm-chair, and could talk to visitors. Those who came to see him found him singularly quiet, responding to their friendly enquiries but initiating no subject of his own. Dr Buren, who visited him daily, saw no reason for immediate anxiety, but also no probability of permanent improvement.

'It's the shock, Miss Quakerley,' he told Joan. 'If he could get over that—if he could be roused—we might look for improvement, but as it is he is just vegetating. Try and interest him in something.'

'That's always been difficult, Doctor,' she responded. 'Andy has no interest outside his garden. Do you think it might do him good if he saw that? Mr Storam has done wonders, and from the *stoep* it now looks quite respectable. I doubt if he would perceive the difference from the *stoep*.'

'He might,' said the doctor, hesitatingly. 'You know he is very quick at that sort of thing, and if he notices that there's anything wrong, it might do more harm than good. If he refers to it ...'

'He used to, constantly, Doctor, when he was in bed. Now he does not seem to remember it, and both Alice and I have kept off the subject. But if he goes out ... and I suppose there's no reason why he shouldn't take the air now, Doctor, is there?'

'No, none at all. He's not very steady on his legs, but I think we can try him on the *stoep* tomorrow. Then we'll watch his reaction. If he remembers, and asks about the garden, better let him have a look at it. I don't think Storam's improvements will deceive him. I see you have moved the piano into the study. Does he care for that?'

'Yes. He likes me to play to him. Or Mr Uhlmann. I think he likes Mr Uhlmann's playing better than mine. Do you think he ought to see Martin, Doctor.'

'I hardly know, Miss Quakerley. You see, he's still under the impression that Martin is dead. I've tried to explain to him, but he does not seem to grasp it. And yet Storam assures me that when he told him that everything would be all right with Martin—you remember, a few days before the trial—he seemed to understand, and looked pleased. That's what worries me about him, Miss Quakerley.'

'Yes, it worries us too, Doctor. I showed him Charlie's photograph last night, but he just glanced at it and didn't seem to take the slightest interest. And the boy was such a favourite with him, Doctor. It made me sad to see him like that.'

'You mustn't get discouraged, Miss Quakerley. And remember that it is perhaps better for him not to realise what has been going on. There are many of us who would like to forget, if we could, what has happened during this year.'

'Oh, but I know, Doctor. In a way I am thankful that if he goes, he'll go like that. I'm sure he would wish it. And that is one reason why I dread his going out and seeing his garden. If it recalls things to him, Doctor ...'

'I doubt if it will, Miss Quakerley. If he does not remember young Crest, I doubt very much if he will remember his garden.'

'And if Martin calls again, Doctor? He comes every morning and afternoon, and I don't know what to say to him. Would it do any harm if he saw my brother, and talked to him?'

'Well, perhaps not. On the whole, I think you might try it. Very likely he will not recognise Martin ...'

'Oh, but he knows people quite well, Doctor. Old Mr Crawley called yesterday morning, and spent quite half an hour with him. He brought him a bunch of wild flowers, and Andrew was so pleased with them. Like a child, Doctor.'

'Well, try it. But better have somebody else present—say, Uhlmann. Or if you like, I'll come—no, I can't come this afternoon. I have to go out. Still, you might ask Mr Uhlmann to come up.'

Andrew lay on his bed. He felt very tired; a few steps round the room, tiny, shuffling steps such as he had taken in the garden when that searing mental pain had tormented him so that he could not see where he was going, tired him, so that he was glad to lie down on the bed. He still at times felt an echo of that pain, but it was no longer insistent, it no longer drove him mad. It made him melancholy; it gave him a feeling of impotent loneliness, so that when he closed his eyes it seemed to him as if he were travelling swiftly on a long, long road that had no ending, a road environed in gloom without a single object on which his mental eye could fix. And when he opened his eyes and looked around at the familiar furniture of his room, there came immediately into his mind the memories of many unpleasant things—of how they had hanged the boy Org, of how they had made a show of Martin, of how it had rained and the court house had been burned down, of how something intolerably worse had happened, somewhere, somehow, something that he could not quite clearly define, but something the mere haziness of which made him shudder for fear that he could remember it more clearly.

That was when he was alone. When visitors came to see him, the memories faded into the background. He was always sensible of their presence, but they did not obtrude themselves, and there were times when he could think quite clearly, and follow the course of conversation. It was all very confusing, but then everything had been so confusing since the war had disturbed the settled order of things and brought chaos where formerly there had been precise arrangement.

And Alice had told him that the war was still going on—after all these years, it was scarcely believable! Alice was growing old; she did not wear well. His mother had always said that that kind of woman wore out sooner than the others. Worrying over little things; taking life as if it were a business of ways and means, rather than an ordained sequence of events, a pattern woven into every man's warp and woof, indelibly fixed. That was Alice's way, and it had annoyed him, irritated him, which again had annoyed him and irritated him, for it was not right that a man should allow such things to annoy and irritate him. He recognised his irritability to be the result of the cumulative infirmity that old age brings, as a sad but inevitable concomitant, like his growing weariness, his forgetfulness, and his impatience with Alice.

Very rarely his thoughts, roaming along strange highways where there were no definite landmarks to be recognised, no special apperceptive masses on which his mind could fix to cull from them memories that could form the nucleus of crystallisation of equally definite concepts, veered towards his immediate environment. Then he remembered, dimly, that into this very room where he now lay on his mother's bed he had sent Martin to dress and shave. Of what happened to the boy after that he had no recollection, and it annoyed him that he could not remember if Martin had escaped or not. Sometimes it seemed to him that Martin had been sentenced, and when he opened his eyes, to escape that ever-present internal sight of a never-ending road with funereal darkness all around, he saw the square in front of the gaol, the posse of soldiers drawn up before the commandant, the lines of armed men keeping back the crowd, the sullen representatives of the District standing with folded arms listening to what was being interpreted to the chief actors.

When he saw that, he quickly closed his eyes again. It was better to be lonely, to feel himself cut off from the world, without one guiding stay which his hand could hold, than to see that scene over again, to live through that half-hour when Martin had been sentenced.

That was why he did not speak about Martin. Joan had mentioned the boy's name, but he had not reacted to it. He had deliberately ignored her hints, just as he had refused to let his mind dwell on the picture of his grandson. It was a good photograph, and he had felt proud of the boy; a real Quakerley, upstanding, with an honest, handsome face, and a fine figure. But he had told himself that it would not do to set his heart on these things. What he had liked and loved, for its beauty, colour, form, contour, scent, arrangement—everything, in fact, that appealed to his innate artistry— had been reft from him, leaving him with his fatigue, his regrets, his loneliness and his confused thoughts that would not clear, but hung about his mind like a heat-haze around a mountain-side. And beyond and above everything that he could think of, there lay something larger, more poignant, which he could not quite remember, a vague sense of unreality that threatened to become clarified into the memory of something much more distressingly painful than even the recollection of the scene on the square.

When Joan came in at eleven o'clock to bring him his morning cup of chicken broth, he was struggling with this intangible, over-burdening pre-sentiment of disaster, which, like Alice's rambling comments on the war, irritated him but, unlike those, also frightened him. And he had always found it wiser to fight fear than to run away from it. He determined to do so now.

'Joan,' he said, and his voice sounded so normal to her that his sister was agreeably surprised, 'I suppose I have been ill quite a long time now?'

'Not so very long, Andy,' she replied, handing him the cup of chicken broth and supporting him as he sat up on the bed. 'And you are getting rapidly better, Brother.'

'I am all right,' he declared, and she was glad to see that the fingers that gripped the handle of the cup were steadier than usual, although still tremulous. 'I should like to go out today. It seems warm and sunny ...'

'So it is, Andy. Drink your broth, my dear. And if you would like Alice or Anna or one of the children ...'

'No, no,' he interrupted, with something of his old querulousness, 'not just yet. Afterwards ... afterwards ... I see you have put the carnations in water ... they are not quite so fine as they were last year. Those are from the lower bed, I suppose. We must give them a little more bone manure, Joanie, but I wonder if that will help. It seems to me they are woody, and it will be better to plant new ones.'

She did not tell him that they were old Crawley's carnations, and that the lower bed no longer existed. She tried to change the subject. 'Would you like me to read to you?' she asked. 'Or shall I play something? Mr Uhlmann is coming presently, so perhaps you'd prefer that he should play to you.'

'Yes. If he would be so kind. There is something I always like to hear, Joanie. You know that bit for a child. I wonder if he would play it to me again?'

She knew to what he referred. Every time Mr Uhlmann came, *The Canon of Alexis* out of Schumann's *Kinderalbum* was played. It was pitiful that he should be so forgetful. Like a child who could not remember. Perhaps it was better so. She decided to hazard Martin's interview.

'There's someone outside who would like to see you, Andy,' she said. 'I am sure it would do you good to have a little talk with him. Shall I ask him in?'

'Certainly, my dear,' he replied with a touch of interested eagerness in his voice. 'If it is someone I know, certainly. You are all so good to me, but I get tired so soon. And I am very tired now, Joan.'

'Never mind. Come, let me take you to your chair. And if you care to go on the *stoep* he will take you. Mr Uhlmann will come presently.'

She assisted him to his arm-chair, and arranged a rug round his knees.

'There, now you are comfy,' she said, encouragingly. 'And the bell is just there,' she indicated it on a little side table. 'Just ring when you want anything, Andy.'

She left him and went into the study, where Martin was sitting, making conversation with Mrs Crest, who was conventionally polite but plainly bored.

'I think you may look in now, Martin,' she said, as he rose expectantly. 'But be careful. Probably he won't know you. If he does, be very careful. Don't upset him. Take him on the *stoep* if he wants to go. We'll come out afterwards and have tea there.'

'I'll be very careful, Miss Joan,' he answered. 'Father told me his mind's gone, but I can't believe that of Mr Quakerley.'

He went alone into Andrew's bedroom. As he entered he was struck by the accentuated leanness of the figure in the arm-chair, so different from the Andrew Quakerley he had known. His mind went back to that early morning when he had come in to report the attack planned on *Kromdraai*. Then his godfather had been flushed with excitement, vibrating with emotion, a strong, hale man, notwithstanding his advanced age. Now he saw before him an old, old man, whose face, with its startling white, neatly trimmed beard, was placid with a calmness from which all emotion seemed absent.

'Mr Quakerley,' he said softly, stretching out his hand and bending over the old man. 'It is I, Martin. I have come to see how you are doing ...'

Andrew took his hand limply, and he felt the long, bony fingers lying in his palm without a responding pressure.

'I am glad to see you,' said the old man, disinterestedly. 'You are from the District?'

'But yes, Mr Quakerley ... I am Martin ... you remember? Martin ...'

'Yes, yes,' old Andrew spoke soothingly. 'Curious that you should have the same name as ... as a young friend of mine. Perhaps you may remember him, young Martin Rekker ... But don't let us talk about him ...'

'But I am he,' said Martin, slightly raising his voice in his eagerness for recognition. 'Does not Mr Quakerley remember me?' He was shocked at the old man's manner, and dimly realised that his father had been right when he had asserted that old Mr Quakerley's mind was no longer clear.

'Well, well,' Andrew's voice was still mildly interested. 'We won't talk about that. I see so many people that I cannot quite place them all. You must forgive me if I can't place you, Nephew,'—he used the old conventional term in which a senior addresses a junior—'you must bear with me, for I am an old man, and we've had so much to upset us these days. You, too, I suppose, have had a hard time of it on your farm?'

It pained Martin to see his attempt at lightheartedness—the wan smile that broadened more over the one side of the face than the other, the little wavering gesture with the bony hand, on which the heavy veins stood out with rounded intensity against the pallor of the skin.

'Yes, Mr Quakerley,' he replied, trying to make his voice even and commonplace. Perhaps it would be best to humour the old man. 'Our place has had its ups and downs, but we'll get it right in time. We're starting thatching the roof on the new homestead ...'

'So. That will be the war, of course,' said the old man, in a matter of fact voice. He made an attempt to rise. Martin bent down and helped him up.

'Would Mr Quakerley care to go outside, on the *stoep*?' the young man asked, mindful of Joan's suggestion. 'It is a very fine day, Mr Quakerley, and it would do you good.'

'So it would. Yes ... but of course,' said the old man, with a little more animation in his voice. 'But you just lend me your arm, Nephew. This illness ... my poor legs run away with me sometimes if I have no one to lean upon.'

Martin supported him as he tottered towards the door. He still moved with quick, stumbling little steps, short, shuffling strides, which gave him the appearance of perpetually trying to avoid losing his balance and falling forward. In the corridor outside he halted for a moment.

'This is as far as I've got up to now,' the old man informed his companion. 'That picture,' he glanced at a framed water-colour hanging on the wall, 'doesn't look straight to me. You might tell them to put it straight. I dislike having pictures askew. But everything is wrong nowadays. You have doubtless noticed it yourself. Did I hear you say that they had burned down your farm? Dear, dear, how sad ... Yes, here's the door. There should be a grass chair near the flower-stand. If you would be so kind ...'

A flood of spring sunshine pouring down through the orange trees mantled the slate paving of the *stoep* with spots of light. On the flower-stand geraniums, cream and white and pink, blossomed in ornamental pots. From the *stoep* could be seen the mass of disordered greenery in the gardens, and far in the distance the imposing mass of the mountain range, hazed with blue.

When the sunlight flecked his tweed coat, old Andrew drew himself upright and glanced round. His figure seemed to stiffen. Martin felt a tremor run through the arm which his own supported, and hurriedly tightened his grasp. Instinctively he was aware that the old man was reacting to some stimulus—some sensory impression that affected him profoundly. He tried to steer him towards the grass chair, but Andrew shook off his arm impatiently. The old man's eyes were fixed on the scene immediately below the *stoep*—on the devastated garden. Mr Storam's gang of picked convicts had worked hard. They had restored some semblance of regularity to the magnificent gardenia hedge; they had put in hundreds of veld bulbs in the beds beyond; they had trimmed the branches of the fine old magnolia tree, which had been sadly damaged by the operations in the garden on the night when Martin had surrendered. They had worked hard, and such supervision of the labour as had been possible had been intelligent. It bespoke the knowledgeableness of amateurs, and to the superficial observer the results that had been achieved would have seemed satisfactory.

But Andrew's swift glance over that makeshift arrangement of beds and borders, hedges and rockeries, was not only that of a trained gardener, but of an artist sensitive to the least blemish, the slightest difference of technique, in the arrangement which he had planned and for years preserved. As his eye swept over the improvised repairs that Mr Storam's gang had effected, he was immediately conscious not only of alterations that were manifestly not improvements, but also of omissions, and, what was infinitely more painful, of glaring gaps where there should have been graceful arrangement. Memory, with its heart-breaking associations, rushed back in a flood, and with it came the cognisance that what had tormented him when he lay in his bedroom, vaguely frightened of some disaster which his mind could not precisely define, lay here before him in dreadful reality, and that once before, in an early, rain-wetted morning, he had seen it with such cruel clearness that it had seared his heart until a merciful unconsciousness had blotted out the sight of it.

Alarmed at his rigidity and the fixed stare in his eyes, Martin dragged him to the chair, the old man resisting feebly, keeping his face turned towards the garden.

'Mr Quakerley, Mr Quakerley,' Martin cried, trying to turn the old man's attention away from what he was looking at, 'don't take it to heart ... don't mind it so much ...'

The sound of his voice seemed to rouse old Andrew, who drew a deep breath and settled down in the chair. His bony hands beat the air tremulously; his pale face was suffused with blood, his lips were slightly bluish. His voice, when it came, was thin and feeble.

'Ah, it is you, Martin,' he said, with a pause between each word, as if he were recollecting himself, trying to frame the sentence he had in mind. 'It is all right, my boy. I'm going to tell the commandant.' His voice became stronger. 'It doesn't matter, Martin. Look, see what they have done to my garden. If I have had to make sacrifice, boy ...'

The voice broke; his arms fell down, and the tremulous, bony hands subsided into quietness. Martin heard him breathe heavily, and saw his head droop.

'Miss Joan,' Martin shouted, jumping towards the study window, 'come quickly. Mr Quakerley ... I don't like the look of him.'

THE MASK

by

C Louis Leipoldt

Chapter 1

The most imposing house in the Village was that of Elias Vantloo. It stood near the end of the main row of residences, fronted by a spacious and well kept garden, where cannas, gardenias, and orange trees blossomed in scented profusion, prodigally watered by the moss-grown furrow that brought water from the mountain stream upon which, by custom and prescription, every resident in the Village had riparian rights. It was overshadowed, in front where its large, trellised *stoep* was made gorgeous in early spring by the wealth of blue wisteria whose tresses daily flung masses of dead petals upon the flat-slate stones, by venerable oak trees planted by the early settlers and still vigorous and splendidly green in their old age. It had rococo gables, neatly white-washed, and outside shutters painted a dull green, a thatched roof spangled with yellow senecio, and massive cedarwood doors, oiled and polished to almost lacquer-like smoothness. Dating back to the early half of the past century, it had been added to and restored so that only its front was really part of the original building, but the alterations had been done with such simplicity that the restoration had not made the modernised building a contemptible thing but rather tended to enhance the dignified solidity of the old design.

That was as it should have been, for Elias Vantloo was, if not the most important inhabitant of the Village, at least one of the three who might be looked upon as aspiring to that dignity. The magistrate, by right of office and authority as the direct representative of the government, took precedence; the Dutch Reformed parson, who lived in the rambling old Dutch parsonage, part of which was falling to pieces because the congregation saw no need of spending money upon it while there was talk of building an entirely new manse, came second; but after these Elias had no competitor who could dispute the third place with him. In wealth he was reputed to be easily first in the District. As usual, popular report exaggerated his possessions, but even when such magnification had been discounted, it was generally agreed that he was by far the wealthiest person in the Village. The proprietor of the Village store, whose ancestors had hawked goods around the District with a donkey-cart and one manumitted slave, had inherited a good business which had greatly and most profitably improved, but everyone knew that a business like that demanded much capital and could not be expected to return more than a moderate interest on the money invested in it. Besides, the proprietor of the Village store had a large family, many current expenses, and had been known to come to Elias for financial assistance. Indeed, many had, in these bad times, turned to Elias for help. He held bonds on most of the farms in the district, notes of hand from many who in times past remembered him as a thin-legged, rather morose and scowling lad, struggling in the matriculation class of the Village school, a boarder whose expenses had been paid in kind by a father who could barely make his holding pay the interest on the first and second mortgages. Now, in his prosperity, Elias gave freely when he was asked, and by giving had earned for himself the reputation that comes from great wealth ostentatiously but skilfully suggested rather than openly displayed. He never gave gratuitously, exacting always a high rate of interest for money advanced, and he never advanced more than half the valuation of the property which he was called in to save. A scrupulous man might have called Elias a usurer, but the Village hesitated to hint at that term. Where the government exacted a hundred and twenty per cent on unpaid taxes, and where security was admittedly, in these hard times, so patently unstable, it was merely good business to lay out one's money to the best advantage.

Time, which had favoured Elias with worldly wealth, had not dealt kindly with his person. The thin-legged adolescent had grown into a fat, heavy, bloated man, whose scowl was accentuated by the wrinkles around his eyes, and whose moroseness, the result of a self-consciousness of social and intellectual inferiority, had given place to a smug complacency expressed in a smile in which self-satisfaction rather than altruistic cheerfulness was dominant. It is an expression often seen on the faces of men who acclaim themselves 'self-made,' implying thereby that they have conquered difficulties by their own worth and work rather than with the assistance of chance and circumstance. The satisfaction of achievement, the sense of power that it gives and the moral fillip that it administers even to characters inherently weak and sometimes as inherently vicious, brings with it a readjustment of social and individual values to which different individuals react differently. In Elias's case it had made him arrogant without eradicating that primitive conception of his own inferiority which had lurked in him at the time when he had chafed under class restraint and envied the facility of younger boys in mastering the subjects for matriculation. In his youth he had learned the advantages of disguising his feelings where such disguise was of benefit to him, and now, in his prosperity, he still aped a humility he really despised but on occasion found exceedingly useful.

His career had contributed to strengthen these temperamental characteristics which in his adolescence he had often admitted to himself were not ornamental or calculated to attract his fellow citizens. He had passed his matriculation, and had gone, as an articled clerk, to a Cape Town firm, where he had worked with that persevering fervour which sometimes is much more useful than knowledgeable application. Very soon he had discovered that a great deal of his fervour was redundant, and that the same, or very much similar, advantages could be obtained by a minimum expenditure of energy and a maximum pretence of interest. Working on these lines, he had soon made for himself a niche in the business into which he had crept, by favour of a personal friend of his father, and when the firm refused his demand for a junior partnership, he had migrated to his old Village and set up for himself as a country attorney. In that capacity he had done admirably well. His local knowledge, and the disposition of the Village and District to turn over their legal affairs to one of their own kind, had considerably helped him, and in the course of a decade he had prospered exceedingly, and, being thrifty, careful, and in a position to apply his knowledge to the best advantage, he had amassed money. He had bought the house of old Martin Rekker, the 'church house' of the family in the Village, and had found it a

profitable investment, if only as an advertisement. He had married, also as an investment, although at the time he had thought that it had been wholly for love, into one of
the best families in the District. His wife brought with her a substantial dowry, to
which, later on, the death of his mother-in-law had added several thousands in trust for
her grandchild, his only daughter. At that stage Elias had taken a partner into his
business, and had devoted himself more closely to higher finance, which necessitated
frequent and lengthy visits to Cape Town and Johannesburg where his activities on the
stock exchange were well known.

In the Village he enjoyed a certain prestige and standing, as much from his reputed
wealth and power as from his popularity. He had never done anything to make himself
unpopular, and on many occasions had displayed positive qualities which had
impressed his fellow Villagers. In the old Colony days he had been too insecurely
established to assert himself in public affairs; his time had been occupied solely in
consolidating his business and social position, and by his assiduous devotion to his
office he had gained the reputation of being a 'solid' man. In the political embroglios
wherein the Progressive and the Bond Parties had become entangled, he had never
definitely taken sides, excusing himself on the ground that as an attorney he had to be
neutral. During the sad days of the Anglo-Boer War, when the Village and the District
were disrupted, and what was practically civil war came up as a sorrowful wave
against every homestead and home, his sympathies were understood to have been with
his own folk, but the curious remembered that he had received a plenary permit when
martial law invaded the Village and when some of the foremost farmers had been
exiled from it. Moreover, it had been noticed that Elias, at about that time, had
organised his transport service, which had been promptly commandeered by the
military authorities, and that, although he had vigorously and vociferously protested
against this high-handed action, he had regularly banked the official cheques which
came every month from the commandant's office in payment for the services of his
teams. When the war ended, he resumed his activities as a lawyer, and started his
money-lending, for there were many whom the war had broken and who were only too
glad to borrow from so accommodating a friend who, notwithstanding the fact that he
too had suffered severely, had yet enough ready cash to take up mortgages on which
the interest was long overdue. In time people forgot that they had had doubts about his
attitude during the war, for Elias blossomed out into a patriot, was offered but
declined a safe seat in Parliament, and through this act of self-abnegation established
himself more firmly in the confidence of his fellow citizens. In the pre-Union days he
had been regarded as one of the upholders of the South African Party, which had
supplanted the Bond Party of pre-war days, and after the consummation of that hasty
and ill-advised fusion of diverse interests and opposing ideals, which he had
wholeheartedly supported and championed on the public platform, he had remained
staunch to his Party until his shrewdness had made him discern that the political vanes
were veering in another direction. Then he had boldly declared himself for
Nationalism, for he was wise enough, and knew his people well enough, to
prognosticate what such a slogan would mean in a District which but ten years before
had been engulfed in the throes of a struggle which had left scars that were still
painful and sensitive. Through his influence the district had returned one of the first
Nationalist candidates to Parliament, and the pendulum had swung over so far that his

old Party no longer possessed the vestige of a hope of regaining the seat. Again he had declined the honour of representing the District in the interests of his new Party. He preferred to work, as he said, as a camp-follower, and his humble attitude won him far more appreciation than he would have gained had he accepted the invitation.

In municipal affairs he had taken a prominent part, and at the time when he had been a staunch South African Party man, when that Party had been in power, he had had his choice of such government nominations as he wished to secure. On the school board, on the divisional council, and on various commissions—these futile and expensive placebos of which his old Party had been so fond—he had sat and done, as most people admitted, good work, though popular opinion did not determine if that work had been solely in the public interest. When he left his Party, to join the newly born Nationalist Party, he had not renounced such appointments as he held, although he humbly declared that he would forthwith do so if popular opinion considered it incumbent upon him to resign, adding that it was perhaps in the public interest that one good Nationalist should sit upon committees preponderantly staffed by adherents of the South African Party. Popular opinion had not insisted upon his resignation, and he had enjoyed his emoluments, and found much satisfaction in reflecting upon the fact that his continued service upon such committees and boards was excellent propaganda for his new Party. Shrewd, well-read, and closely informed upon the shifting currents of political opinion, he steered himself with great skill through the troubled waters at the time of the Rebellion and the Great War; and when the air was full of rumours about a reunion of parties, he had been one of the first to adopt a tentative attitude and to urge that the old wrangles should be forgotten and that a new start should be made. No wonder that the District regarded Uncle Elias as one of its principal men, one of its most trusted and beloved citizens, fashioned of good gold without a carat of alloy, Christian in his humbleness of spirit and exalted in his conception of public and communal duty.

The church had found in him a fine supporter, who had served successively as junior Deacon, senior Deacon, entrusted with the treasury of the church council, Elder, and finally senior Elder, invariably chosen to attend the parson when the latter went south for the quinquennial synod. Although he held mortgages on farms which produced wine in large quantities, and drew dividends from companies which made beer and supported licensed houses, he was regarded as a shining light in the ranks of Good Templary, was indefatigable in his attendance on Lodge nights, and had been elected to the highest official positions to which a follower of teetotal fanaticism could aspire. Indeed, his public interest in prohibition had occasioned his friends some uneasiness, for the District depended for its prosperity to some degree upon its vineyards, and although Elias persistently proclaimed that much more profit would accrue from the planting of sultanas than from the cultivation of pontac and grape vines, such heresy had never been favourably received by either the Village or the District. His teetotalism was held to be a mild fad, not wholly praiseworthy in a man otherwise so level-headed, but not to be condemned so severely in Uncle Elias's case as it would undoubtedly have been anathematised in one less popular than he.

To all acquainted with him it was perfectly well known that Elias Vantloo could retire when he pleased. He had no need to continue his business, for he could easily and most comfortably live on the interest of his investments. He lived well, and to the mind of the District, luxuriously, spending his money easily, entertaining with discrimination, and on occasion giving generously towards something that appealed to him. After the Rebellion he had been one of the first to come forward with a donation towards the 'Help-Mekaar' Fund, established in aid of those who in that miserable fiasco had impoverished themselves. When the fund for the rebuilding of the church had been started he headed the subscription list with a gift of 200 guineas, and when the congregation decided upon presenting the pastor with a motor car he distinguished himself, in a manner about which the District gossiped for a full year, by buying a Ford and donating it to the congregation. Still in the Village street the old signboard swung before his dilapidated office, displaying, in lettering long since faded, the legend 'Vantloo & van Deren, Attorneys & Notaries,' in English on the one side and in Dutch on the other. He still attended at the office and saw clients, who appreciated this courtesy on the part of the senior member of the firm and submitted tamely to whatever he proposed, for such 'forth-coming' makes it difficult to decline a proposition or argue a contrary opinion. The Village accepted service so self-sacrificingly given, and it lauded the servitor who, notwithstanding the fact that he no longer needed to serve, yet busied himself, out of pure friendliness and that neighbourly feeling which the District, by tradition and custom, had learned to value so high, with the affairs of those who could as easily have been satisfied with the advice of his partner.

Chapter 2

In the large dining room of Elias Vantloo's house the morning sun filtered through the thin lace curtains of the *stoep* windows, whose pattern broke the light into filigrees on the polished floor. The room was solidly rather than tastefully furnished. The old fashioned rosewood sideboard, brought years ago from overseas where it had usefully decorated some distinguished country house, bore a load of silver and cut-glass. Elias had bought it at an auction sale for a few pounds, having admired its well-proportioned solidity, and had tried to get other furniture to match it, but had not succeeded in the attempt. The big dining room table was of cedarwood, so beautifully polished that it reflected every glint of light that fell upon it. The chairs were of stinkwood, oiled daily and rubbed so effectively that they seemed to be plated with a lacquer as iridescent as that of the table. There were comfortable club-easies, covered with maroon-red covers, and a large, low-seated Chesterfield, invitingly roomy. On the walls were a few framed oil pictures, landscapes by Naude, a charming still life by Wenning, and a couple of etchings. Over the sideboard hung a gloriously decorative mountain scene by Goodman, and facing it, on the opposite wall, a pastel by Smithard. Elias prided himself on a patriotism that forbade him to patronise alien art, but the pictures had been chosen by his wife, and although he admired them he made no pretence of knowledgeably criticising their merits. For him they stood as a proof of his

Nationalism, a practical expression of the motto 'South Africa First' that he had acquired with his new allegiance.

On the big cedarwood dresser which served as an additional sideboard, and on the dining room table, stood bunches of dahlias, monstrous, treble-petalled flowers, pathetic in their abnormal, hyptertrophic grandeur. They gave a splash of vivid colour to a room that was, even on a sunny autumn day, sombre in its dignified solidity. Over the table hung a massive electric chandelier, with a maroon-red shade in harmony with the covers of the chairs, and the rest of the electric light fittings were of similar substantiality. They gave an impression of luxury more than of homeliness, and of a sober, sedate richness, enhanced by the simplicity of furniture and the absence of any ornamentation of plainly cream distempered walls and cedar-beamed ceiling.

Moving about the room with a duster in her hand was a woman belonging to that large and increasing class of the Cape population which is popularly known as 'Coloured,' in contradistinction to the aboriginal Natives. In this class resort those who are the descendants of White parents who have married or cohabited with non-Europeans, whether the latter be Orientals, recruited originally from Malay slaves or freedmen, or aboriginals belonging to the Koranna, Hottentot or Bushmen tribes. They are distinguished by their lighter colour, approximating in many instances to the white of the European, and while retaining many of the racial features and characteristics of their non-White ancestry, show points of similarity with their more fortunate White co-citizens.

Ayah Mina was in some ways a typical example. She was a moderately tall, lithely proportioned woman, agreeing, as far as bodily shape was concerned, more with the female of the White type than with that of the aboriginal, whose tendency, in later age, is to become ungainly. She carried herself upright, holding her shoulders straight, and walked with a smooth, gliding gait that made her movements graceful. Her plain black dress, and her equally plain, unfrilled cap, a cross between a housekeeper's head-dress and a sun-bonnet, lent dignity to her figure. In her youth her features must have been handsome; in middle age they still possessed some charm, although her face was criss-crossed by innumerable wrinkles, and the close-set eyes and wide cheek-bones considerably detracted from her appearance. Hers was a good-humoured face, but it was one, too, which close observation would have shown to be saddened; her mouth, with its full lips, sagged at the corners.

Ayah Mina, who had no surname to which she responded, could trace her ancestry back to the slaves who had come over from Mozambique, and who had lived in the District since the times of Swellengrebel, long before the Village was founded. Somewhere in that period, one of her ancestors, male or female, must have been European, but Mina had no knowledge which side of her parentage had been responsible for her mixed blood. She had never bothered her head about the matter, for she had been brought up to look upon the White masters as standing in a class apart, where such questions were never publicly discussed, and she knew perfectly well the futility of discussing them. She remembered her grandfather dimly. He had been a slave himself and had known Lord Charles, who had sometimes come to the Village and had taken a great interest in horses. Grand-dad had been a toothless, cataract-blinded old man, but as a child she had listened to his stories of the time when men still held property in man, and her mother had told her much more about these days. In her youth she had been a comely Coloured girl, and had married, properly and not 'behind the bushes,' with a youth from the mission station at Neckarthal. The attractions of service in the Village had lured them into the Village location, where her husband had died. Mina had entered the service of the magistrate, and in the course of time engaged herself to another employer whose daughter Elias had married. With her young mistress she came to live in the Village once more, and had remained with Elias's wife, acting as cook, nursemaid, and indoor servant, until the Master had prospered to the extent of augmenting his staff, and she had no longer to work single-handed. Now she did little work. Elias said his wife spoiled her, but Ayah Mina, though no longer a maid of all work, was by no means idle. She was an under-housekeeper, for the old mistress liked to look after things herself and, much as she wanted to do so, Mina could not induce her mistress to abstain from superintending whatever there was to be done. Nevertheless Ayah Mina was accounted by the other servants the virtual ruler of the kitchen and the yard. It was she who engaged new servants for the house when such were required, and supervised the polishing of the big eight-cylinder Hupmobile car, the pride of Antonie, the coloured chauffeur. She could look back on twenty-four years of faithful and honest service, and she knew that her mistress appreciated her work, her loyalty, and herself, and with that knowledge she was content.

Now as she moved quietly about the room, flicking dust off the furniture with her dusting cloth, she reflected with complacency upon her relations with her mistress. After all these years she had come to regard Elias's wife as the one in whom she took special interest, the one whom she had to guard and shield. The 'old mistress,' who was really not much older than Mina herself—for there was a difference of only a couple of years between them in age—was a weak, delicate woman, frail in health, diffident in her attitude towards life, a woman to be sheltered, coddled, spoiled so far as she, Mina, could spoil, coddle or shelter her. A woman entirely too good for the old master, as a diamond is too good for a leaden setting. The old master, now, was rugged, granite in figure and granite in heart, for all that people believed about his goodness. She, Mina, knew more than people did, and she knew that the old master was very indifferently good, even though the old mistress made an idol of him and thought that butter would not melt in his mouth.

Through the drawing room door, opening into the dining room, came the old mistress. She had the straight, dignified carriage inherited from a long line of ancestors conscious of their race; the regular features, the delicate complexion, the lustrous brown hair, now rapidly greying, characteristic of her family. A woman still good to look upon, though thinned and angular, and aged in appearance by other things than time. In her youth Maria Gerster had been a beauty, and the old wet-plate photographs represented her as a girl with large eyes, long hair, and a frank, engaging smile. They could not reproduce the fresh attractiveness of her colouring, nor the charm of her vivacious eyes, but they showed a young woman of prepossessing appearance. Time had taken its toll from her, time and experience, but Mina, looking at her with eyes which refused to see the obvious, saw nothing more in that sad, wearied face than the marks left by bodily fatigue and advancing old age.

'Why don't you let the maids do that, Mina?' asked her mistress, coming forward into the room as she spoke. I have told you time after time that you must not do these things yourself. What do we keep the maids for?'

'You might well ask that, Old Missis,' answered the old woman. 'They get worse Mevery day. Heavens, to see what a mess they have made of the pantry. They left one of the preserve jars open, and the ants are all over the place, Old Missis. Dreadful! I have to put poison on all the shelves ...'

'I hope you locked the door, Mina. The cat might ...'

'No cat has any business in our pantry, Old Missis. It would serve the dratted beast right if the poison gave it the colic. But I locked it up all right. Will Old Missis have her tea in here or outside on the *stoep*?'

'On the *stoep*, please, Mina. It is such a lovely day. You might put some more cups out, for I expect the young mistress will be back soon. She did not say when she would return, did she?'

'Lord, no! When did the young mistress trouble to declare her out-goings or in-comings to Ayah Mina? She is just like what she was when a child, Old Missis. The wonder of it! And herself a grown woman now, and wanting us to believe that she is a doctor!'

'But she is that, sure enough, Mina,' said her mistress, smilingly. 'She has been abroad all these years, and she has come back a doctor ...'

'Yes, and with her hair cut short like a man's, and her skirts indecently short,' snorted the old woman, in a tone that was meant to be disparaging. 'I do not hold with such things, Missis Maria. The young mistress should get sensible; she is old enough for it.'

'By which I suppose you mean that she should marry Master Eric, eh?'

'And what better can she do, Missis? Haven't they grown up, so to say, together, and isn't he ordained to be her mate? What is the good of dawdling with it?'

'These things do not come as we wish, Mina,' said her mistress, gently. 'It is my wish, as you know, and it is Master Eric's too. But the young mistress has her own mind, and we can only look on ...'

'Yes, and see her make a fool of herself,' declared the old woman, vigorously. 'I don't hold with such goings-on, Missis. Never any good comes of it. If Master Eric had the grit of a Hottentots-god (mantis) in him, he would have taken her by this time.'

'They don't do these things nowadays, Mina. Both have a say in the matter.'

'More's the pity,' grumbled the old woman. 'A foolish young thing like the young mistress does not know what is good for her, and Master Eric does not know what he loses. Ah, the wasted years, Old Missis. The young folk never dream of them ...'

'And we too much, far too much,' said Mrs Vantloo. 'We do no good by it, Mina. God gives us what He thinks meet for us ...'

'Don't you believe it, Old Missis. I am a good Christian—I have had water thrown on my forehead, the same as you, Missis Maria, and though I have not been confirmed like you, I was properly married by the missionary. No one dare call me a heathen. But I say the good Lord does not know half of what goes on in the world. If He did, He would squash most of us like black-beetles ...'

'Probably He would, Mina. But He is judge, not we. Don't be so dreadfully wicked as to question His ways and doings ...'

'If it is wicked, then I am wicked,' insisted the old woman. 'But Old Missis knows quite well that I am talking gospel truth when I say that most of us are no better than cockroaches, and some of us not even so good as they. Why the good little Lord does not burn us all up with brimstone I don't know ...'

'Surely there is something amiss, Mina,' said her mistress, kindly. 'Is Sophy worse this morning?'

'Worse, no. But no better, Missis. The child will never be right again ...'

'Don't say that, Mina. The doctor hopes ...'

'They always hope, the doctors. Even when your eyes break and people are ready to put your chin binder on, they tell you there is hope. The child had a bleeding last night—all over the pillow the blood was, Missis, and for a time I thought she was gone. But she came through, with the help of some brandy and mint tea that I made for her. This morning she is coughing shockingly, Missis, and there is much blood.'

'I fancy the doctor has taken the young mistress round to see her, Mina,' said her mistress. 'Between them they may be able to do something for Sophy. The young mistress is well trained, even though you doubt her ability as a doctor.'

'I don't like to see the young mistress with Sophy,' said the old woman, morosely. 'It is not right that she should be there in the location. Her place is here.'

'A doctor's place is where he is called,' retorted Mrs Vantloo, moving towards the *stoep* door. 'But you, too, should be there, Mina. You should not leave the child alone if she is so ill. Go back now, at once. Yes, I insist, Mina. The maids can bring in the tea.'

'There's time enough later on,' the Coloured woman said. 'Sophy won't die when I am away. I am old enough to know when the signs come, and I shall be there. Now I go fetch the tea for Missis, but first Missis must sit down.'

She followed her mistress on to the *stoep*, and drew forward a comfortable cane deck-chair for her to sit in. From the *stoep* one looked over the gardens, ranging down to meet the river, with the wide stretches of newly-ploughed wheat-lands beyond, and beyond them again the boldly cut outline of the high hills, hazed in the blue of an early winter's forenoon. The scent of blossoming chrysanthemums mingled with the fainter, more delicate perfume of the countless yellow and pink sorrels studding the patches of grass and turf. A crisp chill hung in the air, and from the poplars shading the bath-house in the garden came the cheerful chirrup of the finches swinging with their long, pendulous nests.

Ayah Mina saw her mistress safely ensconced in the deck-chair, brought her the morning papers and her knitting, placed the little table for the tea conveniently close to her side, and hurried indoors to get the tea things ready.

'The old mistress is looking more frail this morning,' she muttered to herself as she entered the kitchen. 'Belike she had the asthma last night, and it has troubled her heart. It is a pity she will not take a glassful of wine. Drat that man.'

This last, apparently irrelevant remark, she uttered with so much energy that she was for a moment almost breathless. But when she observed that the maids had already brewed the tea, and that the tray had been arranged differently from the manner in which she had proposed to arrange it herself, she speedily recovered sufficient breath to give her opinion of such officiousness in a manner as forcible as that in which the apparent irrelevancy had been couched.

Outside on the *stoep* Maria Vantloo knitted patiently, now and then lifting her eyes and staring at the peaceful beauty of the landscape below her. In reality she saw little of its splendours. She knew they no longer had any power to captivate her interest or to soothe her soul's tiredness. Year after year she had seen these innumerable sorrels starring the green all over the Valley, the oleanders blossom in prodigal pink, heard the finches courting in the poplar branches or quarrelling over their nest-building, watched the shadows shortening over the rugged mountain ranges whose weathered cliff-faces glowed with rose and lavender shades, and counted the monotonous strokes of the church clock as it struck the passing hours. She could not even tell if she had loved what she had seen, for she had lost interest in it, too absorbed in her own reflections to take much heed of her environment.

Her life, as the Village saw it, had not been dreary or uneventful. Married to a man like Elias Vantloo, so the Village opined, it could not have been either. She had, it is true, only one child, but such limited fertility was possible of common sense when one remembered, as the Village did, that the Gersters and the Rekkers had inter-married, and that a certain amount of consanguinity, not beyond what the church in its wisdom had decreed as prohibitive of marriage, contributed to it. Almost thirty years ago she had come to live in the Village, a newly wedded woman, with a disposition that was not quite that of which her neighbours had cordially approved. They made allowances—old 'Thunder' Gerster's daughter had been educated at a girls' seminary, somewhere near the capital, and had learned to play the piano, to speak English fluently, and to adopt English fashions and manners. Formerly that would have been accounted so much in her favour, but feeling had hardened in the Village by the time she had married and, although it had by no means been so outspoken as it had become since the Anglo-Boer War, it was yet wholly different from the old times when Gallows-Gecko had been parliamentary representative of the District, and when the beloved Queen's birthday was annually celebrated with much pomp and ceremony on the village square. Many things had encouraged that lamentable change, small things for the most part, but none the less of importance from the point of view of those who disliked the old ways of life and thought, and whose nationalism was as intolerant as it was crabbed. The church had been responsible for something of this change of feeling, even though its influence had been exerted comparatively late. It had introduced the stern Scottish Calvinistic outlook upon daily life, looking askance at pleasure, anathematising dances as being of the Devil, and, by denying the cultural value of aesthetic factors, encouraging a distorted and extravagant conception of sex. In such an environment Maria Gerster's worldly vivacity found few defenders, and soon languished for want of sympathetic support. In time Mrs Vantloo acquiesced in public opinion. She conformed in all things, as a model wife should, and the Village, eminently just and fair in its dealings with repentant sinners, took her to its heart and agreed that as a spouse, apart from that little matter of child-bearing, she left little to be desired. It liked her for her virtues, which were many, and if it was really a trifle contemptuous of her self-effacement, it was scarcely conscious of being so. Gradually she had modelled herself on her husband, and seemed content to let him direct her life as best pleased his inclination and his judgment. She had loyally assisted him wherever she could. In his political life she had changed with him, and had shown no open shame-facedness in so doing. In his Lodge activities she had definitely assisted him, taking an interest in the ritual and mildly proselytising when she found opportunity to do so on behalf of teetotalism. She had been mild, forbearing, self-effacing all through her life. The Village considered her a non-entity.

She had brought Elias a rich dowry; her family was wealthy and related by marriage to the best components of the White population. The Village cordially agreed that Elias had done magnificently well for himself when he married her. In his business dealings she never interfered, and neither her husband nor anyone who knew her would ever have imagined that she could by any possibility have summoned up enough energy or determination to meddle in affairs external to those of the home. Even there, her influence was less tangible than implied. For all practical purposes Ayah Mina ran her household, and whenever there was any difference of opinion it was Elias, and not she, who made the decision.

The one child of their union, Santa, had been, in early childhood, her comfort and solace. Between her and her daughter there existed a relation which was to some extent, though in a different degree, a reflection of the feeling with which she herself was regarded by the community. As the girl had grown older, developing qualities of self-reliance, independence, and initiative that made her more akin to her father than to her mother, the roles of the two had become transposed. Santa loved her mother with the protective, maternal instinct with which one regards a pet dog, upon whom extravagant affection could be lavished in return for a meek and loving subservience, rather than with the fierce, adoring, admiring emotion with which she regarded her father. Spoilt from early childhood, wilful, and fully conscious of her own powers, Santa had triumphantly gone her own way, cajoling her father, ignoring, in that pitiless manner characteristic of a child, her mother, serenely oblivious to the fact that she was typifying the community's attitude towards the two. For the Village also admired, respected, and in a sense loved Elias, and felt a generous, charitable emotion towards Maria.

Santa had had her own way in everything. She had gone to high school, matriculated with honours, entered the University, and in due course declared her intention of qualifying as a doctor. It had cost much argument, petting, and cajoling on her part to obtain her father's consent to this step. Curiously enough, her mother had actively supported her, and it was partly owing to Maria's insistence—an insistence made with patient, unwavering, but at the same time gentle iteration, that had astonished and for a moment impressed her daughter—that she had at last been allowed to go to Europe for her medical education. Elias had urged that she should qualify at a university in Holland, but Santa was aware of her linguistic limitations. She spoke Afrikaans fluently and well, and English with the facility resulting from daily use of that language and excellent training in it at college, but her knowledge of high-Dutch was limited. She had therefore gone to the Royal Free, where she had won high honours, gathering the gold medal in the London MD in her stride, and doing the usual house appointments, and thereafter a year's post-graduate work on the Continent.

On her return, Maria had found her changed in many ways, and Elias had frankly expressed his pride and approbation. Her course of study abroad had made her more self-reliant, self-assertive, and independent than she had been before she had started on her experiment, but those were just the characteristics which Elias valued in his daughter. Santa's regard for her mother was no less sincere than it had been before, but the older woman had noticed, instinctively, that it was merely an exaggeration of the feeling which she had formerly inspired. It was ostentatiously protective, shielding, maternal, rather than filial, and the older woman submitted to it as she had submitted all her life long, uncomplainingly, subserviently, hiding her heart-hunger beneath a pose of mild cheerfulness and pathetic geniality.

Chapter 3

Dr Buren's car stopped in front of the Vantloo house, whither it had been carefully steered, for the front street was narrow and presented many obstructions. The doctor handed out Santa with the dignity of an old fashioned gentleman doing the honours to a great lady. Dr Buren did everything with conscious dignity, a habit that brought him much profit and was calculated to make the Village, accustomed to predecessors who had lacked these high-bred manners, think all the more of his professional skill. He was a short, well-built man, with a neatly trimmed grey beard, a well-dressed, confidence-inspiring general practitioner, who had for years presided over the entrance into and departure from the world of the inhabitants of the Village, had an immense and, on the whole, a lucrative practice, and was fully deserving of all the kind words people spoke about him.

'Here she is, Mrs Vantloo,' he exclaimed, jovially, as he followed Santa up the *stoep* steps. 'A thousand apologies for keeping her so long, but it was worthwhile. Your daughter, ma'am, does you credit.'

'I am glad she has found favour with you, Doctor,' replied Maria, submitting meekly to her daughter's formal kiss. 'Sit down, and have a cup of tea. Mina will bring it in a minute.'

'Yes, let's have tea, Mother,' said Santa, briskly. She was a tall, gracefully proportioned young woman, dressed in tailor-made tweed skirt and jacket, hatless, with her dark brown hair neatly shingled. She carried herself upright, walking with the easy stride of an active, healthy young girl, impressing one by her bodily strength, her perfect health, and her exuberant vitality. Her face, strong rather than beautiful, was attractive in feature and colouring, her complexion strikingly fair and her large, well shaped eyes, neutral grey in tint, and long-lashed.

'And what have you two been doing?' asked Mrs Vantloo, when Ayah Mina had brought the tea. 'Or is it something you cannot tell me about?'

'Oh no. Nothing secret about it, Mrs Vantloo,' said the doctor, genially. 'A difficult confinement case, in which my young colleague here,' he bowed gracefully to Santa as he handed her cup to her, 'was of invaluable assistance. After that a visit to Sophia, Ayah Mina's daughter.'

'How is the girl?' asked Mrs Vantloo. 'Not worse, I hope.'

'No worse and no better,' replied the doctor. But I am afraid there is no question of cure. It is a mere matter of time.'

'Do you know, Mother,' said Santa, 'Sophy is very light. She is almost like a

White girl. I remarked upon it when I saw her this morning for the first time.'

'There is White blood in Ayah Mina, my dear,' said Mrs Vantloo, dispassionately. She spoke in a mild, musical voice, very low in tone, but distinct and clear. 'One does not remark upon it.'

'It's very interesting all the same, Mother,' said the girl, helping herself to bread and butter. 'It's a subject I should like to investigate, Dr Buren. It simply shrieks for investigation.'

'Better let it alone, Miss Vantloo,' remarked the doctor. 'It is one that bristles with difficulties.'

'That's why it's so interesting, Doctor,' retorted Santa. 'I had really no idea that it was so interesting before I returned. Of course I knew all about our Coloured population before I went overseas, but I had never looked at them from the point of view of one who is interested in inter-breeding. Don't you think the subject is well worth taking up?'

'Quite. For someone at the University. But scarcely for a busy practitioner who has his living to make, and who cannot afford to publish anything that will create *animus* against him.'

'I don't see how that will happen,' said Santa, argumentatively. 'After all, they all belong to the past. I mean that sort of thing does not go on nowadays with the same frequency as it did in the past ...'

'That is a matter of opinion,' exclaimed Dr Buren briskly. It is quite true that the number of mixed marriages is decreasing, according to official statistics, but that proves hardly anything.'

'It is not a very nice subject for you to apply yourself to, my dear,' said Mrs Vantloo, mildly. 'Surely there are many others which you can investigate equally well.'

'Poor Mother is still dreadfully frightened of the conventions, Doctor,' remarked Santa, in a tone of voice which the doctor thought too patronising. 'I daren't call my scientific soul my own when she is present.'

'Scientists are not supposed to have scientific souls,' Dr Buren interjected easily. Perhaps your mother is right. It is certainly not a subject which I should advise you to investigate here. To begin with we lack all laboratory conveniences ...'

'Oh, I mean to have a properly equipped lab of my own, Doctor. Father has promised me the money for it. By the way, Mother, Dr Buren made me an offer of a partnership this morning ...'

'That would be very nice for you, Santa,' said her mother, complacently.

'And for me too, I fancy,' laughed the doctor. 'I am by no means as generous as you may imagine, Mrs Vantloo. I shall exact a fair price, and I shall demand good co-partnership service. But from what I have seen of your daughter I am quite convinced that the arrangement will be of mutual benefit. Perhaps I may come over this afternoon and discuss it with your husband.'

'Do, Doctor, Elias is away just now, but he will be back this evening. If you care to drop in after dinner ...'

'That will suit me admirably. Now I must go. May I call for you at two this afternoon, Dr Vantloo?'

'Certainly, Dr Buren. But please bear in mind that my name is Santa. I feel so dreadfully old when you adopt that formal tone towards me.'

'Very well. Two o' clock then, Santa. There is a case of query Malta fever which I fancy might interest and also puzzle you. Good morning, Mrs Vantloo.' The doctor shook hands, climbed into his car, and drove off. Santa poured herself another cup of tea, and settled down in a deck chair by the side of her mother.

'You know, Motherkins,' she said, 'it will really be a splendid thing if I could buy a partnership with Dr Buren. There is no opposition, and his books show a good profit. He suggested a half share at two years' purchase.'

'What does all that mean in plain language, Santa? I am not well up in such things.'

'Probably a couple of thousand. I am not sure, but it won't be more than that. And it will bring an immediate return.'

'Still, it is a very large sum, Santa. I don't know how your father could manage it.'

'Surely I haven't spent all grandma's legacy yet, Mother? And there is your own money. You might lend me some of that, if Father's business can't stand it.'

'I am not sure, Santa, but I think you have spent much more than your legacy. You have been away nearly seven and a half years, you know. Don't think, my dear,' she said hastily, 'that father or I grudge you the money. But father says times are getting hard, and the banks are difficult. Still, I think it may be managed. Your uncle might be able to help.'

'I don't like sponging on Uncle Jerry,' said Santa, pouting. 'And really I do not see why father can't raise such a sum, especially as there will be an almost immediate return. Why, the business must be doing splendidly, if Eric can build himself a house like the one he intends to build.'

'That is really for you, Santa,' said her mother, smilingly. 'He started on the plans as soon as you wrote that you were returning.'

'I wish you would not take it for granted that I am going to marry Eric,' said Santa irritably. 'Since I came back I have heard nothing but Eric's praises. I am getting a little tired of it all.'

'But, my dear, we have always understood ...'

'I know. That is the devil of it. You look upon it as an understanding, and as a matter of fact there is really nothing at all between us. We have never been engaged ...'

'But Eric has asked you, my dear. And, Santa, your language, dear ...'

'Oh, there's nothing in it to bother about, Mother. One gets into the way of using such expressions occasionally, and they are expressive enough. Eric has asked me—he asked me this morning again, as a matter of fact, when I met him in the street—fancy proposing in the street, Mother—and I told him I had no intention of marrying yet. I altogether object to being tied down just when I am about to make a start.'

'Well, my dear, you know your own feelings best. Not that father and I will not be very glad if you were to accept Eric. He is a good boy and will make you a good husband. We both like him very much, and we have known him since he was a boy. You would please us very much ...'

'I won't tie myself to please anybody,' retorted Santa, firmly. 'And I should loathe being tied up just when I have a chance of working on my own. As for Eric, I like him well enough, though I wonder why he is such a favourite with you and father. In politics you are as wide apart as the poles. That is one reason I won't have him.'

'My dear, politics have nothing to do with marriage. Eric is SAP but that does not mean that he is not a good boy. In fact ...'

'In fact he is all the better for being SAP, Motherkins. Oh, I know you are still hankering after the old love.'

'How can you say that, Santa? I have never given you or your father cause to think that my views are different from yours.'

'Oh no. But I can see through you, Motherkins. You are half-hearted in supporting us, and I do believe that you don't want woman suffrage.'

'That is not a plank of your Party platform,' said her mother, smilingly. 'Indeed, I suspect that the Party is as opposed to it as you say I am.'

'But father isn't. He is all in favour of it, while Eric objects to it.'

'Your father sometimes sees further than other people, my dear. But on this point he is possibly mistaken ...'

'Not on your life, Mother. You will see the Nationalists giving us woman-suffrage before we are out of office ...'

'Which you tell me will not be for a very long time yet, my dear. However, by all means support it. I don't mind. Have I ever minded your doing anything which was not patently wrong?'

'No, you old dear, you haven't. But I do wish you would not harp on Eric. It gets on my nerves. He has never done a thing in his life ...'

'My dear, my dear! He is your father's partner; he has done a great deal of good work in the District. He has done splendidly at his profession.'

'That's not what I mean. He has never shown that he has any shred of real greatness or ability in him. Not like father. Father has done great things, and has suffered for his convictions. You know, Mother, if I were to be a man I should like to be just like father. I think he is the nicest, finest, straightest member of the sex I have yet met.'

'But I don't want you to be a man, my dear. I want you to be my girl. I hardly like to see you trying to imitate men. Your father, of course, is all that you say, and even a girl may model herself on him, but, Santa dear, you must bear in mind that we are all old fashioned here. If you become a doctor's partner, you must remember that it does not do to antagonise people ...'

'There you go again, Mother. O, I am sick of it! You are just like the SAP—you are at heart a SAP. We mustn't do this and we mustn't do that for fear of antagonising people. We must commit national suicide to placate people who have never done a thing to please us. Can't you see that the more we do that, the less likely we are to win people's respect? It's just what Lowell said ...'

'What did he say, my dear. And who is Mr Lowell?'

'Lowell is a sentimental American poet. You have him in the drawing room bound in padded leather—one of aunt Gertrude's christmasings to you. He wrote some sensible things, however, and he said:

> 'Conciliate—it just means be kicked
> No matter how you phrase and term it
> It means that you're to set down licked
> And be damn fools and glad to learn it ...'

Something like that, anyhow, although I expect I have got the last line wrong for it doesn't rhyme. But that is the sense of it. I'm sick of it all, and whether the Village likes it or not, I don't care. I shall just go my own way.'

'One can't always go one's own way, my dear,' said her mother, gently. 'And one must respect public opinion. I had to when I first came.'

'You must have had a dev—I'm sorry, Mother—you must have had a bad time of it. Did they really censure you for going to a dance?'

'It was not as bad as that, Santa. And they were worse than that to others. Poor Mr Uhlmann—he was the pastor, you know, before your time. He played on the violin, beautifully, my dear, for he had been well trained in Europe, and at one time he thought of being a professional musician, but his father was set on his becoming a missionary. Then he came out here, for his wife got ill in India and they had to come away. He entered our church and was called here, and the first month he used to play his violin on the *stoep* in the twilight. I often listened to him for he played beautifully. Mozart and Beethoven chiefly, but sometimes Italian things with a lilt in it. But the church council did not like it, and it sent a deputation to ask him to stop playing godless things. I remember there was a squabble. Old Mr Nolte—they used to call him Gallows-Gecko for he had been an executioner in his time—said it was a shame, and got so excited over it that he had a stroke and died the day after the council meeting.'

'What was a shame? Surely they did not mean it?'

'Of course they meant it. Mr Nolte protested against the decision, but the majority was in favour and so they sent the deputation.'

'And what did Mr Uhlmann do?'

'He gave them coffee and cake, and listened to what they had to say, and then he locked up his violin case and never opened it till the day of his death. When he was dying he called for the key, and had the case opened, and he lay fingering the bow when he died.'

'What a ... shame, Mother. But I couldn't do that. I would have given them a piece of my mind. They must have been pretty awful folk.'

'By no means, my dear. They were very nice folk. You can have no conception of what they were like, although you ought to remember some of them.'

'I remember the frumpy old person who was always telling us that her brother-in-law—or was it uncle-in-law—was an admiral of the fleet. She was an insufferable old bore, and she always pawed me, and smelt of some strong scent.'

'That was old Mrs Quakerley, my dear. She used opodeldoc and always wore a tiny bit of ambergris in her brooch. She was rather silly, but very good natured at heart. I remember her father-in-law, old Mr Charles Quakerley. He was one of the early settlers, and a very fine old gentleman, a friend of Lord Charles Somerset, and a great aristocrat. *Quakerskloof* used to be their farm, but it was burned during the war, and subsequently sold.'

'Yes, my dear,' Mrs Vantloo went on, 'you have no idea how friendly people were in those days. There was a large English section here in the District, and they got on very well with us, though very few could speak Afrikaans and fewer of us could speak English. Aunt Gertrude's grandfather, old Uncle Martin Rekker, one of the aristocrats of the District, and Mr Nolte were perhaps the only ones who could speak English fluently. But there was none of that agitation which we have nowadays, for their politics did not lead to quarrelsomeness, and they differed like gentlemen. I remember the old Queen's jubilee in 1887. The Village was illuminated and I went with my father to have a look at the windows. We all sent the Queen a jubilee present—the District subscribed, and they formed committees in every ward, and even the Coloured people had a share in it. But the war changed all that, my dear. If it weren't for the war, and those unhappy things that occurred, then we should have been better off than we are.'

'The war was only one factor,' said Santa, in her argumentative voice. 'And it was a jolly good thing it came. It served to solidify us. The only pity is that we didn't all take a hand in it ...'

'My dear, don't say such dreadful things,' expostulated her mother. 'You have no conception of what we suffered when the commandos came into this District. They had no business here, but they came merely to recruit men from among us ...'

'Quite right, too. Our men ought to have gone in the first place.'

'Then I would say nothing my dear, for it would have been their own look-out. But that is not what happened. The commandos came and forced these men to join them, knowing that as rebels they would have to take a chance of being shot if they were captured by the English. I call that wicked—wicked and cowardly—for those who egged them on were perfectly safe and knew they were. If they were caught they could only be kept as prisoners of war, but every one of our boys stood a chance of being shot. Most of them were ruined, and it makes me angry, my dear, when I think of it.'

'You'll never learn to see things in their right perspective, Motherkins,' declared Santa, unable to argue the point, which had never before been presented to her from this aspect. 'After all, one must make some sacrifice for one's ideals. Didn't Aunt Gertrude's father fight for the Republics?'

'No. He said he would have nothing to do with the commandos, but the English removed him from the farm and sent him to a prison camp. His eldest son was forced to join the commandos, and was shot, I don't rightly know where. But you know what the place is like now, their farm I mean. And in the old days it was one of the show farms in the District. The Governor visited it and stayed with old Uncle Martin many times. It is a great pity, my dear.'

'Never mind, Motherkins. Everything will come right in the end, as President Brand said ...'

'Yes, but he added "if everyone did his duty," and I don't think we are doing our duty today. But don't let us speak any more about it. My chest is troubling me and I think I ought to lie down before luncheon.'

'Would you like me to give an injection, Mother? It stops your asthma, you know, and it is quite safe,' said Santa, solicitously.

'No, my dear. Perhaps tonight. It is chilly of an evening, and cold weather always makes my asthma worse. I shall go and lie down. What will you do?'

'I thought of going to the location to see Sophy again. I am not quite satisfied with her condition. Of course she is Buren's patient, but he won't mind.'

Mrs Vantloo appeared to hesitate, but she made no comment. 'The girl has consumption,' went on Santa, 'and her pulse is bad. I am rather interested in her.'

'Very well. But ...' Mrs Vantloo did not complete her qualifying sentence. She got up slowly from her chair, and Santa took her arm and gently escorted her indoors.

Chapter 4

The Village location, where the Coloured people, reinforced by a number of Natives, lived had, like the Village itself, suffered in the war which, almost thirty years before, had ruined so much that had been beautiful in the Valley. Formerly the location had been something of which its inhabitants and the Village had been proud. Its houses, although unpretentious and poor, had been neat, clean, well thatched and, even in their poverty, dignified, with patches of carefully cultivated garden in front of each, and with trees shading the small, low *stoeps*. The trees had been cut down, the gardens had been destroyed, and the houses themselves had suffered through fire. In the location street there were ruins of walls, the remnants of houses that had never been rebuilt. They stood as glaring momentoes of the time when no one knew what the next morning would bring, when the commandos were scurrying about the Valley, and when martial law ruled in the Village and District. Few cared to remember that time. The location preferred to forget it, as a bad nightmare which had come upon it with unexpected and lamentable suddenness, a visitation from God for sins which they could not specify but had no doubt they had once committed. For the location believed in an anthropomorphic god, in one who took a very personal interest in human affairs and visited with prompt retribution any dereliction from the code which had been drawn up for the wandering desert folk who had fled out of the land of Goshen because the masters had refused to let them make bricks in peace.

In the location lived nearly all the non-European inhabitants of the Village. A privileged few possessed houses lower down near the water furrow, just outside the limits of the location, and although the municipality had tried to oust these, in an attempt to make them reside in the location, they had so far resisted and had succeeded in retaining title to their holdings. How long they would continue to do so was a question they did not care to discuss, for since the war everything was unstable, and there was even talk, nowadays, of taking away their votes from them. The location shook its head when such matters were mentioned, but it felt that its tenure was precarious, and it took good care not to disturb the existing routine of things.

Ayah Mina's house stood at the Village end of the long location street. Like its neighbours it was a low walled, red-thatched house, with a little *stoep* in front on which fuchsias and petunias blossomed in green painted petrol tins. Four pepper trees had formerly shaded the house, but these had been chopped down for firewood in the old war days, and now the sun beat down upon the thatch and discoloured the whitewash of the walls almost as soon as a new coat was applied. Inside were three rooms, a small dining or common room, opening on to the *stoep*, and two small bedrooms. The kitchen was a hang-to structure, made of bricks and sheet iron, and only used for such cooking as could not be done out of doors. The little house was meanly furnished, for Ayah Mina took no pride in it. Formerly she had done so, and she could remember a time when it had been the best house in the location, with a neat little garden in front, skin rugs on the dining room floor, and curtains to the windows. The garden had been destroyed; in front of the *stoep* there was now waste veld, which in winter was passably green and starred with yellow daisies and pink sorrels, and in summer a scorched, barren strip of yellow sand, tortured by the wind and baked into hard clay where the refuse water from the kitchen had been poured upon it. The curtains were still there, but they had not been darned, and their rents flapped when the breeze blew in through the open windows. The house had been looted, and most of the furniture destroyed, and Ayah Mina had not troubled to repair the damage. She lived for the most part at the 'big house' where she had a room, but she still retained her location home because Sophia had to have a place to stay in.

Sophia occupied the larger bedroom, the only room of the three upon which Ayah Mina had lavished some care and attention. Its one small window was curtained with a bit of casement cloth; a strip of linoleum lay on the mud floor. Its furniture consisted of a large, old fashioned bed, whose coverings were clean and neat, an improvised wash-stand made out of petrol cases, with utensils of tin, and a dresser of cedarwood, that had originally decorated the kitchen in the big house. On the walls were framed photographs of the old mistress herself, and of the little missie, a group taken at the mission station when Ayah Mina had been at school there, and a snapshot of a Queen's birthday celebration in the Village—faded, discoloured relics of the past which had found a resting place here in the room where Sophia spent most of her time on the bed.

For Sophia was dying of consumption. Ayah Mina knew that her daughter was too ill for human effort to cure her, and she had long ago given up all hope and resigned herself to the inevitable. Sophia was a relic, like those half-faded photographs. She too was faded, a thin, burned-out lathe of a girl, whose age it would have been difficult to guess. As a matter of fact Sophia was twenty-four years old, four years younger than the little missie, who was now a doctor and had come back to try and do what no self-respecting White missie should do. Ayah Mina had nursed Santa; to her Santa would always be the little missie, whom she had petted and spoiled, and whom she secretly admired as a hen may be expected to admire a swan that it had foster-mothered. Like the hen she wondered at the strange freaks that her pet displayed, but she found herself unable to influence the little missie, and she had long ago decided that it was much better policy to let her nursling go her own way without trying to interfere.

Sophia was different. Sophia was her own daughter, and Ayah Mina had brought her up with a disciplinary strictness which had at times verged on harshness. The girl had had little chance, and by the time she had grown old enough to assert herself she had found herself more than ever dependent upon her mother on account of her illness. A short period of service, away from the Village, had introduced her into a new life and a new atmosphere, but from it she had come back to the location in a state that had thoroughly frightened her mother. Ayah Mina blamed herself, needlessly, for the germs of the disease that had attacked her daughter could scarcely have been defeated by her care, although she imagined that her own harshness had contributed to weakening the girl. At the first examination, four years ago, Dr Buren had shaken his head, and told her quite plainly that Sophia's one lung was affected.

'It is consumption, right enough, Ayah Mina,' he had said, when he and she had talked on the *stoep* afterwards. 'The girl has picked it up down there,'—he swept his hands towards the hills beyond which lay, far off, the capital where Sophia had been in service. 'Here there's little of it, and fortunately our air is pure. Give her as much of it as you can. Feed her up; strengthen her. That is all you can do. Send somebody down for the medicine; I'll give her a draught for the cough, but it's little medicine can do for her, Ayah Mina. It's good food and fresh air she wants, and perhaps we may pull her through, although I doubt it.'

'That is all right, Doctor,' she had answered, tonelessly. 'If it must be, it must, and perhaps it is better so ... for Sophia.'

'I understand,' said the doctor, gravely. 'But while there's life, there's hope, Ayah Mina. And ... I don't want to meddle in your affairs; they are no business of mine; but if you want anything ... if anything happens to the girl ... why, woman, you know what I mean?'

'Doctor means no doubt Sophy's father,' said Ayah Mina, dispassionately. 'That need not be talked of. It is too late for that. Sophia is my child, Doctor, and I can do all that needs doing for her.'

'Quite so. But she'll need more than you can give her, Ayah Mina. And if by any chance there is a likelihood ...'

'There is none, Doctor. It is twenty-five years a-gone. It is too late now. She is my child ...'

'But not your husband's, Ayah Mina,' said the doctor, brusquely. 'I know that. She has far more White blood in her than you have. I have never meddled with these things, but if I can do anything ... I suppose he was one of those who were here at the time, and you have lost sight of him ...'

'No, Doctor is mistaken,' said the old woman, quietly. It was not one of those Doctor means. Nor have I lost sight of him. But that is my business. No one knows but Doctor and myself, so why trouble about it?'

'Well, well, it is your business, not mine. But do your best for the girl. They will help you at the big house. I'll look in again.'

Dr Buren had looked in regularly, but his ministrations had not done Sophia much good. She had weakened, grown thinner, begun to cough up blood, to lose her appetite, to complain of being too wearied to drag herself about. Now she lay there on the big bed, a thin, wasted lathe of a girl, looking whiter than she had ever done before because the tinge of red on her malar bones made her complexion seem less brown than Ayah Mina had always taken it to be. Before her illness Sophia would not have attracted too much attention in a Coloured community where the girls had all shades of complexion; now, when her features were sharpened by disease, it was plain to anyone who looked upon her that she was more than a quarter White. Sometimes, when she lay asleep, breathing more quietly than when awake, her mother felt her hands and noticed how long and shapely her fingers were; felt, too, surreptitiously, the point of her nose and missed the sharp projection of the nasal cartilage which would have proclaimed her pure White. That gave Ayah Mina a sense of satisfaction. Sophia was, after all, more hers than her unknown White father's, whose name she would never know, whose aid Ayah Mina would never call in to save Sophia from a disease which was slowly killing her.

Ayah Mina had never felt any great affection for her daughter. There had been times when she hated Sophia, but these times were past, and now she only felt a great pity which she struggled, unsuccessfully, to change into a protective love. She told herself that she would do everything in her power to make Sophia's passing as comfortable as possible, but she never hid from herself the thought that she considered it better that Sophia should die than that she should continue to live on in a world wherein she was an outsider, a pariah, with less chance of rehabilitation than what her mother had had.

When the little missie had returned from abroad, a fully qualified doctor, Ayah Mina had been glad to hear that Santa had gone to the location to visit Sophia. Santa had known the girl from childhood; the two had played together on occasion when Santa was a small child, and the understanding between them had always been friendly. Santa had been genuinely shocked to hear of Sophia's illness, and much more distressed when she had assured herself that Dr Buren's diagnosis was correct. She had found Ayah Mina's attitude inexplicable, and had commented upon it with her customary outspokenness to her mother.

'Sophy is really very ill, Mother,' she had said, 'and we should try and get her away. I suggested it to Ayah Mina. I offered to pay for it myself. But Ayah Mina seems to want the girl to die. I can't understand it ...'

'After all, Sophia's condition is hopeless,' Mrs Vantloo had argued. 'You yourself say it is only a matter of time. Then why trouble Ayah Mina about it? Naturally she would like to have the girl here. We can do our best for her here, my dear.'

'Yes, but it is so unfeeling, Mother. I was shocked when I saw Sophy. She is so ...'

'Yes, I have seen her. I go to see her sometimes, Santa, though Mina tries to keep me away. She does not like me to go.'

'That's it, Mother. She seems to want the girl all to herself. She almost told me not to come again, but I'll show her that she can't have her own way when it comes to Sophy.'

'Perhaps you'd better not go too much, Santa. Dr Buren looks after her, and you know Ayah Mina does not regard you as a real doctor. She still looks upon you as a child—as her little missie ...'

'I know. That's the ... really, Mother, one does get exasperated when one thinks of it. Everyone looks upon me as a child, and it's getting on my nerves. Only yesterday old Mrs Smith told me I should now let my hair grow ...'

'Yes, my dear. They came to me about it. And the pastor's wife does not like your dress. By the way, she suggested that it was time you saw about your certificate of membership. After all, you were confirmed, Santa.'

'Don't remind me of it, please, Mother. It was just before my matric, and I suppose it had to be done, but I am very sorry that I ever did it. I suppose it'll have to stand, although I don't intend to communicate ...'

'My dear, you will think better of it. Consider what it will mean to us all—to your father, my dear.'

'I should not like to do anything to pain father,' said Santa, reflectively. 'But in a matter like that, Mother, surely I can do as I like.'

'Not here, dear,' said her mother, gently. 'Father is senior Elder of the church and that implies a certain amount of responsibility. I can understand your point of view. I don't say you are right ...'

'You wouldn't,' said Santa, and her mother winced involuntarily at the good natured, protective contemptuousness in the girl's voice. 'You would naturally take their view. But father wouldn't. Father does not really care what people say. He is strong enough to go his own way, and if he agrees it will make no difference to me.'

'Well, my dear, you'd better speak to father about it then. But please bear in mind that father is an Elder of the church, and that he would not like people to think that his daughter dislikes the church. If you really wish to join Dr Buren and stay on here, you should remember that our people have their own conventions. It is not as if you settled at Cape Town. There no one would mind. But here it is different, my dear. Here everyone knows everything about everyone else, and we are easily shocked ...'

'I'll give you something to be shocked about,' declared Santa, laughingly. 'But I'll have a talk to father first. After all, he is the person most concerned, and I should hate to do anything that hurt him. Why, Mother, father has been my hero all through and I should never do anything of which he is likely to feel ashamed.'

'That is right, my dear. That is all I ask of you. And,' Mrs Vantloo was evidently desirous of changing the subject, 'do you really think Sophia is dangerously ill?'

'Of course she is, Mother. Her one lung, or what remains of it, is collapsed. The other is riddled. One more haemorrhage will finish her. Do you know, Mother, Sophia looks almost pure White. I wonder how Ayah Mina ...'

'I think my wheezing is coming on again, Santa,' said Mrs Vantloo, hastily. 'You might get me some of that medicine you put up for me yesterday. It does me good.'

'The ephedrine? I'll run and get it, Mother. But really, you ought to go to the Karroo. You never get asthma there, and you should live there. I'll have to talk to father about it.'

'No, no, my dear. I get asthma everywhere. It is in my system, but your new medicine eases me wonderfully. It is good to have a daughter who is such a clever doctor ...'

Santa talked to her colleague about the case. She pointed out that Sophia should have the chance of dry, dustless air, such as the climate of the high lands; she expatiated upon the value of actinotherapy in tuberculosis, and upon the usefulness of vitamins. Dr Buren, whose acquaintance with these things was largely vicarious, gathered through reading rather than from clinical experience, nodded his head and agreed. And when Santa touched upon the one point that above all others interested her most, Sophia's Whiteness, the doctor switched the conversation round to an abstruse case which had puzzled both of them, and immersed himself in technical details. Santa was annoyed, but she had no opportunity to return to the point.

She visited Sophia frequently. The location, already impressed, greeted her with respectful admiration when she came, and voiced its appreciation in guttural murmurs when she left. Sometimes Ayah Mina was there, watching over Sophia with jealous care, as it seemed to Santa. Ayah Mina's demeanour was always respectful, subservient, submissive, but Santa gained the impression that it was always watchful, suspicious, and a little deprecatory. She appeared to be more concerned about Santa's comfort than about Sophia's sickness. She remained in the room, and when she was not there, another woman from the location, a toothless, withered old woman who acted as the location midwife, nurse and layer-out of corpses, was always in attendance. Sophia was never left alone. Which was as it should have been, for Sophia was dying of consumption and needed all the care that the location could give her.

Chapter 5

Tuesday evening was lodge night, and Elias Vantloo allowed nothing to interfere with his attendance at the lodge meeting. It was a dwindling band of enthusiastic fanatics who gathered in the village schoolroom on Tuesday evenings at eight o' clock, and went stolidly through the ritual prescribed by that particular society to which they owed allegiance. In pre-war years—the Village dating the cessation of its 'war' back to 1902 instead of to 1918—there had been a much larger company, which had included many of the elite of the District, for a teetotal advocate had preached for a week and inscribed all who came forward to take the pledge, making, so far as this simple admission of a determination to give up strong drink was concerned, no difference between White and Black. But when it came to the formation of a lodge, public opinion had rapidly crystallised in favour of separate organisations, times of meeting, and locale. The lodge to which the Coloureds and Natives belonged bore the name of 'Star of Eve,' while that to which the White inhabitants came had been named 'Success.' The ritual of both remained, as it had been in pre-war days, largely English, although Elias had insisted that for the 'Success' lodge Afrikaans should be used on alternate weeks. The 'Star of Eve' affected a cheerful green for its regalia, while its White co-partner favoured a royal blue, edged with gold.

On lodge nights the 'big house' dined early. Formerly it had dined, in conformity with the custom of the Village, in the middle of the day, and there were still inhabitants who remembered the time when the fashionable dining hour had been five o' clock in the afternoon. But that was in the days when the old customs still lingered, and these had now been completely displaced. Elias led the new fashion, and the Village followed tamely. On Sundays, dinner was served at midday, and a cold collation eaten in the evening. As the 'big house' was inclined to linger over its principal meal, which was usually served at half past seven, the dinner hour was advanced to seven on lodge nights so as to give the old master and the old mistress ample time to get ready for the meeting.

On her return from abroad, Santa had been initiated into this household custom which she had found mildly amusing. She had refused to take part in the play, and had expressed her opinion about the mummery of it with tactless sincerity. Neither her father nor her mother had resented her remarks. Elias was used to criticism of his teetotal activities; it was, perhaps, the one thing in which he ran consistently counter to local opinion, which had long since become converted to a saner view than that enunciated by the enthusiastic teetotal preacher who had come crusading from the capital and enlisted old and young under the banner of Good Templary. The Village had repented its initial fervour, and was a trifle ashamed of its activities in the past. The Band of Hope had dwindled, and the members, when they reached the age of discretion, had deemed themselves absolved from their allegiance and reverted to tobacco and wine, instead of coming forward as recruits to the adult lodges. These were now merely remnants of what they had been, and their membership was still dwindling, notwithstanding the example set by Elias Vantloo and his wife. The Village never thoroughly believed in the new gospel, and time had shown that the existence of the two lodges did not make much difference to the community. It had never been a hard-drinking community, and its professional drunkards were safely inscribed on the black list, known to all canteen keepers, and more or less innocuous. Elias Vantloo and his teetotal activities were regarded with philosophic detachment, amounting almost to indifference, which would have been complete were it not for the sneaking respect felt for one who so consistently and courageously persisted in preaching a doctrine which it thought utterly unnecessary and therefore a little vulgar. It never expressed itself in plain language, for the Village was tolerant of many things, and a difference of opinion on matters that did not really matter was one of the things that it agreed to tolerate with equanimity.

To an outsider Elias Vantloo's loyalty to his lodge was one of the puzzling characteristics of a personality which represented many anomalies. Convivial by temperament, a lover of good material things, and a man of the world, Elias was the last person one would have thought capable of riding a hobby to the death of a harmless habit. Everyone in the Village and the District, with the exception of those few who, like him, had sworn to forsake alcohol, took wine or brandy in moderation. Some of the farmers made wine and distilled their own brandy; Elias himself held mortgages on farms whose owners depended on their vineyards for their livelihood. That the Village knew, but no one dreamed of questioning the Elder's sincerity in denouncing strong drink as the root of all evil. Perhaps because he had known, from the first, that no one would delve too deeply into matters in which public interest found no great pleasure in speculating, Elias had persisted in his policy of teetotalism. At any rate he had found such persistence profitable to him in his business. Through it he had obtained the reputation of being a thoroughly sober, conscientious, somewhat straight-laced citizen, whose membership of the licensing board was a benefit to the community which could rest secure and safe, knowing that so long as so conscientious a judge presided over the apportioning of permits for the sale of liquor in the District, no increase of crime from drunkenness need be anticipated.

The 'big house' had dined early, true to its custom on lodge evenings. It had been a family dinner, and Santa had enjoyed the intimacy of it, as she had enjoyed similar dinners since her return from Europe. Mother had sat at the end of the big cedarwood dining table, facing father at the opposite end, and she had sat between them, a vast expanse of empty space on either side of her and a long length of table in front of her. Ayah Mina, an excellent cook, had served a meal worthy of her culinary skill, a simple, well-cooked dinner such as the old master delighted to eat because it not only pleased the palate but pandered also to his nationalistic taste. Home baked bread, crisp edged and loose in the crumb, made from farm wheat ground between stone rollers by the home-made machinery in some oak-shaded farm mill-house where the water splashed monotonously over the slits of the big wooden wheel and the big tarantula spiders twinkled their diamond eyes from between the cobwebs dusty with the powdered flour; white bean soup, richly creamed and served with snippets of black toasted bread; a savoury stew made from the half-opened buds of the scented aponogeton, the white, pink-tinged little water lily that grew in masses on the river ponds; deliciously steamed rice with every grain separate and distinct from its fellow, fully expanded and glistening in its miniver whiteness; sweet potatoes, amber coloured, in a thin syrup; a braized muscovy duck, meltingly tender, stuffed with onions and sage; a salad of cooked beetroot, decorated with hard boiled eggs; and for dessert a baked custard with stewed dried peaches, sun-dried, and flavoured with cinnamon and the peel of tangerine orange. With the coffee, strong, subtly aromatic, for the beans had been freshly roasted and ground that afternoon, there should have been a glass of van der Hum liqueur, or at least of that rich golden muscadel whose taste lingers on the palate. But the 'big house' tolerated no strong drink, and it was Elias's boast that in his cellar there was only ginger beer and vinegar.

Now, as he sat sipping his coffee, Santa found herself looking at him with absorbed interest. She had always found him an interesting personality. As a small girl he had represented all that her conception of a man demanded. His figure was still good, although its curves sagged, and his cheeks were too rounded and full to harmonise wholly with the rest of his face. His eyes, too, were deep set, the lids too fleshy, the nostrils too wide, perhaps, and the chin a shade weaker than she had imagined it to be. His colouring was florid, but that was perhaps from his blood pressure which was no doubt high. Father had always suffered from his heart, although what exactly was the matter with it she had not been able to find out. He had evaded her cross-questioning about his symptoms, and she had not liked to press the matter, especially when he had told her that Buren had recently examined and prescribed for him. His medicine stood on the dresser; every morning and evening he took a dose of it. She had uncorked the bottle and smelt it, but she had not been able to tell what its ingredients were, beyond remarking that it had an odour which was strongly reminiscent of spirit. Probably a liquid extract of gentian with a little strophanthus; that was Buren's standby in such cases, and at any rate it would do no harm. Santa did not believe in drugs. She did not believe in many things, but she had a definite opinion of her own on drugs, and such experience as she had had seemed to her convincingly in favour of the inefficiency of much of the medication which Dr Buren was in the habit of prescribing. She jerked herself back from her reflections to reply to a mild remark of her mother, and resented, unconsciously, the interference which had distracted her from her study of her father. Already she blamed herself for looking at him in the way she had done. She preferred to regard him as she had done when a child, seeing perfection only in his features and form, reading into that smug complacency nothing but a charitable forbearance, a humane kindliness, a determined honesty of expression, agreeable to the soul with which she had dowered him. Whatever blurred the image, those lines that did not fit into the picture, that shifting glance which seemed diffident to meet her own, she knew could only be the result of fatigue, of mental worry and physical tiredness. Father was getting on in years—why, he must be well in the fifties, and the strenuous, exacting life he led ... It was really too bad of Eric. She would have to speak to him about it. To him and to Buren. Father was doing more than his fair share of work. It was just as well that she had come home to look after him ...

'You don't mind, my dear,' her mother's plaintively mild voice droned, 'you won't mind being left alone tonight? Father and I have to attend the lodge—there is an initiation ...'

'Even if there were no initiation,' said Elias, 'it would still be the same. You and I have not missed one single meeting now for five years, Mother.' He spoke in a singularly high pitched voice for one so massive of figure and so thick necked. 'And if

Santa does not wish to accompany us, why then, my little girl must find something to occupy herself with until we return.' Santa came back to the present. What an ungrateful beast she had been to sneer at father's little hobby. If it pleased him to play in the lodge regalia, why not? It was a harmless fad. She repressed her inclination to make a pert remark, and nodded her head instead.

'I shall be all right, Father,' she said cheerfully. 'Eric threatened to call tonight, and perhaps the Doctor and his wife will look in. Don't worry about me. I have plenty to do.'

'Do keep Mrs Buren until we return,' said her mother, 'and Eric too. We might have some music. Telephone Eric and ask him to bring his cello.'

'Very well, Mother. But you are passing him on your way. You might leave a message.'

'I will do so,' said Mrs Vantloo, rising. 'Come, Father, we must get ready.'

Santa went to the drawing room and turned on the electric light. She selected a book from the well-stocked shelf, and came back into the dining room. Her mother and father had already left, and the maids, under the supervision of Ayah Mina, who hovered in the background admonishing and directing with the assiduity of a pernickety overseer, were clearing the table.

'I am going to my room, Ayah Mina,' she said. If anyone calls, come and tell me who it is.'

'It is sure to be Master Eric,' said the old woman. 'Shall I get out the preserves, Missie? There are lovely green figs. Master Eric likes them.'

'Get what you like, Ayah Mina. Only let me know who comes.'

'Shall I bring Missie some coffee? Missie has only had one cup. There is plenty of hot milk.'

'No thank you, Ayah Mina. I have to do some writing. How is Sophia tonight?'

'Just as usual, Missie. The cough plagues her. That stuff the doctor gives us is no good. Won't Missie give her a draught?'

'I'll talk to the doctor about it, Ayah Mina. Let her suck the lozenges; they will ease her cough.'

She went down the corridor to her room, and took out her note books. It was time she wrote some notes, and there would be time before the visitors came to do so. Santa was a quick worker; she had been trained in method in a good school, and her clerking had been commended. Before very long, she was immersed in her work, and had forgotten about her disturbing reflections at dinner.

The maids departed into the kitchen, and Ayah Mina turned down the lights. A door opened and Elias entered the dining room. He was dressed for his lodge meeting, in frock coat and black trousers, immaculately creased, and wore a white tie. Over his waistcoat, suspended by the broad royal-blue ribbon edged with gold, hung his master's jewel, partly concealed by the sash. In his hand he carried the regulation high hat, neatly brushed and ironed.

He went to the dresser and Ayah Mina came forward with a tumbler and a carafe of water. He took up the medicine bottle and poured out a dose, diluted it with water, and tossed it off. Ayah Mina looked at him steadily while he did so, her old, haggard face expressionless.

'It is for the heart, Mina,' he said, apologetically. 'By doctor's orders. Otherwise such poison would not pass my lips.'

'I filled it up this morning,' said the old woman, stolidly. But the bottle is now empty, Old Master. I must have another.'

'You shall have it, Mina. But be secret. I have noticed that Miss Santa smelt it once. You might put some peppermint in it next time.'

'No. Old Master must get some real medicine from the doctor and put some of that in. The little missie is no longer a child. I suspect she knows. Old Master should tell her. It may be that, inadvertently, she says something which may open the old mistress's eye. Old Master would not like that.'

'No, no, Mina. That must not be. But, be quick. Here she comes. Give me another glass of water. And the coffee beans ... no stay, I have a peppermint lozenge. That does better.' He put the bottle back on the dresser, wiped his mouth with a handkerchief, and adjusted his scarf. Mrs Vantloo came into the room, stately in black and lace, with her regalia round her neck, fumbling with her long black gloves.

'Have you taken your medicine, Father?' she asked, and without waiting for a reply went on, 'do take your overcoat. It is chilly outside. Ayah Mina, get the old master's coat. Leave the glass, I want a drink ...'

'I have one for Missis,' said the old woman, quickly. 'This one still has the medicine taste. Here Missis. Now I go fetch the old master's coat.'

'Mina is getting too old for the house,' said Elias, grumblingly. 'We should pension her off, Mother. She's not worth her keep.'

'You promised me, Father, that Mina should stay,' said Mrs Vantloo, her voice a little less mild than usual. 'She has been with us since our marriage. She is a good soul, and she does her best. I don't know what I should do without her, Father.'

'All right, Have it your own way. Perhaps it's as well. Come along, my dear, come along. It won't do to keep them all waiting. Mina, lock the door, and look after the little missie. We shall be back about ten, perhaps a couple of minutes later.'

'You might put out the tea things, Mina,' said Mrs Vantloo, preparing to follow her husband through the door which the old woman held open for them, 'and the preserves, too. Open the fresh jar of chow-chow—the one which came yesterday. And some cake and biscuits ... or make some sandwiches. If Mrs Buren comes, tell her we shan't be long. And let the maids ...'

Her voice trailed off in the night air, and Ayah Mina closed the door, and locked it. Then she went to the table and rinsed the glass from which Elias had drunk, pouring the rinsings into a little pannikin. She took up the medicine bottle, uncorked it and smelt it.

'Hm,' she muttered, 'missie must be stupid if she can't tell what that is. It is pure brandy, that's what it is. The sin of it, and him with his lodge palavering and poison chatter. The sin of it. But he is like that, black to his heart's core, and nobody knows it but I. Though I suspect Master Eric has his suspicions, and that is the worst of it. The sin of it. I thank the little Lord that He made my old missis so simple that she can't see what is just beyond her nose, for it will break Missis Maria's heart, poor thing, if she suspects how he cheats and sins. Damn him ... damn him. But the old missis must never know ... never. I should not mind the little missie knowing—after all she has her years, and she pretends to be so man-like, well then, let her learn what men are really like. But not Missis Maria ... it will break her dear heart for she loves him and she will always love him ... damn him.'

And Ayah Mina replaced the medicine bottle on the shelf with a viciousness that threatened to crack it but fortunately only indented the soft cedarwood planking.

Chapter 6

When Santa came down to the drawing room, in response to Ayah Mina's intimation that 'Master Eric's there, Missie, and I have put out the tea things,' she found her father's partner waiting for her.

'I came early on purpose, Santa,' he said, frankly. 'I knew the old people are away, and I want to talk to you.'

'Sit down, Eric,' she released her hands, both of which he had grasped, and sat down. 'Sit there. If you have a cigarette, give me one, and smoke yourself. Or a pipe, if you prefer it. Mother does not object, even in the drawing room, though father sometimes fusses when he sees me smoking.'

He took out his cigarette case and handed it to her, lighting her cigarette for her, but made no attempt to fill his pipe.

'I came on purpose,' he repeated. 'Won't you have me, Santa? I asked you this morning, as I asked you when you came back, and I ask you now. Let me have the right to protect you, to care for you, Santa. You know I have always wanted you.'

'My dear boy, you have always thought you did,' she responded, briskly. 'But I am not so sure that it will be good for you to get what you want or think you would like. And when you take that high and mighty tone with me, you won't make any progress. Protect me, indeed! What do you think I am?'

'I only know that you are the one woman I want, Santa,' he said, earnestly, 'and that you are not mine. I only know that I cannot protect you—yes, as much as you may dislike it, I repeat it, for I want to have that right. That is the only real right a husband has. Give it to me, Santa.'

She regarded him fixedly, comparing him, just as she had done a few hours previously when she had looked at her father, with the uncertain image she had formed of him in her mind. She had gone away, nearly eight years ago, without any fixed feelings about him. Then he had been merely a clear, wholesome-looking young man, with whom she had associated on terms of equality, whom she had enslaved to her whims and bent to her desires. She had always placed him in the same category wherein she had put her mother, as one belonging to those who were of the earth's weaklings, devoid of that rugged strength of mind and character which she so much admired in her father. She had always assumed a protective, sisterly attitude towards him, just as she had adopted a protective, maternal attitude towards her mother. Neither had openly resented it; neither had given her cause to believe that they were other than what she had taken them to be, and the very fact that they had tacitly acquiesced in the estimate she had formed had strengthened her feeling of conscious superiority.

Had she been wrong after all, in Eric's case? The tall, upstanding man who pressed his suit so insistently was different from the lanky lad whom she had bidden goodbye, without very poignant regret, when she had left eight years before to embark on her great adventure. Eric had filled out; his face had become stronger, in some lights it was positively a handsome face. He carried himself with dignity, he dressed well, though not obtrusively well, and she noted with satisfaction that his tie was immaculately tied, and that his clothes were tailor made. The healthy pallor of his clean-shaven face, the erect figure, and the finely shaped hands reminded her of his ancestry on his mother's side. She had been a Seldon, Eric's mother, a descendant of the very early settlers who had peopled the Valley, and, competing on equal terms with the old established farmers, had won a reputation for honesty and fair dealing. The Seldons were of good yeoman stock, and on his father's side, too, Eric was descended from a race which had proved itself. There was as much English blood in him as there was Dutch, and both were very possibly watered with Scottish, for in the van Deren family as well as in the Seldons there had been ancestors hailing directly from north of the Tweed. She herself could scarcely claim that her descent was so pure. On her mother's side, yes, for the Gersters and the Rekkers were good Frisian and Swedish county folk, who in the old country, before they had emigrated, had held their own lands, and had been entitled to call themselves *armiger*. But on her father's side there was nothing to show comparable to what Eric might submit. Elias Vantloo's father had been a poor farmer; his grandfather still poorer, and his great grandfather had been an employee of the old Company, though what particular avocation he had followed the family tradition did not say. Santa had been interested in the matter and had tried to obtain particulars about her paternal ancestors, but Elias cared little for such things. He had all the arrogance of a self-made man, all the contempt of one who was founding a family for those who had to look backward to find a justification for their own shortcomings. Yes, decidedly Eric had points. She felt no affection for him, beyond the sisterly regard which she retained for an old playmate, with whom she still desired to be on terms of intimate friendship, and his insistence to make the relation between them closer irritated rather than pleased her. It was not her fault that he kept on bothering her. She had told him, clearly and distinctly, that she had no intention of abandoning her independence. Her life was before her, and she had mapped out for herself a professional career. The dull domesticities of married life did not attract her. It was not to savour them that she had slaved for seven years to perfect her knowledge in her art, and it would be rank treason to herself and to her ideals of liberty to surrender at the first assault.

'Sit down, Eric, and be sensible,' she said, motioning him to a chair. He drew it up toward her, and sat facing her, while she made smoke rings in the air. She felt the appeal in his soft brown eyes, reminding her of her mother's mild, wistful gaze, but she steeled herself against it.

'It's useless going on like this, Boy,' she said, speaking, as she had always done since her return when she and Eric talked together, in Afrikaans. It made their conversation more intimate, and gave her at the same time the satisfaction of remaining true to her allegiance. Eric was politically in the opposite camp. It was true he had never been aggressive, and she felt that at heart he was as loyal to true national sentiment as she herself desired to be, but he was certainly lax in upholding those rights which she regarded as sacrosanct and indisputable. Language was one of these, and although Santa spoke English much better than she did Afrikaans, she had rapidly conformed to the prevailing usage in her political circle and asserted, in and out of season, what she was pleased to call her language rights.

'Be sensible, now,' she went on, purposely speaking in as matter of fact a voice as she could assume. When I left there was no understanding between us, and there is none now. None whatever. You must see that, Eric. I know Father would be pleased if I said yes to you, but I have no intention—no intention whatever—of doing so. At least, not for a long time ...'

'It has been a long time waiting for you, Santa,' he pleaded, earnestly. 'And you know I did my level best to get Uncle Elias to let you go. That much I did for you ... I helped you to go and study, although it was sending you away, and ... and you might have married there ...'

'So I might,' retorted Santa, brightly. 'I had three proposals. One from an Australian sheep farmer, fabulously wealthy, my Boy. The second,' she ticked them off against her cigarette, 'from an Oxford boy, who is now somewhere in Burmah, tea planting or teak cutting, I don't know which. How would you have liked me to go to Burmah, Eric?'

'I shouldn't have liked it at all, Santa,' he replied, responding to her playfulness with a wry smile. 'I should only have liked you for myself.'

'Pure unadulterated selfishness, Boy,' said Santa. 'The third, why that was on board, coming back. He is a diamond buyer somewhere about, and he said he would try again. But he had a beard,' she pursued, reminiscently, 'and he was much too old.'

'There must have been many others,' remarked Eric, glumly. 'I should have thought every youngster would have proposed to you when he got a chance.'

'But I didn't give them one, see?' she retorted. 'No, don't fancy I have any wish to get married, Eric. Why, it would be a sheer waste of time and money—all that I spent on my medical course. Have a heart, Eric. You would like me to be a useful member of society, and do things, wouldn't you?'

'I should like you only to give me the right to call myself your husband, Santa,' he said. Aunt Maria, Uncle Elias, they are both growing old. We are neither of us as young as we might be, and our people married long before they were our age ...'

'For heaven's sake, Eric, don't harp on marriage. I have told you repeatedly that I won't ... I won't. Will you take that as final, please, and cease bothering me?'

'No. Not until it is useless bothering you, Santa. Not until you give someone else the right. Then I shall know it is useless. But not until then.'

'You are hopeless, Eric. Don't let us quarrel about it, though. If you are content with the arrangement, let it stand. Let's talk about something else. Doctor and his wife will be here soon, and there's something I want to ask you, and I may not get another opportunity soon.'

'What is it, Santa? Anything I can do ...'

'Well, sit quiet and listen. Do take out your pipe and smoke. I can't offer you a whisky for you know what Father thinks about it. I don't believe there's a drop of the stuff in the house.'

'I can do without it,' said Eric, with a smile. 'And Ayah Mina will be bringing coffee soon. What is it?'

'It's about that partnership with the doctor, Eric,' said Santa, leaning forward, and emphasising her words with the stump of her cigarette. 'He made the proposal himself. A half share, or a third share to start with. It seems to me an admirable thing. I want some experience. Ultimately, of course, I mean to specialise, and for that I will have to go to one of the big centres. But as a beginning, this place would do excellently.'

'Yes. I agree. I am not wholly disinterested, Santa. I should like to keep you here as long as possible.'

'Never mind that, Boy. Detach yourself from the silly sentimental side and look at the matter with the stern business eye of the trained lawyer. You are one, aren't you? Very well then. What about the financial side? I spoke to Mother about it. You see, I have a notion that I have run through grandma's legacy. I went through my books this evening, and I was amazed to find how much I had spent. I must have run through the greater part of two thousand five hundred, though where it all went heaven alone knows. So there cannot be much left ... it was three thousand, wasn't it?'

'About that, Santa. A shade under. I don't recollect the exact figure.'

'Well, doctor would want about fifteen hundred. Mother still has her portion. That was altogether about six thousand, and it must have been accumulating all these years, for father invested it carefully. I thought if mother could lend me that sum, you could draw up a deed or whatever you call it, making it obligatory on my part to pay off so much every year ... the practice would bring in more than I should need ...'

'Why worry about it, Santa? We'll make some plan. If you really want to go into partnership with Dr Buren—and I think it is a good proposal and will be mutually advantageous—there need be no difficulty about finding the money. You know, Santa, if you said yes to me it would not mean that you would have to give up your profession. Then I would be able to pay Buren what he wants and ...'

'And I would be eternally beholden to you, Eric. No thank you. I have never sponged on anybody—excuse the slang, Eric, but you do make a person wild when you suggest these things. Can't you see that I want to be independent? I have been, all my life, and it is quite a different thing taking a loan from mother from what it would be if I took one from you. And it's not very nice of you to suggest that you should buy me ...'

'I had no such intention, Santa,' exclaimed the young man, exasperated. 'I only wanted to ...'

'You only wanted to bring in all that silly sentiment again, Eric. Do be practical. Do you think it could be managed, the way I propose?'

'Certainly, Santa. Leave it to me. I will arrange everything. Tomorrow I'll have a talk with the doctor, go over his books, and find out exactly how much the share is worth. If it is to be a business proposition, we might as well arrange it on strict business lines. Listen, there they are. Shall I go and let them in?'

'Ayah Mina has already done so,' said Santa, rising to greet the newcomers whom the ayah was ushering in. There were three of them, Dr Buren, his wife, a plump, motherly looking lady, diffusing an atmosphere of brisk cheerfulness and cordial geniality, and a small wizened man, nattily dressed in dark-coloured tweeds, a stranger to Santa.

'We have brought Mr Mabuis with us, Santa,' said Mrs Buren, introducing the stranger. 'He is staying with us, but he is leaving again tomorrow and I thought your father might like to see him.'

The stranger bent over her hand and kissed it, a foreign affectation which Eric resented, although the man was presentable enough. Van Deren noted his shrewd, small, coal-black eyes, the little greying goatee on his chin, and the dark complexion. The name recalled vague memories, but he could not place the fellow, whose manners, he had to admit, were irreproachable. Ayah Mina brought in the tea things, and Santa poured out the tea, chatting all the while vivaciously. Eric, after handing round the refreshments, plumped down in a chair alongside the doctor, and was promptly enlightened.

'Mr Mabuis is really no stranger to these parts,' said Buren, impressively. 'You, van Deren, may remember his grandfather—at least you must have heard about him.'

'*Meneer* van Deren surely remembers him,' said the stranger, who spoke in a well modulated voice, enunciating his English crisply, though he talked Afrikaans equally fluently with Santa. 'I never saw him, but he was a legend in the family, with his flute and his French and all that.'

'Are you a grandson of that Mabuis?' asked Eric, astonished. 'The one who married the widow Priem?'

'Even so,' said the stranger. 'He had one son, who went north, as you may remember, and one grandson, myself. And after all these years, Miss Vantloo, I return to the home of my fathers.'

'Mr Mabuis has made a home for himself in the Argentine,' said Mrs Buren. 'He is one of the South American millionaires, and we have been urging him to do something for the home of his fathers. You must help us, Santa. The man does not know what to do with his money.'

'My dear lady,' said the wizened stranger, 'it is much less easy to keep money than to make it. And the inducements to spend some of what I have made in the home of my fathers are not very alluring.'

'There you are, Santa,' said the doctor, teasingly. 'Have at him. There is a victim ready for the arena. Gladys and I will turn down our thumbs if you vanquish him. Go ahead.'

'I am sure it is not really necessary, Doctor,' said Santa, disdainfully. 'If Mr Mabuis has so little love for his own country that he has voluntarily exiled himself from it, one can hardly expect him to be generous to it.'

'Your pardon, young lady. "My country" ... *helas*, it is an expression that every canting demagogue uses. The assumption that because a man happens to be born in a particular part of this ovate spheroid—or is it oblate? My knowledge of these minutiae has sadly dwindled since I took to growing lucerne—in a particular part of it, he is bound to execrate every other part ... that is an assumption so utterly illogical that I refuse to admit it.'

'Then you refuse to admit that there is such a thing as patriotism,' said Santa, belligerently. 'One who has expatriated himself would naturally do so.'

'Zounds, a palpable hit,' applauded the doctor. 'You will find, Mabuis, that my colleague is well up in these political matters.'

'The *seniorita* is merely repeating the catch phrases of the day,' said the stranger, bowing gracefully to Santa as he spoke. 'A man's country, in my most humble opinion, is where he is best off, where he finds the best that life can give, and where life itself offers the best prospects. It is a matter of opinion, but for myself I cannot say the land of my grandfather—let me rather say his adopted land, for he was French, originally, as much expatriated as I am—appeals to me.'

'Why not?' demanded Santa. 'I have seen something of the world, Mr Mabuis, and I have never seen anything better than this. Tell me where you can better it, if you can.'

'If you would come to the Argentine,' said the stranger, smilingly, 'I could show you what you cannot see here. One compares, and one contrasts. That is the only way. I know this country, young lady. I was a *burgher* of the old Republic, and I did my share in the war. But I do not regret that I expatriated myself, and I say to the young men here,' he turned smilingly towards Eric as he spoke, 'expatriate yourselves as soon as you possibly can, for your Union offers you no prospects such as can allure one of our race.'

'Expound, Mabuis, expound,' said the doctor, helping himself liberally to the green fig preserve. 'So long as there are such things as these left, I stay here.'

'Yours is a gastronomic patriotism, Doctor,' said Santa, coldly. 'I daresay we lack many of the comforts which appeal to Mr Mabuis, but he must bear in mind that we are young yet ...'

'The invariable excuse,' proclaimed the stranger, impatiently. 'I meet it wherever I go. And yet you are nearly three hundred years old, and most that you have got dates from a century back.'

'Now, now, Mr Mabuis, be a little more fair,' interrupted the doctor. Look at the difficulties. There's this racial problem, for instance, between English and Dutch.'

'You are English ...'

'He isn't,' exclaimed Mrs Buren. 'He's South African of Irish descent, and please do bear that in mind, Mr Mabuis.'

'Well, Irish then,' said the stranger, glibly, 'and I ... I suppose I am South African of mixed French descent, but we are both of the same race. There is no racial problem between English and Dutch, my dear Doctor. At the most there is an artificially created and politically encouraged cultural antagonism between the two white sections of your community, which is entirely unnatural, for after all the two cultures are basically the same.'

'There is an antagonism of ideals,' interjected Santa, hotly. 'And cultures must recognise these ideals.'

'Quite so, young Lady. But the antagonism of ideal is political, not racial, and not natural. I have heard a great deal about it. Why, I can almost think myself back in the old days, when I was listening daily to the talk of a Dutch Republic from Quoing Point to the Zambesi, for which some of us—I admit I was one of them—were foolish enough to fight ...'

'I should have been proud to have had a chance to fight for it,' exclaimed Santa, impulsively. 'And I should never have turned my back on it, even for the sake of growing lucerne in the Argentine.'

'Many of us hadn't even a chance of doing that,' said the stranger, more gravely than he had spoken before. 'I come back and find that the lesson which we learned then has been forgotten. Most of us seem never to have learned it.'

'What lesson was that?' asked Eric, breaking into the conversation for the first time.

'Toleration, young man, toleration,' said the stranger, impressively. 'What made our war? You tell me Chamberlain and Milner, and I go elsewhere and hear Kruger and Leyds. It is merely confounding effect with cause ...'

'Don't let us speak about the war, please,' said Mrs Buren, apprehensively, for she had noted Santa's eyes flash. 'It was a dreadful blunder, no matter who was responsible for it.'

'All wars are dreadful blunders, *Madame*,' said Mr Mabuis, 'but the world will go on making them, for the world, which delights in cant, has no logic. Thank you, I should like another cup. Delicious—no sugar, please. But it is more dreadful to forget the lessons that a war has taught us, and that is what, as it seems to me, we are doing here. That is why I shudder to think of what is in store for the land of my father, and why I advise you all to expatriate yourselves before the deluge comes.'

'We'll find an Ararat,' said Santa, vehemently. She was beginning to hate the smooth-voiced stranger, whom at first sight she had been prepared to like. 'And our ark will be staffed with those who believe in their ideals.'

'And may one be permitted to ask what these are?' queried the Argentinean. 'I hear such diverse opinions about them. Yesterday I was told it was a White South Africa ... *Pah* ...' he shrugged his shoulders expressively.

'Surely an attainable ideal,' remarked Eric, wishing to help Santa, whose indignation was rendering her almost speechless. 'Australia is working towards that ...'

'Australia!' exclaimed the stranger. 'Australia hasn't got your real racial problem, which is not White versus White, but Native versus White. Believe me, young Sir, there is no future for an exploiting race. You must have effective occupation, else you are doomed. And you haven't got it here, and I see no chance of your getting it unless you take drastic measures. You have an actual population of three or four to the square mile, and you should carry at least thirty; a third of your population are drones who cannot exist unless the remaining two thirds are exploited for their benefit. And you are giving the exploited no chance to become exploiters themselves, thereby stultifying your industrial policy and endangering your own safety. You are entirely dependent for your defence upon foreign aid ...'

'Mr Mabuis probably does not know that we have our own independent status,' said Santa, her voice trembling with indignation. 'We are a sovereign independent state, under the League of Nations, and beholden to no foreign power. I should have thought that everyone knew that.'

'More cant,' said Mr Mabuis, calmly sipping his tea. 'Leagues of Nations and covenants—my dear young Lady, they are like those little scraps of paper to which our lamented friend Bethmann Hollweg so tactlessly referred. The fact remains that we— you see that even though expatriated I still identify myself with my father's country— that we are as much dependent upon England as we were in the days of Lord Charles Somerset. A little more dependent, indeed, than we were half a century ago ...'

'How do you make that out?' asked Eric, interested in the argument. 'We had no status then.'

'You had the status of a civilised community, *Meneer* van Deren,' replied Mabuis earnestly. 'You had a constitution, here in the old Colony, which gave every man an equal chance. Now you have a constitution that favours one class, one race, at the expense of the other. That is hardly civilised. It is a wonder to me that the League of Nations, of which I cordially disapprove, permits a mandate to be held by a country which can hardly claim to have a civilised status in comparison with the authority which it displaces. Germany has a thoroughly representative constitution, the most representative, probably, of any country. Yours—what is it? A botched-up thing into which you were dragged at a time when you were feverishly enthusiastic, and quite unable to forecast the results of that premature step.'

'You have talked enough politics, you people,' said Mrs Buren, placatingly. 'Do let us have some music. Your father is rather late, isn't he, Santa?'

'It is an initiation night at the lodge, Mrs Buren,' said Santa, eager to return to the fray. 'But Mr Mabuis had got us all wrong, and he should be put right.'

'Not tonight, my dear,' said Mrs Buren. 'Mr van Deren, won't you give us some Grieg?'

'I should like to continue the conversation, Mr Mabuis,' said Santa, 'but the votes are against us. You will wait to see father, won't you? Perhaps then we can re-open the subject.'

'It will give me, much pleasure to meet *Meneer* Vantloo again,' said Mabuis. 'And I shall be delighted to discuss these matters with you, young Lady. I still have an interest in this country, even though I have expatriated myself. Now let us behave and listen to the music.'

Chapter 7

Mr Mabuis prolonged his stay in the Village, contrary to his first intention. He found the 'home of his fathers' more attractive than it had appeared to be at first sight, and the attraction of old associations too powerful to be resisted. He visited the family farm, long since alienated from the family of which, indeed, he now believed himself to be the only direct representative. The farm, like so many others in the District, had suffered severely during the war. The homestead had been looted, and part of the outbuildings destroyed, but long before it had become the scene of some of that desultory skirmishing between the regular forces and the Boer commandos which had brought so much misery to the District it had been sold, and since then it had had more than one owner. It was now occupied by a holder who found it extremely difficult to get a living out of the exhausted wheatlands, which had never been properly replenished with the necessary fertilising constituents that generations of tillers, for a hundred years and more, had extracted from the soil by successive crops. To Mr Mabuis, accustomed to the up-to-date agricultural methods which had enabled him to amass a comfortable income from lucerne cultivation in the Argentine, the condition of his father's old home was pitiable.

'Here,' he said to Santa, as he drove her along the corrugated road through an environment of splendidly blossoming veld, whose flowers and greenery seemed to deny the necessity for any admixture of fertiliser, 'here you have an example of the manner in which we live. We exhaust what we possess and we do nothing—nothing whatever, so far as I can see—to put back into the country what we get from it. It is a policy of prodigality, and it must, inevitably, bring disaster.'

'Like most of your criticism,' Santa replied belligerently, 'your comment is based on defective information, Mr Mabuis. This farm is not the only one in the District, and it is in the hands of poor Whites. But all our farms are not like that. If you will go down to the other side of the Valley you will find farmers who spend large sums annually in buying guano and fertilisers for their wheatlands, and get quite good returns. You can hardly call that exhausting the country. And bear in mind, please, that we are only now beginning to realise the advantages of scientific cultivation of the land. If you ask father, he will tell you that there exists an unfortunate prejudice against scientific methods ...'

'I do not need Mr Vantloo's assurance on that point,' exclaimed Mabuis, energetically. 'I know from personal experience how innate the conservatism of our own people happens to be. The expert is still anathema to many of us—and small blame to them, young Lady, for expert assistance has done little in the past to make them realise how valuable it can be.'

'That was because it was given in a manner they could scarcely understand,' contended Santa, animatedly. 'One more reason, Mr Mabuis, why you should not jeer at Afrikaans. Admit that it has done much to benefit us ...'

'I have never for one moment asserted that it hasn't,' interjected Mabuis. 'But admit, on your part, my dear young Lady, that to those farmers who are really progressive, who can and do make use of modern methods, it does not matter very much whether the instruction they receive is in English or Afrikaans. They are proficient in both languages, and it does seem to me that you lay far too much stress on an equality which, like your status, is after all more a matter of suggestion than of essential fact.'

'I don't admit that for a moment,' said Santa, spiritedly. 'A language is the soul of a people—it *is* the people ...'

'Yes, I know,' smiled Mr Mabuis. 'That is another of these cant phrases which politicians use when they have nothing tangible to propose. But consider it; analyse it. In my time, which is unfortunately for me, young Lady, a considerable distance beyond what you can remember, our national feeling was, I apprehend, as strong as yours is today, and Afrikaans was certainly not the people's language in the sense in which it is that today. Those of us who made the least pretence to education and social status spoke, wrote, and read Dutch ...'

'As badly as they did English,' retorted Santa, scornfully. 'That was just the trouble, Mr Mabuis. They spoke two foreign languages, neither of which they properly understood, with the result that their soul was stifled and they had no chance of expressing their cultural aspirations. We are doing only what has been done by other nations—take the Irish, for example. You would not argue that Afrikaans is less useful than Gaelic, would you?'

'I do not know Gaelic,' said Mr Mabuis, warily, 'and therefore I shall not attempt to compare the two. Nor need you confine yourself to instancing the Irish Free State. I can give you a better instance—Serbia. There is, to my mind, considerable analogy between the situation here at present and the condition of Serbia some years before the Great War, and it might be useful for us to remember that analogy. We are rapidly forgetting the lessons of the Great War, just as here we have completely forgotten the lesson of the Boer War. There are many points of similarity between the Serbian situation in 1912 and ours here today. Take the influence of the church ...'

'I don't see how there can be any analogy there, Mr Mabuis. The Serbians were ... really, I don't quite know what they were or are, but certainly not Dutch Reformed.'

'No, my dear young Lady, but Serbian Orthodoxy is not very far removed from Dutch Reformed Calvinism, especially now that we have grafted on it the Scottish interpretation. I would not attempt to speak to others on this matter, but you are, if I may be allowed to say so, sufficiently broad-minded and liberal in your views—as you must be if you wish to cultivate the proper scientific spirit—to appreciate the fundamental difference between Austrian Catholicism, with its strong clericalism evolved for the express purpose of influencing the masses and of denying the individuality of the state, as such, and Serbian Orthodoxy, with its severely practical outlook upon life.'

'I may be dense, Mr Mabuis,' expostulated Santa, 'but I really cannot follow you there. What has Serbian Orthodoxy, to which I have never given a thought, to do with our desire to preserve the individuality of our language?'

'A great deal. Like your Dutch Reformed Calvinism, Serbian Orthodoxy is inimical to culture. Now if you'll permit me to give you a short lecture on Serbian history—it will be a very short one, I promise you—you will grasp my implication.'

'I still do not see what Afrikaans has to do with Serbian. If you want to trail a herring across the path, Mr Mabuis ...'

'Not a herring, my dear young Lady. Merely a language enthusiast. His name was Vuk Karadzic ...'

'I have never heard of him.'

'Nor have many people of Klaas Waarzegger. Consider. Afrikaans started about a hundred years ago, under auspices very similar to those under which Vuk Karadzic mid-wifed the Serbian literary language and spelling about the same time. He was a contemporary of Goethe and a friend of Ranke, the historian, who was immensely interested in the evolutions of a new language. And let me tell you that Serbian had a much harder struggle to win a place than Afrikaans has had. Its use was officially prohibited. Yet in a measure Vuk Karadzic was one of the founders of Serbian nationalism that has done so much to plunge the world into one of the most appalling catastrophes that it was possible to imagine.'

'I daresay,' remarked Santa, unconvinced by an argument of which she could not see the conclusion. 'You would, no doubt, have liked to see Serbia subserviently accept German or Maygar or whatever language Austria wanted to impose upon it. But it did not submit. It had sufficient soul to fight for its own and conquer.'

'At the risk of setting the clock back a hundred years or more. And that is what we are doing here. What is the sum total of what Serbia has given to the world's culture since then? Very little ...'

'I suppose you are in a position to judge,' said Santa flippantly. 'Just like those who criticise Afrikaans and who are not able to read one of our works in it, and in no position to compare its literary results.'

'I happen to know a little Serbian,' said Mr Mabuis, imperturbably. I was with the Serbian forces in the second Balkan War, and I have read a good deal of their literature. And I fancy I am well up in Afrikaans, well enough to compare its literary results with those of contemporary writers in other languages.'

'So you run it down,' cried Santa, passionately. 'Having read one or two, you think yourself competent to judge the whole, just as from one mis-managed farm you conclude that we exploit the rest in the same fashion. There's an old proverb, Mr Mabuis ...'

'You need not quote it. Ornithologically it is entirely wrong, as you must know if you have visited the penguin island and seen how industriously the mother bird selects the dirtiest spot for her brood. But, again, I happen to have read most of your Afrikaans productions written during the last twenty-five years. I laid in a stock of them at Cape Town, when I arrived, just to see for myself on what you based your pretensions to a larger culture. Believe me, my dear young Lady, I have been woefully disappointed. I except half a dozen books, and count the rest as rubbish, literary imitative work, largely based on English models—all the more remarkable as you have that pure well of Dutch to draw upon—without any real originality of thought or facility of expression. How can there be, when you are just evolving a new language and in your enthusiasm confining it into impossible channels where the native soul, as you call it, can find no chance of expressing itself within the limitations which you impose upon it?'

'You are utterly mistaken,' declared Santa. 'Which just shows how little you really know about the subject, Mr Mabuis. Afrikaans is fully able to express what we feel. There is nothing, no subject under the sun, which cannot be just as well handled in Afrikaans, as a medium of expression, as in English.'

'A sweeping statement which you will hardly be able to justify,' commented Mabuis, drily. 'Your own profession, for example. Has it produced anything in Afrikaans which is on a par with what it has produced in English or Dutch?'

'Of course. There have been several treatises—inaugural dissertations, in Afrikaans, and they are just as good, or as bad, as similar publications in English or high Dutch.'

'I have perused one,' said Mabuis, reflectively, and it struck me that the writer constantly fell back upon German. The thesis bristled with Germanisms and Anglicisms, which I believe your Afrikaans critics would much object to. Take colours. Look at that field of sorrels. There must be some twenty shades of colour there, and I suppose every botanist knows how to describe each shade accurately in Latin. I could myself flounder through a description in Spanish or even in Serbian, but my knowledge of Afrikaans is lamentably deficient when it comes to describing colour. Look at that splash over there—now that is a remarkable colour.'

He stopped the car as he spoke and directed her attention to the delicate little flowers which studded in thousands the fields on both sides of the road. It was a gorgeous display, for in the sun-glare the sorrels had unclosed their petals and displayed themselves in their full glory. Mauve and crimson, golden yellow and cerise, orange and ferruginous red, lilac and variegated white, they studded the hard clay, and bloomed in profusion in an environment which held little else but stunted bush, close cropped by the sheep. He got out of the car and picked a few, and held them out to her. 'Now what would you call this in Afrikaans?' he asked, touching a fine red blossom, whose delicate, satiny sheen reflected the light in varying shades so that the tip of its petals was altogether different in colouring from their base.

'Red, I suppose,' said Santa, 'or stone-red, or some combination. What would you call it in English? Come, I imagine you would have some difficulty in expressing it in one word.'

'I should say nacarat,' replied Mabuis, with a smile. 'A good, sound English colour term. Perhaps obsolete, but none the less applicable.' He mounted and let in the clutch. 'It is a wonderful country, all the same,' he said, with a tinge of regret in his tone. 'The pity is that you won't make it more wonderful still, and that you—you see, this time I dissociate myself, for I am a cosmopolitan, my dear young Lady, and as such beyond the pale—that you won't make it better and more wonderful by giving it your active service rather than by canting about its wonders.'

'We are doing that,' said Santa, sturdily. 'It is just by identifying ourselves with it, by evolving our own culture from it, that we are serving it. Our literature ...'

'*Bah*,' interrupted Mabuis, rudely. 'It is as if one heard a child who has just mastered its A B C talking about his literature. Not an original observation, my dear young Lady. Multatuli's. Somewhere in the *Ideas*, which you have doubtless read. No? You do surprise me. That is where you are a constant puzzle to me. If you are really in earnest with your propaganda for Afrikaans, why do you neglect those giants in Dutch literature which should be an inspiration and a constant source of strength to you? An Englishman does not do that to his language. He still reads Carlyle, and he even ventures upon Shakespeare and Marlowe ...'

'Nobody reads Carlyle nowadays, Mr Mabuis.'

'More's the pity. But that is surely no excuse for neglecting Vondel and Verwey and Dekker. You are all dancing *widdershins* around an idea, and you fancy your-selves doing homage to an ideal. To a sympathetic outsider like myself, it is all rather pathetic, my dear young Lady. Your premises are all wrong. You talk of culture, and your greatest cultural influence remains the church which, as I said before, is hostile to culture ...'

'A contradiction in terms, Mr Mabuis. Nor do I see how you make that out—that the church, as such, in this country, is hostile to culture.'

'You will, I think, if you consider what culture, in its best senses, really means. Is it not Life in the fullest conception of the term? The constant adjustment of our internal to our external relations? The cultivation of what is best in ourselves until our morals are transmuted into practice? And does the church ... has it ever practised what it preaches? Does it not give its members, the entire community here, a daily lesson in hypocrisy and dissemblance? It was so in my time, and although I have been long away, now that I have come back I mark much the same tendency.'

'In what way? I don't quite follow you, Mr Mabuis. The church, after all, has a high moral sense. It inculcates practical morality ...'

'And permits the reverse. Surely you, who are scientifically trained, and have learned to observe—that is, after all, the best that medical training gives, the faculty of correct observation: all else is very much illusionary for your medical science is not yet an exact science, although your art of medicine is very much matured. You who have observed, have you found that there is much evidence that the church has developed in its members that nice adjustment of sense to soul which I suppose is culture?'

'You are becoming far too philosophical for me, Mr Mabuis. What exactly do you imply?'

'My dear young Lady, I leave the implication to you. I only ask you to consider such facts as have come under your own observation. You have seen the location. You have noted—you must have; it leaps to the eye—that a percentage of its inhabitants are not pure Native. That percentage must be recruited from a non-Native section. As obvious as the implication.'

'Of course, it is obvious—the fact I mean,' said Santa, argumentatively. 'But I still don't see your obvious implication. If you mean to suggest ... but that is absurd! The church has nothing whatever to do with that.'

'That may be a matter of opinion,' admitted Mabuis. 'But in view of the fact that the church has been the chief cultural factor in this country for nearly two hundred years, I do not see how the church can escape from its responsibility in the matter. I have thought a great deal about the matter, my dear Lady. In South America we have different standards, and we look at it with a less prejudiced eye than we do here. That, again, I think, is due to the church. I am not of it. I have not joined any church, and I do not even belong to that into which I was baptised, which I believe was my father's, the Dutch Reformed. My grandfather, as you doubtless know, was a Roman, but my grandmother was of the Reformed faith, and my father was brought up in that. Possibly because of my grandmother, my father was a trifle more bigoted than his fellow farmers and in my youth I had too much of the church. Altogether too much! So when I became my own master, I fell away from it, and I have never longed for it since. But my experience has taught me that some form of organised religion is necessary for cultural development, that it is at least a factor in such development, and I came back under the impression that here I would find that the church had a greater hold than it had in the past. I am woefully mistaken. It still exists as a force, but its influence is all the other way. It is not a factor any longer in your cultural evolution, simply because it failed in its obligation to promote that culture, through being entirely out of touch with the real factors which have stimulated you to become interested in your own souls.'

'There, perhaps, I am with you,' agreed Santa, whose own views on the subject of the influence of the church coincided with those which Mabuis had expressed. 'The church could have done much more. It opposed where it should have led. It opposed the Great Trek, which was a blunder—the opposition, I mean—and it opposed, until lately, the development of Afrikaans. But that does not necessarily make it hostile to culture.'

'If you take culture to be what I have tried to define, it is obvious that its failure to promote culture results from commission rather than from omission. I am afraid we are talking at cross-purposes. You take culture to be the development of aesthetic perceptions—literature, art, music, culture in the narrow sense of the word ...'

'Indeed, I do not, Mr Mabuis. I have a bigger conception of it than that.'

'I am glad to hear that. Very well, then, if you agree with my definition— admittedly a poor and rather vague one, but sufficiently concrete for purposes of discussion—how can you say that the church has promoted it when today there is not one member of it—except perhaps such as those who, like you, have to a certain extent emancipated themselves from its guiding strings—who dares question the literal interpretation of Scripture or affirm the obvious implications of modern scientific thought? The church exists here as a potent factor in stifling discussion and inculcating intolerance—here more, certainly, than with us in Argentine, where the public spirit is altogether more liberal, simply because the clergy do not possess that authority and prestige which your Dutch Reformed *predikants* hold here. And you must admit that while in the old days the *predikant* was a highly cultured individual who stood as a centre from which practically all culture radiated ...'

'I don't see what difference there was,' remonstrated Santa. 'As a matter of fact, I believe our modern parsons are much more liberal-minded and certainly far better educated than their predecessors.'

'Then you do not know the facts, my dear Lady. Formerly the parson had to have a special dispensation. He was trained to work in the East, and had to obtain his *Acte Classicale* before he could accept a parish here. That meant not only a university education in Europe, with its sound classical scholarship, but also a special preliminary study of Arabic and Syriac. What average *predikant* can look back on such a training today? A little Greek and Latin and a very elementary knowledge of Hebrew—that is all that is necessary, I believe, although on that point I speak subject to correction. Why, I remember that the *predikant* here in my time was reputed a great classical scholar, and one of his successors was a great orientalist who had been offered, but declined, a professorship at a European university. Surely you must see the cultural value of such parsons, and admit that it was far higher than that which is available today?

'Perhaps you are right, Mr Mabuis. I never looked at it from that point of view. But I am sure you are totally wrong when you imply that our cultural efforts are all in vain, and that we should allow ourselves to be swamped by English culture.'

'I never hazarded such an opinion. There is no difference, so far as I can see, between English and Afrikaans culture, and my own impression is that both are merging into a common culture, against which tendency it will be utterly useless for you to strive. After all, that is the direction in which you must work if you are really good South Africans, instead of attempting to be merely sectional South Africans. Take your own case. Here we are discussing abstruse things not in the language which you might say is our mother tongue, but in English. Why? Simply because we both find it easier—nay, it is the truth, young Lady, much as you might dislike it—to express ourselves in English. You wish to make us speak in the future entirely in the mother tongue, but in your efforts to be heroic you lose sight of the fact that in daily life it is not sentiment that counts, but something else.'

'Sentiment does count, Mr Mabuis,' interrupted Santa vigorously. 'Especially with us. If you knew more about your country, you would agree with me that it is sentiment—pure sentiment and nothing else—that has brought about the present state of affairs. It is because the old Party, your Party—for I suppose you are SAP, for only a SAP would talk like that—made no allowance for sentiment, because it thought, like you, that something else counts, that it was swept away and will remain in darkness until it alters its opinion and lives up to its principles.'

'My dear young lady, you take altogether too much for granted. I am not SAP. I belong to no Party, for I am expatriated. Were I living here I rather think I should count myself a Nationalist, for there is today no difference between the principles of the old SAP and modern Nationalism ...'

'Yes, there is. This difference of sentiment.'

'That existed in the old SAP. It exists today among those SAPs who are only restrained from openly joining the Nationalists because they wish to be consistent. My dear Lady, if your Party had a little more common sense, and if your leaders had a little more skill, you might rope in most of us who belonged to the old guard, for your principles are exactly what ours were. The fault with us was that we never lived up to them, and that is going to be your fault as well, for you protested too much and it is impossible for you to live up to your protests. Take the Great War. You protested against that, not because you felt that it was wrong, immoral or unethical, but simply because England was ranged on the side you had to fight on. That was the myrrh in the pill. What binds you together today is that senseless, childish, and to my mind utterly valueless irritation against England. And, for the life of me, I cannot quite understand why you, my dear young Lady, should possess it. I ... well, I was a *burgher* of the old Republic—I even had a vote in the Transvaal, although I came from the Cape. I may claim to have a legitimate grievance against England, because it conquered my country and subdued me by force. But you, who have lived under responsible government all your life, who know as well as I do that whatever England may have done in the past—and she did nothing worse than any other country would have done to its overseas settlements, and infinitely better than the old Company did to our forefathers—she is not going to interfere with you now ... honestly, I can't understand your position. And I should like to understand it. You are a puzzle to me, Miss Vantloo.'

'No more a puzzle, I should think,' Santa answered, 'than father or any other South African who feels himself a Nationalist.'

'Let us leave your father out of the discussion, please. I want your views. I know his, and he is by no means a puzzle. But you are. You have had what in the old days we called "an English education." Now there are separatist schools, and English and Afrikaans children are being divided into different sectional groups, which may in time create artificially a real cultural division. But you went to a school where the medium of instruction was English. English is as much your home language as Afrikaans, which you only talk to assert its rights ...'

'And because I love it, Mr Mabuis. Don't forget that, please. It is not my fault that I received an English education ...'

'You speak as if it is something to be regretted,' observed Mabuis drily. 'But you voluntarily chose to go to England for your medical course. You might have gone to Germany or Holland, yet you went to London. The only reason I can see for your present attitude is the only one I can find for the general feeling of antagonism to English sentiment in this country.'

'And what might that be, pray?'

'I hesitate to tell you. It may sound offensive.'

'Don't hesitate on my account, please. You have already said so much with which I profoundly disagree that one further mis-statement will not matter. Go on.'

'It seems to me that it is merely a reaction—a protective reaction, against your own feeling of ... let me say immaturity. If you had been, as I have, in Germany, in Prussia especially, you would have reacted violently against the Germans, for they give one exactly that sort of feeling. Their thoroughness, their arrogance, their tacit assumption that no one can possibly compete with them, produce that reaction, or it did at least in me. The English produce it less effectively, for at bottom they are more businesslike, and they make no pretence—at least not nowadays—of forcing their culture down other people's throats. And after all, it is merely a matter of cultural development which ranges you in different camps. On essentials you both feel alike. Take the Native problem, for example. What South African, whether English or Dutch, can take an unprejudiced view of it, unless he has been, as I have been, expatriated and has learned that colour by itself, and race by itself, do not really matter in the long run? Yet you Nationalists take it for granted that every English speaking South African holds the old Exeter Hall view of the Native, and every Afrikaans speaking one the South African view. And this while you know that Natal, which is predominantly English-speaking, is the most anti-negrophilistic province of the Union. That seems to me scarcely logical.'

'And consider,' he went on, earnestly, 'what you produce by constantly asserting your rights, as you call them. You imply that these rights are still needing defence, whereas they are enshrined in your Act of Union, and by propagandising for them you merely create the impression that they are still non-existent or at least in jeopardy. That is the way a child looks at things. He imagines all too lightly that someone is trying to rob him of his rights, and as you know that creates one of these peculiar attitudes towards his environment which psychologists declare is a defensive complex, which gives rise to all sorts of reactions.'

'You would have us tamely submit to see those rights whittled away, then?'

'By no means. I have not made myself clear, I am afraid, if that is your impression. Let us take a concrete case, the language. Its equality with English is admitted by statute, isn't it? Very well, why not take that equality for granted, and allow everyone to make his own choice which language he prefers to use? Why propagandise for the one while the other remains content with what it has and by its very inertness, by its abstention from aggressive action, appears—I say, appears, I don't say it actually is so—to justify its superiority? You started that way, but very soon your politicians saw what could be made of the language as a political party weapon, with the result that already Afrikaans has reaped some of the discredit which inevitably attaches to a political subject. Instead of writing, as your pioneers did, purely literary books, you are producing propaganda literature, and you are using your schools, your universities, and your cultural centres for the dissemination of propaganda, not culture.'

'You say that because you refuse to admit that sentiment plays a large part in creating national feeling. I suppose it is propaganda to refer to the war and the concentration camps.'

'You do it for the purpose of creating ill-feeling against the English—as some of your writers do—yes, I do call it that. Your Afrikaans works, written when the writers were under the influence of the war, deal with these matters in a passionate but perfectly legitimate manner, to which no sensible man can possibly object. But do your moderns do that? Do they cull from their own experience and treat these lamentable subjects as objectively as their predecessors did? You know they don't. They go largely on hearsay evidence, and they stress not the wrong *qua* wrong, but the wrong as something peculiarly and especially a wrong done by England against South Africa, or rather against Afrikaans-speaking South Africa. Which, as again you know, is not a fact. There were many of us who, much as they disliked the war, disliked the Transvaal Administration still more. But you slur over these facts. You intend that the younger generation, which knows nothing first hand about these things, shall grow up with the feeling that these wrongs were done deliberately, consciously and purposely by England, and in that way you foster the spirit of ill-feeling and antagonism which was gradually dying down at the time of the Union.'

'It is impossible to argue with you if you really feel like that,' said Santa, with a tinge of contempt in her voice. 'You are utterly out of touch with us Mr Mabuis. You have expatriated yourself so effectually that you no longer belong to us.'

'Pardon me, I still feel that I have some ties left with this country. Which brings me to a matter that I wanted to hear your views about. I was talking to Buren this morning, and he tells me—which is news to me—that there is a good deal of consumption in the location.'

'He is quite right. It is appallingly common.'

'Is that so? Why? Surely you should be free from it here. It was never a formidable disease in the old days. People came from Europe to get cured here. I was wondering if I could do anything. Buren thinks a dispensary ... he tells me his drug allowance is only a bare five pounds a year. I thought it must be a mistake, but I find he is correct. Ought I to give him funds? I can easily do so, although I am not a millionaire as some people suppose. But I should like to do something for these poor folk. After all, most of them have some of our blood in them.'

'There I am wholeheartedly with you,' exclaimed Santa, impulsively. 'If you only could. Let's form a committee and go into the matter. There must be some way in which we can take advantage of your help.'

'Very well. Will you talk to Dr Buren about it? I shall be staying on a couple of days longer. Then I must get north. But I will come back again, my dear Lady, and possibly you may find that the expatriated one is not quite so bloodless as you imagine him to be.'

Chapter 8

Santa found the Argentinean's frank criticism stimulating. She did not agree with his premises, nor did she admit his conclusions, but she was fair enough to acknowledge that some of his observations were justified.

That evening she tackled her father on the subject. Elias Vantloo had enjoyed a good dinner, and had openly taken a dose of his medicine. As he sat in his well furnished study, sucking a peppermint lozenge and lounging back in his club easy chair, he presented the appearance of a comfortable, solid, even benignant elderly gentleman, well preserved, for the subdued reflection of the electric light scarcely served to show all the lines of his face, the sagging of his mouth, and the bagginess under his eyes. Santa seated herself on his knee, as she had done so often in her girlhood days. He had changed since then, and although she rejected the traitorous thought as soon as it entered her mind, she felt that the change was not altogether for the better. He had long ago given up smoking, but the peppermint odour that he now wafted around him was far less attractive than even the scent of stale Havanas had been in the old days.

'Well, Heart's-lamb,' he said affably, playing with her shingled hair, 'it is a long time since you sat on *Papa's* lap. I suppose the favour is not to be too entirely gratuitous, eh?'

'As a matter of fact, I did want to ask you something, Father,' she said, responding to his playfulness.

'I hope it is if you can marry Eric,' he said, lightly. 'If so, you know the answer, Child. There's nothing mother and I would like better than to see you and van Deren mated together.'

'Oh, Father, don't harp on that old thing,' she exclaimed petulently. 'I have told you I won't marry yet ...'

'Well, well, if you won't, you won't,' he remarked, indulgently. 'There is no need to get hot about it, Child. Go your own way. Father has never hampered you, has he?'

'No, indeed,' she said, contritely, kissing his forehead, and noting how his hair was thinning around the bald spot on the top of his head. 'You have been an exemplary Dad, that I must admit. And I do hope you will continue to be one, now that I am here to take you in hand. Doesn't it say somewhere, "Train up your parents in the way they should go that your days in the land may be prolonged"?'

'I wish you wouldn't make sport of scripture,' he said, gravely. 'It is all very well doing so at home, Child, but you are getting into the habit of saying things in company which are not edifying. You must really break yourself of the habit. After all, I have a position to keep up. I am senior Elder of the church.'

'And Grand Master of the Lodge, Dad. But you surely don't intend me to give up an occasional whisky and soda at Dr Buren's, do you? Only occasionally, you know. Nor a cigarette,' she took out her case and lighted one, while he regarded her indulgently. 'That would be too much to ask of me, Dad.'

'I don't, my dear,' he said, confidingly. 'Smoke by all means, if you really like it. But pay some regard to what people think. That has always been my motto, Child. And you know, Heart's-lamb,' his tone became even more confidential, 'I look upon my daughter as if she were my son. In some ways you are that, you know, Santa. It was always a grievance with me that your mother did not give me a son. But I made the best of it ...'

'That was very noble of you, Father,' she said, with a bit of sarcasm in her voice. 'But you know, of course, I don't share your view about the inferiority of my sex.'

'There are exceptions,' said Vantloo, ponderously. 'You are one. That is why I can talk to you as I do now. Most women are fools. Take your mother now. She never sees farther than the tip of her nose, thank God for that. I shouldn't like her to be new-womanish. But I can't discuss matters with her as I can with you. She does not see the necessity for hiding one's feelings sometimes, if you take me. Nor do you either, when it comes to the point. That is a great mistake, Santa. You should guard against that if you want to be successful in your profession. A doctor especially should know how to hide his feelings. He should win people's confidence, and you cannot do that if you outrage their feelings. But I am digressing. What is it you want to ask me, my dear?'

'Many things, Daddy,' she used the old name, and felt for the moment the old sense of intimacy with which she had approached him when a child and when she had wanted to cajole him into consent otherwise unobtainable. 'First, what about that partnership with van Buren?'

'Ah, that,' said her father, hesitatingly. 'That is not a matter for haste, my Child. Eric has it in hand. It is not a little thing to lay one's hands upon a globular sum like that. It will need negotiation. You mustn't mind if there is a little delay. I have many calls upon my purse ... one does not reach the position I have gained without some sacrifice, my dear, and times are hard nowadays.'

'But surely there is my own money, Father? Or mother's?'

'Surely, surely. But you don't imagine that I keep it at fixed deposit at the bank, Child? And one cannot realise investments in a day. It takes time. And there is very little of yours left. Your training has been expensive.'

'I know,' she said, apologetically. 'But it is an asset, and as soon as I start I shall be earning. That is why I want to begin, Father.'

'All right, my dear, all right. Eric will see to it. He is negotiating with Buren. Just give him a little time. Now what else?'

'I have been talking to Mr Mabuis ...'

'Ah,' said Vantloo, and she could not make out whether the ejaculation expressed approval or the reverse. 'That gentleman talks a lot. Just like his lamented grandfather—a notorious drunkard and vagrant, my dear.'

'Did you know him, Father?'

'Not personally. He was dead, then. But I heard a great deal about him. They called him "Tins" and "Teacher," for in his sober moments he taught at the old farm school on Nolte's farm. You remember old Nolte, eh? They called him Gallows-Gecko because he had hanged a man once. Old Mabuis was a vagrant Frenchman whom he had picked up somewhere and who afterwards married the rich old Widow Priem. Your Mr Mabuis is the grandson. He has done very well for himself, my dear, but I apprehend the old traits are in him. Heredity plays a big part in life, my dear.'

'That explains some of his characteristics, Dad. However, he wishes to do something for the location. You know there is a great deal of tuberculosis there. Poor old Ayah Mina's daughter, Sophy, has got it. She is very far gone ...'

'Is she really? How long would you give her?' he asked, with a show of interest.

'That is difficult to say, Dad. Possibly a year, perhaps less. One lobe is quite gone; the other, on the left side, riddled. I am so sorry for her ...'

'If you are going to waste tears over every Coloured woman with consumption,' he said harshly, 'you will have to cry all day long, Child. And you should not go there. You might catch it. I ... I forbid you,' his voice rose and reached an angry pitch. 'You have no business there. What is Sophy to you? Do you hear? ... I don't want you to go ...'

'Why, Father? Why all this fuss?' asked Santa, wonderingly, astonished at his vehemence. 'I can look after myself. It is not the first time I have looked after a tuberculous patient. In Europe nearly every hospital patient is infected. Don't be so childish.'

'No, but I don't like it,' he said grumblingly, and seemingly a little ashamed of his outburst. 'I don't like you going to the location and mingling with them. They are not of your class. Let Buren—he's district surgeon, and it's his work—attend to them.'

'If I'm to be his partner,' said Santa, reasonably, 'I shall have to do some of the work, and after all it interests me. But about Mr Mabuis, Father. He wants to do something for them, and he is rich ...'

'So it is said,' remarked Vantloo, cautiously. 'But is he?'

'That makes no difference if he gives us the money, Father. He wants to give something to start a dispensary for the location. I thought you might bring it before the council. It would be a very good thing to have such a dispensary in the village. There are all these poor Whites—something will have to be done with them.'

'That is the government's business,' said her father, reflectively. 'Tuberculosis is a notifiable disease, and it does not come under the local authority. I must look into the matter, but that is my impression of the Act. Perhaps we might run to a small contribution. But it will have to be considered, my dear, and I can't promise.'

'Surely you have plenty of influence with the government, Father. You could make them do it.'

'It is not so easy as you think,' he declared. 'And it won't do to make a political matter of it. Which reminds me, Santa. You had quite an argument with Mabuis about politics the other night.'

'Yes, Father. He is thoroughly SAP. He said the most awful things, and the worst of it is some of his remarks come uncommonly close to the truth.'

'You must not say that, Child, even if you think it. Remember what I told you about hiding your feelings. Politics is a game, my dear, though some of your age seem to regard it as a sort of religion. It isn't that. It's just skilful anticipation and correct interpretation of which way the wind is going to blow.'

'That's rather a sordid view to take, Dad. I'm sure it's not our view.'

'Of course it is. You surely don't mean to say that you think there is any inherent difference between us Nats and the SAPs? Why, my dear, I was a SAP once—we all were, as a matter of fact—and if it comes to hard bedrock fact, there is no difference between us in principles. Our programmes are very much the same—so much so that it would need a wise man to detect any difference.'

'But, Father, if that is so, why ...'

'Why this difference, my dear? Surely you can see for yourself why we squabble. It is a matter of persons, in the first place, a pure question of personal selfishness. Secondly, it is a matter of prejudice and Party prestige.'

'I can't believe that,' said Santa, indignantly. 'We stand for much more than persons. We stand for principles. There might have been some similarity formerly, but nowadays the SAPs are remnants of the old Unionists.'

'Of course they are, Child. That is just the point. It is the old Party orientation which we had in the Bond days, only then it was provincial, and now it is wider than that. You see, my dear, in politics one must trim, and tack, and take in sail when necessary. That is what you young enthusiasts won't learn, and that is why you make it so difficult for us to save our face sometimes. I wish you had more sense. Why, only last week I had to talk for an hour and more to convince some of our fools that our status is all that we were out to get ...'

'But it wasn't, Father. Our programme distinctly lays down that we should strive for independence, sovereign independence ...'

'Tut, tut, Santa. It's all very well for an uneducated voter to take that line, but you should know better. Every Party has its slogan, which serves for so long as it inspires its followers. But these shibboleths are not immutable. They are changed and modified by circumstances.'

'Not principles, Father. That is the rock on which the old Party came to grief ...'

'Don't you believe it, my dear. The old Party got shipwrecked simply because the ship was leaking, and most of the rats had already swum to shore. I did. Yes, my dear, I am not ashamed of it. I saw how things were going, and I made my choice with my eyes open. Do you think I care a rap for all these fine sentiments you have been proclaiming ever since you came back from Europe? Not a bit. What matters is what the electorate as a whole thinks of the business, and that again is merely what it thinks of the leaders of the two parties.'

'I don't believe it,' said Santa, getting up and depositing her cigarette on the ink tray, there being no convenient receptacle for it in the study of one whose principles eschewed tobacco. 'No Party could come to power, and retain it as we have done, unless it represents the soul of the country.'

'Have it your own way,' said her father, tolerantly. That, indeed, is what we want the public to believe. But as a fact, as soon as any Party gets into power, it forgets about the soul and sentiment and does everything it can to cling to what it has got. It may sound sordid to you, but that's the fact. It's the same with us.'

'Nevertheless we have done far more in our few years of office,' countered Santa, 'than the old Party did in ten years and more. We've carried out some of our principles. We have established our language rights—we have achieved our status, and we have got our own flag. By the way, Father, we must have a flagstaff, and fly it in front of the house. It's deplorable that no one does it here, and we should set them an example.'

'By all means. Get one. I don't know where you can, but if you do, see that it is not one of those things that fade in a couple of days, like the one which is flying on the court house. I can't say it appeals to me, but have it your own way, my dear.'

'It doesn't satisfy my own aesthetic tastes either,' declared Santa, with a smile, 'but it is our own flag, after all, and we should hoist it. You used to hang out a Jack on the King's birthday, didn't you?'

'In Rome ...' Elias shrugged his shoulders nonchalantly. 'But do as you like. It can't do any harm.'

'That's not the way to look at it, Father. We really should be more—more self-assertive. We can't go on being doormats, can we? What have you done about the council minutes?'

'That is a matter of expense, Santa,' said her father, mildly. 'They have always been kept in English ...'

'I know,' said Santa, scornfully, 'and only one member of the council talks English; the others all speak Afrikaans, and your deliberations are wholly in Afrikaans. You should put a stop to it.'

'Now there, my Child,' said her father, confidentially, 'there's just where your impetuosity carries you too far. Why disturb things? Why not let them be? We all understand English, and it will only raise feeling if we insist that the minutes should be kept in Afrikaans ...'

'The principle, Father, the principle. Let them be kept in both languages, and I say nothing. But have them at least alternatively English and Afrikaans. There can be no objection to that.'

'Won't there? Of course there will be objections. The clerk cannot write decent Afrikaans, and we shall have to get clerical assistance. That means extra expense. Remember it is really not a matter of principle, nor of essentials. It is merely sentiment.'

'Don't you recognise sentiment, Father?'

'Of course, my dear, if it hadn't been for sentiment ... but there, you'll never understand some things. You are like your mother in that. And now it is high time for you to go to bed. I shall take one more dose of my medicine ...'

'I'm not sure the medicine does you much good, Father,' said Santa, as he got up from his chair. 'Why don't you get thoroughly overhauled? When you go to Cape Town, you might call in and see ...'

'Now, Child, I will not have you worrying yourself about me. Or about my medicine. It does me a power of good, although you do not believe in it. And there is really very little wrong with me. I saw a specialist when I was last at Cape Town, and he assured me that the medicine was all that I needed.'

He kissed her affectionately and bade her goodnight, closing the door carefully after her. Then he unlocked the drawer of his desk and took out a medicine bottle. It was the same bottle which had been on the dresser in the dining room, but he had thought it was safer to keep it under lock and key. He put it safely away after he had taken a dose from it, and sucked the inevitable peppermint lozenge. It was really not necessary, for Maria never saw further than the tip of her nose, and sometimes, thank God, not even that far.

Then he turned to his desk and absorbed himself in his papers. His face became drawn and anxious as he studied them. He made columns of figures on the blotting pad, and when he added them up their total staggered him. He got up from his chair and paced up and down the room, muttering to himself. Finally, when the clock struck twelve, he locked his desk, turned out the lights, and went to his bedroom.

Maria was still awake, and the bedroom lamp on the little bedside table shed a halo of light around her pale, patient features. She put aside the book which she had been reading, but made no remark.

'I have been talking to Santa,' he said. 'The girl has some queer notions, Wife.'

'She will learn sense in time,' said his wife, mildly. Your pyjamas are on the chair there, Elias.'

'You must keep her away from that damned location,' he said, gruffly. 'There is no call for her to go nosing around it. You must talk to Mina. I won't have Santa attending her girl.'

'I will see what I can do,' she retorted, tonelessly. 'But Santa goes her own way, as you know. You might get the girl away.'

'That is for Buren to do,' he said, savagely. 'He is the district surgeon, not I. What have I got to do with Mina's daughter?'

'I merely suggested it, Elias,' she replied, as tonelessly as before. There is a sanatorium somewhere for consumptive patients. If Sophia could go there, Santa would not need to go into the location.'

'She'd find some pretext to go there, Wife,' he remarked, getting into bed. 'I think, on the whole, we'd better let the thing be. She tells me the girl can't last.'

'I hope she is mistaken,' said Maria, her voice quivering. 'It would ... Mina would feel it, Elias.'

'Mina has no feelings,' he said gruffly. 'Haven't you found that out, Wife? She is a hard old hypocrite, that. I hope you are not going to have asthma tonight. I am dreadfully tired.'

'I hope not,' said his wife. 'I took the medicine. The ephidrene, you know. It really prevents such an attack, I do believe.'

'So much the better,' he said. 'Turn out the light. Good night,' and he turned his face away from her and fell asleep.

Chapter 9

The farm *Eisleben*, the property of Jeremia Gerster, was one of the best cultivated holdings in the District. Originally it had belonged to a German immigrant, a member of the Crimean Legion, who had settled upon it and reclaimed it from the bare veld, making of its rich alluvial a fertile garden, and of its disintegrated sandstone and clay profitable wheat-lands. Its homestead, built in the old fashioned style with over-hanging eaves where the thatching came down over the white-washed walls and rococo gables, was shadowed by sturdy oaks, not yet old enough to be scraggy, but retaining the dignity of trunk and prodigality of leaf belonging to healthy, middle-aged trees. A poplar wood, and a clump of stone pines, a well stocked orchard of deciduous and citrus trees, and luxuriant plantations of tobacco and mealies diversified its environment, and gave varying shades of green to the variegated colour picture on a summer's day. The *Eisleben* oranges, of the sweet seedling variety, had already established themselves on the export market, and competed with the produce of older and better known farms in the District. Jeremia Gerster was known and envied as a successful and highly prosperous farmer in a community keenly critical of agricultural pretensions.

Jeremia was a tall, sun-browned man, with a fierce grey moustache, and a mild, open expression on his good looking features, a representative of the best type in the District, and one who could pride himself on an ancestry second to none among his peers. His wife, Gertrude, had been born a Rekker, a descendant of a well-to-do Swedish official of the old Company, who had been granted extensive holdings in the District, and whose family had for generations maintained their aristocratic standing. She was a small, fragile-looking creature, with a small, fragile face, which utterly belied her energetic, domineering temperament. On the farm, to her Native entourage, she was known as the '*kwaai missis*,' which translated means simply the 'angry mistress,' but in reality implies much more than that, for it connotes qualities of initiative, endurance, determination, and turbulence, and is expressive more of admiration than of deprecatory criticism. That was the reason why the *Eisleben* Natives loved and respected old mistress Gertrude, and submitted to her despotic rule with the good-natured, child-like subservience characteristic of a race descended from slaves who had found slavery not altogether the evil that it is sometimes taken to have been.

The Rekkers had held property in man, like all their contemporaries, but they had held it with a proper realisation of their responsibilities to their human chattels, and when emancipation had come, their slaves had unanimously elected to remain with them, serving voluntarily masters and mistresses to whom they had formerly belonged by rights of purchase. Emancipation had made no great difference in their status, and the Rekkers had continued to live up to their responsibilities. Gertrude had inherited this tradition, a tradition of service, of responsibility and obligation as imperative on the master as its corollary of discipline, subservience and industriousness was upon the slaves. She ruled her underlings with the same standards as those she applied to her husband and her family, and she could point to servants who had been in her employ from childhood and who were likely to remain with her until death had severed all bonds between them. Her Natives loved and respected her, for they recognised that she personified the tradition in which they too had been brought up, although to the younger ones among them it was merely a tradition.

Jeremia Gerster sat in his dining room, at the little side-table placed close to the window, whence he could look down upon the flower garden, and beyond that over the vineyard, until his glance rested on the solid blue mountain wall marking the northern limit of his farm, The room was large, comfortably but simply furnished, with old cedarwood furniture, polished to a resplendent radiancy reflecting every stray beam of light falling upon it.

The floor was of hard clay, smeared with a decoction of dung, according to the old fashion prevailing in the District and followed, in these modern times, by old fashioned housewives like Aunt Gertrude who were conservative enough to retain it. Twice a week the maids brought from the *kraals* the dung, which was stirred into a pailful of clean water, to a thin, porridge-like consistency, and evenly spread over the floor with a sedge broom, where it dried very rapidly and made a smooth, uniformly brown surface with a faint aromatic smell. Some folk mingled ox-blood with the dung mixture, which made it dry more rapidly and gave a warmer brown tinge to the floors, but Aunt Gertrude preferred the simpler way. To anyone not accustomed to such methods the practice may have seemed strange, and even disgusting, but in reality it was not so, for there was nothing offensive in it, and no one would have objected to it who, not knowing on what kind of covering he was treading, had entered the room shortly after it had been smeared and noted the faint, rather pleasant aromatic scent which it exhaled.

On this spring morning, when the blue mountain wall was slightly veiled in light mists creeping slowly from the scarred cliffs and revealing, as it evaporated in the warm sunlight, their variegated colouring, Jeremia was perturbed. He was a mild mannered man, taking refuge, like most weak characters, in strong language when his emotions were stirred; and the communication over which he was now so anxiously pondering had disturbed him to the core of his being. He was beyond words. He could only sit and stare at it. He scarcely saw the scene spread before him outside the window, the early cannas opening their velvety buds, the tall standard roses, the beds of geranium and carnations, the clump of snow-white arums near the fountain. All his attention was concentrated upon the letter.

His wife came in from the garden, carrying her garden scissors and a bunch of roses. She glanced at him sharply, noting his discomfiture, and put her scissors and her gathered roses on the table.

'What is the matter, Jerry?' she asked quickly, imperatively. 'Aren't you feeling well?'

'You-you w-wouldn't feel well, Trui,' he stuttered. He always stuttered when he was stirred. She had tried her best to get him out of the habit, but it persisted in spite of frequent admonitions to draw a deep breath before he spoke, to whistle a bar, or to tap lightly with his index finger on his forehead.

'... if you, you, got such a l-letter as this-this.'

He jerked the paper towards her, but it fell on the floor, and she stooped to pick it up.

'Hm,' she said, brusquely. 'From the bank. What's there to upset you in that, Man? We are solvent, I suppose?'

'Read it, Woman,' he cried, 'read it ... God damn me, read it, Lord my time, can't you-you r-read it?'

'I haven't got my glasses, Man,' she cried. 'They are in the bedroom, and I can't go and fetch them. What's it all about? Don't swear, Husband. It does not become a grown man to go on so. Tell me what it is all about.'

'That, God damn me,' he cried, furiously, 'is just what I can't make out. They w-write to s-say that I have ... that they have ...'

'Come, come, Jerry, don't get so excited. Whatever it is, it must be a mistake if you know nothing about it.' She marched to the sideboard and poured out a glass of water and came back and held it out to him. 'Drink this. Yes, all of it, and take your pipe ... there it is. Fill it. Now light it, and smoke, and then tell me all about it.'

She drew up a chair alongside the table and sat down, smoothing her outdoor apron as she did so. Her small, fragile figure seemed child-like in contrast to his rude, muscular frame; he overtopped her by more than a head as he sat facing her.

'The bank writes,' he explained, more calmly now, 'that a cheque of mine has been handed in. They don't say who handed it in ...'

'Doubtless someone you gave it to. What does it matter? Come to the point, Man.'

'But God damn me ...'

'Stop saying wicked words, Jerry. The Good Lord hears every one of them and puts a mark against you which you will have to work off on judgment day. What does the bank want?'

'It writes to say that it leaves me with an overdraft. I have never had such a thing before. It is wicked—wicked. It can't be, Wife, it can't be.'

'What can't be? Explain, Husband. How much was this cheque?' she asked, practically. 'You have your cheque books. Look up the counterfoil.'

'I never signed one for a thousand pounds this year—never,' said Jeremia, with conviction. 'I must have done so in my sleep, if I did. Whom could I have paid a thousand pounds to?'

'Thousand ... are you mad, Man? What nonsense is this? Here, lend me your glasses. Let me see what I can make of it. You must have misunderstood or misread. Give me the glasses.'

He handed his spectacles to her and she read the letter. Her brows came together as she did so. She read it again, and then she placed the note on the table, keeping her hand upon it.

'It is perfectly clear,' she said. 'You owe the bank forty-two pounds. Last week, you remember, you put in eight hundred. That was for the new car which you were going to buy next week. You then had two hundred—no, wait, you paid Solomon's account which was thirty-six pounds something, I can't remember the exact figures. Get your cheque book, and tell the boy to have the car ready. To go into town, of course. What else for? Don't sit like a fool, Man. Get the cheque book.'

Obediently—he was always obedient when she directed, for he trusted her; she had a head for things, Trui, and could be depended upon—he rose and went to fetch his cheque book and give orders to the boy. He was absent for a short time only, and in his absence she studied the letter again with knitted brows, and made calculations mentally. Something, she felt, was seriously wrong.

'Give them to me,' she said when he came back with the cheque book. She rapidly turned the counterfoils. 'Yes, here it is. Thirty-six pounds fourteen to Solomon, last Friday. And four to the postmaster for the phone. That is forty fourteen, which leaves you—here is the balance two hundred, with one fifty-nine six. That agrees with the overdraft—I see you drew one for ten shillings on the same day, so the bank is correct. I suppose the difference is due to commission or something. Anyway, you had nine fifty-nine balance, and if they have cashed a cheque for a thousand that leaves you forty pounds odd in their debt ...'

'But I never wrote a cheque for forty—I mean for a thousand, Trui. I wouldn't dream of doing such a thing. Not without consulting you ...'

'I should hope not,' said his wife, energetically. 'And anyway, you couldn't have drawn one from this book. And you have no other. And yet the bank says they have cashed one of yours for a thousand. And you have an overdraft of forty odd. Get the bank on the phone. Don't stand there, Man, like a stuck pig. Get the bank, I shall speak to them,'

Jeremia went to the telephone, which was placed in the corridor, and got the connection. His wife came and took the receiver from his hand.

'Is that the bank?' she asked. 'Yes? I want to speak to Mr Marsden, please. It is Mrs Gerster from *Eisleben* speaking. Very well ... Is that you, Mr Marsden? Yes, good morning. Mr Gerster just wished to know ... to whom was the cheque made out ... yes, the large one that you paid out ... Oh yes, it is quite all right. Mr Gerster will see you about the overdraft. Quite so ... and is Mrs Marsden going to the seaside this year? Of course, how can you ask such a question? We'll be glad to see you all, any time. Better come when the watermelons are ripe, then the children will be able to enjoy themselves. Thank you very much. Yes, it's quite all right. Good morning, Mr Marsden.'

She replaced the receiver, and looked at her husband. You must go in and get your pass book and the old cheques, Jerry,' she said, decisively. 'That cheque was paid in by Brother-in-law Elias. It was made out to Vantloo & van Deren. Now don't say a word. Take the car and go in, and get the pass book and the cheques, and put something in for the overdraft. I have some money in my drawer, but best get what the agent owes you for the wheat; it is long overdue, and it must be well over a hundred pounds. Then there is the citrus account—he should be able to give you something on that, say another hundred.'

'But Wife, Elias ... I never wrote a cheque for Elias for that amount ... not for years. You know when he let us down over those shares ... but that was three years ago. How could I have written a cheque for a thousand pounds and not know anything about it ...'

'Never mind that now. And take care you don't talk like that to the manager. You needn't even see him. Just get your pass book in the ordinary way. They put all the paid cheques in the pocket. Pay in the money you get, and come back as soon as you can. Promise me you won't go anywhere else.'

'Very well, Wife,' Jeremia did not know why he should abstain from visiting his sister-in-law when he was in the Village, but his wife's order was peremptory, and he promised.

He drove away in the Ford, and Gertrude saw him off. Then she came back into the dining room, cleaned her garden scissors, put them away, and arranged the roses in a large bowl.

'I expected something of the sort from brother-in-law,' she said to herself, her fragile face assuming a look of stern determination. 'But this time we must put a stop to his tricks. The puzzle is how to do that without letting sister-in-law know what a scoundrel the man is.'

And, still absorbed in the puzzle, she went into the kitchen to give directions to the maids.

Chapter 10

Gertrude Gerster, born Rekker, was a woman of character. Fragile as she appeared to be in form and face, her fragility cloaked a determination all the more decisive because it was apparently so foreign to her appearance.

It was not the determination of impetuousness, for it was born of solid logic and a sense of honour inherited from a long line of ancestors who, through generations, had regarded truth and sincerity as actual, not abstract things.

She took herself and what she stood for seriously. The Rekkers had always been persons of substance who, in all their homeliness and habituation to customs and conventions, engendered in a thoroughly democratic community, had preserved something of the original standards which had demarcated them before they came out as settlers from less noble-born families. They had been, and were still *armiger*, and

Aunt Gertrude liked to tell her children of the family crest and arms which they had really no right to bear, but which still occupied a position of pride in the corridor, facing whoever entered the house of *Eisleben*. She herself regarded her attitude towards her ancestry as venial pride, but in reality it was something more than that, for it was allegiance to tradition, a realisation of what family obligations meant, a scrupulous regard for all that obligation and tradition represented.

It was because she had found Jeremiah responsive, in his slow, lumbering way, to exactly the same feelings which stirred in herself that she had married him, for the young, handsome and wealthy farmer had attracted her more by his innate honesty and sincerity of character than by those qualities which would have appealed to a less sturdily independent temperament than hers.

The marriage had been, in every sense of the word, a happy one, for she had found in him almost a complete complement to herself. At an early stage she had assumed command of him, exercising it so tactfully that he had never been conscious of her superiority to an extent that he could have resented, yet so consistently that in time he had come to depend upon her more than upon himself when it had been necessary to decide any important matter. She had never failed him, and her judgment had invariably been acute, sensible, and fully justified by circumstances. As a result, the partnership between them had never been interrupted by differences of opinion, and she had come to regard it as wholly stable and immutable.

There had been occasions, of course, when they had viewed things from different angles; never, however, irreconcilable. Under his phlegmatic exterior, Jerry concealed feelings which could, as she knew, be stirred into violent upheaval by the thought of injustice done to him or those he cared for. He had the quality of large, indefinite affection, such as is granted to children and dogs, a characteristic upon which she could rely even when she could not entirely control it. There had been the occasion when his sister had fallen violently in love with the young attorney from the Village, and when he had strenuously championed her cause, although Gertrude had pointed out with calm, common-place logic, the unsuitability of the match and the manifest objections to an alliance with a family that could scarcely, from the Rekker point of view, be regarded as a family, because it was of mushroom growth and had not yet established itself. But she had soon seen that nothing that she could say would make any difference to his view and, like a wise and tactful woman, she had ceased her opposition, and Maria and Elias had been married.

Jerry's affection for his sister was deep-rooted and sincere. He had looked upon her, and indeed still looked upon her, as one who was inherently weak, one to be sheltered and protected, petted and indulged. Gertrude had never quite accepted that interpretation of her sister-in-law, whom she too regarded with admiration and love, but here again she had never combated her husband's conception of Maria's character. She had realised that it grew out of the protective affection which an elder brother had lavished upon a sister much his junior, and that Jerry found satisfaction in cherishing it, and never attempted to modify it as the years went by.

Now Aunt Gertrude, with equal clarity, saw before her one of these crises which could not be altogether evaded, even in the most ideal partnership that exists. She felt that the situation was too complex for her to deal with single-handed, and she cast around for someone in whom she could confide, with whom she could take counsel on a matter which, as she knew, might easily lead to complications tending to shake the serenity of thirty years of quiet married life.

'Jerry,' she argued with herself, 'is bound to know the truth this time. Elias—and I have no doubt it is Elias; the thing reeks of him—will not dare to do such a thing without telling him. He must. It is impossible to prevent it getting known. And Jerry will give in, tamely, because he will be frightened at the thought of Maria hearing about it. Maria must be spared—that is all that he will say. And I have had enough of Elias. There must be an end sometime. I shall phone Eric.'

She wasted no time in reconsidering her decision, but marched to the phone and rang up Eric van Deren.

'Yes, it is Aunt Gertrude speaking,' she said, when she had been connected, 'I want you to come out at once, Eric. No, Jerry and I are all right. There is nothing the matter with us. But there is something the matter all the same, and I want your help. Your help and your advice. What's that? Yes, of course, immediately. Stuff, your work can wait. You come out at once. Get the car and drive out. What is that? Oh, the clerks can attend to it. No, I don't want you to say anything to Elias. On no account. Yes? Very well. I shall expect you this afternoon. Yes, it is something serious. I can't tell you over the phone. You will hear all about it when you come. What's that? Bring Santa? No, don't bring her—she can come some other day. I particularly want you not to bring her, Eric. Are you listening? Well, come at once. Don't wait. It is urgent. All right.'

She hung up the receiver, and went back into the dining room and sat down at the little side-table. There were other letters lying on it, for Jerry had been too much disturbed to attend to his correspondence, and had left some of it unopened. She turned the letters over, idly, glancing at the addresses. On one the handwriting was familiar. She drew in her breath with a hissing sound.

'So-o,' she muttered. 'He has lost no time. I may as well see what he says.'

She opened the envelope carefully, and withdrew the enclosure. She felt no compunction in doing so. Jerry had no secrets from her; very often she opened his correspondence for him and read what he received. He would approve, and in the circumstances it was perhaps better that he had not noticed that particular letter.

She read it through with her lips pursed into a thin, straight line. It was from Elias, and it was worded very much as she had expected it to be worded. A thoroughly impudent, hypocritical letter, appealing brazenly to the recipient's feelings, hinting that it would be better if Jerry took no steps, promising, largely, restitution at some indefinite date in the future, when circumstances permitted, expressing perfunctory, wholly inadequate regret.

'*Faugh*,' she exclaimed, throwing the letter on the table and wiping her fingers on her garden apron, although she was not conscious of doing so, 'it is just like him. A hypocrite to his heart's core. But with the sense, at least, to clear up things before they got into a frightful mess. Now what is to be done?'

She resolutely concentrated her mind upon other subjects, but in the midst of her supervision of the maid's household duties she found herself recurring to the puzzle that seemed to deny solution. Years ago she had seen complications looming ahead, she told herself. Oil and water do not mix, or at least it needs a violent agitation to mingle them to an emulsion. No great passion or crisis had stirred the life of Elias and

Maria. A pity, for something of the kind, she reflected, might have changed things for the better. It was pathetic that Maria was so strongly attached to him; in the face of that, very little could be done, and of course it was impossible to risk any open scandal. In so far, she was at one with Jerry. It would be monstrous if the outside public became aware of what was going on. Jerry himself, now ... she wondered if she had acted wisely in sending him in to the village. He might easily, in his blunt, honest, outspoken way, let slip something upon which gossip could fasten, and she knew how avid the busybodies were. Scandal intrigued any community, and the village was no exception to that lamentable rule. It might be better to phone him ... but perhaps the wisest course was to leave well alone.

She speculated on the motives which had forced Elias so stupidly to show his hand. He had always been a cautious, careful player, never divulging a card before he could use it to the utmost advantage. That she would admit to his credit—the man was the reverse of stupid. She had a grudging admiration for the manner in which he had reversed himself in politics; it had been done so agilely, with such a dexterous twist, and with such a semblance of passionate convictions that she herself had been deceived for a while. And the way he had exploited his teetotalism. Much as it shocked her sense of honour and outraged her traditional way of looking at things, she could not but see the ludicrousness of a situation which permitted so vehement an advocate of prohibition to derive pecuniary benefit from the trade he so passionately opposed. He had certainly played his hand well, false-carding constantly but always with a marked advantage to himself, and getting the reputation of a strong, honest player. That was the amazing part of the business. She had watched him for years. She had never believed in his pretensions, for you cannot make silk purses out of sows ears, and who after all were the Vantloos? Blood and race counted, no matter what people said, and if you started, unhappily for yourself, with a false strain in you, time and circumstances would inevitably bring it out. You could not hide these inherited failings. What, otherwise, was the use of being well-born, nobly-bred, imbued with a sense of tradition and obligation?

And Maria? Poor soul, there was no question—there could be none—about her attachment to the man. She was as much in love with him as she had been when they had first 'sat up,' conforming—laughingly—to custom, though courting in a manner considered by the old fashioned indecently hasty. It was rather wonderful, all things considered, that Maria had not found him out by this time. She must have had plenty of opportunity to detect his hypocrisy and realise his innate viciousness. But then Maria was one of those who never could see very far. She was blameworthily blind to some things, and she had set out to spoil her husband from the first, and had disregarded all the warnings, all the suggestive hints insinuated in her direction by those who wished her well. Jerry was just like that. Not practical; too idealistic; too much inclined to take everyone at face value; too averse to test the depth of the gilding that encrusted clay. Even now Jerry would probably make a scene, although the facts were so palpable and the proof so evident.

And there was Santa. The girl adored her father, and she was, after all, a sensible girl. Aunt Gertrude was very fond of her niece, although since Santa's return from Europe she had found her trying on occasions, too impetuous in stating her own opinion, too enthusiastic about matters which are not usually debated with warmth, too

prone to flout popular feelings and assert herself. Nevertheless Aunt Gertrude believed
in her niece's common sense, and saw no great reason why she should not appeal to it.
That was certainly a suggestion that had to be taken into consideration. Jerry, too, was
proud of Santa, in whom he saw, curiously enough, some resemblance to her mother,
and it would be desirable to enlist the girl's sympathy in whatever decision they came
to.

That might not be easy, but with the proofs in their possession and with the case so
damnably clear ...

Aunt Gertrude stepped into the garden, and thence on to the open veld, although
the midday sun was strong and she had forgotten to put on her bonnet. She trod the
brilliant little wine-coloured flowers underfoot, crushing their velvety clyses into the
soft soil as she walked irresolutely towards the road. She had been too busy with her
thoughts to take luncheon, and the maids had removed the dishes and commented in
the kitchen on the fact that the old mistress was annoyed. It did not matter to them, for
her annoyance was not with them, nor would it react upon them. That much they
knew, for the old mistress was eminently just.

Chapter 11

In his spare moments, which in a busy practice were not many, Dr Buren collected
butterflies, a hobby that had earned him the nickname of 'the net-doctor.' The Valley
district did not yield a large number of varieties, but he was in touch with collectors
elsewhere, and went far afield to increase his collection, in which he took a justifiable
pride.

On the morning after the talk with her father, Santa had found the doctor engaged
in sorting out the skippers which he had collected the preceding day. He had spread
them out neatly on the cork setting-boards, pinning down their sturdy, stiff wings with
strips of tissue paper, and tearing out their short antennae with hooked needles.

'Ah, my dear Partner,' he remarked when she came into the dispensary, 'you are a
little early. The car is being oiled and won't be round for half an hour yet. That is why
you find me occupied with such trifles. Not that they are really trifles. For us, natural
history, if diligently and knowledgeably pursued, is a great help. I regret that it is not
taught in the schools. Pure classification—taxonomy, my dear—is very useful to
inculcate the habit of orderly arrangement of one's thoughts. And the identification of
a species—take this Zerites for example—is after all very much like the identification
of a particular disease. It is diagnosis—the study of variations with a view of finding
out the divergence from the norm.'

'I never cared much for it,' confessed Santa. 'My mind is ...'

'Don't apologise,' said the doctor, briskly. 'You are intuitive, like all woman-kind.
You love to jump to conclusions. That is why you sometimes make such amazingly
accurate diagnoses, although you cannot always support your findings. I have a puzzle

for you this morning,' and he proceeded to outline a case which had perplexed him.

'We will go and see it presently,' he concluded. 'Reserve your intuition until you see the patient. Myself, I have not attempted to make any. It is either a myopathy or a myelopathy, and there are clinical signs supporting both possibilities. By the way, you will be glad to hear that everything is going smoothly, and that Mr van Deren will draw up the deed of partnership today.'

'I inferred, from what father said,' began Santa, agreeably surprised, 'that the matter was not yet settled. Eric must have surpassed himself. I understood that there were all kinds of difficulties. Even that my money was exhausted and that I should have to raise a loan from mother.'

'Oh dear me, no,' said the doctor. 'The money side of the matter is the least that bothered Master Eric. His doubts were on the question of your own stability. He does not take you seriously, Santa. You must bear in mind that you are an utterly unusual phenomenon to our community. A lady doctor ... why, do you know that one of the Elders expressed his surprise that I, a sensible fellow like me, could associate myself with such a godless innovation.'

'Then it's high time they came to their senses,' protested Santa, hotly. 'Besides, it's no business of theirs at all.'

'That's as it may be,' remarked Buren, amicably. 'But, my dear Girl, I never go out of my way to antagonise public opinion. It does not pay—I don't mean in a monetary sense, but generally, in practice. I can understand your reforming zeal and all that, but you ought to bear in mind that we live in a backwater, and the eddies that swirl in to us are apt to be disturbing to our calm, old-fashioned ways of life.'

'I have noticed that you are an excellent trimmer, Doctor' said Santa, smiling. 'All these weeks I have been trying to find out where you stand in politics, and I haven't yet discovered which side you favour.'

'Politics, my dear ... Well, in confidence now, although it may shock you, I am still an adherent of the old Party, although, strictly between you and me, I did not record my vote at the last election. I thought it was time the other side had their innings, for honestly, my side hadn't played the game properly. Now they'll be out for a very long time, and your side will bat. I don't see how we are going to get your side out—not with our present team, at least—although your team is not altogether what you take it to be. But it is playing consistently and it is stone-walling with prodigious effect.'

I suppose you have been talking with Mr Mabuis,' said Santa. 'He really does not know about things. He has been away so long, and he has never been in touch with things here.'

'Now there you speak without your intuition,' remarked the doctor, genially arranging his setting boards neatly on the shelf. 'I find Mabuis a singularly well-informed person. You know he was a *burgher* of the old Transvaal Republic, who refused to take the oath of allegiance and went out to the Argentine. He made good there and came back on a visit, but he told me that he saw no reason to regret what he had done.'

'If he really cared for his country,' said Santa, hotly, 'he would come back and help us. He would take his share here ...'

'That is what I told him. But he won't see it and, honestly, I can't blame him. He is very bitter in some ways, though his bitterness is with things, conditions and circumstances, rather than with persons. But he has at least been consistent.'

'So have we, Doctor. I don't see that he has anything to pride himself upon.'

'Well, my dear, I don't like to argue, but I know some of our people who have expressed the same high sounding views—about not taking the oath and all that, you know, and who are now quite the meekest of the meek. I don't say anything against them—every man has a right to his own opinion, as we say here—but it does not strike me as convincing evidence of their consistency.'

'I suppose you agree with him,' said Santa, challengingly. 'In his views about us?'

'You must be more explicit if you want me to answer that question. I really don't know what his views are. We had a good deal of desultory talk, from which I gathered that he thought that we were all degenerating.'

'Yes, that was his chorus. I got tired of the theme, Doctor.'

'Well, perhaps he overdrew the picture. But, seriously, we are not improving. You must have noticed yourself how the old families are dying out, and the newer generation is struggling to keep itself in existence.'

'I can't say I have. I have seen nothing to warrant his conclusions.'

'Oh come, my dear. Why, I remember when I first came here how different things were. We were a settled, contented, harmonious community. Our political squabbles were storms in a tea cup—we were always Bond, you know, and the other side had no real chance, but there was nothing of this racial antagonism that you see now.'

'It was a sheer delight, on Queen's Birthday, to see the old men saluting on the square, and listen to their lusty singing of *God Save the Queen*. None of us felt ashamed of doing that, and none of us thought that we were disloyal to this country because we did it.'

'That was simply because your national consciousness had not been stirred,' declared Santa, with decision. 'You were still content to be doormats, that's all.'

'I don't think you are altogether fair to us,' said the doctor, mildly. 'Take my own case. I went to Edinburgh very much as you went to London, although to be sure I only managed to scrape through my matriculation in the third class. I was there during the First Boer War, and you can have no conception, my dear, how our feelings were stirred. We managed to get up an ambulance, and I came out—too late, however, to take part in the business. And then the First Language Movement ... why, we all subscribed to the *Patriot*, although we found considerable difficulty in reading it. Such queer spelling, you know.'

'Really, Doctor, I had no idea ... I thought you were thoroughly English-minded ...'

'Yes, there you go again. You are obsessed with the idea that if one does not agree with you in all things one must necessarily be antagonistic. Get away from it, my dear. Believe me, some of those whom you call 'English-minded' have done more for this country than many of your fervent Nationalists who have never contributed a scrap to our cultural development. Why,' Dr Buren warmed to his subject, 'there was old Charles Quakerley—his father was county and an MP, and his brother an admiral of the Red, and he deserted his ship in False Bay and married a Dutch girl, and was one of our early settlers here. He built our first school; he gave us our first library—and such a library, my dear, autographed copies of Jane Austen, Sir Walter, Thackeray, and the rest. And a fund for scholarships for boys to go to high school. And he wasn't the only one. There was his son—you must remember his wife, old Mrs Quakerley, who was still alive when you were a girl ...'

'Yes, I do, dimly. She was a frightful old bore. But what became of the library? We haven't one now.'

'Burned, my dear. Destroyed during the war. That was our first great calamity. It changed everything. It killed the good feeling between us, and it made people bitter. You know too little about that chapter, Santa, and perhaps it's just as well. But you do a frightful lot of harm—I don't say you personally, but your Party—when you harp on it and try to make political capital out of that bitterness. Those of us who went through it look back upon it with unutterable regret. Those of you who weren't in it, and who now try to draw vicariously upon it, have no idea what it meant. We may seem old and stodgy to you who think we never had a national consciousness—whatever that may mean—but let me assure you that we felt very passionately in those days, and that we had our own ideals. Ah, my dear, I really don't know why I am telling you all this, for it does not matter now. Now we are in a welter of words, without sincerity and without, usually, much sense, and that to my mind is infinitely worse than anything one could have said about us then.'

'Nobody said anything against you then,' denied Santa. 'I daresay, Doctor, you were justified. You lived in an English atmosphere, and could not be supposed to look at things from our point of view ...'

'English atmosphere be damned,' snorted the doctor. 'Let me tell you this, young Woman, my old dad made me read O'Brien's *When We Were Boys Together* when I was in Edinburgh, and Mitchell's *Jail Journal*. There was precious little we did not know about the wrongs of Ireland, and let me assure you they were, in those days, much more concrete and far less mystical than the wrongs of South Africa ...'

'What about *Slagter's Nek* and the Bezuidenhouts? What about the Raid and Outlander grievances?' demanded Santa, now thoroughly roused.

'What about them?' said the doctor, contemptuously. 'Ask yourself. Would the old Company have acted differently, after the *Nek* rebellion? And Cuyler was American, not English. As for the Raid, Mabuis might have a grievance there, but scarcely you. And down here we knew too much about conditions in the Transvaal to think the Outlanders' grievances entirely a myth. Some of you would like us to think our own grievances today mythical ...'

'So they are. If anybody has a grievance, it is the Afrikaans-speaking citizen. He sees his language constantly slighted, his ideals trod underfoot, his aspirations thwarted ...'

'You should get them to nominate you for the Provincial Council, Santa. And the Party might do worse. But, seriously, my dear young Patriot, no one thwarts you or slights you. It is all in your fertile imagination.'

'My imagination has been fallow since I came back, Doctor. I have only used my eyes and my ears. Both have shown me that it is high time we asserted ourselves, unless we wish to be swamped by English culture.'

'That is because you persist in thinking that English and Afrikaans cultures are necessarily antagonistic. That's the trouble with you all. You cannot think in terms of a common denominator. Your South African nationalism is purely sectional for you refuse to credit us, who do not speak Afrikaans, with an equally strong national sentiment. Yet it exists, and it existed long before you made language and culture the test of a true national South African sentiment. Old Quakerley had it, and his descendants even more so. I have it, although I suppose you would call me a traitor because I don't share my grandfather's hatred of the English, which dates back to the Boyne as yours does to ... well, the Blaauberg fight, I suppose, or the First Occupation. Really, my dear, it is all rather dismally childish. You must realise yourself that there would be very little of this ill-feeling if we could only get away from persons and platitudes and concentrate upon the big things.'

'They are big things to me,' asserted Santa, stoutly. 'Sentiment is a big thing, Doctor. Since I came back I have repeatedly noticed that what you call conciliation— what your old Party harped on in and out of season—is expected from us, not the other side. It's we who have to give everything, and when, once in a while we take things, we are accused of stirring up race hatred.'

'There's something in that,' admitted van Buren. 'But the conciliation business came from what you call the other side. After all, what was it but sentiment that gave us Union? That made Botha our first Prime Minister? I agree it was a mistake, but it came from our side. Yours has done precious little to follow it up, and it has remained very much a one-sided affair. But don't stress it, please. Try and look at things from my point of view.'

'What, after all, is your point of view, Doctor? I have not yet been able to grasp it.'

'It's very simple. My political creed is cast in a Christian mould, much as you might sneer at it. I am a South African, and as such I accept fully and unreservedly the implications which the Act of Union carries. Willy-nilly we are a democratic community—within limits, of course, for we have never had the courage to be logical and to include the Native and the Coloured man in our interpretation of democratic government. That, again, is a legacy from Union. Formerly we did. Our old Colonial government was fully democratic and representative in the best sense of the word. But as a sop to the Transvaal, which has had the major say in our affairs since Union, we grafted on it the illogicality of a representative government which is only sectionally representative. We did that in an excess of fine sentiment, consoling ourselves with the reflection that logic and right must inevitably conquer. I daresay they will, ultimately, for I cannot conceive that a narrow sectionalism will ever prevail against the cultural forces struggling to find expression in this country, but it may take a long time before we reach that stage. Meanwhile you are doing any amount of harm by concentrating your attention upon side issues instead of upon major issues. There, my dear, them's my sentiments.'

'I thank you kindly, Sir,' said Santa, disdainfully. 'Them's not mine. And I've as much right to hold my own view as you have.'

'Nobody denies that. But, to repeat your own question, what exactly is your view? What are you after? Your Party has so often tacked with the shifting political winds that it becomes difficult to understand what your ideals are. Once upon a time, you were out for sovereign independence.'

'Which we have not got,' exclaimed Santa. 'The Declaration of 1926 proves that, at least. You cannot get away from that fact. Our own flag, equality of language and cultural rights, full liberty to express our national sentiment ...'

'All of which you had years ago. Mabuis was perfectly right there. You have exactly the same rights as you held before, and exactly the same obligations though you pretend not to be sensible of them. And you have gained a few externals which really do not appear to have benefited you much. Take your flag. In the old days one saw folk saluting the Jack. They did it as a matter of habit, perhaps, some of the old people, like your Aunt Gertrude's grandfather, because they had the traditional respect for what it implied. Whom do you see nowadays lifting his hat to the flag? The older generation knows that it is the symbol of a Party compromise, in which nine-tenths of the people had no say; the younger does not yet realise what it may stand for. You cannot create tradition by act of Parliament, my dear. Such things grow out of a common sentiment, and in your Party compromise all the factors that go to foster such growth were absent. In the old days, on Queen's Birthday, practically every house flew the Jack; even in the location the Coloured people improvised one or two. Who flies the new flag? Why, even your father who is the chairman of the local branch of your Party, does not flaunt it.'

'I pointed that out to father as soon as I came,' said Santa, apologetically, 'and he is going to have one. We'll fly it on every possible occasion. That is just one of my grievances, that we have been so slack in asserting our rights. I want father to insist that the minutes of the council should be kept in both languages.'

'By all means. I have nothing against it,' remarked the doctor, gathering his instruments preparatory to placing them in his bag. 'But there again you are trying to create a sentiment which is, or should be, the growth of conviction rather than of propaganda. Which reminds me, you have not brought me that interesting Afrikaans book which you promised. Mabuis left some of those he bought at Cape Town behind, and I have been trying to read them, but really, my dear, they seem to me to be inferior to some of the old post-war productions. That must be the car, outside. If you are ready, we might as well go now.'

'I am quite ready. You are incorrigible, Doctor. I shall not try to convert you. I'll only ask you to read some of the better stuff that has been published lately. Of course, it may not be all that one claims for it—I quite agree that chauvinism may be a factor in my own admiration for some of it, but I'm sure you'll find much of it is good writing. Now tell me about that case.'

'You'd better see the patient first. It's out of my depth altogether. I'm afraid I have not kept up my reading as I should have done, but in a busy practice like this one gets so little time. Besides, it's somewhat out of my line. Just now I am interested in constitutional inadequacies—you know, Pende and Viola's work? In that direction. There is a wide field for investigation here. You might try your hand at it, Santa. Plenty of excellent material in the location, and in the Coloured school. By the way, Mabuis has left me some money. I suggested that he should put up funds for an investigation, and he was good enough to give me a cheque. Quite a substantial one too—some millionaires can be generous. I believe he is. You see, there is a strain of generosity in his ancestry. Old 'Tins' Mabuis, his grandfather, was renowned for his free-handedness. Very likely because he did not have the trouble of making money. He merely married it. The rich old Widow Priem. Quite a romantic marriage my dear. Both over fifty, and he without a shilling in the bank, while she had thousands. Before my time. Take care of the step, my dear.'

They drove through the deserted Village street, out into the broad road, the main highway that led from the station, sixty miles away, and went on to the north, the long, yellow road on which, nearly thirty years before, the slow moving ox-wagons had travelled, heavily laden with ammunition and stores, the road on which, more than a hundred years ago, his own forebears had toiled with their goods and chattels, human and otherwise, in their search for a place of settlement. It now traversed veld rich in the splendour of September flowers, the sorrels with their golds, their watered creams and salmon pink, making vivid splashes of colour, the splendour, cerulean aristeas dazzling against the ochre-coloured clays, and the tall-stemmed gladioli and sturdy babianas contrasting boldly with the tender green of grass and stunted sheep-bush. Over the blue mountains shimmered a morning haze, faint beryl in the *kloofs* and darker violet where the shadows fell.

'A beautiful land, this,' said Dr Buren, appreciatively. 'You may think we do not love it, Santa, but you are quite mistaken. You should have heard old Quakerley praising it, or some of those old missionaries who came here at about the same time. All exiles, but all prepared to give to it as much as you would, and perhaps something more, my dear.'

He pointed to a dark patch between the mountains, where the cliffs sheered up into walls of rock, variegated with browns and ferruginous reds. 'That's the way the 1820 settlers trekked,' he said. 'You talk so much about the Voortrekkers. Why don't you give some praise to those who made this part of our world into a settlement? If you only would ... if you only would realise that no section has the monopoly of patriotism ... that English and Dutch have both had a share in making this country what it is ... why, my dear, our partnership would be closer and more profitable to us both.'

Chapter 12

There lingers a legend in the Village, the legend of Etienne Barbier, one of whose quartered limbs was planted, as a warning to rebellious *burghers* and as a symbol of the Company's authority, in the entrance of the *kloof* through which the main road penetrated into the Valley. Tradition asserts, upon what historical evidence no man can say, that somewhere in the Valley, Etienne, that wild, vehement Ishmael whose story no man has yet written, had his lair whence he pounced upon the Company's rangers until he was betrayed to the Company's sheriffs by those in whom he had trusted, and, if tradition is true, had often befriended. Only the oldest inhabitants knew the legend in all its gruesome details, but the sense of it had permeated through to the younger generation which, revelling in such excitements, had embellished it with utterly unsubstantiated and unsubstantiatable addenda. More than one spot was accredited with the shame of having been the depository of Etienne's mangled remains, and many others with associations with his band which were probably equally fictitious.

The Coloured chauffeur who drove Eric van Deren to *Eiseleben* knew all about the legend. He pointed out to Master Eric the exact spot where the White Master's left hand had been nailed to a pole, as they drove over the mountain pass.

'Arrie,' he exclaimed, 'the old Company was quick to punish, Master Eric. My old *tata*, he who is now in bliss, told me the story often enough. *Baas* may rely upon it as upon God's gospel. That was the spot. A nail through the palm of the hand, but the vultures picked the flesh off the bone, my *tata* said.'

'Your *tata* could not possibly have remembered all that,' said Eric. 'It happened, if it happened at all, two hundred years ago, and your *tata* ...'

'Arrie, not him, *Baas*,' said the driver, 'but his *tata's tata* it was ...'

'Even that couldn't be,' explained Eric patiently. 'Not even your *tata's* grand-*tata* could have remembered it.'

'My *tata's* grand-*tata* was wonderfully old, *Baas* Eric,' remonstrated the Native. He was born a slave and bred a slave, which couldn't happen to me, thank the little Lord for that. Now isn't it wonderful how times have changed, *Baas* Eric?'

'I don't remember your grandfather,' said Eric, 'but your father I do remember, and he was never a slave. He was old *Baas* Gert's man, and a much better fellow than you, Jims. He would never have been fined for being drunk and disorderly on a Saturday night ...'

'That was just a little slip, *Baas*,' asseverated the driver, indignantly. 'It is not as if I were a drunkard, now is it? Me that once belonged to the Lodge and wore a coloured scarf round my shoulders. But it was too much, *Baas*, to expect us to leave the wine altogether. The good book says it's well enough for one's stomach, and mine always bothers me since I had the dysentery, *Baas*.'

'Yes, you always have some excuse. Why didn't you stick to the Lodge? Didn't your grand-*tata* tell you that it was the drink that led *Baas* Etienne to rob and burn people's houses?'

'*Baas* Elias did want us all to belong,' said the driver, reflectively. 'But *Baas* Elias only talks like that. He does not really believe in it.'

'You should not say such things, Jims. *Baas* Elias has done a lot for you people, and you've no business to malign him.'

'It isn't maligning him, *Baas*,' replied the driver, earnestly. 'The *Baas* knows it isn't.' He slid into second to breast an incline. '*Baas* Elias gets a good deal out of the drink. Don't we know it, *Baas*. It's he who sells the canteen licences, isn't it?'

'No, he does not sell them,' explained Eric, patiently. 'He sits on the licensing board, and judges if it is right and proper that so-and-so should have a canteen. If the police find that too many of you folk get drunk there, the old master says, "No, you shan't have a canteen there".'

'Aye,' said the Native, 'and then so-and-so comes along with money, and after that *Baas* Elias says, "Very well, you may have a canteen." Don't we know it, *Baas*?'

'Look here, Jims,' said Eric, sternly. 'That is slander. If I tell the old master what you said, you'll be had up before the magistrate and you'll be punished. You must not retail slander that you hear in the location. You Coloured people don't know how things are managed, and you let your imagination run away with you.'

'It's not my imagination, *Baas*,' protested the driver, earnestly. 'And the old master drinks. I have smelt him, although he does chew peppermint to take the smell away ...'

'That's enough, Jims,' said Eric, sternly. 'Don't let me hear another word on that subject from you. I am ashamed of you. If you had lived in the old days they would have tied you to the oak tree and given you a drubbing with the leathern thong. And richly you would have deserved it.'

'They can't do that to me for speaking the truth,' muttered the driver, sulkily. 'As if we didn't know the old master. *Baas Eric* thinks he is all good, but he isn't really ...'

'That's no business of yours.' Eric tried to turn the conversation. 'What is that down there?'

'It's the Ford that was burned last month, *Baas*. The driver was drunk and it was a God's mercy he wasn't killed. He wasn't fit to drive a cart and horses, that boy. And him a member of the Lodge, too.'

Expatiating on the evil-mindedness of the boy who wasn't fit to drive a cart and horses, the chauffeur skilfully steered his car down the sharp incline into the side road which led towards *Eisleben*, and a few minutes later Eric saw the white gables of the homestead shining through the budding branches of the oak trees that surrounded it. The car drew up before the door, and he climbed out and told the driver to wait under the big belombre tree.

Aunt Gertrude awaited him in the dining room. Her greeting was familiarly friendly, for she had always been fond of him, and had looked upon him as a prospective nephew.

'Thanks for coming so quickly, Eric,' she said, motioning him to take the chair at the side-table, where coffee, cake and preserves had already been laid out in readiness. 'You take plenty of milk? And three lumps, no? There, drink first, and try the watermelon. It is fairly fresh still, though the last of last season's batch.'

'What is it you want to talk over with me, Aunt?' he asked, sipping his coffee with relish. It was excellent coffee, freshly roasted and ground, with an aroma that blended with the faint, ethereal reek from the dung-smeared floor.

'A very weighty matter, Eric,' she said, importantly. 'And one on which I want your entire confidence, both as a lawyer and as a friend.'

'But surely, Aunt,' he said, surprised at her gravity. 'Is it Aunt's will, by any chance? I drew one up last year, but women change their minds ...'

'I don't,' she said, tersely. 'I am too old to indulge in whimsies. And as Jerry and I are married in community, it does not much matter—the will, I mean. Ours is a joint one, you know. This is far more important.' She drew out the letter from the table drawer. 'Here is a note from the bank. Read it.'

He took it from her and ran his eye over it.

'Phew,' he said, and pursed his lips into a whistle. 'So Uncle Jerry has decided upon the seven-seated Chrysler. But that means a chauffeur, Aunt.'

'Jerry has decided no such thing,' she answered, crisply. 'I told him that we did not want such a big car. We decided upon a Hudson. Jerry drew no cheque, Eric.'

'But, Aunt, I don't understand. He must have drawn one ...'

'Read that,' she gave him Vantloo's letter, 'Jerry has not seen that yet. I sent him into town to get the cheque. I spoke to the manager over the phone. He tells me ... but read the letter first.'

She watched him as he read it, noted the quick contraction of lips and brows, the angry flush from chin to forehead, the involuntary tightening of the fingers holding the letter. Indignation brought out the character in his face. She reflected with satisfaction that he could look handsome if his emotions were stirred.

He read the letter through twice, before his eyes left the paper and stared over at her. She noted the angry flash in them.

'Take it calmly, Eric,' she cautioned. 'I have felt something like this was bound to happen. Brother-in-law has been altogether too smug of late.'

'But ...' his indignation almost choked him. 'This is forgery ... criminal. And Uncle Elias is my partner. It affects the firm ... not merely him. You must see that, Aunt. Of course, Uncle Jerry shall not lose by it. I will make it up myself ... no, wait, it is not so easy as that, Aunt. Let me think ...'

'Do, Eric. That's what I have been doing all this morning. Jerry will be here in half an hour—he left shortly after you. And we must decide before he comes.'

'But Aunt, it is unbelievable. So utterly stupid ... that is not like Elias ... say what you like, he is never stupid ...'

'No, this is not stupid at all, Eric,' she asserted with conviction. 'He knew that Jerry would never prosecute him; he knew that Jerry would meet the cheque and wait patiently for repayment. That's what he banked upon, Eric. He is by no means stupid. It would have been stupid to have come begging and forging Jerry's signature after Jerry had refused to lend him the money. But now he places Jerry before a thing done. And he knows Jerry will never allow a whisper of it to reach Maria ...'

'Of course not, Aunt. Nor must we. That at all events we must prevent.'

'Yes, Maria must be shielded. Maria must never know,' retorted Aunt Gertrude, impatiently, and with a tinge of bitterness in her voice. 'That has always been the trouble. If Maria had known from the first what an utter scoundrel her man is, she might have done some good. Now she worships him—he is her idol, and of course we must never show her that it has clay fee.'

'No, Aunt, no. Aunt Maria must never know. She is too weak. As Aunt says, she worships Uncle Elias, and it would break her heart ...'

'Women's hearts are not so fragile as that, Eric,' sniffed Aunt Gertrude. 'But I daresay you are right as concerns Maria. She is a poor thing ... No conviction of her own, no backbone, as you might say. By all means let us spare her, if it can be done. But can it?'

'I don't see why not, Aunt. But this, at any rate, must stop. I have for long thought of buying Uncle Elias out. After all, he scarcely does any real work at the office, although his connection is valuable.'

'You have suspected ...' began Aunt Gertrude, tentatively.

'More than suspected, Aunt. I am sorry to say it, but Uncle Elias is a hypocrite through and through. I never thought, however, that he was worse than dishonest in little things.'

'You know about his drinking, of course?' she asked in a matter of fact tone.

'Drinking? Why, no. He doesn't drink, does he?' Eric asked, surprised.

'Then you have not used your eyes—nor your nose,' said the old woman, calmly. 'He swills alcohol whenever he has a chance. Makes the excuse that he feels faint or his heart troubles him. Jerry believes it is as he states; Jerry never sees farther than his nose; in that he is just like his sister. But I know better. And you know of course that he has used his influence to get licences, and has been paid for it?'

'I certainly don't,' said Eric, spiritedly. 'Nor do I believe it, Aunt.' He recalled what the driver had said. 'It is unthinkable. He would not be so stupid as to give someone a chance to blackmail him.'

'I cannot prove it, of course,' she said, shrugging her shoulders. 'But facts are facts. You know Solomon's licence was refused—at first. Why was it allowed afterwards?'

'That I don't know. It may be the police withdrew their objections. There may be some other reason.'

'Cannot you find one, Eric? You know more about his business than I do. But some things I heard made me suspect that there was a basis for what you would very likely call scandal.'

'What you are suggesting is too horrible to be true, Aunt Gertrude,' exclaimed Eric, indignantly. 'I have never taken Uncle Elias's teetotalism very seriously. One never does take these faddists seriously. Indeed, I have more than once pointed out to him that to be consistent he should not hold mortgages on wine farms ...'

'Nor have a financial interest in any place which sells liquor,' she interrupted. 'You know he has, don't you?'

'Well, of course, the firm has,' he admitted, grudgingly. 'That is not quite the same thing, though I agree it looks bad for him. But it is quite another matter when it comes to selling his vote.'

'Is that worse than forging his brother-in-law's signature?' she demanded, shrilly. 'You are deceiving yourself, Eric, if you imagine that there is a spark of honesty left in him. Face facts. Help me to face them. We both want to prevent this matter from becoming public.'

'Yes, Aunt. Aunt Maria and Santa ... they must not hear of it.'

'As far as Maria is concerned, I agree. Jerry will not allow that. But there is no reason why Santa should not hear of it. She is old enough to know the truth, and you know as well as I do that she can't be kept in the dark. That girl is far too shrewd not to put two and two together and make four out of it. Besides, it will do her a world of good to be brought into contact with realities. She lives in a world of her own, wherein her father looms like God Almighty.'

'Aunt is not fair to her. She worships her father, and it would be a shame to disillusion her,' remonstrated Eric, passionately. 'She thinks the world of him, as you know.'

'Of course I do,' said Aunt Gertrude, complacently. 'And very little of you. That should be put right. It is only fair that she should know who paid for her education ...'

'What does Aunt know about that?' demanded Eric, sharply. 'Her education was paid for out of her grandmother's legacy ...'

'Tell that to the fowls,' interjected the old woman, equally sharply, although there was no enmity in her voice. 'I know that her grandmother's legacy went the same way as Jerry's contribution to the great diamond scheme. Frittered away, it was. Don't tell me the contrary. I know, Eric, I know. And I also know whose money it was that kept Santa in Europe all these years.'

'I don't know what you are talking about,' said Eric, in confusion. 'You have no right to draw conclusions where you are not sure of your facts ...'

'But I am sure ... now,' she smiled at him as she spoke. 'You have given yourself away, Eric. I did think that it was her mother's money, but now I know that it was yours. And that makes me suspect that Maria's money has also been frittered away. That letter,' she touched Elias's letter with her index finger as she spoke, 'makes things clear. Santa wants money—I can't imagine for what purpose ...'

'She wants to buy a share in Buren's practice,' interrupted Eric.

'Is that so? That explains things, then. Maria's money has vanished, and brother-in-law must have something to tide over the emergency. Hence the forgery of Jerry's signature. It leaps to the eye, Eric. And it calls for drastic action. You must see that.'

'I do, Aunt,' replied Eric, miserably. He was shocked, outraged, and indignant. He felt himself incapable of coherently considering the situation. The thought of his partner's treachery had overwhelmed him, and yet, as he thought back he remembered incidents and events which, in the light of the revelation which had surprised him that afternoon, should have prepared him for the difficulties which faced him. For years he had mildly resented his partner's hypocrisy, never contemplating it as something that could affect his own credit, but irritated by it because he had thought it childish and ineffectual. Its political possibilities he had grasped. They had amused him, but he had hardly been shocked by them, for politics was a game of which he had seen too much to feel surprise at whatever might result from it. But he had never faced the possibility that his partner's dishonesty might become a tangible liability, not only to the firm but to himself.

'Then pull yourself together,' Aunt Gertrude went on. 'Jerry will be here in a minute and we must have a plan ready to lay before him. He will bluster and swear, of course—it is his way of relieving his feelings, but deep down he will be animated by only one thought, which is how to keep the matter from reaching Maria's ears. We must help him with that. Now the first point I want to discuss is the legal position. Are we doing anything illegal by hushing it up?'

'Strictly speaking, yes, Aunt. It will be condoning. We are supposed not to shelter a criminal, and this act of Uncle Elias is a criminal offence. But it is between us and him; no one else need know, and if Uncle Jerry does not wish to prosecute, the legal position is clear. No one else can.'

'But is it?' her voice was anxious, eager for reassurance. 'Would not the magistrate have to be notified? What is this about compounding a felony, Eric?'

'You have been reading English crime stories,' he said, mildly amused at her insistence, and marvelling that he could extract amusement from a situation so perplexing in its gravity. 'Under our law there is no such thing as a felony. I am not quite certain—I have never had to advise on such a point—but I fancy it is a matter solely for Uncle Jerry to decide. If he does not wish to prosecute, no one can force him to do so. You may take that as definite, Aunt.'

'Very well then. Jerry won't hear of prosecuting. He will do all he can to keep the facts from Maria. And I don't blame him. Elias will get his punishment soon enough, even though the law knows nothing about it. I am thinking more of you and Santa.'

'Santa won't have me, Aunt Gertrude. So far as I am concerned, my mind is made up. I shall ask Uncle Elias to retire—we'll arrange it somehow. I suspect financially we are not so sound as we should be, but I shall have to go into that, and I have some assets which I can realise. Uncle Jerry, at any rate, will not suffer ...'

'Don't be troubled about that, Eric,' she said, firmly. 'A thousand won't break

Jerry or me. I have looked after things, and there is enough, thank God, to tide us over the loss. And something besides, if you find that you need money to break with Elias. But one thing is clear. You must break with him. You must get him to retire completely. He must sever his connection with the firm. He must give up his chairmanship of the Board—yes, that you must insist upon. Why, it is courting disaster to let him go on. You must see to that.'

'I can't think that Uncle Elias has been so criminally stupid as ... you suggest, Aunt. If he has, there will be difficulties, and very likely we won't be able to keep the matter secret. What a fool the man must be.'

'He was never a fool, Eric. But knave, yes. I saw it from the first. That's why I opposed the marriage, but Maria was set on him, and it was no use talking to Jerry. She could twist him round her little finger; she still does. And although I am annoyed with her, I can't help feeling sorry, for she does love the man, in spite of his faults. Of course she does not know how bad he is, but some things she must have noticed, and yet she has been loyal all through. Very well. Tell your driver to put up the car. You must stay till tomorrow, for we must decide this matter tonight, and we can't do that without Jerry.'

Chapter 13

Elias Vantloo came home for luncheon, and met his wife on the *stoep*. He greeted her with the customary salutation. It had become a habit with him to kiss her perfunctorily, but because he knew that her regard for him was still strong and sincere, he always felt, on such occasions when their lips touched, that he was in some measure wronging her. The feeling irritated and annoyed him, for Elias liked to think of himself as outside the pale of criticism. He could not conceive of anyone doubting the full carat value of his husbandship, and the consciousness of doubt in his own mind on this subject was not pleasant.

'Where is Santa, Heart-lamb?' he asked, instinctively modulating his voice into a more pleasant tone than that in which he usually spoke. 'I have a nice little surprise for her.'

'She is away with Dr Buren, Elias,' Maria answered. 'She is indefatigable. But what is it you have for her? Come, let us go in. You can tell me while we are at table.'

'I thought she might like a little car, a small two-seater,' he said, following her into the dining room. 'So I have ordered a baby Morris.' He unfolded his napkin and vigorously attacked his soup. 'Bring me some ginger beer,' he told the maid. 'She should have something of her own to go about in.'

'But can you afford it?' she queried, anxiously. 'Especially now, when there is the matter of the partnership to be settled. Perhaps if you mentioned the matter to Brother Jerry ...'

'Why drag Jeremiah into it?' he retorted. 'Surely I am solvent enough, Wife, to give the girl a car. One of these days I shall sell out. Eric is always asking me to sell my share. I have half a mind to do it, Wife.'

'I wish you would,' her voice was eager. 'You are getting too old to worry about business. Then we could go and live somewhere at the seaside.'

'Not yet, Wife, not yet. I should not like to give up, well, everything we have here. And you must admit we have something. Your old husband has been a bit of a success, now hasn't he? Confess now ... yes, a little more rice, please, Heart-lamb. To go away would mean to sever all my connections here and to give up a large part of my influence.'

'I know that, Elias,' she admitted, 'but after all is it worthwhile? I mean working as you do, so many hours a day, and getting so little for it? Politics, now, don't you think you might drop it, Elias? You know yourself you would not care to enter Parliament ...'

'That I shouldn't,' he said, energetically. 'But I should not like to give up what I now have, the power of deciding who is to go to Parliament. What Elias says goes in this electorate, Heart-lamb; you know that as well as I do, and that is a thing not lightly to be resigned. However, I will think about it. Especially now that Santa is setting up for herself. How stands it between her and Eric?'

'Very much as at first, Elias. You must not hurry them. Santa is keen on her work, naturally. She has the modern young woman's idea of independence and self-help ...'

'That is all nonsense,' he interrupted, contemptuously. 'Women are there to be married. Their proper sphere is the home. I should like to see a grandchild or two. You would yourself, wouldn't you?'

'I don't know, Elias. Sometimes I think ... but it will be very pleasant to have a little one running about the house, one of one's own. But you must not hurry Santa.'

'Do you think she does not care for Eric? In that case we must try and get someone else. I can't think of anyone here, but here is not the world. You must go visiting with Santa; give her opportunities. Here, too, we might do something more. Tennis parties ... there's that new sub-manager, unmarried. I don't place him in the same rank with Eric, but, Heart-lamb, it may be that we are a little too partial towards Master Eric.'

'I should like to see him marry Santa, Elias,' she said simply. 'It is something I have always contemplated as almost an accomplished thing. And I am sure it will happen in time. Not now, perhaps. She is too young to appreciate his sterling worth, and perhaps he does not appeal to her as he should. But I think you may leave them to settle the matter for themselves.'

'Well, you should know. I saw Eric driving out of the village this morning. He did not tell me where he was going, but I fancy it is on some business connected with the auction.'

Ayah Mina removed the soup plates, and the maid brought in the ginger beer. Elias would have been shocked to find that the alcoholic content of the soft drink which he used was appreciable, but in his ignorance of material facts he drank it blissfully, its sharp tang compensating slightly for the tipple he could not indulge in.

'How is Sophie today, Mina?' he asked as the old woman approached his chair.

'Much the same, Old Master,' Ayah Mina replied, tonelessly. 'Shall I get the stewed peaches, Old Mistress?'

'No.' Maria's voice was sharper than usual, and her husband glanced at her curiously, and when the old woman had left the room, asked expectantly, 'Is there anything the matter, Heart-lamb?'

'Nothing, Elias,' Maria responded, in her usual mild tone of voice. 'Why should there be?'

'I thought, perhaps, Mina had presumed, Heart-lamb. She is getting much too uppish—the old, indispensable servant idea, don't you know. But I have told you, it is time to pension her off.'

'Mina will stay with me,' his wife said, with decision in her voice. 'You promised me that, years ago, Elias. Don't let us talk about it. Tell me about the partnership. Are you sure you can manage it?'

'A promise is not irrevocable,' he grumbled. 'There are times when I find her presence trying. About the partnership you need have no doubts. It will be managed all right. Eric will see to it.'

'If it is a matter of money, Elias,' she suggested, timidly. 'Perhaps you might see Brother Jerry ...'

'Now do stop referring to Jeremiah, Wife,' he exclaimed irritably. 'Between Brother Jerry and me there is little love lost, and you know it. Not that he is not helpful on occasion,' he chuckled silently, his irritation apparently dispelled in a moment by some pleasant reflection. 'Yes, he is decidedly helpful at times. You know, Maria, even fools have their uses in the world. This morning I had a deputation. They want to start a new Party, and they are not happy about it. So they came to me. I sent them away with a flea in their ear, but they will be very useful.'

'I should have thought that now, Elias, you would have approved. You have said yourself that it is time for some change. And I am sure they mean well'

'Yes, of course. They always do. But unfortunately they don't think well. They let their feelings run away with their heads. A new Party would benefit nobody; us least of all. A re-alignment—now that is altogether a different thing. We will manage it yet. We'll get rid of Labour; it has served its purpose so far as we are concerned, and the Sappies will get rid of the old Unionist gang ... they too have served their purpose. Both combinations, as you know, my dear, are utterly artificial, but both have been useful and we mustn't complain. But these things have to be managed very carefully, if we are to keep what we have got. You won't understand even if I tell you the ins and outs of the position.'

'I don't want to understand, Elias,' she said, dispassionately. 'I am content to leave these matters to you. Only, at times I am troubled because I think it is so much to be regretted that we can't live in peace and quietness, without all this hateful ill-feeling. It was never like this in the old days.'

'Aye, in the old days it was a one-sided affair. We didn't count. I am afraid you are not a thorough-paced Nationalist, like Santa, my dear.'

'Santa just repeats what she hears,' she said, impatiently. 'She does not remember the old times, and she takes all that people tell her ...'

'That is as it should be,' he interjected complacently. 'Politics, my dear, is largely feeling, and persons and ignorance. With these three you get along splendidly. I have, as you know. Three fourths of the fold hereabouts do not know what we quarrel about, but they vote as I tell them to, and that, after all, is the main thing. They grumble afterwards, but that does not really matter, for by the time another election comes round there is always some new thing to stimulate their feelings.'

'It seems so petty and mean, Elias,' she said plaintively. 'All this bickering and talk. And I am sure there is much that wants doing. Mr Mabuis said ...'

'Aye, Mabuis said a lot of things. We all say a great deal, but when it comes to doing my dear, we all hang back. But don't you worry yourself about that. You leave politics to your old husband—he is still young enough to notice which way the wind veers, and there is still a good thing to be made out of it. As for Mabuis, I am sorry the man left so soon. We ought to have got more out of him. It is sinful for one man to have so much money.'

'We saw very little of him,' she mused. 'I was interested in him, Elias. He must be a very wonderful man.'

'Aye, that he is. So was his grandfather, old "Tins" Mabuis. His father was a poor thing—took after the mother, old Widow Priem. But "Tins" was a character. I remember him when I was a boy, with his flute and his dancing and his queer Frenchified language. A thriftless, vagrant sort of fellow, and unfortunately a great drunkard. A bad example to the District. No wonder his family did so badly.'

'But his grandson appears to have rehabilitated the family fortunes. I hear that Mr Mabuis has given a sum of money for a dispensary here ...'

'Not quite that. He gave Buren a cheque. I don't know for how much. I tried to induce him to buy *Sandvlei* ... that's the old family farm, Heart-lamb; I have a mortgage on it and I could have made some money if Mabuis had been hooked, but he wouldn't look at it. He said that agricultural land was overvalued—I think he is right, too—and that he preferred to invest in Argentinian securities. You can't expect anything else from an expatriated man. But he certainly has money. I made it my business to find out, and I have no doubts on that point. When he comes back from the north—he has gone to the Transvaal and will return via Durban—I shall tackle him again. There's a silly sentimental streak in the fellow—just like his grandfather had. That makes it so miraculous that he has got any money at all.'

Elias retired to his bedroom for his usual afternoon's sleep, and Ayah Mina came in with the maids to clear away. She stopped behind her mistress's chair and bent down over it.

'Old Missie should go and lie down,' she urged, almost tenderly. 'Otherwise the asthma will bother Old Missie again tonight. And Old Missie should not worry. Everything will come right.'

'I am not worrying, Mina.' Maria's voice was listless, and the negation did not impress the old woman. 'Not for myself, that is. A little about you, and about Sophie. Is there nothing I can do? Let me go this afternoon and bring her some jelly ...'

'No, no,' Ayah Mina was imperative in her dissent. 'I will not have old missie doing that. I will myself take her the jelly, but Old Missie must go and lie down. Sophie is all right. She will go on as she has done before. The Old Missie must not worry.'

'But I do, about Sophie,' replied Mrs Vantloo. 'And it seems to me, Mina, that you take the child's condition too lightly. She is seriously ill. Santa tells me, dangerously ill ...'

'I know, Old Missie, I know. But what does it matter? We must all die, and for her, Old Missie, death will come as a relief. She can hardly breathe, and ... There are other things ...'

'Yes, poor thing,' said her mistress with feeling, getting up from her chair and laying her hand affectionately on the old servant's arm. 'We all have our troubles, Mina, but we may lighten them a bit by sharing them with our friends. And you know that you can rely upon us ... upon me ...'

'That I know,' said the old woman, almost brusquely. 'But Missie must go and lie down. Missie must not take everyone's burden upon Missie's own back.'

Maria sighed wearily, and went into the drawing room, where she lay down on the big chesterfield. That was her usual custom, for Elias disliked being disturbed in his siesta in which he indulged until it was time for afternoon coffee. Formerly they had shared a bed for the afternoon sleep, but she rarely slept, and he was easily disturbed. So when he had referred to the example of old Martin Rekker, she had silently acquiesced in the temporary daily separation and had used the chesterfield. She recollected the first occasion when he had broached the subject. He had been in one of his bad humours, disgruntled and grumbling because matters had not run smoothly at the office, and he had complained that his afternoon rest had been disturbed by her entry.

'I shall have to go up on the loft,' he had declared. 'Like old Marin Rekker. He could not stand his womenfolk interfering with his afternoon sleep, so he went up to the loft and slept in his coffin.'

She knew that he had not drawn upon his imagination. In the Valley, in the old days, it had been customary for the wife and husband to give each other a coffin, a shroud, and a couple of old Georgian pennies—heavy discs of alloy and copper to be placed on the eyes of the departed. The coffin, in such rich families as the Rekkers, was of polished cedarwood, cushioned inside with white satin; the shroud of fine linen, with lace ruffles and a lace collar. Martin Rekker had kept his coffin in the loft, where it had been used as a receptacle for bags of seed. These he had taken out, and finding the coffin comfortable and to his liking, he had persisted in sleeping in it every afternoon, and had, indeed, died in it in his sleep.

Now, as she lay on the chesterfield, she thought of those old days, comparing and contrasting them with her own time. They seemed so far away that she had difficulty in persuading herself that her own, intimate recollections of them were real and not imagined. Across her mental picture wandered persons who in those far off days had been personages in the Village; old Charles Quakerley, with his peruke, his prim, old fashioned chivalry; Gallows-Gecko Nolte with his shrewd, effective honesty; Martin Rekker, aristocratic in bearing, a man of real culture and refinement, who could quote Horace, played a masterly game of chess, and spoke in broken English on the occasion when he proposed the annual three cheers for the beloved Queen, Alexandrina Victoria; the Reverend Mr de Smee, a *dominie* of the old school, courteous, suave, a latitudinarian not above a polka with the senior ladies at a wedding feast. Most of these she knew only by hearsay, but she was old enough to remember their lineal descendants, the first and second generations of English, German, and Swedish settlers who had colonised the Valley, and her recollections of them were all kindly, pleasant, and edifying. She remembered that cheerful German missionary family, the Uhlmanns, who had founded and formed the thriving mission station at Neckerthal, and their missionary friends, the stately von Bergmann's, descended from a baron and therefore as *armiger* as the Rekkers. How different things had been then. There had been none of the political squabbles and back-biting so distressing nowadays. Indeed, she wondered how many of the political leaders of today would have been tolerated as equals in the company of such as old Charles Quakerley, Johann Uhlmann, Martin Rekker with his high conception of tradition and the obligations of family, Lodewyk von Bergmann with his rich culture and his wide liberalism, or even old Gallows-Gecko Nolte with his fine sense of humour, his sturdy loyalty, and his passionate nationalism excluding no section, limiting itself to no creed or persuasion. She reflected that her husband, for instance, would have found himself out of place in such company, unable to grasp the meaning of their ideals and what they stood for, and that her well educated daughter would have been totally perplexed by their broad, catholic conception of culture, by the tolerance of their nationalism, and by courtesy that sprang from race and high-bred tradition. Their descendants had degenerated, and to a large extent these old families had died out, or had been merged into others in whom tradition counted for little, and greed, passion, and sordid materialism had displaced much of what she had herself been taught to value above price. She found herself unconsciously trying to find excuses for the present; for its feverish activity, its insistence on things that did not really matter; its negation of the things that counted so much in life. Unsatisfactory, disturbing thoughts kept her from sleep, and after a while she got up and went into the garden, pacing up and down the well kept border paths, and inhaling the scent of the woodbine and roses.

'The Lord will give me strength to bear it all,' she whispered to herself. 'The Lord will give me patience to remain true to myself.'

Chapter 14

Driving home in the dusk from the outlying farm where he had demonstrated his interesting case to his lady colleague, Dr Buren reverted to the subject which they had been discussing immediately before starting on their round.

'Yes, Santa,' he said, familiarly, 'you should revise your opinions. You have been arguing from false premises, my dear. You start from the assumption that only a certain section in this country is really patriotic, and you give to that term a narrow, limited interpretation. But you are altogether wrong.'

'I should be glad if that's the case,' said Santa, with a toss of her head. 'But everything I have been able to observe since my return shows me that I have some justification for thinking so.'

'Yes, because you look at one side of the picture only. You ignore the other side completely.'

'Your side, of course, Doctor. You have had your innings for a century or more, and results speak louder than protestations.'

'Quite right. And just look at results. Now take your basic proposition ...'

'What do you imagine it to be, Doctor?'

'I imagine it to be exactly what you state it is. You have proclaimed it in and out of season. 'South Africa first, last and always ...'

'And an excellent proposition, too, I should think.'

'Quite so. If not carried to extremes, and interpreted in the narrow, intolerant spirit in which you are only too apt to define and practise it.'

'So you think, Doctor. You of course hold that the Empire should come first ...' Santa's voice expressed unutterable scorn. 'The Empire! What is the Empire to us or we to the Empire that we should weep for it?'

'Don't quote out of your context, my dear. Hamlet meant that he had much greater and more important things to think of than Hecuba. But you ... what, after all, have you got that you can be placed co-equal with the Empire? I know you say, glibly, that you are sovereignly independent, but honestly you know that if it were not for the Empire you would not be able to exist for one month. That's as basic a fact as ... as anything.'

'Not to me. The Empire is only a word. It is no longer even an institution. It is a ... an academic expression,' said Santa, belligerently. 'Our status is guaranteed by inter-Dominion agreement, and we are simply one of a number of sovereign independent states consenting, for the time being, to act in concert where common interests are concerned.'

'You really explain it very well,' said the doctor, admiringly. 'And I suppose, in a sense, you are perfectly right. I have never quite fathomed what the position really is. But that makes no difference to the fact that its interpretation is slightly different for ... let me say ... the section to which I belong.'

'Of course. The jingoistic English element will never get away from the leading strings of Downing Street,' retorted Santa, contemptuously. 'That's just our grievance. Instead of helping us to consolidate what we have got, and building up a strong South African nationalism, you crab what we try to do and go bleating for greater interference from England. It's we who must give up everything ... ideas, aspirations, culture, hopes, everything—simply in order not to offend your susceptibilities. Oh, I am sick of it. Hang your susceptibilities. You insult us daily; you ignore our language; you sneer at our culture; you belittle everything which is truly South African; you talk of 'home' and try to substitute a sort of vicarious loyalty to the Empire for the real thing—loyalty to South Africa, to the Union, to ourselves. You are great on shame. You accepted bilingualism and now you are trying to wriggle out of it, on the ground that it is damnably expensive and unbusinesslike. You don't mind us indulging in our ideals so long as such indulgence does not touch your pockets. Oh, I know ... it is trade ... trade, always first with you. You cannot think of these things except in terms of material benefit.'

'There may be some truth in your indictment,' said the doctor, reflectively, 'so far as the press is concerned. But, my dear, don't take the press—either the Afrikaans or the English press for that matter—as representative of public opinion in this country. It isn't. It is representative purely of Party feeling. And try and imagine what people like myself feel and think. Here am I, born and bred in this country. My grandfather was imprisoned in Ireland; my father exiled himself to this country, and in my young days I heard far more harsh things said about England than even your Party now insinuates. I grew up to regard this country as my home; I certainly have had no reason to bless England or to become a proselyte for jingoism. This is my home, just as it is that of my wife, whose grandfather came out with the 1820 Settlers, and whose father was as staunch a South African as I am. You must not take it for granted that Kipling's absurd apology applies to the third or even the second generation of English citizens here. You remember—

> "We learned from our English mothers
> To call old England 'home'."

I certainly did not, nor my wife, and I fancy that also applies to Quakerley's kids, to the Seldons, and if it comes to that, to the Uhlmanns and the von Bergmanns. If it did, what a lot of "homes" we would have. Some of us would have to look to Java, to America, or Greece. But I don't for a moment think that you take that narrow view. If you did, you would have to limit your South African nationalism to those who are of the third and fourth generation, and I doubt if you will find much culture or progress among them. The old families are dying out, as you know. First and second generations will naturally retain some of that sentiment, and can you blame them? They may even be as aggressively sentimental as you say they are ... mind you, I don't admit the accusation, but let that pass. What does it matter? At bottom they are South African, and have been trying to act like South Africans, all along. What you wish them to do is to ...'

'To make them live up to their principles,' exclaimed Santa, vigorously. 'To behave as South Africans, and to admit equality of culture. That's all.'

'Is it? When you make nationalism a plea for rank intolerance, and assume, off-hand, that everyone who is not with you, in your Party, is necessarily an enemy of South Africanism? No, my dear. That is not the way.'

'It is not true,' insisted Santa. 'The intolerance is on the other side. We have been conciliatory all along the line.'

'Pardon me, you know that is not a fact. Just look at what the position is. Take the Boer War. Has any nation ever done what England has done to efface those lamentable mistakes which she made thirty years ago? Why, my dear, we have even made ourselves ludicrous in our eagerness to wipe out any trace of ill-feeling there might be ...'

'What do you mean? The million you gave for repatriation? Surely you don't call that generous? I grant you it was ludicrous ...'

'Now, Santa, you are unfair. You know that it was far more than a million. All told it was nearer six million. But that is not what I am alluding to. I was referring to the grant of a medal, for instance, to those *burghers* who had fought on the Republican side. It is surely a trifle funny that the King should institute a medal for "Faithful Service," if you please, to be awarded to those who fought against him.'

'It was a very noble gesture,' said Santa, indignantly. 'And it is mean of you, Doctor, to question its suggestiveness.'

'I am far from questioning that,' smiled the doctor. 'But it strikes me as distinctly Gilbertian. Time, of course, changes our perspectives, and the pendulum has now swung strongly to the other side. But you don't meet us half-way. Take my own case again. I was against the war ... you have no idea what I had to endure under martial law because I said so frankly and openly. But I was just as much against Krugerism and all it stood for, and it seems to me that we are travelling towards much the same thing nowadays. It's the Transvaal spirit, slowly permeating us, fostered by all this silly talk of an independence that can never be actual until we are strong enough to stand alone. That, my dear, is the main difference between us. That is why I cannot belong to your Party, much as I appreciate that in some things it is better than my own. And let me tell you this, Santa. Once you honestly and frankly confess that our destinies are bound up, radically, with those of the Empire, by which I mean the group of communities concentrated round England and still true to the tradition in which they have been founded—once you do that, my dear, you will have every Englishman who thinks as I do a member of your Party and prepared to work hand in hand with you.'

'There is really nothing now,' began Santa, but he interrupted her quickly.

'In essence, no. But although you have whittled down your aggressive, intolerant ideal of independence to your present contentment with your paper status, most of us feel that at heart you are still unconverted. That is the trouble, and it is damnably difficult for a moderate like myself to make up his mind. The old South African Party still represents, on paper, principles and a programme, such as it is, which I can endorse ...'

'Principles which it never carries out,' jibed Santa 'and a programme which does not exist.'

'Granted,' argued the doctor, patiently. 'We have no constructive leadership. We are bound to persons, and we are too sentimental to make a clean sweep. All the more reason for you to be wiser and make it possible for those of us who feel that the old Party no longer satisfies us to enter your fold. But again you have done nothing to make it possible, or at least easy, for us to do so.'

'We have, at least, been successful in managing the country,' interjected Santa. 'We have managed it without giving up our principles and without disturbance, which is more than your Party can say.'

'Again I admit it. You have, on the whole, done excellently; in some things far better than we did. I frankly congratulate you on that. But go a little further. Wipe out the past. Don't dwell on it as you are doing, simply in order to create ill-feeling. Do a little noble gesturing on your own part. We did in the old days, you know. There was considerable feeling here after the First Boer War, and yet when the Old Lady's jubilee came, in 1887, we all combined and sent her a present.'

'I didn't know about that,' said Santa, her curiosity roused. 'What was it? Do tell me.'

'You'll never guess, my dear. A box of oranges. Contributed by all the farmers. The test was that each selected orange should just fit into the magistrate's tall hat. You never saw such monsters, and, mind you, they were immature, for we had no cold storage in those days, and the fruit had to be sent half-green. But somehow it reached Windsor, and we got a nice letter of thanks which was framed and hung in the court room until our offices were burned down during the war. That was the proper spirit, my dear, and I don't see why we should not resuscitate it. I grant you there must always be a republican Party in the Union. The republican tradition is too strong; it will endure especially among the less cultured—I am not using the term in any derogatory sense, my dear. You remember that even in the old Company's days they started little republics all over the show. It was merely the spirit of intolerance and sectional antagonism, nothing more, but in time it became solidified. A pity in many ways. But I can understand it. I should be a republican myself, my dear, but I am not. Somehow I can't get away from the feeling that it does not really matter under what form of government you live as long as the government is good, and representative of all sections. That is why I welcomed the advent of the Pact. It has done a great deal of good, although I suspect that it has outlived its day.'

'That is very nice of you,' said Santa, surprised. 'The first part of it, at least. I see no reason why we should not go on.'

'No, my dear,' the doctor shook his head, and skilfully negotiated a bump in the road. 'Our rural communities have learned something by the combination. They have realised that Labour is not so bad as it was thought to be after all these strikes and the silly way in which we managed to settle them. That is a point to the good. And the English-speaking working man has also learned something from our rural communities. It is a great pity that Labour, as a Party, is in such a bad way. Again a chance for your Party, if you will only see it and use it. You cannot govern South Africa on the old conservative lines. It is no longer possible. Whatever Party wishes to be the predominant party in the future must go in for a constructive labour policy. It must insist on land reform, which means land taxation, now such an anathema to the rural electorates simply because they do not understand it, and ultimately franchise reform.'

'There I agree,' said Santa. 'I have always urged that. But we must first get woman's suffrage. Then things will come right.'

'Maybe. I don't see how you can get that without greatly changing the whole aspect of politics in this country, but perhaps that is all to the good. It would mean an extension of adult suffrage, I suppose. Not a very promising outlook, for a community with a hundred thousand poor Whites.'

'I don't believe there are so many,' expostulated Santa. 'I haven't seen any here. Of course, poor Coloureds, and that I suppose is a great problem. Indeed, I have been thinking it over, Doctor, and it seems to me that that is the great problem—the Coloured people. I had no idea of their conditions. It is only now when I go into the location ...'

'Ah, my dear, that is a sad mess. Keep away from it, if you can. Not that the matter does not bristle with scientific possibilities, as you have remarked before. But when you touch that, you touch a very large problem indeed, and one that to us seems insoluble. But don't run away with the idea that we have no poor Whites. We have—numbers of them. Some the descendants of good old families, who settled here and flourished. The war created many; poor White-ism is not exactly a legacy from the war, but the war did much to increase its incidence.'

'What is the cause of it, Doctor? There must be some remediable factors.'

'Of course there are. Many. The subject should be properly investigated, but no one thinks of doing that. Another of your missed opportunities, and believe me you might do worse than concentrate on the poor Whites. They are worth reclaiming, but the reclamation must be organised, not sporadic, and it must not be left to the church. The church, my dear ...' he shook his head as if he had no words to express his feelings. 'What you see in the location,' he proceeded, 'can be paralleled in many places. I have had some experience of the diggings—I did a *locum* there once when I was younger. You see most of the poor Whites congregated there. I remember attending a woman. The house was made of sacking, just sacking knotted between four poles with a tarpaulin across the top. It was raining and the floor—bare gravel veld, my dear—was in puddles. She was lying on a bit of sacking, and two small children were on the floor. The child had just been born ... you can imagine the details. I have seen a good many nasty things, but that was one of the nastiest. And yet I found that the husband had contributed to the church building fund—they built a solid stone church, costing several thousands. Wicked, my dear, wicked. Of course, we are better off. Here we have always had good persons, who know the people and who have done a great deal of good. But even we have regular contribution Sundays towards the Soudan Mission Fund. Fancy that. The Soudan Mission Fund when we have a hundred thousand poor White people needing missioning. Wicked, my dear, wicked.'

He accelerated to relieve his feelings, and they raced up the deserted Village street.

'I will take you home,' he said. 'Mrs Vantloo will be getting anxious. Then I shall have to go out again. Do you still want that partnership?'

'More than ever, Doctor,' she answered, firmly. 'It has been a most interesting day. I am sure that it is a case of early *Friedreichs ataxia*, and the boy has only an unresolved pneumonia.'

'Well, time will show,' he retorted, mildly. 'Here we are. Good night, my dear. I'll call for you tomorrow at nine sharp. No thanks, I won't come in.'

Chapter 15

Jeremiah came back to the farm in the late afternoon, much later than his wife had expected him to return. He had dallied on the way, deliberately, for he wanted time to adjust his feelings, time to consider this overwhelming disaster which had intruded itself into his placid, ordinary life.

Jeremiah Gerster was reckoned a shrewd, careful farmer, and the District knew that no agriculturist could reach that reputation unless he was a man who had more than the usual modicum of common sense. It credited Jeremiah with wisdom, with something at least of that cunning in which it delighted so much when that quality was applied to politics. In a community inherently simple, but vitiated through over-worship of political idols, whose petty triumphs seem large when seen through the plain spectacles of ignorance, '*slim*-ness' (or cunning) passes for real cleverness. So, because Jeremiah had never given proof of expert fence-riding, dignified hypocrisy, and hard business-bargaining, people agreed that he was wise but not clever. Which, interpreted into ordinary language, meant that he could be depended upon as a friend, as a debtor or as a creditor, and that he could farm passably well, but that it would be futile to expect him to get the better of a political argument, a neat quarrel about nothing, or a skulduggery agreement wherein the one party tries to circumvent the other. He was a plain, honest, horse-sense sort of man, and the district agreed, tacitly, that much of his good luck was due to the able management of his wife who was accounted far cleverer though no less honest than himself.

For all that, Jeremiah was capable of intrigue, although he lacked the diplomatic facility of conducting it with finesse, and preferred open and bold methods of frontal attack to enveloping tactics. On this occasion, returning from the Village, it appeared to him that open methods were fraught with much danger, and he was acutely concerned in preventing any danger. So far, he flattered himself, he had conducted the matter with some degree of cleverness. He had called at the bank, off-handedly asked the cashier for his pass book and paid in cheques, refused the customary offer to show him in the manager's *sanctum* on the excuse that he was pressed for time, and gossiped in his usual friendly, but not too intimate, manner with the clerk preparatory to the delivery of the documents. When he had received the little parcel he had ostentatiously thrust it into his pocket, although he had been itching to open it and look at the cheques. Outside in the street, he had stopped to chat with a passing acquaintance, and at the garage where he had left his car he had spent a few minutes in neighbourly talk with the mechanic, who had assured him that his choice of a new car was commendable.

It was only when he had left the Village behind him and felt himself reasonably secure from observation that he had halted the car beside a big sandstone boulder which threw a welcome shade over the road, and opened the parcel. He glanced first at the pass book, and saw that he had been debited, the previous day, with a thousand pounds and credited, a few days before, with the money he had banked. Neatly pencilled below the columns he saw his total debit to the bank; later on the figures would be inked in, and already, in the big ledger, he had turned the debit into a credit, for he had taken his wife's advice and deposited more than sufficient to cover his overdraft. He drew the cheques from the pocket in the pass book, and looked them over. They were in order, each neatly cancelled with the bank's rubber stamp. The last was the cheque for a thousand pounds, ostensibly bearing his signature although it was plain enough that he had not filled in the writing. It was a cheque made out to Elias Vantloo, and had been paid in through Vantloo and van Deren's account. The more he looked at it the more perplexed he became, and it did not at first strike him that it was a forgery. The signature was his; it had deceived the teller, who was familiar enough with the way in which he signed, and it deceived him now. He sat with the slip of paper in his hand, his spectacles pushed up on his forehead, his vacant eyes staring at the panorama of blue hills and sun-burnished veld around him, and the more he thought about the matter the more confused he became. Suddenly the solution struck him, and he clenched his hands and nearly tore the cheque in half. But his habitual self control came to his aid, and he carefully replaced the cheque with the others in the pass book, which he put back into his pocket. Then he started the car again and drove on, very slowly, to *Eisleben*.

He wanted time to think it over. Probably Gertrude would have some plan, but Gertrude might make things worse, and at all costs this horrible thing must not come to the little sister's ears. It had been a mistake—he now frankly admitted it, perhaps for the first time in his life, for always he had tried to justify himself for his vehement approval of her marriage with a man whom he had never been able cordially to like— it had been a mistake, that union of the little sister with Elias Vantloo. The man was bad ... bad from top to toe, and perhaps it might have been better to have allowed Maria to suffer sharply nearly thirty years ago in order to prevent her suffering in her old age. Perhaps, too, she might have got over it, and found another and more suitable mate. But what was done was done. It was useless speculating on what might have been, and it would be unmanly for him now to shelve his obvious responsibilities upon a Providence hitherto not invoked. His plain duty was to guard Maria, to shield the little sister from pain and worry, from disgrace and danger, and above all from losing that respect and affection for her man in whom she still believed with passionate confidence and unabated loyalty. Maria had been his favourite. He really thought that he loved Maria as much, although in a different way, as he loved Gertrude. That was understandable, he reflected, for the two characters were so totally dissimilar. The little sister was frail, a woman of feeling and intuition, all heart and emotion, while Gertrude was capable, strong, to be relied upon as one who would never allow her feelings to run away with her, a business-like woman, supremely logical and securely self-reliant. There could be no real comparison between them. His anger against his brother-in-law grew as he reflected upon the difficulties of the situation. That these difficulties would be great he frankly admitted to himself. Elias must be in some sort of hole, otherwise he would never have done such a thing. Jeremiah speculated upon these possibilities and imagined that he saw in some of them a glimmering of hope, a chance of profiting by them to turn the situation, black as it looked, to the ultimate advantage of Maria. These reflections tempered his annoyance, and it was almost in an equable frame of mind that he accelerated the speed of his car so as to arrive home before sunset. He gave the pass book to his wife when he entered the dining room, and flung himself into his arm-chair at the window.

'There,' he said, gruffly. 'You may see for yourself. It is not my cheque. It is a make-believe cheque. I never drew it.'

Only then he noticed Eric, and his face lit up with a smile as he shook hands.

'We shall need a lawyer's *slim*-ness to get us out of this muddle, I warrant,' he chuckled, and both Gertrude and van Deren were relieved to hear his laugh. It made them realise that he had faced the situation on his way from the Village.

'There's a letter from brother-in-law,' said his wife, grimly, handing Vantloo's note to him. 'You overlooked it this morning in your haste, Husband. Read it now.'

He took it and glanced over it, his brows contracting angrily as he did so. 'God damn me,' he said, passionately. 'He presumes too much. With this we ... we could crush him.'

'Exactly,' said his wife. 'And Maria too. That is what he relies upon. Elias is no fool, Husband.'

'Maria,' all his doubts and misgivings assailed him again. 'Do you think Maria need know? Surely we can manage this thing without dragging Maria into it. There must be some way. Come, Eric, let's hear what the lawyer has to say. And God damn me, man, it touches you. The cheque is paid into your firm's account ...'

'On that score Uncle need have no misgivings,' said Eric quickly. 'You will get every penny back. I will see to it myself. I can write you out a cheque for the amount now ...'

'You will do nothing of the kind,' interrupted Gertrude, quickly. 'That would be compounding a felony, even though you assure me there's no such thing in our law.

Jerry can stand the loss; it should be a punishment for his misdeeds in the past ...'

'Aye, Wife, beat me now I am down,' said Jeremiah, miserably. 'Do you think I haven't beaten myself all the way coming here? Perhaps you were right, but then I couldn't see with your eyes. I always ... I always had a sort of fondness for Maria ...'

'A sort of fondness!' said the old lady, almost contemptuously. 'You were infatuated with her. So much the worse for her, Husband. If you had taught sister-in-law to stand on her own legs and to fight her own troubles, she would be better off today than she is.'

'You must not blame her, Wife,' he urged. 'She is not like you. She is a weak vessel, whom we have to protect and shield. Even now. Come, let us put our heads together and make a plan. Eric, what's the use of your being a lawyer and trained to be sharp and look through a brick wall, if you can't help us now?'

'He can and will,' explained the old lady. 'We are taking it for granted that you want this thing kept from sister-in-law ...'

'Therein you are right,' exclaimed Jerry. 'God damn me, Wife, it would break her heart if she were to know ...'

'Women's hearts are not so easily broken as all that, Husband,' said his wife reassuringly. 'But I agree that it is better to keep it from Maria. There is no sense in making her suffer for her man's misdeeds. You spoke to no-one in the Village, I hope?'

'No—that is, not about this matter. I came away as soon as I could. I feared I might run against Elias—not that I knew then. I have thought about it coming home. All the way. When I did not know about his letter, though. That makes things easier, in a way.'

'In a way, yes. But you must make up your mind that this has got to stop, Husband. You and Eric must go tomorrow and have it out with brother-in-law. You must keep the letter and the cheque. That is to have a hold over him in case he jibs. Eric and I have talked it over, and we have made a plan.'

'Is that so?' he said, with some eagerness. 'What is it? But you must promise me that Maria will be kept out of it. And Santa too. I will not have them worried. Maria loves the ground he walks upon, and Santa ... Why, the girl worships him.'

'We'll keep Maria out of it, Man. You need have no fear about that. As for Santa, that's a different pair of boots. The girl is old enough to know things. It would be unfair to her to keep it from her. Sooner or later she will have to hear about it, and better soon than late. Yes, don't interrupt. You will only make things more difficult if you insist. I will come with you if you and Eric think that you cannot manage between the two of you—yes, on the whole I think I should go with you. I shall give brother-in-law an unvarnished sketch of what I think of him.'

'No, no,' said her husband. 'You'd better keep out of it. I don't know what your plan is ...'

'It is simple enough, Uncle,' explained Eric, before Aunt Gertrude could speak. 'We thought we would get Uncle Elias to agree to give up the firm—to give up everything, and to go away. To live somewhere else—he has that house at the seaside, you know, and Aunt Maria is always ever so much better there than at the Village. She does not get asthma there. It will be a good thing for them both. But Uncle Elias will have to promise to keep straight and not meddle with things in the future. There has been far too much of it. Uncle does not know everything.'

'Indeed you don't,' said his wife vigorously. 'You never see farther than your nose, Husband, and you are deaf to what people say. I suppose you do not know that brother-in-law has been using his influence on the licensing board to get licences— Solomon's, for instance. Or that he has made a good thing out of it ...'

'I have heard something about it,' he admitted, frowning. 'But I did not want to listen to it. You know I am not very fond of Brother Elias. I can't help it. But he is Maria's man, and I won't have anything happen to harm her.'

'She will not be harmed,' his wife said, impatiently. 'She will continue to believe her man a little God's pet creature, Man. But then Elias must be made to see that we know what he has been up to. *Bah*, the man disgusts me. I always thought him a clever fool, but I did not know that fools can be so foolish with all their cleverness. Now listen to me, Jerry. Tomorrow we all go into the Village. I shall phone to Maria tonight and say that you and I are coming on a visit tomorrow. That will be all right. We owe them one, and she will not suspect that there is anything amiss ...'

'I can't go tomorrow,' said Jerry plaintively. 'I shall have to keep an eye on the tobacco planting. You know I can't get away tomorrow.'

'Very well then, the day after tomorrow. There is no hurry,' she retorted impatiently. 'That will give us time to calm down a bit, too, I daresay. You, Eric, will have to return tomorrow, and you might explain to him. Tell him that it must be final. We don't want him to do anything until we come, but you can arrange things—draw up some sort of document, you will know what to do ...'

'I shall have to think it over, Aunt,' Eric interrupted. 'It is not going to be easy if he objects ...'

'He won't object,' she declared, confidently. Elias is a coward. When he sees that he is cornered he will hands-up at once. I know his breed,' she spoke with bitter contempt. 'Not one of them is worth powder and shot. He will give in to save his face. Have no fear about that. You can make him sign anything you like, and he will be too frightened to try and get out of it. Yes, I know him. I have observed and studied him all these years, and I have seen how much of a hypocrite he is at heart. But go warily, Eric, go warily. Find out if there is not something else ...'

'What does Aunt mean?' asked Eric, anxiously.

'The man has been treasurer of the church council,' she replied, gravely.

'All these years he has had the control of the church funds. And of the Lodge fund. And I daresay there are other things he has had to play with. Look into all that before you move—look carefully, Nephew Eric.'

'It is unthinkable,' burst out her husband, but he was not allowed to complete the sentence.

'Isn't it unthinkable that he should have forged your name, Man?' she interrupted quickly. 'Isn't it unthinkable that he should have received money for his vote on the court? Or that he should have made himself rich during our war by transport-riding for the English, and now poses as a martyr? He is a white-washed grave, Husband, that's what he is, and we don't know what horrible remnants we may find when we begin to dig. That's why I want Eric to go warily. Maybe there are matters we cannot keep from Maria. You would not like that ...'

'No!' he exclaimed, passionately. 'Whatever he is, he is her man, and she must not suffer through him. It is our duty to see that she doesn't. Mine, at least. I could have prevented her marrying him ... God damn me, why didn't I?'

'Taking the little Lord's name in vain won't help matters, Man,' she said, chidingly. 'Swearing won't help us. Eric must investigate—discretely but quickly. We can't afford to let things grow. Already there is too much that is ... unthinkable. Do you, Eric, go into these matters? I suppose you can have access to the church books. And that reminds me, look into the other matters—Maria's money, for instance, and Santa's. If there is anything left, which I doubt. But the papers should be at the office. You could easily look them over.'

'That I have done,' he said, shamefacedly. 'There is nothing left of Santa's ... I think you know that, Aunt ...'

'Almighty, could the girl have run through all that amount?' asked Jerry in awe-struck tones. 'Three thousand it was that she got from her mother, and all well invested. It should be all there.'

'It isn't, Uncle Jerry. It's all gone. And I am afraid Aunt Maria's too. You see, Aunt Maria signed things. I could not interfere—I had no power. When the *Kaalfontein* boom came on, he bought shares for them both.'

'Just as he did for me,' interjected Jerry moodily. 'I lost a cool four thousand over that, and might have lost more. Lad, look into these things. Do as your Aunt tells you and look into it. It does not so much matter if the money is gone—I have enough for Maria if she wants anything, without wronging my wife or any of my kin. But there may be something else. Look into things, lad. For heaven's sake, don't let us have any scandal. It will break her heart.'

'I will see what I can do, Uncle,' Eric promised. 'But it may be difficult. I may even have to get an order from court, and that none of us would like.'

'No, indeed not,' said the old lady, vigorously. 'You must keep the law out of it, Nephew. We'll manage without the law. Going to law never did any honest folk good, not so far as I know. You should know that yourself. So look into the matter—especially the church funds and whatever trust monies you have under your control. In your own interests, nephew.'

'Certainly, Aunt Gertrude. It touches me too closely for me to neglect any precautions. The only question is if I have not neglected it too long. I never thought Uncle Elias could be so ...'

'Aye, he was too much of a hypocrite for that. I fancy we shall find more than one speck on him. But now you must go and have a wash. It is nearly eating time, and we can talk about it later. Give me the papers. You don't need them. We'll bring them in with us when we come in. Husband, you will find the soap and towel ready for you, and the hot water.'

Jeremiah departed dutifully to tidy himself for supper, and Aunt Gertrude led Eric out on the *stoep*. The maids had entered to lay the table, and private conversation could not be indulged in in their presence.

Outside the rapidly fading twilight had already deepened into the smooth velvety green of night, in which the mountain outline loomed black and massive against the paler, starlit background of sky. The nightjars whirled over the flower beds; the strong reek of aromatic mountain shrubs filled the air; from far off came the lowing of cows, and the yapping of the mongrels round the Native huts.

'Go warily, Nephew Eric,' the old lady said, impressively. 'There is far more to lament than this. Elias is like a stagnant pool where the surface is very quiet, but when you stir it with a stick you find much mud. Be very careful.'

'I will be that, Aunt,' he assured her. 'Not that I think Aunt is right. I can't believe it of Uncle Elias, even though he has forged Uncle Jerry's name. But I don't believe that he is such a scoundrel.'

'I don't believe—I know,' said the old lady, and there was something in the tone of her voice that startled Eric. 'I have known it all these years. I only hope that others will not know it. You and I must keep it from them. Not this. That troubles me but little. Money is of no consequence. If it has been taken it can be replaced. I have enough, and Jerry has enough to cover whatever the man may have stolen. But there are other things about which I am not at all so sure. And those things are of far more importance than money, Eric. So go warily, and if you discover anything let me know before you tell Jerry or anyone else.'

Chapter 16

Santa found her father unusually genial at dinner that night. Elias talked well, displaying an intelligent interest in his daughter's affairs, making practical suggestions she could appreciate, deferring to her judgment, responsive, almost instinctively, to her mood. Only her mother sat silent, mildly smiling, interjecting dull commonplaces, idly crumbling the bread with her left hand, occasionally coughing a wheezy, constrained little cough. Santa found herself contrasting the two—vivacity of the heavy, black-jowled man, with his short, clumsy fingers and his intelligent, alert conversation, and the dejected, dispirited nonchalance of the pale, fragile looking old woman, whose slender, tape-ring fingers trifled with the bread crust. An aimless, nervous trifling, which made one think, involuntarily, of the aimless, nervous fiddling with the bed-clothes of a patient whose days are numbered.

'I wish Mother would pluck up a little spirit,' Santa thought. 'With another wife, father would have been a great man.'

She almost hated herself for the reflection, but she was too honest to suppress it, disloyal though it was. Tonight she only saw her father as her imagination had always pictured him—a virile, strong figure, rough as all self-made men are, but hiding beneath the unhandsome exterior a heart of gold, a character of solid worth. She noted how well his clothes fitted him, and how well he wore them, as if unconscious of them, careless of anything but his comfort. He might not be of mother's family, but like Napoleon he had no need for family. He was sufficient in himself.

'Well, Daughter,' he said, and his thin, throaty voice struck unpleasantly across her reflections. 'Shall we adjourn to the drawing room? Mina might light the fire there, Wife.'

'The maids will do that, Elias,' said Mrs Vantloo. 'Mina is away tonight.'

'Ah, so. Probably with that daughter of hers,' he said, indifferently. 'How long will the girl last, Santa?'

'It is difficult to say, Father. She had a haemorrhage this morning, and she was very bad when I looked in. I think ...'

'You must excuse me, my dear,' interrupted her mother. 'I shall go and lie down. I feel an attack coming on.'

Santa got up solicitously, but her mother waved her back with a smile. 'I shall be quite all right, my dear,' Maria said, mildly. 'Go and talk to father in the drawing room. The fire will be lit by now. Perhaps I will come later on. You can have your coffee there, Elias.'

He did not get up to open the door for her, but drank his ginger beer noisily as she left the room. Santa felt a disturbing twinge of resentment, but fought it down. She lit her cigarette, and blew the smoke across the table.

'Do you do that sort of thing when you are with your patients?' he asked, and she felt the irony in his voice. ,

'Of course not,' she answered shortly. 'One does not smoke when one is examining a patient. Not that it would matter very much, I suppose.'

'It would matter here,' he said, smiling at her. 'You would not have many if you did that.'

'I don't know if you are right,' she retorted, argumentatively. 'Some of them might like it. It would be a novelty, almost as much as I am one. Why don't you smoke, Father?'

'I used to,' he said, and she noticed no regret in his voice. 'But I gave it up even before I joined the Lodge ...'

'What has the Lodge to do with it?' she demanded. 'You don't swear to eschew tobacco, do you? I thought Satan only concerned himself with alcohol, so far as the grown ups are concerned?'

'You should not mock at sacred things,' he parried, gravely. 'It is largely to influence the young souls in the Band of Hope that I set a good example. But don't count me a martyr to my convictions, Santa. Frankly, I don't care for it. So it is no sacrifice to give it up. And it is a good thing, sometimes, not to smoke when the other man does. You have an advantage. You see what I mean?'

'I don't quite, Father. But I suppose you can explain,' she replied, slightly piqued by his tone of raillery. Somehow, since he had refrained from getting up to open the door for her mother, his complacency jarred on her.

'Come into the drawing room, Daughter,' he said, getting up from his chair and leading the way. 'We can talk better there—more quiet-like, you understand.' He ensconced himself in a large easy-chair by the fire, and drew a peppermint from his waistcoat pocket.

'I suppose you think nothing of this sort of thing,' he said, waving the lozenge in the air. 'Sit down, my dear. But it helps me, and I like it just as much as you like your cigarettes—precious little. It is nothing but a habit, and so long as it is comparatively harmless, what of it?'

'Mine doesn't linger,' she smiled. 'Nor is it so penetrating. I think yours is rather a vulgar habit, Father. Why don't you use chewing gum? That at least has no smell.'

'Well, everyone has his own taste,' he said, amicably. 'And we really need not discuss each other's habits, Santa. I have left you a free hand, my dear, and I daresay you will allow me one too. Or is it that you think a parent should be well brought up by the child? That is the modern doctrine, I believe.'

'You are well enough brought up, Father,' she answered, adopting the same tone of raillery though it did not come so easily as she had expected. 'Except for the Lodge. I wonder you don't break out sometimes. You know, I should hate that enforced restraint. A pledge would always be an incitement to me to do just what I had promised not to do. If it was purely a verbal undertaking, I should not like to break it. But that sort of signed nonsense ... And you know you do take alcohol. Your ginger beer contains alcohol, your coffee ...'

'I know, I know, Child. Do you think I am quite a fool? My dear Daughter, now that we are under four eyes, you and I by ourselves, I think it would be as well to have a nice, confidential chat. I have really had no chance since your return to have an intimate conversation with you. And we should have one, you understand. There are some things you ought to know and some things I should tell you. I told you I looked upon you more as a son than as a daughter. You understand—as one who is not weak like your mother. No, don't interrupt. I mean nothing derogatory by saying that. But mother is ... well, an old fashioned woman. And you are ... well, a modern one, young enough to look at some things with common sense eyes.'

'What is all the preface leading up to, Father?' she asked, surprised at the change in his manner. 'Is there anything serious the matter? Do you want me to do something unpleasant? So long as it is not Eric ...'

'Yes, in a fashion it concerns Eric as well,' he said, quickly. 'Sit down. I can't talk to you while you are dropping cigarette ash on my head. It'll soon be bald enough anyhow, and you might drop a spark and burn me. Sit down there, and light another fag. You are spilling that on the carpet. Throw it into the fire. There, that's it. Now we can talk.'

'Go ahead then,' she said, settling herself in the club-easy opposite him. 'But I promise nothing, especially not about Eric.'

'Why don't you take Eric?' he demanded. 'The man is madly in love with you, and he is old enough to know his own mind. It is not as if he were a bloody youngster. He has sown all the wild oats he is ever likely to sow, and will be as staid as an old stager. Besides, Santa, it would help me very considerably if you said yes. Very considerably indeed.'

'I know you and mother want me to marry him,' she said, rebelliously. 'You threw Eric at my head when I was a girl. I had Eric daily ever since I can remember, and I have had about enough of him. I don't like him well enough to marry him, Father. I don't love him, to put it bluntly. So there.'

'Hm. Then it becomes rather difficult to talk to you, daughter. You see, Mother and I looked upon the thing as sort of fixed up ...'

'I know you did. That's where you both made a mistake. If you hadn't looked upon it as the inevitable thing, I might have considered him from a different aspect, Dad. But it's like your pledge. I can't take to it because it seems forced upon me, and I won't have Eric forced upon me. I am old enough to choose for myself.'

'Of that I haven't the slightest doubt. Nor that you will choose rightly when you consider all things pertinent to the matter. That's why I want to talk to you tonight. I think it is time you should understand the matter.'

'I fancy I know all there is to know about it, Dad. Even the ... shall I say, commercial advantages involved? Naturally you want to keep Eric in the firm, and you think he might take it into his head to leave you in the lurch when he gets tired of proposing to me. But that really cannot affect the matter, for you can do without him, or get another partner easily, can't you?'

'Perhaps I could, and perhaps I couldn't, Daughter. But let me put the ... let us say commercial advantages, from another point of view. Here's your partnership with Buren. You are really serious about that, I suppose?'

'Of course I am serious. I told you I should like it, for a few years at any rate. Later on I want to go into consulting practice somewhere. But a few years in general practice would be very good for me.'

'Quite. But a partnership, you understand, means money. In this case it means fifteen hundred down ... that is, Eric tells me, the least that Buren wants. He will stretch a point in your favour ...'

'I don't want any favours, Father. Surely you can find fifteen hundred pounds for me. Why, mother's money and what is left of my own ...'

'Slowly, slowly, Santa. What is left of your own won't pay your church money for the next quarter, if you should desire to go to church, which so far, to my grief, you have not done. And don't be so sure of mother's money, my dear.' He looked her full in the face as he spoke. 'That went years ago. She doesn't know, of course. One does not speak about these things to women who don't understand business affairs, but the plain truth is that she put it into speculative shares—diamond shares, my dear—and they didn't turn out good.' He made the announcement in a perfectly even voice, and for a moment she thought he was jesting, and decided to enter into the spirit of the joke.

'So mother and I are paupers,' she said, lightly. 'And if I don't marry Eric and you die of this mythical heart complaint of yours, we won't know where to turn. Thank you, Dad, I think I could manage to earn some money to support mother and myself for a while until someone turns up.'

'I am not joking!' he expostulated, gravely. 'I am telling you the exact truth. Neither your mother nor you can reckon on anything should I die. People think I am wealthy. I was once, but one speculates, and one does not always have luck. For some years now things have been going badly. I have had difficulties to make both ends meet. I must keep up a certain position, you understand. I have had many calls upon my purse lately, and just now I cannot possibly raise fifteen hundred pounds, even to please you, my dear.'

'But, Father,' she said, aghast, realising with a shock that he was serious. 'It is impossible. Why, you sent me a cheque when I came out. And mother could not have wasted all that money. There must be some mistake. Of course there must. You said it went years ago, and yet here you have been paying for my expenses. I know the firm does very well, but with this house and all your various expenses, you could not ...'

'I didn't, Santa,' he said, evenly. 'That is what I want you to understand. And that is why you must marry Eric. It is his money you have had all these years. A loan from him ...'

'What?' She got up from her chair and, finding that her hands were trembling, threw the cigarette into the fire and turned to free him. 'Say that again, Father?'

'Yes, Santa,' he reiterated, smiling at her. 'It is just as I say. You are indebted to Eric for that. There, my Girl, don't make a fuss about it. Let me give you a piece of advice. Never deny anybody the privilege of doing you a favour. Don't always think that it places you under an obligation. I know what my hot-headed little girl is imagining. But Eric, as you must have discovered by now, is a weak, sentimental fool. You can twist him round your little finger, and he is really very useful sometimes, you understand? Don't get into a huff about it. Yes, I had to turn to him, and I managed the business very creditably to all concerned. He lent me the money under a promise of secrecy, and I regret that it has been necessary to tell you. It would have been better for you to have remained in ignorance of the young man's generosity, though on second thoughts I should not have permitted that. It might have led to complications afterwards, you understand? He might have thrown his generosity at your head when you fell out, and you would not have liked that. No, I am sure my little girl would not have liked that. But now it is different. Now you are forewarned, so to speak. But you should at least consider the matter from another aspect, my dear, now that you know the—shall we continue to say—commercial advantages?'

She felt numbed by her indignation, unable to speak. She heard him pattering on in his thin, squeaky voice that sounded reminiscently of the noise made by the loose bolts of a car wheel. He continued smoothly.

'Yes, he has helped considerably in other matters. This partnership, now. You will get it, but it will be Eric's money—Eric's or that fool of *Eisleben*. So don't worry about it. But it is as well for you to know how matters stand, my Girl. You understand, they don't run smoothly. In time I will tide them over. You may trust me for that. But just now I have too many commitments to be altogether easy, and that is one reason why I should like you to come to an understanding with Eric. You see, my dear, I am talking quite frankly to you—sit down; there is no object in glowering at me. You have really nothing to do with the matter. I acted on my own responsibility, and if I chose to accept money from Eric, it is my affair, not yours.'

She sat down, seething with indignation, but controlling her feelings in a manner that astonished her. It was, of course, Eric's fault. Her indignation was for him, not for her father. Father had probably had money worries, political worries, business worries. It would be a shame to get annoyed with him. She would listen patiently to this rigmarole and get the explanation from Eric afterwards.

'Certainly, Father,' she said, keeping her voice firmly under control. 'It is entirely your affair. Although I fail to see why you did it. I hate to be under an obligation to anyone, and especially to Eric. The loan must be repaid at once, with interest.'

'Easy enough to say that, Daughter,' he replied, sarcastically. 'You don't seem to have followed me. Let me tell you again, and this time I will make it perfectly plain. I am not so rich as you fancy I am. I am, in a sense, a poor man. Have you grasped that?'

'If you say so, Father, I must believe you. But possibly you make a mistake. I can't imagine you poor.'

'There is no mistake. Of course I am speaking comparatively. I do not mean to imply that I am insolvent. That I shall never be, in the ordinary sense of the term. Even if I have to surrender my estate, and there is no question of that yet. But, my dear, I have told you this because I look upon you as my son, because I regard you as your father's child ... you understand?'

His repetition of the query irritated her, but she nodded. He was giving her his confidence, treating her frankly as an equal, confessing his difficulties and entreating her aid.

'Very well. Now look at things sensibly. Think what a mistake it would be for me to fail just now, and consider how much you can help me if you will play up to Eric. You can always change your mind, you know, but honestly, at present you will help me very much if you can get him ... if you can arrange something, you understand? Lately he has been difficult. He has asked inconvenient questions, my dear, and he has meddled with things which are not in his province. And you must remember he is a lawyer ...'

He hesitated, and as she did not speak, he got up from his chair and came to her.

'You think I am asking too much of you, my dear,' he said, caressing her hair. 'But I am asking it not for myself only. I want you to do it for mother. She does not know what I have told you. Imagine her knowing it. Why, Child, it would break her heart. She thinks I am so solid, so ... so everything she thinks I am, and if she were to hear that I ... have been unfortunate ... Why, Child, you would not like her to think that of father, would you?'

'You must give me time to think about it,' Santa said, dully. She still hoped that she had misunderstood him, but the implication of his words was clear enough. He was in grave difficulties. She dared not ask for particulars; she could not follow his argument, but she understood that it was necessary that Eric should, for a time at least, be pacified, cajoled if need be. Well, that would not be impossible; that, in fact, would be comparatively easy, and it would give her time to think the matter over. She no longer felt indignant, for her indignation had given place to an apprehension, a fear, which somehow his final appeal to her had engendered. What lay behind his talk? What did he mean by his confidence to her? She could not find an answer to disturbing thoughts, and though she tried to shake them from her they persisted in recurring.

'Let us say no more about it, my dear,' he said finally. 'I am glad we have had this frank talk. It will make matters easier between us, Santa. You will have to bear with your old father and help him. Then everything will come right and you can do what you like. But for the present you must bear with him, and let yourself be guided by him, if only for a little while. You shall have your partnership with Buren. I daresay I can find the money somewhere, and by and by we will pay Nephew Eric back—yes, with interest. Now don't be too shocked at what I have told you. Believe me, you will hear other things to shock you, but so long as you have faith in your old dad, everything will come right. And now ...' he kissed her as he spoke and she felt the reek of peppermint on her face, 'now I shall have to do a little work. Yes, leave the coffee. I may like a cup later on, even if it is cold.'

The late autumn enfolded the Village with its variegated browns, its lush greens enlivened by the early rain, its passing show of colour blushing in shortened fervour before the coming frosts eclipsed it. On the trellis the bougainvillea still showed belated mauve, and the cassias shed their golden petals on the ground, while everywhere the sorrels opened their fragile beauty to the sun. In the clear, windless air the mountain range loomed in stately grandeur of blue, flecked with carmine where the cliff-face was lichened, against a background of palest amethyst.

From the *stoep* of the Vantloo's house one had a clear view of the picturesque environment in which the Village was set. Once upon a time the Village had been a gem, its thatched houses with their white-washed walls and gables, contrasting boldly but at the same time harmoniously with the greenery of oak, poplar, and orange trees. The war had changed all that. Most of the houses had been burned down, and many of the thatch roofs had been replaced by ugly corrugated-iron painted red, which the scorching sun had blistered and robbed of any beauty they might have possessed. The Village was no longer what it had been in the old days. No longer a gem, but a drab, common-place collection of residences, relieved by no attempt to bring it into harmony with the picturesque environment of mountain, river and sorrel-studded veld. A few of the residents still lavished care and attention upon their gardens, but none could show the magnificent results which old Andrew Quakerley, the son of Charles— who had been a midshipman and had deserted his ship in False Bay to marry a Dutch girl, although his father had been county and had sat in the house of Commons—had attained in his wonderful garden, years ago. The Village still remembered that garden, as one remembers things of which legends speak, things not quite positively proved but so strongly stressed by tradition that belief in them was significant of a liberal toleration.

Sitting on the *stoep*, with the panorama of the hills and mountains before her, Santa found her thoughts straying towards the Quakerley legend. She had other matters to think of, matters of far more importance than the ghost of a garden which she had never seen in its pristine glory. She had been profoundly shocked by what she had heard the evening before, but she had been even more deeply stirred by the realisation that she had been shocked. Hitherto she had believed herself to be liberal, tolerant to the verge of carelessness. She had deliberately set herself to scorn convention, to ignore custom which did not appeal to her, to go her own way, demanding a freedom of action and interpretation which she now found she was not prepared to yield to others. She was annoyed with herself for that. She remembered that Eric had always been like a brother to her, and however indignant she had been the previous evening at his presumption, at what she called his unwarranted interference in her affairs, she was now prepared to make excuses for him. Very likely he had no conception of the enormity of the liberty he had taken, and father was ... well, father looked at these things from a purely business point of view, and it was silly of her to feel outraged at what had been done. The best thing was to treat the matter in a sensible, business-like manner, and to discuss it with Eric without losing her temper or suggesting that it was anything but a perfectly ordinary transaction that could be arranged with very little difficulty. Provided, of course, that Eric did not further presume.

Still, it was unfortunate that such a thing had occurred. It was an affront to her pride and she naturally resented it, and would have liked to tell Eric so. Other folk had had to swallow their pride. The Quakerleys, for instance. How that poor old Andrew must have suffered when the troops camped out in his garden. It served him right in one way. He had been a 'loyalist,' and that was what he had got for his pains. She had no patience with such loyalty, that overlooked present obligations and concentrated upon a misty tradition of the past, effete and outworn, whose very existence was an insult to nationalism. But she could feel for the old man, misguided though he had been. Just because his suffering had been so unjust, so purposeless and so cruel, she could sympathise. She tried to recollect what her mother had told her of the old man, for her own remembrance of him was too dim. A solemn, silent chap he had been, white-bearded, generous, open-handed with his wealth, popular among his peers and inferiors, going his own gait without participating in politics, a neutral, uncertain figure, a gentleman of the old school as his father had been, descended from the best blood of both sections. She imagined him to have been somewhat like mother, weak but well meaning, with no great force of character, but with a capacity for loving his garden like mother loved father. And both with an attachment to that old, worn-out tradition of the past, obsolete, useless, ineffective today. Very much like her own indignation at Eric's presumption. But to be indebted to him ... to feel that he had paid for her ... of course not for the whole, but even for a part of it ... that was too much. She would have to find out exactly how much he had lent father. They would both have to go into business details, for father was obviously getting old. His blood pressure was too high. That, too, she would have to see to. Perhaps she could get mother and father away for a month or two; there was that house at the seaside, and father had been much too busy with exchange speculations. If he could be induced to give them up, things would probably be all right. The firm was flourishing, and she knew that father held many securities. He had himself admitted that his difficulties, whatever they might be, were temporary. Eric would have to go into that ... Yes, they would have a stern, strictly business-like talk, and she would insist that the deed of partnership should be signed that day.

Her mother joined her on the *stoep*. Maria looked frailer, more in need of protection and petting, than she had seen her look before. Santa noticed that the thin, tapering fingers were tremulous, the drooping lines round the mount more sagging. She felt a sudden gush of pity for her mother as she arranged the pillows in the big arm chair.

'Do come and sit down, Motherkins,' she invited. 'Tea will be here in a moment. I told the maids to bring it out. Isn't it a lovely day?'

'They are mostly like that in autumn, my dear,' her mother said mildly, sinking wearily into the chair. 'I like autumn,' she went on, inconsequently. 'I seem to have less asthma then, you know.'

'You should go to the seaside for a bit,' her daughter advised. 'It always does you good, and father works much too much. Both of you will have to go away for a holiday, Mums. I'll see to it. Now that your doctor daughter is here you will have to do as you are told.'

'Yes, that would be nice,' the old lady said, plaintively. 'Your father should take a holiday. He is overworking, my dear. I know it. I said so years ago, but he would not listen to me. You must make him listen, Santa. He pays attention to what you say. You know he always looks upon you as a boy, and he is very proud of you.'

'I wish you, too, were proud of me, Mother,' she said guiltily conscious.

'I am, my dear, I am,' protested Maria, hastily. 'Only you are so impetuous at times, Santa. I get bewildered at you. I suppose it is the modern young woman and I must get used to her.'

'Surely there were modern young women in your day, Mother?' The maid brought the tea, and Santa poured out a cup for her mother and handed it over to the old lady. 'That will be all, Regina,' she said. 'Tell the old master when he comes in that we are having morning tea on the *stoep.*'

'Well, perhaps,' said her mother, reminiscently. 'There were Andrew's daughters. They were not brought up like the rest of us, you know. First their aunt taught them, and then they had their own governess—or rather governesses, for Emily—that was Andrew's wife, my dear, whom you remember ...'

'That queer old bore with the sharp chin who used to slobber over me, and spoke in such a stilted way? Yes, I do, dimly.'

'She was a good soul, for all her mannerisms, my dear. But she was terribly difficult to get on with, and so the governesses did not stay long. Not like Andrew. He was a peaceable, quiet kind of man, though he had a temper. Just like your Uncle Jerry, my dear. Which reminds me, Aunt Gertrude and Uncle Jerry are coming to visit us tomorrow. They must have the spare room, and I should have told the maids ...'

'Never mind that. There is plenty of time. Tell me more about the Quakerleys, Mother. Somehow I've been thinking about them. It must have been terribly hard for the old chap to lose his garden. Not that it didn't serve him right, though.'

'How can you say that, Santa? He never harmed a soul. And he was loyal all through, although his son-in-law and his grand-children were fighting on the Boer side ...'

'Then he shouldn't have been loyal, as you call it, Mother. He should have stuck up for his own folk and for his own country. He was just a trimmer, that's what he was. And I have no sympathy for him.'

'My dear, you wrong him if you think that. You have no conception,' the old lady's voice was impressively grave, and the cup in her hand trembled so that some of its contents spilt on the *stoep* paving. She set it down on the table, and continued earnestly. 'You know nothing about that time. It was awful. For all of us, my dear, but worse, perhaps, for him and those like him. You see, he belonged to both sides, as it were. His mother was Dutch and his father English, and I remember he told us that there were about twenty of his kinsmen fighting on the one side and about the same number on the other side. It was very hard for him, indeed it was.'

'I can't see where the difficulty came in,' said Santa, stubbornly maintaining her conviction that whoever had been against the Republican cause had been—must have been—in the wrong. 'Nothing anybody can say will make me believe that the war was anything but a monstrous iniquity, and that if our people had done more than protest, things would have been different.'

'My dear, that is because you don't know about it,' her mother returned with a tinge of argumentative agitation in her voice. 'From the first it was horribly difficult. It was so unjust—on both sides. We had nothing to do with it, and yet it came here. It ruined so many of us, just as it ruined the Village, and it brought so much misery with it. Andrew was not the only one of the English—though he wasn't really English, my dear; he was just as much one of us as your father is—who suffered. They couldn't do anything but suffer. Things were so terribly difficult, and people made them more difficult still because they couldn't understand our feelings. That is the hard part in life, Santa, people not comprehending how you feel. I pray you may never endure it, but there's nothing that makes you so miserable as to find that what you think much of is of no account to other folk. To have your affection trodden under foot, as it were, my dear, and to have bad motives imputed to you. Then all you can do, my dear, is to suffer, and not let people see what it means to you having to hold your tears back and force a smile. Mr Andrew did that all the time. You see, he was trained that way.'

'Yes,' said Santa, and although she had been impressed by the earnestness in her mother's voice, she could not quite keep out the sneer in her own, 'that is just it. Trained to stand bullying—the English public school spirit. To look on and see two little countries go under just to satisfy England's commercial greed.'

'No, no!' the old lady's voice was entreatingly eager. 'On that point he felt with us. But there was something else. I suppose you might call it tradition,' she pursued, reflectively. "He could not go against that. The von Bergmanns and the Uhlmanns— they were German, you know, and some of them had a very hard time ...'

'That was entirely different,' riposted Santa. 'That was sheer vindictiveness against the Germans, and another proof of England's hypocrisy. I can't conceive of a German-descended Afrikaner doing what some of them did, especially when the others had to suffer for it.'

'But, my dear, you should put yourself in their place. I remember someone writing to your father when the German riots were taking place—you know they wanted to burn down Haefele's store, though poor old Haefele's grandfather had been born here and his great-grandfather had been one of the first *landdrosts* appointed by the English during the Second Occupation. I remember someone writing to point out that the two English ambassadors—I forget their names, my dear, but one was at Berlin and the other at Vienna—were both Germans, just as much as the Uhlmanns and the von Bergmanns are Germans. It impressed father very much; he had never thought about it, and when he told the people about it—he really made a good speech that night, and I was so proud of him—it saved Haefele's store, and General Botha sent him a letter of thanks. I don't know what has become of it; it must be somewhere in a drawer.'

'Mother, you are really an old sentimentalist,' said Santa, laughing. 'I shall never be able to turn you into a good Nationalist.'

'Not if that means thinking ill of our English neighbours, my dear,' said Maria, smiling in her turn. 'But at heart I am just as good a Nationalist as you are, and old Andrew was just as good a one. He loved South Africa, and he did his best for it, and never asked whether a South African spoke English or Dutch. It is different nowadays. Now you seem to imply that one cannot be a good South African unless one speaks in Afrikaans—which you rarely do, Santa, except to the maids and occasionally to father. But it isn't the language,' went on the old lady, shrewdly, 'that makes one feel as one does. It is something else, something you haven't learned yet, my dear. All this talk and ill-feeling do not really matter. We had a great deal of that during the war, and it did not accomplish much except to make bad blood between friends. It is the work that matters, and the spirit, my dear.'

'Then you should give us credit for a great deal, Mother. We've done far more in a few years than the old Party did all the time it was in power. And we have roused the spirit. It always lay dormant, but it is there, right enough.'

'I didn't mean that sort of spirit,' said her mother, wistfully. 'I meant something else. The sort of thing the Uhlmanns and von Bergmanns had, if you know what I mean. A sort of background for one's beliefs. I try to think I have it, but it is difficult, my dear, to live up to it. But when one feels there is something like that behind one, it makes things easier, as it were. One does want something to lean upon.'

'You poor old dear,' exclaimed Santa, petting her. 'Of course you must. You must lean upon me, and father, and not worry your head about politics. You aren't meant for that. Your place, Mother, is in the home. You are the dearest, darlingest example of early Victorian domesticity. Mrs Ewing would have delighted in you.'

'I don't know who the lady might be,' said her mother, gently loosening herself, 'but if she is a friend of yours I shall always be glad to welcome her. I am glad you have some good, married lady friends, Santa. You must tell me more about Mrs Ewing.'

Chapter 18

A full afternoon with Dr Buren gave Santa little chance to indulge in her reflections, and she returned home healthily tired, to find Eric awaiting her in the drawing room. She greeted him coldly, excusing to herself her want of friendliness on the plea that she was fatigued and that he should have called later. But he did not appear to notice her lukewarmness. He was his old self, weakly insistent, solicitous, treating her as if she were superior—a manner of approach which she disliked, although she could give no sound reason for her dislike.

'I have had a busy day, Eric,' she said, throwing herself down on the chesterfield, and lighting the cigarette which he had offered her as she came into the room. 'And I am tired and grumpy. It's your own fault. You should have come this morning when I was free.'

'I, too, have had a tiring day,' he replied, gravely. 'We attorneys sometimes work, you know. And it's not always very agreeable work, Santa. So I thought I would come for a chat. We get so little opportunity of discussing things, an there are so many we ought to talk over.'

'I can't see what there is we have to discuss,' she said, stiffly. 'If you are referring to the partnership, all you have to do is to make out the deed and I'll sign it. I suppose you and father and the doctor can do the rest.'

'The partnership is all right,' he answered. 'You need not worry about that.'

'I am not worrying. Not in the least. Father told me that he would find the money. So that's that. But I have a bone to pick with you, Mr van Deren. Who gave you the right to interfere in my affairs? I mean to offer to lend father money to pay for my medical course?'

'So ... you know,' he said, slowly. 'Well, I suppose sooner or later you would have had to be told. It does not matter, now. You are not angry with me, are you Santa?'

'Of course I am annoyed,' she retorted, briskly, hugging her idea that the matter should be discussed in a business-like spirit. 'You might have had the courtesy to let me know. There was no need for any hanky-panky secrecy about it. That annoyed me, and I think I am justified in being annoyed. If father had asked you ...'

'I did it without asking,' he said, simply. I saw that Uncle Elias had some difficulty, and my money was lying idle. That was all. As for my right, why, Santa, we were boy and girl together, and I have always looked upon you as if you were my sister. That is, so far as these money matters were concerned, and until I realised that you were more to me than any sister could ever be. That is why I have asked you to give me the right to do things for you. Won't you let me? My dear, now more than ever ... now that you know ... won't you give me that right?'

'What right, Eric?' she demanded, affecting not to understand him. 'To lend me more money?'

'Not to lend it, no. To be able to say, "What is mine is yours," Santa. To have the right which every husband has to protect his wife. See,' he slid into soft Afrikaans, 'I have always loved you. It came sort of natural to me, for I have always wanted you, and you alone, Santa. I know there's many a better man you might take, but none who will love you as dearly as I. *Toe, tog,* say yes, and let me be the happiest man on earth tonight.'

'I have told you over and over again, Eric,' she said, gently, for his pleading had impressed her, and somehow she did not like to wound him. His own gentleness, his implied diffidence, and the note of yearning in his voice made it difficult for her to persevere in the strain of bald business-like common-place which she had decided the conversation should take. 'I do not care for you sufficiently to marry you. Won't that be sufficient?'

'Not, it won't,' he said, positively. 'You do care for me. That I know. You have always cared for me, and you do not know how deeply you care for me. I should not ask you unless I felt that you cared for me. And I care so much for you, Santa, that I cannot bear that you should ... that anything should happen to make you suffer while I can help you to avoid it. I love you, Santa, and I want the right to be able to show my love, and to guard you.'

'There is only one thing,' she remarked, reflectively 'that you can help me to guard against, and that is letting mother ... I mean, mother is so set upon the thing that if she knows that it cannot be she would be pained. There you can help. You can let mother know that there is nothing between us, and in time she will become reconciled to it.'

'It lies between you and me, Santa. Aunt Maria has nothing to do with it. Of course I know it would please her, but I am not asking you for that. I am pleading for myself—and for you. Perhaps you are still hurt because I ... because I let Uncle Elias use my money, unbeknown to you. I won't defend that. I know it was not ... perhaps ... just the right thing to do, and I feel now more than before that, having done it, I have placed myself in an unfortunate position, and that you have reason to resent it ...'

'I did not say that I resented it, Eric,' she said, touched by his humility. 'Indeed, I must thank you for what you did, although you might have done it openly and not made a secret of it ...'

'Then Aunt Maria would have had to be told,' he interrupted, 'and all sorts of complications might have arisen ...'

'That is just what I should like to understand,' she interrupted in her turn. 'What complications? I can't imagine why father should have been hard up, ever. Surely the business is profitable enough, and our money is well invested?'

'Investments sometimes turn out badly,' he replied, evasively. 'Uncle Elias had losses. He bought shares and the market collapsed. It sometimes does, you know. We are always like that, and it is not possible to keep a large floating balance on hand.'

'Yet you managed to do so, Eric,' she said, regarding him curiously.

'I? Oh, I haven't got many overhead expenses,' he explained, carelessly. 'I get in much more than I spend, and I have always something that requires investment. As a matter of fact, I am fairly well off, Santa. You know, I do not have to depend entirely on the firm. I have some money in hand, from my father's estate and that brings me in quite enough to live on. But don't let us talk about money matters. Let us get this thing settled. I want you, and I ask you again. Come, give me the right to care for you, Santa.'

She was moved by his appeal, more moved than she had thought it would have been possible for her to be, but she shook her head.

'I like you very much, Eric,' she said, 'very much indeed, but I have told you I don't intend to marry yet. Give me time to think it over. That is all I can say now. Don't press me just yet. Let us see something more of each other, and in time ... well, I'll tell you frankly what I intend to do. But not now, Eric. Now I want to stand on my own feet, even if it is just to show you that I don't need protection ...'

'But you do,' he interrupted quickly. 'You do not know ... No, I did not mean that. I mean that it is best for both of us to come to a decision ...'

'If you think that,' she interjected, 'then I must tell you no—definitely and finally. If you can't give me time—if you don't trust me so far ...'

'I do, I do,' he pleaded, earnestly. 'But what more do you want, my dear? Why not let us decide now ...'

'You mean, why not let us decide in your favour, Eric. But that is just what I can't do, honestly. I have told you how it stands with me. Let us leave it at that.'

He looked so lugubrious that she felt a twinge of pity for him as he turned away to take up his hat.

'It is not as if we were parting for ever,' she said, smilingly. 'We will see each other daily, and there will be lots of chances to ... re-open the subject, Eric. Don't feel huffy about it. Why can't you and I just be good comrades, as we have always been? All this talk and thought of marriage spoils everything.'

'You'll understand some day,' he muttered. 'Now it's no use talking to you.'

'You say that just because you are peeved,' she replied, jestingly. 'And there is really no need for you to go. Stay and have dinner. Aunt Gertrude and Uncle Jerry will be here soon. They are coming on a visit, and you are a favourite of hers.'

He did not like to tell her that he had seen both Aunt Gertrude and Uncle Jerry the previous day, and he hated himself for having to keep that association secret. Sooner or later, he felt, she would have to be told, and he dreaded the telling. Probably Aunt Gertrude would take that in hand, to make things easier. It was obvious Santa had no suspicion.

That morning he'd had a talk with Elias. He had found his partner in a playful, Puckish mood, making no attempt to excuse his fault but treating it as a matter of little consequence. Eric had come away from that interview with mixed feelings, in which a realisation of the fact that Elias was thoroughly amoral predominated.

'My dear chap,' Elias had remarked, laughingly, 'what's the bother about? Jerry can take a joke as well as anyone else, and the fellow can surely spare me a thousand as a loan.'

'Then why didn't you ask him for one, Uncle Elias?' Eric had retorted.

'Because he would have refused,' Elias had replied promptly, as if it clinched the matter. 'But he would not have repudiated his signature. As a matter of fact, it is his signature. I got him to sign a blank cheque some time ago, and used that. I must have the money if we have to pay Buren his fifteen hundred, and that seemed the best way out of a difficulty. Of course he will storm and Gertrude will make a fuss, but it will be all done in strict privacy. Jerry knows quite well that he wouldn't dare to let Maria get word of it.'

'It is just that, Uncle Elias, which I can't understand. You are trading on our affection for Aunt Maria ...'

'Of course I am. I should be a fool if I didn't. Why, man, all my life I have been trading on other folk's sentiments. You must have found that out by now, else' ... Elias had shrugged his shoulders contemptuously, 'you are more stupid than I take you to be.'

In the face of such frank defiance Eric had found himself speechless, partly with indignation and partly with surprise. Elias had continued complacently. 'I suppose you would call it hypocrisy, but, my dear chap, we are all hypocrites. Our daily life is one round of hypocrisy, and a little extra here and there does not matter very much. This I can honestly say, that I have always tried to avoid giving Maria any pain. You know how weak and sensitive she is, and with all my faults—yes, my dear Eric, I admit that I have faults—she loves me dearly, and never questions what I do. When she is gone you can do what you like. But while she is alive we must not worry her with business matters. Jerry would not like that, and it is, after all, a matter purely for Jerry's consideration.'

'The bank may take a different view,' he had hazarded in an attempt to frighten his partner, but Elias had scorned the suggestion.

'Come, come,' he had smiled, provokingly. 'You know perfectly well that the bank has no standing. I, too, am a lawyer, and I know what the position is. Jerry can repudiate the cheque and so force a prosecution, but I know he will do nothing of the kind, and we will refund the money as soon as I have it in hand ...'

'The money was refunded this morning. Do you image I could allow the firm to be implicated, Uncle Elias?'

'I thought you might do something of the kind,' the elder man had said, in a tone of smug satisfaction. 'Naturally you would take that view. And I suppose you can spare the money. It will take some time to pay you back, though. Just at present I find it difficult to meet all claims.'

'You needn't repay it. If you had had the sense to ask me for it, I would have given it to you. There is no sense in ... in doing what you did. I thought a man of your experience would have been shrewder.'

'I think I showed great shrewdness in acting as I did. I place you before an accomplished fact, and that is always the best way to get out of a difficult situation. There was really no danger, my dear chap. I knew it would remain a family affair, and we don't wash our dirty linen in public.'

When Eric had broached the matter of the dissolution of partnership, he had found Elias quite responsive to the idea.

'Certainly! Whenever you like,' the elder man had replied. 'In many ways it would simplify matters, especially so far as Maria is concerned. But you will have to pay me out, and remember that yours is merely a third share, mine two-thirds. Don't for a moment think that this thing is going to make any difference in that. Of course you can debit the thousand pounds you so quixotically paid out for me to my account, but even then there will be a large remainder. You'll have to raise the money somewhere, and I fancy Jerry might help you if you ask him nicely. All that I stipulate is that Maria must not hear of it. She must believe that it is a matter of mutual convenience, and that I am retiring because I am weary and want a rest. She has always pressed me to give up the firm, and now is as good a time as any.'

Eric had left it at that. His disgust, and his sense of shame had prevented him from pressing whatever advantages he felt he possessed, and he decided to wait until Uncle Jerry had arrived on the scene before re-opening the subject.

Chapter 19

The south-west wind, harbinger of rain in the Valley, had swept the dead oak leaves into islands of desolation between the flower beds. The sun went down behind broken clouds, and a thick mist veiled the outline of the mountains. A cold, keen blast blew over the Village, and in the location the Natives hastily stopped up the broken patches in their huts to hold out the rain.

The sudden coming of winter, with its cold and wet, had forced Ayah Mina's sick daughter into the back room of the little house which Ayah occupied in the location. Sophia had spent most of the summer and autumn in the sunshine outside, drinking in the fresh air whose freshness had in it almost an effervescent quality that had counteracted her fatigue and had seemed to give her strength. Nevertheless, the disease had made alarming progress, and the heliotherapy which Dr Buren had so strongly recommended and the new missie doctor had half-reluctantly consented to, had not brought the girl much benefit. Her cough was worse, and her emaciation and lassitude were extreme. The Ayah had no doubt about the seriousness of the symptoms. Sophia was weakening. In a very short time Sophia would be dead.

Ayah Mina contemplated this possibility with a calmness and stolidity which were in inverse proportion to her real feelings. For years she had systematically endeavoured to diminish the affection she felt for her daughter like one who in temporary charge of a treasure feels it advisable wisely to provide against its loss. Ayah Mina had never looked upon Sophia as a treasure. There had been a time when she had regarded Sophia as very much the reverse, when the sight of her infant child had aroused in her feelings too deep for expression, feelings, too, not comparable with the maternal solicitude which she knew should have animated her. At that time she had regretted that Sophia had ever been born. Gradually, however, her feelings had changed. The girl had never appealed to her in early infancy, but when she had returned home from service, a broken, diseased body, something had stirred in Ayah Mina's soul—something which had rooted out all vestiges of early antipathy and had made her sensible of her maternal obligations. Since then she had lavished on Sophia a love that had gradually extinguished all hatred, that had enabled her to bear memories more poignantly painful than she had dared to acknowledge, even to herself, in times past—the memories of disloyalty to herself and to one whom she loved almost as much as she now loved Sophia.

The knowledge that Sophia was dying had not come as a shock to her; she had anticipated it, for consumption killed. It was very prevalent among the Coloured people. The pure Native and the pure White could fight against it, but the half-caste, somehow, did not seem to be able to conquer it. Ayah Mina had seen many of the location dwellers suffering from it, and she knew that nearly all of them had died of it. Died of it, just as Sophia was now dying, just as Sophia would presently die. In the summer months, when the air was so warm that one needed no bed-clothes, and in the autumn and spring when there was an effervescent liquidity in the sunshine, and the sorrels blossomed so profusely, they always appeared better and one hoped against hope that they were getting over it. But with the winter chill Sophia's cough increased, hacking the frail, emaciated body, robbing it of rest, and ending inevitably in the sharp haemorrhage that was a precursor of the end.

Sophia had already had two such bleedings, against which wild absinthe tea and a decoction made of the astringent tops of the sand olive had been perfectly useless. She now lay in the back room, playing with the bed clothes as Falstaff had played with his when commenting on Bardolph's nose. Ayah Mina knew the signs. They were ominous, and her experience told her that death lurked very near. And although it was late at night, and the rain was pattering down on the broken thatch, she sent a small boy to the big house for the little missie. Sophia, who had taken a dislike to Dr Buren, had expressed a wish that the 'missie doctor' should be called in, and she had been so insistent, so querulously anxious, that the old woman, against her better judgment, had humoured her.

'Tell missie that Sophia is dying, Boy,' she had said, 'and that Sophia wants to see her. The missie will come if she can, and you bring her here. They will give you a lantern in the kitchen, or maybe they will drive her up in the car. Go quickly.'

Then she had returned to watch by her daughter's bedside, coaxing Sophia to drink honey and water mingled with vinegar to stop the racking cough, listening to—but hardly hearing—Sophia's half whispered remarks.

'The ... old ... missie came ... this morning when you ... were away, Mother,' the sick girl said, and Mina looked up, startled out of her abstraction. 'She ... was very ... kind. She spoke ... and prayed with me, Mother. It was so nice of her, wasn't it?'

'She had no business to come, Child,' said the old woman, roughly. 'There was no call for her to do so ... Drink some more, Child, and don't talk. It only exhausts you.'

'I won't drink any more. It ... it just makes me sick,' said Sophia, petulantly. 'And I like the old missis to be with me. She ... she was so friendly. She treated me ... like a child. She stroked ... my hair ... and ...'

'That is all fancy,' said her mother, brusquely. 'You were wandering. In delirium one fancies these things, Child. Try and go to sleep.'

'I will when ... when the missie doctor comes,' said Sophia, struggling to suppress her cough. 'She will give me something ... with the little needle, and it will make me sleep. But the old missis ... she was so kind, Mother. She kept on telling me that it would be all right, and that I need not ... worry. About you, Mother ... she mentioned you. She said ...'

'Never mind what she said,' interrupted the old woman, harshly. 'I do not want to hear it. Here, let me shake up the pillow for you; you are dropping down in the bed. This damnable mattress ...'

At the big house they had just finished dinner when the maids came with the message from the location.

'A little boy from Ayah Mina, and would Miss Santa mind coming to see Sophia who lay a-dying and, please, the boy would lighten the way with the lantern.'

'Preposterous,' said Elias, roughly. 'You cannot go out in this weather, Santa.' He cracked a nut as he spoke. 'The girl has lain a–dying these three weeks past and I reckon she'll last until tomorrow. Tell the boy to go back and say missie will come tomorrow ...'

'Certainly not!' exclaimed Santa, rising and putting her napkin on her plate. 'I am going, Father. I promised Ayah Mina I would be there to help.' She looked round the table. Aunt Gertrude sat placidly peeling an apple; Eric and Uncle Jerry toyed with their coffee and looked doubtful. Only her mother, wistfully undecided on ordinary occasions, seemed now to be suddenly eager and peremptory. Her mother's eyes were sparkling, probably from excitement, for death and disaster had rarely entered her life, and such a novelty was quite enough to excite her. She rose together with Santa and her voice, when she spoke, was sharp, commanding.

'Tell the boy to wait, Yesha,' she said to the maid, and then, to the company generally, 'Of course Santa must go. There is no question about it, Elias. Dr Buren is away—you know that. And Santa is, after all, a doctor. It is her duty to go. Eric can go with her—you will, won't you Eric?'

'Certainly, Aunt Maria,' he replied with alacrity, getting up from the table. 'I was just going to suggest it ...'

'Very well. Then get her mack and a couple of umbrellas. They are in the hall stand. Santa, you'd better take your galoshes as well; the location road will be muddy by this time. Yesha, give the lad something to eat in the kitchen and tell him to wait. Missie will be ready in a few minutes.'

'I won't have it!' exclaimed Elias. 'There is no reason why Santa should go out in the rain to attend to Mina's brat. Just sit down again, all of you, and you, Yesha, do as I told you. Tell the boy to go back.'

Santa opened her mouth to speak, but a look from her mother restrained her. Maria seemed to have lost her customary bewilderment; she did not even look to the others for aid, as her habit was. She shook her head, and spoke, very calmly, but Santa could feel that under that calmness lay passionate restraint such as she had never imagined her mother could possess.

'Elias, you will oblige me by not interfering,' she said evenly. 'If Santa wishes to go, she goes. Hurry up, my dear. Eric, run and get her things.'

'Quite right, Maria,' said Aunt Gertrude, leisurely cutting her peeled apple into slices. 'I suppose niece Santa wants to go?'

'Of course I do, Aunt Gertrude. And I think it's very wrong of father ...'

'Never mind about father, Santa,' said her mother, quickly. 'Get along. Let me know if there is anything. Should you want me, send the boy back with a note. Or Eric can come back. In any case send the boy back if you are likely to be long.' She resumed her seat, and Santa noticed that she was trembling.

'Well, well,' said Elias, trying to make his voice sound less responsive to his irritation, 'if everyone is against me, I suppose I must give in. But it is preposterous, all the same. Take care of her, Eric, and bring her back as soon as the ...'

'Stop, Husband!' said his wife, commandingly. 'You may say something you might regret.'

'I?' there was wonder and astonishment in his voice. He had not thought that Maria could speak to him in that tone. Before all the others, too. It surprised him, and it suddenly made him frightened. Was it possible that Maria had heard something? No, that could not be. Her brother and her sister-in-law would never have dared to tell her anything, and at any rate it was foolish to be annoyed at what had occurred. If Santa wished to go, why, let her. It was all very silly, this fuss about a dying half-caste woman, but if they were set upon it, why, he would give way, even though his parental authority had been flouted. He turned, as nonchalantly as he could, to his brother-in-law and started a conversation on some political matter which he knew would interest Jerry. But Jerry was bewildered, unresponsive. He merely sat and looked at his wife, who unconcernedly ate her apple, her fragile face utterly placid.

Santa came round and kissed her mother before she put on her mackintosh. She felt the thin cheek was very cold, and she felt, too, the trembling of Maria's body, but she put both down to the excitement of the moment.

'Never mind, Mother,' she whispered, soothingly, with the patronising protectiveness to which she had become accustomed. 'I'll talk to Father when I come back. I won't have you ordered about like that.'

'It does not matter,' her mother whispered back, returning her caress. 'Do what you can for Mina, my dear. And come away when ... all is over. Tell Mina I ... no, better not say anything, my dear. But be kind to the child, Santa, be kind. Go now.'

She loosened herself gently from the young woman's embrace, and resumed her seat at the table, and Santa took Eric's arm.

'Good night, people,' Santa said, trying to make her voice sound cheerful, although she did not feel cheerful in the least. Her mother's words had surprised her, especially the last admonition to be kind to Sophia. What had made her say them?

As she walked out into the rain, still holding Eric's arm, and preceded by the location urchin who swung the lantern as if it were a play-thing and consequently made it difficult for them to see where to put down their feet, she said as much to Eric.

'I have never seen mother so excited,' she mused. 'It is of course because she is so fond of old Mina. Mina has really been a dear, you know. She has been with mother all these years, and although mother has seen very little of Sophia I believe she was fond of the child. But father was just insufferable tonight. I wonder why he can't realise that people have feelings? I suppose it is just because he is so strong himself, so self-reliant and so utterly free from any silly sentiment that he sometimes overlooks the weakness of others. Don't you think so, Eric?'

'Yes, I suppose Uncle Elias feels like that,' lied Eric valiantly.

'And of course he wanted to spare you the trouble of going out in this infernal rain. It is trickling all down my back.'

'Don't be silly,' she snapped. 'A little rain won't harm a big strong fellow like you. Nor will it harm me. When I was on the district in London I had to go out in all sorts of weather, and it never worried me. I am not made of marzipan though it seems to me you all think that I am. I don't suppose I can do much, but it would be sheer inhumanity to refuse to go when one is called upon to stand to attend a sick person.'

'I suppose it would,' said Eric, reflectively, 'although it has always struck me as rather illogical to call in a doctor to attend to a dying man. They should call me in, or the parson, but what can the doctor do?'

'That's quite true,' she replied, 'but unfortunately the public does not think that. Even when the patient is dead they send for the doctor. That's what is so exasperating, sometimes. If they had called one in before, one might have been able to do something, but ... I am sure that is a pool and we are going right into it. Do tell that youngster not to swing the lantern so much.'

'I'd better relieve him of it,' said Eric, but she demurred.

'Let him enjoy it,' she said. 'It's such a big adventure for him carrying a real ship's lantern. I suppose he's never handled one before, and tomorrow the location will know all about it. Here we are. Now don't come in, Eric. Go straight home and tell them you have seen me safely in Ayah Mina's house. I may be ages, and you won't be able to help a bit.'

'Don't you think I should wait?' he asked, halting on the little *stoep* of Ayah Mina's house. Through the curtained windows the lamp-light glowed dully, and from the eaves a trickle of rain fell down and ran veld-wards in a curling stream that lost itself in the darkness. 'I could easily wait for you.'

'I don't know how long I shall be,' she said, lifting the door latch. 'No, go straight home. Mother will be anxious. And don't trouble to come for me. They boy can show me back, but I daresay I shall have to stay until the morning if I can really do any good. Good night now. Be a good boy and get back.'

'Very well,' he said submissively. He was always submissive, she reflected. Eric was really a very good chap, and the more she saw of him the better she liked him. Perhaps in time her liking might become strong enough to be called love. There would be time enough to think it over later, however, and just now she had other things to think about.

She opened the door of Ayah Mina's house and, entering, closed it softly behind her.

Chapter 20

Ayah Mina was waiting for her in the front room. A worn-out oil stove, a relic of war times when the troopers had shivered in the bare, dismantled houses, gave out little heat and much odour. An aroma of vinegar and buchu hung about the place, and the ill-trimmed oil lamp on the table threw a coarse yellow light upon the rickety bent-wood furniture.

'Missie has come,' she said, and Santa noted that there was no welcome, no relief in her voice, which merely expressed a sense of satisfaction. 'It was Sophia's urge. I should have kept missie away. Missie can do no good.'

'Don't say that, Ayah Mina,' said Santa gently, chilled by the old woman's look of settled despair. 'Who knows what I might be able to do? How is she?'

'She is dying,' said the old woman, tonelessly, helping her off with the raincoat. 'Since this afternoon. She had a bleeding again tonight. It has now stopped.'

'I have brought some things with me,' said Santa, rummaging in her bag. Come, let us go to her. You must not leave her alone.'

The old woman led the way into the next room, where Sophia lay on the bed. As soon as she saw the patient, Santa realised that no ministrations of hers could be of any avail. The girl was manifestly *in extremis*, though fully conscious. She greeted Santa with a wan smile, which changed to a spasm of pain that wrung a groan from her.

'Don't try to speak, Sophia,' said Santa, seating herself on the bed, and feeling the girl's pulse. It taught her that any intervention would be futile, and she felt indignantly resentful at her utter helplessness. She knew what that fluttering, thin, quick-running pulse meant, and she dreaded the final struggle for life, the vehement gasping for air to fill the lung passages, the choking death made painless by no coma but crueller by the consciousness which the sufferer retained until the end. And that end was very close now, too near for her to palliate it by an injection of some anodyne. Still, it was worthwhile trying, and she gave the girl an injection of morphia, hoping it might act before the patient's strength had flickered away.

'You should have sent for me hours ago,' she whispered to Ayah Mina. 'I might at least have saved her this.'

The old woman sat huddled on the other side of the bed. She held one of Sophia's hands, and crooned over it, paying no attention to what Santa did, absorbed in her own thoughts, dry-eyed, but with her wizened old face drawn and pinched. Above the bed, on a wall bracket, stood a glass with some faded flowers in it, chrysanthemums whose drooping petals had once been a glory of white and gold. The dying girl's eyes strayed towards them as she nodded and whispered something. Santa bent close to hear.

'What is it, Sophia?' she asked gently, feeling herself stirred by the appeal in the girl's eyes.

'The old missis was here this morning,' Ayah Mina said to Santa. 'She brought the asters. I wasn't here. I should not have been away. But I was out. I could not help it.'

'I am glad mother came to see her,' said Santa, also in a whisper. 'She was always fond of Sophia ...'

'Not fond,' said the old woman, with a touch of sharpness. 'It is merely Old

Mistress Maria's Christian-like spirit that made her come. Sophia is nothing to her. She should not have come.'

She sat down on the bed and resumed her stroking of the girl's hand, and Santa watched in silence. Sophia's breathing was becoming more laboured; already she was feeling that hunger for air which is the consumptive's final agony. She looked so frail, so delicate, and in the yellow lamp-light the sunburn of her skin showed pale. When Santa opened her night shirt to listen to her heart sounds, the skin showed startlingly pale, almost White. It was a revelation to the young doctor. Santa had regarded Sophia as a half-caste, but had never looked upon her as less than a quadroon who had inherited some of the White blood of a great-grandparent or even a father of a collateral ancestor. But Sophia was almost White, half-and-half at least, and the realisation of this fact came upon Santa with a shock that left her for the moment speechless. A minute later, the effects of her training came to her assistance, and she put the thought that had entered her mind at the sight of Sophia's White skin resolutely from her, and concentrated her attention upon the patient under her care.

It could only be a matter of minutes now. The morphia had had no chance to take effect, and Sophia was still conscious. Her whispered remarks, made at intervals, were too incoherent for Santa to understand, and the painful spasms drew cries from her, cries that could not be properly uttered as her breath failed her. When her struggle for life became more pronounced, more painful to watch, Santa suggested to the old woman that she should leave them, but Ayah Mina shook her head.

'I bore her,' she said dully, 'and I must see her die. Missie can go if Missie does not wish to see it.'

Santa felt inclined to return a sharp answer, but a glance at the drawn, haggard face of the old Ayah stayed the reproof on her lips. She moistened her handkerchief with *eau de cologne* and wiped the sweat off the girl's forehead, and she felt a faint pressure of the thin fingers clasping her hand. A moment later, Sophia opened her eyes—large, brown eyes that had an oddly familiar look in them—and seemed to wish to say something. Santa bent over her. She no longer felt resentful at her helplessness, for her annoyance, which she realised was selfish and out of place, had given way to a great pity for Sophia.

'She is going now, Ayah Mina,' she whispered. 'I am glad the medicine has had some effect. I think she wants you. Come closer.'

The old woman threw herself on the bed, and placed her arm under the dying girl's shoulders. The death struggle had commenced, and Santa, feeling that she could do no more, got up and stood by the side of the bed, holding Sophia's wrist, where she could no longer count the pulse. The final agony which she had dreaded was mercifully short, but it was Ayah Mina, and not she, who realised first that it was over.

'She's gone now, Missie,' said the old woman, who apart from her one frantic effort to give her daughter more air, had shown no great emotion. 'It is best so. Missie must now let me be. I shall have to lay her out, and Missie can do nothing more. Presently it will be daybreak, so Missie had best wait a while in the next room. Then I can go back with Missie.'

'I can't tell you how sorry I am, Ayah Mina,' said Santa, whose heart went out to the dry-eyed old nurse. 'I am only thankful that she did not suffer much at the end.'

'Missie need not sorrow,' said the old woman. 'She is best dead, Sophia is. But I am glad Missie gave her the medicine. See, I will put the old missis's flowers on her breast—so.'

Santa went into the little front room, and sat down on one of the rickety bent-wood chairs. The air was stuffy, for the dilapidated oil stove gave out as much odour as heat, and the windows were closed.

She felt unutterably weary, unspeakably miserable. The long, unavailing struggle with death which she had witnessed, not for the first time but never before under such conditions, had fatigued her, mentally and physically. She felt dissatisfied with herself, annoyed, she could hardly tell why, and irritated with things in general.

Ayah Mina followed her, bringing a basin of hot water, soap, and a clean towel, which she placed on the table.

'Missie had better wash,' she said, in a toneless voice. 'It is a new cake of soap, and the towel is clean.'

Santa got up and dabbled her hands in the hot water. She washed her face in it and her hands, and Ayah Mina stood silently at her side, her eyes fixed on the open door of the room where the dead girl lay.

'Ayah Mina,' said Santa, suddenly. 'What made you do it?'

'What does Missie mean?' asked the woman, with a tinge of interest in her voice. 'What have I done?'

'You know well enough, Ayah Mina.' Santa's voice was hard. Annoyance, irritation, fatigue struggled in it.

'No. Missie must tell me. What is it?'

'You know well enough. Sophia is three parts White. Why ... why ... why?'

'Missie must not ask such questions,' said the old woman, speaking gravely. 'No good comes from it. Missie must let such things be.'

'I am not a child, Ayah Mina,' Santa's voice was indignant, imperative. She resented Ayah Mina's minatory tone. It conveyed a sense of protection, a feeling of superiority that grated upon her. 'I am a grown woman, as you are. And as a woman I ... oh, it is disgusting. Why should you have done it?'

Ayah Mina shrugged her shoulders. 'Missie had better not speak about it. After all, it is many times done, year in, year out, and nobody cares. If the one slips, well, we are all in the good little Lord's keeping ...'

'Keep the Lord out of it, Ayah Mina!' exclaimed Santa, pitched to anger by the old woman's calmness. 'It is yourself ...'

'Missie must not talk so loud with a dead person in the next room,' warned the old woman, sinking her voice almost to a whisper. 'And if Missie really wants to know, why, there are times when one cannot help oneself. That is all, Missie.'

'But Ayah Mina,' Santa laid aside the towel and faced the old woman. 'What made you do it? You were married, you loved your husband, you had children by him. And yet you ... you did this ...'

'No. My husband was dead, then, Missie. Maybe I would not have yielded if he were alive. I do not know. Perhaps yes, and perhaps not. It does not matter now. Best let it alone.'

'It is so dreadful, Ayah Mina. You knew you were doing wrong. You knew what Sophia would have to suffer. The location is full of such children. Why did you do it? I can't conceive what makes a woman do these things. It is so unutterably horrible. It makes one's blood boil. And you too ... you, a woman who have been brought up better than the rest ... you, Ayah Mina, who nursed me ... oh, how could you?'

'It was sudden-like,' said the old woman, reflectively. 'And I was, of course, much younger. One does not regard the consequences, though the little Lord knows I have sorrowed over them all these years. But when it comes sudden-like, and there are complications, why, Missie, it is natural, after all. What are we women made for, but to bear children, whether they be bastards or church children ...'

'For shame, Ayah Mina! It is awful to hear you speak like that. Have you no pride ... no shame? I would sooner be dead ...'

'It is easy for Missie to speak. There are no temptations for Missie. For us there are many. It is not always easy to escape. The masters have a way with them. In the old days it was common enough, Missie, and no one thought very much about it. Now of course it is different, and I do not say I would yield again. Not that there were no compensations ...'

'Compensations? Ayah Mina, do you mean to tell me that you did ... this awful thing, and that you can talk of compensations ... ?'

'Just that, Missie. There is no need to get excited about it. It is my matter,' there was a ring of pride in the old woman's voice, 'my matter alone. If I have made my bed, I do not ask Missie to sleep on it. Let it be. The girl is dead, and there is an end to it. Come, Missie, let us go home.'

She took up the raincoat and held it out to Santa.

'Missie must put this on. It is still dripping outside, and it is harmful to get wet in autumn rain. Come, Missie.'

'What about the funeral?' asked Santa. 'Have you made arrangements?'

'All that is arranged for,' said the woman, soberly. 'It was arranged months ago. We knew she would die, Missie. It is better so. I have money. There will be no difficulty.'

'No, there shouldn't. You must ask father in case you want anything, Ayah Mina. It is a great pity you did not let father know at the time. He ... might have done something.'

'Yes, he might have done something,' the old woman laughed harshly. 'But it was little he could have done, believe me, Missie. These things do not settle themselves easily.'

'He might have made the man marry you, Ayah Mina,' said Santa, with conviction. 'Or settle something upon the child. After all, father is a Justice of the Peace and has influence. He might have seen the magistrate about it.'

'There was no question of marriage,' said the old woman dully. 'That was never mentioned. It is silly of Missie to talk like that. Missie does not know anything about such things—thank the Lord for that—for all that Missie pretends to be a man-doctor in all but the wearing of trousers. Missie is just a silly girl, like what old Ayah Mina used to make candy for ...'

'I am old enough to know that you did a wicked thing, Ayah Mina,' retorted Santa, stung to reply. 'No honest woman would have done it, no self-respecting woman would have done it. She would have thought about the child. I don't care about you, Ayah Mina. All the blame there is rests on you. But I do care about Sophia ... what the girl must have suffered ...'

'And whose fault was that?' said the old woman, her voice tense with emotion, though she still controlled it to a whisper. 'Mine? Or yours ... the White folks that do these things to us, and have no mind when they are done? Was it my obligation to see that the girl came to no harm?'

'You should have made him see to it. You should have gone to the magistrate ... you should have told about it. If it happened to me, I should have made him ...'

'Yes, Missie speaks about what Missie does not know,' came the whisper from Ayah Mina. 'When there is trouble, why make it more? Let those who have had a share in it bear it, even though some of them escape. Why break other people's hearts? It is not Christian-like to do that, Missie.'

'*Faugh*!' Santa made a gesture of disgust. 'Is it Christian-like to let the girl suffer for something she has not done? If the man hasn't the courage ...'

'It is not a matter of courage, Missie.' The old woman's voice was under better control and she spoke gravely, guardedly. 'It is a mater of expedience. Sophia's father ... he, too, has a family ...'

'Ayah Mina,' Santa's voice was horror-struck. 'Do you mean to tell me ...?'

'I did not mean to tell you anything, Missie,' retorted the old woman, quickly. 'No good comes of speaking about these things. Missie imagined that the father was one of these young masters—clerks, shop-servers, farm-hands, belike. It is natural that Missie should think so. But it was none of them. He is ... But there, Missie, let us go home.'

'Ayah Mina,' Santa spoke earnestly. 'Go to father and tell him about it. He will do something. I know he will. He will see that ... that justice is done to you.'

'He? Meneer Vantloo?' the old woman's voice became shrill. 'Missie is mad. He will do nothing at ... at all.'

'I am sure he will and, what's more, I'll tell him myself,' declared Santa. 'Of course, I suppose he knows that Sophia is not your husband's child, but in any case he will know what to do.'

'Missie must do nothing of the kind,' said the old woman, sharply. 'Nobody knows that Sophia is not my church child, although she was born after my husband's death. There was White blood in him as there is in me, far back, and it comes out sometimes—one cannot stay it.'

'That is nonsense, Ayah Mina. Why, if mother knew ...'

'Do not speak of that, Missie, do not speak of that. On no account must the old mistress hear about it. Missie, Missie, promise me that you will not let her hear of it ...'

'Why, Ayah Mina, why should she not hear about it? If I know and father knows— and when I think of that girl lying there, my blood boils, and I get enraged at you both for doing such a thing ...'

'Missie talks like a mad-woman,' said the old Ayah, folding her hands across her breast. 'I told Missie to let the matter be, but I see that Missie will not listen. And I won't have the old mistress harmed. All these years I have watched over the old mistress as a mother watches over her child. Yes, Missie does not know what I have done for Missis Maria, but Ayah Mina knows, and Ayah Mina will not have the old missis harmed. Not by word or deed, not by rumour or belief,' she spoke impressively, and Santa grew apprehensive though she could scarcely fathom the basis of her fear. She stared at the old woman in amazement. Ayah Mina seemed changed in some inexplicable way. Her face looked savage and yet pathetic in its misery, the tears coursing down her cheeks.

'Missie wanted to know ... why and wherefore,' she said, stuttering in her excitement. 'Missie would not leave well alone, and now Missie wants to make unhappiness for the old mistress. That shall never be—not while old Ayah Mina is alive. The old mistress must never know—never, Missie, never. Rather would I go to the gallows for killing him than that it should come out, and it will come out now that Missie is meddling in things which are no concern of Missie's, out of pure mischief-making interference ... Swear, Missie, swear that Missie will say nothing ...'

'I shall certainly not swear anything of the kind,' said Santa, speaking with decision. The woman was getting hysterical. She must be promptly suppressed.

'Missie will swear here and now,' said the old woman, tensely. 'I cannot have Missis Maria harmed. Missis Maria is old, and weak, and she loves—oh, she loves as you will never love or understand, for Missie is now surely a man-doctor who understands all these things. Oh yes, Missie understands everything but what old Ayah Mina knows. Missie understands what no self-respecting woman would do, and Missie wants Sophia's father to marry old Ayah Mina, and Missie does not mind breaking old missis's heart in her old age and bringing sorrow and sin upon Old Missis Maria ... oh yes, oh yes, and all for the sake of interfering in things Missie does not understand. And it is such a little thing Missie does not understand—just a little thing that will break the old missis's heart, and belike Missie's heart as well, even though Missie is a man-doctor and understands all things ... oh yes, oh yes ...'

'Ayah Mina ...' Santa's voice rang through the room but the old woman paid no heed.

'Oh yes, oh yes,' she cried, her own tones becoming shriller, 'Missie would know this and that and the other, and the one thing that matters Missie does not know. Ayah Mina was not going to tell Missie, but now that Missie wants to harm the old mistress, why then Ayah Mina must tell. Missie wants Ayah Mina to marry Sophia's father, now that Sophia is dead and nothing matters, but that is God-impossible, for the old master is Sophia's father ... oh yes, the old master ... the old master ...'

Santa drew back as if she had received a blow, and the clear transparency of her skin reddened under her emotion. Instinctively her hands stretched out and grasped the old woman's shoulders.

'Ayah Mina, you lie,' she whispered, 'you lie ... you lie ...'

The old woman's excitement had spent itself. She swayed and would have fallen, but Santa caught her and lowered her into a chair. She was whimpering, her frame shaken with sobs, and her agitation moved the younger woman more than her passionate excitement had done.

'Ayah Mina does not lie ... Missie knows it is not a lie ... Missie knows ...' the old woman muttered between her sobs, and the girl, looking down upon her, felt intuitively that the assertion was true. Yet she struggled with herself, vehemently rejecting the possibility of its truth. Her father stood on a pedestal, far removed from other men. This degrading, incredible assertion, the fruit of hysterical emotion and perhaps also of malice, could easily be refuted. It was childish of her to take it seriously ...

She went to her bag and took out a bottle of *sal volatile*, poured a few drops of it into a tumbler and handed it to Ayah Mina. 'Drink that,' she said, harshly.

The old woman obeyed, coughed at the drink, but gulped it down, and resumed her whimpering.

'Stop that!' commanded the girl. 'Why did you tell me a lie?'

'It is no lie, Missie,' said Ayah Mina, eagerly. 'Missie knows it is no lie. The birthmark that Sophia caries, Missie carries too, and the old master has it in the same place. And his eyes. It happened long ago ... twenty-three and more years ago. One night, when the old mistress had gone for a visit and the old master was alone in the house. The old master knows all about it. It is his money I have for the funeral. He always took an interest in the girl. He knew who she was ...'

Santa's incredulity gave place to a burning, blind indignation. She scarcely knew what she was doing, but she stepped across to where her mackintosh was lying and put it on. She had no questions to ask ... the statement that her father knew and had acknowledged the relationship, she felt convincing. Ayah Mina would never have made it unless it was culpable proof.

'All these years,' the plaintive voice went on, 'I have hidden it from the old missis. Her heart would break, Missie, if she knew, for she loves the old master with all his faults. She loves him, Missie, and to hear that about him would kill her. He knows, and that is why it has been easy to keep it from her. From you too, Missie, but you meddled with things, and, after all, you are a grown woman, though you do call yourself a man-doctor. I should not mind if it were not for the old mistress. The world can hear about it when she is at rest, but not before. All these years I have shielded her, I have lied to her on his account, and she does not know—she will never know—how bad he is, the old master. Yes, Missie, though he is your father, he is bad, bad all through, from his white skin inwards to his black heart.'

Santa heard her, but made no attempt to stop her whimpering. She wanted to get away, to get into the open air, where the clean cold rain drops could splash on her face, and the chill night breeze ruffle her hair. As she opened the door she felt the old woman's hand clutching at her skirt and she heard the tremulous voice for the last time that evening.

'Swear, Missie, that the old missis will never know. It will break her heart, Missie. It will break her heart, for her love is very great.'

'Mother will never know through me, Ayah Mina,' she said, before she closed the door. 'I swear it, Ayah Mina. Good night.'

Chapter 21

She stumbled her way through the rain-sodden veld intervening between the house where the dead girl lay and the road. There was a grey-green mist around her, for the winter drizzle still continued, and there were no lamps in the location. Instinct, more than premeditation, made her avoid the puddles, for she did not mind squelching through them. Nothing mattered now. She wanted to get back, to think out this thing, to adjust herself to the changed conditions which seemed, in a moment, to have altered her life. Yes, that mattered. That mattered very much, but here, in the drizzle and the dark, she could not think clearly. She must get home.

A shape loomed up through the mist, startlingly big, but she felt no fear, and made merely a movement to avoid it. No one would harm her here, she felt. They all knew her. The location folk were sober, honest folk, and to them she was the little missie. They, at least, knew nothing of what she had just learned. They could not conceive that the dead girl whom she had just left had been ... what? Her sister? She shuddered involuntarily at the thought, and hated herself for the reaction. Whatever happened, she would never blame Sophia for it. Sophia had no part in that sordid, shameful episode. She had been luckily spared all knowledge, all realisation ...

She found Eric at her side, diffidently holding the umbrella over her.

'You?' she said, surprised, but relieved to find that the shape she had tried to avoid was his. 'Surely you haven't been waiting for me, Eric?'

'What is it Santa?' he asked anxiously, taking her arm and leading her on to the hard gravel of the road. 'Heavens, you should not have come. You are trembling, my dear. Was it so very bad? And ... is she dead?'

'It was awful,' she replied, glad that he put her agitation down to what had seemed the obvious cause. 'Yes, she died ... about half an hour ago. You should not have waited. I can easily find my way back, and it is quite safe.'

'I preferred to wait,' he said shortly. 'Come, let us go home. There'll be some hot coffee waiting for us, and probably Aunt Maria will be sitting up for us. I thought you ... were used to such things.'

'I shall never get used to them,' she retorted, and he noticed that she shuddered as she spoke. 'No matter how many I see,' she jerked her thoughts away from the thing that really mattered, and tried to concentrate on the subject he had raised. 'It always seems so futile and pitiful. One does not mind it if the patient is grown-up. He has had a chance, and probably he has made a mess of life, and looks for some compensation. But a child—a young thing, Eric. It always seems to me so unfair.'

'I don't think you can say that of Sophia,' he remarked, gravely. 'There was little she could look forward to, you know, Santa. Apart from her illness ...'

'You mean she was ... part-White, Eric? I suppose that makes a difference. But how did you know?'

'How did I know?' he spoke in surprise. 'It was plain, of course. She was no more Ayah Mina's husband's child than ... than, well it was plain enough. You must have noticed it the first time you saw her, after she came back.'

'I never really noticed it,' she said. 'You see, I knew Sophia when she was a little girl; she used to play with me sometimes, and then I had no idea of ... of such things. Nor had I, indeed, until tonight. I did notice that she was a half-caste, but so is Ayah Mina, and so was her husband. They all have some White blood in them, and I thought Sophia only showed it a little more plainly than others did. It does sometimes show more clearly in some children, even in the third generation.'

'There is no question of that here,' he said with decision. 'Whoever was the girl's father was White. I am fearfully sorry for poor Ayah Mina, but when one takes everything into consideration, this is perhaps the best way out of it. Take care, there's a puddle there.'

'I don't mind mud,' she declared with a fierceness that astonished him. 'It is at any rate clean mud. And I feel dirty, Eric, smudged.' Her voice sharpened and she bit back the words that came involuntarily to her lips. 'No, I am not going to be hysterical, Eric dear,' she continued more calmly, 'but you must be nice to me and not ask any questions. Tomorrow I will tell you. Tonight I just can't ...'

'What is it?' he interrupted, quickly. 'Has anything happened? Did Ayah Mina tell you anything ...'

'No, nothing that you may be thinking of,' she replied, urging him on for he had stopped in his stride. 'Only, one feels like that when one has ... when one is thoroughly tired. What time is it?'

'It is not very late,' he answered. 'It has just gone two. But something has happened, Santa. You are quite upset. Won't you tell me? My dear, even if you do not feel enough for me to do what I ask, you might let me know if there is anything I can do to help you ...'

'Tomorrow, Eric,' she interrupted. 'Tomorrow you and I will have a talk. I can't tell you tonight. If I tried to I should break down ... I feel I shall. Now be a dear and don't ask me questions. Just talk to me, will you?'

'What shall I talk about?' he asked. 'The only subject that interests me you don't want me to talk about? Are you chilled, my dear? You are trembling with the cold ...'

'Well, let's walk quicker. Tell me, when did her husband die?'

'Ayah Mina's? Oh, many years back. I can't say how long ago, but if you know how old Sophia was, you can fix the date more or less. Sophia was a posthumous child. She must be just about a year younger than you, but I am not sure. Why do you ask?'

'Never mind that now. Was she born in the location?'

'That I can't tell you. I wasn't here then. I was at school in Cape Town. I only knew Ayah Mina when I came back here, some ten years ago. I really know very little about her affairs. Only that she was Aunt Maria's maid, and that aunt was always very fond of her.'

'Mother still is,' she said softly. 'You know mother went to see Sophia yesterday. She left some flowers. We put those on Sophia afterwards.'

'She would do that,' he said. 'Aunt Maria is very sensitive. She has a big heart.'

'Yes,' she agreed. 'Mother is sentimental. You saw that tonight. She's like a child in that, but I do wish she had a will of her own, sometimes. I hate to see a woman making a doormat of herself.'

'I am sure you wrong her, Santa,' he said gently. 'She only wants peace and quiet, and ...'

'And that she shall have,' Santa said vigorously. 'I'll see to that from now on. The first thing is to get her away from here. She ought to go to the seaside, and I'll see that she does. Here we are, Eric. Come in and see if there is anything to drink. I daresay mother has put something on the kitchen stove for us, and if not I can easily boil some water for tea in the electric kettle.'

The front door of the big house was not locked, and when they entered the dining room Maria came in to meet them. She was in her dressing gown, and came nervously forward, her pale, aristocratic face set in a studied calmness.

'Take off your mackintosh, Santa,' she said. 'Aunt Gertrude is bringing some hot cocoa. We waited up for you. Father and Uncle Jerry have gone to bed.'

Aunt Gertrude came in, bearing a tray with cups and a jugful of cocoa.

'I am glad you had the sense to wait for her, Eric,' she said, in her shrill, parrot-like voice. 'Now you both drink a cup of cocoa, and then you, Eric, get away home, and we'll put Santa straight to bed. If you'd like a spot of whisky, I'll fetch Jerry's flask, for that's the only supply available in this teetotal household. Now don't look at me like that, Maria. You know perfectly well that Jerry likes a drop for a nightcap, and that I take one too. And you would be all the better for a sip, occasionally, yourself, let me tell you. Sit down, Sister-in-law, and drink your cocoa.'

'It is a marvel to me,' the old lady went on, handing the cups to Eric as she spoke, 'how folk can bear with these outlandish notions. As if we didn't get good money from our wines, and as if God hadn't given us the liquor for our stomach's sake. In moderation, of course. I am not one to favour intemperance, but the way you twist that word, you and your teetotal friends, is positively sinful. Now I daresay Niece Santa will agree with me that a little wine is of real value on an occasion like this, when you are tired and cold and the winter drizzle makes you see things as they aren't really.'

'You should not jest, Trui,' said her sister-in-law, 'when the girl has just come from a death bed. I suppose ...'

'Yes, Mother,' said Santa, setting down her cup. 'She died, about an hour ago. I was there until the end.'

'And Mina?' queried her mother, anxiously. 'How did she take it? Is there anything we can do? Who is with her? Someone ought to go to her. She cannot be left alone ...'

'She preferred to be alone, Mother,' said Santa, soothing her mother who seemed to be still excited and agitated. 'And the neighbours will be there by now. They all knew. There was really nothing more to do ...'

'Are you sure?' Maria's voice was insistent. 'It is terrible to be alone at such a time. You do not realise ... I told one of the maids to go just now. Regina ... she is an old friend. She ought to have been there before you left. Did she come?'

'I think so ... I am not sure,' replied Santa. 'But it is all right, Mother. Ayah Mina was quite calm. She had anticipated the end, and it was not so very dreadful. But I can't tell you about it ...'

'No, certainly not,' said the practical Aunt Gertrude. 'You should be abed, and Master Eric here should go home. We can hear all about it tomorrow, or rather later in the day, for it is already tomorrow. Come along, Maria. So long as we are waiting they will never say good morning.'

She took her sister-in-law's arm, and shook hands with Eric.

'Get home now,' she said, 'and let us see something of you at morning tea. Jerry and I have business matters to talk over with you,' she added significantly, 'and if you have no sleep you will not be in a fit condition to talk. Santa, put the chain on the front door. Come, Maria, let's go to bed.'

In her room, Santa threw herself into the Morris chair after locking her door and turning on the light. She felt no inclination to go to bed, although she was conscious of her physical and mental tiredness. She knew she would not be able to sleep, and it was better to sit in the chair and give her thought full scope, however unpleasant and disturbing it might be. Little incidents, trivialities to which she had paid small heed in the past, recurred to her. In the light of her present knowledge they fell into place, fitting into the mosaic her memory was slowly building up, strengthening probabilities, slowly eliminating that background of doubt to which she still wanted to cling so tenaciously. Since her return home from overseas she had noticed many things which had seemed strange and illogical to her. Her father's rabid teetotalism she had been prepared to accept as a mild fad. She had even told herself that his persistence in the face of popular opposition was a proof of his sturdy independence of character, and had forced herself to respect it because it supported her belief in his innate honesty. From childhood she had cherished that belief in his integrity, his absolute, unequivocal sincerity. Had not the District nicknamed him 'Honest Elias'—'Uncle Honesty'— '*Oom Eerlik*'—and could there be a better testimonial to his rectitude than that? It was that very honesty, that very sturdy uncompromising insistence on principle which had made him such a power in the political life of the Village. She had recognised, since her return, that this characteristic had laid him open to a charge of intolerance and she had bitterly resented, to herself, the obvious implications which his actions and practice carried for one who, like herself, could not agree with his premises. Just in this connection there were little things which now, when she adjusted them in relation to the whole, seemed incongruous and out of place in a character such as she had taken it for granted he possessed. Now she could not reconcile, upon cold consideration, his practice with his precepts. There was, for instance, the question of prohibition. She had thought it mildly amusing that he should take as a medicine a liquid extract which she was convinced was largely alcoholic, and that he was apparently unaware of the fact that his home-brewed ginger ale contained an appreciable amount of the ingredient against which he so constantly fulminated. But now it did not seem to her that there was anything at all amusing in the matter. Moreover, she recollected that when they had discussed financial matters he had referred to his mortgages, and she knew that some of these were on farms owing their existence to and making their profits out of the wine trade. Still less, now that she came to consider things carefully, did she find his political activity to her liking. Less than a month back, she would have been indignant with herself for querying his political sincerity, but now she recollected stray assertions, which she had hitherto put down to the malice of political antagonists, which had been made against him at the time when there had been talk that he would represent the District in Parliament. Assertions whose very vagueness had at that time struck her as convincing proof of their untruthfulness, but which now assumed a different complexion when she was prepared to admit the possibility that they were based on fact. One fact she knew was incontrovertible. She had often discussed it with him, and she had never been quite satisfied with his explanation, any more then she had ever been quite satisfied with the cynical, objective manner in which he had looked at what to her had seemed basic political principles. That was the income which he had drawn from the military authorities during the war when he had allowed his transport teams to be used for war service. He had protested that he had no say in the matter; that he had had to bow to *force majeure*, but even then, she had always felt, he need not have accepted the money. She had argued that with him, and he had told her—she remembered the occasion distinctly—that politics had no place in business transactions. That had shocked her, for her own principles permitted of no trimming or compromise.

And this—this added shame, to which she could give no name, but the thought of which made her writhe with indignation and contempt—was it, after all, so utterly unbelievable? Or, she found herself asking, so utterly unforgivable? She prided herself on her broad-mindedness, her tolerance, at least where her basic principles were not concerned. A man's life was his own ... was it? She saw in imagination her mother's pale face—that mild, gentle-womanly smile, defensive in its placid weakness, like that of a child who tries to deprecate reproof by anticipatory geniality. Mother loved father—passionately, devotedly. Mother had made an idol of him all these years, just as she had idolised him. That was the one patent thing that mattered now. Her own strength was great enough to withstand the shock of her idol's downfall, but with mother it was different. Mother could never survive the disillusionment which would follow when she heard whatever there was to hear. And what possible purpose could be served by proclaiming a thing so sordid and so mean? Santa found herself reflecting on her conduct in the future. She acknowledged to herself that her relations with her father could not be the same as they had hitherto been. But her innate honesty told her that she could not alter them without telling him the reason. That would be a matter between them. She could treat it as if it were something that did not materially affect her, and she could rely upon Ayah Mina to keep the secret. It would be a secret between the three of them, as hitherto it had been a secret between Ayah Mina and him. Mother need not know, and so far as she was concerned, mother would never know. On that point Santa was determined, and by the time she had reasoned herself into a less agitated frame of mind, she had fully convinced herself that the chief thing that mattered was that Maria should be safeguarded, shielded, protected.

'Mother must never know of Mina's wickedness,' she told herself. 'It would break her heart if she knew, and I'll do my utmost to keep it from her. Yes, even if I have to lie to her about it.'

Chapter 22

The morning of Sophia's funeral day dawned in cold and rain—rain that swept through the Village in gusts, and left pools of muddied water in the streets. When the Vantloo family assembled for breakfast, later than usual, the conventional cheerfulness of the occasion was dampened by a feeling of general depression which even Jerry, who thought it his duty to be genial, could not disperse. Elias ate his food in silence, obviously sulky, and Santa, still undecided as to what attitude she should adopt, preferred to breakfast in her room.

'It will be at four o'clock, in the Native cemetery,' said Maria, in answer to a question from Aunt Gertrude. 'If you have no objection, Elias, I should like to go. After all, Mina has been with us all these years, and it is only right that some of us should go ...'

'Go, by all means, if you feel inclined to do so,' her husband replied pettishly.

'Though why you should make such a fuss about Mina's child passes my comprehension. I have other matters to think of.'

'That I can well believe,' said Aunt Gertrude, and he felt the antagonism in her voice and rather liked it. Gertrude would give him some fun. He knew why she and Jerry had suddenly come a-visiting. It was not purely out of neighbourliness. So far they had not referred to the incident of the cheque, but that was obviously the reason. Very well; he would be quite frank and open about the matter, for he knew that Jerry would never dream of letting it go beyond the study door. It would be a private expostulation, confined to the three of them, and he had no fear of what they could say or do. It was not the first time he had crossed swords with brother-in-law and sister-in-law, and so far he had always shown himself to be a much more expert fencer than either. Very well; if they asked for it, they would get it.

'That I can well believe,' went on Aunt Gertrude, buttering her toast. 'You must have your hands full these days, Brother-in-law. What with looking after your wine farm mortgages, and negotiating with Solomons and such-like things, it is a wonder to me that you find time ...'

'Don't concern yourself with matters about which you know nothing, Trui,' he said, drily. 'And bear in mind that there is such a thing as slander. I don't quite know what you mean to imply by that cryptic allusion to Mr Solomons, but, speaking as a lawyer, I should warn you that it is open to an invidious construction.'

He was glad he had made her blush, even though he knew that it was from anger or annoyance rather than from a sense of shame at her unworthy insinuation. But such fencing would have to be postponed until his wife was no longer present. Maria was very much of a fool, but Gertrude sometimes spoke so plainly that even a fool could understand what she meant. And there was no sense in fighting at the breakfast table.

'Take the car if you want to go,' he said generously. 'I shall not require it this afternoon. I suppose Trui and Santa will go with you?'

'I certainly shall,' declared his sister-in-law. 'Just out of respect for Mina. As for Santa, the girl is not up yet, and one cannot very well blame her for sleeping a little later this morning.'

He smiled at that, although he hid his smile with his fingers. Respect for Mina. It was a ludicrous idea, that, if they only knew. He had himself seen Mina that morning, early, before anyone else had stirred. He had gone to the location, and talked to her outside the house. He had refused to go in, and she had not pressed him. The talk had relieved his mind, for Mina had doggedly declared that he was safe. No one would know. No one would ever know. It was true he had been struck by Mina's distrait appearance; she had seemed cast down, woefully depressed, entirely without a spark of her old spirit. She had taken his money calmly, without, however, thanking him for it, but that he had put down to the natural grief under which he presumed she was labouring. In that quarter he was safe, but all the same it was amusing to think that his wife and sister-in-law would attend the girl's funeral out of respect for Mina.

'I am glad you are coming, Trui,' he heard his wife say. 'It is charitable of you. I am sure Santa would wish to come too, and Dr and Mrs Buren will go, I am sure. I have had some flowers brought in from the garden, and some wild smilax the maids have picked in the veld. They are all wet still, but we can easily dry them, and make a couple of wreaths.'

He wondered what they would put on the cards, and afterwards, when the wreaths were lying on the dining room table, he went in and put on his glasses to read what his wife had written. It was as he had expected it would be—nothing in the least compromising, though perhaps a little equivocal. 'With loving sympathy from Santa.' Tut, tut, Maria might have put Miss or Missie in front of the personal pronoun; one had to consider one's status in relation to the location folk, but probably no one would notice that little omission. And the next 'With cordial fellow-feeling from Old Master Jerry and Old Mistress Gertrude Gerster'—that was more seemly, though Jerry, of course, had nothing to do with it, and couldn't be expected to feel any fellow-feeling for Mina. Still, one might let it pass. And finally, a small bunch of white chrysanthemums, just one or two blossoms tied with a white ribbon to which was pinned a black bordered card bearing the inscription, 'The Lord gave and the Lord hath taken away. Blessed be the name of the Lord. Maria Vantloo.' Now that was just like Maria—sentimental all over. What did it matter to Maria what the Lord had given to Mina or what the Lord had taken away from Mina? It would have been much more seemly and edifying to have associated herself with Santa's wreath and to have written on the card 'With sympathy from Old Mistress Maria and Young Mistress Santa.' He felt half inclined to remove the cards and substitute one like that, but he thought better of it and went into the study to read his paper. Maria had gone to her room, complaining of her customary headache. Jerry was somewhere about the premises, but Jerry could look after himself; and any time that sister- and brother-in-law were disposed to talk business with him, they would find him ready.

Jerry was in the spare room, confabulating with his wife. He sat on the bed with his foul cherry-wood pipe, and the room was full of thin blue wreaths of smoke. His wife did not mind that; she was accustomed to the reek of the Cango tobacco. She sat with her hands folded on her lap, a fragile looking but by no means faded old lady, and she did most of the talking.

'We cannot quarrel with him today, Husband,' she said vigorously. 'It would not be fitting, with that dead girl still lying above ground. The talk must wait until tomorrow.'

'I don't see why we can't have it out with him tonight!' he expostulated. 'God damn me, Wife, what about my tobacco plants? Must they await his convenience?'

'Never mind your tobacco plants!' she retorted. Sybrand looks after them just as well as you can. And don't swear in the bedroom. It is not seemly, and in any case at your age you should not swear at all. It will do us no harm to wait and, besides, I am not at all sure that it is wise to talk yet.'

'Curse it,' he declared savagely, 'you don't want me to go back without letting him know what I think of him? Isn't that what we came here for?'

'Aye. But not today. And in any case, Husband, we must go warily. Have you observed how Sister Maria takes it?'

'Takes what?' he asked apprehensively. 'Surely you don't imply that Sister Maria has any inkling of what the scoundrel has done? If she has, by God, I don't know what I shall do to him. I'll ...'

'You'll just do as I tell you, Husband,' she observed placidly. 'And don't jump off the deep end like that. I asked you a plain question, but seemingly you have not had your wits about you, nor used your eyes. I have both. Maria is upset by this death—

strangely upset. I can see it. More, I can sense it, feel it somehow. And that puzzles me. Why should she be upset? It's a funny thing, now I come to think of it, that Maria has always been solicitous about Mina's child. And just now, I tell you, Husband, she is all on edge. I can see that, if you can't. And I tell you plainly that we must go warily. That is to say, if you don't want her to know what kind of creature she has married. My own opinion is that the sooner she knows, the better for all of us ...'

'No, no, no!' he shook his head vigorously, 'that I shall never allow. You must not ask me that. Surely, Wife, you cannot be so cruel? She loves the scoundrel, and even if he is a scoundrel, as he is, and we know it, he is her man, and she believes in him. Let it not be you or I who lift the scales from her eyes, for she will weep herself blind, Wife, blind.'

'That I know as well as you do, Husband. But weeping comes natural to us women, and it does no harm in the long run, provided there is enough strength in a person. And Maria has strength—moral strength, Husband ...'

'No, no,' he interrupted quickly. 'I know her better than you do—after all, she is my sister; I have known her since babyhood. She is weak ... as tender as a bit of gossamer on a winter's morning, Wife. You are different. You are so strong that you cannot conceive her weakness, and you do not make allowance for it. If she hears this, she breaks—breaks, Wife. And that I will not have—that I shall not allow. Rather let him go scot-free than that Maria should suffer for anything he has done.'

'Very well. We have agreed upon that, haven't we? But all the more reason then for us to go cautiously. The slightest error, and sister Maria hears of it. That is why I want you to take your time, and to look out for an opportunity. Obviously we cannot talk to him here. Maria is about. She will get suspicious, and once she is that you may be sure she will discover what we want to hide from her. We must leave it till tomorrow. I have noticed that he is quite aware that we have an apple to peel with him; you could see it in his manner this morning at the breakfast table when he had the impudence to chide me. The brazen effrontery of it, Husband. As if we did not know of his traffick with Solomons, and his mortgages, and the way he tipples ...'

'Almighty, Wife, that is going a little too far. You have no right to say that you know!'

'Ppfew,' she made an indescribable noise, sufficiently expressive of her contempt and disgust. 'I am not talking without my book, Husband. That medicine bottle of his—just go and sniff at it. Pure brandy, which he regularly fills from a bottle of Montagu which he keeps in the garage. Or somewhere. I haven't found it yet, and I don't intend to look for it. I know it is somewhere, for there is nothing but brandy in that medicine. And he takes three doses daily. Quite a good tot, if you ask me. I have nothing against that; you take the same, and it has never done you any harm. But there is no sense in keeping it secret and going on with all this hypocrisy at the Lodge. That should stop, and I mean to stop it.'

'Do you think Maria knows anything about that?' he enquired, anxiously.

'Maria? Of course not. She thinks it is doctor's medicine. She is as rabid on that subject as he is. The wonder to me is that niece Santa has not spotted it, and she a regular doctor, too. But that is always the case. One does not look for what one does not want to find, and Niece Santa believes in him as firmly as Maria does. Do you want that to go on too, Husband?'

'We cannot undermine a daughter's trust in her father,' he began miserably, but she interrupted sharply.

'Certainly, when the father has been untrue. Santa is not a child, Jerry. She is old enough to know the truth, and if you want to keep Maria in ignorance it is absolutely necessary that Santa should know. Just consider. Supposing the girl stumbles upon something about which we know and blurts it out ...'

'We must prevent that,' he said heartily. 'We must get Santa on our side. It should be easy. She has a lot of common sense.'

'Yes, and a lot of flim-flam foolishness,' his wife snorted contemptuously. 'I have little patience with Niece Santa. She has had all her own way these many years, and it is time that she learned something about things.'

'You are hard on the girl, Wife!' he expostulated. 'Remember, she has been away from home, and she does not know.'

'That is just what I do remember,' she retorted. 'If she had common sense she would have found her father out long ago, and prevented all this. But she is foolish and arrogant, and she has no proper sense of duty. You know what I mean. No proper conception of real moral values. How could she have it, Jerry? Brother-in-law brought her up. She has been under his thumb all these years, and Maria has had little doing in shaping her.'

'She is Maria's child,' he argued. 'After all, we are as good as you Rekker folk.'

'Did I say you weren't, Husband? And you with Rekker blood in you, too. But look at the other side. Where do the Vantloos come from? Have they anything to boast of ...'

'I would not boast of my blood,' he said frigidly. 'We are as God made us. He cannot help coming whence he did. Don't throw that against him, Wife.'

'I don't,' she retorted illogically. 'But there is something in blood and race and family, Husband, although we need not boast of them. And he has little, and that little tainted. I warned you from the first ...'

'Don't harp on that, Wife,' he said with some show of irritation. 'You know, by God, I would willingly give half of what I have to unmake their marriage, but things done have no chance of being undone. It is the devil of a mess, and the only thing for us is to consider how to get out of it. Without the little sister knowing that there is a mess,' he concluded.

'Very well. Then let us go cautiously. Do you talk to him about common-place matters. If he refers to the cheque ...'

'He tried to talk about that last night, after Santa had gone, and you and Maria had left the room. I put him off.'

'Go on doing that. I imagine he is not feeling so cheerful about it as he wishes us to believe. And let us get things quite clear before we tackle him. We must have Eric present. Are you still doubtful about the cheque?'

'I have thought and thought about it, Wife, until I don't know what to think. I certainly never signed a cheque for a thousand pounds on that date. On that I can give my affidavit in open court, so help me God. But the more I look at it, the more it seems my signature.'

'But it is not from your cheque book, Husband. Of that I am sure.'

'It might be from an old one, Wife. It is an old cheque form, and I can only think he must have traced my signature. But he admits it is a forgery, and that is all we want, isn't it?'

'I like to be sure of my ground before I charge,' she said reflectively. 'He is as slippery as an eel out of the river, and we must be cautious. That is why I want Eric there. He is a lawyer and will tell us if we go wrong. Now do go and smoke somewhere else. I must have a little rest before we go out. And should you see Santa, tell the girl she might do worse than come and talk to me.'

He got up slowly, and she looked at his stalwart, presentable form with pride.

'You will be careful in what you say to her, Trui?' he said, more as an assertion than as a question. 'She is young, and young folk have no pity. They only see their side of the case, always.'

'Trust me, Husband,' she smiled, propelling him out of the room. 'I will be as careful as a political candidate who does not know his own views.'

He guffawed at that, and bent down to kiss her before he left.

Chapter 23

They buried Sophia in the Native cemetery behind the location, where the yellow dune sand encroached on the veld now verdured by the winter rain. Blue babianas and dark crimson lachenalias, the first of the spring flowers to bud, peeped from the ground between the stone-covered mounds. Coarse Bushman-grass sprouted in tufts between the stunted *kraal*-bush, and myriads of golden sand-sorrels, their petals closely curled because of the rain, bordered the straggling paths. The cemetery overlooked the Village, and from Sophia's grave one could see the Valley, with the River curling round the bend of the Karroo hill and meandering west to join with a mountain stream that entered it miles below. Now the mountains were shrouded in rain and mist, and the outlines of the gardens blurred by the haze which crept low down on the veld and veiled everything afar off in its grey mistiness.

The missionary conducted the simple funeral service. There was a time when Sophia could have reckoned on this final ceremony being performed by the Dutch Reformed parson, but now the Natives and Coloured folk no longer attended the steepled church, although most of them still belonged to the denomination which had built it. They had their own mission congregation and worshipped in a separate church, and were served by a missionary who, although European, had a lower social and ecclesiastical status than the parson. In the big church Natives and Coloured folk were no longer supposed to have any interest, although the sexton, who was also one of the Native constables of the Village, was still a Coloured man. He was looked upon as a privileged individual, but already there was a feeling that he was usurping a place and position which should by rights have been that of a White man and, being aware of this, he had gradually insinuated himself into a somewhat similar office in the mission church. He was an old, wizened Coloured man, whose father and grandfather had officiated as sextons and undertakers practically from the time of the founding of the Village. His father and grandfather had been more than mere sextons. One had been a manumitted slave, and both had been 'cutters for the stone,' and some of the prestige derived from this lithotomical reputation still clung to *Oupa* Berend, though modern developments in medical practice had made his services obsolete. He earned a bare living by his sextonry and a comfortable one as additional constable, and drew largely on his imagination when called upon to tell what had happened in the past.

It was he who had coffined Sophia in a plain cedarwood coffin, and it was he who had taken charge of the ceremonies at the graveside. Those who had gathered there to pay their last respects to the dead girl, included, besides the greater part of the location, who had donned their best clothes for the occasion, a small party of Europeans consisting of Maria, Aunt Gertrude and Santa, Mrs Buren, whose husband had been unable to attend, Eric, and the missionary's wife, who made it an unbreakable rule to be present at every interment, not that, like the Duke and the Duchess, she preferred it, but simply because she thought it her duty to set an example to her husband's parishioners. The little group stood huddled together, under the shelter of their dripping umbrellas, and watched the bearers place the coffin on the planks preparatory to lowering it into the grave. The missionary, an undignified, obese little man, with a straggly beard and uncertain intonation, hurried through the simple service, which could have been made impressive but to which he failed to do justice; the school children sang, pitifully waveringly, a hymn, whereupon the coffin was lowered into the grave, and most of those present drew nearer to cast a handful of rain-soaked soil upon it. That was the customary, age-old tribute which they paid to the dead.

To Santa, whose thoughts still refused to bend to her will, it seemed unutterably drab, common-place, and trivial. She watched Ayah Mina, who, clad in the conventional black decreed for such occasions, stood, as chief mourner, close to the grave, and noted that the old woman's face never relaxed its severity and its studied calmness throughout the ceremony. She watched her mother, who had gradually edged her way closer to the old woman. Her mother's attitude puzzled her. Maria wore a heavy veil, which hid her features completely, but Santa could see that she was far more agitated than Mina. When the coffin was lowered into the grave, Maria had turned closer to the Ayah, and Santa had seen her clasp the old woman's hand. Neither had cast earth upon the coffin, but both had stood silently, side by side, and watched the man shovelling the gravel. Only when the mound had been patted into shape, and most of the spectators had already left, did Maria turn away, still clutching the old woman's arm.

'You will not go back alone, Mina,' Santa heard her whisper. 'You will come home with us in the car.' And Mina had answered, also in a barely audible whisper, 'No, Missie Maria. Not tonight. I go home tonight, Missie Maria.'

'It's sweet to see Mrs Vantloo here,' the missionary's wife had remarked to Santa. 'We all know how fond she was of Sophia. But to come out in this rain—it is a beautiful, Christian-like example to all of us.'

Santa felt annoyed with the woman. What did it matter to her who attended Sophia's funeral? She replied coldly that they had a car, and that Ayah Mina was an old friend.

'Ah yes,' said the missionary's wife. 'We all know that. Such a pity, don't you think, that even these old retainers have no moral sense. Of course you know the girl wasn't Mina's husband's child. That of course makes no difference. You can't visit the sins of the fathers and mothers upon the children, you know, dear Miss Vantloo— but I suppose I must say Dr Vantloo, mustn't I? I have often discussed the matter with my husband ... my dear you are all wet. Perhaps Dr Vantloo will be good enough to give you a lift in their car.'

'Don't trouble at all,' said the missionary, effusively shaking hands. He looked hot and uncomfortable, notwithstanding the chill environment, and he shook hands in a flabby way which Santa found detestable. 'We can easily manage with our umbrellas.'

'I was just saying to Dr Vantloo,' his wife continued, 'that Mrs Vantloo sets us such a fine Christian example, coming out in this rain to attend a funeral, and all because Mina is an old servant. That, of course, does not imply condonation of her wicked sin, and I think, my dear, you might have used the occasion ...'

'I think you are simply hateful,' said Santa, feeling it a relief to express her opinion with sincerity. 'You ought to be ashamed of yourself. What has the poor girl done to you ...'

She turned round and found Eric waiting for her. 'Take me away, Eric,' she said, seething with bitterness. 'These people are simply disgusting.'

'Hoity-toity,' sneered the missionary's wife. 'A pretty how-de-do indeed. One would think Sophia was a church child by the way our very modern young doctor behaves. I told you, my dear, no good would come of Vantloo's sending his daughter overseas. You see for yourself. I daresay she is one of these atheists we read of. You will have to see about it.'

'Perhaps you were a little bit hasty,' he rebuked her mildly. 'She does not know, does she?'

'That Sophia was a child of sin? My dear, who doesn't know it? It stared you in the face when you saw the child. Who do you imagine was the father?'

'My dear, it was long before our time. How should I know?' he remonstrated, unceremoniously pulling her along through the puddles.

'You should make it your business to find out. After all, Mina is of your flock and our dear Lord said "Shepherd my lambs." The man may be anywhere among us. I think it is your duty to have a talk with Mina.'

'Better leave well alone,' he said shortly. 'It's really none of our business. And try to make it up with the doctor, Hessie. We can't afford to be on unfriendly terms with the Vantloos.'

'Oh, that will pass,' she said, more confidently than she felt. 'It was only her new fangled manner. Don't tell me a doctor doesn't know all there is to know about such things. And the Vantloos are no better than they should be, my dear. Take it from me.'

'All the same, I do wish you would not meddle with these things, Hessie,' he insisted. 'You may create difficulties for me.'

Eric drove the car home, and talked trivialities with Santa, who sat next to him, on the way. Maria sat quietly listening to Aunt Gertrude's remarks, her heavy veil hiding her face. When they got out, she took Gertrude's arm and passed into the house without saying a word.

'Mother seems frightfully upset,' said Santa to Eric. 'I have never seen her like that. I must go to her.'

He made no attempt to keep her, and she went quickly to her mother's room, meeting Aunt Gertrude in the corridor outside.

'Your mother is lying down, Santa,' said the older woman. 'I think she has locked her door, but she told me she did not want to be disturbed.'

'Is she all right, Aunt Gertrude?' Santa asked anxiously.

'So far as I can see, yes,' Aunt Gertrude emphasised her words by nodding her head. 'Not crying or hysterical, if that is what you mean. But upset, my dear, upset. You see, she hasn't attended a funeral before. That would account for it, wouldn't it?'

'I suppose so,' Santa's voice was dubious. 'Are you sure she doesn't want me? Perhaps I can do something.'

'Go and knock,' advised the older woman. 'Perhaps it would be as well.'

Santa went to the door and knocked. 'It's me, Mother,' she said ungrammatically. 'Can't I do anything?'

Her mother's voice came back faintly. 'No dear,' it said. 'I just want to be left alone a bit. I shall be all right presently. Don't worry about me, Santa. I am just a wee bit tired.'

Santa went to her room. She too felt tired. She wanted to be alone, and she knew that in the drawing room Aunt Gertrude and Uncle Jerry and Eric would be having coffee. Later on she might join them, but not now. On her way she passed the dining room door, and it opened suddenly. Her father came out, holding a tumbler in the one hand and his bottle of medicine in the other. He almost collided with her, and when he turned she got the reek of brandy from him. She had not seen him since the previous evening, for she had avoided a meeting. Now it was thrust upon her.

He smiled at her, and she thought the smile a leer. His face looked podgy, bloated, the pouches underneath his eyes sagged down, and his lower lids showed red.

'Well,' he asked, 'how did it go off?'

Santa steadied herself with an effort. She took the bottle from him. He made a feeble attempt to resist her, but yielded with unexpected suddenness. 'If you want a brandy and soda,' she said, trying to speak as quietly and calmly as possible, 'why don't you take one? Why do you make such a fuss about it?'

'Ah, you know,' he said eagerly. 'I expected you would find out, sooner or later. One can't keep these little things from such a clever daughter, can one? But you see, my dear, there are difficulties ...'

'Where do you keep the stuff?' she asked, trying hard to keep contempt out of her voice. 'I suppose you have a store somewhere?'

'Just at present in the garage,' he replied, leering at her. 'But they will see me if I go now. They are at coffee in the drawing room, and the window is open.'

'I will get it for you,' she said quietly. 'If you will go to your room, I'll bring it there—no wait, mother is there. Go to mine.'

'I really take it for my heart, my dear,' he said plaintively, and she felt a twinge of pity for him. He had fallen so utterly that his plight no longer filled her with disgust. 'As a medicine, my dear. I am not a drunkard. Don't think that for a moment. Be careful, my dear, be careful. Someone might easily see you.'

He walked towards her room, and she watched him disappear into it. Then she went into the kitchen. From there it would be easy to cross over the yard into the garage. The maid, Yesha, was wiping the coffee cups, and she looked at the medicine bottle in Santa's hand, and came forward obligingly.

'Is it the master's medicine the Missie wants?' she asked naïvely. 'The bottle is in the garage. Shall I get it for Missie?'

'Please,' said Santa, staggered by the request. So even the maids knew about the medicine. How, she wondered, would it be possible to keep the secret from mother.

The maid came running back with the bottle. 'Here it is, Missie,' she panted. 'It's just an ordinary brandy bottle, Missie, and the old master so particular about that sort of thing.'

'Medicine is sometimes kept in brandy bottles, Yesha,' said Santa, lightly. She filled the medicine bottle, and re-corked the supply bottle. 'Take it back,' she said, giving the brandy bottle to the maid, 'and put it where you found it.'

She went to her room, and found her father pacing up and down it. He looked older, heavier, bedraggled, for his hair was in disorder, and somehow his well-cut clothes seemed to have lost their nattiness.

'Here,' she said. You'd better drink it, and then put the bottle back in the dining room.'

He poured out a few fingers breadth of the brandy into a glass and feebly diluted it with water from the carafe on her dressing table. She noticed that he added very little water, and that he drank the 'tot' at a gulp.

'That's that,' he said, jovially. 'I am sure you want an explanation, my dear ...'

'Not now,' she said with decision. 'I must go to them. We can talk things over some other time. Perhaps tomorrow.'

'Quite right,' he said. 'Then I will give you a full explanation. I owe it to you, my dear.' He came closer and moved his arm as if to pet her, but she shrank back, and he let his arm fall. 'I see you are judging me already. That is not fair, Santa. You must give me a chance to explain. It is only my heart, and of course, being Grand Master of the Lodge, it would not do for me to take it openly. A little subterfuge, in the circumstances, is justifiable, eh? Like Mrs Eddy, you know, who used to take something to deaden the pain she did not believe in, my dear.'

He had regained his composure, and was trying to carry off the episode with a high hand. She could see that, and it submerged her pity in a wave of indignation. But she kept herself under control, and merely waved him aside. 'Very well,' she said. 'We can discuss all that later on. Now will you please let me go?'

'Oh, I can see you are displeased with *papa*,' he said, taking out one of his peppermint lozenges and putting it into his mouth. 'You think *papa* is a hypocrite and a fool. But, my dear, you ought not to judge as quickly as all that. I have told you before that it is useful, sometimes, to trade upon sentiment. If you won't understand that, my dear, you'll never make a success of life. In your own profession you will have to prevaricate and tell lies and hide things. It is merely a question of degree, my dear.'

'Don't you think we might discuss all that later?' she asked wearily. 'Is it really necessary to tell me that now?'

'But you are labouring under a total misapprehension, my dear,' he said eagerly. 'I can see that. So much common sense I possess. I can imagine your saying to yourself, "My old daddy drinks in secret, which is very sinful for one who is TT." And it is that misunderstanding I wish to remove, my dear. I do it on doctor's orders. Yes, my dear, I do. The last time I was at Cape Town, I had myself overhauled. The fellow said I had myocardial something or other.'

'Very likely,' she interrupted. 'But he would not have prescribed brandy for that.'

'I assure you he did, my dear,' he asserted eagerly. 'Twice a day. A table spoonful. Which I have never exceeded. That is what I want you to understand, Santa.'

'Quite. But if I stay away so long, Aunt Gertrude will come for me. You would not like her to ...'

'Oh no, my dear,' he said hastily. 'Then I had better be going. But don't misjudge me before you know everything, Santa.'

He walked out of the room, and she closed the door behind him, and stood for a moment holding the knob in her hands. This was not the meeting she had planned, yet she could not imagine how she could have got out of it. She was glad she had not given expression to her feelings while he had been with her; glad that she had overcome her first burst of indignation and disgust, and had been at least ordinarily civil and daughterly towards him. But it could not go on like that. That would be impossible, and the only thing now was to take Aunt Gertrude into her confidence— not of course on that one subject which, more than any other, agitated her when she thought of it, but on the general aspect—and try to keep the knowledge of what her father was from her mother.

Chapter 24

To Santa's relief neither her father nor her mother put in an appearance for dinner. Elias sent word that he had been called out to a meeting and would be back only late that night; they were not to wait for him. Maria declared that she was too tired to take dinner; would Santa send her some soup; that was all she would require that night.

'Now, if your household was not such a terribly faddist one, Santa,' said her aunt when the maid brought the old mistress's message, 'I should advise you to send her a plate of soup and a glass of good old Jeropico. That is the best thing one can take when one is tired ...'

'So should I if we had any Jeropico in the house, Aunt Gertrude,' Santa replied shortly. 'But, as you know, there is none, and it is much too late to get any now.'

'I have some in my bag,' said the old lady. 'I always travel with a bottle of it, just like your Uncle Jerry does with his brandy. Especially when we come here. But it will be useless. Your mother will not take it, and sending it will only give her pain. Now if I were you, Niece, I should try and make her see that it's all nonsense, going on like that. You ought to be able to influence her now. It is not as if you were a young girl, and Elias had all the say.'

'I'll certainly try,' Santa remarked, her face taking on an expression that brought out, startlingly, her resemblance in some features to her father. 'I quite agree with you as to it being nonsense, but it is the sort of nonsense that does an infinity of harm.'

'I am glad you think so, Niece. There is nothing so sinful as turning a virtue into a habit, and that is what these teetotal folk do. They say the most awful things, and they are quite incapable of seeing the other side,' said the old lady, attacking her soup. 'Now this white bean puree would be improved with just a spoonful of wine in it.'

'You might well say that, Wife,' interjected Jerry, glad to be able to share in the conversation. 'It is insufferable the way in which they insult us. Would you believe it, Santa, I came across one of their posters the other day which says that the man who drinks does not think. Now that, to my mind, is an insult, and it is an insult to us wine farmers that the government allows such things to be placarded on public buildings ...'

'They pay for it, Husband,' his wife snapped. 'There are thousands of fools who support them, and that's where they get the money from.'

'Nay, Wife,' he said gravely. 'I would not call them fools. That would be making the same mistake they make. Because a man does not believe in what you believe, that does not prove that he is a born fool. People should behave more kind-like to their neighbours. Then we'd get on better.'

'That's why you'll never be a politician, Uncle Jerry,' jibed Santa, who had always found her uncle totally indifferent to her political enthusiasms. 'One cannot wear kid gloves always.'

'No, not if one does not mind soiling one's hands,' he said, more smartly than she had expected. 'Any kind of dish-cloth will do for politics. Don't you meddle with them, Santa. They are a misery for us. I mind when we had no politics here—or scarce any—and we were much better off then.'

'Yes. Just like the turkeys are much better off just before Christmas!' his niece retorted. She welcomed this opportunity of a sparring match with Uncle Jerry. He was so crudely old fashioned in his outlook, and although at heart he was honest and she had no doubt of his innate loyalty, he laid himself open to any well directed attack. 'Just paying taxes and having no say in any matter, even though it concerned us vitally.'

'There you speak without your book, Santa,' he said mildly. 'Trui here knows better. She will tell you what part we took, since 1854 when we got the vote. But the things that were of vital concern to us then were really things that mattered. Roads and schools and agriculture and such-like things, not foreign ambassadors who can't even sign a passport'—Santa regretted that she had told him about the difficulty she had experienced in getting her passport signed in London, and bit her lip to keep back a flippant retort—'and spend more than our agents-general ever dreamt of spending. But I suppose I mustn't complain. We are moving with the times, they tell me, and I am old fashioned. I can't say I like it, but in any case I should like it better if we did it without stopping to call each other names while we're doing it.'

'Do you really imagine we were better off in these old days, Uncle Jerry?' she asked. 'When we had to speak a foreign language, and a foreign court decided our squabbles, and a foreign army occupied our soil?'

'Aren't we speaking the same foreign language now?' he asked in astonishment. 'Whenever I talk Afrikaans to you, Niece, I find that within five minutes we have both lapsed into English. I don't feel slave-like when I use it, and I don't feel sort of puffed up when I speak Afrikaans ...'

'That, Santa will say, is because you have no national soul, Husband,' his wife reminded him. 'Nowadays one can only express one's soul in Afrikaans. Formerly we expressed it in good Dutch, and some of the Afrikaans we now use was reckoned fit only for the kitchen. But, of course, it is heresy to say so.'

'Of course it is, Aunt Gertrude!' exclaimed Santa. 'Give it a chance. It is just because we continue to speak English, as we are doing here and now, that we fail to cultivate and develop it.' She dropped into Afrikaans and turned to her uncle. *'Oom* Jerry,' she said 'who is that awful missionary woman we saw this afternoon?'

'Oh that,' Aunt Gertrude took upon herself to reply, humouring her niece by giving her explanation in Afrikaans. 'She is of no consequence. A veritable backbiting gossip, a flibbertigibbet, mischief-making woman. It is a great pity. Formerly those who missioned to the Black folk were themselves gentle people, and you still find such at the German mission stations. But the mission congregation here belongs to our church, and I am afraid they do not get of the best.'

'Do you know, Aunt Gertrude,' said Santa reflectively, 'I often wonder what you, and those who like you represent the older generation, really think of that question. We have never discussed it, but I daresay our views are widely dissimilar. You and Uncle Jerry are SAPS, aren't you?'

'Well, yes,' said her uncle haltingly. 'In principle, that is. I can't say I hold by everything the Party has done, and soberly I don't think there is much to choose between us in principle.'

'What your uncle means, my dear,' explained Aunt Gertrude, 'is that he does not like to change his Party, although I confess that, practically, the Party has changed. After all, you Nationalists were all SAPS once, and now you are practically just where we were before our leaders made a mess of things. That is what I am constantly telling Jerry. We would be all right if we could get rid of the leaders, and come together and work together as we did in the old Bond days. But there is too much personal interest in the matter for that to come about just yet.'

'Aye, there is that,' said her husband, moodily. 'I have given up talking about it. Matters just take their own course.'

'But tell me about this Native question,' urged Santa, really desirous of hearing her uncle's views on the subject. It was an opportune time to discuss it, for she felt that inevitably the conversation would drift into more personal channels, and she was not prepared for that. Not yet. Tomorrow other things would have to be discussed, but not now.

'Well, my dear,' said her aunt. 'Your uncle is no great hand at expressing his opinions. But we both know where we stand. I can't exactly say that what we think about the matter agrees with what everyone else does, for we can only speak for ourselves.'

'That's what I want. One so rarely gets a personal opinion, Aunt Gertrude.'

'I daresay you could get them if you tried,' said her aunt drily. 'But you don't usually get them if you express your own views first. I don't know what your views are, and I don't suppose it very much matters. You are not in a position to draw any conclusions for you don't know the facts first hand, and you have had no experience— no experience at all. Uncle Jerry and I have lived among the Black folk all our lives. Your great-grandfather on your mother's side—Jerry's grandfather—bought and sold slaves. Everyone did in his day, and when the first missionaries came they saw no harm in it. Not that there was any harm in it, my dear, though I daresay you can make out a case that it was inhuman and against religion. I am not so sure about that. It seems to me much more inhuman just to neglect them—the Black folk, I mean—as we are doing now, and to recognise no obligations towards them. Your grandfather's father respected his obligations towards his slaves, and when emancipation came they remained with him on the farm and served him faithfully. So did ours, for the Rekkers always had a reputation for treating their folk well. And our obligations went a little further than merely giving them food and looking after their health and welfare. In those days, my dear, you would not have found conditions like those existing in the location now. Grandfather would not have tolerated that. I do not say other masters did likewise, for that would not be true. But the Rekkers and the Gersters, at least, knew what was proper for them and for their slaves, and there were no half-castes among us. No, nor poor Whites in those days.'

'But all that is hearsay, Aunt. You don't remember anything about it. It must have been long before your time.'

'Not the slaves of course. Those I don't remember—as slaves. But I knew them as free men and free women when I was a girl, and I grew up among them, and heard all about them. And my mother taught me something about our obligations to Black folk. I fancy that is no longer taught, more's the pity.'

'Aye, times have changed,' her husband broke in. 'Take the Blacks, too, they have changed. That is the worst part of it.'

'Of course they have!' Aunt Gertrude spoke with decision. 'You cannot expect them to stay children always. And it is natural that some of them should be uppish and arrogant and forget their duties ...'

'But what exactly are their duties, Aunt? Isn't what you call arrogance just simply the reaction against what they were forced to be in the past? I suppose conditions were not everywhere as ideal as at *Eisleben* or on your grandfather's farm. I have heard about other things myself ...'

'Possibly,' said the old lady, unperturbed. 'There were cruel ones among the masters and mistresses, though I fancy all these stories you have heard are greatly exaggerated. Here in the Village they tell of old Mistress Ankus; she used to bury her slaves alive, but that was very long ago, and in those days the Company's authority did not stretch very far. In my grandfather's day, we had a protector of slaves, and the *landdrost* saw to it that none of these things happened. Of course, it all depended on the master. I grant you that. But in our District the masters were, almost without exception, kind and good, and the slaves had a good time on the whole. You saw the proof of it when emancipation came. Most of them stayed, although they got a mere pittance, and were really much worse off than they had been before, for they had to look after themselves. Then the missionaries came, and they were fine men. Old Mr Uhlmann came—he was really young then, for it was way back in 1829, when he founded Neckarthal—and he taught the Black folk well. It was different in those days—there, too, the war has made a change, my dear.'

'And the drink, too, I suppose,' said Santa. 'I'm looking forward to seeing Neckarthal one of these days.'

'It is different now,' said the old lady reflectively. 'But I don't think the difference is the result of the drink. We always gave our Black folk wine; we do still, and I can't say that it hurts them—not if you have taught them properly. My dear, you can't make a child behave by always keeping temptation away from him. That is why I think Elias and these teetotal folk are so dreadfully stupid. You must teach folk to have something they can lean against—something that will help them to overcome temptation. It is the same with that other race, if he is sensible of the obligation he owes to his family, he will not mix his blood. But he does not want a Bible text to tell him that if he holds by tradition.'

'Now she is off on her hobby horse,' murmured Jerry, filling his pipe.

'It is not a hobby,' said his wife sharply. 'It is common sense, and you know it as well as I do. The pity is that so few nowadays, or formerly for that matter, had any tradition to fall back upon. There were some who came from fine stock, but you could count these on your fingers. There were others who had education and culture behind them, and knew what was due to them and theirs. That kept them from making fools of themselves as so many of the others did. But we are wandering away from your question, Niece. I suppose what you wish to know is whether Jerry and I would approve of putting the Black folk on an equality with us.'

'That is what your Party stands for, doesn't it?'

'I don't know about the Party. I can't talk politics with you, but I can tell you what we all thought in 1854—I've often heard father speak about it. He said that no one wanted to put the Black folk on an equality, but that few wanted to keep them permanently where they were. That is why he favoured a high qualification for the vote. And that is where Jerry and I stand today. The Black folk are children, but children grow up, and it would be unfair to deny them their rights when they are no longer children. And some of us White folk are worse than children, for we have fallen behind instead of progressing.

'That's it,' interjected Jerry, blowing volumes of blue smoke across the table. 'The poor White is becoming our master. Look at the latest returns—three fourths of our voters pay no income tax, have no stake in the country to speak of. That shouldn't be. No, God Almighty, that is not fair.'

'Even if it isn't, you need not swear at it,' remarked his wife placidly. 'But he is right, my dear, I said so when I heard that we had given in all along the line to the North. There they view these things differently. They have no tradition; they have no real sense of obligation, for they have no background ...'

'No background, Aunt? With all that history of the Great Trek—all that struggle for existence!' exclaimed Santa, who found such heresy quite intolerable. 'That's merely prejudice.'

'Why should I be prejudiced against my own kin?' the old lady enquired with a tinge of irritation. 'But what is there in all that? Fighting—good gracious, do you think our pioneers did not have to fight? Here in this District against Bushmen, wild beasts, even the soil? Fighting does not give you what I mean. Else soldiers would be the best citizens, my dear. It's another kind of fighting—it's the fight with yourself that makes you see these things in their true light. It's facing facts and dealing with them, and making up your mind to do what is right and proper even though it goes against the grain. And they never did that. I always thought less of them than most folk do because they trekked and didn't stay behind and fight out their own salvation as our own people did.'

'Aye, that was a mistake,' grumbled Jerry in his impassive manner. 'But it was always the way our people went when they couldn't get what they wanted.'

'I honour them for it!' exclaimed Santa, loyal to her convictions. 'They did not intend to have their souls stifled, and so they went out into the wilderness and made good there.'

'Honour them by all means, Niece,' said her aunt, 'but don't look to us to accept their views as gospel. I don't. I was taught differently, and I shall die believing differently.'

'The Rekkers always were obstinate folk, Niece,' commented Jerry drily. 'And your aunt played Samuel to Mrs Uhlmann's Eli.'

'Nor need I be ashamed of it, Husband,' the old lady retorted with spirit. 'Nor frightened to think that the Black folk will crush us unless we keep them down. It is just fear, my dear, that makes people incline to the Northern view and it is just laziness which makes all of us talk so much and do so little. I have never thought the Black folk my equals, and it will be a long time before any of them are anywhere near us. But I am not frightened at the thought that sometime, some day, they may become our equals. Why shouldn't they? After all, they are human beings just like us, and they have just the same rights, and should have the same chances as we have.'

'Then you don't mind giving them the vote—just as you did in 1854?' asked Santa. 'And swamping the White electorate?'

'I should mind, very much,' Aunt Gertrude replied vehemently. 'Just as I mind being swamped, as we are now, by the one man one vote in the North. I don't see much difference between uneducated Black folk and uneducated Whites except that the latter are less to my liking than the former. I should put the qualification so high that only the educated Native or Coloured man could vote. That would exclude a great many of our White folk, though, and no Party would like that, would they?'

'You can't take away what you have already given,' argued Santa, but her aunt caught her up sharply.

'Isn't that just what you propose to do?' she asked. 'Here we had a good constitution. It made, at any rate, some distinction between the vagrant and the fellow who had some interest in the country. You have to hold property and be able to write in order to vote. Up in the North you only had to be passably White; nothing else mattered. And now you want to take away from the Native who has reached that qualification the right you gave him before. You say yourself you can't do it; it's not fair. And yet that is what you propose to do, my dear. Let us go into the drawing room and have coffee there. Perhaps Eric will look in.'

'I shall go for a stroll,' said Jerry, knocking out his pipe. 'The rain has stopped, and I haven't had a chance to stretch my legs. I shall go over and have a talk with Dr Buren. You will not mind, Wife?'

'No. Go, by all means. We can manage to entertain ourselves, eh Santa? We'll probably quarrel violently, but that does not matter. Come, Santa, it's getting cold in here.'

She led the way into the drawing room, where a cheerful fire was burning, and plumped down on the Chesterfield.

'I heard what you said to the missionary's wife,' she remarked, inconsequently. 'I am glad you said it. I had no opportunity to say it for you, my dear, else I should have done it. For I heard what she said.'

'It was vile, Aunt Gertrude. I don't usually lose my temper, but the way in which she said it ...'

'I know, I know. But, my dear, that is what many people would say. It's the world's way, and the world is not very charitable. Mina is in many ways a puzzle to me, and just now I am particularly puzzled. However, that is neither here nor there. I wanted to talk to you about the partnership with the doctor. Yes, your mother told me about that. Now you know that Jerry and I have laid by more than we need for ourselves or the children ...'

'Aunt Gertrude, I don't want you or Uncle Jerry ...'

'Be quiet, Child, and let an old woman speak. I was always told never to interrupt my elders, but I suppose that is no longer the fashion. What I was going to say was that Jerry had definitely laid aside something for Maria's boy. It was a great sorrow to him that she had none. Not that we were not pleased to have you, my dear, but Jerry always wanted Maria to have a boy. But we need not go into that—as there wasn't one—and as I say, the money lies idle, and you may as well have it. No, don't interrupt me. Brother-in-law is, I know, hard-up. You can take it from me that he has always been hard-up. The trouble has been that he has tried to hide his difficulties instead of openly confessing them. We could have helped him, but he ... he went elsewhere. That does not matter, and you need not know about it ...'

'I do know about it, Aunt,' said Santa. 'I know that Eric lent him the money for my study in Europe ...'

'So. I did not know that you knew. I suppose that accounts for Master Eric's despondency these days.'

'No. I have told him that in the circumstances, although I thought his action quite uncalled for, I had decided to look upon the matter as just a business transaction.'

'That is sweet of you,' said the old lady sarcastically. 'It must be paid back, of course, promptly. That is all the more reason why you should make use of the money lying idle. It would have come to you in any case. And this affair with Dr Buren must be put through tomorrow. No, don't interrupt me. I suppose a god-mother may arrange these things for her god-child. That, at least, was regarded as proper in my day. Yes, give me two lumps please, and one green fig. It is a pity you have no van der Hum. I always like a liqueur with my preserve. It is the old fashion, and one does not care to see it fall into disuse. But in a faddist household like yours, one cannot expect to see the old customs honoured. When you have an establishment of your own, I shall expect you to give me a liqueur. And now tell me, why don't you say yes to Eric and have done with it? I do not say you won't get a better man. I am not omniscient, and I suppose there are other Jerry's in the world and you may happen to run across one. But the boy is sound all through, and you would be a fool to reject him, Santa.'

'Even ... even if I did not love him, Aunt Gertrude?'

'Stuff and nonsense!' said the old lady, vigorously. 'I should not ask you if I thought you did not love him. Do you imagine I am feeble-minded, Girl? It would be sinful to take him if you did not love him, and it would be equally sinful for me to urge you to take him.'

'But really, Aunt, I am not at all sure ... how can one be sure? I ...'

'Well, I can't make up your mind for you,' snapped her aunt, viciously impaling a portion of green fig on her fork, 'but I do know what I am talking about. And my advice to you, god-daughter, is that you should say yes as soon as you feel sure about it. You can do your work quite as well when you are married, although you mightn't think so. Now go and play something to me. I want to think, Child.'

Chapter 25

Elias came to breakfast the next morning prepared to give battle to his opponents. But he had determined that the field should be of his own choosing, and he was pleasantly aware of the fact that the one defence he had would be strong enough to resist all attack. A night's rest had amply restored him. He looked his old, self-satisfied, masterful self again. He wore his well-cut tweeds with distinction; his scanty hair was sleekly brushed; his moustache carefully trimmed.

'Well, what is it to be today, you people?' he asked cheerily, deluging his porridge with cream. 'You may have the car. I shall be at the office most of the day. What about a picnic somewhere? It's gloriously fine after the rain, and you might go out somewhere. You'd like that, Mother?'

'I am in their hands,' said Maria, with a wan smile. 'It depends entirely upon Trui and Jerry, my dear.'

'And we came for business,' grunted her brother. 'I have my tobacco plants to look after, Elias, and there are some things we must talk over.'

'Whenever you like, my dear fellow, whenever you like,' said Elias genially. 'But it needn't take the whole day, need it? And your tobacco plants will get on quite well without you. Trui, let me give you a bit of chop, do.'

'Thank you, Brother-in-law, I am doing very well.' Aunt Gertrude's voice was pleasantly polite, but he marked the side glance she flashed at him, and chuckled silently.

'I daresay you would be,' he thought. 'But if you think that you have me in a corner, Sister-in-law, you are very much mistaken.'

Aloud he said, 'Very well. Fix it up between yourselves. Santa, I suppose, is going out with the doctor, eh?'

'Not this morning,' she replied. 'I think I too should talk some matters over with you.'

'Ah yes, about that partnership,' he nodded. 'Quite so. Then we'd better phone Eric to bring the papers along. But it will be very dull for you, Mother. What do you propose doing?'

'If you are going to talk business,' Maria began diffidently, 'I think I shall walk down to the Burens and have morning tea with Mrs Buren. Santa, you might stroll down with me. You can come back as soon as you want to.'

'That will do excellently, Sister-in-law,' said Aunt Gertrude quickly, with a side glance at her husband. 'And there is really no reason why Santa should come back so soon. We may take quite a time over our business matters.'

'Yes,' said Elias, whom this arrangement suited well. This afternoon will do for the doctor's business. He should be there, you know. We can't very well settle it without him.'

'Very well. If that is agreeable,' Maria smiled round the table, and her gaze lingered on Santa, who smiled back and nodded. Santa was anxious about her mother, for the old lady still seemed to be suffering from the excitement of the previous day. Her pale face had its customary mildly deprecating smile, but her eyes seemed more sunken, and now and then a thin, momentary tremor could be observed playing round her upper lip. She scarcely touched her food, but drank her tea with apparent relish. Probably she had had one of her bad asthma attacks in the night. That might account for it, although she had said she was perfectly all right and that she had quite recovered from her tiredness.

Elias talked glibly, ranging over the usual conversational topics, and Aunt Gertrude seconded his efforts with creditable success. She disputed the price of shares with him, and the morning paper had to be consulted to see which of them was correct. The point went to Elias, who immediately launched into a dissertation on tobacco growing, which drew his brother-in-law into the conversation. By the time breakfast was finished, Santa was wondering whether she had not dreamed all that had made her sleep so restless and her mind so disturbed. Her father looked so pleasantly interested, so ordinarily capable, a sturdy, honest citizen, thoroughly at ease in a circle which he seemed to dominate, that she had difficulty in visualising the leering, almost cringing individual whom she had helped the night before. She could feel that there was an undercurrent of repressed excitement around her, but she thought that it came from her alone. Probably father was conscious of what had occurred, and was trying to remove the impression he had made upon her. She had not greeted him in her usual fashion; she had not been able to do that, but he had not seemed to mind. At any rate he had not called attention to the fact that she had not given him a morning kiss, and for that she was grateful.

When they rose from the breakfast table, her mother disappeared into the kitchen to give orders to the maids.

Ayah Mina was already there, supervising the maids, alert and active, reproving as a matter of course, her old self apparently. Santa, following her mother, saw the old coloured woman and paused on the threshold. She had not thought of the complication. Somehow she had taken it for granted that Ayah Mina would not turn up again at the big house, but a moment's reflection told her that she could do nothing. Not yet, at any rate. Afterwards, of course, Mina must go away; it would have to be managed somehow. It was unthinkable that the old woman should remain in daily touch with them all ... unthinkable. She turned away, jarred by her emotion, and went out on the *stoep*.

In the fresh morning air, redolent with the pungent smell of wet earth, the nearby hills looked glossy in their polished green. During the night the clouds had dispersed and the sky was brilliantly blue, the mountain range standing out bold and sharp against the horizon, its weathered cliffs revealing in the morning sunlight their strangely variegated colours. Far away to the north she could see the mountain pass, a blur of shadow against the blue, that led across the range to the mission station in the valley behind.

'I suppose it will have to go on,' she said to herself, clenching her fingers in her palms though she was not conscious of doing so. 'Mina will have to come and go as usual, or mother might get to know. Not that—not that! It would be utterly horribly for mother to know. Even the other thing ... but not that! He must be made to see that ... he must be made to realise that it can't go on.'

By the time her mother came out, ready for the visit to the Burens, Santa had regained her normal poise. Maria found her more than usually attentive, less eager to demonstrate her protective instinct.

'You didn't see Mina, did you?' Maria asked as they walked along the front street, upon which the *stoeps* of the houses looked down. The Burens' house was almost at the extreme end of the row. It had formerly been a fine gabled, thatched residence, but the roof had been burned down during the war, and the gables had been straightened. It now wore a red-painted iron roof, and its woodwork was painted a dull green. On the *stoep*, where Mrs Buren sat enthroned behind the coffee tray, stood green-painted paraffin tins in which bloomed late chrysanthemums and early carnations. In front of the *stoep* stretched a tall hedge of gardenias, whose glossy leaves, washed by the rain, shone almost luminously in the sun.

'The poor thing came down this morning,' went on Maria, without waiting for an answer, waving her hand to Mrs Buren as they strode along. 'I told her not to do any work, but just to have a look around. I wanted her to go away for a bit. She might go to the mission station. There are relations of hers living there, and it would be best for her to be away for a while. Don't you think so?'

'Yes, certainly,' said Santa, wondering why her mother had touched on that topic. 'She is really getting too old for the work. And you, too, must take a holiday, Mother. I am going to take you down to the seaside this week.'

'No, I can't go yet,' said her mother quickly. 'Not just yet. And Mina is by no means old. She is quite strong yet. Why, we are almost contemporaries.'

'She has been with you a long time, Mother,' Santa ventured to observe. Somehow she could not keep Ayah Mina out of her mind. She still felt a grievance against the old woman, a grievance which she knew was based on indignation and contempt which she hoped, unconsciously, that her mother might share.

'Yes. Since my marriage,' answered Maria. 'She nursed you when you were a baby Santa, and she has always been devoted to you. And to me. I owe her a great deal. One does not find her sort too often among our Coloured people. But here we are. Come and have a cup of tea with us. Mrs Buren would like to have a chat with you, I'm sure.'

Santa climbed the *stoep* steps with her. Mrs Buren bustled forward and made them welcome. She chatted incessantly, and under her cheerful geniality Maria gradually lost her preoccupied air of detachment and joined in the conversation.

'They have been delving old Quakerley's garden,' said the doctor's wife. 'I still call it his garden, you know, Mrs Vantloo. We used to spend such happy days there. Old Mr Andrew Quakerley took a pride in it; he did everything himself, and it was a sight to see him going around in the morning with his can of soot and water mixed.'

'It was a little before my time,' said Maria. 'But I have heard about its glories.'

'I suppose it really was a fine garden,' Santa remarked. 'One hears so much about it, but I think people are apt to exaggerate what they saw in the past. I know when I came back and saw the things which I had regarded as something to be proud of, I wondered what I had seen in them to admire.'

'Oh no, it wasn't like that,' Mrs Buren explained animatedly. 'It was really the finest garden I have seen, outside Cape Town. There the old garden at Claremont was better arranged, and larger. But old Mr Andrew's garden was renowned throughout the Colony. People came from all parts to see it. I remember old Sir William Cameron— he was Acting-Governor in those days—coming to see it. It was almost a botanical garden, but nothing like what one usually finds, when all the things have labels.'

'One can scarcely believe it when one sees its present state,' said Santa sceptically. 'It seems too small to have been really a fine garden ...'

'Oh, but every bit of space was utilised,' said the doctor's wife. 'There were terraces and rockeries, and a shrubbery, a pond, and a water-garden, and all sorts of nooks and corners. Four kinds of bougainvilleas—and today there is not a scrap of it left. And twelve different sorts of jasmine, my dear, one kind as big as a small carnation. It came from a South Sea island, I believe, and it had a lovely scent. You should have seen the gladioli in September, and his tulips. They were wonderful, but I always thought that his fuchsias were more wonderful still. The old man was heart-broken when they camped in it. Such a senseless thing to do, my dear, but you know they did all sorts of senseless things. I had no patience with them, myself, and the doctor got frequently into hot water because he objected to their doing them.'

They discussed the war, and Santa was surprised to find how detached a view both her mother and the doctor's wife took of that far-off time. Its episodes roused no fierce resentment in them as it did in her, although she knew of these things only by hearsay, while they had lived through them. Mrs Buren grew reminiscent and described the Quakerleys. Some of their descendants were now getting known. One was a prominent Nationalist, whom Santa knew by reputation, a great upholder of the republican ideal.

'One would not say,' remarked Mrs Buren drily, 'that the man's great-grand-uncle was an Admiral of the Red. But that just shows how things have changed. Look at Mr Mabuis. His grandfather was what one would have called a poor White, although to be sure he had some education and acted as teacher here a while. Then he married a rich widow, and settled down to farm, and did very well. But his son farmed badly and had to sell out and went north. Mr Mabuis grew up in the Transvaal, and went abroad after the war. By the way, he wrote to say that he would pass through here before he sailed. He is still keen on the dispensary.'

'Has he really got much money?' enquired Maria, with some interest.

'Mr Mabuis? Of course. Piles of sheep. He can easily give us something for the location, and it is quite time someone did something there.'

Santa left them discussing the location over their tea, and strolled home. She passed the Quakerley erf and saw the workmen digging in the ruined garden. They were delving, digging a ditch and throwing the soil from it into the parallel ditch they had already dug. In this way the ground was deeply trenched, the subsoil coming on top, where it would be richly manured with *kraal* manure, and made ready for whatever was to be planted there. She crossed the little bridge and went down towards the river. There was only a badly trodden footpath, but here and there she could discern bits of the tiled brick with which the old man had ringed his flower beds. There, too, was all that was left of a once-imposing rockery; between the stones some diminutive blue flowers were growing; a giant stapelia had taken root there and spread its succulent stems decumbent over the clay. There were some exotic trees left, the stump of a big magnolia putting out new leaves, a Pollarded ash, a clump of budding Japanese quince. At the lower end of the garden was what had been the lily pond, now a refuse heap filled with empty tins and broken fruit cases. If the ghost of old Andrew was hovering around, it must have felt poignant sorrow at the sight of all this wreckage, this ruin of what had once been a joy and an inspiration.

The workers touched their hats to her respectfully as she walked past. They all knew the 'missie doctor' and felt a mild respect, co-mingled with a little amusement, for her.

'It's for planting sweet potatoes, Missie,' the man-doer explained as she stopped to enquire what they were trenching for. 'The *baas* says he must get something out of the damned erf before he plants the oranges next year.'

'Have you found anything, *Outa* Tom?' she asked.

'Only some bullets, Missie,' he said, 'and cartridge cases. The khakis camped here, Missie. Arrie, they did a lot of mischief, the tin-dishes did. And *Baas* Andrew's garden was such a wonder, Missie.'

'You never saw it, *Outa*,' she smiled. Tom was much too young to have had first hand knowledge of old Andrew's horticultural experiments, but she gave him the conventional title of *outa* for, like most of the location folk, he had aged early.

'Aye, but I heard much of it, Missie,' he smiled back. 'It's a God's-shame they ruined it. If I were the old master I'd haunt them, I should.'

'Probably the old master does that, *Outa*,' she remarked, nodding to him. What was the use of a posthumous revenge? Would Sophia ...

She walked on quickly, irritated that her thoughts would stray in a direction from that into which she had resolutely tried to turn them. It would be a good opportunity to have a talk with father now. It would be a frank talk without any sentimental frills about it. The presence of Aunt Gertrude and Uncle Jerry at the interview would, she felt sure, conduce to make it a plain, business-like talk, and her mother would be out of the way. Her mother would stay at Mrs Buren's house for some time yet; she would not return much before luncheon, and it was just after eleven now. Father would be in his study, for by this time whatever business Aunt Gertrude and Uncle Jerry might have had to transact with him would be finished. She might just catch him before he went to the office.

She quickened her pace and walked home. When she climbed the *stoep* steps, she heard voices coming from the study and marched straight towards it.

Chapter 26

Elias reserved to himself a room in the big house which he called his study. That term had no euphemistic implication, for whatever Elias could be said to study occupied him in that room, wherein he sometimes gave audience to his friends and where, under lock and key, he kept an additional supply of the medicine which the specialist had recommended for his myocardial trouble. It was unfortunately not such a private apartment as he could have wished, for it was built at the end of the one wing of the house, its main door opening on to the *stoep*, while its inner door gave access to the corridor that led to the dining room. It had two big windows overlooking the front street and the garden and, like all the other rooms in the big house, was roomy and comfortably furnished. One wall was partly hidden by a large built-in bookcase, well stocked with books, for Elias kept most of his law library there and had bought widely, for he had been fond of reading and still delighted to fall asleep over a novel. Works of fiction, theological books, and political or semi-political volumes crowded the shelves, and made an imposing display upon which Elias looked with the satisfaction one derives from a valuable asset which could be made to serve as an advertisement. He had not read half of his diversified stock, and had indeed no intention of reading it, but its dignified appearance impressed those who came to visit him. He had himself noticed how much it had impressed Santa on her return, when he had casually, though with a premeditated casualness, introduced her to his 'little collection' and drawn her attention to such works as Christlieb's *Modern Glaubenszweifel* and Kammerer's *The Unmarried Mother*. He had risen in her estimation, and if his clever daughter was so easily taken in, how much more would the uncultured visitor who came to discuss a loan be impressed by these manifest evidences of literary catholicity?

Another valuable asset hung in a glass case behind his roll-top desk. His Lodge regalia, impressive in colouring, imposing in its ornateness. That, too, was useful, for it tended to make the visitor realise what a position the owner occupied. Throughout his life Elias had studied effect. He had neglected nothing that could give him the advantage which comes from simulating superiority over those who are not in a position to detect the imposture. Invariably he had succeeded in creating the atmosphere which he wanted. That had not been difficult in a community where there were few who could apply the touchstone of knowledge to his pretensions.

In a corner of the room stood a safe, and close to it an old-fashioned, brass-ornamented cedarwood chest. A cedarwood sofa, the seat of which was formed by inter-twined leather thongs, a couple of roomy easy-chairs upholstered in red leather, and two old-fashioned high-backed chairs gave seating accommodation. On the walls hung a few pastel drawings and etchings. On the overmantle above the fireplace were arranged, in silver frames, portraits of Maria and Santa. On the floor was a thick Wilton carpet, patterned in dark red, and the window curtains were of thick, red-coloured material.

The room gave one an impression of comfort, while at the same time the disordered mass of papers on the roll-top desk and on the polished cedarwood table, which adjoined the safe, hinted that it was also a room in which work was done. That was the impression Elias had intended to convey to whoever entered it. He did most of his work at the office, where he considered that he had much more privacy. His study he reserved for occasional work, and especially for interviews, for he felt that he was at his best in an environment which suggested culture, refinement, and a mildly opulent ease. His country callers who saw him there came away with an exaggerated idea of *Meneer* Vantloo's worth. They appraised him as falling into the same category as the doctor, the parson and the magistrate, who all had books in their study, though none so many, nor so finely bound and therefore so imposing, as his. They noticed the quality of the carpet, the distinguished excellence of the cedarwood furniture, and drew their own conclusions. Elias knew that these conclusions were invariably wrong, but it suited him to let his visitors make them, and it was not his business to correct them.

This morning, however, those who faced him were different from the usual type of caller with whom he had to deal. Neither Gertrude nor Jerry was impressed by his surroundings. Both had seen the study too often to be overawed by its cumulative effect; both, too, had no delusions about his culture or his ability to master all that his shelves contained. Aunt Gertrude sat rigidly upright in one of the stiff-backed chairs. She had deliberately refused one of the comfortable easies, and Jerry had only taken one because it gave him more room to spread his legs. Elias himself sat in his swivel chair, behind the roll-top desk, firmly entrenched, with his legs thrust out so that they could see his rubberoid soles.

They had retired to the study as soon as Maria and Santa had disappeared.

'If you have any apple-peeling to do with me,' he had said jauntily, 'now is your time. I don't suppose you wish Maria to get wind of it.'

'That is our intention,' Jerry had answered sombrely. 'Since Sister Maria is away, we might as well have a talk.'

'Well, come into my study,' he had invited. 'We can be private there.'

'Do first ring up Eric, Husband,' his sister-in-law had answered. And when Jerry had fumbled and sworn at the telephone, Elias himself called up the number.

'You might step down here, Eric,' he had said affably. 'Gertrude and Maria are threatening to do all sorts of things to me, and you may be wanted to prevent them going to extremes. Yes, now. Come as soon as you can. And bring along the deed of partnership. We can go into that afterwards.'

'Will that do?' he had asked, and Gertrude, too indignant for speech, had merely nodded. He had led them into the study, and invited Gertrude to take an easy-chair, but she had refused. She sat stiffly upright, her knitting work on her lap, her needles busily flicking against each other. Jerry had stuffed his pipe, and looked a picture of misery.

Elias took his own chair. He felt perfectly composed. It was just like presiding at a meeting, and he had often done that. Sometimes the meetings were stormy, with excitement and passion running high, but he had never failed to rule his audience. He felt he could do that now.

'I suppose,' he said, smiling genially at Gertrude, 'you want to discuss the little affair of the cheque with me. I should have said that there was no need for discussion, especially as I find that the money has been paid back to you, Jerry. Friend Eric has been good enough, I suppose? Yes? What a blessing it is that some people are not ashamed to be sentimental.'

'If there is any shame,' Aunt Gertrude's voice was pitched to a key which showed how deeply she was stirred, '... if there is any shame, Brother-in-law, it will not be on the part of Nephew Eric. You don't seem to realise that what you have done is a crime for which you might be punished by the law, should it become known.'

'Your pardon, Sister-in-law,' he said suavely. 'I have a much better knowledge of the law, first-hand too. Yours is altogether from hearsay, from which, as you doubtless know, many lies come.'

'I know sufficient,' she interjected angrily, 'to know that what you have done is an offence. Indeed, I am not sure that it isn't Jerry's duty to inform the magistrate.'

'By all means do so, if you think any good is likely to come from it, Sister-in-law,' he replied easily. 'I may, however, remind both of you that in such a case there would be a certain amount of ... shall we say publicity? My wife,' he uttered the words reflectively, but both of them felt that it conveyed a warning, 'might not like that.'

'Now God damn me, that shall not be!' exclaimed Jerry violently. 'I have half a mind to ... thrash you, Elias. Almighty, I can't keep my hands off you ...'

'Then put your hands in your pocket!' snapped his wife irritably. 'Can't you see that you are only giving the man cause to jibe at us? Leave him to me. Swearing at him won't do any good, and as for giving him what is his due, we must leave that to the devil.'

'Then why waste so many words upon it?' Elias suggested cheerfully. 'The thing, my dear Sister-in-law, is done. I have already fully explained to you how and why it was done ...'

'The why, not the how,' interrupted his sister-in-law sharply. 'Jerry never signed a cheque for a thousand pounds ...'

'Is he so badly off as that?' Elias sneered. 'I thought he could write one for much more. If you care to know it, Sister-in-law, he did sign that one, although it was blank when he signed.' He chuckled as he played with a pen holder, glancing sideways at his brother-in-law.

'Almighty!' exclaimed Jerry. 'That's how it was, Wife. I remember now ... one day when we were talking about shares. But I did think I had torn it up.'

'I let you think it,' said Elias composedly. 'Well, now that you know all about it, are you still so keen on making a police matter of it? I may remind you that in that case Maria will have to know. And I presume—I only presume, Brother-in-law, for I don't know what your feelings are in the matter—I presume that you would not like her to know. She ... she would be sorry if anything happened to me.'

'That we know very well, Brother-in-law,' Aunt Gertrude replied, recovering her dignity and silencing her husband's intended outburst with a gesture. 'It is for that purpose we are here. There is such a thing as one's good name. Sister-in-law Maria has that. You, Brother-in-law, have never had it. You may yourself think that you have, but what, after all, is there to be said of the Vantloos?'

'Nothing at all, nothing at all,' he retorted quickly, exasperatedly composed. I am the only one that counts. But you might have expressed it a little more politely, Trui.'

'Politeness is wasted on you,' she said icily. 'The time for it has passed. What Jerry and I intend to do ...'

'Yes,' he interrupted, 'tell me that. I am really curious to know what it is you have in mind. It is an interesting situation, don't you think so? You apparently have me at your mercy, and yet, when you come to consider it, Sister-in-law, there is nothing you can lay hold of. You must let the criminal go with an exhortation. It may relieve your feelings, and it won't harm me. *Bah*! You cannot harm me unless you harm Maria at the same time, and I know Jerry will not suffer that. So why make a song about it?'

'Be quiet, Husband,' said the old lady, imperiously silencing Jerry, whose indignation was getting the better of him. 'I can deal with him. But wait,' she added 'there is someone on the *stoep*. It must be Eric. Let him in.'

Jerry rose and opened the *stoep* door to admit Eric, and Elias greeted the newcomer with a nod and a smile.

'You are just in time, Eric,' he remarked. 'My relations by marriage wish to whip me, but they cannot very well do that. Perhaps you might advise them.'

'Yes,' said Aunt Gertrude coldly. 'And at the same time you might give Brother-in-law some sensible advice too. He does not seem to realise his position. You might tell him, for instance, that we know all about him. We know about his negotiations with Solomons, we know what he keeps in that medicine bottle of his, just as well as we know about his dealings with the military long ago when he had a foot in both camps and flourished like a green bay tree ...'

'What do you mean, Woman?' demanded Elias stung out of his superciliousness by her attack. 'You are simply repeating slanders, and you know it. There is not a tittle of proof ...'

'Oh, isn't there, Brother-in-law?' she took him up quickly. 'Fetch your medicine bottle and let Jerry judge—he can tell where you purchased the brandy. Let him ask Solomons how much he paid you for your vote for that new canteen ...'

'Not a penny!' exclaimed Elias. 'It is all lies—lies. You know nothing at all and you are simply retailing ignorant tittle-tattle you have heard. I have told you it is slanderous, and if you repeat such lies ...'

'I am not likely to repeat them,' she said scornfully. 'This is a matter between us— a family affair, Brother-in-law. I have no wish ... Jerry here has no wish to drag our name into the dust, and we are willing to spare you—on conditions.'

'That is what we came for,' growled her husband fiercely. 'I will not have Sister Maria harmed. She must not learn anything about your sinfulness. She still believes in you and, please God, she shall never learn what an almighty scoundrel you are.'

'Eric,' Elias turned to his partner with something of his old air of bravado, 'are you in this too? If not, you might tell them ...'

'Better hear their conditions, Uncle Elias,' Eric said, meeting his eyes squarely. 'The matter has gone too far. You must make some compromise.'

'I suppose you have mapped it all out, planned it beforehand,' sneered Elias, nervously beating the desk with his penholder. The fight was not going as he had anticipated. He did not like Eric's gravity, for he had a certain amount of respect for his partner's shrewdness and legal knowledge. 'Very well. If you have conspired behind my back, I may as well hear what your terms are. Not that I am likely to agree to them,' he added. 'But it would be interesting to hear.'

'Tell him, Eric,' the old lady ordered sharply. 'Don't wrap handkerchiefs round it. Tell him straight out.'

'I have here,' Eric drew some papers from his pocket and advanced to the table where he spread them out, 'a rough statement, Uncle Elias. I went to the office last night and made it out. It is of course merely a rough sort of thing, but as it stands it is serious enough.'

'At the office!' ejaculated Elias in relieved astonishment. 'There's nothing ...' he bit back the words hastily, and resumed. 'Some mare's nest, of course. Let us have it.'

'It may be a mare's nest,' said Eric gravely. 'But you have drawn upon the firm, I find, for private use, to the extent of more than a thousand this year, and you have tried to hide that fact by ... by incorrect entries. You had Santa's money—that was four thousand—and Aunt Maria's over eight thousand. In Aunt Maria's name you have ten thousand Aurora Wests—they are liquidating and I doubt if you will get five shillings a share for them. Of Santa's money there is no trace.'

'God, devil and thunder!' exclaimed Jerry, rising from his chair in his excitement. 'I suspected something of the kind ... you God-damned ...'

'Do not swear, Husband, do not swear!' his wife reproved him chillingly. Let Nephew Eric go on.'

'But it is altogether too damnable,' fumed her husband, subsiding into his chair and vigorously consoling himself with his pipe. 'Maria's money all gone, and that by this ...'

'You have enough for Maria, Husband,' his wife remarked shortly. 'Go on, Nephew Eric.'

'Now there is this letter of yours,' continued Eric earnestly. 'You practically admit that you have forged Uncle Jerry's name. The firm is implicated in that ...'

'Oh, have it your own way!' Elias exclaimed, throwing the pen-holder from him viciously. 'I admit all that. I admit that I used Maria's money and Santa's money. I'll admit the drink too, if you wish it. What does it amount to? Do you want Maria to know all this? Or don't you? That is the only point that need concern us ...'

'Maria need not know anything about it,' interrupted his sister-in-law. 'But there must be an end to it all. There must be an end to your hypocrisy, Brother-in-law, and there must be no chance—no chance whatsoever—of your repeating your ... mistakes. That can all be managed without Maria knowing about it. Although for her it would be better, far better, if she knew and did what she ought to have done long ago, and left you ...'

'No, no, Wife, how can you talk like that?' exclaimed her husband, plaintively. 'I have told you the little sister must not be harmed. It will break her heart—God damn me, it will. I know it to my sorrow. This must remain between us. I will not have it otherwise.'

'Brother Jerry talks common sense,' said Elias, resuming his complacency. 'You are really on the horns of a dilemma, sister-in-law. What do you propose?'

'We propose, Uncle Elias,' said Eric gravely, 'that you should sign a document, which I have prepared. Here it is.' He picked it out from among his papers and held it out to his partner. 'It is a formal acknowledgement of what you have virtually already stated in your letter. It acknowledges that you have ... made mistakes with monies entrusted to your care, and that in consideration of Uncle Jerry not proceeding further in the matter, you will retire from the firm and give up whatever public appointments you hold.'

'A very pretty document indeed,' said Elias sneeringly. 'I might just as well plead guilty in a court of law and have done with it.'

'Your letter is a plea of guilty,' said Eric gravely.

'Ah no, that was in confidence. A joke on brother-in-law.' He spoke lightly, treating the matter as if it was a flippant suggestion. 'And what, pray, is to be done with this ridiculous declaration?'

'It will be put safely away, sealed, in the bank, Uncle Elias,' replied Eric firmly.

'At your death—Uncle Jerry will give you his word for that—it will be destroyed unopened. But it is necessary for us to have it.'

'To have a hold upon you, Brother-in-law,' said Aunt Gertrude grimly. 'What's there to trust a faithless man? And let me tell you that if it were not for the love Maria bears you, neither Jerry nor I, aye, nor Nephew Eric here, would lift a little finger to avoid seeing you stand where you ought to be.'

'You were always a good Christian, Sister-in-law,' he sneered. 'It's lucky for us all Jerry's got some common sense. As for this precious document of yours, the waste paper basket is the proper place for it ...'

'No!' vociferated Jerry, bounding up and snatching the paper, and at the same time clutching Elias by the shoulder. 'Do have some common sense too, Brother-in-law, and sign it. Here, take the pen—it is a good pen. Sign ...'

'You must not coerce him, Husband,' said Aunt Gertrude harshly. 'If he does not want to sign, why, let him leave it unsigned. He knows the option.'

'There is no option, Wife. You know it,' her husband growled. 'Do not talk nonsense. I have told you I will not have Maria incommoded by his wickedness. He must sign, here and now. Eric and you can witness it. Eric is a Commissioner and can attest his signature. Sign. Sign.'

Elias tried to wrench himself loose, but the powerful grasp of the big farmer held him. Calmly, Jerry picked up the pen and forced it into his hands.

'Sign,' he muttered. 'Sign, or God damn me, I shall do you a mischief. I will not have you plague Maria. Sign.'

'I shall certainly not sign such a thing,' Elias blustered, refusing the pen. 'And you, Eric, will bear witness of this assault.'

'I think you had better sign, Uncle Elias,' Eric interjected coldly. He was thoroughly disgusted with the interview. The man's selfishness irritated him and made him feel small, wretched and anxious to get the thing over and done with.

'Yes, and be quick about it,' rumbled Jerry, releasing his grasp, but standing over his brother-in-law in a threatening attitude. 'We have had enough of this nonsense. If you had had your deserts you'd be standing in the dock.'

'Well, if you force me,' replied Elias, making a virtue of necessity, and signing his name with a flourish. 'There you are. Much good will it do you. You will think twice before using that paper. Bear in mind that if Maria has the least suspicion ...'

'Be easy on that score,' said Aunt Gertrude scornfully. 'You are safe enough. You can trust Jerry ...'

'Trust Jerry!' Elias boiled over with wrath and dashed the pen onto the floor. 'You and Jerry can take yourselves off, and never darken my doors again. I have had enough of you and your pious sentiments—yes more than enough.' He raised his voice, which rang more shrilly in his petulant anger. 'You come here and accuse me of things I never did. You slander me and treat me with contempt, and you forget ...'

'I forget nothing,' broke in the old lady coldly. 'Not even the fact that it is a disgrace for Sister Maria to be allied to you. I always said so, but Jerry would not listen, and see what has come of it. You cannot mingle good blood with bad.'

'Hush, Wife,' said her husband anxiously. 'Do not say what you will regret. We have got what we came for. Now let us go.'

'No, by heaven you won't!' exclaimed Elias, snatching at the document which

Eric, who had affixed his signature as a witness, was placing in an envelope. Jerry interposed his massive form, and forced his brother-in-law back, but the latter's rage, which seemed suddenly to have mastered him, made him lunge furiously with his fist, knocking Jerry's pipe to the floor. The big farmer's slumbering indignation, carefully controlled so far as it was possible for Jerry in moments of emotional excitement to restrain himself, woke and he stepped back and drew his arm backwards, when his wife sprang forward and hung on to him.

'Calm yourself, Husband,' she whispered fiercely. 'Here's Santa.'

Chapter 27

On ascending the *stoep* Santa heard her father's voice raised in anger in the study. Her own agitation made her act impetuously, for she walked straight towards the study door, and pushed it open. Her hurried entry had disturbed a quarrel, she felt sure, for the attitude and demeanour of her father and the visitors left no doubt upon the subject. Uncle Jerry, looking very angry and indignant, was subsiding under the direction of Aunt Gertrude; her father, whose heavy, bloated countenance was contorted with rage, stood breathing heavily and holding on to the side of his roll-top desk, while Eric, as flustered as his three companions, hurriedly tried to retrieve an envelope which had fallen upon the carpet. As she came in she caught Aunt Gertrude's warning whisper, and she knew she had intruded upon a scene which she had not been meant to see.

'What is it?' she asked, walking towards her father as she spoke. 'I heard you all quarrelling when I came up the steps. Anyone could have heard you. What is it, Aunt Gertrude?'

'Nothing at all to do with you, Child,' said the old lady, resuming her seat and betaking herself to her knitting. 'We have had an argument, that's all. The matter is now finished and done with.'

'It is really nothing that need concern you, Santa,' interposed Eric quickly. 'We were discussing business matters, and Uncle Jerry and Uncle Elias got a bit excited ...'

'Then there must have been some reason for it,' she interrupted shrewdly. She felt that they were keeping something back from her. Eric's quick interjection had obviously been meant to endorse Aunt Gertrude's easy explanation. Neither satisfied her. And since they were all there—since they could as well know what there was to be known—she made up her mind.

'You have been taxing him,' she pointed to Elias, who had resumed his seat in the revolving-chair behind his desk, but was still breathing heavily, 'you have been accusing him, haven't you? You may as well tell me about it. I know why you are doing it ...'

'That is nonsense,' her aunt put in tersely. 'You know nothing about it, and there is no reason why you should know anything about it.'

'I know something,' Santa said, trying to speak as quietly as possible. She realised that her aunt, whose antagonism to her father she had always suspected rather than admitted, had no animosity towards her. Uncle Jerry, she knew, could be relied upon as a friend. He was passionately devoted to her mother and had proved his regard for her on more than one occasion, while he had always looked upon his niece as his special favourite. Of Eric's loyalty and affection she was no less sure. All three were staunch friends, and at the moment she yearned for the support such friendship could give.

'Very little, perhaps,' she went on, looking at Uncle Jerry, who sat in his chair idly fiddling with his empty pipe, ill at ease and uncomfortable. 'But enough to know that there is something wrong and that you are trying your best to keep it from mother.'

'Aye, aye,' her uncle muttered. 'You are right there. Your mother must not learn anything about it. Where is she, Santa?'

'Mother is having tea with Mrs Buren. She won't come back before luncheon, Uncle Jerry.'

'Then that is all right,' he sighed with relief, and got up. 'Wife, there is nothing more for us to do here. We might as well go.'

'No. Don't go yet, Uncle Jerry,' Santa told him, gently forcing him back into his chair. 'I too have something to say. Perhaps it's about the same matter about which you have been quarrelling ...'

'It can't possibly be,' interrupted her aunt hastily. 'Ours is a business matter about which you know nothing.'

'Yes, purely business affairs, my dear,' her father added. 'Mainly about financial matters which won't interest you.'

'In any case,' her aunt continued, 'it is done with, and there can be no object in re-opening the subject. So far as I am concerned,' she looked fixedly at her brother-in-law as she spoke, and Santa observed that her father made no effort to return that glance, 'it will not be reopened. So far as we are concerned, the matter is finished.'

'Still,' Santa came towards the desk and stood beside her father, resting her hand lightly upon the papers as she did so, 'there is something I want to say, and I should like you and Uncle Jerry to hear it. It also concerns financial matters, and ... and other things. I shall have to say it sometime, and I might as well say it now ...'

'Santa,' Eric's voice had an imploring note in it, and he took a step towards her, but she waved him back. Aunt Gertrude nodded grimly, and clicked her knitting needles more aggressively.

'No, Eric,' Santa went on, keeping her voice steady under her emotion. 'I have made up my mind—probably just as you three made up yours. I suspected you had. Yesterday I knew. Yesterday, when I came back from the funeral ...'

'My dear,' interrupted her father hastily, 'I am sure that is a matter that can wait. I told you that ...'

'I have done with waiting!' Santa cried passionately, so passionately that Aunt Gertrude laid down her knitting and looked at her niece understandingly, and nodded to her husband. 'I want to make an end to all this. I want to get rid of all this make-believe and hypocrisy in which we have been living all these years. I want to start afresh. I want to ...'

'So you shall, so you shall, my Child!' her father exclaimed. 'We can arrange all that. Eric has the partnership deeds ...'

'I want no partnership deeds,' she declared, with a vehemence that made her aunt smile, though the smile was a wry one. Aunt Gertrude loved her niece, and understood. The girl had received a shock when she had heard who had paid for her schooling. It would be better to let her know everything. Half-truths led one astray. They created misunderstandings, engendered difficulties. And it might be advantageous to explain the position to her, otherwise an unguarded allusion to the subject might create suspicions in Maria's mind.

In a flash the old lady saw the possibilities of the situation. She rose from her chair and came towards the desk before either her husband or her brother-in-law was aware of her intention, and took up the statement which Eric had prepared. She held it out to the girl.

'You might glance over that,' she said meaningfully. 'No, Brother-in-law, no.' She gestured Elias away. 'The girl is old enough to judge for herself. Let her.'

Santa took the paper wonderingly. She saw her father sink back in his chair. He seemed to shrink into the same nerveless, pitiable object she had seen scurrying into her room the night before. But this time she felt no pity for him. She scanned the figures on the paper, and looked at her aunt.'

'Will you please explain,' she said helplessly. 'What does it mean?'

'It means simply that your own money and your mother's money—all that Jerry's mother left you—has gone. There is not a penny left,' said the old lady pitilessly. 'And he,' she pointed towards the cringing figure at the desk '... he has spent it all. Speculated with it, stolen it, thieved it ...'

'Wife, Wife,' implored her husband, stirring uneasily in his chair, 'have a care, have a care. She is flesh of his flesh ...'

'But blood kin to you, Husband, and your folk were never cowards,' said the old lady proudly. 'Let her be. She has her age and her sense. Best let her know all there is to know.'

'Yes,' she resumed. 'That is the matter which we came to set right. We did not want you to know, and we do not want Sister Maria to know, even now. You must help us to keep it from Sister Maria. That is why I tell it to you now. See,' she continued, disregarding both Eric and Jerry, who tried to restrain her, and paying no heed to their interruptions. 'For years he has gone on like that, and to crown all—no, Husband, it is fitting that she should be told. It is her duty to bear it—it is her duty to know. That is if you want Maria to be spared ...'

'Yes, Aunt Gertrude,' Santa said dully. 'Mother must be our first consideration. Mother must not know. It would be cruel ...'

'That I shall not tolerate,' her uncle growled. 'I will not have Maria suffer for anything that has been done. Let her abide in her belief in him—what am I saying? Wife, let us go. The matter is finished.'

'No. Now you must tell her all, Husband,' Aunt Gertrude disagreed with decision. 'Give me that paper ... I say give it to me.'

She took the envelope from Eric, who yielded it reluctantly, whispering as he did so, 'Can't you spare her that, Aunt?'

She shook her head. 'If she is what I take her to be,' she said, 'she will not thank me for sparing her. There, Santa, read that.'

The girl took the confession, and as she read it the expression on her face made Aunt Gertrude regret the impulse which had forced her to confide in her niece. Consternation, anger, pain, resentment, emotions struggling for outlet and controlled by a pride which prevented tears or recriminations, shame and the surging passion that is its outcome, mastered Santa for a moment. The old lady looked at her steadily, pitying her distress, but at the same time finding an odd satisfaction in the manner in which she reacted to the shock. Aunt Gertrude had always pitied her sister-in-law, but her pity had been blended with the mild contempt which the strong felt for those weaker than themselves. Maria was a woman of straw; a flare and a flicker and after that formless grey ash, that could not bear the imprint of a finger, that could be wafted away by any wind. About Santa she had had doubts, for her niece's self-confident air, her attitude of complacent superiority, and her domineering manner might be the mask that hid as timid a soul and as sensitive a personality as Maria's. Such a test as that which she had forced upon Santa, she reflected, would have crumpled up her sister-in-law. The woman would probably have fainted right off, and afterwards have had a heart attack from copious weeping. But Santa had some of her grandfather's spirit, which Maria seemingly had never inherited.

Grimly the old woman watched the girl's face. She noted the clenched fingers that involuntarily crumpled the paper they held, the quick in-drawn breath, too noiseless to be a gasp, yet patent enough to those keen watching eyes; the sudden tenseness of the lips and sharply outlined contour of the neck muscles. She noted, too, with satisfaction, the absence of any flicker of the girl's eyelids. Santa, she reflected, was not of the weeping sort, like her mother. She could be depended upon.

With that reflection came reaction. All her pity and love went out to the girl before her, and she put her arm round Santa's shoulder in an attempt to compensate for her cold, almost passionless appreciation by allowing her own emotion to have full play.

The girl shook her off, almost savagely. Santa still held the confession in her hand, but she was no longer looking at it. She had read the few typed lines several times. The words were fixed in her brain; their purport was no longer in doubt. Her eyes were fixed upon her father, who had sunk forwards on the table, his head between his hands. For a tense moment there was unbroken silence in the study. Then Elias lifted his head and looked at his daughter.

'Well,' he said. 'You have seen it all now. And I suppose you condemn your poor old father before you have even heard what he has to say.'

'She need not hear what you have to say,' growled Jerry, but Santa silenced him with a look. She had had time to master her emotion, and great as the shock had been, it had been infinitely less than that which she had already experienced in Ayah Mina's front room.

'I did not need ... this,' she said, finding her words slowly, and speaking with laboured emphasis which disappeared as she went on, and as her emotion struggled with her self-control. 'There was enough to ... to make me feel ... vile. I knew that you were a hypocrite. I did not know you were a ... thief, and ... and a scoundrel, but from a liar one can expect anything ...'

'Santa!' exclaimed her uncle, indignantly. 'Remember, Child, he is your father. The Book says, "Respect Your Parents" ...'

'Respect!' Santa's laugh rang out harshly, and her aunt made a movement to touch her, but the girl warded it off impatiently. 'I am not fit to be touched Aunt Gertrude!' she cried passionately. 'I am ... his daughter. Oh God! His daughter ... the daughter of a drunkard and a thief ... the daughter of Mina's unmarried husband, of Sophia's father ... and you want me to respect him ...'

'Santa!' Aunt Gertrude clutched the girl's arm and shook her. This was not the way a Gerster, one who had some remnant of the Rekker blood in her, should take disaster. It was against all the tradition of the race; it outraged the old lady's conception of family pride. Hysterics—school-girl ravings. It was unworthy of the girl.

Santa shook her off. 'I am not hysterical,' she said. 'Look at him. Ask him to deny it—if he can. Oh, Eric. I feel vile ... vile ...'

Eric sprang towards her and took her in his arms, but she thrust him away and clutched the table to steady herself. Elias had fallen back in his chair and lay with his mouth partly open, a pitiful object, conscious of his guilt and revealing it plainly to Aunt Gertrude's shrewd eyes. Jerry, who had bounced up indignantly when he had heard the girl's passionate accusation, strode over towards him and stood over him.

'By God Almighty, Elias!' he said, speaking with ominous calmness. 'If you have done this evil thing to Maria ... Man, speak up. There is no truth in it ... You were never ...'

'Go back, Husband,' said his wife, coming between them. 'Would you believe him if he denied it?'

'You are ready to think all evil of him,' said Jerry gravely, 'but this is a matter between him and me. If he has done this thing ...'

'Ayah Mina told me,' interposed Santa, recklessly. 'Do you think I ... I imagined it? Do you think I would dare say such a thing unless I had cause? Let him deny it—if he can.'

'Softly, Niece, softly,' said her uncle, still maintaining his position, though both his wife and Eric tried to drag him away. 'What the woman may say is no concern of us. But it is my concern what Maria suffers. I am her brother—she is dear to me, next to Trui here. And I swear by God, if this thing is ...'

'Sit down, Uncle Jerry,' said Eric, asserting himself for the first time. He spoke sternly, authoritatively, for he felt that the big farmer was tense with restrained passion, and he dreaded the explosion that might result when Jerry lost his self-control. He interposed himself between the two older men, and addressed Elias.

'Santa has said something, Uncle Elias,' he began, but Elias interrupted him.

'What use would it be for me to say anything?' he wailed. 'You would all be against me. And what does it matter what a man does when he is young? I warrant neither you nor Jerry can boast that you have never ...'

'God damn me!' Jerry tried to force Eric out of the way. 'While Sister Maria was your wife before God, you dared ... let me get at him, man. Sister Maria that clung to you, that ...'

It was Santa who interfered. She thrust herself between the struggling man and her father, and faced her uncle.

'You would not like mother to hear of this,' she gasped, her voice not yet under control. 'Oh, Uncle Jerry, what does it matter? Think of mother ... of mother alone.'

Her appeal had an effect. The big man dropped his hands from Eric's shoulders and strode back to his chair.

'Aye, she's right,' he muttered, flinging himself down into the chair, and covering his face with his hands. His wife went up to him. She knew what was passing in that slow, lethargic mind, where passion needed a sharp stimulus to evoke it, and where only profound emotion could subdue it. 'Aye,' he whispered when she put her arms around him, 'for the little sister's sake we must bear with him. Though my hands itch to repay him for all the sorrow he has done to her, Wife, we must let him be.'

Santa felt the pain in his voice; it touched her more than his anger had done, for she realised the concentrated bitterness which it hid. She turned to her father and faced him, and spoke harshly.

'If it were not for mother,' she said, and at the contempt her accents expressed Elias quailed before her, 'Uncle Jerry could have his way. Then every one would know you as you are, and for what you are, and they would point their fingers at you as at a despicable thing. I must not do so, for I am your daughter, even though I feel the shame that any daughter of yours ... even that poor girl who never knew you as her father ... must have felt.'

Her aunt gestured to her, but she paid no heed.

'I cannot help it,' she continued, 'that I am your daughter. If I could, I should disown myself, but as that is impossible, you and I must bear our shame. For mother's sake. That is what Ayah Mina said. She too, if it were not for mother, would have spoken. She would have told you what you are, but for mother's sake she has kept silent all these years. She will keep silent. No one will speak about it ... for mother's sake.'

'Aye,' came Jerry's half-stifled voice in interruption. 'Because Sister Maria believes in you, we will keep silent and let you be, though the Good Lord knows you deserve all that can be given you. But I promised mother when she died that I would look after Sister Maria—God forgive me for not having kept that promise, but how could a man think that you would act the scoundrel and break her heart? That shall not be—by heaven, no.'

'I will make up for it,' Elias whimpered, striving to get a little assurance in his voice. 'You are all hard on me. You will make no allowances. Because a man slips once, you judge him and condemn him. But you might think of others, and I am sure that you will not make it harder for us all. I always thought of Maria, and that is why ...'

'Oh be quiet!' Santa exclaimed contemptuously. Her father's attempt at bravado disgusted her more than his previous frank cowardice had done, and in her indignation she made no allowances for his feelings. 'No one thinks of you. The less we think of you, the better. We are only concerned about mother, and about how this awful thing is to be kept from her ...'

'So am I,' he countered, with a return of his old spirit. 'You have said your say, all of you. You have told me what you think of me. Very well. Now let us try and think of the future. Unless you want Maria to know.' Santa's disgust increased as she noted the return of confidence in him and the quick way in which he had managed to seize his one advantage. 'Unless you want Maria to know about this, you will have to co-operate with me. As a matter of fact, you cannot do otherwise. Just consider the position. Maria is infatuated with me. There must be something in me, after all, if that is the case,' he leered at Aunt Gertrude as he spoke. 'She believes in me ...'

'As I believed in you,' Santa interrupted again, raising her voice and heedless of her aunt's warning, 'Steady, Girl, let him have his say.'

'As many others believed in you. Oh, you have been expert at deceiving us all. No doubt Ayah Mina believed in you once, but she has no illusions now. But mother still has, and mother must be protected. How we are going to arrange it, I don't know. Aunt Gertrude, Uncle Jerry, suggest something. There must be some way out.'

She gestured helplessly with her hands. Her indignation had almost spent itself and the reaction left her tired, disheartened, and spiritually weak. Her aunt was quick to see that she was breaking under the strain, and deemed it time to interpose.

'That will be a matter for careful consideration, Niece,' she said gravely. 'Of course, the situation is now altered. Before it was merely a matter of money. Now it is entirely different, and we will have to think it over. My own view is that it would be better to have no secrecy ...'

'No, no,' burst out her husband, looking at her reproachfully. 'To that I shall never consent. Maria must be kept out of it. If she were to know, why her heart would be broken. It will kill her.'

'I do not think so,' said the old lady stubbornly. 'She has your blood, Husband, and as I have already stated, your folk were never cowards. But have it your own way, though I do not think it is the best way. Let sister-in-law continue to believe in her man, and let us four try to hide what we know about brother-in-law'—she stressed the title contemptuously—'for her sake, and for the sake of peace and quietness and the family name. But then we must plan. There must be some definite understanding. The woman Mina,' she spoke with distaste as if the woman Mina were far below the pale of humanity, although Aunt Gertrude had always liked and respected the old Ayah and even now, when she was convinced of the truth of the accusation against Elias, she felt a twinge of pity for the old servant, 'will doubtless keep her own counsel. She, too, loves Maria, and will go through fire and water for her. But let us look at the matter calmly. The old arrangement must stand. Brother-in-law must no longer be a walking sepulchre. We owe that at least to our self-respect—to ourselves and to others. He must give up what he has—no one will grieve about it. The Lodge will not sorrow if it loses its drunken Grand Master ...'

'Keep the Lodge out of it!' cried Elias resentfully, writhing under the scorn in his sister-in-law's tone. 'A little lapse like that does not mean that I have been unfaithful to my pledges ...'

'That,' interrupted Aunt Gertrude, speaking less scornfully than with pitying earnestness, 'that is the misfortune with you, Brother-in-law. You have not in you the power which God gives to some of us, through our parents, to know which path is the right one and which the wrong one. There is nothing within you that tells you when you defile yourself, and warns you against pitch when you are about to touch it. One should not blame you, but rather pity you for what you lack. But,' she went on, almost apologetically, 'one is human after all, and one feels it when, through lack of that which every honourable, honest man has in him, you bring sorrow and shame upon those who are better than you, and who are capable of feeling shame and sorrow.'

'Let it be, let it be, Wife,' urged her husband, rising from his chair. 'It mends nothing that is broken when you speak about it. Words won't heal the harm that he has done, and talk may only make it worse. Let him know that we have done with him. Santa, as well as you and I; and I suppose where Santa goes, Eric will follow.'

'I can stand on my own legs, Uncle,' said Santa, something of her old independence of spirit glimmering through her bitterness. 'Never mind me. I will not live with him any longer. I will not count myself his daughter, and that means that I must go away—somewhere where they don't know the name of Vantloo, and where I can start afresh ...'

'You can do that here, Santa,' said Eric appealingly. 'As my wife. I have asked you many times before to give me the right to protect you. I ask you again. Now more than ever, Santa, I ask you to come with me.'

'Out of pity, Eric?' she said wearily. 'Out of pity because I am Sophia's sister ... out of pity because I am Elias Vantloo's daughter ...?'

'No,' he interrupted fiercely, 'though God knows my heart is bleeding for you, it is not that. It is because I love you, Santa, and would have you for my own, no matter whose daughter or whose sister you are.'

'You think so,' she shook her head, 'and you are thinking of mother as well. So am I—so are we all. But I cannot come to you now—not now, Eric, not now. He,' she pointed towards her father, 'he has made it impossible. There is only one thing left for me now, and that is to look after mother. Mother is so weak, so unprotected, and she as no Eric to take pity on her, and offer her his strength. She has no one to lean upon except me, and I must not fail her now. Mother, when I think of her, when I remember what she is—so weak, so sensitive, so frail—oh Aunt Gertrude,' she turned towards the old lady and met her aunt's responsive caress with child-like eagerness, 'I forgot that I am his daughter, and want to say things which are better left unsaid.'

'There, there, Child,' said her aunt. 'Remember rather that you are your mother's daughter and your grandfather's grand-child, and show that you can bear shame and disaster without breaking under them.'

'For mother's sake, I will,' Santa cried, loosening herself from her aunt's grasp. 'But,' she turned to face her father and spoke with concentrated scorn, all the pent-up bitterness which she had tried so hard to restrain welling up in her, 'for you, though you are my father, I feel nothing but contempt. I believed in you ... worshipped you as mother did. We made an idol of you, mother and I, and now ... now there is nothing left but to shield mother from her idol—to keep mother from knowing—to let her go on believing that you are what you have never been and never will be. Mother ... must not know ... she must never suffer as I suffer ... she must never know ...'

'Mother knows, Santa.' The quiet voice from the doorway struck through Santa's impassioned denunciation with a quavering shrillness that belied its studied calmness. Maria stood there, her thin fragility framed by the green door-posts against a background of sun streaming on to the *stoep*.

They stared at her for a second before Jerry jumped up with an oath and strode forward to meet her. But she brushed him imperiously aside, and walked past him; and stood at her husband's side. Elias, who had been the first to perceive her, had sunk down in his chair, falling forwards on the desk where he pillowed his head between his hands. All his bravado had left him; he lay silently and only an occasional heave of his bent shoulders revealed his agitation. His wife put her hand on his head, stroking his hair, and faced the other occupants of the room. She looked pale, fragile as usual, but there was something in her face that her sister-in-law marked with unutterable satisfaction—a tense, controlled emotion, a look of determination which gave to her delicately-cut features an air of dignity. Santa, who had made a movement to rush towards her mother, found herself restrained by her aunt, and heard the old lady's fierce whisper, 'Be quiet, Child. She knows best.'

'Yes,' Maria said in her gentle, quavering voice, wherein only her sister-in-law detected the undercurrent of suppressed emotion. 'Mother knows about it—all. A wife and her husband have no secrets, even though the one should hide things from the other. I have known—long since. I have known how solicitously you, Brother, and you, Sister-in law, tried to keep me in ignorance, trying to spare me the suffering which a wife must bear if she would be true and faithful to her husband. "Until death us do part," we swore before the pulpit; and you, Brother, should know that we are not of those who make promises only to break them when their fulfilment is too heavy ...'

'I did not know,' her brother muttered, shamefacedly. 'We did it for your sake, little Sister ...'

'Aye, I know,' the gentle voice interrupted. 'You thought of me only as the little girl who cried when someone hurt her, and you thought the grown woman was no different. But you, Sister-in-law, should have known better, for you too have been true to your man, and know what it is to suffer ...'

'I have always thought better of you than that, Sister-in-law,' Aunt Gertrude said, nodding her head vigorously. 'But Jerry would not see.'

'No, Jerry would not see,' Maria repeated. 'His love for me could not rid itself of the sense of protection. Like Santa's here. I saw it all. I knew it and I knew, too, how he would suffer, and she would suffer, if they knew. From the beginning, I knew. No,'— she raised her hand and silenced Santa who had tried to speak—'you think I do not know all, but you are mistaken. I knew that my money had gone ... that Santa's had gone ... that Eric had lent him money for Santa's education. I have known ever since you came, Brother, that there were other and graver matters. Even the worst, which you know for I heard what you said, and though you think that I did not know, I knew. You always wanted a godson, Brother Jerry. You know now why I could not give you one ... not after that. Shortly after Santa came, I knew. And I could not ... not then, Brother. You must forgive me, but it was better so. Better for you, and for me, and for us all.'

'Why ever did you not tell me?' Jerry groaned. She seemed to be speaking to him more than the others, and she answered him gently.

'Because he was my man,' she said, and again only her sister-in-law noted the slight break, the momentary hesitation in her voice. 'His shame was my shame, his honour was mine. Oh,'—the quaver died out from her voice and was replaced by a ring of passion—'do you think I did not feel it? Do you think I was a block of wood, with Mina daily about me, with Sophia lying there a-dying, and with me knowing what they were to him ... what they had been to him? Do you think I did not know how he sold his succour during the war and traded on his patriotism to make money? Do you think I did not know of his subterfuges, his innumerable expedients to hide the truth from me and from you? Oh, I knew it. You cannot tell me anything I do not know, for before you knew it, or of it, I knew. There is nothing you can say of him that I cannot say if I looked at him as you look at him. But you are not his wife; he is not your man. He is mine, and with all his faults, with his sin and his shame, he is mine, whom I loved when I gave myself to him and swore to be true to him until the good Lord breaks the bond between us. I can understand why Santa reviles him—why she finds the shame too hard to bear—for it hurts her pride which has not learned to love as you and I, Sister-in-law, love. But you should have understood. You, Sister-in-law, should have taken my part, for you know what it means to be true to your man and to bear all things with him, even though it is shame that crushes your pride and sin that threatens to break whatever love you have ...'

'I ask your pardon, Sister-in-law,' said Aunt Gertrude humbly. 'You put me to shame. I should have known that your father's daughter was made of better stuff than Jerry would have me believe.'

'Yes,' went on Maria, speaking more passionately. 'You with your family pride— you with your tradition of race! It is not family nor race, Sister-in-law, that makes one bear these things and suffer so that no man is aware how much one suffers. It is the faith that is in one, that comes from the love one bears. You, Santa, pray God you may learn to love so that even if your man shames you, as mine has me—oh, I do not hide it from myself, I have never hidden it, for it was open to me, although you thought I was blind-eyed like a bat—even if your man shames you, the love that is in you is strong enough to make you endure and suffer uncomplainingly. So I loved my man, so I still love him.' She caressed the bent head and the passion died out of her voice, which resumed in gentle quavering tones.

'I tried my best—please God, I shall go on trying—to make him different. But a man is as God has made him ... that ... that ...' her voice broke, and Santa drew nearer and laid an arm round her shoulder, 'is all. But you, Sister-in-law, you ... you should understand.'

'Mother, Mother,' Santa cried. 'I did not know ... I never suspected ...'

Maria shook her off. 'No,' she said gently, 'you never loved me sufficiently to suspect. You never loved anyone but yourself, Child. You admired him for what you thought he was, and you pitied me for what you thought I was, but both pity and admiration came from your own pride. I do not blame you, Child. You will learn to love, and then you will understand. Not now. Now you only judge, and your charity is not great enough to make you a just judge.'

She bent down over the desk and put her arms around her husband's head. He made no movement, and she fell on her knees beside him.

'Come, Husband,' said Aunt Gertrude, softly, and motioned to Eric. 'Take Santa away,' she said. 'Sister-in-law knows best.'

Silently they trooped out of the study. Glancing back as she closed the *stoep* door, Santa saw that her father was sobbing unrestrainedly.

The beginning of summer saw Mr Mabuis back at the Village, though his sojourn in it was of limited duration. He stopped with his friends, the Burens, and told them, with much gesticulation and a spice of humour, of his adventures among his own people, who had cheerfully refused to accept him as an expatriated *burgher* and had frankly enlightened him on many things. He had seen all that there was to see, which had not taken up much of his time. Like the tourist, however, he had made his journey northwards in the swaying, dust-begrimed train which was the admiration and pride of every South African who had no means of comparing it with other and more pleasant means of locomotion. He had eaten the gritty food, and drunk the tepid water supplied, at fairly high prices, on board, and had marvelled at the complacency with which his fellow-students had suffered so indifferent a service. Casting his memory back, to the times when he had been a young fellow travelling down to Cape Town on a holiday visit, he had remembered under what different conditions he had journeyed then by train; how the attendants, mostly Coloured, had been polite and deferential, how the meals had been partaken of, with some measure of ease, at wayside stations, where they served a well-cooked, plain, but attractive dinner at a fair price, and where you could get wine and iced-water equally cheaply.

'I had enough of the railway,' he declared to Dr Buren, as he sat in the doctor's drawing room on the evening of his return to the Village. 'So I came back by car. No more railway travelling for me if it is possible to do my journeying by car. How anyone can endure that long martyrdom to the Falls is a wonder to me; especially when it is just as cheap, and ten times more comfortable, to do it by car.'

'You exaggerate, as usual, Mabuis,' said his friend. 'Millionaires like you may do it as cheaply, but not the ordinary traveller ...'

'I quite disagree,' Mabuis interrupted, vivaciously. 'Count up what you lose in comfort, in health—I found plenty of mosquitoes in my compartment, for there is absolutely no screening and one simply cannot get the insects out—and in temper, and you will grant that no matter what you pay for some other conveyance, it is worth your while. Besides, if you want to see the best of the country—its finest scenery—you must get away from the railway.'

'That is quite true,' said Mrs Buren. 'But the tourist does not know it.'

'Because you haven't a good guide-book,' asserted Mabuis. 'Look here, Buren, I will give you a grant-in-aid of one, if you will compile one ...'

'To your liking, I suppose,' said the doctor with a smile. 'But our tastes possibly differ.'

'I don't think so,' said his guest reflectively. 'From what I have seen of you, I fancy we have many likes in common. Not perhaps as regards sheep or butterflies. There we differ. But the older I grow, Doctor, the more do I become convinced of the fact that people have more common likes and interests than common dislikes and differences. Now I ... I like comfort, ease, and beauty. I suppose I am what one might call a hedonist, although I have worked, and still work, as hard as any man. But I cannot like what is second-rate and inferior when it might just as well be first-grade and superior if someone pays just a little more attention to it ...'

'A back-handed compliment to our railways, I presume,' said the doctor drily.

'Just as you like. I did not mean to apply it to the railways in particular. I think it should apply to the country as a whole,' said Mabuis gravely. 'When I went north, you thought me unduly pessimistic; and now that I am back you will probably think I am mad when I tell you that however pessimistic I was when I arrived, I am still more so now.'

'I know how glumly you look at everything which is not Argentinean,' jeered Buren, more than with the intention of evoking further criticism than in disparagement. 'But there must be some points about us that should carry away your appreciation.'

'There are,' Mabuis admitted. 'But they are precious few. You have mineral wealth and you have, in some parts, admirable country for development. But you are living on capital and doing nothing to exploit the real resources of the country. I am aghast at an industrial policy which expects success to follow when the taxpayer has to put his hand in his pocket for the benefit of a few capitalists. Of course you say—they all told me when I expressed my amazement—that it creates labour, and reduces unemployment. Just as the White labour gangs on the railway are supposed to reduce unemployment. But it merely substitutes one kind of dole for another, and you get no further, while all the while you are drawing upon your reserves. Your real consuming element—the Natives—you do nothing to conserve, improve or study. On the contrary, you go out of your way, foolishly sometimes, to antagonise them. Altogether it is enough to make one despair of this country, and the more I see of the manner in which you manage things the less inclined do I feel to repatriate myself and settle down here. You know, of course, I had some such idea in my head when I came here. I wanted to see the land from which I came.' He crossed to the window and drew back the blind.

'It is unfortunately too dark,' he said regretfully, 'else I could show you the pass my grandfather trudged across when he came here, a vagrant and a vagabond, to find shelter with old Gallows-Gecko. I came back to see that. I had never seen it, and I wanted to see for myself what it was like. I may still buy it, for it is to be had, I am told, for a third of what its real value is.'

'That of course I do not believe. Land values are extravagantly high throughout the Union, and if you want settlers here they must come down. Yes, and you must reform your land laws, fall into line with the rest of the world and admit that land is common property, and that its owners have obligations and duties in rural as well as in urban areas. But to go back to the rather interesting point you raised, Doctor. Common likes and common prejudice, I mean. I have found that most folk out here agree with me in most things, but somehow they haven't got the courage, or the audacity, to proclaim it. There is a sort of political blight over you all, and I find that politics absorbs all your attention. I was surprised to find that you have even miniature parliaments and sham elections among your university students. They, I fancied, would have had enough of such rubbish. By the way, what has become of your intended partner? I rather liked what I saw of that young lady, and looked forward to another tilt with her. It is refreshing to find a political faith so fresh as hers seemed to be.'

'Santa?' said Mrs Buren. 'Yes, she always took her politics very seriously. Much more so than her father did ...'

'Elias never struck me as being a serious proposition,' remarked Mabuis. 'I have no time for him, though he is the political and financial boss hereabouts. But his daughter I liked. And Mrs Vantloo, too. She struck me as being altogether of a different class ...'

'That is so,' nodded the doctor. 'She is a Gerster, and the Gersters and the Rekkers are among our aristocrats. In your grandfather's days they were *the* people here.'

'That I can well believe,' said Mabuis. 'Vantloo's daughter interested me. She seemed capable of better things than the ruck of the folk I met. And you say she has ...'

'We did not say anything,' retorted Mrs Buren. 'As a matter of fact, Santa is away on her honeymoon ...'

'Aha—the intelligent-looking young attorney,' interrupted Mabuis. 'I forget his name, but I saw he was presuming in that direction. So they have made a match of it.'

'Yes, very suddenly,' answered the doctor. 'From what Santa told me, I thought that she had made up her mind not to get married yet. But my own impression was that she was genuinely fond of him, and that it needed merely a little pressure on his part to induce her to consent. They arranged it rather suddenly, a few days after the funeral of Ayah Mina's girl. I fancy her mother had a hand in it. They were married quietly, and have gone away on a motor tour.'

'Santa will be back by the end of the month,' said Dr Buren. 'Then she will enter into partnership with me, and I shall be glad to get her. She really knows her business, for she has been well trained, and that young woman has some original ideas.'

'So,' said Mabuis reflectively. 'Well, I am glad for both their sakes. The father—well, I never cared for him. Perhaps I knew too much about him to take to him, and in any case, I have never cottoned on to a prohibitionist. Doubtless there are many honest ones, but somehow ...' He shrugged his shoulders expressively.

'Ah,' said Dr Buren. Elias has seen the error of his ways. He has resigned from the Lodge and is no longer one of their props. I think his wife made him do that—his wife or his sister-in-law. The old man—you know he is not much older than I am, but he has lately aged very considerably—has given up his firm too. Young van Deren is now solely in charge and the old man has retired. He and his wife have gone to live at the seaside. It was quite sudden, and his decision created a mild excitement in the Village when he announced it. He resigned all his appointments, and left the next day. There's a good deal about the business that puzzles me, but after all it's not my concern; and I don't listen to the local gossip more than I can help doing. The last time I saw Elias, however, he struck me as being very much altered in many ways. You noticed that, my dear, didn't you?'

'Yes, I did,' answered Mrs Buren. 'Strangely enough he seems to have lost all his—how shall I say it—his impudence, if you know what I mean. He was always so assured and so complacent, you know. But lately he has been much milder, and the most wonderful thing is that he seems to defer to his wife in almost everything. She used to be a sort of shadow to him, Mr Mabuis, but now she manages everything for him.'

'I liked Mrs Vantloo very much, from the little I saw of her,' said Mabuis. 'She seemed to me to be the sort of woman one associated with the type that came out here in the past—like my grandmother, only more cultured and more refined in some ways. The sort that in other surroundings, perhaps, one could have regarded as *une grande dame.*'

'Yes, very much so,' agreed the doctor. 'Her sister-in-law, Mrs Gerster, is like that too. But Mrs Vantloo has always been ailing—chronic asthma, you know, and that plays the devil with one's constitution, and I suspect with one's character too. Do you know, my dear,' he addressed his wife, 'before they left, Mrs Vantloo came to see me. She wanted to add a sum of money to the fund we have for the location dispensary. I told her it wasn't necessary. You had given me enough, Mabuis, to go on with.'

'Remind me tomorrow to add to it,' said Mabuis. 'I think you should have enough to pay for up-keep in case the government leaves you in the lurch. Now that I have seen all I wanted to see, I find that there is a little left in the wallet, and I might as well let you have something more.'

'What about your grandmother's farm?' asked the doctor. 'If you mean to buy that ...'

'No, no. What should I do with it if I did?' Mabuis countered. 'If I intended to remain here, then perhaps. But, my dear friends, I have expatriated myself. The Argentine is good enough for me, and, honestly, your squabbling and your talking do not interest me. I shall remain there and get news from you, and if any time I find that you are thinking of reforming yourselves and putting your house in order, why then I might perhaps come over to lend you a hand. But I am afraid that day is far off. You are too self-centred yet, and you are still too personal in your likes and dislikes to try and find out what you have in common with the other man. That is not the way one develops a country like this, and I am too old to bear with it—too impatient, for youth alone, with its sweeping idealism and its lack of perception, can tolerate what you are doing. I am sorry I shall not be able to see the young lady again. I enjoyed our political discussions, and maybe I gave her something to think about. You might remember me to her, Buren. An interesting type ...'

Mr Mabuis departed from the Village, and in due course careered in his car over the steep pass which his grandfather had traversed on foot, and from Cape Town took ship to Rio. He had seen what he wanted to see, and the sight had neither impressed nor stimulated him. But before he left the shores of his native country, which he no longer regarded as his country, he invested in a suitable wedding present which he sent, with a courteously worded covering note, to Mrs van Deren care of Vantloo & van Deren, Attorneys and Notaries.

Santa opened the parcel on her return from the Strand, and found an antiquated silver frame, tarnished with age.

'I send you,' wrote the expatriated one, 'what I have reason to believe is something that belonged to my family in the dim past. It may remind you of our drive among the sorrels; it will, at any rate, remind you of what the past was for some of us, and of the obligations which we owe to it.'

'Oh, I don't want to be reminded of the past, Eric dear,' Santa said to her husband, as she placed the frame on the table. 'The future is before me. Mr Mabuis did say such disturbing things.'

'I don't think he wants to disturb us,' Eric replied thoughtfully, but he means the same sort of thing that Aunt Gertrude has in mind, and your mother, my dear. Shall we run out and see them? They are waiting outside, and Uncle Jerry is burning to show us his tobacco plantation.'

KALAHARI

BECHUANALAND

Molopolole

M

Lobatsi
Ramathlabama
Pitsani

MAFEKING
Lichto

NAMAQUA LAND

Molopo R.

Vryburg

Harts R.

Kuruman o

Taungs

Bloemhof

Border Siding
14 Streams

Vaal

Orange R.

Upington

GRIQUALAND
WEST **KIMBERLEY**

Barkly

O R
Bo

LITTLE NAMAQUA LAND

Griquatown

Modder

Jacobs

rt Nolloth

o Kenhardt

GT. BUSHMAN LAND

Hopetown
Orange R.

Enslin
Graspan
Belmont

auresmith

Buffels R.

Ookiep

Prieska

Jagersfontein

Springbokfontein

Springfontein

Olifants
Vley

De Aar

Philipois

Colesberg

No
Po

Upper Zak R.

Karee Berg

Carnarvon

Hanover

Zuur

St

Olifants R.

CAPE

Victoria West

Naauw Poort

Richmond

Rosmead
Junc.

COL

Calvinia

Doorn R.

Roggeveld Mts.

Fraserburg

Sneeuw Berg

Murraysburg

Graaf
Reinet

Clanwilliam

Nieuwveld Ra.

Beaufort W.

Aberdeen

Somerse

St. Helena
Bay

Piquetberg

GREAT KARROO

Gamtoos R.

F

Saldanha B.

Ceres

Matjesfontein

Zwarte Berg

Prince
Albert Willowmore

Jansenvil

Aliced

Malmesbury

Wellington

Worcester

Robertson
Ashton

Ladismith

Oudtshoorn

Uitenhage

Table B.

Paarl

Breede R.

George

Stellenbosch
Somerset W.

Swellendam

Humansdorp

CAPE TOWN

Simonstown

Riversdale

Knysna

Plettenberg

428 Mile

Fr

Cape of Good Hope

False B.

Chied

Danger Pt.

Bredarsdorp

C. Infanta

Gourits R.

Mossel Ba

Port Elizabeth

Agulhas

Cape Town

SOUTH AFRICA

Statute Miles

0   50   100   150   200   250

REFERENCE

British South Africa
Boer Republics
Foreign Possessions
+++++ Railways ═══ Roads
----- Sea Routes (Distances in Nautical Mile